~~~~~~~~~~~~~~~~~~~~~~~~~~~~~~~~~~~~

ALMOST HUMAN

~ The First Trilogy ~

~~~~~~~

Volume 1: Fatal Infatuation

Part 1 - Captivating Vampires
Part 2 - Tempting Transgressions
Part 3 - Venomous Revelations

Volume 2: Lost Reflections

Part 1 - Persistent Persuasion
Part 2 - Telling Tales
Part 3 - Battles and Bliss

Volume 3: Evolving Ecstasy

Part 1 - Ecstasy Unleashed
Part 2 - Stakes and Sunshine
Part 3 - Evolution of Love

~~~~~~~

Melanie Nowak

~~~~~~~~~~~~~~~~~~~~~~~~~~~~~

Praise for Melanie Nowak's Venomous Vampire series
ALMOST HUMAN ~ The First Series

"An emotional rollercoaster that will have you sitting in suspense one moment, laughing out loud the next, and then crying your eyes out at yet other times. ALMOST HUMAN is definitely a book series that should be read slowly and savored."
– www.NightOwlReviews.com

ALMOST HUMAN
Best Vampire Series 1st place Winner by Public Reader Vote
in The Paranormal Romance Guild 2012 & 2015
Reviewer's Choice Awards

"Ms. Nowak's gifted storytelling weaves a great new tale for vampire lovers. The reader is held breathless as the story twists, turns and evolves along with the relationships. The characters are so real, and the flow of the story so believable, it takes you away."
- www.ParanormalRomanceGuild.com

"This series has continued to be consistently excellent and I have to say I am seriously impressed that the level has remained so outstanding with each book. If you love vampires, and you love great series, then you really should start these as soon as possible!"
- www.NerdGirlOfficial.com

"Melanie Nowak has written her characters in such a way that they keep developing before your eyes, and she keeps you guessing as to what is going to happen next."
– www.2ReadOrNot2Read.com

"The characters are well thought out, with a mature, enjoyable insight, while the storyline captures your attention and keeps it. Melanie Nowak has a vision all her own, that is fun and enjoyable. ALMOST HUMAN was a rollercoaster ride of who I wanted with who, with a surprise ending I did not expect. I love how this author throws you curve balls that completely leave you hooked and wanting more."
– www.ParanormalRomance.org

*ALMOST HUMAN - The First Series was originally published as a trilogy of novels, now broken into novellas as an alternate format. The story is told in a serial succession - not stand-alone books. Each novella is meant to be read in order, as the story unfolds chronologically. Each series will be contained enough to be read on its own, with a certain amount of main storyline closure with the last novella, but there will also be some story-ties leading from one series into the next.

If you enjoy this book, please take a moment to leave a review online, on your favorite book review website! Questions and comments can be directed to: WoodWitchDame@aol.com

You can join author/reader discussions about the series, and get updates on upcoming book releases for this series on the author's web site at:

www.MelanieNowak.com

ALMOST HUMAN
THE FIRST TRILOGY
OMNIBUS EDITION

ISBN: 0-9824102-9-8
ISBN-13: 978-0-9824102-9-5

~~~~~~~~~~~~~~~~~~~~~~~~~~~

A Special Thanks to

~~~

My Mom & Step-Dad, Adele and David Weitzel
who have always given their love and support
~~~

My dearly departed brother, John,
who is loved, and missed each day

~~~

And to my wonderful and loving husband,
Scott,
and our sons, William & Eric,

who had patience when I was obsessed with writing,
gave me never-ending confidence and inspiration,
and for whom I am forever grateful
and blessed to have in my life.
I love you dearly.

~~~~~~~~~~~~~~~~~~~~~~~~~~~

~~~~~~~~~~~~~~~~~~~~~~~~~~~~~~~~~~~
~~~~~~~~~~~~~~~~~~~~~~~~~~~~~~~~~~~
~~~~~~~~~~~~~~~~~~~~~~~~~~~~~~~~~~~

Volume 1

~~~~~~~

Fatal Infatuation

~~~~~~~~~~~~~~~~~~~~~~~~~~~~~~~~~~~
~~~~~~~~~~~~~~~~~~~~~~~~~~~~~~~~~~~
~~~~~~~~~~~~~~~~~~~~~~~~~~~~~~~~~~~

Almost Human ~ The First Series
Volume 1 - Fatal Infatuation

Contents

Part 1 - Captivating Vampires

Prologue

Cain

"Tommy's Place"
A little bar, in a small town, Upstate New York
A Friday night in early June

Cain surveyed the few patrons of the bar with a practiced eye. They were much as he had expected; mostly kids, barely of age. They were probably taking summer classes at the local college. There would surely be more come September. A few older men who looked to be regulars were sitting at the bar, engaged in easy conversation with the bartender. No one was particularly worth his notice; not a killer among them, until...*she* arrived.

Surprisingly enough, it turned out to be a teenage girl that he'd been waiting for. She was heavily made up, to try and disguise her age, but was still quite intriguing and attractive. She had no trouble entering the establishment, the doorman seemed to find her bewitching as well.

She made her way to the bar, walking with a measured stride and an air of aloofness that informed those around her that she considered them beneath her attentions. The man who followed behind gave a glare of warning to any who seemed to find her worth more than passing notice. Once at the bar, her companion ordered drinks for them both as she scanned the room.

Her eyes fell upon Cain and he instantly knew he'd piqued her curiosity...he was the only other like her in the establishment. She obviously intended to grace him with her presence. The man she was with seemed none too pleased when she made it clear that she wanted him to wait at the bar. She hushed him with an artful smile and kiss, which left him grudgingly pacified. Good, Cain was hoping to make her acquaintance privately.

She approached. "Hi there." Her casual tone hardly seemed in accordance with her lofty attitude. "You here alone?" she asked, eyeing him appraisingly.

"I am," he confirmed as he assessed her appearance. "I find myself alone more than not these days." He smiled over her pleasant surprise upon hearing his British accent.

She would be quite fetching without all the paint. Her long, straight hair had been tinted the deepest black. She was scantily dressed to show off her fine, lithe body to its utmost advantage; a little more blatantly than he found necessary, but effective all the same. She definitely had his interest. "I see you're not lacking for company though," he added, with a nod towards the bar.

She gave a little shrug of dismissal. "He's not exactly living up to my expectations."

"Perhaps I could help you do better," he offered, inviting her to join him with a gesture towards an empty chair.

"Perhaps," she repeated with an amused lilt. He wondered if she understood the meaning he'd actually intended. It was clear the other man was under her tutelage, and rather unimpressive, despite her efforts. She was inexperienced, to be sure.

"I'm Sindy." She drew the chair close to him as she sat.

He gave her his name, "Cain."

"I dig the accent, but when I think of old English dudes, I picture them all stodgy. You know, like with a pipe and tweed coat or something. You're actually kind of hot." It was strange to hear her speak like an immature teenager; she had the presence of a queen.

He smiled, noting that she had managed to discern his true age. "Thanks, I guess I'll take that as a compliment. It's true I am older than I look, but I'd like to think of myself as anything but stodgy. I don't smoke, and I hate tweed."

She grinned and peered at him seductively from behind her long lashes. "Planning on staying in town for a while?"

"I don't know... I might. I'm actually here on business."

"Is that so? Well, I'm more of a pleasure seeker myself. Maybe I could show you around; bet we'd have fun."

Unwelcome images of the blood soaked 'fun' she might enjoy invaded his mind as he sought to give her an unconcerned smile. "I must admit, I was hoping you'd offer. I would like to get to know you better, if you don't think your friend would mind." He gave another meaningful glance towards the bar. Her former companion was barely restraining himself from coming over.

"Don't worry about Ernest. He may not look like much, but I've got him wrapped around my little finger. Why don't I ditch him for now, and we could take a midnight stroll?"

"I thought you'd never ask."

Chapter 1 - Firsts

Felicity

The DownTime Café and Bookstore
Upstate New York
A Saturday in early September

Felicity approached the store with a stomach full of butterflies; her first day at her new job. She wasn't used to 'firsts', back home everything had always been pretty much the same. In such a small town, nothing really changed. You always knew what to expect and who you were dealing with. Even when she'd started working at the Quickie Mart after school, it was a place and people she'd known her whole life. Going away to college had sounded like a great idea. She'd been so jealous when her older brother Edmund had gone off to school in Syracuse and she was more than happy to get away from the two younger brothers she was left with at home.

It would be an adventure! And it was; but there were so many people, and she didn't know a single one. She didn't even have a roommate. The lady at the desk had made a big deal about how she was lucky that there was low enrollment this semester, and Felicity would have her own dorm room. Secretly she had been kind of disappointed. It would have been nice to have had an 'instant friend'. Popularity was something she had never aspired to. She had always been far too shy. All of her new classes, new professors, new books and ideas, were a little overwhelming. Now, the new job.

Her parents were paying her tuition, but she had to pay for her own books and half of her living expenses. That was the deal. At least she was here; having to work wasn't so bad, especially since her grades didn't exactly warrant a scholarship. Books were expensive, and she had seen this place when she first came to enroll. She had applied for the job right then and there. Good thing too, so many college kids meant stiff competition for a nice job like this. That is, if it's as nice as it seemed. Only one way to find out.

Before entering, she paused to check her reflection in the glass of the door. She wore a knee length pencil skirt with a blue and white striped tailored shirt, opened a bit to reveal a light blue camisole top underneath. She hadn't really wanted to wear the cami, but she was afraid that if she couldn't leave the top few buttons of the shirt open, it would pull too tightly across her chest. Her friend Deidre was always telling her how lucky she was to have a full and curvy figure, but to Felicity it was usually just something to be self-conscious over. She smoothed her skirt a little and hoped she didn't look too formal.

Her long wavy auburn hair was pulled back from her face with a clip. She'd worn only the usual spare make up that she preferred; a little eyeliner to help bring out the green of her eyes, a hint of blush to her cheeks and some light peach lipstick. After a last glance at her reflection, she resolved not to be shy, to project a confident attitude and hopefully make it through the day without making any embarrassing mistakes. She took a deep breath and opened the door.

The place was bigger than she remembered. It was actually two stores joined together. One side was a cute little café where they sold coffee, cookies and stuff. The other side was a book store; that was where she would be working. Felicity made her way over to the registers, but the line was long, and the pretty blonde behind the counter paid her no attention. Felicity looked for a manager or someone who might know she was coming. The store was awfully busy. What few other employees she saw, were rushing around on one errand or another. No one seemed to notice her; a leftover skill of hers from years of trying to be invisible, most likely. Finally, she saw someone she recognized, it was the man who had given her the job, Mr. Penten.

As soon as she made herself known, she was put straight to work. Mr. Penten was an older man who wore a very dark toupee, which hardly matched his graying eyebrows. He was kind, but had a very business-like attitude. He said the first week of school was always incredibly busy. Most students got their books from the school book store, but they never seemed to have enough to meet everyone's needs. So, then the students came here. It would die down in a few days.

She learned to work the register and help people find what they needed. The day flew by and before she knew it, it was time to close. She was shown how to count out the drawer and record everything. At least that part wasn't all that different from her old job back home. Mr. Penten seemed like he'd be an okay boss, and the job itself was easy enough. She could do this. He had her follow him over to the coffee counter. "You'll be trained to work the café too, in case you ever need to cover a shift for someone." He turned towards the kitchen, calling into the back. "Got a cup of coffee for me Ben?"

"Yes sir, brewed it fresh." A young guy came out from the back and indicated a to-go cup on the counter. "Light and sweet, just fixed it for you." He looked to be barely twenty, tall and slim, with short dark wavy hair. He was very attractive and wore a friendly smile.

"Benjamin here has been with us for…three years is it now?"

"Actually, it was four in June," Ben answered while wiping down the countertop. He paused to flash Felicity a welcoming grin.

"This is Felicity, she just finished her first day." Mr. Penten sipped his coffee as she tentatively nodded hello. "Benjamin manages the café. He's the best employee I've got."

Benjamin laughed as he began to count out the cash register. "Can I use that when I ask for my next raise?" he asked with a smile.

Mr. Penten glanced up from his coffee. "Just as long as it's not tonight. Let's get through hell week first, okay? I've shown Felicity how to close out the cash register, we'll go over it again tomorrow," he assured her, "but you two are closing together Monday, so if she's got any problems, she's coming to you."

Felicity was pleased to hear that she'd be working with Ben. She liked him already. He had such a friendly and casual attitude, but at Mr. Penten's words, Ben looked up anxiously. "I thought Lucy was closing?"

"Nope, she just called. She needs some time off, so you and Felicity are it. Now finish up, I'm closing the office and getting the lights," Mr. Penten answered.

"Damn," Ben muttered as Mr. Penten took the cash register bag and walked away. Not exactly an encouraging response.

"Sorry," she offered quietly.

He glanced up at her. "It's not you," he said, slamming the register closed. "Lucy was my ride home." He walked over and held the door open to the employee lounge, gesturing for her to get her bag. "You don't have a car do you?"

"No," she answered apologetically as she opened the locker and grabbed her purse.

"Great," he muttered sarcastically. His friendly demeanor had quickly fled. He seemed very disheartened by the prospect of losing his ride home. She wondered if it were only that, or if he simply preferred to work with Lucy.

Mr. Penten had returned from the office, and was heading for the front door. "Come on you two, you can get to know each other better on Monday." He held the door open for them. They walked outside and watched Mr. Penten set the alarm. He said goodnight, and left them to go to his car.

There were lots of people around, mostly congregating around a bar called 'Tommy's Place' a little down the street and across the way. Felicity waved as the boss drove off. She looked around, but the lot was now empty. "Are you walking tonight?"

"Yeah." Ben had been looking around too, although if not for his ride, she couldn't tell for what. "You in the dorms?" he asked, as they started across the parking lot.

She nodded. "Wesley Hall. Are you a student too?"

"I'm a junior, but I'm still living at home for now. I grew up here." He put his hands into his pockets and kicked at the rocks on the ground as he walked.

"Oh, so why don't you just have your folks pick you up?"

"My mom passed away a few years ago, so it's just my dad."

"Oh, I'm sorry," she responded awkwardly. From the tone in his voice when he'd said the word 'dad', she could tell family was a topic she should probably stay away from. She wished she could think of something to bring back that winning smile he'd first had.

"Thanks," he replied without looking at her. "Anyway, it's after 10 p.m. That means dad's Jack Daniel's started about 3 hours ago. I'm probably better off on my own."

Felicity was saved from having to comment on that by a terrible noise approaching. An old Bronco came screeching around the corner with music blaring and guys hollering out the windows. It pulled into the lot across the street and the guys piled out to join the line forming in front of the bar. "Is it always so lively around here?" she asked with a little laugh.

"Mostly on the weekends." Ben paused as he noticed a small group of teenagers gathered around a street light up ahead, on their side of the road. He moved a little closer to her and began to pick up the pace. "Come on, let's get out of here." She was given the impression that he would prefer to avoid them if at all possible.

Felicity stole a glance at the kids as they drew near. There were only three, two guys and a girl. They looked like they belonged in a grunge garage band. The guys were wearing baggy clothes that looked like they had been salvaged from Goodwill, and had never been washed. One had a head of long dark curls, fighting their way out from under a knit cap. The other had shaggy blonde hair down to just above his shoulders. Neither looked like hygiene was much of a concern.

In sharp contrast, the girl was stunningly beautiful. She looked like a runway model; with high cheekbones, full pouting lips, and a fine and delicate structure, but she had so much black make-up around her eyes that she seemed to be peering out of twin black holes. Her long straight hair had been dyed the same jet black. Felicity lowered her gaze as they came closer. She could see the girl had on a red micro-mini skirt with fishnet stockings and combat boots.

Ben was giving them pretty wide clearance, when one of the guys approached him; it was the blonde. "Hey man, they're chargin' cover tonight. Think you could spot us a twenty?" Ben just glared the kid a dirty look, and moved around him. The kid turned his attention to Felicity. "What about you babe? Buy me a drink?"

She smiled apologetically and shook her head. "Sorry, not tonight." She tried her best to sound friendly and unconcerned by his approach. Not that she really *should* find them intimidating, not one of them could have been older than sixteen.

Unfortunately, his friends seemed to find their exchange pretty funny. "I don't think she likes you Chris," the girl purred.

He tried again, giving her a creepy smile. "Come on, I'm real thirsty." As usual, Felicity was at a loss for a response in an awkward situation. The best course seemed to be to continue walking. "Guess I'll take a rain check then," he called after her.

Ben took her by the arm, making her very grateful for his presence. "She's with me," he said, after noting Felicity's discomfort. "Let's go." They moved on down the street and left the kids behind, without further event. They came to the corner, and she could see her dorm down the block. Ben looked back towards the street light, and then turned to face her. "I've gotta keep on this way," he said, nodding straight down the street. "You going to be alright? I can walk you to the door if you want."

"No, I'm fine. It's right there," she said, gesturing towards the building. "They're just kids," she said, trying to make herself feel the 'older and more mature' young woman in college, which she was now supposed to be. They probably were a year or two younger than she was, but she still found them intimidating. *You will not act like some little high school girl, terrified of being singled out and criticized*, she mentally chided herself. She smiled at Ben, but he didn't even notice; he seemed pretty eager to get home. She wondered what he thought of her. She couldn't really tell what to think of him yet. "Do you have far to go?"

"Just a few blocks. Walking's not so bad on a Saturday." He turned again in time to see the kids head towards the bar. "Like you said, it's pretty lively tonight. See you Monday."

"Good night. It was nice meeting you." She took a few steps backward toward her dorm, and then turned to head in, after he gave her a wave. Ah well, at least she felt like she knew someone now. So far, all of her classes had seemed to be full of this big crowd of nameless students that she hardly felt a part of. Maybe Ben would ask her to go for a soda or something after work on Monday. Or maybe she should ask him. After all, she had gone away to college to feel like she was starting fresh. She'd spent last night on the phone with her friend Deidre who was away at another school, comparing dorms and classes, and talking about how exciting it was to be able to have a fresh new start. A new start, with people who didn't know Felicity as the quiet little mouse of the neighborhood. She could totally reinvent herself; be more outgoing, a risk taker!

This was definitely an interesting change from the town she grew up in, even if it did sport a few less than desirable types. It was certainly a far cry from the big city, but still... Her hometown had one pub and it was mostly patronized by the same three or four old men every night. At least this place had potential for a little adventure. She smiled to herself as she jogged up the dorm steps. She'd even already met a guy...and he was cute, too!

~~~~~~~~~~~~~~~~~~~~~~~~~~~~~~

It was Monday night and Felicity was only half listening as Ashley tried to explain how to enter special orders into the computer. Ashley was nice enough, but she barely seemed to know what she was doing. In fact, Felicity could already see that she would probably be able to figure it out for herself before Ashley could manage to explain it to her properly.

Ashley pushed a strand of long blonde hair back behind her ear. "I think that should work, but maybe you should ask Mr. Penten to show you again tomorrow, just in case. I'm not really very good with computers. I'm more of a people person," she said, as she turned to smile at Felicity.

You could probably make a good argument for both sides of that statement. Ashley seemed to be one of those endlessly cheerful people, as long as she felt you were worth the effort. Felicity had noted that the young male customers especially, were greeted with a smile worthy of a toothpaste commercial. Ashley was friendly and eager to help them, with more enthusiasm than was strictly necessary, while any guy who seemed over the age of thirty or not particularly attractive, was given minimal service.

Girls seemed to be judged by some other system that Felicity hadn't quite figured out yet. There must be a certain criteria in Ashley's otherwise empty head, which deemed a girl worthy of her friendship. For whatever unknown reason, Felicity seemed to have made the cut. Ashley had taken Felicity under her wing and decided they should 'get to be good friends!' Training with her was like working with 'Cheerleader Barbie'. Thankfully she would be going off shift soon.

"I think I've got it." Felicity returned her smile. "You want me to go put away the new children's books that came in?"

"Well, do you think you know where they go?" Ashley asked.

"In the children's section?"

"Oh, right. Good for you! Sure, I'll stay on register for a while longer, and then I'll come see how you're making out. Okay?"

"Super," Felicity said with feigned enthusiasm. She grabbed a box and headed over to the children's section. She wanted to like Ashley, really. Here was the perfect opportunity to make a new friend. She'd be seeing her at work, and it even turned out that they had a class together. Ashley was a sophomore, but she was taking freshman algebra over again. Apparently once wasn't enough; not exactly a big surprise after witnessing Ashley's computer skills. Math didn't sound like it would be a strong subject for her either.

Considering they would be seeing so much of each other, it would be nice if they got along. In fact, Ashley had said that next class, she would save a seat for her 'new best friend'. She was...nice, but Felicity couldn't help it, this girl just got on her nerves. Ashley joined her just as she finished putting the last of the books away. "Wow, you even divided them by author! I forgot to tell you that."

"It's okay, I figured it out."

"Terrific! There's another box of children's stuff in the storage room. Same thing, I know you can handle it."

"Thanks."

Ashley looked at her watch. "I go off shift soon, but don't worry; we hardly get any customers after 8:00 anyway. If you do, don't worry about putting away the rest of the books. I wouldn't want you to feel overwhelmed."

"Don't worry, I'll manage," she responded. *I'm seventeen, not twelve,* she couldn't help but think to herself.

"I know you'll do great, but if you do have any problems, just ask Ben. He's such a doll!"

"Yeah, we've met. I'm sure I'll be fine."

"Then, I guess I'll see you tomorrow."

"I'm not working tomorrow."

Ashley made a little moue of disappointment. "Oh no. I wonder who I'm on with."

"I'm sure we'll work together again soon," Felicity assured her.

"Sure, and there's always algebra," Ashley said, pretending to shudder. "Hey, are you on Twitter, Facebook or MySpace? I'll add you."

Felicity dropped her eyes to the floor for a moment. "No, I'm kind of technologically challenged at the moment. Only computer I'm on is at the library." Ashley looked as though she couldn't believe it. *Great, now she's going to think I'm some backwoods hick without a clue,* she thought with disdain. "I'm hoping to get a laptop for my birthday," she quickly added.

"Oh, that'd be cool. You know, you can Tweet and do Facebook from your cell," Ashley said helpfully.

"Oh, I didn't know that," Felicity admitted. Explaining that she didn't have a cell phone either was not going to make her look any better, right now. It'd be easier to just end the subject. For the millionth time she wished her parents had more money to set her up with these things, so she could fit in a little better. She felt like such a country bumpkin. "Well, I'll see you in class."

Ashley gave her a sympathetic smile, as though she pitied the poor girl. "Bye."

"Tootles." Felicity gave a little wave as she mentally chastised herself for being sarcastic. Not the way to win friends. It wasn't Ashley's fault Felicity was Internet challenged.

She watched Ashley walk over to the café. She came to the counter just as Ben was coming out from behind it. Rather than wait for him to pass through the entrance, she just turned to the side and squeezed past, rubbing up against him. She did it as if it was nothing, but it seemed awfully familiar to Felicity. Ben certainly didn't seem to mind. Considering the fact that Ashley looked like a swimsuit model, most guys probably wouldn't. Not that there was anything wrong with Felicity's figure. It was far from perfect, but she was okay with it...usually. However, watching Ben notice Ashley did make her feel like eating less burgers and more salad.

She watched Ashley come out of the employee lounge and blow Ben a little kiss goodbye as she left. Could they be dating? She hadn't mentioned it. Could be that Ashley was just like that with every guy. The way she was flirting with some of the cuter customers earlier, it would be like her, but maybe Felicity shouldn't ask Ben to go for that drink after all. She'd have to see how he acted towards her. She didn't want to make things uncomfortable; this was a pretty good job.

The evening passed uneventfully. She had a few customers, but was still able to get all the books put away. Ashley would be so impressed. She glanced over at the café, where Ben was washing tables. Felicity had seen the last customer leave a few minutes earlier. She closed out her register, and everything worked out evenly, just as it was supposed to. She was relieved that she remembered how to do it by herself. It was easy really; this job was a snap. She straightened up the counter and went over to the café. Ben was still counting out his register. Wow, had she actually finished before him? "You're not done yet?" Ben looked up, losing his place . He didn't say anything, but sighed and picked up the money he had put off to the side and began counting…again. "Sorry," she whispered.

He finished and looked up at her. He didn't seem to be in a very good mood. "Did you need help with something?"

"No, I'm done. I guess I'm a quick study." She smiled and hoped that hadn't come out too pretentious.

"Yeah, well *you* didn't still have customers until about ten minutes ago."

"Oh." Where was the Ben who had seemed so approachable and welcoming when she had first met him? Had he decided that he didn't like her? "Well, is there something I can do to help?"

"No, just get your stuff. I'll be done in a sec." He waved her towards the back, distractedly. Felicity went into the employee lounge to get her purse from the locker. Probably not the night to ask Ben out, although he looked like he could use some fun. She wondered if he was twenty-one yet. She didn't think so, but maybe he wouldn't drink anyway, considering what he had said about his dad. Good thing she hadn't asked him to go for a drink, he might think she was being cruel.

She came out from the back just as he turned off the lights. There was only the glow of the light over the front door and a few dim night-lights placed in the back of the store. They walked out front and she waited while Ben set the alarm and locked the door. She wanted to ask if he was dating Ashley, but wasn't sure how to bring it up. She didn't want to sound forward or rude. He didn't seem to feel like talking anyway. Some doll.

Felicity glanced around the empty parking lot. "Couldn't find a ride huh?" she asked, as he put the keys into his jacket pocket.

He gave her a look that made her wish she hadn't asked. "No."

This ought to be a pleasant walk.

He looked up at her apologetically. "Sorry, sore subject. I have a car, it's just not running right now. It's a little more than I can fix myself, so I've been saving up to get it in the shop. It just seems to be taking forever to get up enough cash."

She smiled. "I know what you mean. I'm pretty short of cash myself right now. Stuff's more expensive than I thought it would be."

Ben just gave a little shrug and started walking. They crossed the empty parking lot and stepped out onto the road. It was *so* dark. There were a few street lights in front of the stores, but after their immediate glow the world seemed pitch black. There were no lights on the actual street, and no houses in the area.

Of course, Felicity had grown up in a town even smaller than this one. She was used to the open fields and forests of the country, but she had never done much walking at night. When she first got the job, she kept telling her parents how convenient it would be, that everything was within walking distance. She had never stopped to realize that some of that walking would be in the dark. She was glad Ben was in the same boat. She wondered if he'd drive her, when he got his car fixed.

Not that he was such good company. He seemed out of sorts, walking along the road at a brisk pace with his hands in his pockets. Since they'd left the store, he hadn't said a word. She found herself hurrying to keep up. "Hey, slow down. My legs aren't as long as yours."

He dutifully stopped and waited for her, and then started walking again, though not much slower. "So, what do you do around here for fun?" she asked, eyeing the bar across the street as they walked by. The lot was pretty empty, and the sound of an old country song drifted out an open window to them over the road.

"Not much to do around here."

"This is college, where are all the wild parties and stuff?"

He laughed. "You'll have to find a frat guy to ask. Not really my area of expertise. I'm just trying to get my degree, and save up enough money to move out of this hell hole of a town."

"Oookay. Well, I wasn't really looking for wild parties anyway, just curious, but you must do something besides work and go to school. Isn't there even a movie theater?"

"You want something to do, you have to head over to Binghamton or Oneonta. Without a car, the pickings are pretty slim."

Just then, someone stepped out of the trees from the side of the road. "Oh, I don't know. The pickings seem pretty good to me." It was a kid, one of the guys from the other night in fact. He was dressed the same as before, with a wool hat pulled down low on his head. He went to stand in the middle of the street in front of them.

She heard Ben mutter a curse under his breath as he backed up a step. He spun around at a noise behind them and she turned to see the punk's friend come up to block the road behind. "Guess it depends on your idea of a good time." He looked closer at Felicity; he was the one who had approached her the other night. She remembered his friend had called him Chris. "Hey, don't you owe me a drink?" he asked.

"Leave her alone." Ben said in a strong voice. He was clearly alarmed. Felicity was a bit spooked as well, but what did he think they were going to do? They were just kids.

"Oo, a tough guy," Chris said with a laugh. "Want to know *my* idea of a good time?" Without waiting for an answer, he launched himself at Ben. Ben shoved her out of the way, as the guy tackled him. He pushed Chris off just as the guy with the hat came up behind and tried to grab Ben by the back of the neck. Felicity stood there for a minute in a panic. She had no idea what to do!

The guy with the hat jumped onto Ben's back. As the other came at him again, Ben leaned back against the first and kicked the second square in the chest, knocking the wind from him. Felicity ran over and grabbed the guy on Ben's back by the jacket to try and haul him off, while yelling at them to stop and leave Ben alone. Nobody paid her any attention.

Ben somehow managed to slip out from underneath the guy, and as Felicity let go, Ben turned and punched the guy in the face. He looked at Felicity for a second. "Run, get out of here!" He turned back around just as Chris got up and came running at them.

She was just supposed to leave him here with these guys? She looked around; they were in front of the drug store, but of course everything was closed. They were almost at the corner, right down the road from her dorm. She'd get help. She saw Ben rip something from his pocket just as she turned to run. Did he carry a knife or something?

She ran. She had just gotten to the corner of the building, when she thought she heard someone coming up behind her. Before she could even turn to look, she felt herself being thrown to the ground as someone shoved her in the back. The air pushed out of her lungs in a great whoosh as she hit the grass.

Felicity raised herself up to see the girl from the other night standing before her. She had her hands on her hips and was sneering at Felicity on the ground. "Going somewhere?" she asked in a throaty snarl. She had the superior and condescending demeanor shared by every girl who had ever picked on Felicity back in high school. So much for a fresh start! She was in college now, wasn't this stuff supposed to have been left behind her? Felicity didn't even know this girl or her friends. Did she have a big target painted on her for every bully in the world to see? This girl looked to be at least a year younger than she was. Did they have something against Ben? What did they want?

Felicity was surprised that the girl actually let her get up, when something strange happened. The girl's face changed. Suddenly her cheekbones seemed to shift and her mouth widened into an impossible grin as unnaturally long fangs were revealed. They appeared thin and as sharp at the ends as hypodermic needles. Her eyes glazed over into a bright crimson red, with only a long black slit of a pupil in the center of each. The girl smiled and sprang at her, before Felicity could think to do anything but scream.

The girl knocked her to the ground again, and Felicity found herself trying to hold her off as the girl pressed her to the grass. Felicity gasped and struggled but couldn't get out from under her, as the girl strained to bite at Felicity's neck. Then suddenly, the weight was lifted, and the girl seemed to fly off of her into the street.

There was a man standing over her; he must have thrown the girl. He reached down a hand and pulled her up off of the ground in one strong swift motion. He was very handsome, though in a rugged sort of way. His light brown hair nearly reached his broad shoulders, and he had arresting blue eyes. Before she was barely standing, Felicity saw him turn and run towards Ben.

Ben was in the middle of the street. One guy was lying in the road, and Ben was wrestling with the other; it was the one without the hat, Chris. Suddenly, Chris let out a sharp exclamation of pain, and jumped off of him. Ben still held something in his hand; good, she hoped he'd stabbed the guy. Just as Chris backed off, the one on the ground kicked Ben's feet out from under him and he went down, hard.

Their rescuer reached the road just as the guy who had kicked Ben was getting to his feet. Chris came running at him from the side, but the man reached out an arm and elbowed him in the throat just as he got there. Chris backed off choking as the other guy turned to face his new opponent. Ben got up, but was ignored. Chris joined his friend, and the two guys squared off against their new foe. Ben spotted Felicity standing on the grass and came running. "What happened to you? I heard you screaming. Are you okay?"

The girl! Felicity quickly looked for her, but she was gone. She must have taken off. Felicity looked back to the street in time to see Chris get punched in the head. In the same fluid motion, she saw the man who had helped her, spin around and kick the other guy high in the chest. She turned back to Ben. "That girl, she was... There's something wrong with her! She wasn't human!" She felt herself edging into hysteria. What the hell was she? What was going on?

Ben took her by the shoulders and looked into her eyes, trying to calm her. "I know. Are you okay?"

"I think so. Shouldn't we help him?" she asked, glancing at the fight in the street. Just then, she screamed and stumbled backwards as Chris was thrown by their rescuer. The boy came flying over the pavement to land at their feet. He rolled over and his slightly parted lips revealed fangs fully as long as the girl's.

Ben took her by the arm and pulled her away, while glancing back up at the man who had thrown Chris. "*He* doesn't need any help."

She realized that Ben held not a knife, but a large wooden cross. What in the world was he doing with that? Some slight movement from Chris drew her attention, and she looked down to see his eyes flick open to reveal a bright sickly orange color, with thin upright pupils similar to the girl's. He struggled to his feet. Ben began to approach him, but he got up and ran off into the woods. Felicity looked back into the road and was amazed to see that the other two guys were gone. She spun around nervously. "Where'd they go?"

Ben took a quick glance around and started herding her down the road. "They're gone. Let's just get out of here before they decide to come back."

She let herself be pulled around the corner and ran with Ben down the block to her dorm building. As they reached the lighted porch, she made him let go of her arm so she could turn to face him. "What the hell is going on? What were those things?"

He stood catching his breath, his hand pressed to his side. She suddenly realized that he might be hurt. He looked up at her, shoving the cross back into his pocket. "I still have a few blocks to go. I'd like to get home before they decide to come back for more."

"Are you crazy? Come inside, we should call somebody!"

"No, I'm okay. We'll talk about it tomorrow," he insisted.

"Ben," she fixed him with a concerned stare, "what were those things?"

He looked around, as though mentioning them might bring them back. "Vampires."

"What?" she exclaimed in disbelief.

She was about to say more, when he held up a hand and cut her off. "I have to go. I'll see you tomorrow. When do you have a break for lunch?"

"12:30, but..."

"Good, me too. I'll meet you outside, at the picnic tables."

Before she could say anything else, he turned and took off, down the steps and across the lawn. She watched him go. Every time he passed a bush or a tree, she kept thinking something was going to reach out and grab him, but nothing did. He turned the corner and was out of sight. She slowly turned and opened the door. Vampires?

Felicity entered the parlor and shut the door behind her. No one was around. She turned around and locked the door. You weren't supposed to lock it until curfew - 11:00 p.m., but she wasn't about to leave it open. She slowly climbed the stairs to her room. She heard someone brushing their teeth down the hall. It sounded weird and mundane. She was just attacked by a vampire! She opened the door to her room and slipped inside as if she were in a trance. Vampires?

~~~~~~~~~~~~~~~~~~~~~~~~~~~~~~

College Campus, Outdoor Student Commons
12:30, Tuesday afternoon

It was so warm for September. Felicity sat in a patch of sunlight at a picnic table. She had purposely chosen a table placed away from the stream of students pouring out of the cafeteria. She felt like there was enough buzzing going on in her own head without having to listen to everyone else.

She couldn't have answered a single question about any of her classes that morning. She'd hardly gotten any sleep, and every time she so much as closed her eyes, they were there. She would see that awful girl with the red eyes and those unnaturally long, sharp teeth. Vampires.

When Ben had said the word, you could have knocked her over with a feather. This is New York! Okay, it's the back woods upstate mountains of New York, but still! It's not as if she were going to college in Transylvania or something. This type of thing only happened in really bad horror movies that she never even bothered to watch the whole way through. Maybe she should have stayed awake until the end, then at least she might have some idea what she was supposed to do in a situation like this! But in the movies, the vampire was always some suave mysterious rich guy in a cape, not a pack of teen street thugs who looked like they'd want your wallet more than your blood.

She ripped open her plastic packet of Caesar dressing and began to squeeze it over her salad as she watched the students flow in and out of the building. Where was Benjamin? She needed someone to reassure her of her sanity.

He came up from behind. He put his hand on her shoulder and she managed to squirt dressing clear over the table before she knew it was him. "Ben! Are you trying to give me a heart attack?" she scolded.

"It's a bright sunny day, 'Liss. I think all of the vampires are tucked snugly in their coffins right about now." Ben dropped his lunch tray on the table and swung a leg over the bench next to her.

No one had ever called her 'Liss before. She kind of liked it. It seemed his confident and casual attitude was back. Sure now, when she was not in the mood for it. "How can you make jokes? Aren't you totally wigged out?"

"I'm not joking. They are nocturnal you know; and yeah, I'm a little unsettled, but it's not like it hasn't happened before, unfortunately." Benjamin sat straddling the bench next to her, and began to unwrap his sandwich.

She turned to sit sideways and face him. "They've attacked you before?" she asked, astonished.

"They're not the first in this town, but I've seen that particular group half a dozen times. They've attacked me twice; the girl's name is Sindy. I...used to know her. I think it was in 9th grade that she started spelling it with an 'S'. Pretty stupid huh? Anyway, I don't know the guys, but Sindy ran away from home a couple of years back. Then a few months ago she shows up again, sporting her 'new look'. They hang out in the parking lots of the bars late at night and wait for someone to stumble out after a few too many." He paused to take a bite of his sandwich. "Not a long wait in this town."

"Oh my God! Doesn't anybody else know about this?" She looked around at the oblivious crowd of students eating lunch around them. No one seemed within easy hearing range, or even paid them any attention. She lowered her voice anyway. "Doesn't anyone investigate, like the police? There must be...bodies."

He shrugged. "There was a big scene a little while back; they found a bunch of bodies that'd been dumped, but they never solved it. I guess the fiends got scared off for a little, but they never left. Lot of milk carton college kids around here.

Vampires seem to like this town. You know when they're around, if you pay close attention. Though I must say, it's been awhile since I've heard of anyone missing. No bodies in the paper since early summer. I think they've gotten smart. Now they don't kill you, not usually. They drink you unconscious and then move on. I've seen it happen. You'll wake up after sleepin' it off in the parking lot. Sometimes they'll even put you in your car if they can." He looked around at the college students scattered about. "Think half these guys'd notice?"

"Seen it?" she asked in frightened awe. "Has it ever happened to you?"

He gave her a serious look. "No, I've lived here my whole life, never been bit. I'm too smart for that," he said with a little smile. "They won't bother you if you're careful, and stay out of their way. I wouldn't recommend walking home during the week, but on weekends there are enough partiers around to divert their attention. They like easy targets; people who don't even notice they're different, until it's too late."

"But their faces, that girl, her eyes and her teeth... She was so pale and inhuman." Felicity shuddered just to think of her.

"Oh they were human once, but now, they're just evil dead things. I'm not an authority or anything, I've just been around here long enough to open my eyes." He took another bite of his sandwich.

How could he eat while thinking about this stuff? "They were hideous monsters. Evil dead... wasn't that a movie?"

"Those were *zombies* not vampires. Jeez, don't you know the difference?" he teased. "The movie stuff works though. I mean they can't turn into bats or smoke or anything. At least I don't think so, and I think the garlic aversion is strictly silver screen; but you can hold them off with crosses." He pulled the wooden cross from last night out of his back pocket, where it had been hidden by his shirt. "I don't leave home without it." She noticed he also wore a small gold cross on a thin chain around his neck. "I've also heard holy water burns them like acid, although I haven't tried it myself. Mostly, I just stay in at night."

"Good plan. Thank God that guy was there! Do you know him?"

Ben didn't seem thrilled to be reminded of his rescue; typical prideful guy. "He's been coming into the café almost every night since June, his name's Cain. He buys a coffee and a book, and just sits and reads 'til closing. I'm not proud to say, he's the one who saved my ass the last time I got attacked. I don't get it, he's…"

"Benji!" It was a petite blonde girl from across the commons. At least she used to be blonde, her short wild hair was now streaked with just about every color of the rainbow. She wore a pink t-shirt that would probably fit a five year old and a pair of purple leather pants. She waved and started pulling some guy over by the arm to join them.

"That's Alyson." Ben smiled with obvious affection. "We've been friends since we were like, three. And that's her boyfriend of the month. I think his name is Greg." They made it to the table and Alyson directed her guy to drop an armload of stuff. Two Twinkies, a Yoohoo, a package of mini chocolate chip cookies, a bottle of Sunny D, a squished Devil Dog, and a bag of Raisinettes. They sat down and made themselves at home.

Felicity had never cared for punk hairstyles, but even under that, Alyson was pretty, in an honest and unpretentious sort of way. Apart from the wild colors in her hair, she didn't wear much make-up. Ben and Felicity turned to sit straight again, and face them across the table. "How do you eat all that crap?" Ben asked as they got settled.

"Life's short. You want me to waste it eating salad?" she asked with a smile as she ripped open the bag of cookies and shoved one in her mouth whole. Felicity glanced at her bowl, then back to the girl. Naturally, Alyson was thin as a rail. "No offense, of course," Alyson said around the cookie, wiping her hands on her pants. She reached over the table to shake Felicity's hand. "Hi! I'm Allie."

She shook Felicity's hand, and then ate another cookie. She had a little diamond stud in her nose that glinted as she chewed. "This is Greg." She nodded to her boyfriend who was staring into space while popping Raisinettes. Tall thin guy, with a long, dark mass of hair. He seemed to be in his own world at the moment, or quite possibly every moment from the look of him.

He gave her a nod without making eye contact. "Hey."

She took her hand back. "Hi, my name's Felicity."

"*Really*?" Alyson asked. "You must have died when they came out with the show! Did it give you the urge to go out and get an Ogilvie?"

Ben rolled his eyes and shook his head at Felicity's confused stare. "Felicity just started working over at the DownTime," he added helpfully.

"Oh, that's an exciting job." Alyson began making loud snoring sounds until Ben waved a hand in front of her face.

"Shut up, I make more money than you," he taunted.

"Hey, I am very proud of my job as a professional groupie!" she said, sitting up straighter.

"You wish." Ben muttered, as he turned to Felicity. "Allie waitresses, and works the sound board over at Tommy's…the local chug-a-lug." He turned back to face Alyson. "Any good bands playing this month?"

"Na, just the local red-necks. We never get anybody good anymore."

Ben directed his gaze over to Greg, who looked as though he had fallen asleep with his eyes open. "Hey Greg, aren't you in a band?"

He came out of his daze, it took a minute. "Yeah, the PowerHouses."

"If he could manage to write something original, they might actually get a gig sometime," Allie added accusingly.

"I'm waiting for inspiration."

"It doesn't have to be inspired, it just has to have a beat you can drink to." She leaned over the table as if speaking to Felicity confidentially. "There's only so many times you can listen to 'Shook Me All Night Long' you know? Even the vamps are getting bored."

Felicity almost choked on her diet soda. "Oh my God, you know about them?" Even though Ben knew about them, and had said he'd known Allie well, she just couldn't imagine someone else actually believing in this stuff.

"Who doesn't? Observant much? Freakin' parasites are all over this damn town." Alyson twisted open the Sunny D and managed to swig it all down without coming up for air.

"And you work in a bar, late at night? Aren't you terrified?"

"Fuck that. Lived here all my life. I'm a brown belt, Jui Jitsu. They don't need a piece of me, there's much easier hot lunches walkin' around."

"They still try," Ben cut in, "show her your souvenir."

Alyson pulled down the collar of her tee a bit to show the healing scab of a jagged bite mark on the side of her throat. "That skanky whore Sindy. Kicked her ass, but not before she got a taste of me. It wouldn't have left such a gash, but I was ripping her off me at the time, bitch. I almost wouldn't mind another chance at her alone. I'd love to finish her off."

"Danced with her and her boys last night." Ben sounded awfully nonchalant for someone who had been on the ground the night before.

"No way! And you are just telling me this now? You clown, what happened?" she asked, ripping open a Twinkie.

Ben shrugged, eyes on the ground. "Nothin' really, we got away, but I've gotta get my 'stang runnin'. It sucks not havin' a car in this town, literally. I talked to Penten though, and at least I'm not closing again until next week. Maybe by then Lucy'll be back."

Felicity had wanted to talk more about their attack, when something occurred to her. "Hey, I'm closing on Thursday."

"With Harold?" Ben asked.

She nodded. "I haven't met him yet. Tell me this guy has a car."

"He's got a car, but he's a real jerk," Ben added, looking disgusted.

"You don't think he'd give me a ride?"

"Well, he doesn't give *me* a ride, but he'd probably drive *you* if you asked him." Ben finished his sandwich, while looking at his watch. "I have to get to class."

Greg stood up and looked down at Allie, who had been watching the whole exchange with some amusement. "Let's get out of here."

"Yeah, we should go." Alyson began gathering up what was left of their stuff and shoving it into her purse, which looked more like a small duffle bag.

"Oh, do you have class too?" Felicity asked her.

Alyson let out a sharp laugh. "Oh, we're not students. We just come for the food." She smiled at Felicity's bewildered look, and then glanced over at Ben who was getting ready to leave. "See, ya."

Ben just gave her a nod and turned to face Felicity. "Good luck Thursday. Don't worry; I'm sure you'll be fine. Harold'll drive you home."

Felicity was left staring at her salad. Maybe she should call in sick.

~~~~~~~~~~~~~~~~~~~~~~~~~~~

DownTime Café and Bookstore
Thursday night

Felicity finished shelving the last of the books from the new shipment. She stood, slowly, waiting for the pins and needles to leave her legs, and picked up the empty box. At least it was almost time to go home.

Home...she had gone home for real the other night, for dinner with her family. She had hoped to surround herself with familiar comforts and maybe even broach the subject of not returning to school at all, but it hadn't gone quite as she had hoped. Her mom had gotten called into work. She was a nurses' aide at the local hospital, and they were always short staffed. Her younger teenage brothers had friends over, filling the house with raucous chaos. Even when her dad wasn't playing referee to her brothers, she couldn't really bring herself to talk to him about her concerns. It was hard to talk to him about personal stuff, let alone vampires.

She sat at the dinner table and listened to him complain about his job at the factory and his new jerk of a boss. 'Good thing you're going to school young lady, earn yourself a job where you can get some respect'. After dinner, she tried to get her friend Deidre on the phone. If she could talk to Deidre about things, she knew she would feel better. She and Deidre had been best friends since kindergarten. With Dee, she could talk about anything, but Deidre was away at her own school, and the phone number her mom gave her was busy for a half an hour.

When she finally did get through, some girl told her that Deidre wasn't around, but she would give her a message. Felicity asked the girl twice, to be sure that Deidre called her back. 'It's her best friend, Felicity Snow; please *make sure she calls me.*' She left specific instructions that she would be at her home number this evening, Deidre knew it by heart. She left her number at school too, in case Deidre couldn't call back until tomorrow.

Deidre never did call. After an hour her dad said that he wanted to drive her back to the dorm. He wanted to get home in time to catch the end of her brother Eddie's college football game on T.V., which he also made them listen to on the radio all the way back.

So she found herself back at the dorms, forced back into the routine of school life. She never heard from Deidre. The next time she talked to her mom, she felt that she hardly knew what to say. Her mom apologized for having to run out on their dinner, and then began regaling her with stories of an old friend she'd bumped into at work.

Her parents were wrapped up in their own stuff and busy with her brothers. Now they were supposed to believe stories of vampires? She knew that they loved her, but she felt as though she was pretty much on her own.

So here she was, on her own, with closing time looming ever nearer. Getting home, how was she going to handle that one? Benjamin had been right; Harold was more than willing to give her a ride. He had also been more than willing to help her pin on her forgotten nametag earlier. He seemed to be undressing her with his eyes ever since. He was also very fond of calling her 'sugar'. This was not a ride she was looking forward to.

But what was the alternative? Walking home alone in the dark? Of course, here in the brightly lit store, her memories of Monday night seemed almost dream-like. They weren't really vampires were they? She had turned it over in her mind a million times since it had happened. It seemed so unbelievable, though Ben certainly seemed to believe it. Maybe he was just playing with her, embellishing stories to tease her, but she had *seen* them! There was definitely something wrong with their eyes, and those teeth! Why else did they attack her and Ben like that? Could they really be vampires?

She made her way to the storage room, and tossed the box into the corner, vaguely near the garbage. All she needed to do now was close out the register. She was glad she had gotten this job. Now that classes were under way, it was usually quiet. Most of it was mindless work, but that was okay. She loved to have access to so many books. Sometimes during the evening, she could sneak into the corner with a newly discovered story and lose herself for a little while, but no time for that now, the cash register awaits.

As she worked, she could see Harold across the store in the café. He was in his early thirties. He had a large build, dark greasy hair, and somehow seemed to think women should adore him, even if they weren't good for much else.

He wasn't all that unattractive really, but his attitude far outweighed any appeal he might have had. The worst part of it was that it seemed totally unconscious, as though he had no idea that he was talking down to her, because after all, she really should be flattered that he was talking to her at all. He noticed her looking and grinned. Okay, walking might be the better option here.

Harold glanced over at the corner table, behind the bookshelf. "Hey buddy, you're gonna have to take that somewhere else. I'm tryin' to close here." He must still have a customer.

The man stood up from the table, leaving his coffee and book behind. "I'm finished." She was almost afraid to hope, but as he turned for the door, she saw it was him. The man from the other night, Benjamin had called him Cain.

She wasn't sure what she'd say, but she couldn't just let him leave. He was halfway to the door already. She forced herself to call after her rescuer. "Hey, wait!" He kept walking as if unaware of her. "Cain!"

That stopped him in his tracks. He slowly turned to face her. He looked a little confused, did he even recognize her? She closed the register drawer and came around the counter to him. "Hi, I'm Felicity...from the other night?" His eyes warmed to her and he gave a small smile. "I never got a chance to thank you."

He looked almost embarrassed that she had brought it up. "You don't have to thank me." He had a slight British lilt to his words that she hadn't expected. He was so handsome! It was kind of intimidating. *I will not be shy. I will not be shy!* she kept telling herself.

"Well, of course I'm going to thank you! You probably saved my life. Ben said you've helped him out before too. What is it, like a hobby of yours?"

He studied her for a moment. "More like a self-set obligation, actually."

He was even more attractive here in the light, than when she'd seen him in the dark the other evening. She kept looking at the blonde highlights in his sandy hair and the blue of his eyes. He was definitely older than her, but not much. "Wow," she said, feeling incredibly stupid as it came out of her mouth.

An idea popped into her head, but she was unsure whether she would actually have the guts to ask. *Take a risk!* she thought, trying to goad herself with encouragement. Here it goes... "Um, listen. I know I don't really know you or anything, and you don't know me, but...I was kind of hoping, maybe you could do me a favor...again?"

He simply stood there, patiently taking her in with his eyes. She took a deep breath to try to get up some courage, but her words still came out nervously rushed and rambling. "See, the thing is...I live at the college, in the dorms, which is like right down the road, really, but, um... Well, Monday night kind of freaked me out, and...see... Harold over there," they both glanced into the café, to find Harold staring at them. He winked at her and smiled. "He's my only ride home, and I'm not sure if that's much of an improvement over walking."

Cain took his eyes from Harold to give her sympathetic smile. "I don't have a car."

"Oh, that's okay. I don't mind walking, I just...didn't want to walk alone," she clarified.

"You want *me* to walk you home?" He seemed to think this was strange.

"If you wouldn't mind," she said, hopefully.

He glanced back at Harold. "And you think you'd be safer with me, than with him?" He almost seemed amused.

"Well yes, considering you saved my life the other night, and Harold seems a little too eager to get me alone in his car. So, I think I'd rather walk. You're not going to make me walk home alone, are you?"

He thought about it. "Alright, I'll wait."

"Thank you so much! I really appreciate this. I'll just be a minute."

She quickly ran around the counter and finished tallying up the register sheet. She grabbed the register bag for Harold to put into the safe. "I just have to grab my bag and coat." She crossed the store to the employee lounge behind the café, dropping the moneybag for Harold on the counter as she passed.

"You about ready to go sugar? 'Cause I know I am." Harold was running his eyes up and down her body again as she put on her jacket.

"Actually, I've decided to walk. Thanks anyway." She started back to Cain, who was watching them from the door.

"You sure that's wise?" Harold called after her, casting a disapproving glance at Cain. "A sweet thing like you shouldn't chance talking to strangers."

Couldn't be much stranger than you, she thought. "I'll risk it." Cain opened the door for her as she approached. "Thanks again, really," she said gratefully.

Cain just smiled as they exited the store out into the night. They walked in silence. He seemed so self-assured and at ease. She was a wreck; he was so good looking! She needed to get him talking. Now she wished the dorms were further so she'd have time to think of something witty and mature to say. "Ben says you come into the café a lot, almost every night."

"Yes."

Well, so much for her great conversation starter. They both watched the ground go by as they walked. *Quick, say something before this silence gets longer!* she chided herself. "I guess you have a lot of *'Down Time'*, huh? Get it?" She laughed nervously. "'Cause the name of the café... God, that was so lame."

He chuckled. "I'm around, but not every night, so you should probably find an alternate way home, unless you fancy getting to know Harold much better." He gave her a sidelong glance.

She smiled. "Yeah, really trying to avoid that." She tried to gauge his reaction to her without being too obvious. "I guess I should get myself a can of mace, huh?"

He stared at the pavement flowing under their feet for a moment. "Won't really help...unless you plan to use it on Harold. You ought to learn some self defense." He cocked his head to look into her eyes, lowering his voice in all seriousness. "The running and screaming, very rarely works."

She tore her gaze from his eyes to look back at the ground. "I noticed that."

Okay, she thought to herself. *Time to take a risk for once in your life. This guy is gorgeous, and in about five minutes you will probably never see him again. Do something!* "Hey, maybe you could teach me?" She looked at him expectantly. He didn't answer. "You certainly taught *them* a lesson..." She trailed off into silence. "Okay, that seemed much funnier before it actually came out of my mouth; but you *do* know how to handle yourself, obviously, and I sure don't."

"You'd probably be better off taking a class or something," he said quietly.

Way to throw yourself at the guy. "I'm sorry; I'm not usually this forward. I just thought, maybe...you'd like to..."

They came to the dorm and stopped at the steps. She looked up to find him staring at her with the strangest look of wonder on his face. "I would...like to," he began hesitantly. "I just assumed..." He shook his head. "Where? When?"

She couldn't believe it; maybe he didn't think she was pushy and annoying after all! "I think they keep the school gym open."

"Are you working tomorrow?"

"Yes, but only until eight." She tried to keep the excitement from her voice.

"Alright, then I'll see you at eight." How did he manage to sound so casually in command of the situation and still come off as sweet, and a little vulnerable?

"Great! I'll see you tomorrow!" She wished she could wipe the dumb smile off of her face.

"Good night." He returned her smile, then turned and walked off into the dark.

Chapter 2 – Ice Cream

Cain

School Gym
Friday night

He had forgotten how good this could be, close physical contact with another person; even if he was letting her beat the hell out of him. Not that she could really hurt him, but it was fun letting her try.

Felicity was catching her breath. Rumpled and disheveled in a pink sweat suit, she was bent forward with her hands on her knees. Her long auburn hair was working its way out of a French braid. Minimal makeup, cheeks flushed...she was beautiful.

Cain wore his usual black t-shirt and broken in blue jeans. She had given him a bit of an odd look when she noticed he was wearing boots, but didn't say anything. He didn't own a pair of trainers.

The gym was empty, except for them. There had been a few students there earlier, finishing some kind of aerobic workout. They had left soon after Cain and Felicity had arrived. That was fine with him; he didn't like to be the center of attention.

He was trying to teach her some basic self-defense moves, with limited success. They'd been there for a while, and so far he had managed to establish that she was eager, unafraid of hard work, and totally unaware of how to handle herself in a fight.

The only sound was the hum of the fluorescent lights and her breathing. The gym smelled of sweat and vinyl. It felt an odd place for him to be, and yet she made it seem the most natural thing in the world. She looked up and caught him staring at her, but smiled and didn't seem to mind. She was ready for another go-'round. "All right, try it again. Say a guy comes at you from behind, puts his arm 'round your neck. Ready?" he asked.

She gave him a nod and turned away, planting her feet firmly, bracing herself. He came up from behind as he'd described, putting his arm over her shoulder and around her throat. She grabbed his arm and tried to flip him, but couldn't. He breathed her in, feeling almost intoxicated by her closeness. Her frustration was palpable. "I am never going to get this, I just can't lift you."

He smiled. "It's not about strength, it's about leverage. You're putting your weight on the wrong foot again. You want it to be more like this..." He demonstrated, and then backed off for another try. "Come on, one more time, ready?"

She braced herself again. He waited for a moment, seeing her muscles tense with anticipation, and then came at her the same as before. This time she actually flipped him, although she also managed to throw herself to the ground in the process.

Felicity rolled over laughing. She was lying next to him on the mat, chest heaving with the exertion. She sat up a little to look at him. "I did it!" He had to smile at her innocent excitement. Then her face clouded for a moment. "You didn't *let* me did you?"

He was still lying next to her on the floor, trying not to laugh. "If I'd let you, it would have been a bit more graceful, don't you think?"

She looked a bit sheepish. "I guess I need more practice," she said, getting back to her feet. "Another time though, I think I've punished you enough for one night." She reached down a hand to help him up. He took it, though he felt a bit bewildered. He wasn't used to such casual, sincere camaraderie. She kept catching him off guard.

He looked up to see her noticing the tattoo on the inside of his arm that read 'Genesis 4:7', but she didn't ask after it. She gave him an easy smile. "You want ice cream? I feel like ice cream." He hardly knew what to make of this girl, and found himself following her to a nearby ice cream parlor.

She headed to the walk-up window, glancing back at him. "So, what's your flavor?"

As if he should have any idea what to order. "Oh... um... I don't know, chocolate."

She turned to stare at him from the list of like 50 flavors. "No it's not," she said with disbelief.

"It's not?" he asked, with eyebrows raised.

Now she seemed embarrassed. She was such an innocent combination of bold and unsure. It was rather endearing. "Well, I mean, you just don't seem like a chocolate person. It's so...mainstream," she said, a bit awkwardly.

Mainstream he was not. "So what are you having?" he asked with a smile.

She replied with a little singsong lilt, "I don't know yet." Was she flirting with him? It almost seemed so. It had been so long, and with girls these days, he could hardly tell. She looked at the list as moths and little creatures with gauze wings threw themselves against the lights over the sign. The air still smelled like summer. "Um... I'll have...Butter Rum Ripple," she said, turning back to him with a hint of challenge in her voice, "How 'bout that?"

He had to laugh. Yes, she was definitely flirting. "Well, anything with 'Rum' in the title can't be all that bad, right? Make it two."

Felicity ordered the ice cream, and paid before he could offer. "My treat. It's the least I can do after you let me beat you up all night."

As if it were a chore. "Anytime."

They got their cones and sat outside at a wooden picnic table as Felicity began to lick hers. "I'm glad you don't mind," she said with a laugh, "because I think it's going to take a while before I get it right."

Actually, he hoped she was a fast learner, for her sake. The sooner she learned to handle herself, the less he would worry. Though now that she had his interest, he knew he would never stop worrying. There were so many dangers in the world. "You'll get it, you're doing better," he assured her.

She looked doubtful. "It's a lot harder than I thought it was going to be. Then again, that's the story of my life these days."

Mine too, he thought to himself. "College not exactly what you thought it would be?"

"Oh no, it is. I mean, it's okay. It's just...well, before I came here, people tried to tell me that I'd led a sheltered life, that I was a bit naive." She smiled as he feigned surprise. "I didn't believe them of course, but now that I'm here, I'm thinking...yeah, pretty much, that's me."

He noticed that his untouched ice cream was melting down his hand. He took a few halfhearted licks around the bottom of the cone, just to neaten it up. "Moving *here* would be a big adjustment for anyone, what with the interesting night-life and all."

"So when did you move here?" she asked. She seemed to want to avoid the topic of vampires for now. Fine with him. "I get the feeling you're not 'born and raised'."

Ah yes, the accent. He hadn't quite had the heart to ever work on losing it, although it did tend to set him apart. "No, I was born..." He tried not to think back to those times. He didn't often allow himself to reminisce, no point. "a long time ago..."

Felicity looked to him expectantly as he trailed off into silence. "In...a galaxy far, far, away?"

He smiled. Movie theaters were a favorite refuge of his. He'd seen all of the Star Wars films many times. She was so delightful. "Something like that. Don't worry, you'll get used to it here." She let him off the subject. Good, he wasn't ready to talk about himself. He became mesmerized, watching her mouth as she licked the ice cream. She didn't notice.

"I guess..." She seemed lost in her own thoughts for the moment. "Did you ever feel like you had your whole life all planned out? You thought you knew just what to do, to put yourself on the right track, and have everything under control, and then suddenly, something changes, and now everything is different?"

He smiled to himself and muttered, "Many times."

She seemed heartened by his answer. "Does it ever get easier?" she asked hopefully.

"I'll let you know." He gave her a grin. "But that's just the way it is. Things change, and we're all of us just struggling to keep up, but sometimes change can be good, when you least expect it."

She took the last few delicate bites of her cone and began licking her fingers. "I hope so, because right now I feel like I'm wandering lost in a fog."

"Oh, the fog never lifts," he said with a smile, "you just learn to work through it."

She was leaning a bit forward, listening to him intently when she suddenly straightened. "Work! I have to get going. I have a ton of homework to do if I'm going to have any idea what's going on in class tomorrow!" She looked at his hardly touched ice cream. "You done?"

He glanced down at his melting mess. "Yes."

They got up and ditched their garbage. She seemed to feel bad as she watched him throw away his mostly uneaten cone and attempt to clean his hand with a napkin. "How was it?" she asked tentatively.

Why was such a sweet girl wasting her time with him? "Better than chocolate," he answered sincerely. They shared a smile and walked back to her dorm in silence, stopping at the steps. "So, when can I expect some more punishment?" he asked.

It took her a second to realize what he was talking about. "Oh, the training. I don't know what your schedule's like; I don't want to monopolize all of your free time."

That made him smile; he had absolutely nothing else to do. "I think I can manage to fit you in." She seemed almost surprised. Did she really think he wouldn't want to see her again?

"Okay...how about Tuesday?" she offered. "Is 9:00 too late?"

She had made him smile more times this evening than he could remember smiling in a month. "It's perfect."

"Great! I'm here in Wesley Hall, room 217. It's right at the top of the stairs, just come on up."

"I will." He knew he should leave, but couldn't quite bring himself to go yet. There was an awkward moment of silence. "Thanks for the ice cream."

She finally broke eye contact, blushing. "Good night," she said as she turned and entered the dorm, leaving him standing on the steps. It was a good night indeed.

Chapter 3 - Stupid!

Felicity

Felicity's Dorm Room
Tuesday night

Felicity zipped her sweatshirt over her t-shirt, and sat down on the bed to put on her sneakers. The weekend had gone by in a blur, between working, homework and a quick visit home, she had hardly any free time. Working at the bookstore had turned her on to so many great new books, she couldn't help but spend what little free time she did have, reading. She felt a little guilty that she hadn't made the effort to join some campus activities and make some new friends, but she just couldn't really bring herself to care all that much about anything else.

Right now, all she could think about was Cain. It was amazing how he could make her feel so secure and at ease with herself. Of course, she had been nervous to see him at first. He wasn't like other guys she had known, he made them seem like little boys, but once the initial awkwardness was past, she felt totally comfortable with him.

He made her feel like he valued time they spent together; like she was special. Not that proving her incompetence in the gym and eating (or not eating) ice cream should be considered anything so special, but she got the feeling he didn't care what they were doing. Like he just enjoyed being with her. Maybe it was all in her imagination, wishful thinking, but every time she looked into his eyes...

There was a knock at the door. Felicity glanced at the clock; it was only 8:40. "Who is it?"

"It's Ben, got a minute?"

She got her foot into her shoe and stood up to open the door. "Sure, what's up?" She let him in and sat down to tie her laces, as Ben stood in the open doorway.

"I called earlier, but you weren't in. Someone gave me your room number. I hope you don't mind." Felicity shook her head no. He'd gone through that much trouble to find her? Interesting. "I was wondering if you could cover my shift on Thursday? I'm on from 5 - 9, but I have my first history test Friday morning. If I don't get some study time in I'm doomed." He folded his hands under his chin as if to beg.

He just wanted her to work for him? Much less interesting. "What, and get stuck closing with Harold again?" she teased.

He smiled, bringing out his ace in the hole. "Lucy's back. She said she'll drive you home. Come on, it wasn't that bad was it?" Acting dramatically abashed, he added, "He didn't *compromise* you did he?"

"I survived," she answered drolly, as she stood up from the bed, "but you could have given me better warning!"

"Sorry," he said, stifling a laugh.

"Why don't you just study *now*?" she asked archly.

"Well, I would, except that I have a very important prior engagement. I'm going to the movies with Greg and Allie, and was hoping you might wanna come."

"And Mr. Penten thinks you're so responsible. You're really blowing your image here." She gave him an amused look as she picked up a brush off of the dresser and began to brush out her long hair.

"You think *that's* my image, the responsible café manager? You really need to come with me," he informed her with a smile.

"Thanks, but I already have plans."

"Oh...okay." He seemed kind of disappointed for someone who hadn't bothered to ask her ahead of time. "Well, are you going to help me out Thursday? I promise Lucy won't hit on you, unless there's a lot I don't know about Lucy."

She smiled. "Yeah, I'll do it."

"Thanks, I've gotta go. Greg and Allie are waiting for me downstairs. You need a ride somewhere?" he asked, noticing her sweat suit and sneakers. "Are you going to work out or something?"

"Yeah, that's okay; I'm only going down to the gym. Didn't I tell you? I'm learning self defense." She put up her fists as if to fight him.

Ben backed away laughing. "That's great! Should I warn Harold?"

"Ha, ha. I wish it were only Harold I had to worry about." She grabbed a hair rubber band off the dresser and started putting her hair into a ponytail.

He dropped his smile. "Scared you that bad did they?"

"Well, duh. You've lived here longer than me," she pointed out, "and I don't see you eager to walk home in the dark."

"Learning to fight's good," he said quietly, turning to leave.

"Well, your friend Cain suggested it, and it didn't sound like a bad idea."

Ben stopped dead, his hand on the doorknob. "Wait...who?"

"Cain, the guy who helped us the other night. You said you knew him from the café."

Ben's face went pale. "I said I knew him, I wouldn't call him a *friend* by any stretch. You've seen him since then?" Ben seemed upset.

Strange reaction. Benjamin was attractive, and she'd hoped to start something between them, but she was never sure if he thought of her that way. He was older and far more popular than she was. Why was he acting jealous? He wouldn't want to date a girl like her, would he? "What's the problem? I mean, he sure scared off those things that attacked us. He seemed like a good fighter, so I asked him to show me some stuff." Ben looked disgusted. What was his deal? It wasn't as if *he* had ever even asked her out on a real date or anything, until tonight...if that even counted as more than something casual.

"Oh yeah, Cain's good in a fight. I just didn't think you'd want to hang out with him. The first time you saw a vampire you were all freaked out, calling them 'hideous monsters and evil dead things', and I agree, so..." He trailed off, flustered. "Have you lost your mind? I don't think you want to see what he's got to show."

"What are you talking about? I'm learning to fight, and protect myself, why shouldn't I learn it from Cain? He's been a good teacher, and a perfect gentleman." Ben looked as if he were about to be sick. She tried not to sound too pretentious. "Is this a jealousy thing? Because if you wanted to go out with me, all you had to do was ask."

"What? No, it's not a jealousy thing! It's more like an…'Are You Stupid?' thing! Cain is a vampire, Felicity!"

Talk about self-delusion! "Cain's not a vampire!"

"Yes, he most definitely is!" He looked at her as if pleading for sanity. "Didn't you see him fight the others?"

"Just because he can fight better than you, doesn't make him a vampire," she said matter of factly.

Ben opened his mouth in shocked insult. The sound of a car horn blasted through the window from outside. Ben looked as though he'd like to yell at her, but instead fought to make his voice very calm and serious. "Felicity, this is not about me. I couldn't care less who you date, but Cain *is* a vampire. I've seen him change, fighting one of those things the last time. His face went all…fangs, and his eyes were… Trust me, he's one of them."

"You're wrong. Cain can't be a vampire." But her conviction was wavering. She suddenly felt like a six year old and asking after Bambi's mother, with slightly sick, quiet shock and disbelief. Could it be? How would she know? She'd only seen him at night. This was not happening. How could he have not told her this? "You've been letting me go out alone at night with a vampire?"

"I thought you knew! I figured you'd seen him change like I did. I certainly didn't think you'd be dating him!"

They could hear stomping up the steps and Alyson appeared in the open doorway. "Benji, you'd better get your ass downstairs. Greg is wicked pissed, we're gonna miss the movie." She scowled at him for a minute and then started back down the stairs.

Ben was staring at Felicity, trying to assess if she believed him. "Please don't go see him again, okay?" She felt like she was in a bad dream, she just nodded her head, staring vacantly at the floor.

"Ben! Let's go!" Alyson screamed from the staircase. She was answered with a 'be quiet', and a 'shut up' from down the hall.

"Why don't you come catch a movie?" She gently shook her head; she needed some quiet time to think. "I am so sorry to like, dump this on you and run. I didn't realize, I really thought you knew."

"It's okay."

"Vampire's can't come in unless you invite them. So if I can't get you to join me, just hang tight and we'll talk more tomorrow, okay? Are you going to be alright?" He did seem to be really concerned, but what was she going to say? *Yeah, stay and keep reminding me how stupid I am?*

"Yeah, I'm fine, don't be late."

"Thanks…sorry. I'll see you at lunch, 12:30." With that, he was out the door and Felicity was left trying to decide what to do.

Ben's voice echoed in her mind, 'Vampire's can't come in unless you invite them.' But she *had* invited him, hadn't she? At the time, she had thought it would be nice to have him meet her up in her room. Why hadn't she just told him to go to the gym? She looked at the clock…it was 8:53pm.

Chapter 4 - Are *you?*

Cain

Outside on College Campus
11:00, Tuesday night

The campus was pretty deserted by this time of night. Cain walked the path as it wound between the trees. Very pleasant, but unsafe for anyone alone after dark; anyone except for him of course. Too many places for an attacker to hide. The breeze picked up, and he could smell the coming autumn on the wind.

It would be turning colder soon. He liked the changing seasons. So little in his life changed. He was always the same, just wandering through it all. Questions spun around in his head like the little dust devils playing with the first few fall leaves at his feet. Why did he let himself try to get close to someone again? It always ended badly, he knew better.

Where was she? Had she changed her mind, come to her senses? That seemed the likely explanation. There had been no one in her room, behind the closed door, of that he was sure. She must have decided to go somewhere else, to avoid seeing him, but what if she hadn't? What if she had gone to the gym first, waiting for him? What if something had happened to her, because of him? People were always getting hurt because of him. When would he learn?

He heard faint sounds of music up ahead. The breeze brought him the faintest mingled scent of...feminine perfume, and perhaps fear? It was her...or was it only that he wanted it to be her? He walked faster, it was definitely her.

He came around a bend to see her up ahead. She was sitting perfectly still on a bench by the path. He stopped, watching her. Further down the path a small group of smokers were standing around outside the entrance to the student lounge. Cain scanned the area; no one else seemed near. He saw her take a deep breath and sigh. He was relieved beyond belief. She was alright.

Why was he doing this to himself? He knew he should walk away. He also knew that he wouldn't. How was it that this fragile creature he hardly knew, had such power over him? Pretending to accept him, and then avoiding him, reminding him that he didn't deserve friendship from someone like her. Who was *she* to try and make him hate himself once again? Did she see this as some kind of game?

He approached her. She never turned to him, but stiffened as he drew near. "Out for some air?" he inquired grimly upon his approach. She kept her eyes averted, her shoulders tensed. Oh, was he *bothering* her then?

He felt his fears and concerns quickly turn to annoyance as he came to stand before her. "Where have you been? I went to your dorm, but you weren't there. I went to the gym, no one had seen you. I waited over an hour, and you didn't show. Have you been sitting here all night?" He paused as she turned her gaze on him. "It *is* Tuesday right?"

She stared at him, as though trying to penetrate an illusion. "It's Tuesday." She sounded dazed. Was he too late after all? She seemed unmarked, whole and fine. Why was she out here alone?

"Are you alright? You look as though you've seen a ghost."

She continued to stare at him. "Not a ghost...a vampire."

He scanned the area again, had she been attacked? "Where?"

She blinked, looking up at him with quiet disbelief. "Are *you?*"

Cain relaxed and breathed an exasperated sigh as he realized what she was talking about. It suddenly became clear why she'd been nice to him - she didn't know. Of course she didn't. How could he have deceived himself into thinking it could be otherwise? "Yes."

Her anger momentarily overcame her fear. "You didn't tell me!"

"I don't exactly go about announcing it, besides, I thought you knew. You approached me, remember? You knew my name, and it sounded like your good buddy Ben had told you all about me. Didn't he fill you in on all the sordid details? I know he knows."

Her anger seemed to fade into a feeling of quiet betrayal. "*I* didn't know. How can you be a vampire? Why were you being so nice to me? And we had fun, didn't we?"

He sighed. "What kind of question is that?" At this point, maybe it would just be better if he disappeared. What could he possibly say? She was hardly listening to him anyway. He could tell she was still running it all around in her head; trying to see if it could make sense.

"I can't believe I didn't know, I couldn't tell! It's not as if you ever seemed all angry or evil or anything."

He gave a derisive snort, shoving his hands down into his pockets. "I'm not, but vampires are the 'Great Pretenders'. Do you think we walk around *trying* to look like monsters; calling attention to ourselves, fangs bared? You know better than that, I'm not the first you've encountered. Weren't you paying attention?"

"Well, I *guess* I was too busy trying to keep them from *killing* me to notice!" She suddenly seemed to realize whom, or more accurately, what, she was talking to. Her expression turned disgusted and afraid.

He could see her remembering her fight with the others. She looked around as if someone should come and save her. The trouble was, the only thing vaguely resembling a hero around here was him. "It's a little late to stop trusting me now, don't you think?"

She couldn't meet his eyes. "I just...I thought you were human."

"I was...once," he answered quietly.

This brought her to look at him, sympathetically. He didn't want her pity, he just wanted to take that look of loathing from her face. "What happened to you?" she asked quietly.

He gave her a small, lopsided smile. "I fell in love with the wrong girl."

"She did that to you?" Felicity asked.

He looked at her sadly. She wouldn't understand. He often had a hard time himself. "Funny how one person can make such a big change," he reached out his hand to help her up from the bench. She hesitated a moment, then took it. She dropped his hand as soon as she could. "And now everything is different."

She turned that look of pity on him again. "I'm sorry."

He moved a step away and kicked at the dirt. "I'm not." She looked shocked, and there was an awkward silence. She was obviously waiting for some sort of explanation. Should he even try and justify himself to her? This was really a conversation for another time, but he had to at least try and help her understand a little now. Otherwise, there would not be another time.

"I'm not sorry now, but I used to be. You think I like being one of the 'undead'? You know, dying young and becoming a restless wanderer of the earth was not exactly part of my plan, but eventually, I realized something. *I'm* not the one making the plan.

Some things are beyond our control, but we must have faith that everything happens for a reason. We do the best we can with what we are given. As for the things that we can control...well, we all have choices to make." He gave a little laugh. "Though, some of us have choices more difficult than others. Each day, we must make every effort to do what is right, and pray that we have the strength to do it again tomorrow."

"So, you don't...hurt people?"

"Not today." There was a long moment of silence. He realized he'd frightened her again, but he didn't want her to think he was some valiant champion; a tragic, tortured hero. As much as he would like to be that perfect persona for her. He couldn't really fool himself, he knew better. One day at a time. Still, she needed some reassurance; she looked about ready to bolt. "No one without fangs of their own, not for a long time now.

Don't be too frightened of me. I'm still the same person I was the night I walked you home," he gave her a fond smile, "and the night after that. Why would I hurt *you*? You think anyone else would buy me ice cream?" She tried to give him a little smile, but it never really reached her eyes. Ah well, what did he expect? He tried again. "Look, I think the gym is still open if you'd like..."

She avoided his eyes and stared at the ground. "I don't think so. I think I'm going to go home."

Of course, he'd known before he'd even asked. "I'll walk you."

"You don't have to," she told him quietly.

"I'm not leaving you to it alone. It was a pretty poor decision, you being out here in the first place. What were you thinking? 'I don't want to meet with the vampire, so I'll go sit out in the dark by myself?'"

She rolled her eyes and he could see that she was mentally kicking herself for being so dumb. "I don't know, I didn't even realize. I'm not that far from the commons, really. I went to sit in the lounge, but I needed to come out for some air; everyone was being so noisy. When I got outside everyone was smoking, and it kind of defeated the whole 'get some air' thing, so I came over here to sit. I wasn't thinking, I just...I wanted to be alone."

"Yes...well, you can still be alone with lots of people around. I should know." He turned and started to walk away down the path. Then stopped and turned back to see that she was still standing there. "Are you coming?"

Felicity hesitantly followed and they walked to her dorm in silence. He stopped at the steps, she walked to the door. She turned to say something to him, but he had already disappeared into the night.

Chapter 5 - Find me a book?

Felicity

Down Time Café
Saturday night

Felicity finished ringing up her customer and stole a glance over at the café as he left. Empty. Ben came out from the back with a tray full of sugar dispensers and gave her a smile. She smiled back and went to finish sorting through the latest shipment of books.

They had met for lunch on Wednesday, just as he'd promised. She had found him at a table with Alyson and Greg again, already in the middle of an animated conversation about people she didn't know. She mostly just sat and ate her lunch in silence with a polite nod and laugh now and then. Cain wasn't even mentioned, and she felt unable to penetrate Alyson's rapid-fire tornado of quips and insults in order to bring him up. Before she knew it, she had to leave for class.

As they were gathering their things, she put a hand on Ben's arm and forced herself to ask. "Cain...have you ever seen him...hurt anyone?"

Ben stopped and looked down into her eyes, his smile disappeared. "No. No one human anyway, but he sits at a table and I serve him coffee. Who knows what the hell he does when he leaves."

"But he helped us, and you said he's helped you fight them before. Why would he do that?"

"I have no idea. I guess he's a loner, but that doesn't make him safe. It doesn't change what he is." She tried to picture him as someone to fear, as a monster. It wouldn't come. Ben leaned down a little closer to meet her gaze again. "Are you alright?" he asked earnestly.

She closed her eyes and shook it off. "Yeah, I'll be fine. I just...I've gotta go." She backed away a little and squinted at him as the sun hit her eyes. "Thanks," she said, before she turned and hurried to class.

Felicity covered Ben's shift on Thursday, which worked out alright. She had to give him credit, working the café was definitely much harder than the bookstore. Lucy turned out to be a woman in her forties with shoulder length dark hair, and a friendly demeanor. She drove Felicity home as promised. Felicity was afraid Lucy would ask why she needed a ride for such a short distance, and she wasn't sure how much to say, but Lucy no questions were asked.

On Friday night Mr. Penten asked her to work the café again, and she even made some tips. She closed with Ashley, who was also nice enough to give her a ride. On the way home, Felicity had learned that Ashley didn't believe in dating anyone exclusively. 'It's silly to restrict your options so early in the school year.' So whether Ashley was seeing Ben or not, it couldn't be that serious. Not that she was sure if she was interested in Ben anyway, but...good to know. She hadn't seen Ben again until tonight. She hoped that she could get a chance to talk to him more after closing.

She hadn't seen Cain either, not since Tuesday night. She kept telling herself that was a good thing *(he's a vampire, stupid!)*, but in a strange way she was kind of disappointed. Now that she had gotten over the initial shock of it all, she felt terrible. This was not some nameless creature of the night, lurking in wait for her. He was a real person; and even though he frightened her, she couldn't help but feel that somehow she was the one who had betrayed *his* trust.

Cain said he'd thought that she had known what he was. Could it be that he hadn't meant to deceive her? She knew she should worry that it was all part of some elaborate lie, but somehow she just couldn't bring herself to believe that. It wasn't even really what he said, but more the look in his eyes. It hurt him that she was frightened, she knew it did. She was almost anxious to see him again. The other night felt surreal, but to see him again, without the moonlight and the drama; would he look the same to her? Would there be warning bells going off in her head?

He was so curious...dangerous, yet comforting. She knew from prior experience that it was usually a bad combination. In her hometown there were always guys striving to be 'bad boys'. It was mostly out of boredom, but always led to no good. It motivated them to do stupid things that ended up hurting people like her.

But Cain wasn't like them. He wasn't some schoolboy out to prove something. He was so poised and quiet. He wasn't trying to show off or impress, but she found him impressive all the more, because of it. What was he about? Why didn't he hurt her? She'd certainly given him opportunity with her foolish carelessness. Obviously, that wasn't his agenda or she'd be suffering some considerable blood loss by now.

She couldn't stop trying to figure him out. He seemed honestly interested in her, but why? Shouldn't he be with the other vampires? He'd fought them off to save her and Ben. Was that just to gain their trust, as part of some larger plan? But what would be the point?

She sat on the floor behind the counter, next to a box of recently arrived romance fantasy novels. She pulled one out to look at the cover. A knight in shining armor sat on his noble steed, standing over a fallen dragon. Behind him rode his fair damsel, no doubt recently rescued from distress. If only life were that simple. How did she know the knight was any safer than the dragon? At least the dragon was forthright in its intent.

She would probably be smart to stay well clear of him, maybe even transfer to a different school; preferably, one that was vamp-free. This kind of thing couldn't be going on all over, could it? But damn if she still couldn't get him out of her head. It wasn't that he was good looking, although, hell yeah he was, but it was more than that. It was like...magnetism. She had never really understood that word applied to a person before, but when she was around him, she couldn't help but want to get closer. It was an attraction like she had never felt before. Guys like Ben could be cute, friendly, and fun; but Cain was...desirable.

She put down the book. This train of thought was getting her nowhere. Time to get some work done. She had about two hours to go and no customers. Maybe she could actually get through all of these boxes. She straightened up from behind the counter and let out a yelp of surprise. He was standing right there. Cain.

He tried not to smile. "Sorry, didn't mean to startle you."

"Well…" She was annoyed that he had caught her off guard. "I had finally *stopped* expecting to see you every time I turned around," she said defensively. She studied him a moment. No alarms in her head, just her heart trying to pound out of her chest. He seemed quiet, a little sad. "You haven't been here the last few nights."

He gave a little shrug. "I thought it best if I stayed away."

"Then why are you here now?" she asked him archly.

"There aren't very many places to go in this town at night, and I don't like crowds."

"If you don't like the town, then why do you stay?"

"I'm not finished," he stated matter of factly.

"Finished with what?" She realized that she was firing a barrage of questions at him, but she couldn't help it.

He raised an eyebrow at her directness. "Something I set out to do."

She let out an exasperated sigh, rolling her eyes. "Fine, be all cryptic and mysterious. Does that mean you *didn't* come in here to see me?"

He had to smile. "Well, now *that* is a loaded question, isn't it? I think I'll decline to answer for now, for I do need your help."

She leaned toward him over the counter and lowered her voice, looking around to see if anyone was near. "Are you looking for the other vampires?"

He looked at her quizzically. "No," he answered in a conspiratorial whisper, "I'm looking…for a book."

She leaned back, feeling pretty silly. "There's an OPAC computer right behind you. Just type in the author and title."

"Yes, the thing is…computers don't really like me. Besides, my typing is horrific. Help me out?"

She looked at him in assessment. If she didn't know better she would think he was just a regular guy, trying to get a little extra attention. She wished she knew what was really going on in his head. She let out a little sigh, and decided to play along. "Fine," she said with a tight smile. Perhaps he really did need her help, and if not, a little flirting never hurt anyone, right? She came around from behind the counter to the computer. He looked over her shoulder as she addressed the keyboard. "Author?"

"Max Lucado."

"Title?"

"*It's not about me.*" She gave him a questioning glance. "That's the name of the book, I swear," he said, smiling innocently.

She entered it. "That's weird, it's in the Christian section."

"That makes sense, it's a Christian book."

Now she turned fully to stare at him. "Are you kidding?"

"Is that a problem?" he asked.

"Not for me it isn't, but…what if there's a big cross on the cover?" she asked in disbelief.

"Then I guess I'll have to wear gloves," he replied, with a twinkle in his eye.

He made her think of a remembered line from *Alice in Wonderland…* 'Curiouser and curiouser'. "So what, you're like…a *religious* vampire?" He smiled, but before he could answer, she remembered something. "Your tattoo!"

"What about it?" He almost sounded self-conscious, very unlike him so far.

"Genesis...what was it?"

"Genesis 4:7," he admitted.

"That's from The Bible, right? Was that from, before you...died?" she asked.

"They didn't do much tattooing back in 1692," he informed her with a little grin.

That took a minute to register. "Wait, did you say 16, like in 16 *hundred* and 92?" He gave her a little nod. "But that would make you over 300 years old!" she exclaimed.

"Truth be told, I'm 340. What's the matter, don't you like older men?" he asked playfully.

She had a hard time assimilating this, so decided to put it away for later thought. "What is it?" She gestured toward his arm, though it was covered by a light denim jacket at the moment.

"A reminder."

"So what's it mean?" she asked.

"I think it's pretty self explanatory." She gave him a blank stare. "Been neglecting your studies have you?"

"It wasn't in my curriculum," she said with a smirk.

"Shameful, that. Then let me enlighten you," he said, with a resigned sigh. "The Lord is speaking to Cain, and says 'If you do what is right, will you not be accepted? But if you do not do what is right, sin is crouching at your door; it desires to have you, but you must master it.' Something I thought worth remembering."

She pondered that a moment. "I'm assuming you're not the original, so what kind of name is Cain, anyway?"

"One that fits," he said with a little shrug.

"But not the one you were born with?" she guessed. He gave his head a little shake. "So what's your given name?"

He looked into her eyes, and then wrinkled his nose at her. "I forget."

She laughed. "I know you're supposed to be one of the 'Great Pretenders' and all, but for a vampire, you're a really rotten liar."

He smiled. "I can accept that. Are you going to get me my book, or do I have to cry prejudice?"

"One Christian book, coming up. Maybe I should have you pay first, in case you make it burst into flames or something."

"Very funny. It's true words can carry power, but not in that way. Perhaps I should point out the fact that my arm is still here, burn free."

He followed her to the book in question. No cross on the cover, just a pretty sunset, or maybe it was sunrise. Would that be scary to a vampire? Too weird. She led him back to the register where she scanned the book and handed it over. "$14.95."

He gave her a twenty. "Keep the change; call it a tip for friendly service."

She put his change on the counter. "I'm not allowed to accept tips in the bookstore."

"Then consider it payback for ice cream accepted under false pretenses." He broke eye contact to look down at his book. Had he really thought that she'd known what he was? She felt bad for being so freaked out the other night, even if it was justified.

She studied him for a moment as he read the inside jacket cover of the book. He looked like an ordinary guy. Okay well, maybe not *ordinary*. He looked like an extremely attractive guy. Early twenties probably, broad shoulders, very nice build. How could she be expected to fear someone so achingly gorgeous? His hair fell down into his eyes as he looked at the book and he absently swiped it aside, although it fell back again almost immediately. He was a little pale, but he certainly didn't look supernatural. He looked up from the book to find her staring at him. She quickly searched for something to say. "I suppose you'll be taking it over to the café?"

"Mr. predictable, that's me."

"Right." She had an odd thought as she swept the change from the counter into her pocket. "Do you actually *drink* coffee, or is that just for show?"

He seemed to find her inquiry amusing. She supposed such a direct question might be considered rude, but she couldn't help wondering. "I can drink what I like."

She came out from behind the register and began walking him over to the café. She noticed Ben staring, but ignored him. The presence of the man beside her commanded her full attention. "So what do you do besides drink coffee and read?"

He looked a little sobered by that one. "Fight."

"Other vampires?" she asked quietly.

His gaze travelled over her seductively. "Temptation mostly." She wasn't sure whether to melt or shudder. "But yes, the others as well, when needed."

They reached the counter just as Ben finished pouring a cup of coffee in anticipation of Cain's order. Ben gave her a fierce glance that she pretended not to notice. Cain left a five on the counter and headed towards his table in the corner. He lifted the book towards her. "I'll leave it to you when I've finished. I could never keep them all. In fact, I think Penten puts them back on the shelf when I'm done. Anyway, you should read it. You might learn something."

She didn't like the hint of condescension, but then again, if she were over three centuries old, she might feel she knew more than most people too. She started her way back to the register feeling a bit bewildered. 1692? Could he just be teasing her? She should go find a history text. She couldn't even remember what life was supposed to have been like back then.

"Hey 'Liss," It was Ben. She stopped walking with a sigh. "Can I see you a minute?" She turned back to him as he walked over. He did not look happy. "Why are you talking to him?" he asked in a fierce whisper.

She shook her head and looked up at the ceiling. "I helped him find a book."

"Just don't get too familiar. They get you comfortable, and then catch you off guard. You shouldn't trust him."

"Don't worry, I don't think it was a dangerous book." She smiled but Ben didn't seem to find it funny. "It's not like I bared my throat for him or something."

"Well, that didn't seem far behind, the way you were following him around," Ben said sardonically.

"You know what Ben? I appreciate your concern, but I don't need a big brother," she replied.

"I just think you should keep your distance," he advised.

"You pour him coffee every night!" Felicity pointed out.

Ben gave her a bitter look. "Yes, but I never let myself forget what he is."

"Then maybe you shouldn't be talking bad about him. Don't vampires have excellent hearing?" she asked, with a glance over at the café. Cain was dutifully reading his book and ignoring them. Ben got all flustered. "Maybe the next time you have to walk home, he'll let them eat you."

"I can take care of myself," he muttered.

"Well so can I," she announced.

Ben smirked at her. "Oh yeah, that was real apparent while you were lying on the ground screaming."

"She caught me off guard!" she whispered angrily, trying with difficulty to keep her voice down. "I didn't even know vampires *existed* until she jumped on me! I'd like to see how calm you'd be if you were suddenly attacked by a...a werewolf or something."

Ben shrugged. "I fully believe in werewolves, so it wouldn't surprise me," he said with an air of indifference.

"What?" She gave an exasperated sigh; he was impossible. "There are werewolves now? I should really consider changing schools."

Ben laughed. "Just be careful okay?"

"What are you so worried about me for?"

"You think I want to get stuck working with Harold every night?" Ben asked teasingly. Felicity was about to reply when a girl came up to them.

"Excuse me, miss? I'm looking for a book, but it's not in the computer. It's called *Ariel*, by Steven R. Boyett." Ben gave her another smile and went back to the café.

Felicity gave the girl her attention. "I know that book. It's a good one, but I think it's out of print. Let's see what I can find for you online."

Cain left about fifteen minutes before closing. He didn't even offer to walk her home. He just gave her a little wave goodbye while she was busy in the middle of something. She wasn't sure if she should be offended or relieved. Ben certainly seemed happy. Jerk.

She finished her closing routine before he did, as usual, and went to sit at the counter while he took care of the last details. "Still a pedestrian?"

He looked up from counting, "Yep, but only until Monday. My Mustang's in the shop. I finally saved up enough to get it fixed."

"Congratulations."

"Thanks. I notice your boyfriend didn't stick around to see you home," he replied with a smirk.

"He's not my boyfriend..." she replied curtly, "and shut up."

Ben smiled as he finished up at the register. He held out his hand for her locker key. "Get your stuff?" She tossed him the key and he got their jackets from the back. He handed over her coat and bag. "You know, you should be a little nicer to me if you want me to start driving you next week."

"Maybe I'd rather walk," she answered sarcastically,

"I'll bet you would," Ben muttered in return.

"What is that supposed to mean?"

"I can just see you out in the parking lot doing a 'Sweet Polly Purebred' imitation." He could barely contain his mirth at the thought.

"Who?"

"From 'Underdog', don't you get 'Boomerang'?" He started squealing in a falsetto voice. "Help, Helllp! Save me!" He really seemed to crack himself up.

"Are you five?" she asked, rolling her eyes.

"Come on, like you're not just waiting for some excuse for him to come rushing to your aid again. It's pretty sad," he stated.

"You know what's sad? How much you secretly wish you were just like him! Jealous much?" she asked with a smile.

"No way! Like I'd wish I were some lonely, desperate, old dead guy? Get real."

With quiet consideration she asked, "Do you really think he's lonely?"

"Okay, I'm going to go vomit *outside*, since I just washed the floor." Ben shut the lights and started for the door.

"I'm just saying, you're probably right. I mean, he's in here every night all alone. He obviously doesn't get along with the other vampires," she said thoughtfully.

"Yeah, he's real 'movie of the week' material. Move." He practically pushed her out the door so he could set the alarm. Noise drifted down the street from the crowd in front of 'Tommy's Place'.

"You said yourself that you've never seen him hurt anyone. He told me that he doesn't, and I believe him."

Ben turned to face her. "A vampire like him doesn't have to attack people. Just find some sap like you to feel bad because he's all repentant and alone; soon enough he'll have his own pet blood bank."

"Ew! Would you stop saying stuff like that?"

Ben finished locking the door and turned to study her under the lights of the parking lot. "Question. And this is purely hypothetical, really. If I tried to kiss you right now, would you let me?"

"I don't know." What the hell was he trying to prove?

"Whatever, okay. So, if *he* tried to kiss you right now, would you let *him*?" She was doing her best to look offended and appalled. He didn't even let her say anything. "You would. I *know* you would, so don't even try to deny it. Your view is so totally skewed right now! You see *me* as more of a threat than *him*. How hard do you think it would be from there, for him to get you to let him *take* a little?"

"You're disgusting."

"I'm **right**. He's not *stupid!* It's no wonder the other vampires get all ticked off, he makes it look so easy. Why risk getting your ass kicked every night, when you can find yourself some sweet young thing who's *willing* to be a meal?"

"I'm not going to stay here and listen to this. You're delusional!"

"You think so?" He stood there and let her walk away.

"I hope so," she muttered under her breath as she quickly walked home.

.

Chapter 6 – Rage

Cain

Among the trees outside the
Down Time Café and Bookstore
10:25, Saturday night

Cain trembled as he fought to control his rage. His vision was tinged with red as he glared at Ben speaking to Felicity not twenty-five feet away. How dare he! How dare he try to scare her away from him! It had been decades since he had allowed himself to care about someone who didn't need something from him. This girl had made him remember the first tender feelings of friendship and trust, unmarred by blood in decades.

Felicity knew what he was, and yet she was still accepting and kind to him. He could be himself and enjoy her company, without feeling that he was deceiving her. Every person that he dealt with invariably had an alternate agenda. Every human he had contact with made him feel flawed, a liar, with terrible secrets to hide.

Those who knew, such as Ben, treated him with condescension and thinly veiled revulsion or fear. She did not know his past, but she knew what he was. Yet, now that she had come to terms with the reality of his existence, she still treated him as an equal; neither giving him deference out of fear, nor shunning him from disgust. She saw him as a person. He could win her friendship based on his own merits, disconnected from his vampire nature as much as possible.

Now Ben was going to dare to try and keep her away from him? He clenched his fists so hard that his nails were sure to draw blood from his palms, if he had enough left to flow. He hadn't fed. That wasn't good, it fueled the anger. He felt the muscles in his fore arms cord and tense. The skin of his left arm twitched, a forced reminder of the words printed there. He fought to reign in his fury, to master it.

Ben was a good man, doing what he thought was right to help his friend, but what really touched a nerve, was the fear that the things Ben had told her were true. That he was right. Cain became very still as Felicity approached his hidden refuge. She was walking quickly with her head down. He could practically feel her fear, not of him really, but of her own feelings. *Damn you, Ben.* He closed his eyes and let her scent wash over him. She passed by unnoticing. Beside him, he heard the slightest sigh mingled with the breeze. He steeled himself to look at the others gathered around him, and whispered through gritted teeth. "Touch her and you die."

On his left, the two boys wore undisguised expressions of hunger and lust. It sickened him, but they were so young. They were followers; he could keep them under control, if he could reign in the girl. She was crouched in the bushes to his right, and she was growing impatient. She was young as well, but she had sired the other two, and thought of herself as a leader. That was never good. She grudgingly accepted his superiority, but still was not above testing the boundaries. She normally carried a haughty and superior attitude, but wasn't above a show of supplicance, if she thought it might get her what she wanted.

Sindy turned to him with pleading eyes. "At least let me have Ben. I *deserve* Ben."

"You deserve nothing more than to be a pile of dust ground under my heel. If you had any sense at all, you would stop reminding me of your presence, before I forget why it is I've spared you." To that, Sindy gave a snort of disbelief but was quickly silenced by his glare. His harshness with her was propelled by the worry that she might see how strongly these humans were affecting him. She would never heed him, if she thought him weak. He needed her respect if he ever thought to change her ways.

He'd tried to gain respect through friendship, but she was stubborn and unresponsive. Only his status as her elder kept her at bay. If it was fear she would submit to, then he would do his best to make her fear him, if he could. He made his face into a commanding mask of control. Ben was nearing. Cain stared Sindy down until he had safely passed. The boys shifted anxiously.

"Come on man, I'm so hungry," one of them whined.

It was Sindy who answered; she wanted them to know that she was still in control. "Shut up, Luke. They're off limits." She gave Cain a glance as if to say 'happy?'.

"Well, then let's get out of here and find someone who's not," offered Chris. He fidgeted amongst the scrub and brush where he squatted on the ground, stirring up the thick green scent of plants that did not yet recognize that it was turning to autumn.

Sindy was annoyed that the boys should question her decision to remain here with him. They were spoiled, unused to doing anything other than amusing themselves as they liked, and pleasing her, of course. They had no interest in Cain's teachings. "You got somewhere better to go? You know there won't be an easy mark leaving the bar until at least 1:00, so just chill okay." Sindy noticed the look on Cain's face. "What?"

He wanted to tell them how much their practices disgusted him. They were like vermin. He ran his hands through his hair and schooled himself to see them through the eyes of a teacher. Sindy straightened her clothing and stepped out onto the street. She held herself with the bearing of royalty, although her words always destroyed the image by making her sound like the petulant teenager she still was. She turned back to Cain. "I'll stay and hear what you have to say, but I'm not sitting in the damn bushes all night."

Cain took a deep breath. He was probably wasting his time. Any other elder would have killed them at the outset and been done with it, but that just wasn't his way; although it certainly would have been easier. He still had some hope that they could change. The boys would hardly be worth the effort, but the girl...

He stepped out onto the road and looked back at the boys as they followed. They were both staring at a couple entering the bar a little down the street, across the way. He snapped his fingers for their attention. He was pleased to see that they both jumped guiltily. "This is my town for as long as I choose to dwell within it. You would do well to remember that, and conduct yourselves in a civilized manner.

If you continue to jump people in parking lots," he said with distaste, "you will eventually have all of humanity looking for you. Do you think people are above holding a vampire hunt, just because it's the twenty-first century? You act like foolish children; this isn't one of your teenage horror shows. People are not always as easy to fool as you would believe. Do you have any idea how many people in this town are fully aware of you? It's disgraceful! Your *reputation* drew me here!"

Chris seemed suitably ashamed and lowered his eyes. Luke turned to Sindy, "Cool!"

"You moron," she said mildly, shaking her head.

"The path you are on leads to destruction," Cain continued. "Don't you realize your own potential? You, for whatever godforsaken reason, have been granted eternal life! What do you plan to do with that? Hang out in pubs and watch the world go by? Even if you never do a blessed thing, stop acting like fools, because the wrath you bring down affects us all. If it is coming to that, I shall simply kill you myself."

He said it matter of factly, and it wasn't as though he had never enforced such a threat before. The boys seemed cowed. Sindy knew he wasn't bluffing, but she didn't want to seem intimidated. She stepped closer and met his eyes. Pretty brave, but then, she was still thinking that they outnumbered him. If she really thought that would make a difference, she was mistaken. He'd already dispatched Ernest, her first creation, and he could get rid of these other two as well, if they proved troublesome.

She spoke in a quiet, compromising tone. "You're right. We've made mistakes I'll admit. We'll tone it down, but we'll do it my way, not yours. Do you still think you're human? You live like them, you talk to them and you fool yourself into forgetting what you are. Just 'cause you're old doesn't make you right. We're better than them. We're above them. I'm not gonna cower in the shadows like some dumb animal."

Luke spoke up. "They're the food man. Plain and simple."

"Shut up." She turned her attention back to Cain. "You're better than them. You've been around, you've seen stuff. You're fuckin' immortal! Age and disease can't touch us! How cool is that? But you spend all your time mooning after stupid humans like you're seeking their approval." He stared at her coldly. He usually tried to hold himself aloof from humans, but with Felicity he had obviously failed. Sindy was too observant, and he was losing credibility with her. This would not do.

She glanced down the road after the direction that Ben and Felicity had taken. "She could never understand you. She's human; she may find you morbidly interesting for a little while, but she'll still try to stake you in the end. You don't need her, you need us." She moved in closer until he was enveloped in her perfume. She gave her head a little tilt to the side and tried to give him a fetching smile. "You need *me*."

He marveled at her audacity. So, she still fancied a move up the social ladder did she? Not with him; not now anyway. He had decided that she had a lot to learn and many changes to make before he would begin to look at her in the way that she desired. He wasn't planning on taking this strumpet and her little hoodlum boys under his wing for long, if he could help it. He would deliver the message and move on, as always.

He would do his utmost to make them understand that his way was best. It may take a little longer then he had hoped, but he wouldn't give up on them easily. He had done this many times, and had needed patience before. If he could make them come around, it was worth his effort. What else had he to do?

If they turned on him and attacked him, they would die. He wasn't above having *their* blood on his hands, if there was no alternative. Perhaps it would quiet the beast within him for a while. That might almost be worth it. He leaned in close to her ear. She seemed thrilled by his proximity. "Speak to me like that again, and you will be in hell before the words have finished leaving your lips," he whispered.

She stiffened and drew away from him. She looked back to her boys. "Come on, we're leaving." She avoided his eyes and sauntered off down the street; opposite direction from the bar, he noticed. She wanted to get them away from him before they realized that she was afraid, but she wasn't stupid enough to risk his vengeance by entering the bar; not yet anyway.

He knew her type. After a few days, her boys would begin to chafe against his restraints. Would she be able to hold them back; would she even try? Could she resist it herself? He'd tried to teach them other ways, but they wouldn't listen. The young ones never did. They couldn't resist the thrill, but how could he blame them really? It's not as if he'd never succumbed himself.

Felicity. He tried to catch her scent, but she was long gone. He would stay away from her, for his own good and hers. He tried to summon the resolve to make it a promise to himself, but it wouldn't come. He could appear strong to the others when he had to, but inside he felt so weak. Would his suffering never end? Hadn't he done all that could possibly be expected of him?

Sometimes he craved the peace of death more than the blood. Rest; but his body continued to live, even without the beat of his heart. It was not over yet. When it would be, was not for him to know. 'We must make every effort to do what is right, and pray that we have the strength to do it again tomorrow.' He remembered the old creed he had desperately clung to so often.

He took a deep breath of the cool evening air. He could hear bats hunting for insects in the night. No hunt for him. He put his hands into his pockets and followed the road off into the dark.

.

Chapter 7 – Come see the show!

Felicity

Introduction to Chemistry
College Lecture Hall
Monday afternoon

Felicity was lost. Physically she knew where she was, but mentally she must have zoned out a bit, because she suddenly had no idea what the professor was talking about. 'Introduction to College Chemistry', yeah right. This stuff might make sense to people who have already majored in chemistry for two years. To Felicity, it was hopeless. The lecture ended, and she was left wondering if it was too late to drop this class and take something else.

The girl next to her was gathering her things to leave. She had a notebook full of color-coded tabs and seemed very organized. Felicity looked down at her own mess of papers and sighed. The color-coding and organization gene must not run in her family. Felicity looked up at the girl as she swung her sweater over her shoulders. "Is it just me, or was that very confusing?"

The girl gave her a friendly smile as she fastened her sweater clip. "It's not that difficult a formula really. You just have to break it down into its elemental parts."

"Oh...right." Felicity looked down at her notes with hopeless confusion.

"Do you want to borrow my notes?" she asked, following Felicity's gaze down to her mess. "I take very thorough notes." The girl put down her book and flipped to the blue section. She noted Felicity's grateful smile and unclipped the appropriate pages.

"Thank you so much, I'm sure they'll be very helpful." She stood and took the offered pages. "I'm Felicity."

"Hi, I'm Karen."

"I'll copy these at the library and give them right back. You'll probably want to look at them for the homework."

"Thanks. Do you live on campus?" She asked, as Felicity tried to neaten her stack of papers and make them fit into her folder without shoving them in too crudely. She made sure to neatly put Karen's notes in a separate folder. "I'm in Wesley Hall," Karen added.

"Me too! Room 217." Felicity shoved all of her folders and stuff, into her book bag and slung it over one shoulder.

"I'm in 110." Karen moved out of the row of seats and descended toward the exit as Felicity followed.

"Well, I appreciate you letting me borrow these. I'll bring them back tonight. Where are you headed now?" she asked, pausing in the doorway.

"I have a class in the Hillside building."

"That's on the way to the library, I'll walk with you."

They headed outside into the bright sunshine. Another beautiful day. Felicity had really come to appreciate the sun in the last week or so. Especially now that she knew what lurked in the darkness around here.

Karen seemed like such a confident, organized person. Did she find all of her classes so simple? Felicity wondered if she could get some of Karen's self-assuredness to rub off on her. She should really try to be a better student. She felt so scattered lately.

Just then, they were startled by someone screaming for attention from down the path. "Hey!" As soon as she looked, Felicity wanted to run and hide. It was Alyson.

"Hey!!!" Allie screamed again. She began jogging straight for them. She wore an old 'Judas Priest' concert shirt that she had cut short to expose her belly button ring, and low-waisted, jeans that were more holes and frayed strings than denim.

Karen gave her an odd look and turned to Felicity. "Do you know that girl?"

Before Felicity could answer, Alyson yelled at the top of her lungs. "Felicity!"

Felicity wished she could become invisible. "Yes, I guess I do."

Alyson caught up to them and stood there panting for a minute, while chewing a much too large wad of gum with her mouth open. Then she looked from Felicity to Karen, who both stood there in silence. "Hey," she offered by way of greeting.

Felicity gave her a tight smile. "Hi, Alyson. This is Karen."

Alyson smiled and continued chewing. "How ya' doin'?"

"Hello," Karen said, studying the blue and purple streaks in Allie's hair. They stared at each other in silence for a moment.

Alyson put her hands on her hips and turned to face Felicity. "So here's the deal. Tommy's letting Greg's band play on Wednesday night. Not exactly a prime slot I know, but it's 'ladies night', so you can drink for free. Even if you don't have ID, if you dress slutty, the bartender'll still serve you. So, you gonna come?"

Felicity crossed her arms and stared at the ground. "I don't know."

"Come on, I'm not working, so I get to be on the dance floor. I need someone to hang with while Greg is on stage."

"Why don't you just go with Ben?"

"He's gotta close the café, but he's gonna come by after. I can't hang with another guy or Greg'll be jealous, and I don't have any other girl friends. Girls don't really like me," she said, with a perplexed look and a shrug. "So you have to come, okay? You can bring your friend," she added glancing at Karen.

Karen surprised her by speaking up. "Is there a cover?"

"Five bucks."

Felicity looked at her in surprise. "You want to go?"

"My fiancé Jack is always dragging me to stuff like this. He'd probably want to go."

"Oh, wow. You're engaged?" Felicity tried to sound more curious than jealous.

"Jack and I have been together for a year and seven months." Felicity smiled at her, looking suitably impressed. Alyson just shifted her weight from foot to foot, impatiently. "Are you seeing anyone?" Karen asked Felicity.

"No, not really."

Alyson squinted at Karen. "I don't see a ring." Could this girl be more rude?

Karen didn't seem too off put. "Well, I don't actually have a ring yet, but we are going to get married, he asked me. We're pre-engaged."

"Ookay." Allie raised her eyebrows and then looked back to Felicity. "So you're gonna come right?"

"I guess."

"Cool. They're supposed to play at 9:30, but we have to be there early to set up and stuff. So do you want us to pick you up, or do you just wanna show?"

"I'll just meet you there."

"Jack'll drive us," Karen said with a confident smile.

Alyson beamed back at her, and then turned to Felicity. "Cool, but you'd better show. Don't leave me hangin'."

"I'll be there." Felicity muttered.

"Great, see ya!" Alyson took off back down the way she had come. For someone who wasn't a student, she sure spent a lot of time on campus.

Karen turned, clutching her notebooks. "I have to get to class. I guess I'll see you later."

"Yeah, I'll bring back your notes. Thanks again." She watched Karen head off to class and then turned towards the library.

She looked over Karen's notes while making copies. It was like she had rewritten the textbook - in English. She would have to remember to sit next to Karen every week. She might not have to drop this class after all. She was done for the day and started back to the dorms. It was getting cool, but the sunshine was warm on her face. Days like this were made for walks and quiet reflections. She told herself not to think about Cain anymore though. It was just too confusing, it made her head hurt.

Then she thought about Ben and that was even worse, it brought her thoughts right back to Cain only with annoyance towards Ben too. He was so convinced that Cain was this evil monster and that she was setting herself up as some sort of sacrifice. He couldn't be right about the whole thing, could he? Cain was sincere and well meaning, not some scheming creep out for her blood. She wouldn't believe that. It wouldn't make any sense anyway; he'd had so many chances. She'd been alone with him far more than Ben knew, and he had never even given her cause for alarm, really. That's why Ben couldn't understand. He didn't know about the walks and the ice cream and...was she just being really stupid?

No, she was right. Cain didn't mean her any harm; she truly believed that. Ben couldn't be expected to get it. It was more than just circumstances and words, it was a feeling, like intuition. She knew he was genuinely interested in her. She wasn't sure how, but she just knew it. He needed a friend, someone to talk to.

Of course, she had to admit that she felt far stronger feelings towards him than any 'friend' she'd ever had. He was so damn sexy! That wasn't something she had ever really felt towards a guy before, movie stars and rock singers maybe, but not anyone in *her* life. Guys she'd liked had been attractive, but this was a completely different thing. He just emitted this vibe that made her want him in a way she'd never really felt before. Was it a vampire thing? She hoped not. No, he was just different than the guys she'd dated. He was more mature for one thing...way. Over three hundred years more mature, that was weird.

Felicity stopped in her tracks. The library. She should go back and look up stuff about that era. Was he really from the 17th century? That was so mind-boggling; to think that he had lived through so much. She quickly returned to the library and found someone to help her.

"I wanted to do some research about the late 17th century."

The library assistant was a girl about her own age; she looked up from the computer she was working on. "America?"

"Yes, oh, and maybe England."

"You don't know?"

"Well, it's not for a class. I was just…curious."

"Okay. Well, if I remember my history, there was a lot of migration back then." She did some typing. "The Puritans were leaving England, having been persecuted for their religious beliefs," she read. "That's where a lot of our pilgrims of the area came from."

"Wow, yeah, that sounds right. Could you recommend some books I could look at?"

"Sure, hang on." She typed in some more information, and took a minute to see what came back. "Oh, did you want stuff on the Salem Witch Trials too? Good reading."

"When was that?"

"June, 1692"

She felt chills run down her back. "Okay, yeah. I guess I should check that out." She waited while the girl wrote down various call numbers for her and then headed off to hunt down her books. Witch trials? That wouldn't have anything to do with vampires, would it? She had never been very interested in that sort of thing. Her knowledge of the occult was nil, but the date was too weird. Maybe he was just teasing her, but somehow she didn't think so. Massachusetts really wasn't all that far away. In three centuries he certainly might have moved. In fact, Ben said he'd only showed up here over the summer.

She selected an armful of books from what the library clerk brought. Mostly easy reading educational stuff; 'this is how they dressed, this is what they ate and how they built their houses' sort of books. The witch trial books were far more in depth. She wasn't sure if she'd actually read them, but she felt she had to bring them back to her room. She checked them all out and started back to the dorms again. She almost wished she could just go find Cain and ask, but of course, she had no idea where to even look. He certainly wouldn't be out walking around in the sunshine.

That led to an uncomfortable chain of thought. Where did he go during the day? Didn't vampires rest in cemeteries? The thought of him lying comatose in a coffin somewhere gave her the creeps. Was he asleep, or was it like being dead for twelve hours to suddenly awaken at sunset? Okay, stop it Felicity. This is just going to freak you out.

She got back to her room and dumped everything on the extra bed. She would have liked a roommate, but it was nice not to have to worry about making a mess. She sat down on her own bed and stared at the pile of books. Somehow, she just couldn't bring herself to open them yet. Did she really want to know? The 'Witch Trials' might not even have anything to do with him; maybe it was just a bad year.

Her eyes wandered to her open closet. Now here's a scary thought. What the hell was she going to wear on Wednesday night? She didn't have much 'bar' experience. She was sure anywhere that would have Greg's band play was not something you really dressed up for, but at the same time, she felt the unreasonable urge to look really hot (if at all possible), for no good reason. She was still ticked off at Ben for the things he'd said the other night. She wasn't really trying to attract him; she just felt that if he wasn't going to be on good terms with her, he should at least regret it.

She hated her clothes. Everything she had was so boring, but that's because that was who she used to be. Back home she had shopped to fit in, not stand out. Then her eyes fell on the purple shimmery top she had bought last year. It was dark purple with just a hint of glimmer where the light hit. It was gorgeous, and it had looked good on her too; her best friend Deidre and all the sales girls had said so, but she had never worn it, she didn't have the nerve. It was a little low cut, but not trashy. The back was open, with all strings and ties, so she couldn't wear a bra, and that made her self-conscious. She knew she looked great in it and had planned to wow everyone at a party last year, but then she'd chickened out. She had brought it with her because she had planned to reinvent herself; come out of her shell a bit more. Maybe this was the time. It would be a little dressy, but not too much. Maybe...

She decided to try it on. It still fit, even better than she remembered actually. She turned this way and that, looking in the mirror. She really did look amazing in this top! She could wear it with jeans to dress it down a bit. This might actually work out nicely. Then she pictured herself trying to dance in it. First of all, she was an awful dancer. She hadn't had much practice, and always felt self conscious and awkward. If that weren't bad enough, now she would have to worry about bouncing around without a bra on? No. Don't think so.

But she looked so good! She tried to imagine how satisfying it would be to see Ben get all flustered when she walked into the room. Hey, not just Ben, any guy. Why shouldn't she be the subject of attention for a change? Girls like Ashley were always turning heads. She could turn a few herself, couldn't she? Besides, she knew if she didn't wear it now, she probably never would. She had always been so timid; who was she hiding from anyway? What was she so afraid of?

~~~~~~~~~~~~~~~~~~~~~~~~~~~~~

Wednesday night had arrived. She turned around in front of the mirror again. Yes, it was a good choice. She looked beautiful! She had even found some tiny sparkly purple clips at the drug store to put in her hair. It was mostly down, long and wavy, she had curled it. Now she picked a few artful strands to pull back from her face. This was fun; she hadn't dressed up for anything in a long time. She wore little gold hoop earrings, and after some contemplation selected the small gold cross from her grandma to wear on the chain around her neck. It was a little plain, but she'd been rather partial to crosses these days; it couldn't hurt. She sat down on the spare bed amongst the practically untouched pile of books, to put on her shoes. They were a black pair of wedge sandals that had straps criss-crossing up around her ankle.

She had looked at one of the books earlier today. The pictures were of farmers herding sheep and pilgrim women wearing white aprons and bonnets while baking bread in big stone ovens. Interesting, but nothing too exciting. She certainly had a hard time picturing Cain among them. She hadn't done more than flip through the 'Salem Witch Trials' book either, reading a paragraph here and there. Nineteen people had been put to death as witches after what seemed like ludicrous trials, all because some girls said they saw spirits. She couldn't imagine Cain being involved. The date must have been a coincidence.

She finished lacing up her sandals and went to the mirror to check her makeup. She had just finished putting on some lip-gloss when there was a knock at the door. "Come in."

Karen opened the door as Felicity grabbed her jacket and purse. "Are we too early?"

"No, I'm ready," she said, crossing to the door. She was happy to notice that Karen wore a blue shiny satin shirt with her jeans. She hadn't worn much make-up or done anything with her shoulder length light brown hair, but at least her clothes looked dressed up to just about the same level as Felicity. One less thing to worry over.

Behind Karen stood her first evidence that she looked as good as she'd hoped. Karen's fiancé, Jack, looked as if he'd meant to say something, but forgot to speak after opening his mouth. He recovered quickly, before Karen noticed, to Felicity's great relief. She briefly wondered if she should change after all.

"Felicity, this is my Jack," Karen announced proudly. She clearly sounded as though she were marking her territory. *Fine by me,* Felicity thought. *I don't need someone else's guy, I'll find my own.*

Still, it was nice to know her charms were evident. "Thanks for driving me," she said, donning her jacket.

"No problem," Jack responded with a smile. He looked as though he might have been older than them, but was still quite a way off from 'responsible adult' status. He wore faded jeans and a black button down shirt that was open to reveal a 'Guns N Roses' tee underneath. They headed out to Jack's car. It was an old four-door sedan. It had clearly seen better days, but it was definitely a step up from walking. She sat in the back while Karen got in up front next to 'her' Jack.

Jack looked up at her in the mirror. "So where are we going?"

"Oh, sorry. It's Tommy's, just around the corner."

"I figured, there's only a few places around here. Karen said you know someone in the band?" he asked as they pulled out onto the road.

"Sort of. He's the boyfriend of a friend of a friend, who isn't even a friend really; he's just this guy I work with."

"Oh." She felt kind of silly as he smiled in the mirror. "Does this band have a name?"

"The PowerHouses," she answered.

"Hey, I think I heard them at a party once," Jack replied.

"Were they any good?" Felicity asked.

"I don't remember...good party though," Jack said with a smile.

They pulled into the lot. Not exactly a crowd, but at least there were people there. They paid the cover charge and Jack accepted his 'over 21' hand stamp after showing his ID. It was pretty dark inside and took a minute for their eyes to adjust. There was music playing from the jukebox, but no one was dancing yet. The seats at the bar were pretty full; mostly guys. Funny, she had expected to see more ladies on 'ladies night'. Guess the guys did too. There were some booths up against one wall and a few mostly empty tables pushed up against the other.

She spotted Alyson up on the stage helping the band set up. It wasn't really a 'stage', just a raised platform about three steps up in the back of the room. She looked at the size of the speakers compared to the size of the bar. They were going to be deaf by the end of the evening for sure. Alyson noticed her and jumped down to meet them. "Cool, you came."

"I'm a girl of my word. You remember Karen, and this is Jack." She was tempted to say 'her Jack', but stifled the urge. They nodded hello.

"Not a bad turnout," Allie said as she stuck her hands into her back pockets. She was wearing tight black satin pants and a short white button down shirt with little frills on it that looked like it had been stolen off of a baby doll. "There'll be more later. People mostly come at 11:00 after they stop charging cover. I saved you the big table." They followed Allie over to a big round booth in the corner closest to the band. "Best in the house. You guys want a brew?" Alyson asked as Jack and Karen took off their jackets.

"I'm gettin' a beer, you want anything hon?" Jack asked turning to Karen, who was settling herself in the back of the booth. She shook her head and he left for the bar.

Allie turned to Felicity. "You coming?"

"No thanks, I don't want anything, yet," she answered, leaning against the side of the booth.

Alyson gave her a puzzled look. "You sure? Come on, you're dressed for drinkin'. Let's go."

Felicity crossed her arms self-consciously across her open jacket and glared at her for a moment, as Allie's previous 'dress slutty so they'll serve you' advice came to mind. "No thanks."

"Suit yourself," Alyson said as she left for the bar.

"What did she say?" asked Karen.

"Nothing," Felicity said, while staring daggers at Alyson's back. She couldn't tell just how conscious Allie was of how rude she sounded sometimes. Were they deliberate jibes or just cluelessness?

The band began tuning up. It didn't sound like they were making much progress. Jack and Alyson returned with their drinks, just as the first song started. She didn't know it, but she assumed it was a song. Heavy metal was not exactly her style.

Jack and Karen sat in the booth while Alyson stomped and danced on the floor out in front of the table. Felicity just stayed kind of leaning against the wall on the corner of the booth. After Alyson's 'dressed for drinking' comment, she had lost the nerve to take off her jacket. This may be a long evening.

After about the fifth song, Ben showed up, with Ashley. She looked gorgeous. She had taken her long straight blonde hair, and put sections of long spiral curls every so often. She wore a low cut, chocolate brown spaghetti strapped top that came down to a point in the front and back but was cut rather high on the sides. Her short leather skirt and over-the-knee boots were the same deep chocolate brown. Felicity thought Jack's eyes might pop out of his head.

Ben wore a rather smug look as he said hello. What was he smirking at? It's not like she should care if he was with Ashley. She flashed him a winning smile and took off her own short leather jacket as artfully as possible. She was rewarded by seeing Ben's eyes widen just a fraction as she did. Felicity had the figure of a real woman, not a 'Barbie Doll', like Ashley. She may not have the 25" waist that all the models seemed to think was 'in' right now, but she knew she looked good. She decided she'd be damned if she was going to let Ashley, Alyson, or anyone else make her think otherwise. She usually dressed pretty plainly, but she had to admit, it was fun to be noticed for a change.

Alyson returned and they yelled introductions over the band. Allie slid into the booth next to Karen, and Felicity followed. That left Ben and Ashley to get in on the other side next to Jack. The song ended and they were given blessed silence for a moment.

Jack moved over a bit too eagerly to make room for Ashley, something not lost on his 'fiancé'. "Jack move, I have to go to the bathroom," Karen said, just before Ben could sit down on the end. Ben backed away, Ashley got up, then Jack scooted out and finally Karen. Jack got back in and moved next to Alyson in the back, but before Ashley could get in next to him, Karen quickly pushed her way back in to sit down.

Jack gave her a puzzled look. "Karen, I thought you had to go to the bathroom?"

"False alarm," she said drolly, glancing up at Ashley as she sat down. Obviously she just hadn't wanted Ashley squished in next to *her* Jack. After Ashley slid in next to Karen, Ben sat on the end with a grin.

Felicity looked away trying not to laugh. The jukebox had come back on and a few people were venturing onto the dance floor as the head bangers left for the bar. She turned back to Alyson. "Are they done?" It felt strange not to have to yell. Her ears were ringing.

"No, that's just the end of the first set. They just put the jukebox on while the guys take a break and get a beer."

Karen met Felicity's gaze across the table. "Oh good, there's more," she said with a smile. Felicity turned back to watch the dancers. Yes, it was going to be a long night.

Chapter 8 – I got you something

Cain

Tommy's Place
11:00, Wednesday Night

The guy at the door stamped Cain's hand without bothering to ask for ID. *Guess I'm losing my youthful good looks,* Cain thought with a smile. Of course he hadn't outwardly aged since the day he'd 'died', and that was at the age of 27. He had always looked young for his years, but was certainly no child.

He entered the bar and paused just within the doorway to scan the crowd. Quite a few marked ones, but no vampires that he could see. If there were any others of his kind here, they were well hidden. He'd never met a young one who'd learned that mental trick, unless they'd been taught by Cain himself. As far as he knew, he was the oldest in this neck of the woods. Humans only tonight...until now.

The din coming from the back of the bar was dreadful, but thankfully, it ended as he came inside. This type of place was hardly his first choice to pass the time, but he found himself driven to it all the same. He simply could not bear to be alone with his thoughts any longer, and there was really nowhere else to go. There was only so long he could spend in a diner without attracting attention, and nothing else was open at this hour.

Cain was glad that the 'DownTime' stayed open as late as it did. That was the one place where he could spend a long period of time in the company of others, without really having to interact with anyone too much. The last few nights he'd made sure Felicity wasn't working before he'd entered though. He was trying to keep his distance.

Ben had begun to dislike him ever since he'd discovered Cain's identity. What little camaraderie they had established over the summer was out the window, but at least he was tolerated, however uneasy Ben might now be. Cain usually tried to keep himself from becoming attached to people he dealt with often, but as tough skinned as he thought he was, he couldn't help but feel a bit betrayed by Ben's reversal of attitude. Where Ben was once friendly, he was now cold and suspicious. The young fool would have been dead if Cain hadn't come when he did. Surely Ben knew this, but seemed to offer resentment rather than gratitude. He probably didn't even know of half the times Cain's presence had protected him. That's all right, he never expected thanks, but the dirty looks were getting tiresome.

Enough of that for now. He'd get himself a drink, and find an out of the way table to sit at and watch over the crowd. He wondered if the young ones would show themselves tonight. He was going to have to make a decision soon; he was being too soft hearted. He should finish things one way or another, because he couldn't afford to stay here much longer. Not for any reason other than his own suffering.

He was becoming far too fond of the human girl, and it would only complicate things. He'd let his guard down. He just wasn't used to being treated kindly by someone who knew his true nature. He could blame no one but himself for the position he was in. Always playing with fire. He thought he'd conquered that tendency in himself, for the most part. Yet once he'd discovered her interest in him, however slight, he couldn't help but lead her on.

She was so sweet and innocent, exactly the reasons why she should have nothing to do with him. He could only taint her, he knew that, but try as he might, he just couldn't keep her from his thoughts. He didn't mean to seek her out, but whenever he did see her, he just couldn't tear himself away. Perhaps he could indulge his fancies for just a little longer, as long as the young ones didn't get out of control. He didn't expect anything of her; he knew that would be selfish, but a kind word, or a fond glance, could sustain him for a little while anyway. It was better than feeling invisible, as he was so often called to try to be. He ventured through the dark towards the bar.

"Cain?"

"Felicity." It was she. How did this keep happening? He tried to do the right thing, really he did. Well, she seemed just as surprised to see him. Small towns always made things so difficult.

"Join us." She was sitting at a table full of people, including Ben, who did not look thrilled to see him.

"You have got to be kidding!" Ben said, staring at Felicity as if she had gone insane.

Cain gave Felicity an apologetic smile. "That's alright, I was just passing through." He made as if to move on, but she reached up to him and put her hand out to hold his arm. That light touch kept him rooted to the spot as though he had turned to stone. He wouldn't actually go so far as to pull away from her.

She held his gaze with her large trusting green eyes. "Please, sit down." She turned a hard look towards Ben. "Really."

Cain wouldn't go against her wishes. Although what he would say to these people, he couldn't guess. He recognized the blonde from the bookstore. She didn't really know him, but had flirted with him from time to time. He had always been friendly, but within careful bounds. Would that he had been as careful with Felicity. He noticed Alyson was also among them, she knew him almost as well as Ben did. He didn't know the others, but this would certainly prove interesting. Felicity moved in for him to join her on the bench. It was a tight fit for the seven of them, but they managed.

Ben was obviously quite annoyed. "Right, because what evening would be complete without a visit from our friendly neighborhood..." Felicity cut him off with a look that Cain was happy not to be at the receiving end of. She surely would have kicked him if she could have reached. "Coffee drinker," he ended lamely.

The lovely blonde sitting next to him said sweetly, "You guys must know each other from the café, right?"

"Yes," Ben answered shortly.

"Well, aren't you going to introduce us?" she asked, giving Cain a flirtatious smile.

"No," Ben said while staring at Cain.

"Ben!" Felicity scolded. Then to the blonde, "This is Cain. Cain this is Ashley, Karen, Jack, Alyson, and you know Ben."

He nodded to each of them in turn, including Ben. "Hello."

They all smiled and nodded quiet greetings. "We're here to see Alyson's boyfriend's band." Felicity offered, to fill the silence.

Cain was grateful for her attempt at conversation. "Oh, I think I caught the end of them as I came in. They were very..."

"Loud?" Felicity supplied helpfully.

He laughed. "Yes." He looked to Alyson, who seemed unoffended. He doubted much could offend that girl. "Sorry, not really my thing."

"So, what *is* your *thing* Cain?" Alyson asked, with challenge in her voice.

He smiled at her. He liked this girl, her bold honesty. No doubt she knew that he was no longer fully human. She always gave him a hard time when he came around, but she did it with such spunk, and at least she was honest. "My musical tastes are a bit eclectic, actually."

"I'll bet, with so many decades to choose from," she said with a smile.

"Well, music has changed quite a bit through the years. I'm afraid I haven't quite kept up."

Jack spoke up. "Oh, so you're into the classics. What do you listen to, like…Pink Floyd, Grateful Dead?"

He furrowed his brow. "No, more in the line of Mozart and Bach, to be truthful." He was met with a few strange stares and an awkward silence.

"They're classic," Karen agreed helpfully.

After a moment's thought he added "I do like The Beatles."

Alyson grinned at his datedness. "They broke up you know," she told him almost gleefully, while trying to keep a straight face.

He fixed her with a tolerant smile. "Yes, I know. Terrible tragedy that, and God Bless those no longer with us." He needed to get out of here. This just was not going to work, and he certainly didn't need to give Felicity trouble with her friends. He couldn't just walk out on her though. At least he could go get a drink. He looked to Felicity. "I'm parched. Would anyone like a drink?" he asked of the table.

"You *are* going to the *bar*, right?" Alyson asked him archly.

"Indeed," he answered with a dry smile. "Would you like something?"

"No, just checking," Alyson replied sweetly.

He looked to the rest of the group, and then to Felicity. She gave a small shake of her head. She seemed worried that he would duck out on her. He met her eyes for a moment. "I shall return." He said it lightly, but he knew she needed to hear it. He got up and left for the bar.

He ordered a drink and turned his attention back to the table. He watched as one of the 'musicians' approached the group to speak with Alyson. Apparently, they had a problem with their equipment and would be unable to continue the performance. Pity. Alyson practically pushed Felicity from the booth and stormed off after the man in a wicked temper.

As Felicity returned to her seat the others began to scoot out the other end. It seemed they were going to dance to the music from the jukebox. They asked Felicity to join them, but she declined. She was waiting for him. He wouldn't disappoint her. When he turned to collect his drink, he found he was being given two. The bartender explained that the second was free. He left some money on the bar, then took them both and returned to the table, now empty, except for the girl.

He looked at the empty booth. "Was it something I said?" he asked with a smile.

"No," she answered with a laugh, "they're dancing."

He put one of the drinks down in front of her. "I know you said you didn't want anything, but apparently it's something called '2fers' this evening."

"Oh, two drinks for one. What'd you get?"

He sat opposite her. "Coke." She started to raise it to her lips, but then wrinkled her nose and raised her eyes to him disapprovingly. "Oh, and they may have spilled a little rum in it. They do that sometimes," he added playfully.

She pushed the drink aside with a smile. "Thanks, but I'll pass."

"So, you're not drinking, and you're not dancing. Have you come just to watch the crowd then?"

"Yes, actually. That pretty well covers it."

"Well, then we've something in common, but I must admit, *you* don't strike me as wallflower material. How come you're not dancing?" He allowed himself to run his eyes over her body. "I won't believe no one's asked." She did look particularly luscious this evening. He could see that she wasn't entirely comfortable with that. She crossed her arms over her chest self-consciously.

"I don't dance."

"Neither do I, as a general rule, but for you I think I'd make an exception."

"Oh, I don't just *not* dance, I *can't* dance. Sorry."

He stood and moved to her end of the booth. He'd decided that it was useless to fight it. She was here and so was he, why shouldn't they enjoy each other's company? He certainly wasn't going to spend the evening staring at her from across the room, or even over the table, as her friends looked on. "Well, then it's lucky for you that I'm here."

"Are you a good dancer?" she asked, eyeing him skeptically.

"No, bloody awful really, but on a rare occasion, I do remember how to have a good time. And I would *so* like to see you out from behind that table. You won't make me embarrass myself alone will you?" he asked, holding his hand out to her.

"We're talking multiple levels of embarrassment here. Probably not a good idea."

"Are you worried you'll ruin my reputation? Because I doubt there's any more harm to it *you* could do, than what I've already accomplished myself. You needn't worry about yours. You can blame it all on me; you can say I stepped on your feet."

She was still hesitant, but she allowed him to take her by the hand and lead her to the dance floor. The place had begun to fill up by this time, and there were quite a few people packed into the small bar. Once they found their way to a cleared space, she began to look nervously at the dancers around them. Her friends were dancing a few feet away, but hadn't noticed them. She looked back at him helplessly and yelled over the music. "I don't think I can dance like that."

He moved in closely to speak directly into her ear. "Who are you dancing for?"

"What?" she asked with a puzzled expression.

He whispered to her intimately. "Don't dance for them," he breathed as he glanced at the crowd around them. "Dance for you."

She was still at a loss. "I don't know how."

"Your mind may not, but I'll wager your body does. Close your eyes." She looked at him dubiously. "Close your eyes and move as the music tells you. Dance for you." He took her hands into his own. "Trust me...in this at least. I haven't lost a dance partner yet."

He knew she felt ridiculous, but she did it. She closed her eyes and began to sway. Slowly at first, then to the rhythm of the music. He guided her hands to his shoulders and placed his hands on her hips. This broke her concentration for a moment and he could see the self-doubt creeping back in, but soon he was able to coax her back into the dance. Once again, she lowered her eyelids and a small, secret sort of smile crept over her face. He moved slowly with her, but she was really the only one dancing as he devoured her with his eyes. He noticed the small gold cross she wore around her neck. It made him smile. He'd be careful not to touch it.

With her eyes closed, he finally felt that he had free license to memorize her in his mind; to take in every curve and swell of her body. The soft clean line of her jaw, her slightly parted lips, the way her eyelashes dusted the delicate skin under her eyes... It never ceased to amaze him, how such simple parts came together to make such an incredible being. She was beautiful.

He was terribly conscious of his hands and the gentle motion of her hips. He wanted her so badly, it made him ache, to have such a basic pleasure denied to him. Of course, there were ways for him to take any woman he chose, but he didn't want them like that. That was an urge others had, that he could never really understand.

He knew that other vampires took pleasure in stealing from their victims; their blood and their bodies. To drink and to rape, gave them an unexplainable thrill. That was something he had no desire to explore any further. True, the blood was divine, but his conscience would no longer permit him to take it by force. Rape was such a heinous and abhorrent act. It seemed such an unrewarding violation, pale and distasteful compared to the love of a willing woman. Even those who were willing to give their bodies, for money, or out of simple desperate loneliness, held no pleasure for him. They would never *know* him for what he *really* was, and so their offerings meant nothing to him. They were flesh only, it was empty.

Her eyelids fluttered and he found her gazing into his own blue eyes, as the first song ended and another began. The heels on her shoes made her nearly as tall as he was, and her face was almost close enough to kiss. The world seemed to fall away as he clung desperately to the sweet trust and hope he saw reflected in her eyes. This was worth remaining for. They moved as if in a trance, each mesmerized by the other. It felt as if they were in their own magical universe where the cares of the world were meaningless...

Until he felt a tap on his shoulder, that although gentle, sent shivers down his spine. He was suddenly fully aware of their surroundings and stopped still among the dancers. "Mind if I cut in?" Sindy's query came out in a husky whisper that made the fine hairs on the back of his neck stand on end.

He forced himself to be still and stared at her stonily. "Leave."

Felicity also fought to regain her composure after being caught so off guard. He was proud to see that although she was initially startled to see who it was that had interrupted them, she was now more angry than afraid. "Go to hell," she practically spat at the vixen.

Sindy found this incredibly amusing unfortunately, and laughed. "All in good time honey!" She turned to Cain. "She's feisty! Make sure you keep her on a short leash." She turned her gaze back to Felicity threateningly. "Wouldn't want anything to happen to her."

"Leave *now*." He was sure to be threatening as well. Once again, he marveled at her audacity.

Sindy continued speaking to him as though unaware of his anger. "Because you know what happens when someone finds a pet without a license..." She shook her head with mocked pity. "It's straight to the pound, and that never ends well."

"Are you calling me a dog?" Felicity interjected in angry confusion. Of course, she had no idea what to make of the exchange.

"You needn't explain yourself," he said quickly, pulling back Sindy's attention, "just **go**."

"I don't have to listen to you. This is a public place," she said with a smile of challenge.

He would play these games no longer. She was like a child testing her parents' limits, but there was no underlying love to temper his wrath towards her. She surely felt the waves of rage that must be spilling forth from him by now. Yet still, he would be calm and civilized. He was not some heathen animal such as she. "It will go better for you if you leave," he said with a dead, cold voice.

She finally seemed to realize that she was treading on thin ice. She chose to back pedal with feigned indifference. "Actually, I was just on my way out." She nerved herself to meet his eyes for a last parting blow. "But you know, you really should *mark* your property, just to avoid any unfortunate accidents."

She turned to smile at Felicity and licked her lips. "I'll be seeing you." With that, she disappeared into the crowd.

Felicity seemed to shudder and then looked up at him accusingly. "I am not your *property!*" she stammered.

Great. "Those were her words, not mine."

"Well what the hell was she talking about?"

This was not a subject he wanted broached right now. Of course, Sindy had known that. "Nothing."

"It didn't sound like *nothing!*" She was becoming increasingly angry with him. How was he going to steer clear of this?

"It's nothing that you need concern yourself with, I'll handle it." An answer that had often worked in the past, but these days, women were far too independent for that, and he knew she wouldn't be satisfied.

"Oh right, because being thought of as your unleashed pet shouldn't concern me?"

"She was just trying to rile you up, it didn't mean anything."

"Remember when we talked about what a rotten liar you are?" She wanted explanations he was not entirely prepared to give. Thankfully, they were interrupted.

Alyson stormed up to them looking quite murderous. He was never so happy to see her. "Where is she?" she demanded of him. "Where's your *friend?*"

He raised an eyebrow. "I can assure you, she's no friend of mine."

Alyson looked around distractedly. "Yeah, well I know the bitch is here. She's makin' my freakin' skin twitch."

He looked at her with renewed interest. How had he not noticed before? "You're hers," he stated with quiet astonishment.

"Her worst nightmare!"

He grinned. "I believe she was just leaving," he told her, nodding towards the door.

"Not if I get there first," Allie replied, taking off for the door.

"Alyson!" Felicity yelled, but was paid no heed. "You're just going to let her go?"

"Why not? Alyson's a capable girl, I'm sure she can handle herself," he replied with a smile.

Felicity leaned into him with a harsh whisper. "Against a vampire?"

Again, he smiled. "Sindy may be insolent, but she's not stupid. She won't risk anything too untoward here, in front of all these people."

Felicity wore a look of sheer amazement. "So you're just going to let them have at it?"

"Works for me. Sindy could use to be brought down a notch or two, wouldn't you agree? If Alyson would like to be the one to do it, who am I to try and stop her? Makes my life that much easier." She gave him a very disapproving look. "Eventually Sindy will leave, or Alyson will get tired and *then* I'll step in. It's nothing to be concerned about."

"I am really beginning to worry about your definition of the word 'concern'."

Just then, they heard an ear-splitting shriek from the direction of the door. They moved through the crowd towards the fray. Cain and Felicity made their way to the edge of the space that had been cleared of people near the door. They were just in time to see Sindy grab hold of Alyson's short hair and yank her down hard towards the floor. Allie went down on one knee and the bouncer fought his way through the crowd yelling at them to break it up. Sindy backed off a little, with a wicked smile on her face, and as the large man reached the girls, Allie looked up to practically snarl at him to stay out of it.

Unbelievably, he listened to her and moved away to give her room. He must know her well enough to realize that he would have to physically restrain her if he wanted her to stop. He seemed content to leave them be for now. The bar patrons watched as Alyson charged back at Sindy, who was ready for her, but caught the worst of the attack all the same.

Alyson used the palm of her hand to shove Sindy's face aside, then punched her in the stomach with her other hand, before Sindy even had a chance to regain her composure, Allie brought her knee up to hit Sindy's stomach hard again. Allie grabbed Sindy's long hair and used it to hold her close as she brought the elbow of her other arm down to strike her between the shoulder blades.

As Sindy went down, the bouncer moved in, but before he could do anything Felicity saw a flash of red in Sindy's eyes as she grabbed the wrist that was tangled in her hair. Felicity knew that Sindy had changed as she saw her try to bite Allie's wrist, but no one else seemed to notice in the confusion.

The bouncer was trying to pull Allie off of her, but Allie was fighting him, and screaming for him to leave her alone. Alyson must have felt the fangs graze her wrist, because she suddenly shrieked and pulled her arm away so hard that she and the bouncer fell backwards to the floor.

When Sindy stood up Felicity was relieved to see that her eyes were brown once again, but she still looked wild and ferocious. Felicity looked from the girls to Cain. "That's enough," she said, her eyes pleading for him to intervene.

He put a hand on her shoulder, as she seemed eager to rush to Alyson's aid. "I believe Sindy agrees." As Alyson regained her feet, Sindy slipped out the door. "Wait here, I'll be back," he told her, as he turned to follow after Sindy. Felicity seemed to want to protest, but he never gave her the chance. He hurried to the door, paused just inside, to sense Sindy's whereabouts, and then slipped out.

He could sense her quickly receding. She was gone. He knew she wouldn't stay to face him outside alone. He only hoped she wasn't planning to come back with reinforcements. Not now, he had other things to deal with. As if right on cue, the door to the bar opened and Felicity timidly leaned out to look around. Seeing he was alone, she stepped outside to join him. "Is she gone?"

He turned his eyes from the road to the girl. "I thought I told you to wait inside?"

She gave him a defiant look. "I don't take orders well."

"Why am I not surprised?" he asked with a sigh. He would not be able to put this off any longer. "Are you going to be here for a while?"

"I don't know, why?"

"I want to give you something." She gave him a perplexed look. "I don't have it here, I have to go and get it."

Felicity looked around worriedly. "Why don't I just come with you?"

He sighed again and looked away. He would be a fool to take her, to be alone with her, far from others. The temptation was great and he knew he was going to make an unwise decision, but he was also afraid to drive her too far away from him. She had shown considerable trust in him; he only hoped it was justified.

She mistook his silence. "Oh, I get it. You don't want me to know where you...stay. That's alright. I understand."

He shook his head at his own foolishness. "You'd better go inside and tell your friends you're leaving, so they won't worry."

She smiled and dashed back inside. He would have to exhibit superior self-control, but it wouldn't be the first time. As far as her knowing where he resided, either he was going to trust her or he wasn't. She was trusting him with her life as well.

If he didn't do something to protect her, they would surely hurt her eventually. The danger he'd put her in was already irrevocable. Sindy was the vindictive sort, and if she couldn't get to him directly, she would do it through Felicity. Of course, she wouldn't do anything too inexcusable, not at first anyway. She was still hoping to turn his interest, but she surely wasn't above a drawn out game of cat and mouse with someone he cared for, perhaps siccing her boys on Felicity, pretending their actions were through no fault of her own. She may even decide to simply try and drive her away from him. She'd probably rather hurt him emotionally than physically anyway. That seemed more her style.

Felicity re-emerged from the bar, wearing her jacket. He waited for her to reach him, and then started down the road. She fell into step beside him. "So, where are we going?"

He looked at her for a moment, then straight down the road again. "It's a bit of a walk, but if you want to come with me, I'll have to ask you to be quiet. I need to concentrate, to make sure she isn't coming back...with more."

"You can see her; tell where she is?" Felicity asked.

"Yes. Probably not the way you're thinking, but I can sense if another comes near...if I'm paying attention."

"Sense away, I won't say another word."

Good, at least he would have some time to figure out how much to tell her. They followed the road out of the immediate town and past the few residential houses, into the farmlands. It was quiet once they were away. The muffled music and the buzz from the neon bar lights was gradually replaced by the increasingly loud hum of night insects. The glow of the streetlights eventually gave way to almost complete darkness. There never really was anything quite like country dark. He could see even in complete darkness of course, but the glow of the half full moon surely helped Felicity. She remained true to her word and was silent. Walking any distance in those heels must have been wearing on her, but she didn't complain.

They slowly came upon the edge of the cemetery. They walked down the road past the silent graves on the other side of the fence. Rabbits hopped among the tombstones, feeding on the lush clover. They suddenly froze at the screech of an owl hunting in the distance. He saw Felicity jump at the sound, but when she realized he was unconcerned, she continued walking. As they came to the gate, she noticeably slowed. He kept walking down the road. She seemed puzzled, and then sped up to fall in with him again. Apparently, she had thought that he would like to live with the other dead things. No thanks.

"Where *are* we going?" she dared to ask.

He glanced back and caught her still studying the cemetery. "It's not far now."

About a quarter mile from the cemetery, they came upon a development of homes. All had seen better days, but the drive they turned up belonged to one whose lawn was sorely in need of mowing at the very least. There were no cars parked nearby, only a fine black motorcycle up at the top of the drive. Felicity came up behind him as he approached the door. "Whose house is this?" she whispered, as though fearful of being heard.

He turned a puzzled look to her. "Mine." Did she think him a trespasser now? A common thief?

She looked confused but relieved. "You have a house?"

"I'm renting it." He took the key from his pocket and worked the lock. He held the door open for her as she cautiously stepped inside.

He closed the door behind them and was about to cross the room, when he realized that she would need the lights. He flicked the switch by the door. A bare light bulb hung from the center of the entryway. After the initial foyer, it revealed a large dark living area with bare, dirty wooden floors, bare walls and no furniture. The back of the room and the rest of the house were still swallowed in darkness.

She turned to him with a smirk. "I like what you've done with the place."

He gave her a sheepish grin. "I stay downstairs; less windows."

"Oh...right."

He motioned for her to follow, as he crossed through the living room to the equally bare kitchen. He opened the door to the basement stairs and flipped on the stairwell light. If she thought it seemed less than wise to be following a vampire down a stairwell into the basement of an empty old house in the middle of the night, she gave no sign. She dutifully followed him down the stairs to the equally bare finished basement. At least there was paneling on the walls and carpet on the floor, even if it was old cheap industrial carpet.

The basement was large, the full length of the house, but was also mostly unfurnished. He crossed the room to turn on the light, revealing the lamp to be on the floor next to a small pile of books and a plain queen size bed in one corner of the room. There was also a small built in bar type counter to one side, with a microwave, sink and mini-fridge; and two doors, one leading to the bathroom, the other a laundry room. Nothing else. The few little windows had been covered over with very thick curtains, which were actually hiding the fact that he had boarded them up.

She looked around, then back to him. "It's very...spacious."

He gave her a little lopsided grin. "I'd offer you a chair, but I haven't got one. You can sit on the bed if you'd like." He took off his jacket and threw it on the bar as she walked over and sat down on the bed. He noticed her give the bed a little bounce and begin laughing to herself. "I have a *funny* bed?" he asked.

She tried to cover her embarrassment. "Oh, no. Not at all. It's a very, perfectly normal, nice bed...as beds go."

He broke into a wide grin. "You thought I slept in a coffin, didn't you?"

"No I didn't," she insisted.

"Yes you did!" he accused with a smile.

"Well, have you ever *seen* a vampire movie?" she asked indignantly.

"Well, have you ever *tried* sleeping in a coffin?" he asked.

She thought about that for a moment. "Point taken."

He smiled, shaking his head. "I'll just be a minute," he said as he entered the bathroom, closing the door behind him. Felicity was like a breath of fresh air after being shut up in a cold dark place. He needed more of that in his life. He retrieved the box from the medicine cabinet, and opened the lid. He had prepared this a few nights ago, but hadn't been sure he would actually be able to give it to her, or that he should. Circumstances seemed to have taken the decision from his hands.

It was just as he'd left it. He closed the box again and went back out to her. She had taken off her jacket. To his mild surprise, she had also taken off her shoes and was sitting cross-legged on the bed. The shoes were obviously not made for walking far; he felt a little bad.

"Not much for materialism, are you?" she asked looking around the bare space.

"I hadn't originally planned to be here for long."

"Something change your mind?" she asked.

He chose not to remark on that. He crossed over to her and handed her the box. "I got this for you."

It was a small black velvet box, the kind likely to contain jewelry. He saw the strange and almost hopeful look on her face that it would contain some lovely treasure. "Don't get too excited. You might not like what's inside."

With that warning, she began to open it gingerly, as though it might contain a handful of spiders. The hinge of the box suddenly creaked and it snapped open with a loud click. Inside was something he had found in a little shop that happened to be absolutely perfect for his purposes. It was quite beautiful actually; a glass vial held within a criss-crossing cage of silver made to look like tiny vines, on a thin silver chain. Near the stopper was a little flower of tiny crystals. The vial was of white frosted glass, but it looked almost black at the moment.

She looked up at him. "It's very pretty. What is it?"

He wished he didn't have to say, that he could just slip it over her head and be done with it. "It's blood, *my* blood," he added with a sigh. "It's *protection* is what it is." She was staring at it with her brow furrowed. "You keep it with you, and if ever another vampire were to bother you, you open it. They can smell it; they'd know you were under my protection. That if they mess with you, they must face me."

She looked up at him with some contempt. "Marking your territory?"

He answered her quietly. "You don't have to accept it, I'll throw it away if you'd like. I just thought it might help. It's not nearly as effective as the conventional method, but it's far better than nothing."

"What's the conventional method?"

He wasn't answering that; he shouldn't have said it at all. "Do you want it?"

She studied him for a moment, looking into his eyes. "Thank you." She took the vial necklace from the box, opening the clasp to put it around her throat. "It's beautiful, really," she said as she fastened it.

"So are you." Cain found that the words left his lips in a whisper, although he'd never meant to say them aloud. She looked up at him and there was a long moment of silence, in which he was painfully aware of her heartbeat, and the fact that he had none to match it. "It's late; I should walk you home now."

She raised herself up onto her knees on the bed before him, and before he realized what she meant to do, she put her hands to his shoulders and met his lips with a kiss. It was soft and hesitant at first, but it wasn't long before he lost his resolve; it quickly became heated and passionate as she pressed herself against him. As his hands caressed the soft, warm skin of her bare back, he hoped they didn't feel cold and lifeless.

It was she who pressed her tongue between his lips and he could hardly bear to stop her. Her blouse was so thin that he could feel her breasts crushed against him as though she wore nothing. He could hear the blood rushing through her veins and her heart thudding up against his chest. He wanted her so badly, all of her, her body and her blood.

Suddenly, white-hot pain flashed through his mind and burned his chest. He arched away from her a bit, although she didn't notice. Her cross; he had forgotten. He clenched his eyes shut and willed the beast within him to stay subdued, as he ended the kiss.

Cain regained control of himself and gently pushed her away. He met her eyes and saw that she was not entirely herself for a moment. Yes, he knew the physical effect that his preternatural body would have on someone such as her. He caught her focus and said sincerely, if a bit breathlessly, "It's been a long time since I had a woman in my bed." He bit his lower lip as he chided himself for even bringing her here. "I wouldn't want to forget myself. Let me take you home."

She seemed a little hurt; she was feeling rejected by him. If she only knew the truth, but it was too soon. He wouldn't put that before her until she was fully aware of the true state of things. It wouldn't be fair for him to expect her to think clearly after the fact. Wordlessly, he bent to retrieve her shoes and put them on the bed beside her. She stared very hard at them and he knew she was trying to keep tears from her eyes. She was so young. Had she ever even known a man? She was certainly too trusting by far. Trusting enough that he doubted she had ever really been hurt or betrayed by a man in her life...yet.

He watched as she threaded the straps of her shoes around the tops of her ankles. She had iridescent white polish on each toenail. She wore it on her fingers as well, each painted and filed to a perfect rounded point. She seemed so clean and innocent. Even her name, Felicity, meant honesty and truth, he remembered from somewhere. She stood and put on her jacket without making eye contact, and then headed for the door.

He wanted to stop her, to hold her; to feel his arms around her and bury his face in her hair, but he stood there in silence as she began to climb the stairs. He picked up his own jacket and followed her out of the house. As he turned from locking the door, he saw her at the top of the driveway, trailing her fingers along the seat of his Harley Davidson motorcycle. "Is this yours?" she asked, without looking at him.

"Yes," he answered.

"Then why do you walk everywhere?"

"I like to walk," he said with a shrug. "It takes time; something I've got entirely too much of." She accepted this without further comment and wandered down the drive to the road. He looked again, at what seemed to him, to be painfully high-heeled shoes strapped to her feet. "Did you want to ride?"

Again, without looking, she answered him shortly. "No." They had walked all the way to the cemetery before she said anything else. "Do they go there? More than anywhere else I mean," she asked as she surveyed the various tombs.

"Some do. Not the ones you know though."

"There are more?" She seemed surprised.

"Well, of course. Did you think we were the only vampires in all the world?"

"I hadn't really thought about it," she admitted with a shrug. "Are there *a lot* more?" she asked timidly.

"Humans far outnumber us, if that's what you're asking, but that doesn't really mean anything. They stick to the larger cities as a general rule; it's easier to escape notice. Most small towns are untouched. There are more here, than I've seen in awhile, but I believe that's because Sindy and her friends have shown such lack of restraint."

"Is that why you're here?" she asked tentatively.

He nodded. "I try to show them...alternatives."

"It doesn't seem like they want any."

"Most don't, but sometimes they come around. Most of us never asked for this. We're just trying to get on, live the life we've been given, but that can't mean to just kill anyone who crosses our path. I do think the killing's stopped since I've arrived. That's an improvement, wouldn't you agree?"

Her eyes went a bit wide. "Yes, definitely. Hey, Ben mentioned that too. He said that he thought they didn't kill people anymore; that they'd gotten smart."

"Well, I'm sure he doesn't connect it with me in any way. I doubt he'd like to pay *me* even a 'round about compliment."

"You can't really blame him. I mean, he knows what you are, but he doesn't really *know* you."

"I usually try not to involve people." He stopped walking and took her hands into his own, turning her to face him. "I'm sorry if I've put you in any danger." She looked up into his eyes and ventured a small smile. He could tell she wanted to kiss him again, but because he had pushed her away, she was afraid to try. The moment seemed to stretch on forever.

He closed his eyes and breathed her scent, then opened them to look on her once again. She still waited, patiently, hoping. "You must understand," he began quietly. "It's not that I don't want you. Nothing could be further from the truth, but, I can't. It wouldn't be fair." He watched her struggle to make sense of it. The remembered sensations from the venom in his saliva were still clouding her mind. It was always so hard once they had a taste of it, however slight. Damn this unnatural body of his!

She broke away from him gently and started walking again. "It's okay, I get it."

"No, you don't really. There are things you don't know, about how we affect people. You don't know about..." He broke off suddenly as he became aware of the presence of another, close. He reached out for her arm and held her still. She began to protest, but the look on his face silenced her.

"We're not alone," he informed her quietly. He tried to pinpoint the location. It was only one, blazing brightly in his mind; it must be new. Coming from the cemetery they had just passed. He looked back but saw nothing. Normally he would go investigate, but these circumstances were less than ideal.

"Is it her?" Felicity asked in a whisper.

"No." He concentrated on the other vampire. It seemed to be wandering randomly among the graves from what he could tell. "I don't like this."

"Do you think it's following us?"

"No," he assured her. "I think it's newly risen, and not very well made."

"What does *that* mean?" He could hear a slight tinge of panic in her voice.

"Nothing I can't handle," he said, calmingly. "It's just not a good sign. Someone's decided to increase their ranks, is what it means; someone who's not very good at it."

"Well, that'd be good for us right, that they're not so good?"

He laughed at her peculiar phrasing. "Not really. Turning someone into a vampire is a delicate process. If it's not done with care, you lose the *person* inside. They can become a mindless thing, with only the most basic of instincts. Too much time passes before they re-awaken, and their bodies aren't...preserved. They rise like a living corpse, a true monster."

"Not sounding so good." She looked around nervously.

"It's in the cemetery. Because it's not particularly aware of what it is, I'm sure it also doesn't realize that I can sense it. Most likely, it doesn't even know we're here."

"So, what do you do, when you find these things?"

He gave her a steady look. "I kill them."

"Oh."

"I would never put you in any danger, but it's probably better if I take care of this quickly; send a decisive message to its maker."

"You're not going to leave me here!"

"No, you can come. It's only the one. Just keep out of the way, and be careful." He drew one of the wooden stakes he kept in his boot. It was a little longer and thicker than the size of a pencil, sharpened to a wicked point. "Not very impressive I know, but it does the job.

You have to stake them through the heart though, or they won't die." She took it from him hesitantly, as though it were sticky. "Don't worry; I don't expect you to need it."

Quietly, they returned to the cemetery. Although Cain opened the gate as slowly and steadily as he could, its hinges still let out a piercing shriek. They froze and surveyed the surroundings. In his mind, Cain saw the creature also freeze, and then start towards them. It must have some sense left. He motioned for Felicity to stay behind him as they entered the graveyard and started down the path. He came as close to the thing as he dared without yet having it in sight. He had Felicity crouch down behind a large memorial stone just as the thing topped a rise before them. It started down the hill before it even noticed Cain.

It was truly a hideous sight. It had once been a man, but had clearly not been given enough blood. Its hair had fallen out in patches, and its eyes were glazed over white. Even in the moonlight, he could see dark spots of mold on its skin mingled with the dirt. It must have lain to rot for weeks before what precious little vampire blood it had, could drive it from its grave. The thirst for blood had urged it to rise, but of the man it had been, there was nothing left. Of creatures like this, he could only hope their poor souls had escaped before the vampire blood had forced it to open its eyes once again.

It had been buried, obviously. It was caked with mud and grime, and it wore what was probably once a nice suit. Its hands were little more than bloody lumps. It must have used them to break and dig through the coffin itself, before burrowing its way out of the ground. How things such as this were allowed to come into being he would never understand, but he could not suffer them to live, even hell could not be worse than to walk the earth as such a creature.

As he approached the thing, Cain uncloaked his presence and it finally seemed to take notice of him, although whether or not it could actually see Cain through its clouded orbs, was unclear. It turned to Cain and tried to unsheathe its fangs, to attack him. Cain didn't even give it the chance. He stopped breathing to avoid having to take in the putrid stench of the thing, drew a stake from his pocket and promptly stabbed the corpse in the chest with it. There wasn't even a fight really; the thing never even had time to try to fend him off.

Cain could see that even more amazing to Felicity than the fact that he actually staked the vampiric zombie through the chest, was what happened when he did. The vampire seemed to explode into a great cloud of dust as the wooden stake pierced its unbeating heart.

Felicity recoiled in surprise as the ashes flew into the air. "You...*popped* it," she said as she approached, waving her hands in front of her face to ward off the remaining dust swirling around her.

He stifled a laugh at her description, as he wiped the ash from himself. "That's just what they do. I don't care to look too deeply into the working of it."

"It's weird," she muttered.

"It's convenient. I'd hate to think of the trail of inexplicable corpses I'd leave behind."

She shuddered as she looked at the mounded ash on the ground where it had been. "Yuck. Why would anyone want to make more?"

He stopped to give her a sobering look, trying not to be insulted. "You've no idea what it's like...to be one of us. It's a long, lonely existence."

She looked at him with disbelief. "Have *you* ever made another vampire?"

He kicked at the ground to scatter the rest of the ashes. "Not like that."

"But you *have* made others?"

He could see she was hoping he'd say no. Her expectations of him were far too high. "I've been a vampire for three hundred and thirteen years. That's an awfully long time to be alone."

"I can't help but notice that you still are."

Her words struck him like a blow, but he said nothing. He bent to wipe off his stake on the grass and put it back into his boot. She moved to give him back the one she held. "Keep it." He glanced around. They were alone again. "Let's get out of here. I hate cemeteries." He made his way back to the path and she followed.

Once they had exited the grounds, he closed the gate again. When he turned to face the road, she was standing right in front of him, looking uneasy.

"I'm sorry," she offered. "I didn't mean anything..."

"I know."

They began the long walk back to town. They walked in silence, each lost in their own thoughts. Only once did a car even pass. Its headlights cut through the darkness unexpectedly as it zoomed by and disappeared just as suddenly as it came. They passed a small group of deer feeding in the field just off the road. The animals looked up to watch the intruders pass, ready to bolt at any untoward move. Gradually the fields gave way to trees, and at last, they came upon the first few buildings of the town. The post office, the dollar store, the pizza place, the DownTime Café and Bookstore.

They came upon Tommy's; the parking lot had emptied quite a bit. It was well past two o'clock in the morning. Felicity said she didn't see Jack's car in the lot. Her friends had probably gone home by this time. They kept walking and turned the corner, on towards her dorm building. She stopped to look at him as she reached the front steps.

"Well, here you are, safe and sound," he said.

Her hand went to the vial around her throat. It lay against her skin, just below the cross which was on a slightly shorter chain. In his mind, he pictured them repelling each other like opposite magnets. Of course, they simply lay there, the glass of the vial a protective barrier. She held it out so she could look at it. "Thank you again, for this." She looked up at him and held his gaze.

"You still have to be careful. It only works on someone who's smart enough not to want to make enemies. And of course there are some who won't care."

She smiled. "That's okay. After what I've seen tonight, I don't think I'll ever go outside in the dark without you again anyway."

He laughed. "Good," he said sincerely, gazing into her eyes, "because I worry about you." She was going to be his downfall, but damn if she didn't make him feel human again. "Thank you."

She looked very confused. "For what?"

"For treating me like a man, instead of a monster."

"You're not a monster."

He wished he could agree. "You don't know me very well, but thanks."

She just stood there, staring at him. He wished he could just take her away somewhere, someplace safe and warm; to sit together in front of a fireplace, wrapped in a big fluffy comforter. They could talk all night and he could tell her everything, bare his soul; let it all pour out of him like a secret confession. He could expel it like a poison and never look back. She would nod, and hold him, and tell him that she understood and it would be alright. She could tell him that he was a good man and she loved him; that she would always love him and nothing else would matter.

Of course, she didn't though. She barely knew him, and as much as he might feel that he needed love from one such as her, he never truly expected to obtain it.

A night bird called somewhere off in the trees. The air was cold and the sky was dark, as always. There was no warmth, no comfort, and she was standing there, separate from him; not truly understanding or forgiving as he would wish. It was through no fault of her own, but just because… Because that's the way it would always be. It was nothing but what he deserved. He swallowed back all of the things he would say if he could. He simply looked at her.

She moistened her lips and spoke. "Good night." She stood there. Perhaps she was still hoping for another kiss. No, it was too tempting.

She wouldn't leave until he said something. He fought to keep his voice neutral and steady. It came out as hardly more than a whisper. "Good night."

With that, she went to the door and discovered it locked. She gave a hesitant knock and then turned to look at him for a moment, at a loss as to what to do. Then the door opened behind her. Karen stood there smiling. "Hi, just got in myself. She leaned over to give Cain a wave. "Night." Felicity turned to wave as well and then entered the building. Once again, as he must end every night, he was alone.

Chapter 9 – You're late!

Felicity

DownTime Café and Bookstore
4:15, Thursday afternoon

Felicity paused to catch her breath from running, and then opened the door to enter the bookstore. A quick glance around revealed that only one customer was browsing the shelves and Mr. Penten was nowhere in sight. She turned towards the café and made a beeline for the employee lounge. As she approached, she saw Ben scrubbing the counter-top with a vengeance that made her feel bad for the Formica. He looked up and the strangest mixture of relief and annoyance came over his face as he saw her. "You're late."

"Sorry, *boss*." She heard him throw his sponge into the sink with a wet thud as she went into the back and opened a locker.

"I didn't see you at lunch today," he said, following her.

Felicity turned to look at him questioningly. "Did we have plans?" she asked, putting down her purse.

He turned away. "No, I was just looking for you."

She took off her jacket and shoved it into the locker on top of her purse. "Well, I overslept today, so I spent my lunch taking a make-up for the class I missed this morning." She slammed the locker and shoved the key into her pocket. She turned to leave, but he was standing in the doorway, looking annoyed. "Did you want something?"

"What? No." He went back out behind the counter.

"Then why were you looking for me?" she asked, following.

Ben took the sponge back out of the sink and started scrubbing the counter again. It looked pretty spotless to her. "It was nothing."

She put her hands on her hips and stared at him. Why did guys always use 'nothing' as a code word for 'something really important to me that I don't want you to know'? "What?" she demanded.

Ben turned slowly to face her. He looked like he was trying to read something written in Latin. "You went home with Cain last night didn't you?" he asked accusingly.

She rolled her eyes. "He *walked me home*, yes. And you drove Ashley home, right? So what?"

"So, Ashley's not a blood sucking demon."

She smiled. "You sure about that?"

Ben wasn't amused. "I was worried about you, okay?"

"Felicity?" Shit. It was Mr. Penten. "Weren't you supposed to be on at four?"

"Yes, sir. Sorry, I'm a little behind schedule today," she answered.

"Then maybe you and Ben should continue your conversation later," Mr. Penten advised.

"Yes, sir." She quickly came out from behind the counter and went to the bookstore register.

She was kept busy with customers and sorting books for the rest of the afternoon. She saw Ben once in awhile, across the store, but they hadn't the chance to speak again. As the sun began to set, she couldn't help but wonder when she'd see Cain. She turned to look every time someone opened the door, only to be disappointed. It was still early though.

Chapter 10 – Make me

Cain

Thursday evening

Cain lay in his bed, drifting in and out of sleep. The sun had gone down about half an hour ago, but he hadn't felt like getting up yet. Almost awake but not yet ready to open his eyes, he let his mind wander to thoughts of Felicity. He still had a little time before he should rise to walk her home.

That kiss... Only a small hint of things to come, if he allowed it. There was no question that she would be willing; he had seen how it had affected her. He wouldn't hurt her, not really. He would be careful, show superior self-control.

He could fantasize, but he knew that if he were fully awake, he would have to admit how unlikely it was to end well. Oh, it would work for a little while. It would be hard, but he knew he could resist, but where could it possibly go from there? He had done the right thing to turn her away, but could he trust himself to continue to do so? He let himself drift back into a deeper sleep; one that could hold more dreams and less questions.

Light flared against the backdrop of his closed eyes. For a single, incoherent second, he was certain it was sunlight and it jolted him fully awake, but of course that was impossible. The windows were boarded, and he had felt the sun go down. The light had been in his mind only. It was a new vampire coming into being; another one. He rubbed his eyes and sat up in bed. Another one. What the hell were they doing? Hadn't he put a stop to this yet?

It was nearby, probably not in the cemetery, but closer. What were they doing, burying the things in his backyard now? He would hardly put it past them. Sindy didn't take him nearly as seriously as he would like, but as far as he knew, they didn't know where he slept.

Psychically cloaking his presence was something he had been sure to learn well. Short periods of time were not all that difficult, once you learned the way of it, but to keep a shield over you for every waking moment required superior psychic control and endurance. Over the last century, he'd pretty much perfected it. He hadn't met another who could detect his presence against his will in quite some time. He was fairly certain that it was no longer possible.

He swung his legs over the edge of the bed. He had hoped for a nice quiet evening. Guess not. He grabbed some clothing from the laundry room and got dressed. He pulled a few stakes from the box under his bed, distributing them to the various places he liked to carry them on his person. One in each boot, and one in his back pocket. He put on his light denim jacket as he began to climb the stairs. Couldn't they at least have waited for him to get a cup of coffee? It was another living corpse, he was pretty sure. He headed out to take care of it.

He reached the woods just as the others were arriving, he could sense them. They must be looking for it. He saw the boys' marks clearly in his mind. He could see Sindy's trace as well, but she was flickering. He smiled. She wished she could mask herself as he could. She certainly was trying. She hadn't even known it was possible until the first time he'd snuck up on her and scared her half out of her wits. She was not amused. She'd demanded that he teach her the trick. He'd told her that he could teach her a lot, if she was willing to learn; but it would have to be on his terms, no more killing.

At first, he'd thought she might change. Sindy was very interested in gaining his knowledge, and seemed eager to please. Then the advances had started. Not that she wasn't appealing. She wasn't the kind of girl he was normally drawn to, but after three centuries, one learned to appreciate variety. She definitely had his interest, but he wanted to be sure of her first.

The harder she tried, the less interesting she became, because she obviously thought of her sex appeal as a tool. She thought to wrap him around her finger like the playthings she had made for herself. As he came to know her, he realized that he would get nowhere with her, until he made it quite clear that he had absolutely no interest in extra activities. She didn't take it well.

She did show some promise, though. If she could manage to get over herself a little, she might actually have the stamina to endure the paranormal existence they shared. She was certainly clever and determined, but she would have to accept some limits, and stop behaving as a spoiled child, or it would be her downfall. She had such grand designs for one so young and inexperienced, and a grand temper as well. Her temerity last night was an example.

She knew he had grown weary of her little jabs and games, and simply ignored them now; so she had aimed them at Felicity instead, something she knew he would not ignore.

He had given Felicity the vial of blood to protect her against Luke and Chris, or any others she might meet. It was strong instinct not to touch a victim that belonged to another. Even though he hadn't actually 'marked' her, his intention would be clear, and they would be afraid to go against him so openly, but Sindy herself could be very rebellious, and Felicity was not traditionally marked. If she chose to do something as a message to him, a little glass vial wouldn't stop her. This could take a dangerous turn if not handled properly. He had to find a way to disarm her anger.

Part of him would like to rant and rave, threaten and bully her into submission, but she seemed to thrive on such attention. She would almost certainly call his bluff, and he wasn't quite ready for it to come to that, or to give up on her yet. He also wasn't sure if he could fully protect Felicity at this point. Better to try to reason with Sindy still, although by now he was becoming thoroughly sick of her. It would take her many years of maturing before he would be willing to deal with her again after this was over.

He was walking through the woods, at the edge of the development. The forest would come up against the cemetery eventually. They must have buried the new vampire on their own, just in the wood line.

There they were. The boys were in baggy pants, grungy, over sized t-shirts and army jackets. Their similar actions and demeanor made them seem practically identical, except that Chris had fair straight hair, while Luke's head was topped with an unruly mass of dark curls under the knit hat he wore. Cain didn't think they even bothered to change their clothing anymore.

Sindy of course was much more conscious of her appearance. She had painted both above and below her eyes with her usual black and purple shadows and dark, blood red lipstick stained her lips. Her skin was dead white, with just a slash of red color swiped high on each cheekbone. And of course, she continued to dye her long straight hair that dark jet black that almost looked purple in some lights.

The total effect was very goth-punk, at first shocking and strange, but it actually rendered her seductively exotic. He would find her quite bewitching, if she weren't so persistently irritating him all the time. She had on a tight little red mini dress with fishnet stockings and those clunky boots she so favored. They looked rather ridiculous to him, but she obviously felt otherwise, and he knew from experience that you wouldn't want to receive a kick from them.

The way people dressed never failed to amaze him. He could hardly care less what he wore, as long as it wasn't too conspicuous. Sindy however, had the exact opposite outlook. She adorned herself as though wanting her entire being to scream 'Look at me!'.

He decided to wait and watch them for a moment, before advertising his presence. He spotted the new vampire; it was mostly still in the ground. Either they had buried it awfully deep, or it was too weak to rise on its own. Most likely the latter. The three of them stood and watched in disgust. Sindy threw her hands up in the air and began to pace. "You guys are **so** incompetent!"

The boys both kept their eyes on the corpse as it tried to pull itself from the dirt. It seemed totally unaware of them. Luke looked up at Sindy in annoyance. "We did what you said."

"Barely. Jeez, didn't you give him anything?" Sindy asked.

"He woke up didn't he?"

Sindy backed up a step as the corpse's struggles increased. It really was a sickening sight. In perhaps the same condition as the one from last night, this poor guy had probably been in pretty bad shape even before he'd died. He looked sickly thin, was unshaven, and wearing the mismatched and ill fitted rags that pegged him as one of the homeless. Even from Cain's distance, the smell was horrific to his enhanced senses.

"Ew, look at him! What am I supposed to do with *that*?" Sindy demanded of Luke.

"That's Chris's guy," Luke said defensively.

Sindy looked accusingly at them both. "I ask for back-up and you guys give me *Night of the Living Dead*?" She suddenly wheeled to see Cain approach from the trees. "Oh, and now my evening is complete!" She looked at her boys for a moment, and then stepped towards Cain. "Do you see what I have to work with here?" she asked him conspiratorially. She looked back at Luke and Chris with distaste. "You guys are making Cain look better and better all the time. At least he's not a complete idiot!"

Cain sighed and shook his head as though scolding a precocious child. "What are you doing?"

"Surrounding myself with fools, apparently."

"I thought you understood why this had to stop."

"I know, I know; because of our duty to humankind, and our part in God's plan, and blah, blah, blah. Boy, even when you're dead the Jehovah Witness won't leave you alone!" She turned to share a laugh with her lackey's, then back to Cain, who was not amused. "Lighten up! It's not as if we killed him tonight!" She gave the boys an accusing look. "He's obviously been there for awhile."

He hoped that meant this was the last of them. "Are we finished?" He turned a glare on the boys that should give him a straight answer.

Chris spoke up. "I know I am. I let that skeezy hobo suck on me for *this?*"

Sindy laughed. "It's not my fault you have bad taste!"

"You told me I shouldn't do anyone obvious!"

"You shouldn't have done it at all," Cain interjected, turning to include Luke in the reprimand as well.

"Don't look at me. You snuffed my guy last night," Luke said, as he watched the corpse finally break free of the ground, shaking off the last clods of dirt encasing its feet. It stared blindly into the distance as its motions caused a clump of dirt and a pale, wriggling maggot to come loose from its ear and fall to the ground.

Sindy watched for a moment in disgust and then turned back to Chris. "Get rid of that thing before it makes me puke."

Chris gave her an icy glare. "I was just doing what **you** told me."

She seemed unconcerned at his feeble attempt to stand up to her. "Well, I didn't tell you to do it wrong. Clean up your own mess." She gave him a dark stare, and then suddenly turned to Cain as if all sweetness and light. "Let's take a walk," she said, flashing him a smile.

He followed her into the field alongside the cemetery. She picked wild flowers idly as she walked, as though she hadn't a concern in the world. At least in a mood like this, she might be reasoned with, but he knew her moods to shift as quickly as autumn winds. "Haven't you heard a word I've said?" he asked imploringly.

She stopped walking and laid down in the grass to look at the sky. She held a handful of flowers to her chest for a moment, as though she had been laid to rest. He sat down next to her and she threw the flowers at him playfully.

"I tried to listen, really, I did." She spoke like a pouty little girl and batted her eyes at him. "But the way you live is so boring! And every time I tried to make things even a little interesting," she sat up and leaned into him to make sure he had a nice view of her cleavage, "you got all huffy! And you claimed not to be a stodgy old guy. You could have given me something." She wagged her finger at him as though scolding a puppy. "A girl can't live on blood alone." She gave him her best seductive smile and tried to snuggle into his lap.

He stood up, dumping her onto the ground. "Don't you *have* boys for pastimes like that?" He glanced back towards Luke and Chris, busy doing away with their handiwork.

Sindy got to her feet as she looked at him appraisingly. "Did you want to borrow them?" she asked with a sly smile. "Is that your problem? 'Cause if that's what you're into, they're pathetically stupid, but they're pretty good in the sack." She gave him another grin.

"You make me sick." He shook his head and walked away a pace. She quickly came around in front of him and was in his face.

"No I don't." She placed her hands on his hips and pressed herself up against his body. "I make you hot, and you'd rather die *again* than admit it!"

He let her rub against him while he stared down at her with supreme indifference. "Sindy, you are a spoiled, selfish, child, and I'm getting tired of your games."

She got all pouty again. "Well, what kind of games do *you* wanna play? You want me to be good?"

She looked up at him with her big brown eyes. She had begun to look a little vulnerable, as though she were lowering the emotional shield she usually kept between them. Of course, he knew how skilled she could be at artful manipulation. He paused, seeking the trap. "Yes."

"I can be a good girl. I could be *your* good little girl. Daddy's little girl would do everything you say."

He believed she would be happy to do just that, if it meant he'd keep her. She really did need someone with a strong firm hand to guide her, but right now, he just wasn't interested. He backed away from her a pace. "No," he said mildly.

Her seeming vulnerability abruptly disappeared, to be replaced with scorned annoyance. "Well what do you want?!"

"I want to leave, and I don't want to have to come back."

She dropped herself to lie on the ground, laughing at him. "You are a terrible liar."

He had to smile. "So I've been told."

She lay on her stomach, playing with the flowers and kicking her legs in the air behind her. "You're not in any rush to leave, and you and I both know why."

He sighed. Now at last, we come to the heart of it, he thought; the real reason he'd begun to lose her respect. He knew the conversation would come around to this eventually. He sat down next to her again. "I was not amused by your performance last night."

She smiled up at him mockingly. "What's the matter? Did I scare her? Maybe I made her jealous?"

He smiled at her with disdain. "I think you made her nauseous." That earned him a dirty look. "Leave her alone."

She threw a flower into his lap and gave him a gleeful grin. "Make me." He stared hard at her. He knew exactly what she meant. She smiled sweetly. "Really, I mean it. What are you waiting for? I'm not totally unreasonable. I can play nice and be a good sport. You want her that badly, prove it. Mark her. Put her off limits and I'll never touch her again, I swear." He gazed at the ground, unsure how to answer. "What's the matter, don't you like pets?"

"I don't do that," he protested quietly.

"But you have, it's written all over your face!" He felt shameful that he couldn't deny it. "I would think that's right up your alley, all humane and everything. Although, mine never last for very long. I guess I play too rough."

"I don't need to do it, you know she's spoken for."

She tried to assess how serious he was as she sat up, her eyes never leaving his face. "She's untouched, and that makes her fair game. Any vampire in the world would tell you so. You gonna kill us all?"

"Don't touch her," Cain quietly demanded.

Sindy stood and brushed herself off with a gesture that made him feel as though she were brushing off his wishes as well. "Give me a good reason not to." Before he could think of what to say that might actually penetrate the emotional barrier she had once again constructed between them, she turned and skipped off through the flowers to her waiting toys.

Cain closed his eyes with a resigned sigh. This was not going well. He stood and followed her trail through the weeds and flowers. He noticed that while she was having a conversation with Luke, Chris was standing a bit apart from them, staring at Cain. The unfortunate vampire they had earlier watched struggle to rise from the earth, was now nothing more than a pile of dust on the ground at their feet.

The closer Cain got, the more it seemed that Chris was waiting to speak with him. He glanced back at Sindy and Luke. She was laughing and putting flowers in his hair. He stopped for a moment as the image unkindly reminded him of a girl he'd known in the past; a girl held in much higher regard. It did not sit well with him that someone like Sindy would bring that memory to mind. He shook his head to clear himself of it. Sindy often did silly childish things; it was an unfortunate, but not intentional reminder.

Sindy turned to see if she had an audience, and then began to kiss Luke. Was she trying to make him jealous? He really couldn't care less what she did; Chris certainly had his attention though. Noting that she was fully intent on her charade, he moved close to Chris, who seemed quite thankful to have his ear.

"There's another one," Chris whispered. "Not like this," he nodded towards the ash heap that had once been animate, "one that *she* made." Cain glanced at the amorous couple who seemed unaware of Chris' words. "In a place by the river." Chris abruptly walked away from him as Sindy and Luke disengaged from their kiss.

Sindy looked around for Chris. When she saw that he wasn't even looking at her, she snapped for his attention. He went to her side like a well-trained dog. She caressed his cheek, and then gave it a little slap. "Let's take this elsewhere, shall we?" She turned back to Cain. "Care to join us?" He didn't bother to answer. She smiled and shrugged. "Suit yourself."

He watched them leave as he stretched out his awareness towards the river. It was too far, just beyond his range. He noticed the three of them were headed in the opposite direction, towards town. Should he try to investigate now, while he knew they weren't there? It seemed the smartest decision. He was pleased that Chris had risked Sindy's wrath to tell him. He should use the information while he could. He had no doubt it was true.

He tried to gauge the hour; it had to be close to closing time. He should be at the bookstore, surely Felicity would expect him, but he would barely be able to get there in time now, and he would be giving up his best chance to asses this new one alone. It couldn't be very old; he'd like them to have a chance to talk before Sindy got too deep a hold.

Judging by her present mood, Sindy and her boy toys would be occupied for a little while at least. He shook his head and sighed. He would rather be with Felicity, but this was more important than his own pleasures. He started off across the field towards the river. It would have been nice, to have had a cup of coffee though.

Cain followed the fields until he came to the muddy bank of the river. The moonlight sparkled and gleamed on the running water. He was beginning to sense another vampire in the distance. It was bright and new, just as Chris had said. It was still. Resting, waiting for Sindy's return he assumed.

He wondered if this was where the others stayed as well. Probably not, Chris would be pretty stupid to have told him if it were. Not that Sindy's boys struck him as marvels of common sense, but self-preservation should be a fairly basic instinct.

They had moved around quite a bit since he'd discovered them. It was easy for him to find them when he chose, especially if he knew the general area of where to start looking, so they never stayed in one spot for very long. Sindy must have assumed that he wouldn't find this new one, because he simply wouldn't think to search for it.

She had certainly kept his attention focused on other things. Perhaps that was her whole reason for baiting Felicity in the first place. So that he would become occupied protecting her, and not notice Sindy's other activities. He was not happy about her making others, but at least a being like himself could be reasoned with. Creatures like those living zombies were simply unbearable.

He wondered what kind of man she would have chosen. He had no doubt it was a man, she would never share anything with another woman he was sure. He came upon a little shack in the woods. It was barely more than a shed, or perhaps a child's clubhouse, though it had clearly stood untouched for some time. The weeds and brush had grown up so close around it, that it was very well camouflaged. There was however, a flattened space in the grass in front of the door, from recent use. The subject of his attention was inside.

Cain stepped up to the door. All was quiet. His presence was hidden, so the other would have no idea he was there. How should he approach this? Well, he had come to talk hadn't he? He might as well conduct things in a civilized manner. This creature didn't know him; Sindy might not have even mentioned him. The vampire within could become a valuable new ally, if properly approached.

He knocked on the door. He heard rustling within. Cain decided to stop cloaking his presence as a vampire; it wouldn't be fair to deceive the man of what he was dealing with. The door opened. Framed by the doorway was the largest, most muscular man he had ever encountered. What did she do, go out and turn Arnold Schwarzenegger? "Hello, my name is Cain. I was wondering if I might speak to you..."

The man let out a bellow of rage that sounded as though it should come from a moose. His face evolved into a mask of hate as it changed into its vampire state. He ducked through the doorway and advanced on Cain.

"I take it you've heard of me," Cain said, dancing backwards from the man. The brute took a swing at him with an arm that was easily the size of Cain's thigh. "There's really no need for this." Cain said, ducking out of the way. "I just wanted to talk." The man continued to come after him with mindless fury.

This was not exactly going as planned. The next time the man threw a punch; Cain ducked out of the way and then punched back, right in the stomach. His punch was well thrown, but he felt as though he might as well have been hitting solid rock, for all the effect it had. The guy didn't even seem to notice. He tried again. This time he gave a strong punch to the jaw. It knocked the man back a step, but he didn't seem damaged at all. He just kept coming! Okay, time for a new plan.

Cain reached behind him and pulled the stake from his back pocket, but as soon as he brought his hand back around in front of him, the man grabbed him by the wrist with a grip like iron. The brute lifted him by the arm until he felt himself begin to dangle off his feet like a child. The sheer strength of this man was amazing!

Cain cringed as he expected to hear the fine bones of his wrist begin to snap. He braced one foot against the man's thigh and used the other foot to kick him hard in the solar plexus, hoping to knock the wind from him. Well, it didn't affect him quite as much as Cain had hoped, but at least he let go and backed up a step.

Cain's stake was lost to the tall grass and Cain swore as he flexed his wrist, hoping he could still use the hand effectively. He stooped to take a stake from his boot, but as he did, the man's fist came down on his head. Cain was knocked to the ground, though not unconscious, thankfully. He rolled to the side just as the giant's foot came down where his head had just been. Cain sprang to his feet, but suffered dizziness for it. He staggered to the side a bit, as the man came at him again. This was *definitely* not going as planned.

Cain managed to avoid another blow as he tried to judge his target. Then, as the man was extended from a misplaced punch, Cain came in close and stabbed him in the chest with his stake. He braced his feet as he anticipated the brute to turn to dust, but he didn't. Instead, he yelled and grabbed Cain by the throat.

"I missed? I never miss!" Cain gasped in astonishment.

The man started to throttle him as Cain frantically grabbed for the stake sticking out of his chest to try again. This guy was huge! Was it not in deep enough? He couldn't grab it, and he couldn't stand to be choked any longer to try. Of course, asphyxiation couldn't do him any permanent damage, but it certainly wouldn't do for him to pass out at this point.

He tried to pry the great fists from his throat, to no avail. He then reached up to the man's face and shoved his thumbs into the monster's eyes. That made him let go.
He roared with rage as Cain dropped to the ground gasping. "So much for our little talk." Cain regained his feet and took off. He crossed the fields, vaguely wondering if Chris had set him up, but he didn't think so. He had just blundered into a bad situation by trying to be civilized rather than expect the worst. He should have been better prepared. He hadn't even fed yet. He needed blood to renew his strength. This would have to be dealt with another time.

Chapter 11

I'd go home with the nice human guy, if I were you

Felicity

DownTime Café and Bookstore
Thursday night

Felicity looked out the window for the umpteenth time into empty darkness. She kept thinking she'd see Cain in the entryway, but was always disappointed. The evening passed and as the hour grew late, she still found herself watching the door. Cain never showed; she noticed that Ben caught her looking for him though. He gave no sign, but she was sure he knew that's what she was doing.

Finally, it was time to close. Wasn't he going to come and walk her home at least? Where was he? What else could he possibly have to do? Unless he was out fighting with *her*. Felicity's face twisted into a pinched snarl as she closed out the cash register. Sindy. What had Alyson called her? A skanky whore. That sounded about right. She wondered why Cain didn't just run her out of town, get rid of her.

A horrible thought suddenly occurred to her. What if he didn't want to? She didn't know what their relationship was. What did he really think of Sindy? He didn't seem to like her much, and he had thrown her into the street the first time Felicity had seen him, but did that really mean anything? Felicity didn't know what vampire society was like. He had said there were lots of them. They must have their own little culture, rules of conduct or whatever. He obviously felt superior to Sindy, but that could mean a lot of things. The thought of him with that witch made her blood run cold. Sindy certainly hadn't been afraid to interrupt their dance the other night, like a...jealous girlfriend?

No. He wouldn't be with someone like her. He had more class than that. He really didn't seem to like her much. Felicity could see where a guy might find her kind of alluring though, like something forbidden. She was pretty, in a dark, poisonous kind of way, if you liked that type.

No. He'd even said that it had been a long time since he'd been with a woman, not that she really considered Sindy a *woman*. Oh my God. No. Stop thinking like this. He would never be with her. He's so...

What? Did she even know him really? He said she didn't, implying that he was a monster. She didn't see him that way, but what the hell did she know? She was just some stupid teenager right? The fact that he was good looking and displayed such rakish charm, made him very enticing, but it said nothing of his true character. She didn't really know him. She only knew that she wanted to get to know him.

When she was near him, she could hardly think straight. She found him fascinating, and saw him in a way she had never seen anyone else before. Why should he bring out desires in her that went so far beyond anything she had felt for other guys before him? He had hardly even paid her any real attention honestly. So they had danced together, big deal. They had only ever shared one kiss.

But that kiss! She might be a virgin, but she wasn't totally inexperienced, and she had *never* felt anything like that before. And it was only a kiss! A few kisses like that and she'd probably do anything he asked. Now that was scary.

He hadn't seemed quite as affected by it though. Who was she trying to kid? She must seem like a child to him.

"Aren't you finished?" She jumped. It was Ben.

She quickly resumed counting out the register. "Sorry."

At first he seemed annoyed, but as she finished up, he started to look like he felt bad for her. "Need a ride?"

She looked up at him wearily. She'd really like to say no. She looked out the glass of the front door. No one was in sight. "I guess so." She avoided looking at him as she went to get her stuff.

He didn't say anything as they locked up and she followed him out to his car. She was looking at the ground, watching his feet on the pavement in front of her, when they stopped moving. She looked up at the car.

It was gorgeous, bright yellow, and obviously a classic, though in mint condition. She turned her eyes to Ben, and could tell he was waiting for some kind of reaction. She had to give him a smile. "I like your car."

He grinned like a little kid. "Isn't she sweet? '65 Mustang Fastback."

"I never figured you for a 'car guy'."

"Well, I never figured you for a vampire lover." He said it jokingly, but it really pissed her off. She turned and started walking away, but he grabbed her arm. "Get in."

She turned back around to give him a dirty look, but he was busy opening the door for her. She looked down the dark road, sighed and got in. It really was a beautiful car, inside and out. He got in and started it up. He just sat there for a minute, listening to it run as she put on her seatbelt. He fastened his, but instead of putting the car into gear, he turned to speak to her. "What are you doing?"

She pretended she didn't know what he was talking about. "Nothing." She could use code too.

"He's only going to hurt you, one way or another."

"You don't even know him," she retorted.

"He's not even human 'Liss"

"Are you going to drive, or do I have to walk?" He sighed, put the car in gear and pulled out onto the road. It was quiet. She noticed that the lot at Tommy's held only a few cars; no one was outside.

As they turned the corner onto her block, the headlights swung around to reveal someone standing right in the middle of the road. Ben slammed on the brakes and she was thrown forward as they screeched to a halt. She quickly looked up, but Sindy was gone. Felicity could still see her image like a negative burned onto the backs of her eyelids. She had just been standing there, her skin dead white, her hair jet black. She was wearing red and staring at them with eyes that looked like fiery portals to hell.

Felicity looked out her window and locked her door. Nothing but trees and bushes. She looked around frantically and saw Ben doing the same. "You saw her right?" Ben asked, trying to catch his breath, as he shifted the car into park. He turned and locked his door as well.

"Yeah, I saw her," Felicity assured him.

Ben sat staring out the window for a minute, scanning the wood line next to the road. "I should have run her down."

Felicity couldn't think what to answer to that. She couldn't imagine actually doing that to someone, even Sindy. She wondered if Ben really would have, if he'd known all along that it was her. They sat there in the silence; the sound of their breathing seemed loud in her ears. Her whole body was tense, on edge, waiting for something, anything. There was no other sound, nothing to see, just the dark.

Ben looked at her, then at the gearshift. He put the car back into drive and began to move slowly forward. It seemed like it took forever to get down the road. Finally, they turned into the lot in front of the dorm building. Felicity reached into her shirt at the neckline, and wrapped her fingers around the vial she still wore. Sindy wouldn't care. It'd probably make things worse. Now she wished she'd worn the cross as well. Would that even help? She looked nervously out the window. She'd left the stake in her room. She wouldn't really know what to do with it anyway; as if she'd ever tried to stab anyone in the heart before. Still, at this point, if Sindy jumped her again she might be willing to try.

Ben looked around, and then put the car in park. He turned to watch her for a moment. "Want to stay at my house?"

"No." Felicity sighed and unlocked the door. *She is just trying to freak you out,* she thought to herself. *She wouldn't actually do anything. Cain'd kill her, I hope. She's probably sitting in the bushes laughing her ass off.*

"Sleeping in my car then?" Ben asked.

"I'm going." She took off her seatbelt.

"I'd go home with the nice human guy, if I were you." She turned and gave him a withering look. He smiled. "I'm just saying..."

"Good night." She began to open the door, but then turned back to him with a thought. "Don't leave until I get in the door okay? And keep the headlights on."

He looked at her as though offended. "Give me a little credit. What kind of jerk do you think I am?"

"Good night." She nerved herself to open the door and get out in a calm and casual manner. She'd be damned if she was going to give that bitch the pleasure of seeing her bolt from the car and run across the lawn like a frightened rabbit. It wouldn't help anyway. *If she wants you, you are just going to have to fight her off,* she told herself. She closed the door.

She didn't even look back at Ben, she just started walking. She stared straight at the porch and walked. She imagined Ben staring at her back and yelling at her in his head to hurry up. She heard things rustling in the bushes. She forced herself not to look. She passed the pillars flanking the entrance to the stairway, and started up the walkway steps, one...two...three...four. She crossed the landing, then up two more steps to the porch. She approached the door, reached for the knob...and couldn't get the door open.

For a second her heart stopped and she thought it was locked. *It's not supposed to be locked yet!* she yelled in her mind at the girls of the house. No, not locked, just stuck. It opened. She stepped inside, breathing a sigh of relief. The lights were on, but no one was in the parlor at this late hour.

Suddenly, she heard Ben lean on the car horn with an ear splitting blast, just as she felt something brush her shoulder. She jumped and spun around as though she had been electrocuted, and then stumbled back a few steps further into the house. There was Sindy, standing right at the doorway, almost close enough to touch. She wore her 'vampire face'. Her eyes were a sickly red and she was smiling broadly to reveal her sharp fangs. Felicity was frozen with shock for a minute. Why was she just standing there?

"Aren't you going to invite me in?" she asked, in a hoarse whisper that would surely haunt her nightmares. Felicity was shaken back to reality and slammed the door in her face. She quickly rushed forward and locked it. Then backed away from the door. She saw Sindy's face in the window and stifled a scream. *She can't come in, she can't come in, she can't come in.* She said it in her head like a mantra as she turned around and climbed the stairs. She heard Ben's tires squeal in the parking lot. Just as she reached the top, she heard footsteps in the parlor below. She froze, and then forced herself to turn and look down. It was Maggie, the residence advisor, in her robe and slippers.

"Was that a friend of yours honking outside? Because it's awfully late for that."

"Sorry." She watched Maggie shake her head and start towards the door. "I already locked it!" she yelled, a little too loudly.

Maggie jumped and turned. "Thank you."

"Good night." She finished climbing the stairs and went to her room. She immediately closed her blinds, and collapsed on her bed. It was going to be a long night.

~~~~~~~~~~~~~~~~~~~~~~~~~~~~~~~

Boom, boom, boom. Felicity awoke with a start to someone pounding on her door. She gasped and sat up to see sunlight trying to stream in her window through the cracks of the blinds. Morning, thank God. "Felicity? Phone call," someone yelled from outside the door.

"Coming." She looked at the clock; it was 8:15 a.m. She'd been lying awake on the bed until at least four. She hadn't realized that she'd finally fallen asleep. She got up off the bed and stumbled to the door. She hadn't even bothered to get undressed last night. Out in the hall girls were busy rushing to and from the bathroom. In the hallway was the phone alcove. It was probably originally intended to be a double closet. The doors had been removed and now it held two side-by-side payphones. She saw the receiver of one dangling to the floor. She picked it up. "Hello?"

"Felicity?" It was her mom. "Is everything okay? You missed our Thursday night phone call."

"Oh yeah, sorry." *I was busy being chased by a vampire and frightened for my life,* she thought to herself. "Everything's fine mom. I was working late. I guess I forgot."

"How is that job working out? Are you making enough money?" her mom asked.

"Yeah, it's fine," Felicity assured her.

"Good. How about school?"

"It's fine mom. Everything's good."

"Have you made any new friends?" her mother asked.

"I've made some friends."

"Good, you're always so shy. How about boys, anyone special?" her mom prodded.

"Mom! Yes, I've met some…boys."

"Well, nothing too serious I hope. You keep your mind on your school work."

"Yeah mom, I've gotta go. I have to get ready for class."

"Alright well, you're still coming home Sunday, right? You left me alone in a house full of boys. I need a shopping fix!" her mother pleaded.

"Yeah, sure," Felicity answered, "I'll see you Sunday."

"Okay, your father'll be there at ten, bye honey."

"Goodbye mom." She hung up the phone and slumped down against the wall. She sat for a minute in the hall watching girls rush to and fro in various states of readiness. She hastily pulled her feet in, as a girl in a robe and big fuzzy slippers carrying a toiletry case almost tripped over her.

She got up and went back to her room. What was she supposed to do now, get changed and go to algebra? Sit next to Ashley and listen to what a great time she and Ben had the other night, and how come Felicity didn't stay and dance? She wasn't feeling up for that, and she'd be late anyway. What was she going to do? Things were okay for now, but what about when the sun goes down? At least she had about eleven hours to figure it out.

Things were starting to die down out in the hall as the other students left for their classes. She gathered up her bathroom stuff and went to take a shower. She could barely think straight right now; she needed some time to clear her head.

She came back feeling a little more awake and refreshed, but she still had no idea what to do. She dumped her stuff and lay down on her bed in her bathrobe. Sindy was just trying to scare her - nice job by the way, but let's face it, if she had really wanted to attack Felicity she could have, easily. Her intent was obviously to send Felicity running back to Cain, scared to death. She was probably pissed off at Cain, and using Felicity to get back at him for something, but at some point she might decide to send a stronger message. Felicity had to do something.

She could go to Cain, but then she'd be doing just what Sindy wanted, and that rubbed her the wrong way. But what else was there to do, wait for Sindy to decide to take more drastic measures?

Calm down. She can't come into the dorms; at least she'd established that much. Ben had said that a vampire couldn't enter without an invitation; that much seemed to be true. Even if she managed to get someone to invite her into the building, she shouldn't be able to come into Felicity's room. This was her private space, and she was not about to offer an invitation. At least she wasn't working tonight. She'd go to the rest of her classes, and then stay in her room after sunset. It sounded a little pathetic, but it seemed better than running to Cain for help. She didn't want Sindy to think she was so easily manipulated.

Boom, boom, boom. She was startled up from the bed…again. Couldn't anyone knock without trying to break down the door? Her hair was a damp crazy mess. She tried to run her fingers through it, to make herself look somewhat presentable. Making sure that her robe was well closed, she got up and opened the door. Ben practically burst into the room and closed the door behind him. He turned to her and took her by the shoulders. "You're alright?"

She smiled. "Good morning to you too."

He shoved her shoulders, pushing her back a step. "What is the matter with you?"

"Huh?"

"Generally, when a vampire is chasing you, you **run**! You don't **walk**, you **run**!" Ben exclaimed.

"She wasn't really *chasing* me," Felicity insisted.

"Oh, right. My mistake. She was *stalking* you. Not an improvement!" he declared.

Felicity sat down on the bed. Ben just crossed his arms and stood there looking at her in disapproval. "Ben, we both know that if she wanted me, she could have caught me."

"Kind of the point!" Ben demanded.

"Well, then running wouldn't have made any difference, and I wasn't going to give her the satisfaction," Felicity explained.

Ben looked exasperated. "I'm worried for your life and you're worried about your image?"

"You couldn't have been that worried. I notice you didn't come running with your big cross," she pointed out mockingly.

"Is *that* what you were waiting for?" he asked.

"No, I'm just teasing you. Contrary to popular belief, I am not Sweet Polly whatever her name was. Nor am I some stupid screaming horror flick chick... I think I know what she's doing."

"You do?" Ben asked incredulously.

"Well, yeah. She's got a motive behind this," she told him.

"You mean besides hunger?"

"If she were hungry, she would have caught me. She didn't *want* to catch me, she wanted to scare me," Felicity explained.

"Being caught would have been scary," Ben mumbled.

"This is true, but if she caught me, the game would be over."

"What the hell kind of game are you playing?" he asked.

Felicity clarified, "Not me, her."

Ben shifted his weight and sighed. "So she thinks you're fun to play with?" he asked with a cocked eyebrow.

"She came over to Cain and I at the bar the other night. It was like she was...taunting him. She's only after me to try and piss him off."

"Lucky you. So what are you going to do? Bumping into them once in awhile is bad enough, but to have a vampire actually looking for you, is a very bad thing."

"No kidding," she grumbled.

"So, what are you going to do?"

Felicity put her hands to his shoulders and nudged him towards the door. "You're going to leave, and I'm going to class."

"What?" he asked in confusion.

"I have anthropology in twenty minutes. I have to get dressed," she insisted.

"And this will help save you from the playful vampire, how exactly?" Ben asked.

"I haven't figured that part out yet, but we know she can't come in here, so if I stay in my room after dark, I should be okay."

He laughed. "So, you'll just stay in your room, forever. That's your plan?"

"It needs work, I know. Are you going to be around for lunch?"

"No, it's Friday. I have classes until 1:30, and then I have to get ready for work," he explained.

"What are you doing for dinner?" she asked.

"Eating," he answered smugly.

"Funny."

"I'm working a full shift tonight, my break's at six. Wanna come up to the café?" Ben asked.

"Yeah, okay. I'll be there. As long as I can get back before dark," she added.

"Sunset's at 7:18," Ben provided. She gave him an odd look. "What? When you live in a town full of vampires, you tend to keep track of these things."

She smiled. "Okay, I'll see you at six. Now get out of here, I'm going to be late," she said, pushing him out the door.

She quickly dried her hair and got dressed, to run out into the sunshine and race across campus to class. Amazing how a little sunlight could make everything seem better. She spent the rest of the day going through the motions in class; although it did occur to her more than once that it might be easier just to fail, drop out and go home. Try explaining that to parents who just spent their savings on your tuition.

The day wore on, and the closer it came to sunset, the more she began to think she'd like to be sitting at Cain's house. It might be wimpy, but at least she would feel safe. She should probably at least let him know what had happened, right?

Finally, the time came to go meet Ben. As she entered the DownTime, Ashley looked up from the register and seemed surprised to see her. "Felicity, hi. I missed you in algebra this morning."

"I kind of slept in," Felicity explained.

"Oh. Are you on tonight? Once Harold goes home, I thought it was just me and Ben."

"No, I'm not working; I'm just meeting him for dinner."

"Harold?" Ashley asked, shocked.

"No, Ben." Felicity replied with a laugh.

Ashley seemed a bit taken aback. "Oh."

"I needed to talk to him about something."

Just then, Ben came over from the café. "Hey, you want pizza?"

"Sounds good to me." She looked back at Ashley. "Bye."

"I'll be back." Ben said as they walked out the door.

The pizza place was full of people at the counter, waiting for their orders. Up front there was a family with young kids making a small commotion. She and Ben got their slices and found a table in the back. Ben looked up at her as she started to eat. "How you doin'?"

"I'm okay."

"Sindy's going to open her eyes in about an hour and a half when the sun goes down. Are you getting the heebie jeebies?"

She looked up from her pizza. "Not 'til just now, thanks."

"Come on, like you haven't been thinking about it all day. Do you think she'll come back?"

Felicity shook her head a little. "I don't know. The way I see it, I have three options. Option 1, I go back to my room and spend the entire night there, alone, terrified, and wait for the sun to come up."

"Okay."

"Option 2," she paused to give him a hesitant smile, "I gather some of my closest friends and we wait in the parking lot with stakes and crosses, and waste the bitch."

"Are you serious?" he said a little too loudly. The family up front glanced back at them.

Felicity stifled a laugh. "No, but you're really not going to like option 3, so I thought I'd just throw that one in there."

"What's option 3?" he asked warily.

"I go find Cain, who I'm pretty sure can totally kick Sindy's ass, as well as any friends she might bring. And I sit with him, less terrified, and wait for the sun to come up."

"Okay, yeah. I vote for option 1."

"I thought you might."

"Just how *chummy* were you two the other night?" he asked, leaning back and crossing his arms.

"Not *very*," she answered, defensively, "but enough to know that he wouldn't let Sindy kill me. And I do still have all my blood, so...that's a plus."

"That wouldn't work, even if it wasn't such an incredibly stupid idea. Cain doesn't come in until well after sunset, for obvious reasons. He may come too late. Sindy's never been to the DownTime before, but it *is* a public place. She doesn't need an invitation."

"Well, I wouldn't wait at the bookstore."

"Then how were you planning to find him?" Ben asked.

"I know where he is."

Ben looked at her in shock. "He told you where he sleeps?" She just gave a little shrug. "You've *been* there? Oh my God, you went home with him!"

The family up front glanced back at them again as they were leaving. Felicity turned away from them, embarrassed. "Just to get something. Nothing *happened*. Not that it's any of your business."

He looked disgusted with her, like he had any right to judge. "Fine. So say you do go sit with Cain, Sindy shows up and then they decide to make it tea for two?"

"He wouldn't do that!" she said incredulously.

"How do you know?" Ben asked.

"Because he wouldn't! Call it...intuition"

"Yeah? No offense, but I think your intuition sucks."

"Thanks," she muttered sarcastically.

"Go home, Felicity," he advised her.

"What am I supposed to do all night?" she asked.

"Go home, read a book and go to bed."

Felicity sighed. "I guess, but even if she *doesn't* show up, I just know I'm going to be hearing her scratch at my window and scuffle around outside my door all night and be all creeped out."

He stared at her for a minute over his pizza. "You want to stay at my house? Purely platonic, I swear," he said, raising his hands.

"What about your dad?" she asked.

Ben laughed. "I'm a grown-up. I can have a sleep-over if I want," he said with a smile. "Besides, he's usually out for the evening or passed out by the time I get home anyway."

She lowered her eyes. "Oh." She thought for a moment and then looked back up at him. "You wanna come stay with me, in my room?" she asked hesitantly. "I have an extra bed."

He thought about that for a minute, while he picked a slice of pepperoni off his pizza and popped it into his mouth. "I'm closing tonight, so I wouldn't even get there until 10:30. You don't need me there. You'll probably be asleep by then."

"No, believe me, I won't. It'd make me feel better. I mean, if you want to. Unless you have plans," she added, suddenly thinking of Ashley. "It's Friday night. You and Ashley were probably going to go for a drink or something after work, right?" she asked.

He studied her for a minute. "I don't have any plans."

"It'd just be nice to have someone else in the room, you know?" she said, asking him for understanding.

"Isn't that against the rules or something?" he asked with a smile.

She shrugged. "I've seen other girls do it. At least this is for a good cause, right?"

He grinned. "Yeah, okay. I'll come, if you want. Oh, I almost forgot, I bought you something." He started looking for the pocket of his jacket, which was thrown over the chair.

She looked at him quizzically. "People keep giving me presents. It's not my birthday yet."

He smiled and whipped out a wooden cross about as tall as her hand, like the one he carried. "Something for the *independent*, screaming horror flick chick. Kind of hokey I know, but it does help."

She smiled. "Thanks."

"Don't worry, you're going to be just fine, vampires be damned. I haven't let them get me yet, and I won't let them get you either."

Reassuring...but somehow it didn't seem quite that simple to her anymore. They finished up their pizza and she walked him back to the store. "So, I'll see you later?" she asked. "Definitely."

∽∾∿ ∽∾∿ ∽∾∿ ∽∾∿ ∽∾∿ ∽∾∿ ∽∾∿ ∽∾∿

Part 2 ~ Tempting Transgressions

∽∾∿ ∽∾∿ ∽∾∿ ∽∾∿ ∽∾∿ ∽∾∿ ∽∾∿ ∽∾∿

Chapter 12 ~ Friends and enemies

Cain

DownTime Café and Bookstore
8:00, Friday night

Cain tried to quell his eager anticipation as he entered the bookstore. There was no fooling himself any longer that he'd try to stay away from Felicity. He was a vampire of self-control, and she was a vulnerable human. She needed his protection, although that felt almost like an excuse. After the time they'd spent together the other evening, he wanted her too badly to stay away.

He was annoyed that he'd had to deal with other vampires last night, and lost the chance to be with her. He had spent the wee hours of the morning thinking about her, and decided he would allow himself to spend time with her. When she seemed ready, he would lay all options out before her and see where she stood.

Terrible memories tugged at the back of his mind; this was a plan he had followed before. It had always either failed miserably and left him even more lonely, or had seemed to work and then spiraled out of control, leaving him devastated and heartbroken. Afterwards he would try to resign himself to being alone, but loneliness was a difficult burden to bear. He kept daring to hope that at some point he would find one person with whom it might actually work out, just once.

The young lady Ashley was at the register. She immediately sought to strike a more fetching pose as he approached. She smiled at him coyly. "Well hello again. Did you have fun the other night?"

"It was...an interesting evening," he answered.

"You disappeared awfully early. I thought we'd have a chance to get to know each other better, maybe I'd get a dance out of you," she pouted prettily.

"I had quite my fill of dancing actually."

"Well, maybe another time?" He just smiled noncommittally. He had enough to worry about. Leave Ashley to Ben if he'd like her. Keep him occupied and out of Cain's way for a while. "Can I get you a book?" she asked, trying to keep his attention as he sought to walk away.

"Not tonight, thanks." He moved on into the café, where Ben had been observing their exchange while waiting on a couple at a table. He took their dishes to the sink, as Cain moved to sit at the counter. Ben turned around and just stood there, staring at him haughtily.

"Coffee please," Cain said with a smile. Ben put a cup and saucer down in front of him, with a loud clink that could not have been good for the china. He went back for the coffee pot and stood glowering at Cain as he poured.

"You needn't glare at me Ben; I'm not your enemy." Ben didn't answer, but went to put back the pot. "I take it Felicity isn't working this evening," Cain asked, with a glance back at Ashley.

"No." Ben folded his arms and leaned against the counter behind him, studying Cain. "What do you want with her?"

Cain deliberated on his answer as he fixed his coffee; two packets of sugar, a little cup of creamer. What does any man want with a woman? Better to choose words that would defuse the situation. Ben was obviously not in an understanding mood. Cain looked up at him as he stirred. "Not to hurt her, if that's what you're thinking."

The people at the table got up and left. Cain sipped his coffee and tried to judge Ben's reaction. Ben seemed disgusted with him, even more than usual. "Yeah, well there are a lot of ways to hurt someone."

Cain sighed. "With that, unfortunately, I must agree, but I do need to speak with her. I'm afraid she may be in some danger."

Ben uncrossed his arms and pushed himself off the counter. "You're a little late. Maybe you should have been here last night," he spat out sarcastically.

Cain's coffee cup froze halfway to his lips. He was suddenly stricken with fear. "What happened? Did she walk home alone?"

"No, **I** drove her," Ben said as he crossed his arms again, "and Sindy met her at the dorms." Ben seemed to be enjoying Cain's distress.

At these words, Cain felt himself grow cold with terror. He absently put the cup back down in its saucer. Sindy must have let him assume she'd be occupied and then raced to the dorms to get there in time. What had she done?

Obviously Felicity had survived, or Ben wouldn't be so flip, but what if Sindy had marked her for herself? She wouldn't dare. Sindy must know, for that Cain *would* stake her. "Is she alright? Sindy didn't... Did she...?"

"She's fine." Ben began to realize that Cain was seriously distraught. He seemed puzzled by it. Did Ben think that he wouldn't care, that he was unfeeling? "Felicity seemed to think that Sindy was just trying to scare her, as some kind of message," he added, leaning forward on the counter. "You wouldn't know anything about that, would you?"

Sindy was pushing things too far, rebelling after their little talk. "Oh no," he said with a sudden realization. Cain had discovered and tangled with one of Sindy's new underlings last night. He hadn't killed it, but he'd tried. What would she do when she discovered his stake sticking out of her newest creation? She'd go straight for Felicity if she were angry. "I have to go to her," he said as he began to get up, thinking of protecting Felicity.

Ben grabbed his arm. "Sit down," he ordered mildly. It was the first time Cain could ever remember Ben touching him. He was usually very careful to keep his distance, as though Cain was contagious or something. Cain looked at his hand and then curiously up at Ben.

Ben let go. "She's in her room. Sindy can't come in unless invited right?" Cain acceded with a slight nod of his head. "So, Felicity's not stupid. She'll stay there. I told her I'd go check on her as soon as I'm finished here...and stay the night."

Cain raised an eyebrow. "Well, aren't you valiant?" he observed sarcastically.

"She doesn't need *your* protection," was Ben's disgusted reply.

Cain laughed. "If I don't protect her, who will? You? You were doing such a smashing job of it the last time I came upon you."

Ben shot him a dirty look. "I'm not the bad guy here. If you hadn't decided you wanted to make a new friend, Sindy wouldn't even care about Felicity, would she? Why don't you just leave her alone?"

Cain took a deep breath and let it out slowly. "I regret if I've put her in any danger. That was never my intent."

"Yeah, I'll bet a guy like you is just full of regrets," Ben said.

"You've grown an awfully bold tongue for someone who could still use my help," Cain observed.

"Well, why don't you teach me a lesson? Show her what kind of guy you really are." Cain simply stared at him coldly. Ben backed off a little. "I don't need your help."

Cain smiled. "You must have an awful lot of faith behind that big wooden cross of yours."

Ben lowered his eyes. "It keeps me alive, does the job."

"You could do better." Cain lifted his foot onto the seat next to him and drew a stake from his boot. He handed it to Ben, who stared at it for a moment and then took reluctantly. "Put this through their heart and you won't find yourself fighting the same vampire night after night."

Ben looked back up at him in skeptical disbelief. "You *want* me to kill vampires?"

"Well, I should hope you wouldn't try to use it on me," he said with a grin, "but I do believe that a man has a right to defend himself. Might as well do it effectively."

Cain fixed his pant leg and put his foot back down. Ben was turning the stake over in his hands, probably in his mind as well. He found Cain's assistance unexpected to be sure. Ben looked as if he'd like to argue some more, but was unsure how to proceed. Finally he said, "Why don't you go and tell Sindy that you got her message? And tell her to deliver it to you in person next time."

"I believe I will." Cain tried without full success to keep the amusement from his voice at Ben's sudden fondness for giving him orders. Ben was glaring at him while fingering the stake. "Ben, I've no wish to fight with you, but have care. Foolish heroics have been known to win fair ladies, but they are also a short road to an early death."

"Who says I'm trying to win the lady?"

"Aren't you?" Cain asked.

"No. Not really. Just trying to keep her away from you."

"I appreciate your candor," Cain told him with a chuckle, that quickly ended as his expression grew sternly serious, "but don't find yourself in my way too often." He threw some money on the counter, turned and headed for the door.

So, Ben wanted to stay the night with her? Let him. It wouldn't make much of a difference; Cain knew she would be his when he chose. At least she was safe. He had other things to attend to.

He left the store and turned towards 'Tommy's Place'. There was a vampire there for sure and he was fairly convinced that it was Sindy. That would certainly be convenient. Yes, it was definitely her. As he walked towards the bar he felt his anger build. How dare she try to scare Felicity just to jab at him! And now she'd gone and made some crazed vampire giant for him to contend with as well. His patience with her was growing more than thin.

As he came upon the lot, he realized that the vampire mark in his mind was not actually in the bar, but around back. He circled around quietly. He wasn't about to walk into a bad situation as he had last night. That had been so stupid of him. *I guess that's what you get for trying to be civilized,* he thought to himself. He wouldn't make that mistake tonight.

There was a couple making out up against the back wall of the building. It was Sindy alright, with some gullible human fool. He had no more stomach for her and her insatiable appetites. He simply marched up to them as they groped each other, grabbed her by the collar of her shirt and hauled her off of the man. "We need to talk."

"Hey!" Sindy yelled indignantly.

The man was a bit stunned. He looked to be a working class guy, probably in his early forties. He should be ashamed of himself to be back here with a girl who looked to be a teenager anyway. He tried to focus his eyes on Cain in the dim glow of the street lights from the parking lot, then the guy looked back at Sindy. "Is that your dad?"

Sindy seemed to find this hysterical and couldn't find her voice to answer, as she shook her head no. The man tried to see Cain more clearly through his haze. He turned back to Sindy, in puzzlement. "You didn't tell me you had a boyfriend."

She gave Cain a dazed smile. "I didn't think he cared."

Cain gave the man a threatening glance. "Bugger off."

The man looked from Sindy, back to him. "Hey pal, I don't know what your problem is, but I'm not leaving unless the little lady asks me to."

Sindy grinned. "Yeah," she added gleefully.

Cain narrowed his eyes at them. "I haven't got the patience for this rubbish." Cain let his rage fill him until he felt his face change. His vision blurred for a moment as his eyes lost their human colors and the man's form stood out in orange and yellow heated relief against his cold surroundings. Cain's jaw ached as his fangs extruded and became exposed. He practically growled at the man. "**Go!**" The guy looked like he'd pee his pants. He quickly turned and fled.

"Hey, where are you going?" Sindy called after him. "Way to defend me you wuss!" She turned back to Cain laughing, and then abruptly became sobered and admiring of his obvious vampiric state. "Ooh," she uttered with a sharp intake of breath. "I love it when you're like that!" She reached up a hand to try and caress his cheek.

He changed his face back to human form, chastised, as he slapped her hand away. He usually held himself above such blatant displays. His anger with her was causing him to put aside his common sense. He tried to calm his mind and return to the issue at hand. "I heard you paid Felicity a visit last night."

She backed herself up to a low covered dumpster and jumped up to sit on it. She looked at him with wide eyes and spoke with a scolding tone. "From what I gather, Marcus had a visitor too."

"That thing of yours has a name?"

She looked perplexed for a moment. "I think that's his name. That's what it said on the chart. Anyway, this *is* one of yours, isn't it?" She pulled his stake from the back pocket of her denim cutoff short-shorts. He reached for it but she pulled it back, out of his reach. "I think I'll hold on to it for now, if you don't mind."

He looked at her in disgust. "What did you do to that brute?"

She acted stricken. "Nothing! Apart from the obvious, I mean. He was like that when I found him." She kicked her feet back and forth like a child, giving him a playful little smile. Then she leaned forward with a conspiratorial whisper. "Psychiatric ward. He's totally insane! Isn't he cool?"

He stared at her in shock. "You are unbelievable."

She seemed pleased. "I know, but he likes me!" She played with the stake in her hand absently, twirling it between her fingers and occasionally putting the tip to her mouth the way a person plays with a pen. "You should see him when we are with Chris and Luke. Oh, it is too cute! He's like...King Kong defending Fay Wray! It is absolutely adorable!"

"I'm sure Chris and Luke don't find it as endearing."

"Like I care what they think," she said as she hopped back down from her perch. "I'm getting tired of playing with wimpy teenage boys," she added, eyeing him seductively. "It's about time I had a real man." She abruptly broke eye contact and walked away a pace. "Just because you didn't want the job, didn't mean I wasn't gonna fill the position."

"That thing isn't a real man; it's just a bigger toy."

"The bigger the better, right?" She put the tip of the stake to her lips in a suggestive manner that broke his patience.

He reached forward and ripped the stake from her grasp. He then pointed it at her for emphasis of his words. "Enough of this. Stay away from Felicity. If you touch her again, there will be no coming back from it."

"Ooh, scary." He advanced on her threateningly and she began backing away from him hastily. "I didn't actually touch her. I just...looked at her a little," she said with a laugh. "Now you wouldn't want to do anything rash, or you'll have one very angry Hulk and two pissed off little boys to deal with."

"Is that supposed to stop me?" He stopped about a foot from her and looked at her incredulously.

"It should. Marcus *really* doesn't like you."

Cain smiled, with a touch of delighted malice. "He's got the physique, I'll grant you that, but he's a bit lacking in the neurological department, wouldn't you say?"

"Translation?"

"He's not just insane, he's stupid. Just like all of your boys are stupid, because you don't know how to make them right."

She was offended. "Chris and Luke came out pretty good."

"They're better than the one that came before them, to be sure, but to their credit, I'd like to think they were a little brighter before you got a hold of them."

"So, show me how to do it right."

He laughed at her ridiculous request. "Marcus may be insane, but I'm not."

She eyed him with smoldering anger for a moment and then continued in her usual falsely carefree tone. "Speaking of Marcus, I really should go. He wakes up hungry and if I don't bring him someone to eat, he gets very violent."

He blocked her way before she could enter the back door to the bar. He wasn't finished with her yet. Did she really think she would just go seduce another victim while he stood by and watched?

Perhaps he should just get rid of her now and deal with her creations after. He was beginning to tire of these pointless sparring matches. She had no respect for life at all. Did he care for the lives of others enough to end hers? She tried to run by him but he grabbed her by the throat.

She clawed at his arms but he was far too strong for her. He began to lift her feet clear of the ground while his other hand lifted the stake, whether to use or just to threaten he hadn't decided yet. Her eyes widened as she realized he might actually be through playing with her.

Just then, two men came out the back door, engaged in conversation. They didn't see Cain yet, but as his attention was momentarily diverted, Sindy brought her knee up into his stomach and he involuntarily dropped her to the ground. Once there, she made a terrific show of gasping and crying.

Of course, the men rushed to her aid. They hadn't seen him choking her, but after witnessing her dramatics, they had hardly needed to. She did her best to look like a helpless little girl and stared accusingly at Cain. The men followed her gaze. "Is there a problem here?" one of them asked him.

He smiled innocently at the man as he slid the stake into his back pocket. "Not at all, I was just leaving." *I guess I am going to have to just stand by and watch after all,* he thought. *Either that or beat them both up to save them from her'.* He sighed as he calculated the odds. He could take them, but not without making a racket and drawing attention from the bar.

Most likely, she was only looking for a meal as she'd said. She wouldn't kill them, she knew better than that now. It was much easier to just take what you need and send them off into the night, than to have to deal with bodies.

Sindy took the larger man by the arm and cowered behind him. She really was rather artful at manipulating people. Cain turned and began to walk away. As he was leaving, he heard her speak to them. "I know I shouldn't have stayed out this late, my mom's gonna be pissed. Could you maybe drive me home?"

"I wouldn't do that if I were you," Cain called out over his shoulder as he left. *She loves this. She would never give this up,* he thought. He shook his head; he was fighting a losing battle.

Chapter 13 – Sleepover

Felicity

Wesley Hall Dorm
10:30, Friday night

Felicity sat in the living room with two other girls and Maggie, the R.A., watching television. They didn't seem to notice that Felicity kept straining to look through the arched doorway to the front parlor. She wanted to see headlights in the windows but so far there was nothing.

She looked back to the girls around her. It *was* Friday night, but weren't these people ever going to go to bed? Once Ben did get here, how was she going to do this? Sneaking him in had sounded easy enough, but now she didn't know how she'd pull it off.

Headlights. Should she meet him at the door and tell him to wait until they went to bed? He probably wouldn't be very happy at the prospect of sitting in his car for an hour. She was about to get up when she heard someone at the front door, but they didn't knock. Her heart skipped a beat. The door opened and a girl came through, Bridgette, from the room next to hers. Maggie stood and stretched. "Well, that's everyone in. I'm heading to bed. You girls coming?"

Bridgette turned to lock the door behind her and went upstairs. One of the other girls, Penny, got up off of the couch. "Yeah, I'm beat. Good night."

Maggie looked questioningly to Felicity and the other girl, Regina. "You girls going to stay up for a while longer?"

Regina was intent on the T.V. She barely glanced up. "Yeah."

"Me too. Good night," Felicity answered. Penny and Maggie left for their rooms down the hall. Three down - one to go. She looked over at Regina. She didn't look like she was going anywhere. Oh well, at least Maggie was gone.

"You like MTV2?" Regina asked.

"Yeah, whatever." Felicity got up and went through to the parlor and cautiously peeked out the window. She half expected to see Sindy, but no one was out there. She went back to sit on the couch.

"Waiting for someone?" Regina asked.

Felicity shrugged. "What time is it?"

Regina flipped the channel to check the time. "11:03."

Felicity looked into the parlor again and was rewarded with a flash of headlights across the walls. She stood, looking back at Regina. "Don't say anything okay?" Regina just went back to watching T.V.

Felicity jogged lightly over to the door and peeked out the window again. It was Ben's car. She slowly opened the door and looked around cautiously to be sure no one was on the porch…all clear.

She watched Ben get out of his car with a duffel bag. She looked behind her to be sure no one else was there and then waved him frantically inside. She watched the bushes nervously as he crossed the lawn. He came in and she quietly closed and locked the door behind him. "What took you so long?" she whispered fiercely.

"The car in front of me pulled in here, so I thought I should drive around the block to give them time to get in. You know, to make sure the coast was clear," he said quietly. Just as he finished speaking, he noticed Regina coming in from the other room. "Hi," he said with a sheepish smile.

Regina just smiled back and went upstairs. Felicity shook her head and started up behind her. "Come on."

They entered her room and shut the door. He looked at her bed, which held a few lacy heart shaped extra pillows. He then sat down on the unadorned bed further from the door, putting his bag on the floor. She had cleared everything off of the extra bed earlier and shoved the stuff in her closet.

"Aren't you worried about your reputation?" he asked, smiling.

She shook her head and went to shut her blinds. "My reputation could use a little excitement." She turned back to him and looked at the duffel bag. It looked kind of big and lumpy to contain only overnight clothes. "What's in the bag?"

"Excitement," he said with a little grin.

She looked at him questioningly and he gestured for her to open it. She went over to the bag, unzipped it and pulled out the board game Monopoly. She laughed. "I thought maybe you had brought some weapons or something." She put the game down on the floor next to the bag.

"They're in there too."

She fished around and pulled out a cross, which she laid on the bed. She looked into the bag to see some clothes for the morning, a six-pack of soda (still cold, and the condensation had made his clothes wet), a bag of chips, and at the bottom...she froze for a moment. She pulled out the stake; it was exactly like the one Cain had given her. "Where did you get this?"

"It doesn't matter. We won't need it in here anyway."

"You got this from Cain."

He looked at her like she was psychic. "How did you know?"

She straightened up and pulled her identical stake out from under her pillow, holding it up for him to see. "When did he give you this? Did you see him tonight?" She put her stake back under her pillow and tossed the other one back into the bag as she sat down cross-legged on her bed.

"Yeah, I saw him."

"Did you tell him what happened? What did he say? Where was he last night?"

"Take it easy. I told him. He seemed to agree that you were right. Sindy was just trying to scare you to get at him."

"And?"

"And...it was also said that he ought to stay away from you from now on, so he wouldn't put you in any more danger."

"He said that?" she asked in disappointment. Would it be that easy for him to just not see her anymore?

"No. Actually, that was me."

"*You* said that?" she asked, her voice rising in disbelief.

"Shouldn't I have?"

"Well…that really isn't your call to make! I can't believe you told him to stay away from me!"

"I thought the objective *was* to stay away from the vampires?"

"Yeah, but that doesn't apply to Cain!"

"It doesn't?" he asked with mocking astonishment.

"No!" She was furious with him for taking liberties with her social life, even if he probably was right.

"You know what, you're right. It's really none of my business," he said, standing up from the bed. "You don't really need me here, I'm just going to go."

"Ben," she began in annoyance as he headed for the door.

He turned back to her. "If I see Cain, I'll send him up."

She got up as he began to open the door. "Cut it out." As the door opened, they both heard another girl coming from the direction of the bathroom down the hall. "Close the door!" Felicity whispered harshly as she practically closed it on his hand. She turned to look at him; he seemed completely exasperated with her. "Don't go," she pleaded quietly.

"Why not?" He looked as if he already knew she didn't have an answer he'd want to hear but was too tired to continue arguing.

She looked at him thoughtfully; he was probably getting sick of her mixed signals. She felt her eyes begin to well up inexplicably. If he wasn't prepared to be her confidant in all of this, who else was she going to talk to? She couldn't just keep it all inside, she needed someone to understand. "Because, you're my friend and I need you to stay. Please?"

He searched her face for a moment and then gave a resigned sigh. "Fine, if you really want me to, I'll stay."

"Thank you," she said gratefully.

He sat down on the extra bed and ran a hand through his hair. "You know, if you just ignored him this would all go away. Cain would move on, Sindy would lose interest in harassing you, and that would be the end of it. You'd barely have to think about vampires anymore at all."

She still stood by the door behind her own bed, opposite him. She slumped her shoulders and looked at the floor. "I know. I probably should, but I *can't*." She looked up to see him roll his eyes and shake his head. "I know you don't like him, but Cain isn't this creepy evil guy that you think he is. He's just a guy…who's had some really weird, bad stuff happen to him. He's got no one else, I can't just ignore him."

"Why not? I haven't exactly lived a charmed life, and girls ignore me all the time!" he pointed out heatedly.

She let herself fall forward onto her stomach on the bed with a groan. She laid her head on her outstretched arms. "I know that you really don't want to hear this, but I can't help it!" She picked up her head to hide her face in her hands. "It's like when he comes into the room, everyone else just disappears. Like I can't see anyone but him, and I can't think about anything but him and…" She looked up to see him rubbing his temples as if she were giving him a migraine. "I know, I sound really stupid."

"You sound like you have a crush on a dead guy," he said with distaste.

"I know, but it's more than that. I know I shouldn't encourage him, but no one's ever made me feel like this before. He's like...hypnotizing." She suddenly looked up with frightened shock. "Oh my God! They can't do that can they?"

Ben laughed at her hollowly. "No, I don't think so. It's just you," he added bitterly.

"What is wrong with me?" She asked, burying her face back in her hands.

"You're a teenage girl," he said it as though pronouncing an ailment, although not unkindly. They sat in silence for a minute. Ben eyed the board game on the floor. "I guess we really *will* be playing Monopoly tonight, huh?"

She looked up at him with some surprise. "Was there ever any doubt?"

He smiled. "Not really. Just checking."

She eyed him appraisingly. "Well, just so you know, if I didn't have Cain all up in my head, I probably would've been all over you by now."

He let out a smug little laugh. "Don't worry, I'm not exactly lacking for attention."

She smiled. "I noticed. Think Ashley would totally freak if she found out you were here all night?"

"Yes. Make sure she finds out, okay?"

She laughed and got up off of the bed. "I'm going to go get changed." She went over to her dresser and rummaged through her nightclothes. She looked over at Ben and saw him pull the bag of chips and two soda cans from his duffel bag.

She noticed that he had already changed into sweat pants and a t-shirt at home. All of her nightgowns were just big t-shirts really, far too short. Then she found what she was looking for in the bottom of the drawer. Her sheep pajamas. They were light blue sleep pants with little sheep all over them and a matching light blue tank top with a little sheep jumping over a fence on the front. She gathered them in her arms along with her toiletry case and went to the door. "I'll be right back," she said, as Ben began setting up the board game on his bed.

Felicity changed and brushed her teeth. Then she brushed out her hair and used an elastic headband to keep it back from her face. She looked at herself in the mirror and decided not to take off what little make-up she had on. She wasn't trying to look good for him, but there's no reason to scare the guy, she thought with a mental chuckle.

As she re-entered the room, he looked up from counting out the play money. "Wow," he muttered.

She put her stuff down and looked at him in amusement. "What?"

"Sexy sheep," he said with a smile.

"No they are not! I purposely wore my un-sexy pajamas, thank you very much."

He went back to counting with a little smile. "Well, just so you know...they don't work."

She held up a pillow threateningly but didn't throw it. They'd be picking up game pieces all night if she did. He ignored her. "I thought we had agreed to play Monopoly," she said.

"We are, and I plan to kick your ass at it too. You want the dog, the shoe or the thimble? I'm always the car, and I kind of lost the rest."

"The dog," she said with a tight smile.

They played until almost 3:00 a.m., when Felicity could hardly keep her eyes open any longer. "Doesn't this game ever end?" she asked through a yawn.

Ben yawned as well. "Not really, that's why I brought it."

"Well," she said assessing her dwindling pile of money, "I've been hanging on by a thread for like an hour now. I think I'm going to have to graciously forfeit," she said, bowing her head to him.

"Told ya' I'd win," he said with another yawn. He got up and went to the door.

"Where are you going?" she said with sudden alarm.

"To the bathroom. Don't worry, I'll be quiet." He opened the door and poked his head out into the hall. The hall light was turned to its dimmest setting. All was quiet, so he slipped out.

Felicity watched him go down the hall, suddenly remembering why she had asked him to stay. The thought of Sindy, or any vampire, lurking in the hallway, waiting to attack her was enough to make her wish she'd gone home to her real bedroom to hide.

She stayed in the doorway to her room until Ben reached the bathroom and disappeared inside. She went back and sat on her bed. She got up a minute later and closed the door. She couldn't stand to sit there and look out into the dimly lit hallway. She listened for his return as she put away the board game. It seemed like an eternity until he finally came back, and closed the door behind him.

"Lock it," she whispered.

"She can't even come in the building, 'Liss," he reminded her, but he locked the door.

She turned on the reading lamp next to her bed, and Ben shut the light switch by the door. He then got into his bed and lay there propped up on his elbow, looking at her.

She shut the light and lay down. "Are you working tomorrow?"

"Yeah, 2 to 10. So are you, 12 to 6, right?"

"What, do you know everybody's schedule?" she asked.

"Pretty much," he answered after a slight pause.

She lay there looking at the ceiling. "When is Ashley working?"

He didn't answer. There was only the sound of covers rustling as he rolled over to face the wall. Finally, he said "Good night." She rolled over with a thoughtful smile and went to sleep.

An hour later, Felicity felt herself awaken. She lay in the dark wondering what had woken her up. There was only silence. She had to go to the bathroom. She mentally kicked herself. Why hadn't she gone right after Ben, so he could stand watch? Too late now, he was surely asleep. She could hear his steady breathing. At least he didn't snore.

She quietly got up and tip-toed over to the door. She listened for a moment but heard nothing in the hall. She couldn't wait long. She suffered horrible visions of Sindy standing there as she opened the door, but steeled herself to open it anyway.

The hallway was deserted. She glanced back at Ben, still asleep. She quietly closed the door behind her and darted down the hall to the bathroom. She'd never peed so quickly in her life. She flushed the toilet and went back out into the hall. Still quiet. She dashed back into to her room and closed the door.

Felicity lay back down in bed. She was just getting comfortable, when she heard the door creak. She nerved herself to look. No one was there, but the door was slightly ajar. Damn, she hadn't locked it. Hadn't she closed it all the way? She couldn't remember if it had clicked. She lay frozen staring at the slice of hallway visible through the crack. She kept imagining all kinds of horrible things lurking outside the door. This is stupid. Sindy can't even come in the building, she reminded herself.

Then she had images in her mind of Maggie answering the door while Sindy stood on the porch, looking young and scared. 'Can I come in and use your phone?' Who wouldn't let her in? Without all the make-up, she surely could look like an innocent young girl. Felicity was glad she hadn't thought of that before she went to the bathroom.

She silently sat up and grabbed the stake from under her pillow, without taking her eyes from the door. Still no one there. She glanced over at Ben's sleeping form on the other bed. "Ben?" she whispered hesitantly. He didn't seem to hear her. She wanted to wake him up, but for what? So he could watch her close the door? "Ben?" she whispered again half-heartedly. She sighed. "You're very comforting," she hissed at him, sarcastically.

Felicity slowly got up and went to the door. She reached out tentatively for the knob, like it was going to shock her. Once again she suffered visions of Sindy standing outside the door, waiting to grab her by the wrist as she reached for the doorknob. Finally she nerved herself forward, pushed the door closed and locked it. Ben stirred but didn't say anything. She hopped back into her bed and put the stake back under her pillow.

Just as she was calming her racing heart and trying to drift off to sleep, she could swear she heard something out in the hall. It was probably another girl going to the bathroom. Still, she felt like she couldn't breathe. She lay there frozen, waiting for a sound. She heard it again, a floorboard creaked.

She sat up in time to see a shadow slowly pass in front of the crack under her door…and then pause there. She silently sprang from the bed and went over to Ben's side. She couldn't see the bottom of the door well from where she was now, but heard another creak and then…nothing. The silence seemed to stretch on forever. It had just been another student, she hoped.

She looked at Ben's back; he was on his side, facing away from her. His broad shoulders made his form seem very large and safe compared to her empty bed near the door. She slowly lifted Ben's covers and got into the bed next to him. Just as she lay down, he looked up over his shoulder towards her. "What are you doing?" he asked sleepily.

She put one hand up on his shoulder to keep him from rolling over towards her and snuggled her face down into his back. "Shut up and go back to sleep."

~~~~~~~~~~~~~~~~~~~~~~~~~~~~~

Daylight. Felicity opened her eyes to find herself staring at Ben. He was still asleep. She was stiff and cramped in the same position she'd been in all night, afraid to move. More afraid of vampires or misleading Ben she couldn't say. He must have rolled over though; his arm was draped across her. She carefully slid out from under his arm and the covers onto the floor. She got up to look at the clock. 9:47 a.m. Ben's eyes remained closed. She should let him sleep late; she had about two hours before she'd have to leave for work.

She quietly picked out some clothes and went to take a shower, being careful to close the door behind her. Once in the bathroom, she stood in front of the mirror and looked at the offending sheep pajamas. They were cute, not sexy…weren't they? Maybe the top *was* a little snug.

Whatever. Surely, Cain had taken care of things with Sindy, and Ben would be sleeping in his own house tonight. Not that sleeping next to him hadn't been nice. She had never actually slept with someone before, not since she was a little kid anyway. It was nice to have someone big and warm to snuggle up to, even if she had been scared half to death.

She got into the shower. Her mind wandered to Cain again, as it did so often these days. What would it be like to sleep next to Cain? She thought of the strength she had felt in him when he had lifted her from the ground with such ease that first night. He had a nice, strong build but didn't look overly muscular. She had never liked guys who looked like 'The Hulk', anyway. He was big and robust certainly, but in an understated sort of way. She much preferred the quiet air of power and confidence that seemed to surround Cain, to a more blatant display.

His fairly large frame would certainly be comforting to snuggle up to. Would he be warm? He wasn't technically alive anymore, did that make him cold blooded? Not an appealing thought. Probably room temperature, she decided. She could live with that.

He had certainly felt warm enough when she'd kissed him, but that was probably just because she had generated enough heat for the both of them. That kiss had made her feel as though she had fire racing through her body! She knew she shouldn't even be thinking of him, but it was hard to stop when just the thought of him could send shivers through her.

What would it be like when she saw him again? He had turned her away, but he hadn't really wanted to, had he? He was only trying to do the right thing, to protect her. She would have to convince him that *he* was not the one she needed protection from. Would she see him tonight? He wouldn't stay away from her because Ben had told him to, would he?

She wished there was a way to talk to him before nightfall, but she couldn't bring herself to think that she'd go and disturb him before dark. She was afraid of what she'd find. It was comforting to know that he slept in a bed and not a coffin, but that didn't mean that he wasn't comatose until the sun went down...like a corpse. She pictured him lying there, still like death. That was creepy. She shivered again as she turned the water off, but this time, not in a good way.

She toweled off and then got dressed in the bathroom. She wondered if Ben was awake yet. Would he say anything about her getting into his bed? Would he even remember? He *had* been half-asleep. She hoped he wouldn't mention it; she didn't want to send mixed messages but she was very glad that he had been there. Once she was next to him, it had been much easier to fall asleep. He wasn't as infallible seeming as Cain always came across to her, but he was still a big, strong and protective guy; he made her feel safe.

Where Cain seemed made of the stuff of fantasies, Ben was real; sharing most of the same fears and feelings that she did about the vampires - other than Cain anyway. What was it that she found so appealing about Cain, she wondered? Of course, he was very attractive, but so were lots of guys...including Ben. Was it just that he was different, exciting, that he wasn't human? No, there was also a real connection there. She had felt it. He must feel it too, right?

She opened the door to her dorm room slowly. She stepped inside and closed it behind her. When she turned around, she was surprised to see Ben's bed was empty. Where was he? Just then, she noticed him in the corner, zipping up his jeans. She quickly turned away. He didn't have a shirt on, it was in his hand. "Don't you knock?" he asked. He sounded amused by her surprised reaction to seeing him.

"Sorry, I thought you were still asleep."

"S'okay." He smiled and put his shirt on as she turned back to face him. "I kind of woke up when you got out of bed, actually."

She looked away from him again, embarrassed. "Oh, sorry I woke you."

"No problem. It just wasn't as warm and cozy without you, so I had to get up."

Alright, he was obviously milking her embarrassment for all it was worth at this point. She met his eyes boldly. "Okay, I'll admit it. I freaked out, scared myself out of bed and had to run to you. Just like all those stupid horror movie girls that I hate."

He grinned. "Yeah, but they usually end up having sex and then getting killed. So, I guess we didn't do too bad."

She felt her cheeks heating as she turned away from him and went to brush out her wet hair in front of the mirror. Ben put on his socks and shoes. "Think it's safe for me to leave the room?" he asked.

"Yeah, you could be an early morning visitor by now."

"Right. Is every girl in this dorm as gullible as you? 'Cause that could be valuable information."

She smirked at him and began to dry her hair. He left for the bathroom and she decided to stop with her hair and put on a little make-up quick, while he was gone. She resumed with her hair and he came back just as she finished.

"So, what do you do for breakfast around here? Any coffee?"

"Well, there is a kitchen, but everybody has their own stuff and I haven't really bought much food. No coffee, sorry. They keep the cafeteria open though."

"Weekend school food? Sounds dangerous, but I'm game."

She smiled. "Let's go."

~~~~~~~~~~~~~~~~~~~~~~~~~~~~~

6:00 p.m., the end of her shift. Felicity made her way towards the employee lounge, behind the counter of the café.

After breakfast, she had left Ben to come to work. When he came in later, she hadn't really seen him at all. In a way she was glad, she felt kind of weird around him, self-conscious, but also like they were much closer somehow, although nothing had happened between them.

She was working with Ashley for most of the day. She had noticed Ben staring over at them intently at one point, while she and Ashley were talking by the registers. She knew he was wondering what they were talking about and whether anything was being said about him.

Of course, it was all small talk though. She knew Ben would like to use last night to make Ashley jealous but *she* wasn't about to say anything. She wouldn't lie, she had nothing to hide, but she certainly wasn't going to bring it up. As it was, Ashley had seemed a little off-put by her when she first came in. Probably because she had seen Felicity and Ben go for pizza last night.

Now the day was ending and she found herself in the same dilemma as yesterday. She wasn't about to invite Ben over again, no matter how comforting it might be. That just seemed to be pushing things too far, but she also didn't want to be alone. Should she go to Cain's?

The café was fairly busy. A lot of people liked to stop in on the weekend after dinner for coffee and dessert. Felicity had met the woman who was working the café with Ben, earlier today. Nadine was her name; she usually worked mornings during the week. She was an older woman, with a motherly attitude. She was waiting tables as Ben served people at the counter. Felicity gave Nadine a wave. Ben was busy and didn't seem to notice her as she went into the back for her stuff. She came back out and sat down at the counter. She noticed Ashley watching from the register across the store. *She must be wondering why I'm not leaving,* she thought. Well, let her wonder. Serves her right for stringing Ben along to begin with.

"Hey, want a cup of coffee?" Ben asked, as he made his way over to her.

"No thanks, I'll take one of those cookies though," she said, pointing to a plate on the counter.

Ben got her cookie with a napkin and leaned his elbows on the counter in front of her. "On the house," he said with a smile.

"Thanks," she said, taking a bite.

"So, what are you doing tonight?"

She gave a little shrug. "I don't know yet."

"In case you were wondering, my services are still available."

She laughed. "Thanks but I think I can manage."

"Are you sure? Nothing's changed you know."

"I thought you said that you told Cain about what happened with Sindy stalking and scaring me the other night?"

"I did. So what? You think he ran out and killed her for you?"

She sat playing with the cookie crumbs on her napkin. "I don't know. I hadn't really thought about the details. I just figured he'd...take care of it, somehow."

Ben shook his head. "If he were prepared to do anything drastic, he probably would have done it before now. Sindy's been a pain in the ass all summer. I'll bet he just went and yelled at her. So either she apologized, they've made up and become bosom buddies. Or they argued about it and now she's even more pissed off at you. No way to know which, at this point."

Felicity wore a troubled look on her face. "I don't even know which to hope for."

"Yeah well either way, I wouldn't be breathing a sigh of relief quite yet if I were you. You sure you don't want me to come over again? I have Parcheesi," he said half-jokingly.

"You're just hoping I'll jump into bed with you again," she answered accusingly.

Ben glanced over at Ashley, undisguisedly watching their every move from across the store. "Say that a little louder would you?" Felicity smacked his arm as he smirked at her. "You've got about a good hour of sunlight left. What are you doing, going back to the dorm?"

"I don't know yet." He looked disappointed in her, but she wasn't going to lie. She was still entertaining the notion of walking to Cain's. She had enough time to get there. What she would do once she was there she wasn't sure, but she still wanted to go. "Don't worry about me. I'll see you tomorrow," she said, as she popped the rest of her cookie into her mouth.

"Felicity, don't do anything stupid," he told her shaking his head. Someone down the counter was trying to get Ben's attention. As he went to attend his customers, she got up and left.

She went into the pizza place and picked up a meatball hero for dinner. She stood outside holding the bag for a long time, staring down the road. She had to squint into the setting sun. It wouldn't be all the way down for a while yet, but it was just the right angle to be in her eyes, so she could hardly see. She was trying to remember just how long a walk it was to Cain's. She remembered it was long, but not too bad. She'd have to pass the cemetery, at sunset. That'd be creepy but at least it wouldn't be dark yet. She couldn't even see the cemetery from here, though it hadn't seemed far. Then again, when walking there last time, Cain had taken up most of her attention, so she hadn't really noticed.

What was she thinking? His door will be locked anyway. What was she going to do when she got there, sit on the stoop until night fall? He was 'asleep' in the basement; he probably wouldn't even hear her if she knocked. She certainly wasn't going to break in. This is ridiculous, she decided. Time to go home.

She turned with a resigned sigh and started walking back to the dorms. As she walked by the café window, she wondered if Ben could see her from the counter. The sunlight reflecting off of the glass made it almost impossible for her to see inside. He was probably very happy that she was heading in the right direction.

She took her time, stopping to browse in the drug store. Anything to postpone her confinement. Not that she had anywhere to go anyway, but knowing that she couldn't go out felt so restrictive. The worst part, was that she wouldn't even know if it was necessary. What had happened last night? Had Cain gone to see Sindy? What were things like between them anyway? She wished she could talk to him. Ah, well. She was closing Monday night; maybe she would see Cain then, if not sooner. It would drive her crazy to have to wait, but she'd survive.

Chapter 14 ~ Field trip

Cain

Saturday night

Cain awoke shortly after sunset. His first thoughts were of Felicity, but that was par for the course these days. He showered and dressed. He would go to her, first thing. He could rationalize that she needed to know that Sindy was not planning on backing down as far as he could tell, but if he were to be honest with himself, he really just wanted to see her.

It had been so long since he'd entered into a true friendship with someone, had daily interaction with someone that knew his true nature. He'd only one true friend and that was another of his own kind that he hardly even saw anymore. He wanted to be with someone who could help him to forget his vampire nature for a while; someone with whom he could almost pretend to be human. He wanted to be with Felicity. He craved her attention.

Of course, it'd be fair to say that he'd had such a nightly camaraderie with Ben, but that was before Ben had learned his true identity. He hadn't been seeking a friendship but it was hard not to become friendly with someone you saw on such a regular basis.

He had seen Ashley regularly in the bookstore as well, but had been very strict to keep his distance from her. She was such a flirt for his attention, that he had instantly seen her as a dangerous temptation. His friendship with Benjamin however had caught him a bit off guard.

Not that he and Ben were ever close, but they did hit it off to a certain extent, making friendly small talk over the coffee counter each night...until Cain had sought to defend him one evening.

It was against Sindy's first 'child', Ernest. She hadn't made him very well. He was unflinchingly loyal, but terribly stupid and nasty too. He had attacked Ben in the parking lot of the café. Cain had come to his defense and Ernest had fought hard and dirty. Cain'd had no choice but to finish him off.

Ernest had given him quite the fight. Cain had been forced to go all out in killing him. In doing so, he had let himself change, and Ben saw it. After that, Ben tried to avoid him like the plague.

He supposed he could understand Ben's distress. To suddenly find that a friendly acquaintance was a vampire, had to be a bit upsetting, but it had been weeks now; many weeks of Cain's entering the café with a friendly greeting, being coldly served coffee and then ignored. He had always been there to protect Ben when needed but was never grudgingly accepted or even acknowledged. Ben simply would not associate with him any more than absolutely necessary.

Normally Cain wouldn't care. He usually didn't seek to associate with people much anyway, but this was such a small town, without many options as far as nightly activities. He enjoyed going to the DownTime and even though they had hardly spoken much, it had been nice to imagine Ben as a friend.

Cain was in 'the lonely cycle' again. That was how he thought of it anyway. His life was long and lonely. Sometimes he would go through periods when he enjoyed being alone. It was almost a relief to be an anonymous face in the crowd; to have no one to worry about, or to have to care for. To feel invisible was to feel free, but it never lasted.

After a while, he would begin to feel the pendulum swing the other way and the loneliness would weigh on him again. It started as a slight pull in what was left of his heart whenever he saw couples together, or a loving family. They gave him an ache inside that he couldn't seem to lose until finally it became unbearable. Then he would feel that he couldn't go on without seeking to abate the loneliness.

Interaction with his own kind was always brief and although sometimes rewarding, it just wasn't enough. They never stayed. He would begin to notice humans that he saw regularly, and imagine them as friends. Sometimes they didn't even notice him at all, but that didn't matter. He would watch them and feel that he knew them.

It would help a little, but it was lacking. He would begin to make small talk with people, in bars or at the market. Inevitably, he would enter into a friendship with someone, or perhaps an intimate relationship with a lovely girl such as Felicity. He would feel better for a while, as though they could give him the strength to endure this endless existence, but it always ended badly.

In the end, the relationship would warp and bend until it revolved around the blood. It always ended up being about the blood. How could it not? It was such a basic ingredient of who he was now, of this thing that he had become. It was almost impossible for him to differentiate; the longing for intimacy and the longing for blood were almost one and the same. They were so intricately threaded and woven together, that he could not separate them, no matter how he tried.

So now, once again, he had found someone he felt was worthy of his attention. Felicity was beautiful and lively; trusting and seemingly unafraid. He needed her. Why shouldn't he have her? Why should he continue to torture himself? Didn't he deserve some solace? If he didn't do something soon, he was going to lose her anyway.

To taint her himself would be difficult to live with, but to risk having her touched by another vampire was becoming absolutely unacceptable. He knew that part of it was his vampire instinct taking over, but it was too basic to ignore. He needed to do it, to mark her as his own, and he would have to do it soon.

As he approached the cemetery, he began to feel the familiar but unwelcome sensation of others. Vampires to be sure, but none that he knew. More new ones, at least three. Was Sindy planning to sire an army against him? Perhaps he *should* have killed her last night. Now she had taken the lives of three others instead. Yet another drop of uncertainty and guilt in the ocean of his transgressions.

The closest felt unsteady and slow, the others were just far enough away to make it difficult to tell. More zombies? Who had made them? Sindy usually did better. Perhaps it was Luke and Chris again? Their undead creations were horrible but at least they were easy to deal with. If Sindy had made more though... like Marcus, this could become a bigger problem.

He hoped it was Luke and Chris at work again. At first, he found it hard to believe that they would be brave enough to go against his direct orders again, but then he reminded himself that he was underestimating *her* power over them. They weren't independent or strong, which was probably why they hadn't turned against each other yet to vie for her attention. He actually found it amusing that Chris had been smart enough to try and get him to take Marcus out of the way for them.

Sindy surely made certain that they would be terrified of losing *her*. She had sired them, and the bond they shared was strong. They couldn't think well for themselves because she hadn't made them well enough, so they clung to her desperately. She had said that she wanted to learn how to make a proper consort, but he doubted she would be very happy if she ever actually got one. She wanted someone she could control; to get that you had to accept certain faults, such as a lack of independent thinking and intelligence.

Should he stay and take care of this now? He could try and dispatch them quickly and then go on to Felicity, but look at the unexpected turn things had taken the other night when he'd gone to investigate Marcus. If it took longer than anticipated, he might lose his chance to see her.

If she were working, the DownTime would be closing soon and if she wasn't, surely the dorm did not accept visitors at all hours of the night. Of course, he could easily gain entrance to the building if he chose; she had invited him a few nights after they had first met, but he didn't want to do anything against the rules, and risk making things uncomfortable there for her. He needed to see her now, he had waited long enough. He wouldn't stay, but only check on her and then return to take care of this. Who knows, maybe she would even like to help him.

As he reached the bookstore and started up the walkway to the door, he could see Ashley through the window at the front register. If Ashley was here, then Felicity wouldn't be. It was almost time to close and he knew the store's routine well enough by now to know that there were never more than two people used to close the store. He had already noted that Ben's yellow car was in the parking lot. Good, he would have Felicity all to himself. He turned and kept walking towards the dorms. He hoped she would be there. Of course she would be, she wasn't foolish enough to go out anywhere at night after Sindy's recent antics, he hoped.

It was about 9:45 on a Saturday night, and there were still people coming and going from the building. Everyone must have full evenings planned, he thought. He wished he didn't. He would be perfectly happy to spend the night in her room, as Ben had.

Had Ben really spent the night with her? That was what he'd said he had planned. He didn't know Ben to lie, and believed that if Ben said he would spend the night, then Felicity must have asked him to, but he also felt that he knew her well enough not to think overly much of it. She was outgoing in some ways, but when it came to intimacy with a man, she seemed pretty timid. The kiss she had given him, had come across almost like a bold rebellion; a conscious act of courage against her true nature. Cain was fairly sure that he had stirred something deep within her that other men had not yet seen. She just was not the type to throw her affections around haphazardly.

Of course, strange things had been known to have happened when two people were thrown together in fear or some unpredictable situation. Originally, Cain had dismissed the notion that Ben could ever truly draw her attentions from him, but now he wondered if that was foolish pride.

He knew she liked and trusted Ben. Although Benjamin was still young, and a bit brash, even Cain had to admit that he was a good and trustworthy man. If Felicity chose to give Ben her affections, Cain would have to honor that. If that were the case, he prayed that the beast inside of him could be kept in check and made to understand. He hoped nothing had happened…for Ben's sake.

Vampires were very territorial and possessive when it came to favored victims. The instincts inside of him were so strong, that sometimes he felt as if there were two entirely different beings living within his body. One was the rational, even-tempered and steady man he had always known as himself, but the other was purely an animal, a beast; the vampire creature that lived by instinct and thirsted for blood.

The living corpses he had often seen and killed held only the beast, he was sure. It was all too rare to come across a vampire that had been made well enough to still contain the true person they had been in life. This was why he had such a hard time disposing of Sindy; she was still a real person. She had personality, ingenuity and emotion.

Of course her emotions ran a little too high towards cruelty and lust, but he had seen the real girl inside; in the beginning, before she'd tried so hard to hide it from him. He knew she was really just a frightened young woman, desperate for attention; trying to surround herself with pretend lovers so that she wouldn't feel so alone. Was she really all that different from him? Maybe he was simply better at it; better at fooling himself that he *was* different.

He entered the dorm building without a problem. Felicity had already invited him into it in the past, and the others who lived there were busy with their own affairs. He found her room at the top of the stairs and knocked. He heard her moving within. Felicity began to speak before she had even fully opened the door.

"Ben, I told you not to…" She looked up at him and lost the rest of her sentence. She was staring at him in complete bewilderment. It obviously hadn't occurred to her that *he* might come.

"Hi," he ventured, with a small smile.

"Hi." She still stared at him, dazed.

After a moment of silence under her gaze he asked, "Can I come in?"

"Oh, sorry!" she said, backing away from the door to admit him.

Still he stayed just outside the doorway. He could feel the invisible barrier that blocked him as surely as any door. It was an intangible but flawless force that withheld him from the room; like trying to push against an opposite magnetic field that was seeking to repel him. "You have to actually say it," he reminded her gently.

"Oh! Really?" She looked at him curiously, as though she might be able to see something holding him back.

"Yes," he said quietly.

"Sorry. Come in. Please, come in."

The guise was invisibly lifted. He felt as though the air had thinned and he could move forward once again. "Thank you," he said as he entered the room.

She was still looking at him curiously. "Didn't I already invite you in? I mean, that was before I *knew,* but doesn't it still count?"

He smiled as she settled herself onto her bed and gestured for him to do the same. He remained standing for now, taking in his surroundings as he spoke. "Everything counts, but no, you didn't actually. You said that you were in room 217 at the top of the stairs, and that I should come on *up*, not *in*."

"Oh. Wow, stuff like that must drive you crazy."

"I suppose it could be a nuisance, but I don't usually seek to enter into a place where I'm not welcome."

She seemed to be turning something over in her mind. Finally, she summoned the courage to ask him. "Does it last forever, an invitation?" Before he had a chance to answer, she seemed to think that she shouldn't have asked, and quickly tried to backpedal verbally. "Not that I wouldn't want it to. I mean, of course *you're* still invited. I was thinking of Sindy, really. Like, if she got someone else to invite her into the building."

He smiled. "It's okay; you've a right to know. An invitation lasts for as long as the person who gave it still lives here. Or until they might decide to revoke it."

"I can do that, just...take it back?"

"If you so choose. Although if we're speaking of Sindy, only the person who gave the invitation can revoke it. That might be difficult to accomplish without explanations you may not be prepared to give."

"But what would happen if I *did* change my mind? I mean, would you go flying from the room?"

He laughed. "It's not quite as simple as that, but I'm not really in the mood to experiment, if you don't mind." He sat down on the bed, resting his hand lightly on her leg as he spoke. He felt her tense beneath his fingers, and he withdrew them.

"Oh, no. I was just curious," she said, with a nervous chuckle.

He leaned forward and caught her gaze with his own. "I'm sorry if Sindy frightened you," he said quietly.

She seemed self-conscious to be so close to him. She shook her head a little. "Oh, I'm not scared of her," she said with false bravado. He looked at her questioningly. She smiled. "Okay, that's a really big lie," she said with a laugh, "but I managed to make it through the night."

"With some help, I heard."

She looked slightly alarmed, that he knew. "Ben told you about that, did he?"

"Rather gleefully, I might add." Had something occurred between them?

She looked at him earnestly. "I'm glad you didn't listen to everything that Ben told you."

No, they hadn't been intimate, he was pretty sure. She was just worried it would be misconstrued. She must know Ben was trying to keep him away. He felt a bit guilty, for Ben was probably doing the right thing in that.

He forced himself to say as much. "He's probably right you know, about my hurting you eventually." He looked up, hoping he hadn't frightened her. "Not that I ever *would*, on purpose mind you; but you should know...I don't exactly have a sparkling record." He wanted to be with her so badly and yet part of him felt that he should be urging her to turn him away; to make him leave, before it went too far.

She made an obvious effort to calm her nerves. She let her feet swing back and forth over the edge of the bed a few times and then met his gaze with her own. "That's okay, I'm not scared of you either."

He eyed her appraisingly. "And is *that* entirely true?" *You should be,* he added mentally.

"That's my story and I'm sticking with it."

"Alright then. Perhaps you won't be afraid to go for a little walk."

"Where are we going?" she asked.

"The cemetery," Cain answered.

"Gee, you really know how to treat a lady," she teased.

"Sorry, but I have to check in there. There are some more...things there that need to be taken care of. I thought maybe I should have you come along and make sure that you can actually use that stake that I gave you."

"Those are my choices? Solitary confinement or target practice in the cemetery?"

He chuckled, "It's not exactly my idea of an enchanted evening either but somebody's got to do it. I am sorry about the 'confinement' thing, but it probably is your best course of action right now...unless you're with me of course."

"Of course," she echoed dryly, flashing him an amused smile.

"I did see Sindy last night..." Cain began.

"Oh?" she asked timidly, dropping her smile. She had an odd expectant tone in her voice. Was she actually jealous?

"It didn't exactly go as planned."

"I see." Obviously she didn't, and was wondering just what he might mean by that.

"Don't worry, I'm working on it. In the meantime, I'll understand if you'd rather stay here than come. I'd rather stay here myself." He eyed her meaningfully as his last statement hung in the air. She stared into his eyes and he thought she might try to kiss him again. He pondered how terribly irresponsible it would be, if he were to let her; to simply take her into his arms and kiss her passionately, as he *so* wanted to.

There was a knock at the door that although not loud, shook them both from their thoughts. "Expecting someone?" he asked.

She looked less than pleased. "I wasn't supposed to be." He stood up from the bed as she got up to answer the door. Of course, it was Ben. He didn't see Cain right away. Felicity spoke first. "Hi. Are they just letting in anyone down there?" she asked.

"It's Saturday night, and it's not that late. They don't care if I come visit." He noted her expression; she did not look thrilled to see him. "I know you told me not to come, and I'm not staying. I was just on my way home and I thought I'd..." Now his eyes found Cain in the room, "...check in." He looked back down to Felicity. "Funny, I was under the impression that this room was invitation only."

"It is, he's invited."

"So I see," Ben replied. "Having another sleepover?"

Felicity glared at him dangerously, but it was Cain who answered. "I was just leaving actually. I have some things to attend to," he said, as he moved to meet them at the door. He assessed Ben thoughtfully for a moment. "Perhaps you'd like to come."

"What?" Felicity asked with mild alarm. Both men ignored her.

"Where are we going?" Ben asked warily.

"The cemetery. Give you a chance to use that new stake of yours."

Ben thought about that, as Felicity pleaded with Cain. "This is a really bad idea."

Ben reached a decision. "I'm in."

Felicity returned to sit on the bed. The guys observed her as she reached under her pillow and pulled out her cross from Ben and her stake from Cain. She put one in each back pocket of her jeans. Then she reached down to the floor and began to put on her sneakers. Cain watched her with a smile. "Are you coming then?"

"I think I should, just to make sure the stake ends up in the right vampire."

Cain smiled at Ben. "You needn't worry about that, I can assure you." Ben just squinted his eyes a bit. He still couldn't decide what to make of Cain at this point. He was probably also wondering if he could take him. He couldn't, of that Cain was certain. Not that Ben wasn't capable; Cain had seen him hold his own in fights before. He was also slightly taller than Cain and in strength they were probably almost evenly matched, but there was just no substitute for three and a half centuries of experience.

As they exited the building, Felicity maneuvered herself to walk between them. What did she think they would do, attack each other? Obviously Ben felt threatened by him and he'd wager that Ben had never spoken to Felicity of their slight friendship before his enlightenment.

She probably didn't realize just how well Cain really knew Ben. Cain had been observing him almost nightly for about three months now. He felt he knew Ben rather well and could judge any reaction Ben might have to something, almost before Ben himself knew what he might do. No, he had no fear of Ben. In fact, he hoped to make Ben a valuable ally in all of this, since he had been drawn into it anyway. He was counting on it.

They reached the corner and began to pass Tommy's; there was quite a crowd outside. Felicity eyed the place nervously. "Any *special* partygoers tonight?" she asked Cain.

Ben spoke up. "I didn't see any vamps outside when I passed."

"Cain can feel them," Felicity informed him.

Ben shot her a look of disgust. "Well isn't that special."

"No, only humans," Cain said, answering the question. "If I know Sindy and her lot, they're probably over at Venus. They have better music; she likes to dance."

"Know her well do you?" asked Ben with a smirk.

"What's 'Venus'?" Felicity chimed in.

"It's a club, next town over," Ben looked to her and answered. "It's actually pretty cool. We should go sometime." Both Felicity and Cain turned to look at him strangely, but he had already turned back to look over at Tommy's. "Too bad Alyson's working. She'd love to be in on this."

"In case you hadn't realized, I'm trying to keep this *out* of the public awareness," Cain told him.

"Allie knows more about vampires than anyone else I know." That drew some raised eyebrows. "Present company excluded, of course."

"Maybe she can come on the next field trip," Felicity offered with a smile.

They continued down the road, past the last of the businesses to where the road cut through open fields. No deer out tonight. The moon was at its fullest and Cain was sure his companions could see quite clearly. Good, at least they wouldn't be at much of a disadvantage. As they neared the wood line this side of the cemetery, he began to feel one of their quarry. He paused and then ventured off the road and up the embankment into the trees.

"I thought you said they were in the cemetery?" Felicity hissed after him.

He looked back at her, in amusement. "I guess they decided not to wait."

Ben and Felicity followed quietly until they were well within the woods. He stopped. They could hear it clearly now, as it stomped through the brush.

"Not exactly *stealthy* are they?" Ben asked quietly.

"It's only one," Cain answered.

"That racket is just one guy?" Ben asked incredulously.

It came crashing through the bushes about thirty feet away. It stopped in a patch of moonlight, although it still seemed unaware of them. It was a decaying mess. Disgustingly rotted and filthy, Cain could even see flashes of white bone showing through its left cheek.

"What the hell is that?" Ben asked.

Felicity turned to him. "It's a vampire."

He looked at her in amazement. "You still don't know the difference between zombies and vampires do you?"

Cain turned back to hush them like school children. "Why don't you speak a little louder, I'm not sure he knows we're here."

The creature began to move again, but promptly tripped over a tangled root on the ground and fell forward onto its face with a crash. Ben stifled a laugh. "Oh, that is just sad! I mean, it's nauseating and gross, but on the scare-o-meter, it's really pretty pathetic."

Cain gave him a disapproving look. "Sorry to disappoint you."

"Well, look at it!" he demanded as the thing struggled to right itself. "What *is* that?"

"*That* is the product of poor breeding," Cain replied with a hint of a smile.

"Oh, and what are you, a pedigree?" Ben returned snidely.

"Guys," Felicity cut in, "I think it sees us. Shouldn't we do something?"

The thing had indeed regained its feet and begun lumbering their way. Cain turned to Felicity. "Right, why don't you take care of it then?"

She looked at him as though he had told her to fly away. "I'm not touching that thing!"

Cain smiled, although she probably couldn't see him well in the dark of the trees. "I thought you were coming for some practice?"

"I'll take notes," she replied drolly.

Ben stepped forward, removing his stake from his back pocket as the thing closed on them. "I'll do it."

They backed away as it came closer. Ben seemed to take forever studying its chest for placement of his stake. At first the creature paused in front of him, as if unsure what to do, then its face distorted and tried to change. It was gut wrenching to watch. There wasn't enough proper skin left to stretch around its jaw and the change was accompanied by a sickening ripping sound. Finally, Ben thrust the stake into its chest as it bared its new fangs at him with a hiss. Ben's wrist sunk in with the stake as the soft rotten flesh gave way, before it turned to solidified ash and burst into a cloud of dust in the air.

Ben jerked back his wrist and turned away. He looked as if he were trying to hold down the contents of his stomach. He succeeded, but Felicity didn't quite. She turned away to gag and dry heave over the bushes. She rejoined them, after regaining her composure. "Okay, I think I should have stayed in my room."

Ben was busy trying to wipe his forearm off on a bush. "Ugh! I think I'll have to shower in bleach to get this stench off my arm."

"Lemon juice'll do the job," Cain offered with a smirk.

"Gee, thanks. The dust explosion was pretty cool, but I could have done without the gore. At least I hit the heart the first time, 'cause I wasn't going in again. I think I'd like less gross and more scary."

Felicity paled. "That's okay, let's stick with gross."

Cain shook his head. "You may get more of both. You just have to disconnect yourselves from it and do what has to be done. The others must still be in the cemetery. I can just feel them, and I don't believe they're as far gone as this one was. Be wary."

"Who made these things?" Ben asked. "Sindy and those other guys she hangs with?"

"Luke and Chris are their names. I can't tell. I'd thought they were done, but I hope I was wrong. Otherwise, there's someone else in this equation that I haven't met yet. Better a known threat than an unknown element," Cain replied thoughtfully.

"Whoever made them, we're going to kill 'em right? So let's go!" Ben stuck his stake into his back pocket and rubbed his hands together in anticipation.

Felicity winced and turned to Cain. "I think you've created a monster." Felicity moved to follow Ben, who had started off in the direction the thing had come from, towards the cemetery. Cain had almost smiled at her comment, until it reminded him of past creations he really had made. Of course, he had managed to avoid ever siring a creature like the one they had just destroyed, but suddenly it didn't seem all that funny anymore.

Chapter 15 – The lesson

Felicity

The woods bordering the cemetery
11:30, Saturday night

Felicity followed Ben through the woods towards the cemetery, with Cain coming up behind her. They reached a clearing and Ben turned to Cain. "So, you're the man with the map. Where are we going?" Cain nodded in the direction of the cemetery. "Let's go," Ben said as he started off again.

Felicity gave Ben an odd look. "You're suddenly very enthusiastic. I've gotta tell 'ya, it's kind of creepin' me out a little."

"Would you rather leave those things walking around out here?"

"Well of course not, but you don't have to be so...anxious," she answered.

Cain turned to Felicity, "Don't be too hard on him, Ben's waited a long time for these scales to shift, haven't you Ben?" Ben just gave a little shrug and looked away.

Felicity didn't get his meaning. "What?"

Cain looked at Ben, who wouldn't return his gaze. "Until now the name of the game has been avoidance. It must feel good to finally trade in that cross for a stake. I just can't imagine why it's taken you this long."

Ben turned and stalked over to Cain. "I've lived here my whole life and there have always been vampires in this town. Not usually as many as there are now, but they were around on and off, if you knew how to recognize them. I've had friends that tried to play 'vampire hunter' before. Hell, I was one of them. Some of those friends aren't alive anymore."

Cain looked a little taken aback by Ben's admission. "I'm sorry for your loss."

Ben gave a mirthless laugh. "Loss, that's an interesting choice of words. Yeah, they're lost alright. Well, David they did kill straight off, but Mattie, he's a little *beyond* dead if you know what I mean."

Cain looked stricken. "Mattie, did you say his name was?"

Ben gave him a long hard stare, warning him not to elaborate. "I don't want to know," he said with icy cold intensity. He turned and stomped off through the brush.

Felicity looked askance at Cain who closed his eyes and shook his head. "Now I know why Ben hates me so much," he said quietly.

"Ben doesn't hate you," she assured him.

"It's a difficult thing to find that someone you thought of as a friend, is actually a vampire."

"Gee, I wouldn't know," she answered sarcastically. He realized her point of reference and gave a sad little smile.

She jogged off in the direction Ben had gone. She could barely see his receding back through the trees. "Ben." He kept walking; she could hear him up ahead. "Ben!" She was catching up, but he still wasn't waiting.

"Ben, would you slow down? You can barely see where you're going. You're going to trip and break your neck, and boy would that be a stupid way to die!" He finally stopped and turned to face her. His cheeks were flushed and he looked as if he were trying to control his face to be a neutral mask.

Now that she had caught up to him, she hardly knew what to say. She had felt that he needed a friend; that she should try to understand and make him feel like he had someone he could confide in, but she had no idea how she could make him feel any better. His friends had been killed by vampires. What could she possibly say?

"I'm sorry about your friends," she offered quietly. "It must be awful to lose people you care about like that." Suddenly a horrible thought struck her. "Oh my God, your mom?"

Ben eyes turned small and hard. "Cancer."

"Oh."

"Look, it doesn't matter. Nothing I do *now* matters. I should've done something then," he insisted.

"How long ago was it?" she asked.

"High school," he said.

"Ben, you were kids!" she exclaimed.

"No, we weren't," he muttered in response.

"You were younger than me! Unless you got left back a whole lot of times, and you don't strike me as that stupid," she said.

"Thanks," he replied sarcastically.

"I'm sure you did all you could. I think it was smart that you didn't manage to get yourself killed," Felicity assured him.

"I should have been. You don't know the whole story."

He looked as if he'd like to walk away. She noticed Cain had caught up to them, but was respectfully keeping his distance. "Wanna tell me?" she asked.

He glanced over to where Cain could just be seen among the trees, then back to Felicity. "How about just the 'cliff notes'?" He crossed his arms and leaned his back against a tree. "They got Mattie first actually. He was my best friend, and they changed him."

He saw Felicity's eyes widen a bit. "Not like those *things*," he said, nodding back vaguely towards the direction of the vampiric zombie he'd just killed. "More like...Cain," he said grudgingly. "Anyway, we were out looking for him. I found him about a week or so later, and I'm pretty sure it was him that killed David."

"Your other friend," she clarified.

"Yeah, but it should have been me," Ben muttered.

"Why?" she asked.

Ben faltered for a moment, and then answered, exasperated. "Because, I saw him first. I saw him changed, he spoke to me."

"What did he say?" she asked.

His voice was full of contempt. "That he was still my friend and it wasn't like real death. That he understood things now and it was better than 'human life'. Lies. I had my chance. I should have killed him then."

"He was your friend," she said with sympathy.

"So was David," Ben replied dejectedly.

"What happened?" she asked.

"What do you mean 'what happened'? I took off, and he let me. I should have looked for David, but we'd gotten separated. I didn't know where he went and I was…"

"Afraid?" she asked.

"That Mattie wanted to change me, to be like him."

Felicity fidgeted in the silence. Finally she asked, "Did you ever…think about it?"

"What?" Ben asked.

"About what it would be like. Were you tempted?" she nudged him.

"**No**. I never entertained the idea that becoming a blood-sucking corpse might be fun, but thanks for asking," Ben replied forcefully.

"I just meant that you shouldn't feel bad. That it's okay, if you did. I mean, it's only natural to wonder, right? That…that you shouldn't feel guilty," Felicity answered defensively.

Ben looked ill. "I don't think so. Sort of makes me worry about *you* though," he said, with a pointed look back at Cain.

She ignored it. "Did you ever see Mattie again?"

"No, but that's very probably because I didn't go outside at night again for about two years after that."

"Ben, I hope you don't think anyone would have expected you to kill your best friend. No one ever could have expected that of you."

"Well, maybe when we get to the cemetery, you could go and explain that to David's tombstone for me. You know what? I think I've shared enough for one evening. Let's just go kill these things okay? Better late than never I guess."

He gave an angry glance towards Cain in the distance, and then made his way out through the last of the brush and over to the cemetery fence, which he began to follow around to the road.

Felicity watched him go, then suddenly felt a hand on her shoulder and jumped. Of course it was only Cain, but still her heart was in her throat. She'd still thought him further back; she hadn't even heard him move. "Don't do that!"

Cain looked almost hurt as he took his hand away. "Touch you?" he asked quietly.

She looked at him as if he should know better than to ask that. "No. You can touch me…a little. Just don't sneak up on me like that." She turned to make out Ben along the fence, just stepping out onto the road. "Want me to fill you in?" she asked Cain.

"No need. I seem to remember someone saying that vampires have excellent hearing." He looked at her with a grin. "You were right."

She looked at him with wonder. "You actually *did* hear that conversation?"

He just smiled. "Let's go finish this already, shall we?" He started off after Ben.

She stood there for a moment trying to remember what she had said to Ben about Cain back on that occasion. She hadn't really thought that Cain could hear them. She hoped she hadn't said anything she wouldn't have wanted him to hear. Oh well, too late to worry about it now. She hurried off after Cain.

They followed the fence to the cemetery gate. Ben was just inside, sitting atop a stone memorial. "So counselors, are you finished discussing my case? I think you should recommend immediate therapy. Like working out my aggressions on some hell bound corpses, maybe?"

Felicity went to stand in front of him and put her hand on his knee. "You can kill them all. I didn't really want the practice anyway." She coaxed a smile from him and then turned to Cain. His expression made her drop the smile from her face. She took back her hand, taking an almost involuntary step back from Ben. "What's wrong?"

His eyes were unfocused and she realized that he wasn't even looking at her and Ben, but seeing something within himself. "They're coming. It seems they've picked up a few friends. There are four now."

Ben jumped down and pulled the stake from his pocket. He was looking around warily but Cain just stared off into the distance. Cain then glanced at each of them in turn. "Come on."

They followed him deeper into the cemetery. After a bit, he left the path and went out among the gravestones. He stopped and looked to his companions. "They've split up. They're circling around. They know we're here, I believe."

Felicity turned as though she expected them to be right behind her, but there was no one else in sight. "I thought they didn't really 'know' anything. Aren't they just running on instinct?"

He closed his eyes for a moment, tracking them. "No. These are more like...*real* vampires." He looked to see the effect of his statement. Felicity was suitably wary; to Ben it didn't seem to make any difference. "They'll think I'm human at first. Perhaps I should draw their attack."

Ben looked insulted. "I can handle myself."

"If it comes to a fight, you can have your share, just be careful." He turned his gaze to Felicity. "You'd better mind yourself though. Stay close to us, but not too close. And if you need to..." He put his hand to his throat, to remind her of the blood vial necklace he'd given her as protection. She got his meaning but she hadn't time to say so, before he spoke again. "Here they come." He nodded towards a large stone mausoleum, just behind where Cain and Ben stood.

Felicity looked, but still saw nothing. Then, just as she was about to question Cain, two guys who looked more like linebackers than vampires came running out from behind opposite sides of the structure to circle and attack them from both sides.

By what seemed some unspoken agreement, Ben and Cain moved back to back, as the attackers reached them. Felicity backed away a step and saw the two strangers shift to their vampire states almost simultaneously as they bore down on her friends. Ben's foe simply charged as if to tackle them, and received a strong kick, which sent him stumbling backwards, while Cain's attacker had to arch his back and quickly change his approach to avoid being stabbed with the stake that had seemingly materialized in Cain's hand.

Cain turned to her in his instant's reprieve. "Felicity, behind you!" She was shaken from her trance just as she felt someone's arm come over her shoulder from behind. She was at once alarmed and then heartened as she realized that this was a scenario in which Cain had shown her what to do.

She was aware that her feet were wrong and quickly arranged them properly as she grabbed the arm at her throat. She felt her attacker's expectant hiss of breath on her neck as she momentarily leaned back into him and imagined sharpened fangs about to graze her skin, but she silenced her urge to scream and shrink away. She leaned back and then lunged forward, and actually threw him over her shoulder as she flexed her knee and managed to keep her own feet steady. When she let go and saw the size of the vampire on the ground, she jumped back in surprise. Had she actually thrown him?

He was a large, handsome guy, who looked to be about Ben's age, and she felt a pang of regret as she pulled out her stake and considered trying to use it. As he opened his eyes, his face twisted into a grimace of hate and all regrets she might have had instantly fled. As he sought to regain his feet, Felicity looked down at her pitifully small seeming stake and she thought better of trying to use it.

As she turned to flee, she saw another vampire was running to join the one she had just felled. If these vampires were of Sindy's making, she must have paid a visit to the football team. They were far more than a match for Felicity and although that wasn't saying much, she began to worry for Ben and Cain as well.

She took the cross out with her other hand and circled widely around the ongoing fights to try and put Cain and Ben between herself and the new arrivals.

Felicity backed up against the front of the mausoleum as Cain's first opponent turned to dust, and the guy she had thrown was blocked in chasing her by Cain. She saw Cain and Ben move apart, intent on their own private battles. Ben wrestled with his vampire foe, who kept avoiding Ben's jabs with the stake but she noticed that the vampire's right arm hung limply at his side as though broken, while Ben thankfully seemed unharmed.

Cain engaged his new foe, but of what happened next, Felicity missed almost all. She had been about to try to open the vial of blood that she wore, when she stumbled and fell backwards. Her weight had caused the mausoleum door she had unwittingly leaned against to swing open inward. She fell into the darkness, landing flat on her back on the hard cement floor. She craned her neck up just in time to avoid cracking her skull against the concrete.

She sat up and took a moment to uncork the vial, putting the stopper into her pocket. She then groped in the darkness to find her cross and stake that she had dropped when she fell. As she struggled to rise with full hands, afraid to drop them again in the dark, she looked up to see a figure silhouetted in the doorway before her. Felicity scrambled backwards as she rose, realizing that the outline she saw was not a familiar one.

The man strode towards her as if he could see her perfectly well through the darkness. He seemed to feel that there was no question she would be totally helpless before him. As he came upon her, she lifted her arm to try and stab him but he batted it away with his own hand.

Felicity was almost as surprised as he was, when she realized that the hand she held before him bore the cross and not the stake. As he pushed it away and it connected with his hand, he yelled in surprise and jumped back as though burned. Encouraged by his response, she strode forward with the cross, driving him before her. He seemed confused. She wondered if she smelled Cain's blood from within her vial.

He stumbled backwards to avoid being touched by the cross again, and came up against the doorframe. He paused momentarily and looked to the side to see that in walking backwards and watching Felicity, he had misjudged the door. In his moment of distraction, she lunged forward with her other arm, using all of her strength. She felt the stake sink into his chest, and he burst into a cloud of ash as it penetrated his heart. She continued falling forward, as the resistance of his chest disappeared into thin air, and she was caught by Cain, who was just outside the doorway.

He helped her regain her balance, holding her arms at the elbow. She looked around in amazement to see that the attacking vampire really was gone. "I did it! Did you see that?" She looked past Cain to see that the others had all been taken care of as well. Ben was standing ten feet or so behind Cain, wiping dust from his clothing. The swirl of ash around him told her that he had just dispatched the last of the four. She looked back to Cain, who seemed very relieved to find her unhurt, and repeated, "Did you see that? I killed him! I just killed my first vampire!"

"Congratulations," he answered without much enthusiasm, as he looked back to see that Ben was alright.

Ben looked up at her. "Nice work!"

Felicity hardly heard him though; she was still gazing at Cain. "You don't seem very happy for me. That is why we're here isn't it?"

Now he smiled, but seemed more amused than impressed. She felt like he was laughing at her. "Yes, of course. Just don't get cocky."

She knocked his hands off of her arms and took a step back from him in resentment. She hadn't asked for this! He's the one who wanted her to learn how to defend herself, and now that she had, he would barely acknowledge it? She hadn't really expected praise but, well...yes, she *had* expected praise! She thought she'd handled herself pretty well! It's not as if fighting was something she had any experience in, like him or Ben. "I am not being 'cocky'. I did great! I was totally in control! Well, except when I fell, but I think I made a pretty swift recovery. I staked my first vamp. I even flipped a guy! I was amazing!"

Now he really did laugh at her and considering how non-violent she usually was, she was a little surprised to find that she'd really like to hit him. "My apologies, I must have missed the flip." Cain looked into her eyes in all seriousness and nodded towards the pile of dust in the doorway. "But he was young and stupid."

Over Cain's shoulder, she could see Ben's sympathetic smile to her as he baited Cain in asking, "Friend of yours?".

Cain shot him a withering look and then backed out of the mausoleum entrance gesturing for Felicity to follow, wearing an amused sneer. "Come here."

Felicity eyed him warily. "What?"

Cain continued to back into the open until he was next to Ben. "Come here." She stood her ground and tried to figure out what he was planning. "Come at me the same way that you came at him. I want to show you something." She looked down at her cross and stake, hesitating. "Afraid you're going to hurt me? 'Cause I wouldn't worry."

He wore such a smug smile that she'd almost *like* to shove the cross at him. "Okay, fine," she answered. Ben folded his arms and stepped back with a smile, as though he expected this to be entertaining. She stared straight at Cain and began to advance on him, cross held out in front of her, as he waited patiently.

She walked at a moderate pace and as she neared him he dutifully began to back away, although she really wasn't close enough to touch him yet. Finally, he backed himself against a tree, as though trapped there by her advance. He eyed the cross as she brought it uncomfortably close to his face and began to hold up the stake in her other hand, confident that the cross was holding him at bay. Ben had tracked their progress and was standing a few paces away.

She brought the stake up a bit, as though she would use it. Cain totally surprised her by striking out with his left hand to grab the cross in her left, instead of the stake. She half-heartedly brought the stake down towards him but it was blocked by his arm. He took her hand that held the cross and jerked her forward off balance, twisting her arm behind her back and pulling her into him. This spun her around so that she was pinned with her back against his chest, her arm and cross between them.

He used his right hand to grab hers with the stake, and knocked her wrist against the tree behind them, to make her drop it. She struggled to free herself, but with her arm pinned behind her back, she could do nothing. He let go of her empty hand and used his right hand to wrench the cross from between them, holding it out in front for her to see. Her eyes went wide in disbelief as he held the cross, and tendrils of smoke began to rise from his hand.

"So much for your 'weapon'," he said with disdain, as he let the cross drop to the ground. He still held her pinned, and opened his hand in front of her. His palm and fingers were red and raw with burned skin.

She watched in horror as tiny-bubbled blisters began to form. "Your hand!"

"Will heal. Pain is temporary; it's just a means to an end. That's the fun part of being immortal," he said wryly. "That which cannot kill you, simply hurts like hell. You live long enough, you learn that." He was speaking with a measured, calm voice, although he obviously must have been in some pain. She could see Ben staring at them with the same shocked fascination that she felt, and knew that the 'lesson' had been as much for him as for her. By the look on Ben's face, she assumed Cain held his eyes in a locked stare over her shoulder as he spoke.

He dropped the burned hand down to his side. Some unfathomable change in his presence made her suddenly realize how tempting this position must be for him. She could feel every point at which he touched her body with heightened clarity. Felicity froze as he gently swept aside her hair to expose the right side of her throat and edged over the collar of her shirt. He then let his fingers trail down her shoulder and she suddenly became painfully aware of how helpless she was before him.

She became almost unable to breathe as his words whispered over the back of her neck, just barely still loud enough for Ben to hear. "Pain is a small sacrifice to make...if it gets you what you need." She felt him nuzzle her and give her a small, deliberate kiss on the throat, rather than a piercing bite. She closed her eyes as it caused her heart to flutter and an involuntary shiver to run through her. He then released the slight pressure he still held on her arm, although shock had held her in place more than his grip.

He still held her hand, and used it to spin her around to face him, so that she looked into his eyes. She sought to control her breathing, although her lungs tried to make her gasp as though she had run a marathon. "*He* was young and stupid, but we aren't all." He glanced over her shoulder at Ben once again. "You'd do well to remember that."

She stood staring at him wide eyed and gave a little nod. He let go of her hand and brought his injured one up to his face so he could blow on it. He pulled a bandana from his pocket and used it to pick up the cross from the ground. He offered it back to her and she took it from him in mute bewilderment. He wrapped the bandana about his hand, walked a few paces, then stooped to pick up her fallen stake and gave her that as well.

He moved on towards Ben. "I've always resented having a cross held against me. Bad enough to have my circumstances try and strip me of my faith, without someone waving it in my face now and again. It's an insult more than a weapon really; you should stick with the stake." He walked on past Ben to the path and started back towards the gate.

Ben watched him go, waiting for Felicity. "Are you okay?" She nodded silently. "You know, I was ready. If he'd have changed…I would have been on him before he could break the skin."

"I'm okay," she answered unconcerned, and continued down the path. As she walked, she dug the stopper out of her pocket and closed up the vial. After a moment, Ben fell into step beside her and they caught up with Cain. Felicity fought to regain her composure as she moved next to him and noticed that he held his burnt hand, half-closed, in front of him as he walked. "Going a little far to prove a point, don't you think? You didn't have to go and hurt yourself."

He gave a little shrug. "I heal fast. If I had simply said that a cross was an inadequate weapon, I doubt either of you would have believed me." He looked over at Ben, on the other side of her, who was watching him intently as he spoke.

"It can't do you any permanent damage?" Ben asked.

"Well, I suppose it serves as a decent distraction." He lifted his hand a bit for emphasis. "Don't get me wrong, it's not something I'll be doing again anytime soon, but it can't kill me. Put your trust in the weapons that can."

"What can kill a vampire?" Felicity asked, perhaps a little too eagerly. Cain turned to look at her with some surprise, as if she should know. "I'm still kind of new to all of this. I mean, I know stakes through the heart, and you can't go out in sunlight, but is that it?"

Cain gave her a strange smile. She guessed it did seem sort of odd that she was basically asking how she could kill him, but she did need to know. "You left out intense fire and beheading." He smiled as she cringed.

"What about holy water?" Ben asked.

"That's sort of along the lines of the cross. It hurts like hell. I wouldn't want to drink it or bath in it, but I'd probably live through any lesser amount. I'm not saying you shouldn't use your cross Ben, but you've put far too much trust in it the past. If I *were* your enemy, I would use that to your disadvantage.

Sindy and her friends know you. Eventually they will realize that they aren't quite as restricted as they thought. Don't grab for the cross when you really need the stake. Now if you'd like to chisel yourself a point on the end of that big wooden cross of yours, perhaps you'd have something worth using." They left the cemetery and Cain paused for a moment in the road.

Felicity watched as that 'seeing' look passed over his face again. "Any more?" she asked hesitantly.

"No, not around here. I guess Sindy's out partying somewhere. If these new ones were hers, she told them to expect us, or me anyway."

"What makes you say that?"

"They had to think that I was human at first. I had originally assumed that was why they didn't hesitate to attack us."

Ben spoke up. "You said that before. Why should they think you were human? If you can feel them, can't they feel you? Wouldn't they know you're a vampire?"

"No. I've learned a few useful things over the centuries." Felicity saw Ben look at Cain with new wonder at the word 'centuries', but Cain didn't seem to notice. "I can conceal my presence from other vampires when I choose. A neat trick if you can learn it, a nice advantage. But when *they* attacked us, I let myself be known and they didn't even flinch. Normally that should make them pause. They could tell I was their elder, and usually young ones will defer and at least hear what I have to say, but they were unfazed; in fact, that's when they bared their fangs. No, they had been told to kill me I'm sure, or at least to try."

Felicity smiled to herself. "Nice to know I'm not the only one on the hit list. No offense."

"Guess Sindy never expected that you would've had help," Ben added smugly.

Cain smiled, but there was no humor in it. "I've handled worse." Ben seemed less than pleased not to have his part in the fight acknowledged. Felicity knew just how he felt. Cain seemed totally unaware of their disgruntlement. "I think I ought to go get some wheels and head over to Venus. I've still got about four hours of darkness left. I trust Ben can get you home safely?" he inquired, looking to Felicity.

Ben seemed okay with that, but she wasn't sure if she was. "What are you going to do? What if there's more?"

He smiled at her concern. "Don't waste your worries on me. Not that they aren't appreciated, but they're really not necessary. I've managed to survive this long, haven't I?" He gave her cheek a quick caress and turned to Ben. "It should be a quiet walk home. Thanks for your help." Ben gave a slight nod and Cain went off in the direction of his house before she could say anything else in protest.

They watched a moment as he walked away, then Ben made a snort of disgust. "Gee, should I be honored? He's actually trusting me to walk you home, all un-chaperoned and everything."

"He can still hear you, you know."

"So what?" Ben practically spat the words out in annoyance, but he said nothing else as they watched Cain's back recede into the distance.

"So, you don't have to walk me home if you don't want to," Felicity told him.

"Don't be stupid, of course I'm walking you home, but not because *he* told me to."

"No, that's okay. You don't have to. I'm perfectly capable."

"Cain doesn't seem to think so," Ben said with a smirk.

"Well, it's not up to Cain is it? He doesn't own me."

Ben gave another derisive snort. "Yes he does."

She turned to stare at him. "Excuse me?"

Ben returned it with a long hard stare of his own. "He *totally* owns you. One little kiss on the neck and I thought your knees were going to buckle."

She opened her mouth in shocked protest, but no words would come out. Finally, she found her voice. "I... It was frightening!"

"*I* found it frightening. *You* thought it was exciting."

"He was just trying to prove a point!" she insisted.

"He was just trying to prove his dominance over you, and you loved it."

Unbelievable! "You watch too much 'Wild Kingdom'!"

"I'm not blind, and I haven't conveniently forgotten everything that you told me the other night either. I'm sorry, but you picked the wrong person to confide in, because I have absolutely no sympathy for your situation, whatsoever."

"Thanks." He began walking down the road and she reluctantly followed. "Still, the word '*own*' is a little harsh. He does not own me. You're wrong."

Ben laughed. "It is so funny to me, how you only say that when I am absolutely right on the mark!"

She scowled at him and walked on. Pursuing this with him was obviously pointless. Still, how could he be so unsympathetic? Hadn't he ever...what? Fallen in love? That seemed a little drastic and scary, but quite possible. How could she be in love with a vampire? Still, back to Ben. Hadn't he ever had a crush on someone; known what it was like to be irrational? "So, what are you, totally heartless?" she asked.

That earned her a chuckle. "No."

"Well, haven't you ever been...infatuated with someone before?"

"Infatuation. Good word. Pretty accurate assessment too. You are *infatuated* with him."

"Yeah, I know. So I get extra points for good vocabulary. Answer the question!"

"Who me? Yeah, when I was like twelve!" he answered with a laugh.

"I'm talking post-pubescent here," she clarified with a chuckle.

"No. I don't get 'crushes'. *I* wouldn't let myself act like a fool over some girl."

"Well, that's kind of sad. Hasn't anyone ever had that kind of effect on you?"

He stopped and looked at her as though he couldn't believe she was serious. "I will never understand how girls manage to get themselves so crazed over some guy, that they can't even think straight. I guess men really are from Mars."

"Yeah, or maybe just you." She continued walking. "What's he going to do over at Venus anyway?"

Ben smiled. "See, you still can't stop thinking about him. Oh and nice segue, by the way."

"Thanks."

"Maybe he likes to dance," Ben suggested.

"No, he doesn't," she said confidently.

"He danced with you."

She looked over at Ben, curiously. She hadn't thought anyone had seen them dancing. "For me, he made an exception."

Ben laughed at her. "Oh right, 'cause I've never heard that line before," he said sarcastically.

"It was not a line!" she declared stubbornly.

"Want to go see?" he asked.

"What are you talking about?"

"Let's go to Venus, right now. I'll drive."

"If he had wanted company, he would have asked."

"I know. That's just killing you isn't it?" he asked with an evil little smirk.

She looked at him in disbelief. "You are a terrible friend!"

"No I'm not. I'm an honest friend, the voice of reason. Someone around here should be of sound mind, don't you think? Can I help it if I also like to argue? I'm going to be a lawyer you know. Come on, let's go find out what's really going on. What's the matter, are you afraid to bring down 'The Wrath Of Cain'?"

"No! And really bad pun, by the way. It's like two o'clock in the morning Ben, and I'm going home."

"Because he told you to?"

"Because I'm tired! You wanna go so bad, then go without me!" she said, giving him a little slap on the back. He winced with pain as she did. "Okay, I know I fought pretty well tonight, but I'm not all that strong."

He rolled his shoulders to stretch his back. "Just a wound of war. I'll live."

She stopped to give him a look of concern. "Yeah? I didn't exactly have a ringside seat, but it looked like you guys had quite the tussle going. Are you sure you're okay?"

"Yeah, I'm alright. You should see the other guy," he said with a grin. They had reached the dorm parking lot and approached Ben's car. "So, are we going to Venus or are you really going to bed?"

"Well what's the point of going to a dance club with someone who's too injured to dance?" she joked with a smile. "Go home and take a hot shower, make your back feel better. And use lots of lemon juice!" she added with a chuckle while waving her hand in front of her nose. "Good night."

Ben bowed his head with a sheepish little smile. "Good night." He got in the car, sat and watched as she reached the door. She turned to give him a wave as he drove away and fought off the urge to run after him demanding a ride to Venus after all.

What the hell was Cain going to do there anyway? Confront Sindy? Why wouldn't he want her there for that? She could think of a dozen reasons, some of them were even perfectly good and innocent ones. Besides, it was two o'clock in the morning and even if he was nocturnal, she wasn't. Stop thinking and go to bed! She dragged herself up the steps and prepared to do just that.

Damn, she was locked out again. Either she should stop staying out so late, or she was going to have to find another way to get in. She ended up having to knock. A girl she didn't know came and let her in, groggily. *Sucks to have a room near the door,* Felicity thought, as she entered and whispered an apology. The girl didn't even look at her, but just stumbled back to her room.

~~~~~~~~~~~~~~~~~~~~~~~~~~~

As Felicity walked into Algebra class on Monday morning, she was flagged down by Ashley, who had already saved her a seat. While getting herself settled, she noticed that Ashley wore an overly cheerful smile, which for some reason put Felicity on guard.

"Good morning!" Ashley beamed. "Did you enjoy your day off yesterday?"

"Yeah, it was okay," she answered warily.

"What'd ya do?"

"I went home to see my folks, actually." That was fun...not. Felicity had woken up groggy and bleary eyed, to find her dad at the door. She had totally forgotten he was coming and had to scramble around getting her stuff together. Then she had spent the day at home making small talk about school to her parents, while all the time she couldn't stop thinking about the night before, and wondering what Cain had done after leaving her and Ben.

By the time she got back to the dorms it was well after nine o'clock. The DownTime was closed, and she didn't think it'd be a good idea to try and make her way over to Cain's. So she'd sat in her room, hoping he might come to her, but he never did.

Ashley seemed surprised she had gone home. What did she think Felicity had been doing? "Oh, someone gave you a ride home?"

Felicity gave her a perplexed look. "No, my dad picked me up."

"*Oh*, that's nice," Ashley seemed relieved. Weird.

"What did you do yesterday?"

"I was working. Ben was supposed to work too, but he called in. He said he'd hurt his back, although I closed with him on Saturday, and he seemed perfectly fine to me. So what could he have done between ten-thirty Saturday night and nine-thirty Sunday morning?" Now it was becoming clear. She probably thought Ben had called in sick to spend the day with Felicity. Ben would be so happy to know she cared.

"I don't know," Felicity muttered.

"I do," Ashley leaned closer to her, conspiratorially.

"You do?"

"Well, yeah. I know what's going on." Felicity leaned closer, thinking how amazing it would be if Ashley actually had a clue as to what *was* really going on. "Ben called in sick to work, so he wouldn't have to face me."

"Why?" Felicity asked in confusion.

"Well, he was in such a rush to leave on Saturday night; he must have known that I had a date with Brock Hiller. I'll bet he just wanted to get out of there, so he wouldn't have to be around when Brock came to pick me up. Then Sunday he probably felt all embarrassed about it, isn't that cute?"

She looked at Ashley with confused sympathy. "I guess."

"You know, Ben does have a little crush on me," she said with a knowing smile.

"Really?" Felicity couldn't help but smile back, perhaps a little too broadly. She tried to straighten her face. "How was your date?"

Ashley's features suddenly darkened as if there were a cloud over her head. "He didn't show!" she whispered fiercely. "Can you believe it? The creep stood me up. Who does that? Make a guy captain of the football team and he suddenly thinks he's a god or something! Some people have no respect for other people's feelings!"

Felicity began to have a terrible sinking feeling in her stomach. "Maybe he just forgot," she offered quietly.

"Like that would happen. Oh well, who cares? I still have Ben, right? And there's plenty more guys on the team. Although none quite so yummy as Brock. Jerk!"

Felicity was saved from having to remark on that. A hush fell over the room as the professor entered the class. She gratefully opened her notebook and tried to stop picturing the vampires from Saturday night; the ones that had looked an awful lot like football players, before they had been turned into big piles of dust.

.

Chapter 16 ~ Paranoia

Cain

8:00, Monday night

Cain was in a fierce mood. He welcomed the steady roar and vibration of the motorcycle as he zoomed down the empty country roads. He was trying to drown out all of the thoughts and accusations that were buzzing around in his head.

He couldn't go to the DownTime yet. He'd passed by earlier. He knew that both Felicity and Ben were there, but he hadn't gone in. He couldn't bear the idea of having to patiently listen to their onslaught of questions and his own pathetic lack of explanations.

They were still working, as well. So after the initial telling, he'd have to sit there and do nothing as they watched his every move and waited for it to be time to leave. Better to be out here, blindly riding through field and forest, trying not to curse himself for being a fool.

He had been a fool, he knew. He was forgiving and patient to a fault. All this time he'd thought perhaps Sindy was coming around. He knew she craved a companion just as he always did. He thought that might motivate her to try and please him; and it did, at first, but she seemed to have come to the conclusion that he really wouldn't have her as she was, and to have decided that he was not worth changing for.

To be truthful, he had been so taken with Felicity, that he hadn't given her much reason to try. Cain didn't think that he and Sindy were a proper match, but he still wanted to help her to change. He could teach her to live in a way that would be much less dangerous and hurtful to herself, and those around her, but she was becoming less receptive, and more increasingly hostile.

Still, he hadn't been able to bring himself to kill her. It was just too final. People can change, even the most unpromising ones...he had. He'd thought it would be unkind, to give her what would most likely be false hope, but a kind word, a reason to think that things might someday change, could have made a difference in her attitude. She was growing impatient and so was he.

The problem was that he needed someone. He couldn't be alone any longer. What he really needed was another vampire; one of his own kind, that could truly understand him and share his existence, without being in awe of it. An intelligent and personable vampire was a rare thing to find.

Once in a while, he would meet another male vampire who shared his views and lifestyle closely enough to make them friends, but it wasn't enough. His heart still longed for a mate and his body still longed for a woman to share this unearthly and unending life of his.

However, he'd found that every female of his kind who actually had the stamina and spirit to exist for any amount of time, also tended to be totally unlike anyone he'd want to be with. They were always ruthless and cruel. He supposed they'd had to be to survive, but he just couldn't stand for it. He was inevitably drawn to living women who were all the things that the vampires he had known were not, but this was a doomed venture as well.

A human couldn't truly understand or share in an equal relationship with him for any real length of time. Either they eventually became repulsed by his true nature, or covetous and resentful of it. In the end, he must change them or leave them. Neither choice was ever gratifying.

Those he'd changed had always done one of two things, perhaps not immediately but eventually. Either they would come to hate him for their lives lost, until they parted ways with him or with their very existence; or their personalities would twist and evolve until they became just like the other vampires that he had spurned.

Either way, he was always left alone. Then he would spend a time of atonement, heartbroken and bereft. He would refuse all contact as much as possible. Time would pass and the world would continue to turn and evolve without him, until eventually, he found himself being drawn back into it once again.

Traces of other vampires would come to his attention and he would feel obligated to seek them out. He would find them show them ways to improve the quality of their existence without harming others. He would teach them and guide them…as much as they would let him anyway.

Some practical advice was appreciated, and his teachings were tolerated, but his companionship they never craved. Most of the time they were either loners by choice or already existed in a small coven of two or three. They were content to hear him out and then move on.

He told himself that was as it should be. He would travel to share his enlightenment with as many as he could. Some followed his advice, some did not. He used his status as an elder to impress upon them what he could. Most thanked him for his insight, not wanting him for an enemy, and then went on their way to do as they pleased, far from his scrutiny.

But there were a few…a handful that made it all worthwhile; those who agonized over their nightly habits and knew not what else to do. They were eager for his wisdom and grateful for his help. They let him know in his heart that he was on the right path. If he wasn't here to show them, what would they do? If he did not guide them, would they not be lost? It was his purpose and it was a worthy one.

Still…they never stayed. He showed them how to live, he helped them to find their way in the world, but it *was* out into the world that they went, thanking him and leaving him behind. He was gratified to know that they could exist independently because of him, proud to see them prosper in peace and harmony with humans, but he was still alone.

The satisfaction and fulfillment of a purpose served would only last for so long. While there were always more to be helped, sometimes they did seem few and hard to find. That was a good thing, but then the 'lonely cycle' would return.

Humans would begin to catch his eye once again. A smile, a kind word, something would penetrate the invisible walls he had so carefully constructed; little by little he would feel them crumble and fall away to leave him exposed and desperate for contact, until he sought company and friendship among humans once again.

Why did he continue to ruin the lives of innocents, to try and ease his own suffering? Was he really any better than the other vampires he scorned? True, most of them killed nightly, where he did not, but at least the deaths they brought were quick and painless, without the torture and heartache that seemed to follow him like a shadow, falling over any small light of happiness he might try to bring to himself.

These were gloomy thoughts to be imprisoned with. They were locked inside him always, but tonight they would not let him be. The engine of the motorcycle thrummed and roared beneath him.

Fleeting thoughts of abandoning the whole situation altogether toyed with his heart and made his head hurt; to just keep riding, out of town, out of state, never to look back. It was almost tempting.

Felicity would be hurt, but Ben would surely step in to comfort her, or if not him, some other human man much better suited to her future. The thought made him feel ill. She was his. He felt it as surely as if he'd drunk her blood.

More painful than that, was the knowledge that most likely neither Ben nor Felicity would survive if he fled. Unless they were to leave as well, or lock themselves away each dusk until the danger had passed. Not very likely.

For he *had* seen Sindy on Saturday night. He'd gone to Venus, just as he'd said he would. The setting was as unearthly as its name proclaimed. The walls were painted in fluorescent colors of otherworldly scenes lit by black lights. The dance floor was covered in mist and fog being pumped out by a machine in the corner. There was even another little machine to compliment it, perched up on the balcony to spill bubbles down onto the crowd below.

Colored lights blinked and changed on the dim dance floor, showing the crowd in brief and jerking flashes. It was the perfect place for a vampire to find a midnight snack. Sure enough, Sindy had been there.

He'd seen her dancing and drinking alcohol almost non-stop. If anything more than a momentary effect was to be gained from the liquid, a vampire needed to keep a fast and steady pace. Their body healed them of it quickly, just as surely as if it were any other poison. So she drank and drank, while writhing and undulating to the music on the dance floor. He dared not approach her, for she was not alone.

By the time that he had come to be within a half a mile of the club, he'd begun to have severe second thoughts about entering it at all. The place was practically swarming with vampires. He could sense them, moving about Sindy's trace light in his mind as if they were moths drawn to a flame.

Whether they were of her creation, or simply ones she had managed to call from other places, he had no idea, but one thing was plain to see as he carefully slipped in among the flickering lights and pounding music, they adored her. Not a woman was among them, except for humans of course. Not a great surprise. Marcus was also conspicuously absent, but then he supposed Marcus couldn't be trusted to play well with others.

He stood by the door and took a quick mental count. There were almost a dozen of them. Sindy was on the dance floor with three vampire males, among the human men who vied for her attention while dancing. These vampires' movements alone showed that they were not quite as sapient as Sindy or himself. Perhaps they were below even Chris and Luke's level of awareness. They danced in mindless rhythms, merely echoing Sindy's moves as if on autopilot. Their eyes never left her figure, unless it was to cast a look of unrequited hunger at a human who danced too closely. They never moved to touch anyone though. She must have them well trained at least.

Another, more individual vampire was dancing with a human woman off to one side. Cain spotted Luke and Chris at the bar, looking sullen and annoyed. A group of three sat at a table in the back drinking and watching the floor with blank and eerie stares.

There were two more. One was at the opposite end of the bar from Luke and Chris, apparently trying to chat up the lady bartender. He almost missed the last, as his trace was dim and easy to overlook. He was standing at the rail, up on the balcony with his arms crossed, looking appraisingly down at the crowd.

He was different. He wasn't truly cloaked, but his trace felt purposely dimmed making it easy to dismiss. The man had long dark hair, pulled severely from his face to hang in a ponytail down his back. His skin tone was a little dark for a vampire, though not much. From his features he was Arabic perhaps. In appearance, he looked to be Cain's age, but of course that meant nothing.

He was very unlike the others. He was older, this one. Cain could sense it. Not as old as himself to be sure, but close. Much older than Sindy. He wasn't hers. Cain had never seen him before. None of them other than Sindy, Luke and Chris, were any he had ever known. Each vampire's trace held a certain signature. If he had met one of them before he likely would have recognized it, before even entering the bar and physically laying eyes on them.

Why hadn't he expected this of her? He knew she was smart and resourceful. Did he really think she would continue to accept his reprimands forever? She'd bided her time until she was sure he wouldn't accept her as she was, and then she had made her move. If he didn't want her, she would get rid of him. He'd been fool enough to give her the chance to try.

He could take care of himself, and in the past he had overcome some pretty bad odds, but against a dozen others, alone? Sindy had known that even he would be hard pressed to prevail against so many. And of course, the humans he now cared for had become a serious disadvantage. He felt lucky that they had taken out the four that had attacked them that evening, without Felicity being injured. He could handle himself and Ben he wouldn't really worry for, but Felicity…she was a weakness. She would give them leverage over him, perhaps even get him killed.

How long had Sindy waited for these others to arrive? They couldn't have been here long. They would have to range far and wide to feed. The towns in this vicinity could scarce support Sindy, Luke and Chris without attracting notice, let alone all these others. Some of them may be hers, but not many. He would have known if she had killed so many, so recently. He always checked the papers. He had read of some disappearances, most recently seven boys from the local college football team, but four of those were the boys they had killed in the cemetery, he was fairly sure.

Cain had seen Sindy alone Friday night; these others must have only just arrived. He kept himself inconspicuous and left Venus as quietly as he had arrived. He was sure no one had known of his presence. All the ride home he had seethed with anger over his own stupid lack of foresight.

Sunday night he'd seen no trace of them, not a vampire within range. They must be holed up the next town over, waiting for he knew not what. He was at first panic-stricken that Felicity was nowhere to be found, and even Ben was off somewhere unknown. He had never thought to find out where Ben lived, another stupid oversight.

When Felicity wasn't in her room, he had a flash of annoyance that perhaps they were together, in his. He went back out to the parking lot and found a hidden place to sit and wait. She would be back eventually, he hoped. He had just begun to wonder if she would deign to spend the night with Ben, when an unknown car arrived. He watched unseen as Felicity exited the vehicle, and bid farewell to the man inside.

Her father. She must have spent the day at home. Cain watched with mixed feelings as she gave good-byes and kisses, before she turned to enter the building. He hadn't stopped to think that she would have a family. Of course, he knew she must, but he had never let himself acknowledge that he could be taking her away from others. He wondered if they were very close.

He had thought to approach her before she went in, but her father stayed to see her safely inside. Commendable, but inconvenient. Cain stayed for a little while, playing with the idea of sneaking up to her room, but decided against it. Tomorrow evening would come soon enough.

He had spent the remainder of Sunday night roaming the vicinity, searching for others, but none were to be found. He wondered what Sindy could be doing. He couldn't imagine that the little get together he had witnessed could be something that didn't involve him. If Sindy hadn't called them to help her with Cain, then what else could their reason for gathering be? He had no clue.

So here it was Monday evening, and he was waiting for the DownTime to close so that he could see Felicity. Now he wished he had gone to her alone in her room last night instead.

He was not looking forward to describing the scene that he had witnessed at Venus. He didn't feel like putting up with Ben. He didn't want to have to answer questions or devise strategies. He didn't want to have to admit that he had no idea how to proceed. He had never let himself get close to someone when other vampires were present before. The thought that they could jeopardize his relationship with Felicity was unbearable. He wanted only one thing, to be alone with her.

He began to slowly make his way back into town, when the strangest feeling came upon him. It started as a slight prickle on the back of his neck, that turned itself into chills that made their way down his spine, almost indistinguishable from the vibration of his body on the motorcycle, but he realized that he was feeling something that he had not experienced in decades.

He was being watched. Approached by another of his kind, whose trace he could not read, but somehow he could just feel it. The very idea was preposterous and seemed the product of an overly stressed imagination, but as soon as it was recognized, it shocked him so that he had to stop the bike.

The motorcycle's large engine purred quietly to itself as it awaited further use. The hills and trees were silent and still all around him. Nothing. And yet... He suddenly became acutely aware of the feeling that he was being deceived.

He had the sense that where his mind was telling him there was nothing but unoccupied space, there were actually many beings, watching, waiting. Like a ghost image just out of focus. He could not see them; they were hidden from his physical eyesight. His vampire senses could find nothing, no traces to read, but somehow he just knew they were there.

Stop being a fool, he told himself. Most of those at the club were young and inexperienced; they could never hide their marks the way that Cain could. Even the older one that had been among them, had been uncloaked and visible at the time. If he had known how to conceal his presence, why hadn't he done so then?

Cain had met very few vampires who even knew that it was possible to hide themselves from others' view. He shook his head as if to clear his vision and his mind, and revved up the bike. As he entered town once again, the lights and electric hum brought him a small sense of comfort, but he never quite shook the unease that he had felt.

What if there were others? Older ones that he could not see. What if they had seen him and he had lead them straight here? Straight to Felicity, only to let them take her before she was even truly his?

Ridiculous? Paranoia? There would be no way for him to know, until it was too late.

Chapter 17 – Cruisin'

Felicity

The DownTime Café and Bookstore
9:20, Monday night

Felicity sat at the café counter, as Ben finished straightening up so that they could leave. He walked over to where she sat, with a serving plate in his hand. It held one slightly dried out slice of apple pie. "You wanna eat this? I don't feel like putting it away."

Felicity eyed the lonely slice distastefully. "No thanks, I'm not hungry." He shrugged, threw it in the garbage, and went to rinse the plate in the sink. She watched him stretch his shoulder a bit. "How's your back?"

Ben spoke over the water, finishing with the plate. "It's okay."

"Yeah? 'Cause I heard you called in 'too injured' to work yesterday."

He turned to her with a little laugh as he dried the plate. "Don't worry, I'm fine."

"Oh, I wasn't worried really, but Ashley will be glad to hear it," she informed him.

He raised his eyebrows at her. "*Ashley* will?"

"Uh huh. She mentioned it."

"*Ashley* was concerned about my back?" he asked in disbelief, as he put away the plate. He took her locker key off the counter and went to get their stuff out of the lounge.

She yelled for him to hear in the next room. "No. Actually, she thought that you were lying. She was concerned that you didn't come in to work because you were too embarrassed to face her."

Ben returned with their jackets and her purse, looking very confused. "What? Why?"

Felicity tried not to smile too broadly as she answered. "Well, she seems to be under the impression that you have a little crush on her."

"She *said* that?" Now Ben looked confused and yet pleased at the same time.

"She did. Oh, but don't worry. I totally set her straight. I told her that she must be mistaken, because you don't get crushes. And that *you* would never make a fool out of yourself over some girl."

Ben wasn't quite buying it. He laughed, but he did look a little worried. "You told her that?"

She made him wait for a minute, and then she laughed. "No, but I should have."

Ben smiled. "I don't have a crush on her."

"I know."

"That doesn't mean that if I spent the night with her, we'd be playing Monopoly..." he said with a smile.

Felicity squelched the sudden desire to hit him. She seemed to have developed a real violent streak lately; must be all the vampire hunting. "I doubt *Ashley* could even figure out *how* to play Monopoly."

Ben smiled. "Yeah, but *she* knows lots of *other* fun games."

"Does she?" she inquired archly.

"M-hmmm."

"You *know* this?" she asked. She fixed him with a steady stare, daring him to answer her.

He stared right back at her; a roguish glint in his eye. "I do."

She held his gaze for a moment longer before answering quietly. "Lucky you." He just smiled. "Too bad Brock never got a chance to play," she added as she turned away.

"Who?"

Felicity put on her jacket, grabbed her purse and began to walk to the door. "Do you know a guy named Brock Hiller?"

Ben followed, shutting lights as he went. "Yeah, how do I know that name? Oh, isn't he on the football team?"

"He was, but something tells me we won't be seeing him play next weekend." They went out the door and Felicity turned to face him as he locked up and set the alarm. She shivered as a phantom chill went down her spine. "Those vampires, in the cemetery the other night... Do you think they were all students?"

Ben looked a little unsettled as he put away the keys. When he turned to face her, he looked as though he thought she might need comforting. "They probably were. Did you know any of them?"

"No, *I* didn't. It might not have even been him, but let's just say that if you wanted to ask out Ashley, she's probably free."

That made him look a little sick. After a minute, he shook his head as if to clear it. "Let's get out of here. You coming with me?" he asked, jerking a thumb towards his car.

Felicity looked around, but there was no one in sight. "I thought Cain'd be here. Do you think he's okay?"

"He's practically immortal, 'Liss. What could have happened to him? Besides, you heard the man; he's managed to survive this long." He absently played with the keys in his hand. "How old do you think he is anyway? You didn't really buy that 'centuries' remark, did you?"

"340," she told him matter-of-factly.

Ben looked incredulous and then shook his head. "That is just so wrong."

"It's kind of weird, I know," Felicity agreed.

"I can't believe you like that guy, he gives me the creeps."

"I think you may have mentioned that."

"Well, he didn't show up to walk you home. So, that should be like a demerit or something, right?"

They both looked up at the sound of a motorcycle engine. Cain pulled into the lot on his bike and stopped in front of Ben's car. He was just far enough away to discourage easy conversation. Felicity turned to Ben with a look of triumph. "Ha."

Cain didn't get off the bike; he didn't even shut the engine. He just sat there looking at Felicity with smoldering eyes, as if he were calling her mentally. She thought it a little odd, but wasn't going to question it. She turned to Ben, to say good night. He was staring at Cain with undisguised contempt. "Guess I don't get to hear what happened at Venus," he said quietly.

"I'll talk to you tomorrow." She walked over and hopped on the bike. She was a little awkward at first, figuring out where to put her legs. She'd never ridden on a motorcycle before.

He turned to speak to her over his shoulder. "Sorry, I don't have a helmet. Never really needed one. Put your arms around me and hold on."

He seemed in a very serious mood, but once again, she wasn't going to question it, not yet anyway. She hesitantly wrapped her arms around his waist. "Where are we going?"

Now she could hear some amusement in his voice. "Where did you want to go?"

"I don't know. I've never ridden before, maybe we could just cruise around a little?"

"Your wish is my command." He revved up the bike and Felicity tightened her grip about his waist. They pulled out of the lot and Ben's car followed. Felicity was a little nervous at first, but soon became comfortable with the smooth and confident way that Cain directed the bike. The wind made her hair fly out behind her and she knew it would be hopelessly tangled by the time they were done.

She wondered where she would want to go if he asked again. She wasn't sure. She'd like to be alone and talk. Her room seemed a poor refuge, the dorms being un-private and almost childish. She felt that she could hardly ask Cain to sneak around the way she had made Ben. Cain's place was not a wonderful alternative. Not that she minded it, and she wasn't really afraid to be alone with him there, but for all that, he made her feel as though she would like to melt in his arms. She wasn't sure just how far she should actually let things go. Once there, it might be difficult to keep a clear head.

Cain had headed in the direction of the dorms, but passed the corner. After riding straight for a few blocks, she looked back to see Ben's car turn left, down a side road. Now they really were alone.

How did she know Cain even wanted to be with her, really? He had shown up, so that was a good sign, but maybe he had only planned to drive her home. He had turned her away before, and he certainly was in a solemn mood this evening. She wondered if something might have happened to account for it. Did he really care for her so much?

When she was alone she felt as though he must. She remembered the way he had looked at her when they danced. She thought about the look he usually had in his eyes when they spoke. She always felt that no matter what his words, he was wishing they were in each others' arms, but when actually confronted with him, she had to admit that she didn't always know what to make of him. Why did he act as though kissing her was such a crime?

That kiss! Was she delusional, or was that kiss really as amazing as she remembered? It was just a kiss. Why did it affect her so? She held on tighter and laid her cheek on his back. Stanzas of Michelle Pfeiffer singing 'Coooool Rider' flitted through her head. When the bike stopped and it was time to get off, she knew just how 'Stephanie Zinone' had felt. She wasn't nearly ready for the ride to end and reality to intrude. She looked around as she reluctantly sat up and let go.

They seemed to be in the middle of nowhere. Only fields and a few lonely trees lined the road. Cain put the kickstand down, so she figured they were staying here for a bit. She hopped off, not too ungracefully, and tried vainly to smooth down her wildly wind-blown hair. He got off and then leaned against the bike with his arms crossed. She noticed that he wore a fingerless black glove over the palm of his right hand, and she wondered if it still hurt. He watched her for a moment and then smiled. "So...hi," he said with a little laugh.

She smiled back and suddenly felt very self-conscious. She shifted her weight and looked at the ground. "Hi." A breeze stirred the trees and sent leaves skittering past their feet. "Did you um, go to Venus the other night?"

He sat up and took a step towards her, putting his finger to her lips to silence her questions. "I don't really want to talk about others right now, if that's alright."

She looked up into his deep blue eyes and wondered how she could ever have questioned his feelings for her. Those eyes held nothing but desire, she was certain. She gave his finger a small kiss and he took it away, reluctantly it seemed.

"You're rather determined not to distance yourself from me, aren't you?" He still had that quiet air of melancholy, and she wondered how she should respond. She continued to gaze into his eyes and gave a little shrug. "Little fool. How can I resist you, if your eyes pursue me with such longing?"

He looked as though he wished she didn't want to be with him, and yet he put himself so close to her. She looked down at the ground again and still felt that there was nothing she could say. The other night he had acted a little oddly, but she had never really seen him like this. It seemed strange, as though he were purposely acting his age.

He put his fingers to her chin and lifted her face to look at him. "Consorting with me would be dangerous for you." He looked as though he would say more, but after a moment only took a deep breath and looked away, dropping his hand.

She couldn't think what to do. It didn't seem to matter whether or not he were right, she only felt desperate to convince him otherwise. "I'm not afraid."

He looked back to her with a sad smile. "Yes you are, but you overcome it. That does you credit, foolish though it may be." Suddenly his eyes went wide, although they didn't seem to be looking at anything in particular. "We should leave."

"Is someone here?"

"I...don't know." He looked confused and she found that frightening. She thought maybe he did too. "I don't think so, but let's head back."

Felicity knew better than to argue. She got on the motorcycle and soon they were speeding back towards town, but before they had left the fields entirely behind, Cain skidded the motorcycle to a halt.

When Felicity looked up, she felt a terrible chill run down her back. There was a man in the road. He wore a long black coat and had straight dark hair that fell down to his elbows. It was free and blowing about him in the wind. He looked foreign, dark and mysterious. The wane moonlight cast odd shadows on his thin face.

He wasn't a large man, but something in his demeanor seemed very imposing. He was a vampire, she was sure. His dark eyes seemed normal and there was nothing specific about him to set him apart as inhuman, but somehow, she just knew.

She held tighter to Cain as if she would physically keep him from leaving the bike. Thankfully, he didn't seem to have any intention of doing so. He cut the engine to give them silence, but he said nothing. If this man wanted to have words with them, then let him begin. After a moment, he spoke. "Cain. We must talk."

Felicity wondered if Cain knew him. The man spoke as if they were familiar. His English was very clipped and precise, with a slight middle eastern accent to it.

"And you are?" Cain asked.

The man smiled. "Very interested in your crusade. I would like to hear tell of that, among other things we should discuss."

Felicity was not sure whether to be relieved, that Cain didn't seem to know the man. She wasn't sure why, but she knew she didn't like him. "This is an inopportune time. As you can see, I am escorting my lady home," Cain answered.

The man eyed her as if appraising her value. "I do see the lady. And I must remark that she is not 'yours'."

Felicity felt herself grow cold. Cain had made the words 'my lady' sound like a title of respect, but obviously this man understood it differently. She thought of her outrage at Ben's statement that Cain 'owned' her. Right now, she would be quite content to stand up and proclaim herself as undoubtedly his property. That would be just fine with her. She brought her hands to the base of her throat as inconspicuously as she could, and tried to pry the stopper from her vial.

"I claim her." Cain said with an even, steady voice. Normally she would have been offended by the exchange, but all she could think, was 'Bless him'. "And you haven't given me your name, although you know mine. An unfair advantage."

"True, one that I do not give up easily. With knowledge of a man's name, comes power, and that is not my only advantage, I can assure you."

Felicity could tell that Cain didn't like the man either. He sounded annoyed. "Then you should know that 'Cain' is not my true name," he replied with a chuckle. "You are wasting my time. Have you something to say?"

The man smiled. "You may call me Arif." Cain gave a barely perceptible nod of acknowledgement and the man continued. "It has come to my attention that you have destroyed many of our kind. I believe this girl has ash on her hands as well. While I may find your motives commendable, I feel that your methods may not be."

Felicity felt Cain stiffen. She discreetly worked the stopper loose from her vial and managed to tuck it into the front pocket of her jeans. Neither of the men seemed to notice. *Ride away* she begged Cain silently. Now she wished she'd just had him take her home to begin with.

"I am not seeking anyone's approval, but this is not the time or place for such a discussion. I will say that I have never attacked without provocation, except to put mindless beings from their misery. If you would like to speak more on this, I am certain we can find a more suitable place and time. Now if you'll excuse me, I'll take my leave of you. My lady craves her warm bed, I'm sure."

Arif smiled with an air of menace, but stepped aside with outstretched arms, as if to give them free passage. Cain started up the bike and began to edge slowly forward. Felicity turned away from the man as they passed. He had been staring at her with uncomfortable directness. They picked up a little speed.

As they left the fields and entered the trees, she felt more than heard Cain's gasp of amazement. There, among the trees, stood others. Vampires, to be sure. They did not bare their fangs, but each had eyes that reflected and glowed odd colors in the motorcycle's headlights. They just stood there with an air of quiet intimidation, watching Cain and Felicity pass.

She only saw them for a moment and then the motorcycle was past them, zooming on. It was hard to tell as they flew by, but there seemed to be at least ten. Five on each side of the road, maybe more. Felicity breathed a sigh of relief, that they didn't even try to follow. Suddenly she realized the importance of Cain's surprise. He couldn't sense them! They were right there and he hadn't known!

Felicity put her head down and hugged him tightly. They hit a rough patch of road and as they bumped up and down, she wondered distractedly if there was blood spilling onto her, out of the vial. It couldn't hold much. She wondered how strange it would be, to try and ask him to refill it.

She closed her eyes and tried not to think about anything, lest she frighten herself for no good reason. Maybe she had misinterpreted his surprise...although she knew she hadn't. They would talk when they got home. Finally, she felt them slow and eventually stop. They had reached the dorms.

She got off the bike and waited for him to do the same. After a moment of seeming indecision, he did. Rather than climb the steps to the walkway before the porch, he stopped just shy of them. He stood looking at the building. It was quiet, the lights were all off inside. She walked over to him and leaned against one of the decorative, four-foot stone pillars, which marked either side of the bottom of the wide, cement staircase.

He turned to face her and then stared at her strangely for a moment. She imagined that he must be trying to decide how much to explain to her. Then she realized that he was staring at her throat, at the open vial to be precise. He must know that it's open, she thought. He can probably smell it. She wondered if maybe she shouldn't have opened it. Now she felt stupid for doing so. He had been right there the whole time; maybe it had seemed an insult.

He didn't say anything about it, so neither did she. She thought he meant to give her some explanation for the evening's events, but instead he simply moved closer to her; until their bodies were practically touching and he looked deeply into her eyes. She stood, looking up at him, mesmerized.

"You must know, I would never hurt you," he said quietly.

It seemed an odd thing to say. She nodded mutely, still gazing into his eyes. There were so many things she wanted to ask, but this moment didn't seem made for questions. He leaned closer and she realized with a small leap of joy in her heart, that he meant to kiss her. She closed her eyes and upturned her face to meet his lips.

But the kiss did not come. Instead, she felt his lips graze the side of her throat. She began to have vague feelings of confused alarm when suddenly she felt the sharp points of his fangs touch her skin. She tensed to push away, but his body pressed hers against the pillar and his strong hands held her shoulders in a grip like iron.

She found herself beyond coherent thought as his teeth unmistakably penetrated her flesh. Her mouth opened in protest, but no sound would come, only sharp little gasps for breath she felt she could not control. There was but an instants prick of pain, and then a strange and almost numbing warmth began to spread from her throat and move throughout her body.

She was beyond belief that this could be happening, as though she was trapped in some obscene dream. Her body felt as though it would not obey her commands, although her mind seemed unable to produce coherent thought to command her limbs anyway.

Then it began. She felt a slow and rhythmic pulling against her throat and with each drawing pull she felt what could only be described as a wave of ecstasy. She swooned and her legs would no longer hold her, but Cain held her sure and strong. Her brain could not think to admit that each surging pulse could be anything more than pure pleasure, and the fact that it was also surely her blood leaving her body seemed a trivial aside.

She both felt and heard a low moan escape his lips against her skin and on some disconnected, carnal level, it thrilled her. Every part of her felt as though it were afire with longing for him. Each pull at her throat was an erotic ebb and flow that was entirely unlike any sensation she had ever known.

It seemed that it had barely begun when she felt him withdraw, the wound cold and abandoned. Some locked off section of her mind was filled with horror-stricken relief that it had ended; while at the very same instant, she knew that if she could have spoken, she might have begged him to return to it. It was all she could do, to try not to lose consciousness.

He still held her shoulders, as he leaned back to look at her face. She opened her eyes, but the world seemed unfocused and fuzzy. She found his face and thought she should look for a change there, but as her vision cleared, he looked the same as always. His eyes looked filmed with unshed tears, but the tears may only have been her own.

"And now, you're mine," he said quietly and distinctly.

She was still too unsteady to put words together in her mind, let alone speak them. He let her go and was suddenly gone. She felt herself slide down the pillar to sit on the ground and closed her eyes, as the motion tried to make her dizzy. She heard the motorcycle engine leap to life and then roar off into the distance. Some detached part of her mind understood that he was truly gone.

When next she opened her eyes, she had no idea how much time had passed. She sat there for a moment, staring at the trees against the dark night sky, blowing in the slight breeze, and wondered why she was still outside. Then with a sudden start of shock, her hand shot to her throat. As she pulled it away, she examined her fingers to find a tiny spot of blood there. Hardly anything to be alarmed about…but she remembered. She stared at it for a moment, trying to comprehend its full meaning, when she was startled by someone opening the front door.

She quickly stood, then leaned against the pillar again until a slight wave of dizziness passed. The woman in the doorway noticed her then. It was Maggie. "Felicity, is that you? I thought I heard a car out here. Come inside, it's late. I was just locking up."

He must have only just left, she thought. She hadn't really passed out at all. She started up the steps and found she had no problem, though she didn't trust herself yet to speak. Maggie looked at her with some concern as she approached the door. "Are you alright?" Felicity forced a smile and nodded her head. Maggie didn't look like she was buying it. The woman probably thought she was drunk. She passed into the parlor and straight for the stairs up to her room, without a backwards glance. She felt a bit unsteady but fiercely hoped it didn't show.

Once there, she closed and locked her door and went to stand in front of the mirror. She couldn't even find them at first, the wounds were so tiny; though when she touched the spot, she felt a slight aftershock sort of shiver run through her and the bite felt as though it should be huge.

Everything that the mirror reflected in the room behind her looked strange and unreal. She put her hands down to feel the dresser before her, as if to assure herself of its solidity. She stared wide-eyed, at her reflection. Her eyes found the open vial necklace, still clasped around her throat. She dug into her pocket and found the stopper, placing it on her dresser. She carefully held the vial and took it off. She inspected it to find that it was still about half full. She replaced the stopper to close it and put it away on a shelf.

After a few minutes more of staring at the two perfect, tiny, red marks on her throat in the mirror, she stripped to her shirt and climbed under her covers into bed. There seemed nothing else to do. Sleep came quickly; however, it was anything but restful. Her night was plagued with untoward dreams full of alternating terror, and...avid desire.

Chapter 18 – Self-control

Cain

11:00, Monday night

It was done. He had marked her, and she was undeniably his. It was done, but he knew that it was really only the beginning.

Cain was thankful for the motorcycle's loud and thrumming engine more than ever. He was shaking almost uncontrollably, but it melded with the vibration of the bike into something he could more easily dismiss. The wind in his face, the roar in his ears, the rabbits that froze at the side of the road, with no time to scurry from sight as he passed; these were things he could not even acknowledge or focus on. All he knew was her.

Her scent was still thick in his nostrils, no matter how he tried to let the fresh air carry it away. He could still taste her. It was maddening. He passed his house and continued on. He drove far and fast, because if he didn't, he knew he would return to her for more.

To a vampire, human blood was divine, but to Cain, this was even so much more. It was Felicity. Someone he knew, someone he cared for; someone that he spent almost every waking moment thinking of, analyzing, memorizing, longing for. And now, he had tasted her.

He knew her more intimately than any other being on the earth could ever claim. He had drunk from her, tasted her very lifeblood. In his world of darkness, it was like light itself. Liquid innocence, with fire burning just below the surface. The way she had cleaved to him, the swoon it had put her in, he couldn't get the experience to leave him be. It replayed in his mind until he finally had to stop the bike.

He pulled off to the side of the road, just under an overpass. He walked a few paces from the motorcycle and stood with his hands on his knees trying to clear his head. It had been so long, and he had known that it would be hard, but how sadly he had underestimated the effect that she would have on him. He thanked the Lord that he still retained his own human self along with the beast within him; that he still retained his self-control.

He had set it in his mind that he would have to mark her. He had played it through in his head to be a necessary measure that he would speak to her about and have her understand. She had been frightened by Arif; why else would she have opened the vial? She wanted his protection. It would all be very clinical and done solely for the purpose of safety, or so he had tried to convince himself. Of course, he never really believed that it would play out quite so clinically; he knew that there would undeniably be pleasure in it, but this went far beyond anything he had imagined. When the time came, words had failed him and it had seemed that explanations would come easier after the fact.

The truth was, she needed his bite for protection, he had wanted to do it, and he didn't want her to try and stop him, or to be afraid; so, he just did it. He should have tried to explain, he should have asked her first, but he hadn't. He had violated her trust and stolen her blood. No matter how he tried to hold himself in contempt for it, he couldn't say that he regretted it. He couldn't even try to tell himself so bold a lie. It had been exquisite.

Felicity had responded more strongly than he had expected, and that made it so much harder to end, but he had. That was the one saving grace that he could cling to. He had been able to stop, even though he could have gone on without hurting her for far longer. He knew the limits, but it had been so long, and she hadn't even really fought him. He'd thought it better to end it, before he found himself more caught up in things than he could entirely control.

He stood up and let the wind wash over him. He had stopped shaking, and although he could still taste her on his lips, it no longer summoned him to go back to her. It was done.

He suddenly realized that he had let his guard down in his distraction. He immediately sought to psychically conceal his presence. He felt others approaching, but had no heart for anything else now. He hadn't even let the things said by Arif be fully taken into account yet. How had the man found him? And why had Cain been unable to feel the others? Had Arif somehow stripped him of his psychic abilities? They seemed to be working normally now.

He couldn't think on these things. They seemed unimportant and trivial. All that mattered now was Felicity. He had claimed her as his own and started the cycle that would bring her to him like never before, or drive her far beyond his reach. Either way, he could think of nothing else right now. He would go home and plan what to say when he saw her again. How could he regain her trust? Would she ever be able to forgive him? Should she?

He would have to wait before seeing her again; for a few nights anyway, lest the vampire within him desire too strongly to taste her yet again. Let some time pass, let her blood leave his system. His mark would remain for a while; he could consider her safe from others. He had to be sure she would be safe from him as well. He hoped he had even half as much self-control as he thought he did. It would be inexcusable to underestimate the strength of his inner vampire's need for her blood. The monster inside him fought that control now. It wanted to finish her. It wanted every last drop of blood in her body, but he had conquered that desire in the past and he did again now. He would not succumb to that beast, he would master it.

Cain climbed back onto his Harley, ignored the others approaching and took off back towards town. He couldn't face them now. He outdistanced them easily and fought the urge to continue past his house to rejoin her. Surely she had revived and gone inside by now. Even if she hadn't, she was no longer in any danger from another vampire. No one else would touch her now. Even Sindy would find herself very hard put, to harass a victim not her own. She would know how difficult marking Felicity would have been for him, and she'd surely love to rub it in his face, but Felicity herself was no longer in any danger. He would retire to his room and stay away from her for a while; away from everyone.

Chapter 8 – Aftershocks

Felicity

Felicity's bedroom
Tuesday morning

Felicity awoke to the blare of her alarm clock. She blindly hit the button and rolled over sleepily. As she did, she felt a slight twinge at the side of her throat; just a tight pulling of her skin around the bite as she stretched. It woke her to sit bolt upright in the bed, her hand raised to touch the spot. There was nothing there to be felt; it was even invisible in the mirror from this distance, but her fingers seemed to cause an odd warmth to radiate outward from the bite. She hastily withdrew her hand.

She went over the final events of the evening in her mind. She had thought he was going to kiss her, she had been certain. The look in his eyes was not hunger, or a desire to hurt her, it was...love. She had been absolutely certain at that point that he was falling in love with her.

He had seemed a little hesitant, but not threatening in any way. How could she have been so blind, so thoroughly deceived? Had she mistaken a desire for her blood, as a desire for herself? Was she really that young and stupid? If he had really wanted her for her blood, wouldn't he have taken more of it? However unclear her recollection, he had only really taken a trace amount, she was sure.

Her recollection. She forced herself to face it; the thing she was trying so hard to avoid remembering, that she did not want to admit. Her recollection was very clear actually, although she would like to pretend it was hazy or indistinct. She remembered acutely, every sensation that had passed through her body. The sharp, precise moment that he had actually bitten her and everything that had come after. She had never felt anything so erotically intimate in her entire life.

As it was happening, it had all seemed rather dreamlike, but as she replayed it in her mind, she could call back the feeling as if it had happened only a moment ago. He had bitten her, he had drunk her blood, and she had enjoyed it.

Shame, guilt, disbelief and denial washed over her as she tried to convince herself that she was somehow mistaken. This was unreal. She told herself that what had happened was loathsome and disgusting. Yet if she closed her eyes, she could still feel him there, at her throat, and the memory would produce a shiver of delight in her. Although the very idea horrified her, she couldn't deny it was real.

She grabbed her things, threw on a robe and rushed to the bathroom. She showered until she had rubbed her skin raw. When she emerged, her skin red and her fingers practically too pruned to use, she studied herself in the mirror. She found it hard to believe, that the wound was so small. She had tried not to touch it with her fingers, because that seemed to provoke unwanted phantom sensations on her skin, but she had let the water run over it for a very long time. It seemed gone, effectively invisible to the naked eye, no more than two small freckles on her neck. *She* could see the two perfectly round little punctures at her throat for what they really were, but no one who did not know, would ever notice them.

She had a sudden fierce desire to conduct the rest of her day in as mind numbingly normal a manner as possible. She would dress (being sure to wear her hair down, over her shoulders), go to class, follow her daily routine and put last night behind her. No one would ever know. She would never have to think on it again. She would be perfectly normal. Until sunset.

She couldn't even wrap her mind around the thought of seeing him again. It was too hugely incomprehensible. No, she would not let herself have another thought on the subject. As far as the world was concerned, nothing had happened to her and she would tell herself that as well. She went back to her room and dressed for class.

She immersed herself in her schoolwork with such fervor that her parents would surely be proud. Her attentiveness had been somewhat lacking lately, what with everything else going on. She decided that she would make up for it now, before she fell too far behind. It worked too. She managed to make herself forget what had happened and pretend all was normal, until lunch.

She had chosen a small round table inside the cafeteria, far from the food line. She sat reading a textbook as she ate, hoping that no one she knew would notice her; not that she had made many friends anyway. It didn't work. Ben and Alyson headed straight for her, as though this was where they had planned to meet. They each had a tray of food and were very wrapped up in their conversation as they approached and made themselves at home at her table.

"So then, he grabs the cross with his bare hand," Ben was saying.

"No way!" Allie was obviously quite engaged in the story. Felicity could not think of anything she would like less to be hearing right now. She did her best to ignore them.

"I swear! It was smoking!" Ben continued.

"The cross?" Allie asked.

"No, his hand! You could smell it, it was gross," Ben clarified.

"Sick! I can't believe you guys went without me!"

"You were working," Ben reminded her.

"So? It's not like I've never disappeared for a few hours before."

"Wait, it gets better." Ben put down his tray and as Allie sat in her chair, he knelt on the floor behind her. "He drops the cross, but still has her arm in a lock like this." He demonstrated on Allie while glancing up at Felicity. She still ignored him. He continued, with far too much drama, for her taste. "Then he leans over her shoulder and says 'Pain is a small sacrifice to make, if it gets you *what you need.*' and he kisses her right on the throat." Ben did so to Allie, who's mouth was open in disbelief.

"Get out! He did that?" She looked to Felicity. "That guy's got some set! Did you wet your pants?"

Ben answered for her, with an amused smile. "Sort of."

This was lost on Allie, who was still waiting for Felicity to answer. "Hello, Felicity?"

"What?" Felicity was forced from her silence.

"Were you scared?" Allie asked.

She thought for a moment and shuddered. "I should have been," she muttered.

Allie blew it off with a wave of her hand. "Ah, forget it. Vampires aren't all that scary. So they've got fangs, big deal."

Ben grabbed a chair, sat down next to Felicity and began to eat his lunch. She stared down at her food. "You're right. It's not really their teeth that you have to be afraid of."

This seemed to catch Ben's attention. "Are you okay?" he asked, with a little too much concerned insight for Felicity's comfort.

She forced herself to look at him with a smile. "Yeah, I'm fine." She turned to Allie, to change the subject. "Where's Greg?"

"I've moved on. His band sucks. Besides, he was so boring. That guy's burned out every brain cell he ever had in his head. Even *I* need *some* stimulating conversation!"

Felicity smiled. "You should sign up for some classes. You're always here anyway and it's a great way to meet guys. Just look at all the hotties walkin' around here." She glanced around the cafeteria, her gaze finally landing on Ben. He looked at her as if she were crazy, because of her suggestion for Allie, or because she had never shown an interest in any college guys for herself, she wasn't sure. Allie just laughed at her. "Really, why not?" Felicity pursued.

Alyson looked a little uncomfortable and shrugged. "What would I go for? I could never afford it, anyway."

"They have student loans and financial aid and stuff."

Felicity's attempt at this new subject was apparently just not going to work. Allie just shrugged again and went back to the prior conversation. "So, when are you guys going out again? I wanna stake some vamps!"

"We're not," Felicity said firmly. She knew she looked horrified, but was surprised to see that the look on Ben's face was similar.

"It's not a game Allie. We've had this talk before." Ben reprimanded her.

"Yeah I know, and then you go and break the pact without me, and I'm left sittin' in broad daylight, hearin' about it. What the hell is that?" Allie demanded.

"Alyson, it wasn't exactly something we planned," Ben insisted.

"What pact?" Felicity asked.

Ben answered her. "A bunch of us used to go looking for trouble. After David, we said we wouldn't do it anymore." He looked back to Allie. "Not that it ever stopped you," he added pointedly to her.

"Hey, I don't go lookin'. I work in a bar; the place is like a blood buffet. Trouble finds me."

"Whatever." He thought for moment. "You wanna go out hunting? Fine, let's do it."

"No." Felicity interjected sharply. "You don't want to be out at night. Not now."

"Why? What better time is there? I did some checking, and you were right. Half the football team is missing."

"What?! Well, then you just answered your own question! You wouldn't actually go out looking for them?"

"Why not? Better than them looking for someone else. If you weren't talking about the football team, then why didn't you want us to go? You don't think we should still be scared of Sindy do you? Because to be honest, I'm tired of letting her get to me. And even with those punks of hers, between the two of us, I think we could take her," he said with a smile at Allie.

Felicity sat in silence, as Allie and Ben stared at her expectantly. She decided she had better tell them what had happened, up until...the dorms. She couldn't bring herself to say anything at all about that. "We went for a ride last night," she began weakly.

"Who?" Allie asked.

"Her and Cain," Ben answered distractedly, leaning forward to give Felicity his full attention.

"We met this guy, another vampire. He wasn't like the others. He was old, I think. Like Cain. He was really creepy and he meant business. He said he didn't like the fact that Cain killed other vampires, and he knew that I'd killed one too, although I don't know how. I don't know what he plans to do about it and I don't want to know. I'm done. I'd be perfectly happy to never see another vampire again."

Ben spoke quietly, almost just to her. "Even Cain?"

He was staring, and she knew that he understood something was wrong. "There were more. The missing guys I guess, but not just them, more," she continued, without answering Ben. "They were in the woods, all around us. It was so eerie. They were watching us."

"The old guy, the creepy one, what'd he look like?" asked Allie.

"He didn't look old. He looked like he was in his late twenties, when he died anyway, but he acted old. Like...confident, mature. He was dark, like from the middle east or something. Really long black hair, he said his name was 'Arif.'"

"Never seen him at Tommy's, I don't think," Allie remarked.

Ben pulled his chair closer to her. "What did Cain say to this guy?"

"He just kind of put him off, said they should talk another time, that he was busy," Felicity said quietly.

"With you?" Ben asked.

She tried not to look at him. "That he had to drive me home."

"And the guy accepted that?"

"I guess. He let us leave," Felicity replied.

"Well, at least the guy's somewhat civilized. Let Cain handle him," Ben decided.

"Yes," Felicity quickly agreed, "let Cain do it. Let's just stay out of it all, from now on. It's none of our business,"

"Aren't you worried about Cain, that this guy's after him or something?"

She knew Ben was fishing around for some kind of emotion out of her. She was afraid that he could tell that Cain had her spooked. She had to keep forcing her hands to stay in her lap; they wanted to reach up and feel the bite. "Cain can take care of himself."

Alyson spoke up. "You know, he's pretty cool for a blood sucker. I'm always kind of bitchy to him when I see him at the bar, but it never seems to faze him. You'd think he'd try to scare me, just to get me out of his face by now. He just smiles and takes it."

Ben rolled his eyes at her. "What, are *you* joining the 'Cain fan club' too?"

"I'm just saying, maybe not all vamps are so bad after all. Don't you think it might be nice to have a vampire on *our* side for a change? You've gotta admit, the guy's got class." She turned to Felicity. "You seem awful close with him. You hangin' out regular with this guy?"

She forced herself to sound normal; she didn't want to trigger any alarms in Ben's head. "I see him sometimes. He comes into the 'DownTime' a lot."

Allie smiled. "Yeah, but this doesn't sound like work. These sound like extra-curricular activities to me."

She suddenly remembered that Alyson had been bitten before, by Sindy. She had a terribly unreasonable urge to ask her about it. Instead, she fought to sound casual and just answer the question as shortly as possible. "He just walks me home sometimes. It's nothing."

Ben seemed annoyed. He stood and gathered his stuff off the table. "I'm not workin' tonight, and I know 'Liss has off. You guys wanna do something?"

"Ben..." Felicity warned.

"Something normal. No vampires."

Alyson stood up as she finished the last bite of her muffin. "I have to work. You guys want to come over to Tommy's? I'll steal you some free drinks."

Ben looked to Felicity. "What do you think?"

She tried not to meet his eyes without seeming self-conscious about it. "I've got a lot of homework. I think I'm just going to stay in tonight." *With the door locked*, she added mentally.

She could feel Ben staring at her, but forced herself not to look. She just gathered her garbage onto her tray and put away her book.

Ben turned back to Allie. "I don't know, maybe you'll see me. If not, I'll catch you tomorrow. Same time, same station." He gave a little wave and left.

"See ya," Alyson said, as she headed for the opposite exit. Felicity almost stopped her. She'd like to ask about Alyson's bite from Sindy, without Ben around, but then she decided against it. It would seem strange, and Ben was sure to hear about it later. Instead, she busied herself mentally with wondering exactly how she should go about trying to un-invite Cain from her room.

Chapter 20 - Crusade

Cain

The DownTime café and bookstore
8:45, Tuesday night

Cain took the last swig of his coffee and closed the book that he had been forcing himself to try and read. He had only read the first paragraph, but he had read it about three times. He still had no idea what it really said.

At least Lucy and Harold were working tonight. He didn't even have to pretend to be friendly with them. He was conveniently ignored. When he had first awoken, he had been unsure what to do. He was not ready to face Felicity or any of her friends either, for that matter. He had thought he should find out just what Arif wanted from him, but he wasn't planning on going back to Venus. Why should he seek the man out? *If Arif wants something, he can come to me,* Cain thought. He was sure to feed well this evening though, thinking that he may need his strength, although after the sweet nectar he had tasted last night, anything less was rather difficult to swallow.

He had decided to take the motorcycle into town, just in case he needed to leave in a hurry. As he had approached the DownTime, he'd begun to feel the warm and beckoning sensation of a victim, one of his own; something he had not felt in years. It was Felicity. His mark was on her and he could feel her now, in his mind. Her trace was like a new glowing ember, calling him, begging to be fanned into flame. She was his. His own personal signature seemed to glow around her for all to see; all of his kind anyway.

She wasn't at the café, she was further. Locked away in her room probably. That was just fine with him. He was glad and disappointed at the same time that his house wasn't close enough to feel her always. Although sensing her trace was reassuring at first, he knew it was for the best that there be some distance between them. Eventually it would be a terrible temptation, taunting him, begging him to come to her. It was better that he had a refuge, where he could try and forget for a while.

As he had turned into the lot, he had been relieved to see that Ben's car was not there. He seemed to be having good luck tonight. He was quite happy to be left alone for now. So he had sat, forcing himself to try and read, but for the last hour, all he had really done was scan for others (he found none) and try not to dwell on Felicity (impossible). Closing time was soon, he would have to leave. He would head over to Tommy's, even though he would probably have to put up with Alyson there. Where else was there to go?

There was no band tonight, a fact for which he was very grateful. The place was moderately full. He got a drink and sat at an empty table near the door. He had hardly drained his glass when Alyson inevitably approached.

She came to lean on his table as if they were old friends. "Well, look who decided to show up. I heard about that stunt you pulled."

Cain stared hard at her. The mark she had received from Sindy was fading. Did she know what had happened last night? Had Felicity enlisted her friends in an effort to protect herself from him? He tried to sound non-chalant. "Just which stunt are you referring to?"

"With the cross. I didn't know you were teaching 'Vampires 101'. Is it too late for me to enroll?"

Cain let out a sigh of mixed relief and annoyance. "I came in here to be alone Alyson, so if you don't mind..."

"Sorry, not gonna happen."

"And pray tell, why not?" he asked, imposingly.

Alyson laughed, undaunted. "Cain, this is the twenty-first century. Nobody says 'pray tell'. You should at least *try* to blend," she scolded him.

He bit back his annoyance and tried again. "**Why** will you not be leaving me alone?"

"Oh, it's not me. There's somebody else waitin' to see ya'."

Now he looked around in confusion. Who could she be talking about? Ben was the person who immediately leapt to mind. He knew Felicity wasn't here, but he would be unable to feel Ben. Had he come looking for retribution? "Where?"

"At a table in the back. Oh, don't worry. He hasn't seen you yet. I think it's gotta be that creepy 'Arif' guy though. He fits Felicity's description and he's been sitting there alone since I got here. I figured he must be waiting for you. I guess somebody forgot to tell him that you take your coffee at the DownTime first." He was taken aback that she should know of Arif and that the man was here without Cain's knowledge. Although he shouldn't be so surprised, obviously Arif could cloak himself as well as Cain.

Alyson continued. "Actually it's kind of funny. He doesn't know you're here, and you didn't know he was here; I'm the only one who recognized you both and I don't even know what the hell is going on!"

"You saw Felicity today?"

She seemed puzzled that this was what he should be asking after. She certainly regarded Arif as the matter of importance here. "Yeah, I met her and Ben for lunch. Why?"

Felicity had obviously spoken of *some* of their doings last night and yet Alyson was unafraid of him. She wasn't angry or upset by him at all, in fact she was suddenly quite accepting of him. Had Felicity really not told them what he had done? "No reason. Tell me, have you seen any others in here tonight?"

"I don't think so, but you could probably tell better than me."

Before last night, he would have agreed with her. "Right. Thank you, you've been most helpful."

"No sweat. You want me to keep him distracted while you head for the door?" Allie asked.

Cain smiled. "I don't think that'll be necessary."

"If you want, I could send him over a drink from you. I bet that'd freak him out."

Cain raised an eyebrow at her. "Were you volunteering as the drink?"

The question seemed to catch her off guard. That was fun, Allie was usually pretty un-fazable. "Well, no," she stammered. "That wasn't really what I meant." She recovered her smile. She knew he must be joking, but got the hint. "I guess I should let you handle it, huh?"

He returned her smile. "I think that would be best." She gave him a little nod and moved off into the crowd.

Cain emptied his glass and revisited the bar to refill it, before seeking out Arif's table. He was there, alone, just as Alyson had described. He wore his hair back to expose a small gold hoop earring in one ear and was dressed in a dark midnight blue silk shirt, with a gold chain at his throat. Cain also noticed that he wore what was surely a very expensive gold watch and his hands bore several jeweled rings. Cain had never been impressed by such blatant shows of affluence. Money among his kind really held no meaning, especially since most vampires acquired it through deceit and treachery.

Cain approached slowly, so as not to catch him off guard and make him defensive. It was not long before he was seen. Arif greeted him with a broad smile and gestured for Cain to come and join him. "Cain, I was hoping to see you here. You are a difficult man to find."

Cain took the proffered seat and put his drink on the table. "You didn't seem to have any problem finding me last night."

Arif smiled. "Ah, but you give more credit than I am due. Our meeting last night, was simply a fortunate chance of fate and circumstance." He leaned forward, confidentially. "You may rest assured that your presence remains effectively concealed." Cain tried not to make too obvious his relief. He had grown far too used to the fact that others could not 'see' him. He was afraid that he had become foolishly unwary. Arif sat back with a grin. "You are very good at it actually," he said. "Almost as good as me."

Now it was Cain's turn to grin. "Almost? And the others?"

"As I am sure you had already surmised, they were under my 'protective wing', if you will." Cain could not hide the confusion on his face. He had not known that such a thing was possible. Arif interpreted his expression with some surprise. "You have not encountered this trick before? 'Tis a simple thing, for those of our skill. You could do it, if you tried. Consider it a gift of knowledge. I give it freely, to one who has taken it upon himself to teach so many others."

Cain gave him a tight, thin-lipped smile. He found this man's easy arrogance quite grating. Arif took a sip of his drink, straight vodka from the smell, and continued. "I have heard tell of you many times in the past. You have piqued my curiosity, and so when I found that I was in your vicinity, I thought it only fitting that I should seek you out."

"Is that so?"

"Do not be too flattered. For now that I have found you, I am not yet sure what I shall do."

Cain became impatient. "I can see that you rather enjoy all of this 'cloak and dagger' mysteriousness, but to be entirely honest, *I* find it quite annoying. You wished to speak with me. Here I am. Can you not plainly say whatever it is you have come to say?"

Arif did not even flinch, but regarded Cain in a patient and appraising manner. "Your reputation precedes you. They speak of you in many places. It is said that you alone have taken on a sort of crusade among our kind."

"A *vampire crusade?* Are you sure you've the right man?" Cain asked with some amusement. "I wasn't aware that I'd become notorious. Just what is it you've heard?"

"Some call you an educator. They say that you teach the young ones of our kind, who've no proper mentors of their own. 'The Teacher', they call you. Then, of course, there are others who simply call you a 'pain in the ass'."

Cain smiled. "Yes, well, that does sound about accurate."

"You try to teach the young ones how to feed without killing," Arif clarified.

Cain gave a small nod of agreement. Then added regretfully, "When I must."

Arif smiled. "Then is it also true, that you prefer them not to drink from humans at all?"

"It's not necessary."

"To leave a body that is warm and pulsing, can be difficult enough. When they are young, it is unreasonable to expect them to have the restraint that you and I possess," Arif insisted.

Cain perked up and clung to this last remark. "You also do not drink?"

Arif smirked at his misunderstanding. "I drink, I do not kill. It is a pointless risk. And why deplete the herd?"

At this, Cain was outraged. "It's not 'game management'! It's an aesthetic choice!"

"Do not be offended. I merely state my point of view. Whatever our reasoning, our views coincide." Cain was not so easily mollified. He took a sip of his drink to avoid saying something he might regret as Arif went on. "Then the rumors are true? That your own propensity, is for abstinence from humans? How can you suffer yourself to drink such vile substance as animal blood?"

"It is my personal choice. I didn't ask you to come here and criticize my method of existence," Cain said coldly.

"And yet you criticize every other vampire that you meet, do you not?" Arif said.

"I give them a choice that many are not aware of. We do not need to prey upon humans to survive. Animal blood is a perfectly viable alternative for those who wish it," Cain clarified.

"And those who do not?" Arif asked.

"I teach them control," Cain told him.

"And those who will not learn it, find themselves turned into large piles of ash," Arif concluded.

"That's not true," Cain said sternly.

"You would lie to me? I suppose you would be a fool if you did not," Arif said with a smile.

"I do not lie, and I do not kill without sufficient reason."

"Sufficient for whom? Did you not dispose of four of our kind, just a few nights ago?" Arif asked.

"They attacked me without provocation, and left me no alternative." Arif sighed. "Do you doubt my word?" Cain asked.

"I believe only that which I observe. That is why I am here, but I find myself in a bit of a quandary, to be honest. You see, for all of our differences, we are still of like minds on some things. I find you an interesting entity with whom I might like to discuss much. However, a curious thing happened upon my arrival in this quaint little town of yours. I was immediately beset upon by an acquaintance of recent past."

"Sindy," conjectured Cain.

"None other. I will speak plainly. In other circumstances, she is not one I would invite for association. I do not care for her. I do however, feel that I am somewhat obligated to see to her well-being. It was I, not so long ago, who killed her sire," Arif confided.

Cain lifted his brows in surprise. "So, I'm not the only one with ash on my hands then?"

"Hardly," Arif replied with a smile. "Vampires are immortal, and grudges last long. Killing each other has been a favorite pass time since time began I would suppose. Otherwise we would rule the world." Cain acceded this point, and Arif continued. "He was detestable and I am sure she hardly mourned him, but she was newly made and alone. Now, while it is true that I have allowed a small few carefully chosen women into my coven, this is not for her. She is far too willful and I am not a patient man. So, I took my leave of her. I was quite surprised to encounter her again. She is more resourceful than I had assumed. I had not truly expected her to survive. She comes to me now for protection, from you."

Cain laughed. "Well, it is not her death so much I seek. I wish only to be left alone; me *and mine.*"

"Ah, but here we have conflict. I must point out, that due to your 'aesthetic choice', none here are *yours.*"

Cain gave him a resentful stare. "Sindy knows perfectly well for whom I speak, but there is no conflict. My mark is upon her now."

Arif was evidently astounded by this information. "You have marked *your lady?*" he asked, with a bemused grin. "I must say, this is a most unexpected, yet welcome development. I commend you for your good sense, though I do hope it was not for fear of me," he said with a chuckle. Cain downed the last of his drink, although he would really rather throw it in Arif's face. "And the male?"

"Who?" Cain asked in confusion.

"There is another, a male whom Sindy seeks to claim."

Cain broke into a broad smile. "Benjamin? I'd like to see her try! It would save me further dealing with her."

Arif looked puzzled. "He knows her? Her nature?"

"He does," Cain assured him.

"And he is hostile."

Cain smiled again, thinking of a meeting between the two, now that Benjamin had been given a stake with practice and his blessing to use it in self defense. "Undoubtedly."

"So, am I to assume that you leave him unmarked willingly?"

Cain studied the man for a moment. "For *her* endeavor, yes. I believe the boy can fend for himself. He is unmarked, but make no mistake, I am not leaving him to you."

"Be not alarmed. I bring my own."

Cain tried to hide the sickened disgust he felt at that knowledge. He was not entirely naive to the ways of others, however distasteful he might find them. "Just so we're clear. You may consider her request fulfilled." Cain prepared himself to leave.

"Unfortunately, I must inform you that protection was not her sole request." Cain sighed and gave his attention back to Arif. "She seeks retribution as well."

"*Retribution!* For what; those living corpses she unceasingly thrusts into my path? Those who are wise enough to value what little life they still possess, should refrain from attacking me!"

Arif seemed to be in sympathy with him and laughed. "I have seen that she is not skilled in the art of creation. And it is true also, that she is far too reproductive, but I cannot entirely overlook her entreaty. You yourself have admitted that it has some substance, and I do still consider her my ward. I cannot completely disregard her."

Cain looked at him in disbelief. "I have granted her safety, for as long as she does nothing unwise towards me. I have marked the one that I wish to remain unaccosted. I owe nothing more. I believe that we are finished here." He paused a moment, to see if Arif would dispute him.

Instead, Arif raised his glass to Cain and took his final sip. "I am glad to have met you, whatever the circumstance. I give you my word that I shall not raise a hand against you, for as long as Sindy remains unharmed. I am sure you will be unoffended if I choose to remain hereabouts for a while. Perhaps we shall speak again. Company of our caliber is rare to find." Cain merely gave him an almost imperceptible nod, and left.

Chapter 21 - Interrogating Allie

Felicity

Wednesday morning

Felicity tossed and turned in her bed until she finally awoke. Vague sensual stirrings flitted just beyond reach. She painstakingly avoided trying to remember any dreams she might have had. Instead of lounging in bed for a few minutes, she forced herself to rise and immediately began to busy herself with preparing for the day.

Just as the day before, she dove into her classes with extra attention, trying to give her mind no time to wander. She wasn't entirely successful, having to call back her attention from thoughts of Cain now and then; but by the time lunch came, she was pleasantly preoccupied with thoughts of discussion from anthropology. It was one of the few classes she actually enjoyed and could be counted upon for distraction.

Felicity reached the cafeteria and glanced around, cautiously. The last thing she wanted was to bring down her day with talk of vampires. She considered taking her lunch back to her room, to avoid Ben and Alyson, but finally decided against it. Lunch with them had become a habit during the week. They'd think it strange if she went that far to avoid them. It would be better if she could get them to avoid the topic of vampires and any involvement altogether; better but not likely.

She found Alyson sitting alone at the table they had used yesterday. She still saw no sign of Ben. Maybe this was an opportunity for her. Instead of avoiding the topic, a plan that was unlikely to be successful anyway, she could have a chance to talk to Allie about being bitten by Sindy. She was afraid to broach the subject with Ben around; he was too likely to be savvy about her sudden interest, but Allie would probably remain clueless, she hoped. She went to the table and sat down.

Allie looked up with some relief as she arrived. "I was starting to think I'd be eating by myself today. Where's Ben?"

"I don't know, I haven't seen him."

"I texted him but he's not answering me," Allie replied.

Felicity looked down at Allie's tray, which held a muffin, and an odd assortment of snack cakes and juice. "That's your lunch?"

"No, of course not; breakfast." She laughed at Felicity's raised eyebrows. "I work until four in the morning, sleep 'til noon; come here for breakfast with Ben. Tuesday through Thursday, and every other Monday anyway. Friday's his schedule's all weird."

Felicity smiled at her thorough and precise knowledge of Ben's schedule. "You guys have been friends like, forever huh?"

"Yep, pretty much."

"Have you ever been...more? I mean, you guys practically act like you're married."

"Me and Ben? No. That'd be like dating my brother. Besides, he's way too picky and annoying. He'd drive me nuts. If we ever had sex, he'd probably tell me I was doin' it wrong." She laughed. "We'd kill each other. No. Ben is the guy that I talk to about *other* guys."

Felicity glanced around again, still no sign of him. How could she bring the conversation around to being bitten? Ben would probably show up as soon as she got Allie talking. "It must be nice to have such a close friend; to know each other so well, that you can talk about anything."

"Yeah… Don't you have any good friends like that?"

Felicity shrugged, noncommittally. "I used to, back home. Deidre and I used to be inseparable, but after graduation we kind of got into different things. Now we're in different schools, you lose touch."

"Don't let it fade away - not if she was a good friend. You should call her. You don't get history just anywhere. There's something special about friends you've been through stuff with."

"You're right. Sounds like you and Ben have been through quite a bit. Did you guys really used to go vampire hunting?"

Allie glanced around, looking for Ben, Felicity supposed. Taboo topic. "Yeah, like every weekend since we were old enough to sneak out at night. It started out as kind of a joke, but around here, obviously it got un-funny pretty fast."

"You ever kill any?"

"I have, a long time ago. Earned me some status actually. Me and three guys and I'm the only one who ever accomplished anything. He won't admit it, but I think Ben always kind of resented that."

"Did you ever get...hurt?" Felicity asked.

Allie gave her a slightly puzzled look. "Sure. You saw my latest." She tugged down the collar of her shirt a little. The bite was almost healed, but Felicity could still see the ragged line of raised skin that was surely becoming a scar.

"Oh, right. Sindy bit you." As if she had forgotten. "What was that like? Was it...painful?"

"Not really." Allie sat uncharacteristically still for a moment. Then she shrugged it off. "I was all pumped up on adrenaline. We'd been goin' at it for a while and I screwed up. I did something stupid and she tagged me. It was getting her off me that hurt."

"Was that the only time you ever got bit?"

Allie studied her closely for a minute and Felicity began to wish she hadn't asked. "No." She glanced up behind Felicity and smiled. "Here comes Ben. Nice of you to join us. Not that you'll have any time left to eat. Would it kill you to check your phone once in awhile?"

Ben came up to the table with some books and a sandwich in one hand, and a piece of paper in the other. "Sorry, I kind of got caught up with something," he said with a wave of the paper.

"What's that?" asked Alyson.

"Oh, it's nothing; from my 'Critical Issues' class." He shoved the paper under the cover of one of his books as he put them on the table. "So, what's the topic of conversation?"

Felicity and Allie looked at each other in a way that was sure to be interpreted as incriminating. "Friendship," Allie answered.

Ben gave them a strange look. "Cool subject."

Allie smiled and sat up straighter. "Yeah, but we were just biding our time, until we could get to the real gossip."

"Is that so?" Ben asked, taking a seat. He pulled a water bottle out of his jacket pocket and began to unwrap his sandwich.

Allie smiled at Felicity. "We wouldn't want you to miss anything. Guess who came into Tommy's last night?"

Neither of them seemed to plan on guessing, but Allie paused for dramatic effect. "Arif." Both of them appropriately widened their eyes. "I swear it was him," she said as she looked to Felicity, "and I agree, the word 'creepy' is totally appropriate. I don't think I'd talk to that guy, even if he *were* alive."

Felicity wasn't sure she wanted to know any more, but had to ask. "Was he alone?"

"No. Cain went to keep him company," Allie reported smugly.

Not what she had expected. "He did? What did he say? Did they argue?"

"I don't know, they didn't exactly invite me over."

Ben cut in. "Well, did it look like they were fighting?"

Allie shrugged. "Not really. Cain looked like he got mad once or twice, but they didn't cause a scene or anything."

"Didn't you hear anything they said?" Felicity asked impatiently.

"I couldn't stay close enough, they'd notice. Like I need two more vampires pissed off at me. They talked for almost an hour though, and they both survived. That's *good*, right?"

Felicity struggled with her own worries. "I wish I knew."

Ben didn't seem undecided though. "Let them kill each other. Two less vampires for us to worry about, right?"

Felicity and Alyson both looked up at him in unison. "Ben!"

Ben glared at Felicity. "What?"

It was Allie who answered. "You may not like him, but he's still saved *your* neck once or twice."

"Probably more times than that," Felicity muttered.

Ben continued to glare at her. "You girls are so stupid. If he looked like 'Nosferatu' you would have staked him by now."

Felicity looked at him quizzically. "Who? I've never heard of him. Is that even English?"

Ben laughed. "German, I think. You know, the vampire guy." He twisted his hands into claws and made a horrible face, baring his teeth and trying to bug out his eyes. "From that old movie. Anyway the point is, if you didn't like the way Cain looked so much, he wouldn't stand a chance."

Felicity didn't have the heart to say much. She was offended, but thought that he was probably right. Allie seemed insulted though. "That's not true. I don't judge people by their looks."

Ben answered Allie, but was still glaring at Felicity. "Yeah, well *you're* not the one sleeping with him."

Now that was too much! Felicity opened her mouth in shock and then stood up in a rage. "I am not sleeping with him!"

Her mouth kept moving but the right words just wouldn't come out over her anger. Finally she spat out, "You're such a jerk!" and sat down with a thump in her chair. "You don't know me half as well as you think you do, Benjamin Everheart," she added in disgust.

Ben looked surprised and must have realized he had gone too far, but his stubborn streak wouldn't seem to let him back down. He leaned back in his chair and crossed his arms. "So, maybe you're not. I'm sure it's just a matter of time."

Alyson leaned over and smacked him in the back of the head. "Ben, stop being such an ass." He looked like he'd like to hit her back, but settled for a fierce stare. Alyson ignored him and spoke to Felicity. "Don't listen to him. An 'inter-species' relationship must be a bit of a challenge, but Cain is a pretty cool guy."

Felicity spoke with a quiet, measured voice. "There is no relationship. New subject."

Alyson was happy to oblige. "Okay." She grabbed Ben's book and took out the paper he'd been holding. "Let's see what's got Ben so interested that he was late for lunch."

Ben tried to grab it back from her, but it was too late. Alyson had already seen it and was laughing. She let him have it. "Whoa, not what I expected!" She gave Felicity an amused smile. "It's a phone number. Who's Brenda?"

Ben was a bit flushed and annoyed. "She's in my 'Critical Issues in Law and Society' class."

"New study buddy?" Allie asked with a grin.

"Hardly," he said with a chuckle as he looked over to Felicity. "This is purely social."

"I'm sure Ashley will be devastated," she said sarcastically.

"Ah shit," Ben mumbled mildly, dropping his smile.

Alyson smiled and put her hand on his shoulder, which he promptly swatted away. "Poor Ben, you were never very good at trying to juggle girls."

"I'm not trying to juggle anybody. It's just, I saw Ashley last night, and I have a feeling she thinks that I'm going to take her to the Homecoming Dance on Saturday."

"Did you actually ask her?" asked Allie.

"No, but other than me, Ashley usually dates guys on the football team. That means that the rest of her options are currently sporting fangs, or flying about the cemetery as little motes of dust, courtesy of our field trip the other night. Kind of makes me look like a shmuck."

Felicity answered him quietly. "She doesn't know that, and we didn't kill them, Sindy did. Ashley hasn't got a clue what's going on."

"That's typical," said Allie with a smirk.

"Have you heard half the rumors that have been going around?" Felicity asked.

Ben laughed hollowly. "Somebody told me that the missing guys all took off to Atlantic City on some kind of pre-game road trip or something. People are so stupid."

"Why are they even having a 'Homecoming Dance'?" Allie asked. "Isn't the dance supposed to celebrate winning the football game? How are they gonna play with no team?"

Ben shook his head. "There's a team, just not a very good one, they use second string. They still have the dance, even if we lose."

"People are dying and you're worried about who you're going to take to some dumb dance?" Felicity caught sight of the clock on the wall across the room. "Oh my God! Look what time it is! Now you made me late for chemistry!" Felicity accused them as she started gathering her stuff.

Ben just rolled his eyes at her. Allie held out a hand to stop her before she could leave. "Wait, are you gonna see Cain tonight?"

Felicity gave her a look of agitation. "I don't know."

"Well, are you working?" Allie asked.

"Until eight," Felicity replied.

"He'll probably show up to walk you home, right?" she prodded.

Ben sounded annoyed. "What do you care?"

"I wanna know what happened, don't you?" Allie asked insistently. Ben just shrugged. "It was like trying to watch a soap opera with the sound off."

"He doesn't come every night," Felicity said quietly.

"I'm sure he'll be there," Ben muttered.

"Well, I'm there too," Allie said.

"What are you going to do, hang out in the bookstore all night?" Felicity asked.

"No, she'll hang out in the café and bother me," said Ben.

Felicity gave him a sour look. "Are you closing tonight?

Ben smiled. "Yeah, with Ashley. Should be fun, huh?"

Felicity didn't even answer; she just gave him a parting glare of irritation and hurried off to class.

~~~~~~~~~~~~~~~~~~~~~~~~~~~~~~

The class was almost half over by the time she got there. Luckily, it was a large lecture hall and she was able to slip in unnoticed. Karen had saved her a seat. As the lecture ended, Karen turned to her eagerly. "I was afraid I wouldn't see you."

"Yeah, I got stuck arguing with Ben."

"You guys aren't dating are you?" Karen asked.

Felicity looked at her in amazement. "Oh no; most definitely not. At the moment, I am unquestionably single."

Karen grinned. "So, are we going to hit 'Ladies Night' again?" she asked as she gathered her things.

"What?"

"At Tommy's. I thought maybe we'd go again tonight."

"No, I wasn't going to. I mean, that was just a one-time deal."

Karen stopped, gazing at her in disappointment. "Didn't you have fun last time?"

Felicity just shrugged. "It's just not really my thing."

Karen slumped back down into her seat as the rest of the students emptied out of the class. "Well, that kind of throws a wrench into the works."

"What do you mean?"

"Well, we were supposed to go. Then we were supposed to accidentally/on purpose bump into Jack's friend Todd there."

"Todd?"

"Yeah, he's really cute and sweet, and I know you'd like him. See, he used to go out with this girl, Myra. They were like, our 'couple' friends, you know, that we did 'couples' stuff with. Only, about a month ago Myra pretty much ripped Todd's heart out and stomped all over it.

He's been absolutely devastated, I feel terrible for him. So, I thought it would be good for him to get out. Hang out with somebody different, to make him feel a little better about himself. I really think you'd like him."

"I don't know," Felicity said apprehensively. "I don't want to be 'rebound girl'."

"Oh, you won't. I mean you don't even have to date him or anything. I just thought we could hang out, the four of us - no pressure. You know, you could like, laugh at his jokes and make him feel all witty and attractive. Just so he's not so...suicidal."

"But, no pressure."

"None, really."

"Well, fun as that sounds, I think I'm going to pass. I'm kind of avoiding Tommy's."

"You don't like it there?"

"Well, it's not the greatest, but there's someone I really don't want to bump into and he might be there."

"Oh, like an ex-boyfriend thing?"

"Sort of."

"Well, how about if we go to Venus?"

"No!"

"Ookay. So you don't like Venus either. We could see a movie. Nice and dark, limited possibly for recognition by ex-boyfriends. You wouldn't even have to act like Todd was witty. Which is good, because he's really not. He is sweet though. What do you say?"

"Well, a movie might be okay." She thought about it as she stood and got her stuff together. "But I'm working until eight tonight."

"That's okay, we could pick you up," Karen said eagerly as they made their way out of the class.

"Yeah?" As a matter of fact, this might work out very well. "Could you come and pick me up right at eight?"

"Sure, no problem. In fact, if it's not going to be all 'accidental', I could ask Todd to drive. He has a much nicer car."

"That sounds good. Are you sure? I should expect you at eight?"

"Definitely. Even if it doesn't all work out with Todd, Jack and I will come and pick you up and we'll just go."

"Okay. Great, I'll see you later."

This might work out very well. Karen and company could come and pick her up right from work. Cain hadn't been coming in for coffee, to sit and read the way that he used to. If he were going to come for her, he probably wouldn't come until later.

He wouldn't know what time she was working until. If he assumed she was closing, he might not even show up until almost nine. Maybe she could get out of there without even seeing him. It was worth a try.

Chapter 22 - Staying away

Cain

Wednesday night

Cain paced his room like the caged beast he felt he was. He was unsure how to deal with the past few night's developments. He was overwhelmed and impatient. He felt like the crotchety old man he should surely be at 340 years of age.

He hated that Arif and these others were in his space. Sindy and her boys had been difficult enough to deal with. Now his progress with Sindy, Luke and Chris was destroyed. If Sindy had ever felt the slightest inclination to try his method of existence, it would be gone now. She would never submit to his ways, now that she felt she had others to back her up. If he were going to be honest with himself, she'd seemed pretty inflexible to begin with, but with time and patience, she might have changed. It was a moot point, now he would never know.

That was bad enough, but his real bone of contention was over Felicity. They had made him feel forced to mark her before either of them were ready. He had hoped for more time, to ease into things, in a way she might actually be able to accept. Now he'd panicked and it had been done in a hasty and upsetting manner. He had no idea how she would react when she saw him again.

He hated other vampires. Now Arif and his hoard would be hanging around and he felt obligated to stay out of their way, because at this point he did not want to start a feud that would endanger those humans that he had become accustomed to being with. The whole situation made him sick.

What he really wanted to do was to steal Felicity away to a remote location and forget everyone else. Fear kept him from that. Not fear of another vampire, or for the fate of Ben and Alyson, although that would weigh on his conscience as well. The fear was that Felicity would never forgive him or understand. Without time and finesse, she would surely hate him, that it would all have been for nothing. That put a cold pit of fear into his stomach like nothing else could.

Being hunted didn't bother him. He'd lived with that for ages. He was confident he could win most any fight. If he couldn't, death would almost be a welcome rest, but to be rejected by one he had chosen to open his heart to... that would be unbearable.

He didn't want to go to his usual haunts. His ways were far too methodic. Anyone seeking him would know exactly where to look and he didn't want to deal with anyone tonight. He wanted to let the nights go by in seclusion until he could go to Felicity again.

Right now, he knew it was too soon. He could try to tell himself that he had control enough to see her, but he knew it would not be wise. It was likely that her blood still pulsed within him, just as his venom was within her. If they got close, the connection would be very strong. He would feel almost that she was part of him and he part of her. The need to commune with her, through the blood would be a difficult thing to bear unfulfilled.

He had not drunk from a human in decades. To resist something all but forgotten was not nearly so difficult as it would be now. How hard would it be to keep himself from wanting to repeat the experience of only two nights ago? It was sure to be upsetting, especially if she were hostile towards him. Keeping his vampire nature in check required a delicate balance of self-control and awareness of himself. It was too soon. He might seem in control, but if he was barely restraining himself and then she provoked him with harsh words or physical contact, that balance could easily be upset. Instinct would try to take over. He needed her to accept being with him in private for explanations, and he could not trust himself to be alone with her this soon. He hated the fact that this was so, but at least he was being honest with himself.

So here he was, pacing, secluded away, with nothing to do but wait. It was nearly intolerable, unacceptable…it was too much. The movies. He would go to the theater, his favorite refuge of times past. He had spent whole nights in movie theaters, watching one show after another. Marvelous accomplishments, films of today. As large multiplex theaters were becoming more and more prevalent, he was coming to appreciate them more than ever. They were found everywhere and often open late into the wee hours of the morning.

When they were first introduced, he'd been delighted to have found such a perfect sanctuary. He could spend his entire evening, anonymous and unaccosted, and yet feel as if he were somehow connected to society again. He could better understand people's views and feelings in this almost alien seeming age that was so different from the world he had known when he was alive. Yes, he would lose himself in the movies. He would find one of the big multiplexes and watch every show they had until he felt the coming dawn drive him home. Confident in his solution and finally feeling he had some purpose, he made his way outside to his waiting motorcycle and thundered off into the night.

❦ ❧ ❦ ❧ ❦ ❧ ❦ ❧ ❦ ❧ ❦ ❧ ❦ ❧ ❦

Part 3 ~ Venomous Revelations

❦ ❧ ❦ ❧ ❦ ❧ ❦ ❧ ❦ ❧ ❦ ❧ ❦ ❧ ❦

Chapter 23 ~ Distraction

Felicity

The DownTime café and bookstore
7:45, Wednesday night

Felicity looked up from her register to see Allie enter the store. She had known that Alyson would inevitably show up, but she still had to stifle a groan upon seeing her actually arrive. She didn't want to have to socialize, she just wanted this night to be over. Not that her days were much better lately.

She had tried to keep busy, but still caught herself thinking of Cain sometimes. As bizarre as it might seem, she missed him. She'd find herself thinking of the endearing way he was always swiping the hair back from his face, or how the blue of his eyes seemed so deep and clear, almost iridescent; the rakish hint of a smile he would have, whenever he was teasing her.

Then she would have to stop and remind herself that he was not who she'd thought he was; to try and remember what he had done, without actually reliving it. It seemed almost like he was two different people; the Cain she had enjoyed spending time with and daydreamed about, and the vampire who had bitten her and stolen her blood.

Now here came Alyson to remind her of him yet again. "Hey! Where's Cain?"

She sighed. Couldn't they just let her try to forget him? "He's not here."

"Well the sun went down almost twenty minutes ago, how far away does he live?" Felicity just shook her head and looked up at the ceiling. Alyson continued, with a mischievous smile. "Maybe he likes to have *breakfast* before coffee." Felicity opened her mouth in disgust. "Look at you all shocked and astonished. He's a vampire Felicity; he's got to drink blood sometime."

That was a disturbing thought. "But does he have to? I mean, couldn't he just...refrain?"

Allie chuckled. "Yeah right, and how long could you abstain from eating?"

"But that's different, I'm alive. His body is, well... I just thought he could...do without, if he wanted," Felicity admitted.

"Sorry sweetie, it doesn't work that way," Allie insisted.

"How do you know?"

"Trust me, he's drinkin' somethin'. He needs it. I think I'm gonna go pick on Ben for a while. He kind of expects it and I'd hate to disappoint him," Allie said with a chuckle.

Felicity was still perplexed over the thought of Cain drinking *someone's* blood all this time, even before he'd bitten her. Somehow, she just thought that he could deny himself. And why did Allie just accept it so matter of factly? Didn't the thought even bother her? Maybe Alyson was wrong. Cain couldn't have been drinking people's blood all this time without her knowing, could he? Was she really so easy to deceive? How did Alyson get to be such an authority anyway?

Ah well, at least it was just about time for her to leave. She went to find Ashley in the back of the store, shelving books. "I'm going to get ready to go."

"Oh, is it eight o'clock already?" Ashley asked.

"Almost, and I have friends coming to pick me up."

"Okay, I guess I'll see you in class Friday." Felicity turned to go, when Ashley stopped her. "Hey Felicity, can I ask you something?"

"Sure, what?"

"You and Ben aren't...dating, are you?" Ashley asked hesitantly.

"No." Why did people keep asking her that?

"Oh, I was just wondering. Have you noticed anything wrong with him? He's been acting kind of weird lately."

"Weird how?"

"Well, I let him take me out last night, but he was like, all distracted and preoccupied. I was prepared to be very accommodating, if you know what I mean, but he might as well not even have been there. He was very inattentive. That is *so* not like him, and I can't say I was very happy about it. He'd better step up and take a little better notice of me, or I might not let him take me to the dance on Saturday."

Felicity looked at her wearily. "Ashley, I am the last person you should be asking for insight on Ben. I don't know what is wrong with him and frankly, I don't care. But I will say this, if I were you, I'd find another date for Homecoming. Goodnight."

She made her way reluctantly to the café and the employee lounge to retrieve her jacket and purse. Of course, there was no way to get behind the counter without seeing Ben. She had managed to avoid him for her entire shift. She hoped Karen would arrive on time and save her from having to sit out there and wait.

Alyson was sitting at the counter talking to Ben; they looked up as she arrived. Ben wore a dark expression. "So, do you think your fanged suitor will show up to escort you home?"

She ignored him and went into the back. As she was getting her stuff, Ben came and blocked the doorway. She looked up at him with annoyed impatience for a minute. He didn't move. "What do you want from me Ben? What do you want me to say? Yes, I liked him, I admitted that to you. Now you're going to throw it in my face every chance you get? Grow up. I'm leaving. If Cain does show up, you can tell him that he missed me."

"Take it easy." She didn't reply. She made to push past him, but he caught her by the shoulders and forced her to look at him. She made him let go, but when she did look up into his face, she saw something there that had been missing for a while; that quiet concern that he used to have, when she had thought of him as her friend, back before his sole intent seemed to be harassing her for spending time with Cain and letting her know that he thought she was stupid for doing so.

He stared at her long and hard, seemingly trying to read the look in her eyes. She wondered how he would interpret what he saw there. The only feeling she was aware of, was that of being exhausted by the whole damn thing. He spoke quietly and sincerely. "I'm sorry. I guess I haven't been much of a friend, huh? It's just hard to see someone you...care about, make the wrong choices."

She didn't even know what to say. She realized that he was trying to apologize, and yet she was outraged that he would presume to know what choices she'd made and whether or not they were correct by his standards! He may actually have been right, but *he* didn't know that, and she certainly wasn't planning on telling him.

She had the unreasonable urge to start crying because this was all just too much to deal with right now. She was just so fed up with everything and she felt like she just had to get out of here, before Cain *did* decide to pay her a visit. As if right on cue, she heard Karen out in the café talking to Alyson. "I have to go."

Ben seemed a little hurt that she wouldn't stay and talk to him. Then he heard Alyson call Felicity from out in the café. He stepped aside and she walked past him to the waiting girls.

Karen saw her and waved. "Hi! Ready to go? The guys are waiting in the car."

Felicity noticed Allie and Ben exchange a puzzled look at the word 'guys'. "Yeah, let's get out of here."

Alyson looked confused. "Aren't you going to wait and see if Cain shows up?"

"I'm sure you'll tell me all about it tomorrow, if he does."

Felicity walked out and stood waiting just outside the door. Karen said her goodbyes and followed, passing and then leading her out to a waiting car, a nice new four-door sedan, dark blue. She saw Jack and a guy who could only be Todd, sitting up front. She and Karen climbed into the back.

Karen had spoken truly; Todd was accurately described as 'cute'. He had very curly light brown hair, and an honest and sweet face. Introductions were made and they headed off to the movie theater. Felicity sat silently in the back after a few initial polite comments. She hoped she didn't seem rude, but she really didn't feel like talking.

As they neared the theater she began to feel warm and flushed, as though she had drunk a few glasses of wine, although of course she'd had nothing. As they pulled into the lot, she really felt quite odd. Like she had alternating hot flashes and chills. Was she nearing a nervous breakdown, or coming down with the flu? Wouldn't that just be perfect?

As they left the car, she forced herself to smile at Todd. She tried her very best to radiate accepting and friendly vibes towards him, and make him feel confident. They all bought tickets, popcorn and sodas. She paid for her own and they made their way to their theater.

They found seats and Felicity took off her jacket, settling herself in the aisle seat next to Todd. They made small talk until the lights dimmed and then sat back to watch the movie, Felicity found she couldn't concentrate though.

Her hot flashes and chills had turned into an odd sort of tingling feeling. She felt so odd. It was almost like...static electricity. She had heard somewhere that people who are about to get struck by lightning could feel it before it actually struck; something about the way the particles of their bodies became charged and their hair stood on end. Well, her hair wasn't raised and she highly doubted she would be struck by lightning in the movie theater, but that was the thought this strange sensation brought to mind. She felt...charged, expectant. It was so weird. It had nothing to do with Todd, she was sure. He was very nice, but she didn't imagine there would be any sort of chemistry between them.

For some reason Cain kept coming to mind. Something about how she felt now, that reminded her of the way she had felt when he had bitten her. No matter how she tried to block that from her mind, she just couldn't help but face the truth. It had been an amazingly intimate experience. Just a vague flash of it through her mind could make her shiver. As she thought of it now, she had the inexplicable urge to go to him. As if she needed to experience it again. She fought it back with a chill.

She couldn't say why this odd feeling would remind her of that. Maybe it was just the fact that both feelings were so far removed from anything else that she had ever known, but she had to admit that she suddenly realized how much she missed Cain. She did feel a terrible urge to see him, however unreasonable that might be.

She couldn't help but ponder what Allie had said about Cain needing to drink blood. She felt rather foolish about it really. Of course a vampire needed to drink blood, that was a given. But somehow, when she had first discovered that he was a vampire, he had put her under the impression that he could do without.

What *had* he said really? She thought back carefully. He'd never said that he didn't drink blood; he said he didn't *hurt* people. That gave her a chill, because he had drunk from her, and although she had felt many indescribable things, she knew full well that it hadn't really hurt. There'd been an instant of pain when his fangs had first pierced her flesh, but she'd hardly had time to recognize it before it was soothed by *other* feelings. Even Allie had said it didn't hurt when she had been bitten. Did Cain mean that he drank, but didn't kill people?

That thought produced an inexplicable wave of what she could only identify as jealousy, as bewildering as that may be. She actually felt jealous at the thought of him engaging in the act of drinking blood from someone else, the way that he had from her! What was wrong with her? That was insane!

She had the bizarre mental image of Cain standing before a crowd of girls looking for an intended victim, and all of them raising their hands and screaming 'pick me, pick me!'. Why didn't she just go into the bathroom, slit her wrists and be done with it? She really must be losing her mind!

Felicity realized she must have been fidgeting, because Todd looked over a couple of times, as if trying to figure out why she was so uncomfortable. She made herself sit still and stare at the screen. Still, she couldn't pay attention. Cain kept invading her thoughts as though he were sitting right next to her. She almost felt as if she had a slight 'pins and needles' sensation traveling over her whole body.

For some reason, she began thinking about the night Cain had given her the vial of his blood. More precisely, the kiss they had shared. She kept remembering how passionate it had been, and how it had seemed to almost produce a pleasant sort of 'high' in her.

Her mind was probably embellishing the memory to be more than it really was, but it did make her wish that he were a regular guy, so that things could be different between them. She certainly wouldn't mind a few more kisses like that! She even found herself closing her eyes and reliving the kiss in her mind. *Stop that!* she silently reprimanded herself. *He is not somebody to be fantasizing about!*

Why had he given her that vial anyway, if not to protect her? Why would he do that if he had been planning all along to hurt her? As mixed up as her feelings about the event might be, she still had to consider someone drinking her blood as harmful. Harming her couldn't have been his intention, not from the beginning anyway. She wondered if he'd changed his mind.

The evening passed and the movie finally came to an end. Someone suggested they go for coffee and ice cream. Felicity suffered herself to be brought along and she hoped no one would want to discuss the film. She hadn't really paid a bit of mind to it.

The one thing she was grateful for, was the fact that as they left the theater, that odd feeling that had persisted all evening finally began to fade. By the time they reached the diner, it was all but gone. Todd seemed a bit distracted and she imagined he was thinking about his ex-girlfriend. She herself almost choked over ordering when she saw 'Butter Rum Ripple' on the ice cream menu. She ordered Black Cherry instead. She still had a hard time eating it.

As the evening came to an end, they headed back to the dorms. Felicity had thought the guys would just drop them off at the door, but Jack insisted that they walk the girls inside. As they reached the porch, Felicity stopped to look at Karen as she realized the time. "Oh no, it's after eleven. We'll be locked out and have to knock and wake someone."

"Don't you have a key?" Karen laughed at her blank look. "You're supposed to get a copy key from Maggie."

Felicity shook her head. "Now she tells me."

Karen let them in with her key and she and Jack went off down the hall to her room for a more private goodbye, leaving Todd and Felicity standing alone in the front parlor. No one else was around. How awkward. What was she supposed to say to this guy? She felt bad; she had hardly even looked at him since the movie theater. She hoped he didn't take it personally.

"I had a really nice time," she exaggerated.

He smiled. "No you didn't. It's okay, I know I'm not great company lately. I've kind of had a lot on my mind. Not a great first impression, I know, but thanks for coming."

"You were fine company, *my* head wasn't there. I've kind of got a lot going on too."

"Well, here's a crazy idea. Since neither one of us seems ready to commit our attention fully to someone else right now, well, were you going to the Homecoming dance with anyone? 'Cause if you weren't, but you'd like to go...maybe we could go together. You know, and ignore each other in a more formal setting."

She had to laugh. He was sweet. "I don't know. I wasn't even going to go."

"Well, it's okay if you don't want to. I just thought I'd ask. Considering the dance is only three nights away and I don't have a date, I wasn't going either, but it wouldn't have to be like a real date, if you don't want. I mean, we could just go and keep each other company."

Felicity reconsidered. Why was she saying no anyway? Just because she wouldn't be seeing Cain anymore, why should she stay home? Maybe this was just what she needed. "Well...okay, I'll go."

"Really, you want to?" he asked hopefully.

"Why not? What am I going to do, sit in my room all night?"

"It'll be fun," Todd assured her.

"I don't really dance though," she admitted, apologetically.

"I'm sure we can work around the actual dancing part."

"Cool. Oh, I'm working, until ten o'clock. Sorry, I know the dance starts at nine."

"That's alright, we'll make an entrance. Should I meet you here."

She froze for a moment in indecision. What would be worse, walking home alone, or chancing seeing Cain with Todd around? "No, um, would you mind picking me up at work?"

"Don't you want to come home to change first?"

"I know, it seems weird, but I don't like to leave work alone, if you don't mind. I can get ready there."

"Okay, whatever you want. I'll be there at ten."

"Thanks. I'll see you Saturday."

"Great, I'll see you then. Goodnight."

"Goodnight, it was nice meeting you," she called after him with a wave, as he walked out the door. She headed up the stairs as Jack came into the parlor from down the hall. He didn't notice her on the stairs and went straight out. She went up to her room to get ready for bed.

What was she doing, going to the dance with Todd? Didn't she have enough people to worry about, without adding someone else into the mix? Why was she feeling so out of sorts tonight? The whole movie theater experience had left her feeling all flustered.

As she got beneath the covers and switched off the lights, thoughts of Cain once again tried to invade her mind. She was so tired and weary of fighting them she didn't even try. She just closed her eyes and let them carry her off into sleep.

~~~~~~~~~~~~~~~~~~~~~~~~~~~~~~

Thursday afternoon, she actually did plan on taking lunch up to her room, but Ben found her just outside the cafeteria.

She thought of trying to pretend she hadn't seen him, but he wasn't going to let her. "'Liss!" He was the only one who ever called her that. Originally, she had kind of liked it. Now she thought of asking him not to, but it seemed pointless and hurtful. He caught up to her. "Hi. Can we sit and talk?"

"Why, have you thought of something else you could say to upset me?"

"I wasn't trying to upset you," he said quietly.

"Right, because calling me stupid, questioning my virtue and letting me know that you would like to see someone that you think I care about get killed, shouldn't upset me?"

"Okay, so maybe I was trying a little, but I had good intentions."

She raised her eyebrows at him and then shook her head dismissingly. "Whatever Ben, I don't even want to know. I'm going to go get some lunch." He followed her to the lunch line.

"You *know* I consider you a close friend, don't you?"

She looked at him as if he were nuts. "Is that why I get such special treatment?"

"Yes, because *my* friends are supposed to know better than to get involved with...the wrong kinds of people," he said, glancing around at all of the potential eavesdroppers on the line.

She stopped to stare at him intensely for a moment. No, there was no way that he knew what had happened between her and Cain. "Well big brother, you can happily consider me *un*-involved," she said, as she moved her tray along and selected a chef's salad from the case.

Ben looked unsure whether or not to be pleased with himself. Like maybe she was just trying to pacify him. "Good. What, did you two have a little spat or something?" he asked skeptically.

She sighed. "Something like that."

Ben grabbed a sandwich from the case and they moved on. "Well, it's for the best. You know that, right? And don't call me 'big brother'." They got drinks and paid for their selections. "There's Allie," Ben said, waving across the room.

"Oh good," she replied with a sarcastic lilt.

Ben stopped to give her a wounded look. "Don't you like Allie? I thought you guys were getting along."

"Well you have to admit, she does take some getting used to, but yeah, she's okay. It's just that vampires seem to be her choice subject, and they're not my favorite topic these days."

"So, we'll talk about something else."

They reached the table and sat down as Allie greeted them. "Hi! So Cain never showed last night."

Ben and Felicity shared a glance. Ben answered her. "Yeah, I guess he and Felicity aren't as close as I thought."

Alyson gave Felicity a curious look. "So nobody knows what he and Arif talked about? Well, maybe he'll come see you tonight."

"I'm not working tonight," Felicity told her with a shrug.

"Neither am I," Ben admitted.

Allie knitted her brows and muttered, "Damn. Well, I am. Sometimes he comes into Tommy's, maybe I'll see him."

Ben shook his head disapprovingly. "Alyson, haven't you ever heard the expression 'curiosity killed the cat'?"

Allie smiled. "Cain's the one who's a big pussy cat. He wouldn't bite me." She seemed to watch a little too closely as Felicity flinched. "I'm gonna ask him what happened."

"I should know better than to try and caution you by now. Anyway," he looked over at Felicity, who had been quietly picking at her salad, "I'm sick of vampires. Let's talk about something else."

Allie flashed an impish grin at him. "Okay stud. So, who are you takin' to the dance?" Ben rolled his eyes. "Come on, it's a little late to be leavin' people hangin'."

Ben looked up at her and answered quietly. "I already asked Brenda yesterday."

"Does Ashley know that?"

He shrugged. "I was going to say something last night, but you know, I never actually *asked* Ashley. Why should I feel responsible for what she might have assumed?" Alyson gave him a look of disapproval. "I'll talk to her tonight. What if she really did think I'd take her? I hope she won't be mad. Do you think she'll have time to find another date?"

Allie giggled. "Don't worry Ben. I'm sure she's got a whole bunch of hunks just lined up and waiting to make you jealous."

"I can hardly wait," he answered dryly. "Am I buying you a ticket again?"

"I don't think I'm gonna go this year," Allie told him.

"Allie, you always go to everything," Ben insisted.

"I know, but I'm kind of between boyfriends right now. And you're gonna be all over Brenda, so I'll have no one to dance with."

Ben looked over to Felicity. "You should go with 'Liss. You guys can check out all of those 'college hotties' she was telling you about."

"I already have a date," Felicity said timidly.

Ben was taken aback, Allie smiled. "You do?" they asked.

"Yes," she answered quietly. She cut off Allie's obvious question before she could even ask it. "He's human. Why do you guys seem so shocked? You don't think I could attract a *normal* guy?"

Ben looked properly abashed. "No, of course not. I mean, of course you could. You're...*very* attractive. You just never mentioned anyone."

"His name's Todd," Felicity supplied.

"Oh. Then, I guess I'll see you there," Ben said thoughtfully.

"I guess," she said with a shrug.

Alyson sat back and pouted. "Maybe I should ask somebody. I don't want to be the only one not going, but I'm certainly not going to hang around as the fifth wheel either."

Ben fixed her with an odd look. "Allie, you don't even go to this school. I know we usually go to stuff together, but it's not a big deal."

"Maybe I'll just go to the bonfire," Allie said thoughtfully.

"What's that?" Felicity asked.

Ben answered. "It's a school tradition. They have this big bonfire before the dance. It's supposed to signify roasting the other team or something. It's pretty barbaric if you think about it."

"Oh. Well, I'm working until ten, so we'll just be going to the dance," Felicity told them.

"That sucks." Allie interjected. "Couldn't you switch with someone?"

"I don't mind. We'll just go late," Felicity assured her.

Ben sat up and gathered his stuff. "Speaking of late, it's time to go or I will be." He glanced at Allie. "Maybe I'll stop into Tommy's later, just to make sure you stay out of trouble."

"Like having you around ever stopped me," Allie told him with a smirk.

"Well, God knows what you do when I'm not there."

Allie laughed. "Don't you wish you knew?"

"Not really. Sometimes ignorance is bliss." He turned to Felicity, who was also getting ready to leave. "I'll see you tomorrow night."

"What's tomorrow night?" she asked in surprise.

"We're closing together," he reminded her.

"Oh. Guess I'll see you then, bye." She left for class wondering if she'd done the right thing, accepting Todd's invitation to the dance. It was nice being able to say she had a date, but it wasn't like she was expecting anything to come of it.

At least Todd hadn't seemed too disillusioned either. They were just going to get out and keep each other company - no strings or expectations. Did he really believe that, or was he just trying to get her to go? Oh well, it didn't matter. They'd hang out at the dance together and see what happened. Maybe she'd end up liking him more than she thought...if she could just get Cain out of her head.

Chapter 24 ~ Enduring

Cain

The movie theater
Thursday night

Cain sat in the movie theater and tried to pay attention to the show, again. He could hardly believe his bad luck last night. He had come all the way to the theater to try and keep himself away from Felicity, and she had followed him to the very building.

Of course, she'd had no idea that he was there. He had felt her approaching when she'd entered the furthest extent of his range of perception, which was roughly a mile. It was just before the movie started, he had felt her trace flicker into his mind with a delighted sort of ache; a sudden reminder of her and the intimacy that they had shared.

He had closed his eyes and reveled in her light, but had also reluctantly hoped that she would not come too close. Of course, she had. As the distance had closed, he had felt her glow strengthen in his mind and become more.

He'd been grateful that she hadn't chosen the same room where he sat, but he could feel her through the wall as though she were mere inches away.

He'd closed his eyes and felt himself enveloped in her presence. His blood had practically sung with the knowledge of her proximity. He'd wondered if she felt him. She should, but she wouldn't understand. He'd thought of leaving, so as not to disturb her, but he hadn't been able force himself from his seat. It had been a struggle just to keep from going to find her, endless torture. Nearly two hours of feeling her nearness, but not being able to look upon her, to touch her, to try to explain.

He had seriously considered going to her; taking her from her seat and rushing her to a quiet corner where they could talk, but what if she were afraid of him and caused a scene? And of course, she would not have come alone. That had brought about an unwelcome wave of irritation. Who had she come with? Alyson hadn't been there. Her mark from Sindy was just about gone, but he was fairly sure he would still see it if he concentrated. He didn't know who else Felicity usually socialized with, other than Ben. Did it matter? It was only a movie, but someone else had the pleasure of her company while he was denied.

He remembered how he'd gripped the armrests of his seat with all of his strength and forced stillness upon himself. It had been a long time since he'd had to fight so hard against his instincts. Other than... stopping himself drinking from her. No, he shouldn't even think of it. He could not allow himself to relive that experience while in such a fragile state. He needed to keep himself separate from her. He needed to give himself another night or two.

His body's reaction to her nearness had shown him that he wasn't ready. If he could be assured of her acceptance, it wouldn't matter. In a positive circumstance he was sure he could handle himself, but for her to deny him while his body needed her so badly, could turn dangerous. His will was strong, but he didn't care to test it. Just another night or two and he would have full control again.

His movie had ended and people had begun to leave, but he hadn't dared to move. Surely, she would be leaving soon as well. She had arrived when his own film was only just starting, better to wait her out, than to chance her seeing him.

He hadn't planned on actually leaving the theater, but to stay for another picture, and he couldn't chance hanging about in the lobby while she was here. He'd watched the credits role as people moved around him to the exit. Finally, theater employees had come to collect popcorn buckets and sweep the floor.

A young girl in a red and white striped vest had come to tell him that he must leave before the next showing. He'd assured her that he only needed a moment more to rest; to please excuse him, as he was not feeling well. She'd left him alone, but he'd known she was only going to find someone else to make him leave.

Somehow, he'd endured until he felt Felicity begin to move from the theater. It was almost painful to feel her recede, but the practical side of him was very relieved. When he had been certain that she had left the building, he'd made his way out into the lobby and sat on a bench near the bathrooms. He'd followed her in his mind's eye until she became indistinct and then…she was gone.

He'd spent the rest of the night in the theater, almost afraid to let himself leave, until they closed. Finally, he'd gone home, not having to pass the dorms, for which he was very grateful. For the most part, he was glad because he hadn't wanted to tease himself with her presence again, but a small part of him was actually afraid to pass those dorms and feel that she wasn't there.

If that had happened, he would not have been able to rest until he'd searched for and found her. And if she wasn't in her room by this time of night, it would be much safer for all involved if he did not find where she was. So he'd gone home, safely out of her range and tried to read until morning.

Now here he was again, at the theater, prepared to sit and watch the rest of the films that he had not yet seen, and even those he had again if necessary. Anything to keep himself occupied. He felt secure in the fact that she would not come back so soon. He did find it curious though, that he hadn't felt the presence of any other vampires. Where were they all?

Was Arif keeping them out of his way, or cloaking them? He was unsure what to make of the man, and that worried him. He was unlike most vampires Cain had known. A creature like Sindy might do something surprising from time to time, but basically, he knew what to expect from her and not to trust her.

He had not met many vampires that were past the century mark in their lives, which Arif surely was. Most old ones were either outwardly hostile, or shy and reluctant to even speak with others.

Arif had said that he'd brought his own blood supply, so had no need to hunt the vicinity. Cain had met other, younger vampires who followed the practice of keeping a 'stable' or a 'harem', but they usually did not have much patience for Cain's advice. He disagreed with their ways and had never spent enough time in their company, to really know them. This in turn, meant that he couldn't really speculate on what to expect of one like them, like Arif.

Some vampires came to realize that it was a large risk to prey upon humans night after night, even if they didn't kill, but they were unwilling or uneducated in relying on animal blood for their existence, as Cain did. So they would collect a 'stable' of about a half dozen humans, sometimes called 'pets', to visit repeatedly or keep in their constant care. They would alternate drinking from these, so as to never fully deplete their supply.

Repeat visits to a victim were of course risky in their own right if not properly handled. Most vampires opted to keep their humans secluded from the rest of society. Sometimes they were kept by force, but usually a smart vampire would choose drug addicts who could be kept deliriously high and oblivious to their plight. Whether the vampire realized it at the outset, or learned through experience, the venom they administered with each bite also helped to control them.

Cain had heard rumors of vampires who would steal young children and then raise them to be kept, showering them with material things and keeping them secluded from the outside world. These pets were like so many spoiled rich children as they matured, being allowed to party and play with others at night clubs and such - to a certain extent and always under a watchful eye. They knew nothing of responsibility other than feeding and pleasing their master.

Once in a while, one could even find a human who was happy to be kept, for reasons of their own. They were content to live in a sort of symbiotic relationship with a vampire who would provide for their needs. But that was usually not the case. Usually, a combination of addiction and force prevailed, and whether they realized it or not, those kept were prisoners. That entire arrangement was not something Cain was comfortable accepting.

Along the same lines, sometimes a 'guard' would be kept as well. This was similar to Sindy's practices; although whether she had picked it up from Arif or stumbled upon it on her own he couldn't say.

A vampire might sire other, lesser vampires to do their bidding. They were purposely not made well enough for true independent thinking and then used for protection, sex, or however their sire saw fit. Of course in Sindy's case, the quality of her 'work' was more through incompetence than any purposeful plan, but they served her all the same.

He wondered what Sindy had thought of Arif's meeting with Cain. She had to have questioned Arif over it. She would know that Felicity was now marked and therefore, not to be touched. He also wondered if Arif would mention anything about Ben.

Cain had entertained the thought earlier this evening, of finding Ben to tell him that Sindy wanted him, to give him warning. He had approached the DownTime and seen that Ben was not there. He had felt that Felicity was in the dorms and was glad to let her be. He was content, that at least he knew where she was, but that did not help him find Ben. He certainly wasn't going to go and knock on Felicity's door to see if he was there.

He supposed that if he really wanted to, he could leave a message for him with Alyson, over at Tommy's, but although he could indeed, faintly sense Alyson's presence there, the last thing he wanted to do right now was enter the bar.

He still felt a little jittery, to have Felicity close again. He didn't want to have to talk to anyone; he really just wanted to go off on his own. Ben could fend for himself for a day or two, without Cain's advice. Ben was used to looking out for vampires anyway, so it shouldn't make any difference.

So, he found himself back at the movies again. He briefly wondered how many movies he had seen throughout his lifetime. Probably thousands. Just another night, he kept telling himself. Just make it through another night.

Chapter 25 ~ Look at you!

Felicity

The DownTime café and bookstore
9:45, Friday night

It was almost time to close, and still no sign of Cain. Felicity was quietly relieved, but had to admit, she was starting to stress a little from the tension.

She'd spent last night alone in her room, catching up on homework. She'd also spoken aloud as many phrases as she could think of, all with the sole purpose of trying to un-invite Cain from her room. She wasn't sure if they would work and she didn't really expect him to come anyway…but it couldn't hurt.

She did assume she would see him tonight though. He hadn't been to the DownTime in a while, it was very unlike him. Was he deliberately avoiding her? He must be, but why?

If he was going to attack her, she almost wished he'd get it over with. This anticipation and not knowing what he would do, was driving her crazy. Exactly what *had* happened the night that he'd bitten her? Had he simply lost control, or was it something that he had planned to do all along?

Her instincts kept swinging her back and forth over the issue. First, she would tell herself that she could not possibly have read every single gesture of his, wrongly. She couldn't be *that* gullible. He really had cared for her, genuinely.

Then she would tell herself that she could not judge him by her own standards, because he was not human. Her own methods of reading people's intentions did not apply. He was a totally alien entity that she could not understand and therefore, he was dangerous. She could not hope to guess his agenda. She wished he would make some sort of move, so she would know what to think.

As things stood now, she was frightened by what had happened, but with a few nights of distance, she had a hard time thinking of him in person, as someone to be afraid of. If he attacked her violently and turned out to be a truly evil monster, at least she would *know* that she'd been deceived. Right now, the fact that he had bitten her, just didn't fit with the rest of her feelings towards him. It was very unsettling.

Alyson was there again, and was quite vocal about her disappointment over yet another wasted evening and her unrequited curiosity. She had been very annoyed that Cain had not come into Tommy's again. Now she paced the café and drove Ben nuts. Felicity was glad she had been able to spend most of her evening hiding away in the back of the bookstore, so as to avoid hearing her complaints.

There were no customers, so she began her closing routine a little early. Now as she closed out her register Allie came over to bug her for a while, so Ben could mop the floor. "Why hasn't he come? Did you tell him not to?"

"No. I haven't even seen him," Felicity answered.

"Then where is he? From what you said, there are just too many damn vampires in this town right now. That makes things really unsafe."

Felicity stopped counting her register to give Allie a perplexed look. "Are you worried about Cain?"

Alyson looked confused for a moment. "No. It's not safe for anyone. I just know that vampires don't usually gather in such large numbers unless it means big trouble. They really don't play well together, you know? So this is really weird, and it sounds like something dangerous is going on. If so, I wanna know about it. And right now, Cain is the only vampire around here, that might actually tell me."

"Well, sorry, but I don't think he's coming."

Allie looked at her for a very long time. Then she walked back over to the café, tiptoeing over the wet floor, perched on a bar stool and slumped over the counter. She raked her fingers through her hair, in exasperation. "This sucks!"

Felicity finished her register and went over to join Allie at the counter. Ben came out from the back. "Hey, maybe we can get out of here early tonight. Go flip the sign for me," he said to Felicity, pointing at the open/closed sign on the door. As he did, his face suddenly went pale. Felicity and Alyson noticed his expression and were turning to look, as they heard the little bell ring over the door.

Sindy entered the store. She strolled in wearing a sweet smile, as if she hadn't a care in the world. Her grin grew broader as she witnessed the three of them at the counter. Felicity and Allie had stood from their stools. Ben slowly came out from behind the counter; it was he who found his voice first. "Get out."

Sindy acted as though he hadn't said a word. "Well, looky, looky, the gang's all here. Guess I picked a good night to come visit," she said, stopping on the carpet, just short of the café entrance.

Just then, Alyson seemed to break free of the paralysis that had held her. "Come to get your ass kicked again?" she asked, as she tried to lunge at Sindy.

Luckily, Ben had foreseen her intention, and lurched forward to grab her in a sort of hug from behind. Alyson's feet slid around on the wet floor and she was unable to get any leverage to make Ben let go. Ben widened his stance and managed to hold her while still keeping his feet.

Sindy smiled maliciously. "Hold her tight, Ben. I've got friends outside." She took a step closer and gazed at Allie. "As much as I should take this opportunity to put you back in your place, I won't. Although less witnesses, means that I could have a lot more fun; but, another time. You really aren't the one that I came here to see." She looked around a little, sizing up the place. "So this is Cain's beloved sanctuary. It's funny that he's the only one not here. Do you know why? I'll bet I do."

Ben still held Allie, although she seemed to have calmed down, while watching Sindy intently. "What the hell do you want?" Ben asked.

Sindy shook her head as if in regret. "Oh Ben, don't be disappointed, but I'm not here to see you either. Our time will come, I promise, but for you, I want to plan something special. You're just too good to rush."

Ben looked like he had planned to say something, but Alyson started cursing and struggling with renewed fury, and he was taken with holding her back. Sindy laughed. "But you know, while I have your attention I should ask you something. I know the college is having the Homecoming dance tomorrow. I don't suppose you need a date?"

This so caught them off guard that Ben let go of Allie who immediately burst out laughing. "You have got to be kidding," Ben stated in shock.

Allie tried to reign in her laughter to answer. "Actually, you're a little late, he already has two. Ben, you've become quite the magnet, haven't you? Even the dead girls wanna play."

Sindy looked amused. "Two dates? Well, aren't you the virile young buck? I'll try to make sure none of that gets lost in the process."

Allie stepped forward and made to grab for Sindy, whose eyes flashed red momentarily as she took a step back. Ben held the back of Allie's shirt and gave her a reminding tug. Sindy smiled and continued. "Don't try to tell me you haven't fantasized about us, Ben."

"Actually Sindy, I have. You and me, outside on the grass, watching the sun rise."

He had her going for a second, but her surprise quickly turned to annoyance. "You're so cute; I am really going to enjoy claiming you. Save me a dance." She held up a hand to silence them. "But you have to stop distracting me."

She turned her eyes to Felicity and her smile positively beamed. "Because here, is what I came to see. Look at you! I can't believe it! I had to come and see you for myself!" She stepped closer to Felicity, who edged back towards Ben and Allie.

Sindy's voice took on a soft and soothing quality. "It's okay sweetie, you don't have to be afraid of me anymore. You've got big, strong Cain to take care of you now, don't you?" She dropped her voice to a whisper. "Or maybe *Cain* is the one you should be afraid of."

Felicity froze like a deer in headlights. It was Alyson who yelled, "That's enough bitch. You'd better head for that door, because if you don't, your friends will only be here in time to watch you turn to dust."

Sindy seemed unconcerned. "Relax, I'm going. I've seen what I came to see." She leaned a little closer to Felicity to whisper, "I'll bet he's got a nice touch. Enjoy it while you can." Alyson moved towards her, but she was already heading out the door. Allie followed her and locked it.

Ben took a deep breath and looked at them in confusion. "What the hell was that all about?"

Alyson turned from watching Sindy leave through the glass of the door. "I guess she was feeling nostalgic and wanted a second date."

"A *second* date?" Felicity questioned.

Allie laughed. "Back in tenth grade, Ben took her to the high school Homecoming dance."

Felicity turned to look at Ben. He was staring at her strangely. "She was human then," he explained distractedly. "That's not what I meant. The stuff she said about you and Cain. What was that?"

Felicity gave her head a little shake. Obviously, Sindy must know that Cain had bitten her, but she didn't understand how. She certainly wasn't going to tell Ben that.

Allie strode purposely forward to Ben and took him by the arm, back to the counter. "Who knows? Crazy witch. Finish your stuff so we can get out of here." She glanced back towards the door and Felicity, who began to realize that Allie might not be quite as clueless as she sometimes affected.

Felicity handed Ben her locker key. He was about to say something to her, when Allie spoke again. "Looks like you've got your own personal stalker. Worried?"

"It's nothing new. Sindy's tried for me before. I'll just have to be very careful, that's all."

"Do you think she'll go to the dance?"

Now Ben looked worried. "God I hope not, but I bet she will. And I do not have two dates, by the way. I talked to Ashley; she knows I'm going with Brenda."

"How'd she take it?"

"She acted like she didn't expect me to take her anyway, and said she had another date already. I don't know if that was true, but it works for me." Ben finished the last details and they headed for the door.

Felicity looked out into the dark. "Do you think they're waiting for us?"

Ben pulled out his cross from somewhere and handed Allie his stake. He looked to Felicity, who in turn, reluctantly pulled her own stake from her purse. "We'll see," Ben said.

As Ben got out his keys, Allie turned to Felicity. "Don't worry, you'll be okay," she said quietly.

They exited the building, keeping an extra eye on the nearby bushes and trees. All seemed quiet. Ben locked up and they headed to the cars. Alyson's old dark orange Charger was parked next to Ben's yellow Mustang.

Ben turned to Felicity. "So, what's your ride of choice, my 'stang or you wanna join Allie in the 'General Lee'?"

Allie shook her head and gave Ben an exasperated sigh. "Give it up Ben, I'm never gonna let you paint the '01."

"Come on Allie, how can you have a dark orange '69 Charger and *not* make it the 'General Lee'?"

Felicity looked askance at Allie. "What is he talking about?"

Allie laughed and rolled her eyes. "'The Dukes Of Hazzard'. It's like, a vintage car-guy thing. Anyway, you should let me drive you. You ride with Ben all the time."

Felicity could tell that Alyson must have figured out more than she had let on. She probably wanted a chance to talk to Felicity alone. The thought of trying to talk about Cain biting her, made Felicity grow cold with fear.

She had thought she wanted to pump Allie for information about her bite from Sindy, but discussing the one she had received from Cain was out of the question. She just couldn't do it, not yet. She still didn't even know what to think about it herself. She deliberately took Ben's arm. "Sorry Allie, I'm just a sucker for that smooth ride of his. Thanks anyway."

Ben smiled and then disengaged himself from her to open the door. Alyson squinted at her for a moment, as though she were trying to decipher something. Then she shook her head, got into her car with a wave and left.

Felicity got into Ben's car. He got behind the wheel and stared at her. "What is going on?"

"What?"

"Is he scaring you?" Ben asked.

"Who?" Felicity asked innocently.

"Don't play dumb, you know exactly who I'm talking about. Did Cain hurt you?" Ben asked steadily.

She looked into his eyes, so he wouldn't worry. "No...no." she said quietly. It wasn't really a lie, but it felt like one. She knew what he meant, but she didn't want him to worry, so she looked into his eyes and lied. They were light brown, with little flecks of gold all through them. She felt terrible, she hoped he couldn't tell. After a moment, she let her eyes drop from his. "So, you dated Sindy, huh?"

He snorted derisively. "I saw her for a little while. Then we went to one stupid dance. I was fifteen."

"Did you kiss her?" Felicity asked.

He looked at her with shocked amusement that she should ask. "Yes. In fact, we made it all the way to third base, if you must know."

She tried to remember, "What's third base again? I forget."

He just laughed at her. "Ask Todd," he finally said. She rolled her eyes at him as he started the car and began the drive home. When they turned onto her block, she fully expected to see Sindy in the road, like last time. No one was to be seen. Ben parked in the lot. "Guess I'll see you at the dance."

"Yeah. Thanks for the ride. Goodnight."

"'Night."

He waited for her to get in before driving away. She suffered a brief flashback as she passed the pillar she had leaned against with Cain. Of course she passed it every day, but it looked different in the moonlight. She shivered, ran up the stairs and went inside.

Chapter 26 - Scorned

Cain

Cain's house
8:00, Saturday night

Tonight would be the night. Cain could not wait any longer; tonight he would go to Felicity. Last night seemed to have stretched on forever. He had gone to great pains to avoid her, spending half the night holed up in his room. When he could stand that no longer, he had finally gone out.

It had been safely late enough into the evening that Felicity should be fast asleep in her room. He couldn't bring himself to go and check, but still he made sure to go someplace she was almost certain not to attend. The next town over, there was a pub, just a dank little hole in the wall really, but it was someplace to go and he was sure that he wouldn't meet Felicity there. He had chosen a table where he could sit, inconspicuous and alone, observing people and trying not to think about his own concerns for a while.

About an hour before the bartender would inevitably call for last rounds, Cain saw Arif enter the establishment. He had three human women with him. Foreign beauties, their faces exotically painted and each wearing an ornate bindi jewel affixed to their forehead. Their bodies were heavily adorned with jewelry and scarves of silk bordered in gold thread.

They were quiet and demure, not even speaking to each other. Their only sounds were the musical clinking of their numerous bangle bracelets and the belled anklets that they wore above their slight sandals. Even these sounds would have been lost to the noise of the bar, without his acute vampire hearing.

The crowd parted for Arif and his consorts, as if by magic. He seemed to revel in the small stir that he caused among the patrons. He obviously regarded himself as visiting royalty, like some foreign prince or sheik.

He noticed Cain as he reached the back of the bar. He only momentarily paused in his stride, giving Cain a small smile and a respectful nod. Arif moved on towards a table of his own, settling himself into the back of a large round booth, so that he could easily survey his surroundings.

The girls placed themselves around him and practically draped themselves over him, as if to protect him from any other humans who might dare to approach. Cain had the impression that they would surely have put themselves on the floor at his feet, if it had been possible.

Arif seemed to have had no desire to speak with him that evening, which was fine with Cain. He hadn't the stomach to place himself in the company of such distressingly bound slaves anyway; for slaves they surely were.

Of course, they appeared more than willing, but who could know what former circumstances had brought them to accept their present positions? Perhaps they enjoyed the protection, material wealth and favors of their master. Maybe they had no choice, for surely a human with intimate knowledge of a coven such as Arif's would not be let freely back into society. To play the lovely escort to their master was preferable to being treated as a prisoner.

Most likely, they simply knew of no other life. Cain had tried to release such girls from their emotional bindings in times past. It was a most frustrating and fruitless endeavor. Their hopelessly scarred psyches were doubtless beyond his reach.

Cain had watched them for a moment as they coyly fawned over their master, and then he wasted no time in removing himself from their presence. He had given Arif a parting glance of acknowledgement, and gone back out into the night until dawn had driven him home again.

He was glad to know that the man indeed bore him no ill will, not that night anyway. He couldn't know what the future would bring. Last night's excursion left his mind. For now, he could not look beyond this night. He would allow himself to go to Felicity at last. He took his time to shower, dress and prepare, forcing himself not to rush.

It was Saturday evening and Felicity was most likely working, as usual. He wanted to speak to her in private, without Ben hanging on their every word. He wouldn't arrive until almost closing time, just before ten. That way, he could enter before the doors were locked, and convince her that he had no ill intentions and that they needed to speak alone.

Of course, Ben usually closed on the weekend also, and Felicity would feel that she could leave with him if she wanted, but perhaps it would be good for her to feel that security. Once she felt the choice was hers to make, he was confident that she would see the need for them to speak privately, if he could convince her of her safety.

He thought of waiting at the dorms instead, to remove Ben entirely from the equation. There was always the chance that she had told him, and he would be openly hostile. That was not a situation he wanted to deal with, especially not now, in front of her, but he rejected the idea with the unsettling thought that she might indeed leave work with Ben and not come home at all. That was an unacceptable chance to take.

It had to be at the DownTime, she would feel safe there, besides, waiting at the dorms would remind her of what had transpired between them last; a memory he needed to keep held afar, at least until he could rein in her fear of him.

At last, he felt that he was ready. He had to take the motorcycle. To force upon himself the patience of walking, would be just too much. He drove into town and as he neared the bookstore, he felt her presence, still burning brightly strong in his mind. She was indeed working at the DownTime this evening, as he had presumed; he felt less affected by her mark though. His body and blood recognized her and longed for her, to be sure, but he felt his rational mind was less influenced by it, and was sure he could speak to her without fear of losing control.

As he parked in the lot, he was heartened to see that Ben's vehicle was not even there. Could he be so fortunate, as to escape having to deal with him? He hoped Felicity would still feel safe without Ben's presence. It was important that she feel Cain was not cornering her. He approached the door to find it already locked. He didn't wear a watch, but could see by the clock on the wall inside, that it would only just reach ten in a minute or so.

He did not see Felicity inside, although he could feel her. There was an older woman and a young, well-dressed man, talking near the counter in the café. They hadn't noticed him. He would wait unobtrusively, until Felicity appeared, and then knock. That way, it could be her decision whether or not to admit him. She would feel as though she were in control, and hopefully, unthreatened.

As he watched through the glass, Felicity emerged from the room behind the café counter. Cain was stunned. She looked absolutely exquisite. She wore a modest but truly enticing gown, and her hair had been elegantly swept up and back from her face. She seemed honestly to be the most beautiful vision he had ever beheld. She was also clearly planning to leave with the nicely dressed young man who now took her arm to lead her across the café to the door.

Cain had only a moment to comprehend this new turn of events, before he was forced to rush back to the bike and leave the lot. However badly he would like to see her, it would not be like this. He quickly drove across the street and over into the lot at Tommy's. When he cut the engine, Felicity was still only just entering the young man's car. They had taken their time in exiting the building and locking the door. They hadn't noticed him.

Cain watched, dolefully, as they sped off past him, down the road. Who was it that she was with? He had never seen the man before, he was sure. She had seemed friendly, though not overly familiar with him. Cain hadn't been able to watch them long enough to really tell.

Where were they going? Should he follow? He decided against it. Why torture himself? He wouldn't follow after to try and ruin her evening or demand that she give herself over to him. That would be absurd. He would simply have to accept that she had interests other than him. It did not mean that she would deny him when he finally did approach, he hoped. He would simply have to wait.

He climbed off the motorcycle and entered the bar. It was as good a place to spend the evening as any, and he could definitely use a drink. He peered through the gloom at the various patrons. It seemed an older crowd tonight, not very many of the college students, who usually made up a large part of the customers. In fact it wasn't crowded at all; odd for a Saturday night.

Alyson was also seemingly absent, a fact for which he was grateful. He sat on the stool at the very end of the bar, in the back against the far wall. Upon ordering a rum and coke, he made sure that the bartender was generous with the rum, and understood that his glass was never to remain empty. He left a nice pile of bills to ensure the man's cooperation.

Felicity's presence still flickered in the back of his mind. She was far enough that he could no longer feel her but he could still see her mark easily. He kept waiting for it to recede, but she stayed stubbornly just within reach.

The college, Cain realized. There must be some formal school function that they had gone to. That was why the bar was so empty, and why Felicity had been so charmingly dressed. The college was too close; he would still be able to sense her. So even here, he would be tortured and unable to forget his evening's loss.

He downed his drink and considered leaving. Then the bartender set another glass before him and he decided to stay. What's the difference? At least he would know where she was and when she left. Perhaps he could approach her then. *Before she has a chance to go somewhere else with the stranger she's with.*

He knew he could not suffer to know that she was somewhere private with a man other than him. Not now, not after all of this. His anticipation and hopes for the evening brought to *this* bitter end. At least they were surely at a public function, surrounded by others. He quickly drank the contents of his new glass and tried to find something else to think about.

Unfortunately, the new topic that brought itself to his attention was not one he would have chosen on his own. Sindy approached. She was trying so hard to conceal herself, that he almost felt bad for her. Her trace in his mind blinked on and off like a Christmas tree light. She was making progress though. Eventually, she would learn the trick, and heaven help him when she did.

She was nearing the door. He decided to stand, to make himself ready for her arrival. He wasn't sure if she'd recognize his Harley out front. Although he remained psychically concealed, he wasn't going to try and hide from her physically.

He felt emotionally fatigued and weary, and now that he had settled in, he was becoming comfortable here. He wouldn't let her chase him out. So he stood against the wall next to his seat, with his third drink in his hand, and watched her saunter in.

She looked for all the world, like a cat on the prowl. Every guy in the bar was intrigued by her presence, but she deigned to notice none of them. When she saw Cain in the back of the bar, she made ready to pounce.

He did nothing to inhibit her approach. They were supposedly under truce, for all the authority Arif had anyway; which to Cain's mind was really none, but he felt Sindy would obey the man. She should have been told to leave him alone. So he stood to meet her, trying to decide in his mind if *her* company was better than none.

He chugged the contents of his glass and put it down on the bar, as Sindy approached without the least bit of trepidation. "There you are, I've been searching. I wish you wouldn't cloak your mark all the time. I hate that you always make it so difficult," she said as she closed the expanse between them.

"You know what they say, 'a good man is hard to find'."

Instead of stopping at a respectful distance, she came right up to him, as though they were intimate friends. Personal space was a concept that she consistently ignored. "That's not what *I* say. *I* prefer the saying, 'a hard man is good to find'."

For emphasis, she reached down to rub his groin, at which point he grabbed her wrist. He kept her from touching him as she refused to take her hand away. He increased the pressure on the delicate bones there, but she still would not relent.

She was obviously in pain, but still fought him and forced herself to smile. Her voice betrayed her with a slight tremble. "What are you gonna do, break my wrist? Go ahead, at least I'll finally be giving you some sort of physical satisfaction."

At these words, he promptly let go, and she gave him a token caress there. "Come on Cain. What's the matter? Are you *so* afraid of letting me make you happy, in any way? I know you've got this whole 'passive aggressive' thing goin' on here, but maybe, deep inside your secret self, what you really need is a girl who can actually *take* what you have to dish out."

She lifted her face to his and whispered against his left cheek. "I know there is some major turmoil bubblin' just beneath the surface of that sweet calm face you like to show the world. You need someone to rip into once in awhile? You want to give some of that to me? Go ahead, I like it rough. I know some guys really get off on that kind of thing. Bring it on...if that's the only way I can get you to touch me. I'd take it... from you."

He held himself very still, unwilling to lose his composure. "That's not my style," he told her, his voice quiet, but forceful.

She still persisted, whispering to him, her lips practically at his ear. "And what is your style, Cain? Innocent, doe-eyed little things that wither and die when you touch them? You can bring them nothing but heartache and death, no matter how you try."

He closed his eyes and tried not to let her words land in his heart, where he surely knew them to be true. She reached her hand up to the right side of his face as she placed a small, soft kiss upon his left cheek; the only tender and fragile gesture he had ever known her to make towards him. Her advances in the past had always been brash and bold, like when she had taken the liberty to touch him just before.

This was different, this gesture felt comforting and sincere; as though she knew his tortured heart, and understood. He held himself as unmoving as a statue. Somewhere, in the back of his mind, he wondered if it wouldn't just be better to accept his lot. To accept the fact that Felicity, or any other woman, would only suffer at his hands, and here before him was one who could truly thrive in his hold upon her. Even as he knew it to be true, he refused to accept it.

When next she spoke, her voice quivered with such heartfelt despair that it startled him. "I can give you so much more than they ever could." Surely, there was hope for Sindy yet, to change her ways. But right now, he needed someone sweet and tender; someone who could help him heal the loneliness he suffered from. Sindy could display that gentleness, but it was always fleeting and seldom heartfelt.

He wanted Felicity. He opened his eyes and looked at her with unconcealed heartbreak in his eyes. "You surely could." He saw undisguised hope and relief flash through her eyes for a brief moment, but he continued. "But I can't accept it. Not now."

Her eyes seemed to melt with sorrow, before she brought back the malicious glint he so often saw reflected there. "Well, as a matter of fact, I wasn't here to seduce you anyway," she proclaimed, although she still held herself close to him. He hadn't the resolve to push her away. His words had pushed her far enough. "I was just here to congratulate you. You actually did it."

He realized with a guilty start, what she was referring to, as she went on. "You marked her. I didn't really think you would, but I guess that just proves my point. You can act as civilized and aloof from me as you want, but we're really just the same, you and I. You drank her blood." She sucked in a slow stream of breath. "And I *know* you enjoyed it."

Sindy leaned close to whisper intimately into his ear once again. "Was it good? ...Did she cry?"

That broke him. He shoved her off of him with such force that she overturned the chair behind her. She righted herself and laughed at him, to cover any true feelings she might have. "You still wanna play with humans? I can play too. In fact, I'm gonna have me a good time! You can consider Benjamin **mine.**"

"You're setting yourself up for severe disappointment. He'll never let you take him. Even if he did, no matter what you do to him, no matter what kind of mindless slave you might try to force him to become, the sad truth is, he will **never** love you. You cannot force someone to love you. You poor girl. What kind of past have you endured that you cannot see that?"

She had no words to rebuke him. He had never seen her eyes well with true tears in the way that they did now. He had touched the heart of her sorrow, of her anger.

Perhaps he shouldn't, but he pressed on. "There are other ways to gain approval from people. There are other ways to feel accepted and loved. Surely, your fine body is not the only asset that you possess. Haven't you a fine mind at your disposal as well? Is there truly a heart within you, under all of the scar tissue and pain?"

His words seemed to strike her like blows. She flinched at each syllable until he thought she would finally break down and cry. She did not.

As his last words filled the air, she picked up his glass from the bar and threw it at his face. He jerked aside and it smashed against the wall next to his head. As bits of glass showered him from the side, she turned and fled.

The bar had grown noticeably quiet, as its occupants became aware of their little drama. Cain was unsure how much they had actually heard, and found that he didn't really care. Let them think what they would.

He composed himself and realized that he must go after her. Not to redeem his words, or to confront her, but to ensure that she would not unleash her fury upon the next unlucky soul she met. He brushed the last shards of glass from his hair, and followed her flickering presence out into the night.

Chapter 27 - Revelations

Felicity

The DownTime café and bookstore
Earlier Saturday evening

When Felicity arrived at work for her shift on Saturday, both Harold and Nadine were working in the café. She was in the bookstore with Lucy, who obviously felt bad, when she saw Felicity carry in her dress. Felicity hadn't asked for off. Lucy said she was sorry that she couldn't switch to close for her so that she could leave on time for the dance, but she had plans.

Felicity told her not to give it another thought. She did however, apprehensively ask who she'd be closing with. She eyed Harold distastefully and thought about having to change in the lounge while he waited for her, probably trying to peek in the window.

It was with great relief that she heard Nadine would be the one closing. As the busy day wound to an end, Nadine called her over to the café. Felicity approached with a broad smile, grateful not to be stuck with Harold. "Hi, I was surprised to see you here. Don't you usually have the day shift?"

"Yes, I'm covering for Ben. He has that dance to go to. Don't you go to that school?" Nadine asked.

"Yeah, I'm going to the dance, just a little late. My date's picking me up here actually," Felicity told her.

"Well, I can't pretend I didn't know. I saw your dress hanging up in the back. It's lovely," Nadine replied with a smile.

"Thanks." It *was* a pretty dress; she had worn it to her cousin's wedding. It was a long, champagne colored oriental style dress, sleeveless with a slit up one side. It also had buttons all up that side and a high collar, with a teardrop shaped cut out at the throat, just below the top button. It was demure, but very attractive in the way it hugged her curves.

Nadine folded her hands in front of her and looked at Felicity in the motherly way she usually affected with the younger employees. "You shouldn't be here so late, you should have told Mr. Penten that you had plans."

"That's alright, I don't mind. It isn't really all that important to me, it's just a dance," Felicity told her.

"And the boy?" Nadine asked.

"He's just a guy. It's not like he's my boyfriend or anything. We're okay going late," Felicity assured her.

"Well all the same, why don't you go and close out your register now? You want to be sure and give yourself enough time to get ready."

Felicity looked over at the clock. "It's barely 9:30, I still have customers."

"That's alright. You just tell them to bring their selections over to the café when they're ready. I can ring them up here. It's not like I have anywhere to go."

Felicity smiled. "Thanks."

She was almost ready when she began to feel nervous chills travel over her. Her mind wandered to Cain and she felt a sudden wave of longing for him that astonished her. *Not now!* she thought to herself viciously.

She practically jumped when she heard the bell over the door. It was almost ten o'clock. She peeked out the lounge door to see who it was and let out a small sigh of relief. "That's him, his name's Todd," she told Nadine. "I'm almost ready. Oh, and you should tell him to lock the door behind him," she added, thinking of Sindy the night before.

She tried to shake that odd feeling that seemed to pursue her so often lately. It had grown quite strong and her hands were shaking as she did the last of the buttons on her dress. What was wrong with her nerves? She shook her hands out into the air as if she could free herself through them of the jitters that had taken over her. She heard Nadine and Todd making small talk as she finished fixing her hair. She had put it up in a loose French twist with some curls falling down the side. It looked nice with the high neckline of the dress. She put her earrings on and hurried out to meet him.

He gave her quite a smile when she appeared. "Hi, you look beautiful."

"Thanks." She felt a little awkward, accepting the compliment. He was nice, but she really didn't feel anything special towards him. "Nadine was nice enough to give me extra time to fix my hair and stuff."

Nadine smiled and ushered her out from behind the counter. "That's alright, you two just get going. You're late enough."

Todd obediently took Felicity's arm and led her to the door, but she refused to leave before Nadine was ready. She wanted to see the woman safely into her car. They waited as Nadine finished straightening up, grabbed her coat and shut the lights.

Once the store was locked up, Todd opened the door to his car for Felicity. As she got in, she wondered if Sindy was going to show up as she had implied. She hoped that they could handle it without too much trouble. What if she said something inexplicable to Todd?

Her focus would probably be on Ben though. She felt bad for him, as he'd most likely spend the whole evening looking over his shoulder, unable to enjoy himself. Undoubtedly, that was Sindy's intention all along. It would ruin Ben's evening whether she showed up or not. At least her own inner tremors seemed to be receding.

Todd looked very nice tonight, but there really was no spark between them. Maybe it was because things seemed too complicated right now, but she just couldn't see him as a prospective boyfriend. When they arrived, Todd parked the car and as she began to open her door, he ran around to open it for her. Again, she felt a pang of regret. She hoped he didn't think this would be the start of something.

When they reached the entrance, they needed to purchase tickets, since neither of them had done it ahead of time. Felicity was quick to buy her own. Todd was a little surprised and told her he had planned to buy her one, but she insisted on paying for herself. "It's not really a date; we're just keeping each other company. I'll pay for myself." She hoped she didn't sound too harsh, but she didn't want to give him the wrong impression, and those were *his* words after all.

They entered the ballroom and Felicity was amazed at how beautifully it was decorated. She didn't see Ben, but Karen and Jack found them almost immediately. "You guys look great! Let me get a picture!" Karen quickly whipped a small camera out of her purse. Todd put his arm around her and Felicity obediently posed, although she felt a bit awkward.

"Don't worry; I'll make sure you get copies," Karen said, as she snapped their picture. They all stood and talked for a few minutes and then Todd offered to go and get her a drink. When he and Jack left, Karen practically pounced on the opportunity to fire off a barrage of questions about Todd. "Isn't he nice? Do you like him? You look fabulous! He looks really good tonight too, don't you think?"

"Karen, I don't want to disappoint anyone, but I don't think anything is going to happen between us. I'm just not looking for anyone right now. I hope Todd understands that it's not him." Karen quickly lost her smile, and Felicity felt like a heel. "I'm sorry; I know you wanted me to make him feel better. Maybe I shouldn't have even come."

Karen seemed disappointed, but shook her head. "No. I'm glad you came. Don't worry about it. Todd'll be okay. I mean, still give him a chance; you might change your mind, but don't feel like you have to force yourself to like him or something. If you both just needed to get out, then mission accomplished, right?"

"Yeah." Felicity smiled, grateful that Karen seemed to understand. The guys arrived with their drinks. "Thanks."

They stood and talked until Karen made Jack take her out onto the dance floor. "We'll stay here. I promised Felicity she wouldn't have to dance," Todd explained. Jack and Karen left with a laugh.

Just then, Felicity noticed Alyson across the room. Alyson saw her at the same time, but thankfully she began to walk over, instead of screaming and yelling for her, as Felicity had half expected her to do.

She was wearing knee high black leather boots with the black satin pants she had worn to Tommy's on Ladies' Night. She had paired them with a fitted, shiny pink satin blouse that was not buttoned at all until the very place where it tucked into her pants, being that Allie had such a slight figure, the shirt, although very daring, was at least not embarrassingly so. Felicity still had to stifle the urge to want to button it for her. She also seemed to have added some extra pink streaks to her heavily moussed and wildly shorn hair.

"Hi, I was wondering when you were gonna show up," Allie said as she arrived. She made no pretense as she obviously appraised Todd.

"Alyson, this is Todd. I didn't think you were coming."

"Somebody's got to watch the door for Ben; he's been a little preoccupied."

Felicity followed Allie's gaze to find Ben on the dance floor. He was wearing a really nice dress shirt of a dark golden color, with a black, gold and olive green tie, and black pants. The colors nicely complimented his honey-brown eyes and dark wavy hair. He was clean shaven and actually looked very dashing, but what really caught Felicity's eye, was the woman that he was dancing with.

Brenda was a stunning brunette. She was tall, voluptuous and totally unlike someone that Felicity would have expected to take a class called 'Critical Issues in Law and Society'. Felicity would have to remind herself not to make such preconceived assumptions about people. She wore a classy deep blue silk dress and looked extremely sexy in it. "Wow," she muttered.

"Tell me about it," Allie replied with a chuckle.

Todd seemed to figure out who they were looking at. "Is that your 'ex.'?"

"Oh...no! He's really not. He's just a friend of ours."

Allie smiled. "I don't think her 'ex.' is gonna show. He's not all that sociable."

Felicity gave her a warning look to get off the topic. "He's not my 'ex.'. He's not my anything." She turned back to Todd. "Maybe we should go try and dance, after all." She took his hand and practically pulled him to the dance floor to get away from Allie.

Once there, but not too close to Ben and Brenda, she stopped and looked at him. "You don't mind, do you?"

He laughed. "No, not at all."

They began to dance, hesitantly at first. Felicity had always been terribly self-conscious, trying to dance to fast songs, but she pretty much just copied everyone else and Todd managed to make it kind of fun. After a song or two, she found that she was actually enjoying herself. She was glad she came.

At first it was fine, but soon after they started, she began feeling flushed and getting chills, just as she had earlier and in the theater. When it began, she wondered if it might be because of Todd. He *had* been present each time it occurred, but...no. She studied him for a moment and knew almost instantly that it had nothing to do with Todd.

The feeling settled down into that strangely charged, pins and needles sensation. She felt it growing stronger and found it hard to even sway and dance. It was almost like, a calling; a summons of some kind, as though there were somewhere else she desperately needed to go, although she couldn't say what had put that into her head. The thought frightened her. Mostly because the feeling also brought with it urges of a passionate nature, which seemed to wash over her every now and again.

The feelings were definitely not connected to Todd, but were beginning to make dancing so closely with him, increasingly uncomfortable. She became overly conscious of him touching her and the feeling was growing stronger by the minute. She began to feel inexplicably panic stricken, as though she had to get away from the feeling, even as it called her towards it, though she couldn't say how or why. Maybe it was an anxiety attack of some kind.

Finally, she stopped dancing and looked up at Todd. "I'm sorry. This is nice, really, but I've gotta go. Please don't hate me," she pleaded.

Todd looked at her with confused concern. "I don't hate you, but what's wrong?"

She kept looking around as though she might see the source of her discontentment, but could find nothing to explain it. She wasn't sure how, but she was almost certain it had to do with Cain. She suddenly flinched and backed away from Todd. His hand had brushed down the side of her thigh as he took it off of her hip where it had rested, and it had sent a shiver through her. He looked very hurt and confused. "Nothing's wrong, I just...I need to go get some air."

"Well, let me take you."

"No, that's okay. I..."

Just then, Ben took notice of them and brought Brenda over for introductions. "Hi, you made it."

"Hi Ben, Um, this is Todd," Felicity offered, distractedly.

"Hey, how's it goin'?" Todd asked with a little wave.

"Hi, this is Brenda," Ben answered.

Brenda smiled and offered a "Hello".

Felicity was growing impatient, the odd feeling was as strong as it had been at the theater and it wasn't going away. She didn't know what it meant, but it was very disconcerting. "Nice to meet you. I was actually just stepping out," she said with a little look of apology. She turned to go, but Ben touched her arm, it made her jump.

"Where are you going?" he asked.

"Nowhere, I'll be back," Felicity assured him.

As she walked away, she heard Ben ask, "Is she okay?"

Todd answered. "I couldn't really say."

After that, their conversation was lost as she made her way through the crowded dance floor. She thought she heard Ben call after her, but she kept walking. She thought she could sense the disquieting feeling beginning to fade as she crossed the room. It suddenly occurred to her, that if the feeling was tied to Cain somehow, maybe it meant that he was here. She stopped and looked around again.

Ben caught up to her and gently spun her around. "Where are you going?"

"The bathroom," she lied.

"The bathrooms are over there," he said, pointing back in the direction they'd come. "Where are you really going? Are you okay?"

"I'm fine; I just wanted to get out for a minute."

"Why, what's wrong?" Ben asked.

Allie came jogging over to them. "There you are, I've been looking. Sindy's here."

Felicity looked at Allie in confusion. "*Sindy* is?"

"Were you expecting someone else?" A strange look of comprehension passed over Allie's face. "Oh. Is Cain here too?"

She looked at Allie in agitation. "I haven't seen him." Alyson seemed to think that she hadn't answered the question, and was about to speak again when Felicity cut her off. "I've gotta go get some air."

Ben took her arm again. "Are you nuts? You can't go outside now!" He turned to Allie. "Where's Sindy?"

Allie looked around. "Well, she came in that door," she said with a gesture to the right, "but then I came to find you guys and I guess I'm not as good at keeping track of her as I used to be," she added with a pointed look at Felicity, who wasn't really sure what she meant. She realized that Allie must know Cain had bitten her, but what did that have to do with Sindy?

Ben tried to take control of things. "Look, we're in the middle of a crowded dance floor. Nothing is going to happen to us here. We still have at least two hours left until the dance ends. We might as well try to enjoy ourselves, just keep your eyes open. We left Brenda and Todd just standing there. We really should get back to them. Just keep your cool, okay?" He looked closer at Felicity. "Alright?"

She answered him distractedly. "Yeah, okay."

"Come on." He started back to where they had left their dates. Alyson started to follow, when she noticed that Felicity had become very still and was staring unflinchingly across the room.

Cain, in the far entrance. He was just standing there, unthreatening, unmoving, just watching her. He wore a teal blue dress shirt, half buttoned, over his usual black t-shirt and tucked into a pair of black jeans. He scanned the crowd and then let his eyes fall back to Felicity. She was frozen, watching him. He seemed to be deciding if she would let him approach. After a few minutes, he slowly began to cross the room.

Felicity was panic stricken and thrilled at the same time. She was frightened because she knew that the strange sensations she had been feeling were definitely coming from him and she wasn't sure what that meant, but she also felt relieved to finally see him. Her heart pounded at the mere sight of him and she was more drawn to him than ever, even though her mind tried to fight it. She felt caught between running to him and running away, so she just stood there, unable to move.

Alyson put a hand on her shoulder and spoke into her ear. "It's okay. You're in a room full of people; I'll be right over here." She felt Allie move away a bit and realized that Ben had gone on to Todd and Brenda, without noticing that she and Alyson weren't right behind him.

A room full of people; they might as well not even exist. She felt as though the noise was gone and the lights had dimmed. It seemed she and Cain were in their own private dimension; like she was seeing him with tunnel vision. He finally stopped just shy of her. She realized that he wanted *her* to walk the last few feet to him, to see if she would.

She looked at his face, his eyes. He looked just the way she always pictured him. Gentle, unintimidating and handsome, with just a hint of a jaunty grin playing about his lips. He had such clear and honest eyes, the most beautiful shade of blue she'd ever seen.

She had to go to him. How could she not? She tried to remind herself of what he'd done, but then she thought of what he hadn't. He could easily have killed her. He still could, but she didn't really believe that would happen and the longer she paused the more his eyes began to fill with hurt and sadness. She went to him.

She stopped close enough to talk, without having to yell over the music, but didn't know what to say. He looked at her with a sad little smile. Then he looked aside and she turned to see what he saw. Ben, with Allie, Brenda and Todd, talking, unalarmed. Ben knew they were there and did look over once in a while, but seemed annoyed, more than overly concerned.

Cain looked back to her. "You didn't tell them," he confirmed with pleasant surprise. She opened her mouth to speak, but unsure how to reply, she closed it again. He smiled at her, looking almost apologetic. "We need to talk, I know. This isn't exactly the setting I would have chosen," he said with a glance at the crowd of people dancing around them. "But I was following Sindy. I'll be needing to keep her out of trouble, I imagine."

Felicity found her voice and asked quietly, "She won't do anything here, will she?"

Cain glanced at her friends again. "You mean besides try to ruin Ben's evening? No, nothing too life threatening anyway, but she can be unpredictable at times." He stopped to look into her eyes for a moment, seemingly judging her reaction to him.

She felt as though her skin was humming from his closeness. He hadn't touched her though. She wondered what it would feel like if he did. She was glad when he spoke again, because she had no idea what to say. "Look, we haven't time yet for long drawn out explanations, which I can't really say I'm looking forward to giving." He suddenly looked around distractedly and backed away from her as if to leave. "I've got something to take care of, but I'll be back."

"When?" she asked indignantly. He was just going to show up like this and then leave, without resolving anything?

"Tonight, not long." He turned back to face her with a smile. "You'll know."

He circled around her and as she turned to watch him leave, she was startled to find Allie standing right behind her. "Everything okay?"

She looked back to where Cain had gone, but couldn't see him through the people. "I don't know yet." She sighed and looked at Alyson in resignation. "You *know*, don't you?"

For a second Allie looked as though she might like to make Felicity actually say it, but then spared her. "That Cain bit you? Yeah, I kind of figured that out."

"How did you know? And how did *Sindy* know? And if I can feel Cain like that, does that mean you can feel Sindy?"

Allie chuckled. "I don't mind playing twenty questions, but don't you think we ought to move it off the dance floor?"

Felicity looked around, suddenly aware of all the dancers, although of course they had been there all along. "Oh, right." She looked to find Ben, but saw only Brenda and Todd, dancing together. "Where's Ben?"

Alyson put a hand on her shoulder. "Don't worry, he's talking to Cain. Come on." Alyson took her by the hand and led her through the people to an open doorway.

"I don't think we should leave."

"Don't worry, we're not." Alyson stuck her head out into the deserted hallway beyond the door. "Just trying to get a little privacy." She stepped out into the hall and settled herself against the wall just outside the doorway.

Felicity gave a worried glance around and then stepped out to face Allie. "How did you know?"

"Just perceptive I guess. It's not like you hid it all that well." Felicity became alarmed. "Don't worry, Ben has no clue, but you know, you're not the *first* girl to ever be bitten for reasons other than hunger."

"Other reasons?"

"Guess Cain's explanations didn't get that far, huh? I'll let *him* give you the whys and wherefores, but don't try to tell me it was all bad," she said with a knowing smirk. Felicity was mortified that Alyson might know how she had felt when Cain bit her. She said nothing and Alyson continued. "I'll just say, that the times *I've* been bitten, haven't all been accidents."

Felicity found that appalling. "By *Sindy?*" She was glad to see that Alyson found this revolting as well.

"Ew! No!" She considered a moment. "Not that I have a problem with girls in general, but it wouldn't be her! No, *this* was from Sindy," she said, gesturing to the scar on her throat. "I'm talking about these." Now she moved her shirt collar, to bare the other side of her throat. Felicity couldn't even see anything at first. Then as she looked closer, she began to recognize sets of tiny puncture marks, like she herself had received from Cain. They were healed and very faint, but they crisscrossed and overlapped so that she couldn't even tell how many times Allie had been bitten.

Felicity looked up in disbelief and then felt a wave of indignance pass over her. "Cain?"

Alyson looked insulted. "No, of course not. I hardly even know the guy." She glanced back into the ballroom, to see if they were being overheard. There was no one near. She looked back at Felicity and her voice took on a shy, quiet quality, which Felicity had never heard from Alyson before. "I see Mattie sometimes."

Felicity's mouth fell open in shock. "Ben's friend?"

"He's my friend too! I guess Ben's mentioned him, huh? Well, we've been *more* than friends, before and after, but Ben doesn't know that and you can't tell him, e*ver*."

"I wouldn't. Mattie's still around here? Ben thinks he's long gone."

Alyson shrugged. "He moves around a lot, but he always comes back to visit. He said I'd see him again before Halloween. I hope he's got the good sense to stay away until everything calms down though." Allie looked genuinely worried about him.

Felicity didn't know what to say about Mattie, so she brought up more immediate matters. "Where do you think Sindy went? It doesn't make any sense, her being here. If she were going to do something tonight, then why'd she come warn us about it?"

"I don't think she came to warn us. No, I'll bet she didn't even expect Ben and I to be there last night. She came to see you."

"She said that, but why?"

"To see if you were marked."

"Marked? What is that, vampirese?" Felicity asked in annoyance.

"By Cain. Don't you get it? Cain *bit* you," Allie explained.

"So, what does that mean to anybody else?" Felicity asked.

"It means you are probably the safest person in this place. It's like having a 'get out of jail free' card." Felicity was staring at her in total incomprehension. Alyson started speaking with exaggerated slowness, as though she were talking to a child. "Cain bit you. It puts a mark on you, like you belong to him now. No other vamp is gonna come anywhere near you; you're *his*," Allie assured her.

"Like the blood!" Felicity exclaimed in sudden understanding.

"Okay, now *you've* lost *me*. What blood?" Alyson asked.

"Cain gave me a necklace, a vial of his blood. He said others could smell it and they'd leave me alone," Felicity clarified.

"No way! Does that really work? I gotta get me one of those!"

Felicity just shook her head and laughed quietly to herself. Alyson looked at her questioningly. "Just something Cain said, when he gave it to me. He said it wasn't as good as the 'conventional method'. Now I know what he was talking about."

"I gotta be honest, I'd rather be bit than not." Felicity gave her an odd look. "For practical reasons. There are certain advantages. At least you only have to worry about one vampire getting you, instead of looking out for all of them. And it's not like they can sneak up on you," she said with a knowing smile.

"What *is* that?" Felicity asked.

"I don't know how it works, but it's kind of cool, isn't it?"

"But wait, couldn't you use that to find Sindy?" Felicity questioned.

"Na. Doesn't last forever. It fades," Allie explained.

"Oh, how long?" Felicity asked.

"Three weeks, a month tops. It was kind of useful, but I'm not gonna let her bite me again, just so I can keep tabs on her." They stood in awkward silence for a minute as Felicity tried to assimilate this new information. Alyson got antsy. "Maybe we should go back inside. If Ben comes looking and can't find us, he's gonna freak."

"Yeah, okay." They moved back into the dance hall, when Alyson stopped her just inside the doorway.

"Listen, don't tell Ben any more than you have to. He's very comfortable in the dark. If you put him on overload, I'll be the one dealin' with the fall out."

Felicity nodded. "Don't worry, I won't." She couldn't imagine Ben calmly listening to explanations of 'practical' vampire bites, anyway.

They re-entered the ballroom. It took only a moment for Ben to come and pounce on them. "There you are! I thought you were going to go stay with Todd and Brenda?"

Felicity looked at the couple in question; they certainly looked like a couple too. They were dancing rather closely. She saw Brenda lean in to hear Todd whisper something to her. Then she gave, what looked to Felicity, to be a very well practiced and flirtatious laugh. Felicity gestured for Ben to see them. "They don't seem to miss us much."

Ben was not pleased. "Great. Doesn't that bother you?"

Felicity tried not to smile at Ben's distress. "Not really."

"Thanks a lot."

"Well what do you want me to do? Should I go over there and take him back, get him out of your way?"

Ben looked at her condescendingly. "He is not in my way. I could get her away from him if I wanted."

Both Allie and Felicity chuckled at that boast. "Is that so?"

"I could." He watched Brenda for a few more minutes. "Screw it. We didn't have all that much in common anyway."

Alyson put a hand on his shoulder. "You mean besides both of you being incredibly attractive? What else is there?"

"Very funny."

"Seriously Ben. You set yourself up with these gorgeous supermodel types, then you get all pissed off when they're stunningly stupid and shallow, like you never saw it coming."

"The girls I date are not stupid and shallow!" Ben retorted, but no sooner were the words out of his mouth, than circumstances seemed to conspire to prove him wrong. Who should approach, but Ashley, looking absolutely amazing and with a very handsome and athletic looking hunk on her arm.

Felicity could have laughed at the way she most obviously conspired to guide her date into Ben's path and then affected that she hadn't noticed him until now. "Ben, hi! What a surprise to see you over here. I would have thought you'd be on the dance floor, with…Brenda was it? Oh wait, isn't that her over there? She seems to be having a very good time. I know I am. Enjoy the rest of your evening!" She gave a little wave to include Felicity and Alyson as well and then made her way out onto the dance floor with her date.

Ben watched her sullenly and then turned back to Allie and Felicity. "Okay, maybe Ashley fits the bill," he agreed grudgingly, "but Brenda's not stupid. And she's not all *that* shallow." He looked back over at the girl in question as Allie and Felicity smirked at him. "They're probably better off anyway," he said, turning to Felicity. "If Sindy saw us with them, they'd become targets for sure."

"Where is Sindy anyway? You don't think she left?"

"Cain said he was going to talk to her."

Allie looked steadily at Felicity. "Then we know he's keeping her safely far out of the way. Right?"

Felicity realized what she meant. Cain was definitely not in the building. "Yeah, right. So you probably could go back to your date, if you wanted," she said to Ben.

Ben looked at Brenda again and then shrugged. "What for?" He turned back to Allie and then Felicity. "I've got two beautiful women right here. At least I don't have to worry about turning you two into vampire bait. You come with your own stakes and crosses."

Felicity raised an eyebrow. "Convenient."

Ben smiled. "So, what do we do now?"

"Let's dance," Alyson answered. Felicity gave them both a pained expression which, in concert, they both ignored and dragged her to the dance floor.

After a song or two Felicity thought she might actually be starting to like dancing after all. Karen discovered them and came over; presumably to make sure Felicity hadn't ditched her date. She pulled Felicity of to the side for a moment. "Where's Todd?"

Felicity gestured towards Todd and his newfound dance partner. "They seemed to hit it off, so I thought I'd stay out of the way," Felicity explained. Karen was immediately thrilled for him. She pulled her camera back out and made Felicity, Ben and Allie pose for a few pictures, before finding her way back to Jack.

Another slow dance began. Felicity looked to both Ben and Alyson. "You guys go ahead, I don't really like to dance all that much anyway."

She stepped back as if to leave, but Allie stopped her. "You're gonna have to take Ben, because I've got someone else in mind."

"Who?" Felicity asked.

"See that guy alone at the bar?" Allie asked.

Felicity saw who she meant, and he was definitely dance worthy. "Nice."

"I thought so," Allie answered. "Do you know him?"

Ben and Felicity both shook their heads as Felicity asked, "So what are you going to do?"

"I'm gonna go dance with him," Allie answered.

"Just like that?" Felicity asked.

"Just like that," Allie confirmed.

Felicity smiled. "Good luck."

Alyson seemed undaunted. "Who needs luck?" she answered as she went off to claim her new dance partner.

Felicity faced Ben, hardly believing Allie's confidence. "Not exactly shy, is she?"

Ben gave her a look of disbelief. "Have you *met* Alyson? The girl's got pink hair and no buttons in her shirt. You thought she might be shy?"

Felicity laughed. "Well good for her. I could never do that."

"Ask a guy to dance? Why not?"

She shrugged. "I'm just not good at that sort of thing."

Ben smiled at her. "A girl like *you* doesn't have to be good at that sort of thing."

"And what exactly am I like?"

"You know, different from Alyson," Ben told her.

"Could you be more vague?" Felicity asked with a laugh.

"I just meant that you're more like...my type," Ben clarified.

"Stunningly stupid and shallow?" she asked in mock outrage.

"No! I meant the gorgeous super-model part," he clarified, sheepishly.

"Oh..."

"Hey look, she got him to dance. Way to go Allie!"

Felicity didn't even glance over, she was busy staring at Ben in bewilderment. "Did you just call me gorgeous?"

He looked back at her skeptically. "Do you own a mirror?" She was taken aback by his 'matter of fact' attitude, before she could think of a reply, he continued. "So are we just going to stand here?" he asked, looking at the dancers all around them.

"Oh, right." She hesitantly moved a little closer and he put his arm around her waist. She felt awkward, like she wasn't sure what to do with her hands, but Ben seemed confident and eventually things fell into place. She looked up to find him gazing back at her with a smile. He really did look very handsome tonight. The color of his shirt brought out the golden brown of his eyes. They danced in comfortable silence for a moment, until someone next to them cleared his throat.

"Todd!"

"Hi, I'm sorry to interrupt..." Todd offered hesitantly.

Ben didn't say anything, but seemed annoyed as he dropped his arm from her waist. Felicity turned to address Todd. "I'm sorry we never came back. To tell you the truth, you and Brenda seemed to be hitting it off, so I thought you might rather I...kept my distance."

Todd smiled at her appreciatively. "Thanks. Would you mind if I drove her home?"

Felicity smiled, happy for him. "Not at all."

"Actually, I was asking Ben."

"Oh," she answered sheepishly.

She looked to see that Ben was much less happy, but seemed resigned. "I guess, if she wants you too."

"Well, when you didn't come back..." Todd began.

"I know. Should I go over and..." Ben started to ask.

"No," Felicity and Todd quickly answered in unison.

"I'm sure she understands," added Felicity, as Todd looked at her gratefully.

Ben gave Felicity a strange look and then turned back to Todd. "Okay. I guess you can tell her I said goodnight. I'll see her in class."

Todd nodded to them both. "Thanks, goodnight."

Felicity watched as he left them to rejoin Brenda, who was waiting not far off. Now *she's* gorgeous, Felicity thought. She looked at Ben, who seemed to have a hard time taking his eyes off Brenda. "Sorry. You didn't really like her all that much, did you?"

Ben gave a sharp bark of a laugh. "Have you seen her?" He gave Felicity a timid grin and sighed. "No, not really." He didn't sound very convincing.

The song was ending, but Alyson showed no signs of leaving her new prize. The D.J. made an announcement that this would be the last song of the evening. It was another slow song. Felicity wondered if Ben would want to dance with her again. Especially since they'd hardly even had a chance before Todd had come over, but he didn't even seem to consider it. "I'm going to run to the bathroom before we leave," he said.

"Alone?"

"Did you want to come help?" he asked in amusement.

"I just meant, do you think it's safe?"

He smiled. "I know what you meant. I'm fine. I'll be right back."

As he walked away, she realized that she was feeling Cain's presence again. It was strange. Now that she knew what it meant, it wasn't nearly so disconcerting as before. Where before it had been odd and frightening, now she felt expectant and almost exhilarated. She turned to face the direction it seemed to be coming from. After a moment, he appeared in the doorway.

As he crossed the room, she found that she couldn't take her eyes from him. She was annoyed that he had disappeared before they'd had a chance to talk, but she was surprised to find that she wasn't mad at him. In fact, she had a hard time feeling anything other than an incredible attraction towards him. She wasn't even really upset anymore about the bite, although she felt she should be, she just wasn't. At least she was pretty sure he'd had a noble motive, and not that he was some out of control monster, which she'd had a hard time believing anyway.

He stopped just in front of her, but looked as though he wasn't sure how to begin. So she did, "Last dance," she said simply.

He seemed grateful to be excused from having to explain anything just yet, but was oddly hesitant to dance with her. When he finally touched her she realized why. It was electric. He took her hand and interlaced their fingers and she felt as though no other part of her body mattered; like being in contact with him was the single most important thing to exist for. Her mind rationalized that it must be some kind of weird side effect left over from his bite, but...wow.

She wondered if he felt anything out of the ordinary. He put his other hand to her waist and pulled her in a bit. Her heart was racing and she felt as though she couldn't get close enough to him. *We are only dancing, stop being so ridiculous,* she reprimanded herself mentally.

She purposely did not look at him. She was very annoyed at herself for letting him off the hook so easily and for being so incredibly attracted to him. What he had done to her should be considered inexcusable. Yet still, she found herself almost overwhelmed with desire for him.

Cain let go of her hand and she rested it on his shoulder. He put his finger to her chin and tipped her head up to look at him, his slight touch upon her face giving her a renewed shiver of warmth and butterflies. "I know this doesn't excuse anything," he said, as though reading her mind. She sincerely hoped that he couldn't. "We'll still need to have that talk I've been dreading."

She tried very hard to ignore his fingertip, which trailed along her jaw line, to fall off and move down the side of her throat. He took it away a split second before it reached the bite she'd received from him. She closed her eyes, forcing herself to think clearly. "I can't say I'm not curious to hear what you might have to say."

When she opened her eyes again, he looked miserable. As though he was losing some inner battle. She couldn't have said what he might be fighting for or against, if it weren't about drinking from her…and she wasn't sure that it was. He gazed at her so tenderly and his eyes seemed filled with such anguish, that she felt she needed to give him something else to think about. "Where's Sindy?"

He blanched and she realized she must have picked the wrong subject. "Not here, and that's good enough for me." He shook his head and visibly forced himself not to continue his prior train of thought.

At least she seemed to have brought his mind away from whatever he'd been agonizing about. He smiled at her lovingly. She looked into his eyes and wanted to kiss him so badly. The moment seemed perfect and she knew how amazing it would be. After what he had done the other night, she knew he wouldn't turn her away, but she didn't do it.

She refused to let herself commit anything to him until he was somewhat held accountable for his actions. How stupid would she be to want things to go further anyway? He was a vampire! She had never actually seen him that way, but if she hadn't really believed it before, she full well knew it now. So they only danced. She knew her resolve wouldn't last forever, but at least she could feel somewhat in control for a little while. The song ended all too soon.

Cain sighed. "So, do you want to go somewhere else, or should I begin to beg for your forgiveness here?"

She smiled and looked away, to see Allie and her new friend, deeply engaged in conversation at a table. "I don't know. Where do you want to go?"

She could tell that he was tempted to offer his place, but he must have realized that would be pushing things a bit. "Maybe we could just find a place here that's a little more private?"

She thought for a moment and then took his hand, trying her best to seem unaffected by the thrill of touching his skin to her own. "Come on." She led him out the doors and down a short hallway to the adjacent student lounge. As she held his hand, she was aware of a slight static kind of tingle there, but was growing able to ignore it, almost. The lounge was really just a small sitting area with a lot of big comfy chairs and coffee tables. The overhead lamps were off, but there was a small lamp in the corner on, and the glow from the hall gave a little light. She chose a love seat and he sat next to her.

It took him a long time to say anything. She tried to imagine how she would explain if she were in his position. She almost sympathized. He took a deep breath and began. "I want you to know, that what happened…" He shook his head, as if those were the wrong words. "What I *did*, was not simply for *wanting to*." She raised her eyebrows as if to question him. "I'm not saying that I didn't…want to, mind you. I'm sure you could tell that I did."

He paused for a moment and she couldn't help but remember the soft moan that had escaped his lips as he drank from her that night. It gave her shivers. She hoped he didn't notice. He went on. "But, *wanting* is something which I endure every night. It may be very difficult at times, but I do have control of myself. You must believe that."

She gave a little nod of acceptance. She did believe him. If he didn't have some control, she wouldn't be alive right now. "I did it because I was afraid for you. Afraid of what others might do, afraid that something far worse would happen if I didn't. I know that probably sounds as though I'm just rationalizing and it must be difficult to understand."

She felt bad to make him struggle with words when she did understand the basic idea of the gesture. "I know, about being marked. Allie told me. It's like the blood vial right? Only more...undeniable."

"Exactly." He was obviously very relieved that she accepted that. "When Arif arrived and I realized that Sindy had allies, I was terribly worried for you. Sindy and her creations I can handle, in small numbers, but Arif is different. He is almost as old as I am and has mental abilities that I didn't understand."

That last sentence frightened her. "Well where is Arif now?"

"I don't know, it doesn't matter. We've spoken and I don't think he'd do anything to bother us. He seems happy to stay out of it. It's only Sindy that we need worry about and she's nowhere near here now."

"What does she want with us anyway? Does she just enjoy trying to freak me out, or what?"

"Sindy? No, she doesn't want you at all. She won't even bother me anymore I don't believe. Unfortunately, Ben is the one she's after now, but I've given him warning and weapons, I'm sure he'll be fine."

She had known this already, but it was still upsetting to hear it again from Cain. She was glad that Cain seemed fairly confident that Ben could take care of himself. She did realize however, that he would come back from the bathroom to find her missing. She wasn't at all sure whether Allie had seen her leave the room with Cain. "Ben! I have to get back to him. He'll be worried." Cain seemed very disappointed. "I'm sure you've got more to say, but it'll have to wait."

Cain didn't protest. He stood and followed as she rose and returned to the ballroom. Felicity was very surprised to find that the dance hall was nearly deserted. There was a janitor cleaning off tables and a couple she didn't know in the back. Where were Allie and Ben? Felicity turned to Cain, trying not to feel panicked. "Where would they have gone? Why didn't they wait for us?"

He shook his head non-committedly. "Haven't they their own cars?"

Felicity looked at him in confusion. "That doesn't matter, they wouldn't leave me here."

"They didn't bring you," Cain said matter of factly.

She turned to stare at him. "How would you know?" She became piqued and resentful. "Have you been watching me?"

"No! I mean, I saw you, but not like that! It's not as though I've been spying on you or something. You would know if I were."

She stopped and thought a moment, becoming more upset. "I did know! I've felt you. Not just here tonight, but earlier. And at the movies!"

Cain shook his head wearily. "That wasn't my fault. I was at the theater first. *You* came to me. If you think about it, you'll realize it's true. And I did see you earlier, but not to spy on you! I went to the bookstore to see you, to speak with you. I didn't know you had other plans. I arrived just before you left...and I didn't want to spoil your evening."

She pondered this for a moment and then accepted it. "Well, where are Ben and Allie? I'm sure they didn't just leave."

"Perhaps they only went somewhere to talk, like we did."

She barely acknowledged him; she took off for another doorway. "The bathroom." Cain followed along behind her. She only paused a moment before striding purposefully into the men's room. "Ben?" Empty.

Cain remained standing in the hallway. She came back out and stuck her head into the ladies room quick. "Allie?" She looked up and down the hallway. With the dance over, the building was quickly becoming deserted.

She turned to query Cain. "Sindy's not here?"

He shook his head. "Relax, we'll find them." He didn't seem nearly as concerned as she was. "They're probably just enjoying a rendezvous in a broom closet somewhere," he muttered as he followed her down the hall.

She turned to give him a dark look. "Not likely."

When they re-entered the ballroom there was no one left. Even the janitor had gone somewhere else. Felicity crossed the room to the far exit, with Cain in tow. The double doors opened onto a sort of veranda, looking out onto the athletic field with winding stone steps down to the ground. As they left the building and went out onto the landing, Felicity scanned the parking lot. "Look, Ben's car." At first she was very happy to see it, but then she became even more upset than before. If he hadn't left, then where was he?

"Is there supposed to be something going on in the field?"

She looked to follow Cain's gaze to the athletic field. The remains of the bonfire was there, with streamers and decorations on the bleachers, but that was long over. There was a small group of people out there, on the grass. They were too far off to be recognizable. They were just silhouettes really, mostly obscured by a slight mist that was playing over the field. She felt herself grow cold with fear. She looked at Cain in desperation. "There are no other vampire's around?"

He seemed unsure, but shook his head no. Felicity looked out onto the field again, in time to see someone get punched in the head and go down to their knees. "Ben!" she screamed. She took off and then tripped down the first three steps before stopping to take off her heels.

Cain caught her arm to steady her as she fought to take off the shoes. "Don't worry, she won't kill him."

Was that supposed to be reassuring? She gave him a fierce glare and wrenched herself free of him to run. Felicity practically flew down the rest of the staircase and then began sprinting across the field as fast as the slit in her long gown would let her. Cain was right by her side.

As they approached, she could see Sindy standing out in front of the rest, with her hands on her hips, waiting for them. Behind Sindy, she saw that it was indeed Ben who was down on his knees, backed by the largest, most muscular man she had ever seen outside of a strongman competition on television. There were five others standing around, Luke and

Chris among them. Off to one side there was another figure slumped unmoving on the ground. Allie.

As soon as she recognized Sindy, she slowed. He'd lied to her, he'd lied! He'd said there were no vampires near and here they all were! Had he only been keeping her busy in the school while they'd done this to her friends? She turned to look at Cain but he seemed in shock as well. She couldn't imagine what would happen next, but if Alyson had spoken truly, they wouldn't touch Felicity because of her mark. Only Cain could have her now. She had to get to Ben and Allie.

Ben was obviously conscious, but he wasn't even trying to get up. His hands were tied behind his back and he had a large piece of tape across his mouth. Unthinking of anything else, she tried to run to him, but Sindy reached out as she passed, and grabbed her. Sindy spun her around and threw her back into Cain, who was right behind her. She could have sworn that she heard Cain actually snarl. She fought to stand on her own, apart from him. Sindy smiled. "You'd better watch her, Cain. I can't bite her, but I'll bet I could still kill her if I really tried."

It was Felicity who spoke back. "What do you want?" She felt desperate to get to Ben, and she was afraid to see what they had done to Allie.

Sindy gave her a snort of contempt. "Like I'm dealing with you," she muttered sarcastically. "Cain's the one I've got a little proposition for," she announced with a smile.

Chapter 28 – Let's make a deal

Cain

The college athletic field
2:00, Sunday morning

Cain stood aghast and took in the situation with mute horror. When he had allowed Sindy to approach Ben, he had thought it would be alone, and he didn't think it would be tonight. He'd given Ben ample warning and had been certain the boy could adequately defend himself.

When Sindy did decide to approach Ben, Cain had fully expected him to chase her off. This was the last thing that he had anticipated. Cain had even been sure that he'd felt her leave. He'd had no idea she was here. He hadn't felt the presence of any others, and this was definitely not what he'd had in mind.

Felicity turned to face him accusingly. He realized things looked very bad for him right now, from her point of view. She must think that he had deceived her. How could he have been so stupid? He was the oldest among them and he had been a naive fool.

"Arif!" He yelled into the mist, as he realized the only explanation for the deception. There was a moment of silence and then Arif did appear. He moved closer out of the fog from behind Sindy and her men. Cain was furious. "Arif, do you so easily break your word?"

Arif spread his hands. "I have not raised a hand against you and yours, such was the extent of my oath. I merely have lent my psychic abilities towards the pursuit of my ward's endeavor. A pursuit which you so generously granted her yourself. I leave you to your own dealings now. This does not concern me. I think that Sindy can take care of herself on this occasion."

Sindy stepped forward again as Arif let himself fade back into the fog and was gone. Cain felt the other vampires' trace lights seem to wink into existence in his mind as Arif left. Sindy addressed him in contempt. "Did you really think you were going to give me permission to try for him and I wouldn't get him in the end?" She was quick to pick up on Felicity's confused expression. "That's right. Cain *gave* Ben to me. A little present. I guess he cares for me a little more than he lets on."

Cain practically growled at her. "You know full well, it wasn't like that at all."

"You shouldn't make promises that you aren't prepared to keep, especially when you're playing with other people's lives. Maybe if you weren't so wrapped up in your own martyrdom, you could focus on other people's problems for a change."

"That advice doesn't carry much weight, coming from you."

"Oh, I'm sorry. I forgot. You like to be the one to give advice, be the teacher. What were you gonna teach me Cain? Self-control? I'd say you're a little lacking in that area yourself lately, hmmm? Maybe Felicity could answer that for us. I can't believe you even got her to come near you again! I thought you'd be out of practice, but she's not even nervous around you! Very impressive!"

She came closer to question Felicity. "Did he come whispering promises of eternal life? Or...did you come back on your own, begging for more? Is he that good?"

Of course, Cain knew that Felicity hadn't really fought him when he had bitten her, but they hadn't spoken of it, and he was unsure just how much it had affected her. It was not the same for everyone. Now, Felicity turned away, and Cain could see that she felt degraded that others should know, the experience had indeed pleased her. He was ashamed that she should feel so humiliated because of him.

He took a step forward, but without taking her eyes from Felicity, Sindy raised a hand to make a slight gesture into the air. The result of this was that Chris, who had been poised next to Marcus behind Ben, gave Ben a good kick in the back. It was only a warning, but was unexpected and brought a muffled cry from Ben, which nearly drove Felicity to tears. Cain stood his ground and said nothing. He could see that Ben remained unbitten, although he'd certainly taken a beating.

Sindy dropped her hand back to her side and continued to speak to Felicity, as though uninterrupted. "It was *real* good, I can tell. In fact, I'll bet you loved it, as shameful as you think that is. It's not your fault, if that makes you feel any better."

In the following silence, Cain noticed Alyson beginning to stir. Felicity noticed too and was visibly relieved. Thank God, she was alive! She must have been knocked out and was coming to. She was tied though, just as Ben was, and like Ben she had a large piece of duct tape over her mouth. Cain thought that Sindy had seen Alyson's movements as well, but didn't seem to care. Felicity spoke to take Sindy's attention from Allie, so that she wouldn't decide to knock her out again. "What are you talking about?"

"He didn't tell you did he? Old as he is, he's gotta know. Some vampires don't though. I was lucky, my sire taught me well, before Arif killed him. No hard feelings there though, I kind of count that as a favor. The guy was a horror, but he taught me the tricks of the trade. He taught me about the venom."

She smiled as Felicity's eyes widened. "It's pretty nifty really. It's a narcotic, in the saliva. It's a vampire thing. Not just in the mouth but actually injected with our fangs too. Pretty cool, huh? It's supposed to ease the panic, calm the victim, make things a bit...easier."

She looked to Cain. "You don't mind if I play teacher some more do you? It's kind of fun to have a captive audience and I really would be doing a service to my boys." She turned back and blew a kiss towards Chris, Luke and the rest. Most of them looked too stupid to understand what she was talking about anyway.

"It's a real rush, from what I remember, if you get bit by someone who knows how to do it right. If they drink right away, hardly any of it gets into the system, they suck it right back out. Then it's just enough to keep the victim calm. To be *real* good, they have to know enough to let the venom mix in first, get it runnin' through ya'. Then, it can be a real high, but like any drug, it doesn't work on everyone.

For some people it doesn't do a damn thing. For most, it's just a nice buzz. Fuzz things up, slow their responses." She had been pacing as she spoke, but now she came to stand directly in front of Felicity again. "But I have heard - and stop me if this is just a rumor - I've heard, that some people have a much more intense reaction. That it's something like an...aphrodisiac almost. In fact, I've got a theory that it's a much more common reaction than people let on. Would you agree?

Guys tend to have that reaction to me even *before* I bite them. So I can't say I've encountered real proof of it myself. Until recently, most people I've bitten weren't exactly up for an interview afterwards, if you know what I mean. But I have been experimenting lately and I must say, it's been a lot of fun. I think Felicity knows what I'm talking about.

What d'ya say? Does it get you hot and ready? Is it *better* than sex?" She began to laugh at Felicity's obvious discomfort. "Look who I'm asking, little miss priss. Like you'd have a clue."

Cain had heard enough. "Lesson's over. Are you going to make us stand here all night? What the hell do you want?"

"You know what I want, but you're all convinced that you can't force love, remember? So we're gonna play a little game. See there's this saying I've heard. 'If you love someone, set them free.' Sounds like one of those boring morals you're always trying to instill in me. Except, I don't think you practice what you preach. So here's another saying for you. 'An eye for an eye.' Isn't that Shakespeare?"

"That's from the Bible you twit."

"Oh, right. You'd know, wouldn't you? Anyway, here's the deal. Go ahead and take Felicity, you want her so bad. You like her so much better than me, you think you can make her into a 'proper consort' for yourself? Fine, go ahead. Take her, love her. Set her free. Or...keep her, as a playmate, as a pet. Hell, you can even make her into one of *us* if you want. But know this, anything you do to her, I'm gonna do to Ben. Let's see how great your self-control really is.

In the meantime, I'll be your best student ever. Teacher's pet, if you can picture it, just as you asked. See, I know what you want from me, but why should I behave myself if you're not going to? I think it's a pretty fair deal. More than reasonable, really.

When you finally do get bored with her, or your conscience just won't let you keep her anymore, leave her. Set her free. I'll be here, living by your standards and you'll have to admit, that I've proven myself worthy of your full attention. If you decide to keep Felicity, then I'll keep Ben, everybody wins. There's just one problem. You went and got a head start. So I get to catch up, it's only fair. Especially if I'm gonna have to live like you. Even the condemned get one last meal."

Even from here, Cain could see Ben's eyes widen as he realized what that meant. Cain moved to confront Sindy but she began to raise that hand again. "Cain," she said warningly, "you know I won't kill him, but if you try to stop me, I'm thinkin' even you would be pretty hard pressed to live through it."

He knew she was right. Even without thought for himself, Ben, Felicity and Alyson would die if he made a move. With Ben and Allie tied, it was he and Felicity against Sindy, Marcus and five other vampires. It wouldn't be much of a fight. If he let Sindy do this, she would feel that she had won some ground. They would survive the night and figure out their next move tomorrow. He lowered his head to show he conceded.

Felicity saw him. "No!"

Sindy just laughed. Alyson sat up and looked as though she would struggle, but Luke crouched on the grass next to her and she thought better of it. Sindy just smiled and turned to approach Ben. He was kneeling on the wet grass, with Marcus behind him. He stiffened as Sindy drew near. She knelt on the ground in front of him. He turned away from her.

"I know," she cooed. "I'm disappointed too. This is not how I pictured our first time. You're special, and although I don't really mind an audience, I would prefer to have you all to myself. But sometimes you just have to make allowances. It'll still be good, and if Cain can't control himself, the next time will be even better, I promise. This is just a little something to whet your appetite...and mine, until I can really take you, in private. Besides, this is just like your little fantasy. You and me, out here on the grass. Too bad sunrise is still three hours away, huh?"

Sindy ripped the tape off of his mouth with a quick, rough tug. Ben just stared at her, cold and silent. She tried to kiss him, but he held himself still and unresponsive. She leaned back to look at him and Ben spoke for the first time so far. His voice was a little hoarse, but seemed almost eerily calm. "Don't bother with that. Just do it already and get it over with."

"Oh Ben, aren't you gonna let me relive some of my favorite memories with you? I remember you being so fond of foreplay." She trailed her fingers along the neckline of her shirt, tugging it down a bit, enjoying the feel of her skin and the fact that Ben's eyes seemed hypnotically glued to her breast. "But don't worry, you won't need any. I'm really good."

She leaned into him again and began kissing his neck. Cain couldn't see her change, as she was facing Ben, but he could see Ben tense and all of the muscles down the other side of his neck go taut as Sindy sank her fangs into him. Alyson did struggle then, and was given a hard shove to the ground for it. Felicity turned away, she wouldn't watch.

Ben closed his eyes, trying in vain not to react in any way, but Sindy was taking her time, enjoying her long-awaited feast. Finally, she pressed herself against him until he was forced to lie back on the ground. She lay on top of him writhing in time to the rhythm of her suckling, trying to elicit some response from him.

Cain could imagine how difficult it would be, not to succumb. Her hips pressed firmly against Ben's own, and Cain could hear the rumbling moans of pleasure that issued from deep within her as she fed. As much as it disgusted him, at the same time, he himself could not help but become aroused. He sincerely hoped it was solely the vampire nature within him that was responsible for his body's reaction.

It was going on far too long. "Sindy, don't kill him." He said the words strongly, but they sounded pitifully inadequate in his ears. Some protector he'd turned out to be. Sindy must have heard him though, because she obeyed. She withdrew and covered the wound with little licks and kisses, as though she couldn't bring herself to leave the spot. Cain could see Sindy's trace in his mind, flowing forward into Ben, until he had his own, lesser glow. It had passed into him with the venom, and would mark him until faded by time.

Sindy forced herself up from his neck, although she remained lying on top of him; her elbows poised, holding her up on his chest. She waited a moment for Ben to come around. "Was it good for you?" she asked in a husky whisper.

Somehow, he drew the energy to lean up a bit to look at her. He then spit directly into her face. She jerked back, caught by surprise, but then wiped it away and was unfazed. "Should I expect any other bodily fluids to come my way?" she asked with an amused smirk and a little thrust of her hips. He turned away from her with eyes closed, his mouth set in a hard line.

She practically slithered down his body as she rose from him and returned to Cain and Felicity. She shook herself in a little satisfied shiver and smiled. "Now we're even. Why don't you take your little girlfriend and go have some fun? Keep me apprised of any new developments, hmmm?"

She turned back around to speak to her boys. "You can leave him. I've made my point. He's mine now. No one's gonna keep me from him, if I've got a right to come back." She gave Cain a smug glance. "Arif said he'd see to that for me. Who knows, Ben might even decide to come back on his own. I can be kind of addictive."

She faced Ben; Cain wondered if he was even conscious. "Don't worry lover, you'll know where to find me." She turned and walked towards Cain, pausing first next to Felicity. She leaned forward and when Felicity looked at her, she licked her lips. "He's yummy." She moved on past Cain. "Let the games begin."

Her boys came to follow after her. As Chris and Luke passed by on either side of Felicity, Luke reached out and gave her cheek a caress. Felicity flinched away from his hand and Cain felt an uncontrolled growl spring from his throat. Luke gave him wide clearance as he passed. Marcus came next, dutifully following after his mistress. Cain was happy to see that he had a large cross-shaped burn on the side of his face and numerous bruises and gashes. At least two of the other three that he did not know, had also been stabbed, burned and scratched. Good, at least Ben and Allie had put up a good fight.

Felicity stood frozen until they had all passed. Then, as though suddenly released from paralysis, she flew to Ben's side. He lay on the ground where Sindy had left him. Felicity knelt on the grass beside him and lightly touched his shoulder. He violently jerked himself away from her, presumably thinking it was Sindy again. "Ben, it's me," she said quietly. He stopped trying to arch away from her, but he still wouldn't look at her. She helped him sit up and began trying to untie his hands.

Cain made his way over to Allie. She didn't seem hurt at all, and was miraculously unbitten. Sindy had far better control over her boys than he would have guessed. She must not want to give him extra reason to be angry with her, which was pretty funny, considering the extent to which she'd gone with Ben.

Cain began to try and untie Alyson's bonds, but she began to jerk around to face him and try to get his attention. Oh, the tape. He attempted to take it off her mouth slowly, but she was obviously impatient with that. In the end, he just had to rip it off un-gently, as Sindy had Ben's. "Finally," she said hoarsely. "In my boot." Cain looked at her questioningly. She just pushed her tied feet at him.

He heard Felicity tell Ben apologetically, "I can't get them," as she struggled with the knots tying his hands. He was slumped forward and didn't answer. Cain wondered if he'd passed out.

Cain couldn't take the boot off, because of the ropes that bound Allie's feet together. He slipped his hand down into the boot between her leg and the leather, and then yanked it back out again with a sharp hiss as he burned his hand.

Alyson jerked her leg away in startled reaction. "Sorry, wrong boot," she said ruefully. "That's the cross. Try the other one." He looked at her in annoyance and tried the other leg. Eventually he was able to reach his hand down into it far enough to find what Alyson wanted. It was a knife, a long folded switchblade, held in a little pocket, which had been sewn inside the leg of the boot. He pulled it out and brought it up to cut the ropes.

Felicity had seen him retrieve the knife. "You had that the whole time?"

Alyson looked at her irritably. "I never even saw them coming. I got cracked on the back of the head and knocked out cold. What did you want me to do?"

Cain finished releasing Allie and walked over towards Ben. Alyson followed and held her hand out for the knife. Reluctantly he gave it over to her, although he didn't like the impression that she didn't trust him to do it.

Ben was awake and aware of their approach, but said nothing. Alyson knelt next to him and tipped her head down to make him look at her. "You okay?"

"Great," he answered sarcastically.

Alyson began cutting Ben's ropes. Felicity was still kneeling on the other side of him. She obviously wanted to try and comfort him somehow, but was unsure what to do, and Ben wanted none of it. Cain gave them some space.

Once Ben's hands were untied, he brought them around to rub his wrists where the ropes had chafed. He was still sitting on his feet, from kneeling. When he tried to maneuver himself to bring his feet around, so Alyson could cut those ropes too, he clearly suffered a wave of dizziness. Cain stepped forward. "The effects from the…"

Ben looked up at him sharply. "Shut up." He then closed his eyes and held his head for a minute. Cain took a deep breath, for its calming effect rather than for need of oxygen. This was not at all what he had expected to happen.

Even if Sindy had managed to mark Ben, he hadn't thought it would be so blatantly sinister. He certainly hadn't thought that Felicity would witness it, but of course, Sindy had planned it that way. She had choreographed the whole scene to be as psychologically disturbing as possible. She wanted to be sure that Felicity would never willingly let him near her again.

Alyson cut the ropes binding his legs and then she and Felicity helped Ben to his feet. It was no easy task and took some time. No doubt, his legs were asleep from being folded under him for so long. He accepted their assistance, grudgingly. Sindy had taken her time in feeding from him, and he was sure to have gotten a very full dose of the venom.

Cain wondered if Ben had been greatly affected by it, but was sure Ben would rather die than tell them. He seemed pretty clear headed considering, but his physical reactions were still a bit off. Ben stood for a moment, and then shook their hands off of him. He obviously resented being considered incapable. Felicity turned to look over at Cain. "How could you let this happen?"

"I didn't even know they were here! Arif was mentally hiding them from me, I swear! You don't actually think that I would have agreed to this do you?"

"And just what *did* you agree to?" Felicity asked him dangerously.

Cain shook his head and tried to think desperately of how he could redeem himself in her eyes. It didn't seem likely to be possible right now. He sighed with exasperation. "Nothing. I knew she would try but…It wasn't supposed to be like this." He looked to Ben, who seemed to have regained his composure. "Ben, I did warn you. Tell her. You know I was trying to help. I had no idea those others were here, you have to believe me. I wouldn't have *let* this happen."

Ben only looked at him wearily and began walking slowly towards the parking lot. Alyson watched him for a minute and then faced Cain. "It's not your fault, but you can't expect him to be in a very understanding mood right now. He'll be alright. He's got me." Alyson turned to Felicity. "You coming?"

Ben had stopped a few paces away, waiting for them. Felicity was watching him. She looked as though she wanted to go and help him, but knew that he'd push her away. Not that he had real reason to be angry with *her*. She turned as if to say something to Cain and he could see in her face that she was feeling betrayed and unforgiving. It hurt him more than he would have thought. Cain spoke before she could. "Felicity, you have to stay and let me talk to you." She stared at him as though he were insane to think she'd stay. "Please."

"I can't, not right now."

He felt himself in a desperate panic; he couldn't leave it like this. "Felicity, please. I've less than two hours before sunrise. I can't bear to be imprisoned in that room alone, all day, knowing that you wouldn't even let me speak to you."

She seemed a little surprised at his mention of being shut up inside. Did she think he became unaware during the day? She seemed to waver. Ben was watching her and then turned away in disgust that she might stay. "During the day, can you...? *If* I came to you..."

"Yes!" He pounced on her thread of an offer. "Please. Will you come?"

Ben began to walk away, Alyson followed and Felicity was left standing there undecided. "Maybe." She turned and ran to catch up with them before he could say anything else.

As he watched them leave, a seed of an idea began to form in his head. He would be shut up in his home all day. So would the others. He needed to prove to Felicity that he was not in allegiance with Sindy. Although he couldn't really imagine how that could be unclear. Perhaps he hadn't been as decisively against her as he should have been, but he didn't want to be considered her ally.

They were almost out of range, Sindy and her boys, but he could still sense them. He had never seen Arif's mark, but most likely, he was long gone. In fact, he was probably headed back to his harem and whatever sanctuary they used during the day.

Cain could follow Sindy and the others, inconspicuously. He might have enough time to find where they slept, before he needed to return to his own bedroom for the day. That was their only hope against these others really, to confront them in the day. It would be dangerous, but he'd a feeling that Ben and Allie would be in a dangerous mood.

Cain didn't feel that he had a right to simply slaughter the others. Even if he could, that was never his way. They hadn't really done anything irrevocable, or even against him personally, but if Ben wanted revenge, he had the daylight on his side. If Cain gave their location to Ben, perhaps he, Allie and most importantly, Felicity, would consider Cain redeemed. Then Ben could use the information as he wished, it would be out of Cain's hands. If Ben and Alyson wanted to go vampire hunting, how could Cain be held accountable? As long as he was able to follow the others to their hideaway unseen.

Cain hadn't any more time for conjecture. If he didn't move now, he would lose them. He surmised that dawn was about an hour and a half away. He hoped they would not travel too far from his own resting place. He had never sensed them from the house before, so he knew that they would be at least a mile away. He didn't want to get caught too far from home, but it would be worth it if he could regain Felicity's trust. He would manage.

Contrary to popular belief, vampires could move about during the day when necessary, but it was very dangerous for them. If he were touched by direct sunlight, it would quickly burn and soon kill him.

Once he had been trapped by the day and had used a large umbrella to help get him home. It had seemed ridiculous and flimsy protection from death. Surely, anyone watching would have thought his timid progress and the oddness of his predicament hilarious. He'd thought himself doomed for sure, but he'd made it. He wouldn't care to try it again, but he knew it could be done. Likewise, if the day were very overcast he could go out, but again, at great risk. Following in the shadows of unpredictable clouds was not his idea of a thrill.

He looked up to judge the sky. It did look like it would rain. Maybe luck was with him, better wet than dust. He hurried after the others.

Chapter 29 - Just visiting

Felicity

Sunday afternoon

When Felicity awoke, it was nearly two o'clock in the afternoon. She vaguely remembered someone banging on her door earlier about her mom being on the phone. She had told them she'd call back later.

Alyson had insisted on taking them all home. She wouldn't let Ben drive his own car; they took Allie's. She'd dropped Felicity off first, which didn't seem to matter at the time, but now Felicity realized that she had no idea where either of them lived.

They had never exchanged phone numbers either. She always saw them at school or at work. She had a vague idea of where Ben lived, but she couldn't even go look for his car in the driveway, they had left it in the lot at school. She couldn't stand the idea of waiting around until someone decided to try and contact her. There must be some way she could go and find them.

She threw on some clothes and rushed through a perfunctory call to her parents. Yes the dance was nice, yes she'd had fun and no she didn't think that she and the guy she'd gone with, would be dating. See you next Sunday. Love ya', bye.

She made her way outside. It looked like it had been raining all morning, there were puddles everywhere. Now there was only a damp chill in the air and big fluffy clouds racing across the sky. She stopped at the cafeteria to grab something to eat. She ended up with a ham sandwich and ate it as she walked. Neither she nor Ben were scheduled to work today, but she had the idea that if she went to the DownTime, someone there could give her Ben's address or phone number.

She managed to get Ben's home number from Lucy. She politely fielded questions about the dance and went to call from the employee lounge. No answer. She tried again. After a dozen rings, she realized she would have to give up. She didn't know if Ben was ignoring her or just not home, but she needed a new plan.

Tommy's. She would head across the street and try to get in touch with Allie. She walked over to the bar to find the place locked and deserted. She should have realized. The sign on the door proclaimed that the bar opened at four. She was impatient to wait, but she didn't know what else to do. At least she only had about a half an hour to kill.

She went back to the DownTime, to wait in the café. Unfortunately, Harold was working. She did her best to ignore him and sat at a table by the window. Finally, at about ten to four she saw someone drive up to Tommy's and unlock the door. She wasted no time in getting over there.

There was an older guy behind the bar when she walked in. He looked very surprised to have such an early customer and he didn't appear in a very friendly mood.

"Hi, I'm trying to get in touch with Alyson." She was met with a blank stare. "She's kinda short, pink hair, she works here. I was hoping maybe you could help me?"

"I know who she is. She's on at 8:00."

"Oh…yeah, but I really needed to talk to her now. I thought maybe I could get her phone number? Or an address?"

The guy was shaking his head at her. "I can't give that stuff out."

"Please? It's kind of important. Maybe you could call her for me, I'd really appreciate it."

Just as she thought he'd say no, the guy pulled a phone out from a shelf under the bar. He took out an address book, flipped to the right page and dialed. "Allie? Hey, it's Tom. Yeah I know, there's some girl here for you. Yep." He handed the phone over to Felicity who gave him a grateful smile.

"Hi, it's Felicity. Okay, thanks." She handed him back the phone. "Thanks."

He looked at her oddly, as he hung it up and put it back under the counter. "All set?"

"She's on her way."

"M-hmmm. You want something?" he asked, nodding towards the taps.

She smiled. "No thanks."

He went into the back and she decided to go wait outside. It didn't take long. Alyson explained that she had taken Ben back to her place last night, he was still there now. She said that he wasn't talking much, but he seemed okay.

Allie's place was an apartment converted from someone's detached double garage, behind a house not far from Tommy's. It was a cute little apartment. It was sparsely furnished with what was probably second hand furniture and looked very 'lived in', but cozy.

Allie led her to the bedroom in the back. The room wasn't very large and was dominated by a queen size bed. Ben lay on his side, facing away from them. His nice clothes from the dance were rumpled on the floor in the corner, and he was lying on top of the covers wearing a t-shirt and sweatpants. He looked up at them as they came to the doorway, but put his head back down without a word.

Allie turned back to Felicity. "I'm gonna go make him something to eat. You want anything?"

Felicity gave her head a little shake. Alyson went into the kitchen and Felicity was left staring at Ben's back. She couldn't help but be reminded of the night he'd slept over and she'd climbed into his bed. He was laying just the same way. She walked over to the bed without a word. As lightly as she could, she got on the bed and lay down next to him. She folded her hands under her cheek and snuggled up against his back just as she had that night.

She just lay there for few a minutes in silence, until he finally looked up over his shoulder at her. She peeked up at him and smiled. "Hey." He sighed and then rolled over onto his back. She scooched aside to give him some room. He just lay there, staring up at the ceiling. She propped herself up on one elbow to look at him. "How ya' doin'?" she asked quietly.

He didn't take his eyes from the ceiling. After a moment he said, matter of factly, "Seven."

She stared at him in confusion. "Did you not understand the question?"

"Seven times I have been asked that question today, in one form or another," he clarified.

"Oh."

"Alyson has been hovering over me ever since I woke up. I wish she'd give it a rest already." He finally glanced at her for a second before turning his eyes back to the ceiling. "What are you guys doing, changing shifts?"

"She's in the kitchen making you something to eat."

He rolled his eyes and sat up a little to yell to Allie in the next room. "And I'm still not hungry!" He lay back down with a thump and then winced in pain. He lay still for a few minutes, seemingly contemplating a crack in the plaster overhead, and then asked quietly, "Did you go see him?"

"No," she answered.

He thought about that for a minute. "He bit you," he said with contempt.

"Yeah," she quietly confirmed.

"You didn't tell me." He sounded hurt.

"No."

He turned to face her irritably. "Okay, that's the short version."

She lay back onto the pillows with a guilty sigh. "I'm sorry. I just... I didn't. I'm sorry. I lied to you."

After a moment Ben spoke. "You didn't actually lie."

"Yes I did. A lie of omission is still a lie isn't it? Besides, you asked if he hurt me and I said no."

He lay back again as well. "I get the feeling that it didn't actually hurt all that much." He sounded disgusted. "And no, I don't want to talk about it."

"I didn't ask," she replied. "Anyway, it's all over now. We can just put the whole thing behind us and move on."

Now he sat up on the bed in disbelief. "Were you even there last night? This is not over! This is *so* far from over! We're like...the prizes in some sort of depraved, obscene game of theirs! They're never going to leave us alone!"

She lay calmly looking up at him. "I'm sure Cain will find a way to keep her away from us from now on. Nothing else is going to happen. Cain wouldn't let it."

"Oh, *Cain* wouldn't? Because he was real helpful in keeping things from getting out of control last night, right?"

Now she sat up to face him, indignantly. "What did you want him to do? It was him and me against Sindy and six other vampires! Not to mention *The Hulk!* Did you see the size of that guy?!"

He lay down again in a huff. "Yeah, I managed to get a real close look at him while he was *beating the crap out of me!*" As he was speaking, he pulled up his shirt to reveal his stomach and chest, which were absolutely covered in dreadful greenish purple bruises.

Felicity gasped in horror and her hand hovered lightly over them as if she'd like to try and wipe them away. "Oh Ben! Oh my God! Are you okay?"

He just looked at her wearily for a moment, and then pulled back down his shirt. "Eight. And yes, I'll live. I can't say I've been beaten worse, but at least I don't think they broke anything."

"Are you sure? What if you've got cracked ribs or something? Maybe you should go to the hospital, just to make sure you're alright." She interrupted him just as he looked like he might say something. "And don't you dare start counting at me again."

Just then, Alyson arrived carrying a little tray. "Here you go. Scrambled eggs, soft but not runny, with little bits of cheese in them; just the way you like 'em. Oh, and O.J. of course."

Ben gave her an exasperated sigh. "Alyson, I do not want eggs."

She looked down at the tray, as though wondering what was wrong with them. "Well, what do you want?"

He stared at her for a minute and then propped himself up on his elbows. "I *want* to wake up next to Brenda, to find that this was all some awful nightmare, but I guess *that's* not going to happen, huh?"

Alyson stood there staring at the eggs. After a moment, Felicity inquired disapprovingly, "You'd sleep with her on the first date?"

Ben glared at her for a second. "Thank you Felicity, for putting this in perspective, because my *morals* are the real issue right now!" he replied sarcastically. She shook her head and looked away.

"You have to eat something," Allie demanded. She took the orange juice off of the tray and tried to hand it to Ben, who wouldn't accept it. "Just take it and drink it already! You lost a lot of blood and you need to rebuild your strength."

As she finally managed to shove the glass into his hand, Ben muttered angrily, "You're the expert." As Ben took a sip, Allie looked over at Felicity questioningly. She shook her head and gave a little shrug, to show that she didn't know what he meant.

Alyson questioned him. "Are you mad at me?" she asked, putting the tray down on her dresser.

He looked up from the glass. "Why should I be mad at you?" he asked with another twinge of sarcasm.

"I don't know, but you've been giving me the angry vibe all day. What'd *I* do?"

Ben sat up a little more, beginning to look angry. "Four times."

Felicity shook her head in annoyance. "What is with the new number fetish?"

Ben paid her no attention and continued. "Wasn't it four times at last count?" Allie just shrugged. "You have been bitten four times and you never told me!"

"Told you what?"

"That it was like a drug!" Ben demanded.

"What for?" Alyson inquired with indifference.

Ben became infuriated. "I don't know, as an interesting sidebar? A footnote? My best friend's been bitten four times in three years and I had no clue it was intoxicating! You'd think I would've heard about something like that!"

Alyson spoke calmly and quietly in contrast with Ben's yelling. "What would've been the point?"

"I just...I didn't expect it to be like *that*. I didn't know."

"Well, now you know," Allie said quietly.

"Now I know." He stared at her in resentment for a few minutes, before asking, "Do you have any money?"

She seemed taken aback by the abrupt shift in topic, but dug into her back pocket. "I think I've got a twenty."

"No, in the bank," he clarified.

"About two months rent. Why?" Allie asked.

He didn't answer her, but turned to Felicity. "How about you?"

Felicity spread her hands. "I'm lucky if I've got fifty bucks."

He seemed to be figuring something out in his head. "I haven't got much, since I spent it all on the 'stang, but I've got some. It'll have to do. We're going on vacation."

Alyson laughed. "What?"

"I'm thinking Vermont," Ben informed them.

Felicity stared at him as if he'd lost his mind. "Are you lightheaded? How much blood did you lose?"

He turned to her earnestly. "Allie's told me all about the 'mark' thing. And about the tracking...location vibe. I don't want to feel it. I don't want them to know where we are. I just want us far away from here, the three of us." He turned back to Allie. "How long does it take? Three weeks?"

She shook her head apologetically. "She dosed you up pretty good." He flinched a little at her words. "I'm thinkin' more like four."

"Okay, a month then. And when it's gone, we'll be free. We can go anywhere that we want, they'll never find us. Felicity can go back to her folk's if she wants," he said, turning to Felicity. "They don't know where you live. Allie and I...we'll just have to find someplace else. Or, if it seems feasible, we could come back," he paused to give a meaningful look to Alyson, "and kill them all." Felicity couldn't tell what Allie thought of that. She was just staring at him silently. "But we should stick together at first. Let's go to Vermont."

Felicity took his hands from his lap as she sat next to him on the bed. "Ben, I understand how you must feel, but I'm not going to Vermont."

"Come on," he said with a persuasive little smile. "You'd make a great ski-bunny. Besides, at least you're only dealing with Cain. I can't speak for his motives, but at least he's not a lunatic. Look at who I've got to deal with! Have you seen what she does to those guys? I've got higher goals in life than 'zombie love-slave', I've gotta tell ya'."

Alyson spoke quietly from behind him. "I can't leave."

He turned to face her, dropping Felicity's hands. "Why not? It's not like you have anyone here but me anyway."

"I know but, I don't wanna leave. Besides, they don't even want me," Allie insisted.

"Yes, but if we disappear, who do you think they'll take it out on?" Ben asked.

"I can't leave right now, at least not until after Halloween." Felicity's eyes grew wide as she stared at Alyson over Ben's head. She tried desperately to make her understand that it was a really bad idea to do this now. Allie absently walked around the bed and went to stand in front of the closet door, playing with her fingernails.

Ben was perplexed. "It has to be now, that's kind of the point. We've got big bull's eyes painted on us for the next month. What's on Halloween?"

Allie tried to act non-chalant, but wasn't really pulling it off. "Nothing. I just told someone I'd be around, and I don't want to blow him off."

Ben stood up from the bed and turned to face her. "Are you kidding? You're going to get killed over some guy?" Allie just looked away. "Who is he? That guy from the dance?"

"No, I think Sindy and her thugs probably scared the shit out of him. I'll have to remember to thank her for that."

"Then who? You can't be all that serious, if I don't even know him," Ben insisted.

Felicity gave Allie a desperate look that went totally unheeded. She knew what was coming, but seemed powerless to prevent it. Alyson spoke quietly. "You don't want to know."

"Like that answer doesn't just make it ten times worse. Gimme a name. What is he, a friend of mine?" She gave the slightest nod. "Is it Jeff, Pete, who?"

"Yeah, like any of your yuppie college buddies would ever look twice at me."

"Then who?"

Alyson refused to answer but finally looked up to meet his eyes, pleading silently for him to understand. Ben stared at her uncomprehending. Alyson's hand seemed to rise of its own accord to touch her fingers to the nearly invisible bite marks on her neck. Felicity wasn't even sure if it was a conscious gesture, but it did serve to give Ben a nudge of understanding.

In the growing silence, he suddenly went very pale. He started shaking his head in disbelief and seemed to mouth the word 'no' a few times, silently. Then he stopped to stare stonily at Alyson. "Say it. I dare you to say it."

She seemed to become aware of her hands again and clutched them nervously in front of her. She stared at her finely manicured fingernails as if they were foreign objects. Finally, she whispered, "It's Mattie."

Ben flew into a rage. "It is *not* Mattie! It's a blood sucking demon walking around in my best friend's skin!"

Alyson jerked her head up to look him in the eye. "It *is* Mattie, Ben. I know it is. We've spent time together, we've talked about stuff. I know him!"

"Not as well as I did."

"Better than you do! Even before he died."

Ben's face managed to grow even paler than before. "It's not really him."

"Yes it is Ben. He's just the same. Trust me."

"Trust you? You've been hiding this from me for three years! Longer if you count anything that happened before they got him! If you're so convinced that he's okay, then why'd you hide it from me?"

Another wave of comprehension passed over his face and Ben went from looking resentful, to shocked and then even more enraged than before. He spoke in a quiet voice that was so smoldering with anger, that it frightened Felicity and it wasn't even directed at her. "Is it still four? Is it? Or were those only the ones you couldn't hide? What's the magic number Allie? What else have you been keeping from me?"

Before Alyson could even answer, he crossed the room, grabbed the collar of her shirt and ripped it away from her neck. She tried to protest, but he shoved her up against the closet door and pushed her head to the side so that he could have a clear view of her throat. He stared in silence and then thrust her head to the other side. She just stood there and let him look.

He clenched his hands into tight fists for a moment, and then opened his hand to slam his right palm against the closet door next to her head with a loud bang. "Damn it Allie! You blood whore!" he yelled at her in disgusted disbelief. He pushed himself off the wall away from her and stormed out of the room.

Allie just stood there for a moment with her eyes closed, hearing him stomp around her apartment. She opened her eyes to look at Felicity on the bed. "And that's why I didn't tell him." She ran a hand through her hair and was startled when he bounded back into the room.

"Where are my shoes?"

"Ben, don't go."

"Where are my God damned shoes?"

Allie seemed shaken and quickly stood away from the wall. "Don't go, I'll go. I'm gonna go out for a while. Stay here, please. I'm gonna go over to Tommy's and tell them I'm not coming in tonight. I've got some stuff to do. I'll be back in a little while. You just stay here and chill, okay?" Alyson gave him no time to answer and quickly left. Felicity supposed that Alyson was afraid that if she let Ben leave, he might never come back.

He sat on the bed with his head in his hands, facing away from her. Felicity watched him for a minute. Then she moved closer and tried to lightly put a hand on his shoulder. "She really cares about him, you know."

He jerked away from her touch so violently that it scared her. He turned to face her. "What do you know? Get out." He put his head back into his hands. She got up off of the bed, but couldn't bring herself to leave him so upset. She just stood there, biting her tongue and fighting back tears. Ben spun around angrily to see why she hadn't left. He must have realized that he was frightening her, because he abruptly toned it down, but he was still firm. "I just want to be alone right now."

She didn't say another word, she just turned and left. When she got outside, she saw Allie was just sitting in her car. Felicity bent to knock lightly on the window. Alyson looked up, startled. She was crying. Felicity went around to the passenger door and got in. She looked at Allie, who was wiping her face. "He'll get over it," Felicity offered. "He's just...on overload."

"I know. He can't stay mad at me. He's like my only family; by choice, but still. Ever since his mom died, we take care of each other, you know?" Felicity gave her a tender smile. Alyson sniffled and grabbed a tissue out of the glove compartment to finish wiping her face.

"I keep thinking some girl is gonna come along and finally take him off my hands, but you know Ben, he's never satisfied." She shrugged. "He needs me. Otherwise, I probably wouldn't even be here right now." Felicity looked at her questioningly. "Mattie's offered you know." She nodded towards the apartment. "You think this was bad, Ben would have a total conniption if I told him that. Mattie wants me to come with him, to be like him."

Felicity tried to keep her face carefully neutral. "What did you tell him?"

Alyson smiled. "To ask me again in ten years, before I start gettin' old." She laughed at Felicity's expression of wonder tinged with fright. "Scary stuff."

"Death?"

"Life. All of it. I don't know. I'm not going anywhere right now though, I can tell you that." She pulled herself together, threw the wad of tissues into the backseat and started the car. "I've got some stuff to do. Let him cool off for a while. I'm glad we never went and got his car, he'll stay. You need a ride somewhere?"

Felicity thought about it, as she stared at the car's digital clock. It's little green glowing numbers read 6:09 p.m. It would be getting dark in about an hour, not much time. "You guys are going to stay holed up at your place tonight?"

"Unless I come home to find out Ben's booked us a trip to Vermont. Come back later if you want. Here..." She found a scrap of paper and scribbled down her phone number and address. "Call if you need me to come pick you up."

She smiled. "Thanks. Can you drop me at the cemetery?"

Alyson's eyes widened. "Yeah, sure." She pulled out and started down the road. "Gonna go see him huh?"

"What else is there to do?"

"He doesn't really live in the cemetery, does he?"

"No, just makes for a shorter walk. I don't think it'd be fair for me to..."

"Yeah, that's cool. A vamp's resting place is kind of private. I get that. He must really trust you."

"I guess. Hey, do you want me to ask him anything?"

"Like what?"

"Well I don't know for sure, he didn't say anything, but... He was there, when Ben told me about Mattie. I got the feeling that Cain knows him."

Alyson perked up immediately. "You think?"

She shrugged. "I could ask."

"Just tell him I'm worried."

"I will."

Alyson dropped her off at the cemetery and she walked the rest of the way to Cain's. She wasn't really frightened of him, but she was glad that it was still daylight. She'd thought about things and decided that Cain was telling the truth. He hadn't known what Sindy had planned; he wouldn't have let that happen. If he had expected her to do something like that, he would have been better prepared. Maybe he should have anticipated it, but it wasn't intentional.

She couldn't stop hearing the heartbreak in his voice when he'd asked her to stay and talk last night. It had seemed so important to him, that she not reject him. Did he care for her that much? Was he so desperate to be close with her? She felt that way too, but she kept telling herself how irrational it was. How it would be insane to let him draw her that close to him. Yet, here she was.

She could feel him. As she turned up the driveway, it grew even stronger. She stopped to analyze it for a moment, now that she recognized what it was. It was like the direction in which he lay beckoned her, tried to draw her closer to him. Her body tingled with anticipation.

She thought about Sindy and the others, how they attacked people unaware and then left them. Those people would be walking around the next day feeling this? What would they make of it, how much would they remember? Would they think they were ill? Some might even find it curiously exciting and get close enough to let themselves get bit again, before they understood.

She had memories of a lovely movie maiden, two perfect dots of a puncture wound, dark against her pale throat. Dressed in a beautiful gossamer nightgown, she would awaken in the night, to go out and meet her vampire lover. Felicity had always thought the maiden was so stupid, to let herself be put into such a trance. And yet, here she was. She'd changed from her gown, into jeans and a peasant blouse, but she went to him all the same.

At least it was daylight, she thought with self-assurance. At the instant the thought came to her mind, a large cloud blotted out the sun, placing her in dark shadow. She looked up at the sky, as if she were the butt of some cosmic joke. "That's not funny."

She hung her head in resignation and climbed the steps to the front door. She hesitated for a moment, wondering if he would even hear her knock from down in the basement. He did have very keen hearing, but he was probably sleeping. That made her wonder again, whether it was like normal sleep. She raised her hand to knock, when the door opened from within, startling her.

Cain stood in the shadow of the doorway seeming very relieved to see her. Felicity was struck anew at how handsome he was. She felt as though she were buzzing with excitement at the sight of him. She stood frozen for a second and then dropped her hand back down to her side. "And I was afraid that you wouldn't hear me knock."

He gave her a roguish smile. "I felt you coming from nearly a mile away."

She was a little embarrassed to hear him speak so openly of the amazing bond they now shared. It made her wonder if it were different for him, or if he felt it in just the same way. "I thought you would be sleeping."

"You woke me up." Somehow, he managed to make even that innocuous sentence sound suggestive.

"Sorry." She knew she must be blushing and tried not to meet his gaze. She felt foolish for being so effected by him. He simply stood there, inside the doorway, drinking her in with his eyes. When she did look up at him, she realized something was different. She couldn't put her finger on it. It was most subtle, but he did seem changed somehow. Her curiosity overcame her shyness. "You look...different."

He became self-conscious and she felt terribly rude. "It's nothing. Just a little sunburn."

It took her a second to realize the peculiarity of that statement. "What did you do?"

He smiled sheepishly. "Forgot my umbrella." Just then, the sun poked out from behind a cloud and bathed the porch in sunlight. Cain was protected where he stood, but he still flinched. "Can we talk downstairs?" She didn't answer immediately and he became a little offended. "I wouldn't..." He stopped himself and sighed. "Or we could sit here on the floor by the door, if you'd like."

She felt ridiculous. "No, of course we can go downstairs." He backed away from the door to let her in and then quickly closed it behind her. She couldn't imagine what it would be like, to have something so fatal all around you. She thought it might be rather terrifying. No wonder they slept all day. She began to follow him downstairs. "So, you can be awake during the day, if you want?" Obviously it was true, but it still seemed strange.

"You can be awake during the night, can't you?"

"Yeah, but I always thought vampires were like, comatose until nightfall," she said in defense.

"Would those be the same vampires that prefer to sleep in coffins?" he asked in amusement.

"Yeah, that'd be them," she replied sheepishly.

"I can't say *I* slept much at all, really. I thought perhaps I'd see you sooner."

They entered the basement and crossed the room to sit on the bed. "I was busy," she said with an annoyed tone. She hadn't meant for it to come out so cold, but she wanted to make it clear that she was not so bound to him, that she should put him before all else.

He seemed to get the point. "With Ben, of course. Is he alright?"

"Nothing that time and a whole lot of therapy can't cure."

Cain sat next to her on the bed and looked down into his lap chastened. "Do you believe me when I tell you that it was beyond my knowledge or control?"

"If I didn't, I wouldn't be here," she said firmly.

He nodded his head once, in acceptance. "So, what is Ben planning?"

His business-like attitude threw her off. "Planning?"

"I don't suppose he's just going to wait around to see if she'd like some more. No matter what fool game Sindy thinks she's playing, I know her. Benjamin holds some special significance for her, perhaps because she knew him in life. She sees him as a conquest. I'd like to say that she should be satisfied, having proven herself master to him now. Perhaps she even will attempt to live as I do and leave him alone; I do hope she'll try, but more likely, now that she's had a taste of him, she won't ever quite be able to let him be."

Felicity felt prompted to ask him just *how* he lived. Sindy had insinuated that he didn't usually drink from people, but Felicity was still unsure. It seemed something that she ought to get clear, but Cain continued speaking before she had a chance to ask.

"Also, knowing Benjamin as I do, I don't think he'll give her a second chance. Thoughts of revenge must be running through him even as we speak. I know I've had similar thoughts of my own. So what is he planning?"

Felicity fidgeted a bit on the bed, losing her train of thought. Her own body seemed quite powerfully aware of Cain's physical presence. The urge to touch him, in any way was so strong that it was distracting. She fought to ignore it and answer his question. "Right now the only thing I'm aware that he's planning is a vacation. He wants us to leave; me, him and Allie, for at least a month, maybe longer."

"Until the mark fades. Ben is a smarter man than I give him credit for. Not that I ever doubted his intelligence, but it can be a difficult thing to let your actions be led by your mind and not your emotions. I have a little trouble with that myself sometimes." He looked very thoughtful and a little sad. "When are you leaving?"

"I don't know. Do you think we need to?"

He looked at her for a long time before answering; she began to wonder if he was going to. "I'd like to say no, but I'm having trouble sorting whether that'd be my mind, or my emotions." He fidgeted a bit on the bed and looked away from her, down at the floor. "To be perfectly honest, I'd had that same plan for you myself. Only in my head, I was going with you. Active imagination I've got, eh?"

That brought to mind frightening things that Sindy had said the night before, about Cain wanting to keep Felicity as a 'consort' or maybe a 'pet'. Of course, Sindy had chosen her words carefully; the whole thing had been designed to spook her. To a certain extent, it had worked. She was uncertain how much to believe. She'd be a fool to discount all of it as scare tactics, as much as she'd like to.

As he was looking away, she found herself staring at him, at the side of his face. He had only a hint more color in his cheeks now and across his nose. It wouldn't be noticeable to anyone else really. She wouldn't have even said that he'd looked very pale before, but the fact that the color was there now, made its absence before seem more obvious in retrospect. She suspected that she only noticed because she had spent so much time staring at him and picturing him in her mind.

She found herself reaching out to touch his cheek. Just the slightest, soft caress really, with the backs of her fingers along the new pinkness there. She'd almost forgotten about the heightened sense of touch they seemed to share, since...that night. She was quickly reminded.

He didn't pull away, in fact he seemed afraid to move, but closed his eyes and drew in a slow, soft hiss of breath as she touched him. It gave her chills. "Does it hurt?" He looked at her oddly and she realized that he was thinking of her touch in general. "The sunburn." she clarified, dropping her hand into her lap.

"Not really. It's not that noticeable is it?"

"No, not at all. I think I only see it really because I...know you so well." Then another strange thought popped into her head. "Can you see yourself? In a mirror I mean."

That made him smile. He always seemed amused by her spontaneous and innocent questioning. "What do you think?"

She pondered a moment. "Well," she said as she made so bold as to brush her hand along his cheek again, "you're always clean-shaven." She knitted her eyebrows for a moment as she took back her hand. "But, maybe that doesn't change anymore. Then again, judging by the way that Sindy applies her make-up..."

That brought forth some laughter from him. It made her smile, to see him laugh. He often seemed so sad. "No, we can't see our reflections. And it took me a long time and a lot of bloodshed to learn how to shave this way, I can assure you."

She gazed at him thoughtfully. She had a hard time believing he would ever want to hurt her. She had never had such a sweet and gentle connection with a man she was so attracted to before. Of course, she had never been quite this attracted to anyone else, but the time they shared always seemed so unique. He didn't fit the categories reserved for other guys.

Other guys usually fell into one of two categories. Either they were nothing special to her, like Todd. He was nice, she liked him, but he just didn't do anything for her. There was no spark. Or, the guys she did feel attracted to, also made her feel nervous and uncomfortable. Inevitably she would say and do things that seemed foolish and silly because she was just so infatuated with them, she couldn't be herself.

Then there was Ben. He didn't seem to fit into any category either. He also was unlike any other guy she had known. Mostly because she did feel comfortable around him and could be herself without feeling foolish, even though he was very good looking. Yes, she would definitely consider Ben attractive, but he also seemed to argue with her incessantly, so she hadn't the chance to be nervous around him.

She had used the word infatuation when describing her feelings for Cain to Ben, but that wasn't really true anymore. This had now moved beyond infatuation. Cain was different. Cain made her feel as though she could talk to him about anything, ask him anything, and be herself without repercussions. And yet it was hard to say that she felt *comfortable* around him, because she was so attracted to him that it had driven her to distraction, even before he had bitten her. Now with a heightened perception of it, she felt hard pressed to keep her train of thought. She suddenly remembered what had sparked the question of reflection. "The sunburn...you were outside, in the daytime?"

"I got caught a bit further from home than I'd expected. It's alright, it wasn't for long and luckily the clouds held. I managed to get here none the worse for it."

"But...you were outside, in the daytime?" she repeated incredulously.

"I thought that was made clear. I know, it can be difficult to let go of closely held myths. You have to realize, the rules you've seen in the movies were created for dramatic tension, not authenticity. Only direct sunlight would truly hurt me. Going outside in the day is not a favored pastime, but it can be done. Though I must admit, I've not met many brave enough to test the boundaries. I guess I've grown a bit cocky in my old age."

She stared at him in disbelief. "What were you doing outside?"

"Nothing I'd a right to be. A bit of espionage for the three of you actually. Although I suppose it's for naught. The sun's nearly down already."

"What are you talking about?"

"Last night, well this morning actually, I followed them. They'd no idea I was there. Of that, I'm sure. I thought if I could determine their place of rest, Benjamin might appreciate the information."

She sorted that out in her mind. "Sindy and the others. You followed them to where they live? I don't understand why. Ben, Alyson and I couldn't hope to fight them, even with your help. There's too many of them and they're far too strong."

"We might take them, if we were prepared, but that's not what I meant. You're forgetting, you have a great advantage at your disposal. Sunlight. It's the greatest weapon there is against our kind. If you knew where they slept, you may find a way to bring it down upon them."

As that sunk in she began to feel very uncomfortable with the idea. "That sounds awful."

"It is awful. So is what they'd do to you if they'd the chance. I can't expect you to be thankful that I...marked you, but you should be grateful for its benefits. To think of you in their hands..." He shook his head and looked away from her.

"So you were thinking that Ben should approach them in the day? Just...get rid of them all?"

"Well, I must admit that I hadn't properly thought that through. Self-defense I am usually pretty good at, tactical warfare I am not. Contrary to my undead nature, I haven't much desire or stomach for harming others. Your arrival now makes me realize that Sindy would be fully aware of Ben's approach before he got within twenty feet of her. He couldn't sneak up on her. I don't think her senses have quite the range of mine, but it would be enough to warn her well. I suppose that's what they're for."

"I could do it," she offered.

"**No**," he replied forcefully.

"Allie and I, they wouldn't feel us coming. Allie's mark from Sindy is gone."

"Yours from me, is highly evident my dear. Not just to me, but to all. That's why I gave it to you. I didn't give you nearly as much as Sindy passed into Ben, so it won't last as long, but it's quite clear at the moment."

Felicity felt her cheeks heating again as he spoke of it. The topic must seem an everyday thing to him, but to her it was illicit and risqué. She tried not to be affected by memories of the act, and pressed on. "Alyson then. She could do it," she suggested.

"If she didn't get them all, she'd be marked for death."

"I wonder if she'll live much longer anyway." She hadn't really meant to say that, she had thought out loud, without meaning to. She looked up to find Cain staring at her. "Cain, do you know Mattie?"

He seemed to find this a strange turn for the conversation. "Ben's friend?" She nodded. He gave a slight smile. "Yes, quite well actually. I came across him soon after he was turned. I taught him a few things, and helped him adjust. I like him. He's got commendable strength of will, for one so young. He reminds of my own stubborn abstinence actually."

"He doesn't drink people's blood?"

"No. Well, not without...consent." He had been looking into her eyes as he said it. She wondered if he were trying to imply something. She hoped not; that was a frightening prospect that she wasn't ready to deal with at the moment. He must have noted her reaction. "Don't be so surprised. It's not as uncommon as you might think."

"I'm not, really." She looked away, embarrassed. "In fact, I kind of knew." She looked into his eyes once again. "Alyson is worried for him."

This was clearly something Cain had not expected to hear. "Alyson? That girl does constantly astonish me. I never know what to expect from her. I must admit, it's usually rather annoying, but this is odd news. Does she see him often?"

"He never mentioned her?"

"I haven't seen him in months and it wasn't here. Besides, that's information one does not traditionally share. If she wore his mark, I would know. If she does not, she is fair game for another. To mention her as favored, would merely put her at risk. Not from me of course, but that is usually the way of things."

"He told her he would return soon. She's afraid that he may run into Arif, or Sindy and be waylaid I suppose."

"Well, I haven't seen him, but I will keep watch for his arrival. He would make a welcome ally right now. Although I wouldn't want to have to announce it to Ben."

"Allie told him. It wasn't pretty." She looked at him wonderingly. "Can I ask you a question?"

"You can ask me anything and you often do. It's a little off-putting I must say, but I've come to enjoy it. Ask away," he answered with a mischievous grin.

She smiled, but felt in a much more serious mood than she had been. Something had occurred to her, that wouldn't leave her head. "Ben said something, which I must admit, frightened me more than a little." Cain's smile quickly turned to concern. "I know he's wrong, Allie even said so, but I can't stop thinking about it."

"What is it?"

"When you became a vampire, did it change you? Other than physically I mean. The way you are now, the man you are now, is this who you were? Is this what you were like, in life?"

He became very still, gazing into her eyes. "Everyone changes." He looked away, uncomfortably. "It was a traumatic experience, to say the least. And, more than three hundred years certainly can't pass without leaving their mark, but I don't believe that's what you're asking.

The one who made me was thorough at least, for that I can be thankful. When it's rushed or done poorly, well you've seen the sad results of such attempts. I've got all the memories of my life passed, whether I want them or not. I wasn't aware of any change in that respect. It's not as though another being has completely taken over my body, but I suppose I have changed. For the worse and for the better too, if you can believe it.

I can only tell you this, I don't try to be the man that I was. I didn't much like myself back then, but I don't really think I've lost anything of who I was. There's just been something else added to me. It can be difficult and frightening at times, but I much prefer the being I am now, to the man I was then.

Have you ever seen the cartoons, where someone's got a devil perched upon one shoulder and an angel on the other? I feel as though I walk around with them every moment. The vampire whispers dreadful things in my ear and urges my body to unspeakable longings. Then the new man I long to be, on the other side whispers back, tales of good deeds done and battles yet to fight.

I sometimes wish to close my eyes forever and end it all, just so I might finally have some peace. It would be nice to feel alone in my head for a change. I don't mean to frighten you, but to answer your question. I don't really know. Does it matter? *This* is the man I am now. For what it's worth, I rather hope he meets your approval."

She was gazing into his eyes and without realizing, had leaned a bit forward into him as he spoke, intent upon his every word. She felt anguished over the things he must have endured in his life. He seemed such a sweet and gentle soul, undeserving of such trials.

Of course, who was she to say? She knew nothing of his true past. He seemed to think he deserved what had happened to him. Was he really so despicable in life that he preferred this undead existence? Whatever sort of man he had been in the past, the way in which he conducted his life now spoke volumes, considering how difficult it must be.

Now, as he completed his response to her question, she was suddenly brought back to the present and was more than lightly aware of his proximity. She wanted nothing more than to tilt her face to his for a kiss, long awaited and frequently imagined. A shiver of anticipation went through her as she remembered the last time she'd sampled his lips, and that was before this new heightened sense of touch they seemed to share.

She fought back the urge and very deliberately brought herself to sit fully upright again. He had obviously been very aware of the moment, but let her come to her own decision, watching silently. She felt she should clarify just what he should expect from her. Saying it out loud, might convince her own body to follow her mind's intentions as well.

"I don't want to go away, but that doesn't mean that I'm going to... I don't know what I want, not yet. This all needs to be taken care of, Sindy, Arif and the others. I need to know that's under control and put it all behind us. Then I can think about...other things. Right now, I just... I don't know what I want, except that I want to stay. Is it safe for me to stay?"

He seemed to consider her question for a long time. Then again, maybe he was only memorizing her face, she couldn't tell. He finally spoke in a quiet, confident voice. "I'll make it so."

They stared at each other in silence. This new, magical awareness of his body was nearly overpowering. It seemed masochistic almost, to force herself to sit so close to him without allowing him to touch her. She knew it would be beyond her wildest imaginings, if she surrendered herself to it. She stood and walked away from him a pace, forcing herself to hold firm to her convictions.

"I should go check on Ben and Allie. When I left, things were kind of explosive. If I leave them alone for too long, they might kill each other." She looked back to smile at him. The expression on his face seemed almost to be bewildered admiration. She imagined that he was surprised to see how strongly in control of herself she was and her devotion to her friends.

It had been a very difficult thing, not to succumb to the moment. So much harder than she had expected, that she questioned her judgment in letting herself follow him down here. She had grossly underestimated the temptation. She was afraid that, if he had been so inclined, he could easily have persuaded her to surrender herself to him. In fact, she was almost certain that he could have, but he had not. He had let her be the one to choose. She would not forget that.

He seemed to admire her all the more for her decision, but did look quite forlorn that she was leaving. "Did you want to come?" she asked. She looked around for a window, to see if the sun had gone down yet, but realized that of course they were all covered. "I could wait."

Cain smiled. "The sun has set, but no. As much as it pains me to deny myself your company, I don't think that I'm someone Ben would like to see right now."

Cain had never spoken openly of how he felt about her before today. Of course, it was implied and she'd known that he was attracted to her, but she couldn't remember him ever really saying it, until today. She was flattered to have the full attention of someone who could surely choose any girl he'd like. She tried very hard not to dwell on it, she had other concerns right now.

He continued, "Besides, I think I'll be needing to do some damage control of my own. Discuss my proposition with Ben and Alyson if you'd like. The others may change their location, but what was done once can be done again. Will you be in your room later, if I've any news?"

"I'm not sure. I'm going to stop over at Allie's first, I don't know how long I'll stay. Here, I'll give you the number." She fished around in her purse for a paper and pen to copy the information for him. She found them and quickly did so, although as she wrote, she found it hard to picture him doing something as mundane as calling her on the telephone. She didn't even think it likely that he *had* a phone, but he could call from Tommy's or somewhere.

He stood so close, watching over her shoulder as she wrote. She felt she had to leave...now. She hadn't realized how hard it would be, to be alone in his company for any length of time. It was like a constant struggle not to give herself to him. It seemed to be getting stronger, the longer she stayed. Again, she wondered what he felt, and how he hid it so well.

He followed her as she climbed the stairs and opened the door for her. She turned to say goodbye, but he just looked at her quizzically. "You're not walking all the way back alone."

She looked out the door, up at the sky. Technically the sun had set, but the sky still glowed with shades of pink and orange, more than bright enough to light her way. She nodded towards the receding colors of the brilliant sunset. "That doesn't bother you?"

"It's a bit uncomfortable, but I can handle it. That's why I brought up this." He lifted his arm to show that he'd draped a black leather jacket across it. She noticed he'd brought up his denim as well. "I saw that you didn't bring a jacket, so I took the liberty."

He handed her the denim. She smiled at him and put it on. It was a little big, but she felt inexplicably reassured by it. It smelled lightly of his aftershave. "Thanks. It's not all that cold."

"You'll need it if we take the bike. I'd rather walk, but I suppose that would just be a selfish ploy to stretch out our time together. I guess it's no big secret at this point, that I do cherish time with you. I hope you enjoy it as well. Unfortunately, it's usually spent chasing, fighting and running from other vampires, but I can't think of anyone else I'd rather do it with.

Perhaps one night we can share a quiet evening of pleasant thoughts. However, tonight you need to see to your friends, and I need to check on things as well. As you said, the quicker we get all of this under control and behind us, the better."

He pulled a pair of dark sunglasses from his pocket, put them on and outstretched his hand for her to step out onto the porch. She made her way down the steps to the motorcycle and noticed a new helmet perched on the seat. She turned to him. "Been shopping?"

"I figured your life's been in enough danger lately. Why take a stupid chance?"

Felicity smiled and put it on, as Cain got on the bike. She hopped up behind him and got herself settled, with her hands holding him around the waist. It felt good to be touching him, even through the leather. She wondered just how much of it was her own passion and how much was this strange connection they now shared.

He took off down the road. She was enjoying the ride, even reveling in the little thrill it gave her to be pressed up against him. She wondered if it affected him at all. The feeling from the mark certainly went both ways, he'd indicated as much, but did it really excite him to be close to her? She began to realize that although she did trust him, it might be unfair and maybe unwise to tempt him too much, by being alone with him for too long, or too often. She could guess the things that the imagined vampire perched on his shoulder would be whispering and she'd do better not to press her luck.

He began to slow as they entered town and she realized that he probably didn't know where Alyson lived. As they reached the corner after Tommy's, she gave his left leg a little squeeze with her own, as though she were riding a horse, while also nudging him a bit with her left arm. He understood her perfectly and made the turn without comment. In this way, she directed him, until they reached Allie's. Her car was not there.

Felicity got off the bike and removed the helmet. Cain took it from her and strapped it to the bar on the back of the seat. She watched him and then moved closer, to say goodbye.

She was sorely tempted again to kiss him, but that was something she was better off not starting now. It would be sending mixed signals.

Besides, the last place she wanted to allow herself to kiss him, was in Allie's driveway with Ben probably looking out the window. She settled for lightly resting her hand on top of his, on the handlebar of the bike. She looked into his eyes as a little thrill raced through her at the contact. He looked back into hers, for a long time. Finally, she dropped her hand. "Maybe you should wait until I see if anyone's here. Allie's car isn't back."

"Ben's inside," Cain assured her.

"How do you... Oh," she amended as she realized he could see Ben's new mark.

"I don't think I'll see you later, but I'll find you tomorrow night. Or, if you'd like to come again, sooner..."

She smiled and gave a little non-committal shrug. "Goodnight. Oh…" She began to take off the jacket, to give it back.

"Keep it for now. You can give it back tomorrow." With that he walked the bike back down the driveway, revved the motor and rode off down the road. She quickly found herself alone in the cool night. The breeze had picked up and the clouds were racing across the sky as it turned shades of purple and dark blue with the nightfall.

She started up the front walk, contemplating her receding sense of him. Her body practically ached, to feel him moving away. And he hadn't given her a full measure of the venom? Perhaps it had a more potent effect on her, because she desired him anyway. She didn't know, but it was quite distracting. Poor Ben. She strongly hoped that Sindy did not come anywhere near him tonight.

Chapter 30 - Motives

Cain

An empty field
10:00, Sunday night

Cain sat in the field next to the cemetery, playing with a blade of grass in his hand. He'd been sitting here for some time, unconcealed, waiting. He wasn't sure what else to do. He wanted to speak with Sindy, but another outburst in a public place full of onlookers did not appeal. He didn't want to wander around looking for her. His intentions would surely be misread. He simply wanted to talk, for now.

He had begun to feel that his reaction early this morning was a bit overly dramatic. Would he really have let Ben kill them? He wasn't sure. Undoubtedly, it had all seemed very harsh and tense at the time, but now that it was over, he did see that no serious damage had been done. Ben may not agree, but at least he was alive.

Cain's true motive had been to try to make sure that he did not lose Felicity. She was still receptive to him, though much more poised and in control of herself than he might have thought she'd be. At least he knew she wouldn't entirely shun him. That accomplished, he didn't find himself as furious with Sindy as he probably should have been.

Felicity did still care for him, or she wouldn't have come to see him. Sindy's words may have spooked her a little, but she hadn't completely recoiled from him. He was also sure his bite had produced a potent effect in her; yet she did not let herself bend to its will. That hadn't really been his purpose in biting her, but he was a little surprised. It made her all the more alluring. Much more enticing than if she openly craved his attentions. He had to respect her strength of will as well.

It was always hard to tell how a person would react to being bitten. Of course it wasn't something ever openly studied or recorded. A certain amount of information was passed to a new vampire from their sire, but the venom was almost lost knowledge. Frankly, he was amazed that Sindy knew so much about it. It certainly wasn't something they had ever discussed. That was information Cain usually withheld when possible. Why tempt them?

Most killed when they drank. If their victims felt its effect, it made drinking that much easier, but would hardly be noticed by the predator. As modern times made killing much more difficult to accomplish without notice, more and more vampires were learning to leave their victims still clinging to life.

The mark that came with this was now common knowledge, but as far as Cain knew, mostly it served as a warning to a vampire, to identify one who might give them trouble in knowing their true nature. Or it led a vampire back to a person that they might want to revisit or turn.

It also helped to mark territory. It wouldn't do to have too many hunting the same grounds. The experience itself, of being bitten, was not something many vampires bothered to inquire about of their victims. They had only their own experience to remember.

Cain did know that *his* venom seemed to grow more potent as he aged. It was difficult to gauge, because every person's experience varied. And of course, his experiences with humans were few and far between. But each time, he noticed that their reactions seemed to become more and more pronounced.

Felicity's was the strongest yet. He had made sure to let the venom enter her system, before drinking any of her blood. Once he was sure that his venom was within her, she was marked. He hadn't really needed to drink from her at all, but that was just asking for too much self-control. Even *he* couldn't expect that much of himself, but he had only taken the slightest taste.

He had hardly even fed from her, and yet her reaction had seemed drastically increased, compared to the last person he'd infected. Perhaps she was more vulnerable to it for some reason, but he didn't really think so. It was him; his body's abilities increasing with age. She had clung to him in a way that he had found incredibly arousing and he'd had to summon considerable will to force himself from her. He pushed the memory away, before it led to things that he should not even imagine right now.

Thinking of the venom caused him again to wonder what Ben's reaction had been like. Sindy was newborn compared to Cain, and there was no telling how such things would vary from vampire to vampire, but she had taken her time and been sure to infect him well with her evil serum. Such a dose would certainly have some effect. He was certain that Sindy hoped so. Ben should be well attuned to her.

Felicity was definitely well attuned to him, as he was to her. Admittedly, since the time of the bite itself, he had begun to wonder of its effects. She hid it remarkably well, but today assured him that a heightened desire was in fact there, she simply kept her feelings in check.

That she remained able to hold herself aloof from him still, was almost amazing to him. The beast in the back of his mind coaxed him to realize that this was easily remedied. A fuller sampling would certainly bring her to him, but that was not his desire, not truly. He wanted her, to be sure, but not like that. What would be the point? He could have done that a month ago, if her physical acceptance had been his only aspiration.

He'd been sitting out here alone in the field for some time, pondering these things. Then his mind turned back to Sindy. As angry as she usually made him and as hard as she might try to provoke a reaction, or solicit sexual favors from him, what he found himself feeling for her more and more, was pity. She would be enraged if she ever thought so, but he had begun to see her as someone who had been so hurt, rejected, unloved and abused, that she knew of no other way to gain favor, or at least some attention from others, than the things that she did.

Her actions last night spoke to him not of petty revenge and backlash towards him, although they were certainly so motivated. What it had really seemed to him, was a cry for help. A plea for attention and acceptance. All of her talk about proving herself worthy for him, from a girl with her tenacity of spirit? She was infuriated that she could not gain worth in his eyes, he was sure of it.

Of course, the easiest way for her to meet his approval would be to follow his example, as far as feeding habits were concerned, but she had far too rebellious a nature to give in so easily to his demands. She insisted on having people believe that everything she did was on her own terms. Perhaps she even felt the need to prove that to herself.

The wiles she was most accustomed to using on men had not prevailed with him. She was very used to being valued for her body. He had not accepted her advances. He had turned her away and she didn't know how to bring him back. It tormented her, probably for the principal, more than actually wanting him. She wanted to be in control. Even if she drove him to kill her, at least it would be by *her* actions and decree.

She approached. Marcus was with her. Wonderful. A bodyguard, he supposed. At least she brought no one else. He didn't bother to get up. He was lying back on his elbows, looking up at the stars. Let her see that he had no fear of her; it would probably drive her mad.

She stopped about twenty feet away and smiled at his casual pose. She then turned and placed a firm hand on Marcus's chest, speaking to him quietly. 'Sit. Stay. Good boy,' Cain assumed. Marcus folded his arms and stood, looking sullen and cross. Cain had the childish urge to stick his tongue out at the man. Of course he didn't.

Finally, Sindy sauntered toward him supremely unconcerned, not to be outdone by his lack of alarm. He eyed her for a moment and then asked with quiet sincerity, "Do you *want* to die?"

This rather caught her off guard. She laughed as she dropped herself to the ground, to sit next to him in the tall grass. Not too close, he noticed. "Do you? Here you are, all alone, without your precious psychic shield, just waiting for me. I've got enough manpower now, I'm sure I could take you down. Hell, Marcus there could probably do it alone."

Cain smiled. "I highly doubt it. I could run circles around that gorilla."

"Is that a fact? Then why didn't you finish him off last time? Don't try to tell me that the stake you left sticking out of him was supposed to be some kind of warning, because to me, it looked more like bad aim."

He neatly sidestepped the question. "You don't want to kill me."

"I don't?"

"Oh, heaven's no! You're far too fond of me. You seek my approval. You don't want my death, you want my respect. Which you did not earn last night by the way. All *that* accomplished was to more firmly cement Ben's hatred of you. Probably not wise. I know that you think humans are easily manipulated, but don't push Benjamin and his friends too far, or it will mean your death."

She laughed. "Oh please! What's Ben gonna do?"

"There is a Christian speaker named Beth Moore who once said, that while 'a woman scorned is surely a force to be reckoned with, a man humiliated may yet be far worse'. You don't think he's plotting your demise even as we speak?"

"Even as we speak, I think Ben's probably hiding under the covers, having himself a good wet dream."

She seemed to love trying to shock him; he found it terribly annoying. "Must you always be so crass?"

"What's the matter? Do I offend your prude old English sensibilities?"

He rolled his eyes and pressed on. "The point is, your little performance only shows how sorely you long for my attention. You wouldn't want to kill me, then you'd have no one left to try and impress. I've the feeling Arif is not at all interested. Besides, 'docile harem girl' doesn't strike me as your style."

"All submissive and obedient? Hardly! But you and Arif aren't the only fish in the sea."

"Have you shopped around? A decent vampire is hard to find. We're a rare breed."

"Conceited much? Anyway, 'decent vampire', isn't that a contradiction in terms?" She shook her head and looked up at the sky for a moment. "As flawed as your logic may be, I could still turn it around and say the same of you. You don't want to kill me, or I would have been dead a long time ago. You think you can tame me. I'm like a wild horse that you're just itchin' to break. You want to transform me into something more suitable for your arm. Like that stupid play they made us see in school...*My Fair Lady*."

"Ah, Pygmalion. Fancy yourself Eliza Doolittle do you?" He laughed. "Is that what you think? Well, I'll let you in on a little secret." He paused. Like all girls, she loved secrets and eagerly she hovered close to hear. He wouldn't disappoint her.

He looked into her eyes and spoke slowly and sincerely, with careful attention to each word. "*You* have the potential to become a truly *splendid* creature." He let that soak in for a moment. She wasn't sure how to accept it, whether or not he was teasing her, but she was obviously pleased. "But if you haven't the desire, then I haven't the patience. I am old and I haven't the forbearance to wait around while you play childish games. And now you've made me go and sound like Arif, which I find most disturbing," he finished with a shake of his head.

"Maybe I've decided that you aren't worth changing for."

"*I* never claimed to be. And while I do allow myself a selfish motive now and again, I hadn't really been trying to get you to change for *me*."

"Then why do you try so hard?" she asked.

"For *you*." She gave him a sarcastic smirk. "For your own peace of mind and well being, among other purposes."

"Here we go. What purposes would those be? For God? Are you trying to save my soul? 'Cause you're a little late. We're vampires, honey and no amount of good deeds now, will let you into those pearly gates! You think you're on some kind of holy mission? You're a holy joke! You are like a walking insult to God! If there even *is* a God and he's looking down on you, I'm thinkin' he's got to be pissed!"

"'Do not be deceived: God cannot be mocked. A man reaps what he sows. The one who sows to please his sinful nature, from that nature will reap destruction; the one who sows to please the Spirit, from the Spirit will reap eternal life.' That's Galatians 6:7 and 8. Sindy please, I've argued these points hundreds of times with hundreds of others, far more versed in the gospel than you."

She rolled her eyes at him and shook her head. "You gonna try and tell me you don't ever please that sinful nature of yours?" He began to protest, but she wouldn't let him. "I know, I know. So you don't live off human blood. Give the man a gold star. I'm talking about Felicity and whatever other poor girls you've ruined along the way. You gonna tell me it isn't so?"

"I never claimed to be entirely righteous. We are sinners all. The most we can do is make every effort to do what is right each new day. Anyway, who are you to say that I've ruined anyone? You don't know anything of my life and I've done nothing truly harmful to Felicity."

"Right. And you're what...in suspended animation? Where's it going? Nowhere? Give me a break! There will be a point where you cross the line.

All of this spiritual crap is not really my arena, but physical expression? Now that's something I can tell you about. I've been watching you two; I read the body language. I've gotta tell ya, I'm thinkin' there's not a whole lot goin' on. She likes you and we both know you're hot for her. You've got the chemistry. In fact, the sexual tension between you guys is pretty thick, and isn't that fun? But there are definitely some major boundaries there. So what's the holdup Cain? You wanna take your time, make it all sweet and meaningful? 'Cause anyone you're gonna waste that much effort on, has gotta be more than a passing fling.

You're invested in her. When things reach the limit, where else are you gonna go? You wanna tell me you're not gonna take the next step? You're just gonna walk away? 'Have a nice life.' I don't think so.

If *I* pushed you too far and you lost your beloved self-control and killed me, well that's something that you could probably consider yourself beyond reproach for. I'm not innocent or pure in any sense of the word. Sending my soul to Hell would probably earn 'ya extra credit, but Felicity? You're gonna take her young life and condemn *her* innocent soul? Isn't that a little risky to your precious theology?"

He was shaking his head and dismissing her words before she even finished speaking. "There is no way for us to know the status or condition of one's soul. The best we can do is to conduct ourselves as one would expect a heaven bound soul to act.

I never said that I would change Felicity to become one of us, but even if I did, if it were by her own choice and she were to live as I do, without taking human life, then who are you to say that it's wrong? There are those who see our state, as being in the possession of amazing gifts. If these gifts are used for good, then are we not good as well? Everything and everyone has a purpose, and I will not believe that mine is to be evil."

"So that's the plan? Rationalize a way for you to get just what you want? If that's the plan, then you really *don't* need me, do you? Why bother with me at all? I've got to admit that I do spend a good part of my time trying to think of ways to put you through hell! Why don't you just call it a bad job and leave me alone already? Aren't you getting tired of fighting for a lost cause?"

"'Let us not become weary in doing good, for at the proper time we will reap a harvest if we do not give up.' That's also Galatians, 6:9."

"Don't you get it? It does not apply! We're already damned! It's too late!"

"It's never too late."

"Really? When's the last time you touched a cross? Face it Cain, we are removed from humans and all of their stupid beliefs! That stuff can't help us now. We're outcasts and without each other, we're alone. Other vampires are all we have, and you know what? You're right, I've been around and most of them *are* monsters, but guess what, so are we. We're made to be monsters. Perfect predatory killers. Why fight it?"

"Why not? When is the last time you did something because someone told you to? You think you have to become a killer just because that's what your sire led you to believe? You know already that it's not true.

You've fed without killing. You've the strength of will to live in peace with those around you, if not the desire. I know that you're strong enough. To kill and live off of others is certainly easier and usually more appealing than to have to make it on your own. To live in a responsible and civil manner is sometimes fraught with difficulty, but when isn't sin easy or appealing?

Does it really make you so happy, to hurt others, or is the satisfaction it gives you, fleeting and petty? Is it gratifying to surround yourself with false friends and lovers, so that you can feel secure and accepted, or is it empty and lacking? Doesn't it leave you wanting more? That's why you're never satisfied.

You could surround yourself with hundreds, but if you can't see them as equals... If you can't know that they accept you for who you are, instead of what you may do for them... If you can't deny that they cling to you in fear, whether it's fear of you, or fear of being without you...you might as well be all alone. And if you're going to be all alone, you'd better be able to live with yourself."

Sindy sat and watched him with quiet malice. She was difficult to read. She seemed very capable of suddenly shifting either way. Would she accede his point, finally break down and give in to the hurt and the sorrow that had surely been holding her prisoner? Ask him to help her to start anew? Or would she once again hide behind her rage and build yet another mental wall between them, to keep him out? To keep herself from having to see her own insecurities.

She surprised him by choosing a path level and mature, somewhat down the middle. She was hurt and angered by the things he'd said, because she surely knew them to be true. She did not try to deny them, but she would not set aside her pride, or let him in any way view her as weak. She did have the instincts of a true predator. He was surprised to see that after some thoughtful consideration, her mood seemed compromising.

"You're pretty observant. I'm observant too. I've seen the way you live and I've gotta tell 'ya, the way you dominate the vampire in you is very impressive. I know it's not easy, especially when you've just had such a sweet reminder from Felicity of how good it can be. So I admire your self-control.

I still think it's pointless. Why deny yourself something that you were meant to, *made* to have? But that's your choice, and anything that you feel that strongly about, is worth taking notice of. You are older than me, so maybe you've got more experience than me, but when it comes to strength of will, you are not stronger than me. So I'm gonna stick to what I said. I'm gonna go without for a while, just because I want you to know that I can.

In the meantime, I still think that in playing with Felicity, you are playing with fire. And I'm gonna stand back and watch you get burned. You're not a saint! You aren't meant to be and you can't expect to resist such appetizing fare. She wants you and I know you won't be able to hold out forever.

Maybe you could even make her happy for a while, but guess what? She's got a life! Unlike you, who have nothing else to exist for from night to night, she's got friends and family. She's going to college, so she must aspire to something in her future. Think she'll want a real live hubby too? A couple of snot nosed kids... Well, I guess you could always adopt!" she said with a cruel laugh. "You gonna buy her a house with a white picket fence? Face it Cain, you are from two different walks of life and you just don't mesh. She can't ever really be anything more to you than a plaything or a meal, unless you kill her."

He wouldn't respond. Her words forced him to look into dark truths that he usually shied from. He wouldn't go there now. It was the first time he had ever felt he had made any sort of progress with Sindy, disregarding the parts designed to hurt him. He had to admit that she was uncomfortably close to the mark, but he would deal with his own demons later.

She stood and looked down at him for a moment, then reached a hand down to help him up. It seemed such a strange gesture coming from her, and an uncomfortable one, since it immediately reminded him of his first night in the gym with Felicity. She had reached out to him in the same way, unafraid and wanting nothing more than to connect with him somehow. A simple and sincere gesture. Coming from Sindy however, he eyed it with much more trepidation. He felt like Charlie Brown, wondering whether or not Lucy would pull the football away. Not that he had anything to lose. He accepted her hand and she gently pulled him to his feet with a smile.

"Speaking of playful meals, I think I'll go and pay Ben a little visit. Unless you had something more appealing in mind? I've got a short attention span and I'm done talkin'. I'm in the mood for something a little more physical."

"Why don't you go home to your playthings then?"

"I sent them out hunting. Just 'cause I'm gonna suffer, doesn't mean they should. It wouldn't be fair. Don't worry, I left Chris and Luke in charge. I know you don't approve of my boys, but they are pretty capable, as long as you keep it simple. They know the rules, nobody dies. And Marcus...well I have to admit, he's just not turning out to be as much fun as I thought he'd be. He's useful, sure, but between you and me," she whispered to him conspiratorially, with a quick glance over to her muscle man. "The man's got no staying power." She smiled and shook her head.

She moved in even closer to him and her voice took on the seductive tone he had grown to know so well from her. "But *you* must be feeling awfully *frustrated,* night after night." She openly ran her eyes over his body, lingering here and there. "I could help you out with that; it wouldn't have to mean a thing." He just looked at her with knitted brows. Any kind of satisfaction from their talk, or budding camaraderie he might have felt for her was immediately displaced by her words. Why could she never just let things be?

She assessed his mood and continued. "No, huh? Well, lucky Ben. You don't mind, do you? I wouldn't want you to be jealous."

"I thought you were going to stay away from him now. Wasn't that part of your inane agreement? You should know that I have promised Felicity that she and her friends will not be harmed again. I will enforce that if necessary. As you pointed out, killing you and yours would not be something I would suffer over."

"Oh relax. I'm not gonna *do* anything, unless he begs me to, I mean. You wouldn't expect me to actually *turn him away,* would you? But if you want to get technical, I get what you get, remember? An eye for an eye. Don't tell me you haven't seen her.

Besides, how can you make me miss out on such fun? I've been waiting for Ben to appreciate me for years. He may never admit it, but damn if I'm not gonna make that boy want me!" Cain just rolled his eyes and shook his head. "You know he's safe inside some house somewhere that I can't enter into anyway. So what if I want to sit outside the window? Is that against any of your grand edicts? At least you'll know where I am, and you should be happy that I'm not out wreaking havoc and destruction. Hell, what am I asking you for anyway? I can do what I want. I'm out of here."

She blew him a kiss and returned to Marcus, who had been waiting as a statue the entire time. Cain let her go without a word. He was heartened that she didn't really want to risk his anger anymore. In fact, the entire evening she had conducted herself with a considerable amount of maturity and better thought out arguments than he had ever expected. Perhaps there was hope for her yet.

At the moment, Cain's interest was hopelessly captured by Felicity. An interest, that however unwise, he knew he would find himself unable to ignore. Sindy's words cruelly repeated themselves in his head. *She can't ever really be anything more to you than a plaything or a meal, unless you kill her.* That didn't have to be true…did it? He tried to believe that he was stronger than that, although in truth, he was uncertain.

Felicity had awoken stirrings in his still heart that brought him hope and joy he'd thought forgotten. He *had* to see her again. He could only hope he was making the right decision. He also did believe the prediction he had voiced earlier. Sindy could indeed become a truly splendid creature, with just the right amount of guidance. He wondered if she might even be worth waiting for.

.

~~~~~~~~~~~~~~~~~~~~~~~~~~~~~~~

~~~~~~~~~~~~~~~~~~~~~~~~~~~~~~~

~~~~~~~~~~~~~~~~~~~~~~~~~~~~~~~

Volume 2

~~~~~~~

Lost Reflections

~~~~~~~~~~~~~~~~~~~~~~~~~~~~~

~~~~~~~~~~~~~~~~~~~~~~~~~~~~~

~~~~~~~~~~~~~~~~~~~~~~~~~~~~~

Almost Human ~ The First Series
Volume 2 - Lost Reflections

Contents

CR∞ ∞ CR∞ ∞ CR∞ ∞ CR∞ ∞ CR∞ ∞ CR∞ ∞ CR∞ ∞ CR∞

Part 1 ~ Persistent Persuasion

CR∞ ∞ CR∞ ∞ CR∞ ∞ CR∞ ∞ CR∞ ∞ CR∞ ∞ CR∞ ∞ CR∞

Chapter 1 ~ Morals

Felicity

Alyson's apartment
8:00, Sunday night

As the last blazing colors of sunset faded to deep violet in the sky, Felicity made her way up Alyson's front walk and knocked on the door. It took a long time for Ben to answer, but she trusted Cain's sense that he was still there. He finally appeared, stifling a yawn. She must have woken him. She was glad he'd been able to get some rest and try to recover from his ordeal. She still had a hard time getting the mental image out of her mind, of his chest and stomach covered in bruises from his beating. She could barely even see evidence of Sindy's bite on his throat, but psychologically, Ben probably considered that trespass far worse than any more painful physical injury. "Hi," he said sleepily.

"Hi. Allie's not back yet?" she asked in concern. The sun had only just set, but she didn't find as much comfort in that as she used to. Cain had reminded her that this was real life, not a vampire movie, and she shouldn't be so confident that she knew all the rules of the game.

He shook his head. "No, but she called. She got stuck going in to work. She's going to try and get out early, but I doubt it."

She looked at him appraisingly. "You staying here? No more visions of Vermont?"

"For now. You wanna come in?" he asked.

"Do you want me to come in?" she asked back.

He gave her a look that said he felt bad that she should have to ask. "Of course I do," he answered, backing away some more to let her in. Ben eyed the denim jacket she wore, as she took it off and laid it on a chair. He didn't say anything, but he surely knew who it belonged to.

They went to sit in the living room, on the somewhat lumpy couch. Felicity fidgeted into the corner until she could get comfortable, as Ben sat down quietly next to her. He gave her a sidelong glance. "Sorry I flipped out before."

"It's understandable."

"Yeah, but I shouldn't have taken it out on you."

She shrugged. "It's okay." They sat in silence. She'd like to talk more about what was going on with Alyson and her vampire lover, Mattie, but figured Ben should be the one to start that conversation.

"You went to go see Cain, didn't you?" he asked.

"Yes." He just sat there, waiting for more. "He asked after you."

"I'm touched," he said in sarcasm.

"He thought you might be planning some kind of revenge. He even offered to help." Why had she even said anything? She hadn't really planned to just blurt that out, but she was getting tired of Ben always thinking Cain was against him.

This got Ben's full attention. "What kind of revenge?"

She pondered for a moment whether she should even tell him. His expectant face wouldn't let her think of a way around it. "He knows where Sindy and her coven are sleeping. He followed them, even though it was almost morning and he could have gotten himself killed. As it is, I think he came much closer to being dust than he lets on. Anyway, he figured that if we knew where they were, we could plan to confront them in the daytime. They'd be at a serious disadvantage. Maybe we could even let the sunlight in on them somehow."

Ben was becoming more and more animated as she spoke. "Of course! It'd be easy! All of our problems neatly turned into dust!"

"Hold on there, VanBuren, it's not..." Felicity began.

"Who?" Ben interrupted.

"The vampire hunter," she explained.

Ben groaned. "That's VanHelsing!" he clarified. "VanBuren was a president!"

"Oh. Well you know who I mean!" Ben rolled his eyes. She ignored him and pressed on. "It's not quite as simple as it sounds, this isn't the movies. If Cain can be awake during the day, they can too. What are you going to do, invite them to follow you outside for a stroll? Besides, they'd know you were coming from a mile away." He didn't seem to understand. She spoke as lightly as she could. "You're marked now, remember?"

He flinched and looked a bit sick. "So are you, right?"

She gave a little nod. "Anyway, I don't know about you, but I don't want to play vampire hunter. I just want them to leave us alone."

"Alyson could do it," Ben suggested.

"It's too dangerous," Felicity declared.

"Did she say that?"

"I didn't ask her."

"Didn't Allie go with you?"

"To Cain's?" she asked in puzzlement. "No."

"I saw you leave together," Ben insisted.

"She dropped me off," Felicity clarified.

"You went to see him *alone*?" Ben seemed completely outraged, as though he thought that she had lost her mind.

"I trust him," she said simply.

He looked like he thought she was a fool. "I don't."

"Well, you're not me," Felicity told him quietly.

"He bit you, 'Liss!"

"Once, for a reason. Now that I'm marked, the others have to leave me alone," Felicity told him.

"Oh I see, it was a good deed. That couldn't possibly whet his appetite for more, even though now he's got his own private stock." She shook her head and turned away. "Are you *feeding* him?"

She turned back to him fiercely. "Want to check my neck?" she asked, sharply pulling her collar away from her throat on both sides.

He mumbled, "No," but she noticed that he still looked..

She let go her collar and put her head down into her hands. They sat in silence. After a minute, she looked up to find him staring at her. She stared back at him for a second and then asked, "Think Alyson's got anything good to eat? I haven't had any dinner."

"The Chinese food place delivers."

She turned to him with a smile, relieved to have something to divert their attention. "That sounds wonderful, I'm starved."

He got up and she followed him into the kitchen. "I think Allie's got a menu in here somewhere," he said as he began rifling through a drawer full of papers, scotch tape, scissors and assorted odds and ends. He reached towards the back and winced as he stretched a sore muscle.

"Why don't you go lay down? I'll find it."

He looked at her in annoyance, although he was rubbing his side, under his arm, in pain. "I've been lying down all day. I'm sure I'm capable of getting a piece of paper out of a drawer."

"Sorry." She stood watching him for a minute.

Finally, he looked up at her. "What?"

"Well, I wanted to ask how you were feeling, but I don't want to get counted at."

He tried not to smile. "I'm fine."

She wanted to ask more, but wasn't sure how to phrase it. "You haven't felt anything...weird, have you?"

He took a deep breath and let it out slowly before looking at her to answer. "No, I'm just very, very sore."

"I guess I should tell you..."

He didn't let her finish. "Could we have that talk after we eat?"

"Yeah, sure. Hey, isn't that the menu?" She picked it up off the floor. It must have fallen out when they'd begun their search.

Half an hour later, they were sitting at the kitchen table with a bunch of open cartons. Felicity looked at Ben over her lo mein. She felt terrible about what had happened to him, but she knew he'd be okay. He seemed to have such a strong and confident personality. She wondered if he really was, or if that was just the face he showed the world. When he'd told her about his friend Mattie becoming a vampire, and even when he'd confronted Alyson about being Mattie's secret lover, he'd been angry, but she could see how hurt he'd been inside. He saw her looking at him. "What, is it time for that talk already?"

"What? No. I mean, unless you want to. Actually, I was just wondering something."

He looked as though he thought she was going to ask him something he wouldn't want to answer. He probably thought she was wondering about how he'd felt when he'd been bitten by Sindy last night. She wouldn't pry about that, it was not the kind of thing she thought he'd want to share. "So ask," he said with resignation.

She paused. He just looked at her, patiently waiting. "Would you really have slept with Brenda last night? If she'd let you I mean."

He seemed bewildered, but relieved. "*That's* what you were wondering?" She just gave a little shrug and nod. He smiled and answered, "Yeah." He grinned at her obvious discomfort. "I'm a healthy, young, heterosexual guy and she's really hot. It's kind of a no brainer. I mean, I hope you don't think I'd be pushy about it or anything! But, if the opportunity presented itself? Yeah, I would."

"But you hardly know her."

He gave her a sly grin. "That's part of the allure." She gave him a look of disgust. "Well what did you want me to do, lie? Should I have told you that I would have turned her away, made her wait until we had a solid and lasting relationship? Because any guy who tells you he would have done that, is either lying, or already sleeping with somebody else." She shook her head, dejectedly. "Hey, I never claimed to be anyone's knight in shining armor. I'm just a guy and I'm being honest. I told you men were from Mars."

She looked up at him almost pleadingly. "Doesn't it *mean* anything?"

He gazed at her steadily across the table and his eyes seemed to soften. "Of course it *can*. I'll bet it can be truly amazing, if it's with someone that you really care about." He chewed his lip for a second and then looked back down at his food to begin eating again. "But sometimes, it's just sex."

Felicity was still gazing back at him in puzzlement at his answer. "Have you *ever* been with someone that you cared about?"

"Don't make it sound like I don't care. It's not like I'm out collecting conquests or something; but have I ever been with someone that I might...love?" She gave a little nod. "No, not yet." He shrugged. "It'll happen. Until then, a guy's got to do something to pass the time, right?" She gave him a little smirk at that, just to let him know that she didn't fully agree. "So have you...ever been in love?" he asked. She was taken aback. "What, you get to ask me and I don't get to ask back?"

"No."

"No I don't get to ask, or no to the question?"

"The question. No."

He smiled. "I think that 'no' holds more than one connotation."

She felt herself blushing and looked down, before answering indignantly. "You don't get to ask me that."

He broke into a broad grin. "I don't need to." She played with the last of the food on her plate. "How old are you, eighteen?" he asked.

She looked up at him with an abashed little smile. She couldn't believe she was talking to a guy about this stuff. "Not yet, but I will be in another week and a half. My birthday is on the seventeenth."

He laughed. "Okay, soon to be eighteen then. A beautiful girl like you, remains untouched?"

Felicity's mouth fell open at his insolence. "This is rapidly leaving curious friend territory, and entering rude and obnoxious!" She got up from the table, amazed at his temerity.

"I'm not being obnoxious, I'm just making an observation," he protested with a laugh.

She hadn't planned to say more, but couldn't help herself. "It's not as if I've never had the opportunity." She brought her paper plate to the garbage and came back to begin closing up the cartons of food. Ben was grinning up at her as she moved around him.

He spoke to her as she tried to ignore him. "Now you're all embarrassed and disappointed in me, because you think I've got no morals, right? I may not be celibate, but I still think I'm a pretty decent guy. It's not like I'm out there cleverly tricking girls into being with me. It is a mutual kind of thing, you know? I should be a twenty year old virgin?" He caught her arm and made her stop to look at him. She'd been cleaning up around him, avoiding his gaze.

She looked down at him and smiled. "I don't think you have no morals, and I'm not completely naïve, or chaste..." She added naughtily. He raised an eyebrow and she laughed. She didn't want him thinking she was some kind of prude. "I think you're a good guy, who hasn't met the right person yet. Neither have I. And you're right, it'll happen."

She started to walk away, but he didn't let go of her arm. She looked down at him questioningly to find he'd turned rather serious. "I know this is none of my business. You certainly don't have to listen to me, but since we're on the subject, I might as well give you my opinion, for what it's worth." He took his hand off of her arm, but she stayed, looking down at him solemnly. "If you've waited this long, don't give it up for a dead guy. 'Cause that's just not something that's going to last."

She wanted to be shocked and insulted. Certainly that flashed across her face, but after that first moment, she really wasn't. It was good to have someone to talk to and she saw an opportunity to maybe soften things for Allie as well. She tread gingerly. "How can you know, that it wouldn't last?"

He looked as though he couldn't believe she might defend such a relationship. "He's a vampire. What else is there to know?"

"I know you still don't want to accept it, but it's not like all vampires are these horrible mindless demons. We've seen *them*. Cain's not like that, and from what I've heard, neither is Mattie." He just stared at her coldly. She spoke gently, hoping he would listen, without being provoked to anger again. "I'm not saying it's a good thing, what's been done to them, but bad things do happen to good people. Don't you believe that the good people they once were could still be inside?" He looked away from her, silently. "I'm not saying that there's any kind of future there, as far as a relationship's concerned. To be honest, there's just too much that I still don't know. It's all so strange, but a friendship? Yes, definitely. Everyone needs a friend. Especially when they're going through a difficult time in their life.

What if Sindy had gone too far, Ben? What if it had happened to *you?* What if you felt you were still the same person inside, but now with this terrible curse upon you, this affliction that you never asked for; what would you do? Would you have me turn away from you? Would you take your own life? Or would you do the best you could, to live without hurting others and maybe try to make some kind of difference in the world? You don't have to like Cain, or even Mattie anymore, but I think that you have to accept them as people, instead trying to think of them as some kind of monsters; especially knowing what they mean to us."

"Us? So now I've got Allie *and* you against me, huh?"

"We're not against you. Look, I don't know what Alyson and Mattie's relationship is like, but I can tell she really cares about him."

"Alyson can't keep a relationship going for more than a month!"

"Maybe that's because she's in love with someone that she can't have!"

That seemed to frighten him. He was quiet for a moment. "She can't be." Those were the words that came out of his mouth, but even he didn't seem to believe them.

Felicity had meant Mattie, and she knew Ben also took it that way, but she suddenly wondered if Ben might not be included in that category as well. Alyson certainly loved Ben as a friend. She wondered if Allie was only not interested in Ben romantically, for fear of him rejecting her and ruining their friendship.

Allie *had* been romantically involved with Mattie though, at least she had insinuated that she was. "I don't know, she never actually told me that she was in love with Mattie, but my instincts tell me that, yeah she probably is. They were close before and she still cares now, three years later, after everything. She's so worried about him, Ben. Don't you think she'd know if he were *that* different; if he'd truly changed? Like I said, you don't have to like him. You probably don't even have to see him, but don't punish *her* for it. She needs *you* too, you know. Or at least to know that things are okay between you."

"She knows."

"You talked about it?"

"No, but she knows. What about Cain?"

"What about him?" He just looked at her. "I don't know. I'm not going to tell you that I'm not still attracted to him. I don't know where it'll go, or if I'll even let it go anywhere."

"It's not real."

"What do you mean?"

"The stuff you feel for him. It's not real. It's a drug, it's that... venom. Don't you know that?"

"It's not only that. It couldn't be. I know where the real stuff ends and *that* begins."

Ben laughed, but it was humorless and cold. "You think so? When did he first give you a taste of it? I know it's not all that long ago that he bit you, but what about before that? I wasn't unconscious during Sindy's little speech, as much as I wished I were. It's in their saliva, right? So when did he first kiss you? Isn't that when it really began? Let me tell you something, that's pretty potent stuff."

Somehow, she hadn't made that connection. The thought was both frightening and a relief at the same time. No wonder she had reacted so strongly to their one and only kiss! But at the same time, it showed her more about Cain's character than she had realized, because they had only shared one kiss. She had kissed him and would have again, but he wouldn't let her. Now she knew why. He wanted her to know him, before she became under the influence of the venom. For the second time today, she felt both lucky and grateful at the same time that Cain was indeed a good man.

Of course, Ben didn't know what she and Cain had done together. Just because they hadn't slept together didn't mean she hadn't let him touch her. When Ben had said that Cain had kissed her, she hadn't denied it. She looked up with the thought of telling him of Cain's restraint, but the look on Ben's face made her lose the thought.

Her best guess would be that he was remembering being bitten. He certainly wasn't looking at, or thinking of her. After a moment, he swallowed hard and continued their conversation, although he wouldn't quite meet her eyes. He looked as if he were forcing himself to speak, through great difficulty. It came out as little more than a whisper, as though he didn't really want her to hear. "That stuff is strong poison. If it could make me *want* Sindy so badly... If my hands weren't tied, I can't even tell you what I would have done.

You don't know what's real, you can't. I know you liked him before he bit you. Maybe even before he kissed you, but now? How will you ever know how much is real? How can you ever trust that he's not just using you, bending you to his every whim? Because I haven't the slightest doubt that he could. In fact, the knowledge that he still hasn't, is making me think that maybe he's not such a bad guy after all. But you'll never really know whether it's you, or just some subtle manipulation of you."

She lowered her eyes to the floor and tried to sort out her feelings. It was too difficult right now. She wanted to argue with him, but couldn't even try to think of how she could prove him wrong. She thought she knew how she felt. She wasn't being manipulated in any way right now, but was it just residual feeling, from the overpowering desire she felt for him whenever he was near? Was any of it really her? That was a very unsettling question. She would have to pay close attention to how she felt the next time that she saw Cain.

Until her mark wore off, she probably would have a hard time figuring out what was real. And even then, only if she refrained from kissing him. If she were to remain involved with him, how would she ever avoid the venom entirely? It seemed awfully complicated. She remembered how strongly she had desired him, just after that first kiss.

That thought made her realize that she'd better try to prepare Ben for the evening ahead, just in case. She wasn't sure if Allie had really told him anything. "Sindy may come looking for you later."

"She can't come in," Ben said with assurance.

Felicity drew in a deep breath and sighed. "She may not have to. You'll feel her. It'll...call you."

Ben looked as though she had just taken his security blanket away. "Vermont's soundin' pretty good," he said in annoyance.

"I don't think it's the same for everybody, so I could be wrong, but *I* also didn't get as much venom as you did; and I feel it, pretty strong. I know it's the venom, it's not just me," she confided.

"Great. So what do we do? Tie me to the mast, like Jason and the Argonauts?"

"Who?" Felicity asked in confusion.

"Jason and the Golden Fleece. When he wanted to hear the Siren's song? I've got to sit you down with some movies," he told her.

"Well, I don't think you'll require restraints," she said with a chuckle. "It's just kind of weird and uncomfortable, and I thought you'd want to know. I'd better stay until Allie gets home though, just in case."

"Thanks. Luckily, I kind of like having you around. You certainly make interesting conversation," he said with a mischievous leer. "Are you sure you want to subject yourself to being locked in an apartment with a crazed sex fiend? Could be dangerous," he teased.

She reached out and gave him a quick rap on the chest. It wasn't very hard, but it made him wince from his bruises. "I think I can take you." He gave her a look, which made her realize that her statement could easily be misconstrued. She made as if to hit him again and he backed away laughing. "Sindy probably doesn't even know where Allie lives, and she wouldn't know you'd be here anyway. What is she going to do, walk around the whole town, feeling for you?"

"She certainly could. It's not a very big town, and what else has she got to do?" Ben asked.

"Well, like you said, she can't come in. It may not be the best night's sleep you've ever had, but you'll survive."

Two hours later found them on the couch watching television. At least Ben was watching, Felicity was sleeping, until her head fell to the side and she jerked herself awake for the third time.

"'Liss, why don't you go to bed?"

"What? I'm awake," she said through a yawn.

"Go to bed 'Liss," Ben told her with a laugh.

"What time does Allie get home?" she asked.

"Last call's at 3:30, then she's still gotta clean up and stuff. She won't be back until after four," Ben said.

"What time is it now?" Felicity asked.

"Almost midnight. Trust me, you'll never make it. Don't even try. I'm going to turn in now myself," he told her.

"Okay, goodnight." She laid down and settled herself deeper into the couch, trying to get comfortable as he turned off the television.

"You're not going to sleep out here? This couch sucks. You won't get any sleep. Trust me, I've tried it," he said.

"I'm fine," she insisted.

"Do you want the bed and I'll take the couch?" he asked.

"No. I can't make you sleep out here with bruises like that. You need the bed," she admitted.

"Well, it's a big bed. And it's not like we haven't slept together before." He gave her an impish smile. "You have my word of honor that I will not seek to despoil your virtue," he said with overly dramatic flair. "I'm a little too wounded for such strenuous activity anyway."

"Shut up and go to bed." She didn't get up, or even look at him.

"At least get out of those clothes. Who wants to sleep in jeans?"

Now she sat up. "And just what do you propose? It's not like I brought anything."

"Well it's a good thing. You know how much I like those sheep pajamas of yours." She made good use of a throw pillow. He caught it before it could do any damage. "Wear something of Allie's, she won't care," he said, tossing the pillow back to her.

"Ben, as sweet as it is that you think that I could, Alyson is at least two sizes smaller than me. I don't think so."

"Well, I keep some stuff here. It's mostly tee shirts and sweats, but they should do. Unless you're afraid that you can't squeeze into an extra large." This time the pillow hit him in the head.

He went into the bedroom and came back with the clothing. "I'm not going to lend you my underwear though. And I wouldn't recommend Allie's. I think hers are mostly made out of dental floss."

"How would you know?" she asked with an arched eyebrow.

"She does her laundry at my house," he replied with a chuckle.

"That's okay, I think I'll keep my own," she said, heading into the bathroom to change.

She came back to find that Ben had left a blanket and pillow on the couch. He must have gone to bed already, the lights in the bedroom were off. She arranged everything and shut the light.

"Goodnight." Ben called from the other room.

"Goodnight."

Felicity spent the next half an hour tossing and turning. Ben was right, the couch was awful. She thought maybe she felt Cain at one point, but it was fleeting. He must have just been passing close by. It was so strange to be aware of someone's location without seeing them.

She had classes tomorrow. It seemed weird that she should just resume normal everyday life. She couldn't imagine trying to concentrate on algebra. It was a good thing Cain didn't live very close to the school.

After a bit, she heard Ben get out of bed and come quietly to the doorway. "'Liss, are you awake?" he whispered.

"Yeah."

"I can't sleep. At the risk of sounding like a pervert or a total wimp, I've gotta tell you, I'd feel much better if you came into the bedroom."

She heard something in his voice that made her sit up to look at him. "Do you feel her?" she asked quietly.

She couldn't see his face very well in the dark, but he sounded uncomfortable to have to talk about it. "Yeah. I don't think she's real close by yet, but it's getting stronger, and I've gotta admit that it's freakin' me out a little. I know she can't come in and it's not like I'm scared of her or anything, but it's so weird and I can't sleep." He fidgeted a little in the doorway. "I know you can't be comfortable out here, and it'd just be nice to have someone else in the room, you know?"

She had to smile thinking of when she'd said that to him, the night she had asked him to stay in her room. "Yeah, sure." She got up and followed him into the bedroom. As he flipped on the light, she stood at the foot of the bed, trying to decide which side looked slept in.

He must have mistaken her hesitation. He looked amused. "If you want, I could build a little wall of pillows down the middle."

She laughed. "I don't think that'll be necessary...unless you're afraid I might elbow you or something. I know you're sore."

He smiled. "I'll risk it."

"I just didn't know which side," she explained.

"Oh. I don't care, whatever," he told her.

She climbed in on the left side and then he got in on the right. They both lay on their backs looking at the ceiling after Ben shut the light. She looked over at him in the dark. "What happens when Allie gets home? Where's she going to sleep?" Felicity asked.

"Let her sleep on her own crummy couch. Maybe then she'll finally be convinced she needs a new one. She won't listen to me. Then again, maybe she should just join us in the bed. Would you believe that for *all* my experience, a threesome is something I've yet to be a part of?" Ben asked teasingly.

She elbowed him, which probably did hurt a little, but he laughed. "Behave yourself, or I'm going back out into the living room," she threatened.

"Sorry, but I can't help it. You're fun to tease, and it makes for a good distraction," he said.

She suddenly remembered why he'd asked her in here. "Is it strong?"

"I guess that depends, I don't know how strong it gets. I don't think she's right outside, but I feel her." He turned to face Felicity better. "Do you really feel this every time Cain's around?"

"I don't know if it's the same, but yeah. Only picture how powerful it would be if she were standing right next to you."

"No wonder you're always so distracted."

"Am I?" She could feel him shrug. "You know what's really weird? Whenever he touches me..."

"I don't want to hear about *that*."

"Not like *that*. I just meant, like...regular touching. Never mind."

"I think it's going away," he told her.

"Good, go to sleep," she answered.

They did. For an hour or so, anyway. Felicity was awakened a little while later. Cain was nearby. Not very close, but she could feel him. It didn't bother her anymore really, now that she understood it. It did make her long to get closer to him, but it didn't make her antsy anymore really. As she got used to the feeling, actually it was kind of nice...comforting. She wondered why it had woken her. It didn't seem to be getting any stronger or moving away, so wherever he was, he must be staying there for a while. She thought about where they were and what was close by. Tommy's maybe, that would probably be the only place close by that he would actually stay for any length of time.

She was drifting back to sleep when Ben mumbled something and rolled from his side to his back. He fidgeted restlessly and she realized that he was probably why she had woken up in the first place. He was still sleeping, but very fitfully. He was obviously distressed. Either he was dreaming, or it was Sindy. She was just wondering if she should wake him, when he woke on his own with a gasp. He lay still for a moment, breathing rapidly and trying to calm his nerves. After a minute, she asked, "Are you okay?"

He flinched a little at her voice. He must have thought that she was sleeping. "I'm fine. I was just...having a bad dream. Man, Sindy must be right outside. I'm alright, go back to sleep."

He rolled over, to face away from her and try to go back to sleep. He fidgeted a few more times and Felicity felt bad for him. She remembered how odd and panicky she had felt the first few times she'd sensed Cain. Ben was probably having similar feelings, if not worse.

Sindy had spent an awfully long time drinking from him. He'd probably gotten a lot of venom in his system. She wondered if it was much stronger than what she felt with Cain.

He fidgeted again and his breathing turned a bit ragged. Felicity moved closer to him, up against his back, as she had to comfort herself that night in her room. She put an arm around him, in kind of a hug. He put a hand up onto her arm and gave it a little squeeze. Then after a few minutes, he took her arm up off of him and slid away, out of her reach. "I appreciate the gesture," he said, lying on his back again. "But I think it's better if you stay over there."

"Oh. Okay."

After a few minutes, he hesitantly reached out and took her hand, interlacing their fingers. They lay on their backs, on opposite sides of the bed, each with one arm stretched out to the middle. He didn't let go of her hand, so she gave it a slight squeeze and lay there waiting for sleep to come. She could tell by his uneven breathing that he was still bothered and not sleeping. He squeezed her hand a few times, but he didn't speak to her again. If Ben suffered any other odd perceptions from Sindy, he kept them to himself. Eventually, they slept.

Chapter 2 – We have a problem

Cain

2:00, Monday morning
Tommy's Place

Cain pulled into the lot at Tommy's. He could feel Sindy moving away from him, towards Allie's apartment he assumed. He could feel Ben there, burning with Sindy's new signature upon him. Felicity was still there as well, shining with Cain's own comforting glow about her. They must be staying with Alyson this evening. They would be safe there. If Sindy wanted to sit outside and try to make Ben sweat a bit, then let her. Nothing would come of it, and at least it would give him a respite from her presence.

Cain walked through the front doors of the bar and looked around. There were no other vampires present, a fact for which he was grateful, as usual. It wasn't really crowded, but he was a little surprised to see that there were more than just a few patrons, considering it was late Sunday night. There really wasn't much else to do in a small town.

He didn't bother to visit the bar. He made his way towards the back to find a semi-private place to sit and think about his prior conversation with Sindy. He settled himself at a table and became lost in thought, until he was startled back to attention by someone addressing him from across the table. He looked up to find Alyson standing there with her little serving tray in hand. He was surprised; he hadn't expected to find her working tonight. She was looking at him expectantly with her usual mocking attitude.

"I'm sorry, what?" he asked sheepishly.

"Do you want a drink? From the bar," she added with a smile.

"Right. I'll take a rum and coke." She was turning to go when he called out, "Make it two."

"Two?"

"Save you a trip." She gave him an odd look and went to get his drinks. He stared after her, thinking of Mattie. He was still rather in shock over that. So Alyson was Mattie's chosen one? She had to be; it did seem to fall into place. Mattie had questioned Cain the year before, about how to properly change someone into a vampire. He was very excited, but worried about it. It seemed something that he wanted badly to do, but was frightened to try it. He'd never attempted it before. In fact, he'd never even killed a person that Cain knew of. In that, Cain envied him.

Cain had instilled supreme caution and care into the boy as far as turning someone was concerned. It was not something to be done lightly. Mattie had told Cain of the deep care and devotion he felt toward the one he had chosen. He had never given Cain their name, saying only that it was a childhood friend with whom he was still very close. Cain had never asked, because he'd felt that it was better if Mattie's past life remain somewhat separate. He was going to have to learn to let it go. If he turned his friend, there would be time enough for Cain to meet them then.

Mattie had made it clear to Cain that his affections ran deep for this friend and that he was terrified to fail them, so Cain did something that he had rarely ever done. He gave Mattie detailed and explicit instructions on how to properly turn his friend into a vampire. It was not so difficult to do, but to be careless was to create a horror. Far better to err on the side of caution. Usually he simply advised others against it, but Mattie was different. Cain knew Mattie would never even think of attempting such a thing without the subject's express consent. Mattie was a gentle soul and he deserved the knowledge he asked for. Cain believed he had the good judgment to use it wisely. Mattie was very attentive and somber. He asked numerous questions and had many worries. It was a good sign that he would heed Cain's teachings. Cain was confident that when the time came, it would be done well.

Cain had always assumed from Mattie's attitude, that it was a girl, until that night in the woods with Ben. That had made him wonder. He'd had no idea that this was Mattie's home. He was shocked to find that the young man who had served him coffee nightly for three months, had been one of Mattie's very good friends. He'd begun to worry for Mattie, because if it was indeed Ben whom he wished to change, Mattie would be sorely disappointed. Ben would never want such a life. He gradually came to realize that it could not possibly be Benjamin though. Mattie could never be so blind, as to think that Ben would come around to embrace such an existence. It just was not in him. Besides, Cain had been sure that Mattie was still seeing his friend on a regular basis, whereas Ben said he had only seen Mattie but once since his change. No, it had to be Alyson. Cain approved. Alyson had just the personality to make her tough and strong without being cruel or heartless. He was glad. Mattie needed someone like her.

Cain was extremely proud of Mattie, although Cain had merely shown him the way of things. Mattie's character and way of life were his own accomplishments. Cain felt that only divine intervention could have placed him in the boy's path at so perfect a time in his development. Mattie had been newly turned and horrified at the prospect of living as a creature of the night. He was starved and alone, having run from the ones who had sired him. He had been changed against his will by a brood of vampires who were likely trying to gain advantage over another coven, by increasing their own numbers. Such territorial wars were rare and never lasted long. Most vampires were happy to be left alone with their chosen few companions, and would rather flee than fight, if given a choice. Vampires with warlike tendencies usually managed to kill each other off rather quickly.

Mattie was very lucky to have been so well made. Most vampires were not so careful or thorough, but from what information Cain could glean from the boy, his change had been somewhat of a 'group effort' on the part of several vampires together. It had been a sort of 'gang bang' affair, that they had indulged in for fun as well as to turn him. The result was that Mattie had been drunk from and then fed by his captors many times. His rebirth as a vampire had been traumatic but thorough. He had run from his siring brood as soon as he'd been able. They had surely given chase, but apparently met up with their enemies along the way. There were few survivors after it was done and none were interested in Mattie any longer.

Cain had found him on the steps to the church, of all places, shortly before dawn. His heart had immediately gone out to the boy, who had obviously been contemplating suicide.

He had taken Mattie into his home, seen that he was fed, and had then begun to teach him a new way of life. Mattie had stayed with him on and off for almost a year, traveling every couple of weeks to visit a friend that he'd had in his past life.

Cain had never taken such time with an apprentice, other than those few that he had made himself. In fact, most other vampires simply accepted his suggestions or asked his advice and then encouraged him to move on. Mattie was eager for knowledge and friendship, something that filled a need in Cain also, but once he was confident Mattie could be independent, Cain also felt the need to travel, to continue to help others. He had of course invited Mattie to join him, but had known that Mattie wouldn't care to venture too far from his past home. He still had ties there that he was unwilling to give up just yet.

They had kept in touch, meeting in various places over the next two years, never leaving each other without setting up a place for future contact. Cain had drilled Mattie relentlessly in the art of cloaking his presence from others. Mattie was such a kind and peaceful young man, he could gain nothing from associating with most other vampires, Cain had assured him.

When last they'd spoken, Mattie had told Cain that he would be found in a town nearby this one, come early December. But it was just another town, one of dozens they had inhabited. Cain knew that they were in the general area where Mattie had once lived, but had not thought that he would be in the very spot, with people from Mattie's past. Cain had been traveling in this general direction anyway, following rumors of rogue vampires needing to learn discretion. Those vampires had of course turned out to be Sindy and Ernest. Shortly before he had arrived, Sindy had also added Luke and Chris to her little family. Cain had thought to make contact with Sindy and the others, teach them to lead a less destructive existence and then go on to meet his friend.

So here he was in the local pub, being served drinks by the very girl that he had calmly sat and discussed with Mattie, how to turn into a vampire. He wondered if Mattie had approached her about it yet. Had she turned him down? Or perhaps he had become afraid that it would not go as planned.

Of course, it was possible that Mattie had been thinking of someone else entirely, but Cain didn't think so. Mattie was quiet and shy, and Cain couldn't imagine him being close with more than a few select people. It certainly explained why Alyson wasn't very put off to have found that Cain was a vampire.

Cain watched her move through the crowd to return to him with his drinks, and wondered just how much Mattie had shared with her. She put down two napkins on the table in front of him, and then placed a drink on each. "It's thirteen."

He handed her a twenty-dollar bill and she began to dig into her apron pocket for change. "Keep it," he told her.

She looked down at him with curious appreciation. "Thanks."

He smiled as he took a sip of his drink and then gestured towards the other glass on the table. "You want one?"

Now she really seemed bewildered by his attitude. "I can't, I'm working." She just stood there and watched him for a second. "You're in a friendly mood."

"I've just found out that we've a mutual friend."

Her eyes widened and she quickly looked about to see if she was being watched by her boss. Apparently, she decided it was safe to sit. She took the chair opposite his and leaned over the table towards him, anxiously. "Do you know where he is?"

"No, I'm sorry." He noted her look of concern. "But you needn't worry. Mattie knows how to keep out of trouble."

"I'm surprised you even know him. He usually hides himself from other vampires."

Cain smiled. "Who do you think taught him how to do that?"

Allie stared at him with a look of uncertainty that quickly turned to suspicion. "Are you... Did you *do it* to him?"

"No! No, I'm not Mattie's sire. Just a friend." So, Mattie hadn't told her of his beginnings. Perhaps he hadn't wanted to frighten her, although Alyson was hardly a girl of delicate sensibilities. More likely, Mattie had been afraid that given information about the vampires who had abducted him, Alyson would probably try to hunt them down and kill them. That would only lead to her bringing more danger down upon herself than even she could handle. Cain could see that for all of her oddities and outspokenness, she was a most loyal friend. He wondered how long Mattie'd been away from her. "How long has it been?"

She actually took on a quiet and shy demeanor, very unlike herself. Yes, she and Mattie were intimately close. She didn't even have to think to answer his question. "May. I used to see him at least one weekend a month. Sometimes he'd even stay longer. The last time I saw him, he told me that he wanted to travel around a little, and that he might not be back until Halloween, but it's a long time, you know?"

Mattie must have meant to spend the month here with Alyson before going to meet Cain in December. Cain wondered if Mattie had expected to turn her during that time, and then bring her to meet Cain. It certainly seemed plausible. Cain knew that Mattie had drunk from her, although he had never yet tasted human blood at the time Cain had found him. Mattie existed on animal blood, as Cain did. Cain had certainly hoped that it would remain Mattie's prime source of sustenance, but had spoken to him about having control when drinking from a person, just in case. He was not so naive as to think that Mattie might never be tempted. Better to give him preventative cautions on how to be sure not to hurt the one that he drank from.

Not long after that talk, Mattie had come back to speak to him about it again, almost as a sort of confession. Mattie had told him of the few times he had dared to sample a human's blood. He had told Cain in hesitant whispers of how he'd drunk from his very best friend, a willing offering. Even if Mattie hadn't told him, he might have guessed it from Allie's attitude. Most likely, it had become a regular thing. She definitely cared for him, but there was also a great need in her voice. If the victim were willing, it could be an amazing experience. Cain gave Alyson a sympathetic nod. "It must be difficult. He kept you safe too, didn't he?"

She returned his small nod with one of her own. "I can take care of myself, but things have been getting pretty rough around here." She rubbed the back of her head, where Sindy's thugs had clubbed her, Cain assumed. "It's a little overcrowded in this town, don't ya' think?"

"Definitely."

"I never had to worry much about it before, but lately I feel like I'm seein' 'em every other night." She lowered her voice and seemed as though she were very happy to have someone sympathetic to confide in. "It's gettin' to be nervous business just gettin' home from work, now that my mark's gone."

Cain stared at her long and hard. "Are you... You're not...asking for my protection, are you?"

It took her a second to realize the implication. "No!" She seemed embarrassed to have practically yelled it at him with worried haste. "I mean, no. Um, thanks? I think I'll just wait for Mattie."

He smiled. He found the whole exchange rather amusing actually. He'd thought she might be asking him to bite her and she was basically thanking him for it, while trying to decline without offending him. He wouldn't have anyway, even if he were so inclined. She was Mattie's, marked or not. "Good. No offense. I mean, not that I wouldn't if…but, no. I think it's best if that does not occur. I will keep watch for Mattie though. I'm sure he'll be around soon."

Just then, the bouncer walked by and gave Allie a playful little shove as he passed. "Hey Allie, flirt on your own time."

She looked a little embarrassed as she rose from the table, but still flashed Cain a big smile. "Thanks."

She left, but was sure to keep a full drink in front of him all evening. Cain found himself half listening to the conversation at the next table. Two young men happened to be discussing a movie they must have just seen. It turned out to be a film that Cain had just recently sat through, twice. He soon introduced himself and was drawn into their conversation.

A short while later, he noticed that Sindy was on the move again. He had felt her presence, just barely, all along, but had ignored her. Now she seemed to be striding purposefully straight towards him. Even if she was unsure that he was here, she would find him soon enough. There was nowhere else to go at this hour.

Sure enough, she strode through the door minutes later. She was made to pause for words with the bouncer, who apparently did not like her behavior the last few times she was here. Cain saw that Alyson had noticed her arrival. She looked to Cain, but he gave her a shake of the head to indicate that she should leave Sindy to him. Alyson looked as though she'd rather go throw Sindy out and stake her in the parking lot, but the bouncer seemed to have come to some agreement with her and was letting her enter. Alyson went into the kitchen to avoid trouble.

Cain turned to his newfound friends. "If you'll excuse me gentlemen, I believe we're about to be interrupted."

They looked up to see Sindy bearing down on them. "She can interrupt me anytime," one of them remarked.

"You don't want *her* attentions, believe me," Cain replied as she approached. She looked beautifully murderous.

She stopped directly in front of him and paused to glance at his companions. She turned back to Cain and put her hands on her hips. "We have a problem."

"What else is new? Would you like to have a seat?"

She looked as if the very idea was ridiculous. "No I don't want a seat. I'll take that drink though." Without waiting for him to give her leave, she snatched his full glass from the table and proceeded to chug it down without a breath.

"Help yourself," he remarked, dryly. "Weren't you meant to be out tormenting Ben this evening, so that I might have some peace?"

She finished the drink and slammed the glass down on the table. "Well, I gladly would have, if your slut of a girlfriend hadn't beaten me to him!"

This drew an 'Oooo', from the guys he'd been talking to. He fixed Sindy with an icy glare. "Do you think we might take this outside?" he asked through gritted teeth.

She gave the guys a sharp glance, and stalked towards the back door. "Whatever."

Cain faced the young men who were giving him amused but sympathetic smiles. "Excuse us."

He followed Sindy out the back door and before he was barely outside she spun around to glare at him accusingly. He shut the door behind them and addressed her. "Now, what are you going on about?"

"I am talking about Benjamin. Your little Miss Priss is sleeping with my Ben! I guess she's not as innocent as I thought."

Cain looked at the ground as he stretched out his awareness to them once again. Yes, Ben and Felicity were still together, and of course Alyson was here, but that didn't have to mean anything, did it? Although they were close, their traces were distinctly separate, they did not overlap or even really touch, that he could tell.

Sindy gave a little stomp on the ground and groaned like a child deprived of a treat. He looked up to see her gazing back at him, sullen and forlorn. "Oh Cain, I did him *so* good too. That boy's got me coursin' all through him. I think he must be my best handiwork yet! I'm tellin' ya', I had him squirmin'! Hell, if he'd been alone, I'll bet he would have met me right out on the God damned driveway!"

At this, Cain had to laugh, although she didn't seem pleased by his reaction. "I think you overestimate our abilities, my dear."

She moved closer to wave her finger in his face. "Oh no. Don't you try to tell me." He shooed her hand away with a wave. "This is one area where you have no experience, but since you taught me to leave 'em breathin', this has become my favorite pastime. I know what I'm capable of. If I dose 'em up right, I can call them right out of their sweet safe little houses and into my waiting arms! It's a beautiful thing. I've had guys sleepwalkin' all over this town! But Benjamin is special; Ben is mine! That boy's got the temperament and body of a wild stallion and I'm ready to ride!"

He rolled his eyes at her ridiculous metaphor. "Oh please." He then gave her a hard stare. "So you only agreed not to go after him, because all along you believed that you'd put him in thrall and he'd just come right to you? Well, you'll have to excuse my lack of sympathy that it didn't quite work out for you."

She stared at him resentfully. "It would have worked out just fine. I was feelin' him real strong and I *know* he was feelin' me, but the closer I got, the more I had the sense that something wasn't quite right. I reach the house and lo and behold, what do I see? But your little shinin' star right there with him; in his very bed! I spent over an hour feedin' that boy the best vibes of his life and your little whore is in there reapin' the rewards!"

"Watch your tongue."

"You don't believe me do you? Come and see for yourself! I'm tellin' you we're both gettin' screwed and not in the fun way." She tugged at his arm to follow her closer to Alyson's house, but he shook her off.

"I don't need to go anywhere. I can see them from here."

"That's impossible!"

He raised his eyebrows and gave her a look to remind her that he was over three centuries her senior and she should not presume to know what he might be capable of. "They *are* together. They are still; they're sleeping."

"*Now.* What do you *think* they were doing in bed together?"

Cain took a deep breath and expelled it slowly. She didn't know anything. So they were together, that didn't have to mean they'd had sex. Sindy didn't even know for sure that they were in a bed. So they had been close to each other for a long time, they could be sitting on a couch watching television for all she knew.

Even if they *had* been romantic, as much as Cain wished for that not to be true, he had no right to judge their actions. Whatever his own feelings, he certainly wasn't going to show them to Sindy. He kept his voice neutral and steady. "Felicity has made no pledge of devotion towards me; she may do as she pleases. And certainly neither of them owes anything to you! It's none of our affair."

"Are you kidding? Don't try and act like this doesn't bother you! You've put in a lot of time on that girl and she's obviously steppin' out on you Cain. Doesn't that make you wanna just drain her dry?"

He fought to keep level headed and calm. "Statements like that, will hurt no one but you. The fact that they are together means nothing." She just stared at him mockingly.

Felicity wouldn't have chosen to give herself to Ben, would she? The two did seem awfully close. She'd shown such concern for him last night. Perhaps it was strong feelings for Ben, which gave her such resolve to keep from acting on any desires she might have for Cain. It did seem odd that although she had shown such interest in Cain before, she was now able to hold herself so aloof from him.

Considering what he himself felt for her from the marking, the urges she felt for him from the venom alone, must be at least equally as strong. And she had felt for him even before that, hadn't she? It was she who had kissed him. Had he spent so much time being cautious and worried for her, that she had decided not to wait? Had she become attached to Ben while he had worked so hard to keep himself away, so that he wouldn't hurt her? "Are you telling me that you actually observed romantic activity between them?" Cain asked.

She looked petulant and sour. "Cain, I know Ben. I also know that my feedin' from him was a guilty pleasure that he'll never forget. He *wanted* me Cain, bad. I've got that boy so worked up I could probably get him off with a touch," she said with a lewd little chuckle. "Now I may find Felicity sickeningly sweet on most occasions, but I've got to admit, as far as the physical stuff goes, you've got good taste. Don't think that's lost on my Ben, he's not blind. I've got him all wantin' and you think they're just laying there? Wise up."

He stared at her coldly. "What exactly would you have me do?"

She stopped pouting to give him a hopeful suggestion. "You could *call* her. Make her leave him. It's real easy, you could do it. I could show you how."

"I've no doubt I could accomplish anything *you've* so easily mastered, but I've certainly no need to call a woman from another man's bed. They choose of their own will and that's the end of it."

"You're just going to leave her there?!"

"Sindy, go home and play with your boys. They are yours, as Ben never will be."

She glared at him as though her discontentment was all his fault. "So I get no Ben *and* no hunt, and I suppose *you* still don't want to play?" she asked crossly.

He didn't bother to answer that. "You really haven't fed this evening?"

"From a plastic bag. How do you find *that* at all satisfying?"

"Put it in a glass in the microwave."

She looked disgusted. "I'm talking about the experience! Don't you miss it? You never have any fun! At least I can feed off my boys when they get home."

"That's cheating," he reprimanded her mildly.

She eyed him appraisingly. "You want some?" She moved her long black hair away from the side of her throat and turned her head to expose it to him. "I'd let you."

He never entertained the notion that he actually would, but it was tempting. "Go home Sindy."

She gave him a long time to change his mind, eyeing him wantonly and absently playing with a thin gold chain she wore around her throat, winding it about her finger. He found himself staring at the light glinting off of the chain as though mesmerized. He gave no outward sign, but was a little surprised at himself by how much he actually wanted to drink from her. Marking Felicity had been a dangerous reminder of what he was missing. Drinking from Sindy would be all reward with no regret.

He ignored her as best he could, and turned his attention back to Felicity and Ben. They hadn't even moved; they must be asleep. Sindy eventually gave up on him. He was very glad when she finally left.

The back door opened, rousing him from his thoughts. It was Alyson holding his jacket. She glanced around to see if he was alone. Sindy was gone. "We're closin' up and I'm goin' home. You left this at the table. Nice leather, be a shame to lose it."

He walked over and took it from her. "Thanks."

"Everything alright?"

He sighed. "Besides my usual nightly torment? Fine." Alyson looked at him warily and took an unconscious step back. He looked up and gave her a weary smile. "Relax, you're not my type. Not anymore anyway."

She thought about that for a minute. "Do you...live like Mattie?"

He grinned. "I suppose it'd be more accurate to say that Mattie lives like me, but yes, I buy my blood." He fixed her with a steady gaze. "I have for centuries, but it's not always easy," he added in a whisper.

She studied him for a minute. He wondered what she was thinking. He wanted to tell her more, of what it was like, what to expect. It was not the sort of life that everyone could handle, but he thought that she could, if she chose. However, it was not his place to offer such information unsolicited. Any questions she had, remained unasked. "You'll be alright getting home?" he finally asked. "Sindy was by there earlier, but I don't think she'll return. It's getting late."

"She knows Ben's there."

"Felicity's with him."

"Good, I was hopin' he wouldn't have to ride it out alone. I was thinkin' I'd get out of here earlier, but..." She shrugged. "At least they're okay. I'm sure Ben didn't take it well." Either she didn't think anything would happen between Ben and Felicity, or she just didn't care. The fact that they'd been alone together all night obviously didn't interest her, except in protecting Ben's well being. Alyson stifled a yawn. "Well, I'm gonna split. See ya."

"Goodnight." She went back into the bar and he heard her bolt the door from the inside. He walked around the building to his waiting motorcycle in the nearly empty parking lot. He mounted the bike and sped off towards home.

Chapter 3 - Give her what she wants

Felicity

Alyson's apartment
4:20, Monday morning

Felicity awoke with a start as she heard Alyson come in the front door. She had a terrible wave of guilt as she realized she probably should have waited for her; met her at the door, knowing Sindy was nearby, but she'd fallen back asleep. Ben was also sleeping and Allie seemed to have made it in okay. Maybe Sindy had left. Alyson came to the bedroom doorway and peeked in. Felicity let go of Ben's hand and sat up a little, though she was still half-asleep. "You want your bed back?"

"Na, that's okay." She entered the room and grabbed a nightshirt from her drawer. "Is he alright?"

"Yes, he's finally sleeping."

"Cool, I'll see you in the morning."

Alyson went back out into the living room. Felicity lay back down, but planned to get up and go out to Alyson. She felt as though she should take the opportunity to talk to Allie alone. She was so exhausted, she fell back asleep before she hardly finished the thought.

The next thing she knew, she was hearing what was surely designed to be absolutely the most annoying noise in the world. It was Alyson's alarm clock. It was on Ben's side, he must have set it. She lay there cringing and wondering how Ben could possibly bear to hear that for another minute without shutting it off.

Then a horrible fear came across her, that something was wrong. A fear that Sindy had come back; that somehow she had gotten inside and done something to him. No one could sleep through that horrible noise. She sat up and looked at him in dread. He was still, his features calm and peaceful in sleep. She put a hand on his chest; he was breathing. She felt relief wash over her, and she left her hand there for a moment, feeling his heartbeat. He looked so sweet and vulnerable; she felt bad about his problems with Sindy and couldn't help but feel a bit protective over him. Of course, it was much easier to feel that way when he was sleeping and not arguing with her.

Allie yelled from the living room, startling her. "Somebody shut that damn thing off!" She looked down at Ben again, nothing. It was 7:17 a.m.

Felicity practically had to lie on top of him to reach the alarm clock. It took her a minute to find the right button. She wanted to make sure she didn't just hit snooze, or it would go off again. She finally got it to be quiet and then looked down to find Ben looking back up at her. She hastily withdrew.

"Time to get up I guess," she said a little awkwardly. He just closed his eyes again. She got up and went into kitchen. After some searching, she managed to locate some cereal and a bowl. Alyson got up off the couch and dragged herself into the bedroom. A few minutes later

Ben stumbled into the kitchen, barely glancing at her and looking very weary. He fumbled around at the counter behind her.

"Kicked you out did she?" Felicity asked.

"Coffee?" Ben asked sleepily.

"No thanks," she replied.

He finished setting up the coffeemaker and slumped into the chair opposite her. "How can you be awake with no coffee? You can't have gotten more than a few hours of sleep. I know I didn't."

"Why don't you go back to bed?"

He sighed. She got the feeling he would rather not have to talk until after he got some caffeine. "I've got class."

"You're going to classes today?" Felicity asked incredulously.

"They beat up my body, not my brain." He got up to watch the coffee perk. "Besides, if we're not going to scrap the whole semester and go to Vermont..." He shot her a hopeful glance. She shook her head no. "Then mid-terms are coming up and I can't miss." He got impatient waiting for the coffee and finally just poured what little was in the pot so far, into a mug. He mixed his coffee and stood drinking it at the counter. He turned to face her. "Don't you have Algebra with Ashley this morning?"

"Yeah, at 8:45," she told him.

"Make sure you tell her I had a wonderful time at the dance," he said sarcastically. "Well, I've got until 9:00. I figure that's just enough time to run home for a quick shower and change. I'll give you a ride," he said.

"Your car's still at school," she reminded him.

He grabbed a piece of paper and a pen out of the drawer. "Well, that wasn't *my* idea." He wrote Alyson a note and put it on the table in front of Felicity. It read:

> A-
>
> I'm taking your car. Will pick you up for lunch.
>
> -Ben
>
> (P.S.)
>
> If anything happened to my Mustang, it's coming out of your paycheck!

He looked down at her cereal. "You done?"

"Yeah." She got up and put her bowl in the sink.

She began to walk past him, back out to get her stuff. "Liss," She stopped to look at him. "Thanks, for staying."

She smiled. "Don't mention it."

~~~~~~~~~~~~~~~~~~~~~~~~~~~~~

Lunchtime found Felicity sitting at a table by herself, eating a sandwich and a yogurt. She saw Karen across the cafeteria, rushing on her way somewhere else and gave a quick wave, but no Ben and Allie yet. She wondered if Alyson had even been awake when Ben went to pick her up.

Finally, she saw them enter and stood up with a wave for them to find her. They made their way to the table. Ben dumped his books with a timid 'hey', that made her wonder if he was embarrassed that he'd asked her to stay with him last night. He hardly made eye contact with her, but quickly turned to Allie. "Let's go get something to eat."

Alyson handed him some money from her back pocket and then slumped into a chair, evincing no further plans of moving. "My treat, get me something."

Ben looked surprised she wasn't coming. "What do you want?"

"Whatever. Juice, snack cakes or somethin'. You know, stuff."

"Why don't you just come pick out what you want?"

She looked over at Felicity for a moment and then fixed him with a steady stare. "I don't want to." Ben looked from one girl to the other. Obviously, they planned to talk about him when he left. Alyson waved a hand towards the lunch counter. "Shoo."

Ben looked at her in annoyance. "Just for that, you're getting salad." He turned to leave.

Alyson called after him. "You bring back a salad and you'll be wearing it!" She watched him go and then turned her attention to Felicity.

"Everything okay with you guys, about Mattie?" Felicity asked.

Allie shrugged. "I'm never supposed to mention him again."

"That's it, just avoid the problem?" Felicity asked.

"That's just the way Ben does things, but he also knows I don't listen to him anyway. When the topic comes up, he'll deal. He just wants to be sure I know he doesn't approve. Anyway, enough of that. I've got limited time and lots of questions. All I'm getting from Ben is avoidance and denial, so I need you to fill me in. What happened last night?"

Felicity became flustered. "Nothing! We were sleeping!"

Allie rolled her eyes. "Not with *you*. Ben would've told me if you were *doin' it*. I'm talkin' about Sindy. She came by, right?"

Felicity wasn't sure whether to be happy that Allie believed her, or disgruntled by the fact that Allie was so sure that Ben would've shared it with her. "Oh. Yeah. I felt really bad; we should have warned you that she was there."

"Like I couldn't figure out that Sindy wouldn't pass up the chance to get Ben all hot and bothered? Anyway, she was long gone by the time I got home. So, how'd he take it?"

"He didn't say much. Just that she was there."

"Well of course not. Mr. Prideful. What do you think I'm askin' *you* for?"

Felicity tried not to get annoyed by her attitude. "Well, it must have bothered him, because I started out on the couch, but then he came out and asked me to join him in the bedroom."

Alyson burst out laughing. "Strange behavior! Because there could be no other possible reason, for Ben to have been asking you to join him in the bedroom?"

Felicity gave Allie a withering look and glanced around uncomfortably for Ben. He was still on line. "No. I mean, not that the thought hadn't crossed my mind, but no. Judging by the way he acted once I got there, I'd say he was freaked."

"How'd he act? Come on, I don't have time for subtle! I need details!"

Felicity sighed. "Well, I don't think it was so bad at first, but it must have gotten worse later. It woke him up. He seemed really agitated and kind of spooked. So I moved closer and put my arm around him." Allie began to smirk and raised an eyebrow. "Like to comfort him! But then he pushed me away, like he didn't even want me to touch him."

"Now that's not normal Ben behavior." Felicity looked at her questioningly. "Not that the man can't control himself, but let's face it, I can't exactly see him *fending you off.*"

Felicity became insulted. "Well it's not like I was trying to..." She broke off in a huff as she looked up to find Ben approaching with his lunch tray. He was met with silence as he put it down on the table. It was piled with the usual junk food and stuff Allie would have bought.

"It's always so comforting, when all conversation stops as soon as I arrive."

Felicity looked up at him, ashamed. "We weren't really talking about anything important."

Ben sat down and gave her a condescending smile. "I know exactly what you were talking about, I'm not stupid. We're all adults here and we've all three of us been bitten at one time or another. It's not exactly a big secret." He looked from one to the other of them. Alyson looked almost smug, Felicity felt terrible. Ben continued, "She's going to do that to me every night, isn't she?"

Allie answered. "Yep, I'm sure she will."

Ben looked disgusted. "Great, so I can basically look forward to nightly torture for the next three to four weeks."

Alyson grinned. "Torture? Oh, come on Benji. It wasn't that bad, was it?"

He stared at her coldly. "Don't call me Benji, you know I hate that."

Alyson kept after him, undaunted. "So, is it just like a weird and repulsive blood thing for you, or is it really sexual?"

He glared at her fiercely. "If I didn't answer you in the car, what makes you think I want to talk about it now?" He looked over to Felicity. "We may have all been bitten, but I'm betting that they were three very different experiences.

Alyson still wore a smug smile on her face, but Felicity sympathized with Ben. At least she and Allie had liked the guys who had bitten them. She couldn't imagine what it would be like to feel the effects from a bite from someone you loathed.

That reminded her, she would have to let Allie know that Cain did indeed know Mattie, but this was probably not the time. The next time that she could get Allie alone, she would mention it.

Felicity suddenly realized that Alyson had also been bitten by Sindy once herself. She wanted to remark on that and ask what the effect had been, but didn't quite have the courage. Allie softened her tone and answered Felicity's unasked question on her own. "Come on Ben, I've been bitten by Sindy too, you know. She didn't get me as good as she got you, but I felt it. You wanna talk about unwanted urges? She did you good. I know it must be strong." She gave Felicity a mischievous grin. "I guess Felicity and I will just have to keep you distracted and otherwise occupied nightly for the next three to four weeks."

Felicity looked at her as though she were insane. Ben just smiled. "As delightful as that sounds, I think I'd rather take Cain up on *his* offer."

Allie looked bewildered and amused. "You'd rather sleep with Cain? I didn't think he was your type."

Felicity spoke up about Cain's 'offer' as Ben glared at Allie in annoyance. "You can't do that, it'll never work."

Allie looked over at her. "Do what, sleep with Cain?"

Ben ignored Allie. "It could work, if we're careful."

"What could work?" Allie asked.

"You know she'd feel you coming." Felicity retorted.

"Alyson could do it," Ben suggested.

"**Do what?**" Alyson yelled.

Felicity answered Allie while shaking her head at Ben. "Cain knows where they're sleeping. Ben thinks that we can go over there in the daytime and just open the blinds on them or something."

Alyson looked at Ben with much the same sarcastic attitude as Felicity. "Yeah right, because I'm sure that Sindy has conveniently pushed her coffin up against the window for us, so that we could just open the lid and watch her burn."

"They don't sleep in coffins," Felicity said quietly.

"Some do," Allie corrected her.

"Cain doesn't," Felicity informed her.

"Well neither does Mattie, but that doesn't say anything about Sindy. Some vampires prefer it," Allie replied.

Ben banged a hand down on the table for attention. "Ladies, instead of spending the rest of lunch telling you how disgusted and appalled I am by your thorough knowledge of vampire sleeping habits, I think I'm just going to scrap that whole plan and try something much more simple. Sindy wants me, right?" Alyson looked as though she'd like to make a rude comment, but Ben stared her down. "So tonight when she comes, I'll just give her what she wants."

Allie laughed, Felicity was confused. "What are you going to do?"

"I'm going to go outside," Ben told her.

Allie smiled. "And let off some steam?"

"With a stake," Ben clarified forcefully.

Felicity touched his arm in concern. "You can't do that, they'll kill you. She wouldn't be stupid enough to come alone."

Allie looked thoughtful. "She might. She was goin' on about wantin' to *take* you in private."

Ben didn't look thrilled with her phrasing. "I wonder if she came alone last night? We should have looked out the window."

Felicity shuddered at the thought. "Too creepy. She wasn't alone when she took you from the dance. She knew you'd fight her. What is she going to think, that you had a sudden change of heart? I don't care how much venom is in your system, she knows you hate her."

Ben looked at her thoughtfully. "Yeah, but she doesn't think like you. No matter how much she knows I hate her, she'd still believe I wanna fuck her."

"Ben!" Felicity said in shock.

Allie interjected. "He's right. She would." She gave Ben a disapproving look. "Some guys are like that."

"Well I wouldn't *do it,* but she'd let me get close; close enough."

"Still, she'd probably try to lure you someplace else first, and that's not good. What do you think she's gonna do, let you take her right there out on the lawn, like a dog?" Allie asked.

"She might. She thinks I've got this fantasy about us out on the grass, remember?"

Felicity spoke up. "Ben it's too dangerous. She'll probably bring that huge guy with her. Look what she had him do to you last time! What if you can't get her?"

"Then I guess she'll get me. I'll survive. I did before."

"And if she decides to go a little further this time? We should get Cain. Just for back up, in case things get out of hand and she tries to go too far, or if she sics that guy on you. She wouldn't even have to know that Cain was there unless you needed him." Felicity placed her hand on Ben's arm again, to emphasize her alarm over the issue.

He looked into her eyes and she could tell he appreciated her concern, but he spoke quietly and firmly against the idea. "I don't want Cain's help. Besides, I've got Allie," he added with a smile.

Alyson was caught off guard. "What am I supposed to do?"

"You're the one who spent all of her money on those jui jitsu lessons. Take him out for me," he said with a challenging smile.

"What am I, Buffy the Vampire Slayer?"

Ben laughed. "Relax, it won't come to that. I'm telling you, she'll be alone. Even if she's not, I don't need you to kill anyone, just distract them. If I do it right, I can stake her before she even knows I don't want to play. Then we just have to get into the house, where they can't follow."

Alyson looked as though she might actually be considering it. Felicity tightened her grip on Ben's arm. "Ben, you're going to get yourself killed! Just stay in the house until she goes away. The mark will fade, what's the big deal? Wait it out, please."

"You just don't get it Liss, I can't. You were right. It's like she was *calling* me. And God help me, but I wanted to go to her, *badly.* If you weren't there, I probably would have. I'm not going to let her do that to me every night. I can't. And you can't be anywhere near us. She'll never buy it if you're around. You're marked. She can feel you, so she has to know that you were there last night. She probably figures that's why she couldn't get to me. If you're there again, but I come out, she'll know something's up. You're working tonight anyway. After work, you have to go back to your room and stay there. One way or another, one of us will come and let you know what happened in the morning," he said with a glance to Allie.

"No way!" Felicity said indignantly. "I'm not going to just sit in my room by myself, waiting to find out if you guys got yourselves killed!"

"Then why don't you go sit with Cain?" Ben asked with a sardonic edge. She gave him a wounded look and he softened. "If you come, you *will* get me killed. She has to believe that I'm alone, or she wouldn't think that I'd give in to her. She'd know it was a trap. Stay home, okay?"

"Are you really going to do this?" Felicity asked incredulously.

He nodded. "I feel like I have to."

She looked over to Alyson. "And you're going to let him?"

Allie shrugged. "I may tease him about it and piss him off, but I know it'll kill him if he doesn't do something. He's like my brother, I've gotta back him up."

"You guys are being so stupid!" Felicity sat sulking and looking from Ben to Allie. Obviously, they weren't backing down. She glanced up at the clock. It was almost 1:30 and she should be leaving for chemistry class. Instead, she began calculating how long it would take her to walk to Cain's. She had to be to work at four, but that should give her enough time. It was a long walk, so she wouldn't have enough time for a long visit, but it would be enough. She had to do something. She hoped Karen wouldn't mind lending her the chemistry notes.

Chapter 4 – Persuasion

Cain

2:30, Monday afternoon
Cain's house

Cain was awakened from a deep sleep by a strong surge of hunger, the thirst for blood. He lost fleeting visions of Felicity in a dream he'd been having. It was probably better not remembered. The need for blood washed over him again like a great wave.

Felicity. She was very close, probably at his door. He sat up and rubbed the sleep from his eyes. Her nearness was awakening the vampire within him. It had tasted her before and so it wanted her again, fiercely. He hadn't fed since early the evening before. His body wanted blood and she was right here. The rich, remembered taste of her was tantalizing, beckoning him.

He arose from bed as he heard her knock at the door. He wasn't sure if it was the first time she'd knocked. He fought to suppress his vampire nature, and tried to awaken his humanity instead. He wore only a pair of black sleep-pants. He groped at the end of the bed for his tee shirt, his eyes still half closed in sleep and pulled it over his head as he started for the stairs. She was just knocking again as he opened the door.

Another bright and sunny day. The light made him cringe, as it assaulted his sensitive eyes. He backed away a step and blinked for his eyes to adjust, so that he wouldn't have to squint at her. She was lovely, as always. She wore a simple white gauzy top, a little eyelet pattern worked all around the neckline, with a pair of jeans and white tennis sneakers. Her long hair was falling in beautiful waves over her shoulders. He was so used to seeing her in the darkness of night; he was taken aback by her radiant beauty in the day. The sunlight shone on her, making the usually dark reddish brown of her hair, seem alight like crimson fire. He was so thrilled that she had come to him again, that he hoped he wasn't grinning like an idiot. He was still half-asleep, and hardly thinking clearly.

She looked at him expectantly, seeming unsure of her acceptance here. "Hi." He hadn't even said anything; he'd just been standing there, awed by her beauty.

"Hi. I wasn't expecting you," he said by way of apology for his hesitancy.

"I know. And I woke you up again, sorry," she said timidly.

He smiled. "Don't apologize, come in." She moved inside and he closed the door. He turned back to her with a smile, but quickly realized that she was in a solemn mood. "Is everything alright?"

"I don't know. I hope it will be. I wanted to talk to you...about Ben."

He froze, trying to keep his expression blank. She'd been with Ben the night before. The fog of sleep fled his mind as he remembered. That was why she had come? She wanted to tell him her heart lay elsewhere now? His stomach became a cold hard knot. It almost felt as though the beast inside of him began to pace and want to claw its way out. She was his! She was marked! How dare another touch her and take her away from him! He fought for peace and silence within himself.

She hadn't even been looking at him; she was staring at the floor, lost in her own thoughts. She looked up at him now, distractedly. "Are we going downstairs?"

"Oh. I didn't know if you'd want to." The vampire within him seemed so strong, as it fought for control, he almost wanted to yell at her. *Are you so naïve as to shut yourself down there with me? Don't you know what I am? You plan to put yourself in such a compromising position and then tell me that you're not to be touched! Don't be a fool!* But he couldn't actually bring himself to say anything that might cause her to leave. He clenched his fists and made himself very still, consciously pushing back the vampire within him to the far corners of his mind where he was normally able to keep it locked away.

She did actually stop and think about it for a moment. "It's alright, we can go down." She had such trust in him. He wished he knew if he could trust himself. Why did she cause such an intense reaction in him, that he seemed in such a precarious position? He'd been in similar situations before in his life and he'd always had confidence in his control. His feelings for her were far stronger than he could remember feeling for anyone in quite some time. Truth be told, it frightened him a little. He resolved to start keeping himself better fed, it would help.

She led the way down the stairs and he followed. He tried in vain not to notice her scent as she descended the stairway in front of him. She smelled sweet, of citrus and fresh fruit…some sort of body spray. She spoke to him over her shoulder as she walked. "I don't really have much time. I have to be at work by four and I walked, so I haven't even got an hour before I should leave, but I really needed to speak to you."

She stopped and turned to face him as they reached the bottom of the stairs. It was practically pitch black, with all of the windows boarded. He could see her clearly though. She looked as though she had just stepped out of his dream. He crossed the room and lit the small lamp next to his bed. She came and put down her purse and book bag. Rather than sit, she glanced towards the closed doors at the other end of the room. "Mind if I use your bathroom?" Felicity asked.

"Of course not, go right ahead," Cain answered.

She entered the bathroom, beyond the door that he indicated, and he went to the bar, flipping on its lights. He opened his small refrigerator, as he heard her close the door. The fridge was bare save for a bottle of soda, another of rum and three plastic deli type containers filled with blood. He took out the container of blood that was half-full and put it on the counter.

His thirst for Felicity was so strong, he felt almost tormented by her presence. He could control it, he assured himself, but it was uncomfortable and distracting to say the least. He thought perhaps if he could drink, he could quiet the thirst. If she were here to tell him that she would not return his affections, he did not want his need for blood to fuel his reaction.

He poured the blood into a coffee mug and put it into the microwave for a minute. He put the container away and was just retrieving his cup as she exited the bathroom. He took several large gulps before coming out from behind the bar to her. It seemed so pale and distasteful compared to his memories of drinking from Felicity. There was absolutely no comparison. She observed him for a moment before speaking. "You really need that morning coffee too, huh?" she asked with a smile.

He leaned back against the bar and gazed at her levelly over the cup. "It's not coffee." As comprehension washed over her face, she seemed very confused. As though she'd never imagined he could drink from a cup. How did she *think* he lived? She looked at it as though it were something obscene. He hadn't the patience for discussions of his daily habits at the moment. Other thoughts were far more pressing.

He forced himself to be blunt and to the point. He wouldn't try to stretch out her time here. Let her say what she had come to say, and then leave without further tempting him. "What did you want to say, about Ben?"

She broke her gaze from his cup. "Oh, Sindy was hanging around him last night, outside. He had kind of a difficult time with it. I think she was sending him like a...summons; like she was calling him. It must have been very hard to resist."

Lucky you were there, he thought fiercely. He could hardly blame Ben, but he'd thought her better than to succumb to such urges. She certainly evinced supreme self-control with him. Did she really care for Ben so much?

Suddenly a new and much darker thought occurred to him. What if she hadn't succumbed...willingly? What if Sindy had driven Ben to such desirous distraction that he had taken it out on Felicity, *by force?* Cain would kill him. He hadn't a moment's hesitation at the thought. His reaction scared him a little, but if that were the case, Sindy and Ben would both suffer for it.

He studied her for a moment, as she searched for the right words. She did seem distressed, but she appeared more worried, than degraded or abused. Perhaps he had been right in his first presumptions after all, that she was only worried for his reaction to the news that she belonged to Ben now. She shook her head with a sigh and then looked into his eyes, as if to stop beating around the bush. "He's going to try and kill her."

Cain was momentarily perplexed. This was not the conversation he'd been expecting. "What? Now?"

"No, not *right* now. I convinced him that wouldn't work; he can't try to surprise her in the day. She'd feel him and it's too dangerous, but tonight, if she comes to him... He's going out to meet her, as if... like a trap. I tried to tell him not to, that she wouldn't come alone, but he won't listen. He'll have Allie out in the bushes to help him, *her* mark's gone, but what if Sindy brings that huge guy with her? Ben and Allie'll both get killed."

"Marcus. The huge guy, his name's Marcus. What does Ben think Alyson's going to do?"

"I don't know. Distract him? I know she can handle herself pretty well, but it's still a really bad idea."

"I agree. Ben has no right to ask Alyson to put herself in such danger for him."

"I tried to convince him to ask you for help, but he won't. Cain, you have to go, please. They wouldn't even have to know that you were there, but if things get out of hand, you could...step in. To make sure it works out alright."

He put his mug down on the bar behind him. He did not like where this was going. "You want me to help him kill her?"

Felicity looked contemplative. She seemed to realize that he did not entirely embrace the idea. "I don't really want to kill anybody; I just don't want Ben to get hurt again. The way she bit him was bad enough, but you should see what else they did to him, Cain, the bruises. It was horrible."

He tried to feel badly for Ben, but he couldn't get past the idea of Felicity looking at his body; tending his hurts and showering him with sympathy.

She moved closer to him, seeming desperate for his understanding. She put her hands on his chest and looked up at him pleadingly. "Please, you can't let them hurt him again."

Even through the fabric of his shirt, he could feel the slightly electric tingle of his mark in her touch. He looked into her eyes and breathed in her alluring scent, as he wondered what he should do. He felt as though he would do or say anything to make her happy, and gain her favor. He was such a fool. She was better off without him anyway.

But was he really ready to disregard them all; to leave Felicity, and to let Ben and Sindy kill each other? He certainly couldn't let Alyson be harmed again if he could help it; it would break Mattie's heart. He felt gratefully lucky she hadn't been permanently harmed the last time. No, this could not take place. He would have to do something. He wouldn't promise her Sindy's death, but the safety of her friends he would ensure. He wasn't sure how he'd accomplish that, but he must.

He looked down into her large and hopeful green eyes. They sparkled with unshed tears. She was terribly worried that he would neglect her wishes. She held herself so close to him, innocently, without hesitation. Did she really belong to Ben now? He was no longer so sure. Her words showed great care for Ben, but then she brought herself so close to him, without thought that it might be unseemly. He was certain she was not the type to share her affections with more than one man.

Again, he was incredibly conscious of her body and blood. Memories of marking her flooded his mind. His body was desperate to claim her once again, in any and every way that he could. He fought back the urge to take her into his arms. She implored him once again. "You won't let them hurt him, will you?"

He felt as though he were drowning in need for her. "You have my word." He kept his voice steady and even, although it was little more than a whisper.

Her face brightened and she beamed at him as she breathed a sigh of relief. "Thank you!" She lifted herself swiftly on tiptoe and gave him a quick kiss on the cheek.

He knew that it was just a sweet and simple gesture to her. A spur of the moment thing, but as her lips touched his skin and triggered the thrill of the mark they shared, it made him shiver with wanting her. She had to feel it. As soon as she did it, she stopped to look at him with new awareness of the innocent act. She looked at him for a long time. She wanted him too; he could see it in her eyes. He waited for her to come to his lips, but she only stared at them, longingly and unconsciously moistened her own.

Sindy's words rang in his ears, that he was not a saint, nor was he meant to be. As much as he did not wish to vindicate Sindy in any way, he knew that she was right. He wanted Felicity far too badly.

He could stand it no longer. There were worse things that he could do. How long was he meant to wait? Denying the thirst was bad enough; must he deny his human needs as well?

He pulled her to him and kissed her. He forced himself to be gentle and unthreatening, lest the intensity of his desire frighten her. He needn't have worried. She quickly gave herself over to it and returned his passion with even more fervor than he'd expected. She was not timid or shy as he usually found her to be. She pressed herself against him and kissed him with an urgency that betrayed her own need for him, which she had hidden so well. The vibrant thrill of the mark they shared ran like a current through their kiss, making the experience more charged with desire than he ever could have expected. It seemed to go on forever.

So badly he wanted to scoop her up and bring her to the bed, but he forced himself to accept only what she offered. She crushed herself to him as though she could not get close enough. Surely, she felt how urgently his body longed for her, but she showed no signs of stopping...or of taking things further. He was caught in a pleasant and yet torturous state of purgatory.

It was quite a struggle to keep his lips from moving to her throat. He could hear her pulse pounding as her blood rushed through the veins there, enticing him. Finally, he knew it needed to end. If it would go no further, then he needed to end it now, both his need and his thirst were too great and if she did not leave, one of them *would* be satisfied.

Even as he ended the kiss, she would not leave him. Her lips hovered over his and she covered them with sweet little whispering kisses that finally moved down his chin to his throat as she came down off tiptoe. Even though she was human, this provoked almost a stronger reaction than the kiss. It may only be psychological, but as a vampire, the throat seemed the most vulnerable and sensitive area that one could place their lips. He kept waiting for and wanting the piercing pain of a bite that would never come.

She seemed unaware of his torment and was taken with trying to bring herself back under control. He knew that to taste the venom in his mouth produced a dreamy sort of euphoria. Not nearly the effect of introducing it into the bloodstream, but she certainly felt it. Coupled with the heightened sensitivity of touch brought by her mark and physical desire that seemed as intense as his own, she was surely fighting strongly to keep herself from him. She rested her forehead against his breastbone, as her breaths came in quick little gasps for air. He could feel her heart racing. She turned her head to the side and laid her cheek against the top of his chest. He wondered if she were listening for his heartbeat. She would be disappointed, as he had none to hear.

He tilted his head to look down at her. After a moment, she met his eyes. He knew that his own eyes must be begging her for more, but he said nothing. She looked as though she was having a very hard time, keeping herself from kissing him again. "I have to go." She tried to say the words with a forceful certainty that she obviously did not feel.

He made himself remove his hands from her. "You *really* do." A tremor in his voice seemed to betray his thirst to her. She appeared a little frightened by his bold honesty. She looked as if she would say something, but instead she turned and grabbed her things. He commanded his body to remain standing at the bar, although he could easily see himself rushing to meet her at the bed. She gave him a brief glance and then fled up the stairs.

Instinct wanted him to give chase. He closed his eyes and clenched his fists. *You are a man, not a predator!* he scolded himself. He waited to hear her out the front door, before he opened his eyes. She was safe, outside, bathed in sunlight. He turned and retrieved his mug off of the bar behind him. He forced himself to drink its full contents, although his stomach threatened to reject it entirely. *Be satisfied and leave me alone!* he silently begged his thirst.

He could feel Felicity receding. He wished she would walk faster.

~~~~~~~~~~~~~~~~~~~~~~~~~~~~~~

Would the sun never set? He hadn't been able to go back to sleep. Once Felicity had left he'd tried, but it was hopeless. Every time he closed his eyes, his senses would torment him with vivid reproductions of her.

Her scent would fill his nostrils and he could feel her mercilessly pressed up against his body. The whisper of her lips against the soft, tender skin of his throat was maddening, but when he thought of her kiss, the taste that seemed to flood his mouth was that of her blood. Her kiss had been heavenly torment, but it was nothing compared to drinking her blood. No matter how he tried to separate the two acts, it was impossible. He desired her as a man, but the vampire within him desired her more.

He paced the floor. He tried to read, but could not concentrate. He showered, shaved and dressed. He thought to drink more blood from his refrigerator, to ease his cravings, but could not seem to force it down. It tasted such a poor substitute, when his memories of the sweet nectar flowing through Felicity, were so sublime.

Why was this so difficult? Three hundred and thirteen years he'd been doing this! He'd drunk from humans before and he knew that it was far better than any animal blood that he might buy, but it had always seemed well worth his piece of mind, an educated and civilized choice. He'd never considered drinking from a person *for the blood;* not since his early years anyway. His heady years of shameless excess and selfish slaughter as a novice vampire were quite far behind him now. Now he rarely drank straight from living vein, and never without great care and significance.

He had drunk in passion and for marking, and they were always exquisite experiences, but he had taken them for what they were and then went back to his daily sustenance. Why did she tempt him far more than he was prepared to face? Was it because she was passion and thirst together, undifferentiated? He had dealt with situations like that before, but they'd never been as severe as this.

She would have to choose, and soon. If she wanted to explore a real relationship with him, he could indulge with her, in body anyway. He could be satisfied with that, for a while. Then he'd have more time to approach the question of other experiences with her. If she was open to it, they could have a relationship of unadulterated bliss, for a little while anyway. However sinful it seemed, he must admit to himself, that was where he really wanted to be. He craved that stage in the relationship where she would allow him to drink from her and he could give her pleasures like she would never know again. It would be amazing. Of course, after a time it would become dangerous and they would have other choices to make. That's when things always went wrong.

He began to realize that his young friend Mattie was perhaps far wiser than he in this respect. For surely, he and Alyson had explored the pleasures that he longed for with Felicity, blood and sex went hand in hand for a creature of the night. As far as Cain knew, Mattie and Alyson had been seeing each other for three years now, but Mattie was smart. He never let it go on for more than a few days at a time. Mattie gave Alyson time to live in reality, instead of constantly basking in the venom induced dream state that such relations would surely put her in. Perhaps she'd begun to want it too much, like an addict seeking a fix. Was that why he had left her to travel; to give her time to decide what she wanted with a clear head, planning then to come back with an offer for eternity? Yes, Mattie was far wiser than Cain had ever been, with a woman.

Still, he was not at that point yet. There was much to be considered before such choices were put before them. Felicity had only freely given him a kiss, not her body or her blood; not yet.

She wanted to be with him, but she wanted the troubles around them cleared first. Apparently, she did not want the decision to be reached under such duress. Of course, that's what had happened with the kiss anyway. He had grown weary of fighting his feelings for her. He'd given in, just slightly, to his desires and she had not turned him away. The smallest sign of resistance would have stopped him, he'd like to think; but she had not resisted, quite the opposite. She had been very responsive. However, the tension of the moment, the distress over her friends' safety, and her heightened desire for him through the venom were all factors that hardly made for fair gauges of her true feelings.

Still, as much as he wanted her to desire him for himself and not his vampire nature, his need for her was strong. At this point, he was beginning to think that he would take what he could get. He would never be able to truly remove all of the outside factors that could influence her feelings for him. It would be impossible. He wanted her, if she returned his affections, he would not question her motives and influences. She'd certainly had ample warning to remove herself from the situation.

He would do his best to resolve the problems around them, but in the meantime, he would hold himself back no longer. He was not going to sit here and watch her gravitate towards Ben, just because he was afraid to rush her. He would rather she reject him, than simply choose someone else first. If she came here, it was by her own choice and he would not continue to keep himself from her.

He had always been level headed and calm, slow to anger and never hasty to judge a situation, but lately it had been grating on him. He was becoming impatient. Why could he not take charge of things and put them to rights in his own fashion; chase off Sindy and her boys once and for all, and find a way to convince Arif to leave as well?

Once those outside fears were removed, surely Felicity would find herself drawn back into his arms, unafraid. She wanted to be with him. The passion of her kiss betrayed the desires she had so cautiously kept in check thus far. It was fears placed in her head by Sindy and the others that gave her such caution. Without that fear, Felicity would have given herself over to him by now. She had been attracted to him from the start, but now…his venom within her was too strong a lure for her to fight for long. Why couldn't he just settle everything in the quickest manner possible and bring Felicity to him, unhindered?

He forced himself to halt his thoughts. He knew why, because it was wrong. Sindy and her boys needed his help. He was still unsure whether her boys might be beyond his assistance. They may not have been made well enough to exist independently, but Sindy was desperate for guidance, whether she would ever admit it or not. If he let her be, she would surely drive herself to destruction, taking many more lives along the way. He'd known others like her. He had done this before and it wasn't easy to change a rebellious vampire's ways, but to stand back and let them self-destruct was unthinkable. He could not fail so miserably in the task he had set for himself. If he did not help those in need, who would?

And Felicity, he would not deny himself her company, but it was wrong to let her be so driven to him by his mark. She hardly knew him. Who was he to assume that she should want to completely give herself over to him? Who was he to make that decision for her, the way he had made the decision to mark her?

He wouldn't shun her, but she needed to be given the freedom to determine her feelings uninfluenced by venom if at all possible, or it would be unfair. It was not for him to ordain her future. It was not for him to determine her path. He made himself look down at the tattoo on his arm. Genesis 4:7. '...Sin is crouching at your door; It desires to have you, but you must master it.'

Stop walking down the path of least resistance, he admonished himself, *for surely it will lead to places best you not go.*

It was nearing sunset. He would go to find Sindy. He would try to persuade her to leave Ben alone, for her own well-being. It would be better if he kept one simple and clear goal at a time. Right now, his purpose was to save Ben's life, *again*. That boy caused him more grief for less thanks than anyone he'd ever known, but at least Felicity would appreciate it, even if Ben did not. How he was going to accomplish it, he was still unsure.

He was not going to hide outside Alyson's apartment waiting for Sindy to come and for things to get violently out of hand. That was just not a smart plan. Ben and Sindy would both be feeling the effects of their bond, and both would be emotionally charged and unwilling to back down.

He would go and find Sindy before she ever visited Ben. Somehow, he would convince her to leave him alone. He was undecided what he would be willing to offer her for such a favor, but he would have to work something out, when the situation arose. He was pretty sure that he knew her well enough to be able to turn things to his advantage.

Sunset, finally. He put on his leather jacket and sunglasses, as proof against the sun's dying rays. He set out into the blazing orange sky, started his motorcycle and rode off towards Sindy's last known resting place. As he neared the place the others called home, he could feel them. They were sleeping still. Young ones were always afraid to venture out before full dark. He rarely bothered to inform them that it was possible. Why not keep the advantage for himself? They could wait the hour more.

Now to find Ben. He was a little surprised to discover that Ben was not at Alyson's apartment, but then he realized that Ben was practicing smart tactics. Sindy couldn't feel Alyson anymore, she knew that. If he stayed at Alyson's apartment, Sindy would expect her to be there. Last night was exploratory, but if she were to try again tonight, she would not give up so easily. If Ben wanted her to think that he would succumb to her call, he was best off pretending to be alone.

A little reaching out with his senses helped him to find Ben easily enough; he wasn't far from Allie's. At least now he knew where Ben lived. He assumed that Alyson was there with him, hiding so as to attack from ambush if needed. Cain found a field not far from Ben's house and parked at the edge of it, on the wood line of the forest. The spot where the others lay was still just within his range. He didn't want them to know that he was aware of their exact location, or they would probably move. He just wanted to be sure that he could intercept them before they went to Ben. He could feel Ben as he lay in wait. Cain waited as well.

As the last glow from sunset disappeared and true darkness fell, he felt them awaken and begin to move around. It was interesting to observe, from his limited awareness of their traces in his mind. He could sense Sindy moving about; seemingly visiting each one to give them individual attention. Most likely, she drank a little from each, to more firmly cement their loyalty to her. They did seem to each glow a bit brighter with her signature, mingled with their own as she left them.

It was Chris and Luke she spent the most time with. He knew them well enough to recognize the shape and hue of their marks in his mind. The others were just menials, pawns and bodyguards, to be used for protection. Chris and Luke were the only ones that she had made well enough to be worth his notice. It was questionable whether their intelligence was dimmed by lack of blood, or if this was simply their normal state. Sometimes they did evince some traces of independence. Chris more than Luke, he'd noticed. He knew she'd found them out in the woods doing drugs around a little campfire they had made behind the school. She'd offered them her body and then stolen their blood. She had kept them as pets, before eventually turning them. They were loyal and bound to her ever since. He was unsure whether they had sufficient free will to leave her. Perhaps they stayed by choice, but more likely she made sure that they were terrified to try and live without her.

She seemed to take forever with them. He could imagine what they'd be doing; he tried not to. Finally, they began to move out into the night. None were left behind; there were seven of them in all. Sindy, Luke, Chris, Marcus, and three football players that remained, of those that she had recently abducted.

At the time, he had thought that her taking such a large and prominent group of young men was supremely foolish, an act that would certainly not go unnoticed as foul play, but apparently, he had underestimated the ability of people to concoct explanations for things that they did not wish to face.

Sindy must have had Luke and Chris do something with some of the boys' cars, for they were missing, along with the contents of their football lockers. It would look as though they had taken some things and went on a trip; although where they would go with only gym attire, Cain couldn't guess people should believe. He assumed that a greater investigation was taking place, out of the public eye, but there had been no headlines yet, and for now, people seemed to believe that the young men had gone off on some fool adventure together.

Unfortunately, it was an adventure they would never return from. A fresh reminder of why Sindy should be brought down. Why didn't he just kill her? She had killed so many others. If he had killed her at the outset, he could have prevented those deaths, but he just couldn't do it. When he tried to see her as evil, instead, to his mind she simply seemed lost and in need of help. He'd better do something soon though. He could not allow her to kill again. Things had already gone much further than he should try to justify.

Their marks grew stronger in his mind. He had guessed correctly, they moved in his direction. He waited until they were fairly close and then gradually let his presence be known. They moved in on him as moths to a flame. Eventually they appeared, materializing out of the woods like wraiths in the night. They were eerily silent for such a large group. Sindy went before them, Luke and Chris after her and then the rest ranged out behind.

She looked sinisterly seductive in the waning moonlight. She wore a dress of all black this evening, to match her hair and the dark shadow around her eyes. It made her skin seem all the more pale, as though she were carved from alabaster. The bodice of the dress was cut in a deep V, to show off far more cleavage than was strictly proper. Its belled sleeves were so long that they seemed to be dripping down from her, hiding her hands, but the skirt was very short, to show off her fine legs. Her skin there seemed made up of little white diamond shapes, as it was glimpsed from between the strings of her fishnet stockings.

On the whole she looked ethereal, but in a wicked and sinful manner. Like a succubus, risen strictly to tempt men to surrender to her. The thick-soled black combat boots she wore ruined the effect a bit, but he'd seen other teenagers dressed in similar styles and knew it was the fashion in some circles. Besides, it would be rather impractical to try and hike through the woods in high heels.

She stopped a short distance from him and raised her hand for the others to pause as well. She put her hands on her hips and studied him with a smile. "Well, hello there."

"Good evening." He eyed the others around her warily. If she chose to have them all attack him at once, he would have no choice but to flee. He would never survive such a battle. That's what they were for.

"Can I do something for you?" she asked.

He gave her a seductive smile. "I was hoping," he answered, suggestively. If he was going to get her to dismiss these others, he needed to get her attention; to make her want to be alone with him.

She was pleasantly surprised by his attitude, but knew he was probably teasing her. "What exactly did you have in mind?"

"Well, some privacy for a start."

She laughed. "Can't say I'm not curious, but I'm kind of busy."

He fixed her with a steady smoldering gaze. He tried to make his eyes lie to her, to tell her of how incredibly sexy he found her and how badly he wanted to get her alone. Come to think of it, they weren't really lies. She seemed to be posing for him, inhaling a bit and tilting her head just so. She didn't know what to make of his request. She was too suspicious to believe that he would suddenly give in to her so easily. He gave her a desirous smile. "I'll try to make it worth your while."

That convinced her, that whatever he wanted, he should not be dismissed. She didn't really believe he wanted *her*, but she did know that he was not in the habit of making empty promises. His request was worth investigating. She called out to her boys, although she still gazed at Cain. "Chris? Lukey?"

As they moved towards her, she finally broke eye contact with Cain and turned to them. They stood side by side, and she rested a hand on each of them. "Be good boys and see that these guys get fed, would you?" She nodded her head towards those behind them. Chris was obviously displeased, "You can come and help me play with Ben later," Sindy said soothingly. Cain groaned inwardly. Just as he'd suspected, she had no intention of forgetting Ben.

Luke grinned with excitement. "We get to be in charge again? I like to be in charge." Sindy smiled at him and ran her hand through his thick, unruly curls.

She spoke to Luke with a patronizing tone, treating him like the simpleton that he surely was. "I know you do," she said, as she wrinkled her nose at him and then made as if to snap at him with her teeth.

She looked up to address the others who stood behind, only dimly aware of their surroundings. "Now you behave for Luke and Chris. You know I won't stand for disobedience." Watching her with them made Cain feel ill.

She looked back to Chris and noted the disappointed resentment on his face. He was staring sullenly at Cain until she blocked his view. She moved in front of him and put a hand on his cheek. "Oh, Chris. Don't be sad. I'll see you later." She leaned closer to speak into his ear, although Cain could still hear her clearly. "Feed well. I'm going to be hungry when I get back," she said in a sultry whisper. Chris was apparently thrilled by the prospect of her drinking from him. Most men probably would be. That's what made her so dangerous.

She pressed herself up against Chris and began to kiss him passionately. The others shifted restlessly behind them, but were ignored. Luke was on the other side of her and after a moment, ripped her away from Chris so that he might pull her to him. He didn't kiss her though; he gave her a playful nip on the neck with his human teeth. She seemed pleased. She gave them each a quick parting kiss and moved a step away. "Go on now."

Cain wondered vaguely how she managed to keep them all from killing each other. And wasn't she kept busy enough trying to make them happy? How could she possibly still have desire left to want Cain or Ben?

But Cain knew that it wasn't really sex that she wanted. It was power; the power to make a man want her. That's why she found Cain and Ben so irresistible. They didn't really want her. Easy men she had, she craved a challenge. She wanted to try and rule someone who could stand up to her and prove their dominance over her. It gave him an idea how he might handle things tonight.

Chris looked back at the others in annoyance. His eyes fell upon Marcus. "We don't have to take *him* do we?"

"No, he should stay." She noticed Cain's disapproval. "Cain, you know I can't let him go feed without me. He's not really a team player." The others began to leave and she went over to Marcus and made him understand that he was to stay. He seemed content to just stand there. Cain wondered if he'd any mind left at all. Sindy came back to him and glanced again at Marcus. "Just ignore him. He's useful sure, but you were right, he really is too stupid to know what's going on half the time. It's a good thing he likes me, or we'd have some problem on our hands, huh?" she asked in amusement.

Cain stared at Marcus in distaste. "We?"

Sindy began to walk a little away from where she had left Marcus standing. Cain followed. She stopped and turned to him in expectation. "So, what's so important that you're willing to lower yourself to try and seduce me away from my boys?"

He smiled. "Sindy, if the night comes when I finally do decide to seduce you, I won't have to *try*. And you certainly won't have the presence of mind to question it. I just wanted your full attention."

She seemed amused. "Well, you have me all to yourself now." She glanced back at Marcus. "More or less. So, what do you want?"

"Only what I've asked before. I want you to leave Ben alone."

She rolled her eyes and seemed very disappointed in him. "That's what this is about, Ben? Aren't you over this yet? So I've got yet another college boy pantin' after me like a puppy, big deal."

"You know Ben is different. He knows very well what you are. He is smart, he is resourceful and he won't stand to be made a fool of."

"What's he gonna do? Kill me? I'd like to see him try!"

"Be careful what you wish for."

Sindy widened her eyes with a chuckle. "Well, that's what I've got my boys for, isn't it? Once he comes to me, I wouldn't want him getting cold feet."

"I thought you weren't hunting anymore, anyway. Your resolve isn't weakening already, is it?"

She smiled. "I'm not huntin'. What do you think I want to make sure my boys get so well fed for?" She gave him a sly wink.

"Then why are you visiting Ben?"

"He doesn't count! Besides, it's not really a hunt when they come right to you." He stiffened and gave her a look of warning. "Relax! I don't have to take his blood, I'd accept other offerings."

He lowered his voice and gazed at her steadily. "I promised Felicity that you wouldn't touch him."

She laughed at him. "Well that's your problem, isn't it? You don't really think I'm gonna give up playing with my favorite new toy, do you? I wanna see that boy beg! Or did you put your girlfriend back in his bed, to keep him busy?"

That drew from him a silent pause and a cold stare of contempt, before he spoke again. "Felicity will be sleeping in her own bed this evening, thank you. I don't need *her* to keep you away from him. I'll do that myself."

She actually laughed at him. "Oh please, why am I wasting my time with this crap?" She began to walk past him as though totally unconcerned by anything he might do.

"Don't do it Sindy." He reached out and took hold of her arm. He would not be so easily dismissed.

She looked at him in amusement and then shook her head condescendingly. "Cain, let's face it. I love it when you try to stand up to me! You're so hot when you're all stern and demanding, but we both know by now, that you are all threat and no follow through. There's just no bite behind your bark. I used to think you just hid those tendencies well, but I've come to the conclusion that it's just not in you. You really are the decent vampire that you claim to be. It's kind of boring. So step aside and let me have my fun."

"You're not leaving."

"What, are you gonna try and kill me too?" she asked sarcastically.

He looked into her eyes to catch her full attention. "If I wanted to kill you, I would let you go." It seemed lost on her.

She tried to pull her arm from his grasp, but he wouldn't release her. She turned and glared at him, trying to make him back down. His eyes played over her face, the mocking amusement in her eyes, the fullness of her lips, and then they settled on her throat. She still wore the thin gold chain. He fixed his stare on those delicate links, trying at first, not to look at what lay beneath them.

The hunger rose within him, he still hadn't fed since the cup he'd drunk after Felicity had left. That was hours ago and had barely been enough to curb his thirst for a short while. He glanced up to her face again. She was smirking at him and shaking her head. He had tried to do things his way and she did not take him seriously. Maybe it was time to do things in a way that she would understand and respect. He made the conscious decision to let his thirst come forth.

He willed himself to shift into his vampiric visage and tightened his grip on Sindy's arm as he felt his mouth widen to accommodate his newly unsheathed fangs. He watched Sindy's form begin to take on strange hues as his new vision sought to find heat and blood within her. Other vampires always stood out strangely with his vampire sight. Her body took on cold tones of bluish green, but the vampire blood within her fairly glowed in crimson red, thriving within her, giving her life where none should be.

Her eyes went wide with shock, that he had actually allowed himself to change before her, but he could see that she was not entirely displeased. He was also aware that Marcus had noted his transformation and was bearing down on them both. He quickly pulled Sindy in front of him, so that he held her in much the same way he had held Felicity that night in the cemetery. Sindy was up against him, facing outward to Marcus, as Cain held her arm in one hand, out to the side. He put his other arm around her waist.

"Tell him to leave us, Sindy," he whispered in her ear. She was unsure what to do. Threatening as he must seem, she'd waited a long time for him to take any sort of interest in her, but she was not certain what he had in mind. She knew it would be stupid to let herself be left alone with him like this.

He used the arm around her waist to crush her close against him. Shameful as it seemed, his body was reacting strongly, not only to her blood, but to her own fine body as well, and he wanted to be sure that she could feel it. He was certain that it would please her, to know that she had such an effect on him.

He was right. She felt his body's readiness pressed against her, and it made the decision for her. "Marcus no! It's okay. You can leave us. Cain only wants to play. Go on, go home. Now, go!" He seemed very confused and Cain worried that he wouldn't listen, but Sindy stared him down and finally he turned around dejectedly and left.

He held her fast as he tracked Marcus in his mind, making sure he did not return. She squirmed against him. "So, are you just gonna stand here like this, keeping me distracted for as long as possible, so Ben can get some sleep?" Cain saw that she felt she knew him well enough, that he wouldn't really hurt her.

He released her waist, but not her arm and spun her to face him. She stared with undisguised wonder at his vampire face and smiled. He rarely ever let her see him this way; he knew it turned her on.

She tried to pull away from him again. He knew it was feint, only designed to draw a reaction from him, but he reacted to it all the same. She just wanted to see what he would do, but he couldn't help it, his instincts took over. He pulled her closer by the arm and wound his other hand into her hair. He jerked her head roughly to the side to expose her throat. He stopped himself to look at her face. Now he knew that he had surprised her, by the expression that she wore. Perhaps she had thought that he'd wanted her body more than her blood. She became very still, her eyes wide, her lips slightly parted, not quite believing that he would do, as he seemed to be threatening.

He would. He wouldn't turn back now, he would do this. He would stop her and force her to heed him. She would know that he was serious and he would taste...ecstasy.

He sank his fangs into her throat with a savage snarl. He was not gentle, but he knew she wouldn't want him to be. She let out a sweet moan as his teeth entered her flesh and he began to pull and draw the blood from her body. It was like liquid fire. Human blood was sweet, thick and rich, but this was different. This was the blood of a vampire. It tasted of spice, strength, and the dry smooth fire that vodka and rum could sometimes try vainly to remind him of.

It had been a very long time since he'd drunk from another of his kind. He planned to drink long and well, unlike the little play drinks she was probably used to. She would make him strong as he drained her.

Her free hand grasped and struggled to open his pants but he bit down on her harder with a warning growl. He fought to control himself enough to pull away from her and speak. "Only blood. This is not for your pleasure, but mine."

"But what about yours?" she asked weakly as she groped to feel him hard and ready, restrained by his clothing.

"Sex, I can get elsewhere, your blood I cannot." She tried to answer him but he went back to feeding from her and the words were lost.

She began to swoon beneath him, although he wondered if she were simply choreographing it that way. She wanted to lie down. He indulged her in this; he planned to leave her too weak to stand anyway. She strained to keep herself pressed close against him, as he lowered her to the ground without leaving his feast. She began to writhe and moan beneath him, pressing her hips to him with a force that surprised him. He had denied her the full pleasure of his body, but it seemed his presence at her throat would bring her to orgasm all the same.

He felt her tense beneath him as she climaxed and he fought to hide the fact that it pleased him as well. His body shuddered and his mind was lost to thought. Her blood, it was all consuming. The more he drank the more he wanted. This was exquisite, sinful ecstasy that he had scarcely ever allowed himself. He let it engross him.

She was thoroughly spent and seemed unable to do more than whimper lightly in his ear. This was surely far more than she had expected of him. It would do her good to be under another's control for a change.

Her slight sounds made him wonder if his venom was affecting her strongly. Even her unnatural body would hardly be proof against such poison. He was far older than she was, and was sure that his venom was much stronger than anything she was used to receiving from her younglings. He let her have no respite. She thought that she was experienced in domination? Let her know how truly *he* could master *her*.

He drank still, it seemed unending. He had no need to hold himself back, no fear of hurting *her*. He felt her come to life again beneath him. She tensed and squirmed, but not in pleasure this time. Her struggle renewed and he understood she was trying to gather the strength to shift into her vampire state. He didn't know how he could tell she had shifted, but sure enough, he felt her fangs graze his own throat as she sought purchase there.

He ripped away from the wound at her neck to fiercely admonish her. "No! You don't get to drink *my* blood." She looked up at him, changed. Even like this, she seemed beautiful to him. The humanity left within him, cringed at the thought. Her eyelids were heavy over her bright red orbs as she gazed at him pleadingly. Yes, not only was she suffering lack of blood, she was fighting the venom, and losing.

"Cain, please. I need it. I haven't fed," she begged him in trembling whispers. He was unmoved.

"Good. Perhaps you'll learn some respect. You *will* mind me."

He went back to the wound and she tried to struggle again beneath him. It was hopeless; she was no match for him like this. If it were any other, he would be horrified at himself, guilt ridden, but somewhere beneath her haze, he was certain that she was pleased. She seemed to faint beneath him. She had given up, he would leave her only when *he* would, and not before.

Finally, he could take no more. He left her throat, and let his face return to its human visage, as he licked the wound clean. He looked down at her; she also had lapsed back to her human state, when he would not allow her his blood.

She lay still like death, but she was strong, and he knew that she would recover well before dawn. He was unsure what possessed him to do it, but he placed one soft and tender kiss on her lifeless lips before rising from her.

She startled him by opening her eyes. They were soft and brown, without the feisty spark that usually inhabited her. She looked up at him dreamily. "Cain, please…" she beseeched him. "You can't leave me like this." She hardly had the strength to speak.

"Call someone else to come and give you a drink. I hear you're quite good at it." She simply closed her eyes.

He stood and left her. He walked to his waiting bike, and as he climbed upon the seat, he scanned the area for others. Her boys were not far away, and yet they did not come. She hadn't called them. He had no doubt that she could have. She must still drink from them often. The bond they shared and her hold upon them was strong.

Cain had never explored that effect of the venom himself, but if she could call humans as easily as she boasted, she could surely call her younglings as well, as long as her venom was fresh within them. He looked back at her. She had not moved. He wondered if she would want them to see her like this. She might not even tell them of what had occurred, if she could at all hide it from them.

He wondered how it would change the way she saw him. He began to wonder also how it changed the way that he saw himself. Here he was, engorged with her blood, seeking her submission and obedience. How could he tell himself that he was any different from her? Or from Arif, for that matter? Weren't they really all just the same?

He saw her stir in the grass. She probably didn't even know that he was still there. She hadn't the strength to sit up yet apparently, but she would definitely be recovered before dawn. There were at least six hours left before she would need to seek shelter and he could keep track of her in his mind, to know if she had moved by then.

He had spoken truly to her. If he had wanted her dead, he would have let her go to Ben, but why did he value her life? Was it for the pure and chaste motives that he had so often professed? He could never be happy with one such as her, could he? She needed his guidance, but *he* could gain nothing from her but grief, he was sure.

He started the engine of his Harley Davidson, making her flinch noticeably. She still did not try to rise though. As he left her, he found himself glad that dawn was still half the night away.

He went home. He wanted to shower. He felt dirtied by his actions, inside and out. As he toweled off and went to put on fresh clothing, he knew that he could not stay inside. He had thought to stay home until going to sleep, but he realized now, that he never could. Now that he had left the site of the act, he felt as though he had also left his sinful culpability behind as well. He had done what he needed to; he would no longer dwell on it.

Meanwhile, his body was surging with the power and vitality that he had gained from her. Sindy's blood was coursing within him. It made him feel strong, elated and high almost. It had been a very long time since he had given his body so much blood, and of such quality no less. He felt as if he were an old car, used to running on never more than the most minimal amount of economy gasoline and had now filled his tank with racing fuel. He needed to be outside experiencing the night.

Felicity. At first, he thought it would be distasteful to go to her. Technically what he had done to Sindy would not be considered 'being with another woman', but no matter how he tried not to think on it, in his heart, he felt as though he might as well have raped her.

His conscience was eased by the fact that he knew deep down, Sindy was probably thrilled by the act. In fact, she had even offered it freely the night before. Of course, he was sure she'd never expected him to take things to such extremes, but as he had said to her this very evening, 'be careful what you wish for'.

It's not as if he had given her *his* body or blood, for whatever that was worth. He and Felicity did not even have a relationship or agreement that he could be considered to have been unfaithful to.

Sindy and Felicity lived in two separate worlds. Felicity was human, and he wanted her and treated her as a human woman, worthy of his love and respect. Sindy was a vampire, and he treated her and disciplined her as such.

He loathed the idea that he had behaved like an animal, but it was not by his design that such instincts and patterns were imprinted upon him to bring her under control. He had tried to do it in human fashion first, but he was ignored. He certainly would not be laughed at! Anyway, it did not matter now. It was done and she would take him more seriously from now on. He may even have some slight control over her, strictly through his venom that now invaded her bloodstream. Her body would heal her of it before long, but psychologically, it might be very effective far beyond its physical consequences.

He turned his mind to Felicity again. He realized that while the thought of seeing her did excite him, it did not awaken his thirst. His hunger for blood was thoroughly sated. Visions of her in his mind produced no more than a normal desirous reaction, uncolored by blood lust. Yes, he would definitely go and see her, if only to feel that he could truly relate to her as a man and not have to fight the monster inside him with every fond glance or touch she might bestow.

He should have thought to go to her anyway, just to let her know that things were all right. She surely worried for her friends. It was well after eleven, a little late to her, but the night was long. He was too taken with the idea of seeing her, to resist following through with it now.

He finished dressing and brushed his hair. It was still wet from his shower, but would dry with the wind from the motorcycle ride to her dorm, before long, he was rushing towards her building, feeling her presence. She still moved about, she was not asleep.

He cut the engine just before entering the lot, so as not to disturb anyone. He walked the bike in and parked it, looking up at her window. A dim lamp was lit, as though she were reading in bed. He would not go to the door; it was nearly midnight, too late for open entry.

He thought at first to attempt to call her, as Sindy had suggested last night. Surely, he could, but then he realized that it would probably be regarded as uncouth, after what she had seen Ben go through the night before. It would frighten her and push her away from him. What approach would she look upon fondly?

He looked up again at her window. It would not be easy, but it would be fun. His body seemed eager to use the extra energy it had been given and it's not as though he could really hurt himself.

He set about finding a way to climb up. Eventually he found a tree around the side of the building that would give him access to the roof. He then found his way to the spot over her window and managed to drop down, perching himself on the slight ledge at her windowsill.

Meanwhile, he could feel her within. She had risen from bed, she definitely felt him as well. Her mark was a week old and he hadn't given her much, but although it was beginning to dim, it was still effective.

He endeavored to strike a suave pose, and gave a few slight taps on the window. She was there almost instantly. She looked shocked and amazed as she pulled the string to lift the blinds away, and raised the glass of the windowpane. "Hi," he said, with as much casual charm as he could muster. She was suitably enchanted.

"Hi," she replied hesitantly as she looked around to try and see how he might have gotten there. She was mystified.

"I thought I'd come and let you know that you needn't worry about Ben. Sindy will not be visiting him this evening. I don't think she'll be bothering him any time soon, either."

Felicity was visibly relieved. "Thank you, I was worried. How did you manage that?"

He smiled. "I can be quite persuasive, when I've a mind to be."

She eyed him thoughtfully. He wondered if she was trying to fathom what he might have done, or if she was simply thinking of the times that he had purposely *not* tried to persuade *her*. A little of both, he decided. "I'll bet you can be," she agreed. She looked around again to see if she might gain some clue as to how he had reached her window and gave a little laugh. "This is so weird. I feel like 'Juliet'."

He leaned back a touch, being careful not to fall out of the window, to look her over, as if to assess her. "Oh no, definitely not." Her brow furrowed at his words and he smiled. "Even her description pales next to your beauty. You're far lovelier than anything Shakespeare could have dreamt of." She rolled her eyes and looked away shyly to hide the heat rising in her cheeks. He had to smile. He knew he was being terribly ostentatious, but he couldn't help it. He was so joyful to see her and eager to gain her favor. It felt wonderfully good to be close to her without even really noticing her pulse for a change. He laughed a bit at her bashful pose. "Come now, hasn't anyone ever told you that you're beautiful?"

"Not like that." She laughed a little and shook her head. "Did you want to come in?"

"Unless you'd like to come out."

She peered over the edge to the ground far below. "Not *that* way," she said with another laugh. "Come in, please, before you fall."

She backed away from the window as he began to climb through. He pretended not to notice as she quickly and discreetly fixed her hair and adjusted her clothing before the mirror. She was dressed only in her nightgown. It was a large tee shirt of sorts, with a deep v-neckline and was awfully short. She had very nicely shaped legs, he observed. She had tugged down her hem, self consciously as he was entering the room, but he noticed as he stood that now she seemed transfixed. He realized that she was still peering into the mirror, and that he was not reflected there. She looked to him and then back to her lone reflection again in wonder. She hadn't noticed the oddity the last time that he was here. It was a long-standing habit of his, never to stand near a mirror when he could help it.

As she looked back at him again, he smiled and shrugged. "How do I look?"

She giggled a bit as he tried to comb his hair with his fingers, pretending to preen in front of his invisible image in the mirror. "You look..." she paused, evaluating his appearance, "*really* good."

He gave her a grin and raised his eyebrows as if to question her seriousness. "Well, I guess I'll have to take your word for it." He glanced over to her bed; the covers a rumpled mess. "I hope I didn't wake you."

"No, I couldn't sleep anyway." The mirror kept distracting her. She finally moved to turn her back to it and looked only at him. "Thanks again, for handling things with Sindy. I know you and Ben don't always get along, but I do appreciate your help."

"I've no problem with Ben...that I'm aware of." He looked at her questioningly. She seemed perplexed. "Are you and he, involved?"

Her face brightened as she realized what he was asking. "No," she answered immediately, with a shake of her head.

He smiled at her suggestively. "Then I've no problem with Ben at all." She was blushing again. She was so easy to fluster, he found it adorable. "I want you to know, that when I kissed you earlier..." she became even more flushed at the memory; he went on, "I hope you don't think that you...owed it to me, for my help. They are separate acts." He stumbled a bit for words. "You're not indebted to me, or obligated in any way, for anything. You know that, don't you?"

She smiled in demure appreciation. "Yes, but thanks for saying it."

He gazed at her in silence for a moment. She simply looked back at him, trying not to obviously run her eyes too far down his body. He raked his hand through his hair. "Do you want to go out? We can use the door if you'd like," he said with a mischievous grin.

She seemed a little shocked at the idea. "It's after midnight and I'm not even dressed." She became self-conscious again, trying to smooth down her nightgown with her hands.

He endeavored to keep his eyes from her perfect legs, to avoid making her uncomfortable. "I'd wait. Or else...tomorrow evening?"

She was very happy with the idea. "Yes, I'd like that. I'm working until nine."

"Shall I pick you up at the bookstore?" She gave him a little smile and nod. "Alright then. I should leave; let you get some sleep, now that your mind's been put to ease." He went back to the window and sat on the ledge, making ready to leave.

"You can use the door."

"That's alright, this way has a much more dramatic effect, don't you think? And it's kind of fun." He laughed and she shook her head and smiled. "See you tomorrow."

He spun around to put his legs out the window and perched on the ledge again. He was deciding whether to disappear over the roof or simply try to jump to the ground when she rushed to the window.

"Cain!" He looked back. She gazed at him, unsure what to say. "Goodnight." He realized that she wanted to kiss him. He ducked down to lean his head and shoulders back through the window. She took his face into her hands and met his lips with her own. It was sweet and soft; uncolored by thirst and blessedly normal. Still passionate to be sure, but the intense urgency that had driven him before, was replaced by sincere contentment. Not that he didn't desire more from her, but he could wait. He thoroughly enjoyed it. The kiss ended, and a moment after, he pulled himself up to the roof and was gone.

Chapter 5 - Thanks for bringin' down my day

Felicity

Felicity's dorm room
8:30, Tuesday morning

Felicity found herself singing as she got dressed for class. She couldn't help it, he was still riding a high off of last night's visit from Cain. Brief as it had been, she couldn't wipe the smile from her face. He was so romantic! And overly dramatic and a little silly, but she found him delightfully charming and was very excited to see him tonight.

She put on a lovely skirt and blouse, of hazel green, just the same shade as her eyes. She was just fixing her hair, and was almost ready to leave for some breakfast, when there was a knock at her door. She went and opened it, while trying to clip up her hair with one hand. It was Ben. "Hi," he said with a smile.

She just gave him a casual, "Good morning," and went back to the mirror to finish her hair. From the corner of her eye, she saw him enter the room looking a bit disappointed. Apparently, he had expected a more enthusiastic reception.

"I just figured I should come by and let you know that everything was alright. I mean, in case you were worried...since we weren't at Allie's."

She finished her hair and turned to face him with a smile that hardly matched her scolding tone. "I know. Stayed at your place huh?"

"Yes. And see, that is exactly the reason why. I knew you were going to go over there and I didn't want you getting yourself into trouble."

"I didn't go there. You told me not to, remember?" she reminded him.

"Like you were going to listen to me?" he asked with a smirk.

She smiled. "Well, I actually did listen to you, and I sat here and worried, after I called like twenty times! Thanks for letting me know where you were!"

"Why didn't you try my phone?" he asked.

"Because by the time I realized you weren't answering at Allie's, it was after ten o'clock. I didn't think your dad would be very happy to hear from me."

"Remind me to give you my cell number," Ben told her.

She refused to let him change the subject. "Why didn't you guys just call me and let me know you'd changed tactics?"

"Did you want me to call and wake up the whole dorm? Anyway, she didn't show up."

"I know, Cain told me." Unsurprisingly, he was not thrilled to hear her mention Cain. "And good news, he doesn't think she'll be bothering you again anytime soon either."

"I told you I didn't want his help."

"Well, he wasn't helping *you*. He was doing a favor for me."

"Gee, I wonder why?" he asked sarcastically.

She gave him a look of annoyance. "Look, you wanted Sindy to leave you alone, mission accomplished. So why do you care?"

"Is she still alive?" he asked.

"I would assume!" she exclaimed.

"Well, maybe I wanted to stake her myself!" Ben told her.

"Yes, I'm sure that would have been very satisfying to your bruised ego. It also would have made you very dead! The girl has created her own private army. Do you really think she's going to let herself get killed by someone like *you?*"

"Someone *like me?* What, you don't think I'm capable? I notice you didn't have any problem sending Cain after her!"

"I didn't *send* Cain after her! And all I meant was that you're human! I just didn't want you to get hurt again."

"Thanks, but I don't need you to get Cain to protect me!"

"Ben! It's not so much that I was afraid that you *couldn't* kill her; I was terrified that you would! You're right. She would let you come to her. She would have let you get real close. And you would have staked her, and she would be dust right now," she said.

"Sounds good to me," Ben replied.

"But Ben, no matter how brave, or strong, or clever you are; six to one is just really bad odds. Even if she came alone, Chris and Luke would know it was you. Let me tell you something, the mark that you have from her will fade, but I'm thinkin' their desire for revenge would last a long time. We've seen enough of her guys to know that they're pretty single minded. If you kill their mistress they will hunt you down until the day you die!"

He stared at her for what seemed like a really long time. Finally, he lost the angry scowl he wore and began to look a bit chastened. "Well, I guess that's a pretty good point. Why didn't you just say that yesterday?"

"Like you would listen to me," she answered with a smirk.

"Still, just because she didn't show up last night, doesn't mean she's going to give up so easily," he pointed out.

"Well, Cain seemed pretty confident that we shouldn't worry," she told him. Ben obviously didn't put much stock in that. "If she does try for you again, and you can't manage to keep yourself from going outside, then you can stake her. But for now, let's just wait it out, okay?" Ben still did not seem satisfied. "Was it really so hard to resist?" He just gave her a sullen shrug. She smiled. "Alyson seemed more than willing to help distract you. I bet she'd even tie you to the bed if you asked."

That made him give her a grudging smile. "She probably has her own hand cuffs, but no thanks."

"It'll fade. I think my mark's going away already. I still feel it, but it's not quite as intense as it was in the beginning."

He gave her a level stare. "When did he do it?"

She realized that they were moving into an area that it was probably best not to discuss, but he held her gaze and she felt forced to answer. "It was the night we met Arif," she said, thinking back. "The night after the cemetery, so...Monday? Wow, was it only a week ago yesterday? It seems like longer."

"So...what? Were you like, making out and he just lost control?"

She looked at him with disgusted irritation. "No. It wasn't like that at all. He was afraid that Arif would hurt me. Hell, I'm afraid of Arif too! He is so creepy. He told Cain that I didn't *belong* to him, as if I were up for grabs or something. You should have seen the way that he looked at me," she said with a shudder. "If I'd understood about this whole marking business, I might have *asked* Cain to do it, right then and there."

Ben was very thoughtful, and did seem to sympathize a little. Then he asked, "But you *didn't* know, did you? He just, *did it*. Am I right?" She didn't say anything, but the answer was obvious. "Weren't you scared?"

Why was he bringing this up? Couldn't he just leave it alone? It was over. "I didn't press you for details about Sindy."

"You didn't have to! You had a front row seat." He looked as disgusted as she felt.

"I didn't watch."

He seemed a little surprised, but she thought he appreciated hearing it. "So what happens when it's gone? The mark," he clarified.

"What do you mean?"

"Your mark. Think he'll want to give you a new one?"

That was a disconcerting thought. "Well, things are different now. I think he and Arif have come to some kind of agreement, so I shouldn't really have to worry about him anymore. And Cain did say that Sindy would stay out of our way. So, he shouldn't need to."

"Yeah, let's see what Cain has to say about that in another week or two."

She thought about that for a few minutes in agitation, and then looked up at Ben with a frown. "Thanks for bringin' down my day."

He gave her a sympathetic, half-smile. "Sorry, I try to live in reality. It's a lot less fun, I know." He paused for a moment, as if something had just occurred to him. "Have you ever actually *read* the bible?" She only answered him with a strange look. "Cain was *not* a good guy. Just so you know."

"Look, I'm going to be late for class, as it is I'll have to skip breakfast. I'll see you later, okay?" He held her gaze for a moment longer. He didn't really want her to be able to dismiss the thought so easily, but finally he relented and went out into the hall. She gathered her things and went out to walk to class. She found that he was waiting for her, and they walked together.

~~~~~~~~~~~~~~~~~~~~~~~~~~~~~

Evening. Felicity was working with Ashley in the bookstore, but when Ashley went home, she would be closing with Harold. She was very glad that Cain would be meeting her. Not that she was frightened of Harold, but she certainly didn't relish the thought of spending time alone with him.

She and Ashley were up at the registers around 7:45 p.m., when Alyson entered the store. She wore what Felicity believed was probably one of Ben's tee shirts, which was way too big on her, with a pair of ripped and faded jeans, and big pink basketball sneakers. She leaned on the counter in front of Felicity and pointedly ignored Ashley. "Hey." She glanced over at the cafe and spotted Harold. "Ew, what's the grease ball doin' here?"

"He's working," Felicity said.

"Where's Ben?" Alyson asked.

"Ben's not on tonight," Felicity informed her.

She looked at Felicity in confusion. "But he didn't answer his phone."

Felicity gave her an amused smile. "Maybe he's busy."

"Well, how dare he go and have a life without me!" Alyson's tone was joking, but Felicity suspected that she truly felt that way. "Besides, I even texted his cell! He didn't answer me."

Ashley spoke up. "Alyson, when are you going to give up and realize that Benjamin will never be interested in you?"

Alyson moved to speak to her directly over the counter. "Ben and I are friends Ashley. I realize that's a foreign concept to you, but try to understand. It's when two people hang out and have fun together, *without* having sex. You should try it sometime."

Ashley looked down her nose at Allie. "Of course Ben wouldn't want to sleep with you; you have the body of a twelve year old boy!"

Felicity stepped in. "And you've got the maturity of one." She knew by the look on Allie's face, that if the counter hadn't been between them, Ashley would have been laid out on the floor. "Cut it out, Mr. Penten is here and you're going to get us in trouble."

"I'm goin' for a cup of coffee." Allie began to head for the cafe. "Slut," she muttered as she passed Ashley.

"Freak," Ashley responded mildly. As soon as Allie left, she turned to Felicity. "I will never understand why Benjamin spends all of his time with that refugee from the fashion police."

"They're good friends, Ashley. Not everyone judges people by their appearance."

"Obviously, but that's the worst part; she would actually be pretty if she didn't put ten pounds of multicolored goo in her hair. And did you get a load of those shoes? Ew!"

Just then, a customer approached the counter and Felicity backed away a bit to let Ashley take him. Partly because he was a young cute guy, and Ashley had made it quite plain that customers like that were hers, a point Felicity did not have the patience to argue, but mostly because she had begun to feel Cain approaching.

Sure enough, a few moments later he walked through the door. Her mark must be fading; she hadn't felt him until he was practically here. He looked very handsome this evening. The fairly long layers of his sandy blonde hair had been windswept back from his face with the motorcycle ride. He was dressed much the same as he had been the night of the dance, wearing his black jeans and boots, but his shirt was a deep shade of purple, that made his eyes seem all the more bright, Caribbean blue. He looked to Felicity as though he could have walked right off of the cover of one of the romance novels they sold.

Ashley was still taking her time with her customer, and hadn't noticed Cain. Felicity saw that Allie had gotten her coffee 'to go'. She had definitely seen Cain, and was on her way over. He approached the counter.

"You're early," Felicity said with a smile.

"I couldn't wait to see you," he replied.

Felicity glanced around to see Mr. Penten doing inventory towards the back of the store. He looked up to eye her and Ashley at the counter now and again. "I can't really talk, Mr. Penten's here."

Cain shrugged with a smile. "Then I'll just have to find myself a book to gaze at you over."

Felicity rolled her eyes at him. Ashley's customer left, and both she and Allie gave Felicity and Cain their full attention. "That won't be at all distracting," Felicity said with a sarcastic grin.

"Well, you couldn't expect me to try and read. Your beauty is distracting."

Felicity glanced up at the ceiling as Ashley looked annoyed and Allie snickered. Felicity turned back to Cain. "Aren't you laying it on a little thick?"

Cain smiled at all three girls. "I'm only being honest. So, could you recommend any books for me to *not* read?"

Felicity smiled. "Sorry, all of our books have words in them."

"Well, I guess I'll just go browse the shelves then," he said.

"You do that," she said with a patronizing tone.

As he began to leave, Allie followed and put a hand on his arm for his attention. "Dude, just a tip. I think you're in, stop trying so hard. Your 'aloof' image is gettin' blown to hell." She gave him a pat on the back and then waved to Felicity as she left the store. Cain just laughed and started towards the bookshelves.

"He seems to like you," Ashley muttered.

Felicity smiled as she watched him wander among the aisles. "I guess."

Ashley turned on her, almost viciously. "What did you do?"

"What?" Felicity asked.

"I have been flirting with that guy for *months*, and *nothing!* That does not happen to me! I was starting to think he was gay! Now you've got him coming in here spouting crap about your distracting beauty; what the hell is that?"

"Maybe he just doesn't like blondes?" Felicity asked with a smile.

"As if. You must have done something. When did you first talk to him? How'd you meet him?" Ashley inquired sternly.

Felicity looked at her thoughtfully for a moment. "I was attacked, actually. He rescued me," she answered with a fond smile at Cain, far down an aisle, off to the right. She almost thought she saw him acknowledge the memory with a little smile of his own.

Ashley looked at once relieved and disgusted. "The 'damsel in distress'? How obvious is that? *I* could have done *that!*"

Felicity shrugged. "I certainly didn't plan it that way. That's just what happened."

Ashley sighed in resignation. "You are so lucky. Cain is such a catch!"

Felicity laughed, aware of the fact that Cain could most likely hear their entire conversation, even though to Ashley he probably seemed well out of range. "He is, but everyone has their faults," she said quietly.

"No way! Look at him! Cain is a totally delicious stud! He's so much more mature than any college guy," Ashley observed.

"That's true," Felicity answered.

"And he is so totally cool and confident! Don't you find that just amazingly sexy?" Ashley asked.

Felicity smiled and answered as quietly as she could. "Yeah." She tried not to laugh as she pictured Cain straining to hear her response. He had moved behind a shelf where the girls could not see him, for the moment.

"Not to mention the fact that the man obviously has money!"

That one caught Felicity off guard. "What?" she asked skeptically. "Why would you think that? It's not like he dresses flashy or wears jewelry or anything."

"Real wealthy guys don't have to flaunt it. He always totally over-tips in the cafe, and I know it can't be for Ben's crummy service."

Felicity laughed. "He doesn't even have a car Ashley."

"So, have you seen that sweet motorcycle? Harley Davidson's that fine do not come cheap. And he buys these overpriced books every night and he doesn't even keep half of them. Anyway, I don't need to see material stuff. I'm telling you, the man smells like money!"

Felicity laughed at her again, trying to imagine what Ashley would make of Cain's bare house. "I don't think he's rich, Ashley. That never mattered to me anyway." Another customer came to the counter as they talked. It was an older woman, Ashley gestured for Felicity to ring her. "I thought you liked Ben?"

Ashley smiled and seemed to think about him for a minute. "I do, but you can't expect me to go out with him again, after what he pulled."

"What'd he do?" Felicity asked.

"You know, you were there," Ashley insisted.

Felicity looked at her in confusion as she finished ringing up the books. "$42.25," she told her customer. She looked back to Ashley as the woman paid and Felicity gave her the change. "Are you talking about him not asking you to the dance?"

"Well duh," Ashley said condescendingly.

"Didn't you say someone else had already asked you anyway? Your date certainly didn't look like a 'second choice' kind of guy."

"Well of course I had other offers." She looked at Felicity as though she should know better, and began explaining her 'system'. "All the boys I date for like three weeks before an event invite me to go with them. Then I choose who I want to go with, but I was waiting for Ben. I dated that boy three times before the dance. He owed me an invite!"

Felicity tried not to laugh. "Maybe he didn't like the fact that you were dating all those other guys! Besides, what do you want with Ben? He hasn't got any money!"

Ashley gave her a reprimanding tone. "Oh, come on! Have you seen his car? Besides, Ben is pre-law. That's like being pre-money! He is so suave; couldn't you just see him in a court room?"

Felicity laughed. *Ben, suave?* She always saw him as pushy and argumentative.

Ashley looked dreamy eyed. "Oh yeah! Put that boy in a suit, and he cleans up *real* nice! Didn't you see him at the dance?"

"I guess. I mean, yeah. He's definitely a good looking guy."

"Understatement of the year! Trust me, I've done my share of sampling the stock at this school and that boy is totally top shelf."

Felicity laughed with a little shake of her head. "Isn't 'playing the field' supposed to be a way to find out who you like? Once you like someone, why would you keep dating all those other guys?"

Ashley gave her another condescending look. "Well you can't stop dating other guys right away! Otherwise, the guy you like will know how much you like him! Once he thinks that he means more to you than you mean to him, he's got all the power in the relationship. You have to leave them wanting more."

Funny, Ben had seemed to insinuate that Ashley hadn't left him wanting for much. Felicity knitted her brows. "So, when do you drop the other guys?"

Ashley looked as though she felt bad for poor Felicity, who obviously lacked basic dating skills. "When the guy you like starts buying you jewelry!"

Felicity tried to cover her mouth with her hand and couldn't help but laugh. She knew that she was blushing fiercely, knowing that Cain was listening. Ashley got very serious and made Felicity look at her. "Oh my God! Has Cain bought you jewelry?" she demanded.

Felicity's laughter softened into giggles. "Yes."

"Oh my God! When?" Ashley demanded.

"It was like, almost a month ago," Felicity said, shaking her head dismissively.

Ashley's mouth fell open. "He hardly knew you then! I told you he had money! And you're not even sleeping with him yet, are you?! "

Felicity felt as though her face was on fire and her cheeks hurt from smiling. "I kissed him when he gave it to me."

"Well I should hope so!" Ashley exclaimed.

Mr. Penten began making his way back up to the front of the store; Cain was still browsing, with his back to them. Ashley glanced up at the clock on the wall. "It's eight, I've gotta go."

"Hot date?" Felicity asked with a smile.

"Pretty hot," Ashley answered as she took off her nametag and came out from behind her register. "He's not quite Ben or Cain caliber though. Ah well, better than staying home." She gave a little wave and left to clock out and get her stuff.

Cain came back up to the counter with a book, as Mr. Penten went into the office. Cain was grinning like the cat that ate the canary. Felicity tried to compose herself and not smile too broadly as he addressed her. "Found a book. Look, no words!"

He opened it for her on the counter. It was an art book, filled with prints of famous paintings. He seemed very pleased with himself. Felicity laughed. "You going to buy it? It's $68.95."

"Might as well, being that I'm *rich* and all," he replied with a broad grin.

Felicity shook her head. "You know, it's very impolite to eavesdrop on other people's conversations."

"I know, it really is, but it's rather hard not to when you can hear *everything*," he said apologetically.

"Are you actually buying that?" He put a hundred dollar bill on the counter as he pushed the book towards her. She looked at him questioningly as she rang it up. "You're not really rich, are you?"

He smiled. "I thought it didn't matter to you?"

She gave him back the change. "It doesn't."

"Then you don't need to know." He gave her a little smile as he took the book and went over to the cafe. He spent the rest of the night flipping through his book and making a great show of staring at her whenever she happened to look up. His stares began as smoldering gazes, but as the night wore on, they dissolved into silly faces that became more and more distracting. By closing time, she was barely able to look at him without breaking down into giggles. Luckily, Mr. Penten remained in the office.

At nine, she changed the sign on the door to 'closed' and went back to close out her register. Cain came over to meet her, but Harold followed closely behind. He haughtily announced that only employees were allowed to remain in the store as the registers were counted. Felicity began to protest, but Cain held up a hand to silence her, shaking his head. He didn't want to cause any trouble. He would wait outside.

Felicity was very annoyed, but let him leave. Mr. Penten was still in the office, so it wasn't as if Harold could really bother her. He just wanted to be a prick. Fine, she would be done quickly anyway. She finished in record time and went to get her things to leave. On her way to the lounge, she noticed Cain had left his book on the table. She picked it up and brought it into the back. She'd keep it in her locker for him. When she emerged from the lounge, she saw that Harold looked far from finished. She came out from behind the counter and hardly even paused as she put on Cain's denim jacket to leave. "I hope you don't think you're goin' anywhere," Harold said as she passed.

"I'm done," she told him.

"So? You have to wait until I'm done. That's the rule."

She didn't even bother to argue with him. She gave him an angry glare and then stalked over to Mr. Penten's office and tapped on the door. "Mr. Penten? I'm finished with my register. I know I'm supposed to wait until the cafe is closed out, but since you're still here with Harold, would it be alright if I left?"

"Sure, that'd be fine. Goodnight."

Felicity gave Harold a little smile and a big wave, and was out the door. Cain was leaning against his motorcycle in front of the store. Felicity came out shaking her head. "He acts like such a jerk."

Cain smiled, "Of course he does. Why wouldn't he rather have you in there with him, instead of out here with me?" He patted the seat of the bike and got on.

She looked down at her skirt and then back at the bike. "I didn't plan this very well, did I?"

He looked to see what she meant and smiled. "You could ride 'side-saddle'."

"Yeah right. You have way too much faith in my coordination. I'm a klutz. I'd fall off before we left the parking lot."

He smiled. "I doubt that." He looked at her skirt appraisingly. "But if you aren't comfortable side-saddle, you could always just hike it up. It's cut full enough." He smiled at her chagrin over the idea. "Unless you'd rather walk. Come on, I won't look." He said it teasingly, but did turn to face forward, waiting for her to get on.

She grabbed a handful of material in her hand and got on. She draped and arranged her skirt so that her legs did not really show. "Okay, I'm ready."

He turned to look at her, and laughed. "I don't think so."

"Why not?" she asked.

"Well you look lovely, but this is a motorcycle, not a horse. If you left your skirt like that, it would get caught up in something and be ripped *off* you before we left the parking lot," he informed her.

"Okay, that would not be good." He gave her a smile, which made her think that he might disagree, but he didn't say anything. "So what do I do?"

"You have to tuck it in around you." She fidgeted and attempted to fold it under her. He shook his head and looked at her. "May I?" She was sure her face was red. No one else had ever made her blush so much in her life.

She avoided his eyes while raising her hands into the air as if to surrender, and answered with a smile. "Go ahead." He arranged her skirt for her, tucking it in well under her thighs. He did it very discreetly, but she still thrilled to his touch. He seemed to think it was nothing. It was, but she couldn't help it, she was still blushing.

"Well, it'll be terribly wrinkled when we get there, but at least you'll still be clothed."

"Thank you. Where are we going?" she asked.

"Well, according to Ashley, I should head to another jewelry store," he said with a mischievous grin.

"Very funny, but jewelry will get you nowhere," she said.

"Good. That's why I don't pay much attention to girls like Ashley. We can go anywhere, but I thought maybe you'd like to visit Venus?" He noticed her slight look of apprehension. "Don't worry, it'll be fine. I think you'll like it."

When they entered the club, Felicity was suitably impressed; awestruck was more like it. The place was wild! So far, she'd only been to the little places they had around her town. They were just bars, like Tommy's. This was something entirely different. There was fog, bubbles and flashing lights, brightly painted murals on the walls, great music and an actual dance floor. It was huge! "Wow! This place is so cool!"

Cain smiled as they paused just inside the doorway. "It's not bad. Never been to New York City have you?"

"Twice in my life and not to go to a club, believe me." She couldn't help but worry that she hadn't dressed appropriately, but Cain didn't seem to care. "I've been pretty sheltered, it's pathetic I know."

Cain laughed sympathetically. "The city's not that great. It is convenient for someone like me, who's better off as a face in the crowd, but there is definitely something to be said for quiet country life as well." She had the feeling he was just trying to make her feel better, but it was sweet. "So, are you still shy of dancing?" he inquired.

"I thought *you* didn't like to dance?" He shrugged. "Are there any other... I mean, there's no one else here we should worry about, is there?"

"No. I don't think so," he answered.

"Well, maybe we could dance a little." They made their way to the dance floor and had fun dancing to three or four fast songs. Cain wasn't nearly as 'bloody awful' a dancer as he had originally claimed, but he wasn't nearly so polished a dancer as to make her feel awkward either. It was almost comforting to see him not be perfect at something; it made her feel that they were more on level footing. Sometimes he seemed so impeccably flawless... Well, except for the whole blood sucking thing.

After a while, she motioned to Cain that she needed a break. They made their way off the dance floor and Felicity leaned closer to speak to him. "Maybe we could find someplace to sit for a little." He smiled and took her by the hand. He wove his way through the crowd, to a staircase in the back corner and she followed him up. She hadn't realized that there was a whole upper level. This place was awesome!

There was a balcony that overlooked the dance floor and another bar up here too, but the best part was that further back from the balcony, where the volume was actually conducive to conversation, there were large couches and armchairs scattered all about with little tables for drinks. She was delighted! There were very few people up here. It felt private and cozy. She headed for a little sofa up against the back wall. Cain followed but didn't sit. "Can I get you something?"

"I'll just have a coke. Straight up," she added with a smile, remembering the last time he'd brought her back a drink. He left for the bar and she snuggled back into the overstuffed sofa. All of the furniture up here was done in terribly loud colors and patterns that seemed to have been made to clash. Neon orange and green zebra stripes, yellow and purple polka dots, and other odd hues that glowed in the black lights. There were even colorful lava lamps on many of the tables. If someone had described it to her, she would have thought it sounded hideous, but being here, she loved it!

Of course, she had good company. She was so enjoying being with Cain, she had almost forgotten that he was not just a regular guy. In the past, he had seemed sort of mysterious and gallant, very mature and reserved. But lately he seemed different, freer and less sedate. It was as though he'd stopped trying to present an image, and was just having fun and simply being himself.

He also seemed to be trying to impress her a bit, coming up to her window and saying such flattering things, but she didn't mind, because it was done with a humor that told her he knew he was being a little over the top. He was having fun and being honest about it. He wasn't trying to trick or persuade her. The things he said, no matter how flowery, did seem sincere. He had such a chivalrous manner; it usually put her off guard as to how to react. The boys she was used to associating with just did not act that way. As he came back with the drinks, he looked the perfect gentleman. "Your drink, my lady," he said with a smile. Quite inappropriately, she started laughing. Undoubtedly, it surprised him. "Are you laughing at me?"

She looked up at him abashed, but couldn't quite stop giggling. "Yes. Yes I am."

"Do I want to know why?" he asked hesitantly.

She gave him a smile and put her hand on his arm, to assure him that he shouldn't worry. "I'm sorry, it's just that sometimes you are so...charming."

"That's funny is it?" he asked in amusement.

"No, but I was just thinking about how, here you are, all sophisticated and dignified, but a few hours ago you were sitting in the cafe making funny faces at me from across the room and acting so silly. Then other times, you seem kind of stoic and withdrawn. I never really know what to expect from you. It's kind of disconcerting. Not in a bad way, but I don't know, it just struck me as funny."

He put the drinks on the table as he sat down next to her. "I can't say I mind putting a smile on your face, but I hope you won't be disappointed when you discover that I'm really rather predictable. I just don't get all that much opportunity to actually enjoy myself these days. Have you any idea how long it's been since I've acted truly silly? I hadn't realized how much I miss just having fun. It's not very pleasant having to act the brooding task master all the time."

Task master? "So you basically travel around, looking for vampires who need to be taught a lesson?"

He laughed. "Well, I guess it doesn't sound very nice when you say it like that! I'm trying to stop the killing. Arif calls it my own personal 'crusade'. I try to teach them a way to live their lives without so much violence and torment."

"But I'm thinkin' most of them would probably like you to mind your own business, right? So you end up having to spend most of your time being threatening and scary?"

He seemed to become very serious. "Well, I try *not* to be actually. I don't much like myself that way." She was afraid maybe he didn't really want to talk about it. Maybe she should have let him forget that he was a vampire for a while, if he could. "Though it is true that as a whole, vampires are not exactly a friendly lot," he said with a laugh. "I do my best. Some listen, some don't. I've been attacked, and I've killed when I've had to, but there are those who *are* grateful for my help; those who sorely need it."

He seemed so melancholy, that she felt bad for bringing it up. Time to change the subject. "Would it be alright if I asked you one of my rude and straightforward questions?"

"Wait, let me prepare myself." He took a deep breath, expelled it slowly and smiled. "Proceed."

She giggled at his formal attitude. "Now, it really doesn't matter, but I have to ask. How is it you always have money? Are you working the night shift at Wal-Mart or something?"

He chuckled. "Not at the moment, although I have been known to take the odd job from time to time." He took a sip of his drink and turned to face her more fully. "My father owned quite a large estate back in England; Herald Manor. It's really quite beautiful. You'd like it. Well I don't live there, obviously, but I do still hold the deed. It's been made into sort of a tourist attraction, declared a historical monument and all of that. They hold functions there as well, weddings and whatnot. The gardens alone are absolutely breathtaking.

Anyway, the proceeds are more than enough to take care of the Manor and those who run it for me; the rest goes into my account. I hold other properties as well, here in the states. Houses that I've bought or inherited along the way. I rent them out when I'm not using them. It's enough."

"Then, you *are* rich?" she asked.

"On paper I guess. I've got holdings, properties and such. In a life as long as mine, you do tend to collect things and accrue interest, but as far as liquid assets..." He shrugged. "I try not to take more than I need. I'm not wanting for anything to be sure, but I don't much like money, as strange as that might sound. It's played a part in my life that I'd rather forget. To be honest, I give most of it away."

"To who?" she questioned.

"Other vampires. Young ones who don't know what to do, how to survive. Ones like Mattie, who never even dreamt of such an existence. There aren't that many who need it, unfortunately, but those I do give to, I give all that I can," he explained.

"*Un*fortunately?" Felicity asked in confusion.

"We're talking about beings who steal blood from their victims nightly. Do you think they are above stealing a little money as well? I'm so much more fortunate than most. I've never had to, and even if I had nothing, I'd like to think that I wouldn't do that, but how hard must it be for them?" He seemed to become lost in thought, his expression was kind of sad.

"I'm sorry. Here we've been having a fun evening, the perfect date. And now I'm bringing it down with this dark and depressing conversation."

He looked up at her with a sweet smile. "Darling, I've seen dark and depressing, believe me, this hardly qualifies." He became thoughtful for a moment. "Do you realize that it's been...*decades* since I had an actual date? I hope I'm not too rusty."

"*Decades*? Now that is depressing! Not to mention a little pressure on me," she told him.

"I'm having a wonderful time," he assured her.

"Good. Sounds like you could use a little fun." She found herself gazing into his eyes in one of those moments that seemed to stretch on forever. He was so sweet and so incredibly attractive. How could he actually be interested in *her*, and why did he have to be a vampire?! "Want to go dance some more? I think you've got me hooked." He smiled broadly and stood up, reaching for her hand.

They danced the rest of the night away, until at one o'clock she reminded him that she was in fact not nocturnal, and had classes in the morning. He seemed to feel bad, but she assured him that she had thoroughly enjoyed herself. Unfortunately, it was just time to wind it down. They rode back to her dorm. He cut the engine as they turned in and coasted into the parking lot, as had become his habit, so as not to attract undo attention from those inside.

As they got off the bike and began to walk towards the steps, she noticed that he immediately went straight past the pillars to sit on the third step. It seemed a conscious act, to break any unwanted reminders of the night he had bitten her. That was impossible of course. Here they were in the very spot, under the moonlight. She eyed the pillar for a moment and then went to sit beside him. He had turned and was sitting with his elbows on the step above where he sat, his long legs stretched out in front of him. It seemed a very purposeful pose, as though he was trying to appear as non-threatening as possible. He was watching her as she passed the pillar, and then looked up at the sky full of stars as she came to join him.

She sat next to him in silence for a moment. He looked very casual and at ease, but she imagined he was terrified to do something that she might interpret as menacing. After a few minutes, she very purposefully took his hand. There was still a slight magical sort of tingle there, like a very low voltage current; just the barest humming feeling across her skin. She turned to look at him and he met her gaze with a small smile. "It's almost gone isn't it?" she asked. "My mark."

He looked thoughtful for a moment. Maybe even...ashamed? "The physical aspect fades more quickly. The psychic mark's still got more than a good week left I'd say."

She kept her eyes on the ground, her voice quiet and neutral. "Is that going to bother you? When it's gone, are you going to...feel the need to give me a new one?"

He dropped her hand and in her peripheral vision, she could see him turn to face her. She finally looked up at him. His face seemed to crumple as he looked into her eyes. "You're scared to death aren't you?" he asked in quiet shame.

"No. Should I be?" she asked.

He shook his head and then put his face down into his hands for a moment. "With all of the explaining, running, fighting and dancing, did I ever even tell you that I was sorry?" he asked, looking back up at her. "Did I ever actually ask for your forgiveness?" She just gave a little shrug. "Why do you even grace me with your presence?" He took her hands into his own and made her look into his eyes. "I'm sorry. I am so sorry for the way I handled things. The way that I marked you, it was wrong, unforgivable really. I should have spoken to you, tried to explain my fears, said something! I shouldn't have just..." She almost thought there might even be a sheen of tears over his eyes. "Please, you *must* forgive me. I give you my word, *never* again will I ever touch you, in any way, without your express consent; my solemn promise."

He seemed desperate for her to accept his word. She gave his hands a little squeeze and then let them go, taking her own back into her lap, without breaking eye contact. She wanted him to know her true fears, as much as she could express them. "I believe you. I trust you, but you're not really alone in there, are you?" He looked away from her to the ground. "Will you even have a choice, or will it just be some...overwhelming instinct; the need to let the others know that you think I *belong* to you?"

"I am not an animal. I do have control." He was offended she was sure, but she didn't plan to let it go so easily.

"But is it *total* control, really? Because I would much rather have you tell me now, than find out for myself later. If you were to tell me that it was difficult... If you told me that there were times that it was really hard and maybe it would be better for me to leave, like yesterday; I would respect that and I'd be much more apt to come back, than if you scared me by losing control. But if you pretend that you're infallible and hope for the best... You might pull it off, or the next time, I might not be able to forgive you, if I even survive. That might be a risk you're willing to take. I guess *you* really don't have much to lose, but I hope you'd tell me."

He lost his defensive expression and just stared at her. When he spoke, he had a little smile playing around his lips. "You are a very smart and perceptive girl. And much more accepting than anyone I have ever met, or even deserve to know."

"Why do you always sound like you're carrying out a penance or something? You didn't ask for this did you? Why shouldn't you deserve to have friends or be happy?" He was silent, and she wondered if perhaps his past was even darker than she had imagined. "I don't know what you think you're trying to redeem yourself for and it doesn't matter. From what I know of you, you're a good man now. Aren't you the one who said to me, that we can only try our best to do the right thing each new day? Stop spending all of your time trying to punish yourself for your past. These past few days you finally seem to be happy for a change. Do you always have to be on a 'crusade', or hiding away in seclusion? Can't you just take a break and have a life for a while?"

He gave her a little shrug and a smile. "I suppose I'd like that, though I don't know how attainable it is." He took a deep breath. "One night at a time, right? I will tell you, if I need to; and I can honestly say that I haven't thirsted for you even once this evening. Although I can't say you haven't awakened *other* desires," he said with a mischievous smile. He shook his head and laughed. "Such a weighty discussion, when I was simply hoping for a nice kiss goodnight."

She gave him a coy smile of her own. "Well, *now* you can have one." He had leaned back onto his elbows again and she rested herself on one elbow next to him, as she leaned towards him for the promised kiss. As she came down to kiss him, he didn't come up to meet her, but let her more fully lean into him; so that she felt almost as though she should be lying on top of him. She was amazed at how much she wanted to. She was usually very reserved and almost stingy with her affections, if she were to be honest with herself; intimidated and afraid to act out the daydreams of a romantic teenage girl. But now as she met his lips and lost herself in kissing him, she felt as though things were moving far too slowly for her liking. The caution she had been practicing seemed to fall away, and she could scarce restrain herself from wanting more.

Lying on the steps as they were could not have been very comfortable for him, but the kiss went on and on. He certainly wasn't complaining. In fact, he eventually put his arms around her to pull her over onto him, as she had so wanted to do, but had been afraid to act out. She lay atop him and tried, self consciously, not to push him too strongly into the cement stairs beneath him. She could hardly stop herself from pressing firmly against him as unsated passions awakened within her.

Finally, she broke from him and rolled aside to let him up. She was surprised at herself. She was not usually one for such ardent displays. Obviously, she just hadn't ever been with a guy who warranted such affection from her before. He turned back towards her before she could get up from sitting, and took her face lightly into his hands. He gave her a few more sweet and tender kisses, his tongue only just teasing her lips. She was again amazed at how much she just wanted to pull him to her and love him, unrestrained. She was also aware of the lightheaded haze that his venom was inducing in her, but she was confident that although enjoyable, it wasn't really effecting her thinking at all. This was her, not just the outside catalyst in his saliva causing her desire. Grudgingly he let her go, looking into her eyes. "I hope you had a nice time," he said, sitting up more on the steps.

As if there was any doubt? "You know I did. I'll be sleeping through English Lit. tomorrow, but it'll have been worth it."

"I don't suppose you'd like to stay out a while longer, sleep through a few more classes tomorrow? Or perhaps, blow off the day entirely?"

She laughed at him as her cheeks heated again. "My grades are suffering as it is." She answered, although they both knew that worry over her grades was the furthest thing from her mind right now. She'd almost like to just say, *What the hell?* and give in to being with him, but no, it was far too soon.

"I guess I am a bad influence in that respect. I should leave you to your studies during the week and let you catch up. What are you doing for the weekend?"

Felicity groaned in annoyance. "I have to go home this weekend. Family stuff, birthday party."

"Whose?" Cain asked.

"Mine," she said with a shy and embarrassed little smile. She hated to remind him of how young she was.

"It's your birthday? Why didn't you tell me?"

She shrugged. "It's not until Monday, actually."

"And how old will you be?" he asked with a quiet smile.

"Isn't it impolite to ask a lady her age?"

"Not when the person asking is well over three hundred years older than the lady! No, I don't think that applies. 'Fess up, how old?"

She sighed. "Eighteen," she said quietly.

He leaned in and put his hand to his ear. "What was that?"

She swatted at him playfully. "You heard me perfectly well. I must seem like a little kid to you."

He ran his eyes down her body, seductively. "Hardly. You must be aware that you are far more mature than other young ladies of your age. I love that you are both mature and yet still unjaded and hopeful enough to see the good in people. Funny you should find my 'maturity and cool confidence' sexy," he said, quoting her conversation with Ashley. She was so embarrassed that she couldn't keep eye contact. "It's your quiet and honest insecurity that I'm so drawn to."

He put a finger to her chin, making her tilt her head to look at him, and leaned in to give her a tender little kiss. She looked down again smiling. "I have really got to find you some ear plugs."

He grinned. "Goodnight. I shall do my best to carry on without you. Study hard and I'll see you soon."

"When?" she asked eagerly.

"When I can't manage to keep myself away any longer," he told her with a chuckle. He stood and took her hand, helping her up. "Goodnight."

She started up the steps and turned back to wave, half expecting him to be gone. He still stood just where she'd left him. On impulse, she ran back into his arms to kiss him again. He caught her eagerly and held her tightly as they kissed. After a time that seemed far too short, she pulled back and he let her go. She smiled at him, a little surprised at herself. "Goodnight." She turned and fled up the stairs, this time forcing herself not to look back.

~~~~~~~~~~~~~~~~~~~~~~~~~~~~~

Felicity reached the cafeteria a little earlier than usual. Her class had let out a bit early. She was looking forward to some quite time alone before Ben and Allie would arrive. Once she bought her lunch however, and was walking with her tray trying to find a place to sit, she noticed Alyson already here, sitting alone. Felicity sighed and went to join her.

Alyson sat picking apart, but not really eating a muffin, and seemed grateful to see Felicity heading her way. "Have you seen Ben?"

"No, I've had classes all morning," Felicity told her.

"You haven't talked to him since yesterday?" Allie asked.

Felicity shrugged. "Not since lunch. Why?"

Allie looked very annoyed. "No reason. And what did you do last night?"

Felicity couldn't help but wear a smug smile. "I had a date."

"Oh yeah. Count Cain, right?" Allie joked.

"He's not a Count...I don't think." Alyson rolled her eyes. "Oh, I forgot to tell you, I talked to Cain about Mattie. It turns out that they're pretty good friends," Felicity told her.

"Well thanks for the news flash. I found that out like three days ago," Allie said dryly.

"Oh, sorry. I just didn't think I should bring it up in front of Ben, and you're always with Ben," Felicity explained.

"Speaking of Ben, aren't you just a little worried that we haven't heard from him?" Allie asked.

"We just saw him yesterday Allie, relax. I'm sure he's fine. You don't expect him to keep you apprised of his every move, do you? Cain said we shouldn't worry so much about Sindy anymore anyway. Ben probably had a date of his own."

"Do you know a girl named Regina?" Allie asked her.

"There's a Regina in my dorm, but I don't think she knows Ben," Felicity said in confusion.

"I know *that*, but *you* might wanna avoid her for awhile."

"Why?"

"Well, I called over there looking for you last night."

"So?"

"So, the last time I called it was like one in the morning and she sounded pretty pissed," Allie informed her.

"Great. Why were you calling me at one in the morning?"

"I was looking for Ben," Allie said simply.

"And you thought he'd be in *my* room?" Felicity asked incredulously.

"Wouldn't be the first time," Allie said with a grin.

Felicity let out an exasperated sigh. "He really does tell you everything, doesn't he?"

"Don't bother trying to beat him at Monopoly, he always wins."

"Finally accepted that, have you?" Ben said from behind them. After enjoying their surprise at his arrival, he went around to sit at the other side of the table. "Why are we discussing Monopoly?"

Alyson turned on him with almost furious relief to demand an explanation for his whereabouts. "Where were you all night?!"

Ben was taken aback. "I went over Pete's. He just got a new pool table."

"I thought you were lying dead and drained somewhere, and you were playing pool all night?!"

"What are you, my wife? Allie, what is your problem?"

"I didn't know where you were, and you ignored my texts!"

"So? I forgot to check my phone. Allie, I go out without you all the time. Hell, when you've got a boyfriend, you disappear for whole weekends without telling me, what's the big deal?" he asked.

"The big deal is that I have very few people in my life that I consider important to me. And I would like to know where at least **one** of them is at all times!"

Ben stared at her for a minute. "Ever since you broke up with Greg, you've been hovering over me and making me nuts. You need to find yourself a new boyfriend."

Allie sat back in her chair, folded her arms and took on the expression of a pouting child. "I don't want a *new* boyfriend."

Felicity suddenly realized what the problem was; Mattie. He still wasn't back and Allie was terribly worried. She'd probably broken up with Greg because she was anticipating Mattie's arrival, but he still wasn't here. He must have been gone for a long time, to have her so distressed over it. Felicity felt bad for her, that she couldn't even talk about it with her best friend. Allie shared everything with Ben, but not this. She was all distraught, but couldn't say a thing. It must be hard for her. Felicity thought to try and make her feel better. "Don't listen to him. You don't need anyone else. I'm sure everything will be just fine."

Alyson didn't take kindly to her attempt at comfort. "Easy for you to say. You've got a boyfriend."

Ben gave her a discriminating stare. "Who?"

Allie answered before Felicity could find a way around it. "Who do you think? She's dating Cain."

Ben gave her an angry glare. "You're actually *dating* him?"

"We had one date," Felicity clarified.

Allie smirked at her. "It must have been a doozy!" she laughed, turning to Ben. "She was out well past one, because I called and called."

Felicity looked at her in annoyance. "Thanks for your thorough reporting. See if I'm ever on your side again!"

Allie just shrugged. "Just tellin' it like it is."

Ben spoke quietly and coldly. "You spent the night with him? Couldn't even make it to your eighteenth birthday, huh?"

She stared at him in a mute rage. Finally, she just stood and began to gather her things. Allie and Ben exchanged looks, but said nothing. When she was ready to leave she turned back to them. "You are unbelievable! You know, not everyone sleeps together on the first date! I really don't see how my social life is any of your business, anyway! I'm tired of taking this crap from you guys. Date whoever you want, stake whoever you want. Work out your own stupid problems." She stalked outside to a picnic table, although by this time it was a not so comfortable 60 degrees outside, with the wind making it a little too chilly. At least she was alone.

Chapter 6 - Satisfaction

Cain

DownTime cafe and bookstore
8:30, Wednesday night

Cain sat in the cafe, drinking his coffee and flipping through the art book he'd bought the night before. Felicity had thoughtfully saved it for him. She'd seemed surprised when he'd arrived. "I thought you said I wouldn't see you for awhile? Not that I'm disappointed, but you were going to stay away so I could concentrate on my school work during the week, remember?"

"Actually, my exact words were 'Until I couldn't keep myself away any longer'," he had answered with a smile.

"You couldn't even last 24 hours? And you're always going on about your self-control." She paused to give him a dark smile. "I'm doomed aren't I?"

That had made him laugh. "You aren't doing homework at the moment. I thought you'd appreciate a chaperone to get home safely."

"Oh, I see. You were being self-less."

"Alright, you caught me. I did have an ulterior motive. I really needed a cup of coffee."

She'd given him a big smile and brought out his book, saying for $70 he ought to at least get two nights out of it.

So he sat and thumbed through it as he drank his coffee and tried not to be too distracting to her, although he did find himself gazing at her more than the artwork in front of him. She was beautiful, in body and in personality. Could things possibly progress to a level acceptable to both of them for any lasting amount of time? She made him hope.

She made him want to forget other vampires existed, or that he ever felt the need to perform a service or carry out a duty to others. She made him want to live for himself again. That could be dangerous.

He probably shouldn't have come to see her again so soon, but it was true that he was doing no harm in being here. He spent practically every other evening sitting here reading for an hour or two before heading out into the night. He really didn't plan to keep her out this evening. He would walk her home; that was all. He had other plans for the late hours of the night.

Truthfully, his being here was a bit of a test. He was astounded by the degree to which Sindy's blood had sated him. He had spoken the utter truth when he had told Felicity that he had not thirsted for her last night. He hadn't thirsted for blood *at all*. He had made himself drink a cup before leaving the house to see her last night, as a precautionary measure, but he hadn't really needed it.

He had always drunk only what he badly craved and needed to survive; just enough to keep himself functioning at his normal capacities. A vampire could not really perish from lack of blood, but to deny oneself, was to be weak and incapable. He had never denied himself to that extent, after his initial experiments with his tolerances in the beginning. He knew how much he generally needed, but he had certainly never satisfied his cravings to the extent that he had with Sindy's blood. The benefit from it was still amazing him.

Not only did he feel absolutely wonderful physically, but also his cravings for blood had been non-existent since. A vampire would normally drink at least once every night. It was not uncommon to need to drink two or three times, if the first victim was not drained to death. Cain had drunk from Sindy early on Monday evening. He'd had a cup of blood out of habit more than anything else last night, but had felt no cravings. This would be the third night since he'd drunk a full measure. He had again drunk a cup of blood at home, as a prevention, but that should not be enough to satisfy him.

He'd wanted to come and be near Felicity, to see if she awakened the thirst in him yet. He did feel vague stirrings of it within him, upon seeing her, but they were faint, and he almost wondered if they were the psychological expectation and remembrance of drinking from her, more than the actual craving itself. He almost wanted to spend the whole night with her, just because he could, without fighting for normalcy; as though this were an opportunity wasted if he did not, but no. He did have other things in mind.

Sindy. There had been no evidence of her last night, although he knew she had survived her ordeal. He had kept track of her in his mind for the rest of the evening after he'd left her. She had lain there for some time, in fact he had begun to worry when she still had not moved by four a.m., but just as he had started wondering if he should go to her himself, he had felt Chris move in upon her. He had approached alone, her other boys were heading back to their sanctuary for the day. Chris had gone to her and after a time, they had moved together, to get home before the coming dawn.

She must have drunk from him, just as she had promised him she would. Cain would bet however, that Chris had not been prepared for the thirst his mistress would have had *that* night. Cain hoped that the boy had drunk well before going to her, for Chris' sake.

Tonight he had some experimenting in mind. He'd never had the stomach, or even the desire to test the power his venom provided over a victim. Since Sindy was a vampire, he knew that its effects would not last long. Her body would probably rid her of it in less than a week.

Right now, it was still strong within her though, it had to be. However many times she might let herself become infected by her boys, she could not possibly be immune to poison as powerful as his. He wasn't certain she even let them drink from her anymore. She hadn't been marked, or he couldn't have drunk from her himself. For her it was a power thing. After making her underlings, her blood was probably only given as a special reward, although she probably drank from them often. So while the vampire's she had made were infused with Sindy's venom, it was unlikely she was very used to receiving venom herself.

Cain had certainly given her enough. What little blood he had left within her was surely saturated with it. A new infusion of blood from Chris would try to dilute it, but he knew his venom'd had enough time to entirely infiltrate her body. Long before Chris had gone to her, it'd had a chance to adhere to and infect her nerves and cells where it would not be dislodged, but if he were going to explore its effects, it would have to be tonight. It would begin to fade in the next day or two and after the extent to which he'd drained her, he doubted she would give him the opportunity to try it again anytime soon.

This was not entirely new territory for him. He had, in the past, had vampire lovers; however ill fated their relationships may have been. To drink from another was a very erotic and intimate phenomenon that he had explored on occasion.

He knew from experience for example, that he could not effectively hide himself from her now. Something that he had not really considered before the act, but it probably didn't matter anyway. The ability would return as her mark faded, but for now, although he could still cloak himself from others, *she* would feel him, as Felicity did.

He did have to admit, he was anxious to try out his influence over her. Could he summon her, as she did others? Could he bend her to his will at all; cause her to be unable to go against his wishes? Most vampires elicited very few psychic powers, either because they weren't strong enough, or more commonly, simply because they didn't know it was possible, no one had ever shown them how. He had heard of this power, to hold a victim in thrall, a power bordering on mind control, but he had always dismissed such tales as legends and folklore.

There were so many myths and claims of power that he had found to be untrue, but Sindy's boasts of being able to bring men to her, almost unbeknownst to them, against their will? This was something he thought deserved investigation. He had heard such stories before, but never had the opportunity to truly observe the power in action. He hadn't ever been curious enough to try it on a human victim. Curiosity seemed a poor excuse to go against the careful limits he had set for himself. Of course, Sindy was a poor subject, being a vampire, but he could not even consider that he might experiment with this on a human. Besides, it was time for a visit with Sindy anyway. He wanted to see what her reaction to him would be.

But first, Felicity. Let Sindy do what she would, start her evening off with her boys. He would find her when he chose, the night was young. Felicity eyed him every so often, from across the store. He would smile and return her fond glances with his own. Harold was closing again tonight. He glanced over at Felicity almost as often as Cain himself did. Cain watched him warily and eventually took the opportunity to give the man a warning glare. Harold had better start keeping his attentions to himself, or a more explicit warning might be required. Cain did need to remind himself now and again, that there were other predators in this world besides vampires.

As closing time approached, Cain took his book and went to see Felicity at the registers. "I'll be waiting outside," he informed her gently. He gave a glance back to Harold in the cafe. "Don't let him treat you with anything other than the respect that you deserve." She gave him a little smile and told him that she would try not to be long. He went outside and sat on the stoop under the lights, paying closer attention to the paintings in the book than he had given them in the store.

Eventually she emerged and he walked her home as promised. She seemed a little surprised that he hadn't brought the bike. "We're walking? I've kind of gotten used to the motorcycle," she admitted.

"Used to or spoiled by?" he asked with a chuckle. "I do plan to leave you to your homework this evening, but if I brought the Harley, our time together would be over all too soon wouldn't it? At least this way, I can claim innocent necessity in the time we spend."

"You really expect me to go back to my room and stay there…alone…doing homework? You are a severe taskmaster aren't you?" she asked with a smile.

He gave her a disapproving look that soon melted into a smile. They reached the dorm steps all too soon. This time, he put his book atop the pillar, where he had bitten her that night, and then leaned himself against it. She stood in front of him and awkwardly stared at the ground as two girls passed by on their way into the dorm.

She looked up at him, almost shyly after the girls had left. "I don't have all that much homework," she said with a timid grin.

He laughed and shook his head at her. "Then you'll get a good night's sleep for a change."

She pouted at him. "Wasn't it just last night that you were trying to persuade me to blow off all my classes and stay the day with you?"

He smiled. "It is a very tempting idea, but if I had really been *trying* to persuade you, you probably would have done it, and we wouldn't even be having this conversation."

She pretended to be shocked and disbelieving that he thought that he could indeed persuade her. Then she laughed. "Probably."

"As good as that might sound, I know it's wrong of me to expect you to shirk your responsibilities for me. I've been reflecting on things and I deserve a severe reprimand for endangering your school success. You shouldn't neglect your daytime life in favor of our time spent at night."

"Stop acting mature and responsible, it's annoying," she teased.

He fixed her with a steady and appraising gaze. "I am most definitely a bad influence on you. I *am* leaving you to your studies, so if you'd like a kiss goodnight, you'd better take it, before I go."

She raised an eyebrow at him. "So sure I want one, are you?"

Now he pretended to be the one timid and shy. He tipped his head down and then peeked up at her bashfully. "I was hoping."

She may have thought to tease him, but it didn't last. She moved in to kiss him almost immediately. With the passion of their kiss, he did feel his thirst acknowledge her presence, like a sleepy lion, vaguely aware of the antelope around it, the day after a feast. When the time came, it would seek to pounce, but for now, it was still satisfied.

Another girl approached. She dutifully ignored them as she climbed the steps. Cain had been aware of her all along, but Felicity was startled when she came by, and broke off their kiss in embarrassment. Finally, she looked back up at him. "Will I see you again tomorrow night?"

"Are you working?" Cain asked.

"No. In fact, I can probably even finish all of my school work before nightfall," she told him gleefully.

He laughed at her eagerness to see him. He felt that way himself, but hadn't really expected it from her. "Tomorrow then. Shall I come to your room?"

"Okay, on one condition," she warned.

"What's that?"

"Use the door!" she ordered.

He laughed and kissed her again, and again. Finally, he found himself putting his arms around her waist, holding her tightly to him as they kissed. Maybe he should just forget his experiments with the venom and stay here with Felicity. She did seem anxious for him to remain.

She seemed to read his uncertainty. "Suddenly you don't seem all that eager to leave," she teased him.

"You do make it hard." After a moment, she began blushing fiercely and looked away from him, smiling. He realized the unintended pun and smiled himself. "I thought you were an innocent maiden? You should be naive to such double entendres."

She laughed and nerved herself to face him again. "Who told you I was innocent?"

He blinked at her in surprise. In his day, women defended their virtue, not a lack of it. "I just assumed."

"Because I'm so much younger than you?"

"No. I admit, I may be a little old-fashioned, but I'm not *so* out of touch as to believe that youth promotes innocence. But you, my sweet, have the bearing of a pure and virtuous lady. Whether it is true or not, you needn't reveal. Simply know that *I* see you that way." She smiled and kissed him again. "And not only am I a bad influence on your studies, I seem to have become a corruptive influence as well."

She consciously pressed herself closer to him. "Trust me, I'm not complaining." She gave him a few playful, darting kisses about the lips and then kissed fully him once more.

She certainly was making it difficult for him to leave, but then he began to feel Sindy coming into range, on the verge of his senses. It was the first time since he'd drunk from her, and he was startled by how bright and clear she seemed to be in his mind as she moved closer. She wasn't aware of him yet, but reminded him of his plans.

As delightful as his distraction with Felicity was, he should leave. He knew it was only play; she wasn't really ready to stay the night with him...yet. If he were to test his command over Sindy, it should be now.

He disengaged himself from Felicity's attentions, as gently as possible. "Best we not start what won't be finished," he told her gently. She seemed almost offended that he assumed she *would* leave it unfinished, but after a moment conceded that it was true. She put her arms around him, held herself close for a simple hug for a minute, then let him go, and backed away. She looked as though she thought perhaps he was disappointed in her.

He smiled at her lovingly. "It's alright. I don't mind the wait. Time spent with you has its own worth. No need to look to the future before we're there. *If* and when the time comes, it'll have been worth waiting for." The look in her eyes alone, told him she was swaying towards thinking the time was now. He smiled, it was only the moment. She wasn't ready, and he knew in his heart that if she had reservations about being with him, they were best dealt with before things grew any more serious.

He reached behind him to retrieve his book off of the pillar. "Why don't you keep this for me? I've looked at it all I want, and I'll only have to carry it."

She took it from him with a smile. "Thanks."

"I'll see you tomorrow. As soon as the sun permits."

She nodded and backed up the first few steps. Finally, she gave him a little wave, turned and disappeared inside.

He closed his eyes for a moment, and tried not to think where his spending so much time with Felicity may be going. It was sure to be fraught with difficult decisions, and he wished that he could just be blissfully unaware of the future and live for each night. But that approach was what had caused him to become the man that he was before he died; a man that he never wished to be again.

Sindy was moving again. He was lucky to have found her. He had thought that he might need to go back for his Harley. He'd assumed that she had hidden herself far from town, to avoid him. He knew that she did have access to a car, and had Chris drive them places now and then. Hunting for so many was an endeavor that did require a bit of travel, but he was fairly sure that they never left in hunting parties of larger than three or four.

He had worried that she might bring the entire brood to a different town to inhabit now, just to keep away from him, but fortunately, they were still around. Six guys would probably be difficult for her to move permanently, especially when they were mostly creatures of habit and instinct. Apparently, she wasn't willing to leave them to their own devices.

He began to walk towards her, and pondered what he should do. He didn't really want to *control* her. Even if it was possible, that just did not sit well with him. He just wanted her to stop killing people and to take him seriously.

He thought to try and call her, but then decided that he should get further from the dorms first. He was inexperienced in this sort of thing, and he worried that in being attuned to him, Felicity might somehow pick up some unintended influences. He walked a little further down the street and headed for the woods in Sindy's direction.

He stepped into the dark and silent forest. In moving forward, he was quickly enveloped in its cover and the town was left far behind. Autumn had definitely arrived, as evidenced by the blanket of leaves covering the forest floor. It was almost impossible to walk silently, so he crunched and crackled his way through the trees, stopping every so often to study the silence for evidence of others. Once he had sufficient distance, he decided to try and summon her, as he continued moving towards her.

He wasn't sure how to begin. He cleared his mind and thought of Sindy. He pictured her face and form, her long dark hair, her high and prominent cheekbones and her full and pouting lips. He pictured her large brown eyes and the glint of pride and self-assuredness that was usually reflected there. Having died at little more than the age of sixteen, her body was that of a budding young woman, lithe and thin. Her figure was not quite as fully endowed as it might have been in another year, but it *was* that of a woman, and not a child.

He knew that chronologically she was a little older than Felicity. And she acted as though she were superior to any other she might meet. She was proud and strong; a girl of outspoken temerity and unafraid of a challenge. She was tenacious, beautiful and as much as she would hate it, for now she was *his*.

She wanted to be his, but only on her own terms. Like this, unwillingly, she would hate it. *Good, teach her a lesson*, he thought with a sinister little grin. He wouldn't be cruel. He just wanted to know the effect. It certainly wouldn't hurt her to have a taste of her own medicine.

He imagined a line drawn between her mark in his mind and himself; gossamer thin, yet infinitely strong thread, stretching across the space between them. He imagined the line pulling her to him, reeling her in. He called her mentally, as strongly as he could. He continued to walk through the woods towards her and broadcast his summons. Eventually, reaching a large outcropping of rock, he decided to sit and wait.

The forest around him was silent at first, but once he stopped moving, the night call of insects picked up and sang to him as he waited. He heard slight noises coming towards him, but could not imagine that Sindy could possibly move so quietly. Certainly, she was still some distance away. Sure enough, it was only a raccoon. It came waddling out of the brush, already fat, fur full and ready for the coming winter. It paused to look at him for a moment and then hurried on its way. He stretched out his senses to Sindy once more, tracking her progress and urging her closer.

She was definitely coming to him, although her boys seemed to trail along as well. Disappointed she was not alone, but still gratified by her response, he strengthened his efforts. He imagined himself mentally cajoling and persuading her to come. *I need you to come. I desire your presence, you belong here with me.* He continually sent these messages, although he was unsure exactly what she was receiving.

Finally, he heard her physical approach. She still was not alone, a fact she loudly complained of with a wicked temper. Her brood's obstinate refusal to obey her, coupled with Cain's beckoning call, had put her into a foul mood. Cain decided to fade back a bit, to see if she might actually rid herself of the others so he could approach her alone.

"I don't care where you go, as long as you take them with you! Jeez, can't I ever just be alone? I just want to be left by myself for a while." The others kept a respectful distance, afraid to disobey her, but not sure where to go. Luke seemed to be trying to keep them together and away from Sindy, lest she get even angrier.

It was Chris who kept after her persistently. "Even Marcus? Don't make me take him. He doesn't listen to me."

"There are five of you and one of him. Somehow, you'll manage."

"He doesn't know when to stop drinking, and he gets all pissed off if you take someone away from him. We'll be all night just trying to calm him down again."

"I don't care! Just get the hell out of my sight, **I want to be alone**! I'm sick of all of you!" she screamed. They all seemed to freeze as her voice rang in the silence.

"Even me? You sick of me too?" Chris asked, after a moment. Even Cain felt a little bad for him. He sounded heartbroken. It seemed of all of Sindy's toys, he was the only one smart enough to actually understand and take offense at her outbursts.

She actually did stop and turn to look at him. She too had heard the vulnerability there. Cain suspected that he functioned at a much higher level than she usually gave him credit for. She went to him. "Oh Chris," she cooed quietly in his ear. "I could never be sick of you. You know you're my favorite."

He seemed more perplexed than comforted. "What else did Cain do to you? Why did you let him?"

Sindy stiffened and drew away from him. "You know *why* you're my favorite? 'Cause even though you're smart enough to take care of stuff for me, you're also usually smart enough **not to ask why**." He cringed like a dog expecting to be hit. She abruptly changed her voice to a tone light and sweet, but she still spoke with measured precision that showed she was not to be questioned again. "Take them, and go. I will see you in the morning."

She was trying to stare at them stonily, but seemed very distracted. Chris turned and walked away. "Come on," he said to Luke quietly as he passed. Luke seemed relieved just to be given a direction. They all moved off into the woods and Sindy was finally left alone.

Once they left, she dropped her arrogant facade and was uncomfortable and distressed. It must be difficult to fight, Cain thought. He renewed his efforts once more, just to see if she would come.

She actually did take a few steps towards him, although he was sure that she didn't know he was so close. She could feel him, but she hadn't seen him yet. Finally, she sat down on the same rock where he had sat before, unwilling to move if it killed her. He waited a moment and then came closer, into her view. She noticed him almost immediately. She shot him a look that was perfectly ferocious. He smiled and continued towards her until he was only a few feet away. He did not relent in his summons, but simply folded his arms across his chest and waited for her to respond to him in some way.

"You think you're pretty clever don't you, using my own trick against me?" she asked.

He grinned. "Working well, is it?"

She answered him with another angry glare, until she shuddered and looked away. "I'm right in front of you. You can shut it off now."

"I thought you were to come right into my waiting arms?" he asked, quoting her boast from the other night.

She sneered at him. "Don't hold your breath."

"What's the matter? Didn't you enjoy being there the last time?"

She gave him a thoughtful little smile. "Not as much as you did. Did it *please* that sinful nature, you try so hard to hide?"

He smiled and looked at the ground for a moment before answering. "You have said in the past, that you've only wanted to satisfy me in some way. Congratulations, but as delicious and satisfying as you certainly were, what I did was not only for my pleasure, but also to prove a point. Do not go against my wishes. You will not win. You'll not find safety in numbers either. Next time I'll find my way around them without your cooperation. And don't think running to Arif will protect you; he's no match for me if I truly wished to oppose him. He may be old, but I am older still and I'll not let him think to command me. If you *or* your drones at your behest, should seek to anger me in the future, you'll not find my next reprimand to be so gentle."

"That was gentle?" she asked with an arched brow.

He moved closer, to speak to her more intimately, holding her gaze with his own. "That was only a warning. I know you. I know what you like. I also know what you wouldn't. While it's true that I don't usually care to be cruel or indecent, don't be fooled into thinking that I don't know how. I know you've thought it might be fun to try and awaken the darker side in me, but trust me, it's something you don't want to see. Play your games of being the puppet master, have your fun, but stay away from my friends. That includes Benjamin, and if *anyone* else dies, your ashes will join them." Once he had begun speaking to her, she never took her eyes from him. He wondered if perhaps he *was* holding her in thrall. She didn't move. "Do you understand?" he asked.

She began to nod her head slightly, then blinked and seemed to come back to herself. "Yes," she said quietly.

"Good."

She closed her eyes and shivered slightly. After a moment, she looked back up at him in disgust. "Would you stop already?"

The summons. He hadn't even been aware that he was still projecting it. It must be far easier and stronger than he'd thought. He made a conscious effort to end it. "Not so much fun to be on the receiving end, is it? Just thought you should know what it was like."

"I know what it's like. Trust me." She stood from the rock and began to pace a little as she spoke. "Amos tortured me for weeks before he brought me over. Let me tell 'ya, ain't nothin' *you* could do to me that could be any scarier than what he dished out."

Cain gazed at her thoughtfully. "You never told me."

"Pfft! What for? I already got my revenge. Last thing he saw before Arif turned him to dust was my smilin' face. And if you think I'd be lookin' for your pity, you *don't* know me."

He stood watching her for a minute. Then he became very still, giving no outward sign, but very strongly and clearly in his mind, tried to push her away from him. He had no idea what would come of it, if she even felt it at all. He just wanted to see what would happen. It was nothing dramatic, or even definitive, but she did take a few steps back from him. She didn't even seem aware of it. He wondered if it were coincidence. He now thought to make her sit back down. He gave her very clear and precise mental commands to sit down. She did nothing. She didn't look as though she were resisting him either. Nothing. Ah well, just checking.

Finally, she looked up at him again and sighed. "So, can I go now, or are you gonna be callin' me all damn night?"

He laughed. "I've said my piece. I've certainly no need to force my company on you. One question though, have you fed this evening? Still trying it my way?"

She gave him a sly smile. "I'm not drinkin' anymore of that bagged crap! But no, no humans. Good thing I've got a lot of boys in my brood. Who says it's better to give than to receive? Although I must admit, both have their rewards." She licked her lips and moved the hair from her neck, smiling. She knew how much he'd enjoyed drinking from her, and she loved it. She'd probably remind him of it whenever possible. She stared at his throat and he knew that she wished she could have drunk from him as well. *Sorry, not going to happen,* he thought sternly. She smiled at him.

He could tell that she also thought she had impressed him with her abstinence. "That's still cheating," he said disapprovingly.

"A girl's gotta have *some* fun," she said with a shrug, then turned and walked away. He let her go.

ೞೞ ೞೞ ೞೞ ೞೞ ೞೞ ೞೞ ೞೞ ೞೞ

Part 2 - Telling Tales

ೞೞ ೞೞ ೞೞ ೞೞ ೞೞ ೞೞ ೞೞ ೞೞ

Chapter 7 - Courting trouble

Cain

Sunset, Thursday night
Cain's house

Cain paced the entryway of his house, impatiently waiting for sunset with eager anticipation, so that he could go and see Felicity again. The sun dipped below the horizon and he forced himself to wait a few minutes more, for the blazing hues of the sky to dim. Finally, he couldn't stand it any longer and went out to his Harley, though the fading sunlight still irritated his sensitive eyes and made his skin twitch with the anxious anticipation of pain. He knew he was courting trouble, in more ways than one, as he ducked his head and mounted the bike, but he still couldn't wait to see her. *I'm going to end up with sunburn again,* he thought to himself as he pulled out of the drive and onto the road.

He decided to take a different route to the dorms, so that he might stop for a few things on the way. By the time he reached Felicity it was fully dark. He felt a pang of regret upon his approach, as he saw that her mark was fading. It was still evident though, and she still felt it as well. She opened the door before he even knocked. "Hi, come on in."

He entered the room as she turned to put away the schoolbooks she had left scattered on the bed. He watched her straightening up, amazed at how comforted he felt just to be near her; as though looking upon her loveliness and being in the presence of her pleasant spirits lifted the pall of darkness he could never otherwise seem to shake.

She noticed him watching her, and he sought something normal and practical to say, rather than speaking the phrases of poetry that drifted through his mind like a love-struck fool. "I see you've been working."

"I didn't want you to have any excuses to bring me home early. I'm all done."

"If you were truly done they wouldn't still be out," he responded with a laugh. As he came further into the room and closed the door, the distasteful smell of some fried food assailed his nostrils. He tried to ignore it, but she noticed the unsavory expression on his face. "I'm sorry," he began, "but I have to ask, *what* is that smell?" She seemed startled and sniffed a bit to see what he was even talking about. It must not seem as strong to her.

She giggled in embarrassment. "My dinner, I guess. I'm sorry, does it bother you?"

He got the distinct impression that she thought it might be distasteful to him *because* he didn't need to eat. "Food in general doesn't, but *that* smells only like burnt onions in a great deal of grease."

"It was a Philly cheese steak. Not a stunning example of its kind, I'll grant you, but I can't believe you can even smell it anymore. I finished it over an hour ago."

"I've got a rather keen sense of smell. Lucky me. Remind me to take you out for a real dinner sometime."

She laughed, and then looked horrified. "Oh my God! You'll probably think I smell like that too! I'll be right back." She grabbed a toiletry case and headed out the door, to the bathroom he assumed. He smiled and shook his head. He wandered around the room, which was a bit messy but not terribly so. He loved to look at her things. Scarves and jewelry were strewn about her dresser. Schoolbooks and papers with little doodles around the edges were piled there as well.

Pictures were stuck into her mirror frame. One was of her, with her parents at her high school graduation, another of Felicity and another pretty girl in swimsuits at the beach. Cain's glance lingered on Felicity in a modest but still alluring bronze bikini. She practically glowed with the sunlight upon her, her long hair, blowing in the wind. The other girl was lovely as well, with short dark hair and a mischievous little smirk on her face, but to him, Felicity shown with a radiant beauty unlike any other. To him she was just beyond compare.

He forced his eyes from that photo and moved on to the next. Two others were of her with Ben and Alyson at the dance. In one, they had all posed sedately, wearing their mandatory 'photo smiles', in the other, Ben had an arm around each girl's waist and must have been tickling them both. They were all laughing and both girls seemed to be trying to squirm out of his grasp.

In both pictures, Felicity looked absolutely gorgeous. Cain envied Ben terribly for the fun they seemed to have had. He looked into the mirror, and of course saw only the contents of the bedroom reflected back at him. There would be no pictures of him in her frame. Film wouldn't accept him any better than the mirror itself.

He also noticed that the boy he had seen escort Felicity to the dance, was not in either picture. When Cain had seen the boy there, he hadn't even been with Felicity. Obviously, it had been nothing serious.

He observed a stack of books on the dresser. The top one had caught his eye. It was entitled *17th Century Life, Tales of a Quaker Community*. Curiously, he flipped through a few pages. There were many pictures of a recreated village, with players costumed to the period. It was a very basic description of everyday life in a farming community of the time. It was strange to look at; the village could have been his own.

He closed the book and perused the other titles in the pile, more of the same, with a few witch trial accounts thrown in. He smiled to himself. Homework? He doubted it. She was studying him. He wandered over to the other side of the room and was looking at one of her anthropology texts when she came back through the door.

She returned, smelling of mouthwash and the citrus body spray that she had worn the other day. She came close to him and smiled. "Sorry about that. How do I smell?" She leaned in for him to sample. Of course, stepping in close to a vampire and tilting your head to bare your throat, so that they may *smell* you is normally not a wise thing to do. He knew she was teasing him, seeing how he would take it, he assumed.

He dutifully leaned forward to breathe her in and then whispered into her ear. "Delicious." He chewed his bottom lip a bit, as she looked up at him and smiled. Yes, he was definitely bringing out some new, daring tendencies in this girl. She, who had first struck him as so timid, was now beginning to like a little taste of danger. He glanced about the room again, his gaze lingering a bit on her bed. Indecent thoughts flitted through his head, but no, he would keep to his previous agenda. "Let's get out of here, hmmm?" he suggested.

"We don't have to *go* anywhere. I'd just like to sit and talk."

"You read my mind." He walked in front of the spare bed and took hold of the end of its comforter. "May I?"

She looked confused, but agreeable. "Go ahead."

He pulled it off of the bed and draped it over one arm. He held out the other arm for her to take. "Shall we?"

She laughed and grabbed his denim jacket off the chair before they walked out the door. "What are we doing with that?"

"You'll see."

Chapter 8 - What's in a name?

Felicity

The Dorm Parking Lot
8:00, Thursday night

Felicity took Cain's arm as they made their way out to the parking lot and his waiting motorcycle. He held the comforter draped over one arm, and she wondered where they were going and what exactly he might have in mind. It was a challenge to fold and store it on the bike, while leaving room for the two of them, but they managed. She noticed he had a picnic basket strapped to the back as well; obviously, he had their evening all planned.

He took her to the park, deserted in the darkness. There was an area of grass in front of the little spillway that let the stream fall into a pond for the ducks. To Felicity it all seemed terribly romantic, to be picnicking out here next to the little waterfall alone in the dark, just the two of them. It was like something she would read about in a novel, not actually be out here doing with someone, but then, Cain himself often seemed a little surreal compared to other people in her life. The grass was damp from the mist off the pond, but he had anticipated that. He pulled a plastic tablecloth from the picnic basket to spread on the ground and motioned for her to sit.

"It's a bit colder than I'd hoped, but that's what this is for." He shook out the comforter and draped it over her shoulders. She laughed and then looked at him thoughtfully as he began to unstrap the basket from the back of the bike.

"Do you feel it too, the cold? I mean, does it bother you?"

He stopped and looked at her in surprise. "I feel everything, same as you. I might not notice it quite as much. My body doesn't take the cold as the warning sign that yours does, but I feel it. I'm not going to die of exposure, but I'd rather not sit out here and shiver." She gave him an embarrassed little smile.

Cain put the picnic basket onto their ground cover and began to go through it. He took out a bottle of wine with two glasses, cheese and crackers, a bunch of grapes, some paper goods, a large pillar candle and a book of matches. He wedged the candle into the dirt next to them and lit it. Then he put out the grapes, cheese and crackers before her, on a paper plate with a little plastic knife. She stared at it all for a moment. "Okay, another rude question. Can you actually eat that?"

"Sure I can. Vampires are a sophisticated predator, meant to mimic their prey. Not a very good disguise if they can't do all that the prey can do. Besides, my body really hasn't changed all that much.

I don't know why some things continue while others do not. For example, my hair and nails still grow as always, but my heart no longer beats. Perhaps it's an outward appearance thing. The force that keeps me animate doesn't waste energy on that which doesn't show, but if I eat something, it'll pass through my body normally. I just don't really get anything out of it. Blood supplies all that my body needs now. I don't *need* food and I don't usually bother to eat, but I can."

He sat across from her on the cloth and she held up an end of the comforter, an offer for him to come and snuggle next to her. He gave her a sly smile. "I'm not quite shivering yet, but don't think I won't take you up on the offer later. If I come over there now, I will be sorely tempted to forget my original plans for the evening, and you won't get a chance to ask me all the other questions that I can often see hiding behind your shy smiles. You wanted to talk, and I had planned that we should talk as well. I'm giving you free reign; ask me anything."

She gave an abashed little giggle. Was her curiosity about him so obvious? She thought for a moment and then, leaned forward to swipe his hair back out of his eyes. "Who cuts your hair?"

He looked at her strangely and laughed. "Of all things to ask, that's your question?"

"Well, I can't imagine what would happen if you walked into a salon full of mirrors! They'd faint! Your hair's a little long, but it's nicely cut. It'd be pretty difficult to get such nice even layers when you can't see yourself. I can't even cut my own bangs!"

He chuckled. "There's a woman in Connecticut, she cuts it at her house. She thinks it's against my religion to see my reflection."

"You're teasing me!" she accused him with a smile.

"No it's true! She's not the brightest, but she's sweet. She does the job and she doesn't question it. I pay her rather well not to. When I'm passing through, I stop by her house. Usually about twice a year. Unfortunately, I'll have to find someone else soon though."

"How come?" she asked.

"I've been going to her for over twenty years now."

She was still confused. "So?"

"So, people do tend to notice when two decades go by and I haven't aged at all," he explained.

"Oh, right." He poured her a glass of wine. He almost looked as though he thought she might refuse it. He'd never known her to drink alcohol, but she accepted it without comment. "Wow, you'll never look any different, huh?"

"Nope. Unless I change my hair of course, but you'd be surprised how little such things seem to matter, when you can't see yourself." He poured a glass for himself and put down the bottle.

"How old were you?" she asked.

"27." He didn't even hesitate, he seemed to know just what she meant.

"No you weren't! You don't look it," she insisted.

He shrugged. "So, you've got a birthday coming up, big party at home?"

"Not really, just a birthday dinner. I'd invite you, but besides the obvious obstacles, I wouldn't want to subject you to a weekend with my family anyway."

He laughed. "I'm sure they're delightful."

She rolled her eyes at him and shook her head. "They're okay I guess. So when's *your* birthday?"

"I don't really celebrate it anymore," he told her.

"Why not? Everybody deserves a special day. When is it?"

"To be honest, there's enough celebration going on that day without me. It's Christmas."

"Really? It isn't on the actual day is it?"

"Sure it is. That's where I get my…name." He trailed off and looked seriously shaken. It seemed almost as if he'd forgotten, as though he were human and just having a regular conversation. She was looking at him in confusion. He shook his head a little and sighed as he looked back up at her, as if to apologize. She held his gaze. "Christian. That was my name, before. I was born on the very same day that we celebrate the birth of our Lord Jesus Christ. Guess you can see why I changed it. Not exactly a fitting name for someone who can't even touch a cross."

"Christian." She whispered the name quietly to herself while studying his face, 'trying it on him', as it were. "I like it," she said quietly.

"Me too. Pity it doesn't fit any longer, not that it ever really did."

"Why 'Cain'?" she asked.

He looked as though he'd swallowed something bitter. "Thought that'd be obvious."

She had searched out her mother's bible, the last time she'd been home, and read those few passages in Genesis, regarding 'Cain'. "Because Cain slew his brother, Abel, just as vampires kill humans?"

"I suppose that would loosely fit. Unfortunately, it's much more literal," he said.

She swallowed and forced herself to say it. "You killed your own brother?"

"Charles. Yes, I did. I killed my own brother, after having a very long and sordid affair with his wife," he confessed.

She was staring at him, not judgingly or with horror, just an empty sort of stare, waiting to try and understand why. For a moment, he looked as though he wanted to try to give her some plausible explanation, a justification that would hold the blame from himself, but then he just shook his head in resignation. He took a slow, deep breath. "I don't really want to start the story there, but I thought it best I get it out, before I lost the nerve. Now I'll *have* to tell you, the story complete."

She had prepared herself for this. It was something she had often thought about, lying alone in bed at night and thinking of him. She had assumed there were dark things in his past, he'd even hinted at them before. He was a creature that drank blood to survive and was over three hundred years old. It would be very naive to think that he hadn't a single death on his hands.

She had imagined the time when he might feel close enough to her, to actually trust her with the confessions of his past, but she had never thought it would be this soon. Wasn't he afraid that he would frighten her away from him? He certainly wasn't trying to sugarcoat it. She realized that was the reason he had blurted it out the way that he did, so that he would not have an excuse. So it wouldn't sound like something that could be rationalized into an act that she could sympathize with; it would sound the cold and hideous act that it must have been.

He stared at his wine glass and began to tell her, very slowly and deliberately, about his life. A sentence he had passed upon himself, that she should know the man that he was. "I suppose I should really begin ten years *before* I died. Just after my seventeenth birthday. January 1682, that was when my father disowned me."

"For what?"

"Well, I'm sure he could give you many answers to that question, all of which would be perfectly justified, but to sum it up, I'll just say, for being a rebellious teenager. Of course, that saying would hold a little more weight back in those days. Children were not considered children for long. We were expected to grow up all too soon and rebellion was not accepted. At the age of seventeen, I saw myself as very much a man, even if the reality was that I was a very spoiled and disrespectful child.

We were still in England then and you have to understand, my father was a man of some prestige. He held a title, and connections to the King. He had wealth and power, things that as his son, I enjoyed very well. But with those things came responsibilities, obligations and a certain image to be maintained, all of which I couldn't care less for.

I had always been a troublesome child. Luckily, my older brother Charles could always be counted upon to 'cover my trail', as it were. He would keep father from knowing the full extent of my transgressions when he could. Charles could usually get his hands on enough money when needed, to help smooth over whatever trouble I'd gotten into or replace things broken.

'Round about my sixteenth birthday however, I had discovered that money could buy much more than just material things. It could easily buy the favors of women as well. By the time I reached seventeen, I was living quite the life of sinful excess. My father was too busy with his own business and affairs to tend much to me. My mother had passed away some years before, and although my brother cared for me greatly and tried to advise me, I never listened to him, and he couldn't dictate my actions. He had his own life to keep in order.

Charles was five years my senior, and in fact he was newly married that year, to Maribeth." Cain spoke her name, pronounced with a short 'i', like in the word 'marigold', letting its familiar sound roll off his tongue for the first time in so many years. "She was a delectable young beauty, but from a humble family and had no notable connections. She did have grand designs however, and an unshakable determination. She endeavored to put herself into my brother's path and once he laid eyes on her, he was lost. Charles thought that the sun rose and set in that girl.

I don't know if she ever loved him. Charles was handsome and charming to be sure, but it was clear to me from the start that Herald Manor was her goal. Charles was the eldest son of a Lord, set to inherit title, estate, wealth and status. She was enamored of the idea, more than my brother, I do believe.

But Charles loved her, of that there was never any doubt. So as you can imagine, he was kept rather busy that year, what with the wedding, moving Maribeth in and establishing her as the new Lady of the Manor; introducing her into the social circle of the court and doing all he could to make her happy; far too busy to worry much about me.

Let me try to describe an average day of my life back then for you. On a typical day, I slept and lay about until tea, 4:00 p.m., dressed and attended dinner with the family, then went out for the evening. As a young man of some social status, there was never a shortage of invitations. I spent my early evenings at various social engagements, balls and benefits: my design, to impress the young debutantes there. Often Charles and Maribeth would attend, but I always endeavored to escape them. Then I would wander out to spend the rest of the night with liquor and loose women, until staggering home with the dawn."

"At seventeen?" Felicity asked incredulously.

He shrugged. "Such was my life. One particular evening, there was some party or other that was significant to my father. He was always being invited to attend important events. I don't remember what it was for; in fact, I don't remember much of it at all, but apparently, I arrived drunk out of my skull, with a woman of extremely questionable morals on my arm. I'd probably staggered in straight from the local brothel I imagine."

"They let you into a brothel at seventeen?" she asked in disbelief. She was still having a very difficult time picturing this, especially from Cain.

He let out a breath of a laugh and shook his head. "Things were different then. I was sixteen when I became a regular. The 'ladies' there were quite enamored of me. You can imagine what it did for my ego. They had me convinced that they liked the look of me, and my 'manly charms', but looking back I know it was my father's money that they really liked."

Cain paused to refill his glass, causing Felicity to realize she'd hardly taken a sip of hers. She had been sitting as though spellbound. Now she did take a sip of her own, in fact she drank it half-empty.

"Anyway, I'm sure I said outrageous things and embarrassed father terribly. It wasn't the first time either, but he was determined that it be the last. So he cut me off, kicked me out and told me that I was no longer worthy of the 'Herald' name.

I'm sure he expected only to impress the significance of my actions upon me. Everyone, including father expected me to come crawling back with apologies I'm sure. What else could I have done? I'd no skills or any idea of life in the real world. I'd been schooled by a private tutor of course, so I could read and write, albeit not well. I'd only performed to the absolute minimum that was required of me. Learning was not a love of mine then.

I did gather what little money I could lay my hands upon and take a room at the local inn, thinking to stay there until fallen pride or some unimagined cleverness allowed me to regain my place. While I was there, taking a meager meal downstairs in the tavern, I overheard a conversation that was to change my life. There was a man there, telling another of a journey he was to take. Come the summer, he was to sail to the colonies, to start a new life.

I eagerly introduced myself and asked that I might learn more of his plans. It turned out that he was going to join a community already established, but in need of supplies and eager for growth. It was a modest farming village, but they were prospering, and asked for nothing from new members, but a willingness to assume a productive role in their community. You needn't be a member of a specific branch of the church or have any special skills. They simply wanted the freedom to live a Godly life, apart from the rule of the King. They believed that God would call those who would come, and that they would be joined into the group only if it was his will. They had faith, trust and open hearts to any who would be eager to unite with them.

They would expect me to work and earn my place somehow, if I went, but at the time it certainly sounded more appealing than begging back to my father. I was very prideful and arrogant, and unwilling to accede that I might have gotten just what I had deserved.

And so, the very next day, I snuck back to the estate and pilfered whatever I might get my hands on. After visiting a few pawnshops, I booked myself passage upon 'The Lamb'. It was a ship of Penn's fleet, destined to leave Liverpool the end of June, bound for

Pennsylvania. It was a small ship, mostly carrying cargo for the colony; nails, glass, gunpowder and the like, but they did have some forty passengers or so, and I was to be one of them."

Cain paused for some more wine and Felicity all but finished her own, and then popped a few grapes into her mouth. The evening had taken a far different turn than she had expected, but now she realized that he had probably planned it this way. He would not be telling her his story at this time, if he hadn't truly been ready for her to know. Now she understood that he had conspired to tell her of his past now, purposely, at just this point in their relationship.

The last few times she had seen him, she had begun to think that regardless of the doubt that lay in their future, she still wanted to get closer to him. She couldn't help it. She was so terribly drawn to him; it wasn't anything as unnatural as the venom in his bite or his kiss, it was simply him. However unwise, she was falling in love with him and seemed powerless, even unwilling, to try and prevent it. Her resistance against him was fading even faster than her mark and she knew that soon she would want to take things further than she ever had with another. He must know it too. So he had planned to tell her his past before things went any further. He was such a good and decent man. Could he really have done something as awful as killing his own brother?

She could easily picture him among nobles and debutantes in 17th century England, but patronizing brothels and arriving places so drunk that he could hardly even remember it? That just was not the Cain she knew. She was very glad of that though, because she never had any doubt that he spoke only truth. The fact that these acts seemed so unlike him, showed her how much he must have changed.

But *do* people ever really change *that* much? She remembered her friend Deidre telling her once, that people are incapable of drastic personality change. They may find a way to cover up and hide their tendencies to do things that got them into trouble in the past; but those tendencies never really left them. They always wanted to do the things that were bad, they just controlled the urge or made sure that others never knew. Of course, Deidre had come to this conclusion after her boyfriend had cheated on her…again, but what if it were true?

If that were the case, then just how stupid was she, to think that she would want to get close to a self-professed murderer; someone who had betrayed the trust of people that were close to him and then ended his brother's life?

No, she could not be so rigid as to think that people couldn't change at all. She would have to let him tell her the rest of his story, before she could decide. He'd lived ten more years from where he'd started the narration, before being turned into a vampire. Obviously his life had changed a lot, perhaps his character had too. And if not…well, dying had to change a person for sure. Also, any opinions people might have about the ability to change, were based on humans, in their lifetime. How much more could a person learn, to change their outlook, if they lived centuries longer?

Cain seemed lost in thought himself, and to be drinking quite a bit more wine. She caught his attention and nodded towards the bottle. "Not planning on getting 'drunk out of your skull' tonight I hope?"

He seemed a little embarrassed, but smiled. "It might make for an easier telling and a more interesting story, but I couldn't even if I wanted to. Doesn't work very well on vampires. I feel it a little, but my body cures it in me, like any other disease or poison, before I could ever get more than a slight buzz anyway."

"Oh. So go on. You were planning a voyage on 'The Lamb'," she laughed. "On 'The Lamb'. Isn't that slang for like, 'on the run'? And you were running from your father, that's kind of funny."

"I hadn't thought of that. Of course, that expression didn't even come into being until at least two centuries later. No, I believe the ship was named as 'The Lamb Of God', a sort of humbled sacrifice. There was a saying prevalent back then, that 'God tempers the wind to the shorn lamb'. Meaning that God is merciful to those humble and unassuming, like a lamb. That's why 'The Lamb' is also another title for 'The Christ'." He looked perplexed. "Which also sort of fits, being my name was Christian then," he laughed. "Whatever. I hadn't made any of those connections then; that was just the name of the ship.

Anyway, to tell you the truth, I began having serious second thoughts about even going. As much as I wanted to show my father that I didn't need him, I didn't really want to have to *work* for a living. I began to think that I would try to use the boarding pass as a sort of threat, to get my father to change his mind. I still had over four months before we'd set sail. As tired as my father was of my shenanigans, I was sure he wouldn't want me to partake of such a dangerous journey and perhaps be really lost to him. I was also vaguely aware that the colonies had always been a bit of a sore point with him, although I never paid much attention to his rambling arguments with Charles over dinner. Politics were not an interest of mine either.

I requested a formal dinner invitation, at my own house. Then I sat at the table with my father, Charles, and Maribeth, and announced my plans to voyage to the new world. As I had expected, my father was outraged. He ranted and raved about how he was a staunch supporter of the King, and he thought the colonists were fools who didn't know a good thing when they had it here in the mother country. If they wanted to help expand our borders and bring wealth and resources to England, fine, but he wouldn't have his own son as one of them! I should be reasonable. I should be willing to take on certain responsibilities, conducting myself in a manner befitting a young man of my position. Then he would accept my return.

What I did *not* expect was my brother's enthusiastic response. He thought the whole thing to be an absolutely brilliant idea! He was thrilled at the prospect of beginning anew. Owning and working your own land, edging out to new horizons. He defended me vehemently, and as you can imagine, I was not particularly grateful for his help.

Maribeth seemed to abhor his excitement as much as I, especially when Charles announced that he thought perhaps a move to the new world would be in order for she and himself as well. Father began protesting anew, about a total lack of responsibility in his sons. Maribeth looked at Charles in shock, as though he'd gone insane.

What I did not know at the time, was that Charles and Maribeth had been having their own troubles at home. You have to realize that Charles had been considered quite the catch in our circles. He never cared much for impressing others, but he was one of the most coveted of the eligible bachelors of our time. The debutantes and ladies of class that we knew were none too happy to find that Charles had given his hand to a very young girl of no account. So you can guess how unwelcome she might have been made to feel.

Not only was she the target of much whispered slander and backstabbing among their peers, but as it turned out, the household staff could not stand her either. Apparently, she took her role as 'Lady of the house', much too literally. She was turning the manor upside down to suit her own wishes and the servants were none too happy about it. My father hadn't really paid it mind as of yet, he was always wrapped up in business. Charles had followed along behind her though, trying to smooth ruffled feathers and keep peace. So a change of scenery probably sounded rather good to him right then.

Maribeth had a simple solution to her own problem however, if no one else's. She cut him off about the idea of a move right quick, by taking the opportunity to announce that she could not possibly make such a journey. She was with child.

As she had doubtless expected, this caused quite a stir and flurry of excitement. Charles was beside himself, eager to become a father. My own father also was glad to hear the news. It didn't make much difference to me, but at least it took the focus off my trip for a while. I had accomplished what I'd wanted; I'd laid the foundation of the idea. I knew that I would discuss it again with my father another time, and then let him convince me to stay. I had thought that would be the end of it, but things worked out a bit differently than planned.

Over the next three months, Maribeth's belly began to swell, and she and Charles began to make arrangements for a nursery. Meanwhile, I was still living out of the inn, but was convinced I was making progress with each visit home. Of course, I hadn't changed my ways out of repentance, but without much money at my disposal, I couldn't carry out my old habits anyway. I found my brother had paid the innkeeper, that I might have my room until leaving for the colonies. Charles discreetly gave me a small allowance for food, which I must admit was mostly spent on ale, but he saw I was taken care of. For that at least, I was grateful.

Then, in May, disaster struck poor Charles and Maribeth. She'd begun to bleed. They'd had the best physicians money could call, but there was nothing that they could do. The baby was lost.

Charles was crushed. Maribeth was treated with great sympathy from my family of course, but in society, under the proclamations of sorrow for their loss, there was much whispered contempt and speculation. There were rumors that Maribeth's outspoken manner and lack of self-discipline caused the death of their unborn child. It was whispered that she was so busy trying to be sure that she was in charge of everything at home and arranging various social events to further her own image, that she had put the baby into jeopardy. They speculated that poor Charles would have done better to choose a woman of stronger breeding and proper etiquette, who would have known to rest and take better care of herself. People can be so cruel.

We were still reeling and trying to recover from this terrible loss, when disaster struck our family yet again. My father; he died suddenly, of heart failure. We were left in disbelieving shock. My father had always seemed a strong and unmovable figure, impervious to such things. And yet, now he was gone.

Everything was left to my brother Charles. I was yet to be reinstated; in his anger, my father had been quick to strike me from his will. I wouldn't have inherited as much as my brother anyway. He was the eldest and had first choice of our holdings, including the manor, but I should have received a nice sum for myself. Yet now, I was left penniless.

Of course, I knew my brother would not let me starve. He had always endeavored to take good care of me and guide me in the past. Unfortunately, he was certain that he knew what was best for all of us, whether or not we agreed. When I requested that I return to my rooms at the manor, he declined. 'You may come to pack your things,' he told me. 'But we leave in three weeks to sail for the new world.'

I was confused to say the least. I had truly discarded any adventurous notions I might have had. Living away from home without the comforts to which I was accustomed, for even this short time, had shown me that I would not be eager to try and support myself. Certainly I could, I was a healthy and able young man, even if unskilled, but I had never really worked hard at anything in my life other than impressing women and avoiding real labor. I had fully expected Charles to give me my share of our father's leavings. I would then set myself up in a modest home somewhere and try to find a way to make the rest of that money work *for* me, so that I would not have to.

Charles had evidently anticipated this and announced that I would not be given any money, for I would only waste it on women and wine, and never actually make anything of myself. He declared that purchasing passage on 'The Lamb', was the wisest thing that he had ever known me to do. It was an incredible opportunity to build myself into the fine man that he knew I'd the potential to become.

He was right of course, but I hated the very idea, even if it had originally been my own. Who was he to tell me how to plan my life? He should give me my damn money and sod off! But he wouldn't debate the issue.

In fact, he announced that I should not approach the opportunity with trepidation, for I would not have to start this new adventure alone. He and Maribeth would be joining me. In the wake of all that had happened, he could sense that Mari was unhappy among the Ladies of the court at Canterbury. The baby's nursery at the manor was only a cruel reminder as well. Charles also confessed that he himself was never entirely at ease playing the entrepreneur.

He found the prospect of owning and running a farm very uplifting, if you can believe it. It was something filled with promise and encouragement, when the prospect of trying to take my father's place in society filled him with anxious dread.

He would still hold the deed to the manor, and put some money aside for me into a trust fund. The money would not be accessible to me independently until I reached the age of twenty-one, or until he himself withdrew it and gave it to me.

The manor he would leave in the care of cousins, with the understanding that he would reclaim it if he were to return. In the meanwhile, we would sail to the New World. Charles would use his money to set us each up with a house and to purchase farmland that we would work together. We would give it a go; see how it felt to be independent for a change. Of course, we had a lot to learn, and we would need knowledgeable farm hands and such, until we understood the workings of it all, but it would be good for us, he said; a growth experience.

I was shocked and outraged that my brother would make this decision for me! Then another thought occurred. 'How was Maribeth standing for this?' I wondered. For as difficult a transition as this might be for me, she would surely flounder as a fish deprived of water. Maribeth was young and inexperienced in the ways of the ladies of high society, but a 'farmer's wife', she most certainly was not. She was far too fond of her silk fans and satin slippers. And to be made to give up the manor that she had finally truly obtained? I could not even imagine her response. Harder still was it for me to imagine Charles directly doing something that would so displease her.

I asked Charles as much, and was not surprised to hear that he had not yet advised Maribeth of his decision. He assured me although initially Mari would resist, he must convince her it was for the best. He could stomach society life no longer, and would not bear to watch her suffer the slings and arrows of the ladies of the court. Their slander would kill her spirit far more swiftly than honest work could ever do. He was her husband; where he would go, she would follow.

This was going to be a difficult and interesting venture. We would fail miserably, I was sure, but Charles said we were to give it four years. That was time enough to get crops established and truly figure out what we were doing. If by that time, I was dissatisfied, I could take my money and make myself a life elsewhere. Of course, I was welcome to do whatever I pleased. The money would be mine in four years, on my twenty-first birthday regardless, but what else was there for me to do? He would not allow me to remain at Herald Manor without him. If I went with them, at least he would purchase me a house and supplies. Charles and Maribeth were going, no question. He showed me their boarding passes for my very ship. He was extremely eager for me to join them. I agreed, and our new life began."

Chapter 9 ~ Remembering

Cain

The park
Thursday, 9:30 p.m.

Cain put down his glass, breaking the narration. Once again, Felicity seemed awakened from a dream; she was so entranced by his tale. "It sounds like your brother really cared about you."

Cain tried to smile, an almost painful gesture. "He really did, as much as it provoked me at the time. I'd like to say he was right, that the move was best for us all. It did seem so, at first. Of course, knowing what I do now, I often wonder what might have happened had we simply stayed put, though we probably wouldn't have fared any better. Charles and Maribeth were the people they were, no matter where they would go. Their problems certainly did not start or end with me.

I myself would never have become the man that I am today. I suppose you could argue that to be better or worse, depending upon your point of view, but most likely, had Charles given me any amount of money, I would have lived the life of a 'playboy' until I drank myself to death. They do say that 'there's no great loss without some gain'. I just find it unacceptable to think that my gain might be worth the multitude of loss that purchased it."

Felicity shook her head. "You can't try to analyze things that way. I'm sure things happen for a reason, but we can't think that we know or understand those reasons. I don't know whether the things that happened to you in the past, were a purposeful path to lead you to where you are now. And your life now shouldn't be dictated by actions and deeds from back then. We learn from the past and we shouldn't make the same mistakes over again, but you can't think you know why things work out the way they do. You can call it fate, destiny or God or whatever you'd like, but you can't say that you know for sure why."

"I know you're right. I've said it to you myself, 'I'm not the one making the plan'. It's just hard to accept sometimes. If things had been different, the people's lives that I would *not* have touched... Wouldn't they have been better off never knowing me? A fruitless line of thought I know, but nagging and torturous all the same."

"And what about the people's lives you've touched more recently? How many people would have become just another victim? How many vampires would know of no other way to survive, other than killing people?"

"What do you think I tell myself every night? Those are the thoughts that keep me going. Otherwise guilt and remorse over the past would have weighed me down beyond the capability of carrying on."

Felicity watched him pour the last of the wine, putting back the empty bottle into the basket. "Did we finish that already?"

"You mean did *I*, you've only had one glass. Not to worry though, I came prepared."

He pulled a second bottle from the basket as Felicity took the last sip from her own glass and held it out for a refill. "It's so hard to comprehend; all you've lived through, are things that happened long before my great grandmother was born. It's so very long ago and yet they actually happened, to *you*. Does it get hard to remember? I mean, there's only so much room in our heads, right? Do you forget a lot?"

He'd been struggling a bit with the stubborn top to the wine bottle. Now he finally got it to open and poured her another glass. "Sure, I do. You don't remember every day of your life. I could certainly never remember every day of mine, but I do remember the general succession of my life. Some of my memories are bit foggier than I'd like, but there are days, moments, that are so burned into my memory, that they could have happened yesterday. I can close my eyes and feel them, even now, as though they were happening at this very moment."

"Like what?" Felicity asked.

He sighed; the stronger images were not ones he was ready to share. Their time would come. For now, he would keep to the timeline of his story for her. "Like the day I caught my first glimpse from our ship of these once foreign shores, for one."

Felicity settled her glass onto the ground and then lay back, wrapped in her comforter, to look up at the stars. "Tell me."

Cain closed his eyes and felt transported back in time as he tried to relay for her the feel and excitement of that day. He described for her, his impressions from the image in his mind.

"It was just after dawn when I emerged from below deck, approaching the rail with a stomach full of butterflies. Today would be my first day in the New World. The wind was brisk, the air smelled of salt and I could see land. 'Twas far off in the distance, but looming ever closer through the early morning fog. We should reach it before nightfall. Already it seemed foreign and exotic. I leaned over the rail to try to make something of the dark forests across the water; still too far.

I looked down to the dark waters rushing past, and couldn't help but feel so terribly far removed from everything I had known. But where this had often filled me with fear and dread these past months, I began instead to find myself expectant and excited. Before these four months at sea, I had never been on a ship, much less made a voyage such as this. I wondered if I ever would again. How would our venture fare? Would I be headed home on a ship much like this one, four years into the future; being glad to have this time behind me and eager to return to a life of luxury back in Canterbury? Or would I stay, this foreign land becoming my new home? Would I take to this life well, and meet my destiny here, living simply, as a common man?

Perhaps the woman I was destined to marry awaited me here. That was a sobering thought. Marriage and responsible family living were not notions I had ever seriously entertained, only worries for a far distant future. That was much of my problem. I'd always lived for the enjoyment of the moment, a habit I would do well to leave behind.

I'd spent much time with Charles and Maribeth these last few months. It did make me view them each differently then I had in the past. My brother, whom I had always seen as responsible and level headed, now looked a bit different to me. For although Charles reasoned that this move was something that Maribeth and I sorely needed to revive our deficient lives, I did suspect that for Charles this was nothing loftier than an escape from responsibility. Of course, the endeavor would take much courage, work and planning on Charles' part, but it was running to unknown troubles rather than face the ones he knew.

Charles did not care much for life at court or the effort and canoodling that went into keeping father's investments and contacts working for us. To run the household and carry out father's obligations was something Charles had looked upon with dread. He would much prefer the simple, straightforward challenge of managing fields and livestock, to managing the people and properties of the 'civilized' world. Leave the rest to hired secretaries, accountants and our ambitious cousins. I don't know if I really thought less of him for it, but he no longer seemed my wise and infallible big brother.

Maribeth on the other hand, had gained some slight favor with me as time went on. When first she was introduced to me and for the year after, I had seen Maribeth as a very beautiful, spoiled and manipulative child; very like myself, if I would dare to admit it. We were the same age, she being only a few months my senior. She did exactly as she wished and worked her wiles on my brother to gain anything that she might want, in the very same way that I would do as I pleased and gain things from my father most of the time. That is, until my father had had enough. I wondered if Charles had had enough as well. Was that part of his thinking, when he planned this endeavor? Did he plan to take her out of the world that she knew, so that she might be forced to grow into a woman, instead of remaining a spoiled child?

I had to admit, I'd been rather impressed by the way she'd held her head high, refusing to be beaten down by the attitude of the other ladies of society towards her. Once she'd lost the baby, I'd thought she would be much humbled and broken. It was a terrible thing, to be sure. Maribeth had taken it much harder even than Charles had. She'd seemed so depressed; I'd wondered if she would ever again be herself. Yet, as the time for our journey neared, she picked herself up and carried on with life. It was out of necessity more than anything else, but at least she was more herself again. In that, I thought perhaps Charles was right in saying she needed this new life to focus her energies on.

Yes, Maribeth seemed her old feisty self once again, carrying on with the grace and dignity of royalty, and expecting to be treated as such. However, being that we both were forced upon this journey almost unwillingly, she treated *me* differently now. In the past, she had always viewed me as a person of no importance. If anything, she had seemed to regard me as a nuisance who took Charles' attention away from her, but now, we were prisoners of fate, comrades in our complaints and resentfulness. She had begun treating me more like a secret confidant. Nothing untoward, but someone with whom she could share glances of discontentment and roll her eyes to when Charles went on overly long about his hopes for our future.

But there would be no discontentment today, I decided. One glimpse of that distant shore and I was filled with an excitement that I could not deny. If we were going to do this, I should try to do it right. Maybe Charles would be vindicated. Perhaps we would be successful, building ourselves a new life in which to thrive, instead of living out our stagnant and shallow existences back home. It would be hard work, something I was unaccustomed to, but I resolved to try my best. I figured Charles deserved at least that much from me. I hoped Maribeth would not give him too difficult a time.

I knew my brother and his wife had positively warred over the prospect of coming. It was quite grudgingly that Maribeth had finally let herself suffer to be brought along. Over the time spent on board, she finally stopped her complaints, becoming more accustomed to the idea, but she was still in for a rude awakening. She was stunningly beautiful, but that would not get her very far in running a household on a farm. This girl, who was used to getting things done by giving the right man a hopeful smile and batting her eyes, was in for an education.

The lady of my thoughts appeared on deck, quickly followed by my brother, who immediately rushed to the rail, some distance away. Maribeth, spotting me, ventured to my side, whilst her husband heaved the contents of his stomach into the sea. The waters were a bit rough. Walking was treacherous at times, but she managed without event. I remember her, approaching through the damp and mist, and then the sun cut through the morning fog, to make her red hair shine like a halo of fire. There's something about a woman with red hair that's always piqued my interest. They seem more exciting and passionate somehow."

He was drawn from his thoughts to realize the lovely girl in front of him at the moment was becoming a bit red in the face. Felicity's hair was not nearly the hue of flame that Mari's was, but would definitely be considered a dark red. She was giving him an amused, embarrassed grin. He laughed with a little shrug. He leaned forward to run his fingers through her long hair. He rubbed the ends together between his fingers, holding them to make the candle light shine on them and bring out her hair's auburn glow. "Guess my taste's haven't changed all that much." He dropped his hand and let himself become lost in her eyes for a moment. "But regardless of hair color, who could blame me for being attracted to such an exceedingly lovely woman?" She was giving him an increasingly disapproving stare.

Finally, she leaned back, reminding him coldly, "She was your brother's wife."

He lost his smile and answered her very seriously. "A fact which I was very much aware of at the time. I would have to have been blind not to notice her as a man, but I never treated her with a familiarity unbecoming of our relationship until years hence." He gave her a little grin. "So stop jumping ahead. When I spoke of my attraction to a lovely woman just now, I was talking about *you*."

She was properly abashed and looked down with a smile. "Oh." She took a rather large sip of her wine. After a moment, she looked back up to his eyes, still smiling. "Don't think flattery is going to soften my judgment on you."

She said it teasingly, but it struck a painful cord in him. He took a large swallow of his own wine and prepared to continue. "As well it shouldn't." She seemed regretful of admonishing him and put a hand on his arm. He gently shook it off with a forced smile. It's not as though guilt were new to him.

He began again with strong and measured words. "As I did notice, she was a magnificently beautiful woman, but the only thoughts that came to my mind at the time were that I could only hope that I should find a wife of my own, half as lovely someday. I hailed her with a smile as she approached. 'Good morning. Up for a bit of air?' I asked.

She returned my smile and then turned to look after her husband, still doubled over the side. 'You would think he'd nothing left by now. How much more of this are we meant to endure?' she demanded of me.

'You can see land there, if you look carefully through the mists. I heard Master Tench say that it's only a short while now before we land. You should be stepping onto solid ground by this evening before the sun has even set.'

'Well thank the good Lord in heaven! This has been a bit more than I had thought to be subjected to.'

I gave her a raised eyebrow and a smile. 'Well, I hope you've a bit more left in you madam. This is only the beginning, you know. We are debarking into a new world and it may be quite trying at times.'

'Oh really, Christian! You know as well as I, that this company is simply joining a colony already formed. It's not true wilderness into which we go. I've been speaking to the goodwives of this ship and they all agree that there aren't even any natives living where we'll be. It's really all quite civilized.'

'I can only hope that it will live up to your expectations, my lady.' I said this last with a humorous grin and a little mocking bow. To which she gave me a disapproving little smile and laugh.

My brother staggered over to join us, still looking rather pale. 'How you two are so completely unaffected, I can't begin to understand. I shall never be so pleased as when I might set my feet to solid ground once again.'

I smiled and put an arm around Charles to steady him. 'And what ground it shall be! Look you there brother, it shows even now through the fog. Our new home!' Charles looked a bit surprised at my new found enthusiasm, but as soon as he spotted land, he forgot all else. He was mesmerized. He hung over the rail so that I thought almost we would need to hold him back from falling overboard.

Charles pulled Maribeth to him and squeezed her tightly. 'Have you seen it Mari? Our new home! Doesn't that just sound the most wonderful phrase?' He spun her around and then quickly steadied himself at the rail as he began to look a bit green once again. Maribeth was laughing and I'd felt a bond between the three of us stronger than ever. Hope and excitement tied us together more than sharing a house or family ties had ever done. It seemed such a momentous occasion, a beginning of great times and dreams realized." Cain paused for a moment in thought. "If we had only known what really lay in store."

"Wasn't as good as you'd hoped, huh?" Felicity asked.

"Actually it was, for a little while. We had a few good years anyway. Charles set us up well. He purchased us a good amount of land and had two houses built within walking distance of each other. We did need help getting started, but had no problem finding hired help until we felt sufficient expertise to handle things on our own, with only minimal farm hands. As for the work itself, would you believe I loved it? It sounds bizarre I'm sure, as I'd spent most of my life until then trying to avoid work, but understand that I had never felt the thrill and pride of real accomplishment before. In fact, I don't think I'd ever even broken a sweat, if not through the efforts of pleasing a woman in bed."

He stopped to smile at Felicity's reaction to that comment. He hadn't meant to be crude, but was being truthful. She was so easily shocked; it was rather amusing. He went on to tamer descriptions. "To take bare soil and seeds, and through nothing more than my own efforts, turn them into a viable crop, seemed almost magical! Food for our tables and enough to be sold for profit as well, come right from the ground. It was just amazing to me.

Once I learned the way of things, I threw myself into the work with a passion I'd never felt for anything else. It was a good thing too, besides supporting us, it kept me out of trouble, for at least a little while.

I hadn't ever thought about it, but until then I had taken very poor care of myself. I'd never eaten more than one meal a day and barely picked at that. Not for lack of food, but simply because I spent all my time with alcohol and unseemly activities. For the first time in years, I'd begun eating three square meals of hearty fare. I wasn't drinking anymore, but for ale or wine with dinner. I finally began to fill out my large frame a bit. Running that farm saw me grow from a lank and gangly youth into a well muscled, hard working young man. My face seemed to lose all of its hard and arrogant angles to become that of someone healthy and happy."

Felicity leaned to hold her hand to the side of his face, lovingly. He closed his eyes for a moment, enjoying her touch. Then he turned to give the palm of her hand a little kiss before she took it back. He opened his eyes to see her sweet smile.

"I hope you don't think that I speak of myself this way out of vanity or pride. I'm just trying to help you see the changes that took place in me. Thinking back to those days in England, when I thought I was a man, I realize now that I was really like a large and awkward puppy. I had the height and frame of a man, but not the poise and stature of one who is truly in command of one's faculties.

You know what I look like now, even better than I do, but you should have seen me *then*." He smiled and looked down at himself, shaking his head. "I do remember the reflection in the mirror well enough. I feel a pale shadow of myself now."

She tipped her head to catch his gaze and looked at him in disbelief. "Are you kidding? You look pretty good to me." She actually did run her eyes over his body with a smile, as he laughed. Finally, she took her eyes away to finish her wine and have him refill her glass. He noticed her gaze did still return to travel the length of his body now and again as he spoke.

"Blood does not build muscle. It only maintains the minimum necessary to keep up the 'appearance' of health and provide me with the strength needed to hunt. If you notice, after a time, most vampires do begin to turn quite thin. Never shockingly so, but they would need to constantly exercise their muscles if they want to convince the demon within that they are in fact necessary.

With you, was the first time I'd set foot into a gym...ever. I usually get enough exercise keeping myself from getting killed by young ones who don't like my views, or feel they have something to prove, but maintaining myself is not exactly high on my list of current priorities." He laughed again to see her open admiration of his appearance. Perhaps it was the wine. She usually sought to sneak glances at him when she thought he didn't know.

"The point is, I'd changed. The girls of the village began to notice as well. You can imagine how frustrating that was. Remember, I'd had quite the education with the fairer sex up until our move. Now, I found myself in a Quaker village surrounded by girls of high moral standards and guarded virtue; frustrating to say the least. Their demure glances and shy giggles as I passed were hardly enough to satisfy.

I hadn't found anyone in particular that I thought could hold my interest for more than passing fancy, and I wasn't prepared to offer anything of a more committed nature as of yet. In fact, that may be one of the reasons I threw myself into my work as hard as I did. It proved a welcome distraction. Unfortunately, those girls were not the only ones to notice me. I began to see Maribeth's gaze linger a bit too long upon my form now and again. I ignored her, of course.

Charles worked hard as well, though he didn't seem to have quite the knack with the crops that I did. He took up the care of our small bit of livestock instead and put himself in charge of bringing our excess to town for sale and to barter for things we might need.

Maribeth did have some trouble adjusting at first, as we had feared she would. Cooking and keeping house were not her strong suites, to be sure, but after a few months of floundering difficulty, she did find her place. It seemed that sewing was an art for which she did have great skill. Her mother had been a seamstress in London, and she knew well the ways of cutting and stitching cloth. It came back to her well enough and she soon found her services in some demand as other ladies of the village viewed her fine work. Charles was thrilled that she had found a way for herself to be useful. So he hired a girl, Alice, to come and help with the baking and cleaning, so that Mari could sit and sew to her heart's content. The money earned from her labors paid for the girl and some. It was all working out even better than we might have dared to hope, theoretically anyway.

But Charles and Maribeth had other problems than those of running a household and farm. We lived and ran our farm that way for the next four years. Maribeth conceived children three more times in those four years and birthed none. Each new conception would bring new hopes, only to be dashed as she would find their baby's life running out from between her legs with her blood.

It sorely embittered her towards her husband, who seemed to feel she had failed him. I watched Charles and Maribeth, as their marriage turned cold and they became like strangers living in the same house. Of course, I tried to comfort them in every instance, but there was nothing that I could do. For Charles the best I could help, was to lessen his burden of work, so that he might attend to and comfort his wife. That was something he did less with each loss, I did notice.

Maribeth, at first too proud to let anyone see her distraught, eventually at the end, did cry and sob upon my shoulder of her inadequacies as a wife. She wept of how she was not a true woman, a fact that I thoroughly disputed.

I remember her leaning back to look at me, wiping the tears from her face with the back of her hand. She was so disheveled and broken, but she was lovely still. She was very much a woman of not only beauty, but great strength of character as well. I told her so, though I never meant it in an improper way. She looked at me a bit oddly, and then whispered in a hushed and enticing manner, that I'd no idea how much a woman she could be. That Charles did not appreciate her wiles as he should, for he saw only her shortcomings now, but that pleasing a man was an art she knew well, and if ever I should care to find out just how well... Perhaps she could make me feel more of a man even as I could help to remind her of her worth as a woman.

I gently removed her from my lap as I stood and handed her my handkerchief; one that she had embroidered for me herself in fact, for my last birthday. I told her that I had indeed always admired her for her beauty and spirit, and that there was no doubt in my mind that she could transport a man to heaven and back in her bed if she'd the desire. However, she *was* a married woman. My brother was a fool if he did not appreciate the good fortune that he had, in being wed to such a glorious woman, but that she was still his, all the same. I would forgive her, her transgression and I understood her need for appreciation, but she did need look to her husband, not to me.

Never again did I seek to comfort her, not for years anyway, though my heart did break for her with every unkind glance or harsh word from my brother. I tried to speak to Charles, to convince him to heal his marriage, before he lost her love altogether, but my brother had become bitter and did not take kindly towards the idea that his 'little' brother, five years younger, should think to know more of life than he.

I think Charles resented how well I did adapt to this life. Charles was happy for me, but although he did try hard, it just didn't come as easily for him as it did for me. I think that was grating to him at times. I often wondered if he thought we should return to England. I had decided that I would stay, but when I brought up the prospect of he and Mari returning, he told me to mind my own affairs. He maintained that he would rather live here among true and honest people who shared his ideals. His wife should appreciate that and want him to be happy. She would be happy as well if she weren't more concerned with what others thought, than the happiness of her own husband. There was no talking to him on Mari's behalf and I had to let it alone.

Meanwhile, also during that time, a sweet young girl of the village had caught my attention. She was Elizabeth, daughter of our own Parish Priest. She was a pretty and petite little thing, with long blonde hair and a very quiet and modest demeanor, but every Sunday at services, I would see her, apart from the gaggle of giggling young girls who seemed more eager for my notice. She was different. Her shy smiles seemed far more worth my interest, than the girls who preened and posed for me.

Maribeth did not speak of indiscretions to me again for some time, and I endeavored never to let her find me alone to give her the chance. But after a short time, she did begin to look upon me with improper desire once again, and this time, I couldn't pretend not to understand the intent behind her wanting eyes. As the illicit glances from Maribeth increased in frequency and desire, I became much more aware of the fact that I was sorely in need of a woman of my own. So I did ask Elizabeth's father for her hand, and in due course, we were married."

"Married?" Felicity seemed surprised and almost alarmed.

"Yes," he confirmed.

"She became your wife?" Felicity asked.

"That is how it works." He smiled at her concern. "You needn't worry for your own propriety; she's three hundred years gone, remember?"

Felicity shook her head as though to dislodge her foolishness. "I know. It's just this ingrained thing about staying away from married men, I guess." She took a sip of her wine, and then suddenly seemed to realize what it would mean to him, that she was gone. "I'm sorry. Do you miss her terribly? I mean, is it hard to talk about?"

"Not as hard as it should be, I suppose. Elizabeth was a good woman. She kept a fine house and attended to me, as a wife should. But I had married her because I'd felt that I needed a wife and I liked her better than any others, not because we had fallen in love. I suppose I did grow to love her, but if I'm going to be entirely honest, she never set my heart to racing in the way that Maribeth could.

Just a subtle, but undeniable look of wanting from Mari could make me forget to breathe. And those glances did not stop simply because I became another woman's husband. I always managed to ignore her and to seek solace with my own wife, but it was no easy feat, I can assure you. As I said, Elizabeth was a fine woman, with a pleasing face and figure, but although she never denied me, her own appetite for my attentions and such bed sport seemed sorely lacking. Shortly after we were married however, Elizabeth did find herself with child. We were very happy for the news, of course. And I did rightly assume that having a child would be one of the most changing and wonderful experiences of my life."

Felicity's face immediately seemed to melt into an expression of happy wonder. "You had a child?"

He fought very hard to keep the tears from his eyes, even as an unstoppable smile spread across his face. "A little girl, Amelia." He felt as though he could scarce contain the incredible surge of love and loss that enveloped his heart. Tears were going to flow, but it didn't matter. No one could ever take from him, the amazing love that he would always have for his little girl. He recognized that the proud excitement that was reserved only for Amy was beginning to infuse his voice. "In three hundred and forty years, I have never experienced happiness like she gave me. She was the most perfect and beautiful child. Her hair was like the softest corn silk. Not truly white mind you, but the palest blonde that you ever did see. Her eyes were blue as the sky on a clear summer day, and her smile seemed something that could heal all the ails of the world."

He took a deep breath and sighed. "But I get ahead. I should first tell you of things before she was born. Things between Liza and myself, that's what I sometimes called her, Elizabeth, the depth of our relationship was often less than I desired, yet I endeavored to be a good husband and our lives carried on. Things between Charles and Maribeth grew even more strained. Charles deliberately lost himself in the work of the farm, hardly attending to his wife at all. There were times when I did feel for her, for he treated the serving girl with more warmth.

To her credit, I must say that Maribeth did try to befriend Elizabeth and kindle a strong relationship there. Elizabeth was never unfriendly to her, but she shied away from Mari with an almost instinctive dislike of her. It was almost as if she sensed Maribeth was an influence best kept out of our house. I don't believe she ever witnessed anything to give credence to her suspicions, but our households were kept very separate, even though we still jointly worked the farm.

It was sitting at Charles's table to discuss the sale of crops and purchases of supplies that I most often saw Maribeth. She would hover around us, seeking to serve us tea or something to eat. It was most unlike her and I knew she was just positioning herself to be closer to me. Maribeth had begun to cast those indecent glances my way all too often, after Liza had taken to bed under the burden of pregnancy. I was sure that *I* would never seek to disgrace my brother or my own wife, but Mari was obviously unsatisfied and Charles seemed oblivious.

My own wife refused to let me touch her, once she found that our baby was growing within her womb. I knew that she was terrified to undertake any activity too great, lest she risk losing the child, as Charles and Maribeth had lost all of their own. For her own reasons and distastes, she would never touch me either. As time went on, Maribeth's beckoning glances became almost intolerable.

Finally, I succumbed. Maribeth found me in the barn late one afternoon, storing tools of the field after a day's work. Charles was in town on business and the farm hands had all gone for day's end. Elizabeth was coming near her time and hardly left her bed. We had a young hired girl named Nan in the house to help with her needs. There seemed little risk of being found, and as Mari advanced on me wantonly, her deep blue eyes promised pleasures I'd not known in far too long a time. I found my character weak, and could deny her no longer.

I thought I'd known all there was of the ways of a man with a woman. Indeed, I thought I'd quite the romantic education, but really, what I'd known was anything *but* romance. Even what occurred between Mari and I was not *romantic*. There is very little true *romance* in the world, you know? But still, Mari did give me an experience that I had not known I'd lacked. As I mentioned, Elizabeth was not really one to initiate such play, and the women I had known back home were mostly paid lovers. They surely did earn their money, and I daresay that I made sure they enjoyed their tasks, but Maribeth was different.

I had never been beset upon by a woman with such sheer desire in her eyes. Mari positively *hungered* for me as a man. She was desperate for my touch as no other woman had ever been. The effect was absolutely beyond compare.

Am I embarrassing you?"

Felicity was a bit startled from her trance. She shook her head and remembered to breathe again. Then she smiled. "A little." She took a sip of her wine and stared at the glass. "You're always so, reserved and composed. It's just hard to picture this story being about *you*. Little did I know that the reason you're so passive is because you've already had enough excitement to last three lifetimes."

"*Most* of my life has been very boring, I can assure you."

"Really? Because so far most of it has revolved around sex."

"It hasn't really. I guess it just sounds that way."

"You have probably slept with thousands of women!"

"Not *thousands!*" he replied in defense.

She gave him a disapproving look, daring him to do the math. "Even if you slept with less than ten a year."

He thought about that. "Maybe *a* thousand," he teased, with a grudging smile. "Why does it matter? Just so you know, I may have gotten off to quite the head start in my youth, but in recent *decades*, my life has been rather celibate, if that knowledge makes you feel any better." He stared at her, trying to convince her of his seriousness, until she smiled again.

"How did we end up on this tangent anyway?" she asked.

"Your dirty mind," he supplied teasingly.

"It's *your* story. So you slept with Maribeth, I get the gist. Move on," she told him sternly.

He laughed. "I only wanted you to understand the difference between *that*, and what I had known."

"I get it," she said shortly.

"Do you? Let me phrase it so you'll see what I mean." She rolled her eyes at him and shook her head to show that further explanation was unnecessary, but he carried on, unheeding.

"I've no doubt that your own virtue is more closely guarded than mine was." She gave him a warning look for teasing her. "But surely you have had many suitors, at least; those vying for your *valuable* attentions." She smiled. "And from at least some of those, you must have allowed a kiss." He stared at her with a smile until she acceded this with a nod and a chuckle. "Among those, I'm sure, was an unlucky fellow, whose kiss was simply a touch of the lips and nothing more. And perhaps, there were a few...very few," he added at her raised eyebrows, "whose kisses were sweet; something warm and enjoyable, as a kiss should be. But then maybe...just maybe, you have experienced a kiss filled with such passion...such electric and undeniable fervor, that it begs to go on and on; a kiss after which you can barely restrain yourself from wanting *more*. Might you know what I mean?"

She said nothing, but gazed at him with a hint of longing from over her glass as she sipped her wine and he went on. "Would it be fair to call each of these separate experiences, by the same name, as a kiss?" She looked as though beneath her amused acceptance of his description, she might like to refresh her memory of such kisses again, but she made no move, except to drink more of her wine. He continued with his story.

"And so, I *did* commit adultery with Maribeth. We had sex, but it was *not* like sex that I had ever known before. I found myself unable to resist her charms thereafter. For the last few weeks of Elizabeth's pregnancy, whenever there was a time of opportunity, Maribeth and I would secretly steal away."

"As your wife lay bedridden, pregnant with your child."

He hung his head. "I know. I wasn't trying to justify it, only to help you understand how I could have been so weak. It was unforgivable. I knew it was wrong, reprehensible and lecherous. And yet, she won me over, again and again.

That said, let me describe for you another momentous day in my life. It was September the 23rd, and I was out working in the fields, as always. I had put in a hard day, bundling hay for the livestock over the winter. I'd paused to wipe the sweat from my eyes, yet again. When I looked up, I saw Maribeth, coming out to the fields towards me from the house.

Although she was still far off, I knew her by that flaming copper hair of hers. Even with the condemnation and guilt that her visage brought down upon me, I could not deny that she was still the most beautiful woman that I had ever seen. And as she came to me now, I assumed that her insatiable appetite for my intimacies were what had driven her to the fields.

I felt terribly shamed that I had been so weak in character as to accept her affections these past weeks, but I have to admit that I was still excited by the sight of her nonetheless. It was with mixed feelings that I noted her approach. My guilt had weighed heavily on me of late and I found that although she pleased my eye, she plagued my heart. I thought to tell her that our infidelities should come to an end. I had thought this in the past however and her wiles were always such that I could not bring myself to end it.

As she crossed the fields, the wind tugged and played with her skirts and threatened to unbind her long braid of copper hair. I felt myself tense with the expectation of her advances. Surely, she wanted more of my illicit attentions. Why else would she have come? However, as she drew closer, the stern set of her face convinced me otherwise. I dropped my scythe and went to meet her.

'Mari, what is it, has something happened?' I asked.

"'Tis only your wife, 'Lizabeth. Her time has come at last and she calls for you.' Maribeth was obviously less than pleased to have been the one to bring this news. We did have that young girl Nan, to help care for Elizabeth in these end weeks, but she would certainly be at Liza's side during this time. The other hands of the house and farm were quite busy preparing for the harvest, and so it was Maribeth who was sent to bring the news.

I knew that Mari was sorely covetous of my own wife. As Liza's' stomach grew, it became obvious that she would succeed where Maribeth herself had too many times failed, but until now, I had not seen such undisguised malice on her face. I'd no time for thought on this now however, the baby was arriving!

As I ran back to the house with Maribeth trailing behind, I began to feel my guilt press upon me again. I had wronged my wife terribly, though I hoped she never knew it. I decided things would change. Our baby would come and our marriage would strengthen. My attentions would be for Liza only from now on. Mari and Charles had their own marriage to heal. I would be a new man, a faithful husband and devoted father.

I stopped before we reached the house and turned to tell Mari as much. I didn't want to waste time with many words or explanations, but I wouldn't be too abruptly harsh with her either. I simply told her that things would be different now and that the sins of our past should not be repeated. That she knew I did appreciate what a fine woman she was, but it was wrong for us to be so untrue to our spouses. It was a new time in my life, and perhaps she and Charles could rekindle their own love, even as Elizabeth and I rekindled ours.

She didn't say anything. Not a word. She just gave me a very steady stare. It was vaguely haughty in nature, almost as though she was amused that I should think that Elizabeth could make me happy now. After a moment of silence, I dismissed her from my thoughts and raced home to await the birth of our child.

Some hours later, I sat at Elizabeth's side as she held our new baby girl. She was the most amazing creature that I ever did see. To think that her life came from me, that Elizabeth and I, however imperfect our love might be, had created this truly perfect being! We would name her Amelia Catherine Herald, and she held for me hope that our life would begin anew once again. We would be a true family, and whatever difficulties life held, we would face them together.

The years passed and our family prospered, even as poor Charles and Maribeth conceived and lost yet another babe. In those first few years, I did hold true to the promise I'd made to myself on the day of my daughter's birth. I was a devoted husband and father. Elizabeth and I had no other children as of yet, but we did have hopes of rearing a son one day as well. Although she did not seem any more interested in such pleasures, Elizabeth was the only woman to receive my attentions.

Secretly, I did wish she could be more like Maribeth. In fact, shameful as it was, as time went by I came to find that only remembered visions of Maribeth could please me. So although I stayed true to my wife, I felt an adulterer still. Though I tried to never let it show, Elizabeth surely noted that I was unsatisfied. She didn't seem anxious to fulfill my needs however, and eventually turned all of her attention towards caring for our child and house. I tried to make her feel special. I tried to show her that I felt she was a good wife and mother, but perhaps it was guilt that drove my devotion more than pure love.

I'd no idea how I could turn her to be more like the woman I craved. Most likely, I never could. I guess it was wrong of me to think so, but our marriage was unwell and obviously something needed to be done. I wanted to tell her. I wanted to confess my sins, so that we could purge our relationship of it and move on. I don't think she knew. She never even hinted she might, but she was always a bit colder after Amy was born and I did wonder. Then again, perhaps it was the pain of childbirth that had turned her from wanting to conceive again.

I was afraid to throw myself at her mercy. I was terrified that she would not forgive me, that she might take Amelia and go home to her parents' house, a ruined woman. *That* I could not bear. I'd like to say that I was worried for Liza's emotions and reputation, but really it was my own selfish comfort I thought of. How would I live alone? And what would I do without my precious Amy? Amelia was the light of my life. I could never risk letting her take Amy away. Even if she stayed, I was frightened that she might turn Amelia against me somehow, keep her love from me. So I said nothing.

All of my happiness came from my sweet Amy. I indulged her in everything, though it never spoiled her. No matter how exhausted I was after a long day of work, I always had time for her. We would play for hours. I attended all of her tea parties. I never complained as she dressed me in fancy hats or put flowers in my hair. Her giggles were worth more to me than anything else in life. I used money from my account back home, which I now had the control of, to buy her dolls and dresses. I bought things for Liza too, but she was not one to put much store in material pleasures. She had a good head on her shoulders, my wife. She ran our house as a well-oiled machine; frugal and smart with our expenses so we wanted for nothing. I should have appreciated her more, at the time.

And so, my gifts to her she did accept, but they did not really gain me her favor. I thought I'd done all I could to be a good husband, but I began to feel our marriage turn cold just as surely as Charles and Mari's had. Perhaps if we'd had more heartfelt talks…discussions of our hopes and fears, instead of simply exchanging pleasantries and 'playing house', as it were, things would have been different.

I have to admit that I did begin to treat her more as someone who cooked and kept the house for me, than a woman that I should love. Something that I had rebuked Charles for so many times in my mind years past, but I saw myself as totally unlike him. Charles was lucky enough to have Maribeth, a woman of great passion and beauty. How could he be so foolish as to be blind to her charms? It was his own short sightedness that killed the love in his marriage.

I felt that my own wife however, did bring upon herself any coldness she may have felt from me. For I gave her only that which I received. If she had ever been more loving, and treated me as the prized husband and virile man that I should want her to see me as… Well, perhaps I would have seen *her* differently and treated her differently as well. Or so I told myself. I don't really know what might have been, if either of us had been a bit more giving, but once again I began to notice Maribeth's hopeful glances. As she saw them have effect on me, she tried all the more to lead me astray. After four and a half years, I did finally give in again and our illicit affair was rekindled.

It was late January, not long after my twenty-seventh birthday. Charles was away from home for the day in town, when it suddenly began to snow heavily, out of nowhere. I went over to Charles and Maribeth's barn, to make sure the animals were in, and then I stopped at the house to see if all was well. I knew Charles was not back yet, their carriage was still out, and perhaps *I* should have stayed away as well.

I can't really say what my intent was. I told myself that I was only checking in, as a good brother should be expected to. I did think their girl Alice would be there, so it would be innocent. She'd been sent home however, and Maribeth was alone. I suppose to Mari's eyes, I was there with impure intent. She seemed to expect that I'd come for *her* and she was very glad of it. I did protest, but she wasted no time in stripping me of my defenses, winning me over with kisses and such. I must admit that I did not fight it as hard as I should have.

That tryst was our last transgression. I hated myself when the act was through and I promised myself t'would be the last. As I dressed and readied myself to leave, I became more and more disgusted with our wickedness. I told her that she was to leave me alone thereafter, to look to her own life and stop ruining mine, as though she was the only one at fault in the affair. I was harsh, and it hurt her terribly I'm sure, though she'd never show me.

She wouldn't cry. She held her pride above tears when she could. I guess that's what made it easier for me to keep flinging cruel words at her as I did. In fact, I think I'm the only person who's ever truly seen her cry, other than tears designed for effect of course, but not at that time. I was the one hurting her and so she would shed no tears before me. I called her an evil temptress and threatened that she best stay far away from me from now on. She never even said a word in her own defense. I suppose because she knew that I spoke truly, but still, I was at fault as well and yet I gave her all of the blame. I don't even remember all of the awful things that I said, and I don't really care to. She just took it, until my anger was spent and I stormed away.

Again, I felt as though I should tell Liza, but at the same time, I knew it would only hurt her. If I weren't to commit the sin again, should she still know, or should I try to let it fade into the past? I was undecided.

What happened then, seemed the very next day, although I don't know if it really was, but I know that I was still agonizing over whether to talk to Elizabeth and confess what a poor excuse for a husband I'd been...when it started." Cain felt as though he were growing positively nauseated, but forced his expression blank and his voice steady. "Amy got sick."

Cain could see the fear and foreshadowing of what would be said next, come over Felicity's face. He forced himself to tell the story, instead of just breaking down over his own remembrance of it.

"The winter after Amelia's fourth birthday was a particularly cold one. There had been a wet and ailing summer that had turned the fields to mud and the crops reflected it. We were coming upon hard times, to be sure. The harvest of fish from the sea helped to ease the burden of hunger in the villages, but without the provisions of a strong crop, the winter looked to be long and difficult.

Of course we were far luckier than most. We still had money banked in England that could be used to send for supplies from overseas and that did get us through. We couldn't get much; ships were hesitant to run in the harsh winter. We could have the things we needed bought for us, but getting them sent was a trial. We did get some though. We had dried goods shipped over for our household and were generous as we could be to our neighbors as well, but food was not our community's only problem.

With the cold, the illness came, and no amount of money could keep it from visiting our families just as it plagued the others. It began with a dry harsh cough that racked my daughters' chest and woke us in the night. Soon it developed into a heavy fatigue and ague that affected not only Amy, but Elizabeth and many of the other villagers as well. Fevers raced through the townsfolk and many of them were sent home to the Lord by the time the winter was through." Cain took a deep breath but when next he opened his mouth to speak, no words would come. He could see by her face that Felicity already knew, but this was a story he seldom told, and he felt that he needed to say it aloud, however difficult.

"She was only four. Four short years is all we had together, my sweet Amy and me. She was the light of my life and the sickness put her out. It took her away, just like that. She died, February 12th, 1692." He stopped talking because it seemed there was nothing left to say. A wave of grief he had spent many a night holding at bay, washed over him with such force that he could scarce hold himself silent. Rather than weep he grabbed for his wine.

He drank down the contents of his glass, even as he felt sick from the grief. After it was finished, he threw the glass aside in anger. "Stupid wine doesn't do a damn thing." The weight of loss overcame him then. He did something he had not allowed himself in too long a while. He openly and overwhelmingly mourned the loss of his daughter. He hadn't told anyone of her in so long. Of course, she was always in his heart and he did think of her, but he couldn't speak of her to others usually. Even people he was close with over the years, he usually did not share her with. She was his, his private joy and also his deepest despair.

He'd been so overcome that he had almost forgotten Felicity's presence for a moment. He did not know what it was about this girl that made him want to share his life with her. He had known many others in the past, in longer much more serious relationships, that he had not told, but he wanted to share everything with Felicity. For some reason he felt it very important, that she truly know him right from the start. Maybe that was where he had gone wrong in the past, holding things too dear to share. He had known that he would speak it all to her even before this evening, but now he found the task even more daunting and difficult than he'd expected. He tried to gain control of his sorrow to go on. "She died...and..."

"Oh Cain, come here." He glanced up to see tears streaming down Felicity's cheeks as well. She reached her arms out to him from across the blanket.

He felt so weak and angry with himself for being unable to just tell her, without all of this. He wiped his face, although new tears simply replaced the old ones. "No, I'm fine. I just need a minute. I'm sorry."

"Cain, please." Again, she reached out for him. She tried to wipe his tears and bring him close, but he pulled himself away.

It seemed that she wanted to hug and kiss him. He did not want her kisses right now. "No, I don't need..." She had taken hold of him and did pull him to her, but not to kiss, as he'd assumed. She made him lie down, putting his head into her lap, facing away from her body. He tried to get up, "You needn't..." but she pushed him down again, gently but firmly.

"Just stay." She began to run her fingers through his hair, brushing it back away from his face. She did it over and over in a methodical and strangely soothing gesture. He stopped fighting her and lay there, silent. "Don't say anything else right now. It's late, and you can tell me the rest tomorrow if you want. It's enough for now. Let's just stay quiet for a little."

She kept playing with his hair, and had begun to hum a bit. It felt so odd, that someone should be trying to take care of him. He spent so much of his life worrying about taking care of others. It seemed that others always saw him as strong and removed from emotion. He set it up that way, he knew, for other vampires anyway. To appear weak was to have his advice dismissed. Humans, on the other hand always saw him as some all-powerful creature, good or bad, never as someone in need of comfort.

He lay there for a while, in bewilderment, as the sorrow for his daughter's death took its place back in the corner of his heart where its ache was something he had grown accustomed to and could go on with. His thoughts turned back to Felicity. He turned just a little to look up at her face. He expected to see her studying him, wondering what he was thinking, but she wasn't even looking down at him. Her eyes were closed and her face was tipped towards the sky, as she gently rocked a little and hummed a snippet of some song he'd heard somewhere before. In the candlelight, her cheeks sparkled with the wetness of her tears still, and it gave her a slightly ethereal appearance when seen from below.

She was such a beautiful soul. It wasn't even her physical form he thought of now, although he found that lovely as well, it was her gentle, generous manner. He loved the way she sought to see the good in him and tried to empathize with him. She obviously disapproved of his past, as well she should, but she did seek to understand, honestly, without trying to fit him into some preconceived notion she might have. She made him feel that even where she would disagree with his actions and as the story furthered, surely be horrified by them, she may still forgive him of them. It would change the way that she saw him, but she was a smart girl. She had to have had some idea of things he'd done, by his nature as a vampire at least. She seemed prepared to accept his story and then carry on, as his friend if not more. Many others would have rejected him by now, he knew.

He spent a long time just lying there, gazing up at the stars as she rocked and hummed. Her mark was a pale glow. It was almost gone, but it still seemed to surround and connect them both, and he felt the tingle of it in her fingers when they brushed his skin. She'd ceased stroking his hair and was now just winding her fingers within it, every once in a while taking her hand from it to stroke the side of his face. He couldn't remember a time when he'd felt so at peace. It was probably the greatest gift that she could bestow upon him right now; acceptance and a quiet sharing of his grief. He did hope that she could forgive him when his tale was through, for he knew now if not before, that he truly loved her.

Chapter 10 - A few quarts shy

Felicity

In the park
early Friday morning

Felicity was unsure just how long they sat that way, Felicity sitting on the tablecloth spread over the ground, with her legs curled under her and Cain lying stretched out, with his head in her lap. She stroked his hair and closed her eyes, thinking over all he had said so far. The terrible grief that he'd had for his daughter had broken her heart. She'd felt almost panicked during his telling of it, as though she were desperate to do something to change it. Of course that was foolish, but that was how she'd felt, all the same.

So, she had done all that she could think to do. She had made him lie still and try to be at peace. She had comforted him the only way that she could think how. With someone else, she might have felt inadequate or silly, but somehow, for Cain, it seemed right. He had resisted at first, as though he didn't need or maybe didn't deserve consoling, but she had insisted, and now he seemed content. Every once in awhile she dared to brush her fingers across the side of his face and feel the fading electricity between them from her mark. Of course, there was also still a very real natural spark between them, she thought so anyway. As exciting as the effects of his bite made contact between them, she was glad that it was almost gone. It made things a little confusing, because a kiss from him was wonderful in its own right, just as he had so vividly and accurately described.

She had been almost afraid to let things go further while her mark was in effect. It would be amazing she knew, but a little overwhelming too. The thought of losing her virginity and being with someone as experienced as Cain was scary enough. She was unsure whether she would decide to sleep with him, but would much rather wait for her mark to be gone before she let things go too far. She could too quickly and fully lose herself and all judgment in feelings like that. It would be better to feel somewhat in control.

They had been like this for a while, just quiet and content. She wondered if he was truly happy to remain, or was just waiting for her to allow him up. He'd been so quiet and still, he seemed content to stay with her indefinitely and she certainly wasn't in a rush to end it. She was glad that he seemed calm now. She'd felt so helpless to see him before. Finally, she looked down at him and was very surprised to see him gazing back up at her. "I thought maybe you'd fallen asleep, you've been so still," she said quietly.

He smiled. "No. Just enjoying your quiet company."

She didn't mean to remind him of it, but she suddenly felt tears welling up again over the death of Amelia. "I am so sorry...for the loss of your daughter."

He gave her a watery smile. "Me too. Enough said." He lay there smiling at her for another moment, then sat up and looked at her appraisingly. "It's late, you must be exhausted. Do you have early classes tomorrow?"

"Yes. Why are you suddenly so worried about my education?"

"Because you aren't. Someone should be."

"So I miss a class. It's not that big a deal," she insisted.

"I beg to differ. Your future *is* a big deal. Don't you plan to live in it?" he asked discerningly.

She laughed. "I guess."

"So, it's time I took you back. When do you leave for home?"

"Oh, not 'til Saturday," she assured him.

He seemed relieved. He must have thought she would leave tomorrow. "Alright then, we'll pick it up tomorrow evening."

She smiled at first, but then groaned and tilted her head towards the sky. "I have to work tomorrow night. I'm closing...with *Ben*." She was not looking forward to seeing him again anytime soon. She'd had enough of his judgments and snide remarks.

Cain chuckled. "I thought you liked working with Ben?"

She rolled her eyes and shook her head. "Lately, not so much."

After a thoughtful moment, he smiled. "Good."

Now it was her turn to chuckle. Jealous was he? He shouldn't worry. "You don't like Ben, do you?"

"I like Ben. Ben does not like me." He pondered that for a second. "That's the problem isn't it? Is he giving you a hard time about me?"

She sighed and gave a little shrug. "He's just being...Ben."

"Protective?"

"Sure. You could also add arrogant, aggravating, and annoying, but we can go with protective."

Cain laughed. "Would you like me to speak with him, remind him of his manners?"

"That's okay, I can handle it," she assured him with a smile.

"Alright then, I suppose I'll pick you up at work?" She nodded with a smile. He smiled back and nodded towards the remains of their 'picnic'. "Let's pack this up." He began putting things back into the basket.

"This was nice," she said, gesturing over the tablecloth, and everything, "the way you set this up."

He grinned. "Yes, a very romantic evening, which I wasted no time in turning to tales of deception and depression."

She smiled at him in the waning candlelight. "I'm glad." He looked very confused at that remark; it hadn't really come out right. "I mean, I respect that; that you want me to know, more than you want... Well...that you want me to know." She smiled and blushed at the awkward statement. She hadn't meant for it to come out quite like that, and had a hard time re-wording the sentence halfway through.

He gave her one of his little lop-sided sort of smiles. "I guess it was a bit different from the evening that you'd expected." She just shrugged. "I don't suppose you might grant me a kiss anyway? Come the end of tomorrow night's tale, I certainly don't expect one. In fact, you may decide that I'm not worth your time at all. If I still hold some slight favor with you now, perhaps, just one kiss? Shame to let the wine and candlelight go to waste."

"That depends... How difficult is it going to be, to keep it from turning into something that would make me miss my first class in the morning? Seeing as you're so concerned about my education."

He grinned at that. "I think I can control myself, if I *must*."

She leaned forward a little. "Maybe just a touch of the lips..." she teased. She gave him only a peck on the lips, and then came away to see his reaction. He was obviously disappointed, but made no move. She laughed at him and then leaned in for a more rewarding experience. She teased him with a few more darting little kisses, made into magical little thrills by the remainder of the mark they shared; then she gave him a real kiss. At first, she sought to make it deliberately short and sweet, but the moment it truly began, she realized that would never do.

She knew that she should probably see him differently, in light of the things he had done in the past, but she couldn't help it. It seemed like a story about someone else. He'd changed so much since then, hadn't he? This was not some seventeenth century farmer who was sleeping with his brothers' wife. This was Cain, her strong and confident rescuer, who kept her safe and made her feel so special. Quiet, handsome, mysteriously charming and gentle; this was the man she was falling in love with, not some awful adulterous murderer.

She just couldn't make herself see him that way, not right now. In the candlelight, with her head slightly buzzing from the wine, his kiss was so sweet and disarming. She'd planned to lean over for a short, simple kiss, but she should have known better, before long she found herself melting into his arms. After a moment, she actually found she was lowering herself to their ground cover, and pulling him down to her. It was as if something had come over her and she could not help herself. It might have been the wine, but more likely, it was just him. He lay lightly on top of her, not truly pressing her down with his weight, but she did feel an indecent little thrill as she recognized the hard length of his member stiffen against her. She had never been so sexually aware of someone in her life.

She allowed herself another minute or two of tasting his lips and pressing herself against him, and then she pulled back. As the kiss ended, she felt him take a very deep breath and tip his face up to the sky for a moment. She gave him several parting kisses down the length of his throat, before tucking her head into the crook of his shoulder and just holding him to her for a moment. He rolled over off of her and lay down to look up at the stars with his hands behind his head.

She sat up, thinking to stand, but as she looked at him, she couldn't help but bring herself down for another kiss. He eagerly greeted her lips with his own, wrapping his arms around her, but she forced herself to keep it short. She rose from him and looked down. He was in the most seductive possible pose to her. He lay there unmoving, splayed out and vulnerable, looking up at her with heavy lidded eyes. Those eyes did seem to beg for her attentions, but he left *her* in the position of control. To her that seemed far sexier than boys of the past who tried so hard and always sought to initiate things and be in control themselves. He was so handsome and sweet, no matter what his past. She fought back her urge to lie with him again, stood and lent him her hand to rise. He took it with a smile. He seemed more resigned than disappointed, although he obviously would have been content to stay.

"And so, the evening ends," he said. He rose beside her and then turned and took her face into his hands. He gave her one more very deliberate and seductive kiss, fully tasting and teasing her with his tongue. It wasn't long, but even as he sought to end it, pulling slowly away from her, he sucked just a little on her lower lip. It sent a thrill through her that made her feel as though she should simply like to lie down and pull him onto her again.

That was most likely what he wanted her to feel, but she knew she needed to leave. This was not the night, not yet. She felt a little tipsy from the wine and now the venom of his saliva was beginning to affect her as well. She was very much starting to wonder what she was waiting for. Why not just give in? Was it such a big deal, such an important decision? Maybe not, but if she did it now, she knew that in the morning she would wonder about her real reasons for being with him. Was it only the moment? This was not the time for such a commitment. Let him finish his story, let her have time to think and for her mark to truly fade away.

As he released her, she stepped back from him a bit, almost tripping over the wrinkled edge of the tablecloth that she stood on. He laughed and held out a hand to steady her. "Well, I think that's enough for you, young lady," he teased. "Three glasses of wine and you can barely stand."

"It wasn't the wine; it was *you* that put me over the edge. That venom of yours is dangerous stuff."

She smiled at him, but he seemed a little chastened, as though he was embarrassed by the mention of the unnatural agent in his saliva. She came back to him and gave him another quick kiss on the lips, to try and erase his concerns and show that she was unworried by it. "Not that I'm complaining, but I think that it is time for me to go." He smiled and gave her a little nod.

He walked over to retrieve the larger broken shards from his glass that he had thrown earlier, wrapping them in a napkin and dumping them into the basket. She then helped him to fold up the tablecloth and blew out the candle. She held it out to him and he finished closing up the basket. He could see much better in the dark than she could, she knew, so she let him fasten everything to the bike and then come back for her hand. She could see a little, but he led her carefully to the motorcycle.

On the ride back, she held tightly to him and thought about what he had said. Mostly she pondered his comment about how he thought she would not want to be kissing him tomorrow after hearing the rest of his story. Did he really think that it would affect her so strongly; that she would be so disgusted by his actions? She already knew that he must have killed his brother, what more was there? How much worse could it have been?

She searched her feelings about him now. She knew that he had slept with his brother's wife and then killed his brother. Yet, as absolutely horrible as that was, she still felt she could forgive him and she was certainly still attracted to him. Did that make her a bad person, that she could so easily forgive such horrid acts? Time passed, did not mean that he was any less guilty of the things he'd done. His poor wife. His poor brother! What had they ever done to deserve such treatment? If he'd treated his wife and brother that way, why should she think that he would be any better a person in *her* life?

It was becoming confusingly muddled in her head. The wine, mingled with the loud engine of the motorcycle was giving her a headache. She'd have to think on these things more tomorrow. She may attend her classes in the morning, but she'd a feeling that she would have a difficult time actually paying attention.

He coasted into the dorm lot and she hopped off the back of the bike. He remained in the seat, but turned to watch her as she strapped the helmet back onto the bar on the back. She looked up at him when she was finished, and then moved closer to him, resting her hands on his leg. As she looked into his eyes, he seemed a little sad. She wondered what he'd been thinking about on the ride home.

"Goodnight, I'll see you tomorrow. We close at ten on Fridays."

He grinned. "I know. It'll make for a late start and there's so much left untold. I hope you won't mind being up all night."

"That's alright, I'll take a nap," she said with a giggle.

"Mind if I come early?" She smiled and shook her head. "Alright, then I'll see you tomorrow."

"Can we spend the evening just the same? I mean, go back to the park, and bring some more wine?" He laughed.

"As identical as you like." She leaned in to kiss him, but he turned to make it only a kiss on the cheek. "Sleep well." She was a little bemused by his refusal to kiss her again. She smiled at him and then looked at the comforter on the back of the bike.

"I guess I'll leave that with you, then. Oh, do you want your jacket?" she asked, grasping the collar of his denim she'd worn again.

He gave her a little shake of his head. "Keep it," he said quietly.

She smiled, gratefully. She hadn't really wanted to give it up. She loved wearing it. She loved that it was his. "Thanks. Goodnight," she called as he walked his Harley to the road. He gave her a wave and then started the bike and rode away.

~~~~~~~~~~~~~~~~~~~~~~~~~~~~~

The next morning's algebra class found Felicity in a very tired and grumbling mood. She'd woken up with a bit of a headache. She hadn't gotten nearly enough sleep and she couldn't help but feel that she had far more important things to think about right now. The last thing she was in the mood to do, was fill her head and strain her mind with linear transformations, matrices and determinants.

However, she was unwilling to miss the class because she knew Cain would ask her if she went. She wouldn't lie to him and then he would be disappointed in her for not going. Besides, if she were going to skip class anyway, then she might as well have stayed with him later last night. At least she felt that attending class would help her justify her decision to leave him. She was still a little annoyed with herself for being so indecisive.

Part of her really was bothered by the things that he had done in his past. Cautions and warnings that she would rather not heed, flitted about in the back of her mind. She could not believe that he would ever really hurt her, emotionally or physically, but Charles and Elizabeth had probably thought that too, and look at what he'd done to them. It was disturbing to say the least, but she felt that she knew him now and he was not that same person at all anymore. He was a man who would never do such things again, wasn't he? She hoped she was not just being naive. Although she was unwilling to really admit it to herself, she knew she would be better off to forget about him. There were plenty of other guys in the world, with much less dangerous concerns.

At the very same time, she was so incredibly attracted to him that she could not imagine ever wanting anyone else. If not for his past, she loved everything about him. Alright, maybe not everything. She hadn't really forced herself to come to terms with the vampire issue. Was that really something that could be ignored or worked around? She was being really stupid wasn't she?

But if not for the fangs, he was the most wonderful guy she had ever met. He was so handsome and charming and sweet and...he needed her, didn't he? He was so alone if not for her. He deserved someone that would accept him for what he was. He needed someone he could share things with and not be afraid to be honest with. Of course, the fact that he was so incredibly sexy was something not to be ignored either.

She was becoming impatient even with herself. Physically, their relationship was the most exciting she'd ever had, and they hadn't even really *done* anything yet. What was she waiting for anyway? She had never wanted a man so badly in her life. If he wanted her as well, then why shouldn't they enjoy being together to the fullest extent possible? Was there really anything wrong with that? It's not like she was really waiting for marriage was she? She just wanted to know that it meant something to both of them; that it was not a one night stand or just some passing fling. Cain obviously cared enough for her, to wait until she was ready. She already knew, that however unwise, she was falling steadily and deeply in love with him. What more could she ask for?

She was almost afraid to hear what he had to tell her tonight, because she knew that she would want to be with him, no matter what he said. To find out worse things about him now would only hurt. If she was going to be truthful with herself, she should realize that it was too late to believe that she could just simply walk away from him. She already cared too much. If she really felt that she *had* to leave him, for her own well being, of course she would, but it would not be easy. In fact, she would probably feel devastated. She hoped he had made things out to be worse than they were.

All of these thoughts, combined with a lack of sleep and no lack of wine the evening before, had put her into a fairly grumpy mood. Amazingly, she still made it to algebra on time. Then it turned out that the professor was late anyway. As she slumped into the seat next to Ashley, she hoped she might go back to sleep until class started. Of course, Ashley made that impossible. "Hi!"

She looked over to Ashley, groggily. "Why are you always so chipper?"

"Because *I* recognize and respect the value of a good night's beauty sleep. Look at you. Did you even *go* to bed last night?"

"Yeah, I think I finally got to sleep around three."

Ashley broke into a broad grin. "Out with Cain, huh?"

"Yeah, he's...kind of a night owl."

"Where'd you go?"

"We had sort of a picnic in the park, wine and cheese anyway. You know, by the waterfall."

"Wow, romantic! Finally showing the man some appreciation I hope?"

Felicity tried to look annoyed, but it was ruined by a yawn. "We spent all night talking."

"*Just* talking?"

"Pretty much."

"What a waste! What is wrong with you girl? I've got to be honest, if he ever gets tired of waiting around for you, don't expect me to give you a grace period. That man is so yummy. I am all over that, first opportunity."

"It's not like I ignore him, believe me. It's just, kind of complicated."

"No, it really isn't. He is a totally gorgeous and worthy guy, who I still think has money, no matter what you say, and he totally wants you. All else is secondary and works itself out, believe me."

Felicity just shook her head. She was too tired to try to dispute it. It'd just be easier to get Ashley talking about her favorite subject, herself. "So, I suppose your date book is full for the weekend?"

Ashley gave a sly smile. "Of course it is, full of Ben."

That news was unexpected and woke her up a bit. "Really?"

"*Oh yeah,*" Ashley confirmed.

"Finally decided to let him know that you still like him, huh?"

"I didn't even have to, he called me. I knew he would eventually. He is so hot for me," Ashley informed her.

Felicity tried not to roll her eyes. "Where are you going?"

"Tonight we're going to Venus, one of the few hot spots around here. Then tomorrow he wants to take me to the Debate Luncheon."

"What's that?"

"They do it every year. It's a big fancy lunch at the country club, over in Greene. Ben was chosen as captain of the debate team this year, you know."

"I didn't know that. Although I guess I shouldn't be surprised, he certainly loves to argue. Wait, isn't Ben closing tonight?"

"Yeah, that's okay. It'll give me some time to find an outfit that'll really rev his engine. Ben appreciates that sort of thing, you know? And Venus is the only club around here worth dressing for. You ever been?"

"Yeah, Cain took me once."

"You guys should come," Ashley offered.

Felicity smiled at the thought of she and Cain on a double date with Ben and Ashley. The professor arrived and Felicity gave Ashley a hushed answer as class started. "Thanks, but we have a more private evening planned."

~~~~~~~~~~~~~~~~~~~~~~~~~~~~~~

Felicity arrived for work on time at four o'clock. Thank goodness her school schedule was light on Fridays, and she'd had time for a quick snooze before heading over to the DownTime for her shift. Closing with Ben would probably be aggravating enough, without being tired as well. She also assumed she'd be out late with Cain again and she certainly didn't want to fall asleep during his story.

Friday nights were always pretty busy, so she had Lucy helping her in the bookstore until eight. She noticed that Harold was working with Ben in the café, *oh joy*. She made her way to the counter while both guys were busy with customers, so she could slip into the back without having to address them.

Unfortunately, when she came back out, Ben was standing right there. She wasn't sure if he'd planned it that way. Rather than give her an angry look or a rude comment, he just said 'Hi', as though she weren't mad at him. She stopped for a second, caught off guard, and then returned it with her own 'Hi'. Just then, Harold approached, giving her a look that was an obvious assessment of her body. "Hiii," he cooed in what he seemed to think was a seductive manner. Felicity rolled her eyes and shared a disgusted look with Ben, who then handed Harold an empty dirty bowl he'd been holding.

"Go wash the dishes," he said, nodding towards the full sink. Harold gave him an annoyed glance, but went to the sink as directed.

She didn't say anything else to Ben, but went right over to the registers. At six thirty she had a break for dinner. She'd brought her own sandwich to try to save some money. You weren't supposed to bring outside food into the cafe though. There were two chairs and a tiny table in the 'employee lounge' behind the cafe, where the lockers were. So she resigned herself to having dinner back there, with a magazine. She was about halfway through, when Ben entered the room, with a plate full of pasta salad from the cafe and a drink.

He put his dinner on the table next to hers, although there was barely room for it. Felicity looked at the plate, then up at him. "What are you doing?"

He sat down across from her. "Eating my dinner."

"You bought that here, why don't you just eat it out in the cafe?"

"Do you have a problem with my eating back here?"

"No," she replied defensively.

He just shook his head at her and started eating. After a few minutes of ignoring him and reading her magazine, he started trying to get her to talk, as she'd known he would. Benjamin was just not the type of guy that would let you ignore him. He either made you comfortable or pissed you off, but he just couldn't ever leave things alone. "So, I didn't see you at lunch yesterday. Are you avoiding me now?" She barely looked up from her magazine. "I felt like McDonald's."

"Kind of a long walk, don't you think?" She just shrugged. "Well, if it makes you feel any better, Alyson's mad at me too," Ben informed her.

Lucy came into the break room just then, to get something from her locker. Felicity had been about to speak and wasn't going to let Lucy's interruption stop her. "Gee, I wonder why? Maybe because you're incredibly intolerant and judgmental?"

Ben looked insulted. Lucy seemed to have planned to grab something and leave, ignoring them, but instead stopped to put her hand on Ben's shoulder. "She's right honey. I love ya' but...you are." Without waiting for a reaction, Lucy went back out into the store.

Ben looked at the table with his mouth open in an expression of disgust. "Thanks." Of course, Lucy was already gone. Felicity just chuckled and finished her sandwich. She gathered her garbage and threw it away as Ben spoke. "You know, it's not like I just...don't *like* the guy you're dating. *That* would be judgmental. Sometimes Cain can be an okay guy, I guess. And hell, Mattie used to be my best friend! **But they are not human anymore!** There is something fundamentally wrong with them. Do you get that? Something that could easily get you killed!"

"Cain's not going to kill me," Felicity said dismissively.

"How do you know?"

"Don't you think I would have been dead by now?"

"Maybe he likes to play with his food," Ben suggested.

She stood there for a moment, just glaring at him. "Benjamin, just...stop talking," Felicity replied in disgust.

She walked out the door, but he followed. "You just don't want to admit that I could be right."

She spun around, startling him, because he'd been following closely behind her. "You could be right. You could also be, oh I don't know...jealous?"

"What?" he asked in disbelief.

"Never mind." She turned and began walking away, but he kept following. He put a hand on her shoulder to try to spin her back around, but she planted herself so that he couldn't unless he really forced her. After a minute he took his hand away, then she turned to face him. She crossed her arms and waited for him to speak.

"Jealous of who, Cain? Over *you*? Please! If that were the case, why would I have a problem with Mattie and Alyson? You've got some ego," Ben accused.

"Careful, you're livin' in a glass house," she warned.

"Very cute. Excuse me for not wanting to see my friends in the newspaper as just two more missing girls, found a week later in a ditch, a few quarts shy," he said forcefully.

She sighed. "Not going to happen, so just butt out, okay?" She didn't let him answer, she just turned and went back to work.

Felicity spent the rest of her shift avoiding Ben's annoyed glances from across the store and waiting for Cain to arrive. He said he'd come early, but it was already almost closing time. She kept thinking she felt him, but it was faint and she couldn't really tell if it was just wishful thinking. Where was he?

Ten o'clock arrived, and she went to flip the sign on the door to 'closed'. She paused at the door. Cain was definitely out there. She couldn't see him, but she could feel him. It was slight. Her mark was almost gone, but she was sure he was there. Why wasn't he coming in? She didn't really think that he would stay away because of Ben. Well, all she could do was close out her register and wait.

After she finished she went to look out the door again, nothing but dark. She walked dejectedly over to the cafe to sit at the counter and wait for Ben so she could leave. He was still counting his register. He glanced up as she sat. "Would you go put up the chairs for me?"

She gave him a sour look. "That's not my job." As he looked up at her, she noticed that he looked very pale. She wondered if he felt sick.

"Whatever," he said in annoyance. He slammed the drawer and began to walk around to get the chairs.

She stood and felt bad for being so bitchy to him. He really did look ill. "I got it." She went and lifted all of the chairs to the tabletops as he finished cleaning up behind the counter.

"So, you getting picked up by Count Cain this evening?"

She gave him a condescending look. "Did you get that one from Alyson? You should at least try to be original."

"Thought I was. Good one Allie," Ben said with a chuckle.

"Not really." He stopped what he was doing for a minute to lean on the counter with his head in his hands. "Are you okay?"

He looked up at her and then went back to work. "I'm fine. Cain *is* picking you up though right?" he asked.

She studied him for a minute. Why did he care? "He's already outside."

Now Ben stared back for a moment before answering. "Well, I wish you would have asked him to come alone."

Felicity's eyes widened a bit. No wonder Ben looked so nauseous. "You feel Sindy out there?"

"Nice and strong. Thanks again for not letting me go to Vermont. This is so much more fun," he pointed out sarcastically.

She disregarded him and went to the door. Still nothing. She could still feel Cain though, so they must be close. Just around the side, out of view of the door probably. "Why doesn't he come in? What are they doing out there?"

Ben laughed. "Yeah, I wonder what Sindy could be doing out there, all this time with *your* boyfriend?" She gave him an annoyed glance and then went to the lounge for her stuff, ignoring him. He followed her and went to get his own jacket. "Let's see, either they're killing each other, which *I* would certainly appreciate." He came closer to her with a smile. "Or, they're making nice, which I might also enjoy the results of."

He stood in the doorway. She put a hand to his chest, to lightly push him away. "Very funny, get out of my way."

He backed out the door with a smile and shut the lights for the cafe. "Well, I hope Sindy won't be too insulted if I don't stick around, because I've got plans." He waited for her to come to the front of the store before turning off the rest of the lights. "I still can't believe that you're dating a dead guy."

"At least *he's* got a brain in his head," Felicity said pointedly.

"Are you calling me stupid?"

"Not *you*. You are obviously a pretty intelligent guy, even if you are an obstinate pain in the ass. I'm sure there must be plenty of room for a brain in that swelled head of yours. I was talking about your date."

Ben looked like he was trying to decide whether to be insulted that she thought he was a pain in the ass, or pleased that she thought he was smart. Eventually he decided to dismiss the whole subject of her feelings about him for now. "Why are you always so down on Ashley? She's a very nice girl."

Felicity started laughing. "You barely even like her! But I'm sure you're looking forward to having a *very* nice time tonight all the same. Here's a tip, buy her jewelry."

Ben just gave her a shrewd smile. "Sounds like someone's got some jealousy issues of her own."

She gave him a sharp laugh. "As if. So are we leaving, or are you too afraid to go out into the parking lot?"

"Ladies first," he said with an outstretched arm.

"No problem. Oh, did you want to go get your cross first? I'll wait," she offered snidely.

Ben just gave her a condescending sneer and pushed open the door for her. She made sure to give him a sweet and unconcerned smile as she stepped outside into the dark parking lot.

Chapter 11 - Indiscretions

Cain

8:30, Friday night

Cain started up his Harley Davidson and rode out into the night. He'd awoken almost two hours ago, but he had spent a good deal of time just lying in bed, trying to decide how he would word the rest of his story to Felicity. He truly did want to tell her everything about himself. She should know what she was getting into, in being with him.

At the very same time, he *so* wanted her to stay, that he was afraid to have things come out in too harsh a light. He would be honest of course, but just how detailed did he really need to be, in order to feel that he'd given her a factual and legitimate account of his life? She didn't need to know every detail of his past, did she? It would make for a rather long story and there were aspects of his life that should really have no bearing on her feelings towards him.

For example, his past relationships. Felicity had to know that she was not the first girl he had cared for in over three hundred years, besides his wife and Maribeth, but did she need names, dates, and full accounts? Probably not. Some things should be kept private, he decided. What of the relationships that had ended badly...fatally? Wasn't it his duty to tell of those that had come before her? There had not been many, and most of his relationships had not really failed through fault of his own. As far as those who had trouble adapting to a life like his...he better understood now what kind of personality was necessary to make them strong, to help them bear the burdens of this existence. He would not turn her if she were not suitable, if he did not become convinced that she would indeed thrive. He would not repeat past mistakes, of that he was sure. He sincerely hoped he would also avoid making any new ones.

Truth; this relationship needed to be grounded in truth. He was never a liar in his life, not in words, but he had often refrained from telling girls of the past things they may not look upon fondly. He needed to tell Felicity the truth...all of it. How detailed it should be, he was undecided. He was not thrilled at the prospect of describing certain things to her. He didn't want to frighten her more than necessary, but she had a right to know.

He would tell of his worst transgressions, so he would not feel he had anything to hide. The rest of his life he would then tell in broad generalizations. Did it even matter? He had been quite serious in saying that she may decide after tonight that he was no longer worth her time. What he had to tell her would be bad enough without petty concerns of ex-loves and such.

The very real truth of it was that he might not even see her again after tonight. The thought made him feel a bit ill. It caused a desperation that made him want to edit his narration to his own advantage, but that was why he'd told her the bottom line of it the night before. She knew he was a murderer. There was more to tell of course, but she had the idea of it. At least he felt that if she came back tonight to hear the rest, then he still had a chance. She *had* kissed him after. Then again, that may just have been a combination of her mark and the wine. Now she'd had time to think…

As he approached the DownTime, he was a bit surprised to feel Sindy drawing near. She had thoroughly disappeared after he'd spoken to her on Wednesday night. Last night he hadn't felt her at all. She was purposely staying away from him, he assumed. Yet now, here she was, and alone too! Very strange. She must want something. She seemed to be waiting for him. As he drew near, he saw her sitting on the guardrail at the bend in the road, just before the DownTime. He slowed as he approached her and then cut the engine and rolled up beside her. She stood as he neared. Yes, she'd been expecting him. After a moment's startled realization, he remembered that she could feel him as well as he could feel her, cloaked or not. She was marked...as his.

"Evening," he said with a casual nod.

"Hi there."

"Aren't you missing like, half a dozen people?"

She laughed. "I sent them to follow after Chris for a while. I thought I might want some privacy." She said this last with a coy glance at him that spoke volumes of what she might want that privacy for.

Cain smiled and thought to himself, *sorry luv, not tonight.* "Good luck with that." He got off the bike and began walking it the last of the way to the bookstore.

She followed after him, obviously irked by his lack of interest. "Well, what are *you* doin' tonight?"

He kept walking as she fell into step next to him, on the other side of the motorcycle. "I've got plans."

"With that pet of yours, right?" she pouted.

He stopped to give her a level gaze. "Don't call her that."

Sindy smirked at him. "You can *call* her whatever you want, but we both know that *a pet* is exactly what she is."

Cain stared at her, unmoving. "Considering that you've no protection this evening, in fact even if you had, I rather think that you should be speaking to me with a bit more respect. Wouldn't you agree?"

She stared back at him for a moment. She wasn't really frightened of him, but at least she wasn't smiling. "Sorry."

"I should hope so. Why is it that you've decided to forgo the protection?" he asked, with a slight smile playing about his lips. "Don't you think it's a bit risky for you to be out here waiting for me, all alone? Your boys aren't even within hailing distance, I don't believe."

She shrugged. He started walking again, slowly and she fell back into step beside him as she spoke. "The way I see it, around me you're usually *firm*," she gave him a promiscuously sly smile, just to be sure he caught the double meaning, "but fair. As long as I behave myself, I should be safe, right?"

He smiled. "Indeed. In that case, why don't you just dismiss them altogether? Still planning on misbehaving?"

"I haven't decided yet," she answered with a chuckle, "but you know, I don't think I could get rid of them if I tried. They really like me, and most of them couldn't even survive on their own."

"You should've thought of that before you made them all."

"They do need me, but I need them too. Where else do you expect me to get my evening meals? I've been off humans ever since…Ben." At the mention of feeding from Ben, she gave a little shiver. They were nearing the DownTime. Cain could see Ben's aura bearing Sindy's mark quite clearly. Surely, she felt him very strongly.

He shook his head disapprovingly. "Why do you assume that you're gaining any sort of favor with me this way? How is it that you think feeding off of those boys of yours is any better than feeding off of humans directly? You're just sending six others out to attack people, rather than do it yourself. I'm not impressed. I much prefer to associate with those who do not harm others, in any way."

Sindy furrowed her brow as she thought about that and they crossed the road to the lot of the DownTime. Finally, she gave him a very fond appraising look and declared, "I *could* live like that. It's just boring. Now if you promised to keep me entertained…"

He looked at her oddly for a moment and then lightly laughed. "It was simply meant to be a statement, not an invitation." He kept walking, not waiting for her response.

Cain glanced through the front doors across the lot. He saw Felicity, busy inside. She hadn't noticed him yet. He could just barely feel her. Ben's mark was much brighter. He found that a little depressing. The store was still open for almost an hour yet. He could go right in, but he knew Sindy would be unwelcome there. He wouldn't so blatantly dismiss her yet. Rather than approach the doors, he walked his motorcycle up along the side of the building and parked it there.

Sindy watched him and then sat on the grass next to the building. She seemed to take for granted that he would join her. "Okay teach, I've got a question for you." He went to sit beside her. "What if I were…*involved* with another vampire, exclusively," she eyed him seductively, "and we were in the habit of drinking from one another? You know like, nightly give and take relations." She smiled and eyed his throat, seeming very aroused by the idea. "If neither of us ever drank from anyone else, could we go on that way? I mean, couldn't we just feed off of each other, indefinitely?

"As neatly solved as that sounds, you know it would never work. If you never drank blood from an outside source, eventually you would both become depleted. I don't suppose it would kill you, but you would both become far too weak to function after a time."

She didn't want to accept it, pouting. "How do you know?"

He gave her another level stare, as a smile hovered about his lips. "I've tried it." She seemed very surprised and amused. "Don't look so shocked. A life as long as mine leaves a lot of room for experimentation. I wasn't always as *boring* as you seem to think I am now."

"You know, I always suspected that. You go through a lot of trouble to prove me wrong though."

He laughed. "How else can I ever get you to take me seriously?"

"Because my *salvation* is so important to you, right?"

He didn't answer her, after a moment he just lay down to look at the stars. He spent so many nights staring at the sky. He could recognize practically every constellation at a glance.

Sindy lay down as well and they silently studied the star patterns across the heavens for a while.

This girl was a bit of an enigma to him. They had such an odd relationship. He *was* a sort of teacher to her, and he was so much older and more experienced than she was. Yet in many ways, he felt as though they were almost equals. She was so confident and self-assured. She often did things purposely to anger him, yet she also seemed to desperately seek his approval.

When they'd first met, he'd had it in the back of his mind that she might make an interesting partner for him, someone that he could spend his time with, without fear of bringing her corruption and harm. After being in her company for awhile, he had decided against the idea. He found her personality rather abrasive and irritating at times. He thought that he wanted to assure himself that she would live in a passive manner and then have nothing more to do with her.

He told himself that it was for the sake of her well-being and the safety of others, that he invested so much in trying to teach her to live peacefully. It was for The Lord that he tried to prepare her now. That was what he told himself. It would take patience and be difficult, but eventually she would see the truth in his ways and adopt his more civil practices. He'd no earthly personal stake in her future, though. He didn't really think that she would ever submit to him in any way, not really. He'd believed she could never truly please him as a partner.

He knew now that he had simply not given her enough time to come around. She was proud and stubborn, but she was still all of the things that he had seen in her from the first as well; beautiful, smart, playful, strong and he must remember, she was still very young. As he had once told her, he did believe that she could grow to be a splendid creature as she matured.

But he'd met Felicity. He'd been lonely, vulnerable, and unwilling to wait and distance himself as he should. Now he'd lost his heart to her. Sindy, perhaps someday he could love, but Felicity he loved already. It might sound cruel but in his mind, compared to Felicity, Sindy seemed almost a poor parody of a woman.

But Felicity was human and in that, the problem lies. To keep her, he would probably ruin her life. For all of his beliefs and his desire to be a 'good' man, he must admit that he had worn mental blinders where she was concerned. He was so lonely that he had let his personal desires override his moral responsibilities. It was a pattern that he actually did recognize in himself, after all these years. He tried to change it and did go decades without succumbing to the urge for such relationships, but after awhile he grew weak and managed to deceive himself, that it would be different...*this time.*

At first, he had sought to ignore the fact that she had a true life beyond time spent with him. School and family were things easily dismissed, things to try and distance her from, so as to more easily bring her into his own world. But now, he loved her, he truly did; this was not the sweet infatuation that he had initially felt with her. He really did care for her, with all of his unbeating heart. He was angry with himself for being so intentionally blind! How could he ever risk hurting her? As he fell deeper in love, he was forced to realize that she had a very real future in the world from which he would be taking her away.

That was why he'd almost begun to try to show her that, to hold her at arm's length. His actions and desires seemed almost to yo-yo between bringing her close and pushing her away. He savored her kisses and dearly wanted her body along with her heart, but he would not let her dismiss her schoolwork. He would not try to persuade her to stay with him rather than visit her family. She should remain grounded by the world. It was unfair to expect her to give that up for him.

When he told her the rest of his tale, she might decide that the world was where she belonged and not with him. He was unsure whether he could coexist in her life with everything else. Her world was just not a place where he really belonged. How could he ever think she could live a normal human life with him? How unrealistic was it to think that he could fulfill a need in her life as she did in his?

And, if he did not continue his self-appointed task, of educating other vampires to live a peaceful and non-violent existence, what would he do, 'play house' with Felicity until she grew old and died? What of all the deaths he could prevent in that time, if he were not tied to her? How could he ever justify that to himself? Besides, he could never sit by and idly watch her die of age or disease. He knew that it was not in him. He would feel forced to act, to prevent her from fading away, and doom her to undead eternity instead.

That was an existence that could certainly be rewarding in itself in some ways, and then they could be together, but would she want it? Was it right? It was with an almost masochistic determination that he had resolved to tell her all of his wrongs. As badly as he wanted her, he also almost wished for her to turn him away, so that he couldn't hurt her. No matter how pure his intentions, surely, eventually he would.

As he lay here, looking up at the stars, he found himself doing something that he had not truly done in far too long a time. He prayed. He honestly and unconditionally asked God for guidance. He asked forgiveness as always, and repented past sins, but then he sincerely tried to open his heart and mind. He cleared his thoughts and prayed, for direction, for help.

How would he know The Lord's will from his own selfish wishes? He was unsure and hoped that even if he did, he would have the strength to obey. He took a deep breath to clear himself of these thoughts now and simply prayed for strength and the desire for obedience. He would move slowly and carefully these next days and see what unfolded.

He would see Felicity, and enjoy this night with her, as much as he could, but he would remain true to his intentions and tell her all. Then, if it seemed the only course true to the Spirit, he would steel himself to accept that he must leave her.

He had made some thoughtful insights to Sindy's personality traits the other evening, but her own insights regarding he and Felicity having no real future together had been unfortunately accurate as well. As much as he had not wanted to admit it, Sindy was right. He hated that fact. It messed up their careful relationship; the order of things as he saw them. *He* was supposed to be the elder, the one with the knowledge. *She* was childish, indecent, immoral and she was not supposed to be right!

Sindy brought herself up on one elbow to look at him, as he lay on his back next to her. He noticed that even beneath the garish artificial blush that she wore, she did look a bit flushed. "I don't think I can stay here for much longer. Ben is too close, too tempting. How do you stand it? You see her like, every night don't you? You hold her and you kiss her, and her blood just...calls to you. How do you do it?"

Normally he didn't let himself enter into such conversations with Sindy. It always turned out that she was simply baiting him, verbally trying to turn things to her own ends, but she wasn't speaking in a mocking tone. She seemed to really be asking. She sounded almost in awe of his control. He didn't answer right away and she went on.

"Blood always calls you, no matter who it's in. Isn't it weird? It could be the skeeziest guy. Ugly, dirty and old, it doesn't matter. The blood is always good, no matter what the package, but when it's someone you like, someone you really want, well that's just *special*.

I've known Ben my whole life, you know. I've always wanted him. That's why drinking from him, was sooo good, special. You *know* Felicity. You want her. Drinking from her must have been so intimate, delicious. But you hardly even took any, did you? Even when her mark was new, it wasn't all that strong. How did you stop? How could you control yourself? You must have such command, be sooo strong." She leaned over, slipping her hand under the edge of his open jacket and rubbing it across his chest.

He'd been lying on his back, with his hands under his head, but now he reached out to quickly and firmly grasp her wrist. He gently moved it off of him and let go. "Don't touch me."

She was unfazed. "You didn't seem to mind touching me, when you drank. Was it...*special?*"

He propped himself up, as she was, on one elbow to face her. "Blood always is, no matter the package." As he saw her face crumple, he felt unnecessarily cruel. "But with our kind it's always *extra special*. You know that."

That seemed to mollify her. "It was good wasn't it? Bet I kept you for a while too."

"What do you mean?" he asked.

"Satisfied. Didn't you say you found me very, satisfying?" He just smiled. It was amazing to him and almost a little sad, how badly she wanted please him, in any way. "How could you go back to something packaged in a little plastic container after that?" she asked incredulously.

"That's just what I do. It makes me feel good to know that I'm doing right." He'd made such statements so many times in his life, as explanations to young ones such as her. Why did it suddenly feel so false, as though he were using 'good deeds' to hide larger sins?

She shook her head in disbelief and then sighed up at the sky. "When you drank from me, that was good, at first anyway. Found I don't really care for being...emptied, but thanks for the new experience." He chuckled. "But that was nights ago. Now you're going to see *her*." She nodded towards the store to indicate Felicity. "Hold her and be with her. Won't you wanna drink her?" He lay back down to look at the sky again. "It's gotta be like torture!"

"It can be trying at times," he agreed.

Her voice took on a hushed and hesitant quality. "You know, if you wanted, I could help you out with that. Give you a little, to hold you over. I mean, as long as you promised not to get carried away."

He looked up at her in disbelief, and then laid his head back again and smiled. "No thanks."

"It's not like it would make any difference to anyone. And wouldn't it make things so much easier for you, with Felicity? Besides, I'm already marked by you, so it's not like I can give it to anyone else at the moment."

That was something that hadn't occurred to him. Of course she would be unable to give blood to Chris or Luke, or any of her others. She was his, marked for them to see. She couldn't hide it. "What do they make of that, your boys? I hope I haven't caused you to lose credibility with them."

"Like you care," she said with a huff.

"You're right, maybe I don't, really. Just curious," he added.

She shrugged her shoulders. "They're too stupid to notice."

"That's not true. Not of Chris anyway. Does he feel you've betrayed him? That was not my intent."

"What *he* feels really shouldn't concern you, or me even. He's just a follower, like all the others."

"He's not like the others; don't try to pretend that you can't see it. You made him better, whether or not it was by design. He does understand. Do you care for him at all?"

She shrugged again. He thought she did, but she wouldn't admit it to him. "Not like you care for *her*. Why don't you let me make being with her, easier for you? It's not like *she's* givin' you any." Sindy must have noticed the steady fading of his mark upon Felicity. He wished his personal relations were not so clearly evident to her. She went on baiting him. "You *like* torture? Isn't there a word for people like that?"

"Masochistic. And yes, I suppose at times that does apply to me," he replied with a little laugh. They sat in silence for a moment, as he left her repeated offer unanswered. He certainly had no intention of accepting it, tempting as it was. "I thought you wouldn't remain for long, with Benjamin being so near?"

She lay back down beside him again, very close, but not touching at all. "Guess I'm a little...masochistic myself." He laughed.

They lay there in silence again for a few minutes. The bookstore would be closing soon. He should probably go inside. Felicity would be wondering where he was. She might even have felt him out here by now. He could feel her, although her mark was now faint. He became aware of a change in Sindy. She was shifting; he could feel it. He looked over at her, in slight alarm, though he didn't sit up. "What are you doing?"

She did sit up a bit, but not in a threatening manner. She brought her own wrist up to her mouth and very deliberately, bit it. She tore the skin a little more than usual, to make sure it would bleed easily. Once she had an open wound there, she brought it away from her mouth, holding the inside of her wrist pointed up to the sky so as not to lose the precious blood from inside. He lay there, watching her in disbelief as she licked the blood from her lips.

"Helping out a friend," she said quietly, stretching out her wrist towards his face.

Now he did raise himself up on his elbows, craning his head back a bit, away from her arm. He was uneasy and trying not to obviously stare at her wrist, longingly. "I said I didn't want any."

"You really gonna turn me away?" She placed her wrist to his mouth without waiting for an answer. He smelled the blood there and the change overcame him automatically as it touched his lips. That had never happened to him before, without control. He closed his eyes and forced his hands to remain on the ground, in the grass where he'd been resting them. So badly, he wanted to grasp her arm and crush her wrist to his open mouth, but he barely parted his lips. Very gently and slowly, he let his tongue explore the wound she had made, just barely tasting the blood there.

It was so divine.

He could not do this now, here, with Felicity just inside. It just would not be right...would it? Or did it even matter? It *would* help. He didn't really have much of a choice, his body would not let him move away to refuse her. After an eternal moment of indecision, he sucked a little at her wrist and was rewarded with a few more drops of her exquisite blood. He refused to let himself bite her. He would take only what came. She made it very easy, pressing the wound so firmly against his lips, as though she could force the blood into his mouth.

He drew from her again, more strongly this time. Then, more again. His natural instinct was to bite her himself, to infect her with his venom and renew his mark, but he resisted. As difficult as it was, the blood was what mattered most. It was so good.

It was such pure strong blood, however unpure seeming its source. Drinking from her wrist as he was, it felt pure. Focused, perhaps was a better description. It wasn't colored by sexual intent, as everything associated with Sindy usually was.

The throat was such a sensitive, intimate area. To drink from the throat forced one's body into alignment with the victim's, making the act feel almost sexual by nature. But from the wrist, although still intimate as drinking blood always was, was not nearly the same experience. It was only the blood, nothing else. The blood was enough.

It seemed he spent quite awhile, gently sucking and feeding from her wrist, although he really didn't take all that much. He took only enough to quiet his thirst and give him better control. He shifted back to his human state when he was able. He kissed and then pulled away from her wrist.

She brought it to her own mouth, gave it a little lick and smiled. "Now, isn't that better?" She slowly ran her tongue over her upper lip. "I suppose reciprocation is out of the question?"

He stood, looking back down at her. "You suppose correctly."

She stood as well. "Can't blame a girl for trying." She gave him a quick glance up and down, smiling, as if to show him how much she appreciated his looks. "Enjoy your date."

He smiled back and shook his head at her audacity. "Thanks."

They both turned at the sound of Felicity and Ben emerging from the store. They were around the corner, yet to be seen. Sindy blew him a little kiss and walked up into the tree line behind the store, leaving him to meet them alone.

Ben and Felicity stayed together in front of the store for a moment, locking up he imagined. Once Sindy was gone, he moved around the building to meet them. As soon as he came into view, Felicity went to him, leaving Ben at the door.

"Cain, hi. Why didn't you come in?" She pouted playfully. "I was waiting for you."

"I know. I'm sorry. I was...delayed, talking to someone." She looked down at the ground. Ben finished setting the alarm and began walking towards them, to go to his car. Cain wondered if he had told her that Sindy was there. "Are we still on for the evening?"

"Yes of course. I'm not letting you off the hook that easy."

Ben approached them on the way to his car. Cain glanced up at him, while mumbling to Felicity. "Great... Good evening Ben."

Ben hardly looked at him. "Goodnight." He continued on past.

Cain and Felicity stood in awkward silence for a moment, watching him as he walked. Once he was beyond their range, Cain turned to her and quietly asked, "Is everything alright?"

"Yeah, fine." She stared at him for a moment. "How about with you?"

She seemed a little anxious, uneasy. She had to know that Sindy had been around. He gave her a coy smile. "Wonderful, now that you're here." She smiled and on impulse, he took hold of her and kissed her. She was caught a bit by surprise, but was very responsive all the same. He didn't hold it long, but it was *very* nice. And his thirst was indeed gone, for now.

She gave him a dazed little smile. "I thought the kisses were reserved for the end of the evening?"

"Who made up that dumb rule? You don't plan to hold me to that do you?" She laughed and he suddenly remembered his promise not to touch her without her express permission. "I'm sorry, perhaps I should have asked..."

She laughed. "You're allowed to kiss me! You don't have to ask. I was just pleasantly surprised. You're always so restrained."

"Well, I thought I'd better get my kisses in now, while I still can. You might not be so eager, come the end of the evening."

He'd lost his joyful attitude as he said this last. "You keep saying that. Why don't you let me be the judge?" she whispered, as she stepped closer to kiss him again. Before their lips met however, they were startled by the sound of Ben's tires screeching as he left the parking lot.

After taking a moment to regain her composure, Felicity gave him only a peck on the lips. She then moved out of his arms to look around for his bike. "Are we walking tonight?"

"No, it's 'round the side." He moved towards the motorcycle and she followed. It was loaded just the same as the night before, with the picnic basket and her comforter on the back. "Shall we head back to the park? You wanted 'identical' right?"

"It is pretty spot, but we can go wherever you want. The location isn't exactly the focal point of the evening. All day I feel like I've been waiting for the other shoe to drop."

"Me too. I can't say I'm looking forward to finishing my history for you, but it will be good to have it over with. I don't suppose *you* have any deep dark secrets to share, to make me feel better?"

She smiled. "Sorry, not off the top of my head, but, I'll try and think of some on the ride over."

"Thanks."

~~~~~~~~~~~~~~~~~~~~~~~~~~~~~

Half an hour later found them sitting on the tablecloth spread over the ground, in front of the little waterfall at the pond once again. Cain eyed Felicity playfully as he poured her a glass of wine. "So, out with it, your deepest darkest shame."

She laughed. "You'll be very disappointed, it's pretty tame."

"Well, that's not disappointing. That's a good thing! But I know what you mean. Tell me anyway."

She took a large sip from her glass and put it aside. She took a deep breath, as though preparing herself for a very shameful confession. "I stole a bathing suit once. My friend Deidre dared me. She stole one too. I spent some of last summer in the Hamptons, on Long Island with her family. We were invited to this very important beach party. We didn't have enough money for new bathing suits though. All the really cool guys were going to be there, so you could imagine how vital it was for us to look absolutely amazing. So...we stole them." Cain just smiled and then poured himself a glass of wine. "I know it's kind of dumb, but aren't you even going to say anything? Ask me if we got caught?"

"You did *not* get caught. And you *did* look absolutely amazing," he supplied.

Felicity wore a puzzled expression. "Well no, we didn't get caught, but I don't know how great we looked. We had a lot of fun at the party, but neither of us got a 'cool' boyfriend out of it."

"Those boys must have been blind." He laughed at her as she rolled her eyes at him. "Bronze bikini?" he asked, smiling at the memory of the snapshot in her room.

Now she looked thoroughly shocked. "Yes."

"Deidre's was blue and green. She's very cute, but you... You my dear, looked like a goddess," he told her with a smoldering smile.

Felicity began to look very alarmed. "Okay, you didn't even know me then. Besides, bright sunny day at the beach, so I'm thinkin' you weren't there. Please tell me that you can't read minds."

He grinned. "I can't read minds. There's a picture in your room, on the mirror."

She breathed a too obvious sigh of relief. "Oh yeah, I forgot. You've got a good memory though."

"The way you looked in that bikini, was worth remembering." She smiled and dropped her eyes from his. "Did you really not have a boyfriend?"

She shrugged. "I used to be kind of shy."

"*Used* to?"

"You still think I'm shy? I thought I was making like this conscious effort not to be," she confessed.

"Well, then you must have been positively bashful before! Now, I'd say you're just a little timid," he informed her.

"*Timid?* You think I'm timid?" She pretended to be angry with him and before he knew it, she had lunged herself at him for a kiss. "Is this timid?" He fell back trying to kiss her, laugh and not spill his wine all at the same time. She lay on top of him, until the giggles were gone and a very real kiss took their place.

When she let him up again he made a great show of composing himself. "Thought you might feel compelled to prove me wrong. Worked like a charm." He smiled mischievously and took a sip from his glass. She began to grin as she realized that he'd set her up, but didn't really seem to mind.

She drank some more of her own wine and smiled at him. "It's after eleven. I'm sure you'd much rather spend the evening fooling around, but I want to hear the rest of your story before I have to go home for the weekend."

She was right, though it pained him to admit it. It was time to continue his narration. He could put it off no longer. "I know, alright." He drew a deep breath and took on a more somber composure. "So... I was speaking of the winter ending in 1692. Terrible year. Many people died that winter. My beloved daughter Amelia was among them."

He sighed and spoke slowly, taking his time. "What I did not tell you, was that shortly thereafter, on the twenty first of February, 1692, I lost my wife Elizabeth as well."

"Oh Cain, I'm sorry," she said quietly.

"God forgive me, that I do not shed more tears for her. She was a good woman, my wife. She deserved more of a life than that. I should have tried harder to make things better between us. I should have been honest with her from the start, but now, it was too late. Their deaths weighed heavily on me. I took ill as well, and racked with grief as I was, I could hardly care for myself. In fact, to be perfectly honest, I had no desire to.

I *wanted* to die. I felt I'd brought about the destruction of my family myself. Who was I to deserve a loving family? I had betrayed them! The good Lord giveth, and so the Lord shall taketh away. That I should lose those I loved was fitting punishment. And so I barely cared for myself. I lay in bed and simply waited for the fevers to take me.

Obviously, they did not. I felt the cruel irony in that, but I suppose it just was not my time to die. Although I might have, if not for Maribeth. Once the illness left me, I still wouldn't eat. It was Maribeth who saw to me. Even when I was mostly unaware of my surroundings, delusional with shock, grief and starvation.

Charles and Maribeth had been almost unaffected by the illness. Charles had taken sick for a little in early March, but then the spring came with its green herbs and healing. Charles recovered quickly and he and Maribeth breathed a sigh of relief that their household had been largely passed by.

They had gotten into the habit of coming to check on me each day, after my own family passed. They had wanted me to come and stay with them, so that they could better care for me, but I refused. Then Charles took ill and Mari spent most of her time healing him, but she did get into the routine of bringing me meals each night. Sometimes she would bring their girl Alice with her, the one that helped to keep the house for them. She brought her to keep up the appearance of propriety I suppose. That was rather a joke though, I was so weak.

I barely picked at the food. After awhile I just stopped eating altogether and left the meals untouched. I hardly spoke to the ladies when they came. I wanted nothing to do with Maribeth, or anyone. I was obviously growing thin, wasting away and Mari became worried. She tried to spoon feed me, but I refused her food. She would send Alice over with the morning's fresh bread, but I usually left it untouched. Although the smell was maddening, I still sought to punish myself.

Finally, Maribeth began to bring me a cup of broth along with the usual plate of food that I never touched. She would sit there on the edge of my bed with the cup. The first few nights I ignored her for an hour or so, until I eventually did yell at her to leave and then she would. But finally, one night she sat resolute and pushed the damn cup at me until I drank. After that night, it became like a ritual. Every evening, after seeing that Charles had his dinner, she would bring me a plate, which she left on the table and collect the mostly untouched one from the evening before. Then she would come into the bedroom with my broth and refuse to leave until I'd drunk it. It became easier just to drink the stuff so she would go away and leave me alone. I still wouldn't really speak to her though.

A few of the townsfolk came with Elizabeth's family to pay their respects, but I was unresponsive and cold to them. Once Charles recovered, he came to see me a few times, but I ignored him as well. I just couldn't face him. No one could understand the penance I had set upon myself, except perhaps for Maribeth. I had abused the trust of all those who had loved me. Now I could not even beg their forgiveness. They were gone and I should suffer for it. I did ponder the idea of confessing to Charles, to set things straight with him at least, but I hadn't the spirit for it, I knew that Mari would be the one to suffer. Although I did blame her as well, I had decided that the final choice had ultimately lain with me and *I* had chosen to commit the sin. I wasn't so cruel as to actively seek *her* punishment.

So things went and I suffered in a sort of limbo, if you will. Until one day, it was nearly April by then I believe, Mari had come to me in the evening, as usual. She was alone on this occasion. I lay on the bed, unresponsive as usual. She put down the cup and plate, and stood there, arms folded, staring at me. 'Christian,' she said, "tis time for you to live in the world again.'

I didn't meet her eyes. I don't know what made me answer her, when so many other times I had not, but I did, to tell her that the world held nothing for me now.

She actually seemed to get angry with me. I remember finally looking at her, because I was so very surprised to hear the harshness in her voice, when next she spoke. 'You, Christian Herald, are being dreadfully selfish.' she told me. 'You may not need the world, but there are those in the world who need you. I need you. The truth is, something has happened, something that I cannot face alone.'

I have to admit that I had become accustomed to the sympathy and compassion that people had been speaking to me with, since my family's deaths. To hear her speak to me *this* way seemed a bit shocking. I was cross that she should think that she could pull me back into living for her own selfish reasons, when I'd no desire. I had no idea what she could be talking about.

'I am with child again, Christian,' she said simply.

It took a few moments for the statement to register. Even when it did, all I could think was that it should be a happy circumstance; some joy might come into our lives again, after so much loss. I knew she and Charles would worry whether she could carry the child to completion, but at least we could all hope. 'Mari that's wonderful,' I told her.

She looked at me as though I were truly delusional for such a sentiment. "Tis our undoing! The babe is yours.'

Again, I felt as though we were miscommunicating; that her words needed deciphering before their implications could be understood. It seemed impossible. Our tryst had been before Amy had even fallen sick. It seemed ages ago. 'How can that be? How can you know?' I queried.

She looked rather insulted that I could ask such a question. 'I've loved no one but you. Charles hasn't touched me since months before.'

'Not even once?' I asked, incredulously.

She seemed disgusted to have to admit it. 'Not even.'

'My brother *is* a fool,' I informed her.

'He may be a fool, but he is not a forgiving one. What am I to do?' she asked.

I took only a moment to consider. It seemed a clear sign from God. We must admit our wrong doings, go before my brother, disclose our infidelity and try to put things to rights. The lies would then plague us no further. We should beg forgiveness and carry the secret sins of our past no longer. This I did tell her, though she seemed far less embracing of the idea. 'We are to confess. Charles may be hard hearted of late, but he did love us once. We shall throw ourselves upon his mercy and then you shall get yourself to bed, and stay there. Your only mission is to rest and prepare yourself to birth this child. Don't think and worry on life after, 'tis only the babe that matters now.'

She became very quiet and forlorn. 'Christian, you know that I cannot. My body does not work as it should. 'Twill be only enough to ruin us, not bring forth life.'

I sat up and took her hands into my own, in my lap. 'Mari are you sure there is life within you now? There is no mistake?'

'I am certain.' She stood and flattened her dress against her stomach, that I might see the slight new bulge there. It had been very well hidden amongst her welter of skirts, but it was undeniable, now that she showed it. I know that perhaps she would have expected disappointment, that there was no hiding our deeds of the past, but I could feel nothing but excitement and elation. That was my child! The only thing that had ever truly made me happy, was my daughter, Amelia. Now here was another chance, a baby living within her, so that I might have another chance to be happy again.

She seemed very puzzled by my excited grin. As though she'd expected me to be angry with her. 'Mari, how has he not known already?' I asked.

'He barely looks at me these days.' Again, she looked shamed to tell me.

'He must know immediately! You need to take to bed now, before you've done too much. You must take care of this child, so that it might bring some joy back into our empty lives.'

'*Our* lives? It may be your babe, but I am still his wife, Christian.'

'I don't care if Charles claims the baby for his own, only that I might be a part of its life.'

'Christian, you overestimate your brother's compassion. I do not really want to confess, but I cannot hide who the child came from. 'Twill be obvious in retrospect. Even if I *can* bring this child into the world and *if* Charles accepts to raise it, I would expect that you are the one person that the child will never see.'

'What do you mean?'

'I know him. Far better than you these past years. He's changed. He's not the same man you knew. He has become cold and unforgiving, your brother. He will hate you. He will send you away from us.'

'He can't. Not *my* brother. He would never turn me away. Things will be hard between us, but that needn't concern you any further. As I said, your only worry should be the child now. We shall go and speak to Charles, together. Do not worry.'

She did seem relieved that she shouldn't have to face him alone. 'Christian,' she asked, turning to me, looking quite serious, 'do you love me?' She didn't let me answer though. 'Do not say, 'tis not a fair question. Let us go and do what we must.' She still looked as though she thought I was foolish to think Charles might forgive us. She was right."

"Did you?" Felicity asked.

Cain was startled back to the present. "What?"

"Did you love her? Maribeth?"

After a moment, he smiled. "Yes, I suppose so. Of course, if you'd asked me at the time, I'd have told you no. I cared for her well being, of course, but I'd have said that she was spoiled and stubborn and her personality was totally unlike a woman that I would love. Later on, I might even add conniving and manipulative to the list.

But that's the funny thing about love. They say love is blind, but that isn't always the case. People your heart chooses to love, sometimes have traits you would consider to be glaring faults. You are not blind to them at all, but when you truly come to love someone, those traits simply become part of a larger whole; just a few aspects of someone you love. And because you love them, you can see past those things, to the person inside. You may disagree with their decisions, they may do things of which you disapprove and you may even dislike them a lot of the time, but you don't stop loving them. I know I don't, anyway.

When someone has your heart, 'tis not a simple thing to dismiss. It doesn't even have to be romantic love, in fact it holds true for families a lot of the time, but most people feel that they *must* love their families. They do things for their family more out of a sense of duty, than for love. To *really* give your heart to another, with no obligations, or assurance of its return, is a scary venture. But I do think that's an important lesson in life, to learn how to love. Some people really don't know how, not truly."

"That's so…discerning; perceptive and sad. She loved you too, I'll bet. The way she took care of you and wouldn't give up on you; but I guess it was never meant to be. She was trapped in her marriage with Charles and you had already been so hurt by your loss. Admitting that you loved her would have just made things worse for you. You had already betrayed your wife and brother, and her presence must have just been an awful reminder of that.

I don't think that I would have liked her very much, but I do feel for her. All that she went through, losing all those babies and being trapped in an unhappy marriage. Then to not even be able to hear that someone she loved, loved her back… It's so tragic and depressing, for both of you."

Her eyes looked as though they were tearing and her face held the most forlorn expression. He leaned forward and gave her cheek a quick caress. "Surely you didn't expect the story of *my* life to be a 'feel good' sort of affair, did you? Because I did give you a disclaimer at the beginning, if you remember."

Now she smiled, though it was still a watery sort of grin. "I'm sorry; I guess I'm getting too invested in the characters," she said archly.

"Well, there may have been much trial and heartache along the way, but if you're at all worried, so far, it has a happy ending." That made her laugh. "Shall I go on?"

"Please," she said, eagerly.

They both took a moment to drink from their wine glasses and then he continued. "Well, I don't know how I expected Charles to react. I guess I thought there would be a lot of yelling; a furious rage that would eventually spend itself and then he would calm and we would carry on.

It must sound foolish, I know, that I would think that he could forgive us. You have to realize that I had spent the first seventeen years of my life getting into trouble, and Charles was always the one to bail me out. He was the peacekeeper, the buffer between me and the world. I would have fun without a care for the wrath brought down around me and Charles would help to hide it from father, smooth things over and make things right. I had gone to him for everything, my whole life.

My father was gone now, after having shunned me, even if he had meant it to be only symbolic. I had only Charles. I could never imagine him turning his back on me, even if only for a lesson, as father had tried to accomplish. The greatest betrayal I'd ever felt from Charles, was when he insisted we come here, to the colonies, and even that was for my own good, I could now see. Charles always had my best interest in mind, but it had never before been *him* that I'd transgressed against.

When we told him, he barely even looked at Maribeth. It was as though he had only expected as much from her. He stared at me, long and hard. Then he quietly told me to get out of his house; he never wished to look upon my face again. As I said, I'd been expecting a fight. I was prepared to throw myself at his mercy and agree with terrible accusations and outbursts. I didn't know how to handle this silent anger. He turned from me, and would say nothing more. I tried to engage him in an apology and plead forgiveness, but the only thing he would say was 'get out'." Cain couldn't keep the plea for empathy from his voice, as though Felicity ought to agree that Charles should have forgiven him. He did not really feel that way, but it was difficult not to look for understanding from her.

She was unmoved. "All he had ever done was help you, and you betrayed him. *You slept with his wife*. What did you expect?" Felicity looked as disgusted with him as he felt with himself.

Cain had acceded to his guilt in all of this, in his own mind, long ago. So long ago, that it simply seemed a 'given'. It was something that he'd not really thought of from Charles' point of view in a long while. It was just taken for granted in his memory as something that had *happened*. Other things in his life seemed so much worse. It was true, what he had done in sleeping with Maribeth, was lecherous, but he had let himself forget about it a long time ago, in light of newer sins. "I suppose he had every right to hate me. I should never have expected otherwise.

So, he told me to get out. I wanted to stay, because I was afraid that he would turn his fury upon Maribeth when I left, but I was also afraid to say or do anything more to make things worse. He wanted me out. To stay would only bait him. Mari's eyes pleaded for me to remain, but I left.

I did wait outside a little, ready to come to Maribeth's aid if needed, if Charles' anger got out of hand. I don't know what I thought I would do. I was still so weak from lack of food and grief, but I would not let her take the brunt of it, if I could help it.

He didn't really yell much at her either though. I did hear him call her an ignorant whore. He told her that he thought she was very stupid to have bothered to tell him. That she should have simply waited for the baby to die, like all of the others, and then he need not have known."

"Oh my God, that's horrible!"

"Cruel, I know, but nothing that she couldn't handle. If anything, Maribeth was always strong. I felt for her, but I knew that the hardest thing right now would not be for her to hold back tears, but to hold her tongue. She was more one for vicious arguing than quiet weeping. Thankfully, she was smart enough to keep silent. He sent her to bed and that was the end of it, that night.

I went home. There was nothing more for me to do. Ten days, I waited ten days, desperate to know how she faired. I tried to regain my strength. I made myself some meager meals with what dry stores I had left. I did feel myself slowly beginning to return to health. The illness had left me unharmed, my own refusal to eat or get out of bed is what had kept me weak. From Charles and Maribeth, I heard nothing. I saw no one. They did not even send Alice over with bread any longer. I was afraid to approach their house and rile things up again, so I waited.

Then circumstances did present for me a solution of sorts. I'd gone into town, for something or other. There I saw Nan. You may remember that she was the girl that we had employed some five years before, to help Elizabeth during her pregnancy. Well, she was a *girl* no more. I believe that she was about twenty by then. Still unmarried, but I knew she was being courted. Anyway, she saw me and came to give her condolences over Liza and Amy. She seemed worried for me, I must still have looked terribly thin and pale. She asked if there was anything that she could do.

I told her that as a matter of fact there was. Now that I was alone, I could use someone to cook me a meal each day and take care of some light housework for me. If she could be persuaded, I would pay her well. She and her beau needn't worry for appearances, she could come while I was out at work in the fields. Do some wash and cleaning, then leave me a meal to heat later for supper. It would all be very proper and advantageous to us both.

What I was also thinking about, was that Nan was still friends with Alice, the girl in Charles and Maribeth's employ. I say girl, but that's really untrue. Like Nan, she also had grown. Alice was a married woman now, but still went once a day to help with the baking and such. Once I could re-establish a relationship with Nan, I would explain that Charles and I had had a falling out. She needn't know details, just that I knew Mari was with child and I would be appreciative if she could speak to Alice, and tell me of Maribeth's well being now and again.

Nan did agree and things worked out as I'd hoped. I was able to get news relayed to me every other day or so of the state of things in Charles and Mari's home. Maribeth was indeed still with child and had taken strictly to bed. She seemed to be doing well, although she did ask to call out the doctor for every slight alarm. Charles often became annoyed with her over it.

Confidentially, Nan said that Alice felt bad for Mari, because Charles did not seem hopeful or even very happy for the baby at all. She assumed that he was just worried that the child would not be born. I however, was certain that it was quite the opposite. I don't think Charles had ever expected the child to live. Now that it looked as though Maribeth might succeed with *my* child, when all of his had failed...I did become worried for the future.

In the meanwhile, as my health returned, I began to throw myself back into working the farm. I never saw Charles. He'd hired hands to work in my absence. The spring had come whether I was ready for it or not. We weren't wealthy any longer. We did rely upon our crops, but we had enough money for all the help we needed. My working again did lessen the load, but I never heard anything from Charles about it.

If possible, it seemed I felt my family's loss all the more now. Life was trying to get back to normal, back into routine and yet I was all alone. There was no one for me to come home to, only a covered dish on the table and a note from Nan.

I worked from dawn until dusk when I could. Only when there was work to be done, could I try to forget. Evenings, I would come back to the house and collapse in despair. I tried to force myself to eat whatever Nan had prepared, because if I had no energy, I could not work. If I could not work, I would be trapped in the house with my grief and my worries all day.

I was ever desperate for news of Mari and the child. The baby would be expected mid to late October. Here it was, end of May and she was still well! In my heart, I rejoiced for that, but I also felt an ever-impending doom. Would she really carry to completion? What would Charles do when the baby was born? He still had not spoken to me. I saw him once from afar. He had turned and walked away. Would he really keep this on forever? He had to let me see the child. I felt desperate that he just had to let me be in its life. He knew what it would mean to me, didn't he?

Then, one day soon after sunset, there was a carriage come up my drive and then a knock at my door. I was very anxious as I opened it. No one ever called upon me. I worried something bad had happened.

It was a man in a suit. He introduced himself as being in Charles' employ. He apologized for the hour, but explained that he was told he would only find me at home after dark. He'd a case full of papers that I was to sign. Charles wanted to take over my half of the farm and my house. I was to leave town and find myself a new life elsewhere. I laughed at the man. It was ludicrous!

The man assured me that my brother was fully within his rights, in asking me to leave. In fact, my consent was a mere formality. He could force me to leave if I resisted. You see, it was still his name on the deeds to our properties. In effect, without his grace, I owned nothing! As you can imagine, I was flabbergasted. I would not believe him, but he showed me the legal documents for proof.

Among those papers, I was also dumbfounded to find information on the balance left in my account back in England. It was emptied. At the age of twenty-one, I had gained access to it. I had used the account on occasion, but it was still a joint account with my brother, who had now taken it all. I was penniless, homeless, alone and in total shock over it all. I sent the man away. If Charles thought to rob me of my life, he could bloody well come and throw me out in person!

I know it must seem that I had ruined his life, from his perspective. He felt I'd ruined his relationship with his wife and then gotten her pregnant, branding him a fool, but to be honest, he hadn't a relationship with her anyway. It was still wrong of course, and perhaps I was just feeling selfish, but I couldn't agree to the severity of his reaction. No one else would ever know the child was not his. I didn't know what else Mari might have told him, but as far as I knew, he was only aware of our one tryst, not the ongoing affair we'd had years past.

To be honest, I had no idea really, what he felt. I don't know how I would have felt if our roles had been reversed. I don't think I had ever really felt about someone, the way that Charles had practically worshiped Maribeth when they had first wed, but now their relationship had deteriorated into a hollow facade of a marriage from what I could see. I hadn't been the cause of their troubles. Surely, Charles knew that. It was only true, that I had done an absolutely terrible thing in taking advantage of the fact that his marriage was already weak.

But now he sought to ruin my life in return? What had he to ruin? God had already taken from me the only people I had ever loved! My family was gone! What should I care any longer for money? But he knew I also loved the farm. He saw me out there every day. He knew that it was the only way that I kept myself sane. So he would take that too? Take my livelihood and make sure that I never got to see his wife again, or know of our baby, all in one fell swoop! It was unacceptable! I didn't care how wrong I was or how much I'd hurt him; I would not allow him to do this.

But before anything else, I needed to see Maribeth. I wanted to see her for myself and to know that she and the baby were alright. I had to speak to her of this, find out what she made of it all. She might not even know of Charles' plans. Once I thought it over, I realized that it was very likely that she'd no idea.

I wondered absently if Mari had thought to ask Alice for information on me as I had done over her. I had the baby as motive, but I suddenly realized that perhaps I did care a bit more for Maribeth herself, then I'd previously let myself acknowledge.

It began to take shape in my mind that perhaps the two of us would be happier to rid ourselves of Charles' influence altogether. Run off and start a family of our own, leaving Charles' anger far behind, a distant memory.

Living where and doing what? I was a pauper now. Should I hire myself as a farm hand and work for someone else's profit, leaving Maribeth home alone to sew all day and night so that we might survive? No. There was no way I could consign us to such a life. One thing at a time. I needed to see her.

I waited all the next morning, purposely working in sight of their house, hoping to see Charles' carriage head out for town. Finally, I was rewarded in seeing him leave. I went to Maribeth straight away. Alice met me at the door. She was a bit flustered and apologetic in telling me that she'd specific standing instructions to turn me away if ever I came. Maribeth heard this from the bedroom however. She told Alice to let me in, in spite of what Charles had told her. Alice still had reservations, until Mari threatened that if I were not allowed to come in, then Maribeth herself would be forced to come out. Alice would not have risked hurting the baby. She said she would leave on some errand and know nothing of my visit.

I went to the bedroom and there she lay. I can't say that I felt a rush of romantic love as I saw her, but a great wave of relief did wash over me, that she was indeed alright. Her stomach evidenced that the baby was well also. I just stared for a moment in disbelief. She did look to be doing very well. In fact, upon laying eyes on me, she positively glowed. She put her hands to her belly and beamed at me. 'It's growing Christian. I've never come this far! Do you see? Come, you can feel it!'

I couldn't help it, I had to go and place my hands upon her. How could I not? I remembered doing the very same with my own wife five years before; a magical experience. I felt it too, after a few impatient minutes. I felt the baby move!" Cain had to pause for a moment, a strong smile of remembrance upon his face. "She was so thrilled, we both were. Moments like those...that's what life is all about." He took a deep breath and looked up to see Felicity staring at him intently. Cain had never truly shared his thoughts and feelings on these things with anyone before. As he noticed her gaze upon him, he felt as though her eyes could see into his very soul. He sincerely hoped as he went on, that she would not be too frightened by what she would see there.

"Anyway, I knew that we hadn't much time. We needed to talk. As I had suspected, Mari knew nothing of what Charles had done, in closing my account and trying to strip me of my home. She was appalled, although not entirely surprised. She hadn't known, but she had predicted he would react thusly.

I never mentioned the idea of running off. She was the one who asked me. 'The Manor. Once the baby is born, I want to go back to Herald Manor, Christian. You are a Herald still. If we could wrest it from him somehow, and return to Canterbury, I've had quite my fill of being a farmer's wife. I'm meant for better than this, you know I am, as are you.'

I wasn't so sure of that. Perhaps she did belong elsewhere, but I loved the farm life. Of course, without my family it was a bit empty, maybe a change would do me good. I still could think of the Manor as home. Anyway, it was a moot point. 'The Manor is still in his possession Mari, we cannot gain it from him. He will stand in our way, whatever we were to try and do.'

'Then we must remove him.'

She said it clearly and coldly, as though it was something practiced in her mind. I didn't even know what she could mean at first. When the implication hit me, it was so horrible and yet so like my own thoughts the night before, I knew not what to say. I never would have spoken that myself and I hadn't even thought of it consciously. I'd ideas of leaving him, not *killing* him, but now that it had been said, I had to admit that it seemed to make perfect, if brutal sense. All of our problems neatly solved. It was absolutely dreadful to even consider, but consider it I did.

Then I told Maribeth that I couldn't do it. I told her that our happiness was not worth a man's life. We would have to find another way. She never said another word about it. She didn't try to convince me, she just looked at me for a few moments, thoughtfully. I knew that although I had spoken out against it, she was certain that the idea hadn't left my mind. She knew me well.

I left, telling her that I may come again if I could. I went back to daily life, but every time that I was reminded of my brother, that awful idea surfaced. It wouldn't leave my thoughts. It hovered there, like a poison fog.

The man in the suit came back. He said I had less than a month to collect my belongings and remove myself from the property; preposterous! He had documents and things showing that I would be removed by force if necessary. I had until the first of July. I laughed at that date. Convenient, I had worked all spring to plant, and I would be removed just as work finished. Plenty of time for Charles to find the help he would need for harvest. Then in the autumn, Charles could reap the fruits of my labor. When I told the man as much, he replied to me, off the record, that I could take Charles before a judge on that fact, and be reimbursed for my work, from the profits of the harvest. However, he also said that in dealing with my brother, he knew that this was a highly vengeful situation. He would advise me to let it go. My brother was prepared to be as hurtful and devastating as possible. I should leave for greener pastures and be happy to be rid of him.

Rid of him I would be. I honestly began to entertain the idea. I can't even say that I thought to beset upon him in a rage, killing him in the passion of anger. This was a cold and calculated thought process, of how best to remove this man from my life. I won't tell you of the things that I considered. I never spoke to Maribeth again either. I hadn't the chance to see her alone and I didn't want to provoke Charles any further. I knew that Maribeth would not be distraught if Charles disappeared from our lives. That was all that I felt I needed to know."

Cain was watching Felicity to see her reaction to his words. She said nothing, but stared at him with a rattled discontentment over her wine. Most likely, she had thought that the deaths on his hands had not begun until *after* his change; that his experience as a murderer had come with, and because of his vampire nature. That would indeed have been easier to forgive, he was sure. He was terribly sorry to disappoint her. He continued.

"Of course I had not totally given myself o'er to the plan. I did love my brother still, my brother of the past anyway. I swung back and forth over the issue constantly. I still tried to think of some way that we could simply leave, without finding ourselves destitute, but nothing seemed plausible, and the days were quickly passing. Besides, I could not hope to move Mari in her state. Whatever happened, she would need to remain at home until the baby was safely born.

Finally, I convinced myself that I could not become a murderer. No matter what Charles had tried to do to me, what I had already done to him was bad enough. I would not repay his past years of kindness with death at my hands.

I decided that I would leave peacefully. I would do what I could to set up a new home elsewhere, doing my best to remain in contact with those who could relay information to me of Maribeth. Perhaps I could even convince Charles that if he wanted me to leave, he needed to give me some money for a new start. Once the baby was born, I would return for them. Then we could steal away, Maribeth the baby and I, to live in my new home. I would need to see Maribeth again, to be sure of her, but I knew that she would gladly accept the idea. It may be difficult, and it would certainly not be Herald Manor, but I would care for her and the child. She knew that at least *I* had a loving heart.

I began to prepare my things for a move. I wouldn't bring much really. I finally nerved myself to gather Elizabeth and Amelia's things. I had let no one touch them. Now I brought them to Liza's father, at the church, and asked that he give them to a family who might need them.

I kept nothing of Liza's, although sometimes I do wish that I had. I did however keep Amelia's prized possession, her porcelain doll. I'd bought it when she'd turned three, ordered it from England, although everyone told me that it was too fine a thing for such a little girl. They'd told me that I should get one of cloth, until she was old enough to care for it, but I wouldn't listen. She had carried it everywhere. She treated it like a person and it never got even a chip, she was so careful. The doll's name was Harriet.

So, Harriet went into a box with what few other things I would keep. I went and knocked on Charles and Mari's door, one week before I was to leave. I knew Charles wasn't there. Alice answered once again. I told her that I knew her concerns, as I saw her shaking her head and worrying over disobeying my brother, again, but that I'd be leaving town soon and needed to say goodbye. She couldn't refuse me. I told her to relay to Charles my request for a meeting the next day. She agreed and then left for me to speak with Maribeth in private.

When I told Mari of my plans, she was a little disappointed in staying in the colonies, but as I expected, she professed that she'd be far happier with me than ever she would be with Charles. So it was set. She would write me letters if she could. If not, she would ask Alice to write. Nothing revealing, just a general report of her health and the baby's progress. A few weeks after the baby was born, when Mari felt able to travel, I would come for them.

The next day, the man in the suit returned. I should have known better than to expect Charles himself. I made my proposal, that if Charles should truly hope never to see me again, it was only fair that he give me back the money he had stolen from my account. I would need to buy myself a house and some land elsewhere; otherwise, he could expect to see me here in town, living as a farm hand with a neighbor.

I don't know if perhaps Maribeth had already approached him with the idea or not, but the man was prepared already to do just that. They had anticipated my request and were going to oblige, as long as I promised to leave town. And so, it was settled.

I decided that I should travel some distance from our farm before choosing a place to settle. Not only did I not want any reminders of the past years to intrude, but I also had thoughts that it would make it that much more difficult for Charles to find us, come the time that Maribeth would join me.

I ended up in New York finally. Not far from where we are now, believe it or not. I had just enough money to purchase a modest homestead with a plot of land large enough to work for profit. The house was unfinished and needed much work, but it would do. In fact, I was glad because it gave me something to focus on while I waited for the months to pass.

I sent a letter to Alice at her home, to let her know where I had settled. I asked again for her to please send me any news. I received a response from her not long after, stating that she was glad that I had begun my life anew and wished me all the best. Charles and Maribeth were doing well, her pregnancy progressing nicely. I should rest assured that she would send me updates now and again.

So, time went on. I worked on my house and began to establish myself in this new community. I also prepared a field as quickly as I could, and did some planting, that it was not too late for me to have some small crop come fall. I received another letter from Alice a few weeks later, saying that all was well. It seemed that things would work out as I'd hoped. Then the messenger came.

A messenger arrived with a letter from Alice, highly unusual. I immediately feared the worst, that Maribeth had lost the baby, but once read, it revealed news that might almost be considered worse from my point of view. They were gone! Alice informed me that Charles had unexpectedly sold both of our houses and the farm, and they were leaving for England! By the time I got the letter, they would be on their way. She gave me the name of the ship, port and departure time. They were to sail on the 'Glory' out of Delaware Bay, but they had left at first light yesterday morning. They were gone!

What the hell was Charles doing, making Maribeth travel in her condition? Why were they going back to the Manor *now*? Did he know of our plans? He couldn't. Did it mean so much to him that I be deprived of the pleasure of ever seeing her and my baby again? He was putting her on a ship for such a long and arduous journey...he was going to kill my child!

I hastily scrawled and sent back a short message to Alice, thanking her profusely for the information. I then set about trying to get details about the passage route of the ship 'Glory'. After a harrowing search, I found that luck was with me still. I'd a slight chance to catch them. The ship had three other stops to make before its main crossing. It was scheduled to stop in Keyport, New Jersey. That was not all that far from my new home actually, but they would have landed there today and were going to sail again in the morning. It was very doubtful I could get there in time. The ship would dock again up in Massachusetts however, to drop off some of its cargo to the port at Salem. Then it would stop once more at Kennebunkport in Maine and restock its own supplies before setting out to cross the Atlantic. I would try to meet them in Salem. It would be quite the frantic scramble, but with a good horse and a bit of luck, I might catch them before they were truly gone. It was worth a try. I did not relish the idea of trying to follow them across the sea back to England. I was terribly afraid that my child should not survive it. That was a last resort.

So I chose my fastest horse, a beautiful palomino stallion, packed some supplies for the journey and wasted no time in setting out for Salem, Massachusetts. Once there, if I succeeded in catching up with Charles and Maribeth, and indeed was able to work things so that Mari would return with me, then I would have to purchase a carriage for the return trip. I could never expect her to travel on horseback. I wouldn't bring my own carriage now, for speed was of the essence. I would worry about the return trip once I got that far. My only thoughts now, were of reaching them before it was too late.

I raced through forest and field, from town to town. I won't keep you in suspense, but tell you that I did indeed make the dock the night before they were to set sail, although I was desperately certain the whole time that I wouldn't. In fact, even though I had arrived a few hours before they were to leave, I still could hardly believe my eyes when I saw that the ship was indeed still there.

It was the middle of the night, almost two in the morning. Now that I had actually made it to my destination, I had no idea what to do. I studied the ship from a respectful distance and saw that there was a man there, keeping watch. It was he whom I would have to approach. There was just no way that I might sneak aboard and spirit Mari away, although I would like to. I'd no idea where to find them and surely Charles would be with her. I thought for a moment and then brought with me a small saddlebag as I went to try to gain access to the ship.

I hailed the man and inquired if this was indeed 'The Glory', and whether I might find the Lord and Lady Herald aboard, as it was imperative that I see them at once. Of course, the man was surprised that I should seek to come aboard at so late an hour. He told me that it was out of the question, as only passengers were allowed entrance at this time. The ship would sail at dawn.

At this news, I became quite agitated and told the man that if he had been unaware, the Lady Herald was with child. I was a physician, and had been called to look upon her one last time before they debarked on their journey. I had expected to arrive earlier, but was unavoidably detained. I was quite concerned that perhaps the lady was not well enough for the trip, and I must be allowed to examine her before they set sail. I waved my bag for emphasis, hoping that the dark would help to hide the fact that it was not really a doctor's bag.

This did seem to shake him a bit. He believed me I was sure, and it was obvious that he had noted Maribeth's condition. Still, he was uneasy to allow me aboard to bother them in the middle of the night. After what he said next however, I knew that I must get onboard immediately. He said that although he believed a final examination to be an excellent idea, he really thought that I should wait until Lord Herald came back aboard. He had not yet returned from 'The Ship's Tavern', a local pub, and the man had not been told to expect me.

Charles was not even on board! He'd left Maribeth so he might go and get drunk over his disappointments in us? If only we could leave before his return! I pleaded with the man as to the urgency of my visit. I was due to be somewhere else in the morning, and could not possibly wait for dawn to board this ship. The examination would take only twenty minutes or so. The baby's life could depend on it!

Finally, he decided to risk it. He would accompany me on board and we would inquire whether the lady would see me. When we reached the passenger's quarters, I had him inform her that Doctor Christian wanted to see her. Thankfully, she allowed me in.

I had woken her of course, but she was powerfully pleased to see me. I wanted to interrogate her as to why they were making this journey *now*, or at all! Had she any idea how dangerous this would be for the child? But we hadn't time for any of that now. Charles could return at any moment.

Maribeth knew my thoughts anyway and told me simply that she'd had no choice. Charles had given her no time to find a way to relay the news to me. She was amazed that I'd found my way here. Apparently, Alice had taken it upon herself to inform me, as Mari hadn't even the chance to speak to her before they left.

She was more than willing to leave with me, back to my new farm if that was what I wanted. She wanted only what was best for the baby. Perhaps we could become a real family. I must know that this baby was most important to her. Charles had hired a mid-wife, to make the journey with them, or else he knew Mari would refuse to come. She was asleep in the next room.

I wanted Mari to leave with me straight away, but she began searching the room frantically. It tortured me to see her, more than six months pregnant and rushing about like that. I tried to make her tell me what she was looking for, so that I might find it for her. She wanted a box. Charles had a metal box that he kept their valuables in. It was hidden in the room and there was something that she wanted from it before we left. She wouldn't tell me more, but I helped her search, to no avail. Finally, I persuaded her that we must leave without it. She actually looked undecided for a moment, but I took her hands and kissed them. "Please Mari..." I begged. It was time to go.

As we made to leave the ship, I was concocting in my head some story for the watchman, of how Mari was unfit to travel and I would take her to an inn, but the man was nowhere in sight. We left unseen and made our way off the ship to the dock.

We were so close. The dock was long, and deserted. I had left my horse tied amidst the trees some little distance away. I had thought to take Mari riding gingerly sidesaddle, as I walked the horse to a place where we might camp for the night. Then we would find her a proper carriage the next day and be gone. Unfortunately, it was not to be.

Charles returned, his timing impeccable. He approached the dock even as we stepped off of it. He was drunk. He started yelling at his 'fool woman', daring to come out looking for him in the dead of night. He would return when he was good and ready. Apparently, he'd thought at first that I was just some escort to accompany her, from the ship. It took him a moment to even recognize me. When he did, his eyes went wide, and then his mouth became a vicious snarl and he actually sought to charge at me and knock me from my feet.

I'd never seen rage overtake Charles like that, though I'd seen it in others many a time, back in my more mischievous days. There was a time or two that a man had come rushing at me with fury in his eyes back then, for being in places and doing things I'd no right to be. But it was a decade since someone had come at me that way. I was no longer a child, but truly a man. I backed away in surprise and he actually shoved Maribeth aside as he hit me. He knocked me right off of my feet. His ferocity astounded me. I hit the ground in bewilderment. I hadn't initially planned to fight him, but the fact that he'd put his hands on Mari stifled any empathy I might have felt for his position.

I couldn't even speak to him. He was like an animal fighting blind and started pounding his fists to me, wherever he could connect. Mari, upon seeing him beat me so, became terribly distraught and did the stupidest thing she could have done. She tried to get him off of me.

She began pulling at him and screaming for him to leave me alone. I tried to tell her to get away, but I don't believe she even heard me. I was rather busy just trying to regain my feet before I became too badly injured, so that I might fight back.

Charles turned on her in an absolute fury. He grabbed her off of him and threw her to the ground calling her a filthy whore. Rather than leave it be, she still screamed back at him like a common fishwife and not the lady of noble bearing that she should be.

I flew at him and hit him once or twice, but before he would take notice of me, he kicked Maribeth as she lie there on the ground...hard. Some detached part of my mind saw it and knew that it was a very calculated and intentional strike. Her swelled stomach took most of the blow.

I saw positively red after that, there was no coming back from it. I beset upon him with the sole intent and purpose of killing him. I think he knew it too. We fought brutally. Charles and I were evenly matched in size and strength, but I was five years his junior, and he was still quite drunk. He did fight well though, I must give him that. When it became clear that he wouldn't win, he tried to circle me and find a way to run past, to the ship I suppose. I guess he thought to get help. I don't know how no one heard us, but we remained unobserved. I wouldn't let him by when he sought to pass me. In fact, I gave him a swift punch to the side of the head.

It was then that I heard her, Maribeth. It seemed as though she spoke directly into my ear, although she still lay crying some little bit away. 'Finish him Christian.' I don't know, to this day if I heard it only in my head or if Maribeth actually spoke the words. Charles was dazed and thrown off balance, and before I think I even realized consciously what I was doing, I kicked him over the side.

I don't think I'd meant to do that at first. Truthfully, it all happened so fast, it's rather hard to sort out now, but at the thought of what he'd done to Maribeth, I believe I only thought to kick him back, as he had kicked her. It was only when I heard him hit the water with a loud splash, that I realized what it meant. Charles could not swim. The water was not terribly deep here at the dock, but the tide was coming in and it was deep enough. He was drunk and I'd just punched him in the head hard enough to deliver a concussion. I stood there for a moment in shock, listening to the waves. Then I did think perhaps to go after him, but when I reached the edge, he was gone. I couldn't even see where he had disappeared to under the water. Then I heard Maribeth scream.

It cut through the dazed shock like a knife. I spun to see her digging at her skirts and she screamed again as though she had been stabbed. I ran to her of course, but I knew even before I reached her, what it would mean. She was trying to get the folds of her dress out of the way so that she might see her legs, but had to stop and double over in pain.

There was nothing I could do at first, but hold her until it passed. When she was able, she lifted her skirts away. I'm sure we both expected to see her thighs dark with blood, but that wasn't the case. They were wet though, her skin gleamed in the moonlight. I didn't know much about childbirth, but the doctor and Elizabeth had told me some, before Amelia was born. I remembered that there'd be a rush of fluids to mark the time when the baby would come. Maribeth's water had broken.

This could not be good, it was far too early, but at least it wasn't blood. I lifted her to her feet and we made our way off the dock into the proper town. I helped her walk and half carried her when needed. Twice we had to stop along the way as her body was wracked with contractions. I pounded upon the first door that we came to.

It was a fisherman's home, he and his wife and children awakened by our furious knocking. I quickly made known our situation, and they were kind enough to let us in and give Mari a bed to lie on. The man went rushing out to fetch the local doctor as his wife helped to calm Maribeth. She had her eldest daughter make a tea that she said might help to stave off the labor and soothe her body back to rest. The contractions however showed no signs of slowing, but instead came harder and faster as we waited for the doctor to arrive.

When he finally did come, it was obvious the baby would also be arriving shortly. There was nothing the doctor could do but try to ease the birth." Cain became very quiet and still for a moment, lost in his thoughts. Felicity sipped her wine and waited patiently for him to go on.

"The wait wasn't long, and my second child was born. We had a boy." Cain tried to swallow past the lump in his throat. He would not lose his composure this time, but he resolved that he would not give in to his urge to skip ahead in the story, past the memories he had not called up for himself in so long. His voice became quiet and confidential as he recalled the sad wonder with which he had viewed his little boy.

"He was *so* tiny; perfectly formed, with ten little fingers and toes. He was quiet, but alive, kicking and wriggling, but I knew he was *too* small. Mari knew it too. The doctor only needed to look at us to know that he needn't try to explain.

They have such miracles these days, such modern wonders of technology; special beds and boxes to keep a baby warm and great machines to breathe for a child whose lungs are not quite ready yet. Of course, we'd none of that then. He couldn't breathe well at all, not even to cry properly, and we knew he'd almost no chance of survival.

I held him, while they attended to Maribeth. She was still cramping and bleeding, but they told me not to worry. It was normal and she'd be alright, it would stop soon. As for the baby, he didn't last more than an hour or so. Died in my arms, he did. Maribeth wouldn't hold him, even after she was better recovered.

It was as though she didn't want to become attached to him. She wouldn't even give him a name. I wanted to name him, but she refused to let me. It was as though she was in denial and just wanted to forget it all as quickly as possible.

He died, and they took him away. Maribeth asked them to take care of it for us. She didn't want details. Baby Herald was all they called him. I never told anyone, not even Mari, but...I wanted to name him Daniel. That was his name...Daniel."

Cain paused to wipe the tears that had filled his eyes and to drink more of his wine. Felicity looked silently heartbroken for him. He took a deep breath.

"I guess I wasn't meant to be a father." She didn't say anything, but reached over to squeeze his shoulder for a moment in sympathy. He noticed she said nothing about Charles, not that he'd given her much of a chance. That's how it had happened though. Maribeth had begun labor before he himself had even had a chance to really acknowledge his brother's death in his mind. Charles' death would not remain entirely forgotten at the time however.

"Just after dawn, there was a knock at the door. It was someone come from the 'Glory'. As soon as I realized, terror struck my heart and I was forced to remember the other events of the evening. As I sat quietly by Mari's side, I could hear them from the front room, and they never even mentioned Charles' disappearance. They wanted us to know that the ship would be sailing shortly, with or without us. Maribeth was sleeping, and the man of the house came quietly to fetch me.

For a moment, I feared it would be the watchman from the night before, but I couldn't be *that* unlucky. It was someone that I did not recognize, nor they me. I came to understand that the people of the house had assumed that *I* was Maribeth's husband. Of course they had, why wouldn't they? My name was Herald and I acted 'the father' of the baby. The only person who had seen me approach the ship, knowing that Charles had not yet returned, was the watchman. I don't know what he ever told anyone, but it seemed to have been accepted that Mari left the ship in the night for the baby. Charles was assumed to have met her in town, and now they must have thought me to be him.

The porter who came to us now, brought two suitcases of the Herald's belongings from the ship, and a message from the mid-wife Charles had hired for the journey. I had totally forgotten about her and for a moment, I felt terribly stricken that perhaps if we had gone back to the boat she could have helped us, faster than the doctor in town could. But no, I realized that in all reality she would not have been able to do anything to prevent the baby's early birth. In fact, it was a good thing we hadn't seen her, for she would certainly have been able to tell someone that I was not Charles. As it was, she didn't even know I existed.

She sent word now of her condolences. Unbeknownst to us at the time, when the baby was born, the man of the house had sent word to the ship for us, of our whereabouts and condition. That's why they weren't even looking for Charles. They thought for sure he was here. The mid-wife wanted us to know that she was greatly sorry for our loss, but that she would still be making the passage to England as planned. We could still have our room back aboard the ship if we'd like, but they would sail within the hour.

I was so dazed by the night's events; I could hardly think what to tell them. The doctor gently advised me against continuing the voyage, for Maribeth's condition. She should recover and have time to accept our loss and grieve properly before making such a journey. I simply nodded my head, happy to follow whatever advice I'd been given. I couldn't really expect us to board the ship anyway. They weren't looking for Charles now, but surely *someone* onboard would know that I was not him. How would I explain Maribeth leaving her husband behind to take me in his place?

The porter left and the doctor went to check on Mari. I was about to follow, when the lady of the house put her hand on my arm to stay me. She asked me quietly if I'd seen anything unusual just before Maribeth's labor had begun. I was stunned for a moment and then told her that I had no idea what she could mean.

I was worried of course, that someone had heard the fight that had taken place, so I was quite unprepared for what she said next. She asked if perhaps I had seen a specter or an apparition, the visage of someone hovering above Maribeth, as if to curse or harm her. Mayhap an odd animal or bird had been in the area?

As you can imagine, at this I was thoroughly confused. What on earth could she mean? I apologized, told her that I had seen nothing of the sort and knew not even, what such a thing would mean.

She took me to the corner, as though to whisper a great secret. 'Witches', she breathed. She gave me a knowing nod as she saw my eyes grow quite wide at the word. 'The Devil has been busy, doing evil works here in Salem. 'T'would have been best had you never left that ship of yours, to set foot in this God forsaken hamlet. The Lord help us, but the Devil is run rampant here these past months. Some have hung for it already, but still they've not yet routed him out.'

She said "Twas most likely witches what caused your baby's death.' Did we know anyone here in town? Have we had ill relations with any townsfolk we might have met? Perhaps we'd like to file a formal report?

I hardly knew how to respond. Was she serious? I remembered now that I had heard of a woman being hung for a witch, hereabouts, but I'd dismissed it as foolishness and of course, I'd had more pressing personal matters in mind of late. Finally, knowing not how else to respond, I thanked her for her insight. I told her that I'd no wish to report any mysterious happenings, but that I would surely tell someone if I remembered anything of note.

I returned to Mari a bit bemused. I found she was awake and the doctor had apparently just finished examining her. He announced she was recovering nicely and left us to talk in private. Well, let me tell you, she would ask or say nothing about the baby. I tried to console her, but she would not grieve nor be consoled. She wanted it to disappear into the past, to have never been.

After a time of silence, she fell back to sleep, she was exhausted still from her ordeal to be sure. I sat, trying to understand her affected cold and heartless attitude and then I left that she should rest. The lady of the house invited that I join them in a meal, after which I went back to sit by Mari's side. Before long she did awaken and asked of the state of things.

When I told her about the ship, she grew positively frantic! I thought she should be happy that no one would be the wiser for what had happened. Now we could travel back to my home in New York and try to resume some sort of life. I couldn't understand her desperation.

The box; she still wanted that box that Charles had hidden in the room onboard. She had me search the luggage left for us three times, but of course, it was not there. The ship's crew had packed only those things that were in plain sight. The doctor came to tell us that he'd be leaving and begged for Maribeth to rest, but she shooed him away with barely a glance.

The ship; she demanded that we go after it. I thought she must be mad. What could be so important? I assumed she wanted some family heirloom from the box, a piece of jewelry, or something of sentimental value. I refused to speak to her of going after it until she told me exactly what she was searching for.

Would you believe it was money? I should have known. Wealth and status were always so damn important to her. Charles had put all of the profit from the sale of the farm and our two houses into that box. Bloody stupid if you ask me. He'd never heard of a bank? But they were going back overseas and he wanted to have it with him. He didn't trust anyone on the boat to guard it for him, so he hid it himself. He'd told her so, though she hadn't been privileged enough to know where.

The ship would be docking only one more time before setting out across the Atlantic. It would stop in Kennebunkport Maine, and we would be there to meet it. Maribeth was resolute. If I would not accompany her, she would find her way there alone.

She insisted that physically, she was fine. I didn't quite believe her, for I knew that Liza had needed a few days to recover from Amy's birth, but I also knew better than to challenge her. She would rather die than let me prove her wrong. She said that she would rest in bed until I could purchase her a horse and make ready to go, but she was going. She wouldn't take a carriage, that would tie us to the roads, when through forest may be quicker at times. She was hesitant to try to have my horse carry us both. It would be a close thing and she wouldn't take the chance of weighing him down too heavily to run at full speed.

Maribeth's not a woman easily argued with, and after all she'd been through, I knew better than to try and go against her wishes. A bit of checking did reveal that the ship had left as scheduled, a few hours before. So I found myself looking for a horse and supplies. I ended up purchasing a fine chestnut mare from a man in town. I added a few things to what supplies I already had, including a good map of the area, and made ready to go. I tried to convince her to let me go alone, that she should await me here, but she was adamant that I not leave without her. I think she actually questioned whether I would return!

Before sunset, I stood with much trepidation, and aided Maribeth in mounting her horse. We'd profusely thanked the couple at whose home we'd stayed, and asked that they keep our luggage until we might return for it. I wanted to stay here the night and begin our travels with the dawn, but Maribeth wouldn't hear of it. The ship already had a full days' travel ahead of us. 'Twas a straight easy run up to Kennebunkport from here for sailing, but the boat would stay in harbor for a full two days. We might make it if we hurried.

Once again, I found myself chasing that bloody ship. Warnings rushed about in my head, given by the lady of the house at our departure. 'Stick to the roads and be mindful of spirits and animals of the night. Perhaps they would not be angry with us, for we'd not turned against them to the courts, but the Devil will strike whom he will, with oft' no rhyme or reason. His witches are a wily lot, and know of ways to strike unseen.'

Of course, we paid her no heed, but set off at a harrowing pace. Upon studying our course, I saw that we could not take a direct route, but would often be forced to make detours around inlets and towards bridges over rivers and streams. Maribeth chafed at each setback that I showed her on the map, but refused to be deterred. To be honest, I was much more worried that she not break her neck, than to whether we should catch the ship. At this point, I hardly wanted Charles' money.

In fact, if no one learned of what had happened to Charles and he was simply declared 'disappeared', eventually Maribeth and I would inherit the Manor, and any other holdings he might have had left; a fact that I pointed out to Mari as we traveled, but she was too impatient to wait. What if they discovered that there had been foul play? The money in the box was a sure thing. It was hers, and she wanted it...now.

We didn't get very far. We were still in the outskirts of Salem actually, when our journey met its abrupt detour and eventual end. We had crossed a field and entered a forest, because it was a quicker route than the winding road. The brush was light, and even with the dark we were able to keep a good pace through the tall trees, when our horses suddenly stopped and became terribly skittish, refusing to go on.

A man stepped out from the trees, although I didn't know him for a man at first. He was thin and bald, very withered and old. The wane moonlight that shone through the branches above seemed to bounce off his head and bath him in an otherworldly glow. He seemed so gnarled and old, one would think him a goblin or bogie of the forest, but he stood there and looked at us, and then he did seem only a man.

I don't know why I was so frightened of him, as I said, upon closer inspection, he did *look* human, but the way that he stepped out and smiled at us with an odd and malicious gleam in his eye, told me that he was indeed evil. I didn't know it then of course, but this would be my first encounter with a vampire.

I'm sure it was only a moment, although it seemed to occur in slow motion. He looked at me, gave me an evil grin, and then looked to Maribeth. At that precise moment, her horse became spooked and took off into the woods. The old man grinned at me once again and then took off after her.

Of course, I followed. How such an old man thought he would keep up with a horse, I'd no idea, but somehow they quickly lost me. I was not to learn what he was until much later, and even a vampire is no faster than a man through the woods, but I realize now, that the man must have had some slight telepathic talents and was using them to try and direct Mari's steed.

I've met vampire's who laid claim to such powers, although never anyone skilled enough to do anything truly impressive. The power does not always come with vampirism, as I've never evinced a bit of it myself, if not through venom, but some do have it. I believe that is how he did manage to chase them out of my path. Clouds covered what little moonlight there was and I was left in the dark, picking my way through the forest. I was following the sounds of Mari's mare crashing through the brush, when I heard the animal let out a piercing shriek, and Maribeth herself screamed.

What could have happened? Had he caught up to them? But what could he have done to the horse to make it wail so? I could do nothing but follow the last echo of Mari's scream. All was silence after. I was desperate to find her but knew not what to do. I wouldn't yell to reveal my location, for surely I was close and must surprise them, but...nothing. Finally, I did begin to yell for Maribeth; still, nothing. I searched and searched but could not find sign nor sound of them.

It must have been hours. Dawn arrived, and I had found nothing. I was truly beginning to doubt my own sanity. In fact, a very clear and frightening idea occurred to me. What if I had not caught their boat? What if I'd never re-encountered Charles and Maribeth? The fight, kicking Charles over the side, Mari's labor pains, the baby...what if it were all some grand delusional dream? Here I was alone, wandering through the woods. Could I prove that any of it had ever happened, to anyone...even myself? I was just a lone man riding through the forest, same as two days before, before everything. It was mind numbing to think about.

Then, at last, I came upon Mari's horse, riderless. Thank the Lord that I was yet still sane! I was quite surprised to find the mare alive after the scream she'd let out in the night. I think now, that she must have been rebelling against an overload of mental commands from their pursuer. Or perhaps he had changed before her and she was frightened, knowing him for a predator, for she wasn't greatly injured. She was wandering between the trees, looking for something to graze upon.

The mare seemed totally unharmed at first. Then I did notice upon closer inspection, that she'd a small wound on the side of her neck, a bite of some sort. I'd no idea what would have done that or what it could mean. She seemed none the worse for it. Where was Maribeth?

Then my heart seemed to stop in dread. The saddle...it was covered in blood, but after a moment's reflection, I realized that although it worried me, it was no proof of foul play. It was from Maribeth's riding most likely. Her poor battered body had only just endured the birth of a child, however small. Riding should certainly have been forbidden by the doctor had he known she'd be so foolish. She'd caused herself to bleed again. It was upsetting, but not nearly as much as her continued absence. Again and again, I bellowed her name into the unresponding forest.

Had I any knowledge of vampires at the time, I would surely have realized that it was Maribeth who had drawn the creature right to us. She'd been bleeding rather heavily and the scent must have driven him to follow us like a summons.

I knew not what to do. I wandered the whole day screaming and searching, until finally I had to concede that she was lost. I would not spend the night out here alone. I would go to town and perhaps I could get others to help me search in the morning.

I went not back to Salem, but the next town over, to which I was closer. I thought it best I not return to Salem anyway. If Charles' body had been found, I'd be wanted for questioning. Besides, the last thing that I wanted was to be drawn into some trial over witches killing my baby and now stealing its mother. For I did wonder if witches it was, although I did not care to stand before a court o'er it.

I'd never before heard of a man being called a witch, but he didn't seem merely a man either. Perhaps 'twas Satan himself who'd stolen her away. How else had they so thoroughly disappeared? I was entirely beside myself.

I found an inn at which I could stay, and did gain help in searching for her come the morn'. I don't really know what the men whose aide I enlisted really thought of my tale. They did admit to hearing of many strange happenings of late, but as days went by and we found not a trace of her, I could not ask them to keep looking. At least I had her horse, as some sort of proof that I was not entirely suffering from hallucinations. Maribeth *had* been with me, and now she was gone.

I was aimless and unsure what to do after we stopped looking. Cold as it may sound, I won't say that I missed her terribly as a companion. I worried over what may have happened to her, and I did love her, whether I'd recognize it in myself or not, but ours was never a great romantic love. In fact, our relationship throughout the years had been a strange one indeed, if you stop to think o'er it. It had begun with indifference and even petty jealousy over Charles' attention. Then it ranged through friendly camaraderie, to lust, to angry condemnation and finally a desperate sort of clinging to each other, to help weather the storms of Charles' wrath and simply so we should not be alone in the world. I never saw us as 'soul mates' or two people emphatically in love with one another. We knew each other well and understood each other. Without each other...we each were frighteningly and undeniably alone.

I spent the next week at that inn. My days sleeping late and staring out the windows at the forest, my nights by the hearthside in the tavern. I would scarce notice those around me, but sit and gaze into my ale as though it held great unfathomed secrets of life. I would stay as late as they would let me, and then go to bed and dream of that wrinkled old man and Maribeth's scream mingled with that of her mare.

Until one evening, after the fire had burned low and the serving wench had sent me to bed; I went to draw the shutters closed over the window against the bright, nearly full moon, when I saw something outside that nearly stopped my heart. There was a figure making its way through the woods to come out into the field at the side of the inn. It struck not fear in me, for it stood tall and upright, nothing like the creature that had stolen Mari from me. It was a person moving steadily, and although I could not yet see its features clearly, it was definitely a woman by the long full skirts of the dress she wore.

I could scarce let myself hope for it to be true, until the woman stepped out of the trees into the field under the moonlight. Even in the odd blue light of the moon, I could see a glint of fiery red in the long hair falling over her shoulders. Maribeth!

I could not stop to think of how she could have come here or be unharmed after all these days gone. It was Maribeth! I ran from my room without jacket or hat and through the empty tavern out into the night. As soon as she saw me, she stopped dead in her tracks. I didn't even think it odd that she didn't run to meet me, but when she started to back away, I called to her in confusion.

My calls were unanswered. She was clearly glad to see me, but still she turned and headed back to the cover of the forest. What could I do but follow? Stories floated through my mind of the will-o'-the-wisp, an elusive light or spirit thought to lure people into the woods, to lose their way and vanish never to be seen again. The idea of witches sending out an apparition of a deceased loved one in order to draw the grief stricken into a trap, wanted me to pause for caution.

But this was no glowing spirit. This was no elusive vision of loveliness, garbed in robes of white. Lovely though she was, it was simply Maribeth, just as I'd seen her last, except that her hair had come loose of the braid she had worn. She was real. I saw her clothing snag upon branches she passed and her feet made noise on the forest floor, although slight.

She was just beyond reach and as I put on a desperate burst of speed, I did touch her. She was solid and whole. 'Maribeth stop!' I pleaded desperately as I finally caught her and turned her to face me. She looked into my eyes and seemed dazed and almost terrified. I had no idea what she could have been through, but I tried to console her.

I pulled her to me with such force that it's a wonder I didn't hurt her. I sobbed, and I laughed, and I kissed her hair. I rambled nonsense of how she was safe now, and I would care for her and everything would be over and behind us. Eventually I managed to move her hair away and find her soft skin on which to place my kisses of joy. I don't know how long my lips covered and tasted the place where her throat met her shoulder, but after a time, I felt her kiss the side of my throat as well.

I suppose you can imagine what next I felt."

Felicity was enrapt, her forgotten glass half raised to her lips, her own mouth slightly open and her eyes wide. As Cain's attention fell upon her, she closed her mouth to swallow and she tried to stifle a chill that ran down her back. "She bit you," she whispered.

Cain nodded slowly. He stared at her in thought for a moment. "I won't describe that to you. You *know* what that is." His eyes darted about guiltily for a moment before they settled back on hers. Felicity had still never confided in him, her own impressions of his bite. He wasn't sure how she thought of it, though of course *he* remembered it fondly. He was fairly sure the experience itself had pleased her, although she may not reveal it, but had she also been so frightened that she would not even consider discussing it with him...or repeating it? Smarter to avoid the topic, to be explored another time...or never again. Why couldn't he get that straight in his mind? It should not be repeated, but forgotten.

At least he thought so, but still she asked, "Is it always the same? It's not, is it? Not for everyone."

He forced himself to answer shortly, without emotion. "No, it's similar for most, but in some ways it differs. It's a very personal experience." His eyes could practically read the memory from her own. She'd been thoroughly enthralled and loathed to concede it. He would move on with his tale of the past, to avoid recent events.

"The next I knew, I was in pitch darkness with the cool scent of deep earth all around me. I was unsure if I was even alive. Thought I was dead and buried, I did.

A light flared. There was Maribeth, looking terribly worried, with a lantern, and shelves of jellies and jams behind her. I was so confused, that I had to close my eyes again. My thoughts wouldn't sort themselves. Things were hazy and I felt as though I was drowning in foggy recollections. My body felt terrible heavy and my eyes didn't want to stay open. All I could want was rest.

'Christian?' Maribeth's voice cut through the delirium of half-sleep. I *was* alive then, but where were we, what had happened? I couldn't remember.

'Christian!' This time there was clearly panic in her voice. What was she so worried over? Suddenly I did remember, some. I remembered Charles, the baby, her disappearance, and following her through the woods this very night. Then something had happened...to me, but I could not recall what, the memory stopped there.

'Christian please! You must answer a question for me.'

It seemed terribly hard work just to open my eyes, but I did. Yes, jams and jellies. We were in someone's root cellar, I came to realize. I couldn't fathom how we might have come to be here though. My eyes found Maribeth once again. My, but she did look distraught. The dim light of the lantern made her face look gauntly thin and her eyes were red-rimmed and bright with tears.

'Yes?' I managed to whisper.

'Oh Christian!' She was so relieved that I could still hear and respond to her. I must have been drained very near to death. 'Christian, do you love me?'

I closed my eyes again. She shook me to look at her, and tried to make me sit up. 'Do you love me, Christian?' I couldn't imagine why she'd be asking me this now. In fact, I was so bewildered by everything that it took me a moment before I even realized that she expected an answer. 'Do you?'

I can't really say that I pondered the question. I was hardly in the frame of mind for thoughtful response. I simply know that I opened my mouth and the word that came out was...'yes'. She let me go, and I gratefully dropped myself back to the hay-strewn floor to close my eyes. I very happily would have died just then, but Maribeth wouldn't allow it.

'Drink. Drink, Christian. If you don't, you'll die! Drink it, Christian, I won't let you leave me!'

Maribeth...again. 'Damn that woman' I thought, 'couldn't she just let me be?' Do you know, that I instantly felt as though I had traveled back in time? Funny how our minds seek to protect us from truths. I was positively convinced I had traveled back in time. Maribeth's pregnancy, Charles' death, the loss of yet another child, none of it had ever happened. Of course it hadn't! I was sick, remember? I was grieving over the loss of Amy and Liza. I wanted to die and Maribeth *still* would not leave me alone! All I wanted was to close my eyes and be left to die, and that woman kept pushing at me her bloody broth!

I opened my eyes to tell her just that. I was so powerfully angry! Who was *she* to tell me that she would not let me die! 'I don't want your damn soup!' I yelled at her. Obviously, she found me delusional and then took matters into her own hands. When I did manage to focus my eyes to see what she offered, it was to see not a cup of broth, but her own torn and bloody wrist that she brought to my lips.

I hadn't even the patience with myself to think how odd that was. I simply declared myself insane and closed my eyes again. She pressed her wrist to my lips and forced the blood to my mouth, and then...all else was instantly forgotten and forgiven. I drank."

"You drank her blood?" Felicity's voice was full of quiet awe and revulsion.

"I did. That's how it's done," he confirmed.

"But...you were still human," she said in disgusted confusion.

"I was, at the time," he agreed.

"But, didn't you...resist; find it...appalling?"

Cain gave her a little smile. This was a conversation for a later date. "No. It's not something I can really explain. It's more something you have to...experience." She seemed a little frightened by that remark.

He pretended not to notice, and went on. "Anyway, that is how it is done. To create a vampire, ideally you would want to replace all of the humans' blood with that of their maker. Obviously, this is not an exact science, but to give a person too little vampire blood, is to let their body die. That is how those unfortunate zombie creatures you've seen are created. Lesser amounts can allow the body to become brain dead, produce mild to severe retardation, or simply allow memory loss or a range of cognitive disabilities.

If a vampire is to retain their present state of mind, lucidity, there can be no true death or disruption, but a seamless transition from one state of being to the other. In order to allow this, the candidate must first be as nearly drained of blood as possible, without allowing true death to occur. Then that person is given back all the blood lost, mingled with that of the vampire, but this alone is not enough. For a sure and thorough change, it must be done not just once, but over and over again, until the blood of the vampire and its chosen one are so mixed as to be indistinguishable."

Felicity was still not quite with him. "So you drank her blood, while you were still human, *again and again*? Wasn't there a point when you were recovered enough to think clearly? Wasn't there a time when you thought 'What the hell am I doing?'"

Obviously, she was refusing to understand how he could become caught up in the sheer passion of it all. She wouldn't face her own recollections of being bitten and he was almost afraid to try to describe it to her. Felicity spoke again before he could explain. "She bit you again, didn't she? Only this time, you had to understand what she was, right? Weren't you scared of her?"

He was careful not to show any expression. Had Felicity been scared when he'd bitten her? Her body certainly hadn't reacted in fright. "It was Maribeth," he said with a shrug, by way of simple explanation. "When she bit me the first time, I hadn't seen her change, and truthfully, I didn't really remember it all that well. Too much had happened. I believe I must have been in shock. The second time she bit me, again I didn't see her face.

Until that point, I did *not* know what she was. It was only after she began to draw the blood from my body, that I realized what she had become. I must tell you though, I'd no fear of her. In fact, if you really want to know my thoughts at the time, I realized that she had been transformed, that she was not human any longer. I came to understand that she had instead become something made to prey upon humans. That was clear, and all I could think, was that *even in this, she was magnificent.* I may have seen many faults in her as a person, but as a lover, and as a vampire, I had felt that she was beyond compare. I was not frightened but enraptured that she could even now have such an effect on me."

The way in which Felicity looked at him, was not with understanding or sympathy. She did not pretend to misunderstand him, but rather seemed to deny that she could empathize. Finally, she asked, "When did it happen? Did you know you would become a vampire? How did you *change?*"

"After she drank from me the second time, I would drink again from her. I watched with amazed wonder as she did show me her vampire features and bare her fangs. She did this not menacingly, but as an honest display, so that I might know her now for what she was. Also, so that she might tear her own skin for me, to drink, reopen the wound at her wrist. There were no words spoken, none were needed. It was then that I truly understood. It wasn't as ghastly as I might have thought it should be. It was just like puzzle pieces fell into place, and I understood. She made the tear and I drank without hesitation, it just seemed right somehow, that I should.

When I was done, she drank from me again, and left me severely weakened and empty. It was almost painful to feel the lack of blood within me, although I didn't think that I should die. It wasn't the heavy grogginess that I'd felt when life had been truly slipping from me before, but I knew that I *needed* the blood within her. I was positively desperate for it. She had paused for rest before she would open her vein for me, and I became impatient. Before I could even recognize what was happening, I began to change myself. I felt a sudden fierce ache in my upper jaw and my eyesight grew blurry.

I felt a flash of pain as my jaw exercised its new hinge. It moved for my new fangs to become exposed. The next thing I knew, my gums were tearing to allow new hollow slivers of sharpened bone to come through, and my fangs extended. Then I became terribly disoriented because the colors of the room seemed to suddenly shift, and Maribeth turned blue."

Felicity had been listening with an almost cringing sort of revulsion. Cain almost had the impression that she *felt she ought to* be disgusted, more than she actually was, but this clearly caught her by surprise. She forgot to be disdainful and sat forward with clear curiosity. *"Blue?"*

Cain smiled. "My eyes, they changed. We see heat, and blood, when in our vampire state. I'm sure you've seen such things in movies, or on television, heat vision cameras or whatever, but it's much clearer than that. The details don't suffer nearly as much. I could still perfectly see the expression upon her face. I could count every eyelash if I'd a mind too. They were just the wrong color. Very disorienting as you can imagine.

Maribeth's body was outwardly dead, cold, and so I saw her in blues and greens, but the blood within her stood out with a strong deep red color that beckoned me to come for it. It was as though I could see nothing else. At her throat was a strong thick band of it, just beneath the skin, and I pulled her to me, thinking of nothing but drinking it.

As my fangs touched and then broke through her skin, sliding through her flesh so easily, all I could think was how wonderful it was, that she needn't open the way for me any longer. And so...I was reborn a vampire; all because a woman asked me if I loved her and I was fool enough to say yes.

To be perfectly honest, I don't believe changing me had been her original intent. I don't know exactly what happened to her the night she'd disappeared. She never would speak of it. That remains her story to tell. I don't know how or why the old man changed her, or how it was that she came to be alone after, but alone she was, and just like myself at the time, I think the prospect of being alone terrified her. I believe she came to look for me, only because she knew not to whom else she would turn.

She wanted to see me, to show me and make me understand what had happened to her. I don't think she meant to harm me, but when I pulled her to me and held her the way that I did... I had kissed her very throat. I don't know how much she understood of what she was. I don't believe the one who made her had been much of a teacher. I know that later on, all that we learned of what we had become, we discovered together.

The temptation to drink from me must have overwhelmed her. When she did pull away, she must have been horrified by what she'd done. Do you have any idea how hard it must have been for her to leave me breathing at all? Of course you don't! The will she must have possessed to stop herself...

Anyway, she had taken me to the place she herself must have hidden by day. I can hardly comprehend the strength of will and determination that it must have taken for her to carry or drag me there. I am not a light man and she herself was surely not a woman accustomed to such work, but she knew that we needed to go someplace where we would remain unobserved.

When she saw that I would die, she did the only thing she knew would save me. She did that which had been done to her, when she herself had faced death, but only after I answered her question. Did I love her? Only if I loved her could I forgive her. Only if I loved her, could she feel justified in keeping me with her, instead of letting me go."

Cain gave Felicity a mischievous grin. "I often wonder what she would have done if I'd said no. I very easily could have you know, and Maribeth is not one to take such things lightly. She has a passionate nature and a wicked temper. I've a distinct feeling that I would not be here right now, had my answer not been to her liking. She does rather tend to take things to extremes. Even now, I'm unsure at times, whether she will fly at me in a rage or smother me with her affections."

Felicity's smile of amusement dropped and the narration of his story seemed to come to a screeching halt. *"Even now?"*

"Yes. She hasn't changed much, if anything she's gotten worse."

"She's alive?" Felicity seemed very distraught at the prospect.

Cain smiled. "Well, not technically, but she's around." He furrowed his brow at her confusion. "We're *immortal* luv, remember? Those of us smart enough to stay out of harm's path, anyway."

Felicity shook her head a little, as though trying to dislodge her previous thoughts. "I know, I just...I assumed that something had happened to her. Where is she?"

Now Cain's grin broadened. Felicity looked as though she expected Cain to shout 'behind you!' and have a good laugh as Mari attacked her. "Nevada I think," he answered truthfully. "Last I saw her, she'd quite a spread there, out in the desert, just outside Vegas. Fancy's herself a showgirl now and again. She always was one to want attention.

Of course, that was back in '74...or maybe '73. Early seventies anyway. She may have moved again by now. We do move about. It's never smart to stay anyplace for too long, no matter how fond of it you are." Felicity was quite openly very relieved. She seemed to have worried that he'd still been seeing her or something. "We don't keep in touch. Even when I saw her last, it was by chance. I only stayed the weekend." He added in a confidential whisper, "We don't really get along."

Felicity's face showed seeming understanding. "Oh, because of what she did to you."

"Oh, heaven's no!" Felicity still didn't get it. She saw Mari's changing him as some detestable act of malice. "Not at all! I bear her no ill will! She simply lives differently than I do. It makes it very hard for me to be around her, you know?"

Now true understanding came over her face and Felicity turned a bit pale. "Oh," she muttered. With a start, she suddenly looked down at her watch. Cain couldn't read it from his angle, but he knew that dawn was not far off. He'd been talking all night. She sat up straighter and took the last sip of wine from her glass. "Well, not quite the ending that I was expecting, but I'm glad that you felt you could tell me." She sounded very businesslike and began to put things back into the picnic basket, to prepare to leave.

He almost let her. He watched her begin to clear their things. She stood and brushed off her pants and ran her fingers through her hair. "Wait." She stopped and looked at him, expectantly. "There's more," he said quietly.

"I'm sure there is," she said with a smile. "But it's late. My dad's coming for me in the morning and I have to pack and stuff. You can tell me the rest when I get back."

"I'll see you Sunday then?"

"Sorry, three day weekend. I won't be getting in until late Monday night. I'll see you Tuesday. I'll come to you at sunset and you can take me out for a birthday dinner. Didn't you say you wanted to take me out for a 'real dinner' sometime?"

He smiled a little. "Yes, I did."

"Then it's a date. We'll talk more then, 'kay?"

Again, he almost accepted that. He almost let it go, but no, he had to do this now, and do it right. She deserved to know. She would be away from him for three nights. Her mark would be gone, and she would have time to think. She should know everything now. It was only fair. "No, it's not. I'll keep it brief, but I want you to know...now." She looked a bit shaken by his abrupt seriousness. She sat. "I've killed..." he began haltingly.

She gave him a little smile of understanding. "I know."

"Not just Charles, but others as well."

She took a deep breath, and sighed. "I kind of figured. You were turned into a creature that survives on blood. I assumed there'd been a few deaths on your hands before you figured out...well, how not to."

"No, you don't understand. It's not just a few."

He faced a straight stare. "How many?"

He shook his head. "I don't know."

"Ten? Twenty?...A hundred?"

He looked at the ground for a moment. "Do you remember when you were trying to estimate how many women I've bedded?" She blushed a bit at the memory of that conversation, but then just as quickly paled. "I've killed more than I've loved. Of that I'm sure."

"*Thousands?* You've killed thousands of people?"

"I drank their blood, all of it...and took their lives away. Maribeth and I together, we were like a plague. We left a wake of death behind, wherever we would go. Here, then overseas. We took back the Manor. We lived as horrid demons thriving on the blood of the humans all around us without thought or care for mercy or morality. When we were in danger of discovery we crossed the sea yet again, but still, we brought death with us like a silent companion. Every night of my life, for almost half a century, someone died...because of me."

She just stared at him for a very long time, searching his face as though she could find evidence that what he said was untrue. Finally, she seemed simply to accept it. "I knew. I knew that it had to be. I knew that in the beginning, you had to have killed to survive. For...fifty years? But that means for almost three hundred years, you haven't, right? You were only doing what you thought you had to. You don't hurt people anymore, right? It's okay...it's okay, I can accept that."

She was trying to convince herself. He knew how badly she wanted to. He knew that she would probably tell herself almost anything at this point, just to try to redeem him in her eyes.

He couldn't accept that. It wasn't real to her. "No, you don't understand. When you say 'they died, you killed them', those are just words. You weren't there. You don't know. It was *real*. They were *people*. There were…bodies.

You say that I was only doing what I needed to survive. I suppose I did believe that, but I was a predator, and my prey was mostly young girls; *girls like you*." He was forced to stop for a moment as he actually shocked himself into realizing just how like his old patterns his courtship with Felicity had been. Of course, it was drawn out over weeks instead of one whirlwind night, but still.

No, Felicity was certainly different. He really did love her. In fact, he loved her enough to know that he only wanted her to be happy. He wanted what was truly best for her. That was why this had to end…now. He spoke in a voice that trembled with the desperation of trying to make her understand. "Lovely young women, *so* like you, in the blush of youth, just starting their lives, full of hopes and expectations.

I would charm them, tell them of all the ways in which they were special. I would dance with them, talk with them, sometimes I even…loved them, their bodies anyway. But in the end, whether I bedded them or not, 'twas my deadly kiss they did receive, and it would end their lives.

I told myself it was a necessary evil. That I surely had a fixed place in the scheme of things in the world. God would not suffer me to live if it were not His will. I gave myself leave to prey upon others, night after night, after night.

And each night, when it was finished, I would be left with nothing but an empty shell of a girl; pale and unmoving, never to smile, or laugh, or see her family again. And always before I left them, I would place upon their dead cold lips, a last parting kiss. I would thank them with a kiss, that they had given their blood so that I might survive.

I was a monster. It is two hundred and seventy one years since I have killed someone for my thirst. That's a very long time. And yet, I feel a monster still. All of those lives, gone. For what? For me? There is no possible act more selfish or deplorable. Is it redeemable to human eyes? As I speak to you now, I come to realize something that I have known all along, although at times I do choose to forget. It is not.

There was more, things I'd meant for you to know, but what's the point? What I've told so far is more than enough to make us both realize you would do far better in life without me.

I want to thank you, for being here for me, for giving me a chance to let it out. I've kept these things within me for so long, with no one to tell; no one with a human heart anyway, but I was selfish yet again, in ever thinking that you should try to forgive these things. It's terribly unfair. The only true forgiveness that I can hope to expect is through the Lord now. Who else can truly understand, accept and forgive the burden of *my* sins? Could a young human girl? How horribly wrong of me to lay this on you!

Felicity…the love that I have felt for you, and love it is, it has given me a peace that you cannot know; happiness, to warm this dead heart of mine, something that I had long forgotten. Again, I thank you for that. And I want you to know that I expect nothing more.

I'm going to take you home now. And if you don't mind my asking… If I might beg you to allow me one more selfish act, I'd like to ask that you say nothing else. My story is finished. I don't want to speak of these things any longer. There is nothing you might say or do to try to comfort me. Anything you might utter in understanding or acceptance...well, we both know it cannot help. And if you might have something more harsh to tell me, I can't say that I'd really like to hear that either, although I can't exactly stop you if you've a mind to tell me.

There's not much time left before dawn. I just want to see you home safely. I will return you, whole and sound, to your life, to your rightful place in the world, where I will not seek you again. At least I can do that much."

He stared into her tear-filled eyes for a moment, but it really was only a token pause. He wanted to be gone. He wanted truly to run from her, but he could not be *that* selfish. He gathered the rest of their things as quickly as he could. She stepped away from their ground cover and stood unmoving upon the grass, saying nothing. He was so grateful for that, that he was terrified to even look at her again, lest she speak.

Finally, after what seemed an interminable amount of time, he was ready to mount the bike. She got on behind him, silently and he sped off, to return her home...to her life.

Chapter 12 - Speechless

Felicity

Dorm steps
Just before sunrise
Saturday morning

She was speechless.

Felicity had sat and stared at him with mind numbing bewilderment as he finished his descriptions for her. Then she had stood, moved aside and stared some more, as he shoved the rest of their things into the basket and strapped it to the bike. In mute shock, she was staring at this man she'd thought she knew, trying to figure out how all of his traits and features could come together to form a person who could have done those things.

Two hundred and seventy one years was a very long time. Did that make any difference? Did it matter at all? It's not as though it could ever be *un*-done. He'd had time to change, to repent, to become someone new, someone who would never repeat such horrid acts.

He was right. There was absolutely nothing she could say. She climbed onto the motorcycle and let him drive her home. When they reached the dorms and she dismounted the bike, she realized that she hadn't even thought to put on her helmet. It was still strapped to the back. She stood and stared at it.

He turned and she actually flinched. She hadn't meant to, but she did. He must have seen it, but he wasn't even turning towards her. He was getting her comforter off the back. He thrust it out to her without even looking. It wasn't done *un*-gently but she realized that he was trying to get rid of her as quickly as possible. From what she could see of his eyes, they looked moist and blood shot.

She awkwardly took the bundle into her arms and backed up a step for him to leave. He just sat there at first, staring at the handlebars. She realized that although he wouldn't look at or speak to her, he was waiting to see her safely inside. He was waiting to see her climb the steps to the door with his peripheral vision. She just stood there. She wasn't sure why, but she felt as though she wanted to force him to look at her. She needed to see his face again.

It was obvious that he almost wanted to wait her out. He didn't want to give in and face her, but time was on her side. The dawn was coming fast and he couldn't wait. Finally, he gave her a glance with undisguised guilt and self-loathing in his eyes.

She wasn't ready to leave. She opened her mouth, although she'd no idea what she'd say. He didn't give her the chance. Her revved the cycle to cover any words, and sped away. She watched his back recede until he was lost to her view.

She was still standing there a few minutes later, when she recognized the coming sun. A warm glow began to creep above the horizon in the distance, although all around her, the world was still covered in the odd blue and purple shadows of the night. He hadn't much time. She hoped he'd be alright. She wasn't really worried though. He was riding away from the dawn, shielded by ridges and trees. With the speed in which he'd left, it wouldn't take him long to be home.

She let herself wait to be bathed in the golden light of the sun for a moment, before she fled inside to her room. She collapsed unthinking onto the bed and hoped for sleep to come quickly.

Once again, her father was a bit disgruntled to find that she was not nearly ready for him when he arrived. At least this time she was dressed. Of course, it was still from the night before, but he didn't know that. She didn't think it wise to explain that he should wait while she changed. She simply gathered her things for the weekend, and they left for home.

The ride took over an hour. She spent most of it staring out the window, unable to engage in pleasant conversation or give detailed answers to her father's few probing questions. She told him she'd been up studying most of the night: big test on Tuesday. She felt bad to lie, but at least it explained why she was so tired in a way that her parents would accept without question.

By the time that they actually did arrive home, she was able to put on a joyful face to greet her mom and listen to the latest family news. Her younger brothers made teasing remarks about her new freedom and dorm life. She responded with a few general comments about school and work to satisfy curiosity, and then went to her room for a nap.

Sleep would not come. She was still exhausted, but Cain's story in her mind would not let her rest. She retold the entire tale in her head. Carefully trying to remember and think through each part, each experience, as if she were him. What would she have done? His life before, although certainly not something that she could entirely approve of, she could accept. His affair with Maribeth, even the death of his brother, although awful events in and of themselves, she could live with those things. But what had come after...

He was not human any longer at that point. The things he had done, the *way* in which he had done them, had to have been largely driven by instinct. She had to believe that, but was that only a convenient excuse? Surely, there was more to know, of how he'd lived and the thoughts he'd had. It had to have been frightening and strange for him to discover what he truly was. Had he a choice? Surely he hadn't *enjoyed* killing all those people... No matter what he had felt then, he certainly agonized over it now. What would she have done in his position, driven to desperation by thirst...for human blood? She had no clue.

She wanted to ask him how he had discovered the way in which he could live without surrounding himself with death. How had he learned to live without killing? She forced herself to look at a fact that she had deliberately kept from her conscious mind... She did not really *know* how he lived now.

Of all her questions and curiosities, that was the single most important answer that she never did seek to find. She'd blocked the question from her mind. She was afraid to know. When he had told her that he was giving her 'free reign', to 'ask him anything', the time had been perfect. She knew she should have asked him then, but she'd pushed the question from her thoughts out of fear. She'd queried him about his hair of all things instead.

The memory of the vision she'd had in the movie theater kept haunting her, the one in which she pictured him choosing victims from amongst anxious young girls like herself. Allie's words came back to her also: 'He's drinkin' somethin', he needs it'. The most likely explanation was that he drank from others, as he'd drunk from her, without hurting them.

She didn't know what he did or where he went before he came to her each night, or after. It seemed likely that his thirst was satisfied by others.

Like the night he'd left she and Ben to go to Venus. She had not wanted to go. At the time, she was hesitant to see how he might react to Sindy, if she was there, but she had also worried that perhaps he had gone there planning to find another girl to dance with; a human girl whom he would then bring outside to kiss goodnight, and drink from. It seemed the obvious conclusion. He had all night, every night, until the wee hours of the morning to spend in bars and dance clubs. Someone as handsome and charming as Cain, would not have much difficulty in finding someone to take outside for a moment alone.

The cup; her one clue that she had clung to. When she had gone to his home, to speak to him about Ben, she had observed him drinking from a cup. It had been blood. It had to have been. He had made it quite clear that it was not coffee, and she had known that it was blood, but from where? Where could he get blood like that, to drink from a cup?

All she could think of was the hospital. They asked for people to donate blood all the time. In fact, her own school had just sponsored a blood drive last week. Did he have some sort of arrangement with someone, a worker perhaps? Did he purchase blood from some hospital employee in secret, or steal it even? Murderer or not, she could not picture the Cain that she knew, stealing anything.

It remained a mystery, but at least that idea sat better with her than the thought of him getting blood from another person directly. Would she *ever* know? She wasn't sure that she should see him again, but was terrified by the idea that she might not have the chance. She was horribly afraid that she would return to school to find that he was gone. What if he cleared out and left, disappeared, never to be seen again?

She was distraught over the things that he had revealed, but she was not ready to just let him go, not like this. Surely she needed time to think, and maybe she would decide that she never could look at him fondly again, but she didn't think so, and she didn't want him to take the matter from her hands.

She hoped that he would be there, upon her return. She wasn't frightened of him at all. Even knowing what he had done, she just could not believe that he would ever hurt *her*. Even knowing that there were many young girls, much like herself, who had been deceived by him, she was unafraid. He *had* changed. It might seem unreasonable to anyone else that she should believe it, but she did. She knew that he had. He was *not* that monster anymore. She just wished she knew what had changed him so much, why his life had so totally turned around, into something that seemed selfless and good?

Was it a gradual change, or had something happened to reorder his life with sudden abruptness? There was a word for that...they'd just discussed it in English class. Epiphany. Had it been that way? Had he experienced an epiphany, a sudden flash of insight, an almost religious revealing of another way of life?

He did behave as though he had a great belief and respect for God, like people you sometimes read about who suffered near death experiences and then vowed to change their ways. Well, she supposed you couldn't get much nearer to death than Cain.

Christian; she felt the name suited him better now than ever. Why hadn't he taken it back? She almost instantly knew. The name 'Cain' was a reminder to keep himself in check and be sure that he never sought to forget his past. It would be just like him to force himself to face it every time he gave someone his name.

Felicity was unsure just how long she lay there, but it seemed suddenly that her mom was at the door, suggesting that she should get ready for guests soon, for dinner. Perhaps she'd like to shower and change? Her mom made the request lightly, but Felicity realized that the clothing she wore *was* terribly rumpled. She hadn't even really brushed her hair.

Her aunt and uncle were coming for dinner with her cousins, her older brother Eddie had just arrived home from his college for the weekend, and her mother announced, they were also expecting a surprise guest. After a moment's irrational thought that perhaps it was someone she knew from school, she realized who it had to be. Deidre, finally! Her mother confirmed that it was so. Her best high school friend would be joining them for dinner to celebrate her birthday. She quickly got up to shower and change.

~~~~~~~~~~~~~~~~~~~~~~~~~~~~~~

Deidre didn't arrive until just before dinner, so they hadn't any private time to talk. Felicity's best friend of years past looked a little different from when they'd been together last. She still kept her dark hair in a short and sassy bob, but she had on way too much blue eye shadow and big gold hoop earrings. She was a little shorter than but nearly the same build as Felicity, usually somewhere between a size 12 and 14. Usually that was nice because they could share clothes, but Felicity didn't think she would ever want to borrow tonight's ensemble. Deidre wore a pair of tight and really low-waisted hip-hugger jeans that did nothing to flatter her figure. She had paired them with a short satiny blue shirt that Felicity thought had to have been originally intended to be some sort of petite negligee. A change of scenery seemed to have changed Deidre some, but Felicity was glad to see her old friend again.

Felicity had thought she would be very comforted to be at home, surrounded by friends and family. Familiar and ordinary things and people should be reassuring after spending all of her time talking about, fighting with and trying not to fall in love with vampires. Now that she had become more involved with Cain, she hadn't really wanted to spend time away from him, but the last month had been so unusual that she'd begun to think it might be nice to have some time to be normal again.

It wasn't. It didn't seem comforting or a relief. It seemed boring and mundane, a waste of precious time. It just felt like there were more important things in her life to be focusing on. Even seeing Deidre, which she had waited for as though the girl could solve all of her problems, was a bit of a letdown. She and Dee were still good friends, and she was very glad to see her, but it seemed as though her friend was very caught up in such superficial things. Dee wanted to know what the girls in Felicity's college were wearing, and what kind of music people around her were listening to; questions that Felicity could hardly even answer, as she hadn't really paid any attention to such things.

They hadn't much time to talk alone yet, but she could hardly imagine trying to confide in Dee, the real happenings in her life these days. She could just picture how it would be received, with odd looks, and then excited whispers and acknowledgement. It would be accepted as though Felicity were telling some sort of ghost story, the way that people claimed to believe in things like telepathy and paranormal experience, with an air of 'jump on the band-wagon' fervor and awe. They didn't *really* believe, did they? It was all in fun. It always seemed to Felicity that those same people would probably want nothing but to get as far away as possible, if ever they were really faced with something supernatural.

Maybe Deidre would truly believe. She should give her the benefit of the doubt. Although most likely, her friend would be thinking that Felicity had lost her mind. Felicity did want to talk about Cain, though. Dee's opinion had always meant so much to Felicity in the past. Maybe she would just...leave out a few things. She'd have to feel it out.

After dinner came birthday presents. Her aunt and uncle gave her a cell phone, with her bills paid for the first three months. She thanked them profusely. At least she wouldn't have to sit out on the payphones anymore. Deidre had given her a dress, which actually did seem to suit her perfectly. It was a beautiful tie-dyed silk halter dress done in shades of blue and green. Felicity worried that it must have cost a fortune, but Deidre assured her that she'd bought it with a friend's employee discount and knew that it would look gorgeous on her.

Lastly, her parents informed her that their gift waited outside. She dutifully followed them out front, unsure what to expect. When she saw it, she was happy, relieved and disappointed, all at the same time.

It was a car! She would finally have her own car! It wasn't really much to look at, but it was a car all the same. That meant that she would no longer have to worry about being accosted on the way home from work anymore, but that also meant that Cain would have no reason to escort her home...if he was even still around when she got back, but still, how could she not be excited? It was a car!

It was blue, but faded and a little dented on the passenger door, but for a first car, she couldn't really have expected much better. At least she didn't have to worry overly much about scratching the paint and stuff. Her dad informed her that it was a 1987 Ford Mustang, under his name and insurance, but it *was* really hers. He rode along in the back as she and Deidre took it for a ride. At least the driver's license in her wallet didn't seem so useless anymore. She'd taken driver's ed., and then agonized over and passed her road test, just to be told by her parents that they couldn't buy her a car just yet. College was expensive enough. It had been kind of a letdown.

Finally, they returned to the house for birthday cake and coffee, after which she and Deidre retreated to the kitchen to tackle the mound of dishes in the sink. Over the years, she and Deidre had eaten over each other's houses pretty often. Doing the dishes together was sort of a long-standing tradition. At least they'd have a chance to talk.

Felicity took up her station by the drain board to dry...whoever's house it was always dried - they knew where everything should be put away. Dee got started in the sink, with a smile. "See, it's just like we never left."

Felicity tried to smile back, but couldn't help but feel a little disappointed and annoyed that they hadn't spoken in so long. "I guess...but, I missed you."

Deidre seemed to realize the faux pas. "Oh, I totally missed you too! I'm sorry that I didn't write like I said I would, or return your phone call. I've just been real busy, what with classes and pledging and parties and stuff."

"Oh, did you get into that sorority that you wanted?"

"Yeah! It's so great! The sisters are really nice, and it's like instant popularity...especially with the frat boys! We get invited to parties like every other night! Total party school, my grades are gonna suck." Felicity smiled and gestured towards the running water in the sink, Deidre hadn't washed anything yet. She dutifully picked up a dinner plate to be scrubbed.

"So are you dating any of these frat boys?" Felicity asked.

"Not yet, but I do have a few prospects that are definitely worthy of a future 'maybe'. How about you? I notice you didn't bring a cute college boy home for dinner. Nobody special, huh?"

Felicity took the first plate to be dried and decided she just *had* to talk about Cain. How could she not? "Well, I wouldn't exactly say that..."

Of course, Deidre immediately jumped for the information. "You've been holding out on me? Spill it!"

"Well, he doesn't go to college, and I definitely wouldn't call him a *boy,*" Felicity informed her.

"Ooo, *all man,* I like it! So, how come he's not in college? Does he work with you?"

"No, he's just...kind of *beyond* college," Felicity answered vaguely.

Deidre turned from the sink with a disappointed grimace. "He's *old?*"

"He's not *that* old." Felicity said defensively. "Well, he doesn't *look* old."

"Just how old is he?" Deidre asked skeptically.

"Like...twenty sevenish and he doesn't even look it," Felicity assured her.

"I guess that's okay," Dee said hesitantly.

"Glad you approve," Felicity answered with a chuckle.

"What's his name?" Deidre asked.

Felicity hesitated for a moment. "Cain."

"Cane? Like a stick?" Dee questioned with a raised brow.

Felicity rolled her eyes. "No, with an 'i'."

"Oh. Cain... Different, kind of sexy. I like it," Deidre decided.

All right, if she were going to mention him, she might as well try to get some insight. She wouldn't say anything incriminating, but she did want Deidre's opinion. "Dee, do you still think that people can't change?"

Deidre handed her the next dish with slumped shoulders and a look of disappointment. "He needs to change?"

"No! He already has. He's kind of got a...past," Felicity confessed.

"Who doesn't?" Dee asked with a smile.

"No, this is serious. Serious stuff," Felicity told her.

"Former bad boy, huh?"

"To say the least," Felicity responded quietly, as she put away the plate she'd been drying.

"Well...*how* bad? What'd he do?"

No, definitely not going there! "I don't really want to get into specifics..." Felicity began.

Dee turned to face her again. "It's *that* bad? How long ago are we talkin' here?"

"Oh ancient history," Felicity said with quick assurance. "Really ancient."

"That's good. Do *you* believe that he's changed?"

Felicity thought about it for a moment. "Totally."

Deidre did not seem entirely convinced. "Well, *I* never trust guys like that, but *I've* been known to be wrong...a lot. Is it something that's gonna keep comin' up, like...haunt your future, long term?"

Felicity sighed. "That's another obstacle. I don't really think long term commitment is going to be an option."

"Why? What, is he skittish?" Dee asked.

Felicity stifled a laugh. "No, not at all. It's not his fault, it's just... He's kind of... He's got this...disease."

"Oh my God, he's dying?" Dee asked incredulously.

"No! He's not going to die from it or anything. It's not even a disease, really. It's more of a condition. Like an allergy," she added lamely.

"What's he allergic to?" Deidre asked.

"...Sunlight," Felicity supplied haltingly.

Deidre's mouth fell open in shock. "Oh, I've heard of that!"

"You have?" That was the last thing Felicity had expected to hear.

"Yeah, on the Discovery channel. It's really rare. These people have a deficiency, an absence of pigment or melanin or something in their skin. If they go outside in the sun, they get like instant skin cancer, so they only go out at night."

Close enough. "Wow. Yeah, that sounds pretty accurate."

Deidre scrunched up her nose and asked hesitantly, "He's not like...albino or anything, is he?"

Felicity laughed. "No, he's not albino, and it's not like he's sick or anything. He just has to be careful about some stuff. He's got this drink, like...medication that he has to take every day. Then he's fine."

Her friend looked thoughtful as she washed another dish. "Well, I guess you could work around that, it's do-able. Still, it might be kind of weird, once you have kids and stuff."

"Oh, he can't have kids."

Dee gave her the finished dish and turned to face her disapprovingly. "Alright, wait a minute. This guy's got such a bad past that you can't even tell me about it, he's *old*, he can't go out in the sunlight *and* he can't have kids? You're not givin' me much to work with here, Felicity."

It didn't sound very appealing did it? "I was just getting all the bad stuff out of the way first. There's good stuff too!"

"I should hope so. Is he *hot* at least? I mean, *he'd have to be!*" she said, turning back to the sink.

"Oh yeah! *Very* hot," Felicity assured her.

"Describe..." Deidre demanded.

Felicity closed her eyes for a minute, picturing Cain in her mind, not that it was a difficult image to call up. She felt as though she knew every line of his face by heart. "He's got long, sandy, light brown hair."

"How long? Like, Fabio?" Deidre asked.

"No! More like, surfer dude...except, no tan," Felicity added.

Dee laughed. "Right."

"Shoulder length I guess, in layers. Oh, and his eyes... Deidre, his eyes are the deepest, clearest blue, like the Caribbean sea."

"Yeah, yeah. People always say that."

Felicity looked at her in earnest. "No, *really*. I could drown."

"Oh my God, you're *drowning?*" Dee exclaimed.

"Oh yeah. He is so sweet..." Felicity said dreamily.

"Wait, wait. We're not up to sweet yet. More with the description," Dee interrupted her.

Felicity smiled again. "Um, well...his face is so gentle and disarming, like you would trust him with your life...really. He's got these little lines around his eyes that make him seem so approachable and understanding. Like laugh lines I guess you'd call them."

"Wrinkles. I call them wrinkles," Deidre said with distaste.

"They are not! Would you stop? He does not look old at all, I swear! What else? He's tall. Not very tall, but taller than me. Close to six feet, maybe."

"Okay...body?" Dee asked.

Felicity felt her cheeks heating as she couldn't help smiling. "Nice...*very* nice, broad shoulders, good strong build. Not heavy, but definitely not skinny either. I mean, he's muscular, but not like a body builder or anything."

"That's good. Trust me; never date a guy who loves his weight bench more than you," Dee warned her.

"No weight bench. He's clean shaven and *so* good looking..."

"Mmmm. Okay, now we're up to sweet. Continue."

"Oh, he's kind and quiet, but not shy. He's got this...presence. Like he doesn't even have to say a word, but when he walks into the room, everyone else might as well be invisible! He's so commanding and confident, but he's not like, haughty or arrogant or anything. He's just sweet and unassuming and sooo *sexy!*"

"Felicity! You are *so* smitten! I've never heard you talk like this about anybody before. Usually I'm the one gushing, and then the guy turns out to be a total loser."

"Trust me; he's got his faults, but loser he is not. Oh and Deidre, he is so romantic!"

Dee rolled her eyes. "*Romantic?* Guys are only romantic in the movies. I need an example. Like, where did you go on your last date?"

Felicity thought about how excited and impressed she had been by his thoughtful planning, that first night of their picnic. "The park."

"Cheap," Dee pronounced.

"He is not cheap! In fact, he's got money. Like, independently wealthy – money," Felicity informed her.

Dee stopped washing again to look at Felicity in disbelief. "Are you kidding?"

She just shook her head and smiled. "But he doesn't like to show it off at all, which is cool. And the park was very romantic! It was kind of a picnic, at night. Candlelight, wine and cheese, by a waterfall! Oh, and that's not all. One night, he came to my window...on the second floor! It was like Romeo and Juliet! Only he told me that I was even more beautiful than *Juliet!*"

"He actually said that?" Dee asked.

Felicity tried to ignore Dee's skepticism as she described the occasion. "Not quite in those words. I think he said, 'Even *her* description pales compared to *my* beauty, because I am far lovelier than anything that Shakespeare ever dreamed of."

Dee's mouth fell open, her half-washed dish held under the water, forgotten in her hands. "Holy shit."

Felicity laughed with a nod. "You should hear it in an English accent."

"Hold up...he's *British?*" Deidre demanded.

"Yeah, didn't I mention?" Felicity asked.

"No!" Deidre gave her a playful shove with her shoulder, and then handed her a dish. "You should have told me that first! Guys get extra points for being European! Maybe even enough to see past all that other stuff. Are you sure this guy's for real? I mean, it sounds kind of...James Bond. Romantic British guy with a secret past that only comes out at night? It's a little much to swallow. 'Lovelier than Juliet?' Who talks like that?"

"I know, but he's so sincere, really. It doesn't come off as fake at all." She put away the dish she held and then retrieved the last pot off of the stove. "And he's been so honest. He's told me all about his past and everything, so I'd know just what I was getting into." She stood there in silence for a minute watching Dee wash the final pot. As much as Cain's past bothered her, she felt almost as though it was something that he had done in a past life. He obviously had spent the rest of his life trying to make up for it. He was a different person now. A person that Felicity could not just walk away from, no matter how stupid it might seem for her to stay.

She took the pot to be dried and stared at the floor as she turned it over in her hands with the dishcloth. After a moment, she came to realize that her friend was standing there watching her with concern. "Deidre...I don't know what to do. I don't know if I can really have any kind of future with this guy, but I am really falling for him...hard. And he *so* turns me on, like no one ever has. Every time he touches me, I just..."

Deidre gave a quick glance around to be sure they were alone and whispered fiercely, "*Felicity!* Have you slept with him?"

"Not yet." Felicity put the pot away. "Come on...my room."

They quickly climbed the stairs and secluded themselves in her room, far from parental ears. They both kicked off their shoes and sat cross-legged on Felicity's bed. Deidre shook her head and smiled. "Well, losing virginity is not a topic *I've* dealt with in a while, but oh wow."

"I know. What do I do? This is probably going nowhere, but I can't help it. Whenever we're together, it's like...overwhelming."

"You're still on birth control right? I know you said he can't have kids, but better safe than sorry." She smiled as Felicity nodded yes. "I told you having irregular periods would come in handy one day! Was I right or what? Convince your mom to take you to the gynecologist to get birth control pills - just to regulate, while you're still young. Now that you're older, it's already in place and it's not even an issue. I'm brilliant!"

Felicity just smiled. Getting pregnant was one of the very few concerns she did *not* have at the moment. "I shouldn't even be considering. He even acts like it wouldn't be right. I mean, he definitely would like to, but then he pushes me away. He thinks he's no good for me. He's probably right, but I care about him so much and I'm so attracted to him. I can't just walk away."

Deidre smiled. "Well the sorority sisters have a test, to determine worthiness..."

"Are you kidding?"

"No really. They say if you're going to sleep with a guy, he'd better be a DAMN good man. It's one of those acronym things you use to remember stuff. Check this out:

D -	is for 'discreet'. The guys gotta be, you don't want him going all public with it the next day like a jerk.
A -	is for 'attractive'. Of course you've gotta be attracted to the guy. Sounds like you've got no problem there.
M -	is called the 'mourn' factor. Just how into you is the guy? If you left him, would he mourn the loss, or just move on? and...
N -	is for 'no regrets'. If you sleep with him and then the relationship doesn't work out, will you wish you hadn't? Of course you hope the guy sticks around, but if you're going to do it, you should be able to appreciate the experience for itself, with no regrets.

Not exactly, the kind of standards your mom might appreciate, but...what do you think? Is Cain a DAMN good man?"

"Well, by those standards, yeah. I guess he is," Felicity said.

"Really?!" Dee asked.

"Sure he is. I mean, 'discreet' isn't even a question, neither is 'attractive'. As far as the 'mourn factor' goes...sometimes it's almost like he's in mourning already, in thinking that he shouldn't be with me. I don't know, we left things kind of weird yesterday, but I think that we'd both feel devastated if we didn't see each other again."

"What about the whole no regrets thing though? If you really don't think you have a future with this guy... I mean, this is not your standard situation. We are talking about your *first time*. I don't know if the whole 'DAMN' thing really applies. It's more like a joke than a real determination anyway. Would you really have no regrets?"

Felicity knew it was the kind of thing she should probably consider more carefully, but there was really no question in her mind at this point. "You know, I don't think I'd regret it in the least. Even if I never saw him again, I know how much he cares about me, I just know it. And I know that it would be an incredible experience unlike anything else; which *could* be a drawback when you think about it. If I did sleep with him, I've got the feeling he'd leave some pretty difficult shoes for any other guy to fill."

"Felicity! I can't even believe you are talking like this! It's so unlike you! Just *how* far have you gone with this guy?" Dee asked.

Felicity laughed. "We haven't *done* anything really. It's kind of hard to explain, but when he kisses me...it's like magic."

"*Magic* kisses? I've never had magic kisses," Deidre said poutingly. "The guys I kiss are always too busy trying to figure out how to unhook my bra to concentrate on *magic* kisses. So when are you going to see him again?"

"That's just it. I don't know. I saw him last night, well...this morning. We spent the whole night talking and...I guess we kind of broke up."

"What?" Dee demanded.

"Well, he's so concerned about hurting me, with his past and everything. It's like he's trying to punish himself for things that he did so long ago, like he thinks I deserve someone better. He thinks that I should see him as this horrible person, and maybe I should, but I just don't," Felicity explained.

"Felicity, slow down. It's kind of hard for me to give you advice when I don't even know what you're talking about. Can't you tell me what he did? How bad could it be?" Deidre asked.

"It's bad. Really," Felicity admitted.

"Well, unless he's like a mass murderer or something, I don't see how it could be unredeemable," Deidre tried to assure her.

Felicity stared very hard at the flowers on her bedspread and didn't say anything. How was she going to explain this? Like she was going to try and tell Dee that it didn't count because he was a supernatural monster, being controlled by instinct at the time?

"Felicity? He didn't *kill* somebody...did he?" Felicity looked up, but couldn't quite keep the tears from her eyes, no matter how she tried. "Oh my God Felicity. He killed someone?" She didn't answer. "You have got to stay away from this guy. Do you hear me? This is not the kind of thing that you mess around with, no way. I don't care how charming, romantic or handsome he is, serial killers do not make good boyfriends! Have you gone insane?!"

"You don't understand, Dee. It wasn't really his fault. He's different now, it was so long ago!"

"He's twenty-seven Felicity, how long could it be? What'd he do it when he was ten?" Deidre asked sarcastically.

"Something like that. Look, the details don't matter. I truly believe in my heart that he is a good person. Don't you think a person deserves to be forgiven for past mistakes?" Felicity asked.

"Pretty big mistake! Besides what are you, his priest? Don't get yourself tangled up with someone like that. Even if he wouldn't hurt *you*, it can only lead to problems and heartache. Besides, you only know what this guy has told you himself right? How can you even know if it's the whole truth? I mean, I guess if he were going to lie, he wouldn't have told you at all, but still... Please Felicity, there are so many other guys in the world."

For the second time today, Felicity found herself speechless. Once again, she felt as though there was nothing she could really say. Nothing she could tell Deidre in Cain's defense was very likely to help. She certainly didn't think that trying to explain that he was a vampire was going to earn him any sympathy.

Her whole life she had always been so concerned about what other people thought, but this was different. No matter what Deidre, Ben or even Cain would say to try to dissuade her, she knew that she loved him. She *loved* him.

Felicity believed that the man he was *now* was worthy of her love and respect. She was in love with Cain and all else was secondary. Oh wow, isn't that exactly what Ashley had told her? Who would have thought she'd be following *Ashley's* advice?

She hadn't delusions of trying to spend the rest of her life with him...well not really. Silly fantasies like that did pass through her mind now and again, but she knew that in a practical sense they would probably not last, but Cain was a good man and she did love him. She wanted to be with him and why shouldn't he deserve to have the love and trust of someone who could accept him as he was?

Felicity looked at Deidre's face and had a terrifying thought. Deidre was going to tell her mother. Dee had been her friend since they were little kids. She could read every expression on the girl's face with almost flawless certainty, and she just knew that Dee would be talking to Felicity's mom about this, if she could not handle it herself. That had to be prevented at all costs.

"I guess you're right. We didn't really have much of a future anyway, too complicated," Felicity agreed.

"I'm glad you've come back to earth. Find yourself a nice frat guy to hang out with. They're a little immature but at least their motives are usually pretty clear," Deidre told her.

"Yeah. You know, I probably won't see him again anyway. Like I said, we broke up. In fact, he was only in town temporarily. I got the feeling last night that he was going to leave soon. So I doubt I'll even bump into him again, now that it's over."

"That's good. You sounded pretty hung up this guy though, for someone you thought you'd never see again," Dee said skeptically.

"I know. I had these crazy ideas that I was going to try and go back early, convince him to stay or something, but I know you're right. I should just let him go," Felicity said, carefully observing Dee's reaction.

"It's for the best," Deidre assured her.

She nodded her head and told Deidre not to worry about her. Felicity tried to pacify her friend as best she could, but knew in her heart that she had to go back to Cain. She could never leave things the way that he had. Deidre wouldn't be around for the rest of the weekend, she had stuff to do with her own family, but she did promise to try to keep in better touch. It wasn't long before Dee's mom came to pick her up and they said their goodbyes.

Felicity spent the rest of her time at home closed away in her room as much as possible. She thought about Cain, and just what she would do when she got back to see him again. Maybe she could go back early and surprise him! She thought and planned, and told her parents that she was studying for that test she'd mentioned. She hoped they wouldn't notice that she hadn't brought home any books.

Chapter 13 - Reality

Cain

Cain's bedroom
Monday night

Cain awoke with the sunset, stretched and smiled as he remembered the comforts and pleasures of the day before. Felicity was still sleeping, her naked body soft and warm against his cool skin. He reached his hand beneath the sheets to give her enticingly fully fleshed thigh a loving caress.

He looked up as another approached. It was Ashley, wearing nothing but a cross expression and a filmy negligee. He had spurned her advances and neglected her affections these past months. She was petulant and dissatisfied, but still she sorely longed for him. He gestured for her to join them in the bed, eager to be forgiven.

Felicity awoke as Ashley climbed into their love nest, but simply wriggled against him and gave his bare chest a quick kiss, unthreatened. She knew that the attentions of her body satisfied him well, but she could never hope to slake his thirst alone. His demands were too great, and so she was willing to share.

A sound at the stairway startled him at first, but then he remembered that he had no need for alarm. Ben was standing guard. It was Ben who came to him now, crossing the room in his self-assured, prideful manner, but as he reached the bed, he knelt before his master.

The girls made room for Cain to lean towards Ben, as the boy tipped his chin to the side and upwards in an oft' practiced pose. He wanted Cain to drink, the venom his reward. Cain smiled as Ben closed his eyes, anxiously awaiting Cain's bite. He would not be disappointed.

Cain's lips tasted the salt sweat and bitter aftershave of Ben's skin as his fangs pierced the flesh of the boy's throat. The scent of his body was so different from that of the girls', so strong and masculine. The blood that came rushing to his tongue was rich and sweet. Yes, this was why he kept Ben. The boy gave himself over, utterly subdued and eager to be dominated. It pleased him well.

The girls fought for space, snuggling closer to him, as drinking awakened and aroused his sleepy body; an erection came with the blood.

Cain awoke from the dream with a gasp, as the remembered taste of blood seemed to fill his mouth. He sat up in bed, alone of course. There were no pets beneath his sheets, no willing victim at his throat. Only his erection was real.

He threw back the covers and rose from the bed, disgusted with himself that he should long for such things, even in an unconscious state. No, these were his friends, not his slaves. He wanted nothing from them, not their bodies or their blood, only respect and friendship. He tried desperately to convince himself that it was true, although he probably did not deserve even that. He went to his refrigerator and prepared himself a drink, blood to quench his forbidden cravings and desires, blood to chase his dreams away.

Of course, Felicity was an exception. He *had* wanted *her* body, had he not? But that was different. He wanted her not as a pet, but as an equal. Her love should be a willing gift, not a sacrifice. Was there a difference? It could not lead to anything real. Whether he let himself admit it or not, she would act as his pet in the end, wouldn't she?

Once physical play had been fully explored, blood play would be next. The rewards from such experiments would be so great, how could he resist? How could she? She knew what it was to feel his touch when his mark was upon her. Once her body had been freely given, how could she not ask him to take her blood? The thrill of sex after marking was something he had not enjoyed in many decades, an exquisite experience, beyond description. He knew that once she was in his bed, she would come to greatly anticipate such pleasures. How could he deny her?

No. This train of thought needed to end, now. He had decided that Felicity should be left to her family and her life. He could offer her nothing towards her future. Physical pleasures amidst a euphoric, venom induced haze; these were false comforts and would eventually desert her. Then she would be left wasted and unable to carry on with her life, with nothing to look forward to but death at his hands. Whether it would be death eternal or living death by his side, it was still an unacceptable end.

His relationship with her would end...now. He had spent the entire weekend secluded in his home, grieving the loss of his love. He knew it was necessary, he knew that it was right. Felicity deserved more from life than what he could give her, and *he* did not deserve her at all.

He'd entertained the notion of leaving town entirely, disappearing to take temptation from their path, but he just couldn't do it. He told himself he still worried for Sindy's behavior, should he do such a thing, but he was unsure how much of that was true. He also rationalized that he must stay to protect Alyson. Mattie was his best and really his only true friend. Knowing that the woman Mattie loved may be in danger was an automatic obligation to stay. He would expect no less of Mattie were the situation reversed. So, stay he would...for now.

Besides, staying should not be a temptation for him any longer; he just needed to stay out of Felicity's way until Mattie returned, then Cain would leave. Felicity would certainly not come to seek him out again. He had told her the truths of his past and of the monster, the murderer that he had been. He had scared her away from him now. Felicity was a smart girl with a good level head on her shoulders. He did not flatter himself that she would be seeking him out anymore.

He forced himself to drink the blood from his cup and tried to will his body back to a state of unready rest, but another unbidden feeling came upon him, the closeness of another, one marked as his own. Sindy approached, and his body recognized her with a willing eagerness that undermined his efforts to subdue it.

He cursed the twisted psychological ties that caused the impending opportunity for more of her blood, to be intertwined with his body's physical expression of desire. *His body* saw her as a chance to fulfill its needs. *He* didn't really want to see her at all, but she had found his place of rest at last. He had thought that he might be so lucky as to avoid leading her to his lair. Her mark from him was almost gone, but luck was not with him. Whether she was led by her mark or she already knew her destination, he could feel her coming ever closer.

As usual, he'd worn only sleep pants to bed. Now he found a tee-shirt to pull over his head, hoping it was long enough to disguise his present state of arousal. He mounted the stairs to meet her at the door.

Yes, she definitely knew that he was within. She waited on the porch, not bothering to knock. She was unsurprised when he opened the door, and remained leaning against the rail with arms crossed and a familiar pouting expression upon her lips. He stayed within the doorway. "What do you want?"

She looked strange, different. Her eyes; she had not applied the shadows that she usually wore. He'd never seen her without her face painted. She looked so young! Not a child, but a young fresh maiden in the new bloom of womanhood. He found her extremely appealing this way, and his body fought even harder to express the fact. He changed his stance, self-consciously and tried to keep his face sternly set. He could not judge her mood by her expression. She did not look very happy with him, but that was typical of her. "To talk, can I come in?"

He did his best to look confused and began to leave the house to join her on the porch. He gave a little shrug of nonchalance. "It was only a place to spend the day. What makes you think I've the authority to invite you?"

Now a little smirk came upon her face as she raised her eyebrows at him. "Come on Cain, you obviously live here. You probably even *pay* for it," she added with contempt. "You don't exactly strike me as the squatter type." She uncrossed her arms and stepped a bit away from the rail, expectantly. "So can I come in, or not?"

Cain studied her for a moment. My but she looked lovely without all of the artifice. He chased the thought from his mind. She wanted an invitation into his house. That would certainly not be a wise move on his part. However, it was useless to try to keep up the charade; he could not really deny that he did indeed reside here. "Not." Sindy rolled her eyes and let out an exasperated little huff. He ignored her annoyance. "What do you want?"

She squinted at him as if trying to decide just what to say. "Chris is gone," she finally blurted. He simply stared at her, trying to interpret why she should think this would affect him. He stretched out his psychic awareness. Chris was indeed not within his reach, but that didn't mean anything. They didn't usually sleep within reach of his house anyway. Sindy grew impatient with his silence. "Did you *do* it?" she demanded.

Oh...she meant *gone*. "Why would I harm Chris?"

"Don't play with me Cain! It's not like you haven't threatened him before!" He could hear the tinge of panic and grief creeping into her voice. Yes, she *had* cared for Chris, as he had thought.

He met her eyes, trying to convey the sincerity of his words. "I've done nothing to hurt him, honestly. I haven't had a problem with Chris, for as long as he stayed out of my way and kept out of trouble. He's been smart enough to avoid angering me. Are you certain...did you actually *feel* him die?"

Sindy looked panicked and confused. "I can't feel him at all! Can you?"

"No, but he may just be out of my range. It's further than yours, but not limitless. When did you see him last?"

She looked at the ground, annoyed with his inability to give her instant relief from her worry. "When I woke up last night, he was gone."

Cain sighed and gave her a little comforting smile. "That doesn't mean anything's happened to him." He paused, wondering whether he should call up the memory for her, and then decided that he must. "Remember Ernest?"

Her expression immediately became full of scorn and resentment. "My first apprentice that you heartlessly dusted, after breaking nearly every bone in his body? Yeah, I think I recall."

Cain closed his eyes for a moment and then gazed into her eyes to gauge just how hurt she had been by the act. She hadn't really cared much for the man, he was sure. He had been fairly mindless and very violent. Still, the death of a protégé was always painful. "You know that I hadn't a choice." Her mouth was set in a hard line of discontentment, but he knew that she understood it to be true. "Do you remember the moment that it happened? Do you remember what you felt, the precise moment that my stake entered his heart?"

"Besides my extreme hate for you? Yeah, thanks for reminding me of that torturous moment in time."

He refused to react to her words and instead tried to be comforting to her. "If Chris were truly gone, you would know. You would have felt it...no matter the distance."

She let that sink in for a minute and then gave up trying to be mad at him. Instead, her worry returned, although obviously lessened from before. "Then where is he?"

Cain allowed himself to smile, even if it was slightly at her expense. "Perhaps he was just wanting for a change of scenery...or company."

Sindy looked astonished at such a suggestion. "You mean like...voluntarily? He wouldn't do that! He couldn't do that! He can't leave me!"

"Why not?"

"He's mine! I made him! He needs me! He couldn't live without me, he just couldn't!"

Cain tried not to be cruel, but still could hardly help but smile a bit at her insistence. "Well, if you haven't felt him die, then you will have to concede that he is living, somewhere else...without you."

"Why? Why would he do that?"

A laugh escaped him before he could stop himself. "Is that a serious question? You treat those boys like so much cattle! Obviously you recognize Chris' higher level of intelligence as compared to the rest of your drones, but I've only ever seen you acknowledge it with extra responsibility or through giving him the brunt of your wrath when things are not to your liking.

Do you show him that you care for him at all? You needn't answer, because I can't say I truly wish to know, but answer the question for yourself, in your own mind. Have you ever shown him any sort of real affection? And I am not talking about sex. I mean do you ever even bother to spend any time with him as a person? Talk with him, share some sort of relationship other than that of master and slave?"

Cain's dream immediately sprang to mind and he fought to suppress the memory, the feelings of comfort that it had brought him. That was not the desired order of things! It was sinful, wicked and wrong. These were people not pawns. Vampire or human, they should be treated with respect. Relationships between two people should be built upon mutual fulfillment, trust and admiration for each other. Every relationship Sindy had ever had, had been one-sided, he was sure. Had she ever sought to please another besides him?

She was staring at him thoughtfully, most likely reviewing her bond with Chris in her mind. She knew that Cain was right. Cain knew something as well, although he couldn't say how he could tell. He knew that she was ready to give up all of her guard, get rid of every one of them, and start anew without the safety net of others to support her. If Chris was going to reject her, then she would stifle that hurt by rejecting him as well, by rejecting all of them. She was done with them now. She wanted to learn how to truly share in an equal relationship...with him.

She was only afraid to ask again. Her past pleas to him were always underlied with a mocking tone. She'd always been unwilling to truly distance herself from her boys, in case he would not accept her. After the initial advances she had made upon their acquaintance, she had built an emotional wall around herself. She would not let his rejections truly wound her.

But he could see in her eyes that the wall was gone. Amazing how the absence of make-up made her expression seem so much more open, honest and easy to read. Maybe it was the absence of those shadows that was fooling him, bringing him to these conclusions, but it seemed as though she was just waiting for him to say the word. At his request she would free them all and come to him, in some ways as a student, but hopefully, eventually, as an equal.

She was still staring at him, her eyes softened, her anger gone. He thought of his dream again. Is that what he had to look forward to, if things went further with Felicity? Of course, he assumed that he had better control than to let such a relationship spill over to control the other humans in his life.

But why? Why should he think that it would stop with her? In for a penny, in for a pound. If he was going to keep one pet, why not two, or three? Why stop there? He thought of how Sindy had lived these past months. Human or vampire, what was the difference? Pets to do his bidding, keep him comfortable, fed, pampered and loved. No. He was a good man...wasn't he? He held himself above such temptations.

Sindy almost seemed able to read the conflict within him as she gazed into his eyes. Why did he make things so difficult for himself? Why did he torture himself with people and pleasures that he could not truly allow himself to have? Right here before him was a willing and perfect mistress. Well, maybe not *perfect*, but she would be willing to learn now, wouldn't she? She wanted to please him. She moistened her lips and spoke to him softly, hesitantly. "Cain...you don't like me very much do you?"

She seemed so lost and forlorn. He smiled at her, but didn't answer the question, except for himself. No, he didn't always like her very much, but sometimes you don't much like those whom your heart chooses to love. He wasn't willing to entirely give himself over to the possibility...yet, but it *was* a possibility. He reached to caress the side of her face. At first, she almost stepped back from his touch, alarmed. When she realized that it was meant to be a loving gesture, she seemed very surprised indeed.

She moved forward into his arms and sought to kiss him, but he let her come close while turning his head and resisting her lips. He folded his arms around her in a chaste embrace. It seemed odd that she smelled of nothing really. Usually she was heavily adorned with not only paint, but perfumes as well. The faint scent of shampoo was still in her hair, but that was all. He held her lightly, cool and supple in his arms. There was no pulse or heartbeat to lure him, no living scent of sweat, but she gently pressed herself against him and he felt almost as though she was terrified to make a false move, to cause him to end the embrace.

Could she ever really make him happy? His body desired her, and the memory of drinking from her spurred him to want more, but her charms were so different from those of Felicity. Felicity's ways spoke of sweet, guileless innocent excitement, while Sindy was mischievous and manipulative. He had dealt with more than enough women like that in his life. At this point, women of sly and cunning wiles set off alarms in his head he had learned to heed...the hard way.

Sindy's body, although desirable, was cold as his own, sterile and lacking the reactions that his nearness usually brought about in Felicity. When he held his human love, her heart would pound and her pulse would race; her breaths would come in sweet little gasps that let him know just how truly he did excite her. He could sense her body's physical desire, as it produced for him a welcoming moistness that although he had never directly observed in her, he could smell all the same, with his heightened senses. These memories caused him to long for Felicity far more than he could want the woman in his arms.

It was with stubborn and deliberate refusal to acknowledge the ache in his heart for Felicity, that he leaned back to look into Sindy's eyes. He knew that the physical aspect of a relationship may at first seem the most overwhelming, but it was only a small part of a larger whole. Still, he *did* want Sindy, as a man, and the prospect of drinking her blood made her all the more appealing; something that he could acknowledge in himself without shame. It would not hurt her. She would enjoy it as much as he. Perhaps at some point he would let her drink from him as well, but that would be the final act of submission on his part.

He was most definitely not ready for such admissions. But smaller steps, to repeat actions already completed in previous times? Surely such things held no harm. She stared at him, awaiting his command. She would do anything for him, he knew. He let go of her, stepping back into the doorway of his home. "Come in."

Chapter 14 - Anticipation

Felicity

Tuesday afternoon
Downtime Cafe/Bookstore

Felicity had returned to school driving her own car (!) with her dad following behind, just in case. She had wanted to try to come back yesterday, with the pretense of needing more study time in the library, but her mom had remarked that Felicity was already working too hard, what with staying up all night on Friday to study, and now spending half the weekend in her room to study more. Her mother had insisted on taking her shopping instead.

So now, she was finally back, with her new car, cell phone, some new clothes and a few bags of groceries and things that her mom had thought she would need. All Felicity felt she had really needed was some perspective. With some time away to sort out her feelings, she had been very eager to get back.

At least Tuesday was a light school day for her, with only morning classes. She was at work now for the afternoon, but only from 12 to 4; plenty of time to prepare herself and head to Cain's before dark. Luckily Ben wasn't working, so she wouldn't have to put up with any of his snide comments, not that they could even bother her today. Nothing was going to bring her down. She had done a lot of thinking and finally come to a decision that she felt was long overdue. She was done with anxiety and worrying. That was not how she wanted to live her life. She felt she was finally seeing things clearly and now she could not wait to see Cain.

Felicity had ridden right past Cain's house on her way home last night. Her dad was following close behind though, so she had been unable to stop, and could only slow down as they went by. Her mark was gone now, she couldn't feel him at all, but she still felt an enormous surge of relief as they passed. His motorcycle was still there! It was parked up at the top of the driveway, as always. If he were going to leave town, he certainly would not have walked.

Hopefully he hadn't left after she'd gotten back to the dorms. She hadn't been able to get rid of her dad until late, by then she felt tired and worn out from the car ride and endless contemplation over Cain. She decided that she would just have to trust that he would still be there tomorrow. She wanted time to prepare herself to see him, not to rush over there in the late hours of the night. Tuesday turned out to be a bright and sunny day. As long as she reached him before dark, she felt certain that he would still be there.

She was working with Lucy and the hours seemed to drag, but quitting time would come eventually...it had to! She could hardly wait to go home and change. She was going to wear the dress that Deidre had bought her for her birthday. She'd tried it on at home and it was perfect! It made her look so sexy and appealing, but in a casual and 'breezy' kind of way. As though she hadn't gone through too much trouble and her beauty was unintentional.

She had never really seen herself as beautiful before. She thought that she was pretty, and was never *terribly* unhappy with her reflection, but 'beautiful' was just strong enough a word to make her falter. She had too many flaws for that.

It was kind of odd to look at herself in the mirror and notice all of the good things instead of immediately zeroing in on the bad. In the past, she always tended to focus on things that she saw as drawbacks, upon inspection of herself. She would have to 'psych' herself up and give herself mental encouragements to be excited about how she looked, when she dressed for special occasions.

But as she had looked in the mirror at home, wearing that green dress, she had tried to see herself through Cain's eyes. His eyes always lingered on her as though he could hardly bring himself to look away. From that first night in the gym she had noticed it. He never gawked or stared, it wasn't an obvious or uncomfortable thing, but she did notice that he liked to look at her.

It made her see herself differently. Thinking of how he would see her tonight, made her smile. However, she was still stuck at the register for now, trapped for another interminable half an hour.

Time dragged on. At 3:53 she couldn't take it anymore. It's not like they were busy. "I'm going to get ready to go," she called to Lucy as she headed for the lounge. Lucy didn't argue, not that Felicity gave her much of a chance.

She rushed back to the dorms to get ready. It felt odd to be driving home instead of walking. The DownTime was so close to the dorms that she felt as though she was there in seconds. That suited her just fine, she wanted plenty of time to dress and do her hair, and still arrive at Cain's well before sunset.

She struggled to carry everything in one trip, too impatient to have to go back. When she finally made it into her room, she dumped everything onto the spare bed. She instantly began to undress and throw her clothes onto the floor. She donned her bathrobe and then, after a moment's pause for thought, began digging through one of the bags she'd brought home.

Finally, she found what she'd been looking for. She took the new scented body wash she'd bought while shopping with her mom, stuffed it into her toiletry case and headed for the shower. At least the bathroom was empty at this time of day, so she wouldn't have to wait.

She forced herself to take her time, and shaved her legs...twice. She wanted everything to be perfect. By the time she was back in her room, finishing her hair it was 4:45. A little later than she had hoped, but still at least an hour before sunset. She picked out the only panties she had that she felt looked even vaguely sexy, and got dressed.

By the time she was ready to leave, she felt as though she needed to force herself to stop and relax for a minute. Her heart was racing and she felt terribly rushed. That was not the impression that she was going for. She checked herself in the mirror one more time. She had to smile. She *was* beautiful. She put on a last spritz of perfume and left for Cain's.

Chapter 15 - Detachment

Cain

Tuesday 4:45 p.m.
Cain's house

Cain awoke from his restless sleep, to lie there in the dark of his room. At least there had been no more dreams. Then he remembered the reality of the night before, and that seemed just as bad, if not worse. He had invited Sindy to join him inside. Probably a stupid move tactically, but he was tired of tactics and fighting. If he couldn't defend himself against *her*, then he didn't deserve to live. He couldn't honestly say that he cared anymore anyway.

Her blood...he'd wanted it, and he'd known that it was something she was more than willing to give. He'd wanted to drown his thoughts in her blood and forget all else. So he had invited her in and she had not hesitated. Lying in his bed now, he replayed the events of the evening before in his mind.

Sindy entered his home with an odd glance about, noting his lack of furnishings, but said nothing. He followed, closing the door behind her. He locked it and then stood there, staring at the knob for a moment. He wanted to prepare himself, mentally. He wanted to let go of humanity, call forth the vampire within him to bid the thirst to come and drive out any other consideration. Being a man only brought him heartache and pain; better to be a monster. He did not shift, but confident that he could call it forth at will, he was ready.

When he turned from the door, she was shrugging out of her dress. That was not what he'd planned. He'd wanted only to drink. She had misunderstood...or maybe not. She had understood quite well, when he would not kiss her at the door, but once inside, she didn't think he would have the strength to refuse her.

She was right. He stood, a silent observer as the dress fell and puddled about her feet on the floor. She wore nothing beneath, save her black g-string panty, which stood out darkly against her pale skin. Out on the porch he had been too busy contemplating the lack of make-up on her face to notice that she had dressed sparingly as well. She did not wear her normal stockings and boots, but had only slipped her feet into a pair of flat black shoes. She must have been very concerned over Chris's sudden absence, not to have taken the time to compose her appearance to fit the image of herself that she usually held in her mind. It made her far more approachable and appealing to his eye.

She *was* exquisitely made, he would not deny. Her young, lithe body was tall and thin as was popularly desirable in these times. Her dark straight hair lay full and long down her back, with a few locks straying over her shoulder to partly conceal her left breast. While not very large, her pert breasts were certainly firm and full enough to draw his eye and demand his attention. She stepped out of her dress and shoes, starting towards him, slowly and deliberately. He had plenty of time to speak against her, but found that he had no words to say.

He wanted to be desirous, excited by her, and in fact his body did acknowledge her readily, but he felt sick inside, depressed and cheated that this was not his love, but a poor substitute. If she noticed his lack of enthusiasm, she never let it show. Sindy brought herself to him with the air of an offering. When he did not push her away, she took it as acceptance. She rested her hands lightly on his chest, bringing her lips to his, eagerly. He couldn't help but respond; why shouldn't he? He was a vampire, an undeserving beast plagued by guilt and a thirst for sin. How could he ever fool himself to think he should be allowed happiness with a human girl? Another vampire was the only solace he should dare to hope for. *This* was his destiny, was it not?

He closed his eyes and tried to lose himself in Sindy's kiss. He didn't plan to try to deceive himself that she might be Felicity. Even if that *had* been his intent, it never could have lasted. Sindy's kiss was far more fevered and urgent. Even when taken with passion, Felicity had never sought to nip his lips with her teeth, or so boldly explore his mouth with her tongue. The venom was evident in Sindy's kiss as well, although it was not really all that strong to *him*.

After a moment of kissing him fervently, Sindy began to nip and bite at his lips with increasing frequency and need. He knew what she wanted. She wanted to change. She desired his blood as much, if not more than he wanted hers, but she would not shift without his leave. So she gave him play bites and awaited his consent, afraid to anger him into turning her away. As he hesitated in responding to her playful provocations, she reached up to clasp her hands behind his neck so as to more firmly bestow her attentions. He was increasingly aware of her hardened nipples rubbing up against his chest, but at the moment, the blood within her called to him more strongly than her body ever could.

She left his lips to nip at his throat with teasingly human bites, the pain of which only made him long for more, imploring him to allow her to sample his blood. Cain had already drunk from her twice before, and now he would again; there was no stopping it, but he just was not willing to give himself to her fully yet. He felt that he should, if only to emotionally seal his fate, but it was too soon, he couldn't go through with it. The blood was always so personal, an undeniable bond. He held her back from him for a moment to look into her eyes again. She seemed desperate for his approval, for his permission for her to have him, all of him. It seemed terribly unfair of him, but he would not drive himself to something he was so unready for.

His body. His body he could give her, willingly. It could be disconnected from his heart, to hold no lasting or bonding emotional ties. It would have to be enough. He shook his head gently, to show his dissent. He would not allow her his blood. She seemed very disappointed, but then he shifted to his own vampire state and pulled her roughly to him for another kiss. Apparently, that satisfied her; she accepted and returned it vehemently. Then *he* was the one to nip and bite, but *he* drew blood with his play. He continued to score her lips when he could, but then he found her tongue.

If it was painful, she never let on. It was only a moment. Then he could truly taste her precious blood mingled with the venom in her kiss. It fueled him, brought out desires that he always kept so carefully under control. He spent all of his nights trying to be gentle and kind, punishing himself for past sins, allowing himself only the very slightest of pleasures. Not this time; he had refused to give himself to her emotionally, but that did not mean that she could not please him. She would be his outlet, in her he would satisfy his physical needs, if not his emotional ones.

He pulled back from her suddenly. She was at once startled and chagrinned that he would push her away, but then he pulled off his shirt and she smiled at him with knowing eyes.

He did not speak to her, and was very glad that she followed suit. She simply stripped herself of her thong to reveal the small inverted triangle of dark curls beneath, and then came towards him again. He remained still and silent as she approached and removed the last of his clothing for him. He stood, looking down at her as she helped him free his legs of the sleep-pants he'd worn. She smiled upon seeing him ready for her. She gave his body a few caresses and kisses, taking him into her mouth once or twice, in a well-practiced and expertly pleasing manner, but as good as it felt, it was token. She really wanted *him* to initiate. So after a parting kiss, she then looked up at him with supplicating eyes and simply lay down on the floor, waiting for him. She moved to place his discarded pants beneath her head, a thin and inadequate pillow against the hard wood.

As his passions grew in urgency, he never even thought to take her downstairs. The bedroom was *his* sanctuary. His bed was a personal creature comfort that he was unwilling to share with *her*. This was not for comfort, this was more like a necessary evil; an outlet for his desires and aggressions so that he could remind himself of his true nature, stop pining for a human woman he should not have, and move on.

He needed to release all of the anger, frustration, guilt and remorse that had held him prisoner for so long. If Sindy wanted to bring that out of him, so be it. Her comfort was not his concern. That's what flashed through his mind as he saw her there on the floor. He hated himself at that moment.

Sindy must have seen it in his eyes. She quickly rose and brought her lips to his ear. "It's alright, take it out on me...I can handle it." He closed his eyes and gave her a gentle push away, downward. She dropped back to the floor and he followed, unhesitating. He ran his hands over her breasts and down her torso, smooth, cool and firm. He let his fingers skim the inside of her thighs and stray deeper between to find her already slick with wanting him. He poised himself over her with his fangs at her throat, to take body and blood together.

As he entered her flesh, all concerns fled his mind. He did not need thought. Mindless succumbing to instinct was all that was necessary. He drank her blood and indulged himself in her body, his hips pounding with a rhythm set by the flow of her blood over his tongue. After only a short time, he took his mouth from her throat. Although her blood was sublime, he did not wish to weaken her. His drinks this night were only for play, not for reprimand. There was no deeper meaning, to any of it.

He was blissfully able to ignore any thoughts that these acts should mean more...until he made the mistake of opening his eyes and looking upon her face. What he saw there frightened him. Sindy's eyes were slightly moist and she was looking at him with such a soft expression as he'd never seen from her. She loved him. She really did.

He hastily withdrew and once more, she seemed distraught and forlorn, but he would not disappoint her; he would not send her away. He wished that he could ask her to shift to her vampire state. He did not want to see her as a woman. He wanted her to look like the monster that he felt he was, to assuage his guilt and ease his mind, but he could not ask her to change without offering his blood. She wouldn't understand.

Instead, he raised himself up from her, and gave her a slap on the thigh paired with a tilt of his head. She understood perfectly. He wanted to turn her from him, to be taken from behind. He did not want to see her face. He wanted them not to be lovers, only vampires, creatures of instinct. They should act like the animals he felt they were.

He was able to lose himself then. He entered her once more and become not a man but the beast within. He was never a truly violent creature and wouldn't really hurt her, but he used his body as an instrument to convey all of the unrequited need that he had held for so long. He thrust his fears, frustrations and torment away from him with every forceful, pounding stroke of his body into hers.

Leaning forward a bit, he gently but firmly wound his hand into her hair and pulled her upwards until she arched her back and brought her body up to meet his. He then let go her hair and sank his fangs into her shoulder, that he might taste her yet once more.

He knew that when the blood came, his climax would not be far behind, and did briefly wonder if *she* would be satisfied, but then he felt her fingers gently brush beneath him as the silence was broken with her moans. Her hand left his body for her own, and he realized he needn't have worried for her. If he were unwilling to ensure her pleasure, she would take care of herself. He should have known, it was just like her not to rely upon him, even in this.

The moment came when thought was truly gone and briefly, they were joined as one, both of only one focus, oblivious to the rest of the world. His lips left her shoulder to let her bend forward once again and support herself on all fours. Into her, he poured all of his grief, shame and self-loathing, until he felt an empty shell, incapable of feeling anything else. She tilted her face downward further towards the floor, pressing herself back against him so strongly, that he could scarcely keep upright, and then...it was done.

After a moment or two, she fell forward to the floor and he sat back upon his heels, weary, spent and wanting only to be alone. He watched her change colors as the spectrum of his vision shifted and he became human once again...to the rest of the world anyway.

He stood without a word. Sindy knelt there for a moment on the floor, afraid to look up at him, it seemed. He stepped back from her a few paces. He had a feeling she knew, that he wanted to send her away.

Finally, she stood and turned to face him. He could not really decide if she looked pleased with him, or upset by his harsh and abrupt performance. She said nothing though, thank God. He did not think that he could face sweet sentiments *or* tears, not now. He hadn't really expected either from her but was very relieved just the same.

She just stood there looking at him, as if she were trying to figure him out, and for a moment he feared for what *he* might say to her. He'd no desire to be cruel, but he also had no patience for tenderness right now, should she ask him if she might stay.

She crossed the room to retrieve her clothing, donning her panties and then stepping into her dress. It was a simple garment to pull up and zip. He put his own pants and shirt on as well. It took just a moment, and then they were again fully clothed, as though nothing had occurred. The room smelled not of human sex, but only water and salt, mixed with venom and blood.

Now he did feel awful as looked at her. The guilt he'd thought was gone, was instead trying to return and plague him for yet another sin, but she smiled and came to him before he could say anything. She looked up into his eyes with understanding beyond her years. "You don't have to try and pretend," she said quietly. "It's okay...I know."

Her professed acceptance made it seem all the more disdainful. When had she learned to read him so well? She turned and left. He hadn't even said a word...not since 'Come in'.

~~~~~~~~~~~~~~~~~~~~~~~~~~~~

He had spent the rest of the night at home, alone. He went downstairs to shower, and then lay in his bed, disgusted by his actions, but trying to tell himself that things were as they should be. What should he want with love anyway? It had only ever in his life led him to trouble, grief and heartache. His love for his daughter Amy was the only pure love he could ever claim. Other than that, not even once could he say he had ever loved to a rewarding end, for anyone. Never had he felt that his love had given anyone true joy or happiness, least of all himself, not past the first stages of it anyway. His love always turned others sour and hurtful in the end. Why not just start out that way and be done with it?

He was an inhuman beast, undeserving of human love. Sindy would serve him as a woman when he felt that he needed one. He was not totally unfeeling towards her. On the contrary, he often wondered if he did feel the start of something between them, but compared to Felicity's love that he had lost, it seemed so slight. Although he was loathe to admit it, because of the way that he had treated her, he did believe that Sindy loved him...in her own unguided way. So what if he did not truly love her back, yet? Perhaps that would come in time. If not, maybe love was an unnecessary ingredient for a relationship between dead creatures anyway. Perhaps that was why all of his past loves had failed...he had loved them too much. He could exist in a relationship with Sindy without it.

Or maybe it was better just to be alone.

The day came, and then the night again. He slept, he woke, he drank pale and impersonal blood from his refrigerator. He focused on turning himself back into the disconnected and guarded being that he had been before Felicity had ever come into his life. Human emotions had no place in his existence. If he could not expel them, then he would do his very best to lock them away.

He had an odd thought, a picture in his mind of his body as seen from a knowing perspective. On the outside he appeared human, handsome and finely made. Of course, it was a lie. Inside of himself, he felt as though he were a hollow and false creature behind a clever disguise, empty, and made up of so many rooms, storage spaces and closets, every one with a locking door.

He spent his whole life collecting things to try to fill him, experiences to make him feel whole, but they always turned sour. He found himself filled not with the love and joy that he sought, but with much darker fare. Behind each door was yet another emotional scar, a secret, a sin. Death, sex, sorrow, grief; these were the things that he kept locked away from the world, things he often kept locked away from himself. He was usually so good at that, keeping everything locked up tight and just carrying on.

Now and again, he would meet someone, someone different, special; someone who could touch his heart...someone who had a key. Different people opened different doors. Some made him think of his failed marriage, some made him remember Amy, or Charles. Most simply would bring to mind the face or personality of a victim, long dead and gone, because of him. Yes, he had many closets in his mind filled with those. And then he would visit the secret shame that they exposed. He would take it out, turn it over in his mind, be forced to face it, and remember.

They never stayed, the ones with keys. And in the end, he would be forced to close the doors that they had opened, and carry on. He would spend some time 'tidying up', putting things back to where he could ignore them again. Secluded and shameful, he would do his best to push everything back to where it had come from and go on.

He ought to be pretty good at it by now, but Felicity had opened so many of those damn doors! How had she managed to bring all of that out of him? Why did he let her? Actually, it had been his own stupid idea. He'd thought that perhaps each sin could be revealed and dealt with, so that he could let it go, rather than keep them all. Somehow, in his mind, he had believed that if he emptied everything out for her to see, he could somehow clear it all away and then fill himself with gifts from her instead; gifts of hope and happiness, but he had been thinking only of himself and not the larger picture for her. And now, while all of these things were still exposed to his mind's eye...an emotional mess strewn upon the floor, now he'd gone and started adding more. How could he even have room for yet another sin, another shameful act?

That was the strange picture in his mind of the mess he felt inside. He had thought that long ago he had dealt with all of this. Very purposefully and intentionally he had brought it all out, before the Lord. It was so long ago. September 12, 1734, a date that he did remember well, although it had seemed an evening like all others at the start. The year before, he had begun to feel guilt and remorse with the deaths he caused. It had begun as a slight faltering now and again, but it grew. It got so each time a victim's heart would stop, he felt cold and fearful inside that he had truly become something evil. He became more and more shameful of his actions, until he could hardly carry on.

It was growing difficult to hunt and feed, he felt so convicted of his sins, but he needed the blood and could not go without it. He had tried to speak of it to Maribeth, but she had only laughed and told him to 'stop behaving like a human, with tears in his eyes and worries in his heart. Didn't he realize that he should be beyond such things now?' ...Had she no heart of her own?

Cain had tried to ignore it, but it was becoming increasingly unbearable. He could not just pretend to be above such things, as she seemed so easily to affect. Eventually, there came a night when he just could not do it. He had a willing woman in his arms. He had fascinated and delighted her with pretty words and wine; she would be his to take, it would be so easy. He'd never had much of a problem finding victims. Sometimes he almost felt that they sought him out, it was his honest face he supposed, but when the moment came, he was convicted, forced to see himself as nothing but a bringer of death. Was that his true purpose in the world, to dash the hopes and dreams of others and steal their lives away?

No! He had cried out against it, pushed the girl from him and run. He'd run far from the town through farms and pastures. Finally, he'd found himself among a field of cattle and unable to run further, collapsing upon the grass. What could he do? How could he live?

He'd sat there for hours, pondering his existence. He'd thought of other predators in the world, the wolf, the snake. They had no mercy for their prey. They lived oblivious and carried out their natural course, why couldn't he? He just sat and watched the cows, sleeping on their feet. An interesting memory had come to mind, just a slight snippet of information really, but it changed his life.

A short while back, somewhere in their travels, he and Maribeth had been at a tavern. Once their revisit to England had ended, they'd returned to the new world and had frequented practically every pub and tavern along the eastern coast in their nightly hunts. This one was just like every other, but that evening there was a man there, who considered himself a learned man of animal classification. He was entertaining his fellow patrons with tales of odd discoveries in the animal kingdom. Among the many oddities that he relayed, was the story of a bat recently discovered to live off the blood of animals, biting sleeping cattle and licking the blood from their wounds.

It was only briefly mentioned, a fleeting bit of information meant to impress and shock the others, but it had stood out in Cain's mind. An animal that lived off the blood of other animals. The idea had made him feel a little less alone in the world. It was proof in nature that his existence was not entirely an aberration.

As he had thought of that animal tale, while sitting in the field, an idea had begun to form. Why could *he* not live from the blood of animals as well? It seemed almost amazing that he hadn't thought of it before. He had lived from the flesh of animals as a man. The notion of drinking animal blood was not entirely distasteful. Carrying it out would be another story. He'd stood and approached one of the cows nearby, the animal completely unaware of his presence, in sleep. He had spent a very long time contemplating the animal, and how he could take the blood from within.

Eventually, he'd done it. It was not nearly so graceful or pleasing as feeding from the woman he'd hunted earlier would have been, but the discovery had been made. His body would accept this substance in lieu of the other. It had filled him and quieted his thirst. It would serve.

He'd come home elated, excited to bring Maribeth his news...and she'd thought him positively insane. It was then that he made another startling discovery. She had known. She'd known all along.

That first night, when she had been abducted by the old man, her sire, the night that she had been born to this life, she had learned to drink animal blood. After she'd been turned into a vampire, the man had given her a victim from whom to drink her first blood not his own, her horse. She had drunk from the mare, her very own horse and then sent it out to wander the woods come the dawn. The mark that Cain had seen upon its neck had been from Maribeth's very own new fangs.

He was shocked and appalled. He had completely forgotten the bite upon her horse's neck. Maribeth had known all along that they could prey upon animals to survive, *and she had never told him!* She had seen what he was going through, trying to deal with his remorse. She'd known he would be sorely grateful to have an alternative to their nightly hunts, but the experience of drinking from an animal had been distasteful to her, and so she had never shared it. She'd let him suffer.

That was the beginning of the end for their relationship. He and Maribeth grew further and further apart. He had refined his methods into ways more civilized, and she had thought him a fool. Eventually, they'd parted company. At that point, he could not even say that he would greatly miss her.

So he had continued to live from the blood of animals. His conscience was greatly eased, but the past did haunt him still. It became, yet again, too much to bear. He had been alone in the world at the time. He'd no idea how other vampires might deal with such things. The few he had met, professed attitudes much like Maribeth. They were untroubled by their deeds. He could take no cue from them.

He tried to think of what he would do if he were human. He would go to a priest and confess his sins, but of course, he was *not* human. To do such a thing in this inhuman state would not be wise, but maybe a priest was unnecessary to intercede. Such a confession was between himself and God, was it not?

At first, he'd thought to simply pray by himself at home, but it felt disconnected and false. He would visit a church. He and Maribeth had learned long before that to touch a cross was to feel pain, a very literal translation of the fall from grace that he had perceived within himself. They had never attempted to enter a church.

He had made his way there at nightfall; there were evening services in session. He lost the nerve to go in. Finally, he satisfied himself with sitting outside. He went around back, into the little cemetery there and sat in the grass, listening to the hymns drifting out through the windows from inside.

He wondered at the ability to walk on such hallowed ground, and whether it was proof that to enter the church would not mean his instant destruction. He decided that his intent was pure and his heart set upon repentance and redemption. That being the case, God would certainly show him mercy and allow him entrance.

He didn't try it. He had sat in the cemetery, confessed his sins aloud, wept and prayed over each memory, each transgression. At the time he had felt them taken from him, he really had. He'd become so broken and grief stricken that he had almost believed God would no longer suffer him to live. He'd lain on the ground and waited to be struck down. He had wanted to die. Instead, he had felt as though the weight was lifted, his sins taken away.

He did not receive death at God's will. He received instead, a vision. That was when he had received the notion in his mind to change his life. He must find a way to take the existence that he had, and use it for good.

He had gone home and thought of how he might act on such an idea. The fact that he no longer killed was not enough. He needed a true reversal, a way to give back, that which he had taken. He'd found ways to be useful in the world. Not just protecting humans, that was a short-term goal. He'd begun to seek out other vampires. That was when he had begun to think of himself as a teacher. He'd begun to think of himself as an instrument of God; a servant to help bring about Divine will in the dark and dreadful world of the living dead.

'We must be meant for more', he would insist. He had no idea what that purpose might be, but to him, one thing seemed certain, to stop the killing of humans was the first step. From that might evolve a larger goal at some point. Perhaps that part of the plan was not for him to know, but he'd felt that he had a mission, a duty, and he went to it with unshakable will. At last he'd felt that he was forgiven and his guilt could be replaced with the knowledge that he was doing good works.

Obviously, he had not as fully let go of his guilt as he'd thought. It had come rushing back to him as he'd relayed his tale to Felicity. He used to be satisfied with what he was. Perhaps it was not the sort of life he would have planned for himself, but he was content in the fact that he was doing good, he made a difference. He had a proper place in the world, to his mind.

There were lonely periods, sure. There were times when he transgressed and acted on ideas of his own, and strayed from his goal, but those times had not been allowed to keep him happy. Those transgressions always led to heartache in the end. He would then feel repentant and shameful, and be led back to his cause.

Now he felt so confused. He wanted to do the right thing, really he did. He wanted what was best for Felicity, and he also wanted to keep on traveling and helping others. That required a life separate and apart from human ties. At first his lonely needs had led him into temptation once again, into thinking that maybe she could join him. She could travel by his side, human, or as a creature like himself and they could continue his work together. He deserved that much didn't he? The life of one girl was nothing compared to all of those that she could help, with him.

That was a selfish rationalization. The end did not justify the means. She should not be deprived of her life, on the pretense that it was necessary to help others. It was not a necessary measure; it was a lonely act of selfishness. It was good that he had sent Felicity away and would not see her again, though it made his heart ache. It was the right thing to do. He could find solace in another of his kind, killed not by his hand. Sindy had certainly shown interest in being his companion...even if he didn't love her as he did Felicity. Or, if not, he could carry on alone. That might be better.

He was unsure of how he would face Sindy when next they met. He knew she wouldn't hold anything against him. He suspected she never thought to expect more from a man. Tender expressions of love, were most likely foreign to her. He should seek to change that in her life, not reinforce it.

He would need some time to think upon the course of action that would best benefit them both, and then decide if he could actually carry it out. He needed time. He had no stomach to seek Sindy out again anyway, not for a little while at least. He supposed he should surface to find whether she was planning on keeping her boys, or sending them out on their own. She hadn't mentioned freeing them, that had been his own speculation, but he did need to know her intentions. The last thing he needed to deal with, was six spurned rogue vampires roaming his town. He would have to let her know that if she planned on freeing them, she should seek his help.

Not a favored aspect of the job he had set for himself, but not an unfamiliar one either. If she were to free them, he would need to asses each one on its own merits, as an individual. If he felt it sapient enough to live peacefully, fine; let it go and try to make an existence for itself elsewhere, but if it were functioning on a very low intellectual level, as most of hers were, it should simply have to be destroyed. It might seem cruel, but if they could not discreetly and properly care for themselves, he could not let them endanger others. From what he could tell, only Chris and Luke would make the cut.

Then he remembered, Chris had left. Cain wondered what had finally driven him to independence. Most likely it was Sindy's interest in Cain. She had finally given Cain her blood. Of course, it was not really willingly the first time, but Chris was surely not given details. Cain felt a little badly for causing strife between them, but would not let himself believe that he was the sole contributor to Chris' departure.

He was actually sort of glad for Chris. He'd often felt bad for the boy, although they were usually on opposite sides of an argument. Sindy had always treated him indifferently and he seemed aware enough to deserve better. Luke wasn't given any better treatment, but at least he never seemed to notice or care.

Cain wondered what a difficult time Sindy might have in controlling the rest of them now. He'd noticed that she had begun to leave them in Chris and Luke's care, more and more often as time wore on. She'd been craving more time alone...to spend with him, but in doing so, she had relied upon Chris heavily. Luke was no marvel of common sense and Cain doubted that he could ever handle them alone for any amount of time; probably one of the reasons that she had not been loath to leave so quickly last night, he realized. She had needed to get back, before something went wrong without her.

So these were the thoughts that he busied himself with, as he spent the day alone trying not to think and dwell on his love lost. He was really rather startled when he heard the knock at his door. The sun had not yet set...it was not even six in the evening yet. He stretched his mental awareness, but could find nothing close enough to be on his doorstep. Whoever came was unmarked.

Perhaps it was only a salesman, or someone with a mistaken address. He would ignore it. The knock came again, then again...louder. He waited quietly, with an impending fear coming upon him. There was only one human who had ever knowingly knocked upon his door at this house...

Felicity. Could it be? No, she wouldn't return. She had to have been disgusted and appalled by his account of his actions of the past. He had frightened her away and told her that he would no longer be a part of her life. He'd thought for sure that she would avoid him now. She was a smart girl.

Girl...she was only a girl; that was an aspect of her that he had not really reckoned with. She was sensitive and intelligent, mature for her age and made good decisions most of the time, but there was something that he had not really taken into account, she *was* a teenage girl, in love...with him. Irrational was practically the definition of a teenage girl in love. How unaware and unthinking must he have been not to realize that? She called to him now. "Cain? Please answer. I know you can hear me. Please?" It was definitely her.

He was frozen, unsure what to do. He should have left. He had known it in his heart, and yet he had stayed. He could not see her though, it would be selfish and wrong to give in to such desires. He had sent her away for her own good, and needed to hold firm in his decision. She knocked again.

Had he the detachment to leave her pleas unanswered?

CRECRECRECRECRECRECRECRECRECRECRECRECRECRECRE

Part 3 - Battles and Bliss

CRECRECRECRECRECRECRECRECRECRECRECRECRECRECRE

Chapter 16 - Don't think

Cain

Cain's house
Tuesday, 5:15 p.m.

Cain agonized over his indecision as Felicity knocked upon his door. Why had she come back to see him? She knew he was a murderous monster. He had no choice in being a vampire, and though he did choose now to resist killing humans for blood, it could not erase his past.

She was temptation incarnate, whom he would do better to stay away from, and he could bring a lovely girl such as she nothing but hurt and heartache he was sure. To allow himself to be with her would perhaps endanger her very life.

He knew he shouldn't answer the door. He should shun her, let her go on her way, to live her life. "Please, Cain?" He could hear her call quietly from up on his porch. Did he really think he had the resolve to ignore her?

He waited a few interminable moments and then had to concede that he did not. He could never turn a deaf ear to *her*. He would have to go and talk to her, try to send her away, although he knew that was unlikely to occur.

All of the comforting that he had tried to give himself, consoling himself that he had done the right thing in sending her away...was lost. Truthfully, it was gone and forgotten the moment he'd heard her voice. God, but he was so weak. He went to her. He did not know what he would say or do. He still told himself that he would ask her to leave, but he knew she wouldn't listen without persuasion that he may not be strong enough to carry out.

He opened the door to reveal her standing in the sunlight on his porch. "Hi," she said softly. Once again, he was enraptured by her beauty.

She wore a lovely dress of green and blue, and tiny little sparkling diamonds in her ears. Her hair was wound up off her shoulders, with some sort of oriental hair sticks with green designs on them, just visible towards the back, holding it in place. The dress showed off her smooth shoulders and just enough cleavage to be truly enticing without being too revealing.

Her throat was bare. He tore his eyes from the spot to find her eyes, an earthy green. She gazed at him for a moment and then smiled. "Aren't you even going to say anything?"

He fought to find his voice. "You look...stunning."

Her cheeks flushed gently pink with her pleasure of his compliment. "Thank you," she replied quietly.

He felt so bewildered by her presence, when he had been trying so hard to accept that he would not see her again, and why was she dressed so? "Are you just coming from somewhere?"

Now she rolled her eyes and laughed. "No stupid! It's for you. Aren't you supposed to be taking me out to dinner, for my birthday?"

He vaguely remembered mention of such plans, but that was before he had finished his tale. He'd thought them irrelevant. He hadn't planned to see her again; surely she'd realized? Even if she did think he was taking her to dinner...he was unsure of the time, but the sun was certainly still shining brightly outside. "You're a few hours early."

"I know," she said with a secret sort of smile.

He closed his eyes a moment and tried to gather his strength. That was a smile, hard to resist. He looked at the ground, instead of her face. "I hadn't expected to see you again. I mean, I didn't think we *should* see each other. I thought you'd understood."

"I know." She looked down as he finally did try to meet her gaze, a little uncomfortably, but she then seemed to raise her courage and looked him in the eye. "I've been doing some thinking too. Want to know what I think?" He gazed at her and gave a slight nod, although he was fairly sure what she would say and that it would be better for him to not hear it. He should shut the door and make her go. Of course, he didn't move.

"I think," she said as she moved a bit closer, and he leaned a bit away, "that you and I..." She moved forward again. She didn't wait for an invitation, or for him to even back away for her to enter. She simply began to walk forward as she spoke, causing him to back away almost involuntarily. He was afraid to touch her and he moved back before her more surely even, than when she'd driven him with the cross. He stepped backwards until he met the wall, and she stopped just shy of his body. "We both think too much," she concluded.

She brought her lips to his and he felt powerless to prevent it. He stood stunned and unsure how to proceed, so torn with indecision. He shouldn't, he really shouldn't. She didn't realize where it might lead, how it could ruin her life to be with him.

It also truly bothered him that this was the second time in just as many nights that such a thing had occurred. Her actions so echoed Sindy's that it was frightening. The thought of *his* actions with Sindy made him feel ill.

Felicity sought his attentions now, just as he had so sorely longed for, when Sindy had been the one to approach. It *was* Felicity who kissed him now, and he could hardly even kiss her back. He turned his head away. "I don't think..."

"*Don't* think. Why does everything have to be so well thought out, be perfectly planned, and make practical sense? There are some things in life that I don't want to analyze, I just want to experience."

He looked into her eyes then, with a lump in his throat from the sick feeling he got in remembering the night before. *Now* Felicity wanted this? He didn't deserve her, not in the least. He shook his head sadly. "Not with me," he whispered.

"Yes, with you." She adorned his lips with kisses once again, sweet, soft cajoling little kisses that tempted and persuaded him that nothing else could matter more. This time he stopped fighting her, although he did not really give over to it.

After a few moments, he ended it though. "I can't. I'm no good for you, really. I don't belong in your life."

She wouldn't back away, but instead rested her hands lightly on his shoulders. "This isn't my whole life, it's one day."

He gave a small smile and shook his head. "And tomorrow?"

She smiled back and gave a little shrug. "What's one more day?"

He laughed a bit and shook his head. "No, see living for the moment is really *not* a good thing for me. It's sort of what got me into this mess. I'm trying to avoid repeating past mistakes."

Again, she sought to bring herself to his lips. "It's not a mistake," she whispered as she kissed him.

Again, he felt himself beginning to give over to her, and again he tried to stop it. He should be strong. He knew what was right, even if she didn't. "You should go," he told her quietly.

She stepped back from him, just a bit. She looked very stern and determined. It unnerved him a little, because he knew that she was not planning to leave and he would be rather hard pressed to convince her, without hurting her.

Then he happened to glance at the place on the floor where he had been with Sindy. He hadn't meant to, but as he glanced at the spot, the memory flashed before him. The wonderful young woman before him now, deserved better than someone like him.

She spoke with serious intensity. "Do you really *want* me to leave?" Phrased like that, he could not answer. "Tell you what, I'll go. I'll leave, and I will never come here again...if you can do one thing for me." He made his face a stern mask as he waited for her to continue. "Tell me honestly, that you *don't* love me."

He closed his eyes for a moment, and then opened them to look at the floor. He had to do this; she had to go. He met her eyes, trying to make his own tell her nothing, cold and impersonal. "I don't love you."

Felicity never took her eyes from his, although her own were soon covered with a sheen of tears. She stared at him for a moment, then she tried to smile. "You're a really rotten liar."

As the words left her lips, he felt his face begin to crumple. He had meant to hold on to his stern expression, but it just didn't work. "Yeah, I know."

"You can't send me away." A single tear fell to her cheek as she spoke, and he couldn't take his eyes from it. "Because, I love you."

He just couldn't stand to break her heart. He knew that in the end, to send her away now might be the less painful choice, but he just couldn't do it. He loved her more deeply than any other woman he had ever known. Their future may be uncertain, but he could not deny her now. He took her into his arms. At first, it was only a hug, a crushing embrace. Her heart was pounding against him and he almost felt as though it were trying to pour all of her love out to him in morse code against his chest.

She snuggled her face into his chest and began to kiss him there, through his shirt, but then she raised herself to find his throat. Her kisses moved upwards until her lips found his own and she kissed him with an intensity that surprised him. It was far more urgently seductive than any other kiss he could ever remember receiving from her.

Finally, he made her pull away so that he might speak. "Shouldn't we…"

"Go downstairs?" she asked eagerly.

He laughed. "I was going to say - close the door."

She turned to see the open doorway. The sun had lowered a bit and was sending a slanting slice of sunlight down upon the floor into the house, uncomfortably close to where they stood. An elderly couple was walking past outside. She smiled and giggled. "Oh yeah, sorry." She quickly went to close the door and then rushed back to his arms. "*Now* can we go downstairs?"

He glanced back to the spot where he had been with Sindy and grimaced. He hoped she didn't notice. "Yes, please."

Chapter 17 - No regrets

Felicity

Cain's house
Tuesday, 5:30 p.m.

Felicity eagerly followed Cain downstairs, elated and amazed that she had been brave enough to say the things she had practiced to herself earlier. She had known that he loved her, but had been terribly worried that he would not admit it. He was so bent on protecting her from himself. She had been right too. He had tried to deny his feelings, but she knew. Thank God she'd had the courage to call him on it. He loved her. She'd known.

As he reached the bottom of the stairs, he began to cross the room, to light the lamp next to the bed. She followed right behind him, and as soon as he turned it on, she practically threw herself into his arms. He was very startled. He must have thought that she'd remained by the stairs. Or maybe he just didn't expect her to be so forward.

But she had already decided in her mind that she should surprise him with her boldness. She remembered his story. What stood out in her mind now, were his descriptions of Maribeth. He had obviously been extremely attracted to her. Her brazen desires had most definitely turned him on. Felicity wanted to do the same. She wanted him to find *her* irresistible, in the same way that he could not deny his need for Maribeth. So when she kissed him, it was rushed and urgent, trying to convey impatience for the act she was actually a bit nervous to carry out. She was certain she wanted to, but was nervous all the same.

Her experience with guys was not totally lacking. She'd had some hot and heavy dates out on the cliff over-looking the slate quarry, where kids in her town had parked to make-out, but those experiences only went so far. Cain was an older and *much* more experienced man. She didn't want him to think her naive. She was determined to be bold and unhesitating, as opposed to her usual timid self. She threw herself into his arms and practically propelled him onto the bed. Once there, she pushed him to lie back and moved to lie atop him, as he had caused her to do that night on the stairs. This time she was unafraid of pressing into to him too strongly, letting things go too far. The longer they kissed the more aware she became of his body. She was amazed at how clearly she could feel him. Her silk dress and his thin sleep pants could hardly conceal how badly he longed for her.

With a very deliberate decision to carry on with her boldness, she began to move her hips against him. She brought her hands down to find the hem of his shirt and pushed them up underneath. After only a moment, she came back to the hem and began to tug and pull his shirt up. He sat up a bit to let her, and she pulled it to under his arms, but as it came up higher, she was still unwilling to end their kiss yet. Finally, he sat up fully and broke from her, laughing. He leaned back, with arms up, to let her pull it over his head. She did, and threw his shirt to the floor. His chest was broad and smooth.

Once again, she attacked him with kisses, as though unable to restrain herself. This time it was the waist of his pants that she tugged at, trying to pull them down almost violently. He stopped the kiss and leaned back to look at her oddly. "What are you doing?"

She was a little put off by his question. What did he think? "Taking your pants off."

"Why?"

What kind of question is that? He seemed almost amused. "Because...I want you." After a moment's thought she added, "I *need* you." She was trying her very best to sound desperate and sultry at the same time.

He simply cocked an eyebrow at her. "Really?"

She eyed him for a moment, as he seemed to be trying to read her true feelings. She refused to back down from her plan. She thought of all the things Cain had told her about his past experiences with women. She had paid close attention. He'd thought his wife's 'appetite' for 'bed sport' was sorely lacking and had been thrilled when Maribeth had 'hungered for him as a man' and attacked him with sheer desire in her eyes. Felicity would not disappoint, she wanted to thrill him. "Really. I *need* you, I do."

He gestured for her to let him up. She did, and he stood from the bed. He moved to stand to the side of the bed right next to her and she turned to face him, sitting. He wore a bit of a smirk on his face, but then composed it to be very serious. "You do? Isn't this moving a bit fast for you?"

She looked up at him indignantly, annoyed that he should question her. "I know what I want," she insisted with a confidence she didn't really feel.

He raised his eyebrows a bit. After a moment of thought, he wore a smug smile and said in a commanding tone, "Show me."

She was a little shocked by his attitude, but tried not to let her face convey anything but desire. When she did not immediately respond, he pulled down his pants and was revealed before her. Even though she fought to remain unfazed, she knew that her eyes had gone a bit wide. He was right in front of her face, erect and undeniably, nicely endowed. He took the pants off and then stood there unmoving, waiting for a display of her *need*.

Felicity was very close to trying to please him. Her hand even hovered before his body for a moment, but then she dropped it to the bed and looked up at him in annoyance. He had to know that she hadn't much experience. Exactly what did he expect from her? This was her first time! It was supposed to be romantic, and he was going to stand there and *order* things from her? "Why are you making this so difficult for me?" she asked.

He immediately dropped his stern composure and laughed. He seemed almost relieved. "*There* you are! The Felicity I know and love, who doesn't take orders well. I was hoping you would surface. That domineering girl who was kissing me, while trying to pull the shirt over my head and rip the clothes from my body...I don't know who *that* was, but it wasn't you. Why are you trying to be someone you're not?"

She dropped her eyes to the bed. "I wasn't..."

He spoke to her tenderly. "I know what you were trying to do. I'm glad that you want to please me, but don't. I love you for who you are. Don't do things only to try and impress me." He brought back the stern and commanding voice. "Do you know what I want you to do?"

Felicity kept her eyes lowered, chastened. "What?"

He put a finger to her chin, to tip her face and make her look at him. "Whatever *you* want. That will please me. Have faith." She smiled at him and then as she began to look back down, she turned from him, a little embarrassed. His erection had lessened a bit during their talk, but he was still right in front of her and impossible to ignore. He gave a little laugh. "Now, if you'd like to further your explorations of my body, I'll certainly be happy to oblige, but do you think you might come up here first and give me one of *your* kisses? I do sorely miss them."

She smiled broadly and stood up on the bed. She came into his arms, although the bed now made her slightly taller than him. He wrapped his arms about her waist and they kissed. A comfortable, familiar and wonderful kiss that grew strong with passion unforced. After a few minutes, she gave a little pull for him to lie down with her on the bed. He quickly did so and their kisses continued. She was still fully clothed, but she could easily feel him pressed against her. He was so hard! She was a bit shocked with herself at how much that observation excited her. He stopped kissing her and rolled to the side.

"Your lovely dress is getting all wrinkled," he told her.

She tried to move back towards him. "I don't care," she said with a smile.

"Well, *I* do. Do you think I'm going to take you out to dinner later, looking like a street urchin?" She laughed and he gave her a playful shove to get up from the bed. "Go on and take it off for me, will you? But that's not an *order*, mind you. Just a suggestion," he said with a chuckle.

She stood and moved a few steps from the bed, facing him. After a moment's mental preparation, she reached behind her lower back, and unzipped the dress. The bodice of the dress was tight, but the material was gathered and shirred to a seam that ran up the middle, rather than being smooth. The result was that it created a sort of slanting stripe design. It was beautiful. It also had helped her to be less self-conscious about wearing it without a bra.

The top of the bodice split to create two broad straps that fastened behind her neck, and left her shoulders bare. She brought her hands up behind her neck and opened the hook that held the top closed. She stood there for a second, and then let the dress drop. She wore no bra beneath, but did have on pink cotton bikini panties, and full pantyhose. She looked down at the floor, feeling her face grow flushed.

Finally, she met his eyes and spoke. "Sorry about the plain panties and stockings. I wanted to get sexy ones, you know, like with a garter belt? But I was shopping with my mom, and I didn't want to have to try to explain a purchase like that." He laughed a little and smiled at her lovingly. She took off the pantyhose, but wasn't quite ready to remove her underwear. She left them on, and looked up at him again.

"Well, don't leave it on the floor," he said, nodding towards her dress. She rolled her eyes and picked it up. She moved to drape it across the bar, and then turned back to face him. She just stood there; holding in her stomach a bit and watching him run his eyes over her body. She tried not to be too self-conscious. He hadn't hesitated in the least when revealing his body to her.

He smiled. "So, are you going to torture me further, standing all the way over there as I gaze upon your perfect body, or are you going to come to me?" He still lay on the bed, propped up on one elbow in a very casual pose.

She rolled her eyes, mumbling, "*Perfect* is a little strong a word."

He rose from the bed and went to meet her, since she hadn't immediately come to him. He put a hand on each shoulder, smiled at her and whispered, "No, it's *not*." He then took her into his arms for a kiss. It felt so good to be enfolded in his arms, the absence of clothing making it something special and new. He leaned back again to look at her. "Stop worrying so much about the impression you're making."

She smiled to herself. "Don't think."

He moved his head to make her meet his eyes. "Are you sure this is what you want? Don't feel you need to prove to me, your love."

She snuggled a little closer against him, very aware of his exposed body, pressing against her. "This is definitely what I want. I guess I was just going about it the wrong way. Think we could kind of...start over?"

He laughed. "Well, I don't plan to get dressed again."

"No, that's okay." She began to kiss him again and bravely let her hand wander from his back, down to give his butt cheek a little squeeze. "That really won't be necessary." He laughed a bit, but then their kiss turned much more serious. As passion began to dominate over silliness, she moved her body to the side a bit and let her caresses come around his thigh to find his penis.

He didn't question her boldness this time. His kiss became far more passionate as she let her hand explore him, and then begin to stroke and gently squeeze him in a way that she was sure he would enjoy. After a moment, he did stop the kiss to question her. "Am I meant to believe *that* is an *in*experienced hand?" he asked breathlessly.

She gave a little laugh and met his eyes, while continuing her motions. "I'm a virgin, but I haven't been living under a rock," she answered smugly, glad that she had honestly surprised and impressed him on her own, without artifice.

"Is that so? Because by the look on your face when I disrobed earlier, I would have thought differently." Now he wore the smug smile.

She dropped her eyes with a giggle. "Was it *that* obvious?"

"I found it delightful."

A few more giggles escaped her as she tried to decide how to explain herself. "Well, this is going to seem kind of stupid..."

He spoke with a voice quiet and sincere. "Honest thoughts expressed cannot be stupid."

She stopped giggling long enough to answer seriously. "I've never actually *seen* a man's body before, not in person I mean."

He did look a little surprised. "Are you telling me that the eyes that belong to *that* hand have never seen what they touch?"

She dropped her hand from him as her face turned red. "Well, it's always been in the dark, in a parked car."

"*Always?*" he asked in amusement.

"Three times," she admitted.

"M-hmm." He gave her a little kiss. "Well, I commend you, for your honest admission." That brought forth her giggles again. She felt as though her confession must have sounded absurd to him. He continued. "Feel free to look all you like, but do me a favor?" She tried to compose herself and met his eyes. "Do try to stop giggling first. It's not very helpful to a man's ego." Of course, that only made her giggles worse.

She eventually composed herself sufficiently to speak. "Don't try to tell me that *you're* self conscious? Even *I* can tell that *your* body really is perfect."

He shook his head a little with a modest smile. "I have the same fears and worries as everyone else. I'm just a bit more comfortable in my skin because I've been in it for so bloody long."

"Well, in case you were wondering, I'm very impressed."

He smiled and shook his head again. "I'm glad to hear it, but it's really not about that. I don't want to impress you. I want to love you, fully...unhindered, as I have *so* wanted to these past weeks."

She nodded and said quietly. "Yeah...that sounds *really* good."

"Alright then. Less talk, more kisses." They began their kisses once again and after a moment, he stooped to put his arm under her legs and scoop her off her feet. They continued to kiss as he carried her to the bed. He put her down and then stopped to study her for a moment. She lay in a half-sitting position, propped up a bit by her elbows. She was surprised when he came forward not for another kiss, but to touch her hair. He plucked the sticks from it and let it unwind, down onto her shoulders. He held the hair-sticks up for her to see. "I don't think I'd like to roll over onto one of these," he explained with a smile.

Oh. They were wooden, and each sharpened on one end, like the stakes he used to kill other vampires. She hadn't even realized. "Sorry."

"That's alright. An ounce of prevention and all of that." He put them on the bar, where they would not be lost, and quickly returned to her. "Now...what else might I remove?" he asked teasingly, eyeing her panties.

She smiled, and gave him a slight nod. He hooked one finger into the band at each hip and she lifted herself enough for him to take them off. He pulled them down, let them drop to the floor and came back for more kisses.

She had felt his venom beginning to affect her a bit more with each kiss, bringing about a slight haziness and helping to lower her inhibitions. She worried that it might get stronger, making her feel almost drunk, but as their kisses continued, it seemed to level off, reaching an equilibrium that kept her a little light headed, but not distressingly so.

As he lay down upon her, she couldn't help but tense with nervous apprehension. He noticed and raised himself up a bit to meet her eyes. "Relax. I'm not going to *thrust* myself upon you, unready. We're wanting for pleasure, not pain." He gave her a quick kiss and she smiled. "Have trust, never fear," he whispered. He brought his lips back to hers to continue their kisses.

Before long those kisses did travel from her lips. For a split second she held her breath as they traveled down her throat. He hovered for a moment, at the place where he'd bitten her, but then gave her a kiss there and moved on.

His lips found her breast and he began to kiss and suckle her in a way that she found incredibly arousing. It was unexpectedly exciting, considering the absence of desire she'd felt the few times she had allowed herself to be groped there by boys back home. Her nipple began to tingle and harden a bit as his attentions grew stronger. He moved from one to the other, and then after a few minutes, resumed his travels downward.

After covering her belly with kisses, he gently parted her thighs. Again she tensed in anticipation, but held herself open to him. As he explored her there, with tongue and kisses, she wriggled and thrilled to what seemed such a forbidden act. She felt a warmth come upon her, that she had at first thought to be his breath, but then she sadly realized that he wasn't really breathing.

The venom, she was feeling it on her skin, just as surely as it was in his kiss. It caused only slight warmth and a bit of tingling, but considering where he placed it, it was amazingly effective. Not that it was necessary; she had never felt such desire in her life before this day.

When he came back to her she felt as though she were truly ready for him, although he simply lay atop her lightly and met her lips for more kisses. For a moment, she was startled when she realized that she could taste herself in his kiss, but she decided not to be unnerved, and accepted it as natural to the experience.

His hand found her then, and began to rub and caress the secret and hidden folds above her opening in a way that made her long to take him within her. His mouth left her lips and he spoke quietly. "If you don't mind my asking, has anyone ever ventured into such territory for you?" As he asked, his finger did tease and just barely enter her.

She sucked in her breath and took a moment before answering. She thought of the time she *had* allowed another to touch her there romantically. Unfortunately, it had been anything *but* romantic. It had been ungraceful, bungling and blessedly brief. That uncomfortable experience was far removed from anything she might feel now, she was sure. "Nothing worth remembering."

Surely, he heard the disdain in her voice. She could almost feel his smile as he let out a little breath of a laugh. "Don't be disheartened. This shall erase the past." He didn't have to worry that she was nervous or hesitant. Each touch brought new pleasures she'd never dreamed of and made her want nothing but more.

He brought his lips back to hers and continued to rub his finger against her until she became impatient, in thinking that he would never allow it to fully enter. She *was* beginning to feel the desperate urgency that she had tried to convince him she had felt earlier, but this time there was definitely no artifice necessary. When he finally did let his finger go further, she found she was practically moving herself down upon him, in an attempt to satisfy her need. He removed his hand far too soon for her liking, but then she realized that this was only the beginning.

She found herself very surprised, when rather than lie atop her, he rolled aside and looked up at her, hopefully. "Perhaps you might bestow a kiss or two of your own...to ease the way?"

It took her a moment to understand what he meant. He wanted her to kiss his body and make him wet for her. She moved lower on the bed, to be next to his hips and took then him into her hand. After a few exploratory kisses, she took him into her mouth. It seemed odd that he could feel so soft, smooth and cool, and yet so hard all at once. She did her best to please him, it was a little clumsy and awkward, but he didn't seem to mind. He didn't even let her go on very long really. "It's enough," he said quietly. She was afraid that maybe he was disappointed with her motions, but as she looked at his face, she realized it was quite the opposite. He couldn't wait much longer.

She thought that he would lie over her again, but instead he motioned for her to climb atop him. She was sure that he noted her look of hesitant confusion, but he only smiled and nodded reassurance. She settled herself onto his thighs, thinking that maybe he wanted her to fondle him some more, but he sat up to put his hands to her waist and brought her forward to sit on his stomach instead. He then had her lean down for another kiss. That's when she realized what he really had planned. "But…I thought…I should lie down again," she said uncertainly, as she sat back up.

He smiled up at her doubting expression. "I want *you* to do it. After all, it is your maidenhood, you deserve the honor."

Now she was nervously uncertain at the prospect of being made to take the lead. "But, I can't. I mean, I won't know… It won't be good."

He raised a hand to caress her cheek. "Trust me, it will be wonderful." He looked thoughtful for a moment, and then smiled. "Dance for you."

The sentence almost brought tears to her eyes as she remembered fondly their first dance. It had been so freeing and honest and like something from a dream. She came down to his lips and their kisses, at first sweet and loving, did become increasingly passionate again. He placed his hands upon her hips, and took great care in positioning her just shy of being truly astride him.

He gripped her hips a little more forcefully, and began to give her a rhythm. He moved her ever so slightly forward and back, so that she could feel his manhood press at her opening, and then all but leave her, again and again. His hands then left her hips to wrap gently around her lower back, as she continued the motions on her own.

She was pleased to find that as she moved, the slight friction of his lower stomach rubbing against her, between her legs, brought back the eager desire she had felt when his hand had caressed her there. She became bolder and felt him begin to enter, as she pressed down harder against him with each backward motion. Her body was moist with anticipation as she imagined how it would feel, but she only barely took him within her, taking her time.

She opened her eyes to look at his face. Cain's eyes were closed, but she knew that he was in pleasurable torment. It must seem torture that she would hesitate and tease him so. But then he opened his eyes, and smiled at her with such loving and patient desire, that she knew he would try to wait forever until she was ready, if he could. He needn't worry, she couldn't wait another moment.

With a brazen thrust, she brought herself down upon him. She let out a small cry as her body stretched to accommodate him, but the pleasure far outdistanced the pain. She froze there for a moment, and then tried to go further, but his hands moved back to her hips and stopped her. He moved her upwards instead, and then down, recreating their prior rhythm. His passage into her was much eased this way. With each stroke she let escape a small sigh of amazement and pleasure that he was indeed moving deeper within her. She soon found herself moving faster and further until she was taking him in as fully as possible.

She found rocking motions for her hips and rhythms so pleasing that she felt like an exotic dancer upon him. Twice he brought his hands to her hips again to stop her, and she realized that she was exciting him to the point that he must pause, lest their experience end too soon. She tried to wait patiently for him to let her go on…it was maddening.

He let her continue and she found herself voicing quiet moans of delight that, in her usual shyness, she had never thought she might utter. He answered them with his own, and together they moved until she felt her pleasure grow and build into an unimagined explosion of amazing ecstasy. She cried out, bucking and pressing against him, smothering his throat with kisses. She was shocked at how largely she had underestimated what she would feel.

Just as her own rapture began to subside, his hands again found her hips, to move her strongly upon him a few times, and then he lifted her from him. She swung her leg off him, to lay snuggled next to him on the bed. Felicity watched in amazement, as evidence of their passions spilled out from him, onto his stomach. She held herself pressed as close against his side as she could, while she tried to calm her gasps for breath.

She couldn't help but feel curiously proud as she lay with her head on his shoulder and studied his body. He was obviously well satisfied. She looked up at him and smiled. "Wow," she said with a grin. He opened his eyes and smiled.

"I fully agree." He lay unmoving for a moment, and then turned his head to her for a kiss. "I *do* love you," he whispered.

She felt as though she could not get close enough to him as she continued to kiss his shoulder. "I love you too," she replied.

After studying her with a curiously penetrating gaze, he leaned over her and then moved down her body until his hair brushed her hips while he placed a light kiss upon her abdomen. He ran his hand down her thigh to the knee and then gently edged her legs open as he looked up at her, longing for her consent. "May I?" he breathed.

She was a bit startled when it occurred to her what he might be after, but she simply nodded and lay back to close her eyes. His tongue gently explored her, collecting evidence of her former maidenhood as she felt the comforting warmth of venom renewed once again. She reveled in her newfound lack of inhibition as she allowed herself to be at ease with him there. Just as she thought he might urge her desires to awaken yet again, he took a deep shuddering breath and returned to lie next to her, gazing steadily up at the ceiling. She studied his obvious inner struggle for self-control as she tried to calm her newly racing heart. After a moment, he tilted his head to see her unreservedly running her eyes over his body.

She looked away a bit shyly, to have been caught so obviously observing his anatomy. He reached an arm out to enfold her, but she gently wriggled from his embrace with a smile. "I'll be right back," she explained, as she headed for the bathroom.

"Think you might throw me a towel?" Cain asked.

She quickly found one and tossed it to him, before she ducked into the bathroom for herself. When she emerged, he was lying on the bed facing her, the towel on the floor.

She quickly padded across the room and jumped onto the bed, making him bounce about and laugh. Then she grabbed the sheet and lay down next to him, covering them both. He eagerly took her into his arms for a kiss. After a few minutes, they lay quiet, her head on his chest. She peeked up at him and smiled. "That was...unbelievable." He just smiled. She made her voice stern, teasing him. "Do you realize that all these weeks, we could have been doing that this whole time?"

He laughed. "That thought had occurred, yes." He smiled at her. "It's alright. I told you it'd be worth the wait."

She laughed and kissed him. "Can I ask you..."

"Anything," he assured her.

"Well, just now..." She smiled in thinking of their actions. "Why did you wait, until after I was done? I mean, why didn't you let it happen while you were still...while we were together? And why did you move me away? You couldn't have been worried you'd get me pregnant, right?"

He smiled, a bit sadly she thought. "No. You needn't worry about that with me. Although I do think you might have asked beforehand, if you were wondering."

"I wasn't, until you did that."

"Well, put your mind at ease. The ability to have children is gone in me. This body is no longer equipped. It can't carry diseases either, so that's something else off your mind. No worries." She should have been relieved, but she felt bad for him. It seemed very bittersweet. Truthfully, though it may have been foolish of her, those thoughts hadn't even entered her mind. "As to why I moved you, well...I thought *that* an experience better explored next time."

"What do you mean?"

"The venom. It's in all of my bodily fluids. I understand it can have quite an effect." Her eyes went a bit wide at the thought, he just shrugged a little. "I wanted you to know what it was like, without that. As much as possible, anyway."

She tried to hide her smile at the hint of promise behind his words...next time. She snuggled closer to him for more kisses. "Well, maybe we should do some more experimenting then," she said with a sly smile. He laughed.

"Please, I may not be human, but even my body doesn't regain strength *that* fast."

She laughed as well, but then turned to him, seriously. "I love you. My first time couldn't have been more perfect."

"Well, it's a first for me too, you know."

"Yeah, your first time *with me.*"

"It *is* a first. I've never had the distinct pleasure of de-flowering a virgin before. Well...other than my late wife that is, but she saw such things as little more than her wifely duty. Trust me, that experience was *nothing* like this one. Yours is the only virginity I've tasted as a vampire. In a life as long as mine, *firsts* are rare to come by. The fact that you entrusted the experience to me, is something that I will always look upon with fond memory, and a flush of pleasure." He had seemed so happy and light hearted at first, but after a moment, Felicity could swear he was fighting tears.

"What's wrong?" she asked in quiet concern.

"I wish I could freeze time. Stop things right here and live only in this moment, but things always change in time. Everything but me. Loving you so much, only distresses me more to lose you."

"I'm not going anywhere. In fact, I'm pretty sure I've got at least fifty or sixty good years left in me." She tried to make him smile. It didn't really work.

He swallowed and closed his eyes for a moment, before meeting hers again. "Not planning to live much further beyond that, are you?"

She knew what he meant. She looked down at the bed sheets for a minute, and then looked up with sad seriousness. "Not really...no." She gave a little shrug. "Still...it seems pretty long to me. Could be fun while it lasts." She gazed at him thoughtfully. "No regrets."

He gave a little laugh, as a tear fell onto his cheek. He wiped it away and then took her into his arms again. "It may not be long, but it will be unforgettable, I promise you that." He tickled her beneath the covers, to chase away any impending gloom.

They rolled about, laughing, tickling and kissing until thoroughly exhausted. She lay against him trying to catch her breath, and looked up at him naughtily. "So...when do you think you'll be ready for more?"

He laughed. "What, do you plan to cram all of your experiences into one evening? When I said our relationship may not be long, I didn't mean that I'd be leaving at sunset." He lowered his voice, confidentially. "You know, a certain amount of *blood* is necessary to achieve the readiness you're looking for, and I'm afraid I'm a bit spent at the moment." Her eyes widened as she realized how she had likely awakened his thirst, whether looking to fuel an erection or not. "Besides, I owe you a dinner. You must be starved after such activities."

"Actually yeah, I am. Are *you?*"

He smiled at her concern. "You needn't worry, I'm alright. But I do think a break is in order." He nodded his head towards her clothes at the bar. "Why don't we put some clothes on, and I'll take you somewhere worthy of that beautiful dress?"

She kissed him once more, before leaving the bed. "I'd like that."

Chapter 18 - Reservations

Cain

Cain's house
Tuesday evening, sunset

Cain and Felicity stood in the doorway of his home, arm in arm, watching the sun's brilliant rays dip below the horizon. Cain lightly touched the curls of her beautiful hair, all wound up again with her oriental hair sticks. "Your hair looks so lovely this way, but I hadn't realized, it'll be ruined with the motorcycle ride. Sorry."

She turned to look at him with a smile. "That's okay. I'll drive."

He looked at her in confusion for a moment, and then his eyes found her car, out in front of the house. "A lady of independent means, are you now? Congratulations. Still, now I'll have no excuse to escort you home from work in the evenings."

She gave a little laugh. "That's just what I thought, but it's okay if you still want to come visit. I know how addicted you are to your coffee."

"Trying to trade one addiction for another, I suppose." He took his leather jacket from a closet by the door and then paused, as if to offer it to her. "Do you need it?"

"That's okay; it doesn't really go with my dress," she said with a laugh. "Mine's in the car."

"I suppose I ought to wear something a little more suitable as well." He reached into the closet, trading the leather for a sports jacket.

"Very nice," Felicity said, giving him a smile and a kiss.

As the bright colors of the sunset began to subside, and the sky became shades of lavender and dark blue, Cain took her by the hand, and they went out to the car. Felicity was surprised to learn that she had to invite him into it, just as she had her room. Cain shrugged. "It's your personal space."

"Good to know. Come on in. My space is your space."

He directed her to a restaurant, saying it was a bit far, but surely it would be worth the drive. Honestly, he had no idea where to find a fancy restaurant locally. He'd never had need of such knowledge. The place that he thought of now, he had paused at just before entering this town, back in early June. He had been following rumors and headlines, trying to locate the vampires who turned out to be Sindy and Ernest, wrecking havoc hereabouts, back in the spring.

Normally he would seek out bars and seedy pubs in which he could listen for gossip and scan for other vampires, but as he'd passed this place, he'd been travel weary and wanting for a break from the road. No lesser places offered and he had thought it wouldn't be too extravagant to treat himself to a nicer experience for a change.

It was a very dignified establishment. In fact, he'd paused to take a dress shirt and jacket from his pack, to don before entering. He'd hoped the fact that they'd been terribly wrinkled would go unnoticed.

He'd mostly drunk wine and only picked at the appetizer he'd ordered, but it was nice to feel himself among a more civilized crowd than he was used to. He normally found himself only in the worst parts of towns and cities. Truthfully, he purposely did not treat himself to better on most occasions, as it was not something he ever wanted to get too used to again.

But this time with Felicity, he knew that it would be perfect. He had dressed accordingly and had her stop at an ATM machine along the way, so that he might withdraw some money for the evening. He rarely kept any large amount of cash at his house. He had learned to limit himself; he didn't need it for much more than books and blood anyway.

They reached their destination, Felicity carefully guiding them into the parking lot. Her driving was a bit slow and unsteady, but they did make it in one piece. He had to smile at how much he'd forgotten what it was like to have new experiences in life. To see her having encounters like these for the first time, made him feel young again.

The lot was quite full and as he opened the door for her, he noticed that the restaurant was rather full as well. It was as nice as he remembered and Felicity gave him a surprised little smile. The maitre d' met them at the desk to ask for their reservation.

"As it happens, we haven't got one. I was hoping perhaps you might seat us anyway?" The man was already shaking his head in disapproval as Cain spoke, and telling them that he couldn't possibly find room. Cain took a hundred dollar bill from his pocket and discreetly gave it to the man with a handshake. "I do understand, but I hope you'll check again. It's my lady's birthday you see."

Of course, the man became suddenly quite accommodating and before long they found themselves at a private VIP table a bit away from the dinner crowd. Felicity seemed a little amazed at their service. As Cain ordered them a bottle of the finest wine with two glasses, their waiter became a bit uncomfortable. "I'm sorry sir, but I don't believe she's old enough to be served." He turned to ask Felicity, "Do you have ID miss?"

Felicity looked embarrassed, but before she could answer, Cain spoke to the man. "Terribly sorry, but I believe she's left it at home. It is her 21st birthday though. Perhaps you would be so kind, as to overlook her lack of identification for us?" As he said this, he gave the waiter a hundred dollar bill as well.

Felicity was obviously not comfortable with this. "Cain, it's alright, really. I'll just drink soda."

He wouldn't hear of it. "Nonsense. It's your birthday."

Cain looked back to the waiter, who was very apologetic. "Forgive me, it was my mistake. Obviously the lady is mature enough to order as she likes."

Cain gave a small smile and nodded his head once in approval. "The wine then." He looked to Felicity and she didn't argue, but when the waiter left she looked much less pleased.

"Cain, you didn't have to do that."

He beamed, taking her hands across the table. "It's your birthday."

"I know, but, I just... I'm not very comfortable with the way you're throwing money at people."

He became severely chastened and sought to take back his hands, but she wouldn't let him. "I'm sorry. I just wanted everything to be perfect for you."

"I'm here with you. Being together, *that* makes it perfect."

"You're right, of course. I am sorry. I tend to do that with money, that's why I don't use it all that much." There had been times in his life, when money had easily paved a very tempting path for him, one he had decided a long time ago, not to follow. It was shameful how easily it came back to him. He ventured a smile at her for forgiveness. "I do hope you'll order whatever you'd like for dinner, though. *I* don't plan to eat all that much, so it shouldn't be too outrageously expensive."

"I don't mind if you want to spend *some* money on me. I just feel weird about using it to get people to do what you want."

"Forgive me. I'm just so bewildered," he said with a little laugh. "Being here...with you, this isn't *at all* the evening I had planned. In fact, I still feel very irresponsible for letting you seduce me earlier." Felicity began to blush fiercely and turned her eyes from him with a smile. "I had been trying to resign myself to the fact that I should leave you alone from now on." She met his eyes again, looking a little dejected at his words. "But you *are* irresistible. Please don't think I am at all unhappy at the state of things, I'm just a bit lightheaded I suppose. Everything seems upside-down from the way I'd thought it would be, and old habits are all too easy to fall back on."

"Old habits? Using money to get what you want doesn't sound at all like you. Was that back when you were at Herald Manor?"

"No. Well yes, but I wasn't thinking of when I was human. I was referring to when we went back to England, Maribeth and I...after."

"Oh," she replied quietly.

"After regaining the Manor, we lived rather atrociously for a while, I'm afraid."

The waiter arrived with their bottle of wine in a fancy little bucket of ice on a stand. He put their glasses onto the table, opened the wine for them, and then poured a bit into Cain's glass for him to sample.

Cain did so, and once his approval was given, the waiter filled his glass the rest of the way. The man then made a great show of pouring a glass for Felicity, and waiting to see if she would enjoy it as well. Felicity hesitantly raised the glass to her lips for a little sip. She gave the waiter a small smile and a quiet 'thank you', after which, he said he would return shortly for their dinner order, and left.

The waiter had barely left the table, when another young man came over to fill their water glasses. He was grinning broadly at them the entire time. As soon as he was finished, the waiter returned with a warm loaf of fresh bread, on a little cutting board with a bowl of butter and a fancy little knife. "Have you decided upon your dinner selections?"

Cain smiled at Felicity, who was just staring at the table. She had not even opened a menu yet. "I think we'd like another moment."

"Of course sir, take your time."

The waiter left, and Felicity closed her eyes and shook her head. "What?" Cain asked.

"Now they're going to be tripping over each other trying to serve us and people are going to stare.

"No one's staring," he replied with a little laugh. She just looked at him in disapproval. He shrugged. "I'm sorry, please don't be uncomfortable." He nodded towards the menu on the table in front of her. "What would you like to eat?"

"I don't know," she said sullenly.

"Come on." He tried to get her to smile. "Please? I've been depressed enough for the both of us, believe me. This should be a happy occasion. Don't let me have spoiled this amazing day." She looked up at him with a smile. "You know, most young ladies would be very flattered and excited to have a man throwing money around on their behalf."

Felicity knitted her brows at him. "If you were looking to flatter someone, then you should have asked Ashley."

That brought the dream that he'd had to mind. Odd how the mind unburies and translates improper desires. Felicity was right, what was wrong with him? "You are absolutely right."

"That you should have asked Ashley?" she asked playfully.

"Of course not! I'm behaving terribly. I'm telling you, this unexpected happiness has put me all out of sorts. Brooding really is more my thing. I've had a lot of practice, gotten rather good at it." Now she laughed. He loved to see her smile. "Can we just forget this and start over, like you had asked me earlier?" Every time he even hinted at their earlier activities, it brought a blush to her cheeks. She was so delightful, sweet and innocent. He sorely hoped that they could both still look back on this time fondly, when all was said and done.

"Consider it forgotten," she said quietly.

She opened her menu, but seemed to be having trouble making a selection. "I would offer to order for you," he said, "but it's been so long, that I haven't even a clue what to recommend. Although most say that you can't go wrong with lobster. Do you like lobster?"

"I've never had it."

"Not even a taste? Even *I've* had lobster. Tell you what, order something you know you'd like, then I'll order the lobster, and you can have a bit of both."

"Okay, but you have to eat some too."

He laughed, but agreed. "Anything for the birthday girl."

The rest of the evening went very nicely. The service was impeccable, and although it was a little much at times, Felicity didn't mention it again. She also thoroughly enjoyed the lobster. When she ordered a slice of cheesecake for dessert, the waiter asked him quietly if they should put a candle in it and sing to her, but Cain graciously declined. This sort of place was probably not the type to do such a thing normally, but if Cain had asked, he'd no doubt they would have had every employee in the restaurant, crooning 'Happy Birthday' for them.

Cain knew that Felicity was not one to want such attention. Especially after she had admonished him for seeking special service to begin with. He watched her eat her dessert quietly as he drank his coffee. "Full day of classes tomorrow, I suppose?"

"Yeah. English Lit., Anthropology and Chemistry. And then I get to go to work! The fun just goes on and on."

Cain smiled. "So, you'll be done around 9:30?"

"Actually, I'm off at 8."

"Perfect, I'll only have just woken up a bit before then."

"You are so lucky. You can do whatever you want. It must be nice not to have to answer to anyone, not to have any obligations."

He gave her a serious stare. "No, it's really not. Why else would I have piled so many responsibilities upon myself? Feeling *unaccountable* is a very dangerous state in which to live, believe me."

"I guess, but I don't think carrying the weight of the world on your shoulders is the solution either. Sometimes you sound like you feel responsible for the behavior of every vampire there is. You'll never be able to change them all, you know. Not that it isn't a noble cause, but I don't think you should have to sacrifice your own happiness to do it."

"I remember, you wanted me to 'take a break and have a life for a while', right?"

"Well, yeah. I mean, why couldn't you? Stay here with me for a while. We could hang out, kill a few years..."

He chuckled. "Years?"

"Wow, my friend Deidre is right. She has always maintained that all guys are automatically afraid of commitment, no matter what, like it's preprogrammed or something. *You're immortal.* You have lived for over three centuries, and you're afraid to give up a few years?" She laughed. "Not that I'm like *proposing* or anything. I don't want you to think that because of today I'm going to start expecting stuff from you. I know it sounds like I'm kind of pushing the fast forward button here, but I have to say, your inherent alarm over the idea is kind of funny."

Cain smiled, but this time it was rather melancholy. "You can inform Deidre that she is mistaken. I'm not afraid to give you time out of my life. If I'd the chance, I would stay with *you* for all eternity." Cain was not very heartened by the look on her face. Felicity very suddenly dropped her smile, seriously shaken. Obviously, she wanted to be *with* him, but being *like* him was not an option she was considering.

He had already known. He had sort of hinted at it earlier, and she'd shot him down, but he just couldn't stop thinking about it. Especially since his 'leave her for her own good' strategy, wasn't exactly going as planned. Felicity did not seem open to the idea of changing, to be with him fully. He would have to let it go...for now. They had time. "Be unconcerned, I *do* love you as you are," he said, without giving her a chance to comment. "We should get going. I've been irresponsible enough for one day. I won't be remiss in getting you home at a decent hour on a school night. As far as my 'taking a break' goes...we'll see. I can't make any promises."

"You have to." He raised his eyebrows, questioningly. She held his gaze in grave severity. "Make me one promise, it's all I ask."

"What's that?" he inquired.

Her eyes became moist and she took a deep breath as she looked into his eyes over the table. "Don't ever disappear on me. I know at some point, you're going to feel like you have to leave. I don't know when that's going to be, and I hope it isn't soon, but I can't just pretend the day will never come. I don't *want* you to go, but I guess eventually you'll have to, but you have to tell me. You have to say goodbye. You can't just *disappear*, okay? Promise? I want you to promise."

Of all the things to ask...she was a smart girl. Vampires are notorious for disappearing. Things not going well in a certain town, an identity? Just disappear and go start new somewhere else. It would be very hard for Cain to say goodbye to *her*. If he were going to leave her, disappearing might very well have been his choice, but he had to make the promise and remove that option. He wouldn't refuse her, right now, he would give her anything. "I promise."

~~~~~~~~~~~~~~~~~~~~~~~~~~~~

The evening was at an end. It was decided that Felicity would drop him off at home, but not come in. The temptation would be too great to stay, if she did. They would see each other tomorrow.

As she drove him home, Cain could not help but replay their tryst in his mind. He had to smile at the sweet innocence she had tried so hard to hide. It had been a great pleasure to initiate her into such exploits, but no matter what they did together in times to come, she would always seem chaste and innocent to his mind.

As they neared his house however, any thoughts about chastity or innocence immediately fled his mind. Sindy; he could see her mark and feel her presence growing ever stronger as they drove. When they turned up his driveway, they could both see her standing at the rail up on his porch, waiting for him. Felicity parked the car in the driveway, staring coldly through the windshield. "Looks like you have company."

"Perfect. I should have known that this was going far too nicely to be an evening in *my* life," he muttered drolly.

"What do you think she wants?" Felicity asked.

She was still just standing there...staring at him. She did not look thrilled at his company. He turned to see Felicity staring at him as well. He shrugged. "She probably wants to pout and sulk some more about my not letting her kill Ben."

Her expression immediately softened. "Thanks again for that."

He dropped his eyes from hers. "My pleasure," he mumbled guiltily. "I'll find out what she wants and then send her away. You don't have to stay, I know it's late."

"Did you...not want me to stay? Maybe I should; see if there's anything going on that Ben should know about."

He should have known she wouldn't want to leave. Woman's intuition. "No. You can certainly stay a bit if you want. I just thought you'd like to avoid being subjected to *Sindy's* company if at all possible." She was just looking at him blankly. *Wonderful.* "You coming?" He began to get out, as though everything was fine.

"Yeah, I'll come."

Great. He waited for Felicity in front of the car, as Sindy watched silently from the porch. Felicity came around to him and made sure to take his arm, he noticed. Sindy had remarked on their body language in the past. It shouldn't be very difficult to read now. Surely, that was Felicity's intention, whether or not it was a conscious one.

Sindy just stared at them stonily as they approached. Again, she wore no make-up. It made her look curiously vulnerable, but he knew better than to think she was any less dangerous for it. He prayed that she would refrain from upsetting Felicity too much, or saying anything truly hurtful. It was probably a lot to ask from Sindy though.

They climbed the few steps to his porch, and Sindy uncrossed her arms and gave him a very deliberate knowing look, with a hint of a smile playing about her lips. She knew that she held a lot of power in that moment. She loved it. "Conference over?" she asked. Obviously, they had been discussing her in the car. She had to know that he wouldn't have *told* Felicity though.

He kept his eyes on hers and silently begged for understanding from her. His mark was still upon her, renewed during their tryst, but her body did seem to be learning to fight it; it was not all that strong. He was very glad of that, it would have been very distracting and only made things worse. "Were you waiting to talk to me about something?"

She gave a slight smile. "Yeah. I just came to *talk*." She paused, glancing briefly at the cement beneath their feet, then back to him. "Chris has been gone for three nights, without a trace. You seen him?"

Thank God he did not need to breathe anymore, because he surely would have been holding his breath and then let out a great sigh of relief. She wouldn't say anything, bless you Sindy; he tried to tell her with his eyes. "No. Sorry." He meant that in so many ways.

He wasn't sure if she understood, or accepted it. She certainly didn't acknowledge it in any way. "If he comes on your radar, you'll let me know, right?"

"Yes," Cain assured her.

"Thanks." She folded her arms again and took her eyes from his to look at Felicity. It was the first time she'd really done so, since they came up on the porch. She gave Felicity a very appraising look, and then seemed to notice and appraise Cain's appearance as well. "You guys are all done up nice. Celebrating something?" she asked, with a smirk.

Once again, Cain tried to beg her silently. *Please Sindy, leave well enough alone. Don't spoil it now.* But all he said was, "It's Felicity's birthday." Felicity seemed to squeeze his arm just a bit tighter, though she still did not say a word. He was grateful she would let him handle it. Sindy may be feeling generous towards him, but if Felicity were to bait her, she may decide not to hold back.

Sindy gave a sarcastic sort of laugh and smiled. "No shit. Mine's next week. Although it doesn't really seem to mean as much once you're *dead*." She glanced at Cain. "I won't expect a present." She pushed past him and went down the steps to the driveway. "See 'ya 'round." She gave a dismissive wave over her shoulder without looking, and left.

Cain stood and watched her for a minute as she walked down the road, until Felicity asked, "Think it's anything serious?"

He turned to look at her incredulously. *"What?"*

"She said Chris was missing. You think something happened to him? Something important's going on?"

"Oh. No. If he had died, she would have known. She's his sire." Felicity looked a bit confused. "Sindy *made* him. That makes her his sire, or whatever you call the female equivalent. 'Dam' I suppose, but most vampires just use 'sire', male or female." Felicity was looking at him in amusement. He was rambling, most unlike him. "Anyway, if he'd died...she would know. He probably just got tired of being her 'whipping boy' and left. Can't say I blame him."

"Yeah, who'd want to have to spend eternity following around after her?" Cain tried to smile, but it was an uncomfortable venture. Thankfully, Felicity wasn't even looking at him. "I can't believe how young she looks with no make-up! What is she, fourteen?"

"She's not *that* young. She wasn't all that much younger than you. She certainly was not a child. Anyway, appearance is no indication of age for *our* kind. She's older than you are now." Cain realized he was perhaps protesting too much. He stopped talking and refrained from looking back at the road to search for Sindy's figure in the dark.

He found Felicity's eyes and reminded himself how lucky he was to have such a woman as she, even if it was only temporary. "I won't ask you in, because I know where that would lead. I shall practice restraint, but I will see you tomorrow...and don't expect restraint from me then," he added with a smile.

Now she smiled as well. If she had any suspicions about his relationship with Sindy, they seemed to have been dropped. She came into his arms for a kiss. "I'm looking forward to it," she whispered.

They kissed for a bit longer and then he gently pushed her away. "You had better leave now, or I may not let you."

"Careful, I may call you on that," she threatened.

He pulled her back for another kiss and then whispered, "Good night." She whispered, 'good night' back, turned and left.

He couldn't help but glance back down the road as Felicity entered her car. Sindy had vanished into the woods. Felicity blew him a little kiss and he went inside, closing and locking the door behind him.

Chapter 19 ~ Sympathy

Felicity

10:30, Tuesday night
Felicity's car

Felicity started the car and began her drive home. What a day! As the oddness of seeing Sindy left her mind, she began to think on much fonder memories of the day. They had done it! She and Cain had made love! She was no longer a virgin and no longer felt as though he might see her as a child. It had been so amazing and perfect! Of course, she felt a little silly for trying so hard at first to prove her eagerness to him, but she was glad he had forced her to stop and just be herself, even if he had done it in a slightly disconcerting way.

He was so wonderful, the way that he was with her, once the preliminary awkwardness was out of the way; awkwardness that was all *her* doing of course. She should have just trusted him to lead things to begin with, so that it wouldn't have been awkward at all. He was so gentle, sweet and non-threatening, making everything an amazing new experience instead of something to be intimidated over; like the way he had given her total control over the actual act, so that she would gain confidence in herself and become more comfortable with their actions.

She'd been shocked when he'd wanted her to be on top of him. She never would have dreamt that was how it would be, but he had known that it would be right for her, for this first time. Once they were engaged in it, she felt truly bold and unafraid, no need to pretend. It had been perfect. When their actions had culminated in her orgasm, she had felt as though it was her love for him which was exploding within her, to become something all encompassing and unequaled.

Why did he have to be a vampire? Life was so unfair! She wished they could have a normal relationship. She wished that he were human, so she could introduce him to her friends and family as her boyfriend...or maybe, fiancé. They could have a beautiful wedding, and children, and...a life together. That would never happen. Not with him. She knew that. Still...

No regrets. She could not have chosen a more perfect man to give her 'maidenhood' to. He was so sensitive and loving. The way that he had spoken of it as a great honor...'deflowering a virgin', it had made her smile. She loved the way he spoke, his odd mixture of archaic speech and modern slang, it was so quaint! She did love him, no matter their uncertain future. Sharing the experience of making love with him was something that she would *never* regret. At least they could be together for a little while. He *had* said that there would be a next time... The venom. Oh wow, there was an interesting thought.

She turned into the dorm lot and parked the car. She got out and locked the door, having indecent thoughts and speculating on possible future escapades. When she turned to cross the lot to the dorm, she was more than a little startled to find Luke stepping up to meet her. "Hey pretty girl."

She froze...keys in hand, and wondered what she should do. He didn't advance on her, but stopped a little apart from her and kept talking. "I know you, you're Cain's friend." He smiled. "I remember you from the field. You're pretty." She was just about to take a deep breath to yell for help, but Luke realized what she meant to do and looked curiously desperate and upset. "Wait, wait, take it easy! I just wanna talk, just to talk."

She eyed him warily for a moment. She remembered what Cain had said about lesser vampires sometimes suffering from a kind of brain damage. She wasn't sure how competent Luke was, or what he would do, but she *had* to be smarter than him. If things got physical, she was unsure what would happen, better to let him talk. "What do you want?"

He seemed relieved that she would listen. She studied him as he spoke. He was young...when he'd died. Fifteen or sixteen at most. He had a very handsome young face, cheeks still fleshed out with a little 'baby fat'. Although he wasn't a really heavy guy, he looked solid. He was hardly taller than Felicity, but definitely stronger. His hair was a mess of dark curls, and his brown eyes seemed very large and hopeful. He spoke with a voice nervous and uncertain.

"Chris. You know my buddy Chris? I don't know where he is. Nobody will tell me where he is. I can't find him. Have you seen Chris?"

Her eyes softened towards him, he seemed so lost. "I'm sorry," she said sympathetically. "I haven't seen him."

He moved a step closer and pleaded with her. He spoke with an urgency and cadence to his voice that seemed unnatural. He had always seemed like a regular guy to her, but she'd never spoken to him. Now she realized that he was probably not quite the boy he used to be in life. Of course, she had not known him before, but something about him was just a little *off*.

He went on. "Are you sure? 'Cause, Sindy said he wasn't dead. She swears he's okay, but I don't know where he is. He wouldn't go nowhere without tellin' me." He stopped speaking for a moment to ponder the ground, and then looked up at her as if just noticing her again. "You know Chris, right? He's my best bud. We *always* hang together. Sindy says he left, but he wouldn't leave without me. Only I don't know where he is."

He seemed to be getting more upset as he spoke. Felicity used a calm and reassuring voice, as though he were a child. "Don't worry. I'm sure he'll come back. You should go and wait for him, so he'll know where to find you."

Luke didn't seem to be listening. "You know what *I* think? I think Cain took him. Cain doesn't like us much. One time, when Sindy wasn't listenin' to him, he said she was lucky he didn't turn her into dust. He said that. I remember."

Luke's eyes were beginning to look a little wild; Felicity took a small step back, trying to make her smooth calm voice cut through his growing panic. "It wasn't Cain, Luke. Chris is still alive, he just went somewhere. He's fine. Cain even told Sindy that, just tonight. He's fine."

"Sindy always believes Cain. I think she likes him better than us now. Cain can see us even when we're real far away. He *always* knows where we are. He knows where Chris is, he just won't tell. I'll bet he knows." Luke was beginning to look more than a little upset, more than Felicity wanted to try to handle, but he was standing between her and the dorms. They were still at the bottom of the hill in the lot; a little far to be sure someone would hear her if she yelled. She was sure he could catch her if she tried to run, better to get into the car, where he couldn't follow. She tried to seem casual, as she took a step back towards it.

She'd locked the door! Damn! She'd never be able to work the key in the lock before he was on her if he snapped. She'd have to talk her way out of it. "You know what? Why don't *I* ask Cain for you? I bet he'd tell me. He likes me you know...a lot. Wait here. I'll go ask Cain and then I can find Chris for you, okay?"

Luke got very angry. "You think I'm stupid?" She took another step away as he raised his voice, and was backed up against the car. "You don't like us either, do you? Sindy's the only one ever likes us, and she won't tell me where he is! You probably won't tell me either."

She had found her car key and tried to put it in the lock, but now Luke came forward and grabbed her wrist. "Let go of me." She tried to sound very strong and controlled, although she felt her own panic rising inside. He didn't let go.

"You gonna go see Cain? Cain always tells me 'no'. I'm supposed to stay away from him. I think he knows where Chris is."

"Let me go. I'll find Chris for you, I swear." She tried to pull her wrist back from him as she spoke, but he was too strong for her. His eyes got very wide as an idea seemed to come upon him.

"You could give Cain a message for me. Sindy told me not to ask him. I wanted to ask him about Chris, but Sindy said no. I bet *he* took Chris away. He doesn't like us, but he likes *you*. You could give him a message for me."

"I'll tell him whatever you want, just let go!" She was still trying to pull away, but he held her wrist firm. She couldn't really struggle much without touching his body, he was standing very close. She had the notion in the back of her mind that she should try not to rub up against him if at all possible; she didn't want him getting any other ideas.

He had seemed preoccupied as he'd held her wrist, very strongly but almost forgotten to his attention. Now, he suddenly focused on her face with an eerie smile. "Not *that* kind of message."

That sent a chill down her back. "Luke, think about it, you'd better leave me alone. If Cain knew you were touching me, he'd kill you. I'm *his*."

Luke looked confused. "I can't touch nobody that belongs to somebody else. Sindy told me that, and it makes my head hurt. I don't like that." He looked at her oddly, with new awareness. "But you don't belong to nobody. Maybe Cain doesn't like you so much anymore." He smiled at her new alarm. "I like you." As he finished the sentence, he shifted to his vampire state, smiling broadly to show her his fangs.

She screamed and brought her knee up to his groin as hard as she could. It surely hurt, but he didn't let go. He just squeezed her wrist harder, and pulled her to the ground with him as he fell to his knees.

Felicity's own knees hit the ground hard, and she dropped her keys. She tried to jerk her arm away, while trying also to regain her feet, but Luke still refused to let go. Instead, he used his grip to jerk and twist her arm abruptly backward, so that even as he knelt on the ground in pain, she was thrown onto her back on the ground next to him.

The back of her head struck the concrete, making her see stars. Her free hand went to her hair, expecting to feel blood. What her fingers found instead, was much more promising. Her oriental hair sticks! She grabbed one with her free hand, and pulled it from her hair. Just then, Luke climbed atop her, pinning her legs with his knees. "You bitch, that hurt!" he said it in a dejected tone, as though she should feel badly for him. *Sorry*, she thought, *sympathy's over.*

He still held his tight grip on her arm, and now reached for the other. She jerked both wrist and stick away, knowing that if he got both arms pinned, she'd be done for. He did manage to get a slight hold of her wrist, but it was an awkward grip. She brought the hand down towards her stomach, in close to her body. Luke didn't really fight her motion too hard. He had let go for an instant, to get a better grip around her wrist. He hadn't noticed the stick; he didn't know she had a weapon.

With a desperate prayer that she would have good aim, she strongly thrust the stick upward into his chest with all her might. He yelled and let go of the hand that was over her head, his arm flung out to the side in desperation. His other hand got a better grip on her wrist and tried to pull her 'stake' out of his chest, but he was lying on top of her. It was almost impossible unless he could get up first.

She must not have hit his heart. Not knowing what else to do, she desperately jerked the makeshift stake to the side, even as he fought to get it out. He put his free arm to the ground for leverage, trying to raise himself a bit, to get the stake out. As he did, she violently jerked the stake to the other side...and it broke. She heard it crack and splinter as his hand let hers go, to come away holding half a stick. She looked up just in time to see his face...perfectly formed, of what looked to be solidified ash. He then exploded into a cloud of dust.

She turned away and the other half of the stick fell onto *her* chest, as his disappeared. She lay there for a minute with her eyes and mouth scrunched closed, trying not to breathe. Then she rolled aside as her lungs made her take in a huge gasp for air, causing her to cough and choke on ash. The idea of breathing in Luke's remains nauseated her, and she had to get herself up and away from the spot. As she scrambled to crawl and then stand a few steps away, trying to catch her breath without getting sick, she heard someone coming from the dorms.

"I'm okay." Felicity tried to tell them, as she composed herself. She wasn't hurt really, although her head was pounding and her wrist was very sore.

It was Maggie, in her robe. She came running to Felicity, looking around frantically for an attacker. "Are you alright? What happened? I thought I heard a scream!"

Felicity brushed herself off and tried to think what she could say. She didn't want the police out here, making her give a statement, and searching for an assailant who had already been turned to dust. "I, um...saw a rat," she said lamely.

Maggie looked at her in disbelief, her eyes moving to take in Felicity's messed hair and dusty dress.

"I saw a rat, and I screamed, and then I dropped my keys. Sorry, if I startled you. I think they went under the car, so I was on the ground looking for them. I didn't find them." She just stood there for a minute, looking at the ground and wondering what Maggie would say. Then she saw a glint of metal on the dirty cement by Maggie's bare feet. "Found 'em!" she said as she plucked her keys from the ground. "Thanks."

Not knowing what else to do, she simply started walking inside. Her knees hurt from the fall, but she tried to walk fast, so that Maggie couldn't say anything else. She heard Maggie follow in behind her, but Felicity just kept straight on, up the stairs and into her room, and then closed the door.

She'd killed him. She had killed Luke, just like that. He was...*gone*. She wanted to rush back to Cain's. She wanted nothing more than to be held in his arms. Now that the fight was over and she didn't need to put up a front for Maggie, she felt delayed reaction coming over her. She felt as though she would begin to shake and shiver. She just sat on the bed with her arms wrapped around herself. Cain...she wanted Cain.

A few things kept her from him. First of all, she wasn't sure if she could sneak back out without being seen by Maggie. She was already certain that the woman did not believe her stupid explanation, and she wasn't sure what else she could say.

Secondly, she was still covered in ash; it clung stubbornly to the folds of her dress and made her feel ill. It wasn't as though it was only dirt...it was *Luke*. She felt as though she'd like to take it off and burn it. She needed to shower as well; her hair was also full of dust. She wasn't sure she could stand to be like this a moment longer, certainly not for the whole ride to Cain's.

Lastly, Sindy. Cain had said that Sindy would feel it, if Chris died. That must mean she could feel Luke the same way, right? Sindy must know that he had just died, here in front of *her* dorm. She did not relish the idea of meeting Sindy on the way to Cain's house, covered in Luke's ashes. No thanks.

She would have to wait for the morning. Right now, she would strip and shower - making well sure that the front door was locked and bolted first. Then she would stay in her room, protected by Sindy's lack of invitation, and wait for morning. It was sure to be a long night.

Indeed it was. Felicity's sleep was plagued with dreams that were odd combinations of happiness and nightmare. They seemed to play over and over again, giving her no rest or respite. They began with pleasant memories, bed play with Cain, rolling and tickling beneath the covers, but at some point, he would roll on top of her, and suddenly become Luke. He would smile evilly and try to bite her. She always staked him before he did, but as he died, in that moment when his face had looked ash - he would turn back into Cain. It was then, that she would scream. At one point during her sleep she had thought the screams real. Desperate cries not her own sounded in her ears, but they soon faded from her mind and the dreams returned to replay the scene over, yet again.

Chapter 20 - Comfort

Cain

Cain's house
Tuesday, just after midnight

Cain lay in bed with a book. He wasn't really reading it though, he had too many of his own thoughts, to concentrate on another's. The book lay all but forgotten upon his chest as he replayed the events of the day in his mind.

He'd considered going back out, it was still awfully early, but he had enough to think about without adding to the evening. He just wanted to sit quietly and try to actually be happy for himself for a change. That was such a rare thing for him. *Content* he had been…but excited, eagerly anticipating what each new night would bring, happy? Not in quite some time. Of course it was underlied with the guilty feeling that he was moving in the wrong direction, but how could something that actually made him happy for a change, really be wrong?

Felicity was a constant thought in his mind. She made him happy like no one else ever had. He tried to keep in his mind the fact that their relationship could only go so far and then he would have to leave her, but he still could not quite let go the slim hope that she might change her mind, further into things. Close association with him these next weeks would ease her fears and show her the wonder of the pair they could become, if she might someday ask to be made like him.

It wouldn't be a bad thing, if she chose it for herself, would it? It's not as though he would ever force such an existence upon her. He knew that as an intelligent young woman, she surely had a bright future ahead of her, but if *she* decided her future should be with him… True, it looked unpromising at the moment, but he could not entirely let go of that hope, no matter how selfish and unrealistic.

Even without thoughts of change, their relationship right now had a very promising short-term future anyway. He dreaded the looming thoughts of where they may be a month from now, but right now she wanted to be with him, and he was planning to thoroughly enjoy every moment of it while it lasted.

Thank God, Sindy had chosen not to say anything to upset Felicity earlier. Certainly, she would hold it over him later, but he could handle that. She must have decided that having Cain in her debt would be more rewarding than her immediate satisfaction from telling Felicity of their tryst straight out.

Of course, it's not as though he had *truly* been unfaithful. Although he did spend a lot of time with Felicity, they did not have an expressly exclusive physical relationship…until today. He never would have touched Sindy anyway, out of respect for Felicity and the simple fact that he was with Felicity because he preferred her, but he *had* told Felicity that he would not see her anymore, before he'd let Sindy approach him the other night.

Still, he knew how hurt Felicity would be if she knew. He and Sindy had very long lives ahead of them, if they managed not to kill each other. Sindy must realize that if she let his relationship with Felicity run its course, odds were that eventually he would leave her, or she him. One way or another, Felicity would be out of his life. Then Sindy would have plenty of time to try to pursue her own agenda with him, whatever that might be.

He was just so elated over the prospect of spending the next few weeks loving Felicity, that he did not want to think of anything else right now. He lay back on his bed and replayed the events of the day over in his mind, yet again.

There was a sudden pounding upon his door. He quickly sat up in bed. Could it be Felicity? Was something wrong? He put down the book as the pounding came again. This time he recognized a mark and a voice to go along with it. "Cain!"

It was Sindy. Cain's desire to rush to the door suddenly became much less urgent. She pounded again as he went to put on his boots before answering. He wasn't planning to let her in; he would go outside to talk. She yelled again as he started up the stairs. "CAIN! Open this damn door!"

He was just reaching the top, when he heard the terrible crash of glass shattering. He ran up the last two steps and rounded the corner to see Sindy's boot kick the last of his large front picture window in.

"What the bloody hell do you think you're doing?" he yelled.

She stepped through the remains of his window with clenched fists and an enraged scowl upon her face. He was standing there looking at her with outraged astonishment when she stalked right up to him, and promptly threw two fistfuls of dust into his face.

Of course he stepped back, waving his hands to try and wipe it away, and spitting to clear his mouth. When he looked back up at her in furious anger, she was still standing there glaring at him.

"That was *Luke*, in case you were wondering," she said with seething ferocity. "She killed him! She fucking killed him!"

"Who?" Of course he knew who she must be talking about, but prayed it was untrue.

"Who do you think? Your fucking girlfriend killed my Luke! That bitch is *so* living on borrowed time!"

"Sindy, calm down"

"Calm down? This *is* calm! I think this is a very impressive display of self control. You know why? Because *her* precious heart is *still beating,* just the way *you* like it, while my Lukey is ashes on the fucking ground." As she yelled, her voice had begun to deteriorate from screaming fury into trembling grief. She didn't quite cry, but took a moment to gather and compose herself.

"Sindy, I'm sorry. What happened?"

"I don't know." She practically growled the words at him.

"Well, then how do you know it was Felicity?"

She ripped something from her pocket. "I found *this* in his ashes, in the parking lot next to *her* car. Who do you think killed him?" she asked, as she thrust her find into his hand.

It was the broken top half of one of Felicity's hair sticks. Cain could hardly help but smile a little. "Clever girl."

Sindy smacked it out of his hand to the floor. "You insensitive bastard!"

"I'm sorry, but you know that Felicity isn't one to go looking for trouble. You'll have to admit that if Luke was hanging about in the dorm parking lot, it couldn't have been with pure intentions. She had to have killed him in self defense."

"Thank you. That's very comforting," she spat out sarcastically. "You don't give a shit what happened to Luke, you're just worried about whether or not he sucked her first."

Cain could not help but flinch. "I am sorry. I know how hard this must be for you, to lose Luke just after Chris has left."

"Don't talk to me about him. You said more than enough last night."

"About last night..."

"Whatever." She stood quiet for a moment, and then continued in a softer, gentler tone. "Why'd she have to go and *kill* him? He wasn't the sharpest tool in the shed, but that boy would do tricks like a puppy to try to please me; just to make me happy. Do you have any idea how many people in my life have ever just wanted to make me *happy?*" She glared at him for a moment, but spoke again before he could answer. "I'll give you a hint. It's a real short list," She held up one finger and then pointed it at him. "and *you're* not on it." He turned his face from her to look at the floor. "And once again 'little miss goody two shoes' has taken it upon herself to go and fuck it all up for me."

Her anger was beginning to build again, but she composed herself to look at him with a stone cold glare. "I came to you first Cain. You'd better appreciate that, because you have *no* idea how close it was, how badly I just wanted to...ugghhh. I don't even *want* her blood. I just want to snap her pretty little neck!"

"Sindy, I do appreciate your restraint, but she's surely in her room, where you're uninvited. You couldn't get to her anyway."

Sindy looked at him with an evil smile. "I don't need to get into her room. I just need to get into the building. She's gotta go take a piss sometime, believe me, I'd manage."

He stared at her for a moment. She was probably right. It was by her choice that Felicity lived. "Guess I owe you one."

She dropped herself to sit on the floor with a thump. "Pfft. You owe me more than that. Felicity, Ben, Alyson... I'm keepin' a tab. We live long enough, I figure you've gotta pay me back, eventually." He gave her a little smile and shook his head as he joined her on the floor. The smile quickly left his face however, as he began to worry for Felicity again. What must she have been through? Was she alright?

Sindy seemed to have read his mind. She took a deep breath, presumably to calm herself. "She's not marked."

"What?"

"Felicity, she's not marked. No one in the dorm had Luke's mark on them. *She* must have gotten *him* first. Since you're obviously just itchin' to rush over there and check on her, thought you'd wanna know."

Cain gazed at her thoughtfully and gave a grateful smile. "Thanks. Still, they may have brought her to hospital."

"Na, I didn't hear any sirens, and the place would've been swarmin' with cops. I'm sure she's just *fine*." She couldn't help but add a sarcastic edge to her voice.

"Thank you," he whispered.

"This whole thing is really your fault you know...when you think about it. Luke may have been dumb, but it doesn't take brains to follow instinct. You really ought to mark her again." Cain lowered his eyes, she was right. "What's the matter? Don't tell me she's shy of you. 'Cause you two looked pretty cozy earlier."

Cain looked up at her wearily. "Can't you just *tell* all of them that she's off limits?"

Sindy gave a little laugh. "Cain, have you met them? Sometimes I think that I'm lucky they recognize me."

"Well I don't expect she'll be marked again anytime soon, so try to keep them away from us, will you?"

Rather than take offense at his request, she seemed to find his admission amusing. "Turned you down, did she? What do you see in her anyway? I mean, if she's not even feedin' you..."

"I'd like to think that there's more to life than blood. She makes me happy. Like you said, that's a rare and valuable thing...for any of us." He looked at her meaningfully, for understanding.

She shook her head with a smile. "Won't be for long though. Neither one of you can hold out forever. Even if you did, you'd probably wind up resenting each other for it and that kind of defeats the purpose, don't you think? Doesn't sound like 'happily ever after' is gonna be an option. So...what kind of 'happy' is that?"

"Temporary happiness, better than none. That's the theory I'm going with, anyway. At least our *immediate* future will be happy and satisfying. Even you could understand why I would be hesitant to let that go. I know you've had fleeting glimpses of what a happy relationship can be like. Of course, you'll have to forgive me for saying, you can't have been truly satisfied though, or you wouldn't still be looking for more."

"Yeah well, here's a big surprise. Happy satisfaction, the kind that *doesn't* come at someone else's expense...not something I've had much experience with."

Cain gazed at her sadly. "Come now, there must have some time in your life when you were happy."

"Yeah, like maybe when I was five." He tilted his head with a smile, as though she must be joking. "I couldn't have been much older than that when my dad started makin' me suck his cock every night. When I didn't, he would beat me, so...happiness, not all that familiar a concept."

Cain stared at her for a moment in shocked disgust. That certainly explained a lot about the internal power struggle she seemed to have with every man she knew. Recreating abusive relationships...herself in either role. "I'm sorry."

She chuckled dryly. "So was he, when I came back and sucked him dry."

"And your mother?"

Sindy gave a dismissive little shrug. "She's already got so many holes in her, *I* could never compete. She likes heroin." Sindy watched his face for a moment. "I know what you're thinkin'. No wonder I'm so fucked up, right? Don't worry about it. I'll straighten my shit out eventually. I don't even need *you* to do it." She stared at the floor for a moment and then looked up at him with large, expressive eyes. "Sucks to be alone though. I'm not saying Luke and I had some great relationship or anything. His stupidity *was* pretty annoying most of the time...especially when it came along with its own special guilt trip, knowing that some of it was *my* fault, but we did make each other happy, and now I don't even have him." Cain leaned forward to try to put an arm around her, but she jerked away from him hastily. "I'm not exactly in the mood."

Cain looked at her in disbelief. Couldn't she imagine that he might want to touch her for reasons *other* than sex? "I wasn't planning to... Forgive me, but *that* won't be happening again. I am with Felicity now. I was only going to try and give you a hug."

"What for?" Sindy asked skeptically.

"To comfort you. That's what friends do," he explained.

"Oh, *now* I'm your *friend?*" she asked with a sarcastic smile.

"*You* used the term before *I* ever did," he pointed out.

She furrowed her brow, trying to place the comment. "Oh yeah, back when I fed you that night, from my wrist." She smiled at the memory.

"I suppose *that's* on my tab as well?" he asked with a smirk.

She smiled. "Na, that was a freebie."

He laughed. "Thanks."

She got up from the floor, dusting herself off. "I'm gonna go."

He rose as well. "Back to the rest of your brood? Are they..."

"They're at home. I told them not to go out without me. We've got a TV, they'll stay," she assured him.

Cain laughed at the absurd vision of her nearly mindless zombies sitting eagerly gathered around the television. "I can't even imagine what your home life must be like these days."

She laughed as well, and then looked at him with a sly smile. "Don't even try, I'm sure the reality is more than *you* could handle." She started towards the door to leave, and then turned back to him with a thought. "Keep Felicity out of my way. I mean it. Self control's *not* one of my strong points."

~~~~~~~~~~~~~~~~~~~~~~~~~~~~

Less than a half an hour later, Cain was perched on Felicity's windowsill again. She'd left the window open a crack. At first, he thought it was incredibly careless of her. Then he realized that even though *he* had climbed up here, most humans wouldn't care to try it. And another vampire wouldn't have the invitation to enter this way. Rather than open it, he only reached inside to part the blinds a little, for a clearer view. She was asleep in her bed, safe and sound, just as Sindy had predicted. He sat watching her for a moment, in glad relief.

He thought about Sindy's suggestion, that she should be marked. He wondered what Felicity might think about that? But it would move things forward much faster then he'd like. After the familiarity they had shared with each other's bodies, marking would be a much more intense experience *this* time around. It would be difficult to keep it short and unentwined with physical expressions of their love. It would bring their relationship to a whole new level...and that much closer to its end.

No. He must try to avoid it, for now. Although even without its practical reasons, the idea of marking her again was extremely tempting.

He decided not to wake her. It was the middle of the night, and she seemed fine. Let her rest. Tomorrow would come soon enough. He would wait to see her then, as much as he would rather climb into the bed with her now. More than anything, he wanted to enfold her in his arms, but the morning would come all too soon, and this would not be a safe place to spend the day. She would be alright. Let her take care of her obligations tomorrow, and come to him when she was ready. He blew her a kiss, as she had to him earlier, and left her window, to go back home.

Chapter 21 – Why did you buy me this?

Felicity

Felicity's room
Wednesday morning

Morning was a welcome thing. Cain. She wanted to go to him. She should go to class, but it hardly seemed all that important. She got up and dressed quickly, having showered the night before. She picked out a pair of tan slacks with a matching black, white and tan blouse, more because they were a set outfit requiring no thought, than for any other reason. She already knew it looked fairly nice on her, without having to study her reflection. She was just leaving her room, when she bumped into a girl from down the hall. Her name was Cathy, Felicity vaguely knew her from a class or two that they shared.

The girl quickly pounced on Felicity and wanted to know if she'd studied for their English Literature quiz this morning. Felicity had of course forgotten the quiz entirely and couldn't have even said that she cared right now. The girl walked with her out of the building, speculating about the quiz questions. Felicity was just about to explain that she was planning to miss the class anyway, when she saw their professor approaching from the faculty parking lot, next to the dorm.

"Good morning ladies. All ready for this quiz?" she asked, as she fell in with them to walk to class.

"I guess so," Felicity mumbled, and found herself being drawn across campus. Cain's would have to wait.

After English Lit., she had Anthropology. She figured she might as well go. Daylight had certainly given her a better perspective on things and she no longer felt the desperation that had come upon her when she'd cried herself to sleep last night. She was alright. Lunch would come soon enough and then she could go to Cain's. Now that she had a car, there'd be plenty of time. There shouldn't really be any *need* for him to know what had happened sooner. He, Sindy and any others involved were restricted until nightfall anyway. Besides, at least she actually liked this class. She was pretty sure she'd failed her quiz.

Come the end of Anthropology class, she raced to the cafeteria and bought a sandwich and soda. She then shoved them in her bag and headed to Cain's. She climbed up his front steps, thanking God for the sunlight, when she noticed something rather upsetting on his porch. Glass, there were shards of glass everywhere and his large front window was broken in. She rushed the last steps to the door and pounded on it.

She tried the door, but it was locked. She thought about trying to climb in the window, when the front door opened from the inside. It was Cain, unharmed. She rushed into his arms. He backed away from the door with her and she let him swing it closed again. "Oh Cain, I thought something'd happened to you."

"Easy there. I'm alright. It's you that I've worried for. Thank God you're safe and whole, but I knew that you were, and I'd have braved even the sun if I thought you in danger," he informed her.

"What happened?" she asked, looking at the broken window.

"Suppose *you* tell *me?*" he suggested.

"Oh my God. Last night, Luke...I killed him," she said haltingly.

Cain held her tighter, as though to protect her from dangers already gone. "It *was* you." He leaned back to look into her eyes. "But you're unmarked," he said with obvious relief. "Did he...hurt you?"

"No... well, a little, but I'm okay. I killed him, Cain. I actually killed him." She couldn't get the shock of it from her mind, now that the memory had resurfaced. This was not some nameless monster, 'us' against 'them'. Luke had always been considered an enemy, but still. She'd felt like she knew him a little and the way that he was, was not really his fault, but now...he was dead.

"What did he do?" Cain asked.

"He was all upset, about Chris being gone. I felt bad for him actually. I was trying to make him feel better and hoping that I could just get him to go away, but he had this idea that *you'd* done something to Chris, that you wouldn't tell. That's when he attacked me. He said he was going to give you a message, by biting me I suppose. Maybe he thought that it would hurt you, for not telling him what happened to Chris, I guess. I don't know, he wasn't making much sense.

I warned him not to touch me. I told him you'd kill him, that I was *yours*, but he wouldn't listen. ...I'm not *marked*." She couldn't help but feel panicky tears come to her eyes as she remembered her fear and their struggle.

"Oh Felicity." He hugged her tightly to him again, as he ran his fingers through her hair and kissed the top of her head. "But you defeated him. You defended yourself and kept him from you. It's all over now. You're alright."

She leaned back to look at him excitedly as she spoke. "My hair sticks! I used my hair stick to stake him. You gave me the idea. I'd wear them every day from now on, but I broke one."

Cain smiled. "I'll buy you dozens."

"Guess I should start wearing the vial again too..."

He looked at her thoughtfully for a moment. "Yes."

"What happened to your window?"

"Sindy. She was none too pleased about your ordeal. Not to worry, I've spoken to her. I don't believe she'll bother you over it, but you might want to avoid her for awhile."

"I always do." Felicity shuddered and asked if they might go downstairs. She ate her lunch with Cain, who then sent her back to school. Only kisses were exchanged as he admonished her advances and told her she would see him when work was finished this evening. He offered to meet her, but she assured him that she'd be fine. Now that she had the car, it really wasn't necessary. She promised that she would be extra careful. He reluctantly agreed and said that he'd be home, boarding his window.

So she forced herself to attend Chemistry class, and waited for time to pass. She never believed that it would, but time went on, as it always does. Eventually her class was over, and she was off to the DownTime for her shift.

When Felicity arrived at work, she saw Ben and Harold, both in the cafe. There were a few students at a table being served by Harold, while Ben worked behind the counter. She ignored them both.

Ben was emptying the last of a tray of rice pudding into the new tray, at the far end of the counter as she approached. He finished just as she reached the door to the lounge, and she heard him tell Harold that he was going on break.

She heard the tray clang in the sink as the door swung closed, and she thought for sure that Ben would be entering the lounge right behind her. She put her purse into a locker and quickly took off her jacket. Just as she was wondering why he hadn't come in yet, she noticed something on the table by the phone. It was a present, for her.

The little box was beautifully decorated, gift wrapped at the store, she imagined. There was a card lying next to it on the table, she opened and read it. All it said, in Ben's large, scrawling penmanship was:

Felicity,

  Happy Birthday

                            - Ben

She was stunned. He'd bought her a present? What could he have gotten her? She immediately tore off the paper and became slightly confused as she looked at the small black box beneath. It was obviously from a jewelry store.

She opened the lid. Inside, atop a piece of cardboard covered in black velvet, was a lovely and delicate gold cross on a thin gold chain. It had a tiny diamond chip on the end of each arm and a slightly larger diamond baguette in the center of the cross. It was tasteful, charming and definitely not cheap.

She quickly closed the box and held it clasped tightly in her hand as she went out to find him. He was not in the cafe. Sure enough, she saw him through the window, walking to his car in the parking lot. She rushed to confront him before he could get in.

"Ben!" she yelled as she opened the door. He stopped at his car, slumping his head and shoulders. His hope had obviously been to escape unnoticed. He turned to face her as she stormed up to him, gift in hand. "Why did you buy me this?"

Ben gave a snort of disgust at her reaction. "You're welcome." He turned back around and unlocked his car door.

Felicity put a hand on his shoulder to make him face her again. "Thank you," she said sincerely. "It's beautiful. *It's too much.* You're barely even speaking to me, why would you buy me this?"

He squinted at her in annoyance. "Well, it's not like I bought it *today*." He gave a heavy sigh and dropped his eyes to the ground. "I got it back when I found out your birthday was coming. You know...right after the night we spent at Allie's." He still wouldn't meet her gaze. "I saw it, and it made me think of you. It was pretty and I thought you'd like it." He shifted his feet uncomfortably and then became annoyed again. "I couldn't find the receipt, so I figured I might as well give it to you. Happy birthday." The last was practically spit out, but it made Felicity smile. She was sure he was only pretending to be mad at her.

Ben began to open the car door, but she put a hand out to gently push it closed again. He looked up at her with a scowl on his face. "Thank you," she said again softly. "I love it."

He gave up his pretense of being angry with a little huff of breath and a smile. "Too bad you'll never wear it."

"Sure I will." She immediately opened it, took the chain from the box and fastened it around her neck. "See?"

Ben shook his head with a doubting little laugh. "Yeah, in the daytime."

"*Every* time I leave the house, from now on, believe me." Something in her voice drew his attention. He looked up at her questioningly. "Luke attacked me last night," she explained.

Ben was immediately alarmed, although she was obviously alright. "Oh man, are you okay?"

"I staked him," she said quietly with large eyes. She still could hardly believe she'd done that. It seemed very different from the first vampire she'd killed. It seemed more...real.

"No way!" he said it with quiet disbelief. "He's dust? How'd you manage that? Where was Chris, weren't you double-teamed? They always fight together."

"He was alone; otherwise I wouldn't have stood a chance. Chris is missing, he just up and disappeared. Sindy told us last night."

Ben squinted at her casual use of Sindy's name. "You're sure hangin' with the wrong crowd these days. Enjoy the cross. Sounds like you'll need it. Or of course, you could always ask Cain to bite you again. I'm sure he's just waiting for a good excuse."

She glared at him for a moment, not even dignifying his remark with a response. "Thanks for the gift," she said shortly and turned to walk away.

"Hey," he called out to stop her. She turned back to face him, but he didn't look any less disgruntled. "Sorry I've been such a prick." His expression hardly matched his words, evidenced by the fact that he couldn't leave them stand. "I still think you're being incredibly stupid! But, I'm sorry." It came out short and sarcastic.

Felicity gave him a disbelieving smirk. "Some apology!"

Ben was unfazed. "It's the best you're going to get, so take it or leave it."

"You are so arrogant!" Felicity studied him for a moment. He was trying very hard to affect indifference, but she knew he really did want to make up with her. "But I'll take it."

He looked up in surprise. "Yeah?" he asked hesitantly.

"Are you going to *stop* being such a prick?"

"That depends, are you *done* being stupid?"

She opened her mouth and slumped her shoulders with a short sigh. She was trying to give him an out and he had the audacity to think he would tell her what to do? "If you're asking me if I'm going to stop seeing Cain, the answer is definitely no."

"Then I can't make any promises."

"Why did I even ask? It was stupid of me to expect you to go against your inherent nature!" She turned on her heel and began to leave, as Ben slumped against the car with his arms crossed.

"Do you *really* think I'm a prick?" he yelled after her.

She stopped and stood there for a moment, as though thinking it over. Finally, she returned, eyeing him appraisingly. "No," she said grudgingly as she reached him. "But you sure do a good imitation sometimes." He'd begun to smile, but stopped to roll his eyes at her. "Do you really think I'm stupid?" she asked.

Ben stared at her, assessingly. "You and Cain are getting pretty serious, huh?" She glared at him without answering. "Do I have to answer?"

Felicity crossed her arms as well and shifted her weight to one side, waiting expectedly. "Alright, go ahead."

"What?" he asked.

"Go ahead, I'm waiting," she informed her acidly.

"For what? For me to tell you you're being stupid? I think we already covered that," he said with a chuckle.

"I'm waiting for you to go all 'big brother' on me and give me a lecture on *why* you think I'm incredibly stupid. Tell me how you're just trying to protect me from my own naiveté."

"First of all, I don't *lecture!*" he insisted. Felicity let out a little 'Ha!'. Ben barely contained his annoyance and went on. "Secondly…" he growled, "I'm *not* your 'big brother', so stop calling me that; I hate it!"

Felicity's voice took on a mockingly sweet tone. "Oh, I'm sorry. How terribly insensitive of me! I should have realized that you would worry someone would overhear and think that you might actually be related to someone as dumb as me!"

Ben uncrossed his arms to push himself off the car in outrage, and then ran his hands through his hair as though exasperated. "Felicity! You are *so* far off base, I'm beginning to wonder if you really *are* stupid!"

"What?" she asked in confusion.

He just shook his head with a sigh. "Forget it. Do want to meet for lunch tomorrow?" The question sounded odd, considering he still had a bit of an annoyed growl in his voice.

She stared at him for a minute. "Are you going to lecture me?"

"No," he grumbled.

"Are you going to glare at me disapprovingly the entire time?"

"No," he grumbled again. Then he smiled. "Well, maybe just a little."

She rolled her eyes. "Yeah, okay." She looked back up at him with a smile. "Wanna go to McDonalds? I'll drive."

It took him a second to realize what she meant, and then he smiled back. "Somebody got a car for her birthday!"

She gestured across the lot with excitement. "Yeah, it's over there. The blue one."

He looked to see it and grinned. "You got a Mustang!"

She laughed. "Oh yeah. That's what you've got, right?" She glanced from his car to hers. "So how come they're so different?"

Ben laughed. "Well, duh. Mine's a 1965 Shelby GT-350 fastback, and yours is…"

"A piece of crap?" she interjected, helpfully.

Ben shook his head and smiled. "I'm thinkin' late 80's? 4 cylinder? It's still a Mustang, they're the best."

"It's a 1987 Ford Mustang, and it's blue. That's about the extent of my car knowledge. That and the fact that next to yours, it looks like a scratched and dented piece of junk."

He shrugged. "That's just cosmetic stuff, how's it run?"

Felicity shrugged in return. "I don't know. Okay I guess. Maybe you could check it out for me, let me know if it's any good? Help me fix it up a little?" she asked hopefully.

"Yeah, sure. I love a good project," he said with a quiet smile. "So, where's your last class before lunch tomorrow?"

"Abrams building," she told him.

"Cool, I'm right next door. I'll meet you in lot B, say 12:15?"

"Okay. What about Alyson?" she asked.

Ben looked unhappy that she should ask. "I don't think she'd care to join us."

"You guys still fighting?" she prodded.

Ben just moved his head noncommittally. "I haven't seen her."

"All weekend?" she asked.

"Since Thursday," he clarified.

Felicity became concerned. "Do you think she's okay?"

Ben nodded his head in reassurance. "Oh yeah, I'm sure she's fine. I've seen her car come and go over at Tommy's...I just haven't gone in."

"Why not?"

"I have nothing to say to her." Felicity sighed in disapproval. Ben looked as though he'd like to add something, but was hesitant. Finally, he asked, "Do you know if..." He couldn't finish the question, but she knew what was on his mind.

"Mattie's not back yet. As far as I know, anyway."

Ben nodded thanks for her insight. "Just curious." They stood in silence for a moment. "Cain knows him, doesn't he?"

Felicity gave a little nod. "Yeah."

"What does he say?" Ben asked.

"What do you mean?"

"About Mattie," he clarified. "Does Cain think he's...okay?"

Ben's quiet concern for the friend he had lost, tugged at her heart. "Yeah. Cain likes him. Says he's a 'good kid'," she said with a little chuckle. "Shy, quiet, real nice. And he says he's never killed anybody, not *ever*. So, something else must have happened to David."

Ben winced at the mention of his murdered friend. "How the hell would he know?"

"I guess he wouldn't, really, but that's what he says."

They stood in uncomfortable silence for a moment, staring at the ground. When Ben looked at her again, she almost thought there might be tears in his eyes; not that he would let them fall in front of her. "I don't think I can do this 'Liss. Everybody expects me to just act like this is all okay and it's just not! This has gone so bizarrely *beyond* okay and I'm the only person who can see it! This whole situation has turned so bad and you guys act like *I'm* the one who's gone insane! Do you have any idea the danger you put yourself in every night? I can't just stand here and do nothing! I can't just *watch* while you..."

"Felicity!" It was Ashley, standing in the doorway and staring at them accusingly. Ben didn't turn to look at her. "You were supposed to be on like ten minutes ago! I wanna go on break!"

Felicity barely glanced in Ashley's direction. "Yeah, I'll be right in." Ashley stood there, sullenly for another moment before closing the door. Felicity looked back at Ben, who seemed to have composed himself. "Ben, I'm okay." He just stared into space until she wondered if he'd even heard her. "You should talk to Alyson."

He gave a bitter little smile. "Yeah, not going to happen."

"Why not? Ben?"

He wouldn't look at her. "Whatever. My break's half over and I have to go home for something. We'll talk tomorrow." Without another glance he got in his car. She was forced to back up to let him drive away.

Felicity was still standing there watching him leave, when Ashley leaned out the door again. "Come on Felicity! I wanna go eat!"

"Coming."

~~~~~~~~~~~~~~~~~~~~~~~~~~~

Felicity watched the clock impatiently until finally, at a quarter to eight, she could hardly stand it any longer. It was another slow night, so what if she left a few minutes early – big deal. She headed towards the lounge, taking off her nametag on the way. "Ashley, I'm going to go," she yelled towards the shelves in the back. Felicity was in the lounge getting her stuff before Ashley could even have a chance to answer.

She came back out and gave a little wave to Ben as he was waiting a table, across the cafe. She hadn't had another chance to talk with him once he'd returned from his break, but she had an idea how she would set things right when she saw him for lunch tomorrow. Now, all she could concentrate on was getting to Cain's. She found herself eyeing the sides of the road warily as she drove. She almost expected to see Sindy around every bend, but she made it to Cain's without event. She was so excited to see him! The upset and worry from last night seemed to vanish at the prospect of spending the evening with Cain. In fact, she was planning to spend most of the evening in his bed. She felt so daring and indecent to even be thinking such things, but eager and excited as well. She felt like they had uncovered an entirely new aspect of their relationship. Knowing that it may not last all that long, made her feel as though she wanted to spend every last minute of their time together in his arms.

There was another thought in the back of her mind as well. Now that they had made love together, things were different. She felt as though they were connected in a whole new way. That the bond between them had become stronger than ever, intimate and close, almost like when she'd worn his mark.

Part of her did not really believe that he could leave her, not now, not after feeling *this*. She knew that he had been very up front and told her that he *would* leave, and she did accept that, but there was a small irrational voice in the back of her mind telling her that after he had loved her like that…he could not really go.

She wanted to feel that again, that incredible closeness, that strong and unbreakable bond that she had felt with him…after. *During* was certainly amazing and unforgettable in its own right. Yes, she was certainly looking forward to some more of *that*. But after, lying next to him on the bed, she loved being snuggled close to him and sharing that peaceful satisfaction of being truly together. It made her feel as though she could very happily spend the rest of her life snuggling and giggling in his bed, without a care for the rest of the world.

She had always been so reserved about such things in the past. Loving Cain had been so freeing. It made her wonder why she had wasted so much time being shy in the first place. Of course, a certain amount of decorum was called for. Time to get to know him and to be sure of her feelings, had been necessary. But now that she felt that she knew him so well, what was the point of being timid? She had nothing to hide from *him*. She resolved to stop wasting time with reservations. He knew her...every inch of her. Shyness and hesitation just seemed silly at this point. Subtlety was just a waste of precious time.

She looked around cautiously before leaving her car. All seemed quiet; no one was in sight. As she mounted the front steps, she noticed that he had indeed boarded up his big front window by the door, from the inside. She was actually quite startled when the sound of loud hammering suddenly came from within. Apparently, he wasn't finished. She pictured him, holding up the sheet of plywood and strongly hammering in the nails...maybe with his shirt off. She shook her head, admonishing herself for such silly visions, better to go and see the real thing. She knocked on the door.

The hammering stopped and he opened the door almost immediately...fully dressed. Of course, he was dressed. Felicity smiled at how foolishly disappointed she was. "Honey, I'm home!" she said in a chipper 'playing house' type of voice.

Cain gave her a broad smile. "Hello dear, how was your day?" he answered, copying her tone.

"Better now," she said with a sincere smile.

"What a coincidence, mine too." He took her into his arms for a kiss. They moved inside and by the light in the entryway, Felicity could see his hammer and nails on the floor by the window.

She leaned back to look him up and down. "Look at you, all up and dressed already. That was a very silly thing to do."

He laughed at her. "I had some errands to run. Some work to do," he said, nodding towards the window.

She smiled naughtily. "Well, I suppose we'll just have to get you undressed again, won't we?"

"Well, aren't we bold?" he asked.

"Yeah, it's something new I'm trying." He gave her a little disapproving look. "I'm not trying to be anyone else; I'm just...not going to be shy anymore. Let me know how it works for you." Cain shook his head skeptically, but let her pull him in for another kiss. "Come on, let's go downstairs." She took his hand and began leading him to the stairway. He seemed a bit bemused by her attitude, but suffered himself to be led to his bedroom.

Once at the bottom of the stairs, he went to turn on the light and she followed him into the room. As he turned back to her, she put her arms around his neck and smiled. "Now, where were we?"

This time their kiss went on longer and became far more passionate, until Cain suddenly thrust her away from him. "Ow!"

Felicity felt a slight warmth at her throat and her hand shot to the spot...to find the cross necklace that she still wore. "Oh my God! I am so sorry! Here, I'll take it off!" She began pulling the chain around to try to find the clasp.

Cain was looking at it oddly, while lightly fingering the burn at the base of his throat. "That's new."

"Yeah, I just got it today. I totally forgot that I had it on. I am so sorry! Did it hurt?" she asked in concern.

"I'm alright. It's pretty," he observed.

"Oh, yeah. Ben gave it to me." Felicity was eyeing Cain's throat as she undid the chain and took it off. Cain stretched the collar of his shirt, to keep it from rubbing the spot. "Oh God, it left a burn mark!"

Cain seemed unconcerned with his injury, and was looking at her strangely. "Benjamin did?"

"Uh huh. For my birthday. Do you want some ice?" she asked.

"No, and should I think it odd or be at all concerned, that Benjamin is giving my lady jewelry?"

She brought her gaze from his throat to his eyes, and smiled. "No. It's nothing." She held up the necklace in her hand for emphasis. As they both eyed it between them, she realized that it was too pretty to be so easily dismissed. "Well, I mean, it's not *nothing*. It's...very nice, but it doesn't *mean* anything. It was just...for my birthday."

"Right. Next he'll be spiking my coffee with holy water." Felicity couldn't help but let out a choked little laugh at the idea. "I thought you two weren't getting along?" he asked.

"We made up," she said with a little unconcerned shrug.

"Oh. That's...nice."

Felicity's smile broadened. "Look at you, trying so hard not to be jealous! You're so sweet. You know Ben and I are just friends."

Cain eyed her thoughtfully. "You and *I* used to be just friends."

She looked at him in amazement. "*We* were never *just* friends."

"We weren't?" he asked.

"No! Not in my mind anyway," Felicity informed him.

He raised his eyebrows. "Really?"

"Yeah, where have *you* been? Wasn't it obvious?"

"Best you learn now, that when it comes to reading women, most men are a little slow. I'm glad it's obvious now," he said.

"Me too," she answered.

She shoved the cross necklace into her pocket, and moved to let him enfold her into his arms for another kiss. As the kiss ended, Cain leaned back to look at her again, seeming reassured and satisfied. She had to smile at the insecurity he had shown. As if she would ever want to be anywhere but here in his arms?

"So, you've been straight from school, to work, to me. Have you had any dinner?"

"Not really. I only had a fifteen minute break, during which I wolfed down some pasta salad, but I'm okay. I didn't want to stop for anything after; I wanted to come straight here."

"Are you hungry?" he inquired.

She gave him a sly grin. "Not for food."

She was pleased when he laughed in shock at her statement. "I have thoroughly corrupted you haven't I?"

"Who's complaining?" she replied with a smile.

"You really should eat something," he admonished.

"So, give me *something* to eat," she said with a smirk as she let her hands wander over his body.

He wiggled away from her, seeming a bit off-put. "Alright, this whole 'bold' thing, it *really* doesn't suit you."

"No?" she asked innocently.

"I don't think so. I meant did you want to go to a restaurant?"

"I know what you meant. I kind of wanted to have my *dessert* first. Fits with my whole new bold and un-shy attitude."

"And what was wrong with your old attitude?"

"It was kind of blah. Shy and subtle seems like such a waste of time. Not much fun. This..." She moved closer to let her hands wander again, for emphasis of her words, "is much more fun."

He laughed and shook his head. "I liked your old attitude."

"You called me timid!" She pretended to be cross with him and pushed him down onto the bed.

He allowed it, but made a sad face, as though disappointed. "Yes, but to be honest, I rather liked timid."

She climbed atop him on the bed, straddling him. "Yeah? Do you like this?" she asked, as she came down for a kiss, after which, he gave her a bemused little smile.

"Yes, actually...I think I could grow quite fond of that."

"Quite?" she teased him, smiling.

"Yes. Very, very fond."

She kissed him again and then wiggled her hips against him. "Okay, these jeans...too thick and stiff. I like your P.J.'s way better." She gave him another kiss, pressing herself firmly against him. "Yeah, the denim has definitely got to go." She sat up on him and scootched down his legs to grasp and undo his button and zipper. "Luckily, I can help you out with that."

He reached out to keep her hand from his pants. "Alright. Who are you, and what have you done with Felicity?" She laughed. "This is replaying an awful lot like yesterday. I thought you were going to stop trying to be other people?"

"Alright, I'll admit it. Yesterday, I *was* trying to imitate the attitude of another woman, who really seemed to turn you on." As though he couldn't guess who that might be. "But now, I'm really *not* being anyone else. It's me. Honest. This is just the 'me' that I don't let anyone else see. The side that used to be too shy to come out."

Cain raised his eyebrows and thought about that for a moment. "Intriguing. Right then, carry on."

She laughed and then continued unfastening and pulling down his pants. She threw his jeans to the floor and then went back to remove his underwear. She smiled up at him nervously, but resolved not to hesitate. She kept her eyes on his and not what she was doing, to help ease her nervous butterflies. Unfortunately, that was probably not a good strategy.

She simply pulled his underwear straight down by the band at each hip, and managed to snag them on his erection. She pulled uncomfortably before noticing.

"Ah!" he cried.

"Sorry!" She let go in flustered embarrassment.

"That's alright," he said through his laughter. "At least I know it really *is* you. If you'd managed to undress me too easily, I might wonder where you'd had the practice." She hid her face and shook her head in humiliation.

He reached up to pull her hands away and meet her eyes as he spoke. "Don't waste time and worries on embarrassment. We laugh *with*, not *at* each other. Do you think in three hundred and forty years, I've never had an awkward moment?" She smiled at him, though her face was surely still red. "Now, would you like to try again?" he asked with a chuckle. "Or shall *I* remove those for you?"

She tried to stop giggling. Why did things never go just as she imagined them to? "I think I can do it," she said with a little smile.

~~~~~~~~~~~~~~~~~~~~~~~~~~~~

Felicity snuggled closer under the covers, against Cain in the dim light of his bedroom. She'd thought him sleeping, but as she moved against him in the bed, he opened his eyes and gave her a contented little smile. She smiled back and then rested her head against his chest.

They had spent the evening in his bed, just as she'd fantasized earlier. It was surely well after midnight by now. The hours had seemed to pass in a dreamy haze of laughter, love and new experiences. She was only just feeling the venom fade from her now. He had not bitten her of course, but through his kisses and their love making, her body *had* been thoroughly infiltrated by it. The effects of the venom on her senses never quite reached the level of intoxication that she had felt the night that he *had* bitten her, but it did come close.

She tried never to think of that night. The memory of his bite was something she had tried to block out of her consciousness, not to be confused with the feelings that he stirred in her now. They did seem so similar, the physical desires he brought out in her and those brought about by his bite, but she refused to try to analyze it. The bite was on its way to becoming an indistinct memory, she'd like to think. That was the past, separate and unlike the natural and harmless enjoyments that they now shared.

She lay there, basking in the tender and peaceful contentment of their quiet time together, feeling totally empathetic to his sentiments last night, that he wished time could stop. This moment in time had to be preferable to anything that the future might hold. As though to prove her point, he spoke. "It's late. You should probably go."

She looked up and pouted at him. "I don't wanna go." He just smiled. "You wouldn't actually kick me out, would you?"

He reached around to take hold of her and roll her to lie atop him for a kiss. "You have classes tomorrow."

"So? That's like eight hours away. Can't I stay here, or do you really *want* me to go?"

"What I want and what should be, are two entirely separate matters. I know you must be tired. I however, am nocturnal and will be very much awake for the rest of night. If I were to let you stay, I would be utterly incapable of keeping my hands off of you." He squeezed her bottom to emphasize his point. "You'd get no sleep at all. Then the dawn would come. Knowing that I'll be trapped here alone all day, I really will be loathe to let you leave. You should go now. I won't have you missing classes for me."

"So I take a sick day, big deal."

"Right, and one sick day becomes two and then three... Before you know it, your studies will have been totally neglected and you'll find yourself spending all of your time in my bed."

She cocked an eyebrow at him. "Are you supposed to be discouraging me from this? Because, you're doing a terrible job. In fact, it sounds pretty good to me." She wrapped her legs around him and snuggled her face into his chest. "I could be very happy, right here, cozy in bed with you, forever."

"I myself would be perfectly happy never to leave this bed again. However, *I* would be the only one to survive that scenario. *You* may get hungry after a while," he teased.

"I got a cell phone for my birthday. I'll order pizza."

He grinned and hugged her for a moment, and then gently rolled her aside. She looked up to see him with a quiet sadness in his eyes. He reached up to tap a finger upon her nose with a little smile and then it trail down to her lips for a kiss. "*Forever,* is not a word to be thrown around lightly."

She was a little disgruntled by his statement. They had never discussed it openly, she wouldn't really let him, but she knew that he would change her to stay with him forever, if she'd allow it. She also knew that he understood she didn't want to. Not like that. It was like a little unspoken sore spot between them; one that was better ignored.

Felicity rolled to her side, facing away from him. She felt tears rising to her eyes, because she was not really the kind of woman that he wanted her to be. She knew that he loved her, but she was human and planned to stay that way.

Cain snuggled close to her back and put his arm around her, to hug her from behind. He gave her a kiss on the cheek and whispered in her ear. "But I say you must leave not only for your benefit, but to fix it to be set in my mind as well. You have a life, a future *outside* of my bedroom. That's a wonderful thing for you to look forward to. I'm trying very hard, not to forget that.

Go home, get some sleep. Go to your classes, do the things that you must. Tomorrow evening will come soon enough."

She smiled sadly. He did love her, even if she was human. He would accept her the way that she was. For the hundredth time she cursed the fact that he was a vampire and not just a regular guy. She wiggled herself against him and looked up to him over her shoulder. "Okay, I'll go, but...just one more hour wouldn't hurt, would it?"

He chuckled and pressed himself firmly against her from behind. "Now *that's* something that I might let you convince me of."

~~~~~~~~~~~~~~~~~~~~~~~~~~~~~

The next morning's classes seemed to go quickly, but that might have been because she was half asleep for most of them, by the time she had gotten back to her dorm last night, it was about two o'clock in the morning. She'd had to open the car window, just to ensure she would remain awake on the ride home.

When she had finally made it there, she had held tightly in her hand the new stake that Cain had given her, as she crossed the lot to the dorm steps. She thought about how angry Sindy must be with her and was very grateful that Cain seemed to have intervened somewhat on her behalf. Sindy may not treat her kindly if they came across each other, but at least she was not there waiting in the parking lot.

Now she sat watching the clock and at 11:45, the instant sociology ended, Felicity was out the door again to her car. Ben's beloved yellow Mustang was still in the parking lot, not far from her own. She hoped his class ran late.

Felicity had to pound on Allie's door three times before she finally answered. She was still in her pajamas and stifling a yawn as she opened the door. She was very surprised to find Felicity standing there.

"Hi! Get dressed, we're going to lunch."

"We are?"

"Yes, my treat." Allie backed into the apartment to let Felicity enter. After a minute, she shrugged and went to get dressed.

Felicity wandered over to study some pictures on the wall as she waited. They were photographs; beautifully captured nature scenes of forests and fields, with the odd butterfly in the frame or deer in the distance. At first Felicity assumed that Allie had picked them up at a flea market or garage sale; but when she moved to look at a picture on the opposite wall, she had a strange start of recognition. She recognized the little waterfall near the duck pond at the park, the same one where she and Cain had enjoyed their picnics. Felicity wondered who the photographer was.

"What brought this on?" Allie asked from the bedroom, as she changed her clothes.

"I haven't seen you in a while. Thought we'd talk." Allie stuck her head out the door and looked at her suspiciously.

"About what?"

"Well..." It only took Felicity a second to think of a topic Alyson might take fondly to. "Cain and I have been getting pretty serious. I thought maybe you could give me some insight on some stuff."

Now Allie came out in a t-shirt and jeans. She sat on the couch to put on her sneakers and gave Felicity a sly grin. "Ooh, gettin' hot and heavy are ya? Let me tell you, vampire sex...*best* you will *ever* have. Really. There is no equal."

"Allie! That's not really what I wanted to talk about."

"Why not? That's the fun stuff. It's not like I get to talk about it with anybody else." She sighed. "God I miss Mattie."

"Still no sign of him, huh?"

"No. He's got eleven more days and then I will be officially pissed at him."

"I'm sure he'll show. Are you ready?" Felicity asked.

"Just a sec, I wanna brush my teeth." Allie darted into the bathroom as Felicity impatiently looked at her watch. Only a few minutes before Ben would be waiting for her. Allie came out with the toothbrush still in her mouth. She pushed it to one side and spoke around it. "Are you marked?"

Felicity just stared at her for a minute, until Allie couldn't wait anymore. She went into the bathroom to spit and then came back out, wiping her mouth on the back of her arm. "Are you?"

"No." Felicity opened the front door.

Allie put on and zipped up her sweatshirt as she looked at Felicity's car in the driveway. "That yours?"

"Yes."

"Pretty," Allie replied sarcastically.

"Very funny, get in."

They got themselves settled in the car and Felicity headed back to school. As soon as they left the driveway, Allie started after her again. "So how come you're not marked, you wouldn't let him?"

Felicity glanced at her in annoyance. "He didn't ask."

Alyson rolled her eyes and leaned back to rest her knees on the dash. "Well it's not like you don't know he wants to."

"Allie, I didn't really want to talk about that either."

Now Allie was the one to become disgruntled. "You want to talk about you and Cain, but you don't want to talk about sex, and you don't want to talk about blood. What else is there?"

"Plenty, but I didn't really want to talk about Cain at all. That was just my cover."

"Then who'd you wanna talk about?"

"You and Ben," Felicity informed her.

Alyson slumped down in her seat. "You woke me up for that?"

"Come on, you guys are best friends. You can't stay mad forever," she admonished.

"I'm not mad," Allie said defensively.

"So what happened? You guys had a fight?"

Allie shrugged. "It wasn't much of a fight. It was the whole Vermont scenario again. He wanted me to go away with him before Mattie got back. I said no. He told me not to see Mattie, and I told him to go fuck himself. It was pretty straightforward, really. I'm not mad at him, but I'll be damned if I'm gonna let him tell me what to do. Never have, never will."

"You guys have to talk it out. Somebody has to make Ben see that things are okay," Felicity told her.

"Well, that somebody ain't gonna be me. He won't talk to me; I know how stubborn he is." They pulled onto the college grounds. "Where are we going? You're taking me to school for lunch? Some treat." As they pulled into lot B, Felicity could see Ben at the far end, leaning against his car, Allie spotted him too. "Oh."

Ben was just checking his watch when Felicity pulled up next to him. She put the car in park right in the middle of the lot and got out. Ben spoke to her as she did, but she walked around to the passenger side rather than stop to listen to him. "Where'd you go, I thought we were going to meet here?"

Felicity ignored him and opened the door to pull her passenger out. That's when Ben saw Allie. "Ah, 'Liss what are you doin'?"

Felicity took Allie by the wrist and led her around the car, but she didn't bring her to Ben. She took her to the passenger side of Ben's car and made her get in. Now Ben looked pissed. "Get out of my car." Allie just slumped down in her seat, the same as she had in Felicity's car and wouldn't speak or budge.

Ben looked back to Felicity. "What are you doing?"

"*I'm* not doing anything. *You* and Allie are going to make up."

"Why?"

"Because you and I made up already. You're way better friends with Allie than you are with me. You can't be mad at her for dating a vampire, and still be friends with me while I'm dating one. It wouldn't make sense. You're the one who says he lives in 'logical reality'."

"I'd be more logical to just stop being friends with you again."

"Shut up. I'm going to McDonald's and you and Allie are going to follow me. And by the time we get there, you two better have made up, because I don't have any more classes today, and if you don't make up with her, I'm going to follow you around and bug you until you do."

Ben stared at her for a minute. Alyson spoke up from within the car. "Felicity, being followed around by you all day...not gonna be a big deterrent. Ben, get in the damn car. Otherwise *I'll* follow you around, and I *know* how to be a pain in the ass."

Felicity looked at him pleadingly and smiled. He never looked at Allie, but stayed staring at her for a minute or two longer. "Ben," she asked quietly, "please get in." He didn't say anything.

Allie leaned to look at her from in the car. "Just go to McDonald's, we'll be there"

Ben took his eyes from hers, to look at the ground and sigh. "Go ahead," he said quietly.

She left. Felicity sat in the McDonalds parking lot for fifteen minutes before they finally showed up. When they got out of the car, neither one of them looked very happy, but they didn't say anything.

When they got their food and found a table, she noticed that Ben made a point to sit next to her instead of Allie. They made mostly small talk as they ate their lunch, but at least Felicity got them talking again.

Chapter 7 - Thirst

Cain

Thursday afternoon
Cain's house

Cain lay in bed, waiting for Felicity to arrive. It wouldn't be dark out for a few hours yet, but he couldn't sleep. Their recent time together had made him so happy...it couldn't last. He hated to think that way, but he was becoming aware of an issue that he would have to face. His blood thirst, yet again, was getting in the way. He'd felt the beast within, longing for Felicity, each time they made love. It was getting stronger. It was growing into something difficult to ignore.

In his years of solitude, he drank nothing but animal blood, bought from the butcher, cold and impersonal. His body had become accustomed to that, it expected no more, but in the past three weeks, he had drunk from a victim no less than four times. Starting with Felicity and ending with Sindy, he had given his body blood that, compared to that from his refrigerator was absolutely divine. It truly *was* an addiction, the blood. The more his body had, the more it craved. It knew the difference...it wanted the good stuff.

It served as a good lesson to him actually. It was so long since he'd been in a relationship that allowed him to drink from another regularly. He had forgotten just how difficult it could be, to deny the vampire within what it really wanted. He should not be so hard on the young ones, whom he so often tried to teach. It was harder than he remembered.

In the past, when a blood relationship ended, it was usually tied to emotional heartache as well. When his body admonished him for denial of his thirst, he had usually accounted it to his emotional loss. Purely physical withdrawal was not something he'd really thought much about. Now, his body was remembering the rich rewards of drinking from a host, rather than a cup. It wanted more, but he could not entirely blame his problem on the beast within. He knew that *he* was directly to blame for his blood desires as well.

Old habits die hard. His relationship with Felicity was not moving quite as quickly as things had gone with others in the past. Women that he had shared his bed with he had always drunk from as well. It was something started back in the old days, when he used to hunt. Many of his victims had been 'ladies of the evening'. Thus it was a simple thing to pay them for their services and then take more than they had thought to give.

Even when he had ceased hunting, he'd still drunk from Maribeth during sex. Once that relationship ended, he had gone through the worst withdrawal period of his life, but he'd almost thought that it was the physical expression of his grief over her departure, being that he found it hard to openly emotionally grieve over her leaving.

Over the years he had entered into serious relationships with others, now and again. There weren't many, but they all had one thing in common. For the entire duration of his relationships with those women, be they human or vampire at the time, he had drunk from them during sex. It seemed a natural thing, done not only for himself, but often at their request. They wanted the venom, he wanted the blood. They both came to expect it and often it brought about the climax of their love making, for both of them. His body had come to expect it as well, why shouldn't it? That was only what Cain himself had taught it. The vampire within had come to learn that when his body engaged in sex, blood would be forthcoming.

He had assumed that he could disengage himself from that. That he could make love to Felicity and it could clear the other desires from his mind. Somehow, he had not expected that it would only make them worse. Sindy's blood had helped to quench the thirst for a time, but that blood was just about gone from his system now. He certainly wasn't going to ask to drink from her again. He had planned to drink as much blood from his refrigerator as his body could hold, before seeing Felicity again, but it was not going down very well and he still worried that it wouldn't really help.

He got up from bed now, to try to drink some more. He wanted the evening to be perfect. He was unsure when she would arrive, but she had said she would see him before sunset. She wasn't working tonight, but she did have plans for lunch with Ben and Alyson, before she would come to him.

He tried not to let that bother him. It was a *good* thing that she had a life, outside, in the daylight. If she did not choose to stay with him, (and he had to admit that it seemed likely she would not), then he would eventually have to leave her. She would need friends and outside distractions, to help her to let him go. Still, he wished she had *other* friends. Benjamin, while close with Felicity, would never accept *him* as a friend. Ben could not see past the fact that Cain was a vampire. That made him not a mutual friend, but a sort of wedge between them.

Cain felt as though Ben was constantly speaking against him and doing things to undermine his relationship with Felicity. Giving her a cross for her birthday? It seemed an obvious slap in the face. Not that Cain planned to let the boy get to him, but it would be nice if Felicity did not spend *so* much time with him. It wasn't as though Cain were really jealous of Ben, but anyone who could spend the day outside in the sunshine with her, had something that he did not. The fact that it was Benjamin made it seem that much worse. It was depressing.

But away from petty thoughts and on to more important concerns. Luke's attack on Felicity had brought the blood issue further to his attention. She was not marked. He had decided to try to wait a while longer before marking her again, because he did not want to feed his inner vampire any more than he had too.

However, (and he was loathe to admit this to himself), he could not help but notice with a bit of indignance, that she did not even seem to want him to. He had thought that the experience of Luke's attack would spook her. She understood the concept of marking. She knew that it would help to keep her safe, and yet she had said that she would wear the vial, rather than speak to him of marking her. She did not *want* him to mark her. That should not bother him, but it did.

He knew that she had enjoyed the experience of his drinking from her. She would not discuss it with him and he'd been afraid to question her about it before she was ready, but he *knew.* So why was she so afraid to relive it? She must know that he would not really hurt her and she couldn't have the same concerns as he. She could not foresee how the dynamics of their relationship would change.

Was she in denial? Was she simply trying to pretend that it had not happened, that he was...human? Surely, she wished that he was. Was she unwilling to face the truth? Had she been *that* frightened by the act, scared to realize that he really was *a monster?*

He forced himself to drink the blood from his cup and then went back to bed...to wait. The hours passed, he dozed on and off, listening for her knock upon his door. He got up, showered, shaved and dressed. Finally, she arrived.

She was such a welcome sight to his eyes. Even in jeans and a casual shirt, she was lovely. He greeted and kissed her, and brought her downstairs. He was excited to give her the surprise he'd prepared. She sat on the bed, confused but eager anticipation in her eyes. He felt such silly giddiness as he went to get the package. "Stay there, I'll get it," he said as he went behind the bar.

"What is it? What's the surprise?"

"If I told you, it wouldn't be a surprise," he said with a grin. "I never did give you a birthday present," he said by way of explanation.

"You don't have to give me a present. Besides, you took me out for that expensive dinner."

"That wasn't a present, that was just food."

"It was very nice," she said as he handed her his gift.

It was sadly bundled in newspaper. A child probably could have done better, as he didn't even have any tape. "Sorry, I didn't have any wrapping paper."

She smiled up at him. "You didn't have to go and get me anything."

"Well, I hope you won't be disappointed, but...I didn't. It's something I already had, but I hope you'll like it, I think it suites you."

She smiled at him thoughtfully and unwrapped the paper. There was a black silk scarf, bearing a pink and white floral design inside. "It's pretty."

"The real present's inside the scarf. I didn't have a box either."

Now she unfolded the scarf to find within, an antique hair comb. It was heavily encrusted with beautiful jewels. Tiny little diamonds, sapphires and emeralds in swirling designs, across the top. Her eyes went wide and she was obviously delighted.

He was so glad that she seemed to like it. "Before the thought even comes to your mind, let me say that...no, it did *not* belong to my wife, or Maribeth, or any other ex-girlfriend. Nor did I steal it from any victim long ago. I *inherited* it, from my aunt. It's mine. Shortage of girls in my family. Guess it was thought that I'd give it to my wife someday, but I stuck it in a drawer and forgot about it.

I came across it again, during the estate sale when we cleared out the Manor. You know, we sold everything, before allowing tourists to come traipsing through. Anyway, I ought to have sold it, but it was just so lovely. *I* certainly had no use for it, but I couldn't seem to part with it. So I held on to it, all these years, although I didn't know for whom. As it turns out, it was you. I hope you like it. Happy birthday."

She kept fingering the jewels and turning it this way and that, to shine in the light. "Cain, it's *gorgeous,* but it must be such a valuable antique by now."

"I don't know what it's worth, but the stones are real. And I do think that it's about four hundred years old by this time."

She looked up at him in disbelief. "I can't accept this."

"Of course you can. Please. I *want* you to have it. *If* you do like it, that is." She looked at him as if he'd be crazy to question whether she cared for the piece. He smiled. "Keep it, and when you look upon it, think of me. And make me a promise. If you truly do care for it, then don't leave it locked and hidden away in a safe deposit box somewhere. Wear it, when the occasion warrants. I'm afraid it can't be used for staking ill-mannered vampires, but I know it will look charming in those lovely auburn locks of yours."

She seemed to shake off the shock that had come upon her when first revealing the gift. Now she held it tightly in her hand and leaned to hold and kiss him. "Thank you! Thank you so much! I do love it, really!" He smiled and gladly accepted her kisses and hugs. He tried not to acknowledge the phrase that kept floating through his head...'something to remember me by'.

He took her for dinner, to a more modest establishment this time, and the evening once again ended in his bed. He did not even let his lips wander to her throat this time, the temptation was too great, but their lovemaking did carry its own rewards, and once again, he made it through. Still, he wondered if they would have to speak of his concerns sometime soon.

She trusted him, explicitly. Ever since the first time that she questioned his control. He had promised her that he would tell her, if things became too difficult. He felt his word was sacred. What else did he have if not his word and character? He would tell her, if he *had* to.

To be honest, he had hoped that she herself would have broached the subject by now. They had never even really discussed the bite that she had already received from him in the past. He had believed that once she was fully comfortable with him, physically, it would be something that she would be unafraid to talk about, but she had never even evinced curiosity, or asked for further explanation of the act. He would have to speak to her of it soon, lest he inadvertently make known his illicit desires and make things worse. At least if they talked openly, he would know how she really felt over the issue.

She lay snuggled in his arms and he tried to think how such a conversation could even start, but no words came to mind. The night wore on. Finally, he found himself kissing her goodbye until the morrow. The topic would have to be broached another night.

~~~~~~~~~~~~~~~~~~~~~~~~~~~~~

One night rolled into the next, and before he knew it, a whole week had gone by. He still hadn't brought himself to begin discussions of blood, but he was doing better. He was keeping himself very well fed, no matter how distasteful his meager fare seemed. The vampire in him still wanted more, but the prospect of losing Felicity due to fear, helped motivate him to keep things in check. He drank animal blood until it made him feel ill, refusing to acknowledge his desires to drink from Felicity. It was one of the most difficult things he had ever accomplished.

Their days and nights together seemed to pass in a haze of romantic outings, quiet comfortable evenings at home and ever ardent expressions of love in his bed. She had become confident and playful during their lovemaking, and although the beast within him desired her strongly, the man that he was, was quite well satisfied.

Things were so comfortable now, normal and pleasant. How could he ruin it with admissions of thirst for her precious blood? He told himself that of course he would let her know, if it were truly a problem, but he didn't want to frighten her unnecessarily, he had things under control.

Another solution also came to mind. There was always Sindy. She had strictly avoided him since Luke's death, and he did not seek her out. He was unsure how she was spending her time, but it was not with him. She was still around; he did feel her now and then. She slept in the same location that she and her brood had used back when he'd first gone to find them, to protect Ben, but once the evening was underway, she seemed to prefer solitude. She never strayed all that far from her boys, surely their marks were usually within her range, so she could keep an eye on them he assumed, but she seemed more and more to be seeking physical distance from them.

Sometimes while out with Felicity, he would sense Sindy; though he wouldn't mention it, and they never saw her. He would feel her…alone, near Venus or just out in the woods, on the way from one place to another. He believed he was right in assuming that she was growing tired of her boys. Especially now that Luke and Chris were gone, she did not seem to want to share her company with the others any more than necessary.

He could drink from *her*, that would quiet the beast within him for a longer time. The very idea felt indecent; that he would do so without Felicity's knowledge and that he would *use* Sindy so. It would be wrong, but it would solve his problem, for a while anyway. It was almost as though he needed a separate woman for each of the entities that he was inside; Felicity for the man, Sindy for the vampire.

No, that was not an acceptable scenario. He would have to consider it an option of last resort. For now, he would rely on his own self-control, and hope that it remained strong enough.

Chapter 23 ~ Have a ball

Felicity

DownTime cafe and bookstore
Friday afternoon

Felicity stood at the register, waiting for Cain to arrive. It wasn't even really dark out yet, but she could hardly wait to see him. The last week had been such a romantic whirlwind of new experiences and old comforts, blended together to make the happiest time of her life.

She had seen Cain at his home after school each day, or if she were working, he would come to the DownTime as soon as the sunset permitted. He took her for dinner, dancing, they'd even had another romantic picnic - with no serious or frightening discussion, only happy and wonderful time spent together. She wanted it to last forever.

The finishing touch, to truly make the week perfect...no vampires, not a single one. Except for Cain of course, but she hardly even thought of *him* as a vampire anymore. She had not seen a single vampire since killing Luke, and that suited her just fine. Maybe they were afraid of her now? Probably not, but whatever the reason, she was very happy about it... It couldn't last.

She wore the vial faithfully and the cross from Ben as well. The vial hung a bit lower, on a longer chain than the cross. Together, she thought they looked very interesting; the cross so lovely and traditional, the vial also pretty, but exotic and unique. She had gotten many compliments on them both. She never went out without them and made very sure to take them off, upon arriving at Cain's. He surely noticed this new habit, but never commented on it.

She had worn the hair comb once, for an evening out with Cain. It was so beautiful! It really did work well in her hair and looked absolutely gorgeous. To wear it made her feel like royalty, a princess. She knew that she would treasure it always.

She loved the scarf as well, and wore it often. It had hardly seemed noteworthy next to the comb, but on its own, it was very pretty. She loved that she could wear it all the time, in her hair, or tied about her throat. She loved that it had come from him. She wore the scarf today, holding her long hair in a loose ponytail. It made even such a casual hairstyle, look charming and polished. Even Ashley had commented on how pretty it was, and Ashley was not one to give out compliments often.

Darkness fell and Felicity found herself eagerly watching the door for Cain, as Ashley shelved books. Cain had returned to his habit of walking to the DownTime, when she was working. Then she would drive them back to his house at the evening's end. So she knew that it would take a little longer for him to get there, than when he drove the motorcycle. When he finally did arrive, he met her at the counter for a kiss hello. It began as a simple, and 'workplace acceptable' peck on the lips, but as he sought to back away, she threw her arms around his neck, over the counter, for a longer and much more intimate kiss.

Normally she would never do such a thing, not in public anyway, but whether it was conscious or not, it wasn't just his kiss that she coveted, it was the venom that she wanted as well. She had become quite fond of the dreamy euphoric feeling his deep kisses could produce in her, however short lasting.

They had not seen each other all day, and she had been waiting for that kiss. A simple peck on the lips would not do. The kiss ended, and he backed away from her with a slightly reprimanding look and a small smile. "You're going to get yourself in trouble. I'm going to find a book to read." He gave her a little wink and headed back to the shelves, giving Ashley a quick 'hello' as he passed.

Ashley came to meet Felicity at the registers. "You two certainly seem to have kicked it up a notch." Felicity just gave an embarrassed smile as she turned her eyes from Cain to the floor. "Things finally getting hot?"

"Like molten lava," she whispered with a giggle.

"Ooo. With *him*...I've no doubt." Ashley always persisted in asking her embarrassing questions about Cain, when he was in the store. Ashley assumed he couldn't hear them, and of course he could always hear the entire conversation. It had become almost a game to Felicity and she found herself answering more for Cain than for Ashley, most of the time.

Cain picked out a book to buy and Felicity rung it up with a demure little grin. Cain kept a remarkably straight face, but as Ashley walked away he raised his eyebrows. "Lava?" he whispered with a smirk. She just giggled and sent him over to the cafe.

Ashley came back, very obviously admiring Cain from behind, as he left. Felicity always tried to take Ashley's open attraction for Cain as a sort of compliment. At least Ashley didn't flirt with him in front of Felicity so much anymore, although she had no doubt, the flirting probably still went on when she was not around.

Felicity was certain that a man as handsome and charming as Cain could probably manage to attract the attention of pretty much any girl that he wanted. He was with her because he wanted to be, and by this point in his life, he seemed mature enough not to bother playing games. She didn't really worry about another girl stealing him away. Still, as much as she pretended not to mind Ashley's attraction to Cain, it *was* a bit grating at times.

Felicity decided to give Ashley a little disapproving look as she finally pulled her eyes from Cain. Ashley seemed completely oblivious. "Is he taking you to the Halloween Masquerade Ball?" she inquired.

Sore subject. "No. We're not going." She and Cain had discussed the dance the other night. He had informed her that he definitely would not attend an event centered on such a banal and offensive 'holiday'. She was more than a little disappointed.

Ashley seemed to think it was an outrage. "What?! You totally have to go! I'm on the decorating committee; it's going to be awesome." Felicity just shrugged sullenly. "You have to make him take you."

"I already asked, he said no. He thinks Halloween is distasteful and heathen."

"No it isn't! What does that even mean?"

Felicity shook her head. "It's kind of against his religion."

"Oh. Well that sucks."

Felicity just gave her a little nod. She didn't really think that Cain was listening any longer, but didn't want to say too much about it, just in case. "Are you going with Ben?"

"Of course. I have got that boy wrapped around my little finger. He adores me." Before Felicity had decided whether or not she should comment on that, Alyson arrived. Ashley noted her approach. "Oh look, it's the girl who thinks *every* day is Halloween."

Allie sneered at her. "At least I don't spend all of my time trying to look like a Barbie doll."

"That's funny, because you actually do look just like a 'Barbie' that I used to have, *after* my little sister tortured her with scissors and a magic marker." Allie just gave her a disgusted look and ignored her, thumbing through flyers and bookmarks on the counter. Ashley turned back to Felicity, who had learned to stay out of their frequent insult exchanges. "Anyway, I'm going over to Clarissa's Costume Shop tomorrow, to pick up my outfit. You should come, maybe you'll see something good. If you get the right costume, Cain won't be able to let you go alone."

"Thanks, but I was just going to skip it, really."

Ashley shook her head and rolled her eyes. "See, I tried to tell you. Once you let them think they've got all the power, you're done for." Alyson gave a little snort of a laugh, and went back to browsing through the bookmarks.

"Not everything is a power trip Ashley," Felicity answered. "He just doesn't want to go, and I respect that."

"Okay, but do *you* want to go?" Felicity glanced at Cain, who didn't seem to be paying any attention. She just shrugged. "Did he tell you *not* to go?"

"Well of course not, but I wouldn't go with anyone else. I know you date lots of guys, but I can't do that. I don't wanna go with anyone but Cain."

"So, go alone. It's not like you won't know anyone there."

Felicity just shrugged and decided to try to take the focus off of herself. "So what's your costume?"

Ashley gave her a smug smile. "Jeannie, as in 'I dream of.'"

Alyson snorted at her again. "Original," she said sarcastically.

Her comment was met by a sharp glare from Ashley. "With *my* hair and body, it's the perfect costume."

Felicity spoke up, a little apologetically. "There *are* usually one or two of them at every party."

Ashley seemed unconcerned. "So? It's a classic, and that will just go to prove how much better *I* look in it than *they* do." Ashley glanced from one speechless girl to the other, and then at the registers. She opened one and took out a few twenties. "We need change; I'm goin' over to the cafe." She walked over, money in hand, as Allie and Felicity exchanged looks.

"Is she for real?" Felicity asked.

Allie rolled her eyes. "Unfortunately, and she's spending more and more time with Ben, which frankly, just makes me nauseous."

"He's taking her to the Halloween dance," Felicity told her.

"Well, that's one event that *I* won't be attending," Allie replied.

Felicity watched as Ashley walked behind the counter to the cafe register and promptly began draping herself all over Ben as he made change for her. "I wonder what Ben's going to be."

"You mean besides emotionally abused? Ben's always a super hero. He says he thinks that the girls like them, but I think he's just feeding his inner geek. He used to be big into comic books."

Felicity laughed. "Super heroes huh?"

"Oh yeah, he's been them all. Superman, Batman, Spiderman, various X-Men, the Green Lantern, he's been everybody. He's starting to run out of cool heroes though. I mean really, who's left, *Aqua man?*"

Felicity started to chuckle when she suddenly remembered something and dropped her smile. "Oh no!"

"What?" Allie asked.

"Poor Ben!" Felicity exclaimed.

"What?!" Allie repeated.

"I talked to Karen this morning, and Todd and Brenda are still together," Felicity explained.

"Yeah, so?" Alyson asked.

"So, they're going to the dance...as Captain America and Wonder Woman," Felicity revealed sympathetically.

Allie slammed her hand on the counter with a laugh. "Oh my God! Ben is gonna *die!*"

"I know. Maybe he and Brenda had more in common than I thought. I feel so guilty," Felicity admitted.

"Why? You didn't do anything," Allie assured her.

"I practically threw Todd at her. I feel terrible," Felicity said.

Alyson laughed. "Don't worry about it. Like he said, Ben could have gotten her back if he'd tried. I know he was trying to sound smug, but it's probably true. Ben's a pretty charming smooth talker when he wants to be."

"*Ben* is?" Felicity asked incredulously.

Allie rolled her eyes again. "Well he doesn't waste it on *us*." Felicity laughed and they both turned to watch Ben with Ashley. She had gotten her change but was now obviously working him over for something else. She was really trying hard too, batting her eyes and giving him pouty little kisses, while rubbing against him just so and whispering in his ear. Whatever she was trying to accomplish, Ben did not look very happy about it. It seemed as though he finally gave over, but continued to look very sulky and annoyed.

Allie seemed disgusted. "What could he possibly see in her? She is so vapid and shallow. They've started dating again and he's taking her to this dance, and *I* didn't even think that he liked her all that much."

"That's what *I* said!" Felicity agreed.

"I think the man's gone insane. I mean, I'm sorry, but even sex with *Ashley* can't be worth having to *listen* to her all day."

Felicity shook her head with a smile. "Maybe they have fun together."

Allie chuckled and gestured towards the cafe, where Ben was still looking sullen and aggravated as Ashley tried to make him smile with kisses and tickling. "Does that look like the face of a *happy* man to you? I'd better go rescue him."

Allie turned to leave, but Felicity put a hand on her arm to stop her. "Wait, what are you going to do? I mean, if Ben is dating her, then you really shouldn't say anything. It's none of our business."

"Oh, I'm not gonna say anything. I'm just gonna sit there and smile at her," Allie informed her.

"What's *that* going to do?" Felicity asked.

"Just watch, I'll bet she leaves in under a minute." With that, Allie left for the cafe to prove her prediction. She chose a chair from Cain's table without a word, turned it to face the counter better, and sat. Cain looked up curiously from his book at Alyson's arrival, but said nothing. Allie promptly began to smile at Ben and Ashley. They were probably wondering why she had purposely strode over to Cain's table to ignore him.

It only took a few seconds before Ashley said something to Ben and left, heading back to the registers. She seemed a little displeased when she got there. Felicity looked at her questioningly, but all she said was, "Don't you get another fifteen?"

The question caught Felicity off guard. Oh, her break. "Yeah."

"Well, you'd better take it now, because at eight o'clock, I'm outta here," Ashley informed her.

"Okay." Felicity walked over to the cafe with a bemused expression on her face. She went to Cain's table and gave him a kiss hello. It was just a quick kiss this time, but he quickly pulled back from it, as if to escape her leading him into more. She looked at him as though he'd hurt her feelings.

"Sorry, but I can't be too careful. You've become quite cheeky these days."

She giggled with a slight blush. She *had* been awfully bold with their kiss before. She sat down and stared at him for a moment. "Why do you come here so early? I won't get out for two and a half more hours. Aren't you bored?"

"Well I do have Alyson here, keeping me company."

"Yeah, what am I chopped liver?" Alyson chimed in.

"Did you want something?" Felicity looked up in surprise to find Ben at her shoulder.

"I get *served?*"

"Considering you didn't make it easy for me by sitting at the counter, yeah. You want something?"

"Sorry. Um, yeah. I'll have a cup of coffee."

Alyson chirped up, "Make it three." Felicity gave her a bit of an odd look, that she was ordering for Cain. Since when had they become so familiar?

Felicity spoke to Allie, as Ben left to get their coffees. "So you were right, she left. You didn't say anything?"

"Not a word," Allie answered with a smile. "You may have noticed that Ashley has a hard time being around me, without spitting out some depreciative comment or rude remark."

"I had noticed that, yeah."

"Well, she can't do that around Ben, because he always defends me and then she gets all pissed. So, rather than have to be nice to me, she just leaves."

Felicity and Cain chuckled as Ben returned with their coffee. "There you go," he said, setting one in front of each of them. He then looked pointedly at Cain. "Three coffees, hold the holy water."

Cain looked very annoyed as Allie and Felicity tried to hold in their giggles. Alyson reached up to stop Ben from leaving. "Would you get me a piece of pie?"

"What kind?" Ben asked.

"Whatever's not old," Allie replied.

Cain was staring disapprovingly at Felicity, as Ben left. "You *had* to tell them?"

Felicity smiled. She couldn't help but share Cain's remark, about worrying Ben might spike his coffee with holy water. "It was funny."

"It was a legitimate concern," Cain said defensively.

"Not with Ben!" Felicity insisted.

"Still, you needn't go about giving people ideas," he mumbled.

"I'm sorry, forgive me?" She smiled at him and batted her eyes, feeling a bit like Ashley, in trying to get him to smile. Cain gave her a subtle little amorous look and took her hand from the table, raising it to his lips for a kiss. She was always so thrilled when he did things like that.

Ben dropped Allie's pie plate on the table with a thud. It was pecan. "Is that it?"

Allie questioned his annoyance. "What's *your* problem? It's not like you're busy." The one table of customers Ben'd had, had left a few minutes before.

Ben looked at Cain and then back to Allie. "That's because it's almost eight o'clock on a Friday night. Most people who aren't *required* to be here, have got better things to do."

Allie and Cain shared a glance and a smile, before Alyson answered. "Well, lucky for you, *I've* got the whole evening free. So I'm gonna spend it right here."

"What do you know? Me too," Cain added playfully.

Ben shook his head with a groan and turned to leave. Felicity stopped him. "I heard you're taking Ashley to the Halloween Ball."

"Yeah," he answered shortly.

He didn't exactly sound thrilled. "Who are you going as?" Felicity asked.

"Major Nelson," Ben replied.

"Who?"

"Major Anthony Nelson, the astronaut from 'I Dream Of Jeannie'. Ashley wants us to match," Ben explained.

Allie opened her mouth in indignance. "You don't even get to pick your own costume? That sucks!"

Ben shrugged. "It doesn't matter." It looked to Felicity as though it might matter a great deal to Ben.

She was glad when Allie said something about it. "Ben! You love Halloween! Don't let her wreck it for you! What are you going to wear, a silver track suit and a fishbowl on your head?"

"No! It's a NASA dress uniform," Ben clarified.

"That is *so* lame!" Allie insisted.

"Ashley says I'll look dashing," Ben said defensively.

"Boooring. Ashley must not have ever seen you in the tights." Allie gave Felicity a confidential little smile and informed her, "He looks *really* good in tights."

Cain looked at Ben with an arched eyebrow. "When did you wear *tights?*"

Ben glared at him. "It was a Superman costume." He turned to Allie. "Shut up and mind your own business."

Felicity felt that she ought to say something before they started fighting. "So Allie, what are you going to be?"

Ben answered for her. "Allie doesn't *do* Halloween."

Felicity looked from Allie to Cain. "No wonder you two have been getting along so well."

Cain gave Alyson an amicable grin. "Ah, someone else who doesn't wish to support the celebration of Devil worship and hedonism."

Allie sat staring at him very oddly for a moment before answering. "No. I just think it's *stupid.*"

"Why?" Felicity asked.

"Everybody waits for this one day a year, just so they can get all dressed up in ways that would normally be socially unacceptable and not get criticized for it. It's such a joke."

"Isn't that kind of the point, to dress as something you aren't?"

"But that's just it, people treat it more as a 'come as you secretly are'. It's not like anybody tries to be scary anymore. They choose costumes that are just expressions of their hidden innermost desires. Like Ashley's outfit. You don't think she'd dress like that *every day*, if she could get away with it? Halloween is just a convenient excuse for girls like her to drop their inhibitions without being ostracized for it."

Ben smirked at her. "You should be a psychology major."

"I just speak the obvious truth. I don't have any use for Halloween. I'm *already* out there for everyone to see. I don't have to hide behind some stupid fake holiday. If I want my hair to be pink, I dye it pink. If I *wanted* to walk around half naked, I would and *I* wouldn't have to consult a calendar to do it."

Cain was looking at her with new admiration. "Well said."

"Thank you," Allie answered with a smile.

Ben smiled. "Going as a black cat?"

Alyson's smile disappeared. "Yeah."

Felicity looked to Allie in confusion. "Wait, I thought you didn't dress up?"

Allie sat back in a huff as Ben answered for her. "Tommy always makes Alyson work on Halloween. It's bar policy that all employees *have* to wear a costume." He looked to Allie. "You know he just does that to piss you off, right?"

Allie shrugged. "I wear a head band with ears and pin a tail to my ass, and everybody leaves me alone."

Ashley interrupted them by yelling across the store. "Felicity, it's eight o'clock! Come on, I wanna leave. Some people have a life *outside* of the cafe." She sounded very annoyed and sarcastic.

Alyson beamed a broad smile at Ben. "She is *such* a catch Ben, you must be *so* proud."

"Bite me, Allie."

Ben took Felicity's coffee cup to the sink behind the counter, as Felicity returned to the registers. She offered Ashley a 'sorry', but the girl just brushed past her on the way to the lounge.

A minute later, Ashley came back out with her purse and jacket. She paused to give Ben a quick kiss goodbye, and then headed for the door. Just as she left the cafe, Ben called out to her. "Ashley, wait!"

Ashley turned, looking annoyed. "What?"

He hesitated for a moment, as though searching for something to say. "You can't leave yet."

Ashley was very irritated. "Why not? It's ten after." Ben just looked at her pleadingly for a minute, but she was having none of it. "Ben, I have to go...I have plans."

"Ashley..."

"It's Friday night and you won't be out of here for at *least* two more hours."

Ben now ignored Ashley to stare at Cain, who was deep in a conversation with Alyson. "Cain, go lock the door."

Chapter 24 – Payback's a bitch

Cain

Friday night
DownTime cafe and bookstore

Cain had been very involved in a conversation with Alyson about false personas and hidden identity traits, when Ben ordered him to go and lock the door. He had been very much ignoring Ben's altercation with Ashley, and now wondered why he was being dragged into things, and given orders no less.

Ashley stared at Ben in disbelieving shock. "Ben! Please, let's not make this messy. *You're* the one who didn't want to be exclusive. What, you get to date other people and I don't? It's Friday night!"

Ben was still ignoring her and staring at Cain. He started to come out from behind the counter. Ben's seriousness made Cain get up from the table and start for the door, but why had he asked Cain to do it? Felicity was much closer. As he reached the door and peered outside, a flash of understanding came upon him. Sindy was just outside and had been about to enter. Ben must have felt her coming. Rather than lock the door on her, Cain let her in.

"What the hell are you doing?" Ben yelled from the cafe entry.

Cain ignored him. Sindy seemed very distraught, pained even. She did not seem physically hurt, but she practically collapsed against the wall once inside. Suddenly her trace flared into existence in his mind, and he realized her distress. She'd been cloaking herself, through great mental strain, to get here undiscovered.

She looked up at him, disgusted with her lack of staying power. "I can't hold it. You'd better lock the door."

Cain did as she asked, as Ben came storming up to them. "*Now* he locks it?" Ben yelled to the others with his arms in the air. He stalked right up to Sindy. "Get the fuck out of my store bitch," he growled.

Ashley put one hand on her hip and gestured towards Sindy with the other. "Who is that?" No one bothered to answer her.

Cain gave Ben a warning glance. "Back off." Without waiting for response, he turned his attention back to Sindy. "How far behind you?"

"They didn't know where I was going, they couldn't follow, but I'm too drained to keep up my cover. They'll find me before long."

"Who? What's going on?"

"They're all after me." She glanced at Ben and then back to Cain. "I *can't* go back out there. They'll kill me."

"Good!" Ben practically spat at her.

Cain gave Ben a fierce glare. "Think you might give us a moment?" Ben only backed up a step. "Who?"

Sindy was looking him in the eye, as she leaned her back against the wall. "It's Chris. He came back."

"When?"

"Last night. I went out on my own...shopping." By the way that she said it, Cain knew she meant for blood. He was more than a little surprised; he hadn't thought she was drinking store bought blood. "I was only gone for like an hour, but when I got back to the house, he was there." She glanced down at the floor and he could tell that she would rather not have an audience for her telling. She hadn't a choice. "I thought he wanted to come back, to be like it was, you know? But he started talking about status and stuff. He was all worked up, saying that 'sire or not' he shouldn't have to take orders from a girl. That it just wasn't right." She looked up to find Felicity in the store. Sindy's gaze landed upon her, behind the counter...if looks could kill, it surely would have been deadly. "Then he found out about Luke. Let me tell you somethin' honey. You thought you were livin' dangerously before? He's got *special* plans for *you*."

Cain gave her a little shove on the shoulder. "That'll be quite enough of that, bottom line please?"

"He's turned them against me Cain, all of them! How could he do that? They're *mine*! But they won't listen to me now, not like they listen to him. And he's got them all worked up and thinkin' they'd be better off without me! I take care of them don't I? How could they do this to me?

Chris told them that Luke, and those other dumb jocks that got themselves killed...that it's all *my* fault. Like I'm incompetent or something! He says that *I'm* gonna take orders from *him* for a change. He starts tellin' me to do all this stuff for him, and when I wouldn't he freaked!" She gave Felicity another dangerous glare. "Maybe I should have just done it."

"What did he want you to do?" Cain asked.

Sindy gave an evil little smile. "Like I said, he's got plans for your girlfriend over there. Real specific instructions." She chuckled at Felicity. "Man, you should have left Luke alone."

Cain was staring at her thoughtfully. "You told him no," he said quietly.

She looked up at him and shrugged. "I put it on your tab. Anyway we had this big fight, and he starts threatenin' me, like actually pushin' me around and stuff. So I call Marcus, to make Chris leave me alone, *and he wouldn't come!* Chris starts laughin' at me, tellin' me that *girls* shouldn't be givin' orders.

That's when I realized, they've got his mark Cain. That creep drank from my boys while I was gone! They listen to him; they've always listened to him, but now he's tellin' them to get rid of *me*! They're so stupid, they'll just do anything he says. He wants me out of the way, dusted! And he can make them do it!"

Ben smiled. "Sounds like I'm going to owe that man a favor."

Before anyone else could comment, Ashley approached them at the door, to address Sindy. "Excuse me, hi. Look, I'm real sorry that there's like people trying to kill you and stuff. That really sucks. You should like, call the police or something, but *I'm* late for an appointment. So if you don't mind, I'm just going to slip out to my car, 'kay?"

Sindy just stared at her for a moment in disdain and disbelief. Cain shook his head, as though to clear it and then spoke seriously to Sindy. "You - stay here, don't move and you should probably refrain from speaking as well." Now he turned to Ben. "You - back off and don't do *anything*, until I get back. Understood?" Cain went to take Ashley by the arm. "I'll escort you to your car."

Ashley smiled at Cain as though he were the only sane person in the establishment. *"Thank you."*

Ben moved grudgingly aside, but Sindy stood her ground in front of the door. "Cain, wait. Chris...he can cloak." She looked disgusted to admit it. "Better than *me*."

Cain sighed as Sindy stepped aside for him. "Wonderful." He looked over to Felicity, who hadn't said anything, but was looking rather nervous at the register. "You just stay put, I'll be right in."

There was a nervous moment of silence, as Cain and Ashley stepped outside and glanced around. No one was in sight. He let the door swing closed behind them and turned to Ashley. "Your car, it's the green one?" He nodded towards a little mint green VW Bug convertible.

Ashley began towards it, unconcerned. "Yeah, cute right?"

"Adorable, but you might want to put the top up." They reached her car without event. Cain stood keeping an eye on their surroundings, until he realized that Ashley still hadn't gotten in. She stood there, looking at him for a moment, until Cain opened the door for her.

She gave him a flirtatious little smile and got in. "You know, if you ever wanted to come for a ride...I'd be happy to take you for one."

Cain gave her a benign smile and a light touch on the arm. "Thanks. Goodnight." He tapped her arm before he backed away. "Put the top up."

He watched her as she put up the top and pulled out of the lot. As soon as she was off alright, Cain headed back inside. He approached the glass door to find Sindy against the wall as Ben held a stake to her chest. Alyson was standing behind Ben, arms crossed and Felicity was next to him, obviously trying to talk him into putting away the stake. Sindy stood with remarkable calm, her eyes locked on Ben. She seemed to be concentrating on him intensely. Cain realized that rather than choose a physical rebuttal to Ben's threat, she was using whatever slight mental control she might have left from her mark. Ben looked disgusted and nauseous.

Cain ripped open the door, stalked right up to them and grabbed Ben's wrist. "Can't turn my back on you for a minute, can I?"

Alyson spoke from behind them. "Sindy was eggin' him on. I thought he handled it pretty well. I would have staked her already."

Cain looked from Sindy to Ben, as both still locked in their mental battle of wills. "Now children, let's not fight." He gave a little push on Ben's wrist with the stake, for him to drop the arm to his side.

Ben seemed to notice Cain for the first time, and lowered the stake. "She needs to leave. Why are you even defending her? Don't you actually *care* about Felicity at all?"

"I beg your pardon?" Cain responded in quiet outrage. "How dare you question my loyalties?"

Ben gestured towards Sindy with the stake in his hand. "Don't you see what she's doing? She tells Chris that Felicity killed Luke and then she leads him right to her. So now *her* problem has become *our* problem."

Sindy became indignant. "I didn't even know that Felicity was here!" She looked pleadingly at Cain. "It's not like that at all!"

Cain was just gazing at her steadily, unsure what to believe. "Convince me," he said mildly.

Sindy opened her mouth in disbelief. "I have been dealing with this *without you* since like ten o'clock last night, when I first ran from him. Why wouldn't I have just brought them to Felicity from the beginning?"

Ben was happy to answer and try to make her look worse. "Because she was in her room, where you and Chris couldn't get in. So you had to wait until you could find her in a public place at night. Like...oh, I don't know...**here?"**

Sindy looked as though she'd like to kick him. She turned back to Cain. "Cain, I didn't want to involve you at all, *believe me,* but Arif sent me away, and I don't know what else to do. There are too many of them for me to handle alone."

Cain looked puzzled. "You spoke to Arif of this?"

"Yeah, I went to him last night."

"And...?"

"And..." Her shoulders slumped. Once again, she seemed to loathe having to share her personal business with all of them. "He sent me away." Cain still stared at her, waiting for details. "He told me that while he felt responsible to protect me from *others,* my own brood is my own problem."

Cain raised his eyebrows as Ben spoke. "Sounds fair to me."

Cain gave a little smile. "If I were wise, I'd probably tell you the same." Sindy just stared at him. She didn't bother to try to look hopeful or beg for his help. Apparently, she had decided that he would come to his own decision, and she'd rather hold on to her pride. "Since when does Chris know how to hide his trace?"

Sindy become uncomfortable at the mention of Chris' talent, superior to hers. Her voice was full of contempt. "I don't know. I never saw him do it until yesterday. I guess he's been practicing behind my back or something. I don't know how he got so good at it."

"Sounds to me as though perhaps *Chris* paid a visit to Arif as well. His new philosophies would certainly make good evidence for such a case."

Realization and scorn came over her. "That creep! Turning my own against me and then acting all condescending about it! It's not fair! They were mine! So is Chris! I made him, how can he turn against me like this?"

Ben moved a little closer, enjoying Sindy's distress. "Ain't payback a bitch?" he asked with a smile.

Sindy's anger flared for a moment, but then she fixed Ben with a steady stare and a sweet smile. Strange expressions flashed over Ben's features, before he composed his face into a blank mask. He gripped the stake so hard his knuckles were white and he returned her stare with his own. Cain moved to break their line of sight.

Ben closed his eyes as Cain watched him for a moment. Over Ben's shoulder, Cain noticed that Alyson seemed very interested in the exchange. Normally she became hostile very quickly in Sindy's presence, but right now she seemed to Cain to be curious more than anything else. As though she would really like to understand just what Sindy was capable of and how she did it.

Cain turned to Sindy. By the little smirk on her face, he was certain she was sending Ben the strongest indecent sensations and callings she could manage. "That's enough. End it, *now.*"

Ben brushed past his shoulder to face Sindy again. "She'd better, or I'll find a way to work through it. Keep it up and you're dust," he threatened, lifting the stake in his hand, with a fierce growl in his voice.

Cain let him stare her down for a minute before lightly touching the stake. "Put it away," Cain said quietly.

Ben looked as though he'd like to argue, but thought better of it and slid the stake into his back pocket. "Are you throwing her out or what? She might as well be a neon sign for anybody who wants her and Felicity, right? They can see her? So put her out. Let them chase her around for a while, so Felicity can get home." He suddenly turned to Felicity in apprehension. "Can they...see you too?"

Felicity spoke for the first time during the events of the evening. She seemed a bit shaken. All she said was a quiet 'no'. Ben looked as though he didn't quite believe her.

Alyson spoke up in her defense. "She's not marked."

Both Ben and Cain looked at her curiously. It was Ben who asked. "How would you know?"

"She told me," Allie replied with a shrug.

Cain shook his head and turned back to Sindy. "He's right; you're going to have to hide your trace. It may already be too late, but you should try."

She looked annoyed. "I told you I can't."

"You did it well enough *outside* the door. So unless you'd like me to believe that you *are* purposely leading them here, you'd better do it again now." Their voices began to rise a bit, with the desperate knowledge that every moment lost, was bringing danger closer.

"Cain, I can't! I'm spent."

"It's easy enough. Once you get the correct shape of it into your mind, it can become effortless. I do it almost unconsciously."

"Good for you," she quipped sarcastically.

"Chris learned it quickly enough."

"I guess *he* had a good teacher."

Ben interjected, "We don't have time for this, get rid of her!"

Sindy looked at Cain with degraded contempt in her eyes. "I can't do it. You never taught me."

Cain became impatient. "Well I'm teaching you now!"

Alyson's voice broke through his focus on Sindy. "Too late, school's out." Cain turned to see two of Sindy's football players at the door. In his distraction of breaking things up between Ben and Sindy, he hadn't even locked it again. Not that it mattered much; it was all glass, easily broken.

Cain cursed himself for a fool. He shouldn't have wasted time worrying about hiding Sindy's trace. They'd had time to determine her general location, and Chris wasn't entirely stupid. He had to have guessed where she might come in this area. He should have made Felicity and Alyson get to safety, but he knew that Felicity would be terrified to be far from him, and without her in sight he would worry for a trap. Anyway, too late now.

The two at the door began pushing their way in, as Cain moved forward to shove the door closed in their faces. He locked it, but as predicted, they simply began to kick in the glass. As the first crash sounded, he heard an almost identical crash from across the store. The front window of the cafe came shattering in.

Cain turned to see that Alyson had produced a stake from somewhere, as Felicity raced behind the counter to the employee lounge with Ben close behind, his stake in hand. Sindy watched Cain pull a stake from his own boot, as the two at the door tried to come through. "Got an extra one of those?" she inquired. He tossed her the one from his hand, and took out another from his other boot. He stepped aside, as the two came through the door.

The guy closest to Cain must have been blindly following Sindy's trace. He was so focused on getting to Sindy that he did not even notice Cain, off to the side, until it was too late. Either that, or because of Cain's hidden trace, he simply thought Cain human and therefore of no immediate concern. Cain was able to stake him before the vampire even realized the threat.

Sindy seemed about to stake the one before her, when she suddenly dropped to the floor as though struck. The guy was upon her in a moment, but Cain attacked him from behind. The lesser vampire tried to push him away, but it was hardly adequate resistance. Cain dispatched him easily. As he did, he saw Sindy turn and wince.

He realized the problem. They were her 'children'. She felt their deaths as though it was her own physical pain. She would hardly be much use in this fight. He put out a hand to help her up, as his eyes found the lounge door in the cafe.

Ben and Felicity were emerging from the lounge, with more stakes and crosses. Apparently, the weapons had been with their belongings, in the lounge. What they did not see, was the third football player waiting for them behind the counter. "Felicity, Ben, look out!"

As Cain yelled, the guy sprang at Ben, who had come through the door first. The two became engaged in a struggle as Felicity tried to get out to help. She was blocked in the doorway by their fight, though. Cain tried to imagine if there'd be any doors in the lounge, for someone to come through from behind. He'd never been back there.

Hoping Felicity was safe for the moment, he turned back to Sindy. He'd helped her to her feet, and she stood with the support of his arm. She looked up with a weak smile. "This isn't gonna be much fun."

He turned back to see Ben beating the hell out of his foe. Alyson was moving to join Ben and Felicity, when Ben finally staked the vampire. Cain was forced to turn towards Sindy as she practically broke his arm in her pain. Cain was about to ask after her, when he saw two more vampires coming through the door. They were zombies, filthy, rotten and mindless, but advancing upon he and Sindy with grim determination. He glanced back to Sindy, who hadn't seen them and dragged her back away from the door a step, by her hold on his arm. "Are those yours?"

She looked up to see who he meant, and looked instantly ill. "I do better work than that, give me a little credit."

"Good, then you can fight them." She looked a little offended by his lack of assistance, but he had other worries. Two more zombies had come in by the window to the cafe. They must have followed the guy Ben had killed. Ben seemed eager to tackle one of them. Alyson and Felicity positioned themselves before the other one. They should manage. In fact, as he watched, he saw Felicity remember the vial at her throat. She handed Alyson the cross she'd been holding. Then Felicity quickly opened the vial, and moved Allie aside so that Felicity was directly in front of the thing.

Cain smiled, she was a smart girl, but he was unsure if the vial would help. Hopefully, the instinct driven corpse before her would feel loathe to touch her if she smelled of Cain's blood, but as Felicity was not traditionally marked, there was a good chance that it would not understand the meaning of smelling Cain's blood on her at all. Still, it couldn't hurt. The vampire wasn't decayed enough to suggest that it was totally mindless. It seemed pretty straightforward that the smell of another vampire on a victim should mark ownership...if the thing could even smell it. From what Cain could see, the vampire/zombie they faced must have been through some trying past event. Its face was very disfigured and it hadn't much of a nose left. Cain almost wished Felicity would pour the blood upon herself, to be sure.

Cain left the front entrance registers, moving towards the cafe in case the others needed assistance, but he also had in his mind, the fact that they had not yet seen Chris…or Marcus. *Cain* wanted to be the one to face them, if possible. Cain saw that Ben's foe seemed confused and Cain realized that Ben was still marked. That should serve to help protect him as well. He wished Allie had such assurance. His eyes searched the cafe. Where was Chris?

He heard movement from the back of the bookstore. He spared a parting glance at Sindy, before going to check it out. She had killed one zombie and was struggling with the other. It was a gruesome battle. She couldn't stake it because it was too close to her, holding her in a sort of hug as it tried to bite her. She grabbed at its hair, to try to pull its face back away from herself, but she only came away with a handful of loose hair and ripped scalp.

She pushed and struggled against the thing until she could get out from under it. Cain felt bad to leave her, but it wouldn't do her any permanent damage. It was too stupid to know how to really kill Sindy and it hadn't a weapon anyway.

Cain started towards the bookshelves, looking back to the cafe as he went. Ben had dispatched his 'vampire' and was moving to help the girls. They weren't really in distress. Using vial and cross, they avoided the zombie who was trying to get to them, but they didn't seem to want to touch it. He couldn't blame them.

Cain made his way into the labyrinth of bookshelves. He heard it again, someone was definitely back there. He tried to recall the various windows and exits where Chris might have snuck in. The back door should sound a fire alarm when opened. He approached the corner of each shelf warily, tense with anticipation. He finally reached the back of the store, and as he turned into last aisle he found...a boy. Well, a young man really, although rather short and slight of build; he was certainly not a vampire. He was huddled in the corner, hugging a large book. He wore glasses and was about Felicity's age. Cain sighed in annoyance as the boy spoke. "I was looking something up, for my history paper. Somebody broke the glass door. Did they rob the place? I was going to buy the book, I swear."

Cain shook his head. The boy acted as though he thought Cain might be a cop. "Come on, you don't want to be here." Cain was turning to lead the boy up and out the front, when he sensed four new traces enter the store. Damn, one of them was Marcus. "On second thought, stay here." Cain left the kid to run back up front. He got there in time to see Sindy fighting another zombie. He assumed it was a new one, and she had finished the one from before. This one was definitely better preserved and putting up quite a fight. How many of these things had Chris made?

Well, he knew that there were at least two more. He could feel them...with Marcus. The other two zombies and Marcus were just entering the cafe, after having come through the front door, but Cain's attention was instead instantly drawn to the cafe window. Chris was there. Cain saw him only for a moment. Chris yelled for Marcus, who turned to face him. Chris quickly surveyed the situation and seemed very disappointed that things hadn't gone better for him and his lot. Cain, Sindy and all of the humans within, including Felicity seemed unharmed. Chris certainly must have felt his zombies' deaths, but they would not have been as painful as the deaths Sindy had felt. The better made the vampire, the stronger the blood tie to its sire. Surely, Chris was disappointed.

Chris called insistently again for Marcus and then disappeared from the window. He was indeed cloaked. Cain could not sense where he went. He considered trying to give chase, but then he heard Felicity scream. Marcus was exiting through the window after Chris, but the two zombies had been busy making their way behind the cafe counter. Cain saw that his friends seemed to have killed the one they were fighting before, but Felicity had screamed because a new one had grabbed her by the arm, pulling her close. Ben was trying to beat it off her, so that he might get an open shot at its chest. Meanwhile Alyson was struggling to keep the other one from backing her into a corner. She had out her stake, but seemed to be having a hard time getting to its heart.

Cain sighed; Chris and Marcus would have to wait. He wasn't sure that he wanted to tackle the two of them alone anyway. Marcus was so huge! As he started toward the cafe to help dispatch the last two, he was startled by Sindy. She took his arm at the elbow from behind. "I heard Chris. Is he gone?"

Cain glanced towards the front door. Sindy had finished the zombie that had been there. He stopped to remove her from his arm. "Yes, and Marcus survives also." He looked over to the cafe to see that Allie had killed her foe, and Ben had pulled the other from Felicity. He had it backed up against the counter. Their struggle would certainly be over soon. Cain looked back to Sindy. "We're very lucky to have come out of this unscathed."

She backed away so that he could better see her. "Easy for you to say. You aren't covered in gore and zombie guts! Thanks for your help by the way," she added sarcastically.

Cain turned to face her more fully. "*You should* be thankful, very. Ben was right, you know. I'd have been smarter to put you out, and make you deal with them on your own."

"You mean *kill me;* because you know I couldn't have survived all of this alone."

"Hence the due gratitude."

"Oh. Well yeah, but I could have killed Felicity myself last night. Would have bought me some safety. Just 'cause Chris didn't want to take orders, doesn't mean he didn't *want* me. He'd have been very happy to have me by his side. All I needed to do was take Felicity for him. Then he would have treated me *real* nice. I don't care if she stays where I'm uninvited; I would have found a way. I could have bought some time, done it tonight, or tomorrow. You know I could have."

"That is why you are still alive, but if I find that you knowingly lead harm to Felicity again in any way...I'll stake you myself." Sindy stared back at him in dead seriousness.

"I'm done playing games. Really." Her eyes looked hopefully for his trust.

He hadn't the time or presence of mind to sort such things out now. He simply answered, "Good," and started back to the cafe, where the last of the zombies had been turned to ash floating in the air. Felicity, Ben and Alyson were dusting themselves off.

Sindy stopped him again, her hand lightly on his arm. "I don't suppose I could stay at your place for the day?"

He looked at her as though she must be mad. "No."

She shrugged, looking a bit disappointed, but not really surprised. "Just thought I'd ask."

He stared at her for a moment and then dug some bills from his pocket. He thrust them into her hand. "Go and find a hotel room, and practice your cloaking."

She eagerly tucked the bills into her bra, at the shoulder of her dress. "Thanks."

Ben spoke from behind him, emerging from the cafe. "She leads hoards of angry undead upon us, and you *pay her for it?*" Before Cain could answer, Felicity flew into his arms. She snuggled her face into his chest, and he couldn't help but enfold his arms tightly around her.

Allie reached them, and stopped to take a look around. The front door and large picture window in the cafe were both smashed in, glass was everywhere, and the floor and cafe counter were covered in the ashes of no less than ten vampires. Alyson began laughing, and they all turned to look at her in bewildered curiosity. By way of explanation she said, "Penten's gonna be pissed!"

Just then, they were startled by movement behind them as someone emerged from the back of the store. Everyone made ready for defense by raising stakes and crosses, and preparing themselves to meet...the young man with the glasses, who had been shopping in the back of the store before the attack.

He was still clutching his book, but dropped it to the floor, to put up his hands upon seeing his hostile reception. He stood there for a second in frightened silence, until weapons were lowered with sighs of relief. He looked questioningly at Cain. "Can I go home now?"

~~~~~~~~~~~~~~~~~~~~~~~~~~~~~~~~~~~
~~~~~~~~~~~~~~~~~~~~~~~~~~~~~~~~~~~
~~~~~~~~~~~~~~~~~~~~~~~~~~~~~~~~~~~

Volume 3

~~~~~~~

Evolving Ecstasy

~~~~~~~~~~~~~~~~~~~~~~~~~~~~~~~
~~~~~~~~~~~~~~~~~~~~~~~~~~~~~~~
~~~~~~~~~~~~~~~~~~~~~~~~~~~~~~~

Almost Human ~ The First Series
Volume 3: Evolving Ecstasy

Contents

CRRD ஊ CRRD ஊ CRRD ஊ CRRD ஊ CRRD ஊ CRRD ஊ CRRD ஊ CRRD

Part 1 - Ecstasy Unleashed

CRRD ஊ CRRD ஊ CRRD ஊ CRRD ஊ CRRD ஊ CRRD ஊ CRRD ஊ CRRD

Chapter 1 - You'd better

Felicity

Felicity's car
Friday, midnight

Felicity felt like she was on autopilot driving back to Cain's house. Cain was sitting silently beside her. It had been a long night. After sending home their last 'customer', Felicity had quietly questioned Ben. "What are we going to tell Mr. Penten?"

Ben had surveyed the remains of the vampire attack on the store, and shrugged. "We were robbed…by a gang…they were probably on drugs."

"There's no money missing," Felicity had pointed out.

Ben smiled. "That's 'cause I fought them off."

That's when Alyson had started laughing again. "*You* did? You and Felicity, that's your story?"

"It could happen. Anyway, I guess *you* could have been here, but something tells me that *he* won't want to be involved in questioning," he'd said with a gesture towards Cain. Sindy had already slipped out the door.

Cain answered. "I can have been here if you'd like. I've got valid I.D., and you must admit, it would make your story a bit more credible," he'd added with a smirk.

Ben probably hadn't liked the insinuation that no one would believe that he could have done it with only the help of the two girls, but he kept quiet. Felicity had then brought up another problem. "So where do we say all of the ashes came from?"

After a thoughtful moment, Ben had asked, "Got a blow dryer?"

And so, Cain and Felicity had gone back to her room for her hair dryer. Upon leaving the store, they had been very surprised to find Sindy, sitting out front on the curb.

To Felicity, she had looked very frightened and alone, sitting on the edge of the parking lot, hugging her knees and looking out into the dark. It had been very odd to see Sindy that way. She got up immediately at their approach, trying to put on a brave face it had appeared. Felicity tried to picture how it would feel to have to walk out into that darkness alone, and actually felt sort of bad for her. "You need a ride somewhere?"

Both Sindy and Cain had looked very amazed that she would ask, but of course, Sindy hadn't accepted. "Na, I'm good." She'd quickly walked away and Cain hadn't said anything about it.

They'd gotten into the car and then Felicity had turned to Cain. "You have I.D., like a driver's license?"

"Mm-hmmm."

She'd just stared at him for a moment. "I can't really picture you standing in line at the D.M.V." He'd laughed and pulled his license out of his back pocket for her to inspect. She'd held it up in the light from the parking lot lamps. "Who is that?"

He'd laughed again. "It's supposed to be me. I paid someone to go get their picture taken for me. Tell me that there's some resemblance," he'd added hopefully.

She had studied his face and the picture in turns. "I guess. He does look a lot like you, but you're definitely the better looking of the two."

"Thanks." He'd given her a smile and a kiss, and then she looked at the card a moment longer. It was issued in New York, but listed his address as being in a town that she didn't know. The name read: Cain Herald VI, Sex: M, Eyes: Bl, Ht: 5' 11". He must have seen her looking a bit confused. "Something wrong?"

She'd looked up at him tentatively. "It says 'Cain'."

His eyes had turned downcast as he answered quietly, "*Christian* Herald has been dead for about two hundred and ninety years." She must have still looked confused. "Did you expect me to list my date of birth as December 25th, *1664* as well? It's not always easy, trying to live in the 'civilized' world but I've managed. In order to keep possession of the Manor and keep my bank accounts in order, I do have to *die* now and again, on paper that is."

"What's the VI?"

"That's the roman numeral for six. I am actually considered to be my own great, great, great, great grandson. It gets a bit confusing I know. I've figured out how to keep things going pretty smoothly now though.

Every thirty years or so, I have a fictional girlfriend 'give birth' to a new persona, my son and namesake, to whom I am given sole custody. I give him about twenty years to mature, then I die, and he takes over. It's just a bunch of paperwork really, but you'd be amazed what you can accomplish by giving the right amount of money to the right people. There's probably an easier way to go about it, but I prefer to keep things as legal as possible. I don't like to feel as though I'm hiding anything."

She'd glanced at it once more and handed it back for him to put it away. It also read 'DOB: 12 – 25 – 64'. "According to that you're forty-one."

He'd grinned. "I know. I look pretty good for my age don't I? It'll be time for a new one soon. I start at twenty-one and usually let it go until fifty or so. Much past that and I start drawing odd looks. Of course, I try not to use it unless I have to. It serves."

Just then, Allie had startled them by rapping on the window. Cain had rolled it down for her. "You two haven't even left yet? Let's get this over with and then you can get a room." Cain had just shaken his head with a smile as Felicity started the car and Allie went to get into her own.

They had returned with a blow dryer, to find that Allie had gotten hers as well. They did their best to blow all of the ashes out the broken window and door, while Ben used the attachments on the vacuum cleaner to try to clean up behind the counter. They didn't want it to look 'too' cleaned up before they reported the incident, but at least the ashes were scattered around sufficiently, so as not to be noticeable. Then Ben had called the police and Mr. Penten, trying to sound out of breath and distraught.

They spent a good deal of time answering questions and standing around waiting to be allowed to leave. They had all agreed ahead of time as to the exact events of the evening, so that there had been no discrepancies when reporting to the authorities.

Since there was no money missing and only the windows were broken, they weren't very closely questioned anyway. Mr. Penten was none too pleased about having to close for repairs on a Saturday morning, but at least insurance would cover the windows.

They were finally allowed to go their separate ways. Allie and Ben each left in their cars, as Cain and Felicity got into hers. She'd been about to automatically drive to Cain's house, when he'd turned to her. "You'll probably want to go home, to shower and change. I can walk if it's easier."

Felicity had been behaving normally, cleaning up, answering questions; to everyone else, she must have seemed fine, but she felt as though she was in shock, doing things because she had too, but not really thinking about anything but what had happened and what it might mean for the future. Now that it was finally quiet, all she really wanted was to crawl into Cain's bed and be safe in his arms.

Once he'd mentioned it though, she'd realized that a shower would be a very welcome thing. She'd had little bits of slimy mud, and God knows what else smeared on her from her struggling with the last zombie. She had washed her arms in the sink at the DownTime before the police had arrived, but she'd still felt grossly soiled. She had turned to Cain slowly and asked, "Would you come with me...and wait? I wanna go to your house, after."

He'd looked a little concerned, as though just realizing that she might be upset. He'd given her a little smile and said, "Of course luv, whatever you'd like."

She had driven back to her dorm and left Cain in the car while she went in. She had wanted to have him follow, but Maggie had been standing in the doorway, talking with someone. Felicity didn't feel like being questioned as to Cain's presence.

She'd gone to her room and gathered her things for a quick shower. She'd come back to her room after, and found Cain sitting on her bed. He'd gestured to her open window. "I hope you don't mind. Didn't want people to think I was sitting out there casing the place."

She'd just smiled, giving her head a little shake. Cain had busied himself looking through her schoolbooks, as she'd changed into her sheep pajamas and thrown clothes for tomorrow into a bag. She'd then slipped on some socks and sneakers, put on a sweatshirt over her pajamas, and went to give him a kiss. As much as she wanted to just melt into his arms, she gave him only a quick peck on the lips. She didn't want to be here, Cain's felt safer. "See you at the car."

She'd planned to say she was going home for the weekend if asked, but Maggie was gone. Cain was already in the car when she got there. So now, they were driving back to his house. All was quiet, and she was glad. She couldn't talk anymore right now. She just stared at the road and wanted to be there already.

They entered the house and went straight downstairs. She dropped her bag and unzipped her sweatshirt, dropping it to the floor, while eyeing his bed. Cain looked at her thoughtfully. "Tired?" She just nodded her head, took off her shoes and socks, and went to get in the bed. He took off his boots and followed her. He was gazing at her curiously, as she got beneath the covers. "Are you all right?"

She nodded again, but she could feel the tears welling up in her eyes. Cain must have seen them, because he instantly came to her and wrapped her in his arms. "Oh Felicity, it's all right. It's all right now, you're safe." She drew a deep breath and tried not to cry. He must think she was so weak. She didn't know what to say, until he spoke again. "It's all right, it's over now."

She looked up at him, through watery eyes. "No it's not. You heard her. Chris wants *me*. He wants to kill me...or *worse.*"

He seemed a little shaken by the 'worse', but still tried to comfort her. "You know that I will never let you fall into his hands. Don't be afraid, you're safe now."

"But there were so many of them, grabbing at me..."

He looked almost surprised at her. "You've fought far worse. You killed Luke, and that vampire in the cemetery. These tonight were nothing compared to them."

"But they were so, rotten...and awful."

"They may have seemed the stuff of nightmares, but you've seen them before. They are stupid, slow and easily defeated."

"Yeah, for you. I've seen you fight. You're so good at it."

"Unfortunately, I've had a lot of practice."

"Ben killed like four of them! Allie killed one. Even Sindy, did you see her? She was like, *ripping them apart.*"

"She killed two or three," he said with a little shrug.

"I didn't kill any. All I did was hide behind my vial and scream."

Cain leaned back to smile at her. "You are a gentle soul, who shouldn't be expected to engage in such pursuits, but you have a strong spirit, and have done remarkably well in these situations. You shouldn't reproach yourself for not fighting like the others. Ben seems to have 'hating vampires' in his blood, *that* fuels his efforts. Alyson does usually fight well, but she's had formal training, and still you've done just as well as her in the past. Sindy...well, against mindless zombies, she hasn't much to fear. They can scratch and bite at her all they like, but without a stake and the presence of mind to use it properly..." He shook his head. "They can't really hurt *her.*"

"I guess knowing that, would give a person confidence. They all have something to make them feel confident and strong. I don't have anything."

Cain tipped her chin to make her look at him. "You've got me." She tried to smile, but the phrase 'screaming horror flick chick' kept haunting her. She tucked her head back down into his chest for a hug. She loved the fact that Cain made her feel safe, but still, she didn't want to have to run to him every time that danger threatened.

There was a simple solution. Go home. Go back home where danger wouldn't follow, just remove it from her life. It sounded so easy, but she wouldn't do it. If she left, she knew that she would never see Cain again. He was going to take care of all of this and then leave. Somehow, she just knew it. Felicity was unwilling to let him go, not yet.

Holding the vial out in front of her to ward off that zombie had seemed so flimsy and stupid. She wished she'd had the confidence to fight them like Sindy. Sindy didn't seem to be afraid of anything. Well, she was frightened of Chris and Marcus, but who could blame her for that? Chris may not be all that intelligent, but he was smart enough to dust her for real and get Marcus to help him do it, but Sindy sure wasn't scared of much else. What must it be like, to have the assurance of immortality to fall back on?

Something else came to mind, a solution that she had been very carefully avoiding. She could let Cain mark her again. It wouldn't guarantee anything; Chris may still be able to work around it, but she was pretty sure that it would protect her from any lesser vampires he might make. They were driven by instinct. They should have an overwhelming desire to stay away from her, if she were marked.

In fact, she suddenly realized that Ben had that advantage. No wonder he had managed to kill an impressive three zombies and one real vampire, without getting hurt. They were unable to bite him!

Still, she had kept the experience of being marked by Cain, safely hidden away from her conscious mind. It was not something she had ever thought to consider again. It was so much easier to think of Cain as a man, and not someone capable of such strange things.

He was just holding her quietly, trying to make her feel safe. She looked up at him again, trying to 'see' the vampire in him. It just wasn't there for her to see, not now. He smiled at her. "You needn't worry about Chris. I won't let him get to you."

"I know, but he had so many others."

"Whom we killed."

"He can make more."

Cain looked thoughtful. "I suppose it's possible that he kept a few in reserve, but I doubt it. As for making more, we won't give him the time. Creations such as his, take time to reawaken. Unless he uses a considerable amount of care in making more, they will take a week or two to come back. In fact, judging by the condition of some of them, I'd say he made them more than a month ago."

"Yeah, I guess, but he still has *Marcus*. Cain, no offense but I don't even think that *you* could take *him*."

Cain gave her a kiss on the forehead. "Don't you worry about it. For *you*, I'd fight Satan himself. Now get some rest. I'm going to go and take a shower of my own." He hugged her close for another minute and then got up from the bed. At least she felt safe here. She lay there, feeling very comforted just lying snuggled warm in his bed and watching him move about the room.

She admired his body as he undressed. She had to smile remembering that earlier, in her room, he had purposely *not* watched her as she disrobed to change. He was such a gentleman. She'd been glad at the time. He had seen her body often enough in the past week that she shouldn't be self-conscious, but she still *was* a little. Now she noted that he didn't even seem to notice or care if she watched him. Everyone she knew seemed so much more confident than she was, in every way. He shut all the lights, save those behind the bar, and disappeared into the bathroom. As she listened to the water begin to run in the shower, she drifted off to sleep.

~~~~~~~~~~~~~~~~~~~~~~~~~~~~~

Beep-beep-beep. Felicity awoke, thinking that her alarm clock sounded very odd. That's because it was the microwave. Oh yeah, she was at Cain's. She didn't feel as though she could have slept long. It must still be the middle of the night. She opened her eyes and found Cain in the dim light, coming out of the laundry room to go behind the bar. He'd already showered and his hair was mostly dry. He was dressed in a pair of blue pajama pants, nothing else.

He didn't seem to notice that she was awake. Her eyes lingered on his broad, muscular shoulders as he took his cup out of the microwave and turned to lean on the bar. He was reading the newspaper. She lay there, for what seemed like a very long time, just watching him drink from his mug and read. Even in that unassuming pose he seemed so strong and unshakable; handsome and robust, her protector. And yet, he seemed so incredibly normal, like any guy in his pajamas, reading the paper and drinking his morning coffee...only it wasn't coffee.

She knew that there must be blood in the cup. That seemed so strange to her. She realized that he never drank in front of her. He must purposely drink when she was not around. She wondered how much of it he actually had to drink. Where did he get it all from? How could he actually drink that? She could not imagine voluntarily drinking blood; it seemed so nauseating. It was true that his body had been changed to need it, but still. What did it taste like? He didn't actually *like* it, did he? Did it taste good to him now?

He finished what was in the cup, stood there for a moment finishing the page he was reading, and then put down the mug. Felicity closed her eyes. She wasn't sure why, but she knew he was going to look up at her, and she didn't want him to know that she was awake yet. She liked lying there cozy and sleepy, just watching him.

After a moment, she heard him moving around behind the bar again. She opened her eyes to see him take something from the refrigerator. It looked like a Ziploc bag...of blood. He began to pour it carefully into his mug. She leaned up a little on her elbow to see better. She just couldn't believe that he had *blood* in a bag like that, in the refrigerator. Surely it seemed perfectly normal to him, but it was just so odd.

He saw the movement and looked up to see her awake. He seemed a bit startled, and she was very glad that she hadn't made him spill it. He carefully finished pouring, and then closed the bag.

She was still openly watching him with morbid fascination. He just stood there for a moment, looking back at her. She sat up better on the bed. Finally, she had to ask. "Where do you get that?"

He furrowed his brow and seemed to think that she would already know. "The butcher."

Felicity sighed with realization and relief. "Oh, it's *cows'* blood."

Again, Cain seemed a bit confused at her response. "What did you think, that I robbed the red cross?" he asked with a little laugh. He turned and put the cup into the microwave, setting it for a minute. "Actually this is pig's blood, but sometimes it's cow."

Felicity was looking at him very strangely. "You can tell the difference?"

Cain gave her an odd little smile. He seemed amused that they should be having this conversation. "You'd be amazed." She just stared at him for a moment until the microwave beeped. Cain removed his cup, swirled it around a little, turned to face her and took a small sip. It almost seemed to Felicity, that he did it very intentionally, for her to watch; as though it were high time she faced the truth. He was not human, no matter how well he could pretend to be.

She watched him as he drank some more. "I guess it's a lot different from..." she forced herself to say it, *"human blood."*

Cain gave her a weary little smile. "Water and wine my dear. Water and wine."

So weird. How could the same thing taste so different, just because it came from a different source? "So do different people taste different too?" Felicity suddenly shook her head, becoming disgusted with herself. "Ech, why am I even asking you this? This is so morbid."

Cain gave her a sympathetic little laugh. "It's alright; you're allowed to be curious. I won't tell anyone," he added, conspiratorially. Felicity tried to regain her composure and think of something to change the subject, but before she'd the chance, he answered her question. "If you continue to think of it as 'wine', different people are like different vintages, if you will. Some are similar." He eyed her, a bit hesitantly. "Some are very unique." After a moment, he then gave a little laugh. "I suppose you could consider animal blood to be watered down grape juice in comparison."

Cain had never denied her any information that she'd asked after, but she still felt as though this were a very rare and privileged conversation; one only relegated to the middle of the night in a dimly lit room. It was a conversation that she would not have the courage to continue at another time. She decided that if she was going to satisfy her curiosities, she ought to do it now while she still had the courage. "What's it like for you, when you...feed, from a person I mean? Is it just...food?"

By the look on Cain's face, she could tell that he thought she already knew the answer to that. "What do you think?"

She looked away for a moment, biting her lip and remembering when he'd drunk from her. "I think it's...much more," she answered reluctantly.

He seemed glad that she would admit it. "Much, *much* more." Cain took another sip from his cup, but seemed to find it distasteful now.

Felicity nerved herself to repeat the real question. "So what's it like, for you?"

He came out from behind the bar and leaned against it, in front of the bed. It seemed obvious that this was a topic that she had been avoiding all along. "Are you sure this is a can of worms you want opened, luv?"

Felicity's answer was quiet, but insistent. "I want to know."

He sat down on the bed next to her, with his mug still in hand. Its content was so dark it could almost be mistaken for black coffee...almost. Felicity raised her eyes from it to find him watching her inspect the cup with quiet amusement. She fidgeted a little and rested her hand on his leg.

Felicity was very interested in what he had to say, and yet even through that, she could not help but be very physically aware of his body. He was only half dressed and so close to her on the bed. The temptation was great to try to rebury her questions back into her subconscious mind in lieu of other pursuits. Damn the man was sexy!

She kept her eyes on his face, and chased indecent thoughts from her mind. He had lost his little smile and seemed to exude an odd sense of anticipation, over the conversation of blood and his vampire experiences. As though these were things he had been waiting to discuss. Like he could hardly believe she would finally ask, and was unsure how to answer in a way that she would accept and not be frightened of. "It's kind of hard to explain." He took her hand and kissed it. "It's more the kind of thing you have to..." He then, in a bizarre gesture, dipped one of her fingers into the blood in his cup. "Experience."

He was holding her hand in front of her. She looked at her bloody finger then back at him, thinking 'You're crazy if you think I'm going to taste that'. She moved her hand towards his mouth and looked away from him. Cain sucked the blood from her finger, almost as though it should be something seductive.

He leaned forward to make her meet his gaze. "Perhaps my experiences have caused me to view things differently than most, but it *is* only blood. 'Tis not something vile or distasteful really, just a natural thing. It's in all of us, in one way or another. And to both of us, it means life.

The experience of *drinking* it however, from a vampire's point of view, is something not easily relayed. Kind of like trying to describe sex to a virgin," he added with a grin.

Felicity pulled back her hand, trying to keep her mind from the remembrance of losing her virginity to him in the very bed she now sat upon. "Now you're just teasing me."

He stood up with a little laugh. "Good analogy though." He went to put his cup down on the bar. "You must realize that this is not something I have all that much recent experience in." He looked at her with a fond little smile. "But from what I remember from less enlightened days, most feeds were like...a one-night stand. An intense, erotic encounter with someone you barely knew, that culminated in brief, fleeting ecstasy...Then you left them, and moved on." She did not look very kindly upon that description, however accurate it may be.

He took on a gentler tone. "But then I learned to drink *not* to kill...And then I learned to drink *not* for food...Once I drank, for the *experience... That* was something entirely different. You know that I don't drink human blood any longer, not on a regular basis. You also should know that it is an experience like none other, for me, *and* for you.

To drink from a host, for a vampire, is the ultimate experience; just as sex may be for a human being. Sex is *meant* to be pleasing for you. 'Tis procreation, vital to the continuation of human existence and so, the Lord made it enjoyable as well.

While physical love in the human sense, is enjoyable still to the vampire; blood, *that* is true ecstasy, blood is my ensured continuance, as well as being one half of the act of creating another. And so, acquiring blood is pleasurable to my body, as sex is to yours.

In order to assure cooperation from the one whom a vampire chooses to drink from, there is the venom. That ensures that *your* body will find it pleasurable as well.

Now, in the common order of things...in the world of 'predator' and 'prey', you may consider that a 'dirty rotten trick'," he said with a little laugh. He gently eased himself to sit back down on the bed next to her again. "But *ours* is not a *common* relationship, is it?"

Felicity gave him a shy smile and dropped her eyes to the bed sheets. "I think I see where this might be going."

Cain sighed. "It doesn't have to go anywhere, but I must submit that although it's a comparison that *you* haven't the perspective to fully appreciate...having sex without love, a 'one-night stand' if you will, is like drinking from someone...for the blood. I can't say why there should be a difference, but drinking from someone that you truly care for...that experience is like the difference between *having sex,* and *making love."*

He continued cautiously, as though he knew he was moving into tender territory. "Drinking from you, for your mark...Well, I didn't take much. I didn't want to weaken or overly frighten you more than necessary. I never would have hurt you, but...drinking from you..." his voice dropped to the barest whisper, "was beyond *divine.*

I thanked God for my self-control, because nothing less than iron will, could have pulled me from *your* throat that night." He closed his eyes and seemed to breathe in her scent, to help recreate the moment in his mind. There was a moment of uneasy silence between them, as he recalled the experience.

She couldn't bring herself to speak, so *he* asked the unvoiced question that had always lain between them. "That night...we never have spoken of it, not really. *Your* thoughts, impressions, feelings...and fears. To be honest, I've been afraid to ask."

He seemed suddenly so vulnerable and frightened of her response. He was usually so confident, that those times when he did leave himself open to her, so obviously exposed emotionally, it melted her heart.

She gave a small smile and swallowed nervously. How could she possibly call up that memory again and then try to *describe it?* "I don't think I have the words." She took a deep breath and forced herself to dig out the experience from her memories. She closed her eyes and could feel it as though it were happening again; her rapid pulse, the prick and penetration of his fangs into her throat, the swooning dream state, the waves of...

She raised her eyes to his. "It *was...divine."* Her voice trembled with the whispered confession and she felt choked, tears rising to her eyes. She couldn't have said why, except that she had tried not to face it for so long, hidden it away, but she had known it all along of course.

She looked at him silently, her bottom lip slightly quivering. She knew what he wanted. Did she want it too? She would feel comforted to be marked, but that seemed almost an artificial reason. Part of her wanted to relive that experience, she did. She had just been loath to admit it to herself, until now, but another part of her was still afraid.

Not really afraid that he would hurt her; she trusted him. If he said he had sufficient control, she believed him, but she was frightened that to her mind he would no longer be Cain, her safe and comforting rescuer. That he would become...something else. One of *them... a monster.*

Eventually she made a decision. She knew how to decide what she truly wanted, a way to see how she would feel about it. She told him in a quiet, little girl voice, what she needed him to do. "Change for me."

Cain clearly did not like this turn of things. He was obviously worried to frighten her from him. It seemed as though he worried that, if she saw him that way, their relationship would not recover from the development. He answered her in a mumbling sort of voice, avoiding eye contact. "Oh, I don't have to. I can do it at the last second, you wouldn't even know...until you felt it."

Felicity smiled. "What, you're suddenly shy? I want to see."

He tried to shrug it off. "You've seen others."

"Not up close, not like this. And *they're not you,"* she insisted.

Cain looked very reluctant and still had trouble meeting her eyes. "Sure you can handle it?"

Felicity put one finger to his chin to tilt his head to look at her, as he so often did to her. "Guess we'll find out."

Cain fidgeted on the bed next to her. He'd obviously like to decline, but she was determined not to let him. "You sure?" he asked one last time.

She let out an exasperated huff. "Are we going to do this or not?" Without another word, she watched as Cain closed his eyes, seeming to prepare himself mentally, and brought forth...the vampire within.

He didn't change all that much really. It was a bit unsettling to see his cheek bones begin to move of their own accord. It was slight, but she was paying close attention. She noticed the sides of his face seemed to shift upwards a bit, as his upper jawbone seemed to lengthen. To accommodate his fangs, she assumed. He kept his mouth closed, but his face did look subtly different in shape.

Then, he opened his eyes. Felicity had to force herself not to flinch. His eyes...they were a golden yellow color, rich and bright, like marigolds. They each had a long black pupil, like a cat's. It was very disconcerting to see those golden orbs staring out from Cain's face, where his beautiful marine blue eyes used to be.

Felicity stared at him a moment, then hesitantly reached up to brush the hair from his eyes. She let her fingers trail down the side of his face and then gently part his lips, pulling the corner of his upper lip up to one side, to see his fangs. An incredibly sharp and thin gleaming point was there. She quickly pulled her hand away.

She stared into his eyes a moment and then said in disappointed little voice, "I wish your eyes were still blue."

She felt terrible when he looked down, almost ashamed. "What color are they?" he asked.

Now she looked at him with amazed wonder. "Don't you know?"

He gave a little shrug. "A vampire can't see its reflection. I haven't seen myself since I died."

"They're yellow."

He gave her a small nod. "Figured as much. Maribeth's are a very light golden orange, and most of my...offspring's are light as well, but some vampire's have red. Guess it depends on your...lineage." He became increasingly uncomfortable, as she simply stared at him. "Are you done?"

Felicity couldn't help but become indignant. "No." She looked at him for a moment and then slowly leaned forward, to give him a soft, hesitant kiss on the mouth; sweet, deliberate and unrushed. After an initial startled moment, he began to kiss her back and she even bravely let her tongue very briefly enter his mouth. She was vaguely aware of his fangs, but it wasn't distressing really. It was a kiss...from Cain. She then leaned back and looked into his eyes again. "Yes. I mean, whatever...it doesn't matter. It's still you."

Cain stared at her for a moment and then shifted back to his human face. His eyes began to well up with unshed tears as he looked at her in wonder. "Have I ever told you how incredibly in love with you I am?"

She smiled. "I think you may have mentioned it, yeah." They stared into each other's eyes for a moment longer. "Not that it matters, but *this* is definitely a better look for you."

Cain laughed. He was still looking at her in amazement. As though he couldn't quite believe she was still there, and not frightened away from him. Felicity gave him another shy little smile. "Well, we've got some experimenting to do, don't we?"

Cain became flustered, as though embarrassed to ask it of her at this point. "No, I don't need to…"

"You'd *better,*" she said playfully, trying to bring him around to being his normal self again. "Now who's being timid?" He still looked as if he didn't quite believe her. She knew that he really wanted to, but was afraid to give in to his desires, only to find that she would resent him for it. "I'd be safer if I were marked," she reminded him.

When he did not answer, she gently moved her hair to one side and tilted her head slightly, to expose her throat. He needed no further persuasion. Cain began to lean in towards her, when she hesitated and put a hand up to stop him for a moment. "Self-control right? If it's okay with you, I would like to walk out of here with a heartbeat."

Now he smiled. "As you wish, my lady." He leaned in to her and she let him come first to her lips for a kiss, passionate and deep. After a time, once her head was nicely spinning with the venom of his kiss, his lips left her mouth to move down the side of her neck, until he reached almost the very spot where he had bitten her before.

Her heart began to pound, her pulse to race as she anticipated the feel of his teeth at her throat. She tensed for the pain, but it was another kiss he bestowed upon her skin. He placed one kiss after another, until she was beginning to wonder if he would go through with it.

Then she felt the tips of his fangs pierce her flesh. He did it quickly and decisively in one swift bite, hugging her to him closely. So keen were the points of his teeth, that there was only a moment of pain…and then she felt *the venom.*

It was much more prominent to her senses, now that she recognized it for what it was. She could feel the warmth of it spreading from her throat, to move throughout her body. Her limbs felt heavy and the actual bite seemed almost numb.

Cain held her firmly as the dreamy, euphoric haze that often accompanied his kisses now grew into more and enveloped her mind until she felt almost as though she was floating. That's when he began to drink. At first, just a small and almost hesitant tug at her throat. She felt his lips seal over the spot in a gentle kiss, but then, he truly drank. He sucked strongly at her throat and as before, on the night of her first mark, as her blood filled his mouth she heard him issue a low moan of pleasure. It was almost as though she could feel vibrations of it travel through her body, tugging at nerves that ran deep to secret places within her. His sucking felt like a tide of longing, washing over her, again and again; waves of soothing comfort, pleasure and an ever-increasing desire for more.

She gave herself over to the rhythm of it, swooning in his arms and reveling in her surrender, but after only a few moments, she felt him withdraw. He covered the spot with little kisses and licks, and finally pulled back to look upon her face.

She felt dizzy and abandoned, left teetering on a precipice of passion. She tried to clear her mind and opened her eyes. It took a moment to truly focus upon his face. She wanted to ask why he had stopped, but some part of her mind chastised her for her foolishness. Would she have him drink her to death?

After gazing upon her for a moment with eyes once again blue, he leaned forward and she almost wished she could beg for him to return to her throat, but he only kissed the spot once more and then his lips moved to taste and tickle her ear. He kissed and nuzzled her cheek, and whispered, "I could have gone on far longer. I know how much you can safely give, but I thought it best I take things slowly, test the waters. Are you well?"

"Mm-hmm," was all she could manage to utter. She let herself lean against him, her head on his shoulder, but then he leaned her back so that his lips might meet hers. He tempted her with whispering little kisses at first, his tongue darting about her lips with teasing little licks. Finally, she managed to pull herself from her haze sufficiently to wind her hand into the hair at the back of his head to hold him firm for a true kiss. The kiss was long and grew heated until she needed to lie back, longing to feel him over her.

She wanted to be covered and completely permeated with his presence, outside and in. She wanted him to...*own* her. Never a phrase she would have chosen before, but at this moment, it was a basic and carnal need, an apt description.

He left her lips to pull the pants from her legs and just as quickly discard his own. He then climbed back on the bed to straddle her with a leg on either side of her hips. She looked up at him through heavy lidded eyes. He seemed to tower over her, strong and masculine, dominating, and yet she had no fear of him, none. His words from the first time they had made love drifted back to her. 'Have trust, never fear' and she did have perfect trust.

He put his palms flat to her belly, cool and soft upon her skin, and slid them slowly upwards, to cover her breasts beneath the little tank top she wore. He cupped each breast for a gentle squeeze and then sought to find her nipples to lightly pinch and tease.

His hands left her breasts to support her back and sit her up, so that he might pull off the shirt over her head. Once he removed it, she lay back again and he ran his hands over her breasts once more, his fingers lightly rubbing back and forth and drawing little circles around her nipples.

Cain moved his body and parted her thighs, so that his knees could rest on the bed between them; and then moved down so that his lips might cover the nipple of her left breast. He gently suckled her, and her body responded with warm and wet anticipation between her legs, but her breath caught in her throat when she unmistakably felt the tips of his fangs against the plump flesh of her breast. He did not bite her, but hovered there a minute as she held her breath.

He suckled her for a moment more, allowing her to breathe and then looked up to her pleadingly, with his now golden eyes. She was still unused to seeing him this way, but although it caused her heart to pound, she was not really startled or afraid. It was as though she were allowing herself to discover this new side of him now, not as something to fear, but something interesting and new. After a moment's hesitation, she gave him a quick little nod of her head. Let him do what he would, she was beyond worry over such things.

She lay her own head back to the pillow and could not resist but to move her hips against him and press her body to his, although it was only his smooth stomach the downy hair between her legs rubbed against. He sucked upon and kissed her breast a moment more, before piercing it with his bite.

Felicity felt as though the room was spinning and needed to open her eyes to prove it wasn't so. The warmth and comfort of the venom was renewed within her and his suckling upon her breast to draw her blood, was an experience sensual and exquisite. He did not let it go on long though. As he left the bite, she felt the peculiar mixed sensations of the cold air against her skin and the warmth of the venom pulsing beneath.

This time, when he brought his lips to hers for a kiss, it was with a hunger that was passionate and demanding, as she had never felt from him before. It was tinged with the slightly metallic taste of her blood. She kissed him and wrapped her arms around his lower back, silently begging him to consummate their love once more.

The venom still caused her to feel as though she were floating upon a heavenly plane, when the thrust she had awaited tried to bring her to earth. She only felt connected to her body through the hollow ache inside of it that he now filled with his own.

She wrapped her arms and legs around him, trying to anchor herself to the reality of their bodies intertwined. Desperate to be ever closer to him, she held him as though they could meld into one being. He rocked and moved within her slowly but with ever-increasing speed and intensity, until he began to gently impress his teeth to the tender place between her shoulder and throat. They felt flat and even, the teeth of his human self. Again and again, he gave her little play bites alternated with kisses, until she could hardly stand to feel the barrier of skin between them.

In breathless whispers, she begged him, the barest voice that only he could hear. "Please, do it Cain. Drink from me, **more**." The last was more a demand than a plea and it seemed to ignite his fervor. He began to build his movements to a degree that she had never experienced from him; strong, bold and desperate, where he had always been so gentle and patient before.

It drove her wild. She craned her head aside in a needy attempt to force him to drink from her, before orgasm bore her away. He waited only a moment, and then once more sunk his fangs into her willing throat. With his first pull upon her vein, her body's climax caused her to grip and crush herself to him with all of her strength, though her muscles were surely nothing to his. He withdrew his fangs to let out a cry of his own pure pleasure. He held her firmly as she felt his body fill hers with the warmth and magic of his satisfaction and yet again, she was borne away to ecstasy.

When he loosened his hold upon her, and caused his body to leave hers, he let his lips return to her neck, not to bite, but only to gently kiss and suck upon the wound already there. Her muscles slowly untensed and she felt amazingly comforted by his tender attentions to her throat. Slight shivers and aftershocks of pleasure moved through her now and then from her orgasm and the venom within. Gentle sighs escaped her throat until finally he forced himself to leave her wound and find her lips instead. She felt herself in such a dream-state, that she found it hard at first to find the words she wanted to say. After a moment, she managed to tell him, in a whisper, "You don't have to stop."

He let out a low moan that ended in a little a laugh. "Yes...I do." He rolled onto his back and she quickly moved to keep contact with his body. Even to be only pressed against his side was so much better than to be separate. "The venom, it has a decoagulating agent in it."

As if that explained anything. She felt annoyed that he might expect her to actually *think* at a time like this. She had meant to tell him 'The venom's also got my head reeling at the moment. A deco- what?', but all that seemed to come out was a mumbled… "Huh?"

He laughed and sat up next to her. "It keeps the blood flowing freely, so that it won't clot too soon. Not only have I taken just about as much as I should, but we have to make sure it stops bleeding. My licking and kissing you there, only makes things worse."

She could hardly keep her eyes open as she voiced her disappointment. "Mmmm, but it was so...*nice.*"

He laughed at her again as he softly caressed her cheek. "Yes, I think you've had quite enough." He used his finger to stroke the bite once more and then brought it to his mouth to taste. She watched him, dim and fuzzy, beneath her drooping eyelids. He seemed to inspect the wound at her breast without actually touching it, and then drew the sheets up over her body to her shoulders.

She was half-asleep and hadn't even felt him leave the bed, until he returned with a tissue to gently dab her throat once more. She tried to smile at him as he leaned forward to place a kiss upon her forehead. The next she knew, the world was black.

~~~~~~~~~~~~~~~~~~~~~~~~~~~~~

When next Felicity opened her eyes, it was to see Cain putting a paper bag down on the bar. He was dressed and wearing his leather jacket; he must have gone out. She hadn't even heard him leave. His return had awoken her, not from the noise, but from the feelings that his proximity produced. It was a bit startling, yet oddly familiar to recognize that her body was acutely attuned to his now, just as it had been when she was marked the first time, but now it was so much more. The connection was so meaningful now and emotional as well. She found it very reassuring.

Cain's closeness gave her warm shivers and tingles of anticipation upon her skin, making her long for his touch. It was his venom within her. She belonged to him now. She was marked for all vampires to see...as his. He noticed her awake and spoke as he took off his jacket. "Oh good, I was hoping you wouldn't awaken 'til I returned. I hadn't anything to leave you a note."

"Where'd you go?" Her voice sounded oddly thick and groggy to her ears. She cleared her throat and blinked her eyes to clear the haze of sleep, trying to ignore the odd sensations that his nearness produced in her now.

Cain laid his jacket on the bar and smiled at her. "Well, I figured you might be hungry and I haven't got anything here, so I thought I'd do some shopping."

Felicity suddenly realized that she was rather hungry. She rolled onto her side to see him better, without having to sit up. "What'd you get?"

"Now keep in mind, I couldn't go far. I didn't want to leave you for long and it's nearly dawn. There's not much open around here at this hour." With that disclaimer, he began pulling items from the bag, naming them as he placed them on the bar. "Bag of pretzels, Chocolate chip cookies..."

"Ooh, Entenmann's?" she asked.

"Are they any good?" he inquired.

"Are you kidding?" she asked in disbelief. "What else?"

"Milk and orange juice. I didn't know which you'd want. That's it. Oh, and a beef jerky." He gave her an apologetic little shrug.

"Interesting assortment," she said with a laugh.

"I hope it'll do. The gas station doesn't exactly have a large selection. Besides, orange juice and cookies, isn't that what they give out in hospital when you donate blood?" She giggled and he moved to sit next to her on the bed, gently moving the hair away from her face on the pillow.

He very slowly touched his fingertips lightly to her cheek, trailing them gently downward. As when marked before, she was amazed at the electric sensations that his touch caused on her skin. He leaned forward and gave her a tender kiss, which after a moment turned into lots of little kisses with which he smothered her face and neck, making her squirm and giggle. Each one was made into a magic little thrill by the mark upon her. He ended it by nuzzling the side of her throat and giving it a last very deliberate kiss over his bite there. He inspected the spot for a moment and then looked at her with almost bashful concern. "How are you feeling?"

Felicity smiled at him, instantly touched and amused. "Look at you, you're all concerned and worried about me. You're so cute!"

He stood from the bed. "Vampire's are not *cute.*" He moved to behind the bar, crumpled up and threw away the bag.

"Well, *you* are. Relax, I'm fine...see!" To try to prove her point, she sat up far too quickly and suffered a major head rush. "Whoa." She slowly lay back down.

"Uh huh, think I'll bring the cookies to you. Milk or juice?"

"Milk, and I am fine. I just sat up too fast."

He poured her milk into a mug. "M-hmm."

Doubt tried to creep into her mind. "Why? You don't think I need a transfusion or something, do you?"

Cain laughed and then looked a little insulted as he opened the cookie box. "Of course not. I stopped well above what should be your tolerable level of loss. You just need some rest."

He brought her the milk and open cookie box. She smiled and sat up a little as he handed her a cookie. "You're going to serve me?"

"Always and forever if I could," he said with a very serious and genuine look of love, as he sat on the bed.

She held her cookie and snuggled close to him, as she nibbled it. "After last night, forever's soundin' pretty good. I wouldn't mind a forever filled with nights like *that.*" She suddenly dropped the hand with the cookie back down to her lap, to look at Cain in seriousness. "Except for the zombies. I don't much care for zombies."

Cain laughed. "No zombies, got it." He gazed at her as she finished her cookie and took a swig of milk from her mug. He raised his hand to run his fingers through her hair and gave her a kiss on the cheek. She smiled, but then looked down at her lap in thought. "What is it?" he asked.

She shrugged. "Nothing."

He dipped his head to find her eyes with his own. "What are you thinking about, that's taken the smile from your lovely face?"

"I was just remembering...that night at Tommy's. Remember when Sindy called me a dog without a leash? She said I ought to have a license."

Cain shook his head in disgust. "Why do you think of such things now?"

"Well, I didn't really *get* it then of course, but she was talking about me not being marked...right?" Cain acceded with a slight nod of his head. "Like I was your pet or something. I never really thought about what that could mean...until now, but a vampire could do that, couldn't they? Keep someone, like a pet. Someone to...play with, drink from."

"You're not my pet. I don't think of you that way and I'll thank you not to use the term. It's barbaric."

"I'm sorry. I know *you* don't do stuff like that, but others, vampires like Arif; they do, don't they?" He nodded. "*That,* with him, it just seems creepy. But being with you all the time, that doesn't sound bad at all. Call it whatever you want."

He became very uncomfortable and moved away from her a bit on the bed. "Don't talk like that. Is that what you want? To be shut up down here all the time, with nothing to look forward to but me?"

She smiled. "I'm sure you'd let me go out if I were good."

"Stop it. It's not funny. There are those, like Arif, who do that you know. And it's not always a *voluntary* thing.*"

That caused her to shudder. "Sorry, but that's not really what we're talking about here. Why couldn't I just stay with you? Not like a prisoner, but the way things are now. I think I could be very happy, spending all of my nights with you."

"There's one major obstacle there. You're not *like* me."

"So? That's okay. I can accept that now. In fact, right now, that's seeming like a pretty good thing. I may not have enough in me to feed you all the time, but my body is making more even as we speak." She smiled and spread her arms. "I'm a renewable resource."

Cain rolled his eyes and groaned. "Felicity, the fact that I'm a vampire in itself, is not entirely the problem, but think of what that means. You age, while I do not."

"So...what, you don't like old ladies?" she teased.

"Time is valuable for you, when it means almost nothing to me. Unless you were to decide, that a life like mine was what you really wanted...Well unless that were so, then time spent with me, for you...is time wasted, time from your finite and ever advancing life. To spend all of your time with me, what kind of life is that? To not be accomplishing something, not to be actually doing anything of worth; to have no goals, no career, no family, no future; you deserve more than that."

"I could be with you and still have that stuff, a job or whatever."

"You have no idea how difficult it would be. You don't want to spend your life trying to hide me from your friends and family, or to lie and make excuses for me during every daytime event you attend. You shouldn't have to waste all of your energies on living a lie when you should be focused on your future in the real world."

 "All that stuff seems so important to you. I guess it *should* be important to me too, but right now all I can say really matters to me, is being happy. Being with you makes me happy. Doesn't it make you happy too?"

"Oh luv, what a question. You cause my heart to soar like none other before you. I would very happily keep you with me until the end of my time on earth, but it would be at the price of giving up many of your human ties. I don't know that it's not more than you should be willing to pay.

The life that I lead is certainly fulfilling and worthwhile in its own ways. At least I like to think so, even though it is very lonely much of the time. *If* you were to decide that truly, in your heart, you want to share in that with me...Well, I don't know that I *could* ever turn you away, but you are so young! Too young perhaps, to know what you want from life. You need to live, before you can die, or you will forever resent me for it."

"But why can't we just stay together the way that we are now? Things are good."

He smiled sadly. "Good for *me.*"

"You don't think they're good for me too? I love spending my time with you."

"It all goes back to what I said before. It's time wasted. I can keep you selfishly to myself for a small bit of time, but I could never justify more than a little while. Your life is going by. You can't be content just to let it."

He turned to face her more fully on the bed and took her hands into his own. He raised them to his lips, to kiss her fingertips, and then smiled as he gazed into her eyes as he spoke again. "Somewhere, out there in the world, is another man. A human man, and he's just waiting to fall head over heels in love with you; much as I am now."

"I'll never love anyone the way that I love you," she told him certainly, with a pouting voice.

He gave her a sad little smile. "I'd like to agree, but I have lived through love and heartache as you have not. I know it seems that nothing could be stronger than our love *now.* And I do hope that you will keep my love for you in a special place, always remembered in your heart, but you are a loving young lady, and your heart is big enough to love another as well as me. You'll see.

Someday you'll meet another and *his* love for you will overshadow mine. I can't say I look forward to the prospect, but I know it must be true, as he will be able to give you all of the things which I cannot. I could care for your every need surely, but only he could take you for a walk in the sunlight. He can be a part of your life in the world, not I.

He will love you and protect you; treasure your precious heart and make you happy in all of the ways of which I can only dream. You'll have a place in the world, a career, a happy marriage and a family," he said with a broad smile. "Children, lots of them; you'll make a wonderful mother. You should have a real life." He held back unshed tears and tried to smile, as he continued.

"To stay with me might make you happy for a time. We could probably preserve restraint and safeguard your health through my tender drinks, albeit through great difficulty, but the years will pass and one day you'll look back to see that you've nothing. You'll have nothing in your life, but me; nothing accomplished, nothing achieved, nothing to show for your time spent on earth...with death looming ever nearer. You'll become bitter, vengeful and you will either leave me, to be old and alone for the last of your days...or you will then, beg me for the blood. Even if I were to give it to you, you'll be older then. And I will love you still, but how resentful might you be, to be trapped for eternity in a body no longer in the blush of youth? You will hate me for not giving it to you sooner, but if I did give it to you now, how will you ever know of the life you'll have missed?

No, to stay with me is the wrong decision for you to make in either case. No matter how badly I might long for you to make it. I try to tell myself that we could be happy together always, but as you can see, upon closer inspection, all scenarios seem to fall apart. I can't do that to you. I will leave *because* I love you. I won't take your life away or make you waste it with me for my own selfish ends.

I've tried to be firm in the choice from the beginning, but loving you so does cause me to waver now and again, but when the time comes, I *will* leave you. I'm not yet sure when that will be, but it will come sooner than later. And *you* will have to let me go."

He spoke gently and evenly, with a calm that she almost resented, but she knew that he was right. He was a good man trying desperately to do the right thing, though it break their hearts. Somehow, he remained composed, although she could feel the tears gently rolling down her cheeks.

She almost wanted to beat upon his chest, to tell him that it was cruel and unfair, but anything she might say or do seemed only like a waste of their precious time. And so, she only crushed herself to him for an embrace and prayed that he would stay for as long as he could. After a time, he undressed and joined her under the covers. She held him tightly, as though afraid that he might leave her in the night, although she knew that was foolish. He held her as well, and eventually they slept.

~~~~~~~~~~~~~~~~~~~~~~~~~~~~

Felicity glanced at her watch, and then snuggled closer to Cain to give him a kiss on the cheek. He cracked open an eye to look upon her and then closed it again. "Morning!" she happily cooed in his ear. He gave her a weary smile. "Still tired?"

"I'm usually just heading to bed right about now."

"Oh yeah. Sorry."

He opened his eyes again as he smiled at her remorse. "It's alright. I wouldn't let you leave without properly seeing you off."

"I'm not leaving yet."

"Aren't you expected at work?"

"I was on from ten to four, but Mr. Penten said not to come in until twelve. Give them time to fix the windows, I guess. So that means I've got over two hours to kill before I have to get dressed." She snuggled closer to him and let her hands wander beneath the sheets.

He inched away from her a bit and laughed. "Aren't you tired?"

"Uh-uh," she replied with a smile, still seeking to fondle him under the covers.

He playfully pushed her hand away. "My dear girl, your appetites have become insatiable!"

"Aren't yours?"

He chuckled at her. "No, and you should be very thankful they are not. Otherwise we might have quite an unfortunate situation on our hands."

She smiled. "I didn't mean *that* kind of appetite."

"I haven't the strength for either, and neither should you. We've hardly slept and you haven't even had a proper meal since...when? Early dinner yesterday?"

"More like lunch, dinner was just junk from the café."

"See, you should get dressed and go to breakfast before work," he admonished.

"And don't forget, I also ate cookies," she reminded him.

He laughed at her. "You have to rebuild your strength." He gave her a kiss and whispered in her ear. "If you don't prove yourself to be of a responsible nature, I shall be afraid to repeat that magical experience we shared last night. Please don't take that away from me."

She climbed atop him and leaned down for another kiss. "I'm responsible. I'm going to make love with you and still leave myself a whole hour to eat something before work."

He shook his head with a grin. "Insatiable," he muttered.

"Oh *please,* you love it,*"* she insisted playfully.

He did his best to sound very weary and put out. "I suppose I *might* let you have your way with me..." she raised her eyebrows at him and smiled in amusement at his phrasing, "on one condition. This is serious, really."

She made a great show of trying to look dead serious. "What is it?"

"You can't ask for me to drink from you." She smiled and was about to make a taunting remark when he stopped her. "No really, I mean it. You have no idea the effect that has on me. In the heat of things, to have you begging for me to taste your blood... Well, I'm not infallible, you know. It's too soon. I shouldn't drink from you again, not now. So please, don't ask it. Promise?"

She smirked as though enjoying holding even an imaginary bit of power over him. "Okay, I promise, but can I do anything else I want?"

That startled him a bit. "I suppose," he replied with a smile. "What did you want to do?" She just grinned and disappeared beneath the covers.

~~~~~~~~~~~~~~~~~~~~~~~~~~~~

Felicity left Cain with only a half an hour to get some breakfast, but he wasn't complaining. He had teased her though, in saying that she had better not return until nightfall, as he needed time to recuperate. 'Even a man of his hale and hearty constitution needed some rest,' he'd told her.

She arrived at work to find gleaming new windows already in place, and the glass truck just leaving. Mr. Penten was just leaving as well. He told her again that he was glad for her safety, and thanked her for her dedication and level headedness the evening before. She felt like an idiot as she accepted his praise, remembering herself screaming and shoving the vial out in front of herself for safety.

Ashley was already inside, as well as Harold, working the café. The shards of glass had all been swept away and everything looked clean and perfect again. She still couldn't help but picture filthy walking corpses behind the counter though.

Ashley rushed over to her, gushing with tales of Ben's supposed bravery. Ben had done a great deal to keep things under control, rescuing Felicity and Alyson more than once, but to hear Ashley tell it, he'd single handedly fought off an entire gang of thugs. "I knew that girl was trouble," she said with a disapproving shake of her head. "Did you see how short her dress was? Even *I* have more couth than to wear something like *that.*"

About an hour before the end of Felicity's shift, Ashley was off for the day. She stopped at the counter on her way out. "I'm outta here. When are you done?"

"I'm off at four."

"Cool. I have a manicure, and then I'll come back and pick you up to go check out Clarissa's."

? Oh yeah, the costume shop. "Oh, I don't think so."

"Come on. Even if you don't go to the dance, you're going to have to wear something on Halloween, right?" Felicity shrugged, she didn't quite follow that logic. She liked to dress up for Halloween, but without a party to go to, what would be the point? "Besides," Ashley continued, "I need someone to be there when I try on my costume, to make sure it's perfect. Ben doesn't wanna come." Felicity just shrugged again. "I'll be back."

Sure enough, an hour later Ashley was out front ready to drag her to the costume shop. Felicity glanced at her own car and then back at Ashley's. It wouldn't be dark out for almost two hours yet, and it wasn't like she had anything better to do. She got in.

It was a longer drive than she had anticipated, but eventually they arrived. It was also bigger than she'd expected. Felicity looked at the racks of clothes in wonder as they entered. "Wow, this place has a lot of stuff."

"Best costume shop in the county. Probably also the only costume shop in the county, but still...we're lucky they're so close."

"Yeah, only an hour away," Felicity said in sarcasm.

Ashley affected not to notice. "This stuff is high quality, way better than anything you could get at Party City. I think they mostly rent costumes for like playhouses and stuff, but come Halloween they get pretty cleared out. I ordered my costumes months ago."

Felicity looked at the abundance of clothes in amused amazement, and then stopped to look questioningly at Ashley. "Wait a minute. You ordered both for you *and* Ben, right? How could you have ordered them so far ahead of time? You and Ben weren't even dating then."

"Oh I know. I just ordered the uniform in a size to fit the kind of guys I always go with. I do prefer a certain build you know, tall and trim, broad shoulders. Ben's perfect, it'll fit." Felicity still had trouble believing half of the things that came out of this girl's mouth in genuine seriousness.

They had reached the counter, but no one was around. There was a large photo album filled with pictures of costumes. As Felicity began to flip through it, she noticed that many of the pages had pink 'post-its' on them, proclaiming to be sold out, or yellow ones saying 'on hold'. "Wow, yeah. Looks like most of the cheap ones are already taken, unless I want to be 'Harem Girl'."

Ashley came rushing over in distress. "You *cannot* be a harem girl! Then you and I would have the some pants and I do *not* do the twins thing.*"

Felicity grinned in amusement at Ashley's concern. "That's okay. I didn't really want to be a harem girl anyway."

Just then, a guy about their age in a purple pointed hat and sorcerer's robe came out to meet them. "Hello ladies. The Great Wizard Winterfarthing, at your service." He was pretty good looking, under all the velvet. He noticed Ashley's flirtatious smile and gave her one of his own. "You can call me Brad."

Ashley batted her eyes at him for a moment. "Hi there Brad. I'm a special order," she said, handing him her receipt.

"I'll bet you are." He glanced down to read it and then sized up Ashley some more. "Wow, yeah. You'll look great in that. Assuming you'll be wearing the Jeannie outfit, and not the military uniform." She giggled at him and looked at Felicity, who was thumbing through the photo book with an air of boredom. Brad took back Ashley's attention. "So you got a

'Major Nelson' to wear that, or what?"

She smiled. "Well, the position's filled for tomorrow night, but it's not a permanent post."

He raised his eyebrows at her. "That a fact? Well, I'll just get this out, so you can model it for me, make sure it fits well in all the right places." Felicity rolled her eyes as Brad turned his attention to her. "How about you? You a special order too?"

She stared at him for a moment over the book. "No. I'm just here for moral support."

He laughed and then looked down at the book. It was open to a mermaid costume. "Wanna try that on?"

"No, that's okay," she quickly replied.

Ashley came up behind her. "Why not? What's the fun of coming, if you're not even going to try anything? At least try something on."

Brad smiled at her. "I'll get it for you. What size seashells you want?"

"Excuse me?" Felicity asked.

His grin broadened. "The top. Large?"

She blushed and looked back at the costume. It sported a bikini top made of two large seashells. "Yeah, thanks." Brad disappeared into the back and Felicity turned to Ashley. "I am not going to wear that. And I can't believe the way you are flirting with him!"

"What? He's cute!" Ashley insisted defensively.

"So's Ben," Felicity reminded her harshly.

"Oh big deal. A little harmless flirting never hurt anyone. What do you think Ben does when I'm not around? It's not like we agreed not to see other people or anything. What are you going to do, tell on me? Lighten up," Ashley demanded.

Brad returned with the costumes. "Here you are ladies. The dressing rooms are right over here."

When Felicity was reluctant to go, Ashley pushed her into the booth. "Come on. It'll be fun."

She took it all out and tried to make heads or tails of it...literally. She finally figured out how to put it on, but whoa, was it revealing. The scales for the fish tail didn't start until way low on her hips, far below her belly button. And the seashells were definitely made by someone who had a different interpretation of the word 'large' than she did. There was no mirror in the booth though. She'd have to go out to the big mirror to look at it.

"Felicity, are you done? I need help with this zipper." She heard Ashley call from next door.

It was Brad who answered before she could. "Want me to help you out with that?"

She heard Ashley open her door. "Yeah, thanks."

Felicity stayed huddled in the corner of her room, trying to decide if she should just take the thing back off. She heard Brad again from outside the door. "You look fantastic! Your wish is my command."

Ashley giggled. "That's *my* line silly." Felicity almost groaned aloud. "Felicity, come see. Aren't you done yet?"

"I don't think this is going to work for me," Felicity explained.

"Do you need help?" Ashley asked.

"No!" Felicity quickly replied.

"Then come out already!" Ashley insisted.

Felicity sighed, eased open the door and hesitantly stepped out. Brad let out a long low whistle that immediately made her consider going back in. Then she caught sight of herself in the mirror. Wow! She did look very sexy. She looked much better than she would have thought, but it was *too* sexy.

She noticed Ashley's expression in the mirror behind her. She looked a bit put off by Felicity's appearance. In fact, she got the distinct impression that Ashley was afraid that Felicity looked better than she did. That thought was confirmed by Ashley's negative words and attitude. "You look like a fish," she said sarcastically, taking hold of the end of Felicity's tail.

Brad gave Ashley a skeptical smile. "More like a fisherman's wet dream."

Felicity began to blush again, feeling very uncomfortable. "I don't think I can wear this."

Brad suddenly became the enthusiastic salesman. "Sure you can! A few pearls in your hair, maybe a fishnet shawl. You look amazing!"

Ashley shook her head. "No, you're right. It's really not *you.*"

Felicity turned to look at her in amusement and noticed Ashley's outfit. She really did look perfect. "Wow, Ashley you look great."

Ashley smiled, folded her arms and did the blink thing. "I'll have to do my hair of course." She quickly held her hair up, as if in a ponytail high on her head.

Brad smiled. "Better than Barbara Eden."

Felicity nodded. "You're going to look gorgeous. I have to go and take this off." She quickly stepped back into the dressing room.

"You want me to get you something else?" Brad called from outside.

"No, that's okay."

"I thought you looked super, but if you want something a little more...modest, well, we do have lots of other stuff. Maybe something more...elegant?"

That sounded interesting. Felicity peeked out of the dressing room. "Like what?"

Brad thought a moment and then broke into a big smile. "I've got just the thing! What are you, a size twelve?"

She tried not to grimace. "More like a fourteen."

Brad furrowed his brow. "Well, I only have a ten or a twelve, but don't worry, the twelve'll fit. Don't move." He rushed off before Felicity could stop him and she was left standing there behind the door half dressed.

A minute later Brad came back with the most gorgeous gown she had ever seen. "How about the Medieval Princess?" he asked, holding it up proudly. The dress was the deepest royal blue with silver beads and sequins covering the bodice. It had deeply belled sleeves and the skirt was turned back and fastened with silver clips at a slit in the front, to reveal silver and white lace underskirts beneath. It was absolutely breathtaking.

"It's beautiful!" Felicity exclaimed.

Ashley come back out in her regular clothes, took one look at the dress and then looked accusingly at Brad. "That is the most expensive costume in the store."

Felicity's smile wavered. "How much?"

Brad looked hesitant to tell her, not a good sign. "Well, it's $349."

"Three hundred and forty nine dollars!"

"It comes with a head piece." She had obviously lost any notions of buying it. "We do rent it, though. $50 for the whole Halloween weekend, due back on Tuesday morning."

Ashley scoffed at him. "Fifty bucks? Mine cost forty and I get to keep it."

Brad gave her a sly grin. "Yours uses considerably less material." Felicity couldn't keep her eyes off the gown. Brad held it out. "Try it on."

"It'll never fit."

"One way to find out."

She tried it on. She did manage to get the zipper up without a problem, which was a relief, but even without the mirror, she felt as though she were bursting out the top. The bodice was cut to a low square shape in front. She knew from past experience that the shape was usually a flattering neckline on her, but it was cut so *low*. She came out to look in the mirror. Brad bowed low before her, taking off his hat. "My noble lady."

Ashley was standing with her arms crossed. "I'll bet it weighs a ton."

Felicity looked at herself in the mirror and smiled. "Cain calls me that, 'My lady'."

Ashley looked skeptical. "He *does?*'

Felicity smiled and nodded, admiring her reflection. "M-hmmm."

Ashley just rolled her eyes and pouted as Brad asked, "So I take it you've already got a 'Prince Charming' to go along with that?"

She smiled, thinking of Cain seeing her in the dress. "I sure do."

Ashley eyed the dress some more. "Isn't it a little *tight?*"

Brad seemed to sense Felicity's self-doubt creeping in. "No, it's supposed to be like that. Haven't you ever seen a Shakespearean play?" He turned to Felicity reassuringly. "They all wear them like that, I swear. You look exquisite."

She knew he was just trying to sell her the dress, but he was right. It was perfect. "I'll take it."

"Excellent choice, you won't regret it!" Brad went back behind the counter to ring up Ashley's purchase while Felicity went back inside to change. She came back out and joined them at the register, just as Ashley was signing her credit card slip. "Great. Oh and if you could put your phone number on there as well? For business purposes."

Ashley smiled. "Sure, and um, feel free to use it personally any time."

"Thanks, I sure will." He turned to Felicity. "Oh I forgot to mention, there's a twenty dollar deposit on that dress."

Felicity opened her mouth and slumped her shoulders in disbelief. "So it's *seventy* dollars?!"

"Well, you get the twenty back. It's just in case you pop some beads or sequins, you know? It's an expensive gown."

Felicity grumped at him. "I don't think I have enough."

Brad eyed Ashley, standing nearby. "Maybe you could...borrow it?"

They both looked at Ashley hopefully for a minute, until she caved in disgust. "Oh fine, put it on my charge." She dug out her card to give him back for the transaction, as Felicity gave Ashley her fifty.

"Thank you!" When all was said and done, they gathered up their purchases and receipts and bid the Great Wizard Winterfarthing/Brad farewell.

Chapter 2 - And a large chocolate shake

Cain

Cain's house
7:15, Saturday night

Cain paced the upstairs of his home, waiting to feel Felicity. He'd only been joking when he'd told her not to come back until dark. Actually, he'd expected her to get some dinner after work and then bring it to eat here with him. That had been their usual routine for the past week or so, unless they'd plans to go out. It had been full dark for almost an hour and she still was not even within his range. Neither were Chris or Marcus that he could tell, but that wasn't very reassuring. At least if he could feel them nearby, he would know that they were not near Felicity.

He wondered for the tenth time, if he should try to go out and look for her, but he had no idea where she might have gone. He was afraid that if he set out in the wrong direction, he wouldn't feel her approach and they would miss each other, so he continued to pace and worry.

Finally, he felt her presence begin to flicker into range in his mind. She was moving very fast. Good, she was probably in a car. She turned up the drive as he stood awaiting her in the doorway. She smiled, unconcerned as she walked up to meet him. She tried to give him a kiss hello, but he just gave her an admonishing look. "When I told you not to come back until dark, I didn't think you would actually *listen* to me."

She shrugged. "Sorry, I got caught up with Ashley."

"Do you have any idea the danger you've been in? It's been dark for an hour now. How can I protect you if you go putting yourself into harm's way without me?"

Her face fell downcast as she realized his concern. "Oh. Sorry, but I *am* marked now," she added by way of defense.

He stared at her levelly. "It's not nearly the safeguard you think it is. I haven't had the chance to assess just how seriously committed Chris is to all of this vengeance drama. He may not be able to *bite* you, but that's hardly the full extent of his resources. There are a lot of ways to kill someone. Marking is meant for territorial purposes, not true protection. You have to be more careful, really." The last of his words degenerated from scolding rebuke to anxious relief. He pulled her to him for a hug, gratefully soaking in the delicious feel of his mark upon her. He covered her neck with kisses and then held her back to look upon her face. "Don't worry me like that again," he gently scolded.

She smiled. "Sorry."

"Have you eaten?" he asked.

"No, and for somebody who doesn't need food, you sure worry a lot about it. You're always making me eat, I feel like you're fattening the Thanksgiving turkey," she teased. He looked rather alarmed and insulted at the reference, but she tickled him and made him smile. "Relax, it's a joke. In poor taste maybe, but...lighten up. Come on, let's go out to dinner," she insisted, heading back to the car.

He followed. "So what were you doing with Ashley?"

"Oh, she wanted me to go with her to the costume shop, to pick up her outfit for the dance." They ducked to get in the car and she started it up while he watched her in silence. "I was thinking about it some more, the dance...I'd kind of like to go," she said in a quiet, hesitant voice. She looked up to see him staring at her.

He sighed. "I've already told you, I really don't care to attend."

"Oh I know. *You* don't have to go. If you'd really rather stay home, then I'll just go by myself. Ben and Ashley are going, and Karen and Jack will be there."

He still gazed at her levelly. "Because you had such a wonderful time at the last school function you attended?" She gave him an annoyed look. "By all means, don't stay home on my account. You can certainly do as you like. If it's that important to you, go."

She sat sulking at him. "I got a costume,"

He rolled his eyes and shook his head disapprovingly. "I've seen the costumes young ladies wear these days. What did you get? The 'sexy witch', the 'sexy nurse' or the 'sex kitten'?"

She became indignant. "None of the above."

"Don't tell me you got the little red leotard with the devil's horns and the tail on the back?"

"No! If you want to see my costume, you'll have to come to the Masquerade Ball."

He shook his head again. "A lady of your bearing should be above resorting to such coercions. I'm *not going*. Wear what you like." He nodded towards the gearshift. "We ought to get moving, it's getting late and I've got things to do tonight."

Rather than ask his plans, she sulked for a moment more. "It's a princess," she said quietly. She looked up to see his reaction. "My costume, it's a medieval princess."

He smiled at her tenderly. "Well, I rather *like* the sound of that. I'm still not going though. Perhaps you'll come by and show it to me after."

She still looked a bit sulky, but put the car in reverse and pulled out of the driveway. "Where should we go?"

"Better make it take out; I don't want you out here long." He suddenly remembered something with a start. Arif cloaked his lesser minions. He'd said it was simple. It probably was, Cain had just never tried it before. A marked human should be even easier to hide than another vampire. He concentrated on Felicity's mark as they headed for the McDonald's drive-thru. It was such a simple thing, that he didn't need more than one try. He felt a fool for never attempting it before. At least that was one less worry. They were both invisible to Chris now, as long as they were together. He probably couldn't hold it if she left him. They pulled up to the order speaker and Felicity studied the menu. "I'll have a chicken Caesar salad and a diet coke."

He caught her attention after she ordered. "Just a salad?"

"It's a *chicken* Caesar salad."

Cain leaned to address the speaker. "And a large chocolate shake."

Felicity looked at him in annoyance. "I don't want a shake. "

"That's all." Cain told the speaker. He turned to Felicity in amusement. "It's not for you." She smiled in surprise. Very rarely did she ever see him eat or drink anything other than his nightly coffee. "I treat myself now and then. I'm rather fond of them actually."

"Chocolate huh?"

Cain grinned. "Well, I don't think they come in 'Butter Rum Ripple'."

They got their food and headed home. Once they were unpacked and enjoying their purchase at the bar in Cain's room, Felicity asked, "So what are we doing tonight?"

"Not *we*, me. I probably should have mentioned it earlier, but I didn't want an argument. I'll be leaving you for the remainder of the evening." She began to protest but he held up a hand to stop her. "You can wait here if you'd like, but seeing as I haven't got a tele, you might rather spend the evening at the dorm. Have a girls' night and take your mind off things."

"Tele?" she questioned.

"T.V," he clarified with a laugh.

"Where are you going?" she asked.

He turned quietly sober. "I have to go and find Chris."

"But you can't. He hides himself, how would you find him?"

"Chris can hide but Marcus can't, and he's not exactly the 'self sufficient' sort. If I can find Marcus, Chris will be nearby I'm sure." No matter how well Arif had shown Chris how to cloak, Cain was betting Chris wasn't experienced or strong enough mentally to cover himself *and* another...he hoped.

"Cain, **no.** You can't take them both alone, they'll kill you!"

"Well, thanks for the vote of confidence, but I'm not planning to fight them, if it can be avoided."

"Then what are you going to do?" she asked in concern.

"Negotiate," he replied.

She stared at him for a moment. "Something tells me they aren't going to want to talk." She sounded as though she thought him very naive.

Cain smiled. "Not to worry. It's not as though I've never handled hostile negotiations before." He went to his bed to pull something out from underneath. "In fact, that's what this is for." It was a chain mail vest. Bundled in his hand, Felicity couldn't discern its true shape.

"What's that?"

He held it up for her to better see. "Insurance." He put the vest on over his tee shirt. "Can't say I've used it often in the past. I never much worried over the outcome of such confrontations. I've often wondered why I even keep the thing, but now...now I've got you, for no matter how short a time, and I can't say as I'm quite ready to leave this world yet." He then went to the laundry room to find something to put on over the vest.

"But a stake isn't the *only* thing that can kill you," she called to him in concern.

He came back out, wearing a thin blue cashmere sweater. "My dear, if I can't manage to avoid being *beheaded* or *lit on fire*, then I probably deserve whatever happens to me." He modeled his sweater for her. "I don't look too lumpy do I?" She laughed and came to give him a kiss.

She squeezed his biceps, and then brought her hands around and down to squeeze his buttocks as well. "Only in the right places."

He rolled his eyes at her. "Are you going back to the dorm?"

She quickly shook her head. "No. I want to wait for you here."

"It may take me awhile to find them. Chances are I won't be back 'til almost dawn. I think you're better off at the dorm."

"No. I want to be here when you get back. You'd *better* come back."

"No worries." He gave her a kiss and stooped to reach under his bed and add another stake or two to the one he already carried in his boot. His sweater had tight cuffs at the end of the sleeves, perfect to conceal a stake up his right arm, without having it slide out. He put another in his other boot and one in his back pocket. Felicity was watching him nervously. "Time to go."

She followed him to the door, where he turned to ask her one last time, "You sure you wouldn't rather the dorm?" She didn't even answer but gave him a look that told him not to ask again. "Well, I suppose you should be safe enough here. Read whatever you'd like, I've some books and things about. Stay downstairs; I don't want you near the windows. Chris and any he might bring aren't invited, so you should be all right."

He paused as an uncomfortable thought came to mind. Chris wasn't invited, but Sindy was. No one could issue an invitation but the one who resides in a dwelling, so it wasn't as though Sindy could come and then invite Chris in, but he didn't relish the thought of Sindy herself visiting Felicity, even if she weren't behaving dangerously. She probably wouldn't come...he hoped. Still..."I'm locking the door. If Sindy comes 'round, don't let her in."

"Why would *Sindy* come here?"

"She...bothers me now and again. Just send her away. Better yet, don't answer the door. You've no reason to answer it for anyone. I'll be back before dawn. Alright?"

She looked a little doubtful over the Sindy issue, but didn't argue. Maybe it was just his own guilty conscience. He gave her a kiss and locked the open door. "Don't worry; I've been doing this sort of thing since long before you were born. I'll be back."

He left Felicity, closing and checking the door behind him. He then thundered out into the night on his Harley Davidson Motorcycle. He hadn't really much of an idea where to start and just rode circles around town. Chris probably wouldn't stay within his range, unless he had a specific agenda, but Cain didn't want to chance going too far from Felicity, if Chris lay in wait.

After he felt that Chris was almost certainly not local, he headed out further. As he came upon the next town, he sensed a distraction from his objective. Sindy was nearby and quite obvious about it too. He followed her trace until he came to a motor lodge. She was in room #7.

When she didn't answer after the third knock, he briefly revealed his trace. That brought her to the door after only a moment or two. She opened it fully, without fear. Her hair was dripping wet and she wore only a towel. She was clearly happy to see him and he had a hard time keeping the stern face that he'd thought to use. She was so blatantly thrilled at his presence, although she tried to seem nonchalant as she uttered a throaty, 'Hi.'.

"I see the cloaking isn't coming along very well," he admonished.

She became indignant at his accusation. "I was in the *shower.*"

"So? That's the perfect opportunity. What else have you got to concentrate on in there?"

Now she flashed him a mischievous smile. "You might be surprised."

He resolved to remain business-like, refusing to let her bait him. "Can I come in?"

She kept the smile and moved to admit him. "Please do."

He entered the room and shut the door behind him. As he turned back around, her towel was just hitting the floor. He looked away from her body with a sigh. "Can't I shut a door without you losing your clothes?"

She laughed, drawing him to inadvertently look at her and nodded her head towards the bathroom. "Did you wanna join me?"

He shook his head no, doing his best to divert his gaze. She moved a bit closer to him. Finally, he looked up and did allow himself to run his eyes over her graceful form. His gaze rested upon her face and she gave him a sly smile. He kept his eyes focused on her own as he spoke. "If my heart could beat, it would surely be pounding out of my chest about now, to be in the presence of such a..." he ran his eyes over her lithe body once more, for her benefit more than his own, "desirable and tempting seductress." She was obviously pleased, but wary of the catch. She knew that he was flattering her before the fall. "But I must graciously decline."

She didn't take it to heart; she didn't give up so easily either. "Why? I won't tell. She'd never know."

"I would know."

"So? You said yourself she was only good for *temporary* happiness. You gonna let that get in the way of something that could be *real?*"

"Sindy please, I said no. It won't happen again; not while I'm residing here."

"So when are you movin'?"

He laughed, and tried not to stare at her pert breasts. "I don't know. Maybe not for quite some time and it's not as though I'm asking you to wait around for me. Perhaps we shall decide that we're not properly suited to each other anyway."

"So why'd you give me money for this swell room?"

"For your safety. Did you plan to find yourself a cave in the woods?"

She shifted her weight and put her hands on her hips, drawing his eyes there. "Sure you can't be persuaded? Shame to waste a queen size bed."

He smiled and looked at the floor. "Quite sure."

She shrugged, an interesting movement, considering her lack of clothing. "So maybe you're in the mood for something a little more...liquid?"

He tried not to be annoyed, but looked up at her sternly. "Sindy, when are you going to stop throwing body and blood at me for long enough to show me the *person* you are?" She crossed her arms in a huff. "You are worth far more than only what you may *do* for someone." The words had only just left his lips when he quickly looked down, feeling repentant and ashamed. He forced himself to meet her eyes. "I suppose my actions the night we *were* together didn't do much to substantiate that claim, but it *is* true none the less. Do forgive me. My actions that night were deplorable."

She smirked at him. *"Forgive* you? I waited a long time to get you to give me that night."

Cain's shame was surely written upon his face. "All the more reason for you to be disappointed in me, as I am in myself. It shouldn't have been like *that*. I'm sorry."

"So make it up to me. I'm sure you could do better if you tried," she taunted.

"Get dressed." She only stared at him, amused that he thought to give her orders. "I *am* going to make it up to you. After you cover your body, I will teach you to cover your trace." Now she did smile, genuinely. It seemed she would accept his lack of physical attentions, if he really would teach her to cloak. She had been trying so desperately and discouragingly to accomplish it without him, with such limited success. He smiled back at her. "And don't be all night about it, I have other things to do."

She smiled at him again and went to get dressed, before long she had donned one of her little black dresses and was sitting on the bed next to him. She didn't dry her hair, but brushed it out, to dry long and straight down her back. At first, she did attempt once or twice, to caress him and snuggle close, but he very seriously threatened to leave, and she gave up and lay back on the bed next to him, while he remained sitting.

He turned to face her. "Before we start, I have to ask, you haven't seen or spoken to Chris, I gather?" She just shook her head no. He sighed; he really should be out searching for Chris now, but Sindy was an intelligent girl. Once he showed her the way of things, this shouldn't take long.

"Alright. Cloaking. It's not hard to do, for one who's got decent mental control, but it does require great discipline and stamina. First, let's see what we're working with." She gave him an odd, almost insulted look. "What do you think your range is? How far away can you see the mark of another?"

Sindy shrugged and thought about it. "Like...half a mile I guess."

"All right. I want you to sit up, and clear your mind." She looked annoyed that he should make her change position, but did as he asked. She sat facing him, with her legs folded underneath. "Now, take a deep breath and exhale it slowly."

"Why?" she asked.

"Because I said to."

"We don't even need to breathe Cain, what's the point?"

"Would you stop being so difficult! It's to relax you and help you clear your head. I don't suppose you've any experience with yoga?" Cain inquired.

"You're kidding right?" she asked with a smirk.

"All right, come on, we're wasting time. Be quiet and clear your head. Now, I want you to stretch out your senses and describe to me, the first mark you see."

"The lady in the front office," she quickly answered.

"Don't use your superficial knowledge. Tell me what you can sense *only* from the mark. You only assume it's in the office, but you don't *know*. Use your mental image of the surroundings and not your memory. What do you *know*? Study the mark and tell me everything about it."

"Okay. Judging by the low life energy around the mark, I'd say it's someone alone in a building; hardly any plant or animal life immediately around. Based on direction, and the layout of this place, it's got to be the front office." She stopped to open her eyes and see if he would dispute her.

Cain just smiled patiently. "Go on."

Sindy closed her eyes again to continue. Cain knew that most young ones found it very hard to concentrate without closing their eyes to tune out their surroundings, but he was still impressed by Sindy's display of skill thus far. Marks were fairly easy for any vampire to see, but the surrounding life energies were of a different texture to the mind and usually went unnoticed. The fact that she could decipher them would make cloaking that much easier for her. She went on. "The mark is about a week old I'd say, not all that strong. This guy doesn't know how to use his venom. It's Paulie, he was one of my football guys, but even if I didn't know him, I'd say he's not all that powerful and obviously real young."

"Very good. Read me another."

"Cain, reading marks is inherent, basic stuff. Let's move on."

There was only one more mark that would be within her range anyway. "Just read the other, please."

"Fine. It's kind of far away, but I can see it okay. It's weak; the vampire's a real young one. Maybe one of the zombies, 'cause there was hardly any venom but the mark is real fresh, like from two or three nights ago. The mark itself is poorly lit, not a powerful vampire, gotta be a zombie. Happy?"

"Yes. Whether you know it or not, you read very well. What seems basic to you is difficult for some. Some can only tell the age of the vampire by its mark, and not whether they are well made, or the age of the mark itself. I also suspect your range could be a bit further than you think. With practice and control, you might reach further. Now I want you to read me."

"I can't, you're cloaked."

"Then look at where I *ought* to be. What do you see?"

"Nothing." He watched with a smile as she sat with eyes closed, and realization came over her face. "*Nothing!* It's...too blank, like a black spot was put over the area. There is *no* energy there at *all*. That's like...impossible!

You son of bitch! All of this time you've got me thinkin' that I have to shut my light *off*, when I really just needed to cover it up?"

"I never led you to believe that, you came to your own conclusions. You cannot *shut off* your trace unless you cease to exist. No wonder you've been having such difficulty. That's why it's called *cloaking*. You're trying to hide your light, not put it out."

"Well, thanks for the tip. You could have told me that like three months ago."

"Three months ago I couldn't be sure if you'd use the knowledge to sneak up on me and put a stake through my heart."

She smiled. "And now you're sure I won't?"

"Now I am sufficiently sure if you tried, I could take you out first."

"Thanks," she uttered sarcastically.

"Concentrate on creating a blanket. You want to create a blanket of blackness, with which to cover yourself."

"Wait a minute, I have a question. Now that I know the trick, why couldn't I just notice where the blackness is, and know that there's a vampire there?"

"You see it now because I'm sitting right in front of you. If you were any further than a few steps away, my black spot would melt into the scenery. It would be virtually impossible for you to find me mentally, without actually laying eyes upon me. To be honest, most other vampires don't notice other life energies anyway, or the lack thereof; they only notice marks; another testament to your mental prowess. Trust me, it works. Now see if you can do it."

It took her a few minutes to figure out how to begin, and then to cover her trace entirely, but she was fairly clever and with some proper guidance, she quickly got the way of it. In less than ten minutes, she had herself perfectly cloaked. She gave him a shove on the shoulder. "You jerk, this is so easy! You have no idea how I have been freaking over this."

He chuckled. "Creating the cloak is easy; it's holding it that's the trick. I must say, something tells me stamina won't be much of a problem for you." She grinned. "But have you got focused concentration?"

"What do you mean? I can hold it."

"You are doing well, even through a conversation, but what if you're startled or distracted? Holding it throughout the unexpected, that's the clever bit."

She raised her eyebrows. "Try me."

He laughed. "Well it doesn't prove anything if you're expecting me to distract you, now does it? Let's just practice concentration. All right, let's see. What's twelve times twelve?"

She looked at him as though she were asked to speak Greek. "How the hell should I know?"

He laughed and tried to think of something else to ask of her. "I know, recite me 'Mary Had A Little Lamb'."

"You have got to be fucking kidding me. How about an Avril Lavigne song?"

Cain sighed up at the ceiling and then looked back to her face. "Forget it. Just answer me some questions alright? What's your name?"

"Sindy," she answered, looking at him oddly that he should ask.

"Your *full human name.*" She became annoyed. "Come on, what is it?"

"Cynthia Abigail Applebaum," she answered dutifully.

He raised an eyebrow. "Really?"

"Yes. Use it and you'll be missing teeth," she threatened.

He laughed. "Who was your first grade teacher?"

"Ummmm, Mrs. Beltzer."

"Who was your first date?" Cain asked.

"Robert Melman," she answered, after some thought.

"Who was your first kiss?"

"Benjamin Everheart. This isn't a test, you're just being nosy."

"No I'm not. I *should* be trying to fluster you to make you lose concentration."

She gave him an amused stare. "Cain, I have been living with six guys who have like nothing to look forward to in their nights but sex and blood play with me. It's gonna take a little more to fluster me than 'who was your first kiss'. In fact, it might be fun to hear you try, but don't even bother. You *can't* fluster me."

"You are holding your shield rather well, I must say." He briefly entertained the notion of actually trying. Although he always tried to conduct himself as a civil man, he surely *could* ruffle her if he tried. She had no idea, the true extent of his experiences. "Wait a minute, did you say Everheart?"

"Uh-huh, Ben," Sindy answered.

"The Ben that *I* know?" Cain asked incredulously.

"Yeah, so?"

"Nothing I just…I never knew his last name." Cain paused in contemplation before trying to resume the conversation undaunted. "He was your first kiss, huh?" Cain asked non-chalantly.

"Are we done?"

He smiled. It might be fun to shock her with recounted experiences; in the way she was always trying to fluster him, with the pretext of course, of testing her concentration, but no. He had been irresponsible enough in wasting time here. "Actually yes, I believe we are. You're very good at it," he said sincerely.

"Thanks." She actually became flushed with his compliment. He got the impression that she was unused to true praise for anything other than her body.

"Keep it up, *all the time.*" He gave her a confidential little smile. "Even in the shower."

She laughed at him. "Yes sir." He got up from the bed. "You're not leavin' already are ya?"

"Yes," he told her.

"You don't have to. Stay for awhile. I'll be good, if you *really* want me to be."

"You're wavering," Cain informed her.

"What?" she asked in distraction.

"Your shield. Sorry, I have to go. I've got things to take care of."

She quickly hid her trace again. "Goin' to look for Chris huh?"

He nodded. "You know where I might find him?"

She shook her head 'no'. "Sorry. You want back-up?"

He smiled. "No, but thank you. Stay out of trouble." He walked to the door and turned to see her gazing at him in actual concern. "By the way, the lack of 'soot' smeared about your eyes...it's very appealing." He probably shouldn't have said anything, but he couldn't help but let her know.

She stared at him for a moment, as though trying to decide how to take that. "Chris used to do it for me. Said it made me look like a model, from a big Paris fashion show or something." She took her eyes from his, a bit self-consciously.

Cain smiled sweetly at her. "Chris was a fool to cover up such natural beauty." She looked up in surprise, that he would give her such a genuine compliment. "Besides, Paris girls - very snobby, far too thin and not at all appealing...to my eye anyway. Goodnight." He opened the door to leave.

"Be careful." She said it very 'off the cuff', as though she wouldn't really worry for him, but her eyes spoke differently.

"You too." With that, he left her and closed the door.

He spent the remainder of the night searching to no significant end. Now he had less than an hour left before he would need to head home for the dawn, and there had still been no sign of Marcus or Chris. He felt a bit guilty for letting himself get side tracked by Sindy, but the lesson in cloaking had been very valuable to her, and Cain was pleasantly surprised by her show of mental skill. The visit had also helped to ease the shame he had been carrying over the night that she had come to him and he had not turned her away. He was glad that he'd had the chance to apologize properly, anyway.

Still, it was an hour lost, and he still had no idea where Chris might be, or what he could be planning. He had come across others later in the evening though. Two vampire males, younger than he, but hardly newborn. They were in the parking lot of a restaurant, talking to two human women. Cain didn't really know them, but was fairly sure they had been at

Venus, the first night he had spied Arif. He got the distinct impression that they were Arif's men. They had a very slight aura of Arif's trace about their own. Part of his 'guard' Cain supposed. He couldn't see Arif anywhere about, but that meant nothing.

He thought of intervening, surely the ladies were in for more of an evening than they might expect, but he also did not wish to make enemies; he had enough problems at the moment. He sat watching them a moment more, from his bike across the lot. The men were unaware of his presence.

Cain decided that he just could not leave them in good conscience. He entered the restaurant. He carefully inspected the patrons, half-expecting to see Arif among them, but the man was not to be found. After a few minutes of indecision, Cain approached the payphone. He placed an anonymous 911 call to the police. He gave the address and explained that he had seen two women being attacked in the parking lot.

He quickly returned to his motorcycle, hoping he had remained inconspicuous. A casual glance in their direction showed that they were all still talking. It seemed as though one of the men were trying to convince the women to enter his car. He hoped they were wise enough not to be persuaded. He put on the helmet he had purchased for Felicity; to help mask his identity, in case any glanced in his direction. Unfortunately, the Harley Davidson was not known for its 'subtlety'. He flinched as he started the incredibly loud engine and left, not wanting to be there when police arrived.

He told himself he had done all that could be expected. He hoped it wasn't a foolish move on his part. He didn't want to distress the women, but he almost hoped that the vampires did attack them, so that when the police arrived, there would be no suspicion as to why they'd been called.

That event, and the time spent dawdling with Sindy was the extent of his accomplishments for the night. A bit anti-climactic maybe, but at least he had managed to help Sindy out, while successfully declining her propositions. To her, he probably had seemed steadfast as always, easily turning down her advances. Of course, he did love Felicity. He had no desire to disrespect her, and no need to look elsewhere for attention, but he had to admit to himself, that Sindy had piqued his interest far more than he'd expected her to. All the way home, he tried to analyze why. He loved Felicity, truly. It bothered him that Sindy should be able to turn his head, even though he had not submitted to his urges. It had always seemed a much simpler thing to turn Sindy away in the past. Of course, she'd usually been fully clothed, but he'd thought himself strong enough not to let that make a difference.

Finally, he was able to put his finger on it. In the past Sindy had been sure to have him see her in a certain way. She had always tried to appear confident, controlling and invincible. She still kept the habit of projecting that persona most of the time, but he had seen her briefly, here and there, without artifice. It made a big difference in the way he looked at her now. She'd begun to let down her defenses for him now and then. As he had said to her this very evening, when she was not busy trying to ply him with her body or blood, he could see a bit of the *person* she was. When he wasn't busy fighting with her, or avoiding her advances, she could be rather appealing. In simple times like those, he could see a bit of the human girl left in her.

He pulled into his driveway as the sun was beginning to lighten the eastern horizon. The sky was just a lighter shade of dark in that direction, but he could see the coming dawn for what it was. He would have to continue his search for Chris tomorrow night.

The human girl, who bore his mark within, was still far more appealing to him than any other could be. Even as the thought came to his mind, he chided himself for being a fool. As he had told Felicity himself, their love seemed perfect and unequaled now, but he should know better. Someday soon, things would have to change, but for now, he would immerse himself in her affections. Drinking from her had been everything that he had known it would be, and more. To add that dimension to their bed sport had excited and satisfied him better than he could have imagined. For a rare time in his life, he was very content. For this brief time, he felt that he did not have to struggle so hard to fight his vampire nature, and he needn't be lonely as a man either. The physical pleasures that he shared with her now were amazingly rewarding. He could very easily see how others could desire to keep humans this way.

Unfortunately, many of those vampires *used* the human they kept, unsympathetic to anything but their own greedy desires, and then cast them aside when they died of being poorly cared for, or the vampire simply grew weary of them. Cain would never do that to Felicity. He loved her dearly and would treat her with the respect due a queen if he could keep her with him, but no, he knew what the end results of such an arrangement would most likely be. For the hundredth time he tried to convince himself, if things did not go just right...to take a chance with her life like that was unacceptable.

He had been sure to speak firmly and unwaveringly to her about his eventual departure, but truthfully, he could very easily be persuaded to spend all of his nights, loving and drinking from her. The fact that she had professed a desire for the same startled him to realize that the burden really was on him to end it. Even through his disappointment, he had always felt somewhat comforted by the fact that she did not want him to turn her. Knowing she refused to become his true mate was like a safety net. It was not his burden alone to do the right thing. She would not allow otherwise.

The idea of keeping their relationship going on the way things were now had not really seemed an option to him before. He hadn't spoken to Felicity about his past experiences with others such as she, but it was a scenario that he had played out in the past...more than once. He hadn't seen the need to give her specific examples, but there were women he had stayed with far longer than he should have, before they left him or asked to be turned into vampires themselves. It had never ended well, but somewhere, in the back of his mind, he had begun to think that perhaps it could work this time, with Felicity. He was older now, more experienced. He was better able to discern safe limits for their play. If he filled himself mercilessly with animal blood, their relationship could continue safely for a time.

He'd even considered trying to model his relationship with Felicity, after that of Mattie and Alyson. They had kept things going well for *years*, but there were two major differences between his actions and Mattie's that he should be unwilling to change.

First of all, Mattie and Alyson only saw each other for a few weekends a month normally. Sometimes much more infrequently, even not counting this last long separation. In this way, Alyson was in less danger of losing too much blood, becoming anemic or too dependent on the venom. He couldn't be certain all humans suffered strong physical addiction from it, but certainly it was psychologically addictive anyway. So Alyson and Mattie's time spent apart was probably wise to keep her from losing herself to it, but he could never bring himself to be away from Felicity so often. The other problem was one that he had spoken to Felicity about. Her life was going by. Obviously, Allie did date other men while Mattie was away, but Cain knew that none would satisfy her the way that her vampire lover did. Her heart belonged to Mattie and she would be unwilling to truly give it to another, if there were any prospect of his returning.

Cain could not do that to Felicity. It was terribly unfair. If he could not give her the life that she deserved, he should make way for someone who could. That reasoning is what kept him from trying to carry things on the way they were now. It was pleasurable sure, and he certainly was not going to end it before allowing himself to indulge with her in body and blood many more times to file away with his fondest memories, but his time with her was definitely limited.

It was with a heavy heart, thinking of such detestable truths that he entered his home. He felt Felicity's strong and comforting mark, glowing within; downstairs, burning brightly, beckoning him, though she lay quiet and still. He went down to find her, asleep in his bed. Only his bedside lamp was on and she held a book in her hand, fallen aside as she slept. He moved closer to see what she'd been reading. It was the Bible of all things. That made him smile. Perhaps he should be reading it a bit more often himself these days. At least he could feel that his time with her had been *some* sort of good influence.

He gently took the book from her hand and put it aside as she opened her eyes. Yes, reflected there was the love that he'd been eager to see. He gave her a kiss and stood to undress and join her. He hushed her sleepy questions with more kisses as he joined her in the bed. The morning would come soon enough and explanations could wait for later. For now, he just wanted to lie with her safe, warm and loving in his arms.

~~~~~~~~~~~~~~~~~~~~~~~~~~~~~

They eagerly enjoyed each other's attentions until the time came for Felicity to go back to her own room, to get ready for work. He had even allowed himself to drink from her again - although he was very careful not to take much. At first, he had thought to give her another day to recuperate, but she had actually *asked* it of him. Tentative and almost shyly she had asked if enough time had passed. Knowing that it could be safely done, he could hardly disappoint. She had obviously given herself over to admitting her enjoyment of it. It was an absolutely exquisite experience as before.

She asked him once again if he might reconsider attending the Masquerade Ball, but once more, he declined. She was disappointed but he explained that not only was he not interested in the event, he had much more important concerns. He needed to find Chris and extinguish any other thoughts of revenge that might be brewing. If Felicity was determined to attend the dance, then she had better be sure to stay in the company of her friends *at all times*. 'Even in the bathroom' he added, thinking of Ben's experience. She should be sure to have someone walk her to her car as well. He gave her a key to his house, so that she might enter and wait for him if he were not yet home when she returned. "I know you're disappointed, but I really do feel this is for the best. If you can't be persuaded to keep yourself home safe at the dorm, then I do hope that you'll end your evening here. Give me something to look forward to upon my return," he said, coaxing from her a smile.

She agreed to all of his precautions, still insisting that she would go. There was nothing for him to do but let her. It certainly was not his place to forbid it. Of course, he'd the feeling that if he did, she would obey him, but that was not the relationship he wanted. She was an independent and intelligent young lady, only just learning to be confident in her own decisions. She'd been reminded of the dangers. He could only hope that she would use the utmost care. Hopefully, Chris would be busy elsewhere with Cain anyway.

She left him for the day and he tried to get some sleep before sunset approached. He'd an idea that he wanted to follow up with, and would need to leave just as soon as the sun would allow it. When the sun finally did dip below the horizon, Cain immediately set off on his motorcycle. He inspected the parking lot as he drove by the DownTime. Both Felicity and Ben's cars were there. Of course, he could see their marks as well, letting him know that they were both within. He resisted the temptation to stop in and see her as the sensations from her mark grew strong at his approach. His body acknowledged the venom within her and sorely longed to taste her again. He did his best to ignore it and turned his attentions elsewhere.

He checked Tommy's lot as well when he rode by, but there were no familiar cars there. Good. He made his way through the streets until Alyson's house came into view. There was the car he'd been looking for, luck was with him, and she was at home. She looked very surprised to see him at the door. Especially when she looked up to see the brightly colored sunset still blazing in the sky. She stared at him oddly. "Hi. Did you *know* it's not dark yet?"

He laughed. "It's indirect light. The sun has actually set. No danger." She still just stood staring at him in puzzlement. He was a little surprised that she hadn't learned that from Mattie, but something told him that they spent most of their limited time together *inside* the house. "I wanted to speak with you. Would you like to come out?"

She smiled. "We don't have to stay *outside* to talk, Cain. You can come in."

He returned her smile as he entered her apartment. "Thank you." He hadn't wanted to put her in an awkward position, feeling forced to invite him. As he turned to face her, he noticed that she had plastic gloves on her hands. "Have I caught you at a bad time?"

She followed his gaze to the gloves and then took them off. "Oh, no. That's okay. I was just gonna do my hair. Hey, maybe you could help." She laughed at the look he gave her. "Don't worry, I wasn't gonna make you *do* anything. I just wanted your advice." Surely, he still looked rather doubtful. She continued, unconcerned. "See, I'd put lots of extra pink in, for the Homecoming dance, but it was too much pink. So now I added some green streaks, except it wasn't the color I thought it was gonna be...too dark. Anyway, I tried to get it out, but now it just looks like I had an unfortunate encounter with some pool chlorine. So I have to cover it with something else, but if I do any more pink, I might as well just dye my whole head pink. Didn't really wanna do that."

He was staring at her hair throughout and studying the streaks of pink, purple and 'chlorine green' with bewilderment. "What was wrong with *blonde?*"

She chose to ignore him and kept on. "So I've got this multi-color pack. I haven't got much left though, except a few I've never tried. What the heck is chartreuse? Do you know?"

He chuckled. "It's a yellow/green, like what you've got now."

"Oh. Then what's puce?"

"That's a purple color if I'm not mistaken." He studied her hair again. "What happened to the blue?"

"Oh, I took it out. It didn't really go with what I wore to the dance, but it wouldn't come out all the way either. So then I put pink over it, and that's how I got the purple that's in there now."

He laughed and shook his head. She put her hands on her hips and waited for him to meet her gaze again. He looked back up at her, pushing the hair back from his own face. "You should put back the blue. It'll bring out your eyes."

At first, she seemed to think that he was making fun of her, but he nodded reassuringly. She looked thoughtful for a moment and then smiled. "Thanks. I think I have some blue left." She was still looking at him thoughtfully, when she reached forward and swiped *his* hair out of his eyes again. "When's the last time *you* had a haircut?"

He shrugged. "I don't know, March? Actually April...early April. You know, I had come here to talk to you about things other than hair."

"You should let me cut it for you," she offered.

He smiled, eyeing her wildly shorn locks. "Would I come away looking like you?"

She laughed, unoffended. "Even if you did, I guess you wouldn't know it, huh?" she teased. "No, I'm good with guys' styles, really. I do Ben's hair all the time and Mattie's too. I don't have my license or nothin', but I used to work in a hair salon, as an assistant; 'til I turned twenty-one." She shrugged. "Tommy's pays better."

"I can't. I really can't stay."

"You wanted to talk to me. You talk while I snip, it'll take ten minutes." She moved closer to run her hand across the side of his face. It startled him a little, as Felicity was often prone to such familiar gestures, but Alyson did it with a very business-like attitude. "You need a shave too. Unless you're really goin' for the 'gruff and rugged' look. I've got all the stuff in the bathroom. I shave Mattie. He says I've got a nice touch with it."

He shook his head again as she moved to the bathroom for supplies. "That's alright, really. I can shave later at home, but um...perhaps the haircut. If it really won't take long."

"Not at all." She came out with scissors, comb and a smock, and headed for the kitchen. He followed and watched as she dumped her stuff on the table and pulled out a chair to the middle of the floor.

She eyed him appraisingly and then gestured to the sink. "It'll come out better if you let me wet it first."

He sighed. This was probably a stupid waste of time, but Chris and the others wouldn't even be awake yet. They always waited for well past full dark before venturing out. He let her put the apron over him and dutifully leaned over the sink. She spoke as she began to work her fingers through his hair. "You know, you might as well let me put some shampoo and conditioner in it, if we're going this far."

"Do as you like," he mumbled from under the water.

When she was finished, she toweled off his head and had him sit down so she could comb out his hair; otherwise, she'd never reach. He observed her as she moved around him. She was such a petite little thing. Not something he really noticed when dealing with her; she certainly had a large enough personality, but she could hardly be more than 5'2" and was just a thin little slip of a girl. He found himself marveling at how careful Mattie must be to take *any* blood from her. Surely someone so slight hadn't all that much to spare.

She stood in front of him, brushing down and measuring out the bangs in front of his eyes. Now that they were wet, they hung down well past his nose, practically to his mouth. Allie laughed. "It's a wonder you could see! Why d'ya wait so long?"

He smiled. "I haven't got a proper hairdresser in these parts. Do well and I might give *you* the job."

Allie laughed again. "That's a deal. I've seen the way you tip Ben, and you don't even like him much."

"Just do me a favor, nothing fancy or striking. Just shorten it up. I usually take off as much as possible without getting a crew cut and then let it grow until it's in my eyes again."

"Well that's a dumb system," she said with a smirk.

"It's convenient," he insisted.

"It's silly. You don't have to go half a year before your next cut, just come back to me. Trust me, I'm gonna make you look good. Then if you let me give you a trim every six weeks, you won't need a major cut every time."

He became impatient. "Alright whatever, let's just get started already." He gazed at her levelly for a moment as she came before him with the scissors. "I'm trusting you."

She smiled. "Can I go short in the back?"

"If you want. So listen, about this Halloween Masquerade Ball." Allie began combing and cutting as he spoke. "Felicity seems absolutely set upon attending."

"And *you* still don't want to go."

"It's not that I don't want to go." She met his eyes with a smirk. "All right, I *don't* want to, but it's also true that *I can't.* I spent all of last night looking for Chris, with no sign of him anywhere. I can't assume that he's just given up and moved on. Especially when Sindy professes that he's a specific desire to harm Felicity. I need to confront him and convince him that to do so would be seriously against his best interest. I will not rest until I have dealt with him personally."

"Goin' huntin' huh?" He slumped his shoulders. "Don't move!"

"Sorry. *I* don't do things that way. I just want us to have a chance to talk. I know Chris; he's not really a bad sort."

"No? I find it hard to get to know someone when they're clubbing me over the head, or siccing animated corpses on me, so *I* wouldn't know."

"Well, perhaps he hasn't been all that friendly, but think of what *he's* been through; dying young, without properly being given a choice, having to take orders from Sindy and be treated as some sort of slave. And now with what happened to Luke...losing a close friend is a terrible thing, but he must be made to realize that what he does now cannot bring Luke back. Punishing Felicity or Sindy for past hurts can accomplish nothing. It will only make him enemies, and I am an enemy that he does not want, I can assure you.

He needs a sympathetic ear and to be helped to move past it. I know that he is capable of being far more of a man than Sindy ever gave him credit for. I want to help him to shake off the past, rise above it and begin anew. He needs to leave here and start a new life."

Alyson seemed doubtful of his confidence in Chris' ability to change. "To do what? Live like you? I don't think someone like him has it in them."

"And who are you and I to judge? I won't let him destroy those in his path, to be sure, but if he can manage to live in peace, let him be. He needs a chance to be the man that he never could while under Sindy's shadow. It is his choice what sort of man that will be. If he can find a life that will make him happy without hurting others, that will be a satisfaction far greater than killing these here now. That is what I must make him understand. And of course, I must warn him, that killing Felicity, or even Sindy for that matter, is not an option for him anyway. If he chooses to continue that fight, it will be against me. And he will not win. He should let it go, leave here and start a new life, one without such anger and hatred. I've shown him ways in which he might live without such strife. He must have paid *some* attention."

Alyson stood in front of him for a minute, looking at his face or his hair, he couldn't really tell. "You've got a big heart." He shrugged. "Don't let it get you killed."

"I'll try." He glanced down at the floor. "There's a bloody lot of hair down there."

"Relax. You're gonna look great. Just stay still. I'm not done. So what does any of this have to do with me?"

"Well, I did have a bit of a favor to ask...since I really will be preoccupied, dealing with Chris and all, I can't attend the dance."

"So?" She seemed to know what was coming next.

"So, it still worries me to be so far from Felicity. Even if I've got Chris out of the way, so that he isn't a threat. Look at what happened last time. I can't chance such a disaster again. What if he's got allies, who might try to take her while I'm not there?"

"Cain, I don't wanna go. Besides, what am I supposed to do?"

"I don't expect you to *do* anything. In fact, I would very much prefer that you stay *out* of trouble, but I would feel so much more at ease if I knew that you and Felicity were keeping an eye on each other. I worry for you both so."

"What are you worried about me for?"

"You're all alone. Do you think Mattie would ever forgive me if something happened to you right under my nose?"

"I can take care of myself," she informed him.

"Good, be a dear and take care of Felicity for me as well? Who else can I trust? I don't want you to try to fight anyone for me. Just keep aware of things and keep yourselves out of trouble. Please?"

"Well..." She backed away a bit and then moved to brush her fingers through his hair. "Look at you. How can I say 'no' to such hottie? Alright, I'll go. You're all done. Wow, you do look really hot"

He smirked at her. "That big a difference, eh?"

She chuckled. "You looked good before, but now..." she played with his hair a bit more, "even better. I wish you could see yourself. I'm *good.*"

He laughed and ran his fingers through his hair. It fell down to just above his eyes. "It's still rather long in the front isn't it?"

She put it back as it was and brushed his hand away. "No, it's perfect."

"It'll be in my face again before long," he complained.

"*It's sexy,* leave it alone. It was so long before, how can you even tell? Trust me, it looks good." She took the smock off him and then got out a broom for the floor. As she began sweeping up, he took his wallet out, to see what he could give her. She saw his intent and held up a hand. "Na, first one's on me. You look great. Felicity is gonna flip, although...all that stubble kind of ruins the effect." She put her hand on his chest, as if to keep him in the chair. "Stay." She rushed into the bathroom and came back out with shaving supplies.

"That's really not necessary." He eyed the long straight razor she took out. "You sure you know how to use that thing?"

Alyson gave him a sly grin and struck a pose with her arm raised high in the air. "Are you kidding? At last, my arm is complete again," she quoted.

Cain rolled his eyes at the obvious reference. "I never much cared for Sweeney Todd."

"Relax. It's not like I'm gonna take your head off. You'll survive."

He laughed. "Thanks, very reassuring. You'll go to the dance with her for me?" He allowed her to lather him up with shaving lotion.

"Yeah, don't worry; I'll stick to her like glue. No problem. In fact, I'll tell her I need a ride. That way, she can't ditch me." He couldn't answer, as she had begun to carefully shave him and he didn't want to move. Actually, it kind of felt nice to be fussed over, and she did seem to know what she was doing. It didn't take long. "There you go. Not a knick. You look much better, trust me."

He flashed her another smile. "You have my gratitude. Perhaps I'll see you later. If she doesn't want to return here with you, feel free to join her at my house if you like; or the dorms. Not that you *have* to spend the whole night, but if you don't mind, I'd feel better if you stay together 'til I return."

Allie looked confused. "Shouldn't we pick a place to meet? How are you gonna catch up with us if you don't even know where we'll be?"

He dropped his eyes a moment, though why he should care what Alyson would think, he couldn't say. "I'll find her. She's marked."

"Oh." She stood silent for a moment, and then backed away for Cain to rise from the chair. "Well, it took a *little* longer than ten minutes, but if you could see yourself, you'd agree that it was well worth it." He met her eyes almost shyly, and nodded thanks. "While you're out looking for Chris...Well, you'll keep an eye out for Mattie, right?"

"Of course, but something tells me that when he does come, it's straight *here* he'll be headed."

She looked at him accusingly. "And now I have to spend my night at this dumb dance. If he comes while I'm gone, I'm gonna be pissed."

"Odds are, he won't, but if I see him, I'll tell him to meet you there. I'd better get going. It's full dark by now." He paused once more by the door before leaving. "Thank you."

Allie shrugged. "What are friends for?"

Chapter 3 - Loyalties

Felicity

Alyson's house
9:00, Sunday night

Felicity sat in the driveway at Alyson's and beeped the horn for the third time. Finally, Allie emerged and turned to close and lock the door behind her. She looked as though she were dressed in a regular sweatshirt and jeans. As Allie entered the car, she seemed very impressed by Felicity's gown, but wasn't given time to say anything before Felicity verbally pounced on her. "Allie, where's your costume?"

"I'm wearin' it."

"No you're not. Allie, you said you were dressing up!"

"I did...see." Allie had cut the collar off of her sweatshirt, to widen the neckline. Now she tilted her head to show off the two perfect red dots she had painted on her throat.

Felicity became annoyed. "That is not a costume."

"Sure it is. Isn't it obvious? I'm a vampire victim. I was gonna go with a more gory/open wound sort of look, but I decided to be authentic instead."

"You should have been the cat. Why'd you change your mind anyway? I thought you didn't wanna come."

"Yeah well, what else have I got to do? Besides, I thought it might be fun to hang out and make fun of everybody else's lame costumes. Speaking of costumes, what are you supposed to be, besides *beautiful?!*"

Felicity smiled at the compliment and adjusted her headpiece. It was a little crescent shaped sort of velvet hat that was open to her hair at the top like a crown, with a veil hanging down the back. Felicity had been very pleased when she managed to use the hair comb Cain had given her, tucked into her hair at the base of the veil in the back. "I'm a medieval princess. Do I look good?"

"Let's put it this way, I know Cain hasn't seen you. 'Cause if he did, I don't think he could've pulled himself away! Girl, you are gorgeous!"

Felicity smiled, excited over speculation of Cain's reaction to her costume. "You think? I wish he had come. Why are guys so stubborn?" she asked in disappointment, as she pulled out of Allie's driveway.

"Come on, he's out there trying to take you off of Chris' most wanted list. Give the guy a break. He's only trying to make the world safe for human kind. Don't be so hard on him."

"He didn't wanna come anyway. Wait a minute, how do you know what he's doing?"

Allie shrugged. "I just figured..."

"Uh-huh. And what was wrong with your car again?" Allie was just staring out the window. "Nothing, right? Cain told you to come with me didn't he? I don't need a babysitter."

"I'm not a babysitter. We were just talking, and Cain thought you could use some company. You're supposed to keep an eye on me too. We'll watch each other's backs. That's what friends do. You are like my only girlfriend you know."

"You've said that before. You know, you'd probably have more friends if you weren't so abrasive all the time."

"I do that on purpose, I'm selective. If they can't survive the screening process, they're not worth my time. Who needs a bunch of fake friends anyway?"

Felicity shook her head at Allie's odd logic, but then her jaw dropped as she pulled into the parking lot in front of the school. The entire entrance to the building had been covered in a false facade, made to look like a haunted castle. It had painted 'crumbling' brickwork, complete with cracks. There were even false windows, lit from behind and sporting shadows of spooky figures within. It was amazing!

Felicity parked the car, and she and Alyson got out approaching the castle. Felicity turned to Allie with open-mouthed awe. "Wow."

Allie tried to act unimpressed. "Not bad." Felicity just smiled, and they made their way to the entrance. In front of the actual doors, a giant 'draw-bridge' of plywood had been laid across the sidewalk, 'lowered' by chains attached to the building. The glow from the street lights revealed that day-glow colored chalk had been used to draw the 'moat' on both sides of the bridge over the sidewalk, in beautiful swirls of bright blue and aquamarine. A multi-colored and dangerous looking moat monster had even been drawn. They crossed the bridge into the entryway, which was flanked by two large and appropriately hideous stone gargoyles. Once inside, they paid their entrance fee to a robed and hooded ghoul, who motioned for them to drop it into a smoking cauldron.

The ballroom itself was decorated as well, with cobwebs, spiders and bats hung from every available surface. An eerie mist enveloped their feet, but rather than the spooky sounds one might expect to hear, it was dance music that accompanied them as they entered. After taking a few moments to check out the many costumed guests, Felicity spotted Karen and Jack. She sized up their costumes as she approached.

Karen looked very cute, dressed as a 'roaring 20's' flapper, complete with a feathered headband and mini dress covered in fringe. Jack wore a pinstriped suit, fedora hat and toted a big plastic machine gun. Felicity and Alyson said their 'hellos' and complimented their outfits. Karen positively gushed over Felicity's gown. "You look so amazing! Are you here alone?" she asked in disbelief, looking around for evidence of Felicity's date.

Felicity and Allie shared a glance. "No. I'm here with Alyson."

"Oh, yeah, but I meant like, don't you have a date?"

"No, we're keeping each other company tonight. Our boyfriends couldn't make it." She had to smile at the word boyfriend. It sounded so strange and inadequate applied to Cain. What she and Cain shared was *so* intimate and indescribable. She was sure that Alyson felt the same about what she had with Mattie. *Boyfriend* just didn't cut it.

Karen gave her a sympathetic smile. "You are so daring. I could never come to something like this *alone.*"

Felicity and Alyson shared another amused look as Alyson mumbled. "It's not *really* 1920 hon." Felicity considered reminding Karen that they were not alone, but had each other; and maybe even mentioning that she had planned to come alone in the first place. However, Karen wasn't even paying attention to her anymore.

When Karen finally did turn to her again, it was to point out another couple on the dance floor. Todd and Brenda were dancing nearby, gazing into each other's eyes and completely oblivious to their onlookers. They were dressed as Captain America and Wonder Woman, as promised, and they did look like a picture perfect couple.

"Aren't they just adorable?" Karen asked. "Jack and I have been hanging out with them a lot since Homecoming, and they are just so cute together!"

Felicity hardly spared them another glance. That should be her and Cain dancing and sharing whispered secrets on the dance floor. How depressing. Why did she bother to come without him anyway? "Very cute. I'm going to get a drink." She turned to find Allie eager to follow.

They made it about halfway to the refreshment table when Allie stopped her to say, "Look, there's Ben."

Felicity followed her gaze to find 'Major Nelson' dancing with 'Jeannie' not too far away. Ben wasn't facing Felicity and Allie, and Ashley hadn't noticed them. Felicity could tell that Allie was eager to make her way over there. "Why don't you go say 'hi'? I'll get us drinks and be there in a minute."

"Great." Alyson left to meet Ben while Felicity continued to the refreshments. She ladled out cups of punch for her and Allie, from a cauldron of 'Witches Brew'. As she did, she eyed the odd assortment of snacks assembled there. Among the usual chips and pretzels, there were adorable little 'mummy' hot dogs, wrapped in strips of bread dough with little dotted mustard eyes peeking out, baked potato ghosts were cut in half and painted white with sour cream, and even had little 'O' shaped chives for eyes and mouth. There were munchkin donuts with spider legs and cups of pudding and cookie crumb dirt, inhabited by gummy worms. It was a very eclectic but Halloween worthy assortment.

She took their drinks and joined Ben and Ashley, who had just begun talking to Allie. They still hadn't noticed Felicity. Allie seemed to speak louder for Felicity to hear, upon her approach. "I know, I wasn't gonna come, but then I got an invitation from someone I just couldn't refuse."

Ashley spoke up before Ben could respond. "So where's your date?"

Allie smiled. "Getting me a drink."

Felicity had stopped just behind Ben, and could hear his voice begin to falter as he asked, "Who are you here with?"

"A friend of yours," Allie answered smugly.

That's when she realized what Allie was doing. Ben knew that Allie was eagerly awaiting Mattie's return. Alyson had not been seeing anyone else, in anticipation of his arrival. If she said she had a date, Ben would probably assume that it was his deceased friend. Considering the trepidation with which Ben thought of seeing Mattie again, Felicity decided it seemed rather cruel. She wouldn't let it go on any longer. Felicity leaned lightly over Ben's shoulder and whispered with a loud huff of air, "Boo!"

Ben jumped and spun around, almost making Felicity spill the drinks. She laughed and handed Allie her cup. Felicity then gave Ben a very tender and serious look as she said quietly, *"I'm* Allie's date for the evening."

Ben just stood there, staring at her and apparently trying to calm his racing heart. Felicity eyed him up and down, and then turned to Ashley. "You were right, Ashley. He *does* look dashing."

Ashley only smiled, but Ben seemed to find his voice. "So do you. I mean, you're not *dashing*. You're great. I mean, you look great."

"Thanks."

Ashley spoke up loudly. "I feel bad for you. It must be like a million degrees under all of those skirts. Aren't you roasting in there? Most of the people here are much more lightly dressed, so I know the committee's keeping the heat up pretty high."

Allie took in Ashley's mostly sheer costume with an arched brow. "Maybe people wouldn't be cold if they were actually wearing clothes."

"And what are you supposed to be, 'white trash'?"

Allie smirked at her and pulled her shirt collar aside as she tilted her head to expose her 'bite'. "I'm a vampire victim. Or as Ben so quaintly puts it...a blood whore," she answered, aiming a sweet smile at Benjamin.

Ashley looked disgusted. "Come on Ben, let's go dance." Ben had blanched at Allie's statement, and looked more than happy to be led back onto the dance floor.

After watching them go, Felicity turned to Alyson. "You only dressed like that to bait him didn't you? Why are you giving him a hard time? You know how unsettled he is about the whole 'Mattie' thing."

"If I don't keep shoving it in his face, he'll just try to ignore it forever. Ben does that. Like if he doesn't acknowledge stuff, it'll just go away. If he's gonna stay in my life, he's gonna have to get a grip. I can't go back to hiding stuff anymore.

That's what he wants you know. If I won't stop seeing Mattie, then Ben would like me to do it behind his back. That way he can go back to pretending that Mattie doesn't exist anymore. How can someone I love so dearly, be so dumb?"

"I think we all have stuff that we're dumb about. It's just hard to recognize the dumb stuff when it's your own. I mean, look at *us*. *We're* in love with *dead* guys. How dumb are we?"

Alyson just nodded her head towards Todd and Brenda. "If loving a dead guy's so dumb, than why aren't *you* over there dancing with Captain America?"

Felicity watched them dancing for a moment, and then scanned the crowd. There were plenty of good-looking young guys in the room, but not one of them could hold a candle to Cain in her eyes right now. She couldn't help but remember what she had said to her friend Deidre...Cain was going to leave some pretty big shoes to fill. She looked back to Allie, feeling a bit depressed. "I don't know. 'Cause I'm dumb. You wanna go find somewhere to sit? I don't feel much like dancing."

"Yeah, okay." Allie did not seem very happy to have made her point. They made their way to a table and sat down, not far from two guys dressed as The Mummy, and Frankenstein's monster. The guys looked them over and then asked them to dance. Felicity politely declined to her large green prospective partner. Alyson was a little more blatant about her refusal. She made an unfavorable visual appraisal of the guy dressed as 'The Mummy', and answered "No thanks. I don't like surprises." Felicity shot her a disapproving look as the guys walked away dejectedly. "Well I'm sorry, but just *how ugly* do you have to be to want to cover your face in bandages for a social event?" Allie asked.

Felicity tried not to laugh as she looked back out into the crowd. Her eyes found Ben and Ashley dancing again. Funny, they were dancing together, but neither of them seemed to be paying any attention to the other. Ben was just sort of staring out into space. Meanwhile, Ashley looked to be putting on a show for everyone around her more than she noticed Ben, even though he did look very handsome in his uniform. It was so unlike the way that Todd and Brenda were dancing. *Their* actions reminded Felicity of how she had felt dancing with Cain at Tommy's on that first night that seemed so long ago. It had felt as though they were in their own private world. How hard was that to find with someone? Looking around the room, it seemed depressingly rare.

Felicity watched Ben and Ashley for a few more minutes before turning to speak to Alyson. "Does Ben really do that, ignore stuff? He usually seems like a pretty straight forward and sensible guy."

"He is, as long as it's not about him, or anybody he cares about."

"Well, I think all guys are like that to a certain extent."

"No, Ben is bad. I mean, it took forever for me to get him to believe in vampires," Alyson insisted.

"Allie, be fair. Until I'd seen them, I wouldn't have believed you either," Felicity admitted.

"But Ben is my best friend. He should have taken my word for it. It took years," Allie explained.

"*Years?* How old were you when you first saw one?"

"Eleven. Never forget it. Fucked up my whole life," Allie said.

"Wow. What happened?" Felicity asked.

"I was going to the library with my mom," Allie began.

"You never talk about your family," Felicity observed.

"Yeah, there's a good reason for that. 'Cause they suck. My mom is a total bitch. My dad left us when I was nine, and I have a little brother, Henry, but he's a dick. That's why when they moved, I didn't. That was when I was eighteen, never regretted it.

So anyway, I think it was November. Yeah, it was after daylight savings, 'cause it was only dinner time and it was already dark out. So, it was just my mom and I; I think Henry was at Cub Scouts, and we were goin' to the library. You know, the little one over on Church Street."

"Oh, the one with the cobblestone and the slate roof? It's so cute."

"That's the one. It used to be a church you know. That's how they named the street. Somewhere along the way, it got turned into a library. Anyway, my mom used to work for a publishing company. She was like a fact checker or some shit, you know, before the Internet. So we're goin' to the library, and I'm helpin' my mom carry this shitload of books.

Now, not too long before, this new guy had shown up in town. A real slicker, always in a suit and drivin' a fancy car. He bought this real big house over on Wilshire. It's not there anymore, it burned down, but you should have seen it; the thing was huge, like a fucking mansion. So a guy like *that* in a town like *this* attracts some attention, you know?

So this guy just happens to pull into the lot at the library same time as us. And as we're walkin' to the door, he comes rushing over to give my mom a hand. My mom's kinda hot, and after my dad left, she started dressin' like a real slut. I mean, there's snow on the ground, and she's wearin' a short coat with a mini skirt and freakin' 5-inch heels." Allie shook her head in disgust. "So he's helpin' carry books and he goes to open the door for us, and I just happened to be looking at his face when the guy freaked. I mean he jerks his hand away from the door and drops all the books and his eyes...they turned red. I swear, the guy was looking right at me and I saw his eyes turn totally red."

Allie sounded almost desperate, as though she thought Felicity would question it. "I believe you."

"You're the only one," Alyson informed her.

"What happened?" Felicity asked.

"Well, my mom's all concerned for the guy, and I'm just standin' there in shock. I was totally convinced that I was standin' next to The Devil himself. That's when I dropped all *my* books. So now my mom's all pissed, callin' me a klutz and wantin' to know what my problem is."

"What did you say?" Felicity prompted.

"I couldn't say anything, it's like I just froze. So the guy tells my mom that he got stung by a bee. How lame is that? It's mid-November! And my ditz mom believes him and yells at me to start picking up books."

"So then what happened?"

"Nothin' really. We picked everything up and went inside. The guy didn't come in though. Said he was gonna go put somethin' on his hand, but as we were leavin', I stopped to check out the doorknobs. They're real old, original with the building. They're like brass with all these intricate designs worked all over them. Right in the middle of each one, is a cross. I swear. They're still there; you can go see them for yourself."

"Allie, I believe you," Felicity assured her.

"Later that night, my mom's on the phone with some friend of hers, goin' on about how great this guy is. So I felt like I had to tell her. I mean, the last thing I needed was Satan for a step-dad. So I told her."

Felicity prompted her again, "And?"

"And, she thought I was insane. I was all worked up about it, but she told me to shut-up tellin' her such lies. We didn't see him again and I don't know if I would've said anything else, but then the nightmares started.

Every night, I'd wake up screamin' that The Devil was comin' for me. Stupid nightmares. When my mom tried to tell me to forget them, I'd bring up that guy again. Never did know his name.

So finally, my mom takes me to see some jerk-off psychiatrist. I tell him the story, and he tells my mom that I'm having 'father replacement' issues. Unbelievable."

"That was it?" Felicity inquired.

"I wish. Couple of weeks later we're at the Christmas Parade over in Walton. My brother was on the Cub Scout float. So the guy...he's there, standin' right on the side of the road, with all the regular people! I was already in so much trouble because of this jerk, and then he has the nerve to come over and start hitting on my mom, again! Can you believe it?! There was no way I was just gonna stand there and let that fly."

"What did you do?" Felicity asked uneasily.

"I stood right up to the guy, and I told him that I knew his secret. I told everyone loud and clear that this guy was a demon straight from Hell. I said he'd better stay away from me and my mom or I'd pray that God himself would strike him down with lightning."

"You said that?" Felicity asked in disbelief.

"Uh-huh. Maybe it wasn't the brightest thing to do, but I was only eleven. I wasn't really scared he'd *do* anything, we were in a crowd of people and it'd only prove me right. Still, I thought I was pretty brave. My mom on the other hand, thought I was pretty psycho. That's when she sent me away to Hutchins School."

"What's that?"

"It's a school for troubled kids who need repeat psychiatric evaluations and treatment. Sounds fun doesn't it? That's where *I* spent the second half of sixth grade."

"Oh Allie, that sucks."

"Tell me about it. When they let me come home for the summer, it was Ben who convinced me I should stop talkin' about it all. They all knew, Ben, Mattie, and David. Mattie and Davy said they believed me, but I know they didn't, not really. Ben didn't even try to pretend.

He told me that it didn't matter what I *thought* I saw, 'cause grown-ups just *didn't* believe kids about stuff like that. So I should just keep quiet and try to forget it already, so they wouldn't send me away again.

He was right. Still, I didn't really care if everybody else thought I was crazy, but the guys...knowing that my best friends thought that too, *that* hurt. Ben should have at least tried to believe me. I was closer to him than anybody else in my life, and I don't think the thought ever even crossed his mind that I might be telling the truth. That hurt.

Sure enough, I shut-up and they didn't send me back. I still had nightmares sometimes, but my mom just told me that I'd better figure out how to deal with it. Nice huh?

The guy had left town, something my mom never let me forget was my fault. 'A rich guy took an interest in her and I spooked him'. I probably saved her life, stupid bitch. At least he was gone, but kids never forget stuff like that. Especially since every kid in school thoughtfully reminded me each day by branding me 'Crazy Allie'."

Felicity felt an instant empathy. She also was no stranger to being teased in school. "Kids are cruel."

"*People* are cruel. Why do you think I don't bother with anyone? It's not worth it. I stopped worrying about what other people thought of me a long time ago. 'Cept when it comes to my guys, Ben, Mattie, Davy and I, we were like the Musketeers. We did everything together."

"Like hunting vampires?"

"I'm coming to that. The guy came back. It was on my seventeenth birthday. Some present huh? We were coming out of the movie theater and there he was. Smiled right at me. God, that guy gave me the creeps. Still looked exactly the same too; hadn't aged a bit. I guess he'd decided that things had calmed down enough to return. He didn't go near my mom though. Just went back to livin' in that big old house of his. We'd see him around now and again.

Davy started callin' him 'Drac', you know, like short for Dracula. He thought it was hysterical. I had done some research and the only creature I could find that couldn't touch a cross, was a vampire. I'd only ever seen the guy out at night. It made sense.

The boys had always poked fun at me a little about it. I mean, they're my good friends and I know they love me. So it wasn't hurtful, but they wouldn't quite let me forget it either. You know, like they'd point people out and say 'Gee Allie, that girl's lookin' awfully pale, think she's a vampire?' or 'How about that guy over there, couldn't you just picture him in a cape?'. I was so sick of being teased, that I told them I wanted to find a way to prove it. That's when Davy came up with 'The VanHelsing Club'."

"Are you serious?" Felicity asked with a laugh.

"Oh yeah. He said we should be vampire hunters. They all thought it was a splendid idea. You know, fifteen year old boys don't really need very much persuasion to get themselves into trouble."

"Wait, fifteen? I thought you said you were seventeen?"

"I was. I'm two years older than they are, well Mattie and Ben. Davy was sixteen at the time. Not that it ever mattered, by the time I was twelve they all towered over me, I'm so damn short."

"You're lucky to be so petite. You're like, automatically adorable," Felicity said with a twinge of jealousy.

"Oh please! Ben calls it my 'pixiness'. He used to beg me every Halloween to dress up like 'Tinkerbelle'. I'd like to sock him!"

Felicity laughed. "It *would* look perfect on you."

"Shut up. Anyway, that's when we began sneaking out at night. We started out by snooping around Drac's house, but before we actually did anything, it burned down. The paper said it was faulty wiring, but *I* think it was set by another vampire. Drac must've had bigger problems than us kids.

So then, we started looking for new vamps to uncover. We'd find a likely place, and wait. The back parking lot at the movie theater, the all night gas station, out in the side lot at The Red Barrel; the guys'd sit and watch and I'd be the bait.

Can we just pause for a moment and pay tribute to the fact that I am still alive despite that incredible display of stupidity on my part? I'm a tiny little seventeen-year-old girl. 'Let me go stand out in a dark parking lot in the middle of the night and wait to be attacked.' God I was stupid."

Felicity flinched, thinking of the night she had tried to avoid Cain coming to her in her room, by sitting outside by herself at night. "Everybody does something that they didn't really think through, once in awhile."

"Yeah well, the guys were supposed to be protecting me, but I don't think they were even watching half the time. They'd be sitting in the bushes with a six-pack of beer, comic books and a titty magazine, while Crazy Allie stood out there waiting to prove some kind of point. Even if there were *no* vampires, do you realize how lucky I am? I could have been kidnapped, raped, murdered by some human psycho, the possibilities are endless. And I expected protection from three half-drunk young teenage boys. Stupid."

"So were you attacked by a vampire?"

"Three times," Allie informed her.

"Oh my God!"

Alyson nodded. "Yeah."

"Well, obviously you survived, and at least you proved you were telling the truth."

"You'd think. Here's what happened. I'm standin' out on the side of The Red Barrel mini-mart, and it's like midnight. So, the guys are sitting out behind a dumpster, with their usual entertainments...comics, porn and beer. I'm actin' like I'm waitin' for somebody to pick me up. You know, lookin' around for cars, checkin' my watch and tryin' to look all scared and helpless.

So this guy comes around the side of the building towards me. Looked like a real bum. Dressed in like three layers of dirty clothes, heavy beard, and I thought for sure he's comin' to hit me up for some money. So I'm prepared to chase him outta here, before he scares away the vamps. The bum comes up to me, and freakin' lunges for my throat!

He's got me in a bear hug, tryin' to bite me, and I'm screamin' and tryin to get him off me. Of course, the guys had all the weapons, another testament to my unbelievable stupidity. It seemed like it took them forever to come help. They were totally unprepared. I wish I could've seen them when they first heard me scream. I'll bet it would have been freakin' comical to see them scramblin' over each other and spillin' their beers to come to my aid.

Thing is, soon as they showed, the guy bolted, by the time they got to me, the guy was off in the woods. Davy went to chase him, but he was gone. Meanwhile, I'm tryin' to say I told you so, and they still didn't believe me! All they'd seen was a dirty old bum. Ben says he knows I'm mad 'cause they weren't really watchin', but I don't have to go pretendin' that the guy was a supernatural monster'. If Mattie hadn't held me back I would've punched him right in the face."

"You didn't keep going out after that, did you?"

"Are you kidding? I couldn't wait to go out again. I was right! He was a real vampire! You have to realize, it was six years since I'd seen Drac get burned by that cross. I was almost starting to wonder if I *was* crazy, but now I had proof, even if only for myself. I wasn't just 'Crazy Allie' seeing things, it was real and now I was gonna show them, even if I had to get bit to do it. I was annoyed they hadn't seen it, but at least the incident did make us see how stupid it was, to leave me so vulnerable.

After that, Mattie always stayed with me while Davy and Ben promised to actually glance up at us once in awhile."

"Why always Mattie?" Felicity asked.

"Well, they didn't want to scare the vamps away, and Mattie seemed the most vulnerable of the three guys. Ben and Davy are much...taller." Allie's usual fast and easy cadence of speech seemed to falter as she caught herself. "I mean was...David *was* tall, like Ben." She stopped for a minute, staring vacantly at the dance floor. "David was a pretty big guy, even though he was only seventeen, when he died. They must have ganged up on him." She swallowed hard and continued before Felicity could say anything. "So Mattie was the obvious choice. Not that he's 'little' or anything, but compared to them...I think he's like 5'9" now, and he was shorter then.

Anyway, it took weeks before we saw anything else. We'd go out every Friday night. Mattie and I would hang out and talk while Ben and Davy 'kept watch' with their comics and whatever. As you can imagine, Mattie and I got pretty close. He's so sweet, and I guess he felt like he could talk to me about stuff that he wouldn't ever bring up in front of the guys. One time, we were talking about something, I don't even remember what, but I put my hand on his leg. We were sitting facing each other on the ground, and I put my hand down like just above his knee. He was so cute; he got like hyper conscious of it, and he was all nervous and red in the face. So I'm askin' him what's the matter, and he's tryin' to shake it off like it's nothin', but I see him keep glancing down at my hand.

Mattie's always been kind of shy, and he was sixteen then, but I knew he'd never really had a girlfriend. I was almost eighteen. I'd been out with a few guys, all jerks, but I'd done my share of foolin' around. Mattie was so sweet and innocent, and absolutely adorable. I could tell by the way he was lookin' at me, that I wasn't just 'one of the guys' anymore. It was almost kind of funny, seein' him all flustered, *over me!*"

Felicity smiled. Alyson was practically glowing talking about Mattie. It was obvious how fond of him she was. Love was probably a very appropriate word. "So what did you do?"

"I kissed him. Shocked the hell out of him I'm sure. I know he was a little worried that Ben or Davy would see, but they weren't paying any attention to us. It was really sweet and soft. I mean, it's not like I attacked him or anything. After, he's just lookin' into my eyes with this shocked amazement, like he couldn't believe I did that, but *he's* the one who leaned over for another kiss. It was really nice. I was Mattie's first real kiss you know. I was Mattie's first *everything.*"

"Really?" Felicity smiled as Allie gave a little nod. "Was he *your* first?"

"No, but he's the only one that ever mattered." Allie's eyes had filled with unshed tears, and she stared out at the crowd of dancers again.

Felicity put a hand on her shoulder. "Don't worry. He'll come back."

"I know. He has to. We need each other. You know Ben and I are best friends, and he's like my reality check. He helps me deal with stuff, with life, but Mattie, being with him...he's like my *sanctuary* from the rest of the world, and I think I'm his. He understands me like nobody else does...not even Ben, and I get him too, you know? His life is different now and maybe there's stuff I don't know, but it's still Mattie. I don't know why I ever even bother with other guys. It's like I'm just killin' time. In fact, I'm startin' to think I'd rather just be alone when he's not around."

Felicity and Allie both looked up as Ben and Ashley walked by. Ben was being led by the hand; obviously, Ashley had a certain destination in mind. Ben smiled at them and might have stopped, but Ashley deliberately ignored them and kept walking. Rather than resist her, Ben just gave them a helpless and apologetic sort of grin and kept walking. Watching the two of them, Allie almost seemed nauseous. She turned to Felicity in disgust. "Being alone is definitely preferable to being led by the hand through life, by someone like that."

Felicity watched them for a moment more, and then went back to the prior conversation. "So you said you got attacked *three times?*"

"Yeah. The next time was at the gas station. We were sitting off to the side and back a little, out of sight from the attendant. I was with Ben that night actually. He and Davy were sort of ticked off at each other over some girl. They weren't really fighting, but they didn't want to sit together. So stupid. So Ben came with me, and Mattie stayed with Dave.

Ben and I are talking when all of a sudden this guy comes from out of nowhere and punches Ben in the back of the head!"

"Oh my God!" Felicity exclaimed.

"I know! I must say, that David and Mattie did come pretty quickly that time, but I got him first."

"He was a vampire?" Felicity asked.

"For sure. After he punched Ben, he went 'vamp' and tried to bite him. The guy totally ignored *me,* like I wasn't even worth worrying about! I must say, I was highly insulted. He'll never underestimate me again!"

"What did you do?" Felicity asked uneasily.

"Well, after the last fiasco, it was decided that we should *all* have weapons, even me. And then there was *the pike,"* she said with a laugh.

"What's a pike? I mean, besides a fish?" Felicity asked with a chuckle.

Allie chuckled. "It's a weapon. Sort of like a spear. Davy made it as kind of a joke. It was a long wooden push broom handle with the end sharpened into a wicked point. We decided it should stay with the bait. We'd just leave it on the ground nearby. Considering we were always in back lots near dumpsters and stuff, it just looked like another piece of junk on the ground.

So this vampire had come around in front of Ben and was trying to bite him. Ben was doing a really good job of not getting bit, but he couldn't get away. So I grabbed the pike and put it through the guy's back, to pierce his heart from behind. I hit it too!"

"Wow!" Felicity said in amazement.

"Yeah, but unfortunately I also kind of impaled Ben in the process," Allie admitted.

"What?!"

"I did, but it wasn't my fault! After it hit the guy's heart, he turned into dust and the resistance was gone. I couldn't help but come down harder than I meant to. It didn't go in deep," Allie said defensively.

"Oh my God, Allie, you could have killed him," Felicity said.

"I know, but I didn't. At least he believed me now, and I *did* save his life." Felicity was just looking at her in disbelief that she had come so close to mortally wounding her friend. "It left a scar; he was so pissed. Don't mention it; it's kind of a sore spot with him. It's barely noticeable, but he still makes sure I see it every time he takes off his shirt."

Felicity tried to remember when Ben had lifted his shirt to show her the bruises he'd received from Marcus. She couldn't recall seeing a scar, but it would have been hard to notice under all of the black and blues. "I never noticed the scar."

"Good, do me a favor and pretend you never do. Anyway, I would have been perfectly happy to stop goin' huntin' after that. Ben had seen the guys' fangs up close, and the others had seen him turn to dust. They believed me now, so...mission accomplished. I was never really out to save the world or nothin'.

Mattie wanted to stop because he was afraid one of us was going to end up getting *really* hurt, besides, by that point he and I would rather have spent our Friday nights in private anyway. We had just started to get together alone sometimes during the week, and the guys didn't know. I don't know why we didn't tell them. It's not like we were ashamed or anything, but it might have made things weird for all of us together, you know? Messed up the group dynamic.

Davy on the other hand was psyched up and ready to go. He couldn't wait to stake a vamp. I don't know if Ben was quite as anxious, but that was when his mom got real sick. I think he just wanted to keep going out to get his mind off of things."

"His mom had cancer, right?" Felicity asked quietly.

"Yeah. She went through chemo. She was sick all through Thanksgiving and Christmas. It was real hard on her. At least it worked."

"Wait a minute, I thought she died?" Felicity asked in confusion.

"Well yeah, but not from that. It went into remission. Then she was fine." Felicity was a little confused, but Allie plowed on. "So we said we weren't gonna do it anymore, but then Mattie and I found out that they were still goin' out hunting without us.

They hadn't seen any action. I guess two strapping young men don't make for very good bait. Mattie went off on them, for goin' without us. They didn't want to quit though. So we all started goin' huntin' together again.

We had a few false alarms, but no more vamps. Until all of a sudden in June, we start seein' them. We didn't get any, and there was no proof really, but there were a lot of new suspicious characters around. We'd see them every night, but they always took off on us, before we could do anything. That's when Ben's mom died. They got her right in her own driveway."

Now Felicity sat back and eyed Allie with disbelief. "What? Allie, that can't be right. Ben said his mom died from cancer."

"Well that's what they told *him,* and everybody else for that matter, but she'd been doin' real well, you wouldn't have even known she was ever sick. It was definitely a vampire."

"How do you know?"

"I saw it," Alyson replied.

"You saw her get attacked?" Felicity asked, with frightened awe.

"No. I saw the bite, on her body, at the funeral."

"Are you sure? Why didn't Ben see it?" Felicity asked skeptically.

"They had a lot of make-up on her and her hair was mostly over it, but it was there if you looked close," Allie confirmed.

"Didn't you tell him?" Felicity asked in astonishment.

"Yeah, but Felicity, we were at *his mom's funeral.* Think about that for a minute. He was only sixteen and his mom died. Now I have to try to show him that she was sucked dry by some monster? How fucked up is that? It wasn't until the last night of the wake that I got up the nerve to show him. He wanted to be with her alone for a minute, before they took her away. I made him let me stay, and I showed him."

"What did he say?" Felicity asked.

"He wouldn't believe it. He told me that it was a mark from the hospital equipment or something. He just wouldn't see it. At least he wouldn't admit it to me, but I think he knew, 'cause after that, he started hunting with a vengeance. I think he was goin' out like every night, with or without us. Vamps stayed away from him though. He was on such a mission that he was probably just oozin' a danger vibe. Vampires aren't entirely stupid, they all steered well clear.

There were a lot of them around still though. Somethin' big must have been goin' on, and we couldn't stay lucky forever. There was a night that they went without me. I had to go to my stupid brother's graduation. I don't know exactly what happened, but apparently, they ran into a big gang of vampires who weren't scared of a couple of kids.

The guys took off running, and all of sudden, Mattie wasn't with them anymore. Mattie never came back." Allie was obviously still upset over it, even though Mattie had made it through his ordeal. "They lost him! They said they looked, but it was like he'd disappeared. I could have killed them! They went without me and they let those vamps get Mattie!"

Allie paused for a deep breath. Felicity couldn't say anything. She'd wanted to reassure her that Ben and Davy hadn't meant for that to happen, but Allie already knew that. It was just hard to live with. After a moment, Alyson continued.

"I went lookin' for him. They didn't want me to, said it was too dangerous, but I went anyway. Ben had told Mattie's parents that they were attacked by a gang, so the police were looking for him too, but nobody found anything. Then a few nights later, *we* ran into four nasty lookin' vamps. I don't know if they were the same guys who got Mattie or not, Ben and Davy had said there were at least seven of them that night.

Anyway, I was the only one with a car at the time. I had this beat up old Suburban, so I used to drive us everywhere. I had it parked in a lot about a half-mile away. Seeing that there were more of them than us, I started running for the truck. For some stupid reason the guys ran the other way. So three of the vamps took off after them, and one followed me.

I made it to the truck in record time, closed and locked the doors. It was funny though, as soon as I was in, the guy gave up and took off back for the guys. You'd think he would've tried to break the window or something."

"He couldn't have gotten in," Felicity interjected.

"Why not?" Allie asked in puzzlement.

"A vampire needs an invitation for a car just like a house. It's your personal space," Felicity informed her.

"For real? I never knew that. That explains why he didn't bother. I always wondered about that, but Mattie's been in my car."

"You must have invited him without realizing," Felicity conjectured.

"I guess. So the guy took off, and I didn't know what to do at that point. I wanted to go help the guys, but I was afraid to leave the truck. I couldn't drive to them because they were off in the woods, besides, if I moved the truck, they might not be able to find me if they came back. So I sat and waited. It was awful, just sitting there.

Finally, Ben comes out of the trees, all out of breath and lookin' totally spooked. I'm talkin' white as a sheet and barely able to speak. He just got in the truck and asked 'Where's Davy?'

Obviously, I didn't know. I asked him what happened and he just said they'd gotten separated. That was it, he wouldn't say anything else. So we just sat there and waited. We waited all damn night 'til the sun came up and Davy never showed. We got out, searched and yelled for him, but we couldn't find him anywhere. So Ben said he probably just went home. I don't think he believed that, but he was trying to keep me from freaking out. So we go to his house and his mom checks his room, and he's not there.

Now remember that this was right after Mattie had disappeared. None of us were supposed to be out at all, and his parents understandably freaked. They called the cops, and we showed them where we'd been. We told them we'd been out lookin' for Mattie. They thought we were involved in some kind of stupid gang war or something." Allie's voice became quiet and trembling as she tried to continue without getting too upset.

"They searched the woods, and found Davy's body a little while later. When the vamps were done with him, they'd slit his throat, so you couldn't see the bite marks. I guess it looked weird that there was practically no blood, but the cops didn't make too big a fuss about it, not that *we* ever heard. Ben and I were kind of under 'house arrest' for a little, but they got a fingerprint off a button on Davy's jacket. It belonged to some guy who was wanted for something a few towns over. Must have been one of the vamps.

That's all I knew." Allie stared at Felicity for a moment as a hard cold look came into her eyes. "You know Ben saw Mattie that night? He saw Mattie and *he never told me!* He knew how devastated I was. When we weren't out looking for him, I was crying for him like non-stop for three days. Then the night that Davy died, Ben saw him, and he just came back to the truck and he never told me!"

"Allie, you know Ben was only trying to protect you. If he had told you that Mattie was out there, you would have gone back out to try to find him. You would have gotten yourself killed."

"Felicity, look at me; Ben's like a hundred and eighty pounds and I'm lucky if I'm in triple digits. I think he could have stopped me if he tried. He should have told me."

"He didn't want to upset you," Felicity said in Ben's defense.

"He didn't want me to know, because he knew that I wouldn't turn away from Mattie the way that he did," Allie accused.

"How did you find out, about Mattie?" Felicity asked her.

"Next night, he came tappin' on my window. Oh God Felicity. Talk about overwhelming joy and relief!" Allie's broad smile and tear filled eyes made Felicity feel as though she were seeing the moment again through Allie's eyes. She could imagine the release it must have been, from the helpless devastation Allie must have been going through. "I made him climb through my window so I could smother him with hugs and kisses. I couldn't believe he was there. It was like a miracle.

Then he told me. He told me that he'd changed, but you know what? It didn't matter. It was still Mattie. I *knew* him. He was just the same. I couldn't even see the change. He wouldn't show me, not that night. He put my hand to his chest though, under his shirt. We stood there, silent like that for a long time. At first, I didn't even know what he was doing, but then I realized...no heartbeat.

It didn't matter though. It still doesn't." Allie shrugged. "He's Mattie. You make this big deal about being in love with 'a dead guy', but I don't see it that way. Love is love. Every relationship has obstacles; some are small, some are huge. You just have to decide if your love is worth overcoming them. Sure, being with Mattie makes it kind of hard to lead a normal life. I've been thinking about that a lot. You know what? I can't say I care. How's *my* life normal anyway? All I know for sure about my life, is that it really sucks when Mattie's not in it." Allie sniffled, and took a sip from her drink. She fought back the tears with a deep breath and went on.

"He wouldn't tell me what happened. Mattie's like that sometimes. He's so quiet and keeps stuff to himself. He'll only confide stuff to people he really cares about. And then some stuff, he just won't talk about at all. I asked, believe me, but he just wasn't talkin'. It must have been really awful; I had to let it go.

He did tell me about how he'd seen Ben though. He told me how spooked Ben was and that Ben just didn't understand that he wasn't some inhuman monster. I was enraged! I wanted to kill Ben for not telling me. I couldn't believe it! How could he have seen Mattie and not told me? How could he not see that Mattie was the same? How could he not understand? I told Mattie that we had to make him see. Especially now, after what happened to Davy. We had to make Ben see that Mattie was alright. How could he not be anything but relieved?

That's when I realized that Mattie didn't know what I was talking about. He didn't know...about Davy. I told him what happened and you could just see it hit him like a brick in the face. He didn't know. He was so desperately grief stricken.

Then he realized that it must have happened while he was talking to Ben. That just made things seem worse. If Mattie hadn't told Ben straight off that he'd changed… If Ben hadn't been frightened of him, if only Ben had told him what happened. Mattie and Ben could have gone looking for Davy together and they might have found him in time.

Sometimes I think Ben thinks that too. That's why he blames himself for Davy's death. We never talked about it though. Ben didn't even know that I knew about Mattie until now. Mattie told me not to say anything to him. Ben was just trying to keep me safe and I should try not to hold it against him. He knew it would just push Ben and me apart from each other. He said we needed each other more than ever now. We had to take care of each other. I think he felt bad that he couldn't be around for me.

I wanted Mattie to stay of course, but he said he couldn't, not yet. He couldn't let himself be seen, his folks were better off thinkin' him gone. Ben and I had stuff to do together that he couldn't be a part of. You know, with Davy's funeral and police questions and stuff. He told me that we should keep each other safe and be careful. Mattie promised me he'd come back when he could. He had his own stuff to do. He needed to learn how to live a new life."

Allie looked thoughtful for a moment. "You know, I always thought he was alone, but I guess I should have realized that he would have had a much harder time without help. I have a feeling that I owe *Cain* a really big 'thank you'. Sounds like maybe he took care of Mattie for me. What does he do, run a home for 'wayward vampires' or what?"

Felicity laughed. "I think it's more of a one at a time, case by case basis, but yeah. Something like that."

"He's a good guy," Alyson said admiringly.

Felicity nodded her head and tried to smile but she had a big lump in her throat. Alyson made it seem so straightforward. It made Felicity feel guilty, like the vampire issue shouldn't bother her. Was she really going to let such a wonderful man leave her life? She felt like she was stupid and cruel for not loving him enough to want to be with him…always.

Chapter 4 - Honesty

Cain

9:00, Sunday night

Cain rode his motorcycle through the dark streets of the town, much as he had the evening before. The chain mail that he wore beneath his sweater was a cold heavy weight upon his chest. He'd done a few sweeps of the area, and was confident that no other vampires were within the immediate vicinity at the moment.

He'd felt Felicity's brilliant and beckoning mark over in the direction of Alyson's house. He was grateful to Allie for following through with his wish that they be together. His body recognized the call of his venom within Felicity and urged him to move towards her, but he held his course and stayed clear. As tempted as he was to go and see her, he knew he must resist. She would only plead with him to stay and he really needed to get this business with Chris over with – alone. So he stayed out of her physical range, hoping she would not feel him.

Luckily, his psychic range reached much further, so he could be sure that no other vampires were near – none that he could read. He dearly hoped Chris was keeping Marcus with him. Chris had learned to hide his own trace, but had he realized that he could be traced through Marcus if they stayed together? It seemed a simple conclusion, but common sense was not usually a strength of Sindy's creations. With a silent prayer for Felicity and Alyson's safety, Cain moved on. He had one further stop to make before truly continuing his search. The closer Cain came to the motor lodge in Oxford, the more worried he became. He could not feel Sindy there, not at all; not even a slight telltale slip of her presence. Had she left? Where would she have gone?

He was unsure whether to worry that Chris had found and taken her, or that perhaps she had gone to him willingly. Sindy had told him that she was through playing games, but although he felt fairly certain that she would not seek to harm those Cain had chosen to protect, he had learned from past experiences that such assumptions could be dangerous. She had shown some amount of loyalty to him and he would like to trust her, but he was not a total fool.

He parked the bike out in front of room number seven, and went to the door. He was about to knock, wondering if he was wasting his time, when he heard slight sounds from within. He paused, and then purposefully rapped on the door. The one within was silent a moment, and then seemed to rush to the door, but it was not opened.

Cain stood outside impatient but pleased. It had to be Sindy. She was so perfectly concealed that he had not felt her at all during his entire approach, or even now. It was a wonderful display of psychic control and he could not help but feel almost inordinately proud of her. She still hadn't opened the door though. She had to know that it would be him.

Was she pausing for effect, so as not to seem overly anxious, or was she only being cautious? As he had the night before, he briefly made his identity known, by momentarily dropping his shield. He heard her unlock the door immediately.

Sindy swung the door open wide and seemed to pose, with one arm stretched up to hold the doorframe, the other perched on her hip. Again, she wore the short black mini dress with the long flowing sleeves and a confident little smirk upon her face. No eye make-up. Probably impossible to attempt without a mirror anyway. She wore only lipstick and a hint of blush to accentuate her high cheekbones. She looked amused that he had come to her again, as if she thought he couldn't bear to stay away.

He smiled and was still amazed that she continued to hold herself invisible to his mind so well and for so long. Even upon seeing him, she held it true. "Impressive."

She grinned and opened her arms wide as though to show off her sleek form. "Aren't I always?"

"Your cloaking," he clarified. "It's flawless."

"I know. Look at you, all clean cut and handsome. You didn't get all dandied up for me did ya?"

He raked his hand through his hair. Oh right, the haircut. He'd forgotten. He smoothed his cashmere sweater over his chest, tugged the ends of his sleeves a bit, as though making sure his appearance was suitable, and then gave her a sly smile. "No."

She laughed. "Good, I hate it when guys try too hard. Come on in." She backed away for him to enter.

As he followed her into the room, he refrained from turning to shut the door. "I think I'll let *you* close it," he said with a little smile, remembering the last two times he'd turned his back on her for such a task. She chuckled, closed and locked it he noticed. Perhaps behind her confident demeanor, there was a touch of worry after all. "Any news?"

She shook her head and held to her air of non-chalance tinged with boredom. She was rather good at that affectation he'd noticed. No matter what was happening around her, she always seemed to want him to think that she didn't care. "Nope, life is boring."

He smiled as she walked over and turned off the television program she'd been watching. "Boring also means safe. You're lucky."

She let herself collapse backwards onto the bed. "Yeah, lucky me. Nothin' but a big ol' empty bed and a boob-tube."

Always a bed reference. He wondered fleetingly whether she really did care so much for the physical pleasures of sex, as she liked to claim. Not that she shouldn't, but he'd the feeling that she considered it a priority, mostly because others seemed to. It was something that she considered herself good at, something to be valued for. It should be considered important because it was a commodity and a bargaining tool, more than for the rewards of the act itself.

She sat up and looked at him questioningly. "You don't even *have* a television, do you?"

"I read. I've found the few television programs that I've recently attempted to watch, to be banal and insipid."

Sindy gave him a blank stare for a moment before answering. "If that means they suck, then I agree." She sat up on the edge of the bed as he laughed, and then patted her hand on its coverlet, as though he should join her.

He shook his head to decline. "I'm not staying. I just wanted to check in…see if you needed anything."

She gave him a broad, mischievous smile. "Well, if you're asking…"

He quickly cut off any illicit request she might make. "Have you a refrigerator?"

She studied him a moment, annoyed that he would cut right to practical matters. Even when she knew he would decline, she always seemed to enjoy teasing him with her propositions. After a pause, she nodded towards the far corner of the room where a mini-fridge sat on the floor. "Already stocked. Thanks anyway."

"Microwave?"

She made a face of disgust. "Just a hot plate."

"Whatever does the job. Right then, I'm off."

"Cain, I can't stay here."

He glanced around. The room seemed fairly clean and comfortable. "Why not?"

She glared at him in exasperation. "Because it blows! What am I suppose to do, just sit here alone and watch TV all night?"

Cain sighed. "Well, your cloaking seems reliable enough. You can certainly go out if you'd like." Her face brightened as she smiled at him hopefully. "But you're *not* coming with me."

She slumped her shoulders in a huff. "Why can't I?"

"You know I'm out looking for Chris."

"So? I got your back," she offered.

He let out a little chuckle. "Thank you, but no."

She seemed insulted. "Don't you trust me?"

Now he looked back up at her with mild amusement. "*That* my dear, is another question entirely, but I'm not looking to fight Chris; I only want to speak with him. If I were to confront him with you, he would immediately become defensive and feel that we were ganging up on him. I need to do this alone."

"What for? You're wasting your time. After what he pulled, he doesn't deserve a chance to talk. You know letting him go is gonna come back to bite you in the ass one day. Just dust him."

He shook his head at her in disapproval. "I understand that you feel he's betrayed you, but if you pause for reflection, you might realize that the things you've done to him have been far worse." Sindy looked almost outraged at the idea. He put up a hand to forestall any argument she might have. "To be honest, your own personal quarrels do not concern me.

Now if you are looking for my *protection*, I suppose I might grant you that, but only in the knowledge that you are prepared to let grudges go and be done with it. Otherwise, if you'd both prefer to kill each other, go ahead. Just leave the rest of the world out of it, would you please?" She just rolled her eyes at him.

He pressed on. "Now I plan to go and offer Chris amnesty if he will take his new found freedom and live peacefully elsewhere. Where do you stand?"

She thought about it for a minute, and then shrugged. "Well… I guess I don't really care what he does, as long as he stays out of my face," she replied grudgingly. "But I still think he's a lost cause. He's never gonna listen to you. You should just give up and stake him already, before he gets you first."

Cain gave her an insightful little smile. "I don't give up on people easily…lucky for *you*." She'd no answer for that, but only dropped her eyes to the floor. "Goodnight." Cain undid the lock and opened the door.

"Cain…" He paused, with his hand on the knob. "Can't you stay for a little?"

"No." He stood in the open doorway, looking out into the dark and nearly empty lot. When she didn't say anything else, he turned again to face her. She'd risen from the bed and stood before him. Her confident and superior attitude had disappeared. He stood firm. "I don't like not knowing where he is. I can't dally here."

She obviously still did not want him to go. She seemed almost embarrassed to have stopped him but was having trouble offering an explanation as to why. Finally, she looked up at him with large and honest eyes, although she did drop them to look at the floor now and again almost shyly as she spoke. "It's just… I've… I've never been alone before. I mean really alone. Like…disconnected, from *everybody*. Nobody owns me and I haven't got anybody either. No more shared marks with other vamps, they're all gone. I can't *see* you, or even Chris for that matter. Marcus' trace has Chris all over it now and he doesn't seem all that friendly towards me these days anyway. Only guy wearing my mark is *Ben*, and he'd be very happy to see me dead, so…that's not very reassuring. I've never been so *alone* before. It's kind of…frightening."

Cain gazed at her in wonder for a moment. "Sindy, you have killed *dozens* of men. I have seen you be attacked by animated corpses and rip them limb from limb. And being *alone* is what frightens you?"

She became flustered and turned away. "You think I'm stupid."

He caught her arm to turn her back to face him. "No, I really don't. I think you're being *honest*, and I like that. Just making sure I've got it straight," he said with a sympathetic smile. "But you are an intelligent, independent and very strong young lady. You can stand on your own. Have faith."

She looked away, resentful and unsure. He took her by the shoulders to face him again. He looked into her eyes with a reassuring smile as he spoke. "You *can*, but you don't have to. You're *not* alone." He waited for her to smile back before he continued. "I'm still never sure whether to trust you entirely, but I really don't give up on people easily." She gave him another sly smile and laughed. "However, I can't take you with me, so you're going to have to let me leave now."

She didn't speak, but just bowed her head in acceptance. He knew she was embarrassed for him to have seen her as weak and afraid. As he looked at her now, he made himself realize that no matter how mature and worldly she often pretended to be, chronologically she was really only nineteen.

He let go of her shoulders and turned again to leave. Once more, she stopped him, but her voice sounded so quiet and hesitant that he couldn't be angry with her. "Cain…could you…"

He faced her again, but she wouldn't meet his eyes. After an interminable pause, he prompted her. "What?"

"Would you…" She finally lifted her eyes to his. He'd never seen her look so vulnerable. "Would you mark me?"

He stared at her for a long moment and then dropped his gaze to the floor, a bit uncomfortable with the prospect. She addressed his concern with the idea. "I know you're with Felicity now. That's your choice. Fine, whatever. This isn't about that. It's just…I'm not marked. It's like I don't even matter. I could die before dawn and no one would feel it, no one would even know…or care. I might as well not even exist. It's…scary.

If you marked me, at least I could feel like I'm a part of something, connected to the rest of the world again. It wouldn't have to be sexual. It's not like you'd be cheating on her or nothin'. It's just…a vampire thing. Honest."

He stood there, staring at her for what felt like a very long time, just turning things over in his mind and unsure how to respond. After a moment or two, he could tell that she thought he'd decline. Finally, she turned to move away from him further into the room, her eyes carefully avoiding his own. "Forget it. It was stupid. Go find Chris or whatever, and be careful." He did not speak. She turned to look back at him, and found that he had moved into the room, and was shutting the door behind him.

He came to take her hands into his own and looked into her eyes. "You're not alone."

She looked away and tried to pretend indifference. "Yeah, I know. You'd better get goin'." She tried to move away, but he didn't let go of her hands. She looked back at him questioningly.

"I'll do it, if you want," he said quietly.

Her eyes widened just a touch and she stared at him for a long time, as though she didn't really believe him. He gave her a small smile and a slight nod. The relief was plain on her face. She seemed to ponder things a moment and then turned the inside of her wrist towards him and moved her arm slightly higher, in offering.

Cain felt as though he were seeing her in such a new light. He'd always suspected that there was a frightened little girl behind her fangs and false bravado, but now it was truly plain to see. How scared she must be, to actually admit it to him. She was so young, only sixteen when she'd died and become caught up in all of this. He knew that she was strong and could stand on her own, but being alone *was* frightening sometimes. He knew.

He dropped her hands from his own and opened his arms to her. "Come here."

Her eyes were bright and moist. She looked as if she would like nothing better than to collapse in his arms and cry in relief, but she didn't come to him immediately. Submission was not an easy thing for her. She paused, perhaps wondering if he'd lose respect for her now. Little did she know that he held her display of true feelings in much higher regard than her usual air of fearlessness.

She finally surrendered to him. He enfolded her in his arms for a strong close hug. It took her a moment before she did truly give over to it. He held her for a time, a hug sincere and unrushed that she should feel connected to another; that she should know that he *did* care; and he then moved her back from him to look at her. He lifted a hand to sweep her long hair away from her throat on one side and let it drop down her back. He inched over the material of her dress, to leave her neck exposed and clear.

She seemed a little surprised; maybe she'd thought he would take back her wrist. Not that she seemed to mind. After gazing into his eyes for the space of a second, she closed her own and tilted her head subtly to the side. It was such a demure and supplicating gesture. It was very unlike her and he found it almost *too* appealing.

He gazed at her throat and let the change overcome him. As his vision shifted spectrums, he realized with mild surprise that her eyes remained closed. She wasn't watching him. He knew that to see him change usually excited her. To see him unleash the beast within seemed to give her a thrill. Patiently she awaited his bite. She really *was* trying to keep to her word. She didn't want him to feel that he was betraying his human lover by pleasing another. She held still and silent, her eyelids never lifted.

The last time he had drunk from her throat it was something savage and almost brutal. This would be different. It was not punishment, not foreplay, not even the purely practical act of marking. This was one creature clinging to another to keep them from feeling swept away by the lonely winds of the world.

He wrapped his arm around her waist and bent to her pale throat. She never even flinched as he pierced her skin decisively, with the utmost precision and care. Even as the first drops of blood began to envelope his fangs, he refrained from drinking. First, he would let the venom begin its task. He could feel his poison flowing into her body. She felt it too; she sagged against him a bit, as the first wave of dizziness came over her.

Sindy seemed hesitant to cling to him too strongly, as though he wouldn't want her arms around him. He used his own hold on her waist to crush her closely to him. She spoke, trying to keep her voice neutral and clear, though it wasn't much more than a whisper. "Drink. If you meet up with Chris and Marcus you're gonna need it."

He couldn't wait any longer anyway. Did she really believe his will strong enough to keep him from such ecstasy? He held her tightly and sucked strongly upon her throat. She couldn't help but let out a low moan of pleasure, even as he fought to keep silent himself. Now she did bring her arms up around him. Surely, she would need his support just to keep herself standing through the waves of euphoria his drinking would bring. Her blood was like smooth liquid fire as it filled his mouth. It coated his tongue and burned its way down his throat as his body thrilled to the warm spice of its taste.

Again, he pulled upon her vein and it was almost as though the blood had a life of its own. His mind reeled with lightheaded fulfillment as it moved within him; finding its way through his body to fill not only his stomach, but also every hollow it could reach. It left a trail of warmth and shivers of pleasure in its wake, blood like this could never be confused with something human. It needed not a pumping living heart to propel it; it moved within him of its own accord. It was blood and yet mixed within it was truly something else, something alien and unknown. It was…vampire.

A disease? A separate entity of its own, seeking only a host? Cain did not know, nor did any he had ever met. Right now, it did not matter. It was life, blood, filling and completing him so that he might be a strong and powerful creature again. Her blood was an intoxicating pleasure that although he had not thought to sample again for some time, he had to admit was a very welcome and satisfying gift. His lips covered the wound as his fangs withdrew and he drank long and deep.

After a time, when Sindy seemed too inebriated with his venom to stand any longer, he used his arm to scoop her legs from under her as his other arm supported her waist and he carried her to the bed. He laid her down and forced himself to remove his lips from her throat, although the liquid ecstasy there was something difficult to disengage from. As he rose, she turned her face to try to meet his mouth for a kiss. His lips barely brushed hers as he lifted himself from her.

She looked up at him dreamily, obviously deep in a venomed haze. "Sorry, reflex."

He smiled and gave her a moment to recuperate. Her venom was surely fighting his own even now. He blinked his eyes and straightened, letting the vampire recede so that the man might resurface. He felt almost drunk with her unnatural blood.

Before long, she was sufficiently recovered to look upon him in clarity. He wondered if the fluids within her body saw his venom as an invading toxin or a kindred entity. It was a separate level of their existence he suspected he'd never understand. As long as the vampire within him was satisfied to let the man retain the lead, he was content not to delve further into the philosophy and true mechanics of it all.

He looked down at Sindy lovingly and stepped back from the bed. "I'll be leaving you now," he told her quietly. She only gazed at him with eyes rich and earthy brown like tilled soil. She still seemed loathe to let him go. He retrieved the television remote from the table and threw it to her on the bed. As he turned to leave, he heard it hit the floor as she threw it back at him with a laugh.

He came back to her as she pouted like a child. "TV sucks."

"So read a book," he told her.

"I haven't got any."

He smiled. "Sure you do." He reached to open the drawer of the nightstand next to the bed. Sure enough, a Bible lay within.

Sindy chuckled. "You want me to read *that?*" Her speech was still a bit thick and slurred.

He shrugged. "If you want." He pushed up his sleeve to reveal his tattoo. He tapped the words 'Genesis 4:7' printed on the inside of his forearm for emphasis. "Look it up. It's a good passage." She smiled and shook her head slightly in amusement at him. Without saying anything further, he let himself out. He was only just closing the door as he heard her whisper "Thanks".

෴෴෴෴෴෴෴෴෴෴

Part 2 – Stakes and Sunshine

෴෴෴෴෴෴෴෴෴෴

Chapter 5 – Top of the food chain

Felicity

Masquerade Ball
11:00, Sunday night

Felicity stared out onto the dance floor to try and get rid of that nagging guilty feeling she had over the uncertain future of her relationship with Cain. Allie seemed to think the fact that he was a vampire shouldn't have any bearing on her feelings towards him. Was she just being narrow minded? But Alyson had been involved with Mattie *before* he'd been changed. That made a difference in how she saw things… didn't it? Why did everything have to be so confusing? She and Allie sat quiet for a little, watching the party goers in their various costumes go by.

There was a couple dressed in matching pirate outfits of black, white and red, the guy in pants, the girl in a mini skirt. Another girl was dressed in a red devil leotard much like the one Cain had described when trying to guess Felicity's costume. Felicity was definitely the most elegantly dressed girl there.

She felt stupid. What did she get this dumb gown for anyway? Cain wouldn't even see it. Somehow, she'd thought he would surprise her and come.

As she looked over the crowd, she kept glancing to the door, as though Cain would appear, like she lived in the last scene of some dumb romantic movie. While watching the door, she saw a girl come through. At first, she thought the girl was dressed as 'Morticia', from 'The Addams' Family'. Then she felt an awful chill as she realized…it was Sindy. She spoke to Allie as she kept her eyes towards the door. "What's *she* doing here?"

As Allie followed her gaze, her expression instantly became hostile. "Let's go find out." Sindy knew they were there. In fact, she stood with her hands on her hips and waited for them to approach. Felicity realized that Sindy had seen her mark. Alyson stalked right up to her. "Sorry honey, Ben's dance card's full tonight. Although I have to admit, I almost don't despise you quite as much as I do his current girlfriend. *Almost."*

Sindy smiled and gazed up to unerringly find Ben dancing with Ashley across the large ballroom some distance away. She found him so easily; she must still see his mark in her mind. They were far enough away though, that Ben hadn't noticed them. It seemed the physical aspect of his mark had faded a bit. Sindy smiled at Allie. "I'm not here for Ben. Unless you think he'd like me to be."

Felicity spoke before Allie had a chance to say anything else. "Why *are* you here?"

Sindy gave a little shrug and a smile. "I thought maybe Cain could use some help."

Allie was quick to respond. "He doesn't need any help from *you.*"

"How would you know what Cain *needs*…from me?" She licked her lips and smiled.

Felicity said quietly, "Cain's not here."

Now Sindy turned her attention to appraising Felicity's ornate gown. Felicity knew she looked beautiful, but somehow in front of Sindy she found herself just feeling silly and over done. Sindy smirked at her. "And look at you, all dressed up with no one to show, poor baby. Still, *I* thought Cain'd be here too," she added, glancing around.

"Why? Did you see him tonight? Did he tell you he was coming?" Felicity said, regretting the *too* hopeful anticipation in her voice, as soon as the words came out of her mouth.

Sindy smiled at her maliciously. "Yeah, I saw him, but no, he didn't mention your silly little dance. Sorry. He was looking for Chris."

Alyson spoke up again. "Then why are you *here?*"

"I was following Marcus."

"Marcus is here?" Both Felicity and Alyson asked in alarm.

Sindy slowly finished their thought. "And Cain isn't…"

Allie spoke hopefully as they each glanced around the room. "Well, maybe Cain *is* here, and we just haven't seen him yet."

Both Sindy and Felicity answered her identically, until Felicity faltered upon hearing Sindy echo her. "No, Cain's not here, I would have…felt him." Felicity eyed Sindy in alarmed confusion. Sindy just grinned at her distress.

"Where's Marcus?" Alyson asked Sindy, trying to cut through any new discussion before it started.

Sindy seemed unconcerned as she glanced from one girl to the other. She gestured vaguely off to the left. "He's over that way, and he's not alone, but they're still pretty far off. They're not in the building yet or anything, but they do seem to be on their way here."

Alyson spoke, as Felicity was still uncomfortably staring at Sindy. "Then Cain is probably on his way too. If *you* managed to find and follow Marcus, Cain's probably doing the same thing."

"I don't think so." Sindy smiled thoughtfully. "When I saw Cain earlier, he was nowhere near here. He might have gone in totally the other direction."

"Where were you?" Allie asked.

"Oxford." She turned another smile on Felicity. "In my hotel room." Felicity didn't say anything, but dropped her eyes to the floor.

Alyson rolled her eyes and let out an exasperated sigh. She turned to Felicity. "Don't listen to anything that comes out of her mouth. I don't even know why we're wasting our time."

Sindy laughed. "Believe what you want but if I were you, I'd get anybody you didn't want sucked dry and split, 'cause Marcus is heading this way and subtle is really not his style."

Allie just stared at her for a moment, trying to assess whether she was telling the truth. Sindy glanced over at Ben again, who still hadn't noticed her. "It's time to go. Do you wanna get Ben, or shall I?"

"I'm not going anywhere with *you*. Why should we believe you anyway?" Allie asked suspiciously.

Sindy shook her head and laughed again. "You're right; you caught me. I was just putting you on. Marcus isn't coming here."

Felicity found herself sounding foolishly hopefully again before she could help it. "He's not?"

"Why don't you stay and find out? You guys are so stupid! I'm trying to do you a favor here. I know what's up and whether you'd like to admit it or not, I'm the only person in this room worth listenin' to. So if I say it's time to go, you'd best listen."

Alyson became very annoyed. "Just because you can see things that we can't, doesn't mean you get to order us around. Who the hell put you in charge anyway? I don't even know whose side you're on!"

Sindy stood a little straighter and took on an air of confident superiority. "I'm on *Cain's* side. Unfortunately, that seems to align me with *you,* but I can do whatever the hell I please. Let me let you in on a little secret. *I'm the top of the food chain here.* Vampires are far superior to humans, in every way. I'm the *lioness* in this room, and you guys are just a bunch of little jumpin' gazelles. Get over it, 'cause it ain't never gonna change." She looked up in Marcus' supposed direction. "Now it's time to leave. Let's go."

Alyson glared at her for a moment as Felicity shifted her weight uneasily, watching the door and trying desperately to feel Cain. He was still nowhere near. After an interminable moment, Alyson spoke. "I really don't like you."

Sindy shrugged with a breath of a laugh. "Like I care."

"Stay here. I'll go tell Ben." She turned to Felicity. "Don't go anywhere, I'll be right back."

Felicity watched uneasily as Allie rushed off to get Ben. Then she nerved herself to look at Sindy again. She knew she was better off not saying anything. Sindy would only try to upset her, but she couldn't help but ask. "What makes you think *you* could feel if Cain was here?"

Sindy laughed. "Wouldn't you like to know?" She gave her a level gaze for a moment. "It's a vampire thing. The kind of stuff you'll never understand. When are you gonna realize, you're just not the kind of woman he needs? Cain is a vampire, a pretty powerful one. He needs another vampire by his side, not some whiny little vamp bait like you. Having to protect you all the time's only gonna get him killed. You really ought to step up or step out."

Felicity would like to tell herself that Sindy was only seeking to fluster her, but disturbingly enough, she knew Sindy to be right. Still, she felt compelled to try to stand up for herself somehow. "How do you know I won't...step up?"

Sindy looked her over in amazement. *"You?* You would try to let him make you into a vampire? Ha! You wouldn't last one night!"

"Why not?"

Sindy's voice became falsely sweet and condescending. "Sorry sweetie but you just haven't got what it takes. A pathetic little milksop like you couldn't handle it, trust me. You really ought to go back home where it's safe and leave real life to the big girls." Before Felicity could reply, they looked up to see Alyson and Ben bearing down on them with Ashley following behind.

Ben was obviously pissed off by Sindy's presence. It was also obvious that he was trying to get Ashley to go elsewhere, and was very annoyed when she wouldn't listen. He moved to speak to Sindy, but as soon as Ashley laid eyes on her, she spoke first. "You again! What are *you* doing here? You'd better not have your gang buddies showin' up after you again. The decorating committee laid out a lot of money to rent some of this stuff, and if it gets trashed there won't be enough left in the budget to decorate properly for the Christmas Gala!"

All eyes were on Ashley in bewilderment. Sindy asked Ben, "Is she for real?"

"Fraid so. What the hell are you doing here? I'm really getting tired of paying to come to these things only to have you show up and ruin them."

"Well believe me, unless you leave now, you're gonna think the last one was much more fun." She eyed Ashley again. "Of course, you might think that anyway." She licked her lips and mouthed him a little kiss.

Ashley became offended. "Hey, you know I'm his date and I'm standing right here!"

Sindy glanced at her again but spoke to Ben without bothering to address her. "You should leave her. I'll bet she'd make a nice distraction for Marcus. She looks delicious."

A commotion at the far entrance drew their attention. Frankenstein and the Mummy were standing in the doorway when they yelled in annoyance against someone who simply shoved them aside to move through. As though summoned by his name, Marcus appeared.

"Told you it was time to go," Sindy said with impressive nonchalance. No sooner had Marcus entered, than three other evil looking men came up behind him. They were unmistakably together, and it took only a moment for their gazes to find Felicity across the room.

Ben spoke quickly. "Let's go, something tells me they're not afraid of making a scene. We're not safe here."

As they all moved towards the exit, Sindy spoke in annoyance. "Oh sure, everybody listens to *him*."

Chapter 6 - Connections

Cain

A Motor Lodge in Oxford
Half an hour earlier - 10:30, Sunday night

Cain clicked Sindy's motel room door shut behind him with a smile. He then looked up to his motorcycle to find it flanked by four fairly large men and backed by a long black car. They were vampires, and they were undoubtedly Arif's by the look of their garb and demeanor. Wonderful.

They stood patiently awaiting him. They didn't seem to expect him to run. He would be stupid to try. It would only seem foolish and cowardly. If Arif wanted something, Cain couldn't avoid him for long. If they indeed were Arif's men, better to see what they wanted and get it over with. He briefly considered summoning Sindy as an ally, but quickly dismissed the notion. Not only was she weakened from his drinking, but involving her would probably only make things worse anyway. Surely, Sindy had no idea they were there, as he had not. They were cloaked. He wondered if one of them was projecting it, or if Arif was nearby.

The largest among them spoke. He was a tall, muscular, bald black man with a commanding demeanor. He wore black dress pants with a silk shirt, as did the rest of them. Not one of them wore a jacket, although it was surely below forty degrees. "Arif will see you this evening," the man said in a steady clear voice.

Cain smiled in amusement at his presumptive attitude. "Oh, he *will?*"

"*I* say he will. Do you dispute it?" was the man's reply.

Cain surveyed the four men and then looked back to their 'leader'. "I suppose I've time for chat." Not one of them cracked a smile. Cain glanced at his Harley. "Lead the way."

At this, another of them spoke. He was the shortest of the four, though still stocky and muscular as they all were. The expression on his face told Cain that he was most likely to be the troublemaker of the bunch. The man stared at Cain haughtily. "Leave the bike," he said, and then indicated with a nod of his head, that he expected Cain to get into their car.

Cain gave a snort of amusement. "I don't think so."

"Well *I* do." Now the man smiled and gave the bike a nice shove.

It fell over with a loud crash and Cain had to fight to hold himself still and unresponsive. He prayed that Sindy would not hear it and come out to investigate. Again, he surveyed the men. He locked his eyes upon their leader once more. "Before this goes any further, perhaps you'd like to take a moment to reflect upon just what it is your *master* wants from me." As he said the word 'master', he turned his gaze upon the one who'd pushed his bike. Men like him always hated to be reminded of their superiors. "If Arif desires an exchange of information, perhaps he would also desire that I arrive in an amicable mood. If that is the case, you may lead me to him, or provide the address and time for a future meeting.

But should you expect to force me into your vehicle and bear me away against my will, I can assure you that not one of us will arrive in a condition conducive to conversation. If Arif *does* wish only to talk, I would think that he would be less than pleased."

The leader seemed to be weighing his argument, and coming to think that he was right. Of course, the little one was having none of it. He sneered at Cain in contempt. The black man who seemed to be in charge of the group spoke. "Tony, pick up the man's bike."

Tony seemed outraged. "What for? Let him get in the car. Elric, you let him ride and he's just gonna skip out on us first chance he gets."

A different man spoke quietly from behind Tony. "Tony, this ain't some little chicken shit. Don't you know who this guy is? He's even older than the master."

"So what? He doesn't even keep a court. No guard, no harem, no scouts, nothing. He a rogue."

The black man, Elric, seemed embarrassed that they should squabble before him. "Tony, do it. *Now.*" He turned to Cain, as Tony and the man who hadn't spoken yet, righted his motorcycle. "Follow," Elric said simply, and got into the front passenger seat of the car. The one who had seemed awed by Cain's presence got into the driver's seat, leaving the other two to finish standing his bike. Tony and his friend glared at him haughtily.

Finally, Tony got into the back, leaving the door open for the other. The last man spoke to him with a nasty tone. "You'd better keep up. 'Cause if you try to get lost, we'll find you…and dust you."

Cain smiled in amusement as the man got in the car and closed the door. He mounted his Harley and fired it up. It reverberated loud and echoing in the parking lot. The long black sedan before him pulled out onto the road, and he followed. He never even considered leaving them. Not that he was frightened of any juvenile threat, but he might as well see what Arif wanted, better than to leave it hanging over his head.

He still worried for Felicity though. He felt no sign of Chris or Marcus, but if they were near Felicity, they would be beyond his range at this point. Knowing Alyson was with her did ease his mind a little, but he hoped he could take care of this nonsense with Arif quickly and be on his way.

They wound their way through mountain and forest until they turned onto a private road. Deep into the thickly wooded property, they came upon a very large log cabin type dwelling. It was almost big enough to be considered a lodge. It fit in very well with its wilderness surroundings, but was hardly the type of structure he would picture Arif to live in. Actually, Cain rather liked it.

Separate from the main building was a four-car garage. One of the doors opened as they approached. The car stopped in front of the main house to let out its occupants before the driver took it to be parked. There were other vampires psychically visible inside, although Arif's own trace remained hidden.

Cain parked his motorcycle outside the garage, just to the side. As he dismounted, the driver of the car exited and approached him. He stopped to wait for Cain; it was the man who had been impressed by Cain's age. He was about the same height and build as Cain, with short straight brown hair and an honest face. He looked to have been in his early thirties, though Cain couldn't tell his true age. He couldn't gage much about any of them while they remained psychically concealed.

As though prompted by Cain's thoughts, the marked presence of the four men suddenly became visible to his mind. Cain looked to Elric, the leader. He was most likely the one to have been cloaking them. Undoubtedly, he had dropped the shield to announce their presence to those within.

He was rather old that one, compared to most Cain had met anyway. By his trace, Cain would guess that he'd existed as a vampire for nearly a century. His trace was strong and powerful, he was well made. The vampiric age of the driver was perhaps fifty, while the other two hovered around the twenty-year mark. Although their strengths were fair, none was as clearly potent as their leader.

The man who had driven the car was still standing next to Cain. After a moment's consideration, Cain decided to reveal his own trace as well. It seemed only polite. He could plainly read them. Let them read whom they were dealing with as well. Cain knew that Maribeth had made him well. His mark was clear and bright. His powerful trace would show him to be not only old, but a competent, capable vampire as well; his intelligence and memories unmarred by his death. The vampire within him was strong and he dropped his shield to let it show.

The man next to him stepped back a pace as Cain's mark was revealed. He was obviously quite impressed and practically bowed his head in reverence as he moved his arm to show that Cain should pass him and approach the house.

Cain kept his eyes on the leader as he came near the porch where the men waited. He could swear that a smile was playing about Elric's lips as Cain climbed the few steps. Yes, this man was impressed by him as well. The other two looked only sullen and annoyed. Elric moved to open the door for him, another sure sign of respect.

The house did look to have been a hunting lodge in times past. Warm and inviting, its furniture was rustic and the front room was decorated with many trophies. The heads of large antlered bucks adorned the walls and there were many stuffed and mounted small game animals about. A huge fireplace dominated the far wall, and there were several chairs and ottomans scattered before it. It looked the perfect place for comfortable camaraderie, but the room was unoccupied except for Cain and his escorts.

Elric turned to the man who had driven the car. "Byron, go before us to the master. Tell him that all is well, and we seek audience"

Byron left without question or hesitation. Elric turned to Cain. "I will bring you before Arif shortly, but first, I must ask if you carry any weapons."

Cain smiled. "Of course I do."

Elric returned his smile and then gestured to the man who had helped Tony to lift Cain's bike earlier. "Joseph." He came forward carrying an empty box retrieved from a niche in the wall near the doorway. Elric spoke again to Cain. "No personal weapons are permitted in the presence of the master. You may retrieve them upon departure."

Cain had to smile at the reverent and awesome attitude Arif had instilled in his minions. Cain knew that some vampire elders kept an elaborate social structure around themselves, but he had very rarely encountered it personally. He had certainly never had opportunity to observe it to this degree. It seemed such a silly game to him; to keep oneself surrounded by guardsmen and courtiers, so that you might be constantly reminded of the imaginary status you've decreed upon yourself.

He concluded that he was best off playing along. He had already allowed himself into their presence. If things took an unsavory turn, it was not as though a stake or two would make the difference in helping him to fight his way out. At this point, concealing weapons would only make them mad. If things went wrong later, he would just have to improvise. He could probably cow them with age and attitude anyway. They were obviously well taught to respect their elders, even beyond the degree that their instinct urged them to. It was plain that none of them had ever seen a vampire as old as he before.

Cain withdrew the three stakes he held on his person. He never let on he was wearing the chain mail vest though. Surely they never suspected it and he wasn't about to take it off. It was not a weapon and so he needn't reveal it. He was rather glad he had it on though. He placed his stakes into the box and watched Joseph put the box back into its place by the door.

Elric nodded his approval, and seemed very glad that Cain had not resisted. Cain wondered what they might have done if he had. The men just stood there, arms folded. Apparently, they awaited approval before venturing further into the house.

Cain once again surveyed their surroundings. Everything seemed well maintained and dusted. He wondered how Arif had obtained such a dwelling. Surely it was inhabited by humans until fairly recently and Cain knew that hunting season for big game would begin shortly, in November. The place should be preparing to be filled with guests.

A large stuffed bobcat guarded the door through which Byron had disappeared. Now he returned, and stopped just inside the doorway. He faced Elric and nodded his head in acceptance. Arif would see them now.

Cain followed Elric and Byron through the doorway, while Joseph and Tony trailed behind him. They made their way through the house, passing many closed doors along the way. A few rooms held the traces of lesser vampires within, but none that Cain knew. He could feel seven marked humans in another room ahead that they approached to pass. Even before they neared the door, he could hear dulcet voices and squeals of feminine laughter from within. Elric stopped at the door, gave a sharp rap upon it, and then opened it about halfway.

From the slice of the room visible to Cain, he could see that it was a lushly decorated bedchamber. Two of the girls within were visible to Cain through the opening. One of them had been among the beauties that Arif had brought to the bar the night that Cain had seen him.

The room became immediately silent and the girls lowered their eyes to the floor. Elric said nothing. He only stared at them for a moment, and then closed the door. Apparently, they were meant to conduct themselves in a more demure manner when company was in the house.

Cain and his escorts continued on to the back of the house until they reached a stairway to the basement. They descended into a lower level that was surely as large as the rest of the house, although it was divided into separate rooms, rather than be mostly open as Cain's basement was.

The room that the stairs let out into was decorated with rich wood paneling and made to be a sort of game room. It sported a large pool table with a rack for accessories, two dartboards and a small bar in the corner. They crossed through to a doorway in the back. Elric paused and then knocked respectfully upon the door.

"Enter." Arif's voice came from within.

Elric looked to Byron who then opened and held the door for them. Elric entered the room and Cain followed. When Joseph and Tony had been admitted as well, Byron moved further inside the room and closed the door.

It was an office, albeit a very lavishly appointed one. This room had its own small fireplace also. Arif was not behind the desk that had been pushed into the corner, but reclined in a large armchair before the fire. He gestured for Cain to take the smaller chair next to him. The rest of the men stood awaiting orders.

Arif smiled to Cain. "And so we meet again. Please, be seated. Byron, bring the man a drink. Rum and Coke isn't it?" he asked. Cain gave a light nod as he sat.

Arif turned to Elric. "Thank you Elric, you never disappoint. You may await summons in the parlor."

"Thank you, Master," Elric responded with a nod. He then ordered Joseph and Tony to leave the room before him. As soon as they left, Byron returned to give Cain his drink. They were then left alone.

"Glad you could come," Arif said with a smug smile.

"A less urgent invitation with some notice might have been nice."

"Yes, I understand you are a busy man of late, but I consider *my* business with you this evening more pressing than your dispute with young Chris."

Cain couldn't help but give Arif a resentful look, that he should assume his desire to speak with Cain to be more important than the well being of Felicity. What the hell did he want anyway? "Might I inquire as to just what is so important?"

Arif smiled and turned towards another door at the far end of the room. "Come," he called to those within, before turning back to Cain. "I would like to introduce you to two of my most trusted men." As the vampires Arif spoke of entered the room, Cain had to stifle a groan.

They were the men from the parking lot of the restaurant, the ones that he had reported to the police the night before. He had practically forgotten the incident, as other things had seemed more pressing.

Arif noted the look upon Cain's face as they came to stand at Arif's side. "Am I to assume that you have already met?"

Cain avoided the men's angry stares as he answered. "We haven't been formally introduced."

Arif remained reclining casually in his chair as he gestured towards the men. "Let me do the honors. This is Tomas and Richard, two very highly valued members of my household. In fact, I have been particularly pleased with them of late. To reward this, I had granted them an evening of leave.

They had my blessing to entertain themselves among the local populace, using appropriate discretion of course. Unfortunately, their evening was spoiled by a misunderstanding with authorities. A misunderstanding that they seem to believe was caused *by you*."

Cain did his best to keep his face neutral and unincriminating. "Is that right?"

To their credit, the men said nothing, although Cain was certain that they would love to have leave to speak their minds. They stood silent and let their master speak for them. "In my house disputes are handled swiftly and fairly. I will not have unrest and dissension unsettling my men. So I am certain that you will appreciate the importance of your presence here, so that we might settle the matter expediently. My men should be assured that I consider their requests as matters of importance worth investigating."

Cain lowered his eyes a bit and ventured a small smile as he pondered what to say. Although it was doubtful that his involvement could be proved, Cain decided it would be best not to try to deny his part in the issue.

Not only did he always try to maintain scrupulous integrity, but also if the men already suspected him, he must have been seen. He had no idea by whom or how accurately he'd been identified. It may even have been by Arif himself. Cain took pride in the fact that he considered his word to be unquestionable. He wouldn't let these men think any less of him by trying to dance around this issue. He looked to the two men. "My apologies for any inconvenience you may have endured."

The men only stared at him coldly as Arif spoke. "Then you do admit to playing a part in their misfortune?"

"I do. However, I must submit that any actions taken on my part were motivated not by any political or manipulative desire for vengeance. I act only as my conscience tells me that I must. It's nothing personal against you or yours, but only my own personal obligation to uphold certain standards of conduct. I cannot hold myself blind to that which I perceive as improper. I thought the ladies they courted to be in danger. I regret if I misjudged the situation harshly."

Arif sat up a bit straighter and gazed at him in seeming admiration for a moment. He must have expected denial. Arif then looked back to his men. "Tomas, what say you to this?"

The man's icy glare towards Cain never wavered. "I say that a man's conscience is meant to dictate his *own* conduct and not to judge that of others. If he disapproves of my actions, let him address me of it openly, and not act through humans, like a coward."

Cain could not help but feel ashamed by the man's words. He was well spoken and had valid argument. Cain said nothing.

"Richard?" Arif inquired.

"I agree. Jiminy Cricket should be taught to mind his own damn business. I'd be happy to do the teaching, if you would permit."

Cain could not help but smile, although he was certainly not in the best of positions. How did he manage to get himself into such predicaments? He really never sought such troubles.

Arif waited a moment to see if Cain would respond, but Cain thought it better to remain silent for now. What else could he say? Arif smiled upon him and then turned back to his men. "I do agree that your point is valid and you've every right to anger." His gaze found Cain once more. "Such a trespass upon my men cannot be ignored."

Cain smiled and shrugged. "You know what they say, 'no good deed goes unpunished'."

Arif returned his smile. "To follow conscience can be a challenging and often foolhardy venture, as far as personal welfare is concerned, but it is commendable to some extent all the same."

Tomas and Richard lost their satisfied expressions as they realized that Arif seemed to be looking upon Cain with admiration and acceptance. Arif spoke to them with an air of finality. "I must also conclude that although this act has been inconvenient and unfortunate to be sure, no true harm was done. I have righted the situation with regard to the police, and it will be forgotten to the world.

I must also inform you, that while I may have been inclined to seek retribution for this deed, I have chosen instead to view it as repayment for past actions already taken. In the past, I did grant Sindy aid, albeit in an indirect fashion, against those in the care of this man; and so he has reciprocated with indirect action against mine. It is done, and no further debt is owed. There is no need for hostilities. Do you accept this verdict?"

The men stared coldly at Cain for a moment but then bowed their heads towards Arif in acceptance, albeit grudgingly. "Good. Let no further action be taken against him. You are dismissed." Richard and Tomas left the room through the door they had entered by, leaving Cain and Arif alone again. Arif turned to him now with an air of casual camaraderie. "I hope you will understand the need for such displays. I do seek to keep satisfaction among my ranks. Have you ever kept underlings of your own?"

Cain sipped his drink, glad for the distraction. He did not want his relief over the incident to be too apparent. "No. I've never had the desire to explore such an arrangement. You've quite a large coven."

Arif smiled. "Yes. I think that soon it shall be time to grant a certain number of them leave to part from me. I am thinking that Elric shows great promise as a Lord, though I will miss him. He is loyal and levelheaded. I do not think that I should worry for any problems from those under *his* control, should I allow him freedom."

"He does seem a man of good character. However, I'm not prone to speculation over such political issues. I prefer solitude, or the company of only a select few."

"Yes of course. You need freedom and mobility to carry out your quest." Cain had trouble deciphering if the remark was meant as a sarcastic jibe, or was simply said in earnest.

"If we are finished here, I do have other matters to attend to."

Arif grinned. "Yes I know, but while I have you here, there is something else which I have longed to bring to your attention." Cain looked at him in confusion, wondering what else Arif might have in mind, when the door he had entered by was opened, startling him. It was Elric. Cain was at first very surprised that the man would enter unbidden to interrupt them, but then he realized that Arif seemed unsurprised at his presence. Most likely Arif had summoned the man mentally.

Arif nodded approval at the man's entrance and then turned back to Cain. "Before I explain, I must ask you something. How did you find my men when they approached you?" Cain only looked at him in slight confusion. "Was their invitation polite?"

Cain could see that Elric was a bit apprehensive over his answer. It was obvious at this point, that Arif thought Cain a man due some respect. When first Elric and his men had encountered Cain, perhaps they had not been well informed as to Arif's true feelings about him. After Cain had revealed his trace however, Elric had seemed respectful as well. "It served its purpose," Cain answered.

Arif pressed on. "Were there any among my men who treated you less than cordially?"

Cain only smiled and shrugged. Arif smiled as well. "Noble of you not to say, but I know my men. Elric, I would like you to fetch Tony, Joseph and Kieran, bring them to us in the armory."

Elric seemed a little surprised at the last name, as was Cain; he had never heard of the man. Still, Elric left to his task without question or comment. Arif rose from his chair, gesturing Cain towards the other door used by Tomas and Richard. "Come, I'd like to show you something."

They exited the room into a hallway. A few doors were passed along the way to a final pair of large double doors at the end of the short hall. Arif produced a key to open these doors and reveal a large room that had indeed been turned into quite an impressive armory. It held a few glass cases displaying shotguns and rifles that had no doubt been left by the previous owners of the house, but the rest of the walls had been covered with an amazing array of weapons.

Racks and shelves of all types held swords, axes, crosses and stakes of every description. They ranged in age from modern crossbows to such items as the medieval mace and chain. Cain looked about in wonder and appreciation. There was even a large freestanding covered urn to one side, with an ornate cross depicted on its' cover. Cain assumed there was holy water within.

Arif looked pleased by Cain's open admiration of his possessions. "You approve of my collection? I must admit that it is a bit cumbersome to travel with, but many of the pieces within hold special personal value. I do admire a good weapon, don't you?"

Cain smiled. "Indeed. I had an extensive collection of my own back at my estate in the U.K. Unfortunately, it's mostly been sold to museums and such. You've some intriguing specimens here. Still, I don't see what this might have to do with me. Not to be rude, but I do worry for the humans in my care. I should be going."

Arif seemed unconcerned. "Fear not. I do have those of my own whom I use as scouts. They have been keeping track of the one whom you seek. They will alert us if any troublesome activity ensues. I like to know what goes on around me.

As a matter of fact, that concerns what I would like to show you. You see, I make it my business to know the happenings not only where I reside, but in neighboring provinces as well. As much as practicality permits, anyway." Arif's attention was distracted for a moment. Cain could sense Elric approaching with the others.

Arif addressed the door. "Enter." Elric opened it as bidden, and Tony, Joseph and the one who must be Kieran entered the room. Arif spoke to Elric. "Thank you. You may stay. You might find this of some interest."

Arif continued his conversation with Cain. "As I was saying, I like to be well informed. Kieran is one of my runners. I use him to send messages to others and to scout ahead areas that I plan to visit."

Cain studied the boy. He was young in appearance, perhaps fifteen when he'd died. His trace revealed him to have lived 'undead' for about thirty-five years beyond that. He was a slight young man with long wispy blonde hair and large bright green eyes.

Arif smiled at him. "You should know that I trust him implicitly. That which Kieran reports may be considered unquestionable. He has good insight and judgment of character and he is always invaluable in guiding me, but as I have mentioned in the past, in matters of great consequence I believe only that which I observe. A wise man reserves final judgment of a situation until he has seen it from all sides.

Kieran has informed me of some very interesting developments he observed, prior to my arrival. He is of course very skilled in the art of cloaking his presence, a necessity for my use of him as a scout. No doubt, you were unaware that Kieran surveyed this very area before I did arrive here myself. That which he reported back to me was very odd and interesting. It seems there was some altercation between minions of Sindy's making and yourself with two of your human companions, in the cemetery a while back. Do you know the instance of which I speak?"

Cain thought back. Ah, yes with Ben and Felicity. He'd no idea that they had been watched. He nodded to Arif of his remembrance. The incident had happened shortly before Arif and his brood had arrived. In fact, later that same evening Cain had observed Arif himself for the first time, at Venus with Sindy.

"Kieran tells me that you and your humans fought well, easily defeating her minions. This in itself was not particularly of interest to me. It was that which occurred *after* that I wish to question." Cain furrowed his brow in thought. He'd no idea to what Arif might be referring. Was he seen spying upon them at Venus perhaps? Why should that be of interest to Arif anyway? "I am told that you engaged in a small demonstration for your humans in the cemetery afterwards. Kieran has reported that you were seen *holding* a cross."

Cain laughed. "Oh…yes. I held a cross, that's true enough, but the act was not without repercussions I can assure you. I did only that which any of us might, with sufficient bravery and strength of will."

"Is that so? Would you mind then, demonstrating such an act here for us now?"

Cain could not help but look at them all a bit oddly. What was the point? Surely, they had experienced such things before; they shouldn't need him to demonstrate. Were Arif's children so unversed in the consequences of such an act? Arif could plainly read his speculative thoughts. "Please, humor me. You needn't keep it for long. Tony, bring the man a cross." Tony seemed more than eager to oblige. He went to the wall, donned a thick glove from a lower shelf, and then brought down a particularly large and ornate cross from the rack. He came to stand before Cain with it.

Cain eyed Arif for a moment, who gave him a little nod of reassurance. Fine, he would humor them. He accepted the cross with his left hand. As Tony stepped back to give him room for display, Cain held it out before him. All eyes were trained closely on Cain's hand, awaiting the inevitable reaction. His skin did slowly begin to heat and then burn as he kept contact with the holy object. Cain was sure to keep his face blank and his arm steady. After a minute or so, wisps of smoke began to curl from his skin. Once the smoke was clearly apparent, he looked to Arif. "Satisfied?" Arif smiled and nodded. He seemed incredibly amused, although Cain could not imagine why.

"Thank you." Arif's men seemed rather amazed. "Tony, I'd like to see you do the same." Tony seemed a little startled at the request, but then looked back to the cross in

Cain's hand. Cain still held it out before him, as it steadily emitted a thin trail of smoke, and tried not to let on that he very much hoped to be relieved of it soon.

After a moment's consideration, Tony seemed to decide that he would not let Cain show him up. Arif spoke as the man stepped forward for the cross. "Do keep it until I should take it from you," he said. Arif held out his hand to Tony, who gave him the glove. At his words, Tony seemed much less anxious to take the cross, but he would not back down now.

After a moment, he held out his hand to Cain. Cain gave over the cross with some relief. Tony flinched as he took it, but closed his hand about it. He held his arm out before him as Cain had. Within seconds, smoke began to rise. Still Tony held on to the cross, desperate to prove Cain was no better than he. Cain's eyes widened as an actual tendril of flame arose from the man's hand. Tony stifled a whimper and looked desperately to Arif, who had him hold it for a few seconds more, before relieving Tony of the object. Just as Arif took the cross into his glove, Tony's hand seemed to burst into true ignition with a great whoosh of heat, air and fire.

Tony let out a cry and pulled his hand from the object to smother the flames in the material of his shirt. He brought the hand close in to his chest and managed to put it out. When he held it out again to inspect the damage, his hand proved to be darkly blackened and raw with burns.

Cain stared in amazement and then looked down to his own hand. He brought it higher before his eyes as he observed the small pink and bubbled blisters there. It was damaged certainly, but he had not sustained nearly the injury that Tony had. Yet Tony had held the cross for barely a minute while Cain had held it for at least five.

Cain looked back to Arif in bewilderment. Arif simply nodded with a knowing smile. Cain shook his head in confusion. "I don't understand."

Arif held up a hand for silence from Cain. The other men were already quiet with nearly reverent awe. Tony nursed his hand while glaring at Cain. Arif spoke. "Wait. There is one more experiment I would like for us to undertake, if you will accede." Cain slightly nodded his head in confused uncertainty.

"The Holy Water, if you will. Just a slight touch will do." Cain eyed the urn and then shrugged. He approached it and slid back the lid. Its mechanism allowed for it to be opened without actual removal. Sure enough, clear water was held within. It looked harmless enough, but Cain knew that a priests' blessing could turn it into a painfully acidic fluid to a vampire.

He looked at those gathered around him and then pushed up his sleeves. Using his left hand again, he closed his fist, and then exposed only his pointer finger. He slowly dipped his finger into the water. It felt very warm to the touch. After only a moment, he felt its heat begin to grow. He kept his finger submerged until the water felt as though it should be boiling, although of course it remained calm and clear. Cain could see his finger becoming scalded beneath the surface of the water. He pulled it back out to show the redness of it to the others. It was raw and tender, and he greatly wished there was some plain water that he might immerse it in.

He stepped back from the urn and looked to Arif who wore a broad smile. "Joseph."

The man in question seemed to jump guiltily and was rather hesitant to step forward. He did though, and silently approached the urn. He looked to Arif, who nodded for him to repeat the act that Cain had just completed. Cain found that he was more than a little curious as to what would happen next. He stared intently at Joseph's finger as it dipped below the surface of the water.

Joseph bravely tried to keep it submerged, but could not last long. The second his finger was enveloped in the Holy Water, he seemed to stifle a cry as it immediately became as red and scalded as Cain's was. After less than a minute Joseph jerked it back from the water and cried out in pain. Cain watched in disbelief, as layers of skin from Joseph's finger seemed to slough off into the water and disintegrate. He held his finger in the air and tried in vain to blow on it and end the agony it must have been causing him. It was a truly gruesome sight. Any longer in the water and it would very probably have been stripped to the bone.

Cain stood speechless as Arif addressed his men. "I should think that in the future you would do well to be polite and respectful of your elders, whatever the circumstance. You are all dismissed."

The men filed out and Cain was left staring at his hand in disbelief. He looked to Arif when the door was shut once again. "What does it mean?" Cain asked.

"I had hoped that *you* could tell me. Have you not heard the rumors that circulate about you? Obviously not or you would not be looking so thoroughly perplexed. I had heard stories of your crusade to tame all vampires, to be civil and harmless creatures. With this news, I once heard that you were immune to such Godly weapons as cross and Holy water. I disregarded it of course.

When Sindy told me of your presence here and Kieran reported to me his observation of your doings, I was intrigued. I must admit however that I still had trouble accepting such a thing until witnessed personally. The story I had heard at the first *was* exaggerated, but Kieran's description was as usual infallible."

"I don't understand. Are you telling me that there are none who might do as I have done?"

"None that I have seen," Arif admitted.

"My age perhaps. Am I the oldest that you have encountered? I know that the venom does grow more potent with years, perhaps defense grows as well. I am certainly not fully immune as you can see." Cain held up his slightly injured hand for Arif to see again.

Arif smiled. "I had suspected that theory would hold true…but I was mistaken. You see, *I* am this year 268 years of age. My damage would be identical to that of my men, I have tried it.

I also chanced upon another not very long ago. One almost as old as you. Gwenyfara was her name. 312 she claimed to be, with a strong, old and even mark to convince me it was so. I had not the opportunity to know her well. Apparently, she had some distaste for my lifestyle." Cain had to smile at that, and to refrain from asking Arif where he might find such a lady.

"I did have the fortune however, to observe the effects of a cross upon her fair skin. With only a touch she was quite badly burned. I do not believe age to be a factor."

"What then?" Cain asked.

Arif gazed at him evenly for a moment. "What else is there that would set you apart from other vampires?"

Cain dared not speak as he pondered the implication in his mind. Arif continued. "Might I ask, the name 'Cain', I assume that you chose it for its significance in the Christian Bible, did you not?" Cain nodded slightly. "I wonder if you realize just how well you have chosen.

I like to travel, and I do come across other vampires from time to time. Research into various claims of the powers and origins of our kind interests me. In a life so long, we all need something to peak our interests, no?" Cain smiled. "And so, as I do visit different regions, I like to hear the folklore and myths of each area and the boasts and claims of other vampires. Comparison of such tales often proves quite intriguing, but this is grist for the mill of discussion for another time.

I find your choice of name intriguing also. You must know well the story of Cain and Abel."

Cain gave a bitter smile. "A little too well."

"Indeed. I find it interesting that in punishment Cain is made to be a wanderer of the earth, a vagabond unable to work the ground for its crops. Our kind *are* wanderers by nature, and it is true crops no longer serve us."

"Yes," Cain agreed.

"As you surely know, God did also place a mark upon Cain, that as he walked the earth none should kill him. An interesting idea when applied to a man like yourself – truly marked in his own way, and immortal.

Did you know there is another version of this tale? In Turkey we have a story of the 40 morns and eves, are you familiar with it?" Arif asked.

"No, I can't say I've heard it," Cain admitted.

Arif smiled. "It too includes the story of Cain and Abel. In *this* tale, it is not for slighted praise over crops that Cain kills his brother; it is so that he might take the woman promised to be Abel's wife. It seems Cain did find her fairer than his own."

Cain stared at Arif steadily, trying not to betray the fact that he was a bit shaken by the accuracy of the tale. His face had surely gone a bit pale, but his voice did not falter as he spoke. "No. I had not heard the story." Just how much did Arif know about him? Could he have had his spies listening as he told Felicity of his history? The thought made him feel a little ill that their privacy should have been so intruded upon without his knowledge.

"There is a more interesting version even than that. The Italians also have their own story in which Cain kills his brother Abel. Abel has more money than he and when Cain begs a share, he is refused. He kills his brother and then passes himself off as he to escape reprimand."

Again, Cain felt the odd shock of unforeseen recognition in the story. Hadn't he allowed himself to be mistaken for Charles by authorities to escape punishment of his own? He did not interrupt, but let Arif go on with the tale. "God's punishment of Cain in that instance is what truly stirs my curiosity. I believe the exact phrase is 'Thou shalt be imprisoned in the moon, and from that place shalt behold the good and evil of all mankind.' Do you feel yourself imprisoned in the moon? I surely do, every morn when the moon slips away and I also must flee the coming rays of the sun.

I cannot say though, whether I find myself in a position to behold the good and evil of mankind in better perspective. I do hold myself rather aloof from such things. *You* however, seem very interested in acts of conscience. Mayhap you perceive yourself to be in clearer understanding since your…fall from grace.”

Cain tried to gauge Arif's seriousness. He felt almost as though the man was mocking him; daring him to draw a connection between such strange coincidences. The cross, the Holy Water, his own personal 'crusade'; could there be a connection? “I do consider myself enlightened, in comparison to my past, that much is true. I cannot draw conclusion however as to what tonight's events may insinuate.”

“Perhaps if I better understood the specifics of your existence I could help you to speculate on the occurrences we have witnessed. It was 1692, the year of your transformation?”

Cain looked at him with odd amusement, that Arif should be so bold as to admit to such thorough research into his background. “Yes.”

“And when was it that you chose to no longer take human life? Surely you drank fully at the start.”

Cain eyed him for a moment. “There is a detail in my life of which you've not been previously informed? I was coming under the impression that anything I might divulge had already been reported.”

Arif smiled, unperturbed. “I like to know just with whom it is I deal, be not insulted but see it as a compliment. Most aren't worth the effort of such thorough research.”

Cain gave the man a brief smirk. “1734. After that year I no longer drank deeply or for thirst. Not that I haven't my transgressions mind you, but it was 271 years ago that certain insights changed the way I view the world, and the relationship between the vampires and humans within it.”

“Do you truly believe that you can persuade every vampire in existence to lead their life by your model?”

“Some are very accepting of my ways, and grateful for the knowledge.” Cain replied with a shrug. “Some need a little longer to digest the idea.”

Arif leaned closer with a confidential smile. “I can tell you, there are many who will take a long while indeed.”

Cain grinned. “I've got time.” Cain tore his eyes from Arif to look to the door as they were both distracted by the quickly approaching mark of Kieran. “Master Arif!” he called from the hall.

Arif must have acknowledged him with a mental urging, for the boy quickly opened the door. “I've just received word, the one you watch…Chris, he and his brood are on the move. Their purpose seems to be confronting the girl that Cain owns.”

Cain became distressed, but Arif calmly questioned the boy further. “How long before they reach her?”

“The call came from Peter's post. He says they walk. At least twenty minutes I would think.” Kieran dared to glance at Cain. “You can meet them if you hurry.”

Arif nodded to the scout. “I thank you for the news.” Kieran nodded and left them. Arif turned back to Cain. “It seems you must be going.”

Cain thought to ask for a few men to back him up, but realized that it really was not Arif's responsibility to offer such assistance. *He* had no quarrel with Chris. In fact, he was most likely the one who had taught Chris to cloak. Cain was grateful enough that Arif would report Chris' whereabouts to him. "If I might inquire, how many does he lead?"

"Sindy's mindless behemoth Marcus follows him now. Added to that he has created three others. I must admit that the boy has begun to learn the way of it. He has corrected past mistakes and is creating much more useful allies of late."

Great. Cain eyed his hand once more, hoping it would not impede him. Arif noticed his concern. "Do accept my apologies for your injury. Let me offer compensation." Cain hoped he would send Elric or some other to help, but Arif had something else in mind. He gestured to the wall. "Why don't you choose yourself a gift? Something to keep peace between us."

Aid might have been more welcome, but this was better than nothing. Cain studied the weapons for a moment; very aware that time was of the essence. He was about to just grab anything, when an odd-looking sword caught his eye.

The hilt and shape of the weapon were average enough, but what caught his eye was its sheen. It did not gleam under the lights as the other silver metallic weapons did. Upon closer inspection, he saw why. It was not made from metal. There was a thin keen edge of metal blade running along each side, but the very point of the sword and its main body, from tip to hilt was made from wood. Like a giant stake with a handle and a sword's cutting edge. Against a vampire, it would be a perfect weapon. Cain reached to retrieve it from its place up high on the wall.

Arif shifted weight and sighed, the first unnecessary gesture Cain had ever observed from the man. Cain inspected the weapon in delight. "You have chosen a very unique piece. That is 'Ash bringer' and she is one of very few weapons designed against our kind. I am attached to her, but in respect for you, I will part with her." Arif bowed his head as Cain smiled broadly and experimentally sliced through the air. "Guard her well and make me not regret my gift."

Cain looked up to him. "Perhaps I should take a lesser weapon. This obviously holds personal value."

"No. It is yours, you must accept it or you will insult. Some night you will return that I might tell you of her history." Arif went to the wall and brought down the sheath, that Cain should not carry the blade naked. Cain hooked it to his belt, and housed the weapon within. "Besides, recent events urge me to think that you are a man I would rather not have quarrel with. I wouldn't want to raise hand against you only to be struck by lightning and heavenly wrath!" He laughed and nudged Cain jokingly. Cain could not help but wonder whether Arif might believe the statement to hold a grain of truth. Tonight's events had been odd indeed. "Now go, I have kept you overly long."

Quite right. No time for such philosophic considerations and theology. "My sincerest thanks. For the weapon...and the demonstration."

Arif smiled. "Another time will perhaps permit for further speculation and discussion. Goodnight, Elric shall show you out."

Sure enough, Elric was just approaching as Cain left the room. The man eyed the weapon with some surprise. All humor aside, Cain had the feeling that it had been meant as a sort of 'peace offering'. Age did have its advantages. Before long, he was speeding towards the college. He desperately hoped that he would arrive in time to confront Chris, before Felicity became directly involved.

Chapter 7 ~ Fears, tears and fire alarms

Felicity

Halloween Masquerade Ball
11:30, Sunday night

Felicity, Allie, Sindy and Ben headed to the exit on their side of the ballroom, with Ashley trailing behind them. As they were leaving the room, Felicity turned to observe the actions of Marcus and his new friends. Two faculty members were trying to have words with them as Marcus' eyes were eerily trained on Felicity across the room.

Just as she was turning to follow the others, she saw one of the guys Marcus was with end his heated argument with the faculty by shoving a man roughly to the ground. Felicity turned to grab Ben's arm before he disappeared. "Wait, shouldn't we do something? I mean, what if they hurt someone?"

Ben glanced at her in disbelief and then looked back up to what was very close to escalating into a brawl in the front of the ballroom. "What are *we* supposed to do?"

Sindy gave an amused little chuckle. "In case you hadn't noticed honey, they're here for *you*. You gonna go jump into their waiting arms?"

"Aren't they looking for you too?" Felicity asked.

Sindy laughed. "Sorry sweetie, you're the prime directive. I'm just a bonus at this point. Besides, they can't even see me. You're the one shining like a beacon. They're following you."

Ben stopped to give Felicity a disgruntled look. "You're *marked?*" She looked at him ruefully and gave a little nod. She didn't think 'Seemed like a good idea at the time' would be a well-received answer. He looked disgusted and disappointed in her, but he didn't say anything else about it. He began walking again, pulling Felicity with him. She used one hand to try to gather and hold her voluminous skirts out of the way so she wouldn't trip over them, as Ben didn't seem in a very forgiving mood. After a moment, he spoke to her again over his shoulder as they walked. "If they are following *you,* then if we get the hell out of here, they'll probably just pass through without bothering anyone else. They wouldn't want to lose you."

Ashley caught up and grabbed Ben to stop and look at her. "Wait a minute. We *want* those guys to follow us? What exactly is going on here anyway?" She was trying to look very stern, but it was kind of difficult to take her seriously while she wore a bright pink sheer harem outfit trimmed in gold sequins.

Ben tried to dismiss her and keep walking, but she wouldn't let go of his arm. As they moved out into the hall, he gave an exasperated sigh. "Ashley, you don't want to get involved in this. You should stay here. Go stay with the crowd and no one will bother you. Someone's probably calling the cops as we speak."

"What are you going to do?" she asked.

Ben glanced at the other three girls. "I don't know. I figure if we lead them on a wild goose chase across campus, maybe then we can circle back here in time for the cops to arrive before they catch up to us. Make sure someone calls the police okay?"

"Wait a minute. You're ditching me? I don't think so. You're *my* date and I'm not leaving you to run off with *her*," she said with a pointed look at Sindy, who smiled and mouthed her a little kiss.

Ben looked at Ashley in incredulity. "*What?*"

Allie threw her hands up in exasperation. "We don't have time for this crap!"

Ben looked back to see Marcus and one of his friends slipping through the crowd, as the other two were left fighting and arguing with the man who'd been shoved and those who'd come to his aid. He took Felicity's hand again. "She's right, come on." Ben led them away from the ballroom and down the hall. They were about to make the left turn that Felicity knew led down a corridor to the exit, when Ben stopped dead in his tracks. "Shit." Felicity peered past him to see a metal security gate stretched and locked across the hall, barring their way.

Sindy came up behind them to see the problem. "Nice going fearless leader."

Felicity turned to her, trying to defend Ben's choice of exits. "He didn't know. I guess they want everyone to use the main entrance. How did *you* get in without a ticket?"

Sindy smiled. "Guess the doorman thought I had a pretty face."

Alyson eyed her for a moment and then muttered, "Freakin' succubus." She gave Felicity a little push on the shoulder. "Keep movin'."

Felicity resisted. "If all the doors are locked, we should go back."

Allie turned to look behind her, past Ashley and through the ballroom doors. Marcus and his friend were almost through all the people on the dance floor. They were headed for the doors and gaining fast. "I don't think so." Allie turned to Ben. "What's down that way?" she asked, gesturing further down the way they had been going.

"That's the gym," he answered, although his expression showed that he thought it an unpromising direction.

"Does it have a separate entrance?"

"Yeah, but *it's* probably gated too," Ben said as he reluctantly began to follow Allie, who had started down the hall.

Allie started picking up speed and the others rushed to keep up. "Well there has to be a fire exit or something right?" No one had a chance to answer before they heard a yell from the ballroom behind them. Someone had tried to stop Marcus, and Felicity and the others turned just in time to see the man get thrown through the doorway into the hall. Without further word, they started running. They could hear a commotion coming from the ballroom, but it was doubtful that the vampires within could be delayed for long. They may be hesitant to bear their fangs, but they were hardly worried about following rules or civilized social restraints.

They passed another short hall to an outside exit on their left, but it was gated like the first. "See," Ben said in a huff as Allie passed him to the double doors ahead. Alyson reached the gymnasium and quickly pushed open one of the doors to usher Felicity through.

Ben and Ashley followed and then Sindy entered last, closing the door behind her. "I don't think it has a lock," she said, studying the door.

Felicity turned to face the room and couldn't help but remember the last time she had been in the gym…with Cain. Now she sorely wished she had continued having him teach her self-defense, rather than take her for picnics and dancing. The main gym was a large area of hard floor, half of which was covered by the mat that she and Cain had worked on. Locker rooms were on the left side of the gym and the equipment cage and sign in desk were on the right next to the door. The near left and far right corners of the room each had a staircase that led up to the second floor, which made a sort of balcony that completely circled and overlooked the main gym.

Alyson began looking around near the ceiling of the first floor for an exit sign. "Where the hell is the back door to this place?" The back wall of the room was lined with bleachers, which were mostly folded against the wall at the moment. Allie spotted the red exit light in the far left corner next to the bleachers and rushed over to try the door. Felicity had never spent much time upstairs, but she knew that the weight equipment, stair-climbers and treadmills were up there, and that further back the track circled the room along the walls.

Sindy grabbed hold of a large display rack of health and nutrition pamphlets near the sign in desk. "Ben," she called for his attention to help her drag it in front of the door. Ben pulled his arm away from Ashley to help push the heavy wooden rack of shelves.

Allie stormed back to them in a huff. "It's locked." After a moment, she ran off into the ladies' locker room to look for another door. Felicity went over to the sign in desk and picked up the telephone receiver. She had thought to try to call the police, but despite dialing '9', she couldn't seem to get an outside line.

Just as Ben and Sindy were finished moving the display rack, Sindy quickly backed away. A second later, a loud thump was heard from outside the door. It rocked the rack and some of the pamphlets spilled out onto the floor. The door did not open however. Ashley, who had backed into the left corner near the staircase, screamed and ran up the first few stairs. Felicity dropped the phone and went back out in front of the desk to stand by Ben. He glanced at her and she wasn't very reassured to see that he looked just as worried as she felt.

Allie pushed open the door to the ladies' locker room with a loud bang that made them all jump again. She didn't say anything; she just strode over to the men's locker room and disappeared inside. Apparently, she hadn't any luck finding another exit.

Ben eyed the display rack, and then went to lean up against it, to help it hold the door closed. Sindy watched with a condescending sneer. "This is stupid; we never should have come in here. It's not like we can *hide*," she added with a pointed glance at Felicity.

Felicity flinched at her words. Did Sindy have to keep reminding Ben that she was marked? Not that she was ashamed of it really, but she knew that Ben disapproved. The door was pushed against strongly again from the other side, forcing Ben to push back in order to keep his feet. He glanced up at Felicity standing a few feet away, staring at the entrance in fright. "There's got to be a back way out. Anyway, I thought we could cut through and outrun them, but we're never going to get far enough ahead; they can see your every move." She just looked at him with apologetic worry as he turned back to Sindy. "Isn't there some way to shut off that damn mark? Cain says they can't see him. Can't *you* do that too?" Ben braced himself against the shelf with his back as Marcus pounded against the door again.

Sindy stared at him for a moment. "I've been doing it for me. They probably don't even know that I'm here, but I don't know if I can do it for her too. If we're trapped in this damn gym, it won't make much of a difference anyway. They already know where she is."

Ben looked at her seriously for a minute. "I'm working on that. Please…would you try?"

Sindy almost looked as though she'd like to comment on Ben asking a favor of her, but after a moment's consideration and a sidelong glance at Felicity, she gave him a small smile and nodded. "Sure."

Allie came bursting out of the locker room with a scowl on her face. "Nothing!" No one answered her, so after a moment she stalked back to the far exit again. Felicity started after her as the pounding on the front door became worse. As she rounded the bleachers, she saw that big white letters across the red back door proclaimed it to be a fire exit. 'Do not open – alarm will sound'.

Allie began pounding on the push bar, to no avail. After a few minutes of banging and cursing Alyson turned to Felicity. "It's fucking locked! Can you believe that? I'm gonna sue this damn school. How do you lock a fire exit?" They started back towards the others to try to devise some sort of plan.

Just then there was an incredibly loud crash as the door was pounded against again from the hallway. Ben was taken by surprise and thrown to the floor. The door only opened a crack, but the shelf was knocked over onto Ben and the rest of the pamphlets scattered over the floor. Felicity stifled a yelp of surprise that came to her throat.

Sindy tried to help Ben out from under the display rack, but he jerked his hand back from her in surprise, as though her touch was painful. His mark, it wasn't entirely gone yet. Sindy backed off under his warning glare. As he worked his way out from under the shelf, he seemed more annoyed than hurt and really didn't want her assistance. Felicity went to join Ashley on the stairs. "What do we do?"

Ashley looked at her accusingly. "What do those guys want with you anyway? Why won't anyone tell me what's going on? Ben?"

Ashley was ignored as Allie stalked over to the foot of the stairs and looked up to Felicity. "Still no sign of Cain?" Felicity just shook her head. The pounding against the door continued.

Ben and Sindy were busy trying to right the display rack again, to keep the door from opening. Ben glanced back at Allie. "You *can't* lock a fire exit from the inside, only the outside locks. It must be stuck. Try it again."

"I tried!" Allie glanced around the room and then back to Felicity. "Maybe we can get out a window?" she asked hopefully. Felicity looked up behind her to see the windows Allie meant. She and Ashley quickly ran up the stairs to inspect them, as Alyson went to try the back door again.

As they reached the top of the stairs, Ashley ran off across the track to check the windows on the far left wall. Felicity quickly glanced around to see that the only other windows were at the back of the room over the spot where the bleachers were downstairs. The others were all interior walls. She made her way out onto the track and jogged towards the back wall, but even before she cut through the maze of treadmills, she could see it would be no use. The windows were far too high to ever reach.

After a moment, Felicity heard the front door get slammed against so forcefully, that it knocked over the bookshelf again. She looked down to see that Ben and Sindy had scrambled out of the way to avoid it landing on them. Allie's cursing and banging on the back door below Felicity started again. Ben ran to try to help her.

Felicity looked across the space that was open to downstairs, to see Ashley dejectedly making her way back through the weight equipment. "I can't reach them, unless you want to help me pull a weight bench over."

Felicity glanced up at the windows again. She couldn't even tell how you would open them anyway. She ran and leaned over the railing of the balcony so she could see Alyson and Ben at the back door. "I don't think we can get out from up here. Any luck?"

Ben told Allie to back away as he raised his leg and kicked strongly at the push bar of the door. As he did, Sindy came running towards him. "No, don't open that door!"

Too late. The door bar unstuck and pushed in with a loud click, followed by the wailing of an alarm. Ben was backed up a few steps from the force of his kick pushing off the door. The door only opened a crack, but was caught and opened from the outside by the two vampires that they had left in the ballroom. Having been thrown out of the dance, they must have decided to follow Felicity's mark around the building to this door.

Sindy joined Allie and Ben by the door, giving Ben a scolding glance. She must have seen them coming by their marks, but her warning had come too late. Before anything could even be said, the other door came crashing open. As Ben, Allie and Sindy turned to see Marcus bash through the front door, the other two vampires moved into the room just enough to shut the back door and silence the alarm.

Marcus kicked the front door open further and heaved the display shelf aside. The other vampire he was with came around him into the room and surveyed its occupants.

Surprisingly, none of them seemed to look upstairs at Felicity on the balcony. She glanced back to Sindy and saw that she seemed deep in concentration. She must be doing it; she was hiding Felicity's mark! Felicity never felt so grateful, although it couldn't help for long. She silently prayed that Cain was on his way, and tried to inconspicuously move back a little from the railing to escape notice.

Unfortunately, Ashley had just been coming out from behind the treadmills at the other end of the balcony, when Marcus and his friend had come in. As Marcus was throwing the display rack aside, Ashley screamed, drawing his attention. Marcus looked confused. He was probably unsure what to do, being unable to see Felicity's mark. Upon seeing Ashley flee back from the railing again, he decided to start up the stairs. *Thanks a lot Ashley*, Felicity thought with a frightened shudder. She ducked down behind a stair-master and tried to crawl to where she could still see everyone below, but would hopefully remain hidden. She couldn't see where Ashley had gone and hoped that she was hiding well.

The two vampires by the back door moved forward, preparing to try to push their way further into the room. They only reached the front edge of the bleachers before being blocked by Allie, Sindy and Ben. The other vampire, by the front entrance, looked them over. He seemed to decide that the vamps by the back door needed no help and moved to wait for Marcus at the bottom of the stairs. He didn't seem to realize that there was another staircase in the corner by Felicity. She thought about using it, but once downstairs she could never cross the room to the front door without being seen. She didn't want to leave her friends anyway. She was probably best off staying put for now. She desperately hoped that Cain would come looking for her soon.

Marcus was picking his way through the equipment across the way, to where Felicity couldn't see him well. A second later, he must have spotted Ashley again, because she screamed. So much for remaining hidden. She couldn't just leave Ashley to try to fend off Marcus alone. Felicity crept in and out of exercise machines trying to make her way over to the other side of the balcony unnoticed. As she neared the railing, she saw Ben below. He didn't see her, but neither did the vampires in front of him, so that was a good thing. Ashley screamed again from the other side. "Ben!"

As the vampires by the bleachers moved to come further into the gym, Alyson spoke to Ben. "Go help her, we're alright," she said with a glance at Sindy.

Sindy smiled and stepped up closer to Allie, looking over the two guys and crossing her arms in front of her. "Yeah, we got this."

The vampires looked at the girls in amusement. Ben seemed just as bemused by the girls' confidence as their foes were, when Ashley screamed again. Allie turned to him in aggravation that he was still standing there doubting their competence. "Go, we got it!"

Felicity saw Ashley dart out from behind the weight bench she'd been trying to keep between her and Marcus. She tried to run, but he moved to block her into the back left corner where there was only a small glass front refrigerator, no staircase. Ashley opened the fridge and began throwing water bottles at Marcus, who seemed unfazed and was steadily advancing on her. "Hey!" Felicity yelled for his attention, standing up from behind the treadmill where she'd been crouching. "Weren't you looking for me?"

Marcus turned to face her. Slowly recognition crept across his face. Felicity wondered whether he actually recognized her or if Sindy had stopped hiding her mark, being forced to concentrate on other things. Felicity started backing away and Marcus began to follow her.

As she came closer to the rail of the balcony, she could hear Sindy and Alyson talking to the vampires below. Sindy was all attitude and confidence as she asked, "Who the hell are you guys anyway? What do you want with us?"

"We owe Chris a favor. He wants the girl," one answered.

Sindy laughed. "Well, you may want to go back and tell him that his favor isn't worth your life. 'Cause if you want Felicity, you're gonna have to get through *us* first," she said with a smug grin and a glance at Allie.

The guys laughed at her. Felicity knew that Sindy could be a dangerous and formidable opponent, but her skills hardly looked to lie in the physical combat arena. Of course, Alyson's petite little form was deceiving as well. "No problem." One of the vampire's replied with another chuckle.

Felicity couldn't pay attention to the girl's reply, as Marcus was almost upon her. She'd managed to draw his attention from Ashley, but now what was she supposed to do? Where the hell was Ben? She heard fighting coming from the front left stairs. Ben must still be trying to get past the other vampire that had come in with Marcus. Ben should have used the back right stairs. Maybe he didn't know they were there. Anyway, Ashley's scream had come from towards the front.

She couldn't afford to worry about Ben at the moment, she had her own problems. Marcus stalked up to her with a nasty grin. Even through her frantic thoughts of escape possibilities, Felicity couldn't help but absently wonder whether Marcus had been told to kill her or bring her back to Chris. Would he even know the difference? He didn't look like someone who could handle complex instructions.

Felicity was trying to decide if she would break her legs, should she try to jump over the railing (unfortunately she was not above the mat at this point) when there was a terrible thud and Marcus collapsed to the floor. She looked up in disbelief to see Ashley standing behind him with a dumbbell in her hands. She had whacked him in the back of the head with it.

Ashley smiled and shrugged as Felicity glanced back down at Marcus in bemused relief. Ashley looked to have cracked his head open. His hair was a damp bloody mess. Felicity knew that he'd probably live through it, but he didn't look to be getting up any time soon. "Wow, thanks."

Ashley smiled. "*You* distracted him." She dropped the weight onto the floor with a loud thump and gave Marcus a little kick. "Big dumb oaf. What's his problem anyway?" Ashley backed up a step and looked up to Felicity in sudden worry. "You don't think I…killed him do ya'?"

"No. Definitely not. Don't worry about it. You did great."

Just then, they heard Allie yell "Kiyaa!" followed by what sounded like a man's surprised yell of pain.

Felicity ran to the rail to see Allie beating the heck out of her opponent. She went after him with a flurry of strikes and kicks, and he hardly seemed to know how to respond. He was trying to grab her but she kept slipping away.

His friend had originally seemed to think it was kind of funny that a little girl was beating up a big vampire, but he was suddenly distracted by Sindy who must have changed, because she went straight for his throat. She pierced his skin before he even had a chance to react. It certainly wasn't what he was expecting. "Holy shit, she's a vamp!" he screamed as she pounced on him. Sindy must still have been cloaking herself.

"It's her! It's the other one that Chris wanted." Yelled the guy who was trying to fend off Alyson.

"Well get her off me!" Sindy had wrapped herself around the guy and was surely drinking deeply. He couldn't seem to extricate himself from her and soon fell to his knees. His eyes turned orange and Felicity could see a flash of fangs in his mouth, proving that he had shifted as well. He couldn't seem to summon the strength or leverage to bite Sindy back though. She'd gotten too much of a lead on him. Her venom had probably started to affect his reflexes.

The muscle relaxant in the venom paired with whatever else he might be feeling from her bite, would probably keep him from fighting back very hard anytime soon. After a few moments, Sindy dropped him to the floor and wiped her mouth as she shifted back to her human state. "Mmm. I needed that," she muttered with a smile.

Felicity's attention was drawn from Sindy to see Alyson jump up onto the bottom bench of the bleachers in front of the guy she was fighting. She delivered a kick to his abdomen and then jumped down on top of him as he stumbled backwards and doubled over. Allie's elbow came down to hit him in the shoulder from above and he dropped to his knees. Allie never even gave him a chance to try to use his fangs. She ended the fight by giving him a swift kick to the head. He hit the floor and she pulled out a stake to finish him. He exploded into a big cloud of dust.

Felicity was startled by Ashley strongly grabbing her shoulder. "Oh my God! What did she do to that guy? Where'd he go? Did you see that?"

"Yeah. I think they've got things under control down there. We should see if Ben needs help."

"But…I don't get it. Did you see what happened to that guy? What did she do to him? Why won't anybody tell me what's going on?"

Felicity just started pushing Ashley towards the front stairs. "Ben'll tell you later." As they reached the staircase, they practically collided with Ben running up them, his arms covered in ash.

"Are you girls okay?"

Ashley started rambling in hysterics as she flew into his arms. "Ben, oh my God! Did you see what Allie just did to that guy? And that girl you know, she grabbed the other guy, and I think she *bit* him! It was so bizarre!

That giant dufus was chasing me and then Felicity distracted him and I clonked him on the head with a dumbbell and I knocked him out cold! *I* did! Can you believe it? I hope I didn't kill him!"

Ben glanced up with a smile to see that Felicity was okay, and then put an arm around Ashley to start walking her down the stairs. Felicity was about to follow when she realized that she was beginning to feel Cain's presence, coming from somewhere behind her.

Finally! She stepped towards the rail and leaned over to see Sindy opening the fire door in anticipation of his arrival. He must be outside, coming towards the back door…and Sindy *could* feel him, just as she'd said. Cain was always cloaked, why would *Sindy* be able to feel him?

The door alarm began to wail and Felicity shook off troubled thoughts. At least he was here. She adjusted her headpiece and fluffed her dress in excitement to go down and see him. She headed towards the far right stairs, as they would put her closer to the back door.

She was holding up her skirts as she cut in through the treadmills towards the corner. She had just crossed the track and stopped at the stairwell when suddenly a hand slipped over her mouth. She felt herself grabbed from behind and dragged backwards. She tried to scream but barely let out a thin shriek before her mouth was covered. Surely, no one heard her over the alarm. She shook her hands free of her gowns' sleeves to claw at the arm around her and thought briefly that she should try to flip its owner, but she caught her heel in the lace at the hem of her skirt and could hardly even keep her feet. She was pulled back behind a rack of free weights and then pushed to the ground. The hand was only taken from her mouth for a rag to be shoved into it.

She struggled and looked up in dismay to see Chris leering down at her. He knelt down atop her in the same way that Luke had the night she'd killed him. Unfortunately, Chris seemed much more in control than Luke ever had. He had wasted no time in getting a firm hold of her long flowing sleeves, making her unable to use her hands trapped within. He used the ends of her sleeves to pin her arms to the ground over her head and showed no sign of giving her a chance to twist free. She tried to kick and wriggle from under him, but her legs only became hopelessly entangled in her skirts and it was no use. After a few moments of struggle, she became almost frozen in fear.

Fleeing from the others and taunting Marcus had been different. She had been pumped with adrenaline and surrounded by her friends. She had been scared, but somehow she hadn't really thought anything truly bad could have happened, however naïve that might have been. This was different, back here alone with Chris behind the exercise equipment. Her friends were still nearby, but no one could hear her, no one would see, no one would even know…until it was too late.

But Cain was here, she'd felt him! She didn't think he was in the building yet, but he was certainly close. The alarm was still going off; they must be holding the door open for him. She couldn't even hope for them to hear something with that racket going on, but could Chris possibly hurt her in the few minutes it might take for Cain to get here, even against her mark? What was taking Cain so long?

With a sudden flare of frightened insight, she realized…Sindy was hiding her mark. There was no way for Felicity to know if she'd stopped, but until she did, Cain couldn't see her. He couldn't tell where she was. He would feel the physical awareness of her presence, but without her mark to guide him, it would be vague and hard to follow. She was…alone.

Chris glared at her in hatred and leaned down close to speak into her ear. "You thought you'd kill my best friend and get away with it?" he asked her with a rough shake, knocking her head against the floor. "You thought the 'almighty Cain' could protect you, but you thought wrong." He bared his fangs at her with an evil hiss. She scrunched her eyes shut and turned her head this way and that, trying to keep him from her throat.

As he held the ends of both sleeves pinned down with one hand, he used the other to rip the hat and veil off her. He grabbed a handful of hair on the right side of her head, pinning the side of her face to the floor and leaving the left side of her throat exposed.

Felicity's scalp hurt and her neck ached, her muscles taught from hopelessly pulling away from him to no avail. Chris dipped down to the tender place where her shoulder met her neck but as his fangs touched her skin, he pulled back with an angry snarl. He eyed her in annoyance. "Went and got marked again did ya? Too bad. I was really looking forward to drinking from Cain's private stock." He untangled his fingers from her hair, and then shifted his weight so that he could pull something from his pocket.

He held a shiny silver switchblade up for her to see with an evil smile. "Guess I'll just have to lick it off the floor." She struggled with renewed intensity as he brought the blade to her throat. The blare of the alarm seemed to fill the world as it screamed in her ears and her heart tried to pound its way out of her chest. This could not happen! This was how it would end? She would have her throat slit by this creep while her friends and her love were not twenty feet away?

Felicity tried harder to pull away, but there was no room left to move, she was pinned. Her hands were trapped down in the long sleeves of her dress so that she couldn't use them to get free. Chris sat atop her, a heavy weight upon her stomach and chest so that she could hardly breathe. She scrunched her eyes shut tight as tears began to roll down her face.

Chris put the blade to her throat up high under her ear and she was forced to turn her face aside and strain her head up to keep it from stabbing her. She tried again to scream around the rag in her mouth, as he jerked the knife upwards and the point of the blade poked into her flesh. The cold steel made a puncture sharp and painful, so unlike her lovers bite. It stung as she felt it cut through her skin. He pushed it in deep before beginning to move it across and under her chin.

Felicity opened her eyes to see Chris looking down at her with a cold and sinister grin as he began to slit her throat. Then he jerked forward a bit, his eyes wide and his mouth opened in protest. Before she could wonder why, he seemed to explode. There was nothing left but dust to collapse upon her. The blade in her throat was jerked painfully further upward for a second and then fell dead upon her neck. It snagged there with its point beneath her skin for a painful instant and then dropped onto her chest as the hand holding it was transformed into ash.

She simply lay staring up at the ceiling tiles, through the swirl of dust that still hung in the air above her where Chris had been. Then another face came into view, Ben. He was holding a stake in one hand and holding the other out to help her up. She hardly believed that he was there. He must have come up the stairs while Chris was distracted with her.

Everything in the world seemed reduced to the sting of the cut at her throat and the blaring siren in her ears. Ben was smiling down at her when his face suddenly seemed to collapse upon itself in shock and distress. Her throat...she was bleeding she knew. Ben must not have seen the knife when Chris was in the way.

"Felicity!" He knelt down over her and pulled the rag from her mouth in an instant. She tried to speak, to tell him that she was alright. It was just a cut, it couldn't be that bad, but when first she opened her mouth, no sound would come.

His eyes seemed wide with fear and he grabbed and threw away the blade that had lain upon her chest. She ventured a small smile and he leaned down close to move the hair from her face. He took the rag that Chris had used to gag her, and pressed it against her throat. Maybe she was bleeding worse than she'd realized.

The stupid alarm was still going off. It seemed deafening and she found it hard to even think. She closed her eyes, and then there was suddenly silence. She was frightened for a moment that perhaps she had passed out, but when she opened her eyes Ben was still there and it was the alarm that was gone. They must have finally closed the damn door.

She found herself staring at the shiny buttons on Ben's NASA uniform for a moment before looking back up to his eyes. "Looks like you got to be a superhero after all," she whispered with a smile.

It took him a moment to realize she was referring to his Halloween costume. She was a little surprised to see a tear of relief slide down his cheek. It fell onto her face as he let out a little laugh. She knew that her face was already wet with tears of fear from a moment ago. She blinked as Ben leaned forward and gave her a small kiss on the cheek near the corner of her eye and took her last tear away.

He leaned back and moved the rag to inspect her throat. "It's a nasty slice, but I think you'll be okay." Ben tried to wipe most of the dust pile that had been Chris off her stomach and then helped her gently to her feet, as she moved her own hand to continue holding the rag to her cut. She stood and Ben held onto her strong and sure for a moment as she gained her balance. She looked up at him again, thinking to thank him. He smiled at her with such touching and sincere relief that she was alright, she forgot what she'd meant to say.

"Felicity?" It was Cain, down below. He sounded terribly worried. The others must have filled him in on the evening's events. They had to know of Chris' presence now, for Sindy must have felt him die.

"Oh sorry." Sindy's voice. She must still have been cloaking Felicity, and Cain could not see her. He had to feel her, but that only gave a general sense of direction. Felicity was afraid to yell and hurt her throat.

Ben yelled for her as they moved slowly towards the stairs. "Up here." Cain must have already been on his way up because he was upon them before Ben was hardly done speaking. Before she knew it, Ben had stepped away and Cain was holding her in his arms.

"Careful, she's hurt. Her throat," Ben admonished.

Cain leaned her back to look upon her in concern. He seemed confused. "But...how? He couldn't have..."

Felicity tried not to wince as she swallowed and it caused her throat to burn. "Switchblade," she whispered. Cain looked devastated that she had been hurt without his protection. "I thought you weren't coming," she said lightly, trying to tease him as he her move the rag for him to see and fussed over her wound. He looked into her eyes again as she whispered, "and you're late."

He gave her a lopsided grin. "Yeah I know." He gazed at her with loving concern for a moment, and then seemed to remember something. "But look, I wore a costume." Felicity held the weight rack to keep steady as he let go of her hands for a moment to pull his sweater off over his head, revealing the chain mail vest that he wore underneath. She ran her eyes over him to see that he had added to it a large sword at his belt. He took her hands back into his own and made a little bow. "Your 'knight in shining armor', my lady." He seemed almost choked with remorse as he spoke. "Sorry I didn't get to slay the dragon for you." He glanced over at Ben. "Thanks." Ben just shrugged and looked away.

Felicity gazed at Cain for a moment. She still felt a bit disoriented and the side of her throat was a burning nagging sting that would hardly let her think, but something was tugging at her mind that she couldn't quite place at first. "You look different." Suddenly she placed it. "Your hair! You cut your hair!"

"Oh, yeah." Cain smiled sheepishly and ran his hand through it. "Actually, Alyson cut it for me. Does it look alright?"

At the mention of Allie, Felicity noticed that Ben looked back at Cain in surprise and then became annoyed. He turned from them and went to lean on the rail a few paces away. Felicity surveyed Cain's' newly shorn hair. Allie had done a wonderful job. He looked so sexy! It was very short at the back and sides, but the front was just long enough to still fall forward a bit and look 'casually messy'. It was still 'him', just neatened up and a little more polished. She smiled. "You look really good."

Cain smiled at her adoringly for a moment. "You look lovely as well." She let out a small breath of a laugh, knowing she was probably a terrible mess. He took her gently by the elbows and helped her to the stairs. "Come on princess, let's get you cleaned up."

Felicity looked down at her dress as they began to descend the stairs. It was covered in ash and blood, and was trailing a long ripped swath of lace from the bottom in the back. She looked back up at Cain. "Can I borrow $329?" He gave her a confused laugh and a nod.

Sindy met them at the bottom of the stairs, seeming a bit shaken. She looked up to the balcony, where Ben stood watching them, and then back at Cain. Her eyes seemed to fall on the sword. "Can I borrow that?"

Cain had no time to question her before she pulled it from the sheath at his side. She began to climb the stairs with it as Cain turned to rebuke her. "That's not to play with!"

She called back to him over her shoulder as she topped the stairs. "Don't worry; I'm not planning to enjoy this." Ben eyed her warily as she approached him. "Duck," she said as she closed on him.

"What?" Ben asked suspiciously.

"Duck!" He did, revealing Marcus just coming up behind him. Sindy swung the sword up over her shoulder like a baseball bat and then sharply brought it to swing around over Ben's hunched form. Felicity heard Ashley scream as Marcus' head came flying at them from over the balcony, accompanied by a splattering spray of blood. His face was twisted into a frightening grimace of surprised anger. It turned to dust before it hit the floor. Felicity cringed in surprise and disgust as a few droplets of blood struck her arm, but was even more surprised when they disintegrated into ash as well.

Felicity looked up just in time to see Marcus' body transform into dust and then collapse upon itself in a sort of silent explosion, showering Ben with his ashes. Sindy dropped the sword and fell to the floor clasping her throat.

Alyson had been climbing the stairs to follow Sindy, unsure what she'd had in mind for Ben. Now she ran the rest of the way to reach them. Ben was just sitting up to see what had happened.

Cain had tightened his grip on Felicity's shoulders in surprise. He must have been so worried for her, that he hadn't noticed Marcus moving again. Now he looked down and caught her wincing in pain as she tried to swallow. "You alright?"

Felicity weakly smiled and nodded. She told Cain she just wanted to sit on one of the lower benches of the bleachers for a minute to recuperate. He helped her to sit and after watching her for a moment, presumably to assess whether she really was okay, he turned to examine the vampire that Sindy had left on the floor next to them. Felicity watched as Allie reached Ben on the balcony. Alyson squatted between him and Sindy, with a hand on Ben's shoulder. "You okay?"

"Yeah, what happened?" Ben asked.

"Marcus, behind you." Allie looked over to see Sindy beginning to stir. "She…beheaded him."

Ben stood up with a dazed expression on his face and tried to clear himself of Marcus' ashes. Ashley went running up the stairs to him. "Ben!" She practically tripped over Sindy and threw herself into Ben's arms. "Are you okay? What is wrong with these people? They keep exploding! I thought she was going to kill you! Come downstairs, let's get out of here!"

Sindy opened her eyes to look up at Ben. He met her gaze for a brief moment. "Thank you," he uttered. He looked almost surprised that Sindy would have done that for him. He opened his mouth as though to better express his gratitude, but Ashley pulled at his arm insistently and Ben suffered himself to be led downstairs without another word. He hadn't the chance to say anything else as Ashley fussed over him and dragged him away.

Allie watched them until they disappeared from view and then turned to see Sindy sit up. She looked ill as her eyes met Allie's. "I am seriously starting to reconsider the whole 'be fruitful and multiply' thing. Turns out that pain is a pretty good incentive to keep your blood to yourself," Sindy muttered.

"What the hell are you talking about? No one even touched you!" Allie exclaimed.

Sindy tried to smile, but then shuddered as she looked down at Marcus' ash all around her. "Transferred pain. I made Marcus, so I get my own special sharing experience when he dies."

Allie gazed at her in shock. "You mean you...*felt* it, just like him?"

Sindy nodded. "Uh-huh."

Allie grimaced and looked from the ash back to Sindy. "That sucks."

"Tell me about it," Sindy agreed. Sindy's eyes were trained on Ben downstairs, who was trying to talk to Cain while Ashley alternately smothered him with kisses and pulled at him to leave.

Allie followed her gaze through the railing. "That was cool, that you did that for Ben."

"He doesn't seem too impressed."

"No, I wouldn't think that *you* should expect showers of gratitude from him." Alyson watched him for a minute. He and Cain seemed to be trying to bring around the last vampire on the floor that Sindy had drained. What were they going to do with him? She looked back to Sindy who was still staring at Ben. "But *I* think it was cool. Did it hurt a lot?"

Sindy shrugged. "You had some pretty cool moves down there yourself. Where did you learn to fight like that?"

"I used to take Jui Jitsu. I'm a brown belt. Haven't trained for a while though. Sucks I never got my black. I ran out of cash. My Dojo let's me train for free sometimes, but you know...it's a big commitment. I kind of got side tracked."

"No wonder you always manage to kick my ass."

Allie smiled up at her, amazed that she'd admit it. "I do, don't I? I've seen you pull some interesting tricks though."

"Oh yeah, being a vamp does have its advantages if you know how to use them."

Allie gave her a little grin, intrigued. "Like what?"

A sly smile stole over Sindy's face as she surveyed the people below them. "Keep your eye on Ben."

Alyson looked a bit nervous. "Why?"

"Just watch." Sindy stared at him intently for a moment. Felicity trained her eyes on him as well, wondering what Sindy could possibly have in mind. After a moment, he began to fidget and then gave a violent shudder and stumbled a step in Sindy's direction. He turned to look up at Sindy with an angry glare. He didn't seem hurt at all, just extremely annoyed.

Sindy chuckled as she and Allie moved back from the edge out of Ben's immediate view. Alyson gave Sindy a little shove on the shoulder. "What did you do?"

"Relax, he'll get over it." Sindy peeked over at Ben again, who no longer paid the girls any attention. "He hasn't got much of my venom left in him. I could do much more with the guy on the floor." She nodded towards the vampire who seemed to have come around and was being quietly questioned by Cain and Ben.

"But I don't get it," Allie persisted. "What did you do?"

"My venom is in him. When I'm close enough to him, it recognizes the blood and venom in me. It *wants* to be with me. Just a little urging makes it try to get his body to come to me. It wants us to be together," Sindy explained with a smug little smile.

Allie looked as uncomfortably confused as Felicity felt. "*It* wants? I thought it was just like…a poison."

"I don't really know what it is, but it sure can make things interesting. Since there's hardly any left in him, I haven't got the power for something long sustained and subtle, but if I focus it just right, it's good for a quick burst or two. Not very useful, but still…fun."

Alyson shook her head and stood up. Her expression was a strange mixture of disgust and amusement. "Leave him alone," she said mildly as she started down the stairs. Sindy retrieved Cain's sword from the floor where she'd dropped it, and followed, stopping next to the bleachers by Felicity.

Cain came over to meet them, as Allie went to talk to Ben and Ashley. Sindy handed Cain back the sword. "Where'd you get that thing?"

Cain smiled as he sheathed it at his side. "It was a gift."

"It's *wood*," Sindy said with an odd look.

"Yes, that's kind of the idea." He laughed as he made a motion in the air as though staking a vampire.

Sindy's eyes went wide with comprehension. "Neat."

Cain laughed again and then had Felicity tip her head up and remove the rag so he could see. He shook his head disapprovingly. "It's still bleeding a bit. It looks deep. I think you need stitches. Feeling alright?"

She slowly stood and answered in a low and rasping voice. "I'm a little woozy. It hurts, but I'm okay."

"Yes, I think an ER visit is definitely in order."

Felicity looked up at him in alarm. "I don't wanna go to the hospital." She raised her voice a bit in her distress but the pain immediately made her return to the level of a stage whisper. "What if my folks find out? They'll make me go home."

Cain studied her for a moment. "You *are* going to hospital. I'll pay cash if you like, so you don't have to use your parents' insurance, but you have to see a doctor…now."

Felicity pouted sullenly at the floor but allowed Cain to hold her arm to help her down off the bleacher bench. Sindy caught his attention. "What are you gonna do with him?" she asked, nodding to the vampire that she had bitten. He was still sitting on the floor.

Cain shrugged. "I shouldn't think he'll be bothering us further. Let him be."

Sindy eyed him appraisingly. He was in his mid twenties, kind of good looking actually. Sindy gave Cain a pleading little smile. "Could *I* have him? Like to play with a little? I won't hurt him or try to get him to attack you or nothin'. Promise."

Cain rolled his eyes and shook his head, looking a bit disgusted. "He's certainly not yours or mine to command." Sindy's smile showed that she thought otherwise. After witnessing Sindy's use of venom and psychic control, Felicity was leaning towards agreeing with Sindy. She probably could control him very well if she'd a mind to. Personally, Felicity would be very content to give Sindy someone else to focus her attentions on for a change. Cain just waved her away. "Do as you like, just stay out of trouble."

Sindy grinned, looking at her new catch. "No problem. I can play nice, when I have to." The guy in question got shakily to his feet as she sauntered over to him. At first, he eyed her apprehensively, but relaxed when she stopped a few paces from him. She looked him up and down and then smiled. "Told you that you wouldn't get past me."

He smiled, shaking his head. "I didn't know you were one of *us.*"

Sindy glanced at the spot where a few ashes of the guys' partner could still be seen on the floor. "Was he a friend of yours?"

The guy shook his head with a bit of a shudder. "No, not really."

Sindy gazed into his eyes a moment. He seemed mesmerized. "Wanna make a new friend?"

After taking a second to clear his head, he gave her an odd look and then smiled. He jerked his head towards the fire exit. "Let's get out of here, before the cops show up."

Cain turned to the man as he and Sindy prepared to leave. "Has someone called the police?"

"They threatened us they were gonna, but I don't know if they did."

Cain groaned. "Wonderful. Ben, do me a favor and fetch down the knife that Chris used on Felicity. It must still be up there, right?"

Ben and Ashley had been about to leave by the main entrance. Now Ben stopped and looked annoyed. Felicity couldn't help but think that Cain's use of the word 'fetch' was probably a poor choice. "What for?"

Cain stared at him for a moment as the alarm briefly sounded while Sindy and her new friend left the building. After it was silenced, Cain spoke. "I do spend a decent amount of effort trying to keep things like this out of the papers. We'll have to clean up this mess. Secondly…*you* reached Felicity first." He looked almost pained to acknowledge that fact.

"So?" Ben asked.

"So, did you touch the knife? If you did, it's got *your* fingerprints on it. A detail you may want to take care of before police get a hold of it."

Bens' mouth became a hard line. He made Ashley let him go so he could climb the left front stairs and go find the knife. As he reached the top, Cain yelled up to him. "You might want to try to scatter the ashes up there a bit as well, make them less noticeable." Ben grumbled something that it was probably fortunate they couldn't quite make out.

Allie went over to try to stand up the display rack by the door. As soon as Cain saw what she was doing, he went to help. Once they had it standing, Alyson began replacing the pamphlets. "You should go," she told Cain. "Get her to the hospital. I'll fix this."

He smiled at her in appreciation. "Don't stay too long. You don't want to be the only one here if police do arrive. And Alyson…thank you." She smiled and waved him off.

As Cain turned to leave, he noticed Ashley standing by the front doorway with her arms crossed. Cain watched her a moment and then gave her a smile. "Would you mind?" he asked gesturing towards the flyers and booklets surrounding Ashley's feet.

She glanced down, looking astonished that he would expect her to help. Cain just stood there smiling at her hopefully. Finally, she gave in and started helping Allie with the pamphlets. "There'd better be a good explanation for all of this. You guys ruined my dance." She eyed Allie a bit apprehensively. "And you…you'd better stay away from me. I saw what you did to that guy. That was spooky." Allie just laughed.

Cain returned to Felicity and they made their way to the back exit. Felicity noticed that he tried to kick and scatter the little pile of ash from Allie's kill as they passed. Just before they came to the exit, Ben leaned over the railing above them. "Isn't this your hat?" he asked. He threw Felicity's headpiece down to them, with its veil fluttering behind.

Cain caught it and turned it over in his hands. "It's not a hat, it's a coronet."

Ben left the rail with a 'whatever.' Felicity called up to him. "Thanks." She looked back to Cain curiously. "What's it called?"

"A coronet. Sort of like a tiara made of velvet. High fashion among noble ladies of my day."

Felicity gave him an odd little laugh. Her hand shot up to her head as she realized that she'd been wearing the comb he'd given her as well. It was still there, although hopelessly tangled in her hair. She breathed a sigh of relief. Cain handed her the headpiece and she felt very silly putting something so lovely atop her unruly mop of waves and tangles. She pouted at Cain. "I really did look lovely, honest."

He laughed and gave her a kiss. "You always do. Now stop stalling. If there's one thing I know about, it's blood loss. We've wasted enough time as it is. You've a date with a doctor." As they exited the gymnasium by the back door, Felicity couldn't help but think that she would be very happy never to hear another fire exit alarm again.

Chapter 8 - Fresh air and sunshine

Cain

Arriving at Cain's house
5:45, Monday morning

Cain was very relieved to pull Felicity's car into his driveway and shut the engine. She was sitting silent and still in the passenger seat, probably sleeping. It was becoming uncomfortably close to dawn. He'd thought they would never be done in the emergency room. As it was, they were cutting things rather close. He had less than a half an hour to get inside before the sun would peek over the horizon. More than enough time really, but still, nerve racking after an evening of stressful events.

He looked to Felicity, to tell her that they were home, and was a bit surprised to find that she was awake after all. She sat staring out the window, seemingly deep in thought. She hadn't said much since leaving the gymnasium. He'd been terribly worried and guilt ridden over the fact that he hadn't gotten to her in time. Once in the hospital by her side, holding her hand as they injected her with antibiotics and sewed stitches through her tender flesh had been almost unbearable. He was unused to witnessing such things. In his world, either you healed quickly on your own, or you were dust. Such drawn out and painful intercessions were unnecessary. To see her go through that after her already trying experiences, feeling that he could have prevented it all, was maddening.

Felicity had told the medical staff an unlikely story of pumpkin carving and playing around foolishly with a kitchen knife. She'd said her friends were teasing and chasing her. She'd been running with the knife and then fallen, stabbing herself. For a girl of Felicity's age, it sounded ridiculously irresponsible and unbelievable to Cain, but the nurses barely blinked an eye. It seemed they had dealt with far worse on Halloween's eve.

He turned to her now and wondered if the evening's events had damaged her more emotionally than the physical damage the knife at her precious throat had done. As the evening had worn on, through the hospital ordeal and then the ride home, she had become more and more withdrawn.

"Felicity?" he gently prodded. "We're here." She barely acknowledged him, but then took off her seatbelt. He'd thought she would rather go back to the dorm. She had nothing of her own to change into at Cain's, but she had quietly insisted that she wanted to go to Cain's house. He'd driven her with the car to the hospital of course. Even now, he wouldn't let her drive home. He'd have to return for his motorcycle tomorrow evening, after things had settled.

He left the car and went around to help her from her seat, giving her the car keys to put into her purse. They went up to the house and after he let them in, she passed him and headed straight for the stairs. He worried that she would trip over the welter of skirts her gown sported, but she managed to navigate the stair without event. Once reaching the bottom, Felicity dropped her purse and headpiece. She stood waiting for him to cross the room and turn on a light. He lit the lamp by his bed and turned to face her. She stood quiet and contemplative as he ran his eyes over her once gorgeous gown. Her hair had been pinned up at the sides with only a few curls meant to hang down. Of course, now it was a bedraggled mess, but he was certain that at the start of the evening she had looked every inch a royal princess.

Lovely and demure, she'd dressed so beautifully for him. Why hadn't he just gone to the stupid dance? She'd been so full of innocent excitement when first she'd brought it up, but he hadn't wanted to go. Later he had reasoned that he couldn't go. He'd thought it would be wiser to finish things with Chris before they escalated to a more dangerous level. It seemed almost foolish in retrospect. Why did things never work out the way he planned?

He found her gazing at him in thoughtful seriousness. He tried to coax a smile from her with one of his own, but after a moment, she only yawned and looked at the floor. He went to her. "Here, let's take that gown off and let you have some rest." He took her hands into his own, to spread her arms and look at her one last time. "You look like true nobility. A vision of beauty…under the ash, blood and bandage that is." She did not meet his eyes or smile as he'd hoped. Instead, she only sighed as she dropped his hands and turned around for him to help her remove the dress.

He opened the button at the top and pulled down the zipper. "I don't believe it's entirely ruined. Perhaps I can have it cleaned for you." She only shrugged and turned back around, holding the dress up to her chest. He met her eyes and brought a hand up to gently caress her cheek. She didn't really smile, but did close her eyes and seemed to enjoy his touch. The tingle of her mark *did* make each touch its own special experience.

Cain gently placed his hands upon her shoulders and then slid down the sleeves of her gown. She dropped her arms to her sides, letting him guide it down to reveal her breasts, and then down over her hips to the floor. He was rather surprised as he knelt on the floor and helped her step out of it, to find that over her blue panties she wore a garter belt made with black lace and midnight blue ribbon. It held her thigh high black stockings in place.

He wanted to smile at her for it, but could only feel overcome yet again with guilt and remorse. She'd gone through such trouble to please him and it had all been ruined. Surely she had planned to end the evening here in his bedroom, to be carefully undressed by him as she was now, but this was not the romantic and exciting experience she had surely anticipated. Instead, she was wounded and weary…and he had failed her. He forced upon himself a smile and looked up to meet her eyes after she daintily stepped from the dress with a hand on his shoulder to steady herself. "This is new," he said, running his finger gently over a strap of the garter belt.

She looked down for a moment as though she had forgotten she was even wearing it. She gave him a thin smile. "I went shopping."

"So I see," he said with a playful grin, fingering the lace.

She did not seem in the mood to play however. He could hardly blame her. He removed the gown from the floor at her feet and laid it across the bar. He then came back to her and eyed her hosiery with a smile. She sighed and asked, "Do you know how to take them off?"

Cain couldn't help but let out a little breath of a laugh and give her a sly grin. "Yes." He knelt before her again and slipped the shoes from her feet. Then he undid the clasps that attached the belt to her stockings in the front. She turned around for him to undo the ones in the back and he looked up with a bit of a start to give her a little tap on her bare bottom. "You *do* realize that there's quite a shortage of material back here?" he asked with a chuckle.

When she turned to look down at him over her shoulder, he saw that she'd a slight blush to her cheeks. That made his smile broader. It seemed a long time since he'd made her blush. He always found it so delightful. "It's a thong," she answered with a tinge of bashfulness.

"I see. Can't say I've much experience with one. Perhaps you'll wear it for me again sometime?" She just gave him a weary smile and turned back around.

He completed the task, removing stockings and belt. He left her thong panty for her to remove herself if she'd like. He couldn't help but feel her presumed disappointment weighing on him. By the time he'd brought her hosiery to the bar to leave with the dress, he knew that something must be said. She'd mentioned nothing of the evening's events to him. He'd been filled in a bit by Ben, but he had no idea of what she'd really gone through. He wouldn't ask her to relay it all to him; she would tell him when she was ready. Just the same, she had no knowledge of his doings either.

The things that he had experienced at Arif's were too puzzling and detailed for him to go into now…if at all. He was almost frightened to speculate on their meanings himself. One thing he did know from experience and the reading he had done, was that The Lord *did* work in mysterious ways. Seldom if ever in history was one given concrete evidence of heavenly approval of one's doings. Those who thought to interpret odd phenomenon to such ends were almost always deluded and found themselves following their own praise down a path to destruction.

No, he would not dare to presume that he could understand the meanings behind his partial protection from the heavenly weapons of holy water and cross. He would simply carry on, satisfied in the knowledge that he was living in a manner that he found morally sound. That would have to be enough to sustain him.

He did however want to tell Felicity of his troubles in finding her. She shouldn't think that he'd simply dallied overlong in other pursuits and not reached her in time. The fact that he had arrived *after* the fact seemed inexcusable, a thorn in his side that he felt he needed to justify. He wanted her to understand and not be resentful of it. She'd never said a word to that end of course, but he couldn't help but feel that way. Her quiet demeanor towards him did nothing to help.

He came back to her where she stood unmoving and took her hands into his own once more. After gazing into her eyes for a moment wondering where to begin, he simply poured out what was on his mind. "Felicity, I am so sorry that things turned out this way. I should have done as you asked. I should have gone with you. I had thought that I could prevent such things. I had thought that it was better to find him on my own and reason things out, without putting you into danger, that he could be made to change if given the chance. I worried so much for helping others that I almost lost the one I hold dearest of all. I've failed you terribly haven't I?"

She said nothing. She didn't really seem disappointed in him, only lost in thought. He pressed on. "I didn't think he would go so far. I thought him to hide behind his creations as he did before, afraid to try for you himself. You're marked; safe from his bite or any lesser vampires that he might have made. I hadn't thought things would get so dire in so short a time. I came as soon as I knew his minions to be moving towards you. I thought to reach you before they ever could.

I sped towards you at a breakneck pace but then…you disappeared! Your mark, it was gone! I was beside myself knowing not what to think. I hadn't known Sindy could hide you or ever thought that she *would*. I didn't even know that she was there. A mark can only be truly extinguished by death. Gave me quite a start, I can tell you! But they hadn't reached you yet, I could see them still. They hadn't been quite upon you when your precious light went out. No one had seemed to touch you, unless Chris himself was cloaked and had gone before them, but that just didn't seem to fit.

I reached the dance hall but they wouldn't allow me entrance. I don't know what I would have done, but then I *felt* you. Your mark was still disguised but I could feel your physical presence within, not in the very ballroom, but somewhere beyond. You've no idea the relief that brought! Of course, I don't know if the physical aspect of your mark would remain after death. Never had the unfortunate circumstance to discover that myself, but I had to believe that you were all right, alive and well. Still, it was a difficult task to locate you from the outside. In fact, if it weren't for that bloody fire alarm wailing through the night, I don't know how I ever would have found the door. It was a ghastly racket but I was powerfully grateful for it. That was right clever sounding that alarm. You felt me too didn't you? That's why you had them open the door."

Felicity had been silently staring at him throughout. She gazed at him a moment more before answering quietly. "That was Sindy, actually."

Cain continued on. "That's another thing! I reached the door only to find Alyson, Ashley and Sindy there. I asked for you and Allie said that you were fine, but then Sindy stumbled as though struck and fell to the floor. It took her a bit before she could mumble that it was Chris. It suddenly hit me that if Chris was in difficulty it was most likely over you. That's when I called out for you. Thank God you're alright." She just stared at him strangely. He leaned forward to give her a kiss on the cheek. "Shall I help you to bed?"

She raised her fingers to lightly touch the plastic bandage taped in a rectangle to the side of her throat. "They said I could shower."

"Oh, of course." He gave an awkward glance towards his distressingly small bathroom. "I've only a stall shower though. It's not big enough for two. I'd thought to help you. What if you get dizzy?"

"I'm okay."

"I'll bet there's a tub upstairs. Yes, there's sure to be. We should go up, I'll carry you if you'd like. You can take a bath."

She eyed him for a moment and then left him for the downstairs bathroom. "I can do it." Before he could respond, she'd shut the door. He stood there not knowing what to do. He heard her start the water. After listening to it run for a minute or two, he went to the laundry room.

He came back with a couple of towels and tapped on the door. She couldn't hear him over the water. He hesitantly opened the door a crack. "Felicity, everything alright? I've brought you towels."

"Thanks."

He entered the steam-filled room and put the linens down on the edge of the sink. He was careful to close the door behind him and not let the warmth escape. He noticed that she had left her thong and the hair comb he'd given her on the edge of the sink as well. He touched the comb lightly with a smile. "You want a wash cloth?" She only held her hand out from the curtain for it. He gave it to her and stood there a moment more. "Do you need anything else?"

"No, I'm fine," she replied shortly.

"Careful not to get the bandage too wet." She mumbled an 'uh-huh' through the water. Obviously, she didn't want or need him hovering over her. He left her alone. He went to the bar, thinking to brush off the dress a bit for her. After closer inspection, he realized that it really was in need of professional assistance. Most likely, it was ruined. Not knowing what else to do he went to turn down the bed. He took off his boots and then went back to the laundry room. He found a t-shirt and a pair of his pajama pants for her, and then undressed to don a pair of sleep pants for himself.

The water was turned off and he sat down on the bed, awaiting her. After a few minutes, she emerged from the bathroom, wrapped in towels. She had one around her body and had her hair wrapped up in another on her head. She came to the edge of the bed looking flushed and exhausted. He watched her look at the pajamas and then at him. She picked up the shirt, and went back into the bathroom, leaving the pants behind. She didn't entirely shut the door, but he waited for her on the bed. He couldn't help but feel a little hurt and confused that she didn't want to change in front of him. Then he realized that she'd gone back for her panties.

She returned without the towels, wearing the shirt. It only came down to the very top of her thighs. She was trying to brush through her wet hair with her fingers. She went around the bed to the side that she usually used and sat, slipping her legs beneath the covers. He turned to face her, looking at her long wet hair. "You don't want to go to bed with it wet do you?" She remained sitting and shrugged.

Cain quickly went to the bathroom cabinet and came back with his brush and hair dryer. He plugged it in, put it down on the bed with the brush and then moved to sit behind her on the pillows. "Can I do it for you?"

She shrugged again. "If you want."

He carefully moved the brush through her hair a few times and then turned the blow dryer on. He took his time, just drying and brushing out her hair. She jumped once when he went over a sore spot near the top on the side. She quietly explained that Chris had held her down by the hair. He felt almost enraged to hear it, but sat quiet and still. She offered no further recount of her experience. He refrained from asking for more detail and went back to her hair, being cautious to avoid the spot again. She would talk to him when she was ready, he wouldn't push her.

He didn't really try to style her hair, he'd no clue how he should even try. He just brushed it out long and straight from underneath. In the dim light he watched as it turned from a dark wet chestnut brown, to the beautiful auburn color he so loved. It had a bit of crimson glow where the light touched it. She sat silent throughout. Even when it was fully dry, he spent a few more minutes just brushing and running his fingers through it. Finally, she turned to look at him. "Thanks." She seemed troubled.

"How's your throat?" he asked in concern.

She sighed and raised her fingers to the bandage again. "It hurts a little. I think the stuff they gave me wore off."

He looked at her in concern. "Something I can do?" She just gazed at him thoughtfully. "How about a nice cup of tea?"

"You have tea?" She looked surprised.

He pretended to take offense. "I'm an Englishman; of *course* I've got tea!"

Now she laughed a little. He was glad to see it. "But you always drink coffee."

He smiled and wrinkled his nose at her. "Yes, but sometimes you just need a good cup of tea."

She lightly shook her head. "Maybe later."

"Are you sure? I've got Earl Grey," he said to tempt her.

"No thanks," she told him.

She lay back on the bed beneath the covers and he got in to join her. He reached to shut the light and then turned to give her a kiss. "Sleep well." She lay still on her own side of the bed and he felt obligated to do the same, although he wanted nothing more than to hold her. Finally, she turned towards him and snuggled into his arms, her face buried in his chest. He felt so relieved to have her there. Her attitude had been so oddly cold and he sorely just wanted to wrap his arms around her and feel her melt into him as she did now. He knew she'd been through a lot and didn't want to judge her actions harshly, but he'd been a bit put off that she didn't seem to want him to comfort her at all.

After snuggling with him a bit she wriggled herself up to place a few kisses upon his throat. He wondered if she knew how strongly that always affected him, even if for no good reason. Her lips found his chin, his cheek, and then his own lips. After a few light kisses she moved to have him kiss *her* neck, on the side away from her injury. He gave her the kisses there that she seemed to desire and then once again took back her lips, but she would not give him the deep kiss that he sought. She kept turning away to offer him her throat until it was undeniable that his kiss was not what she really desired. He only kissed her there once more and then leaned back from her, though she seemed desperate to press her flesh to his lips. "Felicity stop."

She seemed confused and hurt as she looked up to his face. "What? I just thought…"

"You're hurt. You need rest, not further trauma." He tried to say it teasingly, hoping he wouldn't sound too stern.

She lay back and seemed to pout. "I can't sleep."

He eyed her for a moment warily, wondering her true thoughts. She enfolded herself back into his arms. He held her close, trying to understand how she must feel. Once again, she brought her lips to his throat. This time not only to kiss, but also to gently suck upon his skin. Yes, she had to know that it thrilled him to feel her there. Yet he knew she was only trying to coax him again to her own throat. Sure enough, before long she thrust her skin to his lips. He pushed her back firmly. "No. You'll not be drowning your worries in venom this night." He couldn't help the slightly harsh tone in his voice. He was annoyed that she wanted his bite more than his other attentions. She seemed very hurt by his words, but to be bitten had obviously been her intent. He spoke to her in a milder tone. "You've lost enough blood for one evening."

She lost her look of aggravation and turned to him hopefully. "You wouldn't have to actually *drink* any."

He stared at her in flustered disbelief. "That's asking a bit *much*, don't you think?"

She glared at him coldly and then rolled over, turning away from him. "I wouldn't think you'd be thirsty for *my* blood anyway. Haven't you had your fill elsewhere?" she asked acidly.

He froze, staring at the back of her head. "What?"

She waited a moment before elaborating, but didn't turn to face him again. "You drink from Sindy don't you?" She spoke again before he could think what to say. "I know you have. She can *feel* you…just like I can."

He closed his eyes and felt his heart sink. No wonder she'd been cold towards him. "I did…drink from her, but there were reasons…" She turned to give him a look that dared him to try and justify it. "…that I'm sure you don't care to hear. I drank from her this evening, but it was only to mark her. It was only blood…nothing more."

She sat up in anger. "Only blood? *Only blood!?* How can you even say that to me? It's never *only* blood. You told me that yourself, remember? *'It's much…much more'* were your exact words, I believe." She gave him no chance to try to defend it. How could he anyway? He'd only meant that he had not indulged in Sindy's body as well, but he couldn't honestly say that her blood hadn't pleased him, even if he hadn't been trying to be untrue to Felicity.

"Is that how you did it?" she asked. He had no idea what she could mean. "Is that what you did, back before I let you drink from me? You told me it was difficult, but that you could keep things under control. Is *that* your control? To quench your thirst for *my* blood by filling yourself with *her*?"

"No! It's not like that at all! I drank from her yes, but it's not like it's been a regular thing." She didn't look like she believed him. "Once. Once I've drunk from her, since you returned to me."

"Returned to you? When did I leave you?"

"It was technically *I* who left. The weekend that you went home, for your birthday. I told you that I wouldn't see you again. I didn't want you to be hurt. I didn't want to ruin your life. I didn't think for a moment that you would return to me. Not after *that*. And it was only after that, when you returned to me that I truly allowed myself to believe we could be together."

"How many times? You drank from her once *since* my birthday. How many times before that?"

She sat looking at him directly, trying to read his eyes. He would never use false words to lie to her anyway. "You came to me asking that I protect Ben from her, do you remember? I drank from her then. I found her and I asked that she leave Ben alone. She wouldn't listen. We argued and then…I drank from her, to control her. I drained her. Drank until she lost consciousness, and left her there, in a field. That's why she wouldn't touch Ben again. It was a warning. I did it for you, to keep your friends safe."

She looked confused, as though trying to place something. "You came to see me that night, at my window."

"To tell you that your friends were safe," he confirmed.

"You were all…giddy and romantic." She looked ill.

"I was relieved that you wouldn't have to worry," he said.

"You were *drunk*…on *her* blood!" He opened his mouth in protest, but again she wouldn't let him speak. She looked disgusted and appalled. "She's got venom too right? Like you. Drinking from her must give you venom and blood. That must be better than drinking from *me* ever could be," she conjectured.

"No, it's really not. Vampire blood *is* different but…it's not like that," he insisted.

"When else?" He began to shake his head. Did she really expect him to recount every instance? "Tell me!"

He gave her a level gaze. "Twice more." She only answered with expectant silence. "There was a night, I was coming to meet you at work. She was there."

"The night of our picnic, right? I knew. Ben felt her. You were out there for a long time and I kept waiting for you to come in, but you didn't. You stayed out there with *her*."

"We were only talking for most of the time…really. Then she offered me her wrist, for my thirst. 'Twas only her wrist and I never asked for it…but I did drink, some. I never meant to hurt or betray you."

"You sure as hell didn't *tell* me!" she exclaimed in disgust. He sat silent, awaiting the inevitable. He couldn't bring himself to offer the information, but he wouldn't withhold it from her. She asked. "When was the last time before tonight? You said twice more, when was the other time?"

He felt almost ill in remembering. "When I sent you away. You went home for your birthday and I told you not to come back, so that I wouldn't hurt you. She came to me then, and I didn't turn her away. I drank from her that night as well."

Felicity stared at him long and hard. Surely, the guilt and loathing he felt for his actions that night were written upon his face. "And was that…*only* blood?" Her eyes were welling with tears. She knew that there was more. "You slept with her didn't you?"

"Once." Her face seemed to crumple. "I thought I had lost you! Look at you. You are so beautiful and innocent; perfectly pure with such a loving heart. I don't deserve someone like you! All *I* could ever do is ruin your life. I tried to tell you, that's why I sent you away. She came to me that night and I let her. I told myself that I deserved nothing more. I was miserable to be without you and I tried to drown my sorrows in her, I did.

Do you think she's who I want? It's *you* that I love, but I can't *have* you, not really, not forever. I thought to resign myself to the truth; to face the fact that I am not human no matter how I may long to be, and that another monster like myself is all that *I* could ever hope to deserve. It was *not* what you might think it was…believe me. But then you came back. Despite the warnings, despite how I tried to turn you away for your own good, you came back to me. You were like a breath of fresh air being offered when I was drowning in sorrow. How could I not breathe you in? How could I send you away to seal my fate?

I tried. I wanted to do the right thing for you, but you wouldn't let me. And God help me but I've never wanted anything more in my life than to show you my love. You came back and you let me. Being with you has been happiness I never thought to know. Since that day, *never* have I touched another with impure intent. It's not as though I haven't opportunity, but it's you that I want. Don't you know that?"

There were tears streaming down her face, but as much as she looked as though she would like to come back to his arms, she held herself still and apart from him as she spoke. "Tonight. Instead of coming to the dance, you went to see her…in her hotel room. Why would you do that without telling me? And now I'm supposed to feel grateful that it was *only* blood!? Have you been spending time with her all along?"

"You're with me always! I was looking for Chris; I've checked with her, thinking that she may have seen him. I've seen her now and again but not for any indecent purpose. I taught her how to cloak, to defend herself. And now, tonight…I marked her. She asked for my protection and I granted it. I spurned her advances but I'm not going to throw her to the wolves."

Felicity turned away from him to look down at her lap. After a moment, she took her legs from the covers. She reached to the end of the bed, where the pajama pants he had left for her lay folded. She picked them up and put them on without saying a word. He kept on. "You must understand. I've only been trying to do right by everyone. I never meant to hurt you. I love you so dearly. I suppose I should have told you, but I've known all along in my heart the strength and loyalty of my love; so I never thought it need be questioned. Felicity?"

She had stood from the bed, taken a glance about and then headed for the stairs. Now, as he called her she stopped to look at him. Her face was streaked with tears, but she didn't seem to be crying any longer. Instead, she had a most disturbing look of confusion and almost panic upon her face. When she spoke it almost seemed that she was talking to herself, as she didn't meet his eyes. "I can't believe this. I can't believe that I should have to question you. I trust you. I trust you with my *life*." Now she did look up at him, her eyes pleading for him to make his admissions untrue, her breaths coming quick and unmeasured. "You're supposed to make me feel safe. You're my protector, my true love, my everything. I have given you *everything*. My body, my blood, I'm yours…*only* yours. And *you* are only supposed to be for *me*. Isn't that how it works?"

She took a deep gasp for breath and suddenly turned again for the stairs as if unsure what else to do. He tried to go to her, to hold her, but she wouldn't let him. She grabbed her purse from the floor by the door and began to climb the stairs as he followed, pleading for her to understand. "I *am* yours. I love you, but I haven't been unfaithful; it's not the same.

I am a vampire. I can't always profess to like it much but it remains a fact. I live in a different world, with different aspects to be considered. The things I've done were for reasons that you may not be able to comprehend. You're human. I love you so, but you have to accept that a vampire must sometimes live by rules that you cannot understand."

They reached the front door and he held her arm to stop her from opening it. Before he could say anything else she asked, "Has she ever drunk from you?"

He closed his eyes for a moment in relief that he could answer something for her without guilt. "No, never. My blood remains my own…for a long time now. I won't share it lightly, but I *would* share it…with you," he told her truly.

He couldn't tell what she thought of that. She only stared at him blankly, although she surely understood the offer. It had always been there, but never so directly voiced. She said nothing. "Felicity please don't go. I love you. I need you."

She gazed at him quietly and he could see the love still in her eyes amidst the tears. He wouldn't lose her, not like this. She wouldn't leave him, she couldn't. She lightly pulled her arm away. She took a very deep breath and exhaled with a shudder. "I love you too, but right now, I think I need some sunshine."

She opened the door and he was forced to back away as the bright early morning sunlight filled the entryway. He barely had the chance to realize that she was actually going to leave, before she moved outside and closed the door.

Chapter 9 - An offer I can't refuse

Felicity

Monday morning
Cain's house

Felicity stepped out into the cold morning air and squinted in the bright sun. She headed straight for her car, never looking back although she heard Cain reopen the door. He didn't call out after her and she hurried to the car, hoping that he wouldn't. She felt as though she were walking on ice as she padded over the cement in bare feet. It was autumn still, but winter was waiting in the wings and up here in the mountains, it wouldn't wait for long. The warmer seasons often seemed fleeting, and winter was always quick to make its presence known and over-stay its welcome. The cold breeze blowing against her tear-wet face made the 35-degree morning feel more like 20.

Short sleeves and no coat, she didn't care. The air felt frigid in her throat as her breaths came out in little gasps of fog before her face. She jumped into her car and slammed the door, trying to cut herself off from the rest of the world. She didn't dare glance back at the house. She dug through her purse for her keys to start the engine, finally found them and started the car. She turned up the heat only to be rewarded with a blast of cold air in the face, forcing her to turn it down until the car had warmed up. The seat felt freezing on her legs through the thin pajamas.

She couldn't wait. She put the car into gear and took off for the dorm. She just wanted to get into bed, pull the covers over her head and cry herself to sleep. She didn't want to think, to reason or try to sort out her feelings. She just wanted to sob and cry unobserved and then sleep all day, but she couldn't be lucky enough to escape turning it all over in her mind on the ride home. His words replayed over and over in her head.

Cain. She kept trying to stare at the road and not hear his voice in her ears. He made his love for her sound so grand and unfailing like something from an epic romance. He made everything he ever did sound so reasonable and understandable, as though she shouldn't be able to help but feel sympathetic and forgiving.

His eyes brimming with tears and his voice trembling to melt her heart; everything he said always made her feel as though he were the wise and mature one and she was unreasonable and cruel not to understand. Like he endured such torture in his daily life that she should feel instant leniency towards anything that would be viewed as a transgression if committed by someone else. As though *she* should be comforting *him* with an arm over his shoulder saying 'of course, perfectly understandable, who could blame you?'.

She'd known that she had to leave. She needed some time alone, to get some perspective. If she had stayed, she only would have forgiven him; how could she not? He was so gentle, loving, charming and persuasive. She would have stayed in his bed and wept in his arms until she'd fallen asleep. After that, things would go on as if no wrong had been done. He obviously felt justified in his actions, even if he wasn't entirely proud of them.

Not to say that she wouldn't *ever* forgive him. The thought of losing him was bad enough, but to give him up before she had to, seemed unbearable. She had a right to be angry though, didn't she? She knew she did, and she wasn't going to let things be smoothed over so easily.

He hadn't told her! To know that he had been with Sindy was just sickening. He'd had sex with her only a day or so before Felicity herself had come to him! To know that haughty, condescending whore had put her hands on Cain's body… That after all of the nights that he and Felicity had spent together dancing and talking and kissing goodnight, building anticipation for the precious moment of their union, he'd gone and fulfilled his desires first by fornicating with that witch!

Felicity understood that he hadn't really thought to see her again. The explanations he gave of his rationale about his misery over losing her and trying to see himself as deserving only another vampire were heartbreaking and believable, but it didn't make it any easier to accept. Just because she could almost understand why he'd done it, didn't mean that she thought he *should* have done it.

Even putting the fact that they'd had sex aside, (albeit with great difficulty), he had drunk Sindy's blood…four times, and he had never told her! She knew about the experience of *drinking* blood, only from what he himself had told her, but judging by the feelings she experienced when being drunk from, she could imagine what it might be like for him. He had called drinking 'the ultimate experience'.

Vampire blood had to be different from human blood. He had even admitted that it was. No matter what kind of rational, logical and unincriminating reasons he might have for drinking from Sindy, he had to have *enjoyed* it. She knew that he must have. To do that without telling her just seemed wrong.

Could things even go back to the way that they were? The thought of him with Sindy made Felicity positively ill. To picture Sindy clinging to him as he penetrated her throat with his fangs and made her feel things that Felicity tried to imagine were only for herself, was crushing. To know that he'd had sex with her as well…how could drinking from her *not* have brought back that memory for him? Just because he didn't repeat the act, should she feel vindicated that he was hers? He had still done things behind her back. Even if sex and blood sharing weren't the same, they *felt* the same to her. It was unacceptable. She'd always thought that Sindy'd had some nerve to act so damn possessive over him, when she shouldn't have any grounds for such an attitude. Now she knew why.

Felicity parked the car in the dorm lot and got out to race across the dew-wet lawn. A few girls were emerging for breakfast before classes. They gave her wide clearance and odd looks as they turned to snicker and whisper to each other as she passed. Crying, barefoot, dressed only in men's pajamas and clutching a dark blue velvet purse; Felicity knew that she must have been quite the odd sight. *Who cares; what the hell do they know about real life anyway?*

Felicity took the stairs two at a time and practically flew into her room, closing the door behind her. She collapsed onto her bed gasping as though she'd run the whole distance home. She wanted to cry, but her tears seemed to have deserted her now and all she could feel was a growing, burning ball of anger in the pit of her stomach.

He'd lied to her! Not with words but with actions. He knew that she believed herself to be the only one to take physical liberties with him. He may try to explain his deeds as innocent, unhurtful and as having practical purpose, but the plain truth was that he had deceived her. She didn't have to be a vampire to know that he must have enjoyed drinking from Sindy. That's why he hadn't told her.

If he was that hell bent on protecting Sindy with his mark, he could have found another way. He could have explained it to Felicity. She wasn't totally heartless. Maybe she could have accepted it if he'd drunk from Sindy's wrist, in Felicity's presence, briefly and only for marking. That would be a truly platonic and wholesome act, but no, he had kissed Felicity goodbye and then snuck off to Sindy's hotel room to enjoy her blood in private.

Cain. She could smell him. It was the pajamas. They smelled faintly of his aftershave. Roughly, she raised herself from the bed and tore the t-shirt off over her head. She didn't want him here, not even in some abstract representation. Not now.

She caught the scent of him again as the shirt came off over her head. With an almost frightening force, she felt a sudden surge of longing for him. It was like a physical need, like being hungry. Her body *wanted* him. She quickly threw the shirt into the corner, as though it were something disgusting. "Go away Cain, I don't want you here!" She yelled, feeling creepily shaken.

She stared at it for a moment, in shock. It was only a shirt, but the smell reminded her of him and the venom in her body must recognize that somehow. Sindy had said it could be like that, hadn't she? Creepy, but apparently true. Her body was infiltrated with his venom. It was all throughout her. She'd never really thought of it as its own entity before. The idea that she was host to something that might try to control her actions was very disturbing. She'd never had cause for concern over it before. She'd never even noticed it as anything more than an interesting and pleasurable addition to her experiences with Cain.

She felt stupid for freaking out, but also leery. She stood for a minute, waiting for further evidence of unwanted urges. Nothing. He wouldn't try to *call* her would he, the way Sindy called Ben? She shuddered remembering how upsetting it had been to be marked the first time, when she didn't understand. To feel compelled to go to him, without realizing why, the panic and anxiety, the hot flashes and chills it had caused her.

But this was different. The first time had been a big adjustment, but she'd gotten used to it and it didn't seem nearly as severe once it was understood. She'd been marked for a while now. She was accustomed to it. Her body was used to feeling him near. Usually it was a comforting thing. Now if she felt it, she would recognize his calling. She felt confident that there was no way that she would be drawn to him against her will. He had to know that trying to summon her would only make her furious. Heaven help him if he tried! No, he wouldn't dare.

It wasn't as though she was frightened of *him*. It wasn't even like she hated him or anything. She was just angry and she wanted the right to be angry. Let him sit there in that dark barren basement alone.

She ripped the pants from her legs and after a moment's thought, she took off the stupid thong as well. She donned new panties from her drawer and found her sheep pajamas in a pile on the floor. Good enough. She just wanted to hide under the covers, forget everything and go to sleep.

At least she probably wouldn't have to worry over having nightmares of Chris and Marcus. They were gone, and now she had what seemed to be much more disturbing fare to darken her dreams.

~~~~~~~~~~~~~~~~~~~~~~~~~~~~

Felicity awoke to a knock at the door. For a second, while half asleep, her heart leapt with joy that it might be Cain. Then she realized not only was that stupid remembered happiness and not really what she wanted right now, but that there was sunlight streaming in the window. It wouldn't be him. Even if by some heroic act he had made his way here through the sunshine, she would have *felt* him. It wasn't him.

"Felicity, you in there?" It was Ben.

"Yeah, come in." She rolled onto her back to stare up at the ceiling.

He let himself in and closed the door behind him. Dropping his stuff on the floor, he turned to face her. "I've been calling your cell all day."

She sat up in bed, offering him a look of apology. "Sorry. I think I turned it off."

He eyed her sheep pajamas with a smile, but didn't mention them. She suddenly realized that the thong she had worn was on the floor right next to the bed, in plain view. She desperately hoped that he wouldn't notice it as he spoke. "I would've come by sooner, but I had classes. To be honest, I wasn't even sure you'd be here."

Felicity gave him a dejected sigh and lowered her eyes. "Here I am."

Ben stared at her for a moment. She knew he was wondering why she wasn't at Cain's, but she certainly wasn't going to tell him. He gestured towards the bandage on her throat. "How are you feeling?"

She almost automatically said 'fine', but then she stopped herself to give him an almost impish smile. "One," she said quietly with a little smirk.

It only took him a moment to remember; back when he'd been injured, he'd answered her query of concern by counting how many times he'd been bugged with the question. He laughed. "One? I can't be the only person to have asked you."

She shrugged. "Do dead people count?"

He avoided answering and sat down on the bed next to her to check out her bandage. "Was it bad?"

"Eleven stitches," she informed him.

"Ouch," he said, wincing in sympathy.

"Yeah," she agreed.

"I didn't think that you were going to feel like going in to work tonight, so I asked Lucy to cover your shift."

Felicity sat up a little straighter, slightly alarmed. "Was I on tonight?"

"3 to 9," he told her.

"What time is it now?" she asked worriedly.

"Almost 4:00," he admitted with a smile.

"Oh. Oops."

Ben laughed. "Don't worry about it."

"Thanks." She suddenly realized that if it was 4:00, Ben should be there now too. He always worked on Mondays. "Aren't *you* closing tonight?"

"Na, I never work on Halloween," he explained.

"Oh yeah, I forgot that was today," she said.

Ben stood and went to the door as though remembering something. He grabbed an orange plastic shopping bag from the floor. It had a picture of a ghost on it and read 'trick or treat' across the top. He brought it to her on the bed and sat back down next to her. "I brought you some candy."

She opened the bag to look at the varied assortment of loose, bite-size candy bars. She looked back up at him with an arched eyebrow. "You went trick-or-treating?"

Ben laughed, shaking his head. "No, I *bought* it. You know, to give to kids. Somebody's got to give the little rug rats their sugar rush. My dad's been out of town. Besides, kids are cute. I like to see their costumes."

Felicity smiled. "Yeah, me too."

"I didn't know what you like, so I gave you a few of everything."

She glanced in the bag again. "That's an awful lot of candy."

"Yeah," he said with a little laugh. "There's a slight possibility that I may have gone overboard."

"Thanks," she said with a chuckle.

"I'm just glad you're okay."

"Thanks to *you*. And to think that all this time I've only known your 'mild mannered alter ego'," she added with a grin.

"Too bad I wasn't a few minutes sooner," he said quietly.

"Good thing you weren't a few minutes later." She gazed at him in all seriousness. "Thank you," she said sincerely. He just shrugged and smiled at her. After a few minutes, she broke eye contact to pull out a candy bar from the bag. She came out with a Butterfinger. "Want one?"

"No thanks," he said.

"So what did Ashley think of everything?" she asked, unwrapping her candy bar and taking a bite.

Ben sighed, shaking his head. "I had to *tell* her."

"Well, yeah," she agreed.

"She…didn't really believe me."

"What? How could she not? She saw at least two of them dusted like right in front of her!"

"Yeah well, she's kind of holding to the theory that it's more something that was done *to* them, than the possibility that they were actually vampires," he explained.

Felicity's mouth opened in disbelief. "What could you possibly do to someone to make them explode into ashes? That is like the stupidest thing that I have ever heard! Then again, look at who we're dealing with." Just after she said it, she realized that she was insulting Ben's *girlfriend*. She looked up at him in embarrassment. "Sorry." Ben just lowered his eyes and slightly shook his head. She could have sworn there was a hint of a smile playing about his lips. "But you tried to convince her right? So if Ashley doesn't believe you, then what does she think…that you're crazy?"

"No! I mean, I don't think so. She still wants to see me tonight," he admitted.

Felicity looked back down at the bed. She felt bad to have said anything derogatory about Ashley, and couldn't help but wonder just how serious Ben really could feel about her. "Where are you going?"

"Well, my annual tradition is to hang out at Tommy's and make jokes about Allie's tail, but…Ashley doesn't want to go. In fact, I think she's kind of scared of Allie now, which is really pretty funny when you think about it," he said with a laugh. "I'll probably just take her over to Venus. They've got a Halloween thing going on. She wants to wear her costume again."

Felicity dropped her eyes. "She did look really great."

Ben gave back an almost embarrassed grin. "Yeah, she did." There was an awkward silence for a moment. Felicity dug into the candy bag again for another bar. She pulled out a Snickers and looked up to find Ben gazing at her intently. "So did you," he said quietly. She tried not to be too obviously flattered and began eating her candy bar. "That dress was beautiful. Did it get ruined?"

She took a bite and shrugged. "It was just a dress."

Ben smiled. "Yeah." They just sat there for a moment as she finished her candy bar. Then Ben took a deep breath and sighed. "Well, I'd better get home before dark or I'm going to have about five pounds of candy left." He stood from the bed with a laugh. "Don't forget to call Mr. Penten and let him know when you'll be back to work."

She nodded. "I will. Thanks for the candy."

He picked up the rest of his stuff and turned back to her from the door. "See ya."

"Bye. Thanks again…for *everything*," she said earnestly.

"Don't mention it," he replied.

~~~~~~~~~~~~~~~~~~~~~~~~~~~~~

Lying on her back in bed, Felicity turned her head to observe the clocks' glowing red display of the time: 12:00 p.m. It was noon on Tuesday… wasn't that part of a song? Oh yeah, Sheryl Crow. 'All I wanna do is have some fun'; not a concept that Felicity felt all that familiar with these days. Fun seemed something long forgotten. It hadn't really been very long since she'd been blissfully happy, spending her nights with Cain; unaware of danger from Chris or deceit from her lover, but it felt like forever.

Halloween night had come and gone without event. Not long after Ben had left, she'd pulled on jeans and a sweatshirt and wandered down to the cafeteria in search of some dinner. Students were running around campus in costume, preparing for parties, acting foolish and generally having fun. She'd gotten some cold chicken and taken it back to her room.

She was up half the night. After sleeping all day, it was difficult to rest all night as well. She was used to staying awake late these days anyway. In fact, if it weren't for forced daytime attendance of her classes, she probably would have adopted a completely nocturnal schedule by now.

She'd sat up half the night trying to catch up on her homework and searching for 'feelings' of Cain. She had thought that she could almost sense him once, but it was fleeting, and slight enough to make her doubt herself. She wasn't really expecting him, and she certainly wasn't hoping for him to try to use psychic influence over her, but she was still a little disappointed not to feel any trace of him at all. As mad as she was, and even unsure whether she'd *like* to see him; shouldn't he at least *try?*

Now it was noon on Tuesday. She was skipping classes again. She had a doctor's note until Wednesday, might as well use it. She sat up in bed. What was she going to do all day though, sit here and feel sorry for herself? One of her first instincts last night had been to call Deidre. They had always been in charge of 'damage control' for each other's love lives in the past, but things were so different now. Deidre could never understand. It would be more frustrating than helpful, but who else could she talk to?

Felicity was startled by an authoritative knock on the door. Curious, she got up to answer it. She opened the door a crack, and then swung it wide upon seeing who it was. "Allie, hi," she said with some surprise.

"Get dressed. I'm taking you to lunch." Felicity just stood looking at her for a moment in slight confusion. "You *can* eat right?" Allie asked, looking at the bandage on Felicity's throat.

Felicity gave her a bemused little smile. "Yeah, I'm allowed to eat. I just thought you might be kind of busy today."

She was met with silence until Felicity backed up to allow her into the room. Alyson stalked inside seeming in a considerably less than cheerful mood. "Yeah well, so did I; yet here it is, another stupid bright and sunny day and I have absolutely nothing else to do. So I'm taking you to lunch."

"Well there's an offer I can't refuse," Felicity mumbled.

Allie gave her a look of annoyance. "Get dressed."

They ended up at the diner picking at tuna salad sandwiches, cole slaw and pickles. Felicity's original thoughts of relief that she might have an understanding ear to confide in were displaced by the fact that Alyson would barely talk to her since leaving the room.

Obviously, Allie was having her own problems, but she wasn't in the mood to share. Mattie must not have showed up yet. Felicity felt bad for her, knowing how long she'd been waiting, but every attempt at conversation was met with a brash comment and then sulking silence. Felicity was trying not to become annoyed, but she felt in just as sour a mood as Allie, and was having a hard time being very understanding.

She took another bite of her sandwich as she watched Allie absently dismantle and destroy hers with a fork. "Allie, why did you even order that?" Alyson just shrugged. Felicity decided to try one more time to get Allie to talk. "Still no word from Mattie huh?" she asked gently.

Allie glared up at her. "What do you think?"

"You don't have any idea where he is? He didn't tell you?"

"If I knew where he was, do you think I'd be wasting my time here?" she asked harshly. After a moment, she looked up in apology. "I'm sorry, but this sucks."

"Halloween was only yesterday. I'm sure he just got delayed." As she said it, Allie looked up in alarm over what kind of 'delay' Felicity might mean. She quickly corrected herself. "I mean like a regular delay. You know, like maybe his car broke down." Allie shook her head lightly and took a big gulp of soda. "Don't worry; I'm sure he'll be here soon. It's got to be difficult, only being able to travel at night and you don't know how far away he's been. He'll be here."

"Yeah well, he'd better be. I already put in for vacation; took two whole weeks off work, starting tonight." A secret sort of little smile stole over Allie's face for a moment. "There's this place, a little bed and breakfast in the Poconos. We go there sometimes, like for long weekends. It's real quiet and secluded. He loves it there. We haven't been in over a year." After a moment, she returned to looking petulant and disappointed. "He'd better get his ass back here soon, because I made reservations."

She looked up at Felicity again while viciously stabbing her fork into the coleslaw before continuing. "I told Cain that Arif and his goons better stay the fuck away from him too. He'd better give them the message, because if I find out they've kept him away from me, I swear I'll stake 'em all."

Felicity watched as the anger drained from Allie's face after a moment and she seemed to shake it off. She took a deep breath and looked back to Felicity with new concern. "Speaking of Cain, enough about my shit and on to *your* problem." Felicity took another sip of her diet Coke, hiding her face momentarily behind the glass. Allie just stared at her until she put it down again. "I saw Cain last night."

Felicity stared into her glass. "Yeah?" she asked sullenly.

"What did you do to that guy?"

"*I* didn't do anything!" Felicity blurted in a huff.

"Well, somethin's goin' on He just holed up at a table in the back right after sunset and drank all night. He didn't even go for coffee first."

"Big deal," Felicity muttered.

"Seven bottles Felicity. When I brought him the first drink, he tells me to hold the sugar water and just bring the rum. He drank seven bottles straight. Well four bottles of rum, then we ran out and I had to switch him to scotch for the last three.

He wouldn't talk to me hardly at all. I told him to keep Arif away from Mattie and he just handed me a pile of money and said he'd do anything I wanted tomorrow, but tonight he just wanted to be left alone with the rum. What happened? It can't be over *that*," she said, pointing at Felicity's bandaged throat.

"No." Felicity took a deep breath and looked Allie in the eye. "He's been drinking."

"Well duh, I just told you," Allie replied.

"*Blood* Allie," Felicity clarified.

"Oh. Well, no kidding. He's a vampire, that's what they do."

"From *Sindy*," Felicity added.

"…Oh…So I guess she wasn't just blowin' smoke, huh?"

"Apparently not," Felicity agreed.

They sat in silence for a moment as Felicity tried to take another bite of her sandwich. She put it back down and pushed it away instead. It just didn't seem very appetizing anymore. Allie seemed to be having trouble deciding what to say. Finally she asked, "Are you sure? 'Cause that just really doesn't seem like something he would do."

"Yes. I'm sure," she said with insulted annoyance. "He drank from her the night of the dance Allie. That very night! I'm sitting at the dance wishing he was there, and he's off sucking on that whore!"

Allie looked surprised and almost amused at Felicity's choice of words, which only pissed her off more. She glared at Alyson who quickly dropped her small smile. "Take it easy. He actually told you that?"

"Not in those *exact* words, but yes," Felicity told her.

It was plain to read on Alyson's face that she thought Cain must be a fool to have told her. "What else did he say? I mean, he must have given you some kind of an explanation."

"Of course he did. He was only marking her, you know, for protection from the others. So even though it was in her hotel room, behind my back, that makes it okay right?" Allie actually seemed to be thinking it over. "It's such a load of crap! It's not like that was even the first time!"

"How many times did he do it?" Alyson asked her.

Felicity glared at her in annoyance that she should even have to ask. "More than once, *does it matter?*"

Allie leaned forward a little to put her hand on Felicity's arm. "I'm just trying to understand. It's hard to picture *Cain* doing something like that. I'm sure he never meant to hurt you."

"Sure, take his side. Hey, you saw him before the dance too, didn't you?" Felicity asked.

"Well yeah, but *I* only gave him a haircut, I swear. And I told you about it, so it's not like I'm hiding anything. Well, I told you I talked to him, but I didn't tell you about the haircut, but only 'cause I thought it'd be a cool surprise."

Felicity rolled her eyes. "I'm not accusing you of anything, but did he say anything to you?"

"You mean like 'Bye, I'm gonna go suck Sindy's blood now'? No, he didn't mention it. He was after Chris, that's all I know," Allie insisted.

"Yeah, until he just happened to bump into Sindy at her hotel room all the way in Oxford? He went there on purpose," Felicity said accusingly.

"Chris was after her too. Maybe he thought Chris'd be there. You know that he couldn't have been there long, 'cause then Sindy showed up at the dance with us," Allie pointed out.

"Yeah, all haughty and full of herself knowin' that Cain had just drunk from her." Felicity stared at the table with a scowl on her face, thinking of the attitude and possessiveness over Cain that Sindy had displayed while talking to she and Allie at the dance. At least Cain hadn't really paid her much attention once he actually got there.

Well, except for the fact that while Felicity was being rescued by Ben from having her throat slit, Cain was busy attending to Sindy who must have collapsed from feeling Chris' death. Good, she hoped it hurt…a lot.

"He's a vampire Felicity. Maybe he had a good reason for needing her blood. You don't know what kind of stuff goes on for them. Mattie's always been pretty solitary, but I think the ones that live in groups have all kinds of social rules and stuff. I think it's kind of like being part of a wolf pack. The Alpha male needs to prove dominance to keep control and stuff."

Felicity had met her gaze as Allie spoke and was staring at her with ever increasing disbelief and disgust. "I can't believe that you are sitting here trying to defend him! *You* know what it's like to get bit. How would you feel if you found out *Mattie* was drinking from some other girl?"

Alyson gave her a steady look before answering. "He prob'ly does Felicity. I don't *ask* him about it or nothin', but I wouldn't be surprised. I mean let's face it, he's a vampire. I'd like to think that he'd rather always take from me, but I'm not going to delude myself into thinking that he's never even tried it from someone else."

Felicity ran her hands through her hair in aggravated frustration. "It's not the same anyway. It's not like you're together all the time. Besides, I haven't even told you the worst part. He slept with her! Try to tell me how *that* was for practical purposes!"

"That night?!" Allie asked in disbelief.

"No, not that night." she admitted, "It was a while ago, but still…"

"Was it after you guys were together?" Allie asked.

"Yes." She said it forcefully, but her conscience wouldn't let her leave the statement stand. "Well, we'd kind of broken up, but it was only for the weekend, and I never really believed we wouldn't see each other again.

I guess technically he did break up with me first, but it's a stupid technicality! He still had sex with her…like right after I left!" At first, Allie did seem to sympathize, but after a moment, a little smile crept over her face. "What the hell are you smiling at?" Felicity demanded.

"I'm sorry, but…did you ever watch 'Friends'?" Felicity stared at her in uncomprehending annoyance. "Ross and Rachel? 'We were on a break!' I'm sorry, never mind. Not really all that funny."

"Allie, you are supposed to be 'the supportive friend' here. You're not helping! You're supposed to sympathize with me and tell me that Cain is a jerk. Get mad and offer to stake him or something."

Allie tried not to smile as she raised an eyebrow. "You want me to *stake* him?" she asked in amusement.

Felicity crossed her arms and sat back in a huff. "No, but it's the thought that counts," she mumbled.

"Look, I'm sorry. I guess I'm just kind of jaded 'cause I've been out with *lots* of guys and they're *all* jerks. Do you realize how very few decent people there are in this world? It's really depressing.

But Cain *is* a good guy. It sucks that he slept with her, and I can't tell you to forgive him for that. It was a shitty thing to do…but everybody fucks up once in awhile.

As far as drinking from her goes, I can't really tell you what to think about that either. I don't really see it like you do, but that doesn't matter, 'cause it's not me.

I guess what you really have to decide is where you want things to go from here. I mean honestly. Are you in it for the long haul, or are you just having a good time? 'Cause if it's not a long-term thing, then you're gonna have to let him look elsewhere eventually. What do you expect?"

Felicity tried not to feel betrayed, but Allie's words reminded her unkindly of the things Sindy herself had said that night at the dance. Alyson was a bit kinder about it, but the concept was the same; 'step up or step out'. What *did* she expect from him? Total devotion, when she wasn't prepared to offer it in return?

No. It's not the same. Just because she wasn't willing to give him eternity shouldn't mean that he couldn't at least give her total devotion for the time that they *were* together.

What he had done was wrong. She knew it and she wouldn't let herself be talked into believing that her own narrow mindedness was to blame.

She sat quietly for a moment, trying not to let her eyes fill with tears. "I expected him to be honest with me, entirely. He had to have known how I would feel. Even if we can't last forever, shouldn't he be only with *me* when he's with me? It's *after* he leaves that life goes on. It shouldn't be going on behind my back."

Allie let that soak in a moment. Then she looked sorry and severely chastened for trying to defend him. "You're right." Allie took a deep breath and sighed. "He's a jerk. You want me to stake him?" she asked quietly.

Felicity rolled her eyes. "No."

"I could you know. I'm tougher than I look," Allie assured her.

"What do I do now?" Felicity asked dejectedly.

"What do you want?" Allie asked. Felicity kind of shrugged, deep in thought. "Do you want to go back to him?"

She looked up at Allie in angry determination. "No." Allie seemed very surprised. "I want *him* to come back to me...begging, on his hands and knees."

Allie smiled. "*Then* do you want to go back to him?"

"No. Then I turn him away because he should suffer more first." Alyson laughed as Felicity described what *should* happen. "But he can't live without me. He begs for my forgiveness like every night. And he *doesn't* give up. And he *doesn't* go back to *her*.

Oh my God, Allie! What if he's with her right now?"

"Relax, he's not," Allie assured her.

"How do you know?" Felicity asked.

"Because it's broad daylight," Allie pointed out.

"So? That doesn't mean anything. She could have been waiting for him when he got home this morning."

"Felicity, let's not get crazy here. He's sitting home alone and depressed just like he should be…with a hangover."

"Vampires don't even get hangovers. How's that for injustice?" Felicity grumped.

"Oh yeah." After a minute, Allie looked back up at her thoughtfully. "So the ball's in his court?"

"I guess. It's not like I never want to see him again, but he's got to know that what he did was *not* okay. I want him to come back; it just shouldn't be so easy. I can't believe he didn't even *try* to come and talk to me last night."

"He probably just figured that you needed some space. At least you know that he wasn't out havin' a 'happy time'."

"None of us seems very happy these days."

"I don't know about that. Ben seems to be getting along okay. He didn't show up at Tommy's last night. He *never* misses Halloween. I figure he must have been over at 'Jeannie's' getting wishes granted or somethin'."

Felicity laughed. "They went to Venus."

Alyson looked up in surprise. "You talked to him?"

"Yeah, he stopped by yesterday," Felicity told her.

"That's just great," Allie muttered sarcastically.

"Why, what's the matter?"

"That means it's only *me*. He's totally avoiding me, Felicity. I thought if I tried to make him face the fact that I'm not gonna give up on Mattie, eventually he'd just accept it, but instead he's being stupid and stubborn, and he's hardly even talking to me anymore. I'm kinda runnin' out of time here you know? Once Mattie shows up I can't be playin' these stupid games. Ben's just gonna have to deal, like it or not.

Why won't he understand? He's my best friend. Does he really think he can make me choose 'Mattie or him', like a friendship ultimatum? I can't do that, it's just not fair! I think that stupid bimbo girlfriend of his must be brainwashing him against me."

Felicity couldn't help but laugh. "I don't think so. He's just being stupid all on his own. He wouldn't let Ashley push him that far. In fact, and this ought to give you a laugh, Ashley's kind of scared of you now."

"What?"

"Yeah, 'cause she saw you dust that vamp. In fact, she's so stupid she won't even believe Ben that they were really vampires. She just thinks you put some kind of whammy on the guy. Even Ben thinks it's pretty funny."

"She is such a moron. How can he stand her?"

"I don't know, but you'd better try and talk to him again before Mattie gets here. In fact, he's the one you should be having lunch with, not me. Go find him. You know his schedule; wait outside his class or something. He'll come around. I know he cares about you enough not to let this stay between you. He's just stubborn."

"Yeah. Stubborn he is, but I didn't think he'd hold out this long. You're right; I should go talk to him. Ashley can't have turned his brain entirely to mush. He'll come to his senses, right?"

"I hope so. Go ahead. I got this," Felicity said, waving her hand over her half-eaten sandwich and Allie's mutilated mess. Allie thanked her, dropping some money on the table anyway, and rushed off to find Ben.

Felicity sat back and sighed, wishing that her problem could be so easily solved. She could go and talk to Cain, but what would she even say? What did she want? She had no idea. She wanted to know that he desired no one but her. She wanted him to love her like he would never love another…and then what did she want him to do? Leave?

He wanted her to stay with him. He'd even offered it, his blood. What he had done behind her back had hurt her, of that there was no doubt, but he *did* love her. She knew that he did. He wished that they could be together, just the two of them, forever. If she went to him… If she asked him to be true to her… If she asked that he pledge unflinching faithfulness and loyalty to her, he would. She knew that he would. He loved her.

He was sorry to have hurt her and she knew that she would forgive him. She had just needed some space, but how much space did she want? Not enough to make him think that she had decided to go on without him. She couldn't lose him like this, it was all wrong. To be angry and wounded and not fix it was unthinkable. She wouldn't leave him like this, she couldn't. Could she even leave him at all?

She had told herself all along that she would, when the time came, but that had always seemed to be something in the far distant future, not a prospect to face now; but why should he stay? He had come to deal with other vampires. Chris and Luke were gone, Marcus was gone...obviously, he and Sindy had come to some sort of understanding, so he really had no reason to stay from the vampire perspective.

Sindy. What would *she* do when Cain left? Go back to her old ways and start causing havoc again? Doubtful; she valued Cain's opinion of her too highly. Felicity knew just what Sindy would do. She would follow Cain. Why not? With Felicity out of the way there'd be nothing stopping her from seducing Cain for herself. She'd done it once, why shouldn't she try again?

Cain would have no further reason to reject her advances. Felicity would be some distant memory of a 'human' that he had dallied with for a short while, hardly anyone of great note in his amazing life. And Felicity herself would be here, left to carry on her mundane existence. To concentrate on school, spend her free time at work and go home for weekends with her family.

Unless…

What would it be like, to be with him…forever? What kind of life would that be? She tried to imagine.

Cain. Handsome, strong, confident, kind, gentle, and adoring. Spending all of his time with her, loving and laughing. They could make each other so happy.

Hardly ever seeing her family, if at all. No sunlight. No career. No children of her own…

No school. No job. No responsibilities. Never worrying for money. They could go anywhere, do anything; travel and explore the world together.

No heartbeat. No reflection. Hiding her true self from the world.

No aging. No disease.

No food, only…blood.

Felicity thought back to the times she had let him drink from her, in his bed. She never would have admitted it to herself before, but now she could almost understand how he could get so caught up in that, how someone could *desire* blood. It was still an imperfect understanding, but somehow it just didn't seem as repulsive as it once had.

He loved her. She loved him. Allie had made it all seem so simple that night at the dance. *Was* it that simple? Aside from the whole prospect of immortality and freedom, they could finally just be happy, together. The decision was in her hands to walk away, or to be with someone she loved, forever. To be together always, what more did she want?

Felicity was startled from her thoughts by the waitress. She approached the table with some trepidation, eyeing the scattered remains of their lunch. She gave Felicity an odd look. "Do you want something else?"

"No, I don't."

Chapter 10 ~ Until we meet again

Cain

Tommy's Place
Midnight, Tuesday

Cain sat staring out into the gloomy bar and tried to drown out the thoughts in his head with another swig of rum. How had things turned out this way? Perhaps he should have been more honest with Felicity from the start, although he'd never really sought to deceive her. He'd never meant to hurt her or be untrue. Once he'd realized that she needed to know about his encounters with Sindy, he had tried to speak the truth in as gentle a manner as possible. He wouldn't try to hide anything from Felicity, but it had hurt her. He knew how she felt about him. He felt the same about her, but he was the first person that she had so completely given her heart to. The fact that he had shared an intimate experience with another was something she could not accept.

Knowing that he had had sex with Sindy was surely a devastating blow to Felicity. In truth, he probably felt almost as bad about it as she did, but he *had* sent Felicity away never to return before it happened. He had tried to convey to Felicity that it truly was an act of self-depreciation more than any sort of illicit reward. He hoped that somehow she could understand and forgive him that, but as much as the sex did disturb her, that did not even seem her main concern. It was the intimacies of blood sharing that seemed to turn her ire most. Something Cain knew she could not fully understand, but he himself did not even really see as a trespass.

If he were to be completely honest with himself, then yes, he had known that she would probably not approve, but he had spoken truly when he had told her that *he* knew all along in his heart that his love for Felicity was strong enough not to be swayed by such things. The blood was an entirely separate matter.

He tried to see things from her perspective, to find an analogy that would help him to understand how she must feel, but the truth was, there was nothing that he could think of that would be the same. She could not drink from another, she was human. Even if she could, he wouldn't be hurt by it. It was not the same as infidelity in a relationship, although she seemed to think that it was.

Cain had never lived as a part of a large group of vampires the way that Sindy and Arif did, but he had lived with a select few at different times in his life. When he had shared relationships with other vampires in the past, sharing blood was a natural thing; with ones' lover, and with other vampires one was close with as well. It was not done lightly, or with someone that you did not care for, but it was not the exclusive act Felicity seemed to think it should be. It was a tie to another, meaning you were allies, friends, family. A blood tie was a serious thing but not an exclusive endeavor by any means.

Felicity could not understand all of the implications and meanings assigned to drinking from someone. Cain wasn't even sure if he did, but it was undoubtedly more than just the physical taking of blood, especially between two vampires. He had drunk from Sindy not only to mark her, but as a connection for her. Instinct played more of a role in the existences of some than others. Whether vampire instinct or human loneliness drove Sindy to crave his mark he did believe she felt incomplete in being alone. It was a basic inherent need to feel a part of a group or family for some. That was most likely the reason lesser vampires subjected themselves to occupying a lower rank in a social structure such as the type that Arif enforced. They could not stand to exist alone. They would rather give up their freedom to obey an elder, than be without family, purpose and security.

The intricacies of blood sharing were complex and almost unexplainable. It was not something he felt Felicity would even try to understand, so he hadn't defended it with explanations. Perhaps he really had been in the wrong not to tell her anyway, but he did feel that he'd had no impure motives. He really did love Felicity enough not to want to endanger her fragile heart, but some things were driven by his vampire nature and that was a command difficult to ignore. Even apart from instinct, his human nature softened his heart to Sindy at times as well. Was that wrong, to feel for another, if it was not sexual in nature? Should he have left Sindy to deal with her own insecurities, knowing Felicity would not understand?

It was beyond debate, it was done. She'd felt betrayed, and had left him. This was not how he wanted things to end, with such an abrupt and unpleasant parting, and that was not the worst part. The awful truth of it was that although she probably wanted him to, he really should *not* go looking to smooth things over. As unforeseen and painful as the other morning had been, it was a catalyst for something he really should have been working up the nerve to do all along. He should leave her. She showed no signs of desiring a life like his and he really had no place in hers. Staying for much longer would only make things that much harder. He should leave now, while she was angry with him. It would probably be easier on her that way.

She really was a creature different than he. He could not fit entirely into her human world without great obstacles to overcome, and she obviously could not handle being with him if he were going to continue to deal with other vampires. Each of their worlds had social complexities that the other could not fully adapt to. Such convoluted thoughts were too much for him now. His attempt to get drunk enough to become blissfully unaware of the situation was only being rewarded with a slight dizziness and the onset of a pounding headache.

He looked up again to survey the crowd around him: young adults drinking, laughing and appraising each other's value as potential mates. Why does everyone have to assign such meaning to everything? Why can't things just be bloody simple for a change? Why can't one just do what *feels* right without worry for what *is* right by social and moral standards? He knew it was the vampire within him, whispering in his ear to be the beast and not the man. Such a strange breed vampires were. Not man, not animal, but something with attributes of each, the instincts and desires of an animal with the mind and nagging conscience of a man. Could something so at war with itself, really have been *meant* to be? Enough philosophy. More rum.

As he drank, his eyes inadvertently tried to focus on a form moving towards him, although his mind was trying to ignore all else in the bar but the glass in his hand. The figure stopped before him and would not be ignored. He put down the glass to make himself look up and acknowledge the face. Alyson. He watched silently as she stood there appraising his state and the table before him. Three bottles of rum, two empty, one still half-full. You'd think it would be taking better effect by now. She smirked at him with her arms crossed before her. "I see you've got another full evening planned."

He gave her a weary smile. "They told me you weren't working."

She sighed. "I'm not, but I couldn't stand to sit home anymore. I left a note on the door." She eyed him for another moment and then gestured to the bottles on the table. "So what's with the stockpile?"

He spoke with a measured, depressive air, as though it were exhaustive to have to explain himself. "No table service tonight. They said you weren't working and that I would have to go to the bar. I don't like having to get up and go to the bar. It inhibits my rate of consumption and interferes with the pathetic attempt I am making to get sodden drunk." Allie laughed at him. He found the very slight fog that had been hovering over his mind was clearing already. Very annoying. "It's not funny. This stupid body of mine nullifies the alcohol so fast that a good stupor is damn near impossible to achieve."

"Well you're gonna need more than that," she said with another gesture towards his bottles.

"That's all they'd let me buy, said I had to leave some for everyone else. Your boss is very annoying. He said if I wanted more I should visit a liquor store."

Allie pulled a chair over from the table opposite and sat down on it backwards with a laugh. "Man, you're even worse off tonight than I am."

He eyed her quizzically. "What's *your* problem?" Allie gave him a pointed look, that he shouldn't be so rude as to make her say it. Of course, he should have realized…Mattie. "Oh. Well at least yours is easily remedied."

She shrugged, with grudging acceptance. "So's yours. She wants you to go to her."

He let out a resigned sigh and answered her quietly. "I know."

"So why are you sitting here?"

He took another large gulp of rum from his glass. "I am trying to drink up the nerve to leave."

She looked at him curiously. "The bar?"

"Town," he clarified.

She didn't seem to take to that well. Neither did he really, hence the rum. "Why do you want to leave?"

"I don't *want* to leave, I have to. It's no good, my being here."

She looked annoyed, although he couldn't imagine why. "Not good enough for who?"

Who did she think, him? "Her."

Alyson leaned down to drag his gaze from the glass before him and make him meet her eyes. "Do you love her?"

"Of course I do," Cain insisted.

"Enough to make it only her?" Allie asked.

He drained his glass. Why was she even asking? It was beside the point. "Yes."

"You sure about that?" she asked with an arched brow.

He gave her an exasperated look and refilled his glass from the bottle. "Devotion is not the problem, believe me."

She nodded and smiled in acceptance. "So…you want her, she wants you… What's the problem?"

He drank almost the entire glass before answering her. Finally, he looked back up to her and put it simply. "She wants *me*, not *it*."

She looked as though she thought he was making a big deal over nothing. "*That's* the problem?"

He became annoyed. "No, that is not the problem. The problem is that I would like for that to be the problem."

She stared at him for a moment, trying to decipher what he meant. "Are you sure you're not drunk?"

He took the last swig of his drink and clunked the empty glass down onto the table. "The real problem is that I should not even offer *it*."

"Why not?" Alyson asked.

"Because, she deserves her life! She doesn't really want *this*." He raised his arms to signify his annoyingly inhuman body. "It's not fair for me to use the love she has for me to sway her towards something that she does not want. Not that I could even sway her if I wanted to. She's no desire to live in darkness and I can't say I blame her. She's a whole future ahead of her and it's not right for me to take that away."

"It's not taking something away, its giving something new, but I don't even know if that's what she wants. I don't think *she* even knows what she wants, but you can't just leave, not like this."

He buried his face in his hands for a moment. "You're right, I can't. I'm not allowed to leave without telling her first, I promised."

"Good, don't." Allie told him.

Why did she have to go and make him promise? She knew how important it was to him to keep his word. That was why. It was going to be hard enough to leave, but to have to face her first… "Does a note count?"

Allie glared at him in disapproval. "No!"

Cain picked up the bottle and poured the last splash of rum into his glass. He put the empty bottle down and was about to raise the glass to his lips, but his hand froze halfway there as he broke into a broad smile. "Speaking of notes…looks like someone got yours."

Alyson's eyes went wide as she interpreted his words. She spun and stood, nearly knocking over her chair to see what Cain saw. It was Mattie, at last. Their friend stood at the entrance trying to reason with the doorman, who was apparently telling him that he was not old enough to come inside. Cain smiled as he could practically feel Allie's relief. She didn't even waste another glance on Cain but began pushing patrons out of the way as she ran to the door.

Mattie did look awfully young. No matter how long he lived, Cain had a difficult time getting used to the fact that vampires did not outwardly age. He had very few long-standing associations with others. Most he dealt with, he knew less than a year. Mattie was different. They always kept in touch. He'd known Mattie since days after his death a little over three years ago. Not a very long time, but in the life of a young living man the difference between seventeen and twenty would certainly be apparent. Cain hadn't seen Mattie in almost a year, yet of course, he had not aged outwardly at all. He'd let his light reddish blonde hair get a bit shaggier than usual. As his skin had begun to pale from lack of sun, it caused the smattering of freckles across his nose and cheeks to become a bit more apparent; but he still looked to be the same young man that Cain had come across newly turned and alone.

The doorman was just stepping away, having decided to allow him in. Mattie smiled, thanking the man, and was just turning to face the room when Allie caught him by surprise. She barreled into him, throwing her arms over his shoulders and challenging him to keep his feet. It took not a moment for Mattie to wrap his arms around her as well. He caught and held her by the waist, letting the force of her rush to him spin them around as he lightly lifted her off the floor. He then let her back down to her feet, but still held her crushingly close. He bent with his face buried in the crook between her neck and shoulder, not to bite, but only to feel her close against him and to breathe in her familiar scent. They seemed to stand there forever, just holding each other.

Not a person in the bar who had noted their embrace could help but smile. The love and relief of reunion after long separation was clearly apparent and would tug at anyone's heart. Cain smiled as well as he watched them from across the room. He too was happy and relieved that his friend had arrived safely. Not that Cain had really worried for him. Other than the misfortune that he had met on the night of his death, Mattie usually had a knack for keeping out of trouble. Mattie was the sort to get along well with people wherever he might go. He usually kept to himself, but he was respectful and polite with such a friendly, easy-going smile, that he always seemed to fit right in.

Although a bit young, Mattie did look to blend rather well with the usual crowd of college students in the bar tonight. He wore the pullover tunic that Cain had bought for him in Mexico two years ago. It was striped with blue, green and black and brought some color out of Mattie's very pale blue eyes. Cain smiled remembering Mattie's insistence that they cross the border for a weekend after they finished business Cain'd had in Arizona.

Since they'd met, Cain had watched Mattie grow from a quiet and shy youth to a young man filled with confidence and inner strength. The first year had been hard as he mourned the loss of his natural life, but once he'd accepted his death to the mortal world, he'd begun to feel liberated, freed from responsibility and unafraid to explore and enjoy the world around him. He was still cautious to be sure, but was eager for new experiences.

Cain had indulged him with plane tickets and spending money, although rarely accompanying Mattie in his travels unless it coincided with business of his own, but of the weekend in Mexico, Mattie had insisted. Cain was glad he'd gone; it was a fond memory. Now Mattie had paired the tunic with a very faded pair of blue jeans that had a hole in one knee bordered by frayed strings, and a pair of brown leather boat shoes with no socks.

Cain was probably the only other besides Mattie himself, who could hear Alyson's mumbled words in Mattie's ear. "I was so worried about you." Mattie held Alyson back by the shoulders so that he could look at her. He ran his eyes over her face and seemed to note the new colors in her hair with a smile. She was grinning from ear to ear, although there was a telltale sparkle of tears in her eyes.

She glanced downward almost shyly for a moment as Mattie looked at her hair again and ran his fingers lightly through it. Then she met his eyes again with a bold reproach. "Don't you ever stay away from me that long again, not ever!"

"That's a promise." He gave her a watery smile as he held back tears of his own. "God Allie, I've missed you," he whispered as he pulled her close for a kiss. It began as a crushing, desperate reunion but after a moment, Alyson threw her arms back around his neck and their kiss turned passionate, unrushed and deep, it went on and on.

Cain turned back to his glass, reminded of his own love soon to be lost. There was only a swallow of rum left. Damn. He downed it and looked up to see Mattie release Allie from their embrace. She smiled up at him adoringly, but then gave him a rough shove on the shoulder. "You said Halloween," she reprimanded, although she couldn't drop the smile for long enough to really appear disappointed in him.

"I know. I'm sorry. It took a little longer to get back than I thought."

"Where were you?" she asked.

Mattie gave her an impish little grin. "Colorado."

"Colorado! What the hell were you doing way out there?"

Mattie smiled and laughed. "Oh it's beautiful Allie, you should see it. I got great pictures. I've been lookin' around a bit, for a good place to settle down, get a house."

Allie took a step back and gave him a very curious look. "You bought a *house*, in *Colorado*?"

Mattie grinned and shook his head. "No. Colorado's pretty, but so are a lot of places. I bought something else…a surprise." Allie just tilted her head, trying to figure out what he was up to. "Come on, it's outside."

Mattie was clearly excited to show her, and took her arm to lead her out, but she stopped him, remembering something. "Wait, before we go…there's a friend I should say goodbye to."

Mattie gave Allie a steady stare for a moment and then began to scan the bar, seeming a bit out of sorts. Cain could guess who he might be looking for. Cain himself was sitting down in the back and was mostly blocked from view by other people. Mattie didn't see him. "An old friend or a new friend?" he asked warily.

Allie gave him a thoughtful smile. "New friend of mine…old friend of yours."

Mattie looked around again seeming very perplexed. "Who?"

Allie took him by the hand with a smile. "You'll see. Come on."

Cain put down his glass and sat up a bit straighter at their approach. Even when Mattie's eyes first fell upon him, it took a moment for recognition. Cain was probably the last person Mattie expected for Alyson to know, and surely he looked a bit different with the new haircut. It was almost odd to finally see the two of them together, these two friends that he had known separately and grown so fond of. They would make an interesting balance of personality, and they were obviously very much in love. Cain definitely approved. As they stopped before Cain's table, Mattie's eyes went wide with shocked surprise. "Cain?" He turned from Cain to Alyson and back a time or two as though completely bewildered.

Cain stood with a grin and took one of Mattie's hands into both of his own. "Welcome back. Always good to see you safe and sound."

Mattie finally gave him a broad smile, but still looked very confused. "What are you doing here? Were you looking for me? Is something wrong?"

"No, no." Cain laughed as he sat back down and Alyson and Mattie took seats at the table. "I'm here on my own business. I arrived back in June and spent the last five months being served drinks almost nightly by this feisty young lady here," he said with a nod and smile at Allie. She had her arm wrapped around Mattie's as though afraid to let go of him. "Wasn't 'till last month that I put her together with you though. Gave me quite the shock, I can tell you."

Mattie looked from Cain to Alyson. He still couldn't seem to believe the two were acquainted. "You really *know* him?" he asked Allie hesitantly.

She laughed. "You mean that he's a vamp? Yeah, I figured that out back in July."

Mattie was suddenly worried as he turned to Cain. "She didn't try to stake you, did she?" Cain laughed and shook his head no. "She does that sometimes. Could have been very embarrassing."

Allie gave him a shove as Cain answered. "Not at all. She's been a good friend," he said with a tender look at Allie. He then realized Mattie, although smiling, might be wondering just *how* good of friends Cain and Allie had been. Cain continued very sincerely to Mattie. "You are a very lucky man to have such a loyal, devoted young lady eagerly awaiting your return."

Mattie gave Allie an adoring smile. "I know."

"And you should not have kept her waiting," Cain added sternly.

Mattie looked properly abashed. "I know, but I'm only one night late. Pretty good considering… I had a good reason." Both Cain and Allie looked to him expectantly. Rather than answer, Mattie stood from his chair and motioned for them to do the same. "It's outside. Come see."

Cain and Alyson shared a curious glance and then followed Mattie from the bar. As Mattie held the door for her, Alyson walked out first into the moderately full parking lot. "What exactly am I supposed to be lookin' at?" she turned to ask Mattie.

He smiled and pointed over to the far side of the lot. "That." It was a very large and obviously brand new, first class motor home.

Alyson looked back at him in surprise. "That's yours?" Mattie just smiled and nodded. "You bought a *motor home*?"

"It's an Alpine Luxury Motor *Coach*. And technically…Cain bought it for me." He gave Cain an apologetic and hopeful look. "You know that bank account that was supposed to be for emergencies?"

Cain gave a little laugh, lightly shaking his head. "What are you going to do with that thing?"

"I'm going to live in it. It's a house on wheels, so I can live anywhere…everywhere. Isn't it great?" He looked back at Allie hopefully. "Please tell me you think it's great."

Allie smiled at his enthusiasm. "Yeah. It's great."

Mattie shook his head impatiently. "Nah… You can't tell anything from out here, wait until you see the *in*side." He took Alyson eagerly by the hand and crossed the lot to the object of his excitement. Cain followed with a little laugh at Mattie's joyful glee over the thing.

Cain followed them inside to a surprisingly spacious living area. It was appointed with rich cherry wood paneling and warm, inviting shades of green, purple and burgundy. It had a couch and recliner facing a large flat television screen. The driver's seat looked like a cozy armchair and was swiveled completely around to face the room, as was the passenger seat, which even had a fold out footrest. There was a little dinette area with a booth type table and benches, and what looked to be a full service kitchen. Cain looked around in amazed wonder as Allie's mouth dropped open. She was obviously quite impressed. "Mattie this place rocks!"

"You like it?" he asked with a broad grin.

"It's awesome!" She walked around running her fingers over the stone kitchen countertop and testing the plushness of the cushions on the couch.

"That folds out into a bed," Mattie informed her.

"No shit? That's the bed?" Alyson asked in surprise.

Mattie smiled. "No, that's *a* bed. *The* bed is back there," he said, gesturing towards the little entryway to the back room.

Allie got up and ran past the bathroom into the bedroom, and by the sound of it, jumped onto the bed with a little scream of joy. "Oh my God, this bed is huge!"

Mattie laughed as Cain turned to face him. "There's nothing left in that bank account is there?" he asked with a resigned little smirk.

Mattie dropped his smile to look at Cain with a little anxiety. "No, not really, but I'll pay you back, I swear. At least I won't have to spend money on hotel rooms anymore."

Allie came back out to them wearing a big smile. "Wow. I totally approve, but you can hardly see out the windows."

As Mattie answered, he and Cain shared a glance. "Extra dark mirror tinted thermal windows; kind of a safety feature for someone like me."

Allie gave them both an awkward smile. "Oh yeah."

"There's really heavy curtains too. And look," Mattie moved to show them a recessed panel door that slid out and across the room behind the driver's seat. "During the day I can close off the drivers cab and make this a separate room. That way I can hang out in here without getting sun through the windshield. Someone else could even drive if they wanted," he said with a smile at Allie.

"Very cool," she answered.

Mattie turned back to Cain, almost fearfully awaiting some sort of response. "Isn't that cool?"

Cain was staring at it in wonder. "Ingenious."

Mattie still seemed apprehensive over Cain's reaction. "It's okay right, that I bought it? It might take me a while, but I'll pay you back."

As if money was an issue. Cain eyed Mattie's hopeful face for a moment. "Consider it a gift," he said with a smile.

Mattie looked very relieved that he wasn't mad. How could he even think that Cain might be? Mattie never asked for much and often worked odd jobs for his own money. Cain had never denied him a request. Mattie smiled in appreciation. "Thanks. I was kinda hopin' you might say that. What do you think of it? Really?"

Cain looked around again in disbelief. He'd never been inside such a thing. He'd no idea how luxurious it could be. He'd thought a motor home to be little more than a glorified bus. "I have never seen the like. And you can actually drive this thing? Live where you please?"

Mattie nodded and smiled at Cain's wonder. "That's the idea. You like it?"

It was so endearing, the way Mattie always looked to him for approval. He often felt like a father figure to the boy. Their relationship actually reminded him a bit of the bond that he and Charles had shared when Cain was a young human of Mattie's age back in England, with Cain now in the role of the older and wiser brother, guiding and sheltering him from harm. Of course, Mattie was much better behaved and far more agreeable than Cain had ever been at that age. 'Let's hope we have a happier ending as well', Cain thought to himself sadly of the relationship. He smiled to Mattie in endorsement of the purchase. "I think that it's a fine investment. Enjoy your new home. I'll still see you at the house though, right?" he asked.

"Yeah, of course."

Alyson looked at them both questioningly. "What house?"

Cain answered. "I've got a house up near Buffalo. Tenants are moving out, end of the month. I'll be staying there for a little. Mattie was originally supposed to meet me there, after his visit here of course," he added with a smile. "Well, you two don't want me hanging about all night. So I'm going to take my leave," he said, turning for the door.

Allie grabbed his arm and stopped him in a commanding tone. "You can't *leave*." She looked at him sternly and he knew just what she meant.

Cain turned back to face her, but it was Mattie who looked at her with raised brows and asked, "Why not?"

Allie realized his confusion. "Oh, he can leave the *trailer*." She turned back to Cain and added in a stage whisper. "I *want* you to leave the trailer."

Cain smiled at her knowingly as Mattie corrected her. "It's not a *trailer*. It's a luxury motor coach."

"Whatever. Cain you *cannot* leave town, not without talking to her."

"I know. I won't."

"And none of this 'quickie goodbye' crap either. You'd better stick around and really talk things out. I mean it." Cain averted his eyes as she pointed her finger at him accusingly. "Because if I come back to find her a sobbing broken mess, I'm gonna hunt you down and stake your ass! Even if I have to go all the way to Buffalo to do it!"

Cain smiled at her phrasing and then sighed and met her eyes again for a long and serious moment. "I will talk to her, but I can't tell you what'll come of it, and one way or another, I *will* be leaving."

He just stared at her silently for a moment, trying not to become emotional about it all. "All I can tell you is that I *do* love her. Whatever you find her emotional state to be when next you see her, most likely mine will be the same. Good or bad, and where that will be, I honestly don't know. We'll just have to wait and see what unfolds."

Mattie was respectfully quiet, although he would surely question Allie later. Alyson looked as though she might cry, but seemed to accept his answer. She gave him a little smile. "So then I guess…this is goodbye."

Cain leaned to give her a fond little kiss on the cheek and then looked into her eyes with a pause for serious reflection. "Until we meet again," he said with a loving little smile.

He then looked to Mattie with sincere precaution. "Take care," he said meaningfully. Mattie gave him a solemn nod. With that, Cain did take his leave of them. Out into the cold dark lot and away into the night. At least for Alyson and Mattie, Cain felt reassured that he knew all would be well. They were lucky to have each other. If only Cain knew what his own future would hold.

Part 3 – Evolution of Love

Chapter 11 – You just don't understand

Felicity

Felicity's dorm room
11:30, Friday night

Felicity hadn't worked tonight. Mr. Penten had seen the bandage on her throat yesterday and told her that she should take some more time to recuperate. She really *was* fine, but she wasn't going to argue.

It had been five whole days since she had left Cain standing in the doorway to his house. Five! This was the fifth night and it was already getting late. Wasn't he even going to *try* to come and see her? After her talk with Allie, Felicity had decided that although she wouldn't rush to seek Cain out, she would certainly be receptive to him when he came to speak to her. Why hadn't he come?

By midnight, she began to worry terribly that he wasn't ever planning to come to her at all. In fact, she suddenly had the terrible fear that perhaps he had packed up and left. She quickly threw on some clothes and went out to her car. Not that she really wanted to go to him. She was still feeling stubbornly angry enough that he should have to come to her, but she just *had* to drive by his house, just to be sure he hadn't disappeared on her. He'd promised he wouldn't, but still…

At first, she was very relieved to see that his motorcycle was still there, at the top of the driveway. He would have taken it if he was going to leave town, but as she slowed in front of the house, she still could not *feel* him at all. Her mark could not be gone already, and she knew from experience that if he were in the house, he would still be in her perceptive range from the street. He wasn't there.

He must have walked somewhere. Where would he go? Only one place came to mind. Tommy's. In fact, now that she thought about it, she *had* felt a flickering tug of his presence when she'd passed the bar on the way to his house, but she'd been so intent upon reaching his house that she'd been going rather fast, and she hadn't paid the feeling proper attention. He must be at the bar. Was he planning to sit at the bar every night until she went to him?

Stupid plan. She wasn't coming. He was the one who had messed everything up, he should come to her. Didn't he realize that?

She drove back, thinking that she would pass Tommy's Place and see if she could indeed again feel him there. Then she had an annoying thought. He could see her mark. Long before she felt him, he would know that she was there. In fact, it was probably already too late to hide the fact that she'd been out looking for him. His psychic range reached pretty far. She wasn't sure of its exact distance, but chances were that from the bar, he had seen her leave the dorm and head off in the direction of his house.

That made her feel kind of dumb. It rather defeated the purpose of the whole 'aloof' image she was trying to achieve. Oh well, too late now. Might as well satisfy her curiosity and see if he was even there.

Allie's. She would drive to Allie's. That way she could pass Tommy's but maybe still try to maintain the illusion that she had concerns other than Cain. What she would pretend to be doing visiting Allie in the middle of the night she didn't know, but that shouldn't matter. She'd just stop at Allie's for a few minutes and then leave. Cain probably couldn't tell if she actually went *in* anyway.

As she neared Tommy's, she slowed the car. Not too much, she didn't want to be obvious, but she couldn't just fly by. Yes, he was definitely there. Her body recognized the feel of his presence with a desirous sort of ache. *Creepy venom* she thought with disgust. Not that she didn't desire him anyway, but it would be nice to acknowledge it on her own and not feel like some other influence was pushing her at him.

When she had first been marked and understood about the venom, it had felt rather nice, like she always had a part of Cain with her, such an intimate and personal connection with each other. She still wanted to see it that way, but ever since overhearing Sindy and Alyson's conversation about it, she couldn't help but feel a little creeped out.

Sindy spoke of the venom as if it were its own separate identity. Like the venom itself had its own motives and desires. That was very unsettling, but it was still something that had come from Cain, and Felicity tried her hardest to see it that way. It was venom, a drug, an inanimate substance. It's not as though anyone was consciously controlling the way she felt. Cain didn't use the kind of powers that Sindy seemed to enjoy playing with. He had never tried to summon or control her. She just felt him when he was near. It was like an addiction, a craving that her body had for more venom, like people had for something like a cigarette. Right?

She kept on to Allie's, wondering if Cain had noticed her closeness. He must have. Even if he had managed to get himself drunk, sensations like those her proximity to him caused could not possibly be ignored. She wished she could see his mark the way that he could see her, to know whether he left the bar to follow her, or what else he might be doing. She sincerely hoped he was alone.

Allie's car was parked out in the street in front of her apartment. Felicity pulled up next to it and sat there for a minute. No lights were on inside. It was after midnight. She could be sleeping, but Felicity doubted it. She knew that Allie was used to working the night shift. Most likely she just wasn't home.

Maybe Mattie *had* come, and they were out with his car. She hoped so, for Allie's sake. Nothing left to do but go back to the dorm. At least she knew that Cain was still around. Of course the fact that he was sitting at the bar instead of coming to see her was aggravating, but it could be worse. She went back to her room, quickly passing Tommy's and feeling Cain's fleeting presence once more, and then went to sleep.

The weekend came and went. Her mom had called, but being unsure how much to say about her throat and visit to the hospital, she ended up saying nothing. The pumpkin-carving story might have gone over alright at the hospital, but her parents were certain to be a bit more discerning. She was afraid that any attempt to give a false account of things would lead her into tripping up her story and making her mom suspicious. It was easier to just pretend nothing out of the ordinary had happened. She'd said that she had to work and had a lot of studying to do, and wouldn't be home this weekend. She hoped when the time did come to go home, her injury wouldn't be too noticeable.

Monday would mean back to work, back to classes, back to routine, but still no word from Cain. How could she possibly just fall back into daily life without him? He *was* her life these days. She felt as though all of her time was spent missing him and keeping herself from going to him.

What was he waiting for? He was the one who had kept things from her and made her feel betrayed. She was emotionally hurt *and* physically injured. Wasn't he even going to try to see her, to make sure she was okay? Could he possibly think that she wouldn't want him to come? She spent her evenings catching up on schoolwork and sitting around the dorm wondering what she should do.

Monday morning she had to miss algebra (not *too* disappointing) to go back to the hospital for a follow up visit, and then she returned to school for lunch. Felicity was just paying for her chef salad in the cafeteria line when she noticed Ben waving at her from a table. He was already eating, alone. Felicity had not seen Alyson since their lunch at the diner on Tuesday and this would be the first time she'd spoken to Ben since then. She wondered how things had gone, and whether Allie might join them for lunch, if Allie was even around.

As the days passed without word from her, it seemed more and more likely to Felicity that Mattie had returned and they were off spending time alone together. How romantic it seemed. Where was *her* romance? Why was Cain being so stubborn? After spending decades alone, was he *that* out of practice in being with a woman that he couldn't figure out that he should come and apologize to her? She almost wished she could send Allie to go and talk to him. Maybe Ben had seen her. She waved back to him and went to join him at his lunch table.

He greeted her as she put her tray down and got settled. "Hey, no more bandage!"

"Yeah. I got my stitches out." She tried not to be self-conscious about it. She had noticed that she'd picked up the habit of raising her hand to her throat as though to cover the spot. She purposely kept her hand on the table. "How's it look? Is it very noticeable?" she asked Ben hesitantly.

"Na. You can hardly see it. Go like that." He tilted his head back to demonstrate exposing the side of his neck. Reluctantly, she did the same. He examined her throat and then shrugged. "It's there, but it's not obvious unless you're lookin' up at the ceiling."

She tilted her head back down and kept her eyes on her lunch. She knew that it was an ugly scar. It was a few inches long, and still a bit puckered and red. The doctor had assured her that it would fade quite a bit as it healed and at least it was mostly under her chin. Hopefully no one would notice it under regular circumstances.

Ben seemed to realize that she was still uneasy about it. "Hey, I have a vampire hunting scar. Well, technically it's not from a vampire though. Allie staked me." Felicity couldn't help but smile, recalling Allie's account of what had happened. "You're smiling? It's true, really. She did."

Felicity chuckled. "I know, she told me."

Ben gave a little nod and chuckle. "I was holding off this vamp and Allie came at him from behind, you know like to stake his heart through the back. She got him, but then she got me. Another inch or two and I could have had a real problem on my hands."

"She said you'll never let her forget it."

"It hurt!"

Felicity smiled. "So let's see it."

Ben looked around, taken aback. *"Here?* In the middle of the cafeteria?"

Felicity smirked at his affected modesty. "I showed you mine."

Ben laughed with an arched brow and then pulled up his shirt. She leaned forward to examine his chest. Now that she was looking for it, it was obvious. Right in the center of his chest was a slightly raised and shiny stripe of scar tissue.

After a moment, Felicity leaned back and looked up at him, unimpressed. "Mine's bigger."

Ben started to laugh as he dropped his shirt. "First time I ever lost *that* contest."

"What? The thing's barely an inch long; you can hardly even see it!"

Ben began laughing hysterically as Felicity gazed at him in confusion. Finally he tried to fill her in. "That was supposed to be a joke."

"I don't get it," Felicity replied.

Ben finished laughing and stared at her for a minute, as though trying to decide whether she really knew what he meant. "I wasn't necessarily referring to the *scar.*"

Felicity went over the exchange again in her head and began to blush fiercely with comprehension as Ben smirked.

She averted her eyes as three guys approached their table. They were clearly friends of Ben's and stopped to say hi. They had lunch trays in their hands, but the table was too small to accommodate them. They only paused on their way to sit elsewhere. After their initial 'hey's and what's up's', one of them turned his attention to Felicity. "Who's your red friend?" he asked Ben with a smile.

Felicity had obviously failed at her attempt not to be embarrassed by Ben's comment, but finally looked up with a smile as he introduced her. "This is Felicity. 'Liss, this is Pete, Jeff and Tim."

She gave the guys a timid 'hi'. They were all older than her, probably juniors and seniors. They turned their attention back to Ben.

"Shouldn't you be in 'research mode'? Don't be slackin' on us," Pete scolded.

"Relax, I've got it," Ben answered.

"I hear Benson's tough," Jeff added.

"I got it. He's toast," Ben assured them, unconcerned. They laughed and headed off to sit at another table a bit away.

Felicity turned back to Ben quizzically. "Got what?"

"Oh, I'm heading a debate later," he said, taking a bite of his sandwich.

Felicity looked back over at the guys, who had settled at their table with much joking and laughter. Felicity looked back again at Ben, quietly eating his lunch. "How come you don't sit with them?"

Ben glanced back at the guys briefly and then went back to eating his lunch. "I see those clowns all day. Lunchtime is always reserved for…Allie."

They sat in awkward silence. Felicity refused to say anything, she only watched him expectantly. Ben was going to have to talk to her about Allie on his own. She was getting tired of playing the mediator and pulling information out of them.

Finally he spoke. "Have you seen her?"

"Not since Tuesday. Didn't she come see you?" she asked.

"Yeah, she cornered me outside my physics class," he said.

"And?" she prompted.

Ben looked as though he'd rather not answer. Finally, he replied grudgingly. "And, the first sentence out of her mouth had the name 'Mattie' in it. So I told her I didn't want to hear anymore and I walked away."

"Ben! You didn't even let her talk? She wanted to talk to you before she went away!"

Ben appeared very distressed by that statement. "Where is she going?"

"She said she was taking some time off work, to go to the Pocono's."

Ben nodded, with a relieved little laugh, as though he should have expected as much. "She does that sort of thing a lot, takes long weekends and stuff. I always used to think it was with *different* guys though. I can't believe she spent the last three years letting me think that she was so…undiscriminating."

Felicity just stared at him for a second in disbelief, as though he were in any position to judge. "Funny, you seemed to accept *that* better than you reacted to the truth."

For a moment, Ben looked as though he would become angry and argue with her. He never took his eyes off her face, but finally he sighed and spoke quietly instead of yelling. "You just don't understand."

"You're right…I don't," she told him.

"You know if it was just some vampire…I would still find it sickening." Felicity gave him a pointed look as he continued. "But the fact that it's *him*. I just can't stomach that."

Felicity tried to put aside the reference to a vampire relationship being 'sickening' and focus on Ben's problem with Mattie. "Can I ask you a question? How would you have felt if you had known they were seeing each other *before* what happened to Mattie?"

"That's another thing! Why didn't they just tell me? They had to hide it? What did they think I would do?" he asked.

"I don't know. I guess they just figured it would make things kind of weird between you," she tried to explain.

"And this has been so much better…"

"Ben." She gave him a look to let him know that she was in no mood for sarcasm.

"I would have been happy for them. Why would I have objected to two of my best friends being together?"

"Why *do* you?" she asked.

"Felicity, you just don't get it. He's not Mattie anymore; he's a vampire *pretending* to be Mattie. That's what they do. Vampires are the 'Great Pretenders'," he said.

Felicity sat very still. "Who told you that?"

"It's what they're made for 'Liss. That's how they survive. They pretend to be human but they're not. Mattie is dead. I went to his funeral! Just because some demon made its way into his blood and reanimated his body doesn't mean I'm going to welcome it with open arms!"

"But it's not like that! Just because he's been changed physically doesn't mean he's not still the same inside."

"How would you know?" Ben asked.

"Allie says he's the same," Felicity told him.

"Allie's being a fool!" he replied.

"Ben, this isn't 'Invasion of the Body Snatchers'! It's like a disease," she insisted.

"No it's not! It's more like an…unexcorcisable possession." Ben just sat there for a minute as she glared over the table at him. "Felicity, *it takes over* a person. It changes them. They may have the same memories, the same mannerisms, but they develop the instincts and priorities of the new creature that they become. They *become* a vampire. Their human life is *over*. It may be more subtle in some than in others, but I refuse to be fooled. They're not the same. They're just *not*. You think you know, but you don't. You don't know any from *before*. I've seen before and after.

Look at Sindy. She has tortured and killed so many guys. You've seen what she's done to them…what she'd like to do to me! She is a manipulative and conniving, heartless bitch, an inhuman, unfeeling predator. Do you really believe that I would have dated someone like that?"

Felicity held his gaze sternly. "I have no great love for Sindy, *believe me,* but isn't that an awfully harsh description of someone who saved your life? If she were just some 'unfeeling predator', why would she do that? Shouldn't she have just let Marcus kill you and had a good laugh over it?"

Ben glared at her for a moment. No doubt, he was unhappy to be reminded of the incident. "Sindy marked me. I'm *hers*. She was just defending her own right to the kill."

Felicity rolled her eyes and dropped her face into her hands for a moment in exasperation. "Oh God Ben, give me a break." It was almost pointless to argue with him. He could find an answer for anything. "Anyway the point is, the fact that *you* dated her once or twice is hardly proof of character. You had some nerve calling Allie undiscriminating, like *you've* got such high standards. You're dating *Ashley*."

Ben opened his mouth in outrage. "That is so unjustified. Ashley may not exactly be…long-term material, but she is a decent person, and at least she's *human*."

Felicity just sat there glaring at him and daring him to say something about her and Cain. He didn't. He went on. "Mattie's not, not anymore. When those things took my friend, *he* became *it*, a vampire. It uses the knowledge of its past life to behave like a human so that it can hunt them. It's a predator…and we are the *prey*."

Ben sat there staring at her over the table, his eyes pleading for her to understand and believe. It was a very convincing argument, except for one thing, Cain. She *knew* him, better than Ben knew any vampire, she'd wager. She didn't know if Cain was any different before he died, and he was definitely host to something other than himself in his body, but it hadn't entirely *taken him over*. He was a good man. No matter what he had done to hurt her feelings and make her angry, she just couldn't think of him as some ruthless animal devoid of emotion. It just wasn't true. He may be a vampire, but he was *also* a man. "Where did you learn that?" she asked Ben quietly.

He shrugged. "I'm observant…*and* I've overheard some conversations that made an awful lot of sense."

"Ben, just because something sounds good, doesn't make it true. Or haven't you learned *that* from the debate team? We are not talking about senseless animals here, we are talking about people. People suffering from…an affliction."

"An affliction that makes them kill other people. I'd say that makes them animals in my eyes."

"Don't be stupid Ben. Stop putting aside your common sense just so you can win an argument. We are not talking about those mindless vampire-zombie things here. You know that Cain isn't like that, and neither is Mattie.

They're not entirely ruled by instinct. They have free will. They have self-control. They don't even live off *human* blood! Did you know that?"

Ben squinted his eyes at her and answered sarcastically. "Yeah, I can tell by the holes in your neck. Or is that just for special occasions?"

Felicity felt a sudden rush of tears welling up in her eyes. She felt overwhelmed and misunderstood. "That's not fair. I can't be expected to sit here and try to defend a whole race of creatures that I don't even fully understand."

"Then don't!"

"But it's *not* the way that you think it is! Cain is a good person, and so is Mattie."

Ben sat forward in alarm. "You've *met* him?"

"No, but I know how Allie feels about him, and I trust her judgment of people. Why can't you just let her be happy?"

Ben held her gaze in silence for a long moment before answering. "Because I love her.

My whole life Allie has been a sister to me. You have no idea what that's been like. It sounds very touching I'm sure, but I've spent the past eighteen years watching her make bad decisions. Look at her life! You don't think I've had higher aspirations for her than 'local barmaid'? She's smart, and strong and she could do so much more, but she gets so passionate about things that she loses all perspective. Trying to talk her out of things only makes it worse. She is so damn stubborn, she would fuck up her whole life just to prove a point!"

"Gee, doesn't *that* sound familiar?"

Ben ignored her. "All these years I have tried to make her recognize a bad choice *before* she makes it and she just won't see. I can't watch her ruin her life 'Liss. It hurts too much. **I** can't do it anymore."

"Well you know what? It's not about **you!** It is *her* life. You want to give her advice, you want to let her know you don't approve? Fine! Have your say, but then she will do what she wants, and if you love her, then you just have to deal with it.

You know, someone once told me that when your heart truly chooses to love someone, you can see past their faults to the person inside. You may disagree with their decisions and they might do things that you disapprove of, but you don't stop loving them. If you love her then you can tell her how you feel, but then you have to let her make her own choices. And if things turn out badly…you'll be there to hold her when she cries, but that's all you can do.

This - what you're doing now, is only making things worse. If you do love her, then she needs to know that. She needs to know that you're still her friend – no matter what."

Ben spent a long time staring at the table before them. The cafeteria around them seemed like nothing more than undefined white noise. Finally, he looked up to her eyes. "You're right."

Felicity was so relieved that he would actually admit it. She gave him a little smile. "I know." She reached across the table to take his hands into her own. "You're going to be a great lawyer someday…but make sure you're arguing for the right side."

He gave a little breath of a laugh and took his hands back. "This doesn't change how I feel about them." Felicity knew that he meant not only Alyson and Mattie, but all vampires in general. She looked down at the table again, wishing she had the right words to make him understand. "But I will talk to her. As soon as she gets back. I will."

"Good."

~~~~~~~~~~~~~~~~~~~~~~~~~~~~~~~

It was Thursday night; this would be eleven nights without hearing from Cain. *Eleven.* She'd non-chalantly checked his whereabouts now and again. He was invariably at Tommy's. She had even thought she might have felt him approaching her now and again, but he always seemed to change his mind and leave before she actually laid eyes on him. It was maddeningly frustrating. She felt heartsick and driven almost to distraction without him. It had been well over a week, almost two! There was no way that she could spend another night just waiting for him. No way, but if she went back to him, would that be sending the message that she'd decided what he had done was okay?

One more night. She would tough out one more night alone and then tomorrow night she would go to him; go to him and give him hell for not pursuing her that way that he should have. Was she *that* easy to ignore?

She had dinner alone and then wandered back to the dorms wondering what she could do to keep herself distracted for the evening. She went up to her room and was rather surprised to find that she was actually all caught up on her homework and had none left to do. She stared at her notebooks in disbelief for a moment. That never happened to her. She always left her assignments until the last minute. It was a bad habit but she didn't expect it to change anytime soon, no matter how good her intentions might be. The combination of having days off from class and work, and not seeing Cain had given her the time to catch up. She thought about trying to study extra…maybe even read ahead.

No. She just couldn't force herself to do it. In fact, she so despised the idea that she cleaned her room instead. That done, she sat on the edge of the bed. She still felt nothing from Cain. It was after eight o'clock already, and daylight savings time had moved sunset to an early 5:30. He certainly could have come to her by now if he'd wanted to, but there were still a lot of hours left in the night.

She found herself knocking on Karen's door.

Karen answered quickly but seemed in a distracted rush, and was very nicely dressed. She must have plans to go out with Jack for the evening.

"Oh, hi Felicity. What can I do for you?" Karen asked.

"I thought I'd see if you felt like hanging out tonight. I guess you've already got plans, huh?" Felicity conjectured.

Karen grabbed earrings off the dresser by the door and began to put them on as she spoke. "Actually I do. Sorry. Jack and I are going out with Terry and Paul. Do you know them?" Felicity just shook her head and shrugged. "I'd invite you, but it's kind of a 'couples' thing."

"Yeah. That's okay, I understand," Felicity assured her.

"I don't really have time to talk. Jack's going to be here any minute, but you know, if you're looking for something to do, I think some of the girls have a T.V. movie planned," Karen said.

Felicity thanked her and Karen smiled, giving a little wave as she closed the door. Felicity looked back down the hall towards the living room. There were a bunch of girls gathered on the couch and love seats. Felicity didn't really know any of them very well though.

In fact, she had been spending so much of her time at work and with Cain that she hadn't made many friends at all. She hadn't cared before, but she was beginning to regret it now. Oh well, at least she knew some of their names.

Hesitantly she left the hall to enter the living room. Not sure whether she should just sit down and join them, or say something first, she stood awkwardly eyeing the girls for a moment. The conversation came to a stop as they noticed her.

There were five girls in the room and all were wearing their pajamas. She knew Regina and Bridgette, who were sitting on the big couch. Both had dark hair, Regina's in a short pageboy cut, Bridgette's long and flowing in beautiful waves over her shoulders. Regina wore a pair of plaid pink and orange sleep pants with a large pink t-shirt, Bridgette had on a long pale green t-shirt style nightgown. They were both Freshmen like herself and had always been friendly to Felicity.

Penny was another freshman Felicity knew by sight but had never really spoken much to. She wore her strawberry blonde curls in childishly cute pigtails and had on red shorts, a white t-shirt with little red hearts all over it and big fuzzy pink slippers. She sat on the love seat with two girls that Felicity didn't know.

The girls she didn't know looked older, sophomores or maybe even juniors. The one perched on the arm of the sofa was a black girl with dozens of long, thin, finely done braids. She wore camouflage patterned pajama pants with an olive green tank top. Felicity remembered seeing her once or twice before.

The other girl sitting with Penny however was much more familiar. Felicity didn't really know her either, but she knew that she was very popular. She certainly had the presence of a 'Queen Bee'. She was tall and thin with shoulder length hair that was originally dark, but was now perfectly highlighted with even streaks of blonde and a warm caramel color. She had it loosely tied back from her face with a headband made from a piece of ribbon. She wore dark blue satin pajamas with matching ballet type slippers. She'd been the one speaking when she noticed Felicity standing there.

Felicity searched for something to say. She focused on the couch with Regina and Bridgette on it. At least she knew that they knew who she was. "Hi, I heard you guys were going to watch a movie?" she began hesitantly, Bridgette smiled but it was the black girl on the other sofa who answered her.

"It's 3-P Thursday," she said, as though Felicity should know what that meant when she obviously didn't.

"3-P?" Felicity asked.

"Pizza, Popcorn, and P.J.'s. How can you have lived here since September and not know that?" the girl inquired haughtily.

Felicity gave an awkward little shrug. "I guess I've been kind of wrapped up in my own stuff."

Regina spoke up. "Anyone who doesn't have plans hangs out down here on Thursday nights. Maggie's got her bridge club, so she's never home until late. She lets us rent a bunch of movies on her. I guess it's her way of trying to keep us out of trouble while she's out. The pizza's all gone, but you can join us if you want."

Felicity gave her back a grateful smile as Bridgette added, "There's still time for you to go put on your p.j.'s before the second movie starts."

"Thanks." Felicity headed back upstairs to change into her sheep pajamas. It was better than sitting in her room by herself worrying about her problems with Cain. She was going to have to get some new p.j.'s though. Her sheep were getting worn just as fast as she could wash them. All of her other nightgowns were over-sized t-shirts that were far too short for her to wear downstairs. She didn't really like to have her legs covered in bed but she was too self-conscious to wear her short nightgowns in front of anyone. Oh well, the 'sheep' would have to do.

She came back down to the other girls who were now sharing two bowls of popcorn as they talked, Bridgette motioned for Felicity to come sit on the big couch. She was glad, because she had been trying to decide if she should do that or sit alone on the other empty love seat.

As she crossed the room, she couldn't help but feel as though everyone was staring at and judging her. Penny smiled and spoke as Felicity sat down. "Those pajamas are cute."

Before she could reply, the girl in blue satin added, "Yeah, *big* improvement over the ones you had on outside last Monday."

It only took a second for Felicity to make the connection. The girl in blue and the one with the braids had been among those out on the lawn when Felicity had come home from Cain's crying, the morning after the Masquerade Ball. *Wonderful.* Penny asked, "Oh, were you the girl outside in her pajamas on Halloween?"

Felicity felt her cheeks grow flushed and began to fiercely wish she had stayed upstairs and read her textbooks. The girl with the braids answered Penny. Felicity noticed that she wore a necklace with her name written in little diamonds. It read 'April'. "They weren't *her* pajamas, they were *men's* pajamas."

Felicity stared at the floor for a minute and then decided that it was better to answer than not, since she wasn't likely to be swallowed into a black hole the way she'd like to be. She looked up at Penny and answered. "Yep, that was me."

It was the girl in blue satin who replied. "So…rough morning, or really lame Halloween costume?"

Felicity averted her eyes and sighed. "Rough morning."

"Don't sweat it," Regina interjected, giving the girl in blue an annoyed glance. "We've all been there. Guys suck."

The girl in blue gave Regina an irritated stare. "Speak for yourself."

Bridgette interjected. "Well of course *you* wouldn't know what it's like Deborah. You've been hooked up with Bobby Gavin since like *forever*. You are so lucky."

Penny quickly turned to Deborah with an excited smile. "Oh my God Debbie, he is so hot!"

Regina answered, looking disgusted at Debbie's smug smile. "Yeah, yeah, we're all very jealous. Maybe you could get him to spring for a room once in a while, so the rest of us can get some sleep?" The girls all seemed very amazed that Regina would actually say that. Felicity was just happy to have the focus off herself. Regina smiled at them all. "Oh come on, somebody had to say it." She fixed Deborah with a steady look and a little grin. "You guys are shameless."

April, the girl in camo spoke up. "So what? We've all of us had a guy in our room at one time or another."

"Speak for yourself," Regina replied, mocking the tone that Deborah had used earlier. "I have a little more class than that."

April made a face at her. "Or a little less opportunity. Don't act like it's so unheard of. If you haven't snuck a guy in, you're the only one."

Penny laughed. "*I* haven't. I'll bet Felicity hasn't either."

"Yes she has!" Regina said gleefully. All eyes turned to Felicity as she looked over at Regina in surprise. "Benjamin Everheart," Regina told them with a grin.

"Oh wow, you're dating *Ben*?" Penny asked.

"No," Felicity quickly replied.

Regina continued. "Maybe not *anymore*. It was weeks ago."

"He came over, but we're just friends, really," Felicity assured them.

"Too bad. Kim Davies used to date him, and boy did she have some stories to tell," Regina said with a smirk.

Felicity wasn't usually one to gossip, but couldn't help but turn to the girl and ask. "Good stories or bad stories?"

Regina grinned. "Good. A little *too* good. They couldn't be true."

Bridgette gave her a light shove on the shoulder. "Shut up." She looked over to Felicity reassuringly. "I know Ben. He's a nice guy. But when it comes to dating, he's kind of known for having a short attention span."

Regina started to chuckle. "It's not the length of his attention span that Kim was telling stories about."

Bridgette stared at her in disbelief. "You are so lewd!"

April tossed a throw pillow that hit Regina in the side of the head – not all that lightly. Regina glared but it was Deborah who spoke. "Ladies please. You're being rude to our new friend. So Felicity, if you're not dating Ben, who's pajamas *were* you wearing?"

Felicity glanced down uncomfortably at the floor. "Oh…he's not a student."

Debbie's eyes seemed to pierce through her for a moment. Then she asked, "Are you sleeping with Professor Eldrige?"

"No! No, you just don't know the guy. My...boyfriend. He's not really from around here."

Bridgette put a hand on her shoulder sympathetically as Debbie asked, "Did you break up?"

"Well..." After a second, she shrugged. The last thing she wanted was to divulge details and run the risk of getting at all emotional in front of these girls. Crying out on the lawn was more than enough of a display. "We had a fight. I don't really want to talk about it."

"That's okay," Bridgette said, and then glanced over to Debbie. "Leave her alone."

Debbie smiled and April held her hand up for a moment as though to stop things. "Wait, wait. I just *have* to ask. What happened to your throat?"

Felicity mentally assured herself that her scar wasn't really noticeable. The girl had seen her with the bandage on Halloween. "I cut myself. On accident," she quickly added. "It was a whole...unfortunate...pumpkin carving thing."

April looked at her skeptically with a raised eyebrow, as though she wanted to laugh. "You were carving pumpkins...and you accidentally stabbed yourself in the neck?"

Regina shifted in annoyance and picked up the remote for the T.V. "I'm starting the movie." Felicity gratefully broke eye contact with April and sat back on the couch. She hadn't even asked what they were watching. Truthfully, she couldn't care less.

It turned out to be a romantic comedy. As long as it wasn't a vampire film, Felicity was happy. About halfway through the movie, they ran out of popcorn. Felicity volunteered to go and make more. She was having a hard time concentrating on the story anyway. She grabbed the bowls and went into the kitchen. The box of microwave popcorn was already out. She put in the first bag and leaned back on the counter as she listened for it to be done.

Was she being stupid...not going to see Cain? Why was *he* being so stupid and not coming to see her? Fears that he was with Sindy popped into her head, as they had when she had spoken to Allie at the diner. No. He wouldn't be with Sindy again, not now. After the argument they'd had, Cain wouldn't see Sindy unless he'd truly decided never to see Felicity again. No, he was just giving her space, spending his time alone. She had to believe that.

The time between pops began to slow down and after a second more Felicity took out the popcorn so that it wouldn't be burned. She put the second bag into the microwave, and then dumped the contents of the first bag into a bowl.

As she was crumpling up the bag for the garbage, a very odd feeling came over her. Like a wave of dizziness. She put her hand out for the counter and paused on her way to the garbage pail. Cain. It *was* Cain wasn't it? After a moment, she felt it again. A slight shiver shook her and she felt a dizzy little wave of longing for Cain wash over her. Yes. It was definitely him, but this was much stronger than the fleeting flashes she'd felt from him now and again in the past week. She threw away the empty popcorn bag and examined the feeling. Where was he?

He didn't feel very close yet, but he was coming closer. Was he coming *here*? It was hard to tell. She was almost too distracted to fully analyze it because her body suddenly seemed absolutely desperate for him. She stood herself fully upright and mentally commanded herself to take control of things. She might miss him, but she wouldn't let her feelings be guided by some superficial addiction.

It was getting stronger. So strong in fact, that for a second she wondered in surprised annoyance if he was actually trying to *summon* her. Would he go so far as to do that? Is that why he hadn't come to her, because he wanted to *make* her come to him?

No. He just wouldn't do that. It must feel so strong only because she'd been away from him and sorely missed him. The microwave beeped and she was startled from her thoughts. As she opened the door, she realized that the smell of burned popcorn was filling the kitchen. *Great.* She quickly poured it into the other bowl and hoped it wouldn't taste too bad.

The strength of Cain's presence had seemed to stabilize and she decided to hand off the popcorn to go up to her room and change. For all she knew, he would be waiting at her window. She headed back out to the girls in the living room. "Here's the popcorn. Sorry it got a little…burned."

Cain. He was standing just inside the front entrance. Apparently, Penny had let him in. She was standing there next to Cain by the door and smiling at Felicity. She seemed very impressed. In fact, all of the girls did, and everyone was staring at Felicity, including Cain. He was standing there looking smolderingly handsome, but in an unintentional, casual sort of way. He wore his usual black jeans, boots and his black leather jacket with a light blue t-shirt underneath. He looked so sexy and yet his expression was very humble and disarming. He was giving her just the slightest smile with large and hopeful eyes. "Hi."

The room was so quiet that you could have heard a pin drop. They must have paused the movie when Penny got up to answer the door. Felicity found her voice, though it was little more than a whisper. "Hi." After a second Felicity glanced down and realized that she still held the two bowls of popcorn. She quickly handed them off to the person sitting closest to where she stood. It turned out to be Deborah, who looked none too pleased to have Felicity shoving popcorn bowls at her. She did take them though. Felicity couldn't care less what she thought, what any of them thought. She wiped her buttery hands off on the legs of her pajamas.

Cain took a step forward and she noticed that he held a single long stemmed red rose in his hand. "I brought this back to you," he said as he lifted it towards her, back? Oh. The stem of the rose was threaded through the tines of the antique hair comb that Cain had given her. She had left it on the edge of the sink in his bathroom. "Be a shame for you to lose it. I really *want* for it to be yours."

She took a few steps towards him and accepted the rose with a 'thank you' that even he might have had trouble hearing. She took it from up high on the stem, near the bloom, without touching Cain's fingers. He seemed very aware that she had purposely avoided his touch, but she didn't want their first electric physical reunion to be in front of a room full of onlookers.

He turned those soulful and heartbreaking eyes of his on her and she thought she would melt. *He was keeping things from you! Sneaking around behind your back!* she tried desperately to remind herself. It didn't seem to matter. As much as she might like the idea of trying to make him unsure of her acceptance of him, she knew that she couldn't deny him for long. She just stood there staring at him, not trusting herself to speak. "Do you think that perhaps we could talk?" he asked her quietly.

She breathed a quiet sigh of relief. Yes, talk. He wouldn't just assume that all was automatically forgiven because he'd brought her a rose, but it did seem terribly romantic and she really just wished she could fly into his arms. She kept herself still where she stood and gave him a shy little smile and a nod of her head. "Yes. I'd like that."

Felicity was startled by the sound of the movie un-pausing, as Penny accidentally sat on the remote. Reminded that they had an audience, Felicity glanced at the girls who were all shamelessly staring at them, and then looked back to Cain. "Maybe we could talk…*up*stairs?"

"As you wish," Cain said with a little grin. He took a step back to let her by as she headed towards the staircase. Cain surveyed the room with a charming smile. "Ladies," he said with a nod of his head, by way of departure. He then turned and followed her up.

She held onto the rose and climbed the stairs, trying not to glance at the girls and very glad that in walking behind her, Cain couldn't see the grin that she could not keep from her face. The other girls in the room were silently smiling as well and Felicity knew that Cain had made quite an impact on them. Of course, the last thing she should worry over at this point was what they would think, but she had to admit, it felt good.

They reached the top of the stairs, out of view of the others and crossed the hall to Felicity's room. She opened the door and entered, Cain following behind her.

Suddenly she heard him let out a quiet but sharp exclamation of pain. "Ah!"

Felicity spun around to find him standing in the hallway. His shoulders were hunched forward and his hands were clenched to his chest in obvious pain. "Cain! Are you okay? What is it?" He looked as though he were having a heart attack.

He took his hands away and shook his head a little as though trying to shake it off. "I'm alright." It was difficult to believe him, as he seemed very disturbed.

Felicity couldn't help but be a little frightened for him. When he finally did look back up at her though, he didn't seem worried or truly hurt anymore, only a bit embarrassed. "What happened?" she asked.

"Apparently, I'm…*un*invited," he answered quietly.

Felicity's eyes went wide. "*I* did that? Oh Cain, I'm sorry. I didn't mean to. You can come in. Of course, you can come in. Please… I invite you. You're *re*invited. Come in." She backed away from the door with her hand held up to the base of her throat feeling absolutely stricken. He tentatively followed her into the room. It seemed to work. The invisible guise was lifted and he had no further problem entering. He still looked kind of hurt though, emotionally. "I am so sorry. I never meant to keep you out, really. I was angry. I was mad at you and…I guess I said some stuff. It wasn't on purpose."

He gave her a little smile as he moved deeper into the room and she passed behind him to close the door. "*Very* angry you must have been, to have been yelling at me aloud when I wasn't even here," he said in an amused but hurt sort of tone.

"I wasn't really yelling at *you*," she said uncertainly. "It was more at your…shirt." He eyed her dubiously, but she felt awkward to try to explain. In any event, her recent distaste for the whole 'venom thing' was beside the point. The evidence of his dis-invitation from the room had brought back the memory of how she had felt that morning. Alone in her room, feeling violated by his venom and betrayed by his actions; feeling completely deceived and distraught because of this man who was supposed to be her 'protector', the man that she loved and who had always made her feel so safe. "Anyway, I think I had a *right* to be angry."

He looked down to the floor with a little smile. "From your point of view, I suppose you did."

She squinted at him in disbelief. "You *suppose?*"

He ventured another smile. "I suppose that was also an unfortunate choice of words."

She stood staring at him with one hand on her hip, the other holding the forgotten rose by her side. "Ya think?" So often she felt that his age and experience gave him better perspective than she had, and gave him an advantage over her in most situations; as though she should automatically defer to him, but this time she refused to be so easily swayed. She would forgive him, but he'd been wrong and he should admit it.

At the same time, his physical closeness to her was distracting almost to the point of over-whelming her. She tried to use the feeling to fuel her stubborn free will and to steel herself not to be too easily persuaded, but…she couldn't remember ever feeling such strong desire.

How could he just be standing there, seeming so unaffected and strong? He was so close to her! How could he stand to be so close to her without kissing her? Didn't his body feel it the way that hers did? Her body was practically screaming for him! All she wanted to do was to forget arguments and past hurts; to hold him, and kiss him, and feel herself pressed up against him and…Uggghhh!!!

In an effort to hold herself still, she unconsciously tightened her grip on the rose and stabbed herself with a thorn. She flinched and broke eye contact with him to pull her thumb loose from the point. Yep, she'd been stabbed pretty good. *Nice going Felicity.* She brought it to her mouth to suck on the small stinging hole there. As soon as the metallic taste of blood filled her mouth, she was reminded of the first night that she had allowed Cain to drink from her. He had kissed her after and had tasted just the same.

She quickly pulled her thumb from her mouth and looked up to find him staring at her. Immediately uneasy and aware of their awkward tableau, she dropped her gaze and walked over to the dresser to put down the rose.

When she turned back to face him, she noticed that he was standing before her other dresser, just opposite the mirror…in which he had no reflection of course. She found herself just staring into the mirror at the reflection of the 'empty' room as she tried to think of what to say.

After a few expectant moments, he looked at the mirror and seemed to become annoyed. "I'm over here," he quipped sarcastically.

She just gave him an irate glance and sat down on her bed. He didn't move at all towards her, but stood his position and crossed his arms over his chest. After a pause, he spoke, sounding must less amicable. "Look, I understand that I've upset you, but I honestly don't think that I've anything to be ashamed of."

She looked up at him in disbelief. *That's how he was going to start?* He continued. "Just because you cannot empathize with my position does not change what I am. I am a vampire and I should act accordingly. You're not, and you shouldn't be expected to understand. In fact, if you search your feelings I'm sure you'll come to agree that this is all for the best. Our relationship was bound to come to an eventual end. T'was inevitable really. Our misunderstanding the other morning was a bit more brash and abrupt an end than I might have liked, but the fact that it should force the issue is actually a bit of a relief."

She just sat there watching his mouth move and trying to figure out what the hell he was trying to say. It sounded almost like rehearsed gibberish. Partly because she didn't want to hear it, but mostly because for every statement that came out of his mouth, his facial expression and body language seemed to be screaming the exact opposite. The desire and pull that she felt towards him with each passing moment was so strong that she was absolutely certain that it had to be more than some passive side effect. He *was* summoning her. Perhaps it was just an unconscious spill over of his true emotions, but it was undeniable.

She stared at him for a moment in disbelief, and finally just blurted out, *"What?"*

He looked at her as though they were acting a play and she'd said the wrong line. "It's time I moved on. I don't want to see you anymore. I'm leaving."

His words came out strongly but his face was so forlorn that she couldn't believe him for an instant. She kept staring at him, waiting for him to take it back. He held firm. Meanwhile, his intangible calling to her grew stronger than she'd thought possible. It was a good thing she was already sitting on the bed. It would have been difficult to keep her feet through the waves of desperate need that seemed to be pouring out of him. She was hardly able to believe that she hadn't thrown herself into his arms already.

Finally, she smiled. He seemed to find that disturbing. Apparently, he'd expected a different reaction. She spoke. "I know that I've told you before what a terrible liar you are, but this is just pathetic. I wish that you could see your face," she said, with a gesture at the mirror. "You look like you're about to fall apart."

She had started with a smile, but as she spoke, emotion began to well up from within her. "You're telling me that you want to leave, and yet even as you say the words…*you're calling me.* Did you know that?

I feel like I'm being smothered in feelings for you. Like I'm hopelessly tangled up in you and you're telling me to go away even as you pull me in. Do you even realize that you're doing that?"

He obviously *hadn't* realized. He seemed almost shocked, and then he did begin to fall apart as she'd predicted. He said nothing, but was having a terribly hard time keeping tears from his eyes. She knew her own were already welling with them. She asked sincerely. "What are you trying to do?"

After a minute, he gave up trying for the 'cold and distant' look that he wasn't achieving anyway. He sat down next to her on the bed and put his head into his hands. "I don't know. I haven't got the words. You've gone and messed it all up and made me forget what I was supposed to say."

She almost would have laughed if she weren't already crying. His nearness to her was overwhelming. She was breathing deeply and trying so hard just to sit still and not move to touch him. God, but his venom must be so strong! She felt as though she wanted nothing more than to drape herself across his lap and bare to him her throat. He looked up with moist eyes and must have seen something in her face that alarmed him. "Are you alright?" he asked in concern.

She closed her eyes for a moment and then whispered to him. "Cain please. The summons. You have to stop. I can't think."

He seemed terribly disturbed and looked closer at her as though perhaps she was teasing him. He sat up straighter and appeared to concentrate. She felt the almost oppressive desire she had for him begin to lift. It receded until she felt that she could talk to him again, but it was only lessened. It never actually left her.

She had raised her eyes to his face as he tried to rein it in. When he looked up at her, he seemed very apologetic. "Sorry. I haven't much practice with that. It's hard to control something that you never use. Looks like it kind of ruined my plan." She raised her eyebrows inquiringly. He explained. "You were supposed to believe that I wanted to go. You were supposed to be mad at me."

"You *wanted* me to be mad at you?" He was staring vacantly into his lap as he nodded yes. "Then why did you bring me the rose?"

He looked almost sheepish and more confused than she was when his eyes found the rose and comb on her dresser, as though he hadn't thought it through. "Well, I wanted you to have the comb back. If I wasn't going to tell you that I was sorry, then it seemed only right that I offer some token of apology. I guess it was a bit contradictory. And when I saw you, I must admit that I almost lost all resolve right then and there. You *are* a sight for sore eyes. I really am bad at this aren't I?"

She looked at him with a confused little grin. Had he really been so socially isolated all these years that he was having such a hard time dealing with his feelings over this? "But why did you want me to be mad?"

She dropped her smile when she realized how exasperated he was with himself. He seemed so hopelessly distraught. As he spoke, his voice wavered with emotional turmoil. "You just don't understand. I spent these past nights trying to find the best way. I drank and I thought and then I drank some more. When that didn't work, I went home and I prayed. I prayed desperately over you but every solution that came to me was unbearable to accept. I couldn't carry it through. I knew that I wasn't strong enough. I just knew it.

So I decided that you should be mad. That's why I stayed away, let you be angry with me, because you see, if you were angry then you could be strong. It would empower you against me and make you fight for yourself, for your life. I need you to be strong…because one of us should be. I am old and powerful as a vampire, physically robust as a man, but my heart… My heart is feeble and weak and it cannot let you go."

A tear slid down his cheek and she found her fingers lifting to it before she'd even thought the act through. As her fingertip touched his face to wipe away the tear, the tingle of his mark upon her was like a warm enveloping current. It shivered through her fingers and traveled down her arm, seeming to land in her heart. She took a long shuddering gasp of breath. After it passed, she exhaled and whispered, "Then don't."

She caressed his cheek again and after a brief moment, he took her face into his hands and came to her lips for a kiss. This time the electricity of his touch ran deeper and further within her. She let herself melt into his arms and give herself over to him as his psychic call had tried to demand and had made her so vividly imagine, but venom or not, she knew that at this moment there was not a thing on earth that she needed more than his touch.

He kissed her with the passion of a love he'd thought lost. She thought that he would lay her back on the bed, but after the initial heat of reunion subsided enough for her to breathe, he leaned back from her with his face turned aside. He seemed to be concentrating on something.

"What is it?"

He gave her a slight smile and glanced at the door. "I believe we have an audience," he whispered. Felicity pulled herself from the haze she was in and looked at the door. She couldn't see any shadow to block the light shining through the space beneath. When she looked back at Cain, he nodded. "They smell like popcorn."

Felicity giggled and sniffed, wiping the tears from her face. "That's probably me."

He fixed her with a very steady gaze and a slight smile. "Yes, you smell delicious...as always," he breathed. She had to drop her eyes, lest she melt back into his arms. "But she..." he nodded once again towards the door, "has the scent of popcorn mingled with cherry lip-gloss and...pepperoni pizza. It's the one who answered the door, with the pig-tails," he whispered so quietly that Felicity could barely hear him.

Felicity looked again at the door and then back at Cain in disbelief. "You can really smell her?"

Cain looked almost ashamed of the ability. He shrugged. "Some talent, eh? Anyway, perhaps we could finish this...conversation back at my place?"

Felicity smiled and dropped her eyes. They still did have talking to do. She planned to chastise him severely for ever keeping anything from her, but she still felt desperate for his touch. She kissed him again. It was softer and sweeter but still just as deep and no less satisfying.

He eyed her for a moment and then stood from the bed. He spoke in a tone that she knew was meant for anyone outside the door as well as for her. "I'll wait downstairs, so you can change in private." He didn't let her speak; he just smiled at her and then went for the door.

He paused a moment more, presumably to be sure the way was clear, and then opened it to step out into the hall. He closed the door behind him.

Chapter 12 - Almost human

Cain

Felicity's dorm
11:00, Thursday night

Cain left Felicity's room, almost grateful to leave her presence for a moment to regain his composure. He'd been rather flustered by how powerfully she affected him. He had stayed away for as long as he could stand in trying to find the courage to end things as he should. He'd told Felicity as much.

What he had not told her was that he'd also hoped for the venom she had received from him to have weakened a bit. Unfortunately, that hadn't worked out nearly as well as he'd hoped. He'd last bitten her almost two full weeks ago. Her mark would still last for another week or two, but the venom itself should have reached its half-life and be on its decline by now, lessening her awareness of its effects. Apparently, he hadn't taken into account just how strong his venom had become. He knew that he really should have waited longer, but he just couldn't stay away. He'd thought that its effect would have at least been weakened by now.

Not only was it disappointing to know that she was still feeling so strongly drawn to him, but he had fiercely underestimated his own need for her. Of course, he missed her and wanted to be with her and hold her, but this was so much more than that. It was thirst. The vampire within him had not been fed human blood for almost two weeks now. It was dissatisfied with the purchased blood that he endeavored to quiet it with, and was thirsting for more gratifying sustenance.

It recognized Felicity and it wanted her, *badly*. It was distracting to say the least. Once he'd found himself alone in the room with her, it was impossible to ignore. He'd focused intently on simply blurting out the things that were necessary to be said, in order to take himself from her presence and end his torment. He had not even realized that he had been sending her a psychic summons throughout. He longed for her in so many ways that he must have broadcast it unconsciously.

The realization shook him and made him realize that he could not do things the way that he'd planned, not that they were working out very well anyway. No, the vampire in him wanted her just as badly as the man and was loathe to leave her, thirst unsatisfied. Her mark was fading, however slowly and he needed to claim her once more. If he did not, the vampire within would never allow him to let her go.

He would give in to desire once more, for a short time. He would make amends with her, love her, and fulfill his needs. Then, when the beast within him was silent and satisfied, he would tell her that he had to go. He would make a swift departure before his inner vampire could rebel against it.

It seemed almost cruel to tease her so, seeking her affections, knowing that he would leave, but it really was the only way. It sat better with him than trying to pick a fight with her anyway. She was a smart and perceptive girl. She saw right through his poor attempt at indifference to her, but she had also known all along that eventually he would have to leave.

Besides, he couldn't honestly say that he didn't relish the idea of having a bit longer with her. He loved her so much and it was going to be heart wrenching to have to leave. To spend a few more days with her would build fond memories and ease their hurt somewhat. They would spend the next few days bathed in lover's bliss, and then, depressing as it may be, he would have to inform her that it was time for it to end.

Cain descended the stairs to the entryway. All five of Felicity's dorm mates who had originally greeted him were obediently sitting on couches in the living room watching their movie, even the one with the pigtails, although Cain could tell she was a bit out of breath. He smiled to himself and stood to wait by the front door. After a moment, he noticed them looking at him expectantly. "I'm just waiting for Felicity. We'll be going out for a bit."

He was met with knowing smiles from the girls. The one in the blue satin pajamas spoke. "Why don't you come and sit? Make yourself at home while you wait," she said, tapping the couch cushion next to her as an invitation to him.

He gave them a small grin and nodded his acceptance. Things were so different these days. Not one of these girls was dressed in any more than her nightclothes, and yet they seemed totally unconcerned. Not that they were really wearing anything very revealing, but it was a far cry from standards of propriety in his day. It still seemed a bit inappropriate to his old-fashioned sensibilities.

As he sat amongst them, they seemed very interested and observant of him, as though they were excitedly expectant to see what he might do. He realized they were using him as a judge of Felicity's status among them. Young girls were such a strange breed. It was like they had their own little society he would never aspire to understand. He hoped his presence had somehow gained Felicity a bit of respect among them. He was conscious to keep his British accent apparent. Ladies always seemed to admire it.

The girl in blue spoke to him again. She seemed to think of herself as the 'leader' of the group. "So, Felicity tells us you're not from around here."

"No, I tend to travel quite a bit," he answered.

"For business?" she asked.

"Mostly."

"So, what do you do?" she pressed further.

Her tone was a bit flirtatious but her main agenda seemed to be information, fodder for future discussion and speculation over him. He hoped that his vague answers would still put him in a positive light. "I guess you could say that I'm sort of a 'Guidance Counselor'. A 'Life Coach', if you will." He was met with a blank stare. "I give advice."

She cocked an eyebrow at him. "To young girls?"

He grinned. "Not usually. No, I have a rather elite clientele, but they're usually very fond of their privacy, so I'm sure you'll understand if I can't get into specifics or name names."

The girl in green with the long dark hair seemed suitably impressed. "A Life Coach. I've heard of that. The big stars use them, like to help them make decisions and stuff. I bet they'd pay anything if you could help them keep up a good image for the tabloids."

Cain just smiled and lowered his eyes as the girls exchanged impressed glances with one another. Only the young lady of color in the camouflage pajamas seemed skeptical. Her necklace proclaimed her name to be 'April'. "Aren't you a little young to be giving people 'life advice'?"

He met her eyes and gave her a charming little smile that seemed to disarm her almost immediately. "I'm a bit older than I look, and I dare say that I've led a rather educational life." He leaned forward to her confidentially. "I can assure you that my disciples are always well satisfied with my credentials." He hadn't really meant for his tone to sound particularly alluring, but was rewarded in seeing he'd actually brought a bit of blush to her perfect mocha complexion.

He really was uninterested in any other here save Felicity, but he had to admit that it was rather fun seeing these young ladies become impressed with him. The girl 'April' seemed of a very strong and confident attitude, uneasy to win over. She was lovely as well. All of them were in their own ways. Silly as it was, he was glad that he seemed to meet their approval.

Unfortunately, although he himself was uninterested in these girls for more than passing conversation, the vampire within him was beginning to recognize them as very appetizing fare. After being awakened by his closeness to Felicity and yet denied, it was eager for a hunt. He would never touch these girls of course, but little things were starting to distract his attention. For one thing, they all smelled very appealing. His keen sense of smell could not help but dwell on the pleasing and varied bouquet of scents that they carried. The way that they giggled and gathered so closely around him, seeming to hang on his every word, was very tempting to the predator within him. The girl in blue sat so close to him that his heightened senses were clearly aware of her heartbeat.

The girl in pigtails worked up the courage to ask, "How old are you?"

He smiled at her tentativeness and tried to keep his mind on making small talk rather than acknowledge his thirst. "Twenty-seven."

The girl in blue reasserted her dominance over the conversation. "You must think we're terribly rude. We haven't even introduced ourselves," she said, leaning forward to rest her hand lightly on his knee in a gesture just a bit *too* familiar. "I'm Deborah." She batted her eyes with a sly little smile. She was definitely flirting now. He must meet her approval. Perhaps she thought it'd be fun to see if she might turn his eye from Felicity. *Not a chance.*

Their attention was drawn to the staircase as they heard the true subject of his desires emerge from her bedroom. Rather than continue his conversation, Cain sat silent with his eyes trained on the stairs in anticipation of her. She descended, dressed in jeans and a peasant blouse of a pleasing paisley pattern done in shades of blue, green and purple. Her beautiful auburn hair was left loose to flow down her back, its lovely waves bouncing as she came down the steps. Cain noticed that she had a winter coat draped over her arm. Good, she'd need it. He'd brought the bike.

He stood from the couch as she entered and surveyed the room. She didn't seem overtly jealous of the girls flocked around him, but he was certain that she was curious as to their conversation. He couldn't resist a parting display for Felicity's sake. He turned back to his hosts. "If you'll excuse me girls, you've been charming company, but my lady awaits," he said with what he hoped was not too much dramatic flair.

He noticed that Felicity had dropped her eyes to the floor and was trying to hide her grin. Hopefully he had made an impression that would please her. He went to meet her with a tender kiss on the cheek. It surely appeared chaste enough, but the bond that they shared through Felicity's mark made even such a simple gesture hold an almost indecent little thrill.

She closed her eyes and breathed deeply as her heartbeat was momentarily quickened. Then Cain took the coat from her arm and helped her on with it. "Shall I drive? I've brought the Harley." She just nodded with a smile. He opened the door for her and gave the ladies in the living room a smile and parting nod goodbye.

~~~~~~~~~~~~~~~~~~~~~~~~~~~~

The ride home was a nice respite from having to try to fight his urges and strive for normalcy. Felicity sat behind him on the bike with her arms wrapped around his waist. Funny how his cravings for her seemed satisfied to let him be for now. His vampire nature still wanted her blood…desperately, but knowing that she was with him seemed to stay it for now. Knowing that he was whisking her away to a place where they could be private, that he had 'landed his prey' seemed sufficient to ease his thirst for the moment. He hoped things would go well between them so that he might silence his inner vampire quickly and simply enjoy being with her as a man.

They reached his house and she dismounted the motorcycle and followed him to the door without saying a word, before long they found themselves in his bedroom. She still said nothing, but went to sit on his bed as he turned on the light. He wished that they could forgo all of the preliminary mediations and just get under the covers to lose their problems in love and laughter.

He thought perhaps she felt that way too. Unfortunately, neither one of them was likely to admit to preferring such physical desires over the discussion of their less tangible obstacles. He had to at least attempt to ease her concerns over the past. She seemed to have the same thing in mind as she spoke. "You kept things from me. No matter what you say you did or didn't do with Sindy, you still hid it from me. That is just unacceptable. You can't do that; you can't hide things from me. We're supposed to be honest with each other always, no matter what."

He sat down next to her on the bed, and looked upon her sweet face. Trying not to notice her alluring scent and the gentle throb of the pulse beneath the skin of her throat, he accepted her accusation. "You're right. Just because I felt justified in my actions does not mean that I should not have shared them. I suppose I knew that you would look upon it unkindly, but my heart has always belonged only to you. And since you came to me to declare your love, I've given no other leave to touch me in any intimate way…no matter what I might have done for them. I hope you'll not judge me too harshly."

She sighed, searching his face for a moment before giving him a little half-hearted smile of acceptance. She wasn't happy about it, but she seemed to have lost the will to fight with him much more. She would forgive him. Thank God, because his desire for her blood was becoming once again difficult to ignore. For probably the hundredth time since his death, he cursed his unnatural body for keeping him from being able to relate to someone without such illicit thoughts and urges.

He made a mental check of himself, to be sure that he hadn't resumed 'calling' to her again. "I am sorry about the whole 'summons' thing. I really never meant to coerce you. I wasn't even aware I was sending it. I guess I just wanted you so desperately, no matter what I might have said."

She gave him another smile. "I figured it was something like that."

She didn't seem at all upset over it. If anything, he thought perhaps she was flattered. Didn't she realize the extent of her effect on him? "It's not troubling you now is it?"

"No, not really. It's still there, but you seem to have gotten things under control," she answered.

With an impish grin, he realized that she actually seemed to like the idea that he found her irresistible. He *had* usually displayed better restraint in the past. Perhaps she didn't fathom the extent of her attractiveness to him. He leaned a bit closer to her and whispered, "It's not easy I can assure you. You bring out longings in me, almost impossible to harness."

She grinned and turned away with flushed embarrassment. Yes, she was pleased, and his closeness was strongly affecting her as well, but she wasn't quite ready to give in to him yet. "Flattery will get you nowhere. I'm still mad at you."

He gently touched her face to turn her back to him. "Are you sure about that? Isn't there some way I might regain your favor? Because I have to be honest, as much as I would never seek to steal affections from you unsolicited…I don't know how much longer I can keep myself from you."

She looked up at him in startled realization. She definitely felt her own urges from his mark upon her, as well as any natural feelings she might have. Now she seemed to study him and try to assess the full extent of his desires for her. How could she not be able to tell that he barely restrained himself? If she hadn't seen it before, she noticed it now. Rather than be disgusted as he had been afraid she might be, it appeared to arouse and excite her.

He implored her with a soft but urgent whisper. "Please, forgive me. I do love you…and I *need* you."

She looked almost shocked to see that she held such power over him. Although the power she held was only by his decree. He could certainly have taken her at any time that he liked. He waited for her assent by his own resolution. He had made a promise to her once. He would never touch her again without express consent. He silently begged her for that consent now.

Rather than answer, she kissed him so vehemently, he felt as though floodgates had been opened to finally unleash all that had been restrained. He kissed her deeply and passionately, but it was not only her kiss that he required. She knew it too. She didn't seem at all disappointed when he ended it. She tilted her head to offer her throat to him without word or hesitation.

He felt a bit guilty to put such desires before all else, but all he could think was to bless her for her generosity. His lips moved eagerly to kiss the skin that covered her willing vein. He paused only a moment, and then let the change overcome him. His eyes had barely finished changing the spectrum of his vision when he pierced her skin with his newly unsheathed fangs. As the first drops of her precious blood touched his tongue, he felt a great wave wash over him of longing and relief rolled into one.

He hadn't the patience to wait for his venom to work its way throughout her system. He knew that she would feel its effects eventually as he fed and it wasn't as though he need worry that she would panic or try to flee from him. She knew the euphoria that would be forthcoming.

Felicity let out a small gasp at his first real pull upon her. He hoped he hadn't hurt her at all. He hugged her closer, forcing himself to be gentle as he drank. Her blood was a thick and rich reward for his wait. Sweet and fulfilling as nothing else could be. This beautiful girl with such an open and giving heart, her blood was love liquefied. He loved her more than he had ever dared to think that he could, not only for her giving nature, but for the fun and simple joys that she brought to him. How was he going to give her up? He knew that he should, but *could* he?

Her blood was a welcome physical reward, a much-needed respite from the desperate thirst that he had faced. Of course, the affections that she displayed for him with her body were pleasurable as well. Yes, their lovemaking was an indulgence that he had denied himself for so many years. He did fully enjoy her attentions, but what he treasured most from her were the plain and simple times that they spent together.

While Felicity had come to appreciate the physical rewards of his vampire nature, she did not love him because he was a vampire; she loved him in spite of it. She had never treated him as anything less than a man. She was truly concerned for his feelings and well-being. She was always there for him. She had listened to his confessions with a sympathetic ear and a consoling manner. She shared her own joys and concerns with him and looked to him for comfort and camaraderie. Just being with her was gratifying in its own right. Time spent with her could be so blessedly normal, just a man and a woman, enjoying each other's company, an indulgence that his life of recent past had been so sorely lacking.

He loved watching her make new discoveries and gain confidence within herself. He loved being a part of that. He loved just sitting with her, anywhere; the café, the park, his own secluded bedroom, it didn't matter. Quiet conversations and fond glances, he loved to make her smile. The way that she would blush and giggle at things that he said, or even at her own newly uncovered boldness at times, those things were so precious to him.

This…this purely selfish act of drinking her blood was sinful ecstasy. It was such exquisite gratification, but her love meant so much more. He needed to pull back from this wicked feast. To keep his senses and be sure that he would please her as well as himself. As soon as he had lessened his thirst enough to regain full control, he made himself disengage from her.

He studied her face, hoping that she hadn't been too startled or disappointed by the abruptness with which he had bitten her. Hopefully his venom was strong enough that it would affect her even without a deliberately full dose. She had been without it for a while, so it shouldn't take much to subdue her pain and bring her the lightheaded contentment to which she had grown accustomed.

As he gazed upon her now, he could see that she did display signs of becoming intoxicated. His venom usually worked rather well on her. That was something for which he was grateful. At least he could feel his guilt over wanting her blood could be eased by the fact that she was gaining some pleasure in the exchange as well. He let her eyes focus upon his own before he spoke. "I'm sorry, I couldn't wait. I didn't hurt you did I?"

She shook her head no and took back his lips to resume their kiss. She kissed him with fervent ardor and passion he would have been surprised to receive from her back in early days of their relationship. Now these expressions of the secret fire within her were a delight he eagerly looked forward to each time they made love. After fully conveying her desires to him through her kisses, she left the bed to remove her clothing. He watched her try to steady herself with a hand upon the bed as she impatiently stripped the material from her body. He undressed himself as well.

Cain had to smile, thinking of the first time that she had disrobed for him. It really was not all that long ago, but what a different girl she had been from the confident woman she was now! She had stood across the room and slowly, shyly removed her dress. She'd been so hesitant and worried over his impressions of her. Now she could hardly wait to bare herself before him.

She removed all save her panties. He wondered at that for a moment, but then he saw why. She had worn the thong for him. The one he had shown an interest in when he'd removed her gown after the Halloween Ball. She gave him a seductive little smile as she climbed back upon the bed to kneel before him where he sat. He gave her an approving little grin of his own as he raised himself to his knees and sought to embrace her for kisses once more. She stopped him with a hand upon his chest and looked up to his eyes. "From now on you have to tell me everything. I mean it."

He couldn't help but smile. Her words were slightly slurred and she looked as though she was having trouble keeping focus on his eyes, but she would not let it go. She continued. "I'm not hiding anything from you."

He moved her hand away from his chest so that he might take her into his arms. He let his hands leave her lower back to explore the edges of the scanty garment she wore. "Well that's obvious," he replied with a teasing grin. She rolled her eyes at him as he cupped and squeezed her fully fleshed and bared derriere. He waited for her attention to come back to his face so he might make her see that he was serious as he spoke, although he did not remove his hands. "Full disclosure, from now on. You've my solemn word."

She seemed pleased but did not answer. She only closed her eyes, took a very deep breath and sighed, after which she leaned her head against his shoulder. As she did, her head was tilted to the side once again baring her throat, although whether it was an invitation or simple chance he could not tell. He graced her bared throat with a small kiss, during which she never flinched. Of one thing he was sure, she was fading fast. His venom must be affecting her very strongly after their hiatus.

"Felicity." He gave her a little squeeze. She looked up at him once again with a dreamy smile. "The night is young and we've other pleasures still to explore. You mustn't leave me yet," he teased. He moved his hands to her waist for some tickling to rouse her.

That brought her around. She giggled and squirmed from him to lay down on the bed. "I'm all right, just give me a minute."

He looked down at her with a smirk and then dropped himself to lie over her legs. He slowly made his way up her body as he spoke, bestowing kisses along the way. "You're going to lie here on my bed, baring this beautiful body of yours before me, smelling of blood and wanton desire, and you expect me to have the discipline to wait?" He reached her lips and took them for a kiss. "I *would* wait until the end of time if you asked it of me, but surely you'll not be so heartless as to torture me so." He teased her with a thrust of his hips as he spoke, though the thin silk of her panties was still between them.

She seemed to be lifting herself from the fog she'd been in. Now she laughed with a playful sparkle in her eye. Yes, he liked that much better. He knew the venom was pleasurable for her, but he'd never been at ease with the notion of bedding a woman drugged into submission. He much preferred her to be lively and spirited in their sport. Once Felicity had overcome her initial inhibitions, she'd learned to tease and pursue him with almost the same enthusiasm with which he sought to please and seduce her. He wouldn't allow her to simply lie in wait for him.

After taking a moment to gather her strength, she pushed against him. He allowed her to roll him onto his back so that she might lie atop him. He knew that while she did like for him to take the lead much of the time, she had also been tentatively discovering her own fondness for assertiveness with him. He did his best to encourage her to have confidence and to be unafraid to make known her desires.

She lay over him now, 'pinning' him to the bed, although of course he could escape her easily if he tried. She lifted herself from him just a bit and pouted at him, trying to hide her slight smile. "I should make you wait… I should torture you. It'd be fitting punishment."

He sighed in exasperation. Would she never let this go? Sindy must be more of a thorn in her side than he'd realized. He stopped his frivolous discontentment with the issue mid-thought. How would he have felt? Maybe sharing blood was a poor example because he did not see that as she did, but what if, unbeknownst to him, she had been spending private time with another, someone who irked him already? Perhaps someone like…Benjamin? He suddenly felt much more sympathetic.

She tormented him with little wriggles against his body and teasing thrusts of her hips now and then as she lay atop him. He closed his eyes a moment and drew breath to subdue his passions. "Felicity, I know that you want us to forget it and enjoy each other, believe me, so do I." She gave him a knowing smile. "But I don't want you to forgive me only because we seek pleasure of the moment. I want this to be right with you. I really do. I'll never keep anything from you. Never again, I promise."

She'd been focused on him intently throughout. She appeared to have cleared herself of her intoxication a bit. He really hadn't drunk from her for long; the initial dose of it had just been a shock to her system.

"Felicity…my love, no one could ever hold a candle to you in my eyes; *no one*. I would have to be mad to seek affections from another. I took refuge in her only after I'd sent you away, to convince myself that I did not deserve you. I would never be with her knowing that I had your love.

I only didn't tell you of more recent time spent with Sindy because I did not see it as private or intimate time really. It was *vampire* time. Time spent pursuing the goal I have set for myself to educate and civilize other vampires. I treated her as a student and comrade, not a lover. *You* are my only love.

I try to keep those details of my vampire life separate from you not to hide them, but because when I'm with you, I can forget...almost. Time spent with you is like… Do you know what it's like in Spring, when you lie out on the grass at mid-day with your eyes closed and the sun shining down full upon your face; the amazing warmth and comfort that it can bring? I do. I *remember* what that's like. It's like being with you. *You're* my sunshine.

I don't want to think of blood and restraint, tactics and lessons in psychic control when I'm with you. When I'm with you the dark parts of my life seem to fall away, and I can be…almost human."

She looked as though she would cry. He felt that himself. Then she became very thoughtful, and worried almost as she asked, "Aren't there…good things? About being a vampire, aren't there *perks?"* They both had to give a little laugh at the way she said it.

She sounded so hopeful, that his life should contain something good and rewarding. "Yes, I suppose there are, but every power I hold, every benefit I enjoy has one horrible drawback: they're all part of something that keeps me from *you.*"

She grinned and gave him a small kiss, seeming to be actually happy with his response, although it seemed an agonizing unfairness to him. She looked into his eyes with a glint of promise that he could not understand. "Let's not worry about that for now."

He wished he could be as optimistic. He felt so cheated and forlorn inside, in knowing that this may very well be their last intimate time together. "I love you."

"Oh Cain, I love you too." She kissed him fervently and then lay back down, holding him close and tight. This was a moment that he wanted fixed in his memory. Something to take out again and remember during long and lonely nights. He held her that way for a very long time, hoping she wouldn't notice the tears in his eyes.

After he let the grief of their pending separation leave him, he decided that they should enjoy the time left. He had always known it, but it seemed from now on every moment would be that much more precious. He began to let his hands caress her lower back, and then once again explore the border of the thong that she wore. She leaned up again to look at his face with a smile as he spoke. "So, do you think that you might remove this for me?" he asked with a playful tug on the strap of her thong.

She grinned and adopted an air of surprised innocence. "I thought you liked it?"

"I think I'd like it better on the floor."

She laughed and began to lift herself from him, smiling and edging herself away from him on the bed. "Is that right? Well, if you want it off…you're going to have to catch me and remove it yourself." He did.

Chapter 13 – Take a break and have a life

Felicity

Cain's house
Friday morning

Felicity awoke from her sleep with a comfortable and contented smile. She rolled over to snuggle against Cain…but he wasn't there. Opening her eyes with a start, she searched the empty bed; then heard a noise and looked up to the bar.

It was the clink of him putting his mug into the sink. He was wearing his pajama pants again and had been behind the bar, drinking apparently. He looked up at her now as he came back to the bed. She sat up a little and asked him sleepily, "What time is it?"

He shrugged. "The sun's been up for about an hour. I was just coming back to bed actually."

Felicity lay back down, rolling onto her side in irritation. "I don't want to get up."

Cain got into the bed next to her under the covers. "Then don't."

She frowned as she lay on her side facing away from him. "I have early classes."

He moved himself up against her back and wrapped his arm around her, leaning forward to whisper into her ear. "Would you be terribly disappointed if I asked you to miss them for me?"

She smiled and looked up at him in surprise. He was usually so adamant about her attendance at school. "Special occasion?" she asked.

He squeezed her close and kissed the back of her neck, just under her ear. "Something like that." He rolled her towards him and tried to kiss her lips but she turned her face away.

"Hold that thought," she said, wriggling out of his embrace. "Got any toothpaste?"

He laughed. "In the bathroom."

"Thanks." She jumped up off the bed and ran to the bathroom to brush her teeth with her finger. Cain spoke to her from the bed as she did.

"Are you working tonight?" he asked.

"Yeah, 6 to 10," she answered with disdain.

"That's not so bad," he assured her.

"Yes it is. I'm closing with Harold," she explained.

Cain laughed. "I'll come and sit with you. How about tomorrow?"

Felicity finished up and came back out to him. "6 to 10 again, with Ben. Mr. Penten's been keeping my hours pretty light since my…accident." She made a quick little gesture to her throat. "Like he thinks I'm in a delicate condition or something. Not that I'm complaining." She sat on the bed close to him and smiled. "*Now* you can kiss me."

He met her lips with his own. After the kiss, he leaned back and inspected the healing wound at her throat. "How is it?" he asked tentatively.

She shrugged. "It still hurts a little, but as long as I don't poke at it, it's all right." He hadn't really asked her about the injury she'd received from Chris until now. She wondered if that was because he knew that she would be self-conscious about it.

"I'm so sorry that you got hurt." He seemed to still feel guilty over it. That's when she realized; he hadn't asked about it not for her self-consciousness but for his. He still sounded worried over it. "How long does something like that take to heal?"

She looked at him a little oddly. It sounded like such a strange…alien question. She had to remind herself that he hadn't dealt with such human concerns in over 300 years. His injuries began to heal almost immediately upon his receiving them. *Must be nice.* "The redness and soreness is supposed to be almost gone. Then it should fade a little every day after that, so it will look better. It'll always be a scar though." She shrugged and tried to pretend that it didn't bother her. "At least it kind of follows the shadow of my jaw line, so you don't really see it. I wear my hair down a lot."

He turned his eyes down to the bed for a moment. There seemed an awkward silence until she leaned forward and kissed him again. "Don't worry about it, I'm fine."

He met her eyes with heartfelt sympathy. "I'm sorry."

"It wasn't your fault. It was just…one those things."

"Right. Just *one of those things*. Every young girl gets her throat slit now and then."

"Cain, it really *wasn't* your fault."

"If you look at the big picture, in the larger scope of things, then yes it really was." She sat looking at his face. He stared right back, unwilling to give up the blame.

"If you want to look at the big picture, then you really should look back at the night we met. If you hadn't been there, Sindy would've drained me dry. Then she would have had her boys hold down Ben so that she could do the same to him. Of course, *he* probably would've gotten a cool new immortal bod in exchange for *his* life, but somehow he doesn't seem the type to appreciate the advantages of something like that. I'm thinkin' over all, it's a pretty good thing that you were there. So – big picture, I'd have to say that *you* have been a pretty *good* influence on my life." She leaned forward for another kiss, and then looked back at him with a smile. "I've enjoyed your influences *a lot*."

The slightest smile came to his face, and just as quickly, his eyes seemed to glaze with unshed tears. He reached a hand up to lovingly caress her face. "That's why I've got to leave now, before I go and spoil it."

Cold fear struck her heart and she dared to hope that she'd misunderstood. "What?"

Cain took a very deep breath and expelled it slowly, eyes closed. When he looked again upon her he seemed very calm, sad and resigned. "I'll have to leave soon. Please don't make me go into all of the responsible rationalizations and arguments over it. 'Cause I just haven't got the heart for that right now. I know that you understand the reasons, however cruel and unjust they may seem."

She dropped her eyes to look down at the bed. *Now? Already?* It seemed like she'd only just regained him! "It's too soon."

He moved his hand against her cheek to make her look at him again. "I'd like to agree, but it isn't only the intangible arguments that chase me to leave. Morals and ethics aside, I would dearly treasure unlimited time with you, but we've more immediate physical concerns as well."

He dropped his hand from her face and sighed. "The vampire within me has been very carefully kept dormant these past decades, scrupulously maintained on the very barest amounts of animal blood.

Now I've awakened it, with you. I would say that I wish I could have waited; held out longer, refrained from drinking your precious blood." He eyed her throat for a moment and she could see the longing in his eyes. "But I don't really think that'd be true. In any case, awakened it is."

He gazed at her with staid gravity, that she might know the severity of his struggle. "The more I drink, the more it wants. It's not very satisfied with animal blood any longer, though I've practically been drowning myself with it. I'm making the local butcher's quite rich, and I've been buying the stuff almost faster than they can get it.

It doesn't seem to help much though. Perhaps it's only in my head, but the stuff just doesn't seem to do the trick the way it used to. It's getting very difficult."

She tried to pout and reject his seriousness. "I'll wear turtle necks."

That did make him smile. "It's not even just *you* anymore. It's becoming hard to be around *anyone*."

"Okay, so then stay away from everyone else." She changed tactics and smiled at him playfully. "I'll feed you. Every day, every drop that I can."

He gave a little laugh. "Right, and quickly become weakened and anemic. And that'd be the least of your problems." He leaned forward and gave her a little kiss. "No.

I haven't told you every bit of my past. There've been others. Few, and none that've touched my heart as deeply as you, but still..." He lightly shook his head with a distasteful frown. "I've tried such arrangements. It never ends well. I can't do that to you. I won't. I have to leave...now, before I start to lose control."

Felicity just sat there staring at the crumpled sheets before her. Her bottom lip began to tremble and she tried so hard not to break down and sob as she'd like. Her vision blurred and turned watery with tears.

After an interminable moment of trying to hold back her grief, she felt it recede as a new calm came upon her. She looked up to his face. He gazed at her with such love, devastated surely, but hopeful that she would not fight him.

She loved him, truly, deeply. What was it worth, not to have to let him go? She just sat there for a moment more, watching him. He looked so human. Was he really all *that* different inside? She knew that he was, and yet how bad could it be?

She put the thought aside. They had to have *some* time, a few more days at least. He waited patiently for her to speak. "Could we just pretend like you don't have to leave, just for the weekend?"

He gave her a watery grin. "That was sort of what I had in mind."

"Then let's not talk about it anymore. 'Kay?"

He nodded his head lightly and reached up to brush her cheek once more. He seemed to be studying her face, memorizing every detail in anticipation of lonely nights ahead. "I love you," he whispered.

"I love you too," she replied.

After the tears began to clear from her eyes, he let his hand wander down to trace her jaw. He seemed to be studying the line of her injury on her throat beneath. "I could do something about that maybe…your scar."

She just furrowed her brow at him, unsure as to what he could mean. He clarified, "There's an old vampire trick Maribeth and I learned back in days of the hunt. Wouldn't do to have a bunch of bodies left behind full of holes. People talk, you know.

A few drops of vampire blood usually did the trick. Vampire blood is quite the odd substance. I do believe it's got a life of its own. Right good at fixing things, it is. Keeps my body working long past what it's any right to. See, the blood regenerates tissue. That's how those awful zombies manage to up and walk around; they're constantly being repaired. In fact, if they manage to survive long enough, getting themselves fresh blood, they can eventually be restored to a life-like appearance…like me. They'd still be brain-dead creatures of instinct though. There are limits as to what can be done.

Anyway, Maribeth and I would put a few drops on a victim's bite and the blood would go to work. We would 'heal' them, as it were." He was quick to banish Felicity's hopeful thought. "They'd still die, blood loss, you know? Only the visible injury would be banished. The blood grows the tissue back together, covers the holes. Doesn't always work perfectly, but it helps."

He seemed to guess her next question before she even asked. "I couldn't have done it to help you, the night it happened. I would have if your life truly depended on it, but the wound would have taken more than a drop or two, and…it was open. It's really better if your blood and my blood never meet, trust me.

But now, it's begun to heal on its own. It's closed and well on its way to recovery. I can't guarantee the results, but a few drops of my blood should help to speed it along. Perhaps it could smooth and fade the mark on your skin, lessen the inevitable scar. I could try…if you'd like."

She looked at him thoughtfully for a moment, and then smiled. "Okay." He smiled back and she knew he was grateful that she would let him try to help. He did take on guilt so easily. She hoped it would make him feel better. She couldn't imagine that it would actually work, but it *would* be nice to look in the mirror without being reminded of Chris lying over her with a knife at her throat. "What should I do?"

"Lie back." She lay back down on the bed with her head on the pillow. Cain closed his eyes and sat very still. She wondered what he would do. Shouldn't he get a knife to cut himself?

He opened his eyes to reveal that they were now a bright golden yellow. Oh. He brought his hand up before his face and used his fangs to puncture the length of his finger.

Felicity just lay there, watching him. It was so strange. It felt like the *first* time that he had changed for her to see. It seemed so long ago. Since then, other times that he had transformed himself before her had been rather surreal. She had always been swooning with passion and the venom of his kisses. She hadn't really looked upon him and studied his change with such a clear head. She also couldn't help but eye him with a new awareness of it now.

What was it like for him? His fangs were only unsheathed when he changed. Where did they go? Up into his jaw apparently, like those of a snake, or a cat's retractable claw, to be kept protected and so unbelievably sharp. Did it hurt when they came out? He didn't look as though it did. It seemed an easy and natural shift. Now that she was unstartled by his alternate appearance, he looked like a natural creature; different to be sure, but not like something monstrous or abnormal.

He brought his finger away from his mouth to reveal two perfect drops of blood there. He'd hardly needed to apply any pressure to produce them, his fangs were so sharp. Now he brought that finger to her throat and lightly rubbed it across the wound there.

It was very sensitive to his touch but she forced herself not to flinch away. Felicity waited expectantly but her skin only felt rather warm as his finger moved across it. She looked up at him as he caressed her wound once more and then took his hand away. His eyes had become blue once again.

She reached out to hold his wrist as he was about to bring the finger to his mouth, presumably to suck and clean away the rest of the blood there. He looked at her a bit strangely, as she stopped him to ask, "What would happen, if my blood met yours? Or if I…drank it? Would that change me?"

He pulled his hand slowly but firmly from her and brought his finger to his mouth to quickly clean it. "Yes and no. You wouldn't become a true vampire. You haven't been drained."

"What would happen? Do you know?" she asked.

She thought perhaps he looked a little ill for a moment. He licked his finger again as a new bead of blood tried to form there. "Unfortunately yes, I do." He looked at her gravely. "You know, there've been others girls…

I hope that you don't feel threatened by that. It'd be hard to live 340 years and never get close to anyone, to never have loved."

He gently brushed the back of his hand across the side of her face as he gazed into her eyes. She loved when he did that. She spoke to him with a smile. "A girl would have to be crazy not to fall in love with you."

"Well, I don't know about that, but I do know that my love for *you* far outshines the rest."

She held his gaze, wanting to think of him selfishly as only her own for a moment before she asked. "So what was her name? What happened?"

"Eileen. Young Irish farm girl, back in 1873," he began.

"You've got some head for dates," she observed.

He shrugged. "It helps to keep things from getting all muddled together. Anyway, we tried it. Thought that since her body was still healthy and alive, she might play host to the blood without losing her humanity; to live in some sort of symbiotic relationship with it, gaining its curative properties without…losing anything.

It worked very well at first actually. With each small drink from me, she gained some of the more useful vampiric traits. Heightened senses, night vision, she even saw marks. It was rather amazing.

'Twas only little drinks I gave her, and they were few and far between. We thought to only sustain her abilities. We hoped that perhaps she might even gain immortality through me that way.

What we hadn't reckoned with was the tenacity of vampire blood's will to survive. We'd thought that it would be filtered through her system and over time, without a new transfusion it would leave her, wear off, as it were. We were wrong.

We should have waited to see, I suppose. Looked for evidence of its passage from her, lessening of its effects, but she was always a bit too eager for more. It can be quite heady, gaining such powers and abilities unknown before. And if vampire blood is tenacious, Eileen was nothing if not its mirror. Always thought she knew just what she wanted that girl did; and wouldn't rest 'til she had it.

As for the blood, she always wanted just a little more, and saying 'no' to pretty girls has never really been a talent of mine. It's something that I had to learn the hard way. Emotional strength and responsibility are not fun traits to wield, but they are necessary at times.

You once told me that you thought I seemed to feel responsible for all vampires and carry the guilt of all of my kind upon my own shoulders. I really don't though. I've enough guilt of my own, believe me."

"So what happened?"

"At some point 'just a little more' became too much. She went through some sort of organ failure. The vampire blood decided she didn't need her internal workings any longer, but her body wasn't quite yet ready to agree. I believe she was in difficulty long before she ever let on to me. Once it was plain that she was in trouble I offered her a true change, but she wouldn't accept it yet. She wanted to wait. She'd thought it would get better, stabilize. That it was only a period of adjustment.

She went into a coma. I did it then. When it was clear she would not awaken on her own, I drained her and gave to her fully of my blood. I should have just let her go."

"Did she ever wake up? Did it work?"

"It did actually, but she was never the same after that. The combination of the slow change and her time unconscious, all she'd been through… I don't know. She couldn't handle things. Her comprehension of the situation seemed imperfect. She was still a sweet and lovely girl but, forgive me for saying, she was a bit…mentally unstable after that."

"What became of her?"

"She had terrible troubles controlling her thirst, as though it tortured her more than I could help her handle. Before long, she simply chose to leave the world rather than face it. She committed suicide."

"How awful! I'm sorry. It must have been hard to deal with."

"I did all that I could to help her. What I really should have done was turned her away before things went too far; quite a lesson in responsibility.

It made me question my own judgment surely. Had I truly believed that she was strong enough, that she'd a desire and a will to live as I did; or was I only feeling guilt ridden and afraid to lose her? Even if my judgment was sound, who was I to proclaim myself in control of her destiny? Who am I to grant eternal life? I am nothing but a lonely and grief stricken man; hardly qualification for such power."

Cain stared at her soberly and Felicity couldn't help but wonder if he might have anticipated her recent ponderings. He spoke to her with a quiet seriousness. "This life of mine is not nearly the exciting and mysterious fight against evil you may imagine it to be. In all reality, it is darkly treacherous, lonely and hard. I would trade it for yours in a heartbeat…if I had one."

What exactly was he trying to convince her of? She refused to be swayed. Besides, he had brought up new interesting ideas. "Still, if you had stopped before things went too far, she would have been okay, right? If you only gave someone enough blood to give them those abilities that you mentioned…to see marks and stuff. That would be wild!"

"I didn't relay the story to put ideas into your head. I don't play around with stuff like that anymore. The costs are higher than I care to pay. I've enough ruined lives on my conscience." He continued his serious gaze for a moment more and then began to smile. "Well, look at that."

He reached out and gently stroked his finger across her throat. "At least this blood of mine's good for something."

She raised her hand to the spot, but of course, she couldn't tell much by touch. She sat up in the bed. "It worked?"

"It's not perfectly healed. There is still evidence of it, but I believe that it's greatly improved over what it would have been, and in time, it still may fade more. Go and have a look for yourself," he said with a gesture to the bathroom mirror.

She kicked her legs from the covers and jumped out of bed to go and see. When she first looked into the mirror, she almost did think that it was gone. It had faded remarkably. Upon closer inspection, it could still be seen, but what a difference! She kept tilting her head this way and that, trying to see it from different angles. It was practically gone!

Felicity jumped as Cain unexpectedly put his hands to her shoulders. She hadn't seen him come up behind her as she'd studied herself in the mirror. She turned to him now and grinned. "Thank you. It's amazing!"

"I know that you'd been affecting that it didn't concern you at all, but just look at how happy you are! I'm glad I could help. When you think back on our time together, that scar really wasn't the memento I'd wanted to leave you with," he told her.

Felicity couldn't help but lose her smile at his mention of being apart. She had an awful lot of thinking to do over the next two days. She gave a quick glance once more at herself alone in the mirror and the indistinct line of a scar at her throat where her injury used to be. Then she turned back to Cain for another kiss.

He was just folding his arms around her when her stomach rumbled, making an embarrassingly loud gurgling noise. She broke off the kiss to look down at the floor with a little self-conscious chuckle.

When she raised her eyes back to Cain, he was smiling as he said, "Being alive can have its drawbacks. I'm guessing it's time for breakfast?"

"Sounds that way doesn't it?" They moved from the bathroom and Felicity gave a glance towards his little refrigerator behind the bar. It was unlikely to contain anything she would want. "Guess I'll have to go out."

Cain gave her an apologetic little shrug. "Let's get dressed and venture upstairs to see what sort of day we've outside."

Once they were ready, she followed Cain upstairs. The windows were letting in little light. It seemed a gray and gloomy day. They opened the door to reveal thick and ominous storm clouds moving in. Felicity flinched as a rumble of thunder sounded from over head. "What a rotten day."

Cain looked at her oddly. "No. Actually, this is a good thing. It means I can take you out to breakfast."

Felicity eyed the sky again and then looked back to Cain in worry. "Are you sure? I mean, do you do this kind of thing often? What if it suddenly clears up?"

He smiled. "Why don't you let me worry about that? Paper said there's a big storm front moving in. We're supposed to have weather like this all weekend. We may even see snow before it's through. I wouldn't worry over unexpected sunny skies. It's not likely, besides, we won't be picnicking," he said with a laugh. "We'll go back and get your car. That way if there's a problem, I'll be somewhat protected until you can drive us home. Alright?"

"Okay," she reluctantly agreed.

The sky remained cloudy and dim as promised. They never actually got rain, but thunder did threaten now and then. As she finished up breakfast, Cain urged her to think of something fun for them to do. She professed to be at a loss. He pressed her some more. "There must be something that you can think of, something whimsical and fun. I don't often do things like that. I want to see you smile and laugh."

An idea popped into her head and he seemed to see it in her eyes, but no, it was silly. It seemed kind of dumb and surely he wouldn't want to. He nudged her arm from across the table. "Come on, I know you've thought of something. What is it?"

She laughed. "Well, there is something that Deidre and I used to do a lot of, but I don't think it'll be your kind of thing."

"Sounds perfect. Tell me!" he insisted.

"Roller-skating?" she mumbled with a smile. "I know it seems kind of childish but it is a lot of fun once you get the hang of it." He chuckled. "You don't want to, do you?"

"I'm sure you'll be surprised to hear it, but I've actually been on skates before."

"No! *You?*" she asked incredulously.

"Well don't sound so shocked. I did live through roller-disco and all of that. I try to hold myself aloof from such things normally, but there are some fads just impossible to ignore. I'm not very good at it, but I'm willing if you are."

"Well, nobody's clumsier than me. It took a lot of practice, but now at least I can keep from falling on my butt most of the time." He laughed. "I can't even imagine you on skates…or living through the seventies…or the eighties even. Did you wear tight leather pants and a sequin glove on one hand?" she teased with a giggle.

"No," he replied shortly.

"Good, that might have been disturbing," she admitted.

He glanced down at his black leather jacket, t-shirt and jeans with boots. "This is pretty standard attire for the last few decades. My wardrobe is boring but timeless. I don't find myself dressing up for much. And things like crazy patterns and loud colors are not really my style. The seventies were an absolute fashion nightmare for someone like me to live through."

She grinned. "Well I like your look. Who was it that decided that vampires should wear tuxedo's and opera capes anyway?"

"The same person who put them into coffins I'd imagine. Very dramatic, but not anything I'm all that comfortable with. Besides, I couldn't very well go skating in a cape could I? I hope that I remember how."

"I'm sure it'll come back to you. The skates are different now though. Most places use all in-line blades." She laughed at his obvious confusion. "You probably used the old skates that were two wheels in front and two in back. We might still be able to rent those, but now they put them all in a line down the middle, like an ice-skate. It takes better balance."

"Well, I'm usually not entirely ungraceful, and it's not as though I'm very worried over breaking anything. I'm sure I'll manage."

She shook her head with a smile. She couldn't believe that this was how they'd spend their day. It would be fun though. "I don't even know where there's a rink around here."

"We'll find one. Come on."

~~~~~~~~~~~~~~~~~~~~~~~~~~~~~~~

They skated, they fell, they laughed and had a wonderful time. The afternoon flew by. Afterwards they sat on a bench unlacing their skates and carefully surveying the sky through the front windows of the roller-rink.

"Looks as though the weather's holding," Cain observed. "Why don't you drop me off at home so that you can change and get ready for work? Then come back for me and if the sun permits, I'll take you for an early dinner before you have to go in."

"Sounds like a plan." Felicity smiled as Cain finished trading the skates for his boots. "Did you have fun today?"

He beamed back at her. "You know I did. I don't think I'll be strapping wheels to my feet again anytime soon…" Felicity laughed. She had actually turned out to be the better skater. It was so endearing, the way that he had needed to cling to her at first just to keep his feet. "But this has been a day that I will always think back upon with a smile."

Unfortunately, Felicity lost her smile all too easily. Why did he have to go and say things like that? 'Look back upon', as though it were crucial that he build these memories now, because he would never see her again.

She couldn't help it when her eyes filled with tears at the reminder of his plans to leave. He noticed and admonished her for it. "You're not allowed to cry," he said firmly.

"Why not?"

His tone softened. "Because if you do, then you'll go and make me cry, and ruin our fun day."

She bit her lip and blinked to force back the tears.

"Where do you want to go for dinner?"

~~~~~~~~~~~~~~~~~~~~~~~~~~~~~~~

After dinner, she dropped him off at home before she left for work. He promised to meet her at the DownTime later. He had a 'date with a butcher' to attend first.

He arrived just before eight to spend the last two hours of Felicity's shift, reading in the café. Friday nights were fairly busy, and working with Harold left her to feel less inclined to spend her time hanging about the café with Cain instead of at her register.

Things were slowing down now. 9:30, they'd be closing soon. She was just finishing ringing up a customer, when she noticed someone new enter the store.

He wasn't at all remarkable in appearance really, just another boy. He was almost sixteen maybe, with shoulder length wispy blond hair. He wore jeans and sneakers with a brown and orange camouflage-hunting jacket.

What struck Felicity as strange, was the fact that he didn't go to browse in the bookshelves as most people did. He stood at the front scanning the store as though looking for someone. He had very bright green eyes that seemed to pierce through every person they rested upon. They barely paused on Felicity though. After a minute or two, he headed directly for the café.

He seemed to be making his way straight to Cain. Sure enough, he reached Cain's table and stopped before it. When Cain looked up at him, Felicity could swear that the boy actually bowed his head to Cain before speaking. Cain offered him a chair and the boy sat.

They treated each other rather formally. Felicity didn't imagine that they might be old friends; it all seemed very business-like. They spent the next twenty minutes or so quietly talking while Felicity tried not to very obviously observe them.

Cain never even glanced in her direction. The boy must have had his full attention. Felicity began straightening her register area and making ready to close as she watched them. She found herself staring hard at the boy. He had to be a vampire. Who else would come to speak to Cain?

It was rather odd that his manner was nothing like the young teenager that he looked to be. She wondered how old he was. Why, he could be a sixty-year-old man for all she knew! How strange and frustrating might it be for him to be forever treated like a kid? Then again, it surely had some advantages as well.

Finally they stood. She saw the boy hand something to Cain. She couldn't really tell what it was; something small, like a business card maybe? Very odd.

The boy started in her direction as Cain began gathering his things to leave. As the boy approached the registers on his way to the door, he turned his eyes on Felicity to meet her gaze for the first time.

He looked at her as though he knew exactly who she was and she could have sworn that he actually gave her a slight smile. It was not malicious in nature but Felicity found it a bit eerie all the same.

Her mark. Of course, he could see it. He must have known she was there and her relationship to Cain all along. He just hadn't spared her a glance at first because Cain had been his priority.

The boy turned away from her and left the store. She just stood there, watching him walk across the parking lot. She was a bit startled when she looked back at the register and found Cain standing before it. She hadn't noticed his approach.

He smiled at her surprise. "I know you're dying to ask, so I'll save you the trouble. Yes, he was undead. He's a messenger, from Arif. They'll be leaving town. He and his horde will be traveling up to Albany.

I must say, I'm rather relieved. I didn't relish the idea of them hanging about after I've gone."

Felicity looked back out the front windows but the boy was gone. She sighed as she turned her eyes down to the counter before her. She had no idea what to say, and once again, the reality of Cain's leaving was a depressing weight upon her.

He seemed to sense her melancholy thoughts and sought to lighten them. "I've been to the market. I bought some ice cream for later."

She looked up at him hesitantly as he tried to make her smile. "What flavor?"

"They didn't have 'Butter Rum Ripple'. Do you like 'Butter Pecan'?" He smiled as she nodded yes. "I also bought whipped cream, chocolate sauce, butterscotch syrup, sprinkles and cherries."

She laughed. "That's an awful lot of toppings. I thought you didn't even really eat ice cream."

"I don't." He leaned forward conspiratorially and spoke quietly with a sly smile. "I'm planning to decorate *you*."

Her eyes went wide and she surely turned very red in the face as she sought to hide her shocked smile. She tried to gather her composure as he leaned closer and gave her a kiss on the cheek. "Sounds sticky," she whispered.

"We'll shower," he whispered back.

She jumped guiltily as Harold yelled from the café. "It's ten o'clock."

Cain just smiled. "I'll see you outside."

~~~~~~~~~~~~~~~~~~~~~~~~~~~~

Saturday night found Felicity at her register again, daydreaming over last night and the day past. The evening before had indeed been quite sticky, romantic, and little silly, but very memorable. Today had been spent in quiet comfort. Cain had taken her out through the pouring rain to breakfast. Then as the rain eased up, they had spent some time walking along the edge of the stream in the park through the drizzle.

It was wet and cold but she'd hardly even noticed. Cain had held a large umbrella over them and they'd watched the ducks playing in the puddles along the bank. All the while, floating through her head was Cain's statement that *she* was his sunshine.

They'd gone home to Cain's, stripped off their wet clothes and made love, slow, tender and almost surreal. She'd allowed him to drink from her again and it had been another intimate and erotic interlude worthy of future daydreams. Just closing her eyes now to think of it could make her head spin.

They'd spent the remainder of the day wrapped in a big fluffy blanket as Cain read her excerpts and recited remembered passages from some of his favorite books and poems. It was so comfortable and soothing just to lie there with him reading to her. It felt like perfect peace and happiness. How could she even question the desire to spend all of her life just so? What more could she want?

It was wonderful to see him become so animated and excited over ideas and questions posed in the literature they perused. They had lively discussions and wistful imaginings and just...talked. He knew so much! It seemed as though there wasn't an idea or a situation that he hadn't already encountered and formed an opinion on. More than ever before, she found him absolutely fascinating.

Tonight. She would tell him tonight. The decision was made. No more nervous wondering or uncertain hesitation. No more depression and grief over future separation. She wanted to be with him, for always.

What good was humanity without someone as marvelous as Cain to share life with? She would let him drain her and then she would drink of his blood, as much and as many times as he thought necessary until it was done. She would become a vampire.

She knew that he could do it without worry over physical difficulties. He was so meticulous and careful about such things. He had sounded disapproving of his power to change others when they had spoken the other night, but that was only regret over past mistakes and resignation over a decision for the future already made.

He'd offered her his blood before, more than once. She had always let him think it was out of the question. She was sure his recent disapproval of the deed stemmed from the fact that he was trying to resign himself to the certainty that she did not *want* to be transformed. How happy he would be, to know she'd changed her mind!

There were certain drawbacks of course, but that was to be expected with any big decision. She was strong. She could handle it. She could get through *anything* with Cain at her side.

She would miss her family, but she could probably still see them once in awhile, in the beginning anyway, before her failure to age became noticeable. She'd just have to be careful, not to let on how she'd changed. She and Cain could get married before them at an evening ceremony, and then he could whisk her away to live elsewhere. She'd tell her parents they'd be moving abroad. Maybe he would even take her to see Herald Manor!

Being a creature of the night wasn't at all what she had originally perceived it to be. So she would no longer be able to walk in the sunlight, big deal. It's not as though she could never see the sun again, it would just have to be from someplace sheltered and protected, a small price to pay for so many magical abilities!

She could live forever! That was almost as scary as it was exciting. Was this the way she wanted to look for the rest of her life, never to grow or change in any significant way? No wrinkles, no gray hair, no disease, she would be forever immune and protected from such things.

She'd be able to see and do all of the things that Cain could do…in time. He would teach her, to see marks and recognize other vampires.

Other vampires…she would have nothing to fear from them now, nothing to fear from anyone. She couldn't help but recall Sindy as she had fought her way through the zombies who had attacked her in the bookstore entrance that night. She had been so fearless. Felicity had found it amazing.

Sindy…and other young vampires; Cain felt a duty to teach and protect them. He would want to continue with that. She could help him. He could teach her the way of things and she could work at his side. Helping others and saving people. That certainly seemed like a worthwhile endeavor to commit one's life to.

It would be scary and new and not at all what she had expected for her life, but she would be with Cain. That was a reward even greater than any strange new magical ability.

Why wasn't he here yet? He'd said that he was coming to meet her just as he had the evening before. Perhaps he had gone to see Arif and his men before they left.

Still, he should be here by now. Doubt and worry had just begun to creep into her mind when she felt him. Yes, he was definitely moving closer, coming to the DownTime. He was moving very fast, he must have taken his motorcycle. She breathed a sigh of relief as she felt the comforting and familiar warmth and shivers of his presence approach and surround her.

Finally, she saw him pull into the lot, riding his bike as she'd surmised. He parked it and entered the store. She gave him a broad smile as he came to her. He gave her a little kiss hello over the counter. "I thought you'd be here sooner," she chastised him.

"Sorry, I had some stuff to do." He glanced about the store; it was fairly empty. They'd be closing in less than half an hour. "Do you think you could steal away for a moment?"

She looked over to see Ben cleaning up after his last customers in the café. They were just putting on coats to leave. "Sure, hang on." She came out from behind the register and called to Ben as he began to head back to the counter with a tray of empty cups. "Hey Ben, I'll be right back, okay?"

Ben did not look very happy, but he didn't say anything. The store was empty, it's not like anyone was going to buy anything else. He'd deal. She turned back to Cain. "Is everything all right?"

"Yeah." He nodded. "Come on." He gestured for her to follow him outside. He held the door as Ben's customers left, and then she went out as well. She folded her arms for warmth in the night chill.

The rain had stopped earlier and now it was just a bit windy. The dark clouds overhead made the night seem oppressive and ominous. Certainly, this was the calm before the storm.

"What's up?"

He moved away from the entrance to the store and she followed. Cain turned to her and reached out to put his arms around her waist and pull her in for a kiss before answering.

"I've got to go."

She stared at him uncomprehending for the space of a second. Then she became indignant. "What? Now? Like *this?* I thought we'd have tomorrow. You can't leave *now!*" She couldn't help but move a step back from him in quiet outrage.

He glanced up at the sky. "There's a big cold front moving in. There's even a blizzard warning out. Not exactly motorcycle weather brewing. If I don't leave now I may get snowed in. And if I were to let myself get snowed in, I might also forget to leave after. I've got to go."

He looked miserable but firm. After her initial shock, she broke into a smile. "No, but see…you don't have to. I've been wanting to tell you something."

He didn't look eagerly expectant as she'd hoped. Perhaps he hadn't guessed. "I want to come with you. I want to do it…let you change me. We can be together, just like you wanted."

First, he looked confused, then very surprised. "But…you don't want to be like me."

"I want to be *with* you."

"It's not the same. You'll have to leave school…your family!"

"I know. I don't care."

He stared at her very closely for a long time. She couldn't tell what he might be thinking. Getting used to the idea she supposed, but he hadn't smiled yet. She was waiting for the broad grin of relief that she had expected. He very slightly shook his head. "You'll lose your *life*."

"I'll have a new life…with you."

"Felicity, you're too young to know what is right for your future."

"No I'm not!" He was going to argue with her? "Do you even remember what it's like to be young? To know what you want and to have everyone around you believe that they know better, like your father or your brother did?"

He gave a little laugh. "Yes, but it turned out that my family really *did* know what was best for me. Your parents want you to have an education and the responsibility of a job to help you develop character.

I want you to *live* life before you die. Not to choose something that you don't even really want or understand just because of me. You'd resent me terribly for it."

"No I won't! I love you! I want to be with you!" She felt desperate to convince him. He had to know that she was resolute.

"I love you too, but you can't even fathom all that you'd be giving up. It's a difficult existence that I lead."

"I'm strong and I'm not afraid to do what I have to."

Cain studied her face for a very long moment. "I know that's true…and it will serve you well." She smiled as he raised his hand to hold the side of her face. He breathed deeply and sighed. "Do you trust me?"

She knew he wouldn't fail her. He would do it right. "Implicitly."

"Then do you promise to do as I say; follow my exact instructions?"

"I promise," she assured him.

"Good." He smiled at her and stroked his thumb back and forth across her cheek as he held her chin cupped in his hand. "Finish school."

"What?" she asked in confusion.

"Find a career doing something that you enjoy, something that does good in the world."

It suddenly dawned on her what he was saying. "No."

He kept on, though his voice slightly trembled. "Don't be afraid to love again. Keep me locked in a little corner of your heart if you will, but then give your love to another."

Her eyes filled with tears. "No!"

His eyes were tear filled as well, yet he did not waiver. "Choose wisely. Find someone who will recognize the amazing young woman that you are and will love you deeply and truly."

"Cain no!" Tears were spilling down her cheeks in earnest now. He would not do this. He could not leave her here!

"Get married, be happy. Have babies. Lots and lots of them! I know you want children. You'll be a wonderful mother." He was smiling through tears of his own and it reminded her of how he'd looked when speaking of his daughter, so full of love and pride.

But he could not do this. He *did* love her didn't he? "Cain, please!"

"*Live* your life."

"Cain no, please! You can't leave me! I want to come with you!"

He took a very deep breath and exhaled it slowly. He gazed into her eyes and then leaned forward for another kiss. He did love her. She knew that he did. His kiss was passionate and true. He would keep her with him. The love in that kiss had to mean that he would.

Their kiss was long and loving. She regretfully gave up his lips as he leaned back to look at her again and speak quietly. "No."

There was no air to breathe. She felt as though her vision was blurred and she couldn't see clearly and his voice was thick in her ears. She could not have heard him right. He let her go and walked to his waiting motorcycle. No.

No? He'd said no! That can't be right. He loved her! He wanted to be with her! He mounted the bike.

Her mouth was open and nothing was coming out. Her cheeks were wet and freezing in the wind. Wait! This isn't how it's supposed to end! She couldn't find her voice to say the words.

He quickly started the engine, loud and thundering. "Cain!" Now the sound leapt from her throat to stop him and was lost in the rolling reverberation of the Harley, but he knew. She shook the seeming paralysis that had held her and began to move towards him. He smiled and mouthed her a kiss.

"Wait!"

He didn't.

He turned to speed away even as she ran to him. It was no use. "Cain wait! Please! You can't leave me!" She screamed after him into the roar of the engine as she ran across the empty parking lot. Even *she* had trouble picking out her voice in the din. No one could have heard her, except for maybe him. It didn't matter.

He was gone.

She just stood there in the empty parking lot. He was gone. He'd left her. He left her! He said no and he left.

He said no.

She had no idea how long she stood there. Time stopped when he was lost to view. He was gone. Nothing else mattered. She stood there staring at the empty road. He was gone.

"'Liss?"

"Felicity, what are you doing? I'm waiting for you to close."

Footsteps behind her. She didn't turn. She couldn't speak.

"It's freezing out here. Do you realize that it's snowing?" Ben reached her and put a hand on her shoulder to turn her to face him. She just stared at him vacantly. His eyes took in her tear-streaked face. His annoyance immediately turned to concern. "'Liss, what's wrong?"

Her eyes didn't really see him. She just stared into the falling snow. She needed to say something but there were only two things going through her head. "He said no. He said no and he left. He *left* me."

"Ah, 'Liss." Now reaction suddenly hit and as Ben used the hand on her shoulder to pull her closer, she began to cry. She stood in the parking lot and sobbed into his chest as he held her.

She cried, and she sobbed, and she mumbled things that he couldn't hear. Ben didn't ask her to clarify. He didn't say a word. He just held her as she cried.

He'd left. He had really left.

Didn't he want to be with her? Didn't he love her? Didn't he think she could do it?

She sobbed until nothing would come any longer but dry gasps for air. Finally, Ben held her back a little and gently swiped the wet hair from her face. "We should go in. You're covered in snow and it's freezing out here."

She didn't say anything, but let him lead her inside.

She felt as though she were in a trance. He'd said no.

They entered the store and her eyes fell on the register. Oh yeah. She was supposed to be working. She started towards it but Ben took her by the arm. "No, that's okay. I'll do your stuff. Come sit."

He steered her into the café and pulled out a chair. She sat and stared out the window into the falling snow.

"You want some coffee?" She didn't look at him but gently shook her head. "No. Of course you don't want coffee."

He watched her quietly for a moment. "I know what you need. I have just the thing. Hot chocolate. You want some hot chocolate?" She just shrugged as she stared out into the snow. "You like marshmallows or whipped cream?" She didn't answer. "I like whipped cream, with a little powdered cocoa sprinkled on top… I'll be right back."

She hardly noticed as he set the cup down before her a few minutes later. "Careful, it's hot underneath."

He just stood there for a minute, watching her stare out the window. "I've got to go finish closing out the registers." He left.

He left. How could he do that to her? How could Cain just leave? Didn't he love her?

He did. She knew that he did. *That's* why he'd left. He thought it was wrong to take her away from her life. He thought that eventually she would be unhappy and regretful.

He was wrong…wasn't he?

It didn't matter.

He left.

"'Liss? I'm done."

Felicity looked up to find Ben standing there with her coat over his arm and her purse in his hand. He put them down on the empty chair next to her. "You done with that?" he asked, gesturing towards her untouched hot cocoa.

"Yeah." She looked up at him as he took the cup. "Thanks," she added belatedly.

He took it back behind the counter and dumped it out into the sink as she put on her coat. When he came back, he had his own coat on as well. He shut the lights and she followed him to the door. He set the alarm and stood under the overhang looking out into the snow for a minute. "You want me to drive you?"

She glanced at their cars. They were dusted with snow, but it wasn't bad yet. "No. I'm okay."

He walked her to her car. She got in to warm it up and he went to start his own. He came back with a snowbrush to dust off her windows. It was light and fluffy snow, not really sticking yet. She just sat there behind the wheel watching Ben brush off their cars. What was she supposed to do now? Go back to the dorm? Go to bed? Wake up and resume her life?

Ben came and tapped on her window. "You're good to go. Are you going to be okay?"

"I'm strong." She had said that to Cain. She'd meant strong enough for him to turn her, not strong enough for him to go.

"You want me to hang out for a little?" Ben was watching her carefully.

"No. I'm all right." She knew where she wanted to be. "Thanks."

He smiled and rested his hand on her arm for a minute. She turned away. He left for his own car. She rolled up the window. He waited for her to pull out of the lot first. Damn.

She drove back to the dorm. She sat in the parking lot for a minute just staring at the steering wheel. Then she turned the car around and went to Cain's. She knew that he wouldn't be there, but she couldn't help it.

No motorcycle in the driveway. No telltale shivers of his presence anywhere. The snow was really coming down now. She could hardly see. She wondered how far he'd gotten before he had to stop.

Crazy notions of driving out blind and trying to 'feel' him flitted through her mind. No. She wasn't *that* stupid. Cain could afford to take chances like that. He had assurance of survival that she did not. She shut off the car and mounted his front steps. The key; he'd given her a spare, for the night of the Halloween ball. She kept it in her purse. She dug it out and worked the lock.

It was dark and barren as always. She closed the door behind her and confidently strode across the room to the basement stairs. There she flipped on the stairwell light and made her way down.

Cain's room. She managed to find the bedside lamp without tripping over anything. She turned it on. The room looked just the same. He hadn't taken anything. There was nothing to take. Just the bed, still messed from when last they'd been in it. The pile of books they'd been reading still lay on the floor.

Felicity dropped her things and stripped off her coat and shoes. She climbed under the covers of the bed and buried her face in the pillow. It still smelled lightly of his aftershave. She shut the light, lay there in his bed and cried herself to sleep.

~~~~~~~~~~~~~~~~~~~~~~~~~~~~~

It was dark when she woke. It was always dark down here. That was the point. She sat up and found the switch for the lamp next to the bed. Her watch showed the time to be 7:30 a.m.

She just sat there on his bed for a few minutes, surveying the room. She got up feeling almost numb. As though her limbs were heavy and she moved in slow motion. He was gone.

She went to the laundry room. Nothing. He'd taken his clothes and left nothing behind. She went to the bathroom. The cabinet was bare. She went behind the bar. The refrigerator was empty and clean. No trace of what it had once held. No one could ever guess.

He wasn't coming back. She'd known, but still…

She wandered over to the books on the floor by the bed. She picked a few of his favorites out of the pile. She would keep them. After donning her shoes and coat, she made her way up the stairs with her purse and an armful of books.

When she opened the front door, she was blinded by the brightness of sunlight on snow. The sky was sunny, the world crisp and clean, covered in white. She was lucky to keep her feet on the stairs as she trudged through the snow without a free hand.

She managed to unstick the icy passenger door of her car and dump the books on the seat before they fell into the snow. She reached across to put in the key and start the engine. Once it caught, she straightened back up to stand outside as she let it run and warm up on its own.

She stood gazing out at the ground and the rooftops, blanketed in fresh snowfall. The branches of the trees were encased in ice, making them seem made of glass. It was beautiful. She wondered if Cain could see it at all, from wherever he was. Would it hurt his eyes? He was probably sleeping.

New tears tried to drip down her face once again as she thought of all that she had lost. She forced herself to try to blink them away…to look at all she had not.

A cardinal was flitting through the branches of the trees nearby; a bright blood red streak and a snippet of song, singing to all the world of how it was good to be alive.

~~~~~~~~~~~~~~~~~~~~~~~~~~~~~~

Felicity found it very hard to agree in the first few days that passed, but alive she was; a fact that wasn't going to change anytime soon she'd imagine. Not that she wanted to die. What had she wanted…really? To be with Cain of course, but beyond that? Had her decision been a foolish one? Should she be thankful that he had neglected her wishes? She found it very hard to feel that way…right now. Maybe someday.

The days passed. Life went on, whether she wanted it to or not. She went to class. Partly because she knew that Cain would want her to, but mostly because…what else was there to do? She didn't want to go home. She had spent all day Sunday alone in her room crying, she certainly needed no more of *that* if it could be avoided. Enough regretful and depressing thoughts filled her head when she tried to fall asleep each night.

She found herself lying in her bed and thinking of him before she could fall asleep. He was probably just waking up. Where was he? Did he miss her? She missed him so bad that it hurt.

At least the last time that they had been apart, she had known that he was there. She could feel him and believe that somehow things would work out. Not anymore. He was gone.

She saw no one, not really. She went to class as though sleepwalking, going through the motions. She took to eating lunch in her room. A yogurt, a sandwich, whatever. Nothing really mattered. She called in sick to work; until Thursday morning. She got a phone call from Mr. Penten begging her to come in if she was at all well. He was having coverage problems. Fine. Whatever. She sighed as she hung up the phone. Time for class.

After History class, she went back to the dorm and headed for the kitchen. She opened the fridge for her yogurt when she realized, yesterday she'd eaten the last one. Damn. She had nothing left. She hadn't done very much shopping to begin with. Her eyes searched the refrigerator, as though something with her name on it would suddenly materialize. No such luck.

Everything else was neatly labeled. Regina, Debbie, Bridgette, Penny… The labels and marker were right there in the door. Everyone used them, it discouraged problems. She briefly entertained the notion of just taking something of someone else's. No one would notice.

A sound behind her made her jump. Deborah stood there with arms crossed. "Are you just going to stand there?" Felicity moved out of the way for her and headed for the door. Cafeteria it is.

She was on line with a chef salad when she noticed Ben. He was sitting with a bunch of guys. Some of them were the ones he had introduced her to early last week. He didn't notice her. She didn't bother to try to make eye contact. She paid for her stuff and headed for an empty table in the corner. She had just settled everything and sat down when Ben came to her table with his tray. "This seat taken?" he asked.

She just shrugged and gestured for him to sit if he wanted. He smiled and sat as he spoke. "I was beginning to think you had given up eating." She just shrugged again and started on her salad. "I would've called but…I figured you just wanted to be left alone for awhile." He tilted his head to meet her eyes. "It's good to see you. I've had to resort to sittin' with *those* guys," he said as he jerked a thumb in the direction of his former lunch companions.

She begrudgingly smiled. "Allie's not back yet?"

He traded his smile for annoyed concern. "No. How long did she say she'd be gone?"

She thought for a moment. "Two weeks. That's how long she said she took off from work anyway."

Ben was obviously counting days in his head. "It has to *be* two weeks by now! When did she leave, Tuesday?"

"So?" Felicity dropped her fork onto the plate and gave Ben a steady stare of irritation. "Ben, she's in the Pocono's with the guy she loves. *She's* happy. I'm sure it's very easy to lose track of time when you're spending it like that." She tried to keep the resentful edge from her voice, but it didn't really work.

Ben just watched her for a moment, and then decided to drop the subject. He began to eat his lunch.

Something suddenly occurred to her. Allie was with Mattie. Mattie knew Cain. They were friends, they kept in touch. Most likely Mattie would know how to find him. She could talk to Allie when she got back…get her to convince Mattie to take Felicity to see Cain. It was a hope…

Felicity looked at Ben again and couldn't help but feel bad. "Waiting to make up with her huh?"

"I just want to get it all over with. Tell her I'm sorry and put it behind us. I don't know what'll happen from there, but waiting around like this sucks."

Ben didn't say any more about it and they ate in silence as cafeteria commotion went on around them.

After a few minutes, Felicity looked back up at him in realization. "Hey, I got a weird phone call this morning. Mr. Penten wanted to know if I'd start taking more hours because Ashley quit!"

Ben went back to eating. "Yeah, I know."

"What's going on?" Felicity asked.

"She's leaving," Ben said quietly.

"Well I get *that*," she told him.

"No, I mean…school, town, she's *leaving*."

"Why?" Felicity asked.

Ben shrugged. "She's transferring schools."

"In the middle of a semester? That's ridiculous! Why would she do that?"

"What do you think? She got her parents to let her go to sunny California. She's been goin' on about how she was really meant for the west coast, but I know it's because of the ever-present blood-sucking population in this town. She's freaked," Ben stated bluntly.

"I thought she didn't believe you?"

Ben gave her a steady look. "You know, Ashley isn't really as stupid as she pretends to be. She just does that because she thinks guys find it attractive. Which really is stupid, so…there's an oxy-moron for you."

"You never seemed to mind," Felicity replied a bit acidly. He dropped his eyes and looked away. Why was she being mean to him? Her unhappiness wasn't his fault. "When does she leave?" she asked gently.

"She already left. This morning," he explained.

She looked at him sympathetically. "I'm sorry."

He gave a little chuckle. "I'm not. I was ready to break up with her anyway, she was drivin' me nuts." Felicity couldn't help but laugh at his confession. He gave her a little nod and then shrugged. "Long term relationships were never really my thing."

"Why not?" she asked.

He seemed to think about it for a minute and then leaned forward to speak to her confidentially. "I'll let you in on a little secret. When it comes to the ladies…" He leaned back again and spread his arms as though very impressed with himself. "I can wine 'em and dine 'em, date 'em and dance with 'em. Spend evenings of questionable morality and all of that," he added with a sly smile. Felicity rolled her eyes and looked away momentarily with a smirk. "But when it comes to every day stuff, routine hangin' out, seeing 'em all the time…it never works. Girls always seem to bore me to tears or drive me insane."

Felicity opened her mouth in disbelief and eyed him for a moment in questioning irritation. "Thanks a lot."

Ben rolled his eyes and smiled. "Well not *you*. You and Allie are like the only normal girls I know." She arched her brow. "Alright, *Allie's* questionable."

She laughed and went back to eating her lunch. Ben did too. He spoke again without really looking at her. "Anyway, I think I'm going to fade back from the whole dating scene for a while. 'Remove myself from the market' as it were."

She laughed as he continued. "No really. I'm going to focus on some more important stuff for a while. Save some money, concentrate on my grades. I'm always so busy thinkin' about my plans for the weekend that I never really spend time planning for the future.

I don't really want to live with my dad forever, you know," he admitted sheepishly. She giggled. "Dating's fun, but I'm starting to think I should take a break from the impractical fun stuff and concentrate more on what's real. You know, take a break and have a life."

She stared at him over the table for a minute. He just smiled and finished his lunch. She answered him quietly. "Yeah, me too."

He spoke to her as he began preparing to leave for his next class. "It's a little hard to swallow, but at some time or another I figure you gotta take the red pill."

"Huh?"

He looked up from packing up his stuff and stared at her over the table. "Don't even tell me that you've never seen 'The Matrix'."

"Nope. I'm guessing there was a pill involved?"

"Unbelievable." He shook his head in contempt and then looked to give her explanation of his attitude. "I watch a lot of movies; I tend to make references. When Allie's here…she *gets* it, but it's not much fun if you never even know what the hell I'm talking about!"

"Sorry," she offered.

"Fortunately, it's fixable. I am hereby placing myself in charge of your cinema education. What's today, Thursday?"

She looked at him dubiously. "Yeah…"

"Cool. From now on, Thursday is movie night. After work, my house, you bring the popcorn, I've got the movies. You in?"

She looked at him blankly for a moment. "Okay…" she answered hesitantly.

"Great. I've gotta go. I'll see you later."

She was still sitting there, watching him leave when she thought to say 'bye'.

~~~~~~~~~~~~~~~~~~~~~~~~~~~~~

Later at work, she finished closing out her register and went to sit at the counter to wait for Ben, wondering how she was going to get out of 'movie night'. Why had she even said she'd go? It wasn't really something she felt up to.

Ben looked up at her from counting his drawer. "So, you know what you wanna watch? I've got just about everything you could think of."

"Oh, you know…I think I'm going to have to pass."

He stopped counting. "How come?"

She looked at him blankly for a minute. "I haven't got any popcorn."

Ben laughed and put down the bills in his hand. He came out from behind the counter and walked to the shelf down in front of the counter to her right. He picked up and handed her a package of 'movie butter microwave popcorn'. "This one's on me."

She rolled her eyes and smiled. "Ben, I'm sorry… I'm just not really in the mood."

He looked disappointed. "Okay. I understand. You probably wanna just sit in your room alone and be depressed…again." She avoided eye contact. "But I wish you'd change your mind and come. *I* haven't got anything else to do." He eyed her hopefully and smiled. "It's just a movie. I promise we won't have *too* much fun."

She sighed. He stood there and wouldn't let her break his gaze until she answered. It would be better than having to endure another '3P Thursday' at the dorm. "All right, I guess."

He just smiled and went to finish closing out. She followed him in her car back to his house. It was a small L-shaped ranch style home. No other cars were in the driveway. He opened the front door with his key and she followed him in.

The house was nice…but a little unkempt. Not very well decorated and definitely in need of a woman's touch. She got the impression that Ben and his dad didn't do very much entertaining.

From the entryway, Felicity could see the dining room; she doubted anyone had eaten in there in the recent past though. The table was piled with what looked like a month's worth of mail and newspapers. The kitchen could also be seen from the entryway. It was nice and fairly clean, but the sink was piled high with dishes.

She glanced around as Ben hung his coat in the hall closet. He reached out to take hers. "Is your dad home?" she asked.

"No, he's away again. He had to go up to Albany for a business meeting."

She walked a little further into the house as Ben hung up her coat. The living room was nice and fairly neat, but every table seemed to have a thin coat of dust over it, as though no one ever even used the room on a regular basis. She took a few more steps in and was about to sit on the couch when Ben stopped her.

"Oh, we're not going to watch the movie out here. My T.V.'s much better." She looked at the old 25" television in the living room and then at Ben, doubtfully. He smiled. "Really. My room's down here," he said with a gesture down the hall.

Now she outright laughed. "Said the spider to the fly."

He realized her thought and laughed himself. "No, it's not what you think. If I were trying to be *slick*, I think I could do better than *this*. I'm on a break, remember? In fact, I'll have you know that you are the only girl – well, besides Allie – who has ever been privileged to even *see* my room."

Felicity eyed him skeptically. "Aren't you supposed to have a reputation as some sort of 'ladies man'?"

He looked a little embarrassed but answered her steadily. "I take them to 'the Hilton'."

She raised her eyebrows with a smirk. "Classy," she murmured.

Ben rolled his eyes and shook his head as he started down the hall. "Come on." He opened the door to his room and stepped aside for Felicity to enter.

Whoa. It was a fairly large bedroom decorated sparsely in various shades of blue. It was impeccably neat, everything clean and organized. It almost looked like an office. This effect was especially heightened by the fact that the entire wall opposite the door was covered with floor to ceiling shelves except for a space in the center that held a huge flat screen T.V.

Most of the shelves were filled with movies; the rest seemed to house video games and plastic sleeved comic books. Felicity walked a few steps further into the room. It looked like a wall from 'f.y.e'. They were even in alphabetical order; and the T.V. was almost too big for the room really. She looked back at Ben. "I'm guessing your dad's not charging you rent."

He gave a sheepish chuckle. "Streaming here sucks, so when the Blockbuster down in town went out of business, I bought a bunch of their stuff cheap. Anyway, I told you my T.V. was better."

"A little *big* isn't it?" She started to grin. "Isn't that supposed to mean you're compensating for something?"

He laughed. "Hardly. When I move out of this dump and get my own place it'll be just fine."

She turned to see the rest of the room. The wall to her far right had a window, with his full-size bed in the corner that met the wall the door was on. It was neatly made with a comforter that had a geometric pattern of blue and white. There was also a desk on that wall with more shelves above it, but these shelves did not hold movies. They were filled with at least two dozen... "You have *toys?*" she asked with a broad smile.

"They're not toys, they're action figures."

"M-hmmm." She went for closer inspection. Comic book personalities, she assumed. She recognized Batman and Spiderman of course, but most of them were of characters that she didn't know. She picked up the figure of a very well endowed and scantily clad woman with an arched brow and a smile. "So what's *her* name?" she asked, bobbing the girl around as though 'playing' with her.

Ben became flustered and walked to retrieve the figure. "Et-dt-dt. Don't *touch* them. All right, please?" Felicity laughed at him as he carefully repositioned the lady in question. "See, this is why I don't let girls in my room."

Felicity giggled some more. "Sorry. Wow, Allie was right. You *do* have an inner-geek."

"I am not a geek! They're collector's items. Graphic novels and comics are cool."

"Well, I don't read comics, but I do like your toys..." She corrected herself as he looked at her warningly, "action figures."

"So what do you want to watch?" She looked at the wall. It was pretty over-whelming, she had no idea what to pick. "Tell you what, why don't we watch 'The Matrix'?" Ben suggested. "It's pretty intense sci-fi for a beginner, but I'll talk you through it. At least you'll get the 'pill' thing."

She laughed. "Okay."

"Make yourself comfortable." He walked over and took the pillows from the head of the bed. He then placed them against the wall, the length of the bed so that they could sit on it like a couch. "I'll go make the popcorn." He was just leaving when he ducked his head back into the room. "And don't touch my stuff."

~~~~~~~~~~~~~~~~~~~~~~~~~~~~~

He was right, it was a good movie. It was also very sci-fi and a little confusing for someone as uninitiated as her, but Ben helped her get it. The red pill represented reality...at least that was one reference explained. She was probably going to have nightmares about robot spiders and things in her belly button, but he was right, it *was* better than sitting alone in her room depressed...again.

She finished the last of the popcorn as the credits rolled. Ben took a swig of soda and then patted her on the back. "So, you are now one movie wiser. Do it again next week?"

"Next Thursday's Thanksgiving."

"Oh yeah. You going home?"

"Of course I am; are you kidding? My parents are ready to kill me! They bought me a car for my birthday and I haven't driven home once since. What are you doing? Do you have like an Aunt or somebody that you visit, or is it just you and your dad?"

"I don't have any other family around here, and since my mom died, my dad's not much for holidays. He always says he'll be around, and then takes off for some last minute work emergency. Usually Allie comes over. She's not a very good cook, but between the two of us we usually manage to concoct something edible."

"That's it? No house full of people, no giant turkey?"

Ben shrugged. "I'm used to it. Thanksgiving's not a big deal anyway."

"It is at my house." What if Allie didn't come back in time? What if Allie didn't come back *at all*? It wasn't something she wanted to bring up to Ben, but it did seem a distinct possibility. She knew that he worried over it too. "You and your dad should come have dinner with us."

"What? No, that's okay," he assured her uncomfortably.

"Really, you should. Why not?" she asked.

"We're not going to just invite ourselves over your house for a major holiday," he explained.

"I thought you didn't think Thanksgiving was a big deal?" she asked him factitiously. "You're not inviting yourself, I'm inviting you."

"You should talk to your mom first. She probably doesn't want extra people for such a big dinner."

"I'll ask, but I know she won't care. You should come, ask your dad." He still looked doubtful. Truthfully, she couldn't stand the idea of having to face her family alone. She didn't want to talk about school or answer questions about what she'd been doing. She'd much rather take the focus off herself. Besides, she came from a fairly large family. Ben's pathetic descriptions of his anticipations for Thanksgiving were depressing. He should come. "My mom's a great cook. I make the stuffed mushrooms and the sweet potatoes. You like mushrooms?"

"Yeah," he admitted with a little smile.

"I put extra Romano cheese in them. And the sweet potatoes…lots of brown sugar, granola and marshmallows on top. They're really good." He didn't answer but he looked like he might sway towards a yes. "My brother Eddie isn't even coming home I don't think, so there's an extra bed right there. And the sofa in the living room opens up too."

"You have a brother?"

She laughed. "I've got three."

Ben looked at her for a moment, and then he laughed too as he seemed to nod his head to himself. "Now I get it."

"Get what?" she asked.

"Why you're always calling me big brother. You miss them."

She let out a sharp laugh. "Hardly!"

"Older or younger?" he asked.

"One older, two younger. Edmund is a junior over at Syracuse. He's on the football team. 'Go Orangemen'. He and my dad are like totally into it. He hopes to go pro. He's going to dinner at his girlfriends' this year. My mom's depressed."

"A junior? So he's *my* age," Ben observed.

She looked at him oddly. "Oh yeah…ew."

"Thanks," he replied with a laugh.

"Then there's Robert. He's 16, annoying, obnoxious and smart as hell. Does way better than me at everything school related and loves making me look like an idiot. He'll probably get a full scholarship and then point out to my parents how much money *I'm* costing them for school.

My little brother Richie is 14. He's sweet…for a teenage boy, I guess. Thank God. One Robbie is bad enough," she assured him.

"I always wished I had brothers."

"Yeah well, come spend the weekend at my house and I guarantee you'll be cured. Ask your dad okay?"

"Yeah, okay. If you clear it at your house first," he told her.

"No problem." She glanced down at her watch. It was after midnight. "I'd better go; I've got Algebra at 8:15 tomorrow morning."

"Yeah, it's late." He walked her to the front door. "I'm glad you came. I hope the movie was…diverting."

"Yeah, thanks. I think I'll still be trying to figure it out tomorrow."

"It does take a few viewings to soak in," he said with a smile as he helped her to put on her coat.

She couldn't help but wonder if Cain had ever seen it, and what he might think. It didn't really seem like his kind of movie on the surface, but she knew the questions it posed and the ideas it explored would be the kind of thing they could spend all night talking about. After a week of misery, she had finally spent over two hours not thinking about and missing him…and now here she was back at square one. Damn.

She sighed and looked back up at Ben as he opened the door for her. "Good night."

Chapter 14 - Have faith

Cain

On the road
Midnight, Saturday

Cain slowed around the curve in the road, wondering again if he should stop for the rest of the night. The weather was likely to get worse before it got better, but he needed to put as much distance between himself and Felicity as possible before stopping; he *really* did. He fought to keep himself from turning back for her even now. He wanted there to be no chance that she might feel and be drawn to him in the coming day.

His love for Felicity seemed a dull and throbbing ache in his heart – its only pathetic and fruitless attempt to beat, irony unfair and cruel. He would gladly trade all of his immortal gifts for a beating heart right now, one that could sustain life and love on its own. If only he had a heart that could beat with no need for unnatural agents designed to persuade and subdue others in a quest for blood; a heart that did not force him to keep himself on a path devoid of personal happiness.

Felicity. He tried again unsuccessfully to force her from his thoughts. She'd said that she had changed her mind. She had wanted to come. She had wanted to give up everything; her family, her friends, her job, her schooling, food, sunlight, her body, her *life*. She was willing to lose it all…for him.

He wasn't worth it.

It had taken every ounce of strength in his body to force himself from her. Oddly enough, it was the vampire within him that had given him the will. It had wanted her. It had wanted to drink from her. It had wanted to drain her. Just being close to her was a struggle now.

The past two nights had been an odd mixture of amazing happiness and torturous temptation. He had drunk from her when she'd allowed, but he had needed to be so careful not to partake beyond the limits. As it was, he was drinking from her far too often to maintain safely for any longer amount of time. The influence of the vampire in him was growing more potent with every drop of human blood that he fed it. He could feel it fighting for dominance within him. He never remembered it being so strong. It was a bit startling.

Most of his life he had been able to ignore the alternate creature within him. He played host to the blood, but he never had to question whether he was in control, while he sustained himself solely on animal blood that is. Human blood seemed to have a more intense effect on his system. It engaged the 'hunting' urges within him. It awoke the predator, and more and more the true vampire was emerging. It was subtle still, as he recognized the warning signs long before an outside eye could observe them, but the vampires' power could grow quickly…he knew.

He was unsure just what made the difference. It was not necessarily the blood itself, but most likely, the act of drinking from a host. He needed to change to drink from a victim, that was a strong determining factor in his control, he was sure. The more he let the vampire out, the more it wanted to be free of his human restraint. There was no need to change his visage when drinking from a cup.

The fact that he was using his venom again fueled the creature within him as well. It gave him territory. It asserted his dominance over other, younger vampires. It gave him a sense of his power.

All of these things contributed to his unsettledness. He was beginning to feel as though his careful hold upon his situation was beginning to slip away. Was it age that strengthened his blood? Perhaps it was the infusions of vampire blood he'd received from Sindy. If some of it stayed within him as he had speculated, rather than dissipating over time, then blood from Sindy would make a difference. Large or slight he was unsure.

The vampire was strong, but he had to have faith in himself and believe that the man in him was stronger. Drinking from Felicity was so difficult now. He felt as though he needed to bargain with his inner beast. He had to fight to stop, before it went too far. *Let her go,* he would command himself, speaking silently to the vampire within. *Let her go, or so help me you will never drink again.*

Sometimes it frightened him to address his alter ego as though it had a mind of its own, but at times like this it often helped, better to have an adversary to fight. He was unsure if the perception was valid. It didn't matter, so long as he won in the end.

He had done it. He had left. Felicity would live, assuming her rightful place in the world. He wanted to feel proud of his strength and a sense of accomplishing something good and right. At the moment, the only feelings he was aware of, were thirst and despair.

The snow was coming down thickly now. The road before him was lost behind a sheet of white. Time to stop. He tried to think where he would stay. He had hoped to get further than this. Perhaps it would only be a short delay before he could travel on ahead of the dawn.

He pulled to the side of the road as an unsettling but necessary thought came upon him. Sindy; she really was the very last person that he wanted to think of or see right now, but he was leaving. He would not return to this town, not for a very long time, if ever. He couldn't return, the temptation to visit Felicity would be too great. She needed time to move on, and so did he.

But he couldn't just leave without giving Sindy some sort of clue as to where he might be found in the future. He had thought of this earlier, but hadn't wanted to see Sindy until after everything with Felicity was complete. Now he wished he had just spoken to her days ago and been done with it. He really had no desire to see her tonight, but he couldn't just leave. Vampires are nomads by nature and not easily tracked down once separated by great distance. However much he did not want her with him now…forever was a long time.

He sighed, fought the sick feeling inside him, and set about trying to find a way to bring her to him. Sindy no longer carried his venom within her, so this would not be easy to accomplish quickly. He revealed his trace; although it was doubtful he would just happen to be in her range. He was not in the habit of letting his presence be known, so anyone who wanted to see him would hopefully take notice and come to him now; not something he wanted to rely on though. He could wait all night without her coming into range. He wanted to get this over with and leave.

Perhaps he should try to summon her psychically. He had originally assumed that this was not an option because his venom was gone from her now, but what about blood? He had never allowed her to drink from him; she carried nothing of him now, but what did he have of her? He had drunk from her…many times. Most of her blood should be gone from him by now, but what if some of it *did* stay? There must be some accumulative effect. Otherwise, little drinks over time should not have been so devastating to Eileen, as he had relayed in his story to Felicity. He had even speculated earlier that perhaps some part of Sindy's blood had stayed with him, strengthening the vampire influence already so firmly entrenched in his body.

A blood tie was a thing not easily broken. Perhaps it would give him the connection that he needed to bring her to him now. Nothing to do but to try. He would do his best to summon her and see. The force and turmoil of the emotions within him at the moment certainly should help. His despair over leaving Felicity lent power to his call even as he tried his best not to think of and dwell upon his loss. Even if not well controlled, just the fact that he was uncloaked and the force of his sorrow should be strong enough to draw some notice. He worried briefly that Felicity might somehow 'pick-up' the summons that he was sending out, but then dismissed it from his mind. He knew that he was not very psychically skilled and Felicity wasn't at all, if not through his venom – which did have a definite and limited range. He was a fair distance from Felicity now.

But Sindy was a vampire, and a very psychically skilled one at that. She did not give herself very much credit for having great range, but Cain thought that she was mistaken in that. He was certain that she had psychic skills far greater than she had yet realized. He had known many vampires, and almost none of them ever realized their potential; but those few who did, truly amazed him. He'd a feeling Sindy was going to enter that category some day, if she didn't get herself killed first. She certainly knew more of summoning skills than he did. He would try his best to attune his summons only to her and hopefully she would receive and acknowledge it.

This was probably going to take a while. He walked his motorcycle to the overpass just ahead and parked underneath it so that he would not continue to be covered in snow. The wait seemed interminable. All the time, he tried to think of Sindy and his need to see her before he left. He tried to convey his impatience and the strength of his desire to accomplish his will and be done. He tried to concentrate on the task at hand, to keep from calling up the image of Felicity to his mind, but his hope to speak with Sindy was poor substitute to cover how badly he felt about abandoning Felicity. Even when he sought to call up Sindy's image for the summons, only Felicity's sweet tear streaked face came to mind.

She had cried. He'd known she would, but worse than that, she had seemed desperate and betrayed. She had run after him in a display of recklessness resulting from her despair. Somehow, he had remained strong, but to see her so drastically stricken by his decision had broken his heart.

He stood huddled under the overpass, leaning against the warm engine of his bike. He had the sudden strong desire for a cigarette. Not that he had one, but if he did, it might help. He hadn't smoked in years. It was never something that he had been seriously committed to, but had only sampled during grief stricken periods in his life, or more precisely, times when he had needed to consciously fight against the thirst. It was usually worst after a blood relationship ended. Smoking helped…a little. He didn't find it very pleasant really. It's not as though he was worried over lung cancer or emphysema, he just didn't really care for it; but it was something to do, something to focus on, a diversion. Nicotine was a poison for the vampire blood to withdraw and expel from his body, like the alcohol he sometimes drank. He almost imagined it as a device to keep the vampire blood occupied, so that other cravings might go unnoticed.

He would have to pick up a pack of cigarettes the next time he passed a mini-mart. Where the hell was Sindy? He really just wanted to get this over with so that he could leave. Although where he would be able to go in this storm, he was unsure. He tried to have patience. He had to trust that she could sense him. He certainly did not relish the idea of having to actually go and seek her out. She had to know he was here waiting for her; she just *had* to feel his call. Even if she did, she was probably delayed by the snow as well. He would wait just a little longer. It's not as though he could get very far until the snow stopped anyway.

He suddenly had the fear that *she* had left without informing him. Perhaps she had left town and was already some great distance away. He hadn't seen Sindy since the night in the gym when Felicity had been attacked. Her cloaking had become flawless, so he had not sensed her since. The vampire she had left with (his name had turned out to be Roger) had kept her company for a while he was sure, but while Cain had felt Roger's presence here and there afterwards, he hadn't been around at all recently, not that Cain had paid much attention to him. Sindy could be with him now someplace far from here, or they might have parted company. He had no way to know, and couldn't say that he cared, except that he was disturbed by the idea that he might never see her again.

He tried to analyze why. He couldn't really convince himself that he cared all that much for her. Things might be easier if he did, but it was Felicity that he loved. No one else would fill that need for him now, but he did care about Sindy as a person. Truthfully, although she would probably never want to admit it, he suspected that she needed him. She had shown some small flicker of desire to change her life. Surprisingly, as far as he knew, she wasn't drinking from humans any more. That was a great accomplishment, worth being proud of.

He had shown her the way, just as he had countless others but she had actually listened. Most other vampires did not follow his advice as he would hope. They might sample butcher-bought blood to appease him, but always found it lacking. The hunt satisfied not only their thirst, but relieved their boredom as well. The most he could accomplish with the majority of those he met, was to teach them not to kill. He would help them to master the art of leaving a victim before drinking them to death, and living off two or three little drinks a night instead of one kill. It was distasteful to him, but better than the alternative. At least their victims were left alive.

Actually, Sindy had been a vampire that he had been almost convinced that he could not change. He had taught her not to kill, but he'd never dreamed that she would follow his practice of surviving off purchased animal blood. As strong as she was, if she were to attempt to continue her abstinence from humans, she would probably need some support now and then. He needed to be there for her. She had proven herself to be so much stronger a person than he had ever expected. He did have faith in her ability to change, but he could not just disappear and hope for the best. It would undermine all he had worked for. He wished she would show up already.

Thoughts of Felicity again tried to creep into his unoccupied mind. He hoped she could be happy. She would be. Of course, she would. Was he so pompous and naïve as to think that she couldn't be happy without him?

But could *he* be happy without *her?*

That didn't matter. That had never mattered. Happiness was not his goal. He was doing the right thing. He was doing what was right for her and he was going back to his own self-appointed duties as well.

He would find those in need of help and he would guide them; that in itself should be fulfilling. It did bestow some small happiness to know that he was making a difference. He was doing good in the world. He was doing the right thing. He should just forget Felicity now, but somehow he knew that although he might travel the globe... Though he might meet and change the lives of many others that he would encounter... No one would make him happy the way that she did. All of the grand sights and experiences of the world would not compare to time spent snuggled next to her, sharing whispered secrets and laughter under the covers in his bed. She saw him differently than others did. She seemed to see through everything...his power, his age, his venom, his guilt, his sins...she looked right through it and saw the man inside.

A sad little smile came to his face before he could try to reprimand himself and hide his feelings away again. She loved him. *Him.*

Irrelevant. It was good that he was leaving, good for her. She thought she knew what she wanted, but she had such limited perspective. To live for eternity as a vampire, giving up her human life... He could not let her make such a decision based on young love and naiveté. It would be irresponsible and selfish on his part. She was unready. But maybe...someday...

He tried to squash the thought even as it came upon him, but it was too late. The seed of the idea was already there within him.

Give her time. Let her *live*. She should have a chance to experience life on her own as he had intended, and she would.

But that did not mean that he should *never* see her again.

What if he did come back, just to *see* her, to see that she was alright, that she was getting along well in the world as he had hoped she would?

Not right away of course. Even *he* could not inflict such torture upon himself, but at some point in the future. He could come back, to see what she was doing with her life, to see that she was happy.

Just to...look in on her from time to time. Once she was older, once she knew more about what the world really had to offer...what if she *wasn't* happy? What if she really did wish that he had chosen otherwise? Well, things might be different *then*, might they not?

"You called?"

Sindy's voice cut through the blustering wind like a sultry whisper in his ear. He barely managed to steel himself not to jump with a guilty start.

He turned, expecting to see her in one of her revealing little dresses. Although vampires could feel the cold, it didn't trouble them much. Most younger ones didn't bother to dress for it. Stupid give away on their part. Any human would have found the lack of a coat very inappropriate out here in the snow. Sindy was smart; she must have come to the same conclusion. She was covered in a very long and sumptuous black fur coat. The thing looked inordinately garish on her in his eyes.

She smiled at him as she clutched it closed at the top near her throat against the wind. He got the impression she liked the feel of the fur in her fingers more than she truly held it against the weather. "What are you pullin' me all the way out here for? Would it have killed you to get a room first?"

He looked away from her into the snow as his despair tried to return. How could he have ever believed that he could spend his time with *her* and be satisfied? But that was unfair. Those had been the thoughts in his mind before he had ever laid eyes upon or let himself get close to Felicity. He had not really seen Sindy that way in a long time. The feeling showed no signs of returning at the moment. He looked back upon her face.

At least his call had worked. She was obviously pleased to be summoned by him, no matter how she might complain or pretend to be annoyed. His unhappiness was not her fault. She was just a young girl trying to find her way; however misguided she may have been in the past. It was his duty to teach and help her just as he did for others like her.

"So, you just gonna stand there and look at me? Not that I mind, but if you want, I could give you a little more to see." She gave him a sly smile and seemed to threaten that she would open her coat. Just what was she wearing under there anyway?

He shook his head at her lightly. He glanced about to see how she might have arrived, but the night held no clue. "You here alone?"

"Yeah. I like to have you all to myself."

He let out a small breath of a laugh. "And Roger?"

"Oh, I lost him nights ago. Too wishy-washy. Turns out he was just lookin' for someone new to follow. You know, someone to give him orders and tell him what to do with his life."

"Sounds like you were a perfect match."

She chuckled. "Yeah, you'd think, but it's getting' old. I told him if he was lookin' for a leader, he should pay Arif a call. I'm outta the biz. Turns out I prefer a man who already knows where he's goin'."

He dropped his eyes to see the tips of her toes just poking out from beneath the hem of her fur coat in the snow. Hadn't she bothered to don shoes? "I'm leaving."

He definitely caught her interest with that news. It took a moment for her to realize the implication. Then the artifice left her features and she looked at him with honest interest. "Is that right?" She gave him a small but hopeful smile. "Want some company?"

"No. I really don't."

He felt cruel as her face fell. She quickly composed herself again into the confident seductress she liked to portray. He spoke again before she even had the chance to try to tempt him with some indecent proposition or lewd remark. "*Right now,* I just want to be alone in the world." He sighed. "But the world is a big place. It's all too easy to lose someone. Unfortunately, losing *myself* to anonymity is a luxury that I haven't got at the moment. Right now, I have others who count on me. Perhaps you're one of them." He felt himself getting tangled up in words. He stopped speaking and stared out into the night to clear his mind. Keep it simple. He reached into his pocket and drew out the paper he had written earlier. He handed it over to Sindy who looked at it rather oddly.

The gesture very much reminded him of Arif's man Kieran, giving him the card with a cell phone number printed on it. A direct line to Arif's coven, should he ever again wish contact. He wondered by the look on Sindy's face if Arif had treated her to the same information. She looked as though she were experiencing déjà vu.

His note did not hold a cell phone number though. He never carried electronic devices. Silly as it seemed, recent technologies rather scared him. It was too much, too fast. Looking into store windows filled with computers, i-Pod's, and fax machines made him feel so alien and disconnected from society. He had a basic understanding of their purpose, but shied away from such things when possible. He had no desire to understand that aspect of the world. His habit of reading the newspaper to scan for evidence of vampire activity kept him current enough. Leave the technology to those who wished it. He had no need for such 'modern conveniences'.

Sindy studied the scrap of paper as he spoke to explain it. "It's a house address. I own it. As much as I would prefer to go into seclusion for a while, I'll have to be there for a bit. I'm meeting someone. Something tells me that I may be called upon to play the mentor for a while longer. If you'd like, you can join us.

Make no mistake; it's an invitation for knowledge and camaraderie…nothing more. I won't be there until December. I do need *some* time for myself, but after that, I'll be playing teacher again. You should stop by. I have a feeling you might find it very…interesting.

Or don't. I can't say how long we'll stay. Not more than a month or two, I'd imagine. Still…if you come, I can give you an idea as to where I might be found in the future. If you ever need help…or if you just want to talk. I don't know, perhaps you would rather I just be lost." He lowered his eyes, unsure what else to say. It's not as though he were offering her much. Actually, it probably sounded rather arrogant and rude considering…

"Thanks. You'll see me again. Not that I *need* anything…but maybe *you* need someone. I'm not gonna pretend I'm a very good listener but…I could be there for you, if you want. Who knows, maybe there's a thing or two that *I* could teach *you*."

He had a hard time meeting her eyes. He didn't want to think about the future. The present was bad enough. "I've gotta go."

He didn't really wait for a response. He got on the Harley and started up the engine. The snow seemed to be drifting off now and it looked as though he would be able to continue riding until the dawn.

He still didn't really know where he was going, just away. He would drive until the dawn forced him to seek shelter and then he would continue the journey tomorrow night. He would travel and spend his time clearing his head, preparing to move on. He would be 'the wanderer' until the time came to go and meet Mattie and he was forced to deal with the world again.

He revved the engine and looked back to see Sindy standing there watching him silently. It was only then, that he thought to wonder again where she had come from. How had she gotten here? He'd called her out onto this desolate road that led out of town into nowhere.

She was just standing there clutching her fur coat and looking stark and black against the white snow. "You need a ride?"

She just stared at him for a minute, her lips pursed and her expression contemplative. She looked like she was trying to figure him out. A little smirk came upon her face. Perhaps she already had, and found him amusing in some way. "No."

She turned and walked off into the night, her long black fur coat making a little sweeping arc, and then a trail in the snow. He watched her progress towards town until he could no longer pick out her black form, swallowed by the darkness.

He turned to face his own path forward. The road before him looked very dim and unpromising, but he had faced such roads before in his life. He never knew where they would lead…but he had faith. This was his path, chosen for him with a higher purpose. However difficult it was to accept, he had to believe that everything happens for a reason.

He would make every effort to do what he felt was right, and pray that he would have the strength to do it again tomorrow.

Chapter 15 - Things change

Felicity

Felicity's dorm room
11:30, Monday night

Felicity lay in bed trying to fall asleep. She'd actually come to bed over an hour ago, but sleep wouldn't come. It was the same every night. All she could think of was Cain.

Where was he now? Nine nights he'd been gone, nine whole nights. He could be almost anywhere by now; someplace far, far away. Did he think about her? Did he miss her even half as much as she missed him?

It was getting better. Not that she really *wanted* to let him go, but everyday life was getting a little easier. She was going to class, going to work, keeping busy and forgetting to be depressed for a while, but night-time…night-time sucked. She would lay awake in bed and that's when her heart would ache. Somewhere he was waking up, getting dressed and getting ready to head out into the night. Where was he going? Who was he with? Was he alone? She didn't want him to be unhappy, but she really hoped that he was alone. Was that cruel?

Maybe she should be hoping that he had someone else. A friend. Someone to talk to, to take his mind off things and help him go on, but she knew him. He didn't have things in his life to divert him the way that she did. He isolated himself from others, on purpose. The only friend she knew he had was Mattie, and obviously *he* was still off with Alyson. Eventually Cain would look for other vampires who might need his help, but right now, she was almost certain that he was alone. Her tragic and tortured hero…that was what he seemed in her mind.

Of course, every time she came to this conclusion and convinced herself that he was sitting alone somewhere, depressed and missing her, another darker thought tried to intrude... Sindy.

Those first few nights after Cain had left, she could think of nothing but the heartache and unfairness of losing him, but soon after, she had begun to wonder where all of the other vampires had gone. She knew that Arif and his followers had left, Cain had told her so, but were there others? Would she ever see another vampire?

She was still marked; she would be for a while, so she really hadn't anything to worry about on that level. She'd certainly gotten quite a bit of venom into her system before Cain had left. Her mark shouldn't fade until mid-December probably. She still had the vial as well. So come the time that her mark did fade, she could always start wearing the vial again. There was no one left who should be interested in her anyway.

But what about Sindy? She wouldn't have gone with Arif. She had seemed very angry with him over the whole 'Chris thing'. She had left the gymnasium with another vampire. Where were they now? Were they still hanging around here? As unsettling as that might seem, she almost hoped that they were. She wished she would spot them somewhere, just so that she would know, because if they weren't here, then there was a chance that they had gone off to follow Cain.

Felicity knew that Sindy wanted him. No matter who else she was with, Sindy wanted Cain. Even if only to prove that she could get him to want her back, and then move on. It's not that Felicity never wanted Cain to ever look at another woman…well, okay, she didn't really want him to, but she knew that eventually he would. She could grudgingly accept that…but *Sindy*?

Then again, what if Sindy wasn't following Cain? What if she was hanging around here? Felicity would be happy to know that they weren't together, but having her here would not really be such a good thing either. What if now that Cain was out of the way, Sindy decided to renew her quest to turn Ben? Or what if she went after Felicity, just for spite?

No. She couldn't think that way. Sindy didn't want to risk Cain's disapproval. She wasn't here anyway. Felicity would have seen her. If there were any other vampires in the area at the moment, they were keeping themselves well hidden. That was just fine with her.

Cain's friendship with Mattie came to mind again. How close were they? Did they see each other regularly? Probably not often, but Cain did say that they kept in touch.

After Allie got back, maybe Felicity could even meet Mattie. She could talk to him and convince him that she needed to see Cain again. She could have another chance.

A chance for what? For Cain to tell her no again?

What if he didn't? What if seeing her again after being apart was enough to wear him down, enough for him to agree to change her? What then? Was that really what she wanted? Cain had said no for a reason. He had really felt that he was doing the right thing. Shouldn't she trust his judgment…even though it hurt?

One thing at a time. She didn't even know if she would get to see Mattie. What if she didn't? What if Allie wouldn't take her to meet him? What if Allie didn't come back at all?

That made her think of Ben. Poor Ben, waiting all this time to fix things between him and Allie. What if she didn't come back? He'd be devastated. It was his own stupid fault for being so stubborn and not talking to her before she left, but Felicity knew that in a way it was only because he cared so much that he'd been angry with Allie in the first place. She hoped Allie came back.

In the meantime, she would have to convince Ben that he and his dad should have Thanksgiving at her house. Allie didn't seem likely to return in time and Felicity couldn't stand the thought of Ben having Thanksgiving dinner alone with his dad. They didn't seem to have a very close relationship and Alyson's absence would stand out that much more, making things so hard on him.

Besides, she had spoken to her mother on the phone about it the other night. Her mom was fine with the idea. In fact, she was very happy to have guests, since her brother Eddie wasn't coming home for the holiday weekend.

Felicity would be very happy to give her parents someone else to focus on as well. It had been hard enough getting out of having to come home this weekend. Her parents were getting suspicious that she had been totally avoiding them. Maybe Felicity should have just gone home, but she really didn't want to have to deal with questions about what she'd been so busy doing these past weeks. The scar on her throat was much improved – thank you Cain! – but you could still see it if you really looked. If she waited until Thanksgiving, her aunt and uncle would be there with her cousins for added distraction and things would be too busy for anyone to notice. She didn't want anyone to try to really sit her down for serious questioning. If she brought home guests to take some of the spotlight, so much the better.

She'd have to speak to Ben about it at lunch tomorrow. She hadn't seen him today; he had an extra physics lab every other Monday.

These thoughts buzzed around her head and before she realized it, Felicity had fallen asleep. For the first time since he had left, she had fallen asleep without tears in her eyes over Cain.

~~~~~~~~~~~~~~~~~~~~~~~~~~~~~~

Felicity woke up in a fairly good mood. She attended her English class and somehow managed to do very well on a pop quiz, leaving the class in reasonably good spirits. Then she got to History class. She took one look at the board and wished she could leave.

They were beginning a new topic. 'England in the 17th Century: The Struggle between King and Parliament'. It didn't really sound like anything she would be all that interested in, but that was not the problem.

17th Century England. How was she going to study that and not think of Cain? He was born there, that was the start of his life! He had sat and had discussions at his dinner table with his father and brother over the very topic! It was why his father hadn't wanted him to leave England. Not only was this going to be difficult and frustrating, she couldn't help but wish that they could have studied it earlier. Then she could have just asked him what had happened and been done with it! This was not going to be a class to look forward to.

When the professor finally let them go, her mind was hopelessly muddled with thoughts of Cain again. 'What was the social climate of England at that time? What do you think the common man thought of such controversies? How about Nobles and Lords? And how did religious beliefs come into play?' *Thanks a lot teach.*

Ben had already gotten them a table when she arrived at the cafeteria. She dumped her stuff with barely a word and got on line.

She came back with her sandwich tray and sat down with a thud.

Ben just watched her for a moment. When she started to unwrap her sandwich and it was obvious that she wasn't planning to exchange pleasantries, he decided to go first. "Hi!"

"Hi," she replied with barely a glance.

"How ya' doin'?" he asked.

"Fine," she answered shortly.

He stared at her for a minute while she started eating her lunch. "What's new?" he asked with a humorous little lilt to his voice. He was teasing her for her clipped response. She didn't answer, she just gave him an annoyed look and took a sip from her water bottle. "Not much for conversation these days are ya'?" She just shrugged and took another bite of her sandwich. "That's okay. It's still better than sittin' with *them*," Ben said, jerking his thumb towards his friends at another table across the room.

They looked like they were laughing and having fun. She felt bad that Ben felt obligated to sit here and try to cheer her up instead. "Sorry. I'm just having a rough morning. You probably would be happier sitting with them," she said, as she looked away and took another bite from her sandwich.

"Na, spoil my lunch. You're much easier on the eyes."

She tried to smile but it didn't really work with a mouth full of chicken salad. She knew he was just trying to distract her, to make her feel better and take her mind off things. She resolved to let him. After she swallowed, she looked up and gave him a real smile. He seemed relieved to have pulled her out of her funk. He gave her a smile back, and then went on with a new conversation…business as usual.

"So remember when you first got your car, you asked me if I'd help you fix it up?"

"Oh yeah. You don't have to, it's okay. I'll probably just ding it up anyway. The parking here is impossible."

He laughed with a little cringe. "Remind me to never lend you *my* car. I was thinkin'…I know it's minor but, what kind of stereo have you got?"

She shrugged. *What kind?* "I don't know."

"CD?" he inquired.

"Tape deck," she clarified.

He nodded as he ate his sandwich. "Well I got a new one a little while back. You want my old one?"

She shook her head a little, as she finished a gulp from her water bottle. "That's okay."

"You might as well take it. It's got a CD player and it's just sittin' on a shelf in my garage. There's nothin' wrong with it."

"So why'd you get a new one?"

"Multi-disc."

She grinned. "Was that before or after you decided to start saving money and concentrating on important stuff?"

He responded to her little smirk with a steady gaze and a little smile of his own. "Before. You want it? I'll put it in for you."

"Okay. If you don't mind. Thanks." With her mind off history, she suddenly remembered what she had been waiting to tell him. "I talked to my mom last night, about Thanksgiving. She's fine with it."

Ben immediately seemed to avoid her eyes and concentrate a little too intently on his food. "Oh, yeah...I don't know."

"Did you ask your dad?" she asked.

"I mentioned it," he told her vaguely.

Her shoulders slumped. "He's not cool with it, huh?"

"Are you kidding? He was relieved. See, if I have another offer, then he doesn't even have to pretend to feel guilty when something comes up at the last minute and he has to skip out."

"On *Thanksgiving?*" she asked incredulously.

"He does that. It's no big deal. It's just Thanksgiving. Some people don't even see it as a real holiday."

She stared at him across the table. "People *I* know do."

He looked back at her with a derisive little laugh. "You know people who were *at* the first Thanksgiving."

"Funny. You're off by a couple of decades, but nice try. So are you coming?" she nudged.

He went back to trying to be evasive and very interested in his lunch. "I don't know. I might just hang around here."

"What for? If your dad's not even going to be around…" He wouldn't look at her. She changed to a softer tone and tried to get him to meet her eyes. "You're still hopin' Allie'll show up, aren't you?"

He finally did look up at her. He seemed very sadly hopeful, like a little kid asking if there really was a Santa Claus. "I know she's late, but she's got to come back for Thanksgiving right? We *always* spend it together, it's like a tradition." Oh, wow. He almost looked as though he were holding back rising tears. "We make stupid stuff like chicken fingers and macaroni and cheese."

Felicity couldn't help but laugh a little at the thought, but was quickly sobered again by his forlorn and hopeful look. "I don't know."

Ben began to really look upset. "I went to Tommy's after work last night. Allie quit."

"She came back?" Felicity asked anxiously.

"No, over the phone. She wouldn't even tell him anything. She just said 'it was time to move on'. What does that even mean?"

"I don't know," she admitted quietly.

He sat up a little straighter and seemed to pull it together. "Her rent's paid up for the next two months, and all of her stuff is still there…I have a key." Felicity just sat looking at the table. Did that really mean anything? Ben continued, looking for reassurance. "So she's gotta come back, right?" Felicity shrugged. What could she say? Ben gazed at her, desperately serious as he asked, "Would *you* have?"

She couldn't look at him. She thought of the night Cain had left. Ben had found her out in the parking lot and tried to comfort her. What had she told him? She could barely remember the words. She knew she had been hysterical. She had told Ben that Cain had left. What else had she said? She was pretty sure that in her daze she had told Ben that 'he said no'. Would Ben even remember or know what that meant? Probably. He was pretty savvy.

As he looked at her now, he seemed shaken. "Let me guess, you don't know."

They sat in awkward silence for a moment as she avoided his eyes. There was no point in saying any more on the subject. There was nothing to say. She forced herself to start eating again, instead of giving over to tears as she'd like. Thinking of that night had made her eyes go all watery and brought a lump to her throat. She stared at the table until her vision cleared and wouldn't look at Ben until he continued with his lunch as well.

After a few minutes, she went back to the original question as though uninterrupted. "I doubt my mom would be keen on chicken fingers, but I can make macaroni and cheese if you want." She finally lifted her eyes to meet his. He didn't seem to want to accept her attempt to lighten things. "You've got to come to my house for Thanksgiving Ben."

"Why? Because you feel bad for me, sittin' alone in my empty house waitin' for somebody who might not even show?"

"No. I do…but that's not why I want you to come."

He just sat there looking at her for a second. "It's not? Then why?"

"Because, Thanksgiving is supposed to be for spending time with people that you care about. And if you don't have other obligations, then I'd like you to come."

"Really?"

"Well, sure. I know I haven't been very good company lately. I've been kind of moody. I hardly talk to you these days and when I do I'm either distant or I snap at you. I'm surprised you take it."

"I've had a lot of practice… I'm friends with Allie," he reminded her.

They both laughed. "Well you're a good friend, and I'm kinda thankful for that. If it means anything, you'll notice that you're the only person that I actually *sit* with while I eat my lunch in a bad mood and ignore everyone."

He nodded. "I was kind of hoping that counted for something."

"It counts for a lot. Thanks…for understanding…and being my friend." She thought again, of how he'd tried to comfort her after Cain had left. He really was sweet. She was lucky to have such a good friend. He'd never even asked her to talk about it. "Although I must say…there *is* something that's been kind of bothering me."

"What?" he asked.

"Well, about Cain… I've been waiting for you to say '*I told ya' so.*' It's been hanging over my head. Makes me very 'on edge'. You should just say it and get it over with."

He gave a little laugh at her abrupt tone. He looked at her quietly for a moment before answering. "I wasn't going to. You'd think I'd like to… but to be honest I just feel really bad that it's been so hard on you. Kinda sucks the fun out of it." She shook her head with a little laugh. "So, you can consider yourself 'off edge'."

She gave him a tentative smile. "Well that's a relief," she said jokingly. "So, I have to leave tomorrow night. You coming?"

"I have to work. I'm closing with the new girl."

"Oh yeah. Have you met her?"

"Yeah. Her name's Candy, or Brandy…something like that."

Felicity giggled. "Mr. Penten said it's Mandy. Lucy trained her, so if she screws up don't blame me." Ben chuckled. "What's she like?"

He just shrugged. "She's okay I guess. Anyway, I don't know if you want to get such a late start tomorrow night. Maybe you should just go without me."

"Trust me; I'm not all that eager. A late start sounds just fine. Unless you really don't *want* to come.

Ben thought about it for a minute. "All right. Mr. Penten's going to have to do some schedule shifting, but if you really want me to, I'll come."

She grinned. "Good. Ask your dad again too. Maybe he'll surprise you."

"Yeah, I doubt it. Where do you live anyway, is it far?"

"A little under two hours."

"We're talkin' farm country right?"

"A little, but we're on kind of a steep mountain, so it's mostly woods."

"Dirt roads?" he inquired.

She looked at him oddly that he should ask. "A few."

"Yeah okay, let's take *your* car."

She laughed. "Okay but if you want to listen to decent music you'll have to put the stereo in tonight."

"I can't I'm closing with you, remember? That's okay. I guess I can suffer through two hours of actually having to talk, as long as you promise not to be all moody."

She smiled and nodded. "Promise".

~~~~~~~~~~~~~~~~~~~~~~~~~~~~~

Ben was right, his dad wouldn't come. He'd said that since Ben had other plans, he was going to spend the long weekend in the city and get some extra work done. That's what Ben told her anyway. Felicity never actually met him. According to Ben, his dad had a little apartment there. He worked late hours, so he did overnights a lot. Felicity couldn't imagine why anyone would want to commute all the way to New York City from here anyway.

So it was just she and Ben. He insisted that they stop at Allie's before they left so that he could tape a note to her door with Felicity's phone number on it. He said he'd taped one to his door at home and his window as well. That sounded kind of odd, but he assured her that if Allie came around, *that* was the note she'd see. She usually came over late and she never went to the door. She'd been climbing in his window for years.

By the time they got home to Felicity's house, it was almost eleven-thirty. After introductions, Felicity was able to set Ben up in her brother's unused room and then go right to bed.

The next day was busy as expected. Her aunt and uncle arrived with her cousins, 9-year-old twins John and Jenna and 6-year-old Kevin, turning the house into happy chaos. Felicity was given cooking tasks to help her mom and aunt with, so Ben was left to socialize with the guys. They had the football game on. She felt a little bad for Ben; he said he liked football, but she knew he wasn't *that* into it. She hoped he wasn't bored.

Her dad was such a sports fanatic. When they'd arrived last night, he'd asked Ben what sort of team he was on at school. Felicity had tried to cover any awkwardness for him. "Dad, not everyone is a sports nut."

Ben had seemed unfazed though. He'd just answered 'the debate team', with a smile. Now her dad and her uncle were parked in front of the TV watching football games as her brother Richie tried to teach her cousins how to play a card game on the floor. From the kitchen, Felicity could see that Ben had resorted to talking to *Robbie*.

After a while, Ben came into the kitchen to see if they needed any help. Her mom had given him a big smile and told him they were just fine and he should go relax. Felicity caught his arm to whisper to him before he left, "Unless you're lookin' for something to do. I hope you're not too bored."

"Not at all. I've been talking to Robbie. We're getting along great."

Felicity looked at him dubiously and she noticed that her mom seemed a little surprised as well. Robert usually had to be forced to be social with guests. In fact, even her mom would admit that he was often rather rude. "Really? What are you talking about?"

"His criminal justice class. He's a smart kid," he answered, and then returned to the living room to finish their discussion.

Felicity gave a pained look to her mom and aunt. "Oh no. He's been turned."

Her aunt laughed. "Maybe it's the other way around. Maybe your friend Ben has found a way to tame the beast."

Her mom laughed as well. "I'd say that makes him a keeper."

Felicity just rolled her eyes and shook her head. Both her mom and aunt knew very well that she and Ben were just friends.

Dinner went well, with easy conversation and delicious food. Felicity couldn't help but be delighted by Ben's grin when she brought out macaroni and cheese along with the other side dishes she had made.

The next morning at breakfast, her mom began asking questions. She wanted to know how Felicity was doing in school and remarked that she hoped all of the extra studying she had been doing would reflect in her grades. Felicity quietly murmured that she hoped so too. Although for her grades to reflect the number of times she had used studying as an excuse not to come home would take a miracle. Ben tried to soften things for her. "The first semester is always the hardest. I know she's got some tough professors."

Then her mom remarked to Ben that Mr. Penten must be pretty tough as well…demanding such long hours every weekend. Felicity had tried to cover Ben's confused look. "Yeah, the store's been kind of short-handed."

Felicity stood and looked to Ben, who seemed done with his breakfast. "You finished?" He nodded and she took his plate and brought it to the sink.

Her mom seemed to know that she was trying to avoid any more conversation. "You kids have plans for today?"

"Yes, actually we do."

Ben looked understandably confused. "We do?"

"Uh-huh. Come on."

He looked at her questioningly as they left the kitchen. She smiled. "You owe me a Monopoly rematch."

Ben laughed as she led him to the upstairs hall game closet. She stood before it with her hands on her hips in annoyance. "It should be in here. I know we have it."

"That's okay. We can play something else."

Just then, Robert came up the stairs and began to head towards his room when Felicity stopped him. "Robbie, don't we have Monopoly?"

He stopped to give her an irritated look as though she were keeping him from something. "Yeah."

"It's not in here," she told him.

"Do I care?" he asked facetiously. Felicity gave him a withering look. Robbie glanced at Ben and then back to Felicity. "What do you want it for anyway?"

"*For to play it.*"

"Yeah right. Pretty flimsy cover. Why don't you just go make out in your room like normal people?"

He turned and stalked down the hall to his bedroom as Felicity felt her face quickly turning red. She spoke quietly to Ben without really looking at him. "Okay, let's pretend like that wasn't at all embarrassing."

Before Ben could answer, Richie approached. Felicity was grateful for the distraction. "Richie do you know where the Monopoly game is?"

"Yeah, it's in my room. You want it?" he asked.

"Please."

Richie brought the game out to them and then looked very surprised when they asked if he wanted to play, as though he didn't think that they would want to include him. Felicity assured him that it was fine, and the three of them played together. It took the better part of the afternoon but they had a good time.

Actually, it was Richie who won. Felicity suspected that Ben had let him, but he wouldn't admit it. She lost miserably…again. Something Ben had fun teasing her over. She pointed out that *he* hadn't won either, but he said that the important thing was that he hadn't lost *to her*. Men.

Come Saturday afternoon, they were watching TV when the phone rang. Felicity's mom called into the living room that it was for her. Over the course of the weekend, Felicity had noticed that Ben had checked his cell phone dozens of times and always seemed to freeze at the sound of the house telephone. He was waiting to hear from Allie. Now he looked at her with hopeful expectancy as she picked up the phone.

"Hello? Oh…hi Deidre." She gave Ben an apologetic little shrug and he sat back down by the TV as she took the call. Deidre was determined that they get together tonight. When Felicity explained that Ben was there, Deidre became very excited at the prospect of Felicity having a new boyfriend. Although she was disappointed that they probably wouldn't want her tagging along if they went out tonight.

Felicity explained that she and Ben weren't romantically involved and Deidre became excited again. They should all go out together, for pizza or something! It would be good to get out of the house. Felicity agreed to talk to Ben about it and call her back. Ben had told her that he was up for anything she wanted…so pizza it was.

Later, when they picked Deidre up, Felicity was happy to see that her friend had toned down the eye shadow a bit from the last time they had seen each other. Her sweater was rather tight, with a very low cut v-neck, but actually, Deidre looked very pretty tonight. She was obviously quite impressed with Ben. She proceeded to flirt with him madly over the entire course of the evening.

At first Felicity wasn't really sure what Ben thought of her friend. He was very friendly to her and didn't seem to mind the attention, so Felicity tried to fade back a bit and give them more of a chance to talk; Ben kept pulling her back into the conversation though.

Before long it became clear to Felicity that Ben was just being nice to Deidre, and he really wasn't interested. Unfortunately, Deidre didn't seem to get the message. Felicity discreetly tried to get her friend to tone it down but Deidre refused to acknowledge her.

At one point, Deidre actually *asked* Ben if he had a girlfriend. She then went on before Ben could answer. "Obviously you don't or you wouldn't be coming home with *Felicity* for Thanksgiving, but still…" She sucked in a little hiss of breath and gave Ben her best seductive smile. "You're a really good lookin' guy Ben. You're a Junior right? Freshman girls must be positively falling all over themselves for you."

Ben looked down with a humble little smile. Felicity answered sarcastically for him, "Yeah. It's a wonder no one's been injured." She gave Deidre a little warning glare to cut it out and then rolled her eyes as Ben laughed.

Deidre went on as though she hadn't noticed Felicity's ire. "So how is it that a hottie like you isn't already taken?"

"I had a girlfriend. We broke up."

Deidre was instantly all sympathy. "Oh, how come?"

"She moved."

"Her loss."

Felicity shook her head with a weary sigh, by the end of the night she felt terribly embarrassed and was very grateful that the evening was over. She pulled into Deidre's driveway to drop her off and they said their goodbyes. Deidre was in the front, which put Ben in the back. Deidre turned to Felicity and gave her a quick hug. "We really have to keep in better touch. Call me."

Then Deidre turned to Ben in the back seat and gave him a hopeful smile. "You too Ben. Call me sometime. Have Felicity give you my number." Felicity could have died. She didn't turn around to see Ben's face and was afraid to try to meet his eyes in the rearview mirror, although she did wonder what he thought of the offer. He didn't say anything. He must have smiled though. Deidre didn't seem disappointed by his lack of response. She turned to smile at Felicity again and then left the car to go into the house.

Felicity just sat there with her cheeks burning. Deidre was always far more outgoing then she was. Usually it left Felicity feeling as though she was too shy. She had always been glad in the past that Deidre had been brave enough to talk to guys and try to get them double dates when Felicity didn't dare, but somehow, between this year and last, it struck her differently than before. For some reason Deidre's behavior came off as immature, brash and far too forward. Maybe it was just Felicity's perspective that had changed.

She was a little startled when the passenger door opened again. It was Ben. She hadn't even realized that he'd gotten out to switch seats. He settled himself next to her and put on his seatbelt. She turned to look at him with a small smile of apology. "I am so sorry about tonight."

He actually looked like he didn't know what she was talking about. "Why? I had fun."

She put the car into gear and began driving them home. Maybe she had read things wrong. Maybe Deidre's outgoing and 'in his face' approach *was* the way to get a guy's interest. Felicity was certainly no expert. "You want Deidre's number?"

Ben looked at her very strangely indeed and then he laughed. No, she hadn't read him wrong. "No, thanks."

Felicity gave a little laugh of her own. "Not exactly subtle is she?"

"It's okay. She's cute. I'm just not lookin'."

Something about the way he said 'cute' made her realize that Ben was almost three years older than she and Deidre. She had thought about that once or twice before, like when he'd mentioned being the same age as her older brother. Was it odd that they had gotten to be such good friends? Did he think of her as being *younger?* "Cute like *a kid?*"

He gave her that strange look again. "No." He shrugged. "You know…just cute."

She nodded with a little smirk. "Oh. Cute like one night at the Hilton and then she'd drive you insane, cute."

He actually looked shocked. "I don't do one night stands."

"You *don't?*"

"*No*. I may not have mastered the 'long term' relationship but it's not like I wake up next to a girl and run the other way! Besides, I'm not doing that sort of thing anymore, remember?"

"Oh right, because of the whole 'get serious and concentrate on real life' thing." He laughed and nodded. "So this new responsible life of yours involves celibacy?"

Again, he looked shocked. Felicity was a little shocked at herself. She never would have spoken to a guy about such things…but talking to Ben was different. She felt like she knew him so well. She could tease him about things she wouldn't dare utter to any other guy. He laughed. "No. I'm just going to be a little more…discriminating."

"M-hmmm. According to Allie you're already *way* too picky when it comes to girls."

He nodded with a smile. "Yeah, I am, but there's a big difference between being picky about a girl you want to spend a lot of *real* time with… and being picky about a girl you just want to take to the Hilton a few times."

She tried not to be embarrassed by his candor. She smiled and chuckled, shaking her head a bit. "Oh. I get it."

He turned to look at her steadily for a moment as she drove. "Do you?"

She laughed. "Yeah. You're *waiting*…to fall in love."

He gave a little chuckle and then looked back out the window with a sigh as they pulled into the driveway. "I'm not really…waiting…"

~~~~~~~~~~~~~~~~~~~~~~~~~~~~

And so the weekend passed. Felicity was very relieved that no one had noticed the faint scar at her throat. In private, Ben had even remarked that it was miraculously faded. She hadn't told him what Cain had done. She'd just smiled and agreed that she was glad it looked so much better.

The time came to go back to school and Felicity promised her parents that she would try to make it home more often. They said goodbye and assured Ben that he was welcome to come back anytime.

Life goes on. It's funny how quickly 'routine' can set in and take over when you're not looking; school, work, regular everyday stuff. At one point Felicity was actually shocked to realize that whole days had gone by without her thinking of Cain even once. At first, she felt horribly guilty, but that passed. What did she plan to do, mourn his leaving her forever?

Her plans of begging Mattie to take her back to Cain were fading. Not that she wouldn't, but it didn't seem likely that she would ever have the chance. It was the first week of December, a whole month since Allie had left, and she was nowhere to be found.

Ben put the CD player in her car for her and they resumed their Thursday night movies. It was pretty much the only 'social' thing she did. Karen was always busy with Jack, so she didn't see her all that much. At one point, she thought that maybe she would attempt to get closer with Bridgette and Regina from her dorm, but they only regaled her with questions about Cain.

The new girl at work was nice, but didn't seem very interested in ever getting together socially. She was twenty-one and liked to go dancing at Venus. She was never rude, but Felicity got the impression that she thought going out with a 'minor' would cramp her style.

Mandy was also absolutely beautiful and single. She probably didn't want Felicity hanging around when she was out meeting guys. Honestly, Felicity was a bit surprised that Ben wasn't at all interested in her. He must really be serious about the whole 'taking a break thing'. Mandy was pretty friendly to him, but from what Felicity could see, Ben totally ignored her.

So, humdrum life carried on. Weeks went by and they weren't exciting or mysterious. She didn't save anyone's life or fight the forces of evil. She had no night vision or special psychic abilities. In fact, she found she was rather afraid of the dark these days. *This* is what Cain had been loath to take her away from? For *this* she should be grateful?

Thursday night again and it was snowing, hard. Third time this week. They were sure to have a white Christmas. Felicity sat in the car waiting for Ben to leave the parking lot before her. He'd freak if he thought she didn't let it warm up enough first. Men.

She followed him home past houses decorated with cheery Christmas lights and parked behind him in the driveway. His house was dark and unadorned. No other car outside; his dad must be away…again. He hadn't been home last Thursday either, so she still hadn't met him. Ben said he usually only bothered to come home for the weekends these days.

He popped the popcorn as she studied the 'movie wall'. She pulled out an older DVD as he came back into the room. "Ooh, how about this?"

"You've never seen 'Romancing the Stone'?" he asked.

"Bits and pieces, but I never got to see it all the way through. I always miss the end." Ben sighed. "Come on, you picked the last two. After 'The Matrix' and 'Predator' I think you could humor me with something *human* for a change. You don't like it? It's *your* movie."

"No, it's a good one. Go ahead, put it in."

So they sat and watched Kathleen Turner cry as she wrote romance novels and Michael Douglas fight an Alligator for a jewel. It was great, until they neared the end. Kathleen Turner's character was struggling with the villain of the film when the man shoved her to the ground, climbed atop her and tried to slit her throat with a knife. Felicity had been sitting back and casually hugging her knees as she sat on the bed, but now she found herself shrinking down behind her legs and unwittingly guarding her throat with her hands. She watched in horror as chills ran down her back and phantom stinging sensations regaled her throat where Chris had tried to kill her in the very same way.

Ben must have noticed her distress. He didn't say anything, but moved closer and put his arm around her. She gratefully leaned into him and watched in cringing fascination as their heroin fought the man off. When it was finally over she breathed a great sigh of relief and even gave a small smile to Ben as she realized just how rigidly tense she had been throughout the scene.

He looked down at her in apology. "Sorry. I totally forgot about that part."

"I'm okay." She sat up straighter to watch the rest of the movie and Ben removed his arm. He seemed to look over at her once or twice more, but he didn't say anything else. She kept her eyes on the screen, enthralled with the story and wondering how it would end. The conclusion was so terribly romantic that Felicity found herself crying almost uncontrollably. She knew Ben probably thought she was being silly, but she couldn't help it. It was so melodramatic; something in it just struck a very personal emotional chord in her.

What was wrong with her? Movies never affected her this way, but she was in a pretty fragile emotional state these days. She looked up to see Ben smiling at her, and realized that she must look like a sentimental fool. "I thought it was mostly an action movie," she said with a sniffle. "I hadn't realized it was such a *romance*."

"It's called '*Romancing* the Stone', 'Liss."

"Oh yeah," she mumbled sheepishly as she tried to wipe her eyes with her sleeve.

Ben smiled as he got her a tissue from the box on his dresser, and then sat back down next to her on the bed. "You do realize that it was a happy ending?" he teased.

She took the tissue with another sniffle as the credits rolled on a sailboat heading down the New York City streets. "I know, but it was just so romantic. The way he came back at the end…" *Why do they always do that in movies?* she thought. *Guys don't pleasantly surprise you in real life. It never happens that way, love just swooping in to save the day when you least expect it.*

"You're crying all over my bed."

She quickly tried to use the tissue again, but it was already soaked. She crumpled it up in her hand and leaned to place it on his nightstand. She looked up in apology. "Sorry."

He laughed at her a little. He'd only been teasing. "It's okay." He quickly leaned forward and before she knew what he meant to do, he had touched her cheek, under the corner of her eye with his lips, kissing a tear away.

It was almost exactly what he had done after saving her from Chris. She'd been crying in fear and he'd leaned over her, crying in relief that she was alive. He had leaned down and kissed her tear away in just the same motion, but this was different. This was not a life or death moment. It was just a movie. And here in his room, it felt a little different. A little *too* familiar…intimate. He knew it too.

He slowly leaned back and stared at her in awkward silence. He looked almost desperate to explain himself. In a poor attempt at humor to cover any embarrassment, he licked his lips and tried to smile. "Salty," he offered weakly.

She just sat there and stared at him. Ben, her best friend, he had saved her life, more than once. He had made her laugh when she was sad and made her argue with him until she wanted to smack him. He had been there through it all. He'd tried to warn her about losing her heart to Cain and he had held her as she cried when he left. Through everything and even now, he had been her best friend; and he seemed perfectly willing to let things go on that way, indefinitely, but was it possible that he wished they were…*more?*

He sat perfectly still. It was almost as though he was aware that she was seeing him differently for the first time, and he was terrified to ruin it. He sat frozen and gazed at her, awaiting her response; looking for some small sign of her acceptance, waiting to follow her lead as to what he should do. She had no doubt that if she laughed and then went on with regular conversation, he would accept that. It would be like nothing had ever happened. *Was* that what she wanted to do? She tried to analyze the moment as she watched him watching her.

The wait must have seemed interminable. She sat there and studied his face and looked at him with new eyes. Ben, so handsome and smart, older, charming… She knew that there were lots of girls who wished he would invite them to spend time with him. But he wasn't spending his time with anyone else, was he? He was sitting here giving his hopeful smiles to her. Her heart began to pound as she sat up a little straighter and then leaned ever so slightly closer to him.

He didn't move. She almost would have laughed if watching from another perspective. He held himself still like a man afraid to spook a hesitant horse. After another moment, she raised her lips to his for a kiss.

Tentative and sweet, her lips touched his. It only took that first touch for her to know that she wanted more. She moved closer still, to kiss him again. It was thrills and butterflies, and excitement that she had thought forever lost.

But although her heart was racing, she didn't entirely give herself over yet. She ended the kiss and leaned back to see his reaction. He grinned. "It's about time."

She leaned back in open-mouthed awe at his audacity. "You are *so* arrogant!" she said in amused disbelief.

He was unfazed. He spoke quietly and seductively as he leaned in for another kiss. "Yeah, I know." She didn't pull away, but she didn't quite kiss him back either…although she was surprised how much she actually wanted to. He moved to meet her eyes again. "But you have to admit, I've been *very* patient. That's not usually my strong suit."

He smiled at her and then leaned forward to kiss away a tear on the other side of her face. He kissed another further down her cheek and then his lips chased a tear that had slid down the side of her throat.

Before she could help it, Felicity had jerked back from him. It was *that* spot. *Cain's* spot.

Ben looked at her oddly. "Take it easy. I don't bite."

For a moment she was upset by the obvious reference, but after searching his face she wondered if he had really meant it that way, or if it had just been an unfortunate choice of words. He seemed to realize his mistake. He didn't say anything else, but he obviously hadn't meant it maliciously. Slowly, he gave her a tentative little smile.

It touched her to see the ever confident and self-assured Ben that she knew, looking so hopeful and vulnerable. She couldn't resist coming back to his lips again for another kiss. She kissed him and let him wrap his arms around her lower back. He gently teased her lips with his tongue until she permitted it to enter her mouth.

Wow. He was a *really* good kisser. Her head was spinning. She found herself almost amazed that he hadn't venom of his own. After a few minutes though, he pulled back from her as though uncertain about something. "Wait, 'Liss…maybe this isn't such a good idea." She looked at him in disbelief. *Now* he was having second thoughts? He saw the look on her face and sought to reassure her. "I want to, believe me. I *really* want to, but are you sure you're ready, to move on I mean? It's just, I don't want to be the 'rebound guy'."

She began to smile as she studied his face. He meant it. He really cared about her, she *knew* he did. And she was more than a little surprised to realize just how much she cared back. When did this happen? She gave him a reassuring smile, full of new and slightly bewildered comprehension. "You're not. *You're* the guy I should have been kissing all along."

Now Ben smiled too. "Well, *I* could have told you that."

She laughed as he took her back into his arms to resume their kiss. What had started out as so hesitant and exploratory quickly became passionately urgent. She kissed him with heated fervor that he returned with equal passion if not more.

It seemed almost amazing to her that this was Ben, her best friend these past months. She had grown to know him so well, yet this was a side of him that she had never known before. The way that he anxiously drew kisses from her lips was surprising and exciting, and yet even while discovering this new part of him, he seemed so familiar and comfortable that it just felt right somehow. Even more amazing to her than the fact that he seemed eager for her kisses, was the fact that she so desperately wanted his. Once given over to it, the feelings he brought out in her were so strong that they astonished her. Restraint was like trying to hold back an avalanche.

She found herself wanting to feel his skin. It was an irrational desire, but she just had to feel her hands on his skin. She pressed her palms against his chest as they kissed and then slid them down until she found the hem of his shirt. Without a moment's hesitation, she slid them up underneath. Her hands ran up the ridged plane of his stomach and onto his smooth broad chest under his shirt. His skin felt so hot it was like he was burning with fever. Some disconnected part of her mind came to realize that she had expected him to feel like Cain. Although Cain had never felt cold to her, Ben's body was noticeably hot to the touch in comparison.

Ben's body was warm and pulsing, brimming with life. His heart pounded in his chest every bit as fast as hers and his skin felt so warm and inviting to her caresses. His chest rose and fell with ever quickening gasps for breath in his growing excitement over her; little details that she might not have even noticed before, but now…they spurred her own excitement that much more.

He leaned back from her and pulled his shirt off over his head. That startled her for a moment. She hadn't really been suggesting for him to do that, but she *had* wanted to feel his skin. She looked at his bared chest and wondered just *what* she wanted.

She couldn't help but feel the sexual tension build within her as she gazed at him. For someone who wasn't into sports, he certainly had the body of an athlete. Her eyes lingered for a moment on the slight scar just below the very center of his breastbone. Then she ran her eyes over his broad pecs, took in the few little wisps of hair that framed his nipples, and the toned muscles of his arms. He wasn't terribly muscular, but fairly filled out and well defined. Fighting off vampires must be good exercise, she thought to herself with a smile.

He was about to lean in to kiss her again, when she lifted her own arms above her head in invitation. He looked at her a bit uncertainly, but she only waited patiently for him to remove her shirt as well. He took it off her and threw it onto the floor next to his own, revealing her bra underneath. He went back to kissing her then, as his hands caressed the newly bared skin of her back.

His hands wandered over her bra strap once or twice, but he never paused to unhook it. Maybe he was unsure if she would want him to. She reached back and undid the clasp herself, impatient at the fabric between them. She wanted to feel his skin pressed up against her.

As she unhooked the back, he stopped kissing her to meet her eyes. He seemed very surprised at her. Not disappointed of course, but surprised. She didn't care. She wanted him to hold her, skin to skin, so that she could feel the warmth of his embrace. He watched as she brought her hands up to the straps at her shoulders, poised to slide them down to remove her bra and reveal her breasts beneath.

He didn't let her. He covered her hands with his own on her shoulders to stop the motion. He kissed her fervently and then, to her great astonishment he used his hands on her shoulders to give her a playful shove down to the bed. As her head hit the pillow, she gasped in surprise at his forcefulness. Truthfully, she found it thrilling. It ignited her desire for him in a way that she wouldn't have expected. She raised her eyebrows and gave a surprised little laugh. He smiled at her acceptance of the act.

Ben looked at her with such undisguised longing, but it seemed with agonizing slowness that he brought himself down to her. She eagerly wrapped her arms around him, feeling the warm closeness that she had longed for. It felt better than she had even imagined it would, even with her bra still between them.

He kissed her again as he lay atop her lightly. This time it was not only his kiss that excited her. He held himself from pressing against her very strongly, but the bulge in his jeans was becoming impossible to ignore. She was amazed that he found her so alluring; his arousal over her was clearly evident. His lips left hers to anoint her jaw line with little kisses that traveled to her ear. She almost forgot to breathe as he tickled her with his tongue and gently sucked upon her lobe.

His kisses moved downward…and then paused. She knew that he had been about to kiss her neck, but was afraid of her reaction. No, this would not do. She had always enjoyed having her throat kissed and she could not let it become a memory that was only of Cain. If she was going to move on, then she should do it right. She needed to feel that she could give herself over fully; otherwise, it would become a barrier between her and Ben. It was best broken now, swiftly. She would have to get past it.

She ran her fingers through the hair at the back of his head and then gently pressed him downward, permission to go on. He continued, letting his kisses trail down her throat, but they did not linger. He moved them to the center of her chest, where he placed a tender kiss between her breasts, just above the fabric of her bra. He looked up at her with a fond smile and she returned it with her own.

He raised himself from her a bit and eyed her bra. He slipped his hand beneath the strap at one shoulder and slid it down without yet revealing her breast. He was obviously savoring the moment. He removed his hand from the strap and slowly slipped it inside the bra, closing his eyes and caressing her with a gentle squeeze. He held her cupped in his hand as he slowly grazed his thumb over her hardening nipple. Finally, he opened his eyes and lifted her breast free of her bra as though he were unwrapping a greatly anticipated prize.

He dipped his head down to meet her skin and took her nipple into his mouth. She could not help but let a small moan escape her and he looked up at her with a slight smile in his eyes as he suckled her gently. After a moment, he repeated his actions almost identically for the other breast as she played her fingers over his shoulders and held him close.

Finally, he left her breasts to remove her bra and toss it onto the floor. He came back to kiss her tenderly. Their kiss grew in intensity and her desire for him swelled until she wondered how it was possible that she hadn't longed for this from him before.

Ben left her lips to place kisses down the center of her torso, until he reached the rim of her jeans. She closed her eyes in anticipation and waited to see what he would do. He tickled the top of her belly with licks and kisses, making her again meet his eyes. He looked up at her playfully, but after a moment, his expression grew serious. "Do you think we're going too fast?" *Oh God, don't stop now.* She didn't say that of course, but that's what went through her mind.

Was that wrong? Did he think less of her, that she had become so uninhibited? She looked at him questioningly. "Do *you?*"

He laughed that she should even ask. "*I've* been fantasizing about this for months. *You're* the one who's just getting used to the idea."

She sat up a little to see him better. "Months?" He lowered his eyes a bit sheepishly. She grinned. "You've been fantasizing about me?"

He actually looked almost bashful as he met her eyes again. He smiled. "Don't let it go to your head."

She gave a little laugh. He dipped down to place another kiss on her abdomen and then silently looked askance of her. *What the hell.* She gave a little nod towards the waistband of her jeans. "Go on," she whispered. He looked a little undecided. He obviously wanted to, but was afraid to push her too far too fast. He was so sweet. She gave him a nod of reassurance. "Really, I want you to."

He crinkled his nose at her dubiously. "You sure?"

She laughed and wiggled her hips against his chest. "Yes."

Ben grinned. He took the edge of the denim just over the buttonhole into his teeth. He then gently tugged upwards and then down again, pulling it free of the button. She watched in amazement as he used his tongue to flip up the tab of her zipper. He then took the material into his teeth again and yanked it sideways, causing the zipper tab to slide down and open fully. She laughed at him in surprise. "Show off."

He gave her a sly grin and then grasped her jeans in his hands at each hip and tugged them down. She lifted herself to let him pull them free. He brought them down to her ankles, removed her shoes and socks and then her jeans. They landed on the floor next to their shirts.

She wore plain cotton bikini panties. He didn't even look at them really. He paused to take off his own sneakers. She had thought he might remove his jeans as well, but instead he brought himself back to lay with her for more kisses.

Once again, he let his lips travel down her body. He smothered her belly in kisses, and then placed one firm kiss upon the little cotton triangle of her panties. Rather than continue there, he sat up, parting her thighs and positioning himself on the bed between them.

He ran his hands down her left leg to under her knee and then to her ankle as he lifted it from the bed. He had her leg raised high as she pointed her toe like a dancer. He gently caused her to bend and flex her leg at the knee as he held her ankle in one hand. He ran his other hand down her leg, pausing to kiss and admire the contours and shapeliness of it.

He rested her foot on his shoulder as he kneaded the full meat of her calf and thigh with almost as much attention as he had given each of her breasts, his caresses alternated with gentle, pulling little kisses. She had never thought of her legs as all that appealing, but she found his obvious appreciation of every inch of her body incredibly sexy. He let her bring her left leg to rest only to turn and fondle the right. His attention to detail was almost maddening.

Just when she thought she couldn't wait any longer, he came back to kiss her again. He lay down beside her as his fingers caressed the inside of her thigh and then came up to slip down beneath the cotton of her panties. They seemed to leave a trail of fire on her skin beneath them as they slid between her legs. There he found clear evidence of her eager anticipation of him. Even as he began to stroke and massage her, Felicity found her own hand groping blindly to find the button of his jeans.

He paused in his attentions to inch away from her reach. Her fingertips brushed the denim restraining him but she couldn't maneuver to free his body for her. "Take it easy," he teased. "*I've* waited this long, *you* can show a little patience."

She looked at him in confusion. "Why?"

He smiled and wrinkled his nose at her again. "I'm shy," he whispered teasingly.

She looked at him in odd amusement, but before she could question him further, his attentions to her body were strongly renewed. His fingers moved against her and within her until she was absolutely mad with desire. She could barely even think. His motions brought her so close to climax that she had to arch away from him lest she become carried away.

"Ben!" With only his name, she demanded that he stop so that he might undress and attend to her properly. He understood perfectly. He gave a little laugh and leaned down for another kiss before he let her go.

He left the bed to approach his tall dresser across the room. He opened the top drawer and fumbled through it for a moment as she waited impatiently. Finally, he found what he was looking for…and he didn't look happy. "Oh shit."

"What?" she asked.

"Shit!" he repeated.

She sat up to look at him. "What?"

"This…being with you, it was kind of unexpected." As he spoke, he raised his hand for her to see. He held a box of condoms. The bold print across the front proclaimed them to be Magnum X-tra Large.

She stifled a laugh. How many guys bought them just for the prestige of the title on the box? It seemed a ridiculously blatant display. That couldn't be what Ben was showing her could it? "So?"

"So… I'm not exactly…prepared." He shook the box a little and she realized that it was open on its side…and nothing was falling out.

"Oh." He looked so disappointed it was almost funny. She smiled. "It's okay."

"No. It's not," he insisted in somber defeat.

"I'm on the pill," she informed him.

Ben looked at her in hopeful amazement. "*You're* on birth control?"

She smirked at him a little. "Well, it wasn't originally *for* that, but yeah, I am."

He looked as though he wouldn't quite dare to believe that he shouldn't be deprived of enjoying her body. He eyed her doubtfully. "Still, I always use a condom. *Always.*"

She thought for a moment and then sat up a little more in confidence. "Well good. Then we know you haven't got anything. And the only guy that I have ever been with is *incapable* of carrying disease. So there's no problem."

Ben looked annoyed and ill. "You're right. Now we really don't need one, 'cause boy did *that* just kill the mood."

She sat up fully to stare at him. "Well it's not like you didn't know."

"That you were sleeping with a *dead guy*? Yeah, I guess I mentally blocked it out."

"Ben! It's not like I was with one of those zombie things! Cain's body is just like any other guys'."

"Does he have a *heartbeat?*" he asked her almost viciously.

She dropped her eyes to the floor. "Well he didn't *seem* dead," she mumbled.

"I guess you had to *be* there," he said factitiously.

Her face crumpled and she felt like she would cry. Why was he doing this? He was ruining everything! She grabbed the end of the comforter and pulled it up to cover herself. "You're such a jerk!"

How could she have opened herself to him? How could she have let herself believe that it would be a good thing? She was so emotionally charged it seemed almost instantly that she'd been drawn from one extreme to the other. She huddled under the blanket and cried. She heard him come closer but she didn't look.

"You're right." He sat next to her. "I *am* being a jerk."

He put a hand on her shoulder but she shrugged him off without looking. "Don't touch me," she mumbled from under the blanket.

"I am so sorry 'Liss. It's just that…you have no idea how hard it's been. To see you with *him* and to know that he was kissing you and loving you…"

She looked up at him accusingly. "Just because he's a vampire?"

"A little, but mostly…because he wasn't *me.*"

That made her pause. Had he really wanted to be with her all of this time? She had thought that maybe he had begun thinking about her when Cain had left, but she'd had no idea that *all along…* She thought back again over all of the time that she'd known him. That first night that Ben had told her that Cain was a vampire, it seemed so long ago. He had come to her room and asked her to go to the movies with him. He'd tried to make it seem very casual and non-chalant, but…had he been attempting to get closer to her even then? She thought of other times, little things that should have shown her how he felt about her. The necklace that he'd bought her for her birthday, the way that he had danced with her at Homecoming, his concern over her on Halloween… Had he really been waiting all this time?

She looked up to study his face again, but he wasn't looking at her. He sat on the edge of the bed in only his jeans and put his head down into his hands with his elbows on his knees as he spoke. "This is all wrong. Why'd I start this now? It *is* too soon, and now I've gone and messed it all up. I'm sorry. Please don't hate me 'Liss. I don't blame you for being upset, but you *have* to forgive me." He looked up at her in atonement. "I know you're prob'ly thinkin' this was all a big mistake. Nothing else matters to me now as much as your friendship, I don't want this to mess that up. How can I make this right?" She lowered her eyes in contemplation.

He kept on. "I have to know that when I see you tomorrow, at work or at school…I have to know that we're okay. It can't be all awkward and weird. You have to let me fix it."

She still didn't say anything. "I'm sorry 'Liss. Please, forgive me?" He watched her for a moment and then put his head back down into his hands. "I wish I could just take it all back."

She thought of the way he had savored the moment before removing her clothing and how she had felt when he'd kissed and caressed her. He turned his head to look at her, his eyes pleading forgiveness. She sat up again. "You don't really want to take back *all* of it…do you?"

He just looked incredibly relieved that she was going to talk to him. Then he seemed to realize what she had said. "Were there some parts that you wanted to keep?" he asked hesitantly.

She grinned and leaned a little closer to him. "Yeah." She moved to kiss him and as her lips touched his, she felt their passion reignited. "*Oh yeah.*" She kissed him again. He found his way beneath the blanket to wrap his arms around her.

After the kiss ended, he looked at her with serious concern in his eyes. "Are you sure it's not too soon? I could wait. It might kill me, but I could try."

"No." She laughed and kissed him again. "It's right. Just do me a favor? Try not to say anything else stupid, okay?"

"Maybe you'd better just shut me up." He laid her back on the bed as they began to kiss again. They were all tangled in the blanket and his jeans were rough against her hips. After a few moments, she could tell that he was having a very hard time keeping from rubbing himself strongly against her. She pressed herself firmly against him as well. This was unbearable. "Ben, you know… If you're really uncomfortable about not using a condom… Well, we could make each other happy in *other* ways."

He leaned back to eye her with a grin. "Yeah?"

"I know I sure wouldn't mind some more of that *special attention* you were givin' me before," she admitted.

He gave her a sly smile. "You liked that huh?"

As though he had to ask. She smiled. "And um… *I* can give special attention too." She licked her lips suggestively and he looked as though he couldn't believe her boldness.

"Are you really on the pill?" he asked incredulously.

She nodded. "Uh-huh."

He gave her a last brazen kiss before he disengaged himself from the blanket to leave the bed. He stood back a few steps and then began to take off his pants. She watched him with a silent smile as he pulled them from his legs. As he bent to take his socks off, her eyes were illicitly drawn to his underwear. The bulge hidden there looked awfully large. As Felicity lay there, half covered by the blanket she stared harder at him. He straightened and then removed his underwear to reveal his body to her.

Felicity's eyes widened as she saw him. He was *huge*. She had thought that Cain was a well made man, but this was something entirely different. "Oh my God."

She hadn't meant to actually say that *out loud*, but it seemed to spring from her lips uncontrollably. Ben looked as though he couldn't believe she had said it out loud either. "Thanks. Now I'm not at all self-conscious or uncomfortable."

She gave him a look of apology. "I meant that in a good way," she said, trying to cover her shock.

"Uh-huh," he muttered.

She peeked up at him with a little smile. "I'm sorry, but Ben… *oh my god,*" she repeated in a little whisper.

He rolled his eyes at her. "Sorry. It's a birth defect."

She felt terrible. "Come here."

He came and sat down next to her on the bed. She tried very hard not to stare. She was certainly not an experienced judge, but this was obviously beyond normal. He was just *so* big. Any desire she had felt had immediately fled. She knew that women were supposed to want size in a man, but to her he seemed absolutely terrifying. She hoped it wasn't too obvious.

"You're gettin' all intimidated on me now, aren't you?" he asked. He said it with a playful edge, but it was true. He didn't seem too surprised though. She couldn't be the only girl to have had this reaction. He smiled at her and leaned down to give her a little kiss on her cheek and whisper in her ear. "I know it's a bit *much*. We can stick with the *special attention* plan if you want." He started kissing her ear again, and she couldn't help but snuggle closer against him. "It's okay…" he whispered breathlessly between kisses. "Really, it's your call." He leaned back to look at her again. "But you have to know, that I would *never* hurt you."

She froze for a moment. He couldn't know of course, but that was almost exactly what Cain had said to her…just before the first time that he'd drunk her blood. She found herself gazing into Ben's eyes. "I know you wouldn't." She gave him a little kiss. "I want to."

He didn't say another word. He kissed her passionately and then moved down to take off her panties. He kissed the inside of her thighs until she couldn't help but try to hold her legs more open to him. His kisses traveled up between them until the heat of his breath and the teasing licks of his tongue made her squirm.

She was so ready and eager with anticipation that it seemed torture to have to wait any longer, but when he came back to lie over her, she felt the broad tip of his penis press against her gently and she couldn't help but tense. "Ben, wait. I…" she struggled to find words to voice her concern. She didn't *want* to be frightened of him but… "I don't think it'll fit."

He started laughing. It didn't make her feel bad though. It was a comfortable and loving little laugh. He bent to kiss her again before he whispered, "Don't worry, I'll fit. It just takes a little…coaxing. I'll be gentle, I swear. Do you trust me?"

"Uh-huh." He kissed her and tried to bring her back into the moment as he pressed against her again. Passion returned with his kisses and her body was undeniably eager for him. Her lips moved down the side of his throat, and as he began to enter her, she couldn't help but close her teeth lightly on his shoulder. She gripped him with a force like iron, but he was ever gentle as promised. It was like slow, passionate torture.

Back and forth, slowly he made his way further as her doubts fled before the promise of gratification. He straightened his arms to hold himself up from her, to give himself better leverage and she was forced to let him go. As she lay back on the bed, he felt so far away. She wanted to feel him lying down on her, to wrap her arms around him and share more kisses, but he seemed afraid to let himself press down on her too strongly as he whispered, "Don't let me hurt you. You tell me."

"Uh-huh." She looked up at him but he had closed his eyes. He seemed so hesitant and afraid to harm her that he was in pleasurable torment. Each slight motion from him drew a moan from her that voiced her delight even as it pleaded with him to come back to her lips. She needed him close, she needed his kiss, she needed more…

He pressed slightly deeper within her and she moaned louder. He instantly looked down in concern. "Liss, you okay?"

She quickly nodded her head against is fears, but this was not working. She couldn't let him go on with this affection that was like interminable agony. To feel so close to satisfaction and yet be kept from truly being with him... "Ben?"

He withdrew in concern. "I'm sorry." Wow, he was so worried for her, how could he even enjoy it?

"No, I'm fine. It's just... Do you think that maybe... *I* could be on top?" she asked hesitantly.

He looked very amazed and aroused that she would ask, but then he grew doubtful. "You might have kind of a hard time."

She grinned and gripped his shoulders as she brought herself up to him for a kiss. Then she startled him by turning and pushing him down on his back roughly to the bed. She smiled at him with a sparkle in her eye, thinking of the excitement that *she* had felt when he had pushed *her* down before in almost the same way. She sat astride his belly and leaned down over him, smiling playfully. "No, I won't."

He had seemed very aroused by her actions, but was a bit sobered by her words. "Had a lot of practice, have you?"

She looked down at him in annoyance, but before she said anything harsh, she realized that it was just a defense mechanism. He was feeling inadequate – odd as that might sound for a man of his proportions. She looked down at him sternly and refused to be baited. "Shut up."

She kissed him before he could respond and he didn't fight it. Now she was the one to let her kisses travel down *his* body. She placed a small very deliberate kiss on the scar on his chest, and then moved downward over his stomach.

She had originally thought to savor and show appreciation for his body in the way that he had for hers, but in practice, she just hadn't the patience. She moved herself down between his legs and took his penis into her hand. She was very aware not to hesitate in the least. Her kisses moved down his stomach and followed the light line of hair there, to the smooth skin surrounded by downy curls below.

Felicity caressed and kissed him gently in her hand with a care that she hoped would make him feel that his body was something she treasured, and was not afraid of. Then she took him into her mouth briefly, though he barely fit. The rumbling moans that emerged from deep within his chest begged her for more as she covered him with licks and velvet kisses. She was sure to leave him good and wet for herself.

He looked at her through a haze of ecstasy as she came up to set herself astride him. She positioned herself carefully and began to let her weight down upon him, but the angle wasn't quite right and she quickly lifted herself with a hiss.

"Liss stop. You don't have to, really."

She lifted her hips upwards away from him, and then lay down flat upon his belly and chest as she brought her mouth to his lips for a kiss. "I thought I told you to shut-up," she whispered teasingly. She kissed him and then used her hand to help position him between her legs where she lay.

She gently moved herself down onto him and drew in another hiss of air as he began to enter her body, before Ben could protest she took his lips again with her own. This was good, this was right. He was so warm and close against her as she moved her hips to take him further.

She had to end their kiss for a gulp of air. She couldn't help but cry out as her body stretched to accommodate him fully, but it was so good to feel him deep within. *This* is what she had been wanting when his hesitant motions before had teased her so. Her gasps for breath came in time to her movements down upon him until the hollow ache inside of her was entirely filled with him. A missing piece to make her complete.

She looked into his eyes to see such wonder and affection in them as he gazed back at her. She smiled and cupped the side of his face with her hand as she kissed him again. He was such a mixture of boldly headstrong confidence and quiet vulnerability. So stubborn and willful and yet now he gave himself over fully to her control.

How could she have known him so well, and yet never *known?* His kisses held such loving desire for her and she drank up his passions as though she'd been starved without them. It fit so perfectly that her best friend should be her lover as well.

She was amazed at how acutely aware she was of each new sensation. In being with *Cain,* the venom had certainly held its pleasures, but she'd never realized how much it also must have clouded her mind. *Now* with Ben, each slight bit of friction, every touch seemed so raw and intense.

She began to build her movements faster upon him and it seemed to drive him wild. He began kissing any part of her that he could reach with his lips. She arched her body upwards until he found her left breast. He took her into his mouth and sucked strongly upon her in time to the rhythm of her pulsating hips.

She thrust herself down upon him mercilessly as a wave of ecstasy caused her to lose control. He released the nipple of her breast to cry out as climax overcame him and she clenched her muscles tight around him as she was carried on that wave to the same perfect fruition.

Felicity held him tightly until she lost all strength and collapsed upon his chest gasping for air. She lay and gave him tender kisses on his throat and shoulder until finally, she began to lift herself from him. She sucked in a long deep hiss of breath as he left her body and then she collapsed once more, rolling to the side of him onto her back.

They lay there in recuperative silence for a moment, and then Ben propped himself up on one elbow to face her. She smiled up at him as he gazed upon her with blatant adoration.

The strange thing was…she'd seen him look at her that way before. Maybe not the *exact* same expression, but so similar that she must have been blind not to see it for what it was earlier. Odd times, during conversation or just sitting quietly at lunch. How had she never recognized it before?

He leaned down to kiss her. She pursed her lips but it was the corner of her eye that he kissed, once, twice, and then lots of little pecks all over her cheek and her eye. She laughed. "No more tears."

"Good." He smiled at her and then dipped down to give a little lick between her breasts. She had to laugh at the absurdity of it. "Still salty though."

She cringed and shook her head with a grin. Of course, her body was covered with a thin sheen of sweat from their exertions. "I work hard for my rewards," she responded in justification.

Ben gave her a sly smile. "I noticed." He lay back on the bed next to her as though completely exhausted. "Oh my God, 'Liss." He looked over at her again in concern. "Are you okay?"

She giggled. "I'm fine." Actually, she *was* a bit sore, but she certainly wasn't going to tell him that, besides, it was worth it.

"I have never been with a girl like that."

She lay there looking up at the ceiling in confusion. It seemed kind of an odd thing for him to say. "What do mean?"

"I've never been with a girl who likes to be in charge. I mean, not that the position's new, but usually it doesn't really work out…on account of my *birth defect*."

She rolled her eyes and gave him a little shove. "Stop calling it that."

"No really. Most girls seem to find me pretty intimidating. They're never assertive like that. They always seem to want to follow my lead, like I wouldn't ever want to let them take charge of things."

Felicity smiled. "Well you are kind of bossy."

He laughed a little and shook his head. "*Thanks*, but I always end up having to kind of…hold back. I mean let's face it, if I ever really *came down* on a girl the way I'd like to…I'm always afraid I'd hurt them. So, it's good, but it's always kind of…restrained."

He leaned up again on his elbow to look at her. It seemed odd to be having this conversation with him about other girls, but as his *friend,* she felt like he needed to get it off his chest. It was like a confession that he'd needed to talk out, but who could he ever really talk about it with? Allie? Maybe…but it didn't sound like it. She lay quiet and still, afraid to say the wrong thing to make him feel ill at ease.

She looked up to see him gazing down at her with that adoring look again. He moved her hair aside, gently stroked her cheek, and then smiled with widened eyes. "But with *you*… That was unbelievable! So honest and real, that was *no holding back*. It was absolutely *amazing*." He paused in gently stroking the side of her face to smile at her again tenderly. "You know *why* it was so amazing?"

She eyed him dubiously. "Because I have good rhythm?" she offered with a grin.

He broke out into laughter. "No! Well…*yes*, but no. It's because it was *you*. You're my 'Liss. You *know* me. I don't intimidate you…not really. You're not afraid to stand up to me and you don't take my shit. You're there for me when I need someone to set me straight.

Even just *every day*, I enjoy being with you, and you're fun, and you're beautiful, and you're smart, and…and I love you," he looked at her with sudden concern. "You *know* that right? I love you."

She gazed up at him with wide eyes. "I am so stupid."

"Okay, not really the response I was hoping for."

"I *am* stupid," she repeated.

"No you're not," he insisted in confusion.

"Don't argue with me, ask me *why* I'm stupid."

"Okay…" he began hesitantly. "Why are you stupid?"

"Because I love you too."

He looked at her oddly that *that* should make her stupid. "I don't know if I like where this is going."

"I mean, why didn't I see it before?" she asked.

"You were kind of…distracted."

"Yeah, I guess I was, but I *do* love you. Part of me has loved you all along. Even when you were arguing with me and driving me crazy. I've always felt close to you. It's just, I never realized that it could be like *this*. What is wrong with me?"

Ben smiled. "You're a teenage girl." She laughed and he gave her a soft, sweet kiss. "I love you."

"I love you too."

"Now *that's* what I was hopin' to hear." He grinned from ear to ear and kissed her again. "I am so in love with you!"

She giggled. "I think you may have mentioned that."

"I know. I can't stop saying it. It feels good. I love you Felicity Snow."

"I love you too Benjamin Everheart. I really do."

~~~~~~~~~~~~~~~~~~~~~~~~~~~~~

Felicity was pulled from sleep by a noise. She opened her eyes to see what was making that faint 'whirring' sound. Oh, the man on TV was trying to sell a blender.

Ben was still sleeping. She snuggled closer to him and watched with heavy lidded eyes as the man on the infomercial shoved in various vegetables to make an oddly colored, 'nutritious' concoction.

Then she heard another noise. It didn't come from the television, but from the window that shared the wall with the headboard of the bed. That's what had woken her. Her pulse began to race in alarm as she watched the glass slide slowly upwards.

She was about to wake Ben, when she heard someone talking outside. The voice was familiar. She cautiously sat up in bed. They weren't even talking to her, but to someone else outside in the dark…seeming completely unconcerned with anyone in the room at the moment. "I know. You don't have to. I won't take long."

The covers slipped from Felicity as she moved, and she realized that she was still nude. Her eyes quickly searched the floor and found Ben's tee shirt. She grabbed it and quickly put it on as she tried to see the face that belonged to the arm on the windowsill. "Allie?"

Alyson turned to face her through the window as Ben sharply sat up, nearly knocking Felicity from the bed. "Allie!"

Allie's eyes widened as she took in the occupants of the room and their state of undress. "Oh my God, *you guys*…" She was grinning broadly. "Is this a bad time? You want I should leave?"

Ben sat up further and Felicity shoved the sheet into his lap, as he seemed completely oblivious to his nudity. "Alyson Freeman, don't you dare! You get your ass in here right now!"

Allie grinned and climbed in the window with a laugh as Ben continued to reprimand her. "Where have you been? I've been worried sick about you!"

Allie had barely finished climbing in the window when Ben began to climb from the bed to meet her for a hug. Allie briefly eyed him up and down and then turned away slightly with a little smirk. "Jeez, Ben. Put some clothes on."

Ben realized his nakedness and grabbed the sheet to cover himself in annoyance as his eyes searched the floor for his pants. They were across the room. He turned instead to rifle through the drawer of the nightstand.

Felicity got up with a smile and went to give Allie a hug hello. She was glad Ben was tall, his tee shirt hung down far enough on her to preserve modesty. Allie whispered in her ear. "When did *this* happen?"

Felicity grinned shyly at the floor. "Just tonight."

Allie made her look up and met her eyes after a glance at Ben and a smile. "You guys are gonna be great."

Allie turned back to Ben who was finishing putting on some boxer shorts he'd dug up. She spoke louder for him to hear too. "Sorry to barge in. I climb through Ben's window all the time, but I've never interrupted something before. What…was the Hilton booked?" she asked with a sly smile.

Ben came over and grabbed her for an embrace. He hugged Allie's tiny frame so strongly, Felicity was surprised he didn't crack her ribs. "Thank God you're back. What'd you go and quit Tommy's for? You scared me to death."

Allie shrugged as he loosened his hold. "Time for somethin' new."

Ben held her by the shoulders and beamed, that she was really there. "I'm so glad you came back. I'm sorry about everything. It's not fair that I'm always tryin' to tell you what to do. You know I love you…no matter what. Still friends?"

"Of course."

He hugged her again tightly. "You're back," he repeated with a smile.

She leaned back to make him let go. "I can't stay," she said quietly.

The happy relief on Ben's faced turned to confusion. "What? Why not? Of course you can. *It's okay.* You can see whoever you want. I won't say a word, I swear. It's going to be hard but…you don't have to go."

Allie smiled at him sadly. "I love ya' Benji, but yes…I do." Ben began to protest again but she just shushed him and grabbed his hand. She made him open it flat as she pressed it to her slight chest.

That's when Felicity realized.

It was freezing outside…there was still snow on the ground. Yet Allie wore only a thin 'Judas Priest' concert shirt.

Ben stood there in confusion with his hand on her chest. He was about to speak again when something in Allie's eyes stopped him. That's when it hit him. Felicity watched in silence as his eyes went wide and his face drained of color. He pressed his hand strongly to her chest and moved it over a little, searching. He tried again desperately, but Felicity knew…he wouldn't find a heartbeat.

She watched him as the look on his face turned to horror and he silently mouthed the word 'no' a few times before he found his voice. When he did, it was quiet and trembling. "What did you do? *What did you do?* Oh my God Allie, no! What did you do!?" His voice became raised with a mix of hysteria and tears. "You are so stupid! Oh my God Allie! You are so stupid! What did you do?!"

He took his hands off her and held them before her as though pleading for the obvious not to be true. "Your whole life! This is your whole life! Why? Why would you do this?! Oh my God, no! Allie!" He closed his eyes and then covered his face with his hands for a moment. The way he was gasping for air, Felicity was afraid that he might hyperventilate. Allie just stood there and watched him.

Suddenly he looked up in new distress. "You let me hold you; you let me think you were… Oh my God, you *tricked* me. You got me to invite you into my house! Into my room!"

Allie looked confused and then moved forward to put a hand on his shoulder in reassurance. "Ben, it's still me."

Ben smacked down her hand and backed away. "No! You're not…" He looked as though he couldn't figure out what to believe.

Felicity moved to go to him, to say something, but Allie looked up at her and slightly shook her head no. This was between her and Ben. It was obvious to Felicity that Allie's spiritual essence was unchanged even if her body was not quite the same, but Allie wanted Ben to come to his own conclusion.

Ben started to cry. He just looked at Allie and cried. After a moment, Allie tried again to hold him, but as she neared, Ben's sorrow turned to rage. "Don't touch me! Oh my God…*you fucking demon! Get out!* Get out of my room! *Get out!*" As Ben yelled the last he turned away from her. He looked like he wanted to punch and break something, but nothing was in reach but Felicity. He grabbed her in a crushing hug and cried.

Even as he did, Felicity's attention was drawn to Allie. Ben didn't see it, but as his last words rang through the air, Allie stumbled as though physically struck. She was shoved back against the windowsill with only the force of Ben's words and his rescinded invitation.

The look on her face was a mixture of shocked distress and hurt betrayal. She opened her mouth as though in pain and unable to breathe. Felicity tried to take a step to go to her, but Ben held her tight as he faced the other way.

Allie reached backwards blindly to grab the edge of the window frame against which she'd been thrown. She hopped herself up onto the sill and ducked her head to lean a bit outside. Once there she was obviously much relieved. It only took her a second to compose herself. She took a deep shuddering breath to help restore calm, and looked back to Ben and Felicity again.

Felicity's gaze met Allie's as Ben still hugged her tight with eyes shut, unwilling to face his childhood friend. Allie was fighting back tears as she tried to smile. She knew him. She had to have known that he wouldn't be able to accept it. Felicity felt like she wanted to shake him, yell at him and make him see that Allie was okay.

Alyson seemed to read her mind. She gave her head a little shake and blinked back her tears. She spoke so quietly, Felicity could only just pick out her words over Ben's quiet sobbing at her shoulder. "It's okay. Take care of him for me."

Felicity tried to smile and nodded as Allie blew her a little kiss and turned to hop down out of the window onto the lawn outside. Felicity stared at her as she did…comprehension of Allie's new vampire state still just sinking in. Was she really…

Another thought came to mind as well. *That could have been me.* She wasn't sure how she felt about that.

Allie turned back for one last look. She was crying now. Her face seemed to crumple as she met Felicity's eyes, and then she just turned and ran. As Felicity's eyes followed her outside she saw someone else standing out on the grass. For one unreasonable second her heart stopped as she searched the face for recognition…but no. She didn't know him. A young man stood outside waiting. He looked as though he wanted to catch and hold Allie but she wouldn't let him.

As she ran past, the young man turned and looked through the window. Even from out on the lawn, too far away for real clarity, Felicity could feel his eyes meet hers.

It was Mattie. It had to be. He looked disappointed and resentful. He stood there and watched her holding Ben for what was probably only a second, although it seemed like an eternity.

Half a dozen haphazard thoughts seemed to rush through Felicity's mind in the space of that second.

She wanted to run out and assure him that Ben was only temporarily blinded with grief.

She wanted to make Ben see that his grief was unnecessary. Allie would be happy now. This was what she wanted.

She wanted to make Ben turn and face his lost friend. To reconcile them somehow. To make what seemed to Ben an awful tragedy, somehow change into a reunion…something good.

She wanted to go and comfort Allie.

She wanted to find Allie and hug her and talk to her and ask her what it was like. Was she happy?

The last thing that flashed through her mind almost made her feel numb. It was Mattie! She had been waiting, hoping to see him! She could go to him. He could take her to Cain. And if he wouldn't, surely Allie could convince him.

In fact, if she worried that Cain would turn her away for guilt, she could take the matter from his hands. Allie was one of them now. *She could do it*…if that was what Felicity really wanted.

Obviously, Mattie was capable. He and Allie could do what was necessary. She could come to Cain already changed… At that point, he would never turn her away. This was the chance she'd been waiting for.

Mattie only met her eyes for a moment. Then he turned and began to walk away.

She let him go.

Ben gasped at her shoulder like a drowning man coming up for air. Something in him suddenly realized that Allie was really gone. "Allie!"

He turned to face the rest of the room, but of course, she was no longer there. "Allie!" His eyes found the window and he rushed to look out into the night. His eyes must not have found them. "Allie!" They were gone.

Ben turned to Felicity with a look of wild desperation. "She's gone! Oh my God, she's gone! She left! I made her leave…and I didn't get to say goodbye! She's gone! She thinks I hate her. She left and I didn't get to say goodbye." He started to break down again and Felicity went to hold him. The realization of it all was just too much. "Liss I yelled and said awful things. She thinks I hate her and she's gone."

"It's okay. It's okay Ben…she knows. She knows you didn't mean it. She knows."

"But she's gone. She's not even… Oh my God, 'Liss. Her *life* is gone! I didn't even get to say goodbye. At school, we argued, and she left, and now she's…" He had no more tears but just a desperate sort of hysteria that shook him with dry sobs.

Felicity tried to speak with a voice of calm authority. She made him meet her eyes. "Ben, she's okay. She really is. She's happy now. It's what she wanted. She's okay."

Ben looked like he wanted so desperately to believe her, but was having a very hard time reconciling her words with his conjectures of the past. His old perceptions and opinions of things were hard to let go. He needed time. He stared at her with the frightened and unseeing look of a deer in headlights.

"Ben, it's okay. You've got me."

He finally focused on her face. Recognition seemed to seep in as his anguish slowly drained away. He looked so grateful for her presence, her steadfast support…for her love. He loved her, and he needed her, he really did. He drew her into his arms, not a blind grasping hold to reality as before, but a tender, loving embrace.

How had *she* turned into someone that others looked to for confidence? How had she become the calm voice of reason and the pillar of strength in the midst of emotional turmoil? Wasn't she Felicity Snow…the quiet little mouse, afraid of her own shadow and always with a stomach full of butterflies?

A vision came back to her, a memory of her and Cain, outside eating ice cream on a warm September night. She could see him clearly and almost hear his words to her then. 'Things change and we're all of us just struggling to keep up, but sometimes…change can be good – when you least expect it.'

"I love you Felicity." It was Ben, holding her close and kissing the side of her face.

Maybe things really do happen for a reason. "I love you too."

Epilogue

Felicity

Ben's bedroom
Friday morning

Felicity awoke to a cardinal singing outside the window in the early morning sunlight. She opened her eyes to see that Ben was already awake. He gave her a little smile and snuggled closer to her in the bed. "Morning."

"Morning."

He lay there quiet for a few minutes. She could almost see all of last night's happenings going through his head. He took a deep breath and sighed. "I feel like I spent last night on an emotional roller coaster."

She shook her head with a little chuckle. "The ride started back in September for me."

"I hate roller coasters. They always make me sick." He gave her a weary, hopeful sort of look. "Think the ride's over?"

"Are you kiddin'? We're just switchin' tracks," she answered with a laugh. She lay there playing her eyes over his face for a minute. Yeah, she loved him. She really did. "I'll try not to make you throw up."

"I appreciate that." He seemed to make a decision to carry on, past it all. He gazed at her with a smile, and she returned it with her own, happy to concentrate on new beginnings.

Ben rolled over for some space and rubbed the sleep from his eyes. They still looked a bit bloodshot from last night. She scooched up closer to him and kissed his cheek up near his eye, as he had done to her the night before. He grinned at her a bit weakly. "There has been entirely too much crying going on in this room."

"I thoroughly agree," she said with a smile.

"Well then…new rule. Crying is no longer allowed."

"Really?" she asked in amusement.

"So sayeth King Ben."

"*King* Ben?" she asked with a raised eyebrow.

"My room, my rules," he clarified.

She sat up and thought about that for a moment. "I think you should know…I'm not a big fan of absolute monarchy."

"No?" She wrinkled her nose at him and shook her head. He nodded. "I can accept that. How about an equal partnership?"

She grinned. "Equal?"

"Absolutely. Except…" he leaned forward and whispered to her conspiratorially. "You can still boss me around during sex if you want. I kind of liked it."

She laughed. "I'll try to keep that in mind."

"Speaking of which…how you doin'?" he asked tentatively.

704

She smiled at his concern. "I'm fine."

He looked unconvinced. "It's *me* you're talkin' to here 'Liss. Come on." He lowered his voice again although there was no one else to hear. "I know you've gotta be sore."

She shrugged. "Maybe a little."

"Sorry," he offered quietly.

"I'm not," she said with a sly grin.

"Well just so you know, you don't always have to do that. I mean, I know it's a lot to ask. It's okay if sometimes you're not up to it. I'll understand." He gave a little laugh. "Besides, you give good *special attention."* She laughed as she felt her cheeks turning red. He watched her with a grin of his own. "I love to make you smile."

She'd been about to comment on his own adeptness and skills when she was startled by the noise of a door slamming from somewhere else within the house. "What was that?"

Ben listened for a moment before answering, but seemed unconcerned. "My dad's home." Felicity froze as though caught in the midst of an indecent act. Ben noticed and quietly laughed. "It's okay that you're here." He became very thoughtful for a moment. "In fact…I'd like you to meet him."

Felicity sat up further in alarm. *"Now?"*

Ben laughed again. "You can get dressed first. Then I'll make us breakfast and introduce you…my *girlfriend."* He seemed kind of tickled by the word. "When he takes Friday off it usually means he's had a rough week. He'll probably just say hello and then leave to go sleep all day."

Felicity still couldn't help but feel a bit uncomfortable, but Ben seemed insistent. He'd already met all of her family. Maybe he just felt that this was the next step. He did seem to be positively glowing over her. It was kind of nice that he wanted to introduce her as his girlfriend. She got dressed and he led her to the bathroom to freshen up before they joined his dad, who seemed to be in the kitchen. The smell of fresh coffee was drifting down the hall.

As Felicity brushed out her hair before the mirror, she couldn't help but wonder what Ben's dad might be like. Truthfully, she hadn't a very complimentary mental picture of him. All she'd ever heard about him from Ben was that he was never home, drank far too much and seemed to live only for his work. He was some sort of stock trader or something.

She rejoined Ben, following him hesitantly into the kitchen. Ben's dad was sitting at the table with a cup of coffee reading the paper. He looked nothing like Felicity had pictured at all.

He was a very good-looking older man. He looked a lot like Ben really, but with a swath of gray streaked through his hair at the temples on each side, and careworn little crinkles about his eyes. He looked quite distinguished and handsome. He wore a smoky gray turtleneck sweater with a black pair of slacks. She saw that a black and gray sports coat lay draped over the empty chair next to him.

He didn't even look up as Ben entered the kitchen with Felicity just a bit behind him. "Morning, dad."

"You're up early. Classes?"

"Not yet. Dad, I'd like you to meet someone." Now he did look up as Ben took Felicity's arm to guide her more fully into the room. "This is Felicity."

Ben's father looked up at her and seemed to narrow his eyes a bit. Felicity was instantly uncomfortable. It was as though he was looking right through her. After a moment though, he smiled.

He looked up at Ben with a sly smirk. "I had a feeling you weren't in there alone." Ben shifted a little in embarrassment for Felicity as his father stood to approach them.

He stood before Felicity and gave her a warm grin. "Do you know that you are the first girl that Benjamin has ever *introduced* to me? So with his twenty-first birthday quickly approaching, I must presume that either my son is incredibly socially awkward...or *you* are a very special young lady. Judging by the number of times I have been awakened by the comings and goings of the opposite sex through his bedroom window at night...I would venture to guess that it's the latter."

Ben rolled his eyes and shook his head in annoyance. "Dad, you know that's only Alyson."

"Has she had a sex change that I'm unaware of?" Ben just glared at him. Ben's father seemed completely unconcerned with his son's ire. He smiled and took one of Felicity's hands into both of his own. "It is a pleasure to meet you Felicity."

Felicity tried to smile and keep herself from shyly averting her eyes. After a moment, he dropped her hands and went to take his place back at the table.

Ben spoke to Felicity as he turned to the refrigerator. "How does bacon and eggs sound?"

She was just nodding her head as Ben's father answered. "That sounds wonderful. I'm starved."

Ben looked very surprised and gave Felicity an apologetic look that his dad was planning to join them. She just smiled and shrugged. Rather than go sit, she stood by the counter with Ben as he got things started.

Ben's father spoke from the table. "So Felicity, are you a student?"

She answered a bit timidly. "Yes sir."

He raised his eyes from his paper to train them on her for a moment. "A *college* student?"

Ben sighed in exasperation. "Yes dad. She's legal."

Barely, Felicity thought uncomfortably as she averted her gaze. She began to fiercely hope that Ben's father would decide against breakfast and retire to the bedroom as expected.

The sound of a telephone rang from down the hall, drawing Ben's attention. "Oh, that's mine. 'Liss, would you watch the bacon?"

"Sure."

It seemed the moment that Ben left the room, his father's eyes left his paper again to study her. "How are you?" he asked. He seemed very direct and sincerely concerned for her.

She shifted awkwardly. "I'm fine." She looked down the hall after Ben and resolved to be confident. Ben *loved* her. That was all that mattered...right? She turned back to his father with new confidence. "Great actually," she said with a smile.

He smiled in return. "I'm glad that my son makes you happy, but if ever you need to talk... If there's a *problem* that you'd like to share..."

She looked at him oddly. "Problem?"

He stood and moved a bit closer to her. "If I'm not mistaken, it was a few weeks back." He gestured to her throat as he approached.

Her eyes went wide and she self-consciously raised her hand to the light scar there. "Oh this? It's nothing."

"Actually, I was referring to the *other* side." She froze. He could only be referencing the slight marks left by Cain, but they were barely visible! How could he have noticed them?

He seemed to misread her distress. "Never fear dear. It's no reflection on you. One never knows when or where those beasts will strike."

"But how…" she began in bewilderment.

"Their bite leaves an aura about the victim. A 'mark', if you will. I'm rather skilled at reading them. And judging by yours, I'd say you're very lucky indeed to have escaped with your life. You were attacked by a *very* old and powerful creature."

Felicity just stood there with her mouth open in shock. He went on. "Not to worry. It's nearly faded, so if he hasn't returned by now, I shouldn't think you'll see him again. These creatures seldom linger in such rural areas, but should you ever be in need of assistance, don't hesitate to ask."

He seemed to realize her disquieted astonishment at his words. "Let me introduce myself properly." He took back her hand in both of his own, as he had held it before. "Bernard Everheart – Vampire Hunter," he said with a little nod, "at your service. Just…be a dear and don't mention it to Benjamin. I've been very fortunate in keeping him shielded from this sort of thing. I'm afraid it would be a bit of a shock."

She stood staring at him in open-mouthed awe. He dropped her hand and retreated to the table as Ben re-entered the room.

"Liss? The bacon's burnin'."

~~~~~~~~~~~~~~~~~~~~~~~~~~

To Be Continued

in

ALMOST HUMAN ~ The Second Series

Born to Blood

Part 1 ~ Vampiress Rising

~~~~~~~~~~~~~~~~~~~~~~~~~~

If you enjoyed this series, please take a moment to leave a review
on your favorite book review website!

You can join author/reader discussions about the series,
and get updates on upcoming book releases for this series
on the author's web site at: www.MelanieNowak.com

www.ingramcontent.com/pod-product-compliance
Lightning Source LLC
Chambersburg PA
CBHW080941020726
47505CB00009B/2109